THE WORLD'S CLASSICS

Arabian Nights' Entertainments

Edited with an Introduction by
ROBERT L. MACK

Oxford New York
OXFORD UNIVERSITY PRESS

Oxford University Press, Walton Street, Oxford OX2 6DP
Oxford New York
Athens Auckland Bangkok Bombay
Calcutta Cape Town Dar es Salaam Delhi
Florence Hong Kong Istanbul Karachi
Kuala Lumpur Madras Madrid Melbourne
Mexico City Nairobi Paris Singapore
Taipei Tokyo Toronto
and associated companies in
Berlin Ibadan

Oxford is a trade mark of Oxford University Press

First published as a World's Classics paperback 1995

British Library Cataloguing in Publication Data
Data available

Library of Congress Cataloging in Publication Data
Arabian nights. English.
Arabian night's entertainments / edited with an introduction by Robert L. Mack.
p. cm. — (The World's classics)
Includes bibliographical references and indexes.
I. Mack, Robert L. II. Title. III. Series.
PJ7715.M27 1995 398.22—dc20 94-39408
ISBN 0-19-282832-0 (pbk.)

3 5 7 9 10 8 6 4 2

Printed and bound in Great Britain
by Biddles Ltd,
Guildford and King's Lynn

CONTENTS

ACKNOWLEDGEMENTS

I would like to thank the Princeton University Library for permitting me to reproduce the texts upon which this edition is based; I am grateful too to the librarians of the British Library, the Bodleian Library, the Henry W. and Albert A. Berg Collection of the New York Public Library, and the Jean and Alexander Heard Library at Vanderbilt University in Nashville, Tennessee, for their help and assistance. A generous grant from the University Research Council of Vanderbilt University permitted me to spend two summers of research, writing, and editing in Great Britain in 1992 and 1993. In the course of the long and at times arduous process of preparing this edition for the press, I have naturally incurred more than a few debts of gratitude. I would like to take this opportunity to thank the following individuals for providing continued help and support: Misty Anderson, John Bomhoff, Margaret Anne Doody, William E. Engel, Sam B. Girgus, Allan Hepburn, Allegra Huston, Ivo Kamps, Lynn Meloccaro, Judith Luna, Clark Piper, Mark Schoenfield, Florian Stuber, and Sarah Zimmerman.

INTRODUCTION

With the exception of Ovid's *Metamorphoses* and—obviously—the Bible, few works have had such a profound and lasting influence on the English literary tradition as the *Thousand and One Nights* or, to use the name by which the volumes were more commonly known in England throughout the eighteenth and nineteenth centuries, the *Arabian Nights' Entertainments*. Like Ovid's exhaustive compilation of Greek and Roman mythology (and, indeed, to some degree like the Bible itself) the *Nights* is not a single tale, but a generically diverse and kaleidoscopic *collection* of tales; like the *Metamorphoses*, it shuns singularity and revels in multiplicity, never allowing its readers to rest content and inactive on any one narrative shore. Like Ovid's collection, too, the *Nights* not only celebrates the power of stories, but offers a vision of the very act of story-telling itself as nothing less than an art form which offers both its practitioners and its listeners an opportunity to order, comprehend, define, and delimit (at least temporarily) an otherwise chaotic and incomprehensible world of experience. It is by telling stories and by hearing stories told, the *Nights* seems to say, that we come to know our world, each other, and—ultimately—our own selves.

Some characters in the *Nights* tell tales simply because they find it difficult ever to keep still or to keep silent. They narrate fables, fairy tales, travel adventures, crime stories, romances, and even family anecdotes simply because they are compelled to articulate—articulate both in the sense of speaking and expressing themselves, but also in the more etymologically precise sense of joining or uniting, of making intelligible the raw 'stuff' of existence. For other characters, however (including the central figure of Scheherazade herself), story-telling is nothing less than a matter of life and death. Again and again in the collection we encounter individuals whose lives depend upon the responses of their listeners to their tales. If, in the frame story which structures the entire body of narratives, for example, Scheherazade fails to persuade the sultan Schahriar to rescind his pledge to execute each of his new wives on the morning following their marriage, she will not only forfeit her own life, but effectively will be Schahriar's accomplice in sentencing an untold number of young women to a similar fate. Her plight is reiterated and reflected in many other tales in the *Nights*. The diversion or entertainment provided by a well-told story can mitigate a sentence or even prevent an execution; narrative itself often serves as a placating salve to the impatient or to the wicked as well as a healing, consolatory balm for the wounded. For characters like Scheherazade, then, story-telling is both a dangerous and a paradoxical activity. After all, their tales must—in order to satisfy the curiosity of their listeners—be novel and unusual, yet the tellers must take care at the same time not to disrupt or disturb these listeners *too* much, not to push them too far. Their stories need to be at once both profoundly original and playfully derivative, both capable of stunning and compelling innovation, while at the same time remaining endlessly familiar and reassuringly self-referential. What ultimately brings both kinds of story-tellers together, and what finally emerges as the common denominator of all the tales in the *Nights* itself, is the fact that story-telling—the telling of tales and the desire to listen to the tales of others—is the consuming human activity. Story-telling, simply put, is the quality which defines mankind.

Many of the stories brought together in the *Nights* are ancient. Like the Homeric epics to which the West has so often looked as the foundations of its literary traditions, these stories no doubt circulated for years—many centuries even—before being written down at all. As is the case with the classical works, too, it remains uncertain who decided to set them down in the first place; in this instance we lack even a fictional 'Homer' to provide us with a possible point of origin. We do, however, possess some basic information. The earliest written fragment of the *Nights* which has come down to us, relating an Arabic version of the 'Introductory Tale' or frame story of Scheherazade and the sultan Schahriar, dates from about the late ninth century AD and indicates that the basis of the collection is probably of Persian and, ultimately, Indian origin (the names of both Scheherazade and her sister Dinarzade—in the earliest sources 'Shirazad' or 'Shahrazad' and 'Dinizad' or 'Dinazad'—are Persian and appear in Persian legends; the name 'Sindbad', for example, is Indian).[1] In the tenth century an Arabic historian named al-Mas'udi, in a discussion of the popular fiction and writing of the day included in his history *Murudj al-Dhahab* or 'Fields of Gold', disparagingly mentions an early collection of stories which he calls the *Alf Layla* or 'Thousand Nights'. It is clear from al-Mas'udi's brief description of the narrative material that this collection forms the basis for the body of stories eventually known throughout the Islamic world as *Alf Layla wa Layla*, a title meaning literally 'the thousand nights and one night'. Al-Mas'udi's observations reinforce the suggestion that many of the stories in the 'Thousand Nights' are of Persian origin. He even mentions a Persian original—the

[1] For details and discussion of the origins and early textual history of the *Nights* in Arabic see Enno Littmann, 'Alf Layla wa-Layla', in H. A. R. Gibb, J. H. Kramers, *et al.* (eds.), *The Encyclopaedia of Islam*, 2nd edn. (Leiden, 1954–), 358–9; Mia Gerhardt, *The Art of Story-Telling* (Leiden, 1963), 9–36; Robert Irwin, *The Arabian Nights: A Companion* (Harmondsworth, 1994), 48–51.

Hasar Afsana or *Hazar Afsaneh* (the 'Thousand Legends' or 'Thousand Stories')—from which, he claims, the tales had first been drawn and translated into Arabic as the *Alf Khurafa* or the 'Thousand Entertaining Tales'. A bookseller named Ibn al-Nadim, writing at about the same time as al-Mas'udi, similarly makes a reference to the *Hasar Afsana* in his *al-Fihrist* (an ambitious catalogue of all the books written up until his own day), again taking the time to disparage this earliest glimpse of Scheherazade—here 'Shahrazad the Story-teller'—as 'a coarse tale, without warmth in the telling'.[2]

As they were told and retold, the stories were constantly being transformed and rewritten. As one recent translator of the *Nights* has observed, the narratives were not only 'modified to conform to the general life and customs of the Arab society that adapted them and to the particular conditions of that society at a particular time', but were also endlessly modified 'to suit the role of the story-teller or the demand of the occasion'.[3] The body of fictions finally known collectively in the West as the *Arabian Nights' Entertainments* or the *Thousand and One Nights* brings together three main levels or sources of narrative material. The first—and this includes the frame story itself—includes those tales of Persian origin already being circulated both orally and in manuscript (in Arabic) by the end of the tenth century AD. These stories, in other words, are those first described by historians such as al-Mas'udi and Ibn al-Nadim, the origins of which reach deep into the ancient Persian and Indian past. A second body of narratives consists of a group of tales which probably originated in Baghdad in the tenth to twelfth centuries AD. Baghdad, home to the Abbasid Caliphate from AD 750, was the economic and intellectual centre of the Islamic world in the European Middle Ages, and many of the narratives in the *Nights* reflect this cultural hegemony. This second body of tales includes, for example, the popular adventures of the caliph Haroun Alraschid (more properly Harun Al-Rashid) and his prime visier Giafar (or Jiaffar), both of whom were well-known figures in Islamic history. A third and final body of stories appears to have originated in Cairo from about the twelfth to the fourteenth century AD. Many of the tales from this last group are set in Cairo, rather than in Baghdad or Balsora (Basra), and some include narrative tropes and motifs which can be traced as far back as the stories and folk tales of ancient Egypt. Most of the tales in the collection featuring clever tricksters, talismans, demons, genies who are the servants of signet rings, and other magical objects are from this Egyptian source; many of the stories often referred to

[2] Ibn al-Nadim, *The Fihrist of al-Nadim*, trans. Bayard Dodge (New York, 1970), ii. 713–14; repr. in Irwin, 50.

[3] Husain Haddawy, 'Introduction' to *The Arabian Nights* (London and New York, 1990), p. xi.

as 'bourgeois romances' and novels also belong to this last group. All three bodies of stories circulated orally, and then began to be pulled together and written down in various forms from the twelfth to the fourteenth century. The extraordinarily lengthy period of time over which the collection was thus assembled, and the geographically and culturally wide range of Eastern, Islamic, and Mediterranean civilization from which the tales finally included in the sequence were culled, leads to a fascinating and at times thoroughly bewildering blend of fictions. As one commentator has observed of the *Nights*, 'there are stories of king Solomon, of the kings of ancient Persia . . . of the caliphs and sultans on one side, and stories in which guns, coffee, and tobacco are mentioned on the other side'.[4] Readers alive to the extended genesis of the collection will not get very far into the work before encountering some perplexing narrative 'impossibilities'. The opening sentence of the *Nights*, for example, informs us that the 'Introductory Tale' itself is an ancient story first recorded in the chronicles of 'the Susanians, the ancient kings of Persia'. These 'Susanians', as the Explanatory Notes to the present edition explain, were in fact the Sassanians, an ancient dynasty which ruled in Persia and eastern Asia from AD 226 to 641. Yet within the boundaries of that same tale Scheherazade goes on to relate to Schahriar many narratives which include references to the paraphernalia and historical events of later eastern cultures. If we needed any reminder that the *Nights* was never to be bound by the more chronologically scrupulous conventions of the European novel, Scheherazade's seemingly proleptic or prophetic imagination would alert us to the fact that we are closer here to the world of magic realism than to that of literary naturalism.

As a collection the *Nights* poses other, unique problems for literary scholars as well. No systematic or authoritative Arabic edition of the *Nights* would be available until the early nineteenth century, when a cluster of important editions—known, respectively, as Calcutta I (1814–18), the Bulak or Cairo Edition (1835), the Breslau Edition (1825–38), and Calcutta II (1839–42)—were made available to scholars.[5] Our usual notions of just what constitutes literary 'influence' are thus muddied by the fact that standard European versions of the *Nights* had been circulating in the West for well over a hundred years before the literary culture which gave birth to the tales in the first place produced an authoritative or canonical textual point of origin *for* those French and English collections. Moreover, as we shall see, some of the most popular stories in the *Nights* (the so-called 'orphan stories',

[4] Littmann, 'Alf Layla wa-Layla', 358–9.

[5] On Arabic editions of the *Alf Layla wa Layla* see ibid. 360; on the role of these editions in subsequent European translations of the *Nights* see Gerhardt, *Art of Story-Telling*, 67–71; Irwin, *Arabian Nights*, 9–41.

including 'Aladdin; or, the Wonderful Lamp') appear never to have been part of the 'real' Eastern collection at all, and were for a long time thought to have been the intrusive products of the Western imagination. Nevertheless, it is doubtless a testament of sorts to the sheer power of the *Nights* as an ancient body of narratives that even before the collection was written down and translated as a coherent group of fictions tied together by the frame story, fragments of the cycle seem to have made their way into the traditions of European literature. Indeed, at times the two traditions—the Arabic and the European—seem inextricably, if inexplicably, linked. It has long been recognized, for example, that the third voyage of Sindbad tells a story of the legendary sailor's encounter with a cyclops which bears a startling resemblance to Odysseus' adventure with the giant Polyphemos in Book IX of Homer's *Odyssey*; the Sindbad story cycle may have borrowed some of its narrative incident from the *Odyssey*, or it may share a common source with the Homeric epic. There are several other noticeable instances of such literary 'cross-pollination'. Readers of Chaucer will recognize in 'The Story of the Enchanted Horse' a possible source of the motif of the mechanical horse which makes its appearance in 'The Squire's Tale' in *The Canterbury Tales* (*c*.1388–1400). Similarly, 'The Story of the Sleeper Awakened', which tells the tale of a simple Baghdad merchant who is deceived into believing that he is himself the caliph or 'Commander of the Faithful', appears to have been known in some form to William Shakespeare, who uses a similar conceit of the 'awakened sleeper' as the framing device for his *The Taming of the Shrew* (*c*.1592); the same plot device would be used to different effect by Calderon de le Barca in his *La vida es sueño* or 'Life Is a Dream' (1635). Finally, the larger introductory tale and the traditions of Arabic framing devices may have been known to Italian authors such as Giovanni Sercambi and Boccaccio (and, again, to their English descendant, Chaucer); the episodes in the frame story concerning the sultan Schahriar and his brother were certainly known in some version to Ludovico Ariosto, who rewrites them as the story of Astolfo, told by Rodomont, in Canto 28 of his *Orlando Furioso* (1532). Before ever appearing in Europe, then—in some cases before ever being written down at all—the power of Scheherazade's nocturnal fables was already becoming embedded in the shared narrative heritage of both East and West. 'Good stories', as the novelist and commentator on the *Nights* Robert Irwin has observed, 'pay little attention to cultural or linguistic frontiers.'[6]

The *Nights* were first translated from Arabic into French by Antoine Galland at the beginning of the eighteenth century. Galland, who was to

[6] Irwin, *Arabian Nights*, 65.

distinguish himself among a growing number of orientalists working in Europe in the late seventeenth and early eighteenth centuries, came from a modest background. Born in the small town of Rollot in Picardy, he had begun studying classical and oriental languages at the nearby Collège de Noyon before enrolling at the Collège du Plessis in Paris (see Chronology).[7] In 1670, at the age of 24, he became secretary to the marquis de Nointel, who was then serving as Louis XIV's ambassador in Constantinople. While in service in the East, Galland furthered his earlier study of Turkish and Arabic, and was presented with the opportunity to meet and talk with experienced travellers such as Jean Chardin. Galland himself eventually travelled throughout Syria, Greece, and what is now Israel, working for some time as a purchaser of various artefacts and rarities for French collectors; he would not return permanently to France until almost twenty years had passed. When Galland did return to Paris he embarked on a series of publications which would have profound consequences for the course of European orientalism in the eighteenth and nineteenth centuries. He first completed and published, in 1697, Barthélémy d'Herbelot's *Bibliothèque orientale*, a work originally conceived as an encyclopedic guide to the customs and manners of the East; he would eventually, in 1710, translate the Koran into French. Even while he was engaged on this more scholarly work, however, Galland found the time to begin translating some of the many other manuscripts and unidentified fragments which he had brought back with him from Constantinople. Among these was a version of the seven voyages of Sindbad the Sailor, which Galland translated from Arabic and published in 1701. Intrigued and excited by the Sindbad stories, Galland ordered to be sent to him four volumes of the *Alf Layla wa Layla*. The particular volumes he received and subsequently worked from appear to have been assembled in Egypt. They were originally purchased at Aleppo and date from the fourteenth or fifteenth century; they are, with the exception of the tenth-century fragment already mentioned, the oldest known manuscripts of the *Nights* and are generally thought to contain one of the best surviving texts. These volumes—three of which are still in the possession of the Bibliothèque Nationale in Paris—were to provide the material for the first instalments of Galland's translation of *Mille et une Nuit*. To this original collection Galland appears to have added the Sindbad stories and one additional tale ('The Story of the Amours of Camaralzaman, Prince of the Isles of the Children of Khaledan, and of Badoura, Princess of China') from an unidentified manuscript. The first volume of Galland's *Mille et une Nuit* appeared in 1704, and within two years a total of seven volumes had

[7] Biographical information on Antoine Galland is drawn partly from Raymond Schwab, *L'Auteur de Mille et une nuits, vie de Antoine Galland* (Paris, 1964).

been published. Galland had by that point run through the original four volumes of his Arabic source text. The series was proving so popular, however, that his publisher—much to Galland's own annoyance—brought together a tale which he had earlier rendered into French with some supposed translations from other Arabic sources by Galland's fellow orientalist Francois Pétis de la Croix. These three tales (Galland's 'The History of Ganem, Son to Abou Ayoub, and known by the Surname of Love's Slave' along with Pétis de la Croix's 'The History of Prince Zeyn Alasnam, and the King of the Genii' and 'The History of Codadad and his Brothers') the bookseller published together as volume VIII of *Mille et une Nuit*. In the same year Galland himself was introduced by his friend, the traveller Paul Lucas, to Hanna Diab, a Syrian Maronite Christian from Aleppo who was visiting France. Hanna was able to provide Galland with enough material to fill out a further four volumes, bringing the total number—including the spurious eighth volume which was to become an inextricable part of the collection—to twelve. Some of the material which Hanna transmitted to Galland appears to have been in the form of Arabic manuscripts, while at other times Galland seems simply to have transcribed the stories as they were told to him, feeling free to elaborate on or alter the narratives as he saw fit. It is worth remembering, then, that the completed series of *Mille et une Nuit*, as it appeared in Europe, includes: (i) at least two stories 'translated' from a Turkish manuscript by Pétis de la Croix which may never have belonged to the genuine story cycle of the *Alf Layla wa Layla* in the East; (ii) a number of independent tales (including the Sindbad stories) which Galland himself appears to have inserted in the collection; and finally (iii) a group of stories supposedly told by Hanna to Galland—including, most memorably, 'orphan stories' such as 'Aladdin; or, the Wonderful Lamp' and 'The Story of Ali Baba, and the forty Thieves destroyed by a Slave'—which do not appear ever to have been part of the *Nights* cycle. In other words, the most frequently reprinted tales in the West's *Arabian Nights* traditions may well not have been part of the East's *Alf Layla wa Layla* at all.

The dubious canonicity of some of the tales drawn together in Galland's collection has proved a major stumbling-block for later translators of the Arabic *Alf Layla wa Layla*; estimations and evaluations of Galland's artistic achievement in the *Mille et une Nuit* have varied as well. Galland was described earlier this century as 'a born story-teller' who possessed both 'a flair for a good story and a knack for telling it'.[8] Likewise, observing that while 'translation' may be 'too precise a word' for the manner with which the author treated his Arabic sources, E. F. Bleiler similarly noted that Galland, faced with a vast and daunting amount of narrative material, in the end

[8] Littmann, 'Alf Layla wa-Layla', 359.

nevertheless 'turned out to be a very fine storyteller'.[9] Others, however, have offered more qualified praise or criticism. The moral philosopher and literary critic James Beattie, writing in the eighteenth century, doubted whether the stories in the collection were 'really Arabick' at all. 'If they be oriental,' he noted suspiciously, 'they are translated with unwarrantable latitude; for the whole tenor of the style is in the French mode; and the Caliph of Bagdat, and the Emperor of China, are addressed in the same terms of ceremony which are used at the court of France.' Edward William Lane, who produced his own translation of the *Nights* in 1838–41, similarly grumbled that Galland had 'excessively perverted the work', again asserting that the Frenchman's understanding of Arab customs and manners were 'insufficient always to preserve him from errors of the grossest description'.[10] Lane obviously had his own axe to grind (and his own book to sell), but others similarly complained of the liberties Galland had seemingly taken with his sources. (One recent translator of the *Nights* echoed his nineteenth-century predecessors when he qualified Galland's version as 'not a translation, but a French interpretation, or rather a work of his own creation'.)[11] To this day questions still remain concerning the true origins of many of Galland's narratives. The popularity of the collection, however, was certain. Although subsequent translators (the most important of whom include Edward Lane, John Payne, and Sir Richard Burton) would alter and enlarge upon Galland's version of the *Nights*, it would be his collection more than any other which would influence generations of European readers—readers who, as the bibliographer James Hanford put it, 'could quote from memory phrases which must have come from his version and no other'.[12] The shape the *Nights* assumed in the history of European literature is that first imprinted upon it by Antoine Galland.

The several volumes of Galland's *Mille et une Nuit* seem to have been translated from French into English almost immediately. This anonymous 'Grub Street' translation circulated widely throughout the earliest years of the eighteenth century. Long after the appearance in English of the twelfth and final volume of the collection in about 1721, the stories continued to provoke a strong response from British readers.[13] Some derided what they

[9] E. F. Bleiler, 'The Arabian Nights', in id. (ed.), *Supernatural Fiction Writers: Fantasy and Horror I, Apuleius to May Sinclair* (New York, 1985), 22.

[10] See Irwin, *Arabian Nights*, 17, 24.

[11] Haddawy, 'Introduction' to *The Arabian Nights*, p. xvi.

[12] James H. Hanford, 'Open Sesame: Notes on the *Arabian Nights* in England', *Princeton University Library Chronicle*, 26 (Autumn 1964), 50.

[13] On the general influence of the *Nights* on English literature see Peter L. Caracciolo's superb and comprehensive 'Introduction' to *The Arabian Nights in English* (New York, 1988), 1–80.

perceived to be the prevailing 'Moorish fancy'. As early as 1711 the Earl of Shaftesbury mocked the narrative landscapes of the *Nights* as 'idle deserts' which were capable of transforming even the most sober philosopher or wit into the 'silliest woman or merest boy'. Peter Caracciolo and others have pointed out that the tales were in fact often criticized for being too 'feminine'. It was all very well for women to waste their time on such stuff, we hear again and again, but a serious and discerning (male) reader would do well to avoid them. Bishop Atterbury, one of the most famous preachers of the early eighteenth century, in fact blithely dismissed several volumes of the collection sent to him (a gift of the poet Alexander Pope) as in all likelihood 'the product of some Womans [*sic*] imagination'. Still, even in the early eighteenth century some few readers spoke favourably of the *Nights* and of the ensuing fashion for oriental tales of all types and varieties. Pope himself read and enjoyed the collection, even recommending it to Sir William Trumbull as 'proper enough for the Nursery'. Later in the century Edward Gibbon, recalling his own reading as a child, would couple the *Nights* with Pope's translation of Homer as the two books which 'will always please by the moving picture of human manners and specious miracles'.

However much the more serious-minded critics might have blanched to see Galland's collection thus coupled with the *Iliad* and the *Odyssey* as landmark works of narrative fiction, there was no denying its enormous popularity on both sides of the Atlantic. Before the last volumes had even been translated from the French, English authors had begun writing their own Arabian or pseudo-Oriental tales. Joseph Addison was among those who led the way in his *Spectator*, with stories such as 'The Vision of Mirza' and 'The Story of Shalum and Hilpa' (1711). Throughout the century other periodical authors—among them Richard Steele, John Hawkesworth, Samuel Johnson, and James Austen—found the form a congenial one, and frequently resorted to the oriental landscape when the need arose for a moral apologue. The inclusion of at least one oriental tale in an author's output seems by mid-century to have become almost *de rigueur*. Samuel Johnson, of course, returned to the form most famously when, under pressure to pay the expenses of his mother's illness and subsequent funeral, he wrote and published *The History of Rasselas, Prince of Abbyssinia* in 1759. Johnson's friend and former colleague John Hawkesworth produced the influential *Almoran and Hamet* in 1761; another friend, Oliver Goldsmith, had published his *The Citizen of the World*—a collection of pseudo-oriental correspondence modelled on Baron de Montesquieu's *Lettres persanes* (1721)—in 1760. Montesquieu was not the only European author to prompt insular imitators. The extended collections of French writers such as Pétis de la Croix and Thomas Gueullette were promptly translated into English, and in turn inspired collections such as the Revd James Ridley's *Tales of the Genii* (1764). The later eighteenth century saw the publication of oriental fables by authors such as Frances Sheridan, Horace Walpole, Clara Reeve, Robert Bage, and of course William Beckford, whose *Vathek* first appeared in 1786. Nineteenth- and early twentieth-century authors whose works would be influenced by Galland's *Nights* and—to a lesser degree—by the later translations of the collection by Lane, Payne, and Burton, include Maria Edgeworth, Sir Walter Scott, Jane Austen, Elizabeth Gaskell, William Makepeace Thackeray, Charles Dickens, Charlotte Brontë, Robert Louis Stevenson, Joseph Conrad, H. G. Wells, and James Joyce. A list of more recent writers indebted to the *Nights* would prominently include Jorge Luis Borges, John Barth, Robertson Davies, Naguib Mahfouz, and Salman Rushdie.

The *Nights* also, of course, became a corner-stone in those traditions of children's literature which had begun taking shape in the late eighteenth and early nineteenth centuries. Moralized and at times rather savagely edited versions of Galland's text began appearing in about 1790, and for well over a hundred years volumes with such titles as *The Oriental Moralist, or The Beauties of the Arabian Nights' Entertainments* (1790), *Oriental Tales, Being Moral Selections from the Arabian Nights Entertainments calculated both to Amuse and Improve the Minds of Youth* (1829), *The Arabian Nights' Entertainments, Arranged for the Perusal of Youthful Readers* (1863), and—somewhat startlingly—*Five Favourite Tales from the Arabian Nights in Words of One Syllable* (1871) made their way into nurseries throughout Britain and North America. Such volumes often found it necessary to observe that while the *Nights* was a collection 'unsurpassed in weird fairy lore', its tales are often nevertheless 'of questionable delicacy'. One early editor of the *Nights* for children, the 'Rev'd Mr Cooper' (in fact the hack writer Richard Johnson) commented in the preface to his translation and abridgment that he first read Galland's *Nights* in French simply to pass the time while stranded at a rural inn. 'It struck my imagination', he observed,

> that these tales might be compared to a once rich and luxuriant garden, neglected and run to waste, where scarce anything strikes the common observer but the weeds and briars with which it is over-run, whilst the more penetrating eye of the more experienced gardener discovers still remaining, though but thinly scattered, some of the most fragrant and delightful flowers.[14]

'Full of this idea', he continues, 'I determined to turn florist'. Johnson's idea of narrative gardening unfortunately involved snipping the frame story almost out of existence (tales of marital infidelity no doubt being unsuitable

[14] Rev'd Mr Cooper [Richard Johnson], *The Oriental Moralist or The Beauties of the Arabian Nights Entertainments* (London, 1790), 2.

for 'the most delicate readers'), and in general concluding each tale with a moral which pointed ploddingly and unimaginatively to the virtues of industry, fortitude, and trust in providence. While young readers seem to have enjoyed the stories in whatever form (and in whatever spirit) they were offered, some of the prefatory material and textual apparatus which began to surround the tales in these redactions began to smack of narrative terrorism. One so-called 'preface' addressed explicitly to young children reads:

When reading these stories, all children will do well to remember the following:

First of all, they are only for good boys and girls; and if you, small reader, do not happen to be good, then put the book down at once and go to bed.

Secondly, if you have already gone to bed, and are reading there, then you must know that you are not doing the right thing; so close the book as well as your eyes and go to sleep.

Thirdly, they are not to be read in bed in the morning, when all should be up and getting ready for breakfast.

Fourthly, you must not cry at the stories, nor laugh too loud; or, perhaps, they will be taken from you.

Fifthly, and lastly, you are not to turn up the pictures before reading the stories; or you will be like the boy who picked out all the plums from his cake, and did not care to eat it afterwards.[15]

Such anxious restrictions—attempts as they are to contain or to control the threateningly boundless narrative energy of the collection—seem on some level doomed to failure. At least one editor, George C. Baskett, who published his revision of selected stories in the series Bell's Reading Books, attempted to comfort parents with the consolation that while the tales themselves may offer a fanciful vision of the world 'to the total exclusion of moral and didactic teaching', nevertheless 'the important influence they have had on much modern European literature makes an acquaintance with them a matter of no small value to any intelligent mind'.[16] 'Boys in England', another edition had sighed several years earlier, 'will read them as long as England lasts.' The prolific novelist Mary Elizabeth Braddon, who revised three of the tales for publication in 1880, was somewhat more even-handed in her estimation of the influence of the collection. 'The day when a boy *or girl* first opens this volume of wonders', she wrote of Galland's *Nights*, 'is a day never to be forgotten.'[17]

Not surprisingly, Galland's *Nights* would survive all its editors and would also go on to have a uniquely profound effect on other art forms as well. Musicians and composers have been particularly drawn to the tales. Rimsky-

[15] *Child's Arabian Nights* (London, 1903), pp. ix–x.

[16] George C. Baskett, *Selections from the Arabian Nights, Rewritten from the original English version* (London, 1885), pp. vii–viii.

[17] *Aladdin; or the Wonderful Lamp, etc., Revised by M. E. Braddon* (London, 1880), preface.

Korsakov's symphonic suite *Scheherazade* (1889) is undoubtedly the most widely known lyrical adaptation of the collection. Other indirect references to or quotations from the *Nights* are contained in a number of operas, including Mozart's *Die Zauberflöte* (1791), Weber's *Abu Hassan* (1810–11), Peter Cornelius's *Der Barbier von Bagdad* (1858), Bizet's *Djamileh* (1871), and Puccini's *Turandot* (1920–6). The popularity of the *Nights* as material for the nineteenth-century British pantomime—and the obvious theatrical potential of fables which deal so spectacularly with enchanted objects, titanic rivalries, and romantic passions assisted by the supernatural—likewise paved the way for a number of successful dramatic and musical adaptations in our own century, including Broadway productions such as *Kismet* (1953) and Cole Porter's *Aladdin* (1959). Film references to the *Nights* of course include Alexander Korda's *The Thief of Baghdad* (1940)—itself a remake of Raoul Walsh's 1924 adventure classic starring Douglas Fairbanks—several versions of the Sindbad stories (most memorably *The Seventh Voyage of Sindbad the Sailor*, 1958), and the Walt Disney studio's stunningly successful 1992 animated musical feature, *Aladdin.*

The ever-changing artefacts of popular culture have thus ensured that very few readers of English and American literature need to have references to such characters as 'Sindbad the Sailor', 'Aladdin', or 'Ali Baba' identified for them; even this late in the twentieth century phrases such as 'Open Sesame' and 'New Lamps for Old' still ring familiarly in our ears. Similarly, it has often been noted that descriptions such as 'like a fairy tale straight from the *Arabian Nights*' or 'as beautiful as a scene in the *Thousand and One Nights*' signify, to most of us, something easily pictured and recognizable. Yet what exactly do we mean when we use the *Nights* as this kind of cultural or aesthetic touchstone? Why is it that the *Nights* has proved so perennially popular? Why, most often encountering them first as children, do we continue to reread these stories and rewrite them as adults? What is it—finally—that draws these tales together?

Critics of children's literature such as Bruno Bettelheim have speculated as to why the *Nights* has proved so consistently appealing to (at least) younger readers. Bettelheim himself fits the tales neatly into his larger paradigm of the ways in which *all* fairy tales have rich psychological meaning for their readers, particularly allowing children to confront and at least begin to resolve and overcome 'basic human predicaments'.[18] The *Nights*, Bettelheim further suggested, have perhaps remained especially resilient thanks to the fantastic exaggeration of the oriental landscape (an exaggeration which nevertheless accurately represents and bodies forth pressing psychological

[18] Bruno Bettelheim, *The Uses of Enchantment* (New York, 1976), 8.

realities) and—always an important point in Bettelheim's assessment of the efficacy of fairy tales—its unflinching portrayal of the chaotic, angry, and violent side of human experience.

Bettelheim's assessment to some degree holds true not only for children, but for readers of all ages. Many of the stories retold in the *Nights* are what formalist critics such as Northrop Frye would call 'archetypes'—stories, that is, which imaginatively and symbolically present to their readers those central, recurring myths which detail the most profound and deep-seated fears and desires of our shared experience as human beings. The system of 'narrative categories' or literary modes by means of which such critics attempted to impose order on the infinite re-imaginings of these myths could be applied quite easily to almost all of the tales included in Galland's collection. We find in the volume ritual quests ('The Story of the Three Calenders, Sons of Kings', for example, or the voyages of Sindbad), and tales both of actual and of figurative 'rebirth' (as in 'The Story of the Little Hunch-back' or 'The Story of the Two Sisters who envied their Younger Sister'), as well as the seemingly universal fairy-tale motifs of maturation and fulfilment (for example, 'The History of Prince Zeyn Alasnam, and the King of the Genii' and 'Aladdin; or, the Wonderful Lamp'). If literature is indeed, as critics like Frye have contended, one of the arms of that greater 'civilization' which attempts to impose order on or to contain *all* nature and humanity, then what better figure than Scheherazade—and what more suitable or appropriate structure than the discrete, nocturnal instalments of her never-ending story—to represent 'the total dream of man'?[19]

The psychological approach of Bettelheim and the anthropological or pseudo-scientific formalism of archetypal critics such as Frye thus provide at least two ways of making sense of the *Nights*. However, for those who, like the folklorists Iona and Peter Opie, feel that such all-embracing theories have tended to 'pour darkness on their subject rather than light', there are also more straightforward explanations for the appeal of the collection.[20] One is the sheer adaptability of these seemingly indestructible tales. Each generation has been able to create its own version, its own retelling, of these stories. The tremendous size and near-biblical scope of the collection allow for an infinite number of local alterations; the fundamental themes of the *Nights*, however—its basic fables of transgression and punishment, growth and understanding, perseverance and reward, guilt and penitence—remain unchanged. Alternatively, many readers have been drawn to the *Nights* simply by the picture it presents of life in the Muslim East. Much of this picture may well be the deliberately seductive product of the eighteenth- and nine-

[19] Northrop Frye, *The Anatomy of Criticism* (Princeton, NJ, 1957), 119.

[20] Iona and Peter Opie, 'Introduction' to *The Classic English Fairy Tales* (Oxford, 1974), 21.

teenth-century European imagination. Yet, as the Arabic historian Albert Hourani has pointed out, that imagination, 'working on the knowledge or half-knowledge derived from travel and scholarship', nevertheless produced an important vision of the Orient as 'mysterious, enticing, and threatening, cradle of wonders and fairy tales, which fertilized the arts'.[21] While critics such as Edward Said are at least partly correct in their assessment of this 'vision' and its subsequent influence as a discourse consciously constructed by European culture in order to gain in strength and identity 'by setting itself off against the Orient as a surrogate or even underground self', the fact remains that the *Nights* is for many readers their first and most impressive introduction to the East and to Islamic civilization in general.[22] Although the picture of the medieval Caliphate which emerges from some of the tales (for example, 'The Story of the Three Apples') may be 'that of a cruel and capricious tyrant, wielding unfettered power and living in the luxury and vice of the harem', scholars other than Said admit that there is 'a certain element of truth in that picture'.[23] In any case, most readers seem very quickly to move beyond the stereotypical image of imperious sultans and impatient genies to which the *Nights* perhaps first gives rise, to develop a genuine interest in the history, social customs, and rituals of Islam which are everywhere documented in the text. Western readers leave the *Nights* at least having begun to learn something about the belief and practice of Muslim religious life—about the central importance of the *Koran*, for example, or the essential obligations of the Five Pillars of Islam (the practice and relevance of prayer, or the rituals of the fast of Ramadan). The folklorist and scholar of fairy tales Jack Zipes has observed that one of Scheherazade's most serious functions in the *Nights* is to 'socialize the Muslim readers of her time and all future readers, who may be unaware of Muslim custom and law . . . Without disregarding the entertaining and humorous aspect of these stories, they are primarily *lessons* in etiquette, aesthetics, decorum, religion, government, history, and sex.'[24] Just as Scheherazade's tales in the collection are drawn together by the unstated purpose of *educating* her listeners, so too we as readers of the *Nights* are drawn together by what we learn. We carry away from the work not simply a collection of stock characters and narrative tropes, but a coherent and compelling vision of a fascinating, alternative culture.

[21] Albert Hourani, *A History of the Arab Peoples* (Cambridge, Mass., 1991), 300.

[22] Edward Said, *Orientalism* (New York, 1979), 3.

[23] C. E. Bosworth, 'The Historical Background of Islamic Civilization', in *Introduction to Islamic Civilization*, ed. R. M. Savory (Cambridge, 1976), 20.

[24] Jack Zipes, 'Afterword' to *The Arabian Nights* (New York and London, 1991), 587–8.

Other recurring themes and motifs, finally, serve similarly to draw the *Nights* together and to create for the reader a sense of the collection not merely as a haphazard or accidental jumble of narratives, but rather as a unified—even epic—undertaking. Once again it is the central figure of Scheherazade who pulls together and transforms the tropes of her subsidiary narratives into something of greater moment and consequence. Each of the stories in Galland's collection is effectively an echo of the 'Introductory Tale'. Even the physical violence or mutilation which is so prominently featured in some of the narratives (as in, for example, 'The Story of the Three Apples' or the cycle of tales related within 'The Story of the Little Hunch-back') serves to recall and to reinscribe the imminent sentence of death under which Scheherazade is performing. More importantly, just as the characters in the tales are so often mesmerized or motivated by the prospect of an enigma or a mystery—by the force of curiosity—so too the sultan Shahriar and, indeed, we ourselves as readers, are drawn through the collection by our own insatiable desire for narrative awareness, for understanding, comprehension, and knowledge. Curiosity in the *Nights* is, on a few occasions, punished ('The Story of the Husband and Parrot' or 'The Story of the Grecian King and the Physician Douban'), but it is far more frequently rewarded (as in 'The Story of Sindbad the Sailor', 'Aladdin; or, the Wonderful Lamp', or 'The Story of Ali Baba, and the forty Thieves destroyed by a Slave'). The dual concepts of Time as a devourer on the one hand and as a near-apocalyptic revealer of 'truth' on the other are likewise combined in these tales to further the suggestion that the curiosity which produces artistic achievement and the curiosity which furthers the attainment of genuine understanding necessarily occur simultaneously. The sands of the hour-glass and the ticking of her sister Dinarzade's 'pendulum' recall to Scheherazade the pressure under which she is narrating, but alert her as well to the gradual approach of her goal and to the grand, cumulative power of her achievement. The stories in the *Nights* ultimately chronicle not merely a series of individual romances and adventures, but together offer a profound and far-reaching vision of the transformative powers of narrative, and the constructive, conciliatory power of art.

NOTE ON THE TEXT

This edition is based on the text of Antoine Galland's twelve-volume *Mille et une Nuit* (1704–17) as it was originally rendered into English by the anonymous 'Grub Street' translator, from about 1706 to 1721. The immediate source for this text has been Henry Weber's three-volume *Tales of the East* (1812), a collection which conveniently reproduced in a slightly modernized version (for example, eliminating the long eighteenth-century 's' and attempting to standardize much typography, orthography, and italicization) the text of the *Nights* as it appeared in England throughout the eighteenth and well into the nineteenth century.

Readers wishing a more complete account of the extraordinarily complex publishing history of the *Nights* in Europe are referred to D. B. Macdonald's 'A Bibliographical and Literary Study of the First Appearance of the *Arabian Nights* in Europe' and James H. Hanford's 'Open Sesame: Notes on the *Arabian Nights* in English'; a brief and readable discussion of the earliest translations and editions of the *Nights* in France and England is also included in Robert Irwin's *The Arabian Nights: A Companion* (see Select Bibliography).

As noted in the Introduction (pp. xiv–xv) Galland's *Mille et une Nuit* was published in France over a period of thirteen years, from 1704 to 1717. English editions of the earliest French volumes probably began appearing in about 1705–6, when the bookseller Andrew Bell (at the sign of the Cross Keys and Bible in Cornhill) first began publishing Galland's collection under the title *Arabian Winter-Evenings' Entertainments* or *Arabian Nights' Entertainments.* Bell and his successors continued to publish English translations of Galland's work as it appeared through to the eighth volume of *Mille et une Nuit* in 1709 (which in fact contained only one story translated by Galland and two by his fellow orientalist Pétis de la Croix originally intended for his own collection, competitively entitled *Mille et une Jours*: see Introduction, p. xv); some time afterwards a group of publishers led by W.Taylor 'at the ship in Paternoster Row' obtained the copy for subsequent material and eventually undertook the publication of the final four 'instalments' of the series. The twelfth and last volume appears to have been printed in English in about 1721. The rights to the entire collection seem eventually to have passed into the hands of the enterprising publishers Robert Osborne and Thomas Longman, who continued to hold the copy throughout the eighteenth century, by the end of which the original English translation of Galland's text had reached about twenty editions.

Changes have been made in the printed text according to the following general principles:

1. The spellings in the text (e.g. 'croud', 'gulph', 'sattin') have been retained as in the original, with the exception of some very few instances in which the sense or readability of a passage was impaired (for a modern reader, at least) by the orthography. Obvious misprints, misspellings, and anacoluthon have been silently corrected.

2. The titles of the individual stories in the collection have been brought into conformity with the titles as they appear in the copy text's Table of Contents.

3. A single line indicating a break between tales which begins appearing only midway through the copy-text has been eliminated throughout. On a few rare occasions (for example, pp. 13, 178) a space or break has been added to the text better to distinguish between the end of one tale-within-a-tale and the resumption of the central narrative.

4. Within the tales are included several epistles, few of which are introduced or treated in the same typographical manner. The typography of these epistles has been brought into conformity, the better to distinguish them from the main text and thus avoid any possible confusion for the reader.

5. Quotation marks are not generally used in the collection; on the few occasions when they are employed, they have been systematized to conform with modern custom.

SELECT BIBLIOGRAPHY

Editions and Translations

BURTON, RICHARD FRANCIS, *The Book of the Thousand Nights and One Night. A Plain and Literal Translation of the Arabian Nights' Entertainment*, 10 vols. (Benares, 1885–6).

DAWOOD, N.J., *Tales from the Thousand and One Nights* (London, 1955).

GALLAND, ANTOINE, *Les Mille et Une Nuit, contes arabes*; nouv. edn. corrigée (Paris, 1726).

GAULMIER, JEAN (ed.), *Les Mille et une Nuits: Contes arabes*, traduction d'Antoine Galland (Paris, 1965).

HADDAWY, HUSAIN, *The Arabian Nights*, based on the Fourteenth-Century Syrian Manuscript edited by Muhsin Mahdi (New York, 1990).

LANE, EDWARD WILLIAM, *A New Translation of the Thousand Nights and a Night; Known in England as the Arabian Nights' Entertainments* (London, 1838–42).

LANG, ANDREW, *The Arabian Nights Entertainments* (London, 1898).

MARDRUS, J. C., *Le Livre des Mille Nuits et Une Nuit; trad. litterale et complete du texte Arabe* (Paris, 1900–4).

MATHERS, POWYS, *The Book of the Thousand Nights and One Night, Rendered from the Literal and Complete Version of Dr. J. C. Mardrus* (London, 1923).

PAYNE, JOHN, *The Book of the Thousand Nights and One Night* (London, 1882–4).

MAHDI, MUHSIN, *The 1001 Nights (Alf Layla wa-Layla) from the Earliest Known Sources* (Leiden, 1984).

ZIPES, JACK (ed.), *Arabian Nights: The Marvels and Wonders of the Thousand and One Nights*, adapted from Richard F. Burton's unexpurgated translation (New York, 1991).

Bibliography and General Criticism

BETTELHEIM, BRUNO, *The Uses of Enchantment: The Meaning and Importance of Fairy Tales* (New York, 1975).

BLEILER, EVERETT FRANKLIN, 'The Arabian Nights', in id. (ed.), *Supernatural Fiction Writers: Fantasy and Horror I, Apuleius to May Sinclair* (New York, 1985).

CARACCIOLO, PETER (ed.), *The Arabian Nights in English Literature: Studies in the Reception of* The Thousand and One Nights *into British Culture* (New York, 1988).

CLINTON, JEROME, 'Madness and Cure in the *1001 Nights*', *Studia Islamica*, 61 (1985), 107–25.

CONANT, MARTHA PIKE, *The Oriental Tale in England in the Eighteenth Century* (New York, 1908).

GERHARDT, MIA, *The Art of Story-Telling: A Literary Study of the Thousand and One Nights* (Leiden, 1963).

HANFORD, JAMES H., 'Open Sesame: Notes on the *Arabian Nights* in English', *Princeton University Library Chronicle*, 26 (1964–5), 48–56.

HOLE, RICHARD, *Remarks on the Arabian Nights' Entertainments* (London, 1797; repr. New York, 1970).

IRWIN, ROBERT, *The Arabian Nights: A Companion* (London, 1994).

LITTMANN, ENNO, 'Alf Layla wa-Layla', in H. A. R. Gibb, J. H. Kramers, *et al.* (eds.), *The Encyclopedia of Islam*, 2nd edn. (Leiden, 1954–), 358–64.

MACDONALD, DUNCAN B., 'A Bibliographical and Literary Study of the First Appearance of the *Arabian Nights* in Europe', *Literary Quarterly*, 2 (1932), 387–420.

NADDAFF, SANDRA, *Narrative Structure and the Aesthetics of Repetition in the 1001 Nights* (Evanston, Ill., 1991).

SAID, EDWARD, *Orientalism* (New York, 1979).

A SELECT CHRONOLOGY
OF THE LIFE OF ANTOINE GALLAND AND THE APPEARANCE OF THE *ARABIAN NIGHTS' ENTERTAINMENTS* IN EUROPE

1646 Antoine Galland born 6 April in the small village of Rollot, near Montdidier, in France.

1661 Enrolls in the Collège du Plessis in Paris, having first studied at the Collège de Noyon; remains in Paris for nine years, studying both philosophy and classical and oriental languages.

1670 Becomes secretary to the marquis de Nointel, Louis XIV's Ambassador to the Ottoman Empire. Arrives in Constantinople with Nointel on 21 October. He there perfects his knowledge of Turkish, Persian, and Arabic, and meets several famous travellers to the East, including Guillaume-Joseph Grelot, Jean Chardin, and Cornélio Magni.

1673 20 September, begins a lengthy journey throughout the Middle East, passing through the Greek isles, Syria, and Palestine, and including extended stays in Jerusalem, Aleppo, and Athens. Galland does not return to Smyrna until 8 January 1675.

1675 Returns to France, where his travels and experience in the East gain him access to the learned circles and literary salons of influential Parisian scholars, numismatists, and collectors of antiquities.

1677 Leaves Paris for a several months' visit to Smyrna, where he negotiates the purchase of antiquities for the collection of King Louis XIV. Returns to Paris in September 1678.

1679 Again leaves France for an extended stay in the East, remaining in Constantinople for more than five years. Travels throughout Greece and Egypt collecting coins, medallions, manuscripts, and other curiosities. Returns in December 1688, to spend the remainder of his life in France.

1689 Enjoys the patronage of Melchissedech Thévenot, the Bibliothèque du Roi. Begins a series of translations of Arabic texts.

1694 Engaged by Barthélémy d'Herbelot, a well-known specialist in oriental languages and professor at the Collège Royal, to assist in the preparation of his *Bibliothèque orientale, ou Dictionnaire universel contenant généralement tout ce qui regarde la connaisance des peuples de l'Orient*, a compendium of European knowledge of the geography, history, religion, literature, and customs of the East.

1695 December, death of Barthélémy d'Herbelot. Galland continues work on d'Herbelot's nearly completed *Bibliothèque orientale*, finally publishing the encyclopedic dictionary in February 1697.

1697 Enjoys the patronage and support of both Thierry Bignon and subsequently, in Caen, of Nicolas-Joseph Foucault, both orientalists famous for their libraries and collections.

1702 Begins translating, from an Arabic manuscript, the tale of 'Sindbad' and the stories which will form the earliest volumes of *Mille et Une Nuit*.

1704 January, publication of volume I of *Mille et Une Nuit*, by 'la Veuve de Claude Barbin'. Six more volumes of the collection appear by 1706. English translations of Galland's volumes appear very soon after their publication in French.

1706 September, returns permanently to Paris, still in the employ of Nicolas-Joseph Foucault.

1709 On 7 June named Professor of Arabic at the Collège Royal. An eighth volume of *Mille et Une Nuit*, containing some material translated by Galland and other stories rendered into French by fellow orientalist Pétis de la Croix, is published by 'la Veuve Ricœur' in the 'boutique de Claude Barbin'. On 25 March of the same year Galland had met a Maronite of Aleppo, called 'Hanna', at the home of the Eastern traveller Paul Lucas. For over two months Hanna provides him with further material for the final four volumes of *Mille et Une Nuit*.

1710 Translates the Koran into French.

1711 Completes his translations and retelling of the material to be included in volumes X and XI of *Mille et Une Nuit*; volumes IX and X are published the following year.

1715 17 February, dies in Paris aged 70.

1717 Publication of volumes XI and XII of *Mille et Une Nuit*. As was the case with Galland's earlier volumes, the tales are translated almost immediately into English.

ARABIAN NIGHTS' ENTERTAINMENTS

CONTENTS

(*Tales related within other stories have been indented*)

ARABIAN NIGHTS' ENTERTAINMENTS

THE chronicles of the Susanians,* the ancient kings of Persia, who extended their empire into the Indies, over all the islands therunto belonging, a great way beyond the Ganges and as far as China, acquaint us, that there was formerly a king of that potent family, the most excellent prince of his time; he was as much beloved by his subjects for his wisdom and prudence, as he was dreaded by his neighbours, because of his valour, and his warlike and well disciplined troops. He had two sons; the eldest, Schahriar, the worthy heir of his father, and endowed with all his virtues. The youngest, Schahzenan, was likewise a prince of incomparable merit.

After a long and glorious reign, the king died, and Schahriar mounted his throne. Schahzenan being excluded from all share of the government by the laws of the empire, and obliged to live a private life, was so far from envying the happiness of his brother, that he made it his whole business to please him, and effected it without much difficulty. Schahriar, who had naturally a great affection for that prince, was so charmed with his complaisance, that, out of an excess of friendship, he would needs divide his dominions with him; and he gave him the kingdom of Great Tartary. Schahzenan went immediately, and took possession of it; and fixed the seat of his government at Samarcande, the metropolis of the country.

After they had been separated ten years, Schahriar, having a passionate desire to see his brother, resolved to send an ambassador to invite him to his court. He made choice of his prime visier * for the embassy, sent him to Tartary with a retinue answerable to his dignity, and he made all possible haste to Samarcande. When he came near the city, Schahzenan had notice of it, and went to meet him with the principal lords of his court, who, to put the more honour on the sultan's minister, appeared in magnificent apparel. The king of Tartary received the ambassador with the greatest demonstrations of joy; and immediately asked him concerning the welfare of the sultan his brother. The visier having acquainted him that he was in health, gave him an account of his embassy. Schahzenan was so much affected with it, that he answered thus: Sage visier, the sultan my brother does me too much honour; he could propose nothing in the world so acceptable; I long as passionately to see him, as he does to see me. Time has been no more able to diminish my friendship, than his. My kingdom is in peace, and I desire no more than ten days to get myself ready to go with you. So that there is no necessity of your entering the city for so short a time; I pray you to pitch your tents here, and I will order provisions in abundance for yourself and your company.

The visier did accordingly; and as soon as the king returned, he sent him a prodigious quantity of provisions of all sorts, with presents of great value.

In the mean while Schahzenan made ready for his journey, took orders about his most important affairs, appointed a council to govern in his absence, and named a minister, of whose wisdom he had sufficient experience, and in whom he had entire confidence, to be their president. At the end of ten days his equipage being ready, he took his leave of the queen his wife, and went out of town in the evening with his retinue, pitching his royal pavilion near the visier's tent, and he discoursed with that ambassador till midnight: But willing once more to embrace the queen, whom he loved entirely, he returned alone to his palace, and went straight to her majesty's apartment; who, not expecting his return, had taken one of the meanest officers of the household to her bed, where they lay both fast asleep, having been in bed a considerable while.

The king entered without any noise, and pleased himself to think how he should surprise his wife, who he thought loved him as entirely as he did her; but how strange was his surprise, when by the light of the flambeaus, which burn all night in the apartments of those eastern princes, he saw a man in her arms! He stood immoveable for a time, not knowing how to believe his own eyes: but finding it was not to be doubted,—How! says he to himself, I am scarce out of my palace, and but just under the walls of Samarcande, and dare they put such an outrage upon me? Ah! perfidious wretches, your crime shall not go unpunished. As king, I am to punish wickedness committed in my dominions; and as an enraged husband, I must sacrifice you to my just resentment. In a word, this unfortunate prince, giving way to his rage, drew his scymetar,* and approaching the bed, killed them both with one blow, turning their sleep into death; and afterwards taking them up, threw them out of a window into the ditch that surrounded the palace.

Having avenged himself thus, he went out of town privately, as he came into it; and returning to his pavilion, without saying one word of what had happened, he ordered the tents to be struck, and to make ready for his journey. This was speedily done; and before day he began his march, with kettle-drums and other instruments of music, that filled every one with joy except the king, who was so much troubled at the disloyalty of his wife, that he was seized with extreme melancholy, which preyed upon him during his whole journey.

When he drew near the capital of the Indies, the sultan Schahriar and all his court came out to meet him: the princes were overjoyed to see one another; and alighting, after mutual embraces and other marks of affection and respect, they mounted again, and entered the city, with the acclamations of vast multitudes of people. The sultan conducted his brother to a palace he had provided for him, which had a communication with his own by means of a garden; and was so much the more magnificent, for it was set apart as a banquetting-house for public entertainment, and other diversions of the court, and the splendour of it had been lately augmented by new furniture.

Schahriar immediately left the king of Tartary, that he might give him time to bathe himself, and to change his apparel. And as soon as he had done, he came to him again, and they sat down together upon a sofa or alcove.* The courtiers kept at a distance, out of respect; and those two princes entertained one another suitably to their friendship, their nearness of blood, and the long separation that had been betwixt them. The time of supper being come, they eat together; after which they renewed their conversation, which continued till Schahriar, perceiving that it was very late, left his brother to his rest.

The unfortunate Schahzenan went to bed; and though the conversation of his brother had suspended his grief for some time, it returned upon him with more violence; so that, instead of taking his necessary rest, he tormented himself with cruel reflections. All the circumstances of his wife's disloyalty presented themselves afresh to his imagination, in so lively a manner, that he was like one beside himself. In a word, not being able to sleep, he got up, and giving himself over to afflicting thoughts, they made such an impression upon his countenance, that the sultan could not but take notice of it, and said thus to himself; What can be the matter with the king of Tartary, that he is so melancholy; Has he any cause to complain of his reception? No surely; I have received him as a brother whom I love, so that I can charge myself with no omission in that respect. Perhaps it grieves him to be at such a distance from his dominions, or from the queen his wife: Alas! if that be the matter, I must forthwith give him the presents I designed for him, that he may return to Samarcande when he pleases. Accordingly next day Schahriar sent him part of those presents, being the greatest rarities and the richest things that the Indies could afford. At the same time he endeavoured to divert his brother every day by new objects of pleasure, and the finest treats; which, instead of giving the king of Tartary any ease, did only increase his sorrow.

One day, Schahriar having appointed a great hunting-match, about two days journey from his capital, in a place that abounded with deer; Schahzenan prayed him to excuse him, for his health would not allow him to bear him company. The sultan, unwilling to put any constraint upon him, left him at liberty, and went a-hunting with his nobles. The king of Tartary being thus left alone, shut himself up in his apartment, and sat down at a window that looked into the garden: That delicious place, and the sweet harmony of an infinite number of birds, which chose it for a place of retreat, must certainly have diverted him, had he been capable of taking pleasure in any thing; but being perpetually tormented with the fatal remembrance of his queen's infamous conduct, his eyes were not so often fixed upon the garden, as lifted up to heaven to bewail his misfortune.

Whilst he was thus swallowed up with grief, an object presented itself to his view, which quickly turned his thoughts another way. A secret gate of the sultan's palace opened all of a sudden, and there came out at it twenty women, in the midst of whom marched the sultaness, who was easily distinguished from the rest, by her majestic air. This princess, thinking that the king of Tartary was gone a-hunting with his brother the sultan, came up with her retinue near the windows of his apartment; for the prince had placed himself so, that he could see all that passed in the garden, without being perceived himself. He observed, that the persons who accompanied the sultaness threw off their veils and long robes, that they might be at more freedom; but he was wonderfully surprised when he saw ten of them blacks, and that each of them took his mistress. The sultaness, on her part, was not long without her gallant. She clapped her hands, and called Masoud, Masoud; and immediately a black came down from a tree, and ran to her in all haste.

Modesty will not allow, nor is it necessary, to relate what passed betwixt the blacks and the ladies. It is sufficient to say, that Schahzenan saw enough to convince him, that his brother had as much cause to complain as himself. This amorous company continued together till midnight, and having bathed altogether in a great pond, which was one of the chief ornaments of the garden, they dressed themselves, and re-entered the palace by the secret door, all except Masoud, who climbed up his tree, and got over the garden-wall the same way as he came.

All this having passed in the king of Tartary's sight, it gave him occasion to make a number of reflections. How little reason had I, says he, to think that no one was so unfortunate as myself? It is certainly the unavoidable fate of all husbands, since the sultan, my brother, who is sovereign of so many dominions, and the greatest prince of the earth, could not escape it. The case being so, what a fool am I to kill myself with grief? I will throw it off, and the remembrance of a misfortune so common shall never after this disturb my quiet. So that from that moment he forbore afflicting himself. Being unwilling to sup till he saw the whole scene that was acted under his window, he called then for his supper, eat with a better appetite than he had done at any time since his coming from Samarcande, and listened with pleasure to the agreeable concert of vocal and instrumental musick, that was appointed to entertain him while at table.

He continued after this to be of a very good humour; and when he knew that the sultan was returning, he went to meet him, and paid him his compliments with a great deal of gaiety. Schahriar at first took no notice of this great alteration; but expostulated with him modestly, why he would not bear him company at hunting the stag; and without giving him time to reply, entertained him with the great number of deer and other game they had killed, and what pleasure he had in the sport. Schahzenan heard him with attention, gave answers to every thing, and being rid of that melancholy, which formerly over-clouded his wit, he said a thousand agreeable and pleasant things to the sultan.

Schahriar, who expected to have found him in the same condition as he left him, was overjoyed to see him so cheerful, and spoke to him thus: Dear brother, I return thanks to heaven for the happy change it has made in you during my absence; I am extremely rejoiced at it; but I have a request to make to you, and conjure you not to deny me. I can refuse you nothing, replies the king of Tartary, you may command Schahzenan as you please: pray speak, I am impatient till I know what it is you desire of me. Ever since you came to my court, replies Schahriar, I found you swallowed up by a deep melancholy, and I did in vain attempt to remove it by diversions of all sorts. I imagined it might be occasioned by reason of your distance from your dominions; or that love might have a great share in it; and that the queen of Samarcande, who, no doubt, is an accomplished beauty, might be the cause of it. I do not know if I be mistaken; but I must own, that this was the particular reason why I would not importune you upon the subject, for fear of making you uneasy. But without my being able to contribute any thing towards it, I find now, upon my return, that you are in the best humour that can be, and that your mind is entirely delivered from that black vapour which disturbed it. Pray do me the favour to tell me why you were so melancholy, and how you came to be rid of it.

Upon this the king of Tartary continued for some time as if he had been in a dream, and contrived what he should answer; but at last replied as follows: You are my sultan and master; but excuse me, I beseech you, from answering your question. No, dear brother, said the sultan, you must answer, I will take no denial. Schahzenan, not being able to withstand these pressing instances, answered, Well then, brother, I will satisfy you, since you command me; and having told him the story of the queen of Samarcande's treachery, this, says he, was the cause of my grief: pray judge, whether I had not reason enough to give myself up to it.

O! my brother, says the sultan (in a tone which shewed that he had the same sentiments of the matter with the king of Tartary) what a horrible story do you tell me! How impatient was I till I heard it out! I commend you for punishing the traitors who put an outrage upon you. Nobody can blame you for that action; it was just: and for my part, had the case been mine, I could scarce have been so moderate as you, I should not have satisfied myself with the life of one woman; I verily think I should have sacrificed a thousand to my fury. I cease now to wonder at your melancholy. The cause of it was too sensible, and too mortifying, not to make you yield to it. O heaven! what a strange adventure! nor do I believe the like of it ever befel any man but yourself. But in short, I must bless God, who has comforted you; and since I doubt not but your consolation is well-grounded, be so good as to let me know what it is, and conceal nothing from me. Schahzenan was not so easily prevailed upon in this point, as he had been in the other, because of his brother's concern in it. But being obliged to yield to his pressing instances, answered, I must obey you then, since your command is absolute; yet am afraid that my obedience will occasion your trouble to be greater than ever mine was. But you must blame yourself for it, since you force me to reveal a thing which I should otherwise have buried in eternal oblivion. What you say, answers Schahriar, serves only to encrease my curiosity. Make haste to discover the secret, whatever it be. The king of Tartary, being no longer able to refuse, gave him the particulars of all that he had seen of the blacks in disguise, of the lewd passion of the sultaness and her ladies; and to be sure, he did not forget Masoud. After having been witness to those infamous actions, says he, I believed all women to be that way naturally inclined; and that they could not resist those violent desires. Being of this opinion, it seemed to me to be an unaccountable weakness in men to make themselves uneasy at their infidelity. This reflection brought many others along with it; and, in short, I thought the best thing I could do was to make myself easy. It cost me some pains indeed, but at last I effected it; and if you will take my advice, you shall follow my example.

Though the advice was good, the sultan could not take it; but fell into a rage. What! says he, is the sultaness of the Indies capable of prostituting herself in so base a manner? No, brother, I cannot believe what you say, except I saw it with my own eyes: yours must needs have deceived you; the matter is so important, that I must be satisfied of it myself. Dear brother, answers Schahzenan, that you may without much difficulty. Appoint another hunting-match, and when we are out of town with your court and mine, we will stop under our pavilions, and at night let you and I return alone to my apartment; I am certain that next day you will see what I saw. The sultan approving the stratagem, immediately appointed a new hunting-match: and that same day the pavilions were set up at the place appointed.

Next day the two princes set out with all their retinue: they arrived at the place of encampment, and staid there till night. Then Schahriar called his grand visier, and without acquainting him with his design, commanded him to stay in his place during his absence, and to suffer no person to go out of the camp upon any account whatever. As soon as he had given this order, the king of Grand Tartary and he took horse, passed through the camp incognito, returned to the city, and went to Schahzenan's apartment. They had scarce placed themselves in the same window where the king of Tartary had seen the disguised blacks act their scene; but the secret gate opened, the sultaness and her ladies entered the garden with the blacks, and she having called upon Masoud, the sultan saw more than enough to convince him plainly of his dishonour and misfortune.

O heavens, cried he, what an indignity! what horror! can the wife of a sovereign, such as I am, be capable of such an infamous action? after this, let no prince boast of his being perfectly happy. Alas! my brother, continues he (embracing the king of Tartary) let us both renounce the world; honesty is banished out of it; if it flatters us the one day, it betrays us the next; let us abandon our dominions and grandeur; let us go into foreign countries, where we may lead an obscure life, and conceal our misfortune. Schahzenan did not at all approve of this resolution, but did not think fit to contradict Schahriar in the heat of his passion: Dear brother, says he, your will shall be mine; I am ready to follow you whither you please: but promise that you will return, if we can meet with any one that is more unhappy than ourselves. I agree to it, says the sultan, but doubt much whether we shall. I am not of your mind in this, replies the king of Tartary; I fancy our journey will be but short. Having said this, they went secretly out of the palace by another way than they came. They travelled as long as it was day, and lay the first night under the trees; and getting up about break of day, they went on till they came to a fine meadow upon the bank of the sea, in which meadow there were tufts of great trees at some distance from one another. They sat down under those trees to rest and refresh themselves, and the chief subject of their conversation was the lewdness of their wives.

They had not sat long, before they heard a frightful noise, and a terrible cry from the sea, which filled them with fear; then the sea opening, there rose up a thing like a great black column, which reached almost to the clouds. This redoubled their fear, made them rise speedily, and climb up into a tree to hide themselves. They had scarce got up, still looking to the place from whence the noise came, and where the sea opened, when they observed that the black column advanced, winding about towards the shore, cleaving the water before it. They could not at first think what it should be; but in a little time they found, that it was one of those malignant genies,* that are mortal enemies to mankind, and always doing them mischief. He was black, frightful, had the shape of a giant, of a prodigious stature, and carried on his head a great glass box, shut with four locks of fine steel. He entered the meadow with his burden, which he laid down just at the foot of the tree where the two princes were, who looked upon themselves to be dead men. Mean while, the Genie sat down by his box, and opening it with four keys that he had at his girdle, there came out a lady magnificently apparelled, of a majestic stature, and a complete beauty. The monster made her sit down by him; and eyeing her with an amorous look, Lady (says he,) nay, most accomplished of all ladies who are admired for their beauty, my charming mistress, whom I carried off on your wedding day, and have loved so constantly ever since, let me sleep a few moments by you; for I found myself so very sleepy, that I came to this place to take a rest. Having spoke thus, he laid down his huge head on the lady's knees; and stretching out his legs, which reached as far as the sea, he fell asleep, and snored so that he made the banks to echo again.

The lady happening at the same time to look up to the tree, saw the two princes, and made a sign to them with her hand to come down without making any noise. Their fear was extraordinary, when they found themselves discovered; and they prayed the lady, by other signs, to excuse them; but she, after having laid the monster's head softly down, rose up, and spoke to them with a low but quick voice, to come down to her; she would take no denial. They made signs to her that they were afraid of the Genie, and would fain have been excused. Upon which she ordered them to come down, and if they did not make haste, threatened to awake the genie, and bid him kill them.

These words did so much intimidate the princes, that they began to come down with all possible precaution, lest they should awake the genie. When they had come down, the lady took them by the hand, and going a little farther with them under the trees, made a very urgent proposal to them. At first they rejected it, but she obliged them to accept it by her threats. Having obtained what she desired, she perceived that each of them had a ring on his finger, which she demanded of them. As soon as she received them, she went and took a box out of the bundle, where her toilet was, pulled out a string of other rings of all sorts, which she showed them, and asked them if they knew what those jewels meant? No, say they, we hope you will be pleased to tell us. These are, replies she, the rings of all the men to whom I have granted my favour. They are full fourscore and eighteen of them, which I keep as tokens to remember them; and asked yours for the same reason, to make up my hundred. So that, continues she, I have had an hundred gallants already, notwithstanding the vigilance of this wicked genie, that never leaves me. He is much the nearer for locking me up in this glass box, and hiding me in the bottom of the sea; I find a way to cheat him for all his care. You may see by this, that when a woman has formed a project, there is no husband or gallant that can hinder her putting it in execution. Men had better not put their wives under such restraint, if they have a mind they should be chaste.—Having spoke thus to them, she put their rings upon the same string with the rest, and sitting her down by the monster, as before, laid his head again upon her lap, and made a sign for the princes to be gone.

They returned immediately by the same way they came; and when they were out of sight of the lady and the Genie, Schahriar says to Schahzenan, Well, brother, what do you think of this adventure? Has not the Genie a very faithful mistress? And do you not agree that there is no wickedness equal to that of women? Yes, brother, answers the king of Great Tartary; and you must also agree, that the monster is more unfortunate, and has more reason to complain than we. Therefore, since we have found what we sought for, let us return to our dominions, and let not this hinder us to marry again. For my part I know a method by which I think I shall keep inviolable the faith that any wife shall plight to me. I will say no more of it at present, but you will hear of it in a little time, and I am sure you will follow my example. The sultan agreed with his brother: and continuing their journey, they arrived in the camp the third night after they left it.

The news of the sultan's return being spread, the courtiers came betimes in the morning before his pavilion to wait on him. He ordered them to enter, received them with a more pleasant air than formerly, and gave each of them a gratification. After which he told them he would go no farther, ordered them to take horse, and return speedily to his palace.

As soon as ever he arrived, he ran to the sultaness's apartment, commanded her to be bound before him, and delivered her to his grand visier, with an order to strangle her; which was accordingly executed by that minister, without enquiring into her crime. The enraged prince did not stop here; he cut off the heads of all the sultaness's ladies with his own hand. After this rigorous punishment, being persuaded that no woman was chaste, he resolved, in order to prevent the disloyalty of such as he should afterwards marry, to wed one every night, and have her strangled next morning. Having imposed this cruel law upon himself, he swore that he would observe it immediately after the departure of the king of Tartary, who speedily took leave of him, and being loaded with magnificent presents, set forward on his journey.

Schahzenan being gone, Schahriar ordered his grand visier to bring him the daughter of one of his generals. The visier obeyed; the sultan lay with her, and putting her next morning into his hands again, in order to be strangled, commanded him to get him another next night. Whatever reluctance the visier had to put such orders into execution, as he owed blind obedience to the sultan his master, he was forced to submit. He brought him the daughter of a subaltern,* whom he also cut off next day. After her he brought a citizen's daughter; and in a word, there was every day a maid married, and a wife murdered.

The rumour of this unparalleled barbarity occasioned a general consternation in the city, where there was nothing but crying and lamentation. Here a father in tears, and inconsolable for the loss of his daughter; and there tender mothers dreading lest theirs should have the same fate, making the air to resound beforehand with their groans. So that instead of the commendations and blessings which the sultan had hitherto received from his subjects, their mouths were now filled with imprecations against him.

The grand visier, who, as has been already said, was the executioner of this horrid injustice against his will, had two daughters, the eldest called Scheherazade, and the youngest Dinarzade; the latter was a lady of very great merit; but the elder had courage, wit, and penetration infinitely above her sex; she had read abundance, and had such a prodigious memory, that she never forgot any thing. She had successfully applied herself to philosophy, physic, history, and the liberal arts; and for verse, exceeded the best poets of her time; besides this, she was a perfect beauty, and all her fine qualifications were crowned with solid virtue.

The visier passionately loved a daughter so worthy of his tender affection; and one day, as they were discoursing together, she says to him, Father, I have one favour to beg of you, and most humbly pray you to grant it me. I will not refuse it, answers he, providing it be just and reasonable. For the justice of it, says she, there can be no question, and you may judge of it by the motive which obliges me to demand it of you. I have a design to stop the course of that barbarity which the sultan exercises upon the families of this city. I would dispel those unjust fears which so many mothers have of losing their daughters in such a fatal manner. Your design, daughter, replies the visier, is very commendable; but the disease you would remedy seems to me incurable; how do you pretend to effect it? Father, says Scheherazade, since by your means the sultan makes every day a new marriage, I conjure you by the tender affection you bear to me, to procure me the honour of his bed. The visier could not hear this without horror.—O heavens! replied he, in a passion, have you lost your senses, daughter, that you make such a dangerous request to me? You know the sultan has sworn by his soul, that he will never lie above one night with the same woman, and to order her to be killed the next morning; and would you that I should propose you to him?

Pray consider well to what your indiscreet zeal will expose you. Yes, dear father, replies the virtuous daughter, I know the risk I run; but that does not frighten me. If I perish, my death will be glorious, and if I succeed, I shall do my country an important piece of service. No, no, says the visier, whatever you can represent to engage me to let you throw yourself into that horrible danger, do not you think that ever I will agree to it. When the sultan shall order me to strike my poniard into your heart, alas! I must obey him; and what a dismal employment is that for a father? Ah! if you do not fear death, yet at least be afraid of occasioning me the mortal grief of seeing my hand stained with your blood. Once more, father, says Scheherazade, grant me the favour I beg. Your stubbornness, replies the visier, will make me angry; why will you run headlong to your ruin? They that do not foresee the end of a dangerous enterprise, can never bring it to a happy issue. I am afraid the same thing will happen to you, that happened to the ass, which was well, and could not keep himself so. What misfortune befel the ass? replies Scheherazade. I will tell you, says the visier, if you will hear me.

The Fable of the Ass, the Ox, and the Labourer

A VERY rich merchant had several country-houses, where he had abundance of cattle of all sorts. He went with his wife and family to one of those estates, in order to improve it himself. He had the gift of understanding the language of beasts; but with this condition, that he should interpret it to nobody on pain of death; and this hindered him to communicate to others what he had learned by means of this gift.

He had, in the same stall, an ox and an ass; and one day as he sat near them, and diverted himself to see his children play about him, he heard the ox say to the ass, Sprightly, O how happy do I think you, when I consider the ease you enjoy, and the little labour that is required of you! you are carefully rubbed down and washed; you have well dressed corn, and fresh clean water. Your greatest business is to carry the merchant our master, when he has any little journey to make; and were it not for that, you would be perfectly idle. It is scarce day-light when I am fastened to the plough, and there they make me work till night, to till up the ground, which fatigues me so, that sometimes my strength fails me. Besides, the labourer, who is always behind me, beats me continually. By drawing the plough my tail is all flea'd; and in short, after having laboured from morning till night, when I am brought in, they give me nothing but sorry dry beans, not so much as cleansed from sand, or other things as pernicious; and to heighten my misery, when I have filled my belly with such ordinary stuff, I am forced to lie all night in my own dung; so that you see I have reason to envy your lot.

The ass did not interrupt the ox, till he had said all that he had a mind to say; but when he had made an end, answered, They that call you a foolish beast do not lie: you are too simple, you let them carry you whither they please, and shew no manner of resolution. In the mean time, what advantage do you reap by all the indignities you suffer? You kill yourself for the ease, pleasure, and profit of those that give you no thanks for so doing. But they would not treat you so, if you had as much courage as strength. When they come to fasten you to the stall, why do not you make resistance? why do not you strike them with your horns, and shew them that you are angry, by striking your foot against the ground? and, in short, why do you not frighten them by bellowing aloud? Nature has furnished you with the means to procure you respect, but you do not make use of them. They bring you sorry beans and bad straw; eat none of them, only smell to them, and leave them. If you follow the advice I give you, you will quickly find a change, for which you will thank me. The ox took the ass's advice in very good part, and owned he was much obliged to him for it.

Dear Sprightly, adds he, I will not fail to do all that you have said, and you shall see how I shall acquit myself. They held their peace after this discourse, of which the merchant heard every word.

Next morning betimes, the labourer comes to take the ox: he fastened him to the plough, and carried him to his ordinary work. The ox, who had not forgot the ass's counsel, was very troublesome and untowardly all that day; and in the evening, when the labourer brought him back to the stall, and began to fasten him to it, the malicious beast, instead of presenting his horns willingly as he used to do, was restive, and went backward bellowing; and then made at the labourer as if he would have pushed him with his horns: in a word, he did all that the ass advised him to. Next day the labourer came as usual, to take the ox to his labour; but finding the stall full of beans, the straw that he put in the night before not touched, and the ox lying on the ground with his legs stretched out, and panting in a strange manner, he believed him to be sick, pitied him, and thinking that it was not proper to carry him to work, went immediately and acquainted the merchant with it.

The merchant perceiving that the ox had followed all the mischievous advices of the ass, whom he thought fit to punish for it, he ordered the labourer to go and put the ass in the ox's place, and to be sure to work him hard. The labourer did so; the ass was forced to draw the plough all that day; which fatigued him so much the more, as he was not accustomed to that sort of labour; besides, he had been so soundly beat, that he could scarce stand when he came back.

Mean while, the ox was mightily pleased, he eat up all that was in his stall, and rested himself the whole day. He was glad at the heart that he had followed the ass's advice, blessed him a thousand times for it, and did not fail to compliment him upon it, when he saw him come back. The ass answered him not one word, so vexed was he to be so ill treated; but says within himself, It is by my own imprudence I have brought this misfortune upon myself; I lived happily, everything smiled upon me. I had all that I could wish, it is my own fault that I am brought to this miserable condition; and if I cannot contrive some way to get out of it, I am certainly undone; and as he spoke thus, his strength was so much exhausted, that he fell down at his stall, as if he had been half dead.

Here the grand visier addressed himself to Scheherazade, and said, Daughter, you do just like the ass; you will expose yourself to destruction by your false prudence. Take my advice, be easy, and do not take such measures as will hasten your death. Father, replies Scheherazade, the example you bring me is not capable of making me change my resolution; I will never cease importuning you until you present me to the sultan to be his bride. The visier perceiving that she persisted in her demand, replied, Alas then! since you will continue obstinate, I shall be obliged to treat you in the same manner as the merchant I named just now, treated his wife in a little time after.

The merchant, understanding that the ass was in a lamentable condition, was curious to know what passed betwixt him and the ox; therefore, after supper, he went out by moon-light, and sat down by them, his wife bearing him company. When he arrived, he heard the ass say to the ox, Comrade, tell me, I pray you, what you intend to do to-morrow, when the labourer brings you meat? What will I do? says the ox; I will continue to do as you taught me. I will go off from him, and threaten him with my horns, as I did yesterday; I will feign myself to be sick, and just ready to die. Beware of that, replies the ass, it will ruin you: for as I came home this evening, I heard the merchant, our master, say something that makes me tremble for you. Alas! what did you hear? says the ox; as you love me, hide nothing from me, my dear Sprightly. Our master, replied the ass, had these sad expressions to the labourer: since the ox does not eat, and is not able to work, I would have him killed to-morrow, and we will give his flesh as an alms to the poor for God's sake; as for his skin, that will be of use to us, and I would have you give it to the currier* to dress; therefore do not fail, but send for the butcher. This is what I had to tell you, says the ass. The concern I have for your preservation, and my friendship for you, obliged me to let you know it, and to give you new advice. As soon as they bring you your bran and straw, rise up and eat heartily. Our master will by this think that you are cured, and no doubt will recall his orders for killing you; whereas if you do otherwise, you are certainly gone.

This discourse had the effect which the ass designed. The ox was strangely troubled at it, and bellowed out for fear. The merchant, who heard the discourse very attentively, fell into such a fit of laughter, that his wife was surprised at it, and said, Pray, husband, tell me what you laugh at so heartily, that I may laugh with you. Wife, says he, you must content yourself with hearing me laugh. No, replies she, I will know the reason. I cannot give you that satisfaction, answers he, but only that I laugh at what our ass just now said to our ox. The rest is a secret, which I am not allowed to reveal. And what hinders you from revealing the secret, says she? If I tell it you, answers he, it will cost me my life. You only jeer me, cried his wife; what you tell me now cannot be true. If you do not satisfy me presently what you laugh at, and tell me what the ox and ass said to one another, I swear by heaven, that you and I shall never bed again.

Having spoke thus, she went into the house in a great fret, and setting herself in a corner, cried there all night. Her husband lay alone, and finding next morning that she continued in the same humour, told her, she was a very foolish woman to afflict herself in that manner, the thing was not worth so much; and that it did concern her as little to know the matter, as it concerned him much to keep it secret: therefore I conjure you, said he, to think no more of it. I shall still think so much of it, says she, as never to forbear weeping till you have satisfied my curiosity. But I tell you very seriously, replied he, that it will cost me my life, if I yield to your indiscretion. Let what will happen, says she, I do insist upon it. I perceive, says the merchant, that it is impossible to bring you to reason; and since I foresee that you will occasion your own death by your obstinacy, I will call in your children, that they may see you before you die. Accordingly he called for them; and sent for her father and mother, and other relations. When they were come, and heard the reason of their being called for, they did all they could to convince her that she was in the wrong, but to no purpose: she told them, she would rather die than yield that point to her husband. Her father and mother spoke to her by herself, and told her that what she desired to know was of no importance to her; but they could gain nothing upon her, either by their authority or intreaties. When her children saw that nothing would prevail to bring her out of that sullen temper, they wept bitterly. The merchant himself was like a man out of his senses; and was almost ready to risk his own life, to save that of his wife, whom he loved dearly.

Now, my daughter, says the visier to Scheherazade, this merchant had fifty hens, and a cock, with a dog that gave good heed to all that passed; and while the merchant was set down, as I said, and considering what he had best to do, he sees his dog run towards the cock, as he was treading a hen, and heard him speak to him thus: Cock, says he, I am sure heaven will not let you live long; are you not ashamed to do that thing to-day? The cock standing up on tiptoe, answers the dog fiercely, And why should I not do it to-day as well as other days? If you do not know, replies the dog, then I tell you, that this day our master is in great perplexity. His wife would have him reveal a secret, which is of such a nature, that it will cost him his life if he doth it. Things are come to that pass, that it is to be feared he will scarcely have resolution enough to resist his wife's obstinacy; for he loves her, and is affected with the tears that she continually sheds, and perhaps it may cost him his life. We are all alarmed at it, and you only insult our melancholy, and have the impudence to divert yourself with your hens.

The cock answered the dog's reproof thus: What! has our master so little sense? He has but one wife and cannot govern her; and though I have fifty, I make them all do what I please. Let him make use of his reason, he will speedily find a way to rid himself of his trouble. How, says the dog, what would you have him do? Let him go into the room where his wife is, says the cock, lock the door, and take a good stick and thrash her well, and I will answer for it, that will bring her to her right wits, and make her forbear to ask him any more what he ought not to tell her. The merchant had no sooner heard what the cock said, but he took up a good stick, went to his wife, whom he found still a-crying, and shutting the door, belaboured her so soundly, that she cried out, It is enough, husband, it is enough, let me alone, and I will never ask the question more. Upon this, perceiving that she repented of her impertinent curiosity, he forbore drubbing her; and opening the door, her friends came in, were glad to find her cured of her obstinacy, and complimented her husband upon this happy expedient to bring his wife to reason. Daughter, adds the grand visier, you deserve to be treated as the merchant treated his wife.

Father, replies Scheherazade, I beg you would not take it ill that I persist in my opinion. I am nothing moved by the story of that woman. I can tell you abundance of others, to persuade you that you ought not to oppose my design. Besides, pardon me for declaring to you, that your opposing me would be in vain; for if your paternal affection should hinder you to grant my request, I would go and offer myself to the sultan. In short, the father being overcome by the resolution of his daughter, yielded to her importunity; and though he was very much grieved that he could not divert her from such a fatal resolution, he went that minute to acquaint the sultan, that next night he would bring him Scheherazade.

The sultan was much surprised at the sacrifice which the grand visier made to him. How could you resolve upon it, says he, to bring me your own daughter? Sir, answers the visier, it is her own offer. The sad destiny that attends it could not scare her; she prefers the honour of being your majesty's wife one night, to her life. But do not mistake yourself, visier, says the sultan; to-morrow, when I put Scheherazade into your hands, I expect you should take away her life: and if you fail, I swear that yourself shall die. Sir, rejoins the visier, my heart without doubt will be full of grief to execute your commands: but it is to no purpose for nature to murmur: though I be her father, I will answer for the fidelity of my hand to obey your order. Schahriar accepted his minister's offer, and told him he might bring his daughter when he pleased.

The grand visier went with the news to Scheherazade, who received it with as much joy, as if it had been the most agreeable thing in the world: she thanked her father for having obliged her in so sensible a manner; and perceiving that he was overwhelmed with grief, she told him, in order to his consolation, that she hoped he would never repent his having married her to the sultan; but that, on the contrary, he would have cause to rejoice in it all his days.

All her business was to put herself in a condition to appear before the sultan; but before she went, she took her sister Dinarzade apart, and says to her, My dear sister, I have need of your help in a matter of very great importance, and must pray you not to deny it me. My father is going to carry me to the sultan to be his wife; do not let this frighten you, but hear me with patience. As soon as I come to the sultan, I will pray him to allow you to lie in the bride-chamber, that I may enjoy your company this one night more. If I obtain that favour, as I hope to do, remember to awake me to-morrow, an hour before day, and to address me in these or some such words: My sister, if you be not asleep, I pray you, that till day break, which will be very speedily, you would tell me one of the fine stories of which you have read so many. Immediately I will tell you one; and I hope by this means to deliver the city from the consternation they are under at present. Dinarzade answered, that she would obey with pleasure what she required of her.

The time of going to bed being come, the grand visier conducted Scheherazade to the palace, and retired, after having introduced her into the sultan's apartment. As soon as the sultan was left alone with her, he ordered her to uncover her face, and found it so beautiful, that he was perfectly charmed with her; and perceiving her to be in tears, asked her the reason. Sir, answered Scheherazade, I have a sister, who loves me tenderly, as I do her, and I could wish that she might be allowed to be all night in this chamber, that I might see her, and bid her once more adieu: Will you be pleased to allow me the comfort of giving her this last testimony of my friendship? Schahriar having consented to it, Dinarzade was sent for, who came with all possible diligence. The sultan went to bed with Scheherazade upon an alcove raised very high, according to the custom of the monarchs of the east; and Dinarzade lay in a bed that was prepared for her near the foot of the alcove.

An hour before day, Dinarzade being awake, failed not to do as her sister ordered her. My dear sister, cries she, if you be not asleep, I pray, until day-break, which will be in a very little time, that you will tell me one of those pleasant stories you have read; alas! this may, perhaps, be the last time that ever I shall have that satisfaction.

Scheherazade, instead of answering her sister, addressed herself to the sultan, thus: Sir, will your majesty be pleased to allow me to give my sister this satisfaction? With all my heart, answers the sultan. Then Scheherazade bid her sister listen, and afterwards addressing herself to Schahriar, began thus.

THE FIRST NIGHT.

The Merchant and the Genie

SIR,—There was formerly a merchant, who had a great estate in lands, goods and money. He had abundance of deputies, factors,* and slaves. He was obliged from time to time to take journies, and talk with his correspondents; and one day being under a necessity of going a long journey, about an affair of importance, he took horse, and put a portmanteau behind him, with some biscuits and dates, because he had a great desart to pass over, where he could have no manner of provisions. He arrived without any accident at the end of his journey, and having dispatched his affairs, took horse again, in order to return home.

The fourth day of his journey, he was so much incommoded by the heat of the sun, and the reflection of that heat from the earth, that he turned out of the road to refresh himself under some trees that he saw in the country. There he found at the root of a great walnut tree, a fountain of very clear running water; and alighting, tied his horse to a branch of the tree, and sitting down by the fountain, took some biscuits and dates out of his portmanteau, and as he eat his dates, threw the shells about on both sides of him. When he had done eating, being a good Mussulman,* he washed his hands, his face, and his feet, and said his prayers. He had not made an end, but was still on his knees, when he saw a Genie appear, all white with age, and of a monstrous bulk; who advancing towards him with a scymitar in his hand, spoke to him in a terrible voice thus: Rise up, that I may kill thee with this scymitar, as you have killed my son; and accompanied those words with a frightful cry. The merchant, being as much frightened at the hideous shape of the monster, as at those threatening words, answered him trembling: Alas! my good lord, of what crime can I be guilty towards you, that you should take away my life? I will, replies the genie, kill thee, as thou hast killed my son. O heaven! says the merchant, how should I kill your son? I did not know him, nor ever saw him. Did not you sit down when you came hither? replies the genie; did not you take dates out of your portmanteau, and as you eat them, did not you throw the shells about on both sides? I did all that you say, answers the merchant, I cannot deny it. If it be so, replies the genie, I tell thee, that thou hast killed my son; and the way was thus: when you threw your nut-shells about, my son was passing by, and you threw one of them into his eye, which killed him; therefore I must kill thee. Ah! my lord, pardon me! cried the merchant. No pardon, answers the genie, no mercy. Is it not just, to kill him that has killed another? I agree to it, says the merchant; but certainly I never killed your son, and if I have, it was unknown to me, and I did it innocently: therefore I beg you to pardon me, and to suffer me to live. No, no, says the genie, persisting in his resolution, I must kill thee, since thou hast killed my son; and then taking the merchant by the arm, threw him with his face upon the ground, and lifted up his scymitar to cut off his head.

The merchant, all in tears, protested he was innocent, bewailed his wife and children, and spoke to the genie in the most moving expressions that could be uttered. The genie, with his scymitar still lifted up, had so much patience, as to hear the wretch make an end of his lamentations, but would not relent. All this whining, says the monster, is to no purpose; though you should shed tears of blood, that shall not hinder me to kill thee, as thou killed'st my son. Why, replied the merchant, can nothing prevail with you? Will you absolutely take away the life of a poor innocent? Yes, replied the genie, I am resolved upon it.

As Scheherazade had spoke those words, perceiving it was day, and knowing that the sultan rose betimes in the morning to say his prayers, and hold his council, Scheherazade held her peace. Lord, sister, says Dinarzade, what a wonderful story is this! The remainder of it, says Scheherazade, is more surprising; and you will be of my mind, if the sultan will let me live this day, and permit me to tell it out next night. Schahriar, who had listened to Scheherazade with pleasure, says to himself, I will stay till to-morrow, for I can at any time put her to death, when she has made an end of her story.

So having resolved not to take away Scheherazade's life that day, he rose and went to his prayers, and then called his council.

All this while the grand visier was terribly uneasy. Instead of sleeping, he spent the night in sighs and groans, bewailing the lot of his daughter, of whom he believed that he himself should be the executioner. And as, in this melancholy prospect, he was afraid of seeing the sultan, he was agreeably surprised, when he saw the prince enter the council-chamber, without giving him the fatal orders he expected.

The sultan, according to his custom, spent the day in regulating his affairs: and when night came, he went to bed with Scheherazade. Next morning before day, Dinarzade failed not to address herself to her sister, thus: My dear sister, if you be not asleep, I pray you, till day-break, which must be in a very little time, to go on with the story you began last night. The sultan, without staying till Scheherazade asked him leave, bid her make an end of the story of the Genie and the Merchant, for he longed to hear the issue of it; upon which Scheherazade spoke, and continued the story as follows.

THE SECOND NIGHT.

WHEN the merchant saw that the genie was going to cut off his head, he cried out aloud, and said, For heaven's sake, hold your hand! allow me one word, be so good as to grant me some respite: allow me but time to bid my wife and children adieu, and to divide my estate among them by will, that they may not go to law with one another after my death; and when I have done so, I will come back to the same place, and submit to whatever you shall please to order concerning me. But, says the genie, if I grant you the time you demand, I doubt you will never return. If you will believe my oath, answers the merchant, I swear by all that is sacred, that I will come and meet you here without fail. What time do you demand then, replies the genie? I ask a year, says the merchant; I cannot have less to order my affairs, and to prepare myself to die without regret. But I promise you, that this day twelve months I will return under these trees, to put myself into your hands. Do you take heaven to witness to this promise, says the genie? I do, answers the merchant, and repeat it, and you may rely upon my oath. Upon this the genie left him near the fountain, and disappeared.

The merchant, being recovered from his fright, mounted his horse, and set forward on his journey: and as he was glad, on the one hand, that he had escaped so great a danger; so he was mortally sorry on the other, when he thought on his fatal oath. When he came home, his wife and children received him with all the demonstrations of a perfect joy. But he, instead of making them answerable returns, fell a-weeping bitterly; from whence they readily conjectured, that something extraordinary had befallen him. His wife asked the reason of his excessive grief and tears; We are all overjoyed, says she, at your return, but you frighten us to see you in this condition; pray tell us the cause of your sorrow. Alas, replies the husband, the cause of it is, that I have but a year to live; and then told what had passed betwixt him and the genie, and that he had given him his oath to return at the end of the year, to receive death from his hands.

When they had heard this sad news, they all began to lament heartily: his wife made a pitiful outcry, beat her face, and tore her hair. The children being all in tears, made the house resound with their groans; and the father, not being able to overcome nature, mixed his tears with theirs: so that, in a word, it was the most affecting spectacle that any man could behold.

Next morning, the merchant applied himself to put his affairs in order; and, first of all, to pay his debts. He made presents to his friends, gave great alms to the poor, set his slaves of both sexes at liberty, divided his estate among his children, appointed guardians for such of them as were not come of age; and restoring to his wife all that was due to her by contract of marriage, he gave her, over and above, all that he could do by law.

At last the year expired, and go he must. He put his burial-cloaths in his portmanteau; but never was there such grief seen, as when he came to bid his wife and children adieu. They could not think of parting, but resolved to go along and to die with him; but finding that he must be forced to part with those dear objects, he spoke to them thus: My dear wife and children, says he, I obey the order of heaven in quitting you; follow my example, submit courageously to this necessity, and consider that it is the destiny of man to die. Having said those words, he went out of the hearing of the cries of his family; and taking his journey, arrived at the place where he promised to meet the genie, on the day appointed. He alighted, and setting himself down by the fountain, waited the coming of the genie with all the sorrow imaginable. Whilst he languished in this cruel expectation, a good old man, leading a bitch, appeared, and drew near him: they saluted one another, after which the old man says to him, Brother, may I ask you why you are come into this desart place, where there is nothing but evil spirits, and by consequence you cannot be safe? To look upon these fine trees, indeed, one would think the place inhabited; but it is a true wilderness, where it is not safe to stay long.

The merchant satisfied his curiosity, and told him the adventure which obliged him to be there. The old man listened to him with astonishment; and when he had done, cried out, this is the most surprising thing in the world, and you are bound by the most inviolable oath; however, I will be witness of your interview with the genie; and sitting down by the merchant, they talked together.—But I see day, says Scheherazade, and must leave off; but the best of the story is yet to come. The sultan, resolving to hear the end of it, suffered her to live that day also.

THE THIRD NIGHT.

NEXT morning Dinarzade made the same request to her sister as formerly, thus: My dear sister, says she, if you be not asleep, tell me one of those pleasant stories you have read: but the sultan, willing to understand what followed betwixt the merchant and the genie, bid her go on with that; which she did as follows:

Sir, while the merchant, and the old man that led the bitch, were talking, they saw another old man coming to them, followed by two black dogs; after they had saluted one another, he asked them what they did in that place? The old man with the bitch told him the adventure of the merchant and genie, with all that had past betwixt them, particularly the merchant's oath. He added, that this was the day agreed on, and that he was resolved to stay and see the issue.

The second old man, thinking it also worth his curiosity, resolved to do the like: he likewise sat down by them; and they had scarce begun to talk together, but there came a third old man, who addressing himself to the two former, asked why the merchant that sat with them looked so melancholy. They told him the reason of it; which appeared so extraordinary to him, that he also resolved to be witness to the result, and for that end sat down with them.

In a little time, they perceived in the field a thick vapour, like a cloud of dust raised by a whirlwind, advancing towards them, which vanished all of a sudden, and then the genie appeared; who, without saluting them, came up to the merchant with his drawn scymitar, and, taking him by the arm, says, Get thee up, that I may kill thee, as thou didst kill my son. The merchant and the three old men being frightened, began to lament, and to fill the air with their cries.—Here Scheherazade, perceiving day, left off her story, which did so much whet the sultan's curiosity, that he was absolutely resolved to hear the end of it, and put off the sultaness's execution till the next day.

Nobody can express the grand visier's joy, when he perceived that the sultan did not order him to kill Scheherazade; his family, the court, and all the people in general, were astonished at it.

THE FOURTH NIGHT.

TOWARDS the end of the following night, Dinarzade failed not to awake the sultaness. My dear sister, says she, if you be not asleep, pray tell me one of your fine stories. Then Scheherazade, with the sultan's permission, spoke as follows:

Sir, when the old man that led the bitch, saw the genie lay hold of the merchant, and about to kill him without pity, he threw himself at the feet of the monster, and kissing them, says to him: Prince of Genies, I most humbly request you to suspend your anger, and do me the favour to hear me. I will tell you the history of my life, and of the bitch you see: and if you think it more wonderful and surprising than the adventure of the merchant you are going to kill, I hope you will pardon the poor unfortunate man the third of his crime. The genie took some time to consult upon it; but answered at last, Well then, I agree to it.

The History of the first Old Man, and the Bitch

I SHALL begin then, says the old man; listen to me, I pray you, with attention. This bitch you see, is my cousin, nay, what is more, my wife: she was only twelve years of age when I married her, so that I may justly say, she ought as much to regard me as her father, as her kinsman and husband.

We lived together twenty years without any children, yet her barrenness did not hinder my having a great deal of complaisance and friendship for her. The desire of having children only, made me to buy a slave, by whom I had a son, who was extremely promising. My wife being jealous, conceived a hatred for both mother and child; but concealed it so well, that I did not know it till it was too late.

Mean time my son grew up, and was ten years old, when I was obliged to undertake a journey: before I went I recommended to my wife, of whom I had no mistrust, the slave and her son, and prayed her to take care of them during my absence, which was for a whole year. She made use of that time to satisfy her hatred; she applied herself to magic, and when she knew enough of that diabolical art to execute her horrible contrivance, the wretch carried my son to a desolate place, where, by her enchantments, she changed him into a calf, and gave him to my farmer to fatten, pretending she had bought him. Her fury did not stop at this abominable action, but she likewise changed the slave into a cow, and gave her also to my farmer.

At my return, I asked for the mother and child: Your slave, says she, is dead; and for your son, I know not what is become of him: I have not seen him these two months. I was troubled at the death of the slave; but my son having only disappeared, as she told me, I was in hopes he would return in a little time. However, eight months passed, and I heard nothing of him. When the festival of the great Bairam* happened, to celebrate the same, I sent to my farmer for one of the fattest cows to sacrifice; and he sent me one accordingly. The cow which he brought me was my slave, the unfortunate mother of my son. I tied her, but as I was going to sacrifice her, she bellowed pitifully, and I could perceive streams of tears run from her eyes. This seemed to me very extraordinary, and finding myself, in spite of all I could do, seized with pity, I could not find in my heart to give her the blow, but ordered my farmer to get me another.

My wife, who was present, was enraged at my compassion, and opposing herself to an order which disappointed her malice, she cries out: What do you do, husband? Sacrifice that cow, your farmer has not a finer, nor one fitter for that use. Out of complaisance to my wife, I came again to the cow, and combating my pity, which suspended the sacrifice, was going to give her the fatal blow, when the victim redoubling her tears, and bellowing, disarmed me a second time. Then I put the mell* into the farmer's hands, and bade him take and sacrifice her himself, for her tears and bellowing pierced my heart.

The farmer, less compassionate than I, sacrificed her; and when he flayed her, found her nothing but bones, though to us she seemed very fat. Take her to yourself, says I to the farmer, I quit her to you; give her in alms, or which way you will; and if you have a very fat calf, bring it me in her stead. I did not inform myself what he did with the cow; but soon after he took her away, he came with a very fat calf. Though I knew not that the calf was my son, yet I could not forbear being moved at the sight of him. On his part, as soon as he saw me, he made so great an effort to come to me, that he broke his cord, threw himself at my feet, with his head against the ground, as if he would excite my compassion, conjuring me not to be so cruel as to take his life; and did as much as was possible for him to do, to signify that he was my son.

I was more surprised and affected with this action, than with the tears of the cow: I found a tender pity, which made me concern myself for him, or rather nature did its duty. Go, says I to the farmer, carry home that calf; take great care of him, and bring me another in his stead immediately.

As soon as my wife heard me say so, she immediately cried out, What do you do, husband? Take my advice, sacrifice no other calf but that. Wife, says I, I will not sacrifice him, I will spare him, and pray do not you oppose it. The wicked woman had no regard to my desire, she hated my son too much, to consent that I should save him; I tied the poor creature, and taking up the fatal knife—Here Scheherazade stopt, because she perceived daylight.

Then Dinarzade said, Sister, I am enchanted with this story, which bespeaks my attention so agreeably. If the sultan will suffer me to live to-day, answers Scheherazade, what I have to tell you to-morrow will divert you abundantly more. Schahriar, curious to know what would become of the old man's son that led the bitch, told the sultaness, he would be very glad to hear the end of that story next night.

THE FIFTH NIGHT.

WHEN day began to draw near, Dinarzade put her sister's orders in execution very exactly: who being awaked, prayed the sultan to allow her to give Dinarzade that satisfaction, which the prince, who took so much pleasure in the story himself, willingly agreed to.

Sir, then, says Scheherazade, the first old man who led the bitch, continuing his story to the genie, the two other old men, and the merchant, proceeded thus: I took the knife, says he, and was going to strike it into my son's throat; when turning his eyes, bathed with tears, in a languishing manner, towards me, he affected me so, that I had not strength to sacrifice him, but let the knife fall, and told my wife positively that I would have another calf to sacrifice, and not that. She used all endeavours to make me change my resolution; but I continued firm, and pacified her, by promising that I would sacrifice him against the Bairam next year.

Next morning, my farmer desired to speak with me alone; and told me, I come, says he, to tell you a piece of news, for which, I hope, you will return me thanks. I have a daughter that has some skill in magic: Yesterday, as I carried back the calf, which you would not sacrifice, I perceived she laughed when she saw him, and in a moment after fell a weeping. I asked her why she acted two such contrary parts at one and the same time. Father, replies she, the calf you bring back is our landlord's son: I laughed for joy to see him still alive, and I wept at the remembrance of the sacrifice that was made the other day of his mother, who was changed into a cow. These two metamorphoses were made by the enchantments of our master's wife, who hated the mother and son. This is what my daughter told me, said the farmer, and I come to acquaint you with it.

At these words, the old man adds, I leave you to think, my lord genie, how much I was surprised: I went immediately to my farmer, to speak with his daughter myself. As soon as I came, I went forthwith to the stall where my son was; he could not answer my embraces, but received them in such a manner, as fully satisfied me he was my son.

The farmer's daughter came: My good maid, says I, can you restore my son to his former shape? Yes, says she, I can. Ah! says I, if you can, I will make you mistress of all my fortune. She replied to me, smiling, You are our master, and I know very well what I owe to you, but I cannot restore your son into his former shape, but on two conditions: The first is, that you give him for my husband, and the second is, that you allow me to punish the person who changed him into a calf. For the first, says I, I agree to it with all my heart: Nay, I promise you more, a considerable estate for yourself, independent of what I design for my son: In a word, you shall see how I will reward the great service I expect from you. As to what relates to my wife, I also agree to it: A person that has been capable of committing such a criminal action, deserves very well to be punished: I leave her to you, only I must pray you not to take her life. I am just a-going then, answers she, to treat her as she has treated your son; I agree to it, says I, provided you restore my son to me beforehand.

Then the maid took a vessel full of water, pronounced words over it that I did not understand, and addressing herself to the calf, O calf, says she, if thou wast created by the Almighty and Sovereign Master of the world, such as you appear at this time, continue in that form; but if thou beest a man, and art changed into a calf by enchantment, return to thy natural shape, by the permission of the sovereign Creator. As she spoke these words, she threw water upon him, and in an instant he recovered his first shape.

My son, my dear son, cried I, immediately embracing him with such a transport of joy, that I knew not what I was doing; it is heaven that has sent us this young maid to take off the horrible charm by which you were enchanted, and to avenge the injury done to you and your mother. I doubt not, but in acknowledgment, you will take your deliverer to wife, as I have promised. He consented to it with joy; but before they married, she changed my wife into a bitch; and this is she you see here. I desired she should have this shape, rather than another less agreeable, that we might see her in the family without horror.

Since that time, my son is become a widower, and gone to travel; and it being several years since I heard of him, I am come abroad to inquire after him; and not being willing to trust any body with my wife, while I should come home, I thought fit to carry her every where with me. This is the history of myself and this bitch, is it not one of the most wonderful and surprising that can be? I agree it is, says the genie, and upon that account, I forgive the merchant a third of his crime.

When the first old man, Sir, continued the sultaness, had finished his story, the second, who led the two black dogs, addressed himself to the genie, and says to him: I am going to tell you what happened to me, and these two black dogs you see by me, and I am certain you will say that my story is yet more surprising than that which you have just now heard, but when I have told it you, I hope you will be pleased to pardon the merchant the second third of his crime. Yes, replies the genie, provided your story surpass that of the bitch. Then the second old man began in this manner. But as Scheherazade pronounced these words, she saw it was day, and left off speaking.

O heaven! sister, says Dinarzade, those adventures are very singular. Sister, replies the sultaness, they are not comparable to those which I have to tell you next night, if the sultan, my lord and master, be so good as to let me live. Schahriar answered nothing to that, but rose up, said his prayers, and went to council, without giving any order against the life of the charming Scheherazade.

THE SIXTH NIGHT.

THE sixth night being come, the sultan and his lady went to bed. Dinarzade awaked at the usual hour, and calling to the sultaness, says, Dear sister, if you be not asleep, I pray you, until it be day, to satisfy my curiosity; I am impatient to hear the story of the old man and the two black dogs. The sultan consented to it with pleasure, being no less desirous to know the story than Dinarzade; and Scheherazade continued it as follows:

The Story of the second Old Man, and the two black Dogs

GREAT prince of genies, says the old man, you must know that we are three brothers, I and the two black dogs you see: Our father left each of us, when he died, one thousand sequins;* with that sum we entered into the same way of living, and became merchants. A little time after we had opened shop, my eldest brother, one of those two dogs, resolved to travel and trade in foreign countries. Upon this design, he sold his estate, and bought goods proper for the trade he intended.

He went away, and was absent a whole year, at the end of which, a poor man, who I thought had come to ask alms, presented him before me in my shop. I said to him, God help you. God help you also, answered he, is it possible you do not know me? Upon this I looked to him narrowly, and knew him: Ah, brother, cried I, embracing him, how could I know you in this condition? I made him come into my house, and asked him concerning his health, and the success of his travels. Do not ask me that question, says he; when you see me, you see all; it would only renew my grief, to tell you all the particulars of the misfortunes that have befallen me, and reduced me to this condition since I left you.

I immediately shut up my shop, and carrying him to a bath, gave him the best cloaths I had by me; and examining my books, and finding that I had doubled my stock, that is to say, that I was worth two thousand sequins, I gave him one half. With that, says I, brother, you may make up your loss. He joyfully accepted the proffer, recovered himself, and we lived together as before.

Some time after, my second brother, who is the other of these two dogs, would also sell his estate: I, and his other brother, did all we could to divert him from it, but could not. He sold it, and with the money bought such goods as were suitable to the trade he designed. He joined a caravan,* and took a journey. He returned at the end of the year, in the same condition as my other brother; and I having gained another thousand sequins, gave him them, with which he furnished his shop, and continued to follow his trade.

Some time after, one of my brothers comes to me to propose a trading voyage with them; I immediately rejected their proposal. You have travelled, says I, and what have you gained by it? Who can assure me, that I shall be more successful than you have been? They represented to me in vain, all that they thought fit, to prevail upon me to engage in that design with them, for I constantly refused; but they importuned me so much, that after having resisted their solicitations five whole years, they overcame me at last: but when we were to make preparations for our voyage, and to buy goods necessary to the undertaking, I found they had spent all, and that they had not one farthing left of the thousand sequins I had given each of them. I did not, however, upbraid them in the least with it. On the contrary, my stock being six thousand sequins, I shared the half of it with them, telling them, My brothers, we must venture these three thousand sequins, and hide the rest in some sure place; that in case our voyage be no more successful than yours were formerly, we may have wherewith to assist us, and to follow our ancient way of living. I gave each of them a thousand sequins, and keeping as much for myself, I buried the other three thousand in a corner of my house. We bought our goods, and after having embarked them on board of a vessel, which we freighted betwixt us three, we put to sea with a favourable wind. After a month's sail—But I see day, says Scheherazade, I must stop here.

Sister, says Dinarzade, this story promises a great deal; I fancy the rest of it must be very extraordinary. You are not mistaken, says the sultaness, and if the sultan will allow me to tell it you, I am persuaded it will very much divert you. Schahriar got up as he did the day before, without explaining his mind; but gave no order to the grand visier to kill his daughter.

THE SEVENTH NIGHT.

When the seventh night drew near a close, Dinarzade awaked the sultaness, and prayed her to continue the story of the second old man. I will, answered Scheherazade, provided the sultan, my lord and master, do not oppose it. Not at all, says Schahriar; I am so far from opposing it, that I desire you earnestly to go on with it.

To resume the thread of the story, says Scheherazade, you must know that the old man who led the two dogs, continued his story to the genie, the other two old men and the merchant, thus: In short, says he, after two months sail we arrived happily at a port, where we landed, and had a very great vent for our goods. I, especially, sold mine so well, that I gained ten to one: and we bought commodities of that country, to transport and sell in our own.

When we were ready to embark, in order to return, I met, upon the banks of the sea, a lady handsome enough, but poorly clad: She came up to me presently, kissed my hand, prayed me with the greatest earnestness imaginable to marry her, and take her along with me. I made some difficulty to agree to it; but she said so many things to persuade me, that I ought to make no objection to her poverty, and that I should have all the reason in the world to be satisfied with her conduct, that I yielded. I ordered fit apparel to be made for her; and after having married her, according to form, I took her on board, and we set sail. During the navigation, I found the wife I had taken, had so many good qualities, that I loved her every day more and more. In the mean time, my two brothers, who had not managed their affairs so well as I did mine, envied my prosperity, and their fury carried them so far, as to conspire against my life: so that one night, when my wife and I were asleep, they threw us both into the sea.

My wife was a fairy, and by consequence, genie, you know well, she could not be drowned: but for me, it is certain, I had been lost, without her help. I had scarcely fallen into the water, till she took me up and carried me to an island. When it was day, the fairy said to me, You see, husband, that by saving your life, I have not rewarded you ill for your kindness to me. You must know, that I am a fairy, and that being upon the bank of the sea, when you were going to embark, I found I had a strong inclination for you; I had a mind to try your goodness, and presented myself before you in that disguise wherein you saw me. You have dealt very generously with me, and I am mighty glad to have found an opportunity of testifying my acknowledgments to you: But I am incensed against your brothers, and nothing will satisfy me but their lives.

I listened to this discourse of the fairy, with admiration; I thanked her as well as I could, for the great kindness she had done me: But, madam, says I, for my brothers, I beg you to pardon them; whatever cause they have given me, I am not cruel enough to desire their death. I told her the particulars of what I had done for them, which increased her indignation so, that she cried out, I must immediately fly after those ungrateful traitors, and take speedy vengeance on them; I will drown their vessel, and throw them into the bottom of the sea. No, my good lady, replied I, for the sake of heaven do not so; moderate your anger, consider that they are my brothers, and that we must do good for evil.

I pacified the fairy by those words; and as soon as I had spoke them, she transported me in an instant from the island where we were, to the roof of my own house, which was terrassed, and disappeared in a moment. I went down, opened the doors, and dug up the three thousand sequins I had hid. I went afterwards to the place where my shop was, which I also opened, and was complimented by the merchants, my neighbours, upon my return. When I went to my house, I perceived two black dogs, which came to me in a very submissive manner; I knew not what it meant, but was much astonished at it. But the fairy, who appeared immediately, says to me, Husband, do not be surprised to see these two black dogs by you; they are your two brothers. I was troubled at those words, and asked her by what power they were transformed. It was I that did it, says she, at least I gave commission to one of my sisters to do it, who at the same time sunk their ship. You have lost the goods you had on board, but I will make it up another way. As to your two brothers, I have condemned them to remain five years in that shape. Their perfidiousness too well deserves such a penance; and in short, after having told me where I might hear of her, she disappeared.

Now the five years being out, I am travelling in quest of her; and as I passed this way, I met this merchant, and the good old man that led the bitch, and sat down by them. This is my history, O prince of Genies, do not you think it very extraordinary? I own it, says the genie, and upon that account, remit the merchant the second third of the crime which he had committed against me.

As soon as the second old man had finished his story, the third began, and made the like demand of the genie, with the two first; that is to say, to pardon the merchant the other third of his crime, provided the story he had to tell him exceeded the two he had already heard, for singular events. The genie made him the same promise he had done the other two. Hearken then, says the old man to him,——But day appears, says Scheherazade, I must stop here.

I cannot enough admire, sister, says Dinarzade, the adventures you have told me. I know abundance more, answers the sultaness, that are still more wonderful. Schahriar, willing to know if the story of the third old man would be as agreeable as that of the second, put off the execution of Scheherazade till the next day.

THE EIGHTH NIGHT.

AS soon as Dinarzade perceived it was time to call the sultaness, she says, Sister, I have been awake a long time, and have had a great mind to awake you, I am so impatient to hear the story of the third old man. The sultan answered, I can hardly think that the third story will surpass the two former ones.

Sir, replies the sultaness, the third old man told his story to the genie; I cannot tell it you, because it is not come to my knowledge, but I know that it did so much exceed the two former stories, in the variety of wonderful adventures, that the genie was astonished at it; and no sooner heard the end of it, but he said to the third old man, I remit the other third part of the merchant's crime upon the account of your story. He is very much obliged to a three of you, for having delivered him out of his danger by your stories; without which, he had not now been in the world. And having spoke thus, he disappeared, to the great contentment of the company.

The merchant failed not to give his three deliverers the thanks he owed them. They rejoiced to see him out of the danger; after which he bid them adieu, and each of them went on his way. The merchant returned to his wife and children, and passed the rest of his days with them in peace. But, sir, added Scheherazade, how pleasant soever these stories may be that I have told your majesty hitherto, they do not come near that of the Fisherman. Dinarzade, perceiving that the sultan demurred, says to her, Sister, since there is still some time remaining, pray tell us the story of the Fisherman, if the sultan is willing. Schahriar agreed to it, and Scheherazade, resuming her discourse, pursued it in this manner.

The Story of the Fisherman

SIR,—There was a very ancient fisherman, so poor, that he could scarce earn enough to maintain himself, his wife, and three children. He went every day to fish betimes in a morning; and imposed it as a law upon himself, not to cast his nets above four times a-day. He went one morning by moonlight, and coming to the sea-bank, undressed himself, and cast in his nets. As he drew them towards the shore, he found them very heavy, and thought he had a good draught of fish, at which he rejoiced within himself; but in a moment after, perceiving that instead of fish, there was nothing in his nets but the carcase of an ass, he was mightily vexed. Scheherazade stopt here, because she saw it was day.

Sister, says Dinarzade, I must confess, that the beginning of this story charms me, and I foresee that the result of it will be very agreeable. There is nothing more surprising than the story of this fisherman, replied the sultaness, and you will be convinced of it next night, if the sultan will be so gracious, as to let me live. Schahriar being curious to hear the success of such an extraordinary fishing, would not order Scheherazade to be put to death that day.

THE NINTH NIGHT.

My dear sister, cries Dinarzade, next morning at the usual hour, if you be not asleep, I pray you go on with the story of the fisherman; I am ready to die till I hear it. I am ready to give you that satisfaction, says the sultaness; but at the same time she demanded leave of the sultan, and having obtained it, began the story again as follows:

Sir, when the fisherman, vexed to have made such a sorry draught, had mended his nets, which the carcase of the ass had broke in several places, he threw them in a second time; and when he drew them, found a great deal of resistance, which made him to think he had taken abundance of fish; but he found nothing except a pannier* full of gravel and slime, which grieved him extremely. O Fortune! cries he, with a lamentable tone, do not be angry at me, nor persecute a wretch, who prays thee to spare him. I came thither from my house to seek for my livelihood, and thou pronouncest death against me. I have no other trade but this to subsist by; and notwithstanding all the care I take, I can scarcely provide what is absolutely necessary for my family. But I am in the wrong to complain of thee; thou takest pleasure to persecute honest people, and to leave great men in obscurity, whilst thou shewest favour to the wicked, and advancest those who have to virtue to recommend them.

Having finished this complaint, he threw away the pannier in a fret, and washing his nets from the slime, cast them the third time, but brought up nothing except stones, shells, and mud. Nobody can express his disorder; he was within an ace of going quite mad. However, when day began to appear, he did not forget to say his prayers, like a good Mussulman, and afterwards added this petition: 'Lord! you know that I cast my nets only four times a-day: I have already drawn them three times, without the least reward for my labour: I am only to cast them once more; I pray you to render the sea favourable to me, as you did to Moses.'*

The fisherman having finished this prayer, cast his nets the fourth time, and when he thought it was time, he drew them as formerly, with great difficulty; but instead of fish, found nothing in them but a vessel of yellow copper, that by its weight seemed to be full of something; and he observed that it was shut up and sealed with lead, having the impression of a seal upon it. This rejoiced him: I will sell it, says he, to the founder, and with the money arising from the product, buy a measure of corn. He examined the vessel on all sides, and shook it, to see if what was within made any noise, and heard nothing. This circumstance, with the impression of the seal upon the leaden cover, made him to think there was something precious in it. To try this, he took a knife, and opened it with very little labour; he presently turned the mouth downward, but nothing came out, which surprised him extremely. He set it before him, and while he looked upon it attentively, there came out a very thick smoke, which obliged him to retire two or three paces from it.

This smoke mounted as high as the clouds, and extending itself along the sea, and upon the shore, formed a great mist, which we may well imagine did mightily astonish the fisherman. When the smoke was all out of the vessel, it reunited itself, and became a solid body, of which there was formed a genie twice as high as the greatest of giants. At the sight of a monster of such an unsizeable bulk, the fisherman would fain have fled, but was so frightened that he could not go one step.

Solomon, cried the genie immediately, Solomon, the great prophet,* pardon, pardon; I will never more oppose your will: I will obey all your commands.—Scheherazade, perceiving it day, broke off her story.

Upon which Dinarzade said, Dear sister, nobody can keep their promise better than you have done yours. This story is certainly more surprising than the former. Sister, replies the sultaness, there are more wonderful things yet to come, if my lord, the sultan, will allow me to tell them you. Schahriar had too great a desire to hear out the story of the fisherman, to deprive himself of that pleasure; and therefore put off the sultaness's death another day.

THE TENTH NIGHT.

DINARZADE called her sister next night, when she thought it was time, and prayed her to continue the story of the fisherman; and the sultan being also impatient to know what concern the genie had with Solomon, Scheherazade continued her story thus:

Sir, the fisherman, when he heard these words of the genie, recovered his courage, and says to him, Thou proud spirit, what is that you talk? It is above eighteen hundred years since the prophet Solomon died, and we are now at the end of time. Tell me your history, and how you came to be shut up in this vessel.

The genie, turning to the fisherman with a fierce look, says, You must speak to me with more civility; thou art very bold to call me a proud spirit. Very well, replies the fisherman, shall I speak to you with more civility, and call you the owl of good luck? I say, answers the genie, speak to me more civilly, before I kill thee. I have only one favour to grant thee. And what is that, says the fisherman? It is, answers the Genie, to give you your choice in what manner thou wouldst have me to take thy life. But wherein have I offended you, replies the fisherman? Is this your reward for the good service I have done you? I cannot treat you otherwise, says the genie; and that you may be convinced of it, hearken to my story.

I am one of those rebellious spirits that opposed themselves to the will of heaven; all the other genies owned Solomon, the great prophet, and submitted to him. Sacar and I were the only genies that would never be guilty of so mean a thing; And to avenge himself, that great monarch sent Asaph, the son of Barakhia, his chief minister, to apprehend me. That was accordingly done, Asaph seized my person, and brought me by force before his master's throne.

Solomon the son of David commanded me to quit my way of living, to acknowledge his power, and to submit myself to his commands: I bravely refused to obey, and told him, I would rather expose myself to his resentments, than swear fealty, and submit to him as he required. To punish me, he shut me up in this copper vessel; and to make sure of me, that I should not break prison, he stampt (himself) upon this leaden cover, his seal, with the great name of God engraven upon it. Thus, he gave the vessel to one of the genies who submitted to him, with orders to throw me into the sea, which was executed, to my great sorrow.

During the first hundred years imprisonment, I swore that if one would deliver me before the hundred years expired, I would make him rich, even after his death: But that century ran out, and nobody did me that good office. During the second, I made an oath, that I would open all the treasures of the earth to any one that should set me at liberty; but with no better success. In the third, I promised to make my deliverer a potent monarch, to be always near him in a spirit, and to grant him every day three demands, of what nature soever they might be: But this century ran out as well as the two former, and I continued in prison. At last, being angry, or rather mad, to find myself a prisoner so long, I swore, that if afterwards any one should deliver me, I would kill him without pity, and grant him no other favour, but to chuse what kind of death he would die; and therefore, since you have delivered me to-day, I give you that choice.

This discourse afflicted the poor fisherman extremely: I am very unfortunate, cries he, to have come hither to do such a piece of good service to one that is so ungrateful. I beg you to consider your injustice, and revoke such an unreasonable oath; pardon me, and heaven will pardon you; if you grant me my life, heaven will protect you from all attempts against yours. No, thy death is resolved on, says the genie, only chuse how you will die. The fisherman perceiving the genie to be resolute, was extremely grieved, not so much for himself, as for his three children; and bewailed the misery they must be reduced to by his death. He endeavoured still to appease the genie, and says, Alas! be pleased to take pity on me, in consideration of the good service I have done you. I have told thee already, replies the genie, it is for that very reason I must kill thee. That is very strange, says the fisherman, are you resolved to reward evil for good? The proverb says, 'That he who does good to one who deserves it not, is always ill rewarded.' I must confess, I thought it was false; for in effect, there can be nothing more contrary to reason, or the laws of society. Nevertheless, I find now, by cruel experience, that it is but too true. Do not let us lose time, replies the genie, all thy reasonings shall not divert me from my purpose: Make haste, and tell me which way you chuse to die.

Necessity is the mother of invention. The fisherman bethought himself of a stratagem. Since I must die then, says he to the genie, I submit to the will of heaven; but before I chuse the manner of my death, I conjure you by the great name which was engraven upon the seal of the prophet Solomon, the son of David, to answer me truly the question I am going to ask you.

The genie finding himself obliged to a positive answer, by this adjuration, trembled; and replies to the fisherman, Ask what thou wilt, but make haste. Day appearing, Scheherazade held her peace.

Sister, says Dinarzade, it must be owned that the more you speak, the more you surprise and satisfy. I hope the sultan, our lord, will not order you to be put to death till he hears out the fine story of the fisherman. The sultan is absolute, replies Scheherazade, we must submit to his will in every thing. But Schahriar, being as willing as Dinarzade to hear an end of the story, did again put off the execution of the sultaness.

THE ELEVENTH NIGHT.

SCHAHRIAR, and the princess his spouse, passed this night in the same manner as they had done the former; and before break of day, Dinarzade awaked them with these words, she addressed to the sultaness: I pray you, sister, to resume the story of the fisherman. With all my heart, said Scheherazade, I am willing to satisfy you, with the sultan's permission.

The genie (continued she) having promised to speak the truth, the fisherman says to him, I would know if you were actually in this vessel? Dare you swear it by the name of the great God? Yes, replied the genie, I do swear by that great name that I was, and it is a certain truth. In good faith, answered the fisherman, I cannot believe you; the vessel is not capable to hold one of your feet, and how should it be possible that your whole body could be in it? I swear to thee, notwithstanding, replied the genie, that I was there just as you see me here: Is it possible, that thou dost not believe me after this great oath that I have taken? Truly not I, said the fisherman; nor will I believe you, unless you shew it me.

Upon which the body of the genie was dissolved, and changed itself into smoke, extending itself, as formerly, upon the sea-shore; and then at last, being gathered together, it began to re-enter the vessel, which it so continued to do successively, by a slow and equal motion, after a smooth and exact way, till nothing was left out, and immediately a voice came forth, which said to the fisherman, Well now, incredulous fellow, I am all in the vessel; do not you believe me now?

The fisherman, instead of answering the genie, took the cover of lead, and having speedily shut the vessel, Genie, cries he, now it is your turn to beg my favour, and to chuse which way I shall put thee to death; but not so, it is better that I should throw you into the sea, whence I took you; and then I will build a house upon the bank, where I will dwell, to give notice to all fishermen, who come to throw in their nets, to beware of such a wicked genie as thou art, who hast made an oath to kill him that shall set thee at liberty.

The genie, enraged at these expressions, did all he could to get out of the vessel again, but it was not possible for him to do it; for the impression of Solomon's seal prevented him; so perceiving that the fisherman had got the advantage of him, he thought fit to dissemble his anger. Fisherman, says he, in a pleasant tone, take heed you do not do what you say; for what I spoke to you before was only by way of jest, and you are to take it no otherwise. O genie! replies the fisherman, thou who wast but a moment ago the greatest of all genies, and now art the least of them, thy crafty discourse will signify nothing to thee, but to the sea thou shalt return: If thou hast staid there already so long as thou hast told me, thou mayst very well stay there till the day of judgment. I begged thee, in God's name, not to take away my life, and thou didst reject my prayers; I am obliged to treat you in the same manner.

The genie omitted nothing that could prevail upon the fisherman: Open the vessel, says he, give me my liberty, I pray thee, and I promise to satisfy thee to thy own content. Thou art a mere traitor, replies the fisherman, I should deserve to lose my life, if I be such a fool as to trust thee; thou wilt not fail to treat me in the same manner as a certain Grecian king treated the physician Douban. It is a story I have a mind to tell thee, therefore listen to it.

The Story of the Grecian King and the Physician Douban

THERE was in the country of Zouman, in Persia, a king, whose subjects were originally Greeks. This king was all over leprous, and his physicians in vain endeavoured his cure; and when they were at their wits end what to prescribe him, a very able physician, called Douban, arrived at his court.

This physician had learned his science in Greek, Persian, Turkish, Arabian, Latin, Syrian, and Hebrew books; and besides that he was an expert philosopher, he fully understood the good and bad qualities of all sorts of plants and drugs. As soon as he was informed of the king's distemper, and understood that his physicians had given him over, he clad himself the best he could, and found a way to present himself to the king. Sir, says he, I know that all your Majesty's physicians have not been able to cure you of the leprosy; but if you will do me the honour to accept my service, I will engage to cure you without drenches,* or external applications.

The king listened to what he said, and answered, If you be able to perform what you promise, I will enrich you and your posterity; and besides the presents I shall make you, you shall be my chief favourite. Do you assure me then, that you will cure me of my leprosy, without making me take any potion, or applying any external medicine? Yes, Sir, replies the physician, I promise myself success, through God's assistance, and to-morrow I will make trial of it.

The physician returned to his quarters, and made a mallet, hollow within, and at the handle he put in his drugs. He also made a ball in such a manner as suited his purpose, with which next morning, he went to present himself before the king, and falling down at his feet, kissed the very ground.—Here Scheherazade perceiving day, acquainted the sultan with it, and held her peace.

I wonder, sister, says Dinarzade, where you learn so many fine things. You will hear a great many others to-morrow, replies Scheherazade, if the sultan, my master, will be pleased to prolong my life farther. Schahriar, who longed as much as Dinarzade to hear the sequel of the story of Douban, the physician, did not order the sultaness to be put to death that day.

THE TWELFTH NIGHT.

THE twelfth night was far advanced, when Dinarzade called, and says, Sister, you owe us the continuation of the agreeable history of the Grecian king and the physician Douban. I am very willing to pay my debt, replies Scheherazade, and resumed the story, as follows:

Sir, the fisherman, speaking always to the genie, whom he kept shut up in his vessel, went on thus: The physician Douban rose up, and after a profound reverence, says to the king, he judged it meet that his majesty should take horse, and go to the place where he used to play at the mell. The king did so, and when he arrived there, the physician came to him with the mell, and says to him, Sir, exercise yourself with this mell, and strike the ball with it until you find your hands, and your body in a sweat. When the medicine I have put in the handle of the mell is heated with your hand, it will penetrate your whole body; and as soon as you shall sweat, you may leave off the exercise, for then the medicine will have had its effect. As soon as you are returned to your palace, go into the bath, and cause yourself to be well washed and rubbed; then go to bed, and when you rise to-morrow you will find yourself cured.

The king took the mell, and struck the ball, which was returned by his officers that played with him; he struck it again, and played so long till his hand and his whole body were in a sweat, and then the medicine shut up in the handle of the mell had its operations, as the physician said. Upon this, the king left off play, returned to his palace, entered the bath, and observed very exactly what his physician had prescribed him.

He was very well after, and next morning when he arose, he perceived, with as much wonder as joy, that his leprosy was cured, and his body as clean as if he had never been attacked with that distemper. As soon as he was dressed, he came into the hall of public audience, where he mounted his throne, and shewed himself to his courtiers; who, longing to know the success of the new medicine, came thither by times, and when they saw the king perfectly cured, did all of them express a mighty joy for it. The physician Douban, entering the hall, bowed himself before the throne, with his face to the ground. The king perceiving him, called him, made him sit down by his side, shewed him to the assembly, and gave him all the commendation he deserved. His majesty did not stop here; but as he treated all his court that day, he made him to eat at his table alone with him. At these words, Scheherazade perceiving day, broke off her story. Sister, said Dinarzade, I know not what the conclusion of this story will be, but I find the beginning very surprising. That which is to come is yet better, answered the sultaness;

and I am certain you will not deny it, if the sultan gives me leave to make an end of it to-morrow night. Schahriar consented, and arose very well satisfied with what he had heard.

THE THIRTEENTH NIGHT.

DINARZADE, willing to keep the sultan in ignorance of her design, cried out as if she had started out of her sleep: O dear sister, I have had a troublesome dream, and nothing will sooner make me forget it than the remainder of the story of the Grecian king, and the doctor Douban. I conjure you by the love you always bore me, not to defer it a moment longer. I shall not be wanting, good sister, to ease your mind; and if my sovereign will permit me, I will go on. Schahriar, being charmed with the agreeable manner of Scheherazade's telling her story, says to her, you will oblige me no less than Dinarzade, therefore continue.

The Grecian king (says the fisherman to the genie) was not satisfied with having admitted the physician Douban to his table, but towards night, when he was about dismissing the company, he caused him to be clad in a long rich robe, like unto those which his favourites usually wore in his presence; and besides that, he ordered him two thousand sequins. The next day, and the day following, he was very familiar with him; in short, this prince thinking he could never enough acknowledge the obligations he lay under to that able physician, bestowed every day new favours upon him. But this king had a grand visier, that was avaricious, envious, and naturally capable of all sorts of mischief; he could not see without envy the presents which were given to the physician, whose other merits had begun to make him jealous, and therefore he resolved to lessen him in the king's esteem. To effect this, he went to the king, and told him in private, that he had some advice to give him, which was of the greatest concernment. The king having asked what it was? Sir, said he, it is very dangerous for a monarch to put confidence in a man whose fidelity he never tried. Though you heap favours upon the physician Douban, and shew him all the familiarity that may be, your majesty does not know but he may be a traitor at the same time, and come on purpose to this court to kill you. From whom have you this, answered the king, that you dare tell it me? Consider to whom you speak, and that you advance a thing which I shall not easily believe. Sir, replied the visier, I am very well informed of what I have had the honour to represent to your majesty, therefore do not let your dangerous confidence grow to a farther height: If your majesty be asleep, be pleased to awake; for I do once more repeat it, that the physician, Douban, did not leave the heart of Greece, his country, nor come hither to settle himself at your court, but to execute that horrible design, which I have just now hinted to you. No, no, visier, replies the king, I am certain, that this man, whom you treat as a villain, and a traitor, is one of the best and most virtuous men in the world; and there is no man I love so much. You know by what medicine, or rather by what miracle, he cured me of my leprosy. If he had a design upon my life, why did he save me? he needed only to have left me to my disease; I could not have escaped; my life was already half gone; forbear then to fill me with unjust suspicion: Instead of listening to you, I tell you, that from this day forward, I will give that great man a pension of a thousand sequins per month, for his life; nay, though I did share with him all my riches and dominions, I should never pay him enough for what he has done me: I perceive it is his virtue, which raises your envy; but do not you think that I will be unjustly possessed with prejudice against him. I remember too well what a visier said to king Sinbad, his master, to prevent his putting to death the prince, his son.—But, sir, says Scheherazade, day-light appears, which forbids me to go any farther.

I am very well pleased that the Grecian king, says Dinarzade, had so much firmness of spirit, as to reject the false accusation of his visier. If you commend the firmness of that prince to-day, says Scheherazade, you will as much condemn his weakness to-morrow, if the sultan be pleased to allow me time to finish this story. The sultan, being curious to know wherein the Grecian king discovered his weakness, did farther delay the death of the sultaness.

THE FOURTEENTH NIGHT.

AN hour before day, Dinarzade awaked her sister, and says to her, You will certainly be as good as your word, Madam, and tell us out the story of the fisherman. To assist your memory I will tell you where you left off: It was where the Grecian king maintained the innocence of his physician, Douban, against his visier. I remember it, said Scheherazade, and am ready to give you satisfaction.

Sir, continues she, addressing herself to Schahriar, that which the Grecian king said about king Sinbad, raised the visier's curiosity, who says to him, I pray your majesty to pardon me, if I have the boldness to demand of you what the visier of king Sinbad said to his master, to divert him from cutting off the prince his son. The Grecian king had the complaisance to satisfy him. That visier, says he, after having represented to king Sinbad that he ought to beware, lest on the accusation of a mother-in-law, he should commit an action, which he might afterwards repent of, told him this story.

The Story of the Husband and Parrot

A CERTAIN man had a fair wife, whom he loved so dearly, that he could scarce allow her to be out of his sight. One day, being obliged to go abroad about urgent affairs, he came to a place where all sorts of birds were sold, and there bought a parrot which not only spoke very well, but could also give an account of every thing that was done before it. He brought it in a cage to his house, prayed his wife to put it in the chamber, and to take care of it, during a journey he was obliged to undertake, and then went out.

At his return, he took care to ask the parrot what had passed in his absence, and the bird told him things that gave him occasion to upbraid his wife. She thought some of her slaves had betrayed her, but all of them swore they had been faithful to her; and they all agreed that it must have been the parrot that had told tales.

Upon this, the wife bethought herself of a way how she might remove her husband's jealousy, and at the same time revenge herself of the parrot, which she effected thus: Her husband being gone another journey, she commanded a slave, in the night time, to turn a hand mill under the parrot's cage; she ordered another to throw water, in form of rain, over the cage; and a third to take a glass, and turn it to the right and to the left before the parrot, so as the reflections of the candle might shine on its face. The slaves spent great part of the night in doing what their mistress commanded them, and acquitted themselves very dextrously.

Next night the husband returned, and examined the parrot again about what had passed during his absence. The bird answered, Good master, the lightning, thunder, and rain, did so disturb me all night, that I cannot tell how much I suffered by it. The husband, who knew that there had been neither thunder, lightning, nor rain, that night, fancied that the parrot, not having told him the truth in this, might also have lied to him in the other; upon which he took it out of the cage, and threw it with so much force to the ground, that he killed it. Yet afterwards he understood by his neighbours, that the poor parrot had not lied to him, when it gave him an account of his wife's base conduct, which made him repent that he had killed it.—Scheherazade stopt here, because she saw it was day.

All that you tell us, sister, says Dinarzade, is so curious, that nothing can be more agreeable. I shall be willing to divert you, answers Scheherazade, if the sultan my master will allow me time to do it. Schahriar, who took as much pleasure to hear the sultaness as Dinarzade, arose and went about his affairs, without ordering the visier to cut her off.

THE FIFTEENTH NIGHT.

DINARZADE was punctual this night, as she had been the former, to awake her sister, and begged of her as usual to tell her story. I am going to do it, sister, says Scheherazade; but the sultan interrupted her, for fear she should begin a new story, and bid her finish the discourse between the Grecian king and his visier, about his physician, Douban. Sir, says Scheherazade, I will obey you; and went on with the story as follows:

When the Grecian king, says the fisherman to the genie, had finished the story of the parrot; and you, visier, adds he, because of the hatred you bear to the physician Douban, who never did you any hurt, you would have me cut him off; but I will take care of that, for fear I should repent it, as the husband did the killing of his parrot.

The mischievous visier was too much concerned to effect the ruin of the physician Douban, to stop here. Sir, says he, the death of the parrot was but a trifle, and I believe his master did not mourn for him long. But why should your fear of wronging an innocent man hinder your putting this physician to death? Is it not enough that he is accused of a design against your life, to authorise you to take away his? When the business in question is to secure the life of a king, bare suspicion ought to pass for certainty; and it is better to sacrifice the innocent, than to spare the guilty. But, sir, this is not an uncertain thing; the physician Douban has certainly a mind to assassinate you. It is not envy which makes me his enemy; it is only my zeal, and the concern I have for preserving your majesty's life, that makes me give you my advice in a matter of this importance. If it be false I deserve to be punished, in the same manner as a visier was formerly punished. What had that visier done, says the Grecian king, to deserve punishment? I will inform your majesty of that, says the visier, if you will be pleased to hear me.

The Story of the Visier that was punished

THERE was a king, says the visier, who had a son that loved hunting mightily: He allowed him to divert himself that way very often; but gave order to his grand visier to attend him constantly, and never to lose sight of him.

One hunting-day, the huntsmen having roused a deer, the prince, who thought the visier followed him, pursued the game so far, and with so much earnestness, that he was left quite alone. He stopt, and finding he had lost his way, endeavoured to return the same way he came, to find out the visier, who had not been careful enough to find him, and so wandered farther.

Whilst he rode up and down, without keeping any road, he met, by the way side, a handsome lady, who wept bitterly. He stopt his horse, asking who she was? how she came to be alone in that place? and what she wanted? I am, says she, daughter to an Indian king; as I was taking the air on horseback in the country, I grew sleepy, fell from my horse, who is got away, and I know not what is become of him. The young prince taking compassion on her, asked her to get up behind him, which she willingly accepted.

As they passed by the ruins of a house, the lady signified a desire to alight on some occasion. The prince stopt and suffered her to alight, then he alighted himself, and went near the ruins with his horse in his hand: But you may judge how much he was surprised, when he heard the lady within it say these words, Be glad, my children, I bring you a handsome young man, and very fat; and other voices which answered immediately, Mamma, where is he, that we may eat him presently, for we are very hungry.

The prince heard enough to convince him of his danger; and then he perceived that the lady, who called herself daughter to an Indian king, was a Hogress, wife to one of these savage demons called Hogres,* who stay in remote places, and make use of a thousand wiles to surprise and devour passengers; so that the prince being thus frightened, mounted his horse as soon as he could.

The pretended princess appeared that very moment, and perceiving she had missed her prey, she cries, Fear nothing, prince; Who are you? Whom do you seek? I have lost my way, replies he, and am seeking it. If you have lost your way, says she, recommend yourself to God, he will deliver you out of your perplexity. Then the prince lifted up his eyes towards heaven. But, Sir, says Scheherazade, I am obliged to break off, for day appears.

I long mightily, says Dinarzade, to know what became of that young prince; I tremble for him. I will deliver you from your uneasiness to-morrow, answers the sultaness, if the sultan will allow me to live till then. Schahriar, willing to hear an end of this adventure, prolonged Scheherazade's life for another day.

THE SIXTEENTH NIGHT.

DINARZADE had such a mighty desire to hear out the story of the young prince, that she awaked that night sooner than ordinary, and said, Sister, pray go on with the story you began yesterday: I am much concerned for the young prince, and ready to die for fear that he was eat up by the Hogress and her children. Schahriar having signified that he had the same fear, the sultaness replies, Well, sir, I will satisfy you immediately.

After the counterfeit Indian princess had bid the young prince recommend himself to God, he could not believe she spoke sincerely, but thought she was sure of him, and therefore lifting up his hands to heaven, said, Almighty Lord, cast thine eyes upon me, and deliver me from mine enemy. After which prayer, the Hogress entered the ruins again, and the prince rode off with all possible haste. He happily found his way again, and arrived safe and sound at his father's court, to whom he gave a particular account of the danger he had been in through the visier's neglect: upon which the king, being incensed against that minister, ordered him to be strangled that very moment.

Sir, continues the Grecian king's visier, to return to the physician Douban, if you do not take care, the confidence you put in him will be fatal to you: I am very well assured that he is a spy sent by your enemies to attempt your majesty's life. He has cured you, you will say; but, alas! who can assure you of that? he has perhaps cured you only in appearance, and not radically; who knows but the medicines he has given you, may in time have pernicious effects?

The Grecian king, who had naturally very little sense, was not able to discover the wicked design of his visier, nor had he firmness enough to persist in his first opinion. This discourse staggered him: Visier, says he, thou art in the right: he may be come on purpose to take away my life, which he may easily do by the very smell of some of his drugs. We must consider what is fit for us to do in this case.

When the visier found the king in such a temper as he would have him, Sir, says he, the surest and speediest method you can take to secure your life, is to send immediately for the physician Douban, and order his head to be cut off as soon as he comes. In truth, says the king, I believe that is the way we must take to prevent his design. When he had spoke thus, he called for one of his officers, and ordered him to go for the physician; who knowing nothing of the king's design, came to the palace in haste.

Know ye, says the king, when he saw him, why I sent for you? No sir, answered he, I wait till your majesty be pleased to inform me. I sent for you, replied the king, to rid myself of you, by taking your life.

No man can express the surprise of the physician, when he heard the sentence of death pronounced against him. Sir, says he, why would your majesty take away my life? What crime have I committed? I am informed by good hands, replies the king, that you came to my court only to attempt my life; but to prevent you, I will be sure of yours. Give the blow, says he to the executioner, who was present, and deliver me from a perfidious wretch, who came hither on purpose to assassinate me.

When the physician heard this cruel order, he readily judged that the honours and presents he had received from the king had procured him enemies, and that the weak prince was imposed upon. He repented that he had cured him of his leprosy, but it was now too late. Is it thus, replies the physician, that you reward me for curing you? The king would not hearken to him, but ordered the hangman a second time to strike the fatal blow. The physician then had recourse to his prayers: Alas! sir, cries he, prolong my days, and God will prolong yours; do not put me to death, lest God treat you in the same manner. The fisherman broke off his discourse here, to apply it to the genie. Well, genie, says he, you see what passed then betwixt the Grecian king, and his physician, Douban, is acted just now betwixt us.

The Grecian king, continues he, instead of having regard to the prayers of the physician, who begged him for God's sake to spare him, cruelly replied to him, No, no; I must of necessity cut you off, otherwise you may take my life away with as much subtleness as you cured me. The physician melting into tears, and bewailing himself sadly for being so ill rewarded by the king, prepared for death. The executioner bound up his eyes, tied his hands, and went to draw his scymitar.

Then the courtiers, who were present, being moved with compassion, begged the king to pardon him, assuring his majesty that he was not guilty of the crime laid to his charge, and that they would answer for his innocence; but the king was inflexible, and answered them so, as they dared not to say any more of the matter.

The physician being on his knees, his eyes tied up, and ready to receive the fatal blow, addressed himself once more to the king. Sir, says he, since your majesty will not revoke the sentence of death, I beg, at least, that you would give me leave to return to my house to give order about my burial, to bid farewell to my family, to give alms, and to bequeath my books to those who are capable of making good use of them. I have one particularly I would present to your majesty; it is a very precious book, and worthy to be laid up very carefully in your treasury. Well, replies the king, why is that book so precious as you talk of? Sir, says the physician, because it contains an infinite number of curious things, of which the chief is, that when you have cut off my head, if your majesty will give yourself the trouble to open the book at the sixth leaf, and read the third line of the left page, my head will answer all the questions you ask it. The king being curious to see such a wonderful thing, deferred his death till next day, and sent him home under a strong guard.

The physician, during that time, put his affairs in order; and the report being spread, that an unheard-of prodigy was to happen after his death, the visiers, emirs,* officers of the guard, and, in a word, the whole court, repaired next day to the hall of audience, that they might be witnesses of it.

The physician Douban was soon brought in, and advanced to the foot of the throne, with a great book in his hand; there he called for a bason, upon which he laid the cover that the book was wrapped in, and presenting the book to the king: Sir, says he, take that book, if you please, and as soon as my head is cut off, order that it be put into the bason upon the cover of the book; as soon as it is put there, the blood will stop; then open the book, and my head will answer your questions. But, sir, says he, permit me once more to implore your majesty's clemency; for God's sake, grant my request, I protest to you that I am innocent. Your prayers, answers the king, are in vain; and were it for nothing but to hear your head speak after your death, it is my will you should die. As he said this, he took the book out of the physician's hand, and ordered the executioner to do his duty.

The head was so dextrously cut off, that it fell into the bason, and was no sooner laid upon the cover of the book, but the blood stopped; then to the great surprise of the king and all the spectators, it opened its eyes, and said, Sir, will your majesty be pleased to open the book? the king opened it, and finding that one leaf was as it were glued to another, that he might turn it with the more ease, he put his finger to his mouth, and wet it with spittle. He did so till he came to the sixth leaf, and finding no writing on the place where he was bid to look for it, Physician, says he to the head, here is nothing writ. Turn over some more leaves, replies the head. The king continued to turn over, putting always his finger to his mouth, until the poison, with which each leaf was imbued, came to have its effect; the prince finding himself, all of a sudden, taken with an extraordinary fit, his eye-sight failed, and he fell down at the foot of his throne in great convulsions. At these words, Scheherazade perceiving day, gave the sultan notice of it, and forebore speaking. Ah, dear sister, says Dinarzade, how grieved am I that you have not time to finish this story! I should be inconsolable if you lose your life to-day. Sister, replies the sultaness, that must be as the sultan pleases; but I hope he will be so good as to suspend my death till to-morrow. And accordingly, Schahriar, far from ordering her death that day, expected next night with much impatience; so earnest was he to hear out the story of the Grecian king, and the sequel of that of the Fisherman and the Genie.

THE SEVENTEENTH NIGHT.

THOUGH Dinarzade was very curious to hear the rest of the story of the Grecian king, she did not awake that night so soon as usual, so that it was almost day before she called upon the sultaness; and then said, I pray you, sister, to continue the wonderful story of the Greek king; but make haste, I beseech you, for it will speedily be day.

Scheherazade resumed the story where she left off the day before: Sir, says she to the sultan, when the physician Douban, or rather his head, saw that the poison had taken effect, and that the king had but a few moments to live: Tyrant, it cried, now you see how princes are treated, who, abusing their authority, cut off innocent men: God punishes soon or late their injustice and cruelty. Scarce had the head spoke these words when the king fell down dead, and the head itself lost what life it had.

Sir, continues Scheherazade, such was the end of the Grecian king and the physician Douban; I must return now to the story of the Fisherman and the Genie; but it is not worth while to begin it now, for it is day. The sultan, who always observed his hours regularly, could stay no longer, but got up; and having a mind to hear the sequel of the story of the Genie and the Fisherman, he bid the sultaness prepare to tell him it next night.

THE EIGHTEENTH NIGHT.

DINARZADE made amends this night for last night's neglect; she awaked long before day, and calling upon Scheherazade, Sister, says she, if you be not asleep, pray give us the rest of the story of the Fisherman and the Genie; you know the sultan desires to hear it as well as I.

I shall soon satisfy his curiosity and yours, answers the sultaness: and then addressing herself to Schahriar, Sir, continued she, as soon as the fisherman had concluded the history of the Greek king and his physician, Douban, he made the application to the genie, whom he still kept shut up in the vessel. If the Grecian king, says he, would have suffered the physician to live, God would also have suffered him to live; but he rejected his most humble prayers; and it is the same with thee, O genie. Could I have prevailed with thee, to grant me the favour I demanded, I should now have had pity upon thee; but since notwithstanding the extreme obligation thou wast under to me for having set thee at liberty, thou didst persist in thy design to kill me, I am obliged, in my turn, to be as hard hearted to thee.

My good friend fisherman, replies the genie, I conjure thee once more, not to be guilty of so cruel a thing; consider that it is not good to avenge one's self, and that, on the other hand, it is commendable to do good for evil; do not treat me as Imama treated Ateca formerly.* And what did Imama to Ateca, replies the fisherman? Ho! says the genie, if you have a mind to know it, open the vessel; do you think that I can be in a humour to tell stories in so strait a prison? I will tell you as many as you please, when you let me out. No, says the fisherman, I will not let thee out, it is in vain to talk of it: I am just going to throw thee into the bottom of the sea. Hear me one word more, cries the genie, I promise to do thee no hurt; nay, far from that, I will shew thee a way how thou mayst become exceeding rich.

The hope of delivering himself from poverty prevailed with the fisherman. I could listen to thee, says he, were there any credit to be given to thy word; swear to me by the great name of God, that you will faithfully perform what you promise, and I will open the vessel; I do not believe you will dare to break such an oath.

The genie swore to him, and the fisherman immediately took off the covering of the vessel. At that very instant the smoke came out, and the genie having resumed his form, as before, the first thing he did, was to kick the vessel into the sea. This action frightened the fisherman: Genie, says he, what is the meaning of that? Will not you keep the oath you just now made? And must I say to you, as the physician Douban said to the Grecian king, Suffer me to live, and God will prolong your days?

The genie laughed at the fisherman's fear, and answered, No, fisherman, be not afraid, I only did it to divert myself, and to see if thou wouldst be alarmed at it: But to persuade thee that I am in earnest, take thy net and follow me. As he spoke these words, he walked before the fisherman, who having taken up his nets, followed him, but with some distrust: They passed by the town, and came to the top of a mountain, from whence they descended into a vast plain, which brought them to a great pond, that lay betwixt four hills.

When they came to the side of the pond, the genie says to the fisherman, Cast in thy nets and take fish; the fisherman did not doubt to catch some, because he saw a great number in the pond; but he was extremely surprised, when he found they were of four colours; that is to say, white, red, blue, and yellow.* He threw in his nets, and brought out one of each colour; having never seen the like, he could not but admire them, and judging that he might get a considerable sum for them, he was very joyful. Carry those fish, says the genie to him, and present them to thy sultan; he will give you more money for them than ever you had in your life. You may come every day to fish in this pond, and I give thee warning not to throw in thy nets above once a-day; otherwise you will repent it. Take heed, and remember my advice; if you follow it exactly, you will find your account in it. Having spoke thus, he struck his foot upon the ground, which opened, and shut again after it had swallowed up the genie.

The fisherman being resolved to follow the genie's advice exactly, forbore casting in his nets a second time; but returned to the town very well satisfied with his fish, and making a thousand reflections upon his adventure. He went straight to the sultan's palace, to present him his fish.—But, Sir, says Scheherazade, I perceive day, and must stop here.

Dear sister, says Dinarzade, how surprising are the last events you have told us! I have much ado to believe that any thing you have to say can be more surprising. Sister, replies the sultaness, if the sultan, my master, will let me live till to-morrow, I am persuaded you will find the sequel of the history of the Fisherman more wonderful than the beginning of it, and incomparably more diverting. Schahriar being curious to know if the remainder of the story of the Fisherman would be such as the sultaness said, put off the execution of the cruel law for one day more.

THE NINETEENTH NIGHT.

TOWARDS morning, Dinarzade called the sultaness, and said, Dear sister, my pendulum* tells me it will be day speedily, therefore pray continue the history of the Fisherman; I am extremely impatient to know what the issue of it was. Scheherazade having demanded leave of Schahriar, resumed her discourse as follows: Sir, I leave it to your majesty to think how much the sultan was surprised, when he saw the four fishes which the fisherman presented him. He took them up one after another, and beheld them with attention; and after having admired them a long time, Take those fishes, says he to his prime visier, and carry them to the fine cook-maid that the emperor of the Greeks has sent me. I cannot imagine but they must be as good as they are fine.

The visier carried them himself to the cook, and delivering them into her hands, Look ye, says he, there are four fishes newly brought to the Sultan, he orders you to dress them; and having said so, he returned to the sultan, his master, who ordered him to give the fisherman four hundred pieces of gold of the coin of that country, which he did accordingly.

The fisherman, who had never seen so much cash in his life-time, could scarce believe his own good fortune, but thought it must needs be a dream, until he found it to be real, when he provided necessaries for his family with it.

But, Sir, says Scheherazade, having told you what happened to the fisherman, I must acquaint you next with what befel the sultan's cook-maid, whom we shall find in a mighty perplexity. As soon as she had gutted the fishes, she put them upon the fire in a frying-pan, with oil, and when she thought them fried enough on one side, she turned them upon the other; but O monstrous prodigy! Scarce were they turned, when the wall of the kitchen opened, and in comes a young lady of wonderful beauty, and comely size. She was clad in flowered sattin, after the Egyptian manner, with pendants in her ears, necklace of large pearl, and bracelets of gold, garnished with rubies, with a rod of myrtle in her hand. She came towards the frying-pan, to the great amazement of the cook-maid, who continued immoveable at this sight, and striking one of the fishes with the end of the rod, says: Fish, fish, art thou in thy duty? The fish having answered nothing, she repeated these words, and then the four fishes lift up their heads all together and said to her, Yes, yes: if you reckon, we reckon; if you pay your debts, we pay ours; if you fly, we overcome, and are content. As soon as they had finished these words, the lady overturned the frying-pan, and entered again into the open part of the wall, which shut immediately, and became as it was before.

The cook-maid was mightily frightened at this, and coming a little to herself, went to take up the fishes that fell upon the earth, but found them blacker than coal, and not fit to be carried to the sultan. She was grievously troubled at it, and fell a-weeping most bitterly: Alas! says she, what will become of me? If I tell the sultan what I have seen, I am sure he will not believe me, but will be mightily enraged against me.

Whilst she was thus bewailing herself, in comes the grand visier, and asked her if the fishes were ready? She told him all that had happened, which, we may easily imagine, astonished him mightily; but without speaking a word of it to the sultan, he invented an excuse that satisfied him, and sending immediately for the fisherman, bid him bring four more such fish; for a misfortune had befallen the others, that they were not fit to be carried to the sultan. The fisherman, without saying anything of what the genie had told him, in order to excuse himself from bringing them that very day, told the visier he had a great way to go for them, but would certainly bring them to-morrow.

Accordingly the fisherman went away by night, and coming to the pond, threw in his nets betimes next morning, took four such fishes as the former, and brought them to the visier at the hour appointed. The minister took them himself, carried them to the kitchen, and shutting himself up all alone with the cook-maid, she gutted them and put them on the fire, as she had done the four others the day before; when they were fried on the one side, and that she turned them upon the other, the kitchen wall opened, and the same lady came in, with the rod in her hand, struck one of the fishes, spoke to it as before, and all four gave her the same answer. But, sir, says Scheherazade, day appears, which obliges me to break off. What I have told you is indeed very singular, but if I be alive to-morrow, I will tell you other things which are yet better worth your hearing.

Schahriar, conceiving that the sequel must be very curious, resolved to hear her next night.

THE TWENTIETH NIGHT.

NEXT morning the sultan prevented Dinarzade, and says to Scheherazade, Madam, I pray you make an end of the story of the Fisherman; I am impatient to hear it. Upon which the sultaness continued it thus:

Sir, after the four fishes had answered the young lady, she overturned the frying-pan with her rod, and retired into the same place of the wall from whence she came out, the grand visier being witness of what passed: This is too surprising and extraordinary, says he, to be concealed from the sultan: I will inform him of this prodigy; which he did accordingly, and gave him a faithful account of all that had happened.

The sultan being much surprised, was mighty impatient to see this himself. To this end, he sent immediately for the fisherman, and says to him, Friend, cannot you bring me four more such fishes? The fisherman replied, If your majesty will be pleased to allow me three days time, I will do it. Having obtained his time he went to the pond immediately, and at the first throwing in of his net, he took four such fishes, and brought them presently to the sultan, who was so much more rejoiced at it, that he did not expect them so soon, and ordered him other four hundred pieces of gold. As soon as the sultan had the fish, he ordered them to be carried into the closet, with all that was necessary for frying them; and having shut himself up there with his visier, that minister gutted them, put them in the pan, upon the fire, and when they were fried on one side, turned them upon the other: then the wall of the closet opened; but instead of the young lady, there came out a black in habit of a slave, and of a gigantic stature, with a great green battoon in his hand. He advanced towards the pan, and touching one of the fishes with his battoon,* says to it, with a terrible voice, Fish, art thou in thy duty? at these words the fishes raised up their heads, and answered, Yes, yes, we are; if you reckon, we reckon; if you pay your debts, we pay ours; if you fly, we overcome, and are content.

The fishes had no sooner finished those words, but the black threw the pan into the middle of the closet, and reduced the fishes to a coal.—Having done this, he retired fiercely, and entering again into the hole of the wall, it shut and appeared just as it was before.

After what I have seen, says the sultan to the visier, it will not be possible for me to be easy in my mind. These fish, without doubt, signify something extraordinary, in which I have a mind to be satisfied. He sent for the fisherman; and when he came, says to him, Fisherman, the fishes you have brought us make me very uneasy; where did you catch them? Sir, answers he, I fished for them in a pond situated betwixt four hills, beyond the mountain that we see from hence. Know you that pond, says the sultan to the visier? No, sir, replies the visier, I never so much as heard of it; and yet it is full sixty years since I hunted beyond that mountain and thereabouts.—The sultan asked the fisherman, how far the pond might be from the palace? the fisherman answering, It was not above three hours journey: Upon this assurance, and there being day enough beforehand, the sultan commanded all his court to take horse, and the fisherman served them for a guide. They all ascended the mountain, and at the foot of it they saw to their great surprise, a vast plain, that nobody had observed till then; and at last they came to a pond, which they found actually to be situated betwixt four hills, as the fisherman had said. The water of it was so transparent, that they observed all the fishes to be like those which the fisherman had brought to the palace.

The sultan staid upon the bank of the pond, and after beholding the fishes with admiration, he demanded of his emirs, and all his courtiers, if it was possible they had never seen this pond, which was within so little a way of the town.—They all answered, that they had never so much as heard of it.

Since you all agree, says he, that you never heard of it, and as I am no less astonished than you are, at this novelty, I am resolved not to return to my palace, till I know how this pond came hither, and why all the fish in it are of four colours. Having spoke thus, he ordered his court to encamp, and immediately his pavilion and the tents of his household were planted upon the banks of the pond.

When night came, the sultan retired under his pavilion, and spoke to the grand visier by himself, thus: Visier, my mind is very uneasy. This pond transported hither; the black that appeared to us in my closet, and the fishes that we heard speak; all this does so much whet my curiosity, that I cannot resist the impatient desire that I have to be satisfied in it. To this end I am resolved to withdraw alone from the camp, and I order you to keep my absence secret; stay in my pavilion, and to-morrow morning, when the emirs and courtiers come to attend my levee, send them away, and tell them, that I am somewhat indisposed, and have a mind to be alone; and the following day tell them the same thing till I return.

The grand visier said several things to divert the sultan from his design: He represented to him the danger to which he might be exposed, and that all his labours might perhaps be in vain; but it was to no purpose, the sultan was resolved on it, and would go. He put on a suit fit for walking, and took his scymitar; and as soon as he saw that all was quiet in the camp, he goes out alone, and went over one of the hills without much difficulty; he found the descent still more easy, and when he came to the plain, walked on till the sun arose, and then he saw before him, at a considerable distance, a great building: He rejoiced at the sight, in hopes to be informed there of what he had a mind to know. When he came near, he found it was a magnificent palace, or rather a very strong castle, of fine black polished marble, and covered with fine steel, as smooth as a looking glass. Being mightily pleased that he had so speedily met with something worthy his curiosity, he stopt before the front of the castle, and considered it with abundance of attention.

He afterwards came up to the gate, which had two leaves, one of them open; though he might have entered when he would, yet he thought it best to knock. He knocked at first softly, and waited for some time; but seeing nobody, and supposing they had not heard him, he knocked harder the second time; but neither seeing, nor hearing any body, he knocked again and again; but nobody appearing, it surprised him extremely; for he could not think, that a castle so well in repair was without inhabitants. If there be nobody in it, says he to himself, I have nothing to fear: and if there be, I have wherewith to defend myself.

At last he entered, and when he came within the porch, he cries, Is there nobody here to receive a stranger, who comes in for some refreshment as he passes by? He repeated the same two or three times; but though he spoke very high, nobody answered.

This silence increased his astonishment; he came into a very spacious court, and looking on every side, to see if he could perceive any body, he saw no living thing. But, sir, says Scheherazade, day appears, and I must stop.

Ah! sister, says Dinarzade, you break off at the very best of the story. It is true, answers the sultaness, but, sister, you see I am forced to do so. If my lord the sultan pleases, you may hear the rest to-morrow. Schahriar agreed to this, not so much to pleasure Dinarzade, as to satisfy his own curiosity, being mighty impatient to know what adventure the prince met with in the castle.

THE TWENTY-FIRST NIGHT.

DINARZADE, to make amends for her neglect the night before, never laid eye together, and when she thought it was time, awakened the Sultaness, saying to her, My dear sister, pray give us an account of what happened in the fine castle where you left us yesterday.

Scheherazade forthwith resumed her story, and addressing herself to Schahriar, says, Sir, the sultan perceiving nobody in the court, entered the great halls, which were hung with silk tapestry, the alcoves and sofas were covered with stuffs of Mecca, and the porches with the richest stuffs of the Indies, mixed with gold and silver. He came afterwards into an admirable saloon, in the middle of which there was a great fountain, with a lion of massy* gold at each corner: Water issued at the mouths of the four lions, and this water, as it fell, formed diamonds and pearls, that very well answered a jet of water, which, springing from the middle of the fountain, rose as high almost as the bottom of a cupola, painted after the Arabian manner.

The castle, on three sides, was encompassed by a garden, with flower-pots, water-works, groves, and a thousand other fine things concurring to embellish it; and what completed the beauty of the place, was an infinite number of birds, which filled the air with their harmonious notes, and always staid there; nets being spread over the trees, and fastened to the palace to keep them in. The sultan walked for a long time from apartment to apartment, where he found every thing very grand and magnificent. Being tired with walking, he sat down in an open closet, which had a view over the garden, and there reflecting upon what he had already seen, and did then see, all of a sudden he heard the voice of one complaining, accompanied with lamentable cries. He listened with attention, and heard distinctly these sad words: O Fortune! thou who wouldest not suffer me longer to enjoy a happy lot, and hast made me the most unfortunate man in the world; forbear to persecute me, and by a speedy death, put an end to my sorrows. Alas! is it possible that I am still alive, after so many torments as I have suffered!

The sultan being affected with those pitiful complaints, rose up; and made towards the place where he heard the voice; and when he came to the gate of a great hall, he opened it, and saw a handsome young man, richly habited, set upon a throne raised a little above the ground. Melancholy was painted in his looks. The sultan drew near, and saluted him: The young man returned him his salute by a low bow with his head; but not being able to rise up, he says to the sultan, My lord, I am very well satisfied that you deserve I should rise to receive you, and do you all possible honour; but I am hindered from doing so, by a very sad reason, and therefore hope you will not take it ill. My lord, replies the sultan, I am very much obliged to you for having so good an opinion of me: As to the reason of your not rising, whatever your apology be, I heartily accept of it. Being drawn hither by your complaints, and afflicted by your grief, I come to offer you my help; would to God that it lay in my power to ease you of your trouble; I would do my utmost to effect it. I flatter myself that you would willingly tell me the history of your misfortunes; but pray tell me first, the meaning of the pond near the palace, where the fishes are of four colours? what this castle is? how you came to be here? and why you are alone?

Instead of answering these questions, the young man began to weep bitterly. O how inconstant is Fortune! cried he: She takes pleasure to pull down those men she had raised up. Where are they who enjoy quietly the happiness which they hold of her, and whose day is always clear and serene?

The sultan, moved with compassion to see him in that condition, prayed him forthwith to tell him the cause of his excessive grief. Alas, my lord replies the young man, how is it possible but I should grieve? And why should not my eyes be inexhaustible fountains of tears? At these words lifting up his gown, he shewed the sultan that he was a man only from the head to the girdle, and that the other half of his body was black marble.—Here Scheherazade broke off, and told the sultan that day appeared.

Schahriar was so much charmed with the story, and became so much in love with Scheherazade, that he resolved to let her live a month. He got up however as usual, without acquainting her with his resolution.

THE TWENTY-SECOND NIGHT.

DINARZADE was so impatient to hear out the story, that she called her sister next morning sooner than usual, and says to her, Sister, pray continue the wonderful story you began, but could not make an end of yesterday morning. I agree to it, replies the sultaness, hearken then.

You may easily imagine, continues she, that the sultan was strangely surprised, when he saw the deplorable condition of the young man. That which you shew me, says he, as it fills me with horror, whets my curiosity so, that I am impatient to hear your history, which, no doubt, is very strange, and I am persuaded that the pond and the fishes make some part of it: therefore I conjure you to tell it me. You will find some comfort in it, since it is certain, that unfortunate people find some sort of ease in telling their misfortunes. I will not refuse you this satisfaction, replies the young man, though I cannot do it without renewing my grief. But I give you notice before-hand, to prepare your ears, your mind, and even your eyes, for things which surpass all that the most extraordinary imagination can conceive.

The History of the young King of the Black-Isles

YOU must know, my lord, continued he, that my father, who was called Mahmoud, was king of this country. This is the kingdom of the Black-Isles, which takes its name from the four little neighbouring mountains; for those mountains were formerly isles; The capital, where the king, my father, had his residence, was where that pond you now see is. The sequel of my history will inform you of all those changes.

The king, my father, died when he was seventy years of age; I had no sooner succeeded him, but I married, and the lady I chose to share the royal dignity with me was my cousin. I had all the reason imaginable to be satisfied in her love to me; and for my part, I had so much tenderness for her, that nothing was comparable to the good understanding betwixt us, which lasted five years, at the end of which time, I perceived the queen, my cousin, had no more delight in me.

One day, while she was at the bath, I found myself sleepy after dinner, and lay down upon a sofa; two of her ladies, who were then in my chamber, came and sat down, one at my head, and the other at my feet, with fans in their hands to moderate the heat, and to hinder the flies from troubling me in my sleep. They thought I was fast, and spoke very low: but I only shut my eyes, and heard every word they said.

One of them says to the other: Is not the queen much in the wrong, not to love such an amiable prince as this? Ay, certainly, replies the other; for my part I do not understand it, and I know not why she goes out every night, and leaves him alone. Is it possible that he does not perceive it? Alas! says the first, how would you have him to perceive it? she mixes every evening in his drink, the juice of a certain herb, which makes him sleep so sound all night, that she has time to go where she pleases, and as day begins to appear, she comes and lies down by him again, and wakes him by the smell of something she puts under his nose.

You may guess, my lord, how much I was surprised at this discourse, and with what sentiments it inspired me; yet, whatever emotions it made within me, I had command enough over myself to dissemble it, and feigned myself to awake, without having heard one word of it.

The queen returned from the bath; we supped together, and before we went to bed, she presented me with a cup full of such water as I was accustomed to drink; but instead of putting it to my mouth, I went to a window that stood open, and threw out the water so privately, that she did not perceive it, and I put the cup again into her hands, to persuade her that I had drunk it.

We went to bed together, and soon after, believing that I was asleep, though I was not, she got up with so little precaution, that she said, so loud as I could hear it distinctly, Sleep, and may you never wake again. She dressed herself speedily, and went out of the chamber.—As Scheherazade spoke those words, she saw day appear, and stopt.

Dinarzade had heard her sister with a great deal of pleasure; and Schahriar thought the history of the king of the Black-Isles so worthy of his curiosity, that he rose up full of impatience for the rest of it.

THE TWENTY-THIRD NIGHT.

An hour before day, Dinarzade being awake, failed not to call upon the sultaness, and said, Pray, dear sister, go on with the history of the young king of the four Black Islands. Scheherazade calling to mind where she had left off, resumed the story thus:

As soon as the queen my wife went out, continues the king of the Black-Islands, I got up, dressed me in haste, took my scymitar, and followed her so quick, that I soon heard the sound of her feet before me, and then walked softly after her, for fear of being heard. She passed through several gates, which opened upon her pronouncing some magical words; and the last she opened was that of the garden, which she entered: I stopt at that gate, that she might not perceive me, as she crossed a plat,* and looking after her as far as I could in the night, I perceived that she entered a little wood, whose walks were guarded by thick pallisadoes.* I went thither by another way, and slipping behind the pallisadoes of a long walk, I saw her walking there with a man.

I gave very good heed to their discourse, and heard her say thus: I do not deserve, says the queen to her gallant, to be upbraided by you for want of diligence; you know very well what hinders me; but if all the marks of love that I have already given you, be not enough, I am ready to give you greater marks of it: You need but command me; you know my power. I will, if you desire it, before sun-rising, change this great city, and this fine palace, into frightful ruins, which shall be inhabited by nothing but wolves, owls and ravens. Would you have me to transport all the stones of those walls, so solidly built, beyond mount Caucasus, and out of the bounds of the habitable world? Speak but the word, and all those places shall be changed.

As the queen finished these words, her gallant and she came to the end of the walk, turned to enter another, and passed before me. I had already drawn my scymitar, and her gallant being next me, I struck him in the neck, and made him fall to the ground; I thought I had killed him, and therefore retired speedily, without making myself known to the queen, whom I had a mind to spare, because she was my kinswoman.

In the mean time the blow I had given her gallant was mortal; but she preserved his life by the force of her enchantments, in such a manner, however, that he could not be said to be either dead or alive. As I crossed the garden, to return to the palace, I heard the queen cry out lamentably, and judging by that how much she was grieved, I was pleased that I had spared her life.

When I returned to her apartment, I went to bed, and being satisfied with having punished the villain that did me the injury, I went to sleep; and when I awaked next morning, found the queen lying by me.—Scheherazade was obliged to stop here, because she saw day.

O heaven! sister, says Dinarzade, how it troubles me that you can say no more? Sister, replies the sultaness, you ought to have awaked me more early; it is your fault. I will make amends next night, replies Dinarzade, for I doubt not but the sultan will be as willing to hear out the story as I am: and I hope he will be so good as to let you live one day more.

THE TWENTY-FOURTH NIGHT.

DINARZADE was actually as good as her word, she called the sultaness very early, saying, Dear sister, if you be not asleep, pray make an end of the agreeable history of the king of the Black-Isles, I am ready to die with impatience to know how he came to be changed into marble. You shall hear it, replies Scheherazade, if the sultan will give me leave.

I found the queen lying by me then, says the king of the Black-Islands: I cannot tell you whether she slept or not; but I got up without making any noise, and went to my closet, where I made an end of dressing myself. I afterwards went and held my council, and at my return, the queen was clad in mourning, her hair hanging about her eyes, and part of it pulled off; she presented herself before me, and said, Sir, I come to beg your majesty not to be surprised to see me in this condition; three afflicting pieces of news I have just now received all at once, are the cause of my heavy grief, of which the tokens you see are but very faint resemblances. Alas! what is that news, madam, said I? The death of the queen my dear mother, answers she; that of the king my father killed in battle; and that of one of my brothers, who is fallen headlong into it.

I was not ill pleased, that she made use of this pretext to hide the true cause of her grief, and I thought she had not suspected me to have killed her gallant. Madam, says I, I am so far from blaming your grief, that I assure you, I am willing to bear what share of it is proper for me. I should very much wonder, if you were insensible of so great a loss. Mourn on, your tears are so many proofs of your good-nature; but I hope, however, that time and reason will moderate your grief.

She retired into her apartment, where, giving herself wholly up to sorrow, she spent a whole year in mourning, and afflicting herself. At the end of that time, she begged leave of me to build a burying-place for herself, within the bounds of the palace, where she would continue, she told me, to the end of her days: I agreed to it, and she built a stately palace, with a cupola, that may be seen here, and she called it the Palace of Tears: when it was finished, she caused her gallant to be brought thither, from the place whither she had made him to be carried the same night that I wounded him; she had hindered his dying, by a drink she gave him, and carried to him herself, every day after he came to the Palace of Tears.

Yet, with all her enchantments, she could not cure the wretch; he was not only unable to walk, and to help himself, but had also lost the use of his speech, and gave no sign of life, but only by his looks.—Though the queen had no other consolation but to see him, and to say to him all that her foolish passion could inspire her with; yet every day she made him two long visits: I was very well informed of all this, but pretended to know nothing of it.

One day I went out of curiosity to the Palace of Tears, to see how the princess employed herself, and going to a place where she could not see me, I heard her speak thus to her gallant: I am afflicted to the highest degree, to see you in this condition; I am as sensible as you yourself, of the tormenting grief you endure; but, dear soul, I always speak to you, and you do not answer me. How long will you be silent? speak only one word: alas! the sweetest moments of my life are these I spend here, in partaking of your grief. I cannot live at a distance from you, and would prefer the pleasure of always seeing you, to the empire of the universe.

At these words, which were several times interrupted by her sighs and sobs, I lost all patience; and discovering myself, came up to her, and said, Madam, you have mourned enough; it is time to give over this sorrow, which dishonours us both; you have too much forgot what you owe to me and to yourself.—Sir, says she, if you have any kindness or complaisance left for me, I beseech you to put no force upon me, allow me to give myself up to mortal grief, it is impossible for time to lessen it.

When I saw that my discourse, instead of bringing her to her duty, served only to increase her rage, I gave over, and retired. She continued every day to visit her gallant; and for two whole years, gave herself up to excessive grief.

I went a second time to the Palace of Tears, while she was there; I hid myself again, and heard her speak thus to her gallant: It is now three years since you spoke one word to me, you return no answer to the marks of love I give you, by my discourse and groans. Is it from want of sense, or out of contempt? O tomb! have you abated that excessive love he had for me? Have you shut those eyes that shewed me so much love, and were all my joys?

No, no, I believe nothing of it. Tell me rather, by what miracle you become intrusted with the rarest treasure that ever was in the world.

I must confess, my lord, I was enraged at these words; for, in short, this gallant, so much doated upon, this adored mortal, was not such an one as you would imagine him to have been; he was a black Indian, a native of that country. I say, I was so enraged at that discourse, that I discovered myself all of a sudden, and addressing the tomb in my turn, O tomb! cried I, why do you not swallow up that monster in nature, or rather, why do not you swallow up the gallant and his mistress!

I had scarce finished those words, when the queen, who sat by the black, rose up like a fury. Ah, cruel man, says she, thou art the cause of my grief, do not you think but I know it. I have dissembled it but too long; it is thy barbarous hand which hath brought the object of my love to this lamentable condition; and you are so hard hearted, as to come and insult a despairing lover. Yes, said I in a rage, it is I who chastised that monster, according to his desert; I ought to have treated thee in the same manner; I repent now that I did not do it, thou hast abused my goodness too long. As I spoke these words I drew out my scymitar, and lifted up my hand to punish her; but she stedfastly beholding me, said with a jeering smile, moderate thy anger. At the same time, she pronounced words I did not understand; and afterwards added, By virtue of my enchantments, I command thee immediately to become half marble and half man. Immediately, my lord, I became such as you see me, already a dead man among the living, and a living man among the dead. Here Scheherazade perceiving day, broke off her story.

Upon which Dinarzade says, Dear sister, I am extremely obliged to the sultan, it is to his goodness I owe the extraordinary pleasure I have in your stories. My sister, replies the sultaness, if the sultan will be so good as to suffer me to live till to-morrow, I shall tell you a thing that will afford as much satisfaction as any thing you have yet heard. Though Schahriar had not resolved to defer the death of Scheherazade a month longer, he could not have ordered her to be put to death that day.

THE TWENTY-FIFTH NIGHT.

TOWARDS the end of the night, Dinarzade cried, Sister, if I do not trespass too much upon your complaisance, I would pray you to finish the history of the king of the Black-islands. Scheherazade having awaked upon her sister's call, prepared to give her the satisfaction she required, and began thus:

The king, half marble half man, continued his history to the sultan, thus: After this cruel magician, unworthy of the name of a queen, had metamorphosed me thus, and brought me into this hall; by another enchantment, she destroyed my capital, which was very flourishing, and full of people; she abolished the houses, the public places, and markets, and made a pond and desert field of it, which you may have seen; the fishes of four colours in the pond, are the four sorts of people, of different religions, that inhabited the place. The white, are the Mussulmen; the red, the Persians, who worshipped the fire;* the blue, the Christians; and the yellow, the Jews. The four little hills were the four islands that gave name to this kingdom. I learned all this from the magician, who, to add to my affliction, told me with her own mouth, those effects of her rage. But this is not all; her revenge was not satisfied with the destruction of my dominions, and the metamorphosis of my person; she comes every day, and gives me over my naked shoulders an hundred blows with ox pizzles,* which makes me all over blood; and when she has done so, covers me with a coarse stuff of goat's hair, and throws over it this robe of brocade that you see, not to do me honour, but to mock me.

At this part of the discourse, the young king could not withhold his tears; and the sultan's heart was so pierced with the relation, that he could not speak one word to comfort him. A little time after, the young king, lifting up his eyes to heaven, cried out; Mighty Creator of all things, I submit myself to your judgments, and to the decrees of your providence: I endure my calamities with patience, since it is your will it should be so; but I hope your infinite goodness will reward me for it.

The sultan, being much moved by the recital of so strange a story, and animated to revenge this unfortunate prince, says to him, Tell me whither this perfidious magician retires, and where her unworthy gallant may be, who is buried before his death? My lord, replies the prince, her gallant, as I have already told you, is in the Palace of Tears, in a tomb in form of a dome, and that palace joins to this castle on the side of the gate. As to the magician, I cannot precisely tell whither she retires, but every day, at sunrising, she goes to see her gallant, after having executed her bloody vengeance upon me, as I have told you; and you see I am not in a condition to defend myself against so great cruelty. She carries him the drink with which she has hitherto prevented his dying, and always complains of his never speaking to her since he was wounded.

Oh, unfortunate prince! says the sultan, you can never enough be bewailed! Nobody can be more sensibly touched with your condition than I am; never did such an extraordinary misfortune befall any man; and those who write your history will have the advantage to relate a passage that surpasses all that has ever yet been writ. There is nothing wanting but one thing, the revenge which is due to you; and I will omit nothing that can be done to procure it.

While the sultan discoursed upon this subject with the young prince, he told him who he was, and for what end he entered the castle, and thought on a way to revenge him, which he communicated to him. They agreed upon the measures they were to take for effecting their design, but deferred the execution of it till the next day. In the mean time, the night being far spent, the sultan took some rest; but the poor young prince passed the night without sleep, as usual, having never slept since he was enchanted; but he conceived some hopes of being speedily delivered from his misery.

Next morning the sultan got up before day, and, in order to execute his design, he hid in a corner his upper garment, that would have been cumbersome to him, and went to the Palace of Tears. He found it enlightened with an infinite number of flambeaus of white wax, and a delicious scent issued from several boxes of fine gold, of admirable workmanship, all ranged in excellent order. As soon as he saw the bed where the black lay, he drew his scymitar, killed the wretch without resistance, dragged his corpse into the court of the castle, and threw it into a well. After this, he went and lay down in the black's bed, took his scymitar with him, under the counterpane, and lay there to execute what he had designed.

The magician arrived in a little time; she first went into the chamber, where her husband, the king of the Black-Islands, was, stripped him, and beat him with bulls' pizzles, in a most barbarous manner. The poor prince filled the palace with his lamentations, to no purpose, and conjured her, in the most affecting manner that could be, to take pity on him; but the cruel woman would not give over, till she had given him an hundred blows. You had no compassion on my love, said she, and you are to expect none from me. Scheherazade perceiving day, stopped, and could go no farther.

O heaven! says Dinarzade, sister, this was a barbarous enchantress indeed! But must we stop here? Will you not tell us whether she received the chastisement she deserved? My dear sister, says the sultaness, I desire nothing more than to acquaint you with it to-morrow; but you know that depends on the sultan's pleasure. After what Schahriar had heard, he was far from any design to put Scheherazade to death; on the contrary, says he to himself, I will not take away her life, till she has finished this surprising story, though it should last for two months. It will always be in my power to keep the oath I have made.

THE TWENTY-SIXTH NIGHT.

As soon as Dinarzade thought it time to call the sultaness, she says to her, How much should I be obliged to you, dear sister, if you would tell us what passed in the Palace of Tears? Schahriar having signified that he was as curious to know it as Dinarzade, the sultaness resumed the story of the young enchanted prince, as follows:

Sir, after the enchantress had given the king, her husband, an hundred blows with bulls' pizzles, she put on again his covering of goat's hair, and his brocade gown over all; she went afterwards to the Palace of Tears, and as she entered the same, she renewed her tears and lamentations; then approaching the bed, where she thought her gallant was, What cruelty, cries she, was it to disturb the contentment of so tender and passionate a lover as I am? O thou who reproachest me that I am too inhuman, when I make thee feel the effects of my resentment! Cruel prince! does not thy barbarity surpass my vengeance? Ah traitor! in attempting the life of the object which I adore, hast thou not robbed me of mine? Alas! says she, addressing herself to the sultan, while she thought she spoke to the black, my soul, my life, will you always be silent? Are you resolved to let me die, without giving me so much comfort as to tell me that you love me? My soul! speak one word to me at least, I conjure you.

The sultan, making as if he had awakened out of a deep sleep, and counterfeiting the language of the blacks, answers the queen with a grave tone, 'There is no force or power but in God alone, who is almighty.' At these words, the enchantress, who did not expect them, gave a great shout, to signify her excessive joy. My dear lord, cries she, do not I deceive myself? is it certain that I hear you, and that you speak to me? Unhappy wretch, said the sultan, art thou worthy that I should answer thy discourse? Alas! replies the queen, why do you reproach me thus! The cries, replied he, the groans and tears of thy husband, whom thou treatest every day with so much indignity and barbarity, hinder me to sleep night and day. I should have been cured long ago, and have recovered the use of my speech, hadst thou disenchanted him. That is the cause of my silence, which you complain of. Very well, says the enchantress, to pacify you, I am ready to do what you will command me; would you that I restore him as he was? Yes, replies the sultan, make haste to set him at liberty, that I be no more disturbed with his cries.

The enchantress went immediately out of the Palace of Tears; she took a cup of water, and pronounced words over it, which caused it to boil as if it had been on the fire. She went afterwards to the hall to the young king, her husband, and threw the water upon him, saying, 'If the Creator of all things did form thee so as thou art at present, or if he be angry with thee, do not change; but if thou art in that condition merely by virtue of my enchantments, resume thy natural shape, and become what thou wast before.' She had scarce spoke these words, when the prince, finding himself restored to his former condition, rose up freely, with all imaginable joy, and returned thanks to God. The enchantress then said to him, Get thee gone from this castle, and never return here, on pain of death. The young king, yielding to necessity, went away from the enchantress, without replying a word; and retired to a remote place, where he immediately expected the success of the design which the sultan had begun so happily. Meanwhile the enchantress returned to the Palace of Tears, and supposing that she still spoke to the black, says, Dear lover, I have done what you ordered, let nothing now hinder you to give me that satisfaction, of which I have been deprived so long.

The sultan continued to counterfeit the language of the blacks. That which you have just now done, said he, signifies nothing to my cure; you have only eased me of part of my disease; you must cut it up by the roots. My lovely black, replies she, what do you mean by the roots? Unfortunate woman, replies the sultan, do not you understand that I mean the town, and its inhabitants, and the four islands, which thou hast destroyed by thy enchantments?

The fishes every night at midnight raise their heads out of the pond, and cry for vengeance against thee and me. This is the true cause of the delay of my cure. Go speedily, restore things as they were, and at thy return I will give thee my hand, and thou shalt help me to rise.

The enchantress, filled with hopes from those words, cried out in a transport of joy, my heart, my soul, you shall be soon restored to your health; for I will immediately do what you command me. Accordingly she went that moment, and when she came to the brink of the pond, she took a little water in her hand, and sprinkling it,—Here Scheherazade saw day, and stopped.

Dinarzade says to the sultaness, Sister, I am much rejoiced to hear that the young king of the Black Islands was disenchanted; and I already consider the town and the inhabitants as restored to their former state; but I long to know what will become of the enchantress. Have a little patience, replies the sultaness, you shall have the satisfaction you desire to-morrow, if the sultan, my lord, will consent to it. Schahriar having resolved on it already, as was said before, rose up, and went about his business.

THE TWENTY-SEVENTH NIGHT.

AT the usual hour, Dinarzade called upon the sultaness, thus: dear sister, pray tell us what was the fate of the magician queen, as you promised us. Upon which Scheherazade went on thus: The enchantress had no sooner sprinkled the water, and pronounced some words over the fishes and the pond, but the city was restored that very minute. The fishes became men, women, and children; Mahometans, Christians, Persians, or Jews; freemen, or slaves, as they were before; every one having recovered their natural form. The houses and shops were immediately filled with their inhabitants, who found all things as they were before the enchantment. The sultan's numerous retinue, who found themselves encamped in the largest square, were astonished to see themselves in an instant in the middle of a large, fine, and well-peopled city.

To return to the enchantress: as soon as she had made this wonderful change, she returned with all diligence to the Palace of Tears, that she might reap the fruits of it. My dear lord, cries she, as she entered, I come to rejoice with you for the return of your health; I have done all that you required of me, then pray rise and give me your hand. Come near, says the sultan, still counterfeiting the language of the blacks. She did so. You are not near enough, replies he, come nearer. She obeyed. Then he arose up, and seized her by the arm so suddenly, that she had not time to know who it was, and with a blow of his scymitar he cut her in two, so that the one half fell one way and the other another. This being done, he left the carcase upon the place, and going out of the Palace of Tears, he went to seek the young king of the Black Isles, who waited for him with a great deal of impatience; and when he found him, Prince, says he, embracing him, rejoice, you have nothing to fear now; your cruel enemy is dead.

The young prince returned thanks to the sultan in such a manner, as shewed that he was thoroughly sensible of the kindness that he had done him, and in acknowledgment, wished him a long life and all happiness. You may henceforward, says the sultan, dwell peaceably in your capital, except you will go to mine, which is so near, where you shall be very welcome, and have as much honour and respect as if you were at home. Potent monarch, to whom I am so much indebted, replies the king, you think then, that you are very near your capital. Yes, says the sultan, I know it is not above four or five hours journey. It will take you a whole year's journey, says the prince; I do believe, indeed, that you came hither from your capital in the time you spoke of, because mine was enchanted; but since the enchantment is taken off, things are changed: however, this shall not hinder me to follow you, were it to the utmost corners of the earth. You are my deliverer, and that I may give you proofs of my acknowledging this during my whole life, I am willing to accompany you, and leave my kingdom without regret.

The sultan was extremely surprised, to understand that he was so far from his dominions, and could not imagine how it could be. But the young king of the Black-Islands convinced him so plainly, that he could no more doubt of it. Then the sultan replied, It is no matter, the trouble that I shall have to return to my own country, is sufficiently recompensed by the satisfaction I have had to oblige you, and by acquiring you for a son; for since you will do me the honour to attend me, and that I have no child, I look upon you as one, and from this moment I appoint you my heir and successor.

This discourse between the sultan and the king of the Black-Islands concluded with most affectionate embraces; after which the young prince was wholly taken up in making preparations for his journey, which were finished in three weeks time, to the regret of his court and subjects, who agreed to receive at his hands one of his nearest kindred for king.

At last the sultan and young prince began their journey with an hundred camels laden with inestimable riches from the treasury of the young king, followed by fifty handsome gentlemen on horseback, perfectly well mounted and dressed. They had a very happy journey; and when the sultan, who had sent couriers to give advice of his delay, and of the adventure which had occasioned it, came near his capital, the principal officers he left there came to receive him, and to assure him, that his long absence had occasioned no alteration in his empire. The inhabitants came out also in great crowds, receiving him with mighty acclamations, and made public rejoicings for several days.

Next day after his arrival, the sultan gave all his courtiers a very ample account of all things, which, contrary to his expectation, had detained him so long. He acquainted them with having adopted the king of the four Black-Islands, who was willing to leave a great kingdom, to accompany and live with him, and, in short, as an acknowledgement of their loyalty, he rewarded each of them according to their rank.

And for the fisherman, as he was the first cause of the deliverance of the young prince, the sultan gave him a plentiful estate, which made him and his family happy the rest of his days.

Here Scheherazade made an end of the story of the Fisherman and the Genie. Dinarzade signified, that she had taken a great deal of pleasure in it; and Schahriar having said the same thing, the sultaness told them, that she knew another which was much finer; and, if the sultan would give her leave, she would tell it them next morning; for day began to appear. Schahriar bethinking himself that he had granted the sultaness a month's reprieve, and being curious moreover to know if this new story would be as agreeable as she promised, got up, with a design to hear it next night.

[ADVERTISEMENT.* The readers of these Tales were tired in the former editions, with the interruption Dinarzade gave them: this defect is now remedied; and they will meet with no more interruptions at the end of every night. It is sufficient to know the Arabian author's design, who first made this collection: and for this purpose we retained his method in the preceding nights.

There are of these Arabian Tales, where neither Scheherazade, sultan Schahriar, Dinarzade, nor any distinction by nights, is mentioned; which shews that all the Arabians have not approved the method which this author has used, and that a great number of them have been fatigued with these repetitions. This, therefore, being reformed in the following translation, the reader must be acquainted that Scheherazade goes now on always without being interrupted.]

The Story of the three Calenders, Sons of Kings; and of the five Ladies of Bagdad

In the reign of Caliph Haroun Alraschid, there was at Bagdad, the place of his residence, a porter, who, notwithstanding his mean and laborious business, was a fellow of wit and good humour. One morning as he was at the place where he usually plied, with a great basket, waiting for employment, a young handsome lady, covered with a great muslin veil, came to him and said with a pleasant air, Hark ye, porter, take your basket, and follow me. The porter, charmed with those few words, pronounced in so agreeable a manner, took his basket immediately, set it on his head, and followed the lady saying, 'O happy day, a day of good luck.'

The lady stopped presently before a gate that was shut, and knocked: a Christian, with a venerable, long, white beard, opened the gate, and she put money into his hand, without speaking one word; but the Christian, who knew what she wanted, went in, and in a little time after, brought a large jug of excellent wine. Take this jug, says the lady to the porter, and put it in your basket. This being done, she commanded him to follow her; and as she went on, the porter says still, 'O happy day! this is a day of agreeable surprise and joy.'

The lady stopped at a fruit-shop, where she bought several sorts of apples, apricots, peaches, quinces, lemons, citrons, oranges, myrtles, sweet basil, lilies, jessamine, and some other sorts of flowers and plants that smell well; she bid the porter put all into his basket, and follow her. As she went by a butcher's stall, she made him weigh her twenty-five pounds of his best meat; which she ordered the porter to put also into his basket.

At another shop, she took capers, cucumbers, and other herbs preserved in vinegar: at another shop, she bought pistachios, walnuts, small nuts, almonds, kernels of pine apples, and such other fruits; and of another she bought all sorts of confections. When the porter had put all these things into his basket, and perceived that it grew full, My good lady, says he, you ought to have given me notice that you had so much provision to carry, and then I would have got a horse, or rather a camel, to have carried them; for if you buy ever so little more, I shall not be able to carry it. The lady laughed at the fellow's pleasant humour, and ordered him still to follow her.

Then she went to a druggist, where she furnished herself with all manner of sweet scented waters, cloves, musk, pepper, ginger, and a great piece of ambergris, and several other Indian spices; this quite filled the porter's basket, and she ordered him to follow her. They walked till they came to a magnificent house, whose front was adorned with fine columns, and which had a gate of ivory: there they stopped, and the lady knocked softly.

While the young lady and the porter staid for the opening of the gate, the porter had a thousand thoughts; he wondered that such a fine lady should come abroad to buy provisions; he concluded she could not be a slave, her air was too noble for that, and therefore he thought she must needs be a woman of quality. Just as he was about to ask her some questions upon that head, another lady came to open the gate, and appeared so beautiful to him, that he was perfectly surprised, or rather so much struck with her charms, that he was like to have let his basket fall, for he had never seen any beauty that came near her.

The lady who brought the porter with her, perceiving his disorder, and the occasion of it, diverted herself with it, and took so much pleasure to examine his looks, that she forgot the gate was opened. Upon this, the beautiful lady says to her, Pray, sister, come in, what do you stay for? do not you see this poor man so heavy loaded, that he is scarce able to stand under it?

When she entered with the porter, the lady who opened the gate shut it, and all three after having gone through a very fine porch, came into a spacious court encompassed with an open gallery, which had a communication with several apartments on a floor, and extraordinarily magnificent. There was at the farther end of the court a sofa richly adorned with a throne of amber in the middle of it, supported by four columns of ebony, enriched with diamonds and pearls of an extraordinary size, and covered with red satin, embroidered with Indian gold of admirable workmanship. In the middle of the court there was a great fountain, faced with white marble, and full of clear water, which fell into it abundantly out of the mouth of a lion of brass.

The porter, though very heavy loaden, could not but admire the magnificence of this house, and the excellent order that every thing was placed in; but that which particularly captivated his attention, was a third lady, who seemed to be a greater beauty than the second, and was set upon the throne just now mentioned; she came down from it as soon as she saw the two former ladies, and advanced towards them: he judged by the respect which the others shewed her, that she was the chief, in which he was not mistaken:

This lady was called Zobeide, she who opened the gate was called Safie, and Amine was the name of her who went out to buy the provisions.

Zobeide says to the two ladies, when she came to them, Sisters, do not you see that this honest man is like to sink under his burden? why do not you ease him of it? Then Amine and Safie took the basket, the one before, and the other behind, and Zobeide also lent her hand, and all three set it on the ground; then emptied it, and when they had done, the beautiful Amine took out money, and paid the porter liberally.

The porter, very well satisfied with the money he had received, was to have taken up his basket, and be gone; but he could not tell how to think on it; do what he could, he found himself stopped by the pleasure of seeing three such beauties, who appeared to him equally charming; for Amine having now laid aside her veil, was as handsome as either of them. That which surprised him most was, that he saw never a man about the house, yet most of the provisions he brought in, as the dry fruits, and the several sorts of cakes and confections, were fit chiefly for those who could drink and make merry.

Zobeide thought at first that the porter staid only to take his breath; but perceiving that he staid too long, What do you wait for, says she, are you not well enough paid? And turning to Amine, says, Sister, give him something more, that he may depart satisfied. Madam, replies the porter, it is not that which stays me. I am over and above paid; I am sensible that I am unmannerly to stay longer than I ought, but I hope you will be so good as to pardon me, if I tell you, that I am astonished to see that there is no man with three ladies of such extraordinary beauty; and you know that a company of women without men is as melancholy a thing as a company of men without women. To this he added several very pleasing things, to prove what he said, and did not forget the Bagdad proverb, That one is never well at table, except there be four in company: And so concluded, that since there were but three, they had need of a fourth.

The ladies fell a-laughing at the porter's discourse; after which, Zobeide says to him very gravely, Friend, you are a little too bold, and though you do not deserve that I should enter into particulars with you, yet I am willing to tell you, that we are three sisters, who do our business so secretly, that nobody knows any thing of it. We have too great reason to be cautious of acquainting indiscreet persons with it; and a good author that we have read says, Keep your secret, and do not reveal it to any body. He that reveals it, is no longer master of it. If your own breast cannot keep your secret, how do you think that another person will keep it?

My ladies, replies the porter, by your very air, I judged at first that you were persons of extraordinary merit, and I conceive that I am not mistaken; though fortune has not given me wealth enough to raise me above my mean profession, yet I have not failed to cultivate my mind as much as I could, by reading books of science and history: And allow me, if you please, to tell you, that I have also read in another author, a maxim which I have always happily practised: We do not conceal our secrets, says he, but from such persons as are known to all the world to want discretion, and would abuse the confidence we put in them; but we make no scruple to discover them to prudent persons, because we know they can keep them. A secret with me is as sure as if it were in a closet, whose key was lost, and the door sealed up.

Zobeide perceiving that the porter did not want sense, but conceiving that he had a mind to have a share in their treat, she replies to him, smiling, You know that we are about to have a treat, and you know also that we have been at a considerable expence, and it is not just that you should have a share of it without contributing towards it. The beautiful Safie seconded her sister, and says to the porter, Friend, have you never heard that which is commonly said, If you bring any thing with you, you shall be welcome; but if you bring nothing, you must get you gone with nothing?

The porter, notwithstanding his rhetoric, must, in all probability, have retired in confusion, if Amine had not taken his part, and said to Zobeide and Safie, My dear sisters, I conjure you to let him stay with us: I need not tell you that he will divert us, you see well enough he is capable of that: I must needs tell you, that without he had been very willing, as well as nimble, and hardy enough to follow me, I could not have done so much business in so little time; besides, should I repeat to you all the obliging expressions he made to me by the way, you would not be surprised at my protecting him.

At these words of Amine, the porter was so much transported with joy, that he fell on his knees, kissed the ground at the feet of that charming person, and raising himself up, says, Most beautiful lady, you began my good fortune to-day, and now you complete it by this generous action; I cannot enough testify my acknowledgement for it. As to what remains, my ladies, says he, addressing himself to all the three sisters, since you do me so great honour, do not think that I will abuse it, or look upon myself as a person that deserves it. No, I shall always look upon myself as one of your most humble slaves. When he had spoke these words, he would have returned the money he had received; but the grave Zobeide ordered him to keep it. That which we have once given, says she, to reward those who have served us, we never take again.

Zobeide would not take back the money from the porter, but said, My friend, in consenting that you stay with us, I must forewarn you, that it is not only on condition that you keep secret what we have required you, but also that you observe exactly the rules of good manners and civility. In the mean time the charming Amine put off the apparel she went abroad with, put on her night-gown that she might be more easy, and covered the table, which she furnished with several sorts of meat, and upon a sideboard she set bottles of wine and cups of gold: Soon after, the ladies took their places, and made the porter sit down by them, who was overjoyed to see himself at table with three such admirable beauties. After they had eat a little, Amine, who sat next the sideboard, took up a bottle and cup, filled out wine and drank first herself, according to the custom of the Arabians,* then she filled the cup to her sisters, who drank in course as they sat; and at last she filled it the fourth time to the porter, who, as he received it, kissed Amine's hand; and before he drank, sung a song to this purpose: That as the wind brings along with it the sweet scents of the perfumed places through which it passes, so the wine he was going to drink, coming from her fair hands, received a more exquisite taste than what it had of its own nature. This song pleased the ladies so much, that each of them sung another in their turn. In short, they were extraordinary merry all the time of dinner, which lasted a long while, and nothing was wanting that could make it agreeable. The day being almost spent, Safie spoke in the name of the three ladies, and says to the porter, Arise, and be gone, it is time for you to depart. But the porter, not willing to leave so good company, cried, Alas! ladies, whither do you command me to go in the condition I am in? I am quite beside myself, by what I have seen since I came hither; and, having also drank above my ordinary, I shall never find the way home: Allow me this night to recover myself, in any place where you please; for no less time is necessary for me to come to myself; but go when I will, I shall leave the best part of myself behind me.

Amine pleaded a second time for the porter, saying, Sisters, he is in the right, I am pleased with the request, he having already diverted us so well; and if you will take my advice, or if you love me as much as I think you do, let us keep him, to pass away the remaining part of the night. Sister, answered Zobeide, we can refuse you nothing; and then, turning to the porter, said, We are willing once more to grant your request; but upon this new condition, that whatever we do in your presence, relating to ourselves, or any thing else, take heed you do not once open your mouth to ask the reason of it; for if you ask questions about that which does not belong to you, you may come to know that which will be no way pleasing to you: Beware therefore, and do not be too curious to dive into the motives of our actions.

Madam, replied the porter, I promise to observe this condition with such exactness, that you shall have no cause to reproach me with the breaking it, and far less to punish my indiscretion; my tongue shall be immoveable on this occasion, and my eye like a looking-glass, which retains nothing of the object that is set before it. And, to shew you, says Zobeide, with a serious countenance, that what we demand of you is not a new thing among us; rise up, and read what is over our gate in the inside.

The porter went thither and read these words, written in large characters of gold: 'He who speaks of things that do not concern him, shall hear of things that will not please him.' Returning again to the three sisters, Ladies, says he, I give you my oath, that you shall never hear me speak any thing which does not concern me, or wherein you may have any concern.

This agreement being made, Amine brought in supper, and after the room was set round with tapers, that were mixed with aloes and ambergris, which gave a most agreeable scent as well as a delicate light, she sat down at table with her sisters and the porter. They began again to eat and drink, sing and repeat verses. The ladies took pleasure to fuddle the porter, under pretext of causing him to drink their healths, and abundance of witty sentences passed on both sides. In short, as they were all in the best humour in the world, they heard one knocking at the gate.

When the ladies heard the knocking, they all three got up to open the gate; but Safie, to whom this office did particularly belong, was the nimblest; which her other two sisters perceiving, sat down till she came back to acquaint them who it could be that had any business with them so late. Safie returning, said, Sisters, we have here a very fine opportunity to pass a good part of the night with much satisfaction, and if you be of the same mind with me, we shall not let it slip. There are three calenders* at our gate, at least they appear to be such by their habit: but that which you will most admire at, is, they are all blind of the right eye, and have their heads, beards, and eye-brows shaved; and, as they say, are but just come to Bagdad, where they never were before; and it being night, and not knowing where to find any lodging, they happened by chance to knock at this gate, and pray us, for the love of heaven, to have compassion on them, and receive them into the house: They care not what place we put them in; provided they may be under shelter, they would be satisfied with a stable. They are young and handsome enough, and seem also to be men of good sense; but I cannot, without laughing, think of their pleasant and uniform figure. Here Safie fell a-laughing so heartily, that it put the two sisters and the porter into the same mood. My dear sisters, says she, are you content that they come in? it is impossible but with such persons as I have already described them to be, we shall finish the day better than we began it; they will afford us diversion enough, and put us to no charge, because they desire shelter only for this night, and resolve to leave us as soon as day appears.

Zobeide and Amine made some difficulty to grant Safie's request, for reasons they knew well enough. But she having so great a desire to obtain this favour, they could not refuse her. Go then, says Zobeide, and bring them in, but do not forget to acquaint them that they must not speak of any thing which does not concern them, and cause them to read what is wrote over the gate. Safie ran out with a great deal of joy, and in a little while after returned with the three calenders in her company.

At their entrance they made a profound bow to the ladies, who rose up to receive them; told them most obligingly that they were very welcome, that they were glad to have met with an opportunity to oblige them, and to contribute towards relieving them from the fatigue of their journey, and at last invited them to sit down with them.

The magnificence of the place, and the civility of the ladies, made the calenders to conceive a mighty idea of their fine landladies: But, before they sat down, having by chance cast their eye upon the porter, whom they saw clad almost like one of those other calenders, with whom they are in controversy about several points of discipline, because they neither shave their beards nor eyebrows; one of them said, Look here, I believe we have got one of our revolted Arabian brethren.

The porter being half asleep, and having his head pretty warm with wine, was affronted at these words, and with a fierce look, without stirring from his place, answered; Sit you down, and do not meddle with what does not concern you. Have you not read the inscription over the gate? Do not pretend to make people live after your fashion, but follow ours.

Honest man, says the calender, do not put yourself in a passion; we should be very sorry to give you the least occasion; but on the contrary, we are ready to receive your commands. Upon which, to avoid all quarrels, the ladies interposed, and pacified them. When the calenders were set at table, the ladies served them with meat; and Safie, being most pleased with them, did not let them want for drink.

After the calenders had eat and drank liberally, they signified to the ladies, that they had a great desire to entertain them with a concert of music, if they had any instruments in the house, and would cause them to be brought them. They willingly accepted the proffer, and fair Safie going to fetch them, returned again in a moment, and presented them with a flute of her own country fashion, another of the Persian sort, and a tabor. Each man took the instrument he liked, and all three began to play a tune. The ladies, who knew the words of a merry song that suited the air, joined the concert with their voices; but the words of the song made them now and then stop, and fall into excessive laughter.

At the height of this diversion, and when the company was in the midst of their jollity, some body knocks at the gate; Safie left off singing, and went to see who it was. But, sir, says Scheherazade to the sultan, it is fit your majesty should know why this knocking happened so late at the lady's house, and the reason was thus: The caliph Haroun Alraschid was accustomed to walk abroad in disguise very often by night, that he might see with his own eyes, if every thing was quiet in the city, and that no disorders were committed in it.

This night the caliph went out pretty early on his rambles, accompanied with Giafar his grand visier, and Mesrour the chief of the eunuchs of his palace, all disguised in merchants habits; and passing through the street where the ladies dwelt, he heard the sound of music, and great fits of laughter; upon which he commanded the visier to knock, because he would go in to know the reason of that jollity. The visier told him, in vain, that it was some women a-merry making, that without question their heads were warm with wine, and that it would not be proper he should expose himself to be affronted by them. Besides, it was not yet an unlawful hour, and therefore he ought not to disturb them in their mirth. No matter, said the caliph, I command you to knock. So it was that the grand visier Giafar knocked at the lady's gate by the caliph's order, because he himself would not be known. Safie opened the gate, and the visier perceived by the light that she held in her hand, that she was an incomparable beauty; he acted his part very well, and with a very low bow and respectful behaviour, told her, Madam, we are three merchants of Moussol, that arrived about ten days ago with rich merchandize, which we have in a warehouse at a khan (or inn)* where we have also our lodging. We happened this day to be with a merchant of this city, who invited us to a treat at his house, where we had a splendid entertainment; and the wine having put us in humour, he sent for a company of dancers: Night being come on, and the music and dancers making a great noise, the watch came by in the mean time, caused the gate to be opened and some of the company to be taken up; but we had the good fortune to escape, by getting over a wall. Now, saith the visier, being strangers, and somewhat overcome with wine, we are afraid of meeting another, and perhaps the same watch, before we get home to our khan, which lies a good way from hence. Besides, when we come there, the gates will be shut, and not opened till morning: Wherefore, Madam, hearing as we past this way, the sound of music, we supposed you were not yet going to rest, and made bold to knock at your gate, to beg the favour of lodging ourselves in the house till morning, and if you think us worthy of your good company, we will endeavour to contribute to your diversion what lies in our power, to make some amends for the interruption we have given you; if not, we only beg the favour of staying this night under your porch.

While Giafar held this discourse, fair Safie had time to observe the visier and his two companions, who were said to be merchants like himself, and told them that she was not mistress of the house; but if they would have a minute's patience she would return with an answer.

Safie acquainted her sisters with the matter, who considered for some time what to conclude upon: But being naturally of a good disposition, and having granted the same favour to the three calenders, they at last consented to let them in.

The caliph, his grand-visier, and the chief of the eunuchs, being introduced by the fair Safie, very courteously saluted the ladies and the calenders: The ladies returned them the like civilities, supposing them to be merchants. Zobeide, as the chief, says to them with a grave and serious countenance, which was natural to her, You are welcome. But before I proceed farther, I hope you will not take it ill if we desire one favour of you. Alas! said the visier, What favour? We can refuse nothing to such fair ladies. Zobeide replied, It is, that you would only have eyes, but no tongues, that you put no questions to us about the reason of any thing you may happen to see, and not to speak of any thing that does not concern you, lest you come to hear of things that will not please you. Madam, replied the visier, you shall be obeyed. We are not censorious, nor impertinently curious; it is enough for us to take notice of that which concerns us, without meddling with that which does not belong to us. Upon this they all sat down, and the company being united they drank to the health of the new comers.

While Giafar entertained the ladies in discourse, the caliph could not forbear to admire their extraordinary beauty, graceful behaviour, pleasant humours, and ready wit; on the other hand, nothing was more surprising to him than the calenders being all three blind of the right eye. He would gladly have been informed of this singularity; but the conditions so lately imposed upon himself and his companions, would not allow him to speak. This, with the richness of the furniture, the exact order of every thing, and neatness of the house, made him to think it was some enchanted palace.

Their entertainment happening to be upon divertisements, and different ways of making merry, the calenders arose, and danced after their fashion, which augmented the good opinion the ladies had conceived of them, and procured them the esteem of the caliph and his companions.

When the three calenders had made an end of their dance, Zobeide arose, and taking Amine by the hand, said, Pray, sister, rise up, for the company will not take it ill if we use our freedom, and their presence need not to hinder our performance of what we are wont to do. Amine, by understanding her sister's meaning, rose up from her seat, carried away the dishes, the tables, the flasks, and cups, together with the instruments which the calenders had played upon.

Safie was not idle, but swept the room, put every thing again in its place, snuffed the candles, and put fresh aloes and ambergris to them, and then prayed the three calenders to sit down upon the sofa on one side, and the caliph, with his companions, on the other. As to the porter, she says to him, Get up, and prepare yourself to serve in what we are going about: a man like you, that is one of the family, ought not to be idle. The porter being somewhat recovered from his wine, gets up immediately, and having tied the sleeve of his gown to his belt, answers, Here am I, ready to obey your commands, in any thing. That is very well, replied Safie, stay till you are spoke to, you shall not be idle very long. A little time after, Amine came in with a chair, which she placed in the middle of the room; and so went to a closet, which having opened, she beckoned to the porter, and says to him, Come hither, and help me; which he obeying, entered the closet, and returned immediately, leading two black bitches, with each of them a collar and chain; they looked as if they had been severely whipped with rods, and he brought them into the middle of the room.

Then Zobeide rising from her seat, between the calenders and the caliph, marched very gravely towards the porter; Come on, says she, with a great sigh, let us perform our duty; then tucking up her sleeves above her elbows, and receiving a rod from Safie, Porter, said she, deliver one of the bitches to my sister Amine, and come to me with the other.

The porter did as he was commanded; the bitch that he held in his hand, began to cry, and turning towards Zobeide, held her head up in a begging posture; but Zobeide, having no regard to the sad countenance of the bitch (which would have moved pity) nor her cries (that sounded through all the house) whipped her with the rod, till she was out of breath; and having spent her strength, that she could strike no more, she threw down the rod, and taking the chain from the porter, lifted up the bitch by the paws, and looking upon her with a sad and pitiful countenance, they both wept: after which, Zobeide, with her handkerchief wiped the tears from the bitch's eyes, kissed her, returned the chain to the porter, bid him carry her to the place whence he took her, and bring her the other. The porter led back the whipped bitch to the closet, and receiving the other from Amine, presented her to Zobeide, who bid the porter hold her as he did the first; took up the rod and treated her after the same manner; and when she had wept over her, dried her eyes, and kissed her, returned her to the porter: But lovely Amine spared him the trouble of leading her back into the closet, and did it herself. The three calenders, and the caliph with his companions, were extremely surprised at this execution, and could not comprehend why Zobeide, after having so furiously whipped those two bitches, that by the Mussulman religion are reckoned unclean animals, should cry with them, wipe off their tears, and kiss them; they muttered among themselves, and the caliph, who being more impatient than the rest, longed exceedingly to be informed of the cause of so strange an action, and could not forbear making signs to the visier to ask the question; the visier turned his head another way: but being pressed by repeated signs, he answered by others, that it was not yet time for the caliph to satisfy his curiosity.

Zobeide sat still some time in the middle of the room, where she had whipped the two bitches, to recover herself of the fatigue; and fair Safie called to her, Dear sister, will you be pleased now to return to your place, that I may also act my part? Yes, sister, replies Zobeide, and then went, and sat down upon the sofa, having the caliph, Giafar, and Mesrour on her right hand; and the three calenders, with the porter, on her left.

After Zobeide sat down, the whole company was silent for a while; at last, Safie sitting on a chair in the middle of the room, spoke to her sister Amine, Dear sister, I conjure you to rise up, you know well enough what I would say; Amine arose, and went into another closet, near to that where the bitches were, and brought out a case covered with yellow sattin, richly embroidered with gold, and green silk; she came near Safie, and opened the case, from whence she took out a lute and presented her; and after some time spent in tuning it, Safie began to play, and accompanying it with her voice, she sung a song about the torments that absence creates to lovers, with so much sweetness, that it charmed the caliph and all the company. Having sung with a great deal of passion and action, she said to lovely Amine, Pray take it, sister, for I can do no more; my voice fails me; oblige the company with a tune and a song in my room. Very willingly, replied Amine, who, taking the lute from her sister Safie, sat down in her place.

Amine, after a small trial, to see whether the instrument was in tune, played and sung almost as long upon the same subject, but with so much vehemency, and was so much affected, or rather transported with the words of the song, that her strength failed her as she made an end of it.

Zobeide, willing to testify her satisfaction, said, Sister, you have done wonders, and we may easily see that you have a feeling of the grief that you have expressed so much to the life. Amine was prevented from answering this civility, her heart being so sensibly touched at the same moment, that she was obliged, for air, to uncover her neck and breast, which did not appear so fair as might have been expected from such a lady as she; but, on the contrary, black and full of scars, which frighted all the spectators. However: this gave her no ease, but she fell into a fit.

While Zobeide and Safie ran to help their sister, one of the calenders could not forbear to say, We had better have slept in the streets than have come hither, had we thought to have seen such spectacles. The caliph, who heard this, came up to him and the other calenders, and asked them what might be the meaning of all this? they answered, Sir, we know no more than you do. What, says the caliph, are not you of the family? nor can you resolve us concerning the two black bitches and the lady that fainted away, and has been so basely abused? Sir, said the calenders, this is the first time that ever we were in the house, and came in but a few minutes before you.

This increased the caliph's astonishment. It may be, says he, this other man that is with you, may know something of it. One of the calenders made a sign for the porter to come near; and asked him, whether he knew why those two black bitches had been whipped, and why Amine's bosom was so scarred? Sir, said the porter, I can swear by heaven, that if you know nothing of all this, I know as little as you do. It is true. I live in this city, but I never was in the house till now, and if you are surprised to see me here, I am as much to find myself in your company; and that which increases my wonder is, that I have not seen one man with these ladies.

The caliph and his company, as well as the calenders, supposed the porter had been one of the family, and hoped he could inform them of what they desired to know, but finding he could not, and resolving to satisfy his curiosity, cost what it would, he says to the rest, Look ye, we are here seven men, and have but three women to deal with; let us try if we can oblige them to satisfy us, and if they refuse it by fair means, we are in a condition to force them to it.

The grand-visier Giafar was against this method, and shewed the caliph what might be the consequence of it; but without discovering the prince to the calenders, addressed him as if he had been a merchant, thus: Sir, consider, I pray you, that our reputation lies at stake; you know very well upon what conditions these ladies were ready to receive us, and we also agreed to them. What will they say of us if we break them? we shall be still more to blame if any mischief befal us, for it is not likely that they would demand such a promise of us, if they did not know themselves in a condition to make us repent the breaking of it.

Here the visier took the caliph aside, and whispered to him thus: Sir, the night will soon be at an end, and if your majesty will only be pleased to have so much patience, I will take these ladies to-morrow morning, and bring them before your throne, where you may be informed of all that you desire to know. Though this advice was very judicious, the caliph rejected it, bid the visier hold his tongue, and said he would not stay till then, but would have satisfaction in the matter presently.

The next business was to know who should carry the message. The caliph endeavoured to prevail with the calenders to speak first; but they excused themselves, and at last they agreed, that the porter should be the man. And as they were consulting how to word this fatal question, Zobeide returned from her sister Amine, who was recovered of her fit, drew near them, and having overheard them speaking pretty loud, and with some passion, says, Gentlemen, what is the subject of your discourse? what are you disputing about?

The porter answered immediately, Madam, these gentlemen pray you to let them understand wherefore you wept over your two bitches after you whipped them so severely, and how that lady's bosom, who lately fainted away, comes to be so full of scars? This is what I am ordered to ask in their name.

At these words, Zobeide looked with a stern countenance, and turning towards the caliph and the rest of the company, Is this true, gentlemen, says she, that you have given him orders to ask me this question? All of them, except Giafar, who spoke not a word, answered, yes. On which she told them, in a tone that sufficiently expressed her resentment. Before we granted you the favour of being received into our house, and to prevent all occasion of trouble from you, because we are alone, we did it upon condition, that you should not speak of any thing that did not concern you, lest you might come to hear that which would not please you: and yet, after having received and entertained you as well as possibly we could, you make no scruple to break your promise. It is true, that our easy temper has occasioned this, but that shall not excuse you, for your proceedings are very unhandsome. As she spoke these words, she gave three hard knocks with her foot, and clapping her hands as often together, cried, Come quick. Upon this, a door flew open, and seven strong sturdy black slaves, with scymitars in their hands, rushed in; every one seized a man, threw him on the ground, and dragged him into the middle of the room, in order to cut off his head.

We may easily conceive what a fright the caliph was in; he then repented, but too late, that he had not taken his visier's advice. In the mean time, this unhappy prince, Giafar, Mesrour, the porter, and the calenders, were upon the point of losing their lives by their indiscreet curiosity. But before they would strike the fatal blow, one of the slaves says to Zobeide, and her sisters, High, mighty, and adorable mistresses, do you command us to cut their throats? Stay, says Zobeide, I must examine them first. The frightened porter interrupted her thus: In the name of heaven, do not make me die for another man's crime. I am innocent, they are to blame. Alas! says he, crying, how pleasantly did we pass our time! those blind calenders are the cause of this misfortune; there is no town in the world but goes to ruin where-ever these inauspicious fellows come. Madam, I beg you not to destroy the innocent with the guilty, and consider, that it is more glorious to pardon such a wretch as I, who have no way to help myself, than to sacrifice me to your resentment.

Zobeide, notwithstanding her anger, could not but laugh within herself at the porter's lamentation: but without answering him, she spoke a second time to the rest: Answer me, says she, and tell me who you are, otherwise you shall not live one moment longer. I cannot believe you to be honest men, nor persons of authority or distinction in your own countries; for if you were, you would have been more modest and more respectful to us.

The caliph, who was naturally impatient, was infinitely more impatient than the rest, to find his life depend upon the command of a lady justly incensed; but he began to conceive some hopes, when he saw she would know who they all were; for he imagined she would not take away his life, when once she came to be informed who he was; therefore he spake with a low voice to the visier, who was near him, to declare speedily who he was: but the visier, being more prudent, resolved to save his master's honour, and not to let the world know the affront he had brought upon himself by his own weakness; and therefore answered, We have what we deserve. But if he would have spoken in obedience to the caliph, Zobeide did not give him time; for, having turned to the calenders, and seeing them all three blind of one eye, she asked if they were brothers. One of them answered, No, madam, no otherwise than as we are calenders; that is to say, as we observe the same rules. Were you born blind of the right eye, replied she? No, madam, answers he, I lost my eye in such a surprising adventure, that it would be instructive to everybody, were it in writing. After this misfortune, I shaved my beard and eyebrows, and took the habit of a calender, which I now wear.

Zobeide asked the other two calenders the same question, and had the same answer; but he who spoke last, added, Madam, to shew you that we are no common fellows, and that you may have some consideration for us, be pleased to know, that we are all three sons of kings; and though we never met together till this evening, yet we have had time enough to make that known to one another; and I assure you, that the kings from whom we derive our being, made some noise in the world.

At this discourse Zobeide assuaged her anger, and said to the slaves, Give them their liberty a while, but stay here. Those who tell us their history, and the occasion of their coming, do them no hurt, let them go where they please; but do not spare those who refuse to give us that satisfaction.

Scheherazade demanded leave of the sultan, and having obtained it; Sir, says she, the three calenders, the caliph, the grand-visier Giafar, the eunuch Mesrour, and the porter, were all in the middle of the hall, set upon a foot carpet in the presence of the three ladies, who sat upon a sofa, and the slaves stood ready to do whatever their mistresses should command.

The porter understanding that he might rid himself of his danger, by telling his history, spoke first, and said, Madam, you know my history already, and the occasion of my coming hither; so that what I have to say will be very short. My lady, your sister there, called me this morning at the place where I plied as porter to see if any body would employ me, that I might get my bread; I followed her to a vintner's, then to an herb-woman's, then to one that sold oranges, lemons, and citrons, then to a grocer's, next to a confectioner's and a druggist's, with my basket upon my head as full as I was able to carry it; then I came hither, where you had the goodness to suffer me to continue till now: a favour that I shall never forget. This, madam, is my history.

When the porter had done, Zobeide says to him, Go, march, let us see you no more here. Madam, replies the porter, I beg you to let me stay; it would not be just, after the rest have had the pleasure to hear my history, that I should not also have the satisfaction to hear theirs. And having spoken thus, sat him down at the end of the sofa, glad to the heart to have escaped the danger that had frightened him so much. After him one of the three calenders, directing his speech to Zobeide, as the principal of the three ladies, and the person that commanded him to speak, began his story thus:

The History of the First Calender, a King's Son

MADAM, in order to inform you how I lost my right eye, and why I was obliged to put myself into a calender's habit, I must tell you, that I am a king's son born; the king my father had a brother that reigned as he did, over a neighbouring kingdom; and the prince, his son, and I, were almost of an age.

After I had learned my exercises, and that the king my father granted me such liberty as suited my dignity, I went orderly every year to see my uncle, at whose court, I diverted myself during a month or two, and then returned again to my father's. These several journies gave occasion of contracting a very firm and particular friendship between the prince my cousin, and myself. The last time I saw him, he received me with greater demonstrations of tenderness than he had done at any time before; and resolving one day to give me a treat, he made great preparations for that purpose. We continued a long time at table, and after we had both supped very well: Cousin, says he, you will hardly be able to guess how I have been employed since your last departure from hence, now about a year past. I have had a great many men at work to perfect a design I have in my mind; I have caused an edifice to be built, which is now finished, so as one may dwell in it: you will not be displeased if I show it you. But first you are to promise me upon oath, that you will keep my secret, according to the confidence I repose in you.

The love and familiarity that was between us, would not allow me to refuse him anything. I very readily took the oath required of me: upon which he says to me, Stay here till I return, I will be with you in a moment; and accordingly he came with a lady in his hand, of singular beauty, and magnificently apparelled. He did not discover who she was, neither did I think it was manners in me to make inquiry. We sat down again with this lady at table, where we continued some time, entertaining ourselves with discourses upon indifferent subjects; and now and then a full glass to drink one another's health. After which the prince said, cousin, we must lose no time, therefore pray oblige me to take this lady along with you, and conduct her to such a place, where you will see a tomb newly built in form of a dome; you will easily know it, the gate is open, go in there together, and tarry till I come, which will be very speedily.

Being true to my oath, I made no farther inquiry, but took the lady by the hand, and by the directions which the prince my cousin had given me, I brought her to the place, by the light of the moon, without missing one step of the way. We were scarcely got thither, when we saw the prince following after, carrying a little pitcher with water, a hatchet, and a little bag with plaister.

The hatchet served him to break down the empty sepulchre in the middle of the tomb; he took away the stones one after another, and laid them in a corner. When all this was taken away, he digged up the ground, where I saw a trap-door under the sepulchre, which he lifted up, and underneath perceived the head of a stair-case leading into a vault. Then my cousin, speaking to the lady, said, Madam, it is by this way that we are to go to the place I told you of. Upon which the lady drew nigh, and went down, and the prince began to follow after; but turning first to me, said, My dear cousin, I am infinitely obliged to you for the trouble you have been at, I thank you; adieu. I cried, Dear cousin, what is the meaning of this? Be content, replied he, you may return back the same way you came.

Madam, says the calender to Zobeide, I could get nothing farther from him, but was obliged to take leave of him; as I returned to my uncle's palace, the vapours of the wine got up into my head; however, I got to my apartment, and went to bed. Next morning, when I awaked, I began to reflect upon what befel me the night before, and after recollecting all the circumstances of such a singular adventure, I fancied it was nothing but a dream. Being full of these thoughts, I sent to see if the prince, my cousin, was ready to receive a visit from me; but when they brought back word that he did not lie in his own lodgings that night, they knew not what was become of him, and were in much trouble about it, I conceived that the strange event of the tomb was but too true. I was sensibly afflicted at it; and stealing away privately from my people, I went to the public burying-place, where there was a vast number of tombs like that which I had seen. I spent the day in viewing them one after another, but could not find that I sought for; and thus I spent four days successively in vain.

You must know that all this while the king, my uncle, was absent, and had been a-hunting for several days. I grew weary of staying for him, and having prayed his ministers to make my apology to him at his return, I left his palace, and set towards my father's court, from which I had never been so long absent before. I left the ministers of the king, my uncle, in great trouble to think what was become of the prince, my cousin; but because of my oath I had made, to keep his secret, I durst not tell them any thing of what I had seen or knew, in order to make them easy.

I arrived at my father's capital, the usual place of his residence, where, contrary to custom, I found a great guard at the gate of the palace, who surrounded me as I entered. I asked the reason, and the commanding officer replied, Prince, the army has proclaimed the grand vizier king, instead of your father, who is dead; and I take you prisoner in the name of the new king. At these words the guards laid hold of me, and carried me before the tyrant: I leave you to judge, madam, how much I was surprised and grieved.

This rebel visier had entertained a mortal hatred against me of a long time, upon this occasion: When I was a stripling, I loved to shoot in a cross-bow; and being one day upon the terrace of the palace with my bow, a bird happening to come by, I shot, but missed him, and the ball, by misfortune, hit the visier, who was taking the air upon the terrace of his own house, and put out one of his eyes. As soon as I understood it, I not only sent to make my excuse to him, but did it in person; yet he always resented it, and, as opportunity offered, made me sensible of it. But now, madam, that he had me in his power, he expressed his resentment in a very barbarous manner; for he came to me like a madman, as soon as ever he saw me, and thrusting his finger into my right eye, pulled it out himself; and so, madam, I became blind of one eye.

But the usurper's cruelty did not stop here; he ordered me to be shut up in a box, and commanded the executioner to carry me into the country, to cut off my head, and leave me to be devoured by the birds of prey. The hangman and another, carried me thus shut up, on horse-back, into the country, in order to execute the usurper's barbarous sentence; but, by my prayers and tears, I moved the executioner's compassion. Go, says he to me, get you speedily out of the kingdom, and take heed of ever returning to it, otherwise you will certainly meet your own ruin, and be the cause of mine. I thanked him for the favour he did me; and as soon as I was left alone, I comforted myself for the loss of my eye, by considering that I had very narrowly escaped a much greater danger.

Being in such a condition, I could not travel far at a time. I retired to remote places while it was day, and travelled as far by night as my strength would allow me. At last I arrived in the dominions of the king, my uncle, and came to his capital.

I gave him a long detail of the tragical cause of my return, and of the sad condition he saw me in. Alas! cried he, was it not enough for me to have lost my son; but must I have also news of the death of a brother I loved so dearly, and see you also reduced to this deplorable condition? He told me how uneasy he was, that he could hear nothing of his son, notwithstanding all the diligence and inquiry he could make. At these words, the unfortunate father burst out into tears, and was so much afflicted, that, pitying his grief, it was impossible for me to keep the secret any longer; so that, notwithstanding my oath to the prince my cousin, I told the king, his father, all that I knew.

His majesty listened to me with some sort of comfort, and when I had done, Nephew, says he, what you tell me gives me some hope. I knew that my son ordered that tomb to be built, and I can guess pretty near at the place; and with the idea you still have of it, I fancy we shall find it: but since he ordered it to be built privately, and you took your oath to keep his secret, I am of opinion, that we ought to go in quest of it alone, without saying any thing. But he had another reason for keeping the matter secret, which he did not then tell me, and an important reason it was, as you will perceive by the sequel of my discourse.

We both of us disguised ourselves, and went out by a door of the garden which opened into the field, and soon found what we sought for. I knew the tomb, and was so much the more rejoiced at it, because I had formerly sought it a long time in vain. We entered, and found the iron trap pulled down upon the entrance of the stair-case; we had much ado to raise it, because the prince had fastened it on the inside with the water and mortar, formerly mentioned: but at last we did get it up.

The king, my uncle, went down first, I followed, and we went down about fifty steps. When we came to the foot of the stairs, we found a sort of anti-chamber, full of a thick smoke, and ill scent, which obscured the lamp that gave a very faint light.

From this anti-chamber, we came into another, very large, supported by great columns, and lighted by several branched candlesticks.* There was a cistern in the middle, and provisions of several sorts standing on one side; but we were very much surprised to see no body. Before us there appeared an high sofa, which we mounted by several steps, and over this, there appeared a very large bed, with the curtains drawn close. The king went up, and opening the curtains, perceived the prince, his son, and the lady, in bed together; but burnt and changed to a coal, as if they had been thrown into a great fire and taken out again before they were consumed.

But that which surprised me most of all, was, that though this spectacle filled me with horror, the king, my uncle, instead of testifying his sorrow to see the prince, his son, in such a frightful condition, spit on his face, and says to him with an air, 'This is the punishment of this world, but that of the other will last to eternity;' and, not content with this, he pulled off his sandal, and gave his son a great blow on the cheek with it.

I cannot enough express, madam, said he, how much I was astonished when I saw the king, my uncle, abuse the prince, his son, thus, after he was dead. Sir, said I, whatever grief this dismal sight is capable to impress upon me, I am forced to suspend it, on purpose to ask your majesty what crime the prince, my cousin, may have committed, that his corpse should deserve this sort of treatment? Nephew, replied the king, I must tell you, that my son (who is unworthy of that name) loved his sister from his infancy, and so she did him. I did not hinder their growing love, because I did not foresee the pernicious consequences of it. This tenderness increased as they grew in years, and came to such a head, that I dreaded the end of it. At last I applied such remedies as were in my power; I not only gave my son a severe reprimand in private, laying before him the foulness of the passion he was entertaining, and the eternal disgrace he would bring upon my family, if he persisted in such criminal courses; but I also represented the same thing to my daughter; and besides, I shut her up so close, that she could have no conversation with her brother. But that unfortunate creature had swallowed so much of the poison, that all the obstacles which, by my prudence, I could lay in the way, served only the more to inflame her love.

My son being persuaded of his sister's constancy, on pretence of building a tomb, caused this subterraneous habitation to be made, in hopes to find one day or other an opportunity to possess himself of that object which was the cause of his flame, and to bring her hither. He laid hold on the time of my absence, to enter by force into the place of his sister's confinement; but that is a thing which my honour would not suffer me to make public. And after so damnable an action, he came and inclosed himself and her in this place, which he has supplied, as you see, with all sorts of provisions, that he might enjoy his detestable pleasures for a long time, which ought to be a subject of horror to all the world: but God, that would not suffer such an abomination, has justly punished them both. At these words, he melted into tears, and I joined mine with his.

After a while, casting his eyes upon me, Dear nephew, cried he, embracing me, if I have lost that unworthy son, I shall happily find in you what will better supply his place. And upon some other reflections he made on the doleful end of the prince and princess, his daughter, we both fell into a new fit of weeping.

We went up the same stairs again, and departed at last from that dismal place. We let down again the trap-door, and covered it with earth, and such other materials as the tomb was built of, on purpose to hide, as much as lay in our power, so terrible an effect of the wrath of God.

We had not been very long got back to the palace, unperceived by any one, but we heard a confused noise of trumpets, drums, and other instruments of war. We soon understood by the thick cloud of dust, which almost darkened the air, that it was the arrival of a formidable army. And it proved to be the same visier that had dethroned my father, and usurped his throne, who with a vast number of troops, was also come to possess himself of that of the king, my uncle.

That prince, who then had only his usual guards about him, could not resist so many enemies: they invested the city, and the gates being opened to them without any resistance, they very soon became masters of the city, and broke into the palace; where the king, my uncle, was, who defended himself till he was killed, and sold his life at a dear rate. For my part, I fought as well as I could for a while; but seeing we were forced to submit to a superior power, I thought on my retreat and safety, which I had the good fortune to effect by some back ways, and got to one of the king's servants, on whose fidelity I could depend.

Being thus surrounded with sorrows, and persecuted by fortune, I had recourse to a stratagem, which was the only means left me to save my life; I caused my beard and eye-brows to be shaved, and putting on a calender's habit, I passed, unknown by any, out of the city: after that, by degrees, I found it easy to get out of my uncle's kingdom, by taking the bye-roads.

I avoided passing through towns, until I was got into the empire of the mighty governor of the Mussulmen, the glorious and renowned Caliph Haroun Alraschid, when I thought myself out of danger; and considering what I was to do, resolved to come to Bagdad, intending to throw myself at that monarch's feet, whose generosity is every where applauded. I shall move him to compassion, said I to myself, by the relation of my surprising misfortunes; and without doubt he will take pity on such an unfortunate prince, and not suffer me to implore his assistance in vain.

In short, after a journey of several months, I arrived yesterday at the gate of this city, into which I entered about the dusk of the evening, and standing still a little while to revive my spirits, and to consider on which hand I was to turn, this other Calender you see here next to me, came also along; he saluted me, and I him. You appear, said I, to be a stranger, as I am. You are not mistaken, replied he. He had no sooner returned this answer, but this third Calender, you see there, overtook us. He saluted us and told us, he was a stranger newly come to Bagdad; so that as brethren we joined together, resolving not to separate from one another.

Mean while it was late, and we knew not where to seek a lodging in the city, where we had no acquaintance, nor had ever been before. But good fortune having brought us before your gate, we made bold to knock, when you received us with so much kindness, that we are incapable to return you suitable thanks. This madam, (said he,) is, in obedience to your commands, the account I was to give you why I lost my right eye, wherefore my beard and eye-brows are shaved, and how I came to be with you at this present time.

It is enough, said Zobeide, you may retire to what place you think fit. The Calender made his excuse, and begged the ladies leave to stay till he had heard the relations of his two comrades, whom I cannot (says he) leave with honour; and till he might also hear those of the three other persons that were in company.

The story of the first Calender, seemed very strange to the whole company, but especially to the caliph, who, notwithstanding the slaves stood by with their scymitars in their hands, could not forbear whispering to the visier, Many stories have I heard, but never any thing that came near the story of the Calender. Whilst he was saying this, the second Calender began, addressing his speech to Zobeide.

The Story of the Second Calender, a King's Son

MADAM, said he, to obey your command, and to shew you by what strange accident I became blind of the right eye, I must of necessity give you the whole account of my life.

I was scarce past my infancy, when the king, my father, (for you must know, madam, I am a prince by birth,) perceived that I was endowed with a great deal of sense, and spared nothing that was proper for improving it. He employed all the men in his dominions that excelled in sciences and arts, to be constantly about me.

No sooner had I learned to read and write, but I learned the alcoran* from the beginning to the end by heart; that admirable book, which contains the foundation, the precepts, and the rules of our religion; and that I might be thoroughly instructed in it, I read the works of the most approved authors, by whose commentaries it had been explained. I added to this study, that of all the traditions collected from the mouth of our prophet by the great men that were co-temporary with him. I was not satisfied with the knowledge alone of all that had any relation to our religion, but made also a particular search into our histories. I made myself perfect in polite learning, in the works of poets, and versification. I applied myself to geography, to chronology, and to speak our Arabian language in its purity; not forgetting, in the mean time, all such exercises as were proper for a prince to understand. But one thing which I was mightily in love with, and succeeded in to admiration, was, to form the characters of our Arabian language, wherein I surpassed all the writing-masters of our kingdom, that had acquired the greatest reputation.

Fame did me more honour than I deserved, for she had not only spread the renown of my parts through all the dominions of the king, my father, but carried it as far as the Indian court, whose potent monarch, desirous to see me, sent an ambassador with rich presents, to demand me of my father, who was extreme glad of this embassy for several reasons; he was persuaded that nothing could be more commendable in a prince of my age, than to travel and see foreign courts; and, besides, he was very glad to gain the friendship of the Indian sultan. I departed with the ambassador, but with no great retinue, because of the length and difficulty of the journey.

When we had travelled about a month, we discovered at a distance a great cloud of dust, and under that we saw very soon fifty horse-men well armed, that were robbers, coming toward us at full gallop.

As we had ten horses laden with baggage and other presents, that I was to carry to the Indian sultan from the king, my father, and that my retinue was but small, you may easily judge that these robbers came boldly up to us; and not being in a posture to make any opposition, we told them, that we were ambassadors, belonging to the sultan of the Indies, and hoped they would attempt nothing contrary to that respect that is due to them, thinking to save our equipage and our lives; but the robbers most insolently replied, for what reason would you have us shew any respect to the sultan your master? We are none of his subjects, nor are we upon his territories. And having spoke thus, they surrounded and fell upon us. I defended myself as long as I could; but finding myself wounded, and seeing the ambassador with his servants and mine lying on the ground, I made use of what strength was yet remaining in my horse, who was also very much wounded, and separated myself from the crowd, and rode away as fast as he could carry me; but he happening all of a sudden to fall under me, by weariness and the loss of blood, he fell down dead; I got rid of him in a trice; and finding that I was not pursued, it made me judge the robbers were not willing to quit the booty they had got.

Here you see me all alone, wounded, destitute of all help, and in a strange country. I durst not betake myself to the high road, fearing I might fall again into the hands of these robbers. When I had bound up my wound, which was not dangerous, I marched on the rest of the day, and arrived at the foot of a mountain, where I perceived a passage into a cave: I went in, and staid there that night with little satisfaction, after I had eaten some fruits that I gathered by the way.

I continued my journey for several days following, without finding any place of abode, but after a month's time I came to a large town well inhabited, and situated so much the more advantageously, that it was surrounded with several rivers, so that it enjoyed a perpetual spring.

The pleasant objects which then presented themselves to my view, afforded me some joy, and suspended for some time the mortal sorrow with which I was overwhelmed, to find myself in such a condition. My face, hands, and feet, were all tawny and sun-burnt, and by my long journey, my shoes and stockings were quite worn out, so that I was forced to walk bare-footed; and, besides, my cloaths were all in rags. I entered into the town to inform myself where I was, and addressed myself to a taylor that was at work in his shop; who perceiving by my air, that I was a person of more note than my outward appearance bespoke me to be, made me sit down by him, and asked me who I was, and from whence I came, and what had brought me thither? I did not conceal any thing of all that had befallen me, nor made I any scruple to discover my quality.

The taylor listened with attention to my words, but after I had done speaking, instead of giving me any consolation, he augmented my sorrow. Take heed, says he, how you discover to any person what you have now declared to me; for the prince of this country is the greatest enemy that the king your father has, and he will certainly do you some mischief, when he comes to hear of your being in this city. I made no doubt of the taylor's sincerity, when he named the prince; but since that enmity which is between my father and him, has no relation to my adventures, I must beg your pardon, madam, to pass it over in silence.

I returned the taylor thanks for his good advice, and shewed myself inclinable wholly to follow his counsel, and assured him that his favours should never be forgot by me. And as he believed I could not but be hungry, he caused them to bring me somewhat to eat, and offered me at the same time a lodging in his house, which I accepted. Some days after, finding me pretty well recovered of the fatigue I had endured by a long and tedious journey, and besides, being sensible that most princes of our religion did apply themselves to some art or calling, that might stand them in stead upon occasion, he asked me, if I had learned any thing whereby I might get a livelihood, and not be burthensome to any man? I told him that I understood the laws, both divine and human; that I was a grammarian and poet: and above all, that I understood writing perfectly well. By all this, says he, you will not be able, in this country, to purchase yourself one morsel of bread; nothing is of less use here than those sciences: But if you will be advised by me, says he, dress yourself in a labourer's habit; and since you appear to be strong, and of a good constitution, you shall go into the next forest and cut down firewood, which you may bring to the market to be sold; and I can assure you, it will turn to so good an account, that you may live by it, without dependence upon any man: And by this means you will be in a condition to wait for the favourable minute, when heaven shall think fit to dispel those clouds of misfortune that thwart your happiness, and oblige you to conceal your birth; I will take care to supply you with a rope and a hatchet.

The fear of being known, and the necessity I was under of getting a livelihood, made me agree to this proposal, notwithstanding all the meanness and hardships that attend it. The day following the taylor brought me a rope, a hatchet, and a short coat, and recommended me to some poor people that gained their bread after the same manner, that they might take me into their company. They conducted me to the wood, and the first day I brought in as much upon my head as brought me half a piece of gold, which is the money of that country; for though the wood is not far distant from the town, yet it was very scarce there, by reason that few or none would be at the trouble to go and cut it. I gained a good sum of money in a short time, and repaid my taylor what he had advanced for me.

I continued this way of living for a whole year; and one day that by chance I was gone farther into the wood than usual, I happened to light on a very pleasant place, where I began to cut down wood; and in pulling up the root of a tree, I espied an iron ring, fastened to a trap-door of the same metal. I took away the earth that covered it, and having lifted it up, saw stairs, which I went down, with my axe in my hand.

When I was come to the bottom of the stairs, I found myself in a large palace, which put me in a mighty consternation, because of the great light, which appeared as clear in it as if it had been above ground in the open air. I went forward along a gallery, supported by pillars of jasper, the bases and chapiters of massy gold; but seeing a lady of a noble and free air, and of extraordinary beauty, coming towards me, this turned my eyes from beholding any other object but her alone.

Being desirous to spare the lady the trouble to come to me, I made haste to meet her; and as I was saluting her with a low bow, she asked me, What are you? a man or a genie? A man, madam, said I: I have no correspondence with genies. By what adventure, said she, (fetching a deep sigh) are you come hither? I have lived here these twenty-five years, and never saw any man but yourself, during that time.

Her great beauty, which had already smitten me, and the sweetness and civility wherewith she received me, made me bold to say to her, Madam, before I have the honour to satisfy your curiosity, give me leave to tell you, that I am infinitely satisfied with this unexpected encounter, which offers me an occasion of consolation in the midst of my affliction; and perhaps it may give me an opportunity to make you also more happy than you are. I gave her a true account by what strange accident she saw me, the son of a king, in such a condition as I then appeared in her presence; and how fortune would have it that I should discover the entrance into that magnificent prison, where I had found her, but in an uneasy condition, according to appearance.

Alas! prince, said she, (sighing once more,) you have just cause to believe this rich and pompous prison cannot be otherwise than a most wearisome abode; the most charming place in the world being no wise delightful when we are detained there contrary to our will. It is not impossible but you may have heard of the great Epitimarus, king of the isle of Ebene, so called from that precious wood it produces in abundance; I am the princess, his daughter.

The king, my father, had chosen for me a husband, a prince that was my cousin; but on my wedding-night, in the midst of the rejoicing there was in the court and the capital city of the kingdom of the isle of Ebene, before I was given to my spouse, a genie took me away. I fainted at the same moment, and lost all my senses; but when I came to myself again, I found myself in this place. I was a long time inconsolable, but time and necessity have accustomed me to see and receive the genie. It is twenty-five years, as I told you before, that I have continued in this place, where, I must confess, I have every thing that I can wish for necessary to life, and also every thing that can satisfy a princess that loves nothing but fine dresses and fashions.

Every ten days, says the princess, the genie comes hither to lie with me one night, which he never exceeds; and the excuse he makes for it is, that he is married to another wife, who would grow jealous, if she came to know how unfaithful he was to her: Mean while, if I have occasion for him by day or night, as soon as I touch a talisman, which is at the entrance into my chamber, the genie appears. It is now the fourth day since he was here, and I do not expect him before the end of six more; so, if you please, you may stay five days and keep me company, and I will endeavour to entertain you according to your quality and merit. I thought myself too fortunate, to have obtained so great a favour without asking it, to refuse so obliging a proffer. The princess made me go into a bagnio,* which was the most handsome, the most commodious, and the most sumptuous, that could be imagined; and when I came forth instead of my own cloaths, I found another very costly suit, which I did not esteem so much for its richness, as that it made me look worthy to be in her company. We sat down on a sofa covered with rich tapestry, with cushions to lean upon, of the rarest Indian brocade; and some time after, she covered a table with several dishes of delicate meats. We eat together, and passed the remaining part of the day with very much satisfaction; and at night she received me to her bed.

The next day, as she contrived all manner of ways to please me, she brought in at dinner a bottle of old wine, the most excellent that ever was tasted, and out of complaisance, she drank some part of it with me. When my head grew hot with the agreeable liquor, Fair princess, said I, you have been too long thus buried alive: come follow me and enjoy the real day, from which you have been deprived so many years, and abandon this false light that you have here. Prince, replied she, with a smile, leave this discourse, if you out of ten days will grant me nine, and resign the last to the genie, the fairest day that ever was, would be nothing in my esteem. Princess, said I, it is the fear of the genie, that makes you speak thus; for my part, I value him so little, that I will break his talisman, with the conjuration that is wrote about it, in pieces. Let him come then, I will expect him, and how brave or redoubtable soever he be, I will make him feel the weight of my arm. I swear solemnly, that I shall extirpate all the genies in the world, and him first. The princess, who knew the consequence, conjured me not to touch the talisman, for that would be a means, said she, to ruin both you and me; I know what belongs to genies, better than you. The fumes of the wine did not suffer me to hearken to her reasons; but I gave the talisman a kick with my foot, and broke it in several pieces.

The talisman was no sooner broke, but the palace began to shake and was ready to fall, with a hideous noise like thunder, accompanied with flashes of lightning, and a great darkness. This terrible noise in a moment dispelled the fumes of my wine, and made me sensible, but too late, of the folly I had committed. Princess, cried I, what means all this? she answered in a fright, and without any concern for her own misfortune, Alas! you are undone, if you do not escape presently.

I followed her advice, and my fears were so great that I forgot my hatchet and cords. I was scarcely got to the stairs by which I came down, when the enchanted palace opened at once and made a passage for the genie. He asked the princess, in great anger, What has happened to you? and why did you call me? A qualm in my stomach, said the princess, made me fetch this bottle which you see here, out of which I drank twice or thrice, and by mischance made a false step, and fell upon the talisman, which is broke, and that is all the matter.

At this answer, the furious genie told her, You are a false woman, and a liar. How came that ax, and those ropes there? I never saw them till this moment, said the princess. Your coming in this impetuous manner has, it may be, forced them up in some place as you came along, and so brought them hither without your knowing it.

The genie made no other answer but what was accompanied with reproaches and blows, of which I heard the noise. I could not endure to hear the pitiful cries and shouts of the princess, so cruelly abused; I had already laid off the suit she made me put on, and took my own, which I had laid on the stairs the day before, when I came out of the bagnio. I made haste up stairs, being so much the more full of sorrow and compassion, that I had been the cause of so great a misfortune; and that by sacrificing the fairest princess on earth to the barbarity of a most merciless genie, I was become the most criminal and ungrateful of mankind. It is true, said I, she has been a prisoner these twenty-five years; but, setting liberty aside, she wanted nothing that could make her happy. My madness has put an end to her happiness, and brought upon her the cruelty of an unmerciful devil. I let down the trap-door, covered it again with earth, and returned to the city with a burden of wood, which I bound up, without knowing what I did, so great was my trouble and sorrow.

My landlord, the taylor, was very much rejoiced to see me; your absence, said he has disquieted me very much, by reason you had entrusted me with the secret of your birth, and I knew not what to think. I was afraid somebody had known you; God be thanked for your return. I thanked him for his zeal and affection, but never a word durst I say of what had past, nor the reason why I came back without my hatchet and cords.

I retired to my chamber, where I reproached myself a thousand times for my excessive imprudence. Nothing (said I) could have paralleled the princesses good fortune and mine, had I forborn to break the talisman.

While I was thus giving myself over to melancholy thoughts, the taylor came in, and told me, An old man, said he, whom I do not know, brings me here your hatchet and cords, which he found in his way, as he tells me, and understood by your comrades that go along with you to the woods, that you lodge here. Come out, and speak to him, for he will deliver them to none but yourself.

At this discourse I changed colour, and fell a trembling. While the taylor was asking me the reason, my chamber-door opened at once, and the old man, having no patience to stay, appeared to us with my hatchet and cords. This was the genie, the ravisher of the fair princess of the isle of Ebene, who had thus disguised himself, after he had treated her with the utmost barbarity. I am a genie, said he, son of the daughter of Ebis, prince of genies. Is not this your hatchet? said he, speaking to me, and are not these your cords?

After the genie had put the question to me, he gave me no time to answer, nor was it in power; so much had his terrible aspect put me beside myself.

He grasped me by the middle, dragged me out of the chamber, and mounting into the air, carried me up as high as the skies, with such swiftness, that I perceived I was got so high without being able to take notice of the way he carried me in so few moments. He descended again in like manner to the earth, which he caused to open with a knock of his foot, and so sunk down at once, where I found myself in the enchanted palace, before the fair princess of the isle of Ebene. But, alas, what a spectacle was there! I saw that which pierced me to the heart, this poor princess was quite naked, all in blood, and laid upon the ground, more like one dead than alive, with her cheeks all bathed in tears.

Perfidious wretch said the genie to her, pointing at me, is not this your gallant! She cast her languishing eyes at me, and answered mournfully, I do not know him: I never saw him till this moment. What, said the genie, he is the cause of thy being in the condition, thou art justly in; and yet darest thou say thou dost not know him? If I do not know him, said the princess, would you have me make a lie on purpose to ruin him? Oh, then, said the genie, pulling out a scymitar, and presenting it to the princess, if you never saw him before, take the scymitar, and cut off his head. Alas! replied the princess, how is it possible that I should execute what you would force me to do? My strength is so far spent, that I cannot lift my arm; and if I could, how should I have the heart to take away an innocent man's life, and one I do not know? This refusal, said the genie to the princess, sufficiently informs me of your crime. Upon which, turning to me, And thou, said he dost thou not know her?

I should have been the most ungrateful wretch, and the most perfidious of all mankind, if I had not shewn myself as faithful to the princess as she was to me, who had been the cause of her misfortunes. Therefore I answered the genie, How should I know her, that never saw her till now? If that be so, said he, take the scymitar, and cut off her head. On this condition I will set thee at liberty, for then I will be convinced that thou didst never see her till this very moment, as thou sayest thyself. With all my heart, replied I, and took the scymitar in my hand.

Do not think, madam, that I drew near to the fair princess of the isle of Ebene, to be the executioner of the genie's barbarity: I did it only to demonstrate by my behaviour, as much as possible, that as she had shewn her resolution to sacrifice her life for my sake, that I would not refuse to sacrifice mine for her's. The princess, notwithstanding her pain and suffering, understood my meaning; which she signified by an obliging look, and made me understand her willingness to die for me; and that she was satisfied to see how willing I was also to die for her; Upon this I stepped back, and threw the scymitar on the ground. I shall for ever, says I to the genie, be hateful to mankind, should I be so base as to murder, I do not only say a person whom I do not know, but also a lady like this, who is ready to give up the ghost; do with me what you please, since I am in your power; I cannot obey your barbarous commands.

I see, said the genie, that you both out-brave me, and insult my jealousy: but both of you shall know by the treatment I give you, what I am capable to do. At these words, the monster took up the scymitar, and cut off one of her hands; which left her only so much life as to give me a token with the other, that she bid me for ever adieu. For the blood she had lost before, and that which gushed out then, did not permit her to live above one or two moments after this barbarous cruelty; the sight of which threw me into a fit. When I came to myself again, I expostulated with the genie, why he made me languish in expectation of death. Strike, cried I, for I am ready to receive the mortal blow, and expect it as the greatest favour you can shew me. But instead of agreeing to that, Look ye, says he, how genies treat their wives whom they suspect of unfaithfulness; she has received thee here, and were I certain that she had put any farther affront upon me, I would make thee die this minute; but I will content myself to transform thee into a dog, ape, lion, or bird; take thy choice of any of these, I will leave it to thyself.

These words gave me some hopes to mollify him. O genie, said I, moderate your passion, and since you will not take away my life, give it me generously; I shall always remember your clemency, if you pardon me, as one of the best men in the world pardoned one of his neighbours that bore him a mortal hatred. The genie asked me what had passed between those two neighbours, and said, he would have patience till he heard the story, which I told him thus: And I believe, madam, you will not take it ill, if I also relate it to you.

The Story of the envious Man, and of him that he envied

In a considerable town, two persons dwelt next door to one another: one of them conceived such a violent hatred against the other, that he who was hated resolved to remove his dwelling farther off, being persuaded that their being neighbours was the only cause from whence his animosity did arise; for though he had done him several pieces of service, he found, nevertheless, that his hatred was nothing diminished; therefore he sold his house, with what goods he had left, and retired to the capital of that kingdom, which was not far distant. He bought a little spot of ground which lay about half a league from the city; he had a house convenient enough, with a fine garden, and a pretty spacious court, wherein was a deep well which was not in use.

The honest man having made this purchase, put on a dervise's or monk's habit,* to lead a retired life, and caused several cells to be made in the house, where, in a short time, he established a numerous society of dervises; he came soon to be publicly known by his virtue, through which he acquired the esteem of a great many people, as well of the commonalty as of the chief of the city. In short, he was extremely honoured and cherished by every one. People came from afar to recommend themselves to his prayers; and all those who came to live with him, published what blessings they received through his means.

The great reputation of this honest man having spread to the town from whence he came, it touched the envious man so much to the quick, that he left his house and affairs, with a resolution to go and ruin him. With this intent he went to the new convent of dervises, of which his former neighbour was the head, who received him with all imaginable tokens of friendship. The envious man told him that he was come on purpose to comunicate a business of importance to him, which he could not do but in private: And because that nobody shall hear us, let us, says he, take a walk in your court, and seeing night begins to draw on, command your dervises to retire to their cells. The head of the dervises did as he required.

When the envious man saw that he was alone with this good man, he began to tell him his errand, walking side by side in the court, untill he saw his opportunity; and getting the good man near the brink of the well, he gave him a thrust, and pushed him into it, without any body's being witness to so wicked an action. Having done thus, he marched off immediately, got out at the gate of the convent, without being known of any one, and came home to his own house, well satisfied with his journey, being fully persuaded that the object of his hatred was no more in this world; but found himself highly mistaken.

This old well was inhabited by fairies and genies, which happened luckily for the relief of the head of the convent; for they received and supported him, carried him to the bottom, so that he got no hurt. He perceived well enough that there was something extraordinary in his fall, which must otherwise have cost him his life; whereas he neither saw nor felt any thing. But he soon heard a voice, which said, Do you know what honest man this is, to whom we have done this piece of service? Another voice answered, No. To which the first replied, Then I will tell you. This man, out of charity, the greatest that ever was known, left the town he lived in, and has established himself in this place, in hopes to cure one of his neighbours of the envy he had conceived against him; he has acquired such a general esteem, that the envious man, not able to endure it, came hither on purpose to ruin him, which he had performed, had it not been for the assistance which we have given this honest man, whose reputation is so great, that the sultan, who keeps his residence in the neighbouring city, was to pay him a visit to-morrow, and to recommend the princess, his daughter, to his prayers.

Another voice asked, What need had the princess of the dervise's prayers? To which the first answered, You do not know, it seems, that she is possessed by Genie Maimoun, the son of Dimdim, who is fallen in love with her. But I know well how this good head of the dervises may cure her; the thing is very easy, and I will tell it you. He has a black cat in his convent, with a white spot at the end of her tail, about the bigness of a small piece of English money; let him only pull seven hairs out of this white spot, burn them, and smoke the princesses head with the fume, she will not only be presently cured, but be so safely delivered from Maimoun, the son of Dimdim, that he will never dare to come near her a second time.

The head of the dervises remembered every word of the discourse between the fairies and the genies, who were very silent all the night after. The next morning, by break of day, when he could discern one thing from another, the well being broken down in several places, he saw a hole by which he crept out with ease.

The other dervises, who had been seeking for him, were rejoiced to see him. He gave them a brief account of the wickedness of that man to whom he had given so kind a reception the day before, and retired into his cell. It was not long till the black cat of whom the fairies and the genies had made mention in their discourses the night before, come to fawn upon her master, as she was accustomed to do: He took her up, and pulled out seven hairs off the white spot that was upon her tail, and laid them aside for his use when occasion should serve.

The sun was not high, when the sultan who would leave no means untried that he thought could restore the princess to her perfect health, arrived at the gate of the convent. He commanded his guards to halt, whilst he, with his principal officers went in. The dervises received him with profound respect.

The sultan called their head aside, and says, Good sheich, it may be you know already the cause of my coming hither. Yes, sir, replies he very gravely; if I do not mistake it, it is the disease of the princess which procures me this honour that I have not deserved. That is the very thing, replied the sultan.—You will give me new life, if your prayers, as I hope they will, can procure my daughter's health. Sir, said the good man, if your majesty will be pleased to let her come hither, I am in hopes through God's assistance and favour, she shall return in perfect health.

The prince, transported with joy, sent immediately to fetch his daughter, who very soon appeared with a numerous train of ladies and eunuchs, but masked so as her face was not seen. The chief of the dervises caused a pall to be held over her head, and he had no sooner thrown the seven tufts of hair upon the burning coals, but the genie Maimoun, the son of Dimdim, gave a great cry, without any thing being seen, and left the princess at liberty; upon which, she took off the veil from her face, and rose up to see where she was, saying, Where am I, and who brought me hither? At which words the sultan overcome with excess of joy, embraced his daughter and kissed her eyes; he also kissed the chief of the dervises hands, and said to his officers, Tell me your opinion, what reward does he deserve that has thus cured my daughter? They all cried, he deserves her in marriage. That is what I had in my thoughts, said the sultan; and I make him my son in law from this moment. Sometime after, the prime visier died, and the sultan conferred the place on the dervise.—The sultan himself died without heirs male; upon which the religious orders and the militia gathered together, and the honest man was declared and acknowledged sultan by general consent.

The honest dervise, being mounted on the throne of his father-in-law, as he was one day in the midst of his courtiers on a march, he espied the envious man among the croud of people that stood as he passed along, and calling one of the visiers that attended him, whispered him in his ear thus: Go bring me that man you see there; but have a care you do not frighten him. The visier obeyed, and when the envious man was brought into his presence, the sultan said, Friend, I am extremely glad to see you. Upon which he called an officer, Go immediately, says he, and cause to be paid this man out of my treasury one hundred pieces of gold: let him have also twenty load of the richest merchandize in my store-houses, and a sufficient guard to conduct him to his house. After he had given this charge to the officer, he bid the envious man farewell, and proceeded on his march.

When I had finished the recital of this story to the genie the murderer of the princess of the isle of Ebene, I made the application to himself thus: O genie! you see here, that this bountiful sultan did not content himself to have forgot the design of the envious man to take away his life, but treated him kindly, and sent him back with all the favours which I just now related. In short, I made use of all my eloquence, praying him to imitate such a good example, and to grant me pardon: but it was impossible for me to move his compassion.

All that I can do for thee, said he, is, that I will not take thy life; do not flatter thyself that I will send thee safe and sound back; I must let thee feel what I am able to do by my enchantments. With that he laid violent hands on me, and carried me cross the vault of the subterranean palace, which opened to give him passage; he flew up with me so high, that the earth seemed to be only a little white cloud; from thence he came down again like lightning, and alighted upon the ridge of a mountain.

There he took up a handful of earth, and pronounced, or rather muttered, some words which I did not understand, and threw it upon me. Leave the shape of a man, says he to me, and take on thee that of an ape. He vanished immediately, and left me alone, transformed into an ape, overwhelmed with sorrow, in a strange country, not knowing if I was near unto, or far from my father's dominions.

I went down from the height of the mountain, and came into a plain country, which took me a month's time to travel through, and then I came to a coast of the sea. It happened then to be a great calm, and I espied a vessel about half a league from the shore: I would not lose this good opportunity but broke off a large branch from a tree, which I carried with me to the sea-side, and set myself astride upon it, with a stick in each hand to serve me for oars.

I launched out in this posture, and advanced near the ship. When I was nigh enough to be known, the seamen and passengers that were upon the deck thought it an extraordinary spectacle, and all of them looked upon me with great astonishment. In the mean time I got aboard, and laying hold of a rope, I jumped upon the deck, and having lost my speech, I found myself in very great perplexity; and indeed the risk I ran then, was nothing less than when I was at the mercy of the genie.

The merchants, being both superstitious and scrupulous, believed I should occasion some mischief to their voyage, if they received me; therefore, says one, I will knock him down with an handspike; says another, I will shoot an arrow through his guts; says a third, let us throw him into the sea. Some of them would not have failed to have executed their design, if I had not got to that side where the captain was; when I threw myself at his feet, and took him by the coat in a begging posture. This action, together with the tears which he saw gush from my eyes, moved his compassion; so that he took me into his protection, threatened to be revenged on him that should do me the least hurt; and he himself made very much of me. And on my part, though I had no power to speak, I did, by my gestures, show all possible signs of gratitude.

The wind that succeeded the calm was gentle and favourable, and did not alter for fifty days, but brought us safe to the port of a fine town, well peopled, and of great trade, where we came to an anchor. It was so much the more considerable, that it was the capital city of a powerful state.

Our vessel was speedily surrounded with an infinite number of boats, full of people, that either came to congratulate their friends upon their safe arrival, or to enquire for those they had left behind them in the country from whence they came, or out of curiosity to see a ship that came from a far country.

Among the rest, some of the officers came on board, desiring to speak with the merchants, in the name of the sultan. The merchants appearing, one of the officers told them, The sultan, our master, hath commanded us to acquaint you, that he is glad of your safe arrival, and prays you to take the trouble, every one of you, to write some lines upon this roll of paper; and that his design by this may be understood, you must know that he had a prime-visier, who, besides a great capacity to manage affairs, understood writing to the highest perfection. This minister is lately dead, at which the sultan is very much troubled, and since he can never behold his writing without admiration, he has made a solemn vow, not to give the place to any man but to him that can write as well as he did. Abundance of people have presented their writings; but to this day, no body in all this empire has been judged worthy to supply the visier's place.

Those merchants that believed they could write well enough to pretend to this high dignity, wrote one after another, what they thought fit. After they had done, I advanced, and took the roll out of the gentleman's hand; but all the people, especially the merchants, cried out, He will tear it, or throw it into the sea; till they saw how properly I held the roll, and made a sign that I would write in my turn. Then they were of another opinion, and their fears turned into admiration. However, since they had never seen an ape that could write, nor could be persuaded that I was more ingenious than other apes, they offered to snatch the roll out of my hand; but the captain took my part once more. Let him alone, said he, suffer him to write. If he only scribbles the paper, I promise you, that I will punish him on the spot. If, on the contrary, he writes well, as I hope he will, because I never saw an ape so handy and ingenious, and so apprehensive of every thing, I do declare that I will own him as my son: I had one that had not by far the wit that he has. Perceiving that no man did any more oppose my design, I took the pen, and wrote, before I had done, six sorts of hands used among the Arabians,* and each specimen containing an extemporary distich or quatrain in praise of the sultan. My writing did not only outdo that of the merchants, but I dare say, they had not before seen any such fair writing in that country. When I had done, the officers took the roll, and carried it to the sultan.

The sultan took little notice of any of the other writings, but considered mine, which was so much to his liking, that he says to the officers. Take the finest horse in my stable, with the richest harness, and a robe of the most sumptuous brocade, to put upon that person who wrote those six hands, and bring him hither to me. At this command the officers could not forbear laughing; the sultan grew angry at their boldness, and was ready to punish them till they told him: Sir, we humbly beg your majesty's pardon; these hands are not written by a man, but by an ape. What do you say, says the sultan? Those admirable characters, are they not writ by the hands of a man? No, sir, replied the officers, we do assure your majesty that it was an ape, who wrote them in our presence. The sultan was too much surprised at this account not to desire a sight of me; and therefore says, Do what I command you, and bring me speedily this wonderful ape.

The officers returned to the vessel, and shewed the captain their order, who answered, the sultan's command must be obeyed. Whereupon they clothed me with that rich brocade robe, and carried me ashore, where they set me on horseback, whilst the sultan waited for me at his palace with a great number of courtiers, whom he gathered together to do me the more honour.

The cavalcade being begun, the harbour, the streets, the public places, windows, terraces, palaces, and houses, were filled with an infinite number of people of all sorts, who were curious to come from all parts of the city to see me; for the rumour was spread in a moment, that the sultan had chosen an ape to be his grand-visier; and after having served for a spectacle to the people, who could not forbear to express their surprise, by redoubling their shouts and cries, I arrived at the palace of the sultan.

I found the prince seated on his throne, in the midst of the grandees. I made my bow three times very low, and at last kneeled and kissed the ground before him, and afterwards sat down in my seat in the posture of an ape. The whole assembly admired me, and could not comprehend how it was possible that an ape should understand so well to give the sultan his due respect; and he himself was more astonished than any man. In short, the usual ceremony of the audience would have been complete, could I have added speech to my behaviour; but apes do never speak, and the advantage I had of having been a man, did not allow me that privilege.

The sultan dismissed his courtiers, and none remained by him but his chief of the eunuchs, a little young slave, and myself. He went from his chamber of audience into his own apartment, where he ordered dinner to be brought. As he sat at table, he gave me a sign to come near, and eat with him. To shew my obedience, I kissed the ground, stood up, sat me down at table, and eat with discretion, and moderately.

Before the table was uncovered, I espied an ink-horn, which I made a sign should be brought me; having got it, I wrote upon a large peach some verses after my way, which testified my acknowledgement to the sultan; who having read them after my presenting him the peach, it increased his astonishment. When the table was uncovered, they brought him a particular liquor, of which he caused them to give me a glass. I drank, and wrote some new verses upon it, which explained the state I was in, after a great many sufferings. The sultan read them likewise, and said, an ape that was capable of doing so much, ought to be exalted above the greatest of men.

The sultan caused them to bring in a chessboard, and asked me by a sign if I understood that game, and would play with him? I kissed the ground, and laying my hand upon my head, signified, that I was ready to receive that honour. He won the first game, but I won the second and third; and perceiving that he was somewhat displeased at it, I made a quatrain to pacify him; in which I told him that two potent armies had been fighting very eagerly all day, but that they made up a peace towards the evening, and passed the remaining part of the night very peaceably together upon the field of battle.

So many things appearing to the sultan, far beyond whatever any one had either seen or known of the behaviour or knowledge of apes, he would not be the only witness of these prodigies himself, but having a daughter called the Lady of Beauty, to whom the head of the eunuchs, then present, was governor; Go, said the sultan to him, and bid your lady come hither: I am willing she should have a share in my pleasure.

The eunuch went, and immediately brought the princess, who had her face uncovered, but she was no sooner got into the room, than she put on her veil, and said to the sultan, Sir, your majesty must needs have forgot yourself; I am very much surprised that your majesty has sent for me to appear among men. How, daughter! said the sultan, you do not know what you say. Here is nobody but the little slave, the eunuch your governor, and myself, who have the liberty to see your face; and yet you lower your veil, and would make me a criminal in having sent for you hither. Sir, said the princess, your majesty shall soon understand that I am not in the wrong. That ape you see before you, though he has the shape of an ape, is a young prince, son of a great king; he has been metamorphosed into an ape by enchantment. A genie, the son of the daughter of Ebis, has maliciously done him this wrong, after having cruelly taken away the life of the princess of the isle of Ebene, daughter to the king Epitimarus.

The sultan astonished at this discourse, turned towards me, and spoke no more by signs, but in plain words, asked me, if it was true what his daughter said? Seeing I could not speak, I put my hand to my head to signify that what the princess said was true. Upon this, the sultan said again to his daughter, How do you know that this prince has been transformed by enchantment into an ape? Sir, replied the Lady of Beauty, your majesty may remember that when I was past my infancy, I had an old lady waited on me; she was a most expert magician, and taught me seventy rules of magic, by virtue of which, I can transport your capital into the midst of the sea in the twinkling of an eye, or beyond mount Caucasus. By this science, I know all enchanted persons at first sight: I know who they are, and by whom they have been enchanted: therefore do not admire, if I forthwith relieve this prince, in spite of the enchantments, from that which hinders him to appear in your sight what he naturally is.—Daughter, said the sultan, I did not believe you to have understood so much. Sir, replied the princess, these things are curious and worth knowing; but I think I ought not to boast of them. Since it is so, said the sultan, you can dispel the prince's enchantment. Yes, sir, said the princess, I can restore him to his first shape again. Do it then, said the sultan, you cannot do me a greater pleasure; for I will have him to be my visier, and he shall marry you. Sir, said the princess, I am ready to obey you in all that you shall be pleased to command me.

The princess, the lady of beauty, went into her apartment, from whence she brought in a knife which had some Hebrew words engraven on the blade: She made us all, viz. the sultan, the master of the eunuchs, the little slave, and myself, to go down into a private court adjoining to the palace, and there left us under a gallery that went round it. She placed herself in the middle of the court, where she made a great circle, and within it she wrote several words in Arabian characters, some of them ancient, and others of those which they call the character of Cleopatra.*

When she had finished, and prepared the circle as she thought fit, she placed herself in the center of it, where she began adjurations, and repeated verses out of the alcoran. The air grew insensibly dark, as if it had been night, and the whole world about to be dissolved. We found ourselves struck with a panic fear, and this fear increased the more when we saw the genie, the son of the daughter of Ebis, appear all of a sudden in the shape of a lion of a frightful size.

As soon as the princess perceived this monster, You dog, said she, instead of creeping before me, dare you present yourself in this shape, thinking to frighten me? And thou, replied the lion, art thou not afraid to break the treaty which was solemnly made and confirmed between us by oath, not to wrong or do one another hurt? Oh, thou cursed creature! replied the princess, I can justly reproach thee with so doing. The lion answered fiercely, Thou shalt quickly have thy reward for the trouble thou hast given me to return. With that he opened his terrible throat, and ran at her to devour her; but she, being on her guard, leaped backward, got time to pull out one of her hairs, and by pronouncing three or four words, changed herself into a sharp sword, wherewith she cut the lion through the middle in two pieces.

The two parts of the lion vanished, and the head only was left, which changed itself into a large scorpion. Immediately the princess turned herself into a serpent, and fought the scorpion; who, finding himself worsted, took the shape of an eagle and flew away: But the serpent at the same time took also the shape of an eagle that was black and much stronger, and pursued him, so that we lost the sight of them both.

Some time after they disappeared, the ground, opened before us and out of it came forth a cat, black and white, with her hair standing upright and keeping a fearful miauling; a black wolf followed her close, and gave her not time to rest. The cat, being thus hard beset, changed herself into a worm, and being nigh to a pomegranate that had accidently fallen from a tree that grew on the side of a canal, which was deep, but not broad, the worm pierced the pomegranate in an instant and hid itself, but the pomegranate swelled immediately, and became as big as a gourd, which mounting up to the top of the gallery, rolled there for some space backward, and forward, fell down again into the court, and broke into several pieces.

The wolf, who had in the meantime transformed itself into a cock, fell a-picking up the seeds of the pomegranate one after another; but finding no more, he came towards us with his wings spread, making a great noise, as if he would ask us, whether there was any more seed? There was one lying on the brink of the canal, which the cock perceiving as he went back, ran speedily thither; but just as he was going to pick it up, the seed rolled into the river, and turned into a little fish.

The cock jumped into the river, and was turned into a pike, that pursued the small fish; they continued both under the water above two hours, and we knew not what became of them; but all of a sudden we heard terrible cries, which made us to quake, and a little while after, we saw the genie and princess all in flames. They threw flashes of fire out of their mouths at one another, until they came to it hand in hand; then the fires increased, with a thick burning smoke, which mounted so high, that we had reason to fear that it would set the palace on fire. But we very soon had a more pressing occasion of fear, for the genie having got loose from the princess, came to the gallery where we stood, and blew flames of fire upon us. We had all perished, if the princess, running to our assistance, had not forced him, by her efforts, to retire, and defend himself against her, yet, notwithstanding all her diligence, she could not hinder the sultan's beard from being burnt, and his face spoiled, the chief of the eunuchs from being stifled, and burnt on the spot, nor a spark to enter my right eye, and make it blind. The sultan and I expected nothing but death, when we heard a cry, Victory, victory! and, all of a sudden, the princess appeared in her natural shape, but the genie was reduced to an heap of ashes.

The princess came near to us, and that she might not lose time, called for a cup of cold water, which the young slave who had got no damage, brought her: She took it, and after pronouncing some words over it, threw it upon me, saying, If thou art become an ape by enchantment, change thy shape, and take that of a man, which thou hadst before. These words were hardly uttered till I became a man, as I was before, one eye only excepted.

I was preparing myself to give thanks to the princess, but she prevented me by addressing herself to her father thus: Sir, I have got the victory over the genie, as your majesty may see; but it is a victory that costs me dear; I have but a few minutes to live, and you will not have the satisfaction to make the match you intended; the fire has pierced me during the terrible combat, and I find it consumes me by degrees. This would not have happened, had I perceived the last of the pomegranate seeds, and swallowed it, as I did the others, when I was changed into a cock. The genie had fled thither, as to his last entrenchment, and upon that the success of the combat depended, which would have been successful, and without danger to me. This slip obliged me to have recourse to fire, and to fight with those mighty arms as I did between heaven and earth in your presence; for, in spite of all his redoubtable art and experience, I made the genie to know, that I understood more than he: I have conquered and reduced him to ashes, but I cannot escape death, which is approaching.

The sultan suffered the princess, the lady of beauty, to go on with the recital of her combat: And when she had done, he spoke to her in a tone that sufficiently testified his grief. My daughter, said he, you see in what condition your father is; alas! I wonder that I am yet alive! Your governor, the eunuch, is dead, and the prince whom you have delivered from his enchantment has lost one of his eyes. He could speak no more; for his tears, sighs, and sobs, made him speechless; his daughter and I were exceedingly sensible of his sorrow, and wept with him.

In the mean time, while we were striving to outdo one another in grief, the princess cried, I burn; Oh, I burn! She found that the fire which consumed her, had at last seized upon her whole body, which made her still to cry, I burn, until death had made an end of her intolerable pains. The effect of that was so extraordinary, that in a few moments she was wholly reduced to ashes, as was the genie.

I cannot tell you, madam, how much I was grieved at so dismal a spectacle: I had rather all my life have continued an ape or a dog, than to have seen my benefactress thus miserably perish. The sultan being afflicted beyond all that can be imagined, cried out piteously; and beat himself on his head and stomach, until such time as being quite overcome with grief, he fainted away, which made me fear his life. In the mean time the eunuchs and officers came running at the sultan's cries, and with very much ado brought him to himself again. There was no need for that prince and me to give them a long narrative of this adventure, in order to convince them of their great loss. The two heaps of ashes, into which the princess and the genie had been reduced, was demonstration enough. The sultan was hardly able to stand upright, but was forced to be supported by them till he could get to his apartment.

When the noise of the tragical event had spread itself through the palace and the city, all the people bewailed the misfortune of the princess, the lady of beauty, and were sensible of the sultan's affliction. Every one was in deep mourning for seven days, and a great many ceremonies were performed: The ashes of the genie were thrown into the air, but those of the princess were gathered into a precious urn, to be kept, and the urn was set in a stately tomb, which was built for that purpose, on the same place where the ashes had lain.

The grief which the sultan conceived for the loss of his daughter, threw him into a fit of sickness, which confined him to his chamber for a whole month. He had not fully recovered strength when he sent for me: Prince, said he, hearken to the orders that I now give you, it will cost you your life, if you do not put them in execution. I assured him of exact obedience; upon which he went on thus: I have constantly lived in perfect felicity, and was never crossed by any accident; but by your arrival all the happiness I possessed is vanished; my daughter is dead, her governor is no more, and it is through a miracle that I am yet alive. You are the cause of all those misfortunes, for which it is impossible to be comforted; therefore depart from hence in peace, but without further delay, for I myself must perish, if you stay any longer: I am persuaded, that your presence brings mischief along with it. This is all I have to say to you. Depart and take care of ever appearing again in my dominions; there is no consideration whatsoever, that shall hinder me from making you repent of it. I was going to speak, but he stopt my mouth by words full of anger; and so I was obliged to remove from his palace, rejected, banished, thrown off by all the world, and not knowing what would become of me. Before I left the city I went into a bagnio, where I caused my beard and eye-brows to be shaved, and put on a calender's habit. I began my journey not so much deploring my own miseries, as the death of the two fair princesses of which I have been the occasion. I passed through many countries without making myself known; at last I resolved to come to Bagdad, in hopes to get myself introduced to the commander of the faithful, to move his compassion by giving him an account of my strange adventures. I came hither this evening, and the first man I met was this calender, our brother, that spoke before me. You know the remaining part, Madam, and the cause of my having the honour to be here.

When the second calender made an end of his story, Zobeide, to whom he had addressed his speech, told him, It is very well, you may go which way you please; I give you leave; but instead of departing, he also petitioned the lady to shew him the same favour she had vouchsafed to the first calender, and went and sat down by him.

The third calender, perceiving it was his turn to speak, addressed his speech, as the rest had done, to Zobeide, and began in this manner:

The History of the third Calender, a King's Son

Most honourable Lady,

THAT which I am going to tell you, very much differs from what you have heard already. The two princes that spoke before me, have each lost an eye by the pure effects of their destiny, but mine I lost through my own fault, and by hastening to seek my own misfortune, as you shall hear by the sequel of my story.

My name is Agib, and I am the son of a king, who was called Cassib. After his death, I took possession of his dominions, and resided in the same city where he lived before. This city is situated on the sea coast; has one of the finest and safest harbours in the world, and an arsenal large enough for fitting out fifty men of war to sea, that are always ready on occasion, and light frigates, and pleasure boats for recreation. My kingdom is composed of several fine provinces upon Terra-Firma, besides a number of spacious islands, every one of which, lie almost in sight of my capital city.

The first thing I did was to visit the provinces; I afterwards caused to fit out and man my whole fleet, and went to my islands to gain the hearts of my subjects by my presence, and to confirm them in their loyalty, and some time after I returned, I went thither again. These voyages giving me some taste of navigation, I took so much pleasure in it, that I resolved to make some discoveries beyond my islands: to which end I caused only ten ships to be fitted out; embarked on board them, and set sail.

Our voyage was very successful for forty days together, but on the forty-first night the wind became contrary, and withal so boisterous, that we were like to have been lost in the storm: About break of day the wind grew calm, and the clouds were dispersed, and the sun having brought back fair weather, we came close to an island, where we remained two days to take in fresh provisions; this being done, we put off again to sea. After ten days sail, we were in hopes of seeing land, for the tempests we had gone through had so much abated my curiosity, that I gave orders to steer back to my own coast; but I perceived at the same time, that my pilot knew not where we were. Upon the tenth day, a seaman being sent to look out for land from the main-mast-head, he gave notice, that on starboard and larboard he could see nothing but the sky and the sea, which bounded the horizon; but just before us, upon the stem, he saw a great blackness.

The pilot changed colour at this relation, and throwing his turban on the deck with one hand, and beating his breast with the other, cried, Oh, sir, we are all lost; not one of us will escape; and with all my skill, it is not in my power to prevent it! Having spoke thus, he fell a crying like a man who foresaw unavoidable ruin; his despair put the whole ship's crew into a terror. I asked him what reason he had thus to despair? he told me, the tempest which we had outlived, had brought us so far out of our course, that to-morrow about noon we shall come near to that black place, which is nothing else but the black mountain, that is a mine of adamant, which at this minute draws all your fleet towards it, by virtue of the iron and nails that are in your ships; and when we come to-morrow at a certain distance, the strength of the adamant will have such a force, that all the nails will be drawn out of the sides and bottom of the ships, and fastened to the mountain, so that your vessel will fall to pieces and sink to the bottom. And as the adamant has a virtue to draw all iron to it, whereby its attraction becomes stronger, this mountain on the side of the sea is all covered over with nails, drawn out of an infinite number of vessels that have perished by it; and this preserves and augments its virtue at the same time.

This mountain, continued the pilot, is very rugged: On the top of it there is a dome of fine brass, supported by pillars of the same, and upon the top of that dome, there stands a horse of the same metal, with a rider on his back who has a plate of lead fixed to his breast, upon which, some talismanical characters are engraven. Sir, the tradition is, that this statue is the chief cause that so many ships and men have been lost and sunk in this place; and that it will ever continue to be fatal to all that have the misfortune to come near it, until such time as it shall be thrown down.

The pilot having ended his discourse, began to weep afresh, and this made all the rest of the ship's company to do the like. I myself had no other thoughts, but that my days were there to have an end. In the mean time every one began to provide for his own safety, and to that end, took all imaginable precautions; and being uncertain of the event they all made one another their heirs, by virtue of a will, for the benefit of those that should happen to be saved.

The next morning, we perceived the black mountain very plain, and the idea we had conceived of it, made it appear more frightful than it was. About noon we were come so near, that we found what the pilot had foretold, to be true; for we saw all the nails and iron about the ship fly towards the mountain, where they fixed, by the violence of the attraction, with a horrible noise; the ship split asunder; and sunk into the sea, which was so deep about that place, that we could not sound it. All my people were drowned; but God had mercy on me, and permitted me to save myself by means of a plank, which the wind drove ashore just at the foot of the mountain: I did not receive the least hurt, and my good fortune brought me to a landing place, where there were steps that went up to the top of the mountain.

At the sight of these steps, for there was not a bit of ground either on the right or left, whereon a man could set his foot, I gave thanks to God, and recommended myself to his holy protection, as I began to mount the steps, which were so narrow, rugged, and hard to get up, that had the wind blown ever so little, it would have thrown me down into the sea; but, at last, I got up to the top, without any accident: I came into the dome, and kneeling on the ground, gave God thanks for his mercies to me.

I passed the night under the dome, and in my sleep an old grave man apeared to me, and said, Hearken, Agib, as soon as thou art awake, dig up the ground under thy feet; thou shalt find a bow of brass, and three arrows of lead, that are made under certain constellations, to deliver mankind from so many calamities that threaten them. Shoot the three arrows at the statue, and the rider shall fall into the sea; but, the horse will fall down by thy side, which thou must bury in the same place from whence you took the bow and arrows. This being done, the sea will swell and rise up to the top of the mountain: When it is come up so high, thou shalt see a boat with one man and an oar in each hand. This man is also of metal, different from that thou has thrown down; step on board to him, without mentioning the name of God, and let him conduct thee. He will in ten days time bring thee into another sea where thou shalt find an opportunity to get home to thy country, safe and sound, provided, as I have told thee, thou dost not mention the name of God during the whole voyage.

This was the contents of the old man's discourse. When I awaked I was very much comforted by the vision, and did not fail to observe every thing that he had commanded me. I took the bow and arrows out of the ground, shot them at the horseman, and with the third arrow I overthrew him, and he fell into the sea, as the horse did by my side, which I buried in the place whence I took the bow and arrows; and in the mean time, the sea swelled, and rose up by degrees. When it came as high as the foot of the dome that stood upon the top of the mountain, I saw afar off a boat rowing towards me, and I returned God thanks that every thing had succeeded according to my dream.

At last the boat came ashore, and I saw the man was made of metal, according as I had dreamed. I stepped aboard, and took great heed not to pronounce the name of God, neither spoke I one word at all: I sat down, and the man of metal began to row off from the mountain; he rowed without ceasing till the ninth day, that I saw some islands, which put me in hopes that I should be out of all the danger that I was afraid of. The excess of my joy made me forget what I was forbidden to do: God's name be blessed, said I, the Lord be praised.

I had no sooner spoke those words, but the boat sunk with the man of metal, leaving me upon the surface; I swam the remaining part of the day towards that land which appeared nearest to me.—A very dark night succeeded, and not knowing whereabout I was, I swam at a venture; my strength began at last to fail, and I despaired of being able to save myself, when the wind began to blow hard, and a wave as big as a mountain threw me on a flat, where it left me, and drew back. I made haste to get ashore, fearing another wave might wash me back again. The first thing I did was to strip and wring the water out of my cloaths; I then laid them down to dry on the sand, which was still pretty warm by the heat of the day.

Next morning the sun dried my cloathes betimes; I put them on, and went forward to see whereabouts I was: I had not walked very far, till I found I was got upon a little desart island, though very pleasant, where there grew several sorts of trees and wild fruits, but I perceived it was very far from the continent, which much diminished the joy I conceived for having escaped the dangers of the seas. Notwithstanding, I recommended myself to God, and prayed him to dispose of me according to his good will and pleasure; at the same time I saw a vessel coming from the main land, before the wind, directly to the island. I doubted not but they were coming to anchor there, and being uncertain what sort of people they might be, whether friends or foes, I thought it not safe for me to be seen: I got up into a very thick tree, from whence I might safely view them. The vessel came into a little creek, where ten slaves landed, carrying a spade and other instruments fit for digging up the ground; they went towards the middle of the island, where I saw them stop, and dig the ground a long while, after which I thought I saw them lift up a trap-door. They returned again to the vessel, and unloaded several sorts of provisions and furniture, which they carried to that place where they had broken ground, and so went downward, which made me suppose it was a subterannean dwelling.

I saw them once more go to the ship, and return soon after with an old man, who led a very handsome young lad in his hand, of about fourteen or fifteen years of age; they all went down at the trap-door, and being come up again, having let down the trap-door, and covered it over with earth, they returned to the creek where the ship lay, but I saw not the young man in their company; this made me believe that he staid behind in that place under ground, at which I could not but be extremely astonished.

The old man and the slaves went aboard again, and the vessel being got under sail, steered its course towards the main land. When I perceived they were at such distance, that they could not see me, I came down from the tree, and went directly to the place where I had seen the ground broken; I removed the earth by degrees, till I found a stone that was two or three feet square. I lifted it up, and saw it covered the head of the stairs, which were also of stone: I went down, and came into a large room, where there was laid a foot-carpet, and a couch covered with tapestry, and cushions of rich stuff, upon which the young man sat, with a fan in his hand. I saw all this by the light of two tapers, together with the fruits and flowerpots he had standing about him. The young lad was startled at the sight of me; but to rid him of his fear, I spoke to him as I came in thus: Whoever you be, Sir, do not fear any thing, a king and the son of a king, as I am, is not capable of doing you any prejudice. On the contrary, it is probable, that your good destiny has brought me hither to deliver you out of this tomb, where it seems, they have buried you alive, for reasons unknown to me. But that which makes me wonder, and that which I cannot conceive, (for you must know, that I have been witness to all that hath passed since your coming into this island,) is, that you suffered yourself to be buried in this place without any resistance.

The young man recovered himself at these words, and prayed me, with a smiling countenance, to sit down by him; which when I had done, he said, Prince, I am to acquaint you with a matter so odd in itself, that it cannot but surprise you:

My father is a merchant jeweller, who has acquired, through his ingenuity in his calling, a great estate; he hath a great many slaves, and also deputies, whom he employs to go as super-cargoes* to sea with his own ships, on purpose to maintain the correspondence he has at several courts, which he furnishes with such precious stones as they want.

He had been married a long while, and without issue, when he understood by a dream that he should have a son, though his life would be but short, at which he was very much concerned when he awaked. Some days after, my mother acquainted him that he was with child, and the time which she supposed to be that of her conception, agreed exactly with the day of his dream. She was brought to bed of me at the end of nine months, which occassioned great joy in the family.

My father, who had observed the very moment of my birth, consulted astrologers about my nativity, who told him, your son shall live very happy till the age of fifteen, when he will be in danger of losing his life, and hardly be able to escape it: but if his good destiny preserve him beyond that time, he will live to grow very old. It will be then (said they) when the statue of brass that stands upon the top of the mountain of adamant, shall be thrown down into the sea by prince Agib, son of king Cassib; and, as the stars prognosticate, your son shall be killed fifty days afterwards by that prince.

As the event of this part of the prediction about the statue agrees exactly with my father's dream, it afflicted him so much that he was struck to the very heart with it. In the mean time, he took all imaginable care of my education until this present year, which is the fifteenth of my age; and he had notice given him yesterday, that the statue of brass had been thrown into the sea about ten days ago, by that same prince I told you of. This news has cost him so many tears, and has alarmed him so much, that he looks not like himself.

Upon these predictions of the astrologers, he has sought, by all means possible, to falsify my horoscope, and to preserve my life. It is not long since he took this precaution, to build me this subterrannean habitation to hide me in, till the expiration of the fifty days after the throwing down of the statue; and therefore, since it was that this had happened ten days ago, he came hastily hither to hide me, and promised, at the end of forty days, to come again and fetch me out. As for my own part, I am in good hopes, and cannot believe that prince Agib will come to seek for me in a place under ground, in the midst of a desert island. This, my lord, is what I have to say to you.

Whilst the jeweller's son was telling me this story, I laughed in myself at those astrologers who had foretold, that I should take away his life; for I thought myself so far from being likely to verify what they said, that he had scarce done speaking, when I told him with great joy, Dear sir, put your confidence in the goodness of God, and fear nothing, you may consider it as a debt you was to pay; but that you are acquitted of it from this very hour. I am glad, that after my shipwreck I came so fortunately hither, to defend you against all those that would attempt your death: I will not leave you till the forty days are expired, of which the foolish astrologers have made you so apprehensive; and in the mean while I will do you all the service that lies in my power: after which I shall have the benefit of getting to the main land in your vessel, with leave of your father and yourself; and when I am returned into my kingdom, I shall remember the obligations I owe you, and endeavour to demonstrate my acknowledgments in a suitable manner.

This discourse of mine encouraged the jeweller's son, and made him have confidence in me. I took care not to tell him I was the very Agib whom he dreaded, lest I should put him into a fright, and took as much care not to give him any cause to suspect it. We passed the time in several discourses till night came on. I found the young lad of a ready wit, and eat with him of his provisions, of which he had enough to have lasted beyond the forty days, though he had had more guests than myself. After supper we continued some time in discourse; at last we went to bed.

The next day, when we got up, I held the bason and water to him; I also provided dinner, and set it on the table in due time: after we had done, I invented a play to divert ourselves, not only for that day, but for those that followed. I prepared supper after the same manner as I had prepared dinner; and having supped, we went to bed as formerly.—We had time enough to contract friendship: I found he loved me; and for my part, I had so great a respect for him, that I have often said to myself, those astrologers who predicted to his father, that his son should die by my hand, were impostors;

for it is not possible that I could commit so base an action. In short, madam, we spent thirty nine days in the pleasantest manner that could be in a place like that under ground.

The fortieth day appeared: and in the morning, when the young man awaked, he says to me with a transport of joy that he could not restrain, Prince, this is the fortieth day, and I am not dead, thanks to God and your good company. My father will not fail to be here anon, to give you a testimoney of his gratitude for it, and shall furnish you with all that is necessary for your return to your kingdom; but in the mean time, said he, I beg you to get ready some water very warm, to wash my whole body in that portable bagnio, that I may clean myself, and change my cloaths, to receive my father more chearfully.

I set the water on the fire, and when it was hot, put it into the moveable bagnio. The youth went in, and I myself washed and rubbed him. At last he came out, and laid himself down in his bed that I had prepared, and covered him with his bed cloaths. After he had slept a while, he awaked, and said, Dear prince, pray do me the favour to fetch me a melon and some sugar, that I may eat some and refresh me.

Out of several melons that remained, I took the best, and laid it on a plate; and because I could not find a knife to cut it with, I asked the young man now if he knew where there was one? There is one, said he, upon this cornice over my head: I accordingly saw it there, and made so much haste to reach it, that while I had it in my hand, my foot being entangled in the covering, I fell most unhappily upon the young man, and the knife ran into his heart in a minute.

At this spectacle I cried out most hideously: I beat my head, my face, and breast, I tore my cloaths, I threw myself on the ground with unspeakable sorrow and grief. Alas! I cried, there were only some hours wanting, to have put him out of that danger, from which he sought sanctuary here. And when I myself thought the danger past, then I became his murderer, and verified the prediction. But, O Lord, said I, lifting up my face and my hands to heaven, I beg thee pardon, and if I be guilty of his death, let me not live any longer.

After this misfortune I would have embraced death without any reluctance had it presented itself to me. But what we wish to ourselves, whether good or bad, will not always happen. Nevertheless, considering with myself, that all my tears and sorrows would not bring the young man to life again, and the forty days being expired, I might be surprised by his father, I quitted that subterrannean dwelling, laid down the great stone upon the entry of it, and covered it with earth.

I had scarce done, when casting my eyes upon the sea towards the main land, I perceived the vessel coming to fetch home the young man. I began then to consider what I had best do: I said to myself, if I am seen by the old man, he will certainly lay hold on me, and perhaps cause me to be massacred by his slaves. When he has seen his son killed, all that I can alledge to justify myself, will not be able to persuade him of my innocence. It is better for me then to withdraw, since it is in my power, than to expose myself to his resentment.

There happened to be near that subterrannean habitation, a large tree with thick leaves, which I thought fit to hide me in. I got up to it, and was no sooner fixed in a place where I could not be seen, but I saw the vessel come to the same place where she lay the first time.

The old man and his slaves landed immediately, and advanced towards the subterannean dwelling, with a countenance that showed some hope; but when they saw the earth had been newly removed, they changed colour, particularly the old man. They lifted the stone and went down; they called the young man by his name, but he not answering, their fears increased; they went down to seek him; and at length found him lying upon the bed with the knife in his heart, for I had not power to take it out. At this sight, they cried out lamentably, which increased my sorrow; the old man fell down in a swoon. The slaves, to give him air, brought him up in their arms, and laid him at the foot of the tree where I was; but notwithstanding all the pains they took to recover him, the unfortunate father continued a long while in that condition, and made them oftener than once despair of his life; but at last he came to himself. Then the slaves brought up his son's corpse dressed in his best apparel, and when they had made a grave, they put him into it. The old man supported by two slaves, and his face all covered with tears, threw the first earth upon him, after which the slaves filled up the grave.

This being done, all the furniture was brought out from under ground, and with the remaining provisions, put on board the vessel, the old man overcome with sorrow, and not being able to stand, was laid upon a sort of litter, and carried to the ship, which put forth to sea, and in a short time sailed quite out of sight.

After the old man and his slaves were gone with the vessel, I was left alone upon the island. I lay that night in the subterrannean dwelling, which they had shut up; and when the day came, I walked round the isle, and stopped in such places as I thought most proper to repose in when I had need.

I led this wearisome life for a month together, after which I perceived the sea to be mightily fallen; the island to be much larger; and the main land seemed to be drawing nearer me. In effect the water grew so low, that there was but a small stream between me and terra firma. I crossed it, and the water did not come above the middle of my leg. I marched so long upon the slime and sands, that I was very weary; at last I got upon ground, and when at a good distance from the sea, I saw a good way before me somewhat like a great fire, which gave me some comfort, for, said I to myself, I shall find some body or other, it not being possible that this fire should kindle of itself; but when I came near hand, I found my error, and saw that what I had taken to be fire, was a castle of red copper, which the beams of the sun made look at a distance as if it had been in flames.

I stopped near the castle, and sat down to admire its admirable structure, and to rest awhile. I had not taken such a full view of this magnificent building as it deserved, when I saw ten handsome young men coming along, as if they had been taking a walk; but that which most surprised me was, that they were all blind of the right eye; they accompanied an old man who was very tall, and of a venerable aspect.

I could not but wonder at the sight of so many half blind men all together, and every one of the same eye. As I was thinking in my mind, by what adventure all these men could come together, they came up to me, and seemed to be mighty glad to see me: after the first compliments were passed, they inquired what had brought me hither? I told them my story would be somewhat tedious, but if they would take the trouble to sit down, I would satisfy their request. They did so, and I related to them all that had happened unto me since I left my kingdom, which filled them with astonishment.

After I had ended my discourse, the young gentlemen prayed me to go with them into the castle; I accepted the proffer, and we passed through a great many halls, anti-chambers, bed-chambers and closets, very well furnished, and arrived at last into a spacious hall, where there were ten small blue sofas set round, and separate from one another, upon which they sat by day, and slept by night. In the middle of this round, there stood an eleventh sofa not so high as the rest, but of the same colour, upon which the old man above-mentioned sat down, and the young gentlemen made use of the other ten; whereas each sofa could only contain one man, one of the young men says to me, Comrade, sit down upon that carpet in the middle of the room, and do not enquire into any thing that concerns us, nor the reason why we are all blind of the right eye; be content with what you see, and let not your curiosity go any farther.

The old man having sat a little while, rose up, and went out; but he returned in a minute or two, brought in supper to those ten gentlemen; distributed to each man his proportion, by himself, and likewise brought me mine, which I eat by myself, as the rest did; and when supper was almost done, he presented to each of us a cup of wine.

They thought my story so extraordinary, that they made me repeat it after supper, and this gave occasion to discourses that lasted a good part of the night. One of the gentlemen observing that it was late, said to the old man, You see it is time to go to bed, and you do not bring us that with which we may acquit ourselves of our duty. At these words the old man arose, and went into a closet, from whence he brought upon his head ten basons, one after another, all covered with blue stuff: He set one before every gentleman, together with a light.

They uncovered their basons, in which there were ashes, coal-dust, and lamp-black;* they mixed all together, and rubbed and bedaubed their faces with it, in such a manner that they looked very frightful.—After having thus blacked themselves they fell a-weeping and lamenting, beating their heads and breasts, and cried continually: This is the fruit of our idleness and debauches.

They continued thus almost the whole night, and when they left off, the old man brought them water, with which they washed their faces and hands; they changed also their cloaths, which were spoiled, and put on others; so that they did not look in the least as if they had been doing so strange an action.

You may judge, madam, how uneasy I was all the while; I had a mind a thousand times to break the silence which those young gentlemen had imposed upon me, and ask questions; nor was it possible for me to sleep that night.

After we got up next day, we went out to walk and then I told them, Gentlemen, I declare to you, that I must renounce that law which you prescribed to me last night, for I cannot observe it. You are men of sense, and all of you have wit in abundance, you have convinced me of it, yet I have seen you do such actions as none but madmen could be capable of. Whatever misfortune befals me, I cannot forbear asking, Why you bedaubed your faces with black? How it comes that each of you has but one eye? Some singular thing must certainly be the cause of it, therefore I conjure you to satisfy my curiosity. To these pressing instances they answered nothing, but that it was none of my business to ask such questions, that I should do well to hold my peace.

We passed that day in discourses upon different subjects, and when night was come, and every man had supped, the old man brought in the blue basons, and the young gentlemen bedaubed their faces, wept and beat themselves, crying, This is the fruit of our idleness and debauches, as before, and continued the same actions the following night. At last, not being able to resist my curiosity, I earnestly prayed them to satisfy me or to shew me how to return to my own kingdom; for it was impossible for me to keep them company any longer, and to see every night such an odd spectacle, without being permitted to know the reason.

One of the gentlemen answered in behalf of the rest, Do not wonder at our conduct in regard to yourself; and that hitherto we have not granted your request, it is out of mere kindness, to prevent you the sorrow of being reduced to the same condition with us. If you have a mind to try our unfortunate destiny, you need but speak, and we will give you the satisfaction you desire. I told them I was resolved on it, let come what will. Once more, said the same gentleman, we advise you to restrain your curiosity, it will cost you the loss of your right eye. No matter, said I, I declare to you, that if such a misfortune befal me, I will not impute it to you, but to myself.

He farther represented to me, that when I had lost an eye, I must not hope to stay with them, if I were so minded, because their number was complete, and no addition could be made to it. I told them, that it would be a great satisfaction to me never to part from such honest gentlemen, but if there was necessity for it, I was ready to submit; and let it cost me what it would, I begged them to grant my request.

The ten gentlemen perceiving that I was so positive in my resolution, took a sheep, and killed it, and after they had taken off the skin, presented me with the knife, telling me it would be useful to me on a certain occasion, which they should tell me of presently. We must sew you into this skin, said they, and then leave you; upon which a fowl of a monstrous size, called a roc,* will appear in the air, and taking you to be a sheep, will come down upon you, and carry you up to the very sky; but let not that frighten you, he will come down with you again, and lay you on the top of a mountain. When you find yourself upon the ground, cut the skin with the knife, and throw it off. As soon as the roc sees you, he will fly away for fear, and leave you at liberty: Do not stay, but walk on till you come to a prodigious castle, all covered with plates of gold, large emeralds, and other precious stones: Go up to the gate, which always stands open and walk in: We have been in the castle as long as we have been here; we will tell you nothing of what we saw, or what befel us there, you will learn it of yourself; all that we can inform you is that it hath cost each of us our right eye, and the penance which you have been witness to, is what we are obliged to do, because we have been there. The history of each of us in particular is so full of extraordinary adventures, that a large volume would not contain them. But we must explain ourselves no farther.

When the gentleman had ended this discourse, I wrapt myself in the sheep's skin, held fast the knife which was given me; and after those young gentlemen had been at the trouble to sew the skin about me, they retired into the hall, and left me on the place. The roc they had spoke of was not long a-coming; he fell down upon me, took me up between his talons like a sheep, and carried me up to the top of the mountain.

When I found myself upon the ground, I made use of the knife, cut the skin, and throwing it off, the roc at the sight of me flew away. This roc is a white bird of a monstrous size, his strength is such that he can lift up elephants from the plains, and carry them to the tops of mountains, where he feeds upon them.

Being impatient till I reached the castle, I lost no time, but made so much haste, that I got thither in half a day's journey, and I must say that I found it surpassed the description they had given me of it.

The gate being open, I entered into a court that was square, and so large, that there was round it ninety-nine gates of wood of sanders and aloes, with one of gold, without counting those of several magnificent stair-cases that led up to apartments above, besides many more I could not see. The hundred doors I spoke of, opened into gardens or store-houses full of riches, or into palaces which contained things wonderful to be seen.

I saw a door standing open just before me, through which I entered into a large hall, where I found forty young ladies of such perfect beauty, that imagination could not go beyond it; they were all most sumptuously apparelled; and as soon as they saw me, rose up, and without expecting my compliments, said to me with demonstrations of joy, Noble sir, you are very welcome. And one spoke to me in the name of the rest thus: We have been in expectation a long while of such a gentleman as you; your mein assures us that you are master of all the good qualities we can wish for, and we hope you will not find our company disagreeable or unworthy of yours.

They forced me, notwithstanding all the opposition I could make, to sit down on a seat that was higher than theirs, and though I signified that I was uneasy. That is your place, said they, you are at present our lord, master and judge, and we are your slaves, ready to obey your commands.

Nothing in the world, madam, did so much astonish me as the passion and eagerness of those fair ladies, to do me all possible service. One brought hot water to wash my feet, a second poured sweet-scented water on my hands, others brought me all sorts of necessaries, and change of apparel; and others brought in a magnificent collation; and the rest came with glasses in their hands, to fill me delicious wines, and all in good order, and in the most charming manner that could be. I eat and drank; after which, the ladies placed themselves about me, and desired an account of my travels. I gave them a full relation of my adventures, which lasted till night came on.

When I had made an end of my story, which I related to the forty ladies, some of them that sat nearest me staid to keep me company, whilst the rest seeing it was dark, rose up to fetch tapers. They brought a prodigious quantity, which made such a marvellous light as if it had been day, and they were so proportionably disposed, that nothing could be more beautiful.

Other ladies covered a table with dry fruits, sweet-meats, and every thing proper to make the liquor relish: And a sideboard was set with several sorts of wines and other liquors. Some of the ladies came in with musical instruments; and when every thing was prepared, they invited me to sit down to supper. The ladies sat down with me, and we continued a long while at supper. They that were to play upon the instruments, and sing, rose up, and made a most charming concert. The others began a sort of ball, and danced by two and two, one after another, with a wonderful good grace.

It was past midnight before those divertisements ended: At length one of the ladies says to me, You are doubtless wearied by the journey you have made to-day; it is time for you to go to rest; your lodging is prepared; but before you depart, make choice of any of us you like best, to be your bedfellow. I answered, That I knew better things than to offer to make my own choice, since they were all equally beautiful, witty, and worthy of my respects and service, and I would not be guilty of so much incivility, as to prefer one before another.

The same lady that spoke to me before, answered, We assure you, that the good fortune of her whom you chuse shall cause no jealousy; for we are agreed among ourselves, that every one of us shall have the same honour, till it go round; and when forty days are past, to begin again; therefore make your free choice, and lose no time to go and take the repose you stand in need of. I was obliged to yield to their instances, and offered my hand to the lady that spoke; she, in return, gave me hers, and we were conducted to a sumptuous apartment, where they left us; and then every one retired to their own apartment.

I was scarce dressed next morning, when the other thirty-nine ladies came into my chamber, all in other dresses than they had the day before: They bid me good-morrow, and enquired after my health; after that they carried me to a bagnio, where they washed me themselves, and, whether I would or no, served me in every thing I stood in need of; and when I came out of the bath, they made me put on another suit, much richer than the former.

We passed the whole day almost constantly at table; and when it was bed-time, they prayed me again to make choice of one of them to keep me company. In short, madam, not to weary you with repetitions, I must tell you, that I continued a whole year among those forty ladies, and received them into my bed one after another; and during all the time of this voluptuous life, we met not with the least kind of trouble. When the year was expired, I was strangely surprised that these forty ladies, instead of appearing with their usual chearfulness, to ask how I did, entered one morning into my chamber all in tears: They embraced me with great tenderness, one after another, saying, Adieu, dear prince, adieu! for we must leave you. Their tears affected me: I prayed them to tell me the reason of their grief, and of the seperation they spoke of. For God's sake, fair ladies, let me know, said I, if it be in my power to comfort you, or if my assistance can be any way useful to you. Instead of returning a direct answer, Would to God, said they, we had never seen or known you. Several gentlemen have honoured us with their company before you; but never one of them had that sweetness, that pleasantness of humour, and merit, which you have; we know not how to live without you.—After they had spoken these words, they began to weep bitterly. My dear ladies, said I, be so kind as not to keep me in suspence any more: Tell me the cause of your sorrow. Alas! said they, what other thing can be capable of grieving us, but the necessity of parting from you? It may so happen, that we shall never see you again; but if you be so minded, and have command enough over yourself, it is not impossible for us to meet again. Ladies, said I, I understand not your meaning; pray explain yourselves more clearly.

Oh then said one of them, to satisfy you, we must acquaint you, that we are all princesses, daughters of kings; we live here together in such manner as you have seen, but at the end of every year, we are obliged to be absent forty days, upon indispensible duties, which we are not permitted to reveal; and afterwards we return again to this castle. Yesterday was the last of the year, and we must leave you this day, which is the cause of our grief. Before we depart we will leave you the keys to every thing, especially those belonging to the hundred doors, where you will find enough to satisfy your curiosity, and to sweeten your solitude during our absence: But for your own welfare, and our particular concern in you, we recommend unto you to forbear opening the golden door; for if you do we shall never see you again; and the fear of this augments our grief. We hope, nevertheless, that you will follow the advice we give you, as you tender your own quiet, and the happiness of your life; therefore take heed that you do not give way to indiscreet curiosity, for you will do yourself a considerable prejudice. We conjure you therefore, not to commit this fault, but to let us have the comfort of finding you here again after forty days. We would willingly carry the key of the golden door along with us; but that it would be an affront to a prince like you, to question your discretion and modesty.

This discourse of the fair princesses made me extremely sorrowful. I omitted not to make them sensible how much their absence would afflict me: I thanked them for their good advice, and assured them that I would follow it, and willingly do what was much more difficult, in order to be so happy as to pass the rest of my days with ladies of such rare qualifications. We took leave of one another with a great deal of tenderness;

and having embraced them all, at last they departed, and I was left alone in the castle.

Their agreeable company, the good cheer, the concerts of music, and other pleasures, had so much diverted me during the whole year, that I neither had time, nor the least desire to see the wonderful things contained in this enchanted palace. Nay, I did not so much as take notice of a thousand rare objects that were every day in my sight; for I was so taken with the charming beauty of those ladies, and took so much pleasure in seeing them wholly employed to oblige me, that their departure afflicted me very sensibly; and though their absence was to be only forty days, it seemed to me an age to live without them.

I promised myself not to forget the important advice they had given me, not to open the golden door; but as I was permitted to satisfy my curiosity in every thing else, I took the first of the keys of the other doors, which were hung in good order.

I opened the first door, and came into an orchard, which I believe the universe could not equal; I could not imagine, that any thing could surpass it, but that which our religion promises us after death;* the symmetry, the neatness and admirable order of the trees, the abundance and diversity of a thousand unknown fruits, their freshness and beauty ravished my sight.

I ought not to forget, madam, to acquaint you, that this delicious orchard was watered after a very particular manner; there were channels so artificially and proportionably digged, that they carried water in abundance to the roots of such trees as wanted it, for making them produce their leaves and flowers. Others carried it to those that had their fruit budded: Some carried it in lesser quantities to those that had their fruit growing big, and others carried only so much as was just requisite to water those which had their fruit come to perfection, and only wanted to be ripened. They exceeded the ordinary fruits of our gardens very much in bigness; and lastly, those channels that watered the trees whose fruit was ripe, had no more moisture than just what would preserve them from withering.

I could never be weary to look at and admire so sweet a place; and I should never have left it, had I not conceived a greater idea of the other things I had not seen. I went out at last with my mind filled with those wonders: I shut that door, and opened the next.

Instead of an orchard I found a flower-garden, which was no less extraordinary in its kind: It contained a spacious plot, not watered so profusely as the former, but with greater niceness, furnishing no more water than just what each flower required. The roses, jessamines, violets, dills, hyacinths, wild-flowers, tulips, crows-foots, pinks, lillies, and an infinite number of other flowers which do not grow in other places but at certain times, were there flourishing all at once, and nothing could be more delicious than the fragrant smell of this garden.

I opened the third door, where I found a large volary,* paved with marble of several fine colours, that were not common. The cage was made of sanders and wood of aloes; it contained a vast number of nightingales, gold-finches, canary-birds, larks, and other rare singing-birds, which I never heard of; and the vessels that held their seed and water, were of the most precious jasper or agate.

Besides, this volary was so exceeding neat, that considering its extent, one would think there could be no less than a hundred persons to keep it so clean as it was; but all this while not one soul appeared, either here or in the gardens where I had been; and yet I could not perceive a weed or any superfluous thing there. The sun went down, and I retired, being perfectly charmed with the chirping notes of the multitude of birds who then began to perch upon such places as were convenient for them to repose on during the night; I went to my chamber, resolving to open all the rest of the doors the days following, excepting that of gold.

I failed not to open a fourth door next day, and if what I had seen before was capable of surprising me, that which I saw then, put me in perfect ecstacy. I went into a large court surrounded with buildings of an admirable structure, the description of which I will pass by to avoid prolixity.

This building had forty doors, wide open, and through each of them was an entrance into a treasury, several of which were of greater value than the largest kingdoms. The first contained heaps of pearls; and what is almost incredible, the number of those stones which are most precious, and as large as pigeons eggs, exceeded the number of those of the ordinary size: in the second treasury, there were diamonds, carbuncles, and rubies: In the third, there were emeralds: in the fourth, there were ingots of gold: in the fifth, money: in the sixth, ingots of silver: in the two following, there was also money. The rest contained amethysts, chrysolites, topazes, opals, turkoises, and hyacinths, with all the other stones unknown to us, without mentioning agate, jasper, cornelian, and coral, of which there was a storehouse filled, not only with branches, but whole trees.

Being filled with amazement and admiration, I cried out to myself, after having seen all these riches, Now, if all the treasures of the kings of the universe were gathered together in one place, they could not come near this: What good fortune have I to possess all this wealth with so many admirable princesses!

I shall not stay, madam, to tell you the particulars of all the other rare and precious things I saw the days following; I shall only tell you, that thirty-nine days afforded me but just as much time as was necessary to open ninety-nine doors, and to admire all that presented itself to my view, so that there was only the hundredth door left, the opening of which I was forbid.

I was come to the fortieth day after the departure of those charming princesses, and had I but retained so much power over myself as I ought to have had, I should have been this day the happiest of all mankind, whereas now I am the most unfortunate. They were to return next day, and the pleasure of seeing them again ought to have restrained my curiosity; but, through my weakness, which I shall ever repent, I yielded to the temptations of the evil spirit, who gave me no rest till I had thrown myself into those misfortunes that I have since undergone.

I opened that fatal door, which I promised not to meddle with, and had not moved my foot to go in, when a smell that was pleasant enough, but contrary to my constitution, made me faint away: Nevertheless, I came to myself again, and instead of taking this warning to shut the door, and forbear satisfying my curiosity, I went in, after I had stood some time in the air to carry off the scent, which did not incommode me any more: I found a large place, very well vaulted, the pavement strewed with saffron; several candlesticks of massy gold, with lighted tapers that smelled of aloes and ambergris, lighted the place; and this light was augmented with lamps of gold and silver, that burnt with oil, made of several sorts of sweet-scented materials.

Among a great many objects that engaged my attention, I perceived a black horse, of the handsomest and best shape that ever was seen. I went nearer the better to observe him, and found he had a saddle and bridle of massy gold, curiously wrought. The one side of his trough was filled with clean barley and sessems,* and the other with rose water: I took him by the bridle, and led him forth to view him by the light: I got upon his back, and would have had him move, but he not stirring, I whipped him with a switch which I had taken up in his magnificent stable; and he had no sooner felt the stroke, than he began to neigh with a horrible noise, and extending his wings, which I had not seen before, he flew up with me into the air, quite out of sight. I thought of nothing then, but to sit fast; and considering the fear that had seized upon me, I sat very well. He afterwards flew down again towards the earth, and lighting upon the terrace of a castle, without giving me any time to get off, he shook me out of the saddle with such force, that he made me fall behind him, and with the end of his tail struck out my right eye.

Thus I became blind of one eye, and then I began to remember, the predictions of the ten young gentlemen. The horse flew again out of sight. I got up very much troubled at the misfortune I had brought upon myself; I walked upon the terrace, covering my eye with one of my hands, for it pained me exceedingly, and then came down and entered into the hall, which I knew presently by the ten sofas in a circle, and the eleventh in the middle, lower than the rest, to be the same castle from whence I was taken away by the roc.

The ten half-blind gentlemen were not in the hall when I came in, but came soon after with the old man; they were not at all surprised to see me again, nor at the loss of mine eye; but said we are sorry that we cannot congratulate you upon your return as we could have desired; but we are not the cause of your misfortune. I should be in the wrong to accuse you, said I, for I have drawn it upon myself, and I can charge the fault upon no other person. If it be a consolation to the unfortunate, said they to have fellows, this example may afford us a subject of rejoicing; all that has happened to you, we have also undergone; we tasted all sorts of pleasure during a year successively; and we had continued to enjoy the same happiness still, had we not opened the golden door, when the princesses were absent: You have been no wiser than we, and you have had likewise the same punishment; we would gladly receive you among us, to do such penance as we do, though we know not how long it may continue: But we have already declared the reasons that hinder us; therefore depart from hence, and go to the court at Bagdad, where you shall meet with him that can decide your destiny. They told me the way I was to travel; and so I left them.

On the road I caused my beard and eye-brows to be shaven, and took on a calender's habit. I have had a long journey; but at last arrived this evening in this city, where I met these my brother calenders at the gate, being strangers as well as myself. We wondered much at one another, to see that we were all three blind of the same eye; but we had not leisure to discourse long of our common calamities, we had only so much time as to come hither, to implore those favours which you have been generously pleased to grant us.

The third calender having finished this relation of his adventures, Zobeide addressed her speech to him and his fellow-calenders thus: Go wherever you think fit, you are all three at liberty. But one of them answered, Madam, we beg you to pardon our curiosity, and permit us to hear those gentlemen's stories who have not yet spoke. Then the lady turned to that side where the caliph, the visier Giafar, and Mesrour stood, whom she knew not; but said to them, it is now your turn to tell me your adventures, therefore speak.

The grand-visier Giafar, who had always been the spokesman, answered Zobeide thus: Madam, in order to obey you, we need only to repeat what we have said already, before we entered your house: We are merchants of Moussoul, that came to Bagdad to sell our merchandise, that lies in the khan where we lodge. We dined to-day with several other persons of our profession, at a merchant's house of this city; who, after he had treated us with choice dainties and excellent wines, sent for men and women dancers, and musicians. The great noise we made brought in the watch, who arrested some of the company, and we had the good fortune to escape; but it being already late, the door of our khan is shut up, we know not whither to retire. It was our hap, as we passed along this street, to hear mirth at your house, which made us determine to knock at your gate. This is all the account that we can give you, in obedience to your commands.

Zobeide having heard this discourse, seemed to hesitate upon what she should say; which the calenders perceiving, prayed her to grant the same favour to the Moussoul merchants, as she had done to them. Well then, said she, I give my consent; for you shall all be equally obliged to me: I pardon you all, provided you depart immediately out of this house; and go whither you please.

Zobeide having given this command in a tone that signified she would be obeyed, the caliph, the visier, Mesrour, the three calenders, and the porter, departed, without saying one word; for the presence of the seven slaves with their weapons kept them in awe. When they were out of the house, and the door shut, the caliph said to the calenders, without making himself known, You gentlemen strangers, that are newly come to town, which way do you design to go, since it is not yet day? It is that which perplexes us, Sir, said they. Follow us, replies the caliph; and we will bring you out of danger. After saying these words, he whispered to the visier, Take them along with you, and to-morrow morning bring them to me; I will cause their history to be put in writing; for it deserves a place in the annals of my reign.

The visier Giafar took the three calenders along with him; the porter went to his quarters, and the caliph and Mesrour returned to the palace. The caliph went to bed, but could not get a wink of sleep, his spirits were so perplexed by the extraordinary things he had seen and heard: But above all, he was most concerned to know who Zobeide was, what reason she could have to be so severe to the two black bitches, and why Amine had her bosom so mortified. Day began to appear whilst he was thinking upon these things; he arose and went to his council-chamber, where he used to give audience, and sat upon his throne.

The grand-visier came in a little after, and paid his respects as usual. Visier, said the caliph, the affairs that we have to consider at present are not very pressing: That of the three ladies and the two black bitches is much more so. My mind cannot be at ease, till I be thoroughly satisfied in all those matters that have surprised me so much. Go bring these ladies and the calenders at the same time; make haste, and remember that I do impatiently expect your return.

The visier, that knew his master's quick and fiery temper, made haste to obey, and went to the ladies, to whom he communicated, in a civil way, the orders he had to bring them before the caliph, without taking any notice of what had passed the night before at their house.

The ladies put on their veils, and went with the visier; as he passed by his own house, he took the three calenders along with him, and they, in the mean time, had got notice that they had both seen and spoke with the caliph, without knowing him. The visier brought them to the palace with so much diligence, that the caliph was mighty well pleased at it. This prince, that he might keep a good decorum before all the officers of his court that were then present, made those ladies be placed behind the hanging of the door of the room that was next his bed-chamber, and kept the three calenders by him; who, by their respectful behaviour, gave sufficient proof that they were not ignorant before whom they had the honour to appear.

When the ladies were placed, the caliph turned towards them, and said, Ladies, when I shall acquaint you that I came last night, disguised in a merchant's habit, into your house, it will certainly alarm you, and make you to fear that you offended me; and perhaps you believe that I have sent for you to no other end, but to shew some marks of my resentment; but be not afraid, you may rest assured, that I have forgot all that is past, and am very well satisfied with your conduct. I wish that all the ladies of Bagdad had as much discretion as you have given proof of before me. I shall always remember the moderation you made use of, after the incivility we had committed. I was then a merchant of Moussoul, but am at present Haroun Alraschid, the seventh caliph of the glorious house of Abbas, that holds the place of our great prophet. I have only sent for you, to know who you are? and to ask you for what reason one of you, after severely whipping the two black bitches, did weep with them? and I am no less curious to know, why another of you has her bosom full of scars?

Though the caliph pronounced these words very distinctly, and that the three ladies heard him well enough, yet the visier Giafar did, out of ceremony, repeat them over again.

Zobeide, after the caliph by his discourse encouraged her, satisfied his curiosity in this manner:

The Story of Zobeide

COMMANDER of the Faithful, says she, the relation which I am about to give your majesty, is one of the strangest that ever was heard. The two black bitches and myself are sisters by the same father and mother; and I shall acquaint you by what strange accident they came to be metamorphosed. The two ladies that live with me, and are now here, are also my sisters by the father's side, but by another mother; she that has the scars on her breast, her name is Amine, the other is Safie, and mine is Zobeide.

After our father's death, the estate that he left us was equally divided among us; and as soon as these two sisters received their portions, they went from me to live with their mother. My other two sisters and myself staid with our mother, who was then alive, and when she died, left each of us a thousand sequins. As soon as we received our portions, the two elder, (for I am the youngest) being married, followed their husbands, and left me alone. Some time after, my eldest sister's husband sold all that he had, and with the money and my sister's portion, they went both into Africa, where her husband, by riotous living and debauchery, spent all: and finding himself reduced to poverty, he found a pretext for divorcing my sister, and put her away.

She returned to this city, and having suffered incredible hardships by the way, came to me in so lamentable a condition, that it would have moved the hardest heart to compassion. I received her with all the tenderness she could expect; and inquiring into the cause of her sad condition, she told me with tears, how unhumanly her husband had dealt by her. I was so much concerned at her misfortune, that it drew tears from mine eyes: I put her into a bagnio, and cloathed her with my own apparel, and spoke to her thus: Sister, you are the elder, and I esteem you as my mother: During your absence, God has blessed the portion that fell to my share, and the employment I follow to feed and bring up silk worms. Assure yourself there is nothing I have but what is at your service, and as much at your disposal as my own.

We lived very comfortably together for some months; and as we were often discoursing together about our third sister, and wondering we heard no news of her, she came in as bad a condition as the elder; her husband had treated her after the same manner; and I received her likewise with the same affection I had done the former.

Some time after, my two sisters, on pretence that they would not be chargeable to me, told me they had thoughts to marry again. I answered them, That if their putting me to charge was all the reason, they might lay those thoughts aside, and be very welcome to stay with me; for what I had would be sufficient to maintain us all three, answerable to our condition: But, says I, I rather believe you have a mind to marry again; which if you have, I am sure it will very much surprise me: After the experience you have had of the small satisfaction there is in wedlock, is it possible you dare venture a second time? you know how rare it is to meet with a real honest man. Believe what I say, and let us stay together, and live as comfortably as we can. All my persuasion was in vain, they were resolved to marry, and so they did; but after some months were past, they came back again and begged my pardon a thousand times for not following my advice. You are our youngest sister, said they, and abundantly more wise than we; but if you will vouchsafe to receive us once more into your house, and account us your slaves, we shall never commit such a fault again. My answer was, Dear sisters, I have not altered my mind with respect to you since we last parted from one another; come again, and take part of what I have. Upon this, I embraced them again, and we lived together as we did formerly.

We continued thus a whole year, in perfect love and tranquility; and seeing that God had increased my small stock, I projected a voyage by sea, to hazard somewhat in trade. To this end, I went with my two sisters to Balsora, where I bought a ship ready fitted for sea, and laded her with such merchandise as I brought from Bagdad. We set sail with a fair wind, and soon got through the Persian gulph; and when we got into the ocean, we steered our course for the Indies, and saw land the twentieth day. It was a very high mountain, at the bottom of which we saw a great town, and having a fresh gale, we soon reached the harbour, where we cast anchor.

I had not patience to stay till my sisters were dressed to go along with me, but went ashore in the boat by myself; and making directly to the gate of the town, I saw there a great number of men upon the guard, some sitting, and others standing, with battons in their hands; and they had all such dreadful countenances that it frightened me; but perceiving they had no motion, nay, not so much as with their eyes, I took courage, and went nearer, and then found they were all turned into stones. I entered the town, and passed through the several streets, where there stood every-where men in several postures, but all unmoveable and petrified. On that side where the merchants lived, I found most of the shops shut, and in such as were open, I likewise found the people petrified. I looked up to the chimneys, but saw no smoke, which made me conjecture that those within, as well as those without, were all turned to stones.

Being come into a vast square, in the heart of the city, I percieved a great gate, covered with plates of gold, the two leaves of which stood open, and a curtain of silk stuff seemed to be drawn before it; I also saw a lamp hanging over the gate. After I had well considered this fabric, I made no doubt but it was the palace of the prince who reigned over that country; and being very much astonished that I had not met with one living creature, I went thither in hopes to find some: I entered the gate, and was still more surprised, when I saw none but the guards in the porches, all petrified; some standing, some sitting, and some lying.

I crossed over a large court, where I saw a stately building just before me, the windows of which were inclosed with gates of massy gold: I looked upon it to be the queen's apartment, and went into a large hall, where stood several black eunuchs turned into stone. I went from thence into a room richly hung and furnished, where I perceived a lady in the same manner. I knew it to be the queen, by the crown of gold that hung over her head, and a necklace of pearl about her neck, each of them as big as a nut; I went up close to her to view it, and never saw any thing finer.

I stood some time and admired the riches and magnificence of the room; but above all, the foot cloth, the cushions, and the sofas, which were all lined with Indian stuff of gold, with pictures of men and beasts in silver, drawn to admiration.

I went out of the chamber where the petrified queen was, and came through several other apartments and closets richly furnished, and at last came into a vast large room, where there was a throne of massy gold, raised several steps above the floor, and enriched with large enchased emeralds, and a bed upon the throne of rich stuff, embroidered with pearls. That which surprised me more than all the rest, was a sparkling light which came from above the bed: being curious to know from whence it came, I mounted the steps, and lifting up my head, I saw a diamond as big as the egg of an ostrich, lying upon a low stool; it was so pure, that I could not find the least blemish in it; and it sparkled so bright, that I could not endure the lusture of it, when I saw it by day.

On each side of the bed's head there stood a lighted flambeau, but to what use I could not apprehend: however, it made me imagine that there was some living creature in this place; for I could not believe that these torches continued thus burning of themselves. Several other rarities detained my curiosity in this room, which was inestimable, were it only for the diamond I mentioned.

The doors being all open, or but half-shut, I surveyed some other apartments that were as fine as those I had already seen. I looked into the offices and store-rooms, which were full of infinite riches; and I was so much taken with the sight of all these wonderful things, that I forgot myself, and did not think on my ship or my sisters; my whole design was to satisfy my curiosity: mean time, night came on, which put me in mind that it was time to retire. I was for returning by the same way I came in, but I could not find it; I lost myself among the apartments and finding I was come back again to that large room where the throne, the couch, the large diamond, and the torches stood, I resolved to make my night's lodging there, and to depart the next morning betimes, to get aboard my ship. I laid myself down upon the couch, not without some dread to be alone in a wild place; and this fear hindered my sleep.

About midnight I heard a voice like that of a man reading the alcoran, after the same manner, and in the same tone, as we use to read it in our mosques. Being extremely glad to hear it, I got up immediately, and taking a torch in my hand to light me, I passed from one chamber to another, on that side where the voice came from: I came to the closet door, where I stood still, no-wise doubting that it came from thence. I set down my torch upon the ground, and looking through a window, I found it to be an oratory. In short, it had, as we have in our mosques, a nich, that shews where we must turn to say our prayers.* There were also lamps hung up, and two candlesticks with large tapers of white wax burning.

I saw a little carpet laid down like those we have to kneel upon when we say prayers, and a comely young man sat upon this carpet reading the alcoran, which lay before him upon a desk, with great devotion. At the sight of this, I was transported with admiration; I wondered how it came to pass that he should be the only living creature in a town where all the people were turned into stones, and I did not doubt but there was something in it very extraordinary.

The door being only half-shut, I opened it, and went in, and standing upright before the nich, I said this prayer aloud: Praise be to God, that has favoured us with a happy voyage; and may he be graciously pleased to protect us in the same manner until we arrive again in our own country. Hear me, O Lord and grant my request.

The young man cast his eyes upon me, and said, My good lady, pray let me know who you are, and what has brought you to this desolate city: and in requital, I will tell you who I am, what has happened to me, why the inhabitants of this city are reduced to that state you see them in, and why I alone am safe and sound in the midst of such a terrible disaster.

I told him in a few words from whence I came, what made me undertake the voyage, and how I safely arrived at the port, after twenty days sailing; and when I had done, I prayed him to perform his promise, and told him how much I was struck by the frightful desolation which I had seen in all places as I came along.

My dear lady, says the young man, have patience for a moment. At those words he shut the alcoran, put it into a rich case, and laid it in the nich.—I took that opportunity to observe him, and perceived so much good nature and beauty in him, that I felt such strange emotions in myself, as I never had done before. He made me sit down by him, and before he began his discourse, I could not forbear saying to him, with an air that discovered the sentiments I was inspired with, Amiable sir, dear object of my soul, I can scarce have patience to wait for an account of all those wonderful things that I have seen since the first time I came into your city; and my curiosity cannot be satisfied too soon; therefore pray sir let me know by what miracle you alone are left alive among so many persons that have died in so strange a manner.

Madam, says the young man, you have given me to understand, you have the knowledge of a true God, by the prayer you have just now addressed to him. I will acquaint you with the most remarkable effect of his greatness and power. You must know that this city was the metropolis of a mighty kingdom, over which the king, my father, did reign. That prince, his whole court, the inhabitants of the city, and all his other subjects, were magi, worshippers of fire, and of Nardoun, the ancient king of the giants who rebelled against God.*

And though I was begotten and born of an idolatrous father and mother, I had the good fortune in my youth to have a woman-governess, who was a good mussulman. I had the alcoran by heart, and understood the explanation of it perfectly well. Dear prince, would she oftentimes say, there is but one true God; take heed that you do not acknowledge and adore any other. She learned me to read Arabic, and the book she gave me to exercise upon was the alcoran. As soon as I was capable of understanding it, she explained to me all the heads of this excellent book, and infused piety into my mind, unknown to my father, or any body else. She happened to die, but not before she had perfectly instructed me in all that was necessary to convince me of the mussulman religion. After her death, I persisted with constancy in the belief I was in; and I abhor the false god Nardoun, and the adoration of fire.

It is about three years and some months ago, that a thundering voice was heard all on a sudden, so distinctly, through the whole city, that nobody could miss hearing it: the words were these, Inhabitants, abandon the worship of Nardoun, and of fire, and worship the only God that shews mercy.

This voice was heard three years successively, but nobody was converted; so the last day of the year, at four o'clock in the morning, all the inhabitants in general were changed in an instant into stone, every one in the same condition and posture they happened then to be in. The king my father had the same fate, for he was metamorphosed into a black stone, as he is to be seen in this palace; and the queen my mother had the like destiny.

I am the only person that did not suffer under that heavy judgment, and ever since, I have continued to serve him with more fervency than before. I am persuaded, dear lady, that he has sent you hither for my comfort, for which I render him infinite thanks, for I must own that this solitary life is very uneasy.

All these expressions, and particularly the last, increased my love to him extremely. Prince said I, there is no doubt but providence hath brought me into your port, to present you with an opportunity of withdrawing from this dismal place; the ship that I am come in, may in some measure persuade you that I am in some esteem at Bagdad, where I have left also a considerable estate, and I dare engage to promise you sanctuary there, until the mighty commander of the faithful, who is vice regent to our prophet whom you acknowledge, do you the honour that is due to your merit. This renowned prince lives at Bagdad; and as soon as he is informed of your arrival in his capital, you will find that it is not in vain to implore his assistance. It is impossible you can stay any longer in a city where all the objects you see must renew your grief: my vessel is at your service, where you may absolutely command as you shall think fit. He accepted the offer, and we discoursed the remaining part of the night about our embarkment.

As soon as it was day we left the palace, and came aboard my ship, where we found my sisters, the captain and the slaves, all very much troubled for my absence. After I had presented my sisters to the prince, I told them what had hindered my return to the vessel the day before; how I had met with the young prince; his story, and the cause of the desolation of so fine a city.

The seamen were taken up several days in unloading the merchandise I brought along with me, and embarking, insteed of that, all the precious things in the palace, as jewels, gold, and money.—We left the furniture and goods, which consisted of an infinite quantity of plate, &c, because our vessel could not carry it; for it would have required several vessels more to carry all the riches to Bagdad, that were in our option to take with us.

After we had laden the vessel with what we thought fit, we took such provisions and water aboard as were necessary for our voyage, (for we had still a great deal of those provisions left that we had taken in at Balsora); at last we set sail with a wind as favourable as we could wish.

The young Prince, my sisters and myself, enjoyed ourselves for sometime very agreeably. But alas! this good understanding did not last long; for my sisters grew jealous of the friendship between the prince and me, and maliciously asked me one day, what we should do with him when we came to Bagdad? I perceived immediately that they put this question to me, on purpose to discover my inclinations; therefore resolving to put it off with a jest, I answered them, I will take him for my husband; and upon that, turning myself to the prince, Sir, I humbly beg of you to give your consent, for as soon as we come to Bagdad, I design to offer you my person to be your slave, to do you all the service that is in my power, and to resign myself wholly to your commands.

The prince answered, I know not madam, whether you be in jest or no; but for my own part, I seriously declare, before these ladies, your sisters, that from this moment, I heartily accept your offer, not with any intention to have you as a slave, but as my lady and mistress; nor will I pretend to have any power over your actions. At these words my sisters changed colour, and I could perceive afterwards that they did not love me as formerly.

We were come into the Persian Gulf, and not far from Balsora, where I hoped, considering the fair wind, we might have arrived the day following; but in the night, when I was asleep, my sisters watched their time, and threw me overboard. They did the same to the prince, who was drowned. I swam some minutes on the water; but by good fortune, or rather miracle, I felt ground. I went towards a black place, that by what I could discern in the dark seemed to be land, and actually was afloat on the coast; which, when day came, I found to be a desart island, lying about twenty miles from Balsora. I soon dried my clothes in the sun: and as I walked along, I found several sorts of fruit, and likewise fresh water, which gave me some hopes of preserving my life.

I laid myself down in a shade, and soon after I saw a winged serpent, very large and long, coming towards me, wriggling to the right and to the left, and hanging out his tongue, which made me think he had got some hurt. I arose, and saw a serpent larger than he, following him, holding him by the tail, and endeavouring to devour him: I had compassion on him: and instead of flying away, I had the boldness and courage to take up a stone that by chance lay by me, and threw it at the great serpent with all my strength, whom I hit on the head, and killed. The other finding himself at liberty took to his wings, and flew away. I looked a long while after him in the air, as being an extraordinary thing; but he flew out of my sight, and I lay down again in another place in the shade, and fell asleep.

When I awaked, judge how I was surprised to see a black woman by me, of a lively and agreeable complexion, who held two bitches tied together in her hand of the same colour. I sat up, and asked her who she was? I am, said she, the serpent whom you delivered not long since from my mortal enemy. I knew not how to acknowledge the great kindness you did me, but by doing what I have done. I knew the treachery of your sisters, and, to revenge you on them, as soon as I was set at liberty by your generous assistance, I called several of my companions together, fairies like myself; we have carried all the lading that was in your vessel into your store-houses at Bagdad, and afterwards sunk it.

These two black bitches are your sisters, whom I have transformed into this shape: But this punishment is not sufficient, for I will have you to treat them after such a manner as I shall direct.

At those words the fairy took me fast under one of her arms, and the two bitches in the other, and carried me to my house at Bagdad, where I found all the riches which were loaden on board my vessel in my store-houses. Before she left me, she delivered me the two bitches, and told me, If you will not be changed into a bitch, as they are, I ordain you in the name of him that governs the sea, to give each of your sisters every night a hundred lashes with a rod, for the punishment of the crime they have committed against your person and the young prince whom they have drowned. I was forced to promise that I would obey her order. Since that time I have whipped them every night, though with regret, whereof your majesty has been a witness, I give evidence by my tears, with how much sorrow and reluctance I must perform this cruel duty; and in this your majesty may see I am more to be pitied than blamed. If there be any thing else, with relation to myself, that you desire to be informed of, my sister Amine will give you the full discovery of it, by the relation of her story.

After the caliph had heard Zobeide with a great deal of astonishment, he desired his grand visier to pray fair Amine to acquaint him wherefore her breast was marked with so many scars.

Upon this Amine addressed herself to the caliph, and began her story after this manner.

The Story of Amine

COMMANDER of the faithful, says she, to avoid repeating what your majesty has already heard by my sister's story, I shall only add, that after my mother had taken a house for herself, to live in during her widowhood, she gave me in marriage, with the portion my father left me, to a gentleman that had one of the best estates in this city.

I had scarce been a year married when I became a widow, and was left in possession of all my husband's estate, which amounted to ninety thousand sequins. The interest of this money was sufficient to maintain me very honourably. In the mean time, when my first six months mourning was over, I caused to be made me ten suits of cloaths, very rich, so that each suit came to a thousand sequins; and when the year was past I began to wear them.

One day, as I was busy all alone about my private affairs, there came one and told me, that a lady desired to speak to me. I ordered them to bring her in: She was a person well stricken in years; she saluted me by kissing the ground, and told me, kneeling, Dear lady, pray excuse the freedom I take to trouble you, the confidence I have in your charity makes me thus bold; I must acquaint your ladyship, that I have a daughter, an orphan, who is to be married this day; she and I are both strangers, and have no acquaintance at all in this town; this puts me in a perplexity, for we would have the numerous family with whom we are going to ally ourselves, to think we are not altogether strangers, and without credit: Therefore, most beautiful lady, if you would vouchsafe to honour the wedding with your presence, we shall be infinitely obliged to you; because the ladies of your country will then know that we are not looked upon here as despicable wretches, when they shall come to understand that a lady of your quality did us that honour. But, alas! madam, if you refuse this request, we shall be altogether disgraced, and dare not address ourselves to any other.

This poor woman's discourse, mixed with tears, moved my compassion. Good woman, said I, do not afflict yourself, I am willing to grant you the favour you desire; tell me what place I must come to, and I will meet you as soon as I am dressed; the old woman was so transported with joy at my answer, that she kissed my feet, without my being able to hinder it. Good charitable lady, said she, rising up, God will reward the kindness you have shewed to your servants, and make your heart as joyful as you have made theirs. It is too soon yet to give yourself that trouble; it will be time enough when I come to call you in the evening: So farewell, madam, said she, till I have the honour to see you again.

As soon as she was gone, I took the suit I liked best, with a necklace of large pearl, bracelet, pendents in my ears, and rings set with the finest and most sparkling diamonds; for my mind presaged what would befal me.

When night drew on, the old woman came to call me with a countenance full of joy: She kissed my hands, and said, my dear lady, the relations of my son in-law, who are the principal ladies of the town, are now met together; you may come when you please, I am ready to wait on you. We went immediately, she going before, and I followed her, with a good number of my maids and slaves very well drest: We stopped in a large street, newly swept and watered, at a large gate with a lanthorn before it, by the light of which I could read this inscription over the gate in golden letters, 'Here is the abode of everlasting pleasures and content.' The old woman knocked, and the gate was opened immediately.

They brought me to the lower end of the court, into a large hall, where I was received by a young lady of admirable beauty; she came up to me, and after having embraced me, and made me sit down by her upon a sofa, where there was a throne of precious wood, beset with diamonds: Madam, said she, you are brought hither to assist at a wedding; but I hope this marriage will prove otherwise than what you expected. I have a brother, one of the handsomest men in the world; he has fallen so much in love with the fame of your beauty, that his fate depends wholly upon you, and he will be the unhappiest of men, if you do not take pity on him. He knows your quality, and I can assure you he is in nowise unworthy of your alliance. If my prayers, madam, can prevail, I shall join them with his, and humbly beg you will not refuse the offer of being his wife.

After the death of my husband I had no thought of marrying again: but I had no power to refuse the offer made by so charming a lady. As soon as I had given consent by silence, accompanied with a blush, the young lady clapped her hands, and immediately a closet door opened, out of which came a young man of a majestic air, and so graceful behaviour, that I thought myself happy to have made so great a conquest. He sat down by me, and by the discourse we had together, I found that his merits far exceeded the account his sister had given me of him.

When she saw that we were satisfied one with another, she clapped her hands a second time, and out came a cadis or scrivenor,* who wrote our contract of marriage, signed it himself, and caused it to be attested by four witnesses, he brought along with him. The only thing that my new spouse made me promise was, that I should not be seen, nor speak with any other man but himself; and he vowed to me, upon that condition, that I should have no reason to complain of him. Our marriage was concluded and finished after this manner; so I became the principal actress of a wedding, where-unto I was only invited as a guest.

After we had been married a month, I had occasion for some stuffs; I asked my husband's leave to go out and buy them, which he granted; and I took that old woman along with me, of whom I spoke before, she being one of the family, and two of my own female slaves.

When we came to the street where the merchants dwell, the old woman told me, dear mistress, since you want silk-stuffs, I must carry you to a young merchant of my acquaintance; he has of all sorts, and it will prevent your wearying yourself, by going from one shop to another. I can assure you that he is able to furnish you with that which nobody else can. I was easily persuaded, and we entered into a shop belonging to a young merchant, a man likely enough; I sat down, and bid the old woman desire him to shew me the finest silk-stuffs he had: The woman bid me speak myself; but I told her it was one of the articles of my marriage-contract, not to speak to any man but my husband, which I ought to keep.

The merchant shewed me several stuffs, of which one pleased me better than the rest; I bid her ask the price. He answered the old woman, I will not sell it for gold or money, but I will make her a present of it, if she will give me leave to kiss her cheek. I bid the old woman tell him, that he was very rude to propose such a thing. But instead of obeying me, she said, what the merchant desires of you is no such great matter: you need not speak, but only present him your cheek, and the business will soon be done. The stuff pleased me so much, that I was foolish enough to take her advice. The old woman and my slaves stood up, that nobody should see it, and I put up my veil; but instead of a kiss, the merchant bit me till the blood came.

The pain and surprise was so great, that I fell down in a swoon, and continued in it so long, that the merchant had time to shut his shop, and fly for it. When I came to myself, I found my cheek all bloody: The old woman and my slaves took care to cover it with my veil, that the people that came about us could not perceive it, but supposed it to be only a fainting fit.

The old woman that was with me, being extremely troubled at the accident, endeavoured to comfort me: My dear mistress, said she, I beg your pardon, for I am the cause of this misfortune, having brought you to this merchant, because he is my countryman; but I never thought he could be capable of such a villainous action. But do not grieve; let us make haste to go home, I will give you a medicine that shall perfectly cure you in three days time, so that the least mark shall not be seen. The fit had made me so weak that I was scarce able to walk: But at last I got home, where I had a second fit, as I went into my chamber. Meanwhile, the old woman applied her remedy, so that I came to myself, and went to bed.

My husband came to me at night, and seeing my head bound up, asked the reason. I told him, I had the headache, and hoped he would enquire no farther; but he took a candle, and saw my cheek was hurt: How comes this wound? said he. And though I was not very guilty, yet I could not think of owning the thing: besides, to make such confession to a husband, I thought was somewhat indecent; therefore I told him, that as I was going to seek for that stuff you gave me leave to buy, a porter, carrying a load of wood, came so close by me, as I went through a narrow street, that one of the sticks gave me a rub on my cheek; but it is not much hurt. This put my husband into such a passion, that he vowed it should not go unpunished; for I will to-morrow give orders to the lieutenant of the police to seize upon all those brutes of porters, and cause them to be hanged. Being afraid to occasion the death of so many innocent persons, I told him, Sir, I should be sorry that so great a piece of injustice should be committed. Pray do not do it; for I should judge myself unpardonable, if I were the cause of so much mischief. Then tell me sincerely, said he, how came you by this wound? I answered, that it came through the inadvertency of a broom-seller upon an ass, who coming behind me, and looking another way, his ass gave me such a push, that I fell down and hurt my cheek upon some glass. Is it so? said my husband; then to morrow morning before sun-rising the grand visier Giafar shall have an account of this insolence, and he shall cause all the broom-sellers to be put to death. For the love of God, sir, said I, let me beg of you to pardon them, for they are not guilty. How, madam, said he, what is it I must believe? Speak, for I am absolutely resolved to know the truth from your own mouth. Sir, said I, I was taken with a giddiness, and fell down; and that is the whole matter.

At these last words, my husband lost all patience. Oh! cried he, I have given ear to your lies too long; with that, clapping his hands, in came three slaves: Pull her out of bed, said he, and lay her in the middle of the floor. The slaves obeyed his orders, one holding me by the head, another by the feet; he commanded the third to fetch him a scymitar, and when he had brought it, Strike, said he, cut her in two in the middle, and then throw her into the Tigris to feed the fishes. This is the punishment I give to those to whom I have given my heart, if they falsify their promise. When he saw that the slave made no haste to obey his orders, Why do not you strike? said he, who is it that holds you? what are you waiting for?

Madam, then said the slave, you are near the last moment of your life; consider if you have any thing to dispose of, before you die. I begged leave to speak one word, which was granted me. I lifted up my head, and looking wishfully to my husband, Alas, said I, to what condition am I reduced! must I then die in the prime of my youth? I could say no more, for my tears and sighs prevented me. My husband was not at all moved, but on the contrary went on to reproach me; so that to have made answer would have been in vain. I had recourse to intreaties and prayers; but he had no regard to them, and commanded the slaves to proceed to execution. The old woman that had been his nurse, came in just at that moment, fell down upon her knees, and endeavoured to appease his wrath: My son, said she, since I have been your nurse, and brought you up, let me beg the favour of you to grant me her life; consider, that he who kills shall be killed, and that you will stain your reputation, and lose the esteem of mankind. What will not the world say of such a bloody rage? She spoke these words in such a taking way, accompanied with tears, as she gained upon him at last.

Well, then, says he to his nurse, for your sake I will spare her life; but she shall carry some marks along with her, to make her remember her crime; with that, one of the slaves, by his order, gave me so many blows, as hard as he could strike, with a little cane, upon my sides and breast, that he fetched both skin and flesh away, so that I lay senseless: After that, he caused the same slaves, the executioners of his fury, to carry me into a house, where the old woman took care of me. I kept my bed four months; at last I recovered; but the scars you saw yesterday, against my will, have remained ever since.

As soon as I was able to walk, and go abroad, I resolved to go to the house, which was my own by my first husband, but I could not find the place.—My second husband, in the heat of his wrath, was not content to have razed it to the ground, but caused all the street where it stood to be pulled down. I believe such a violent proceeding was never heard of before; but against whom should I make my complaint? The author had taken such care, that he was not to be found, neither could I know him again if I saw him: And suppose I had known him, is it not easily seen that the treatment I met with proceeded from absolute power? how then dared I make any complaints?

Being desolate and unprovided of every thing, I had recourse to my dear sister Zobeide, who gave your majesty just now an account of her adventures; to her I made known my misfortune; she received me with her accustomed goodness, and advised me to bear it with patience. This is the way of the world, said she, which either robs us of our means, our friends, or our lovers; and oftentimes of all at once: And at the same time, to confirm what she had said, she gave me an account of the loss of the young prince, occasioned by the jealousy of her two sisters; she told me also by what accident they were transformed into bitches: And in the last place, after a thousand testimonials of her love towards me, she shewed me my youngest sister, who had likewise taken sanctuary with her, after the death of her mother.

Thus we gave God thanks, who had brought us together again, resolving to live a single life, and never to separate any more, for we have enjoyed this peaceable way of living a great many years: And as it was my business to mind the affairs of the house, I always took pleasure to go myself, and buy in what we wanted. I happened to go abroad yesterday, and the things I bought I caused to be brought home by a porter, who proved to be a sensible and jocose fellow, and we kept him by us for a little diversion. Three calenders happened to come to our door, as it began to grow dark, and prayed us to give them shelter until next morning: We gave them entrance, but upon certain conditions, which they agreed unto; and, after we had made them sit down at the table by us, they gave us a concert of music after their fashion, and at the same time we heard knocking at our gate. These were the three merchants of Moussoul, men of a very good mein, who begged the same favour which the calenders had obtained before: We consented to it upon the same conditions, but neither of them kept their promise; and though we had power as well as justice on our side to punish them, yet we contented ourselves with demanding from them the history of their lives, and consequently bounded our revenge with dismissing them, after they had done, and depriving them of the lodging they demanded.

The caliph Haroun Alraschid was very well satisfied with these strange stories, and declared publicly his astonishment at what he had heard.

The caliph having satisfied his curiosity, thought himself obliged to give some marks of grandeur and generosity to the calender princes, and also to give the three ladies some proofs of his bounty. He himself, without making use of his minister, the grand visier, spoke to Zobeide: Madam, this fairy, that shewed herself to you in the shape of a serpent, and imposed such a rigorous command upon you, did she not tell you where her place of abode was? or rather, did she not promise to see you, and restore those bitches to their natural shape?

Commander of the faithful, answered Zobeide, I forgot to tell your majesty, that the fairy left with me a bundle of hair, saying withal, that her presence would one day stand me in stead; and then, if I only burnt two tufts of this hair, she would be with me in a moment, though she was beyond mount Caucasus. Madam, says the caliph, where is the bundle of hair? She answered, Ever since that time I have had such a particular care of it, that I always carry it about me: Upon which she pulled it out, opened the case a little, where it was, and shewed it.—Well then, said the caliph, let us make the fairy come hither; you could not call her in a better time, for I long to see her.

Zobeide having consented to it, fire was brought in, and she threw the whole bundle of hair into it: the palace began to shake at that very instant, and the fairy appeared before the caliph in the shape of a lady very richly dressed.

Commander of the faithful, said she to the prince, you see I am ready to come and receive your commands. The lady who gave me this call by your order, did me a particular piece of service; to make my gratitude appear, I revenged her of her sisters' inhumanity, by changing them into bitches; but if your majesty commands it, I will restore them to their former shape.

Handsome fairy, said the caliph, you cannot do me a greater pleasure; vouchsafe them that favour, and after that I will find out some means to comfort them for their hard penance: But besides, I have another boon to ask in favour of that lady, who has had such cruel usage from an unknown husband: And as you undoubtedly known a great many things, we have reason to believe that you cannot be ignorant of this; oblige me with the name of this barbarous fellow, that could not be contented to exercise his barbarous cruelty upon her person, but has also, most unjustly, taken from her all the substance she had; I only admire how such an unjust and inhuman action could be performed in spite of my authority, and not come to my ears.

To serve your majesty, answered the fairy, I will restore the two bitches to their former state, and I will cure the lady of her scars, that it shall never appear she was so beaten; and at last I will tell you who it was that did it.

The caliph sent for the two bitches from Zobeide's house, and when they came, a glass of water was brought to the fairy, upon her desire; she pronounced some words over it, which nobody understood; then throwing some part of it upon Amine, and the rest upon the bitches, the latter became two ladies of surprising beauty, and the scars that were upon Amine vanished away. After which the fairy said to the caliph, Commander of the faithful, I must now discover to you the unknown husband, you enquire after; he is very nearly related to yourself, for it is prince Amin, your eldest son, who, falling passionately in love with this lady by the fame he had heard of her beauty, he, by an intrigue, got her brought to his house, where he married her. As to the strokes he caused to be given her, he is in some measure excusable; for the lady his spouse had been a little too easy, and the excuses she had made were capable to make him believe she was more faulty than really she was. This is all I can say to satisfy your curiosity; and at these words she saluted the caliph, and vanished.

The prince being filled with admiration, and having much satisfaction in the changes that had happened through his means, did such things as will perpetuate his memory to all ages. First, he sent for his son Amin, and told him, that he was informed of his secret marriage, and how he had wounded Amine upon a very slight cause. Upon this the prince did not wait for his father's commands, but received her again immediately.

After which the caliph declared, that he would give his own heart and hand to Zobeide, and offered the other three sisters to the calenders, that were kings sons, who accepted them for their brides with a great deal of joy. The caliph assigned each of them a magnificent palace in the city of Bagdad, promoted them to the highest dignities of his empire, and admitted them to his councils.

The town-clerk of Bagdad being called, with witnesses, wrote the contract of marriage; and the famous caliph Haroun Alraschid, by making the fortunes of so many persons that had undergone such incredible calamities, drew a thousand blessings upon himself.

The Story of Sindbad the Sailor

DINARZADE having awaked her sister, the sultaness, as usual, and prayed her to tell her another story, Scheherazade asked leave of the sultan, and having obtained it, began thus:

Sir, in the reign of this same caliph, Haroun Alraschid, whom I formerly mentioned, there lived at Bagdad a poor porter, called Hindbad. One day, when the weather was excessive hot, he was employed to carry a heavy burden from one end of the town to the other. Being very weary, and having still a great way to go, he came into a street, where the delicate western breeze blew on his face, and the pavement of the street being sprinkled with rose-water, he could not desire a better place to rest in. Therefore, laying off his burden, he sat down by it, near a great house.

He was mightily pleased that he stopped in this place, for an agreeable smell of wood of aloes and of pastils, that came from the house, mixing with the scent of the rose-water, did completely perfume and embalm the air. Besides, he heard from within a concert of several sorts of instrumental music, accompanied with the harmonies of nightingales, and other birds peculiar to that climate.—This charming melody, and the smell of several sorts of victuals, made the porter to think there was a feast, and great rejoicings within. His occasions leading him seldom that way, he knew not who dwelt in the house; but, to satisfy his curiosity, he went to some of the servants, whom he saw standing at the gate in magnificent apparel, and asked the name of the master of the house.—How, replied one of them, do you live in Bagdad, and know not that this is the house of signor Sindbad, the sailor, that famous traveller, who has sailed round the world? The porter, who had heard of Sindbad's riches, could not but envy a man whose condition he thought to be as happy as his own was deplorable; and his mind being fretted with those reflections, he lifted up his eyes to heaven, and says, loud enough to be heard, Almighty Creator of all things, consider the difference between Sindbad and me.—I am every day exposed to fatigues and calamities, and can scarce get coarse barley-bread for myself and family, whilst happy Sindbad profusely expends immense riches, and leads a life of continual pleasure. What has he done to obtain from thee a lot so agreeable? and what have I done to deserve one so miserable? Having finished his expostulation, he struck his foot against the ground, like a man swallowed up with grief and despair.

Whilst the porter was thus indulging his melancholy, a servant came out of the house, and taking him by the arm, bid him follow him, for Signor Sindbad, his master, wanted to speak with him.

Your majesty may easily imagine, that poor Hindbad was not a little surprised at this compliment; for, considering what he had said, he was afraid Sindbad had sent for him to punish him: Therefore he would have excused himself, alledging, that he could not leave his burden in the middle of the street. But Sindbad's servants assured him they would look to it, and pressed the porter so, that he was obliged to yield.

The servants brought him into a great hall, where abundance of people sat round a table, covered with all sorts of fine dishes. At the upper end there sat a grave, comely, venerable gentleman, with a long white beard, and behind him stood a number of officers and domestics, all ready to serve him; this grave gentleman was Sindbad. The porter, whose fear was increased at the sight of so many people, and of a banquet so sumptuous, saluted the company trembling. Sindbad bid him draw near, and setting him down at his right hand, served him himself, and gave him excellent wine, of which there was good store upon the side-board.

When dinner was over, Sindbad began his discourse to Hindbad; and calling him brother, according to the manner of the Arabians, when they are familiar one with another, he asked him his name and employment. Signor, answered he, my name is Hindbad. I am very glad to see you, replies Sindbad, and I dare say the same for all the company; but I would be glad to hear from your own mouth, what it was you said a while ago in the street: For Sindbad had heard it himself through the window, before he sat down at table; and that occasioned his calling for him.

Hindbad being surprised at the question, hung down his head, and replied, Signor, I confess that my weariness put me out of humour, and occasioned me to speak some indiscreet words, which I beg you to pardon. Oh, do not think I am so unjust, replies Sindbad, to resent such a thing as that; I consider your condition, and, instead of upbraiding you with your complaints, I am sorry for you; but I must rectify your mistake concerning myself. You think, no doubt, that I have acquired, without labour and trouble, the ease and conveniency which I now enjoy. But do not mistake yourself, I did not attain to this happy condition, without enduring more trouble of body and mind, for several years, than can well be imagined. Yes, gentlemen, adds he, speaking to the whole company, I can assure you, my troubles were so extraordinary, that they were capable of discouraging the most covetous man from undertaking such voyages as I did, to acquire riches. Perhaps you have never heard a distinct account of the wonderful adventures and dangers I met with, in my seven voyages; and, since I have this opportunity, I am willing to give you a faithful account of them, not doubting but it will be acceptable.

And because Sindbad was to tell his story particularly upon the porter's account, he ordered his burden to be carried to the place appointed, and began thus:

His First Voyage

My father left me a considerable estate, most part of which I spent in debauches, during my youth; but I perceived my error, and called to mind that riches were perishable, and quickly considered, that, by my irregular way of living, I wretchedly mispent my time, which is the most valuable thing in the world. I remembered the saying of the great Solomon, which I frequently heard from my father, That death is more tolerable than poverty.* Being struck with those reflections, I gathered together the ruins of my estate, and sold all my moveables in the public market to the highest bidder. Then I entered into a contract with some merchants that traded by sea; I took the advice of such as I thought most capable to give it me; and resolving to improve what money I had, I went to Balsora, a port on the

Persian gulph, and embarked with several merchants, who joined me to fit out a ship on purpose.

We set sail, and steered our course towards the East Indies, through the Persian gulph, which is formed by the coasts of Arabia Felix* on the right, by those of Persia on the left, and, according to common account, is seventy leagues in the broadest place. The eastern sea, as well as that of the Indies, is very spacious. It is bounded on one side by the coasts of Abyssinia, and is 4500 leagues in length to the isles of Vakvak.[1] At first I was troubled with the sea sickness, but speedily recovered my health, and was not afterwards troubled with that disease.

In our voyage we touched at several islands, where we sold or exchanged our goods. One day, whilst under sail, we were becalmed near a little island, even almost with the surface of the water, which resembled a green meadow. The captain ordered his sails to be furled, and suffered such persons as had a mind, to land upon the island, amongst whom I was one.

But while we were diverting ourselves with eating and drinking, and refreshing ourselves from the fatigue of the sea, the island trembled all of a sudden, and shook us terribly.

They perceived the trembling of the island on board the ship, and called to us to reimbark speedily, or we should all be lost; for what we took for an island, was only the back of a whale. The nimblest got into the sloop, others betook themselves to swimming; but, for my part, I was still upon the back of the whale, when he dived into the sea, and had time only to catch hold of a piece of wood that we had brought out of the ship to make a fire. Meanwhile, the captain having received those on board who were in the sloop, and taken up some of those that swam, resolved to improve the favourable gale that was just risen, and hoisting his sails, pursued his voyage, so that it was impossible to recover the ship.

Thus was I exposed to the mercy of the waves, and struggled for my life all the rest of the day, and the following night. Next morning I found my strength gone, and despaired of saving my life, when a wave threw me happily against an island. The bank was high and rugged, so that I should scarcely have got up, had it not been for some roots of trees, which fortune seemed to have preserved in this place for my safety. Being got up, I lay down upon the ground half dead, until such time as the sun appeared. Then, though I was very feeble, both by reason of my hard labour and want of victuals, I crept along to see for some herbs fit to eat, and had not only the good luck to find some, but likewise a spring of excellent water, which

[1] These Islands according to the Arabians, are beyond China; and are so called from a tree which bears a fruit of that name. They are, without doubt, the isles of Japan; but they are not, however, so far from Abyssinia.

contributed much to recover me. After this I advanced farther into the island, and came at last into a fine plain, where I perceived a horse feeding at a great distance. I went towards him between hope and fear, not knowing whether I was going to lose my life, or to save it. When I came near, I perceived it to be a very fine mare, tied to a stake. While I looked upon her, I heard the voice of a man from under ground, who immediately appeared to me, and asked who I was? I gave him an account of my adventure; after which, taking me by the hand, he led me into a cave, where there were several other people, no less amazed to see me than I was to see them.

I eat some victuals which they offered me; and then, having asked them what they did in such a desart place? they answered, that they were grooms belonging to king Mihrage, sovereign of the island; and that every year, at the same season, they brought thither the king's mares, and fastened them as I saw that mare, until they were covered by a horse that came out of the sea, who, after he had done so, endeavoured to destroy the mares, but they hindered him by their noise, and obliged him to return to the sea, after which, they carried home the mares, whose foals were kept for the king's use, and called sea-horses. They added, that we were to get home to-morrow, and had I been one day later, I must have perished, because the inhabited part of the island was at a great distance, and it would have been impossible for me to have got thither without a guide.

Whilst they entertained me thus, the horse came out of the sea, as they had told me, covered the mare, and afterwards would have devoured her; but upon a great noise made by the grooms, he left her, and went back to the sea.

Next morning they returned with their mares to the capital of the island, took me with them, and presented me to king Mihrage. He asked me who I was? by what adventure I came into his dominions? and, after I had satisfied him, he told me he was much concerned for my misfortune, and at the same time ordered that I should want nothing; which his officers were so generous and careful as to see exactly fulfilled.

Being a merchant, I frequented men of my own profession, and particularly inquired for those who were strangers, if perhaps I might hear any news from Bagdad, or find an opportunity to return thither.—For king Mihrage's capital is situated on the bank of the sea, and has a fine harbour, where ships arrive daily from the different quarters of the world. I frequented also the society of the learned Indians, and took delight to hear them discourse; but withal, I took care to make my court regularly to the king, and conversed with the governors and petty kings, his tributaries, that were about him. They asked me a thousand questions about my country; and I being willing to inform myself as to their laws and customs, asked them every thing which I thought worth knowing.

There belongs to this king an island named Cassel; they assured me, that every night a noise of drums was heard there, whence the mariners fancied, that it was the residence of Dagial.[1] I had a great mind to see this wonderful place, and in my way thither saw fishes of an hundred and two hundred cubits long, that occasion more fear than hurt; for they are so fearful, that they will fly upon the rattling of two sticks or boards. I saw likewise other fishes about a cubit in length, that had heads like owls.

As I was one day at the port after my return, a ship arrived, and as soon as she cast anchor, they began to unload her, and the merchants on board ordered their goods to be carried into the magazine.—As I cast my eye upon some bales, and looked to the name, I found my own, and perceived the bales to be the same that I had embarked at Balsora. I also knew the captain; but being persuaded that he believed me to be drowned, I went, and asked him whose bales these were? He replied, that they belonged to a merchant of Bagdad, called Sindbad, who came to sea with him; but one day, being near an island, as we thought, he went ashore with several other passengers upon this supposed island, which was only a monstrous whale, that lay asleep upon the surface of the water: But as soon as he felt the heat of the fire they had kindled on his back to dress some victuals, he began to move, and dived under water; most of the persons who were upon him perished, and among them unfortunate Sindbad. Those bales belong to him, and I am resolved to trade with them, until I meet with some of his family, to whom I may return the profit. Captain, says I, I am that Sindbad whom you thought to be dead, and those bales are mine.

When the captain heard me speak thus, O heaven, says he, whom can we ever trust now-a-days! there is no faith left among men. I saw Sindbad perish with mine own eyes, and the passengers on board saw it as well as I, and yet you tell me that you are that Sindbad: What impudence is this! to look on you, one would take you to be a man of probity; and yet you tell a horrible falsehood, in order to possess yourself of what does not belong to you. Have patience, captain, replied I, do me the favour to hear what I have to say. Very well, says he, speak: I am ready to hear you. Then I told him how I escaped, and by what adventure I met with the grooms of king Mihrage, who brought me to his court.

He began to abate of his confidence upon my discourse, and was soon persuaded that I was no cheat: For there came people from his ship, who

[1] Dagial to the Mahometans is the same with Antichrist to us.—According to them, he is to appear about the end of the world, and will conquer all the earth, except Mecca, Medina, Tarsus, and Jerusalem, that are to be preserved by angels, which shall be set round them.*

knew me, made me great compliments, and testified a great deal of joy to see me alive. At last, he knew me himself, and embracing me, Heaven be praised, says he, for your happy escape, I cannot enough express my joy for it; there are your goods, take and do with them what you will. I thanked him, acknowledged his probity, and, in requital, offered him part of my goods as a present, which he generously refused.

I took out what was most valuable in my bales, and presented it to king Mihrage, who, knowing my misfortune, asked me how I came by such rarities? I acquainted him with the whole story: He was mightily pleased at my good luck, accepted my present, and gave me one much more considerable in return. Upon this, I took leave of him, and went aboard the same ship, after I had exchanged my goods for the commodities of the country. I carried with me the wood of aloes, sanders, camphire, nutmegs, cloves, pepper, and ginger. We passed by several islands, and at last arrived at Balsora, from whence I came to this city, with the value of one hundred thousand sequins.[1] My family and I received one another with all the transports that can happen from true and sincere friendship. I bought slaves of both sexes, fine lands, and built me a great house. And thus I settled myself, resolving to forget the miseries I had suffered, and to enjoy the pleasures of life.

Sindbad stopped here, and ordered the musicians to go on with their concert, which his story had interrupted. The company continued to eat and drink until the evening, that it was time to retire, when Sindbad, sent for a purse of one hundred sequins, and giving it to the porter, says, take this, Hindbad, return to your home, and come back to-morrow to hear some more of my adventures. The porter went home astonished at the honour done him, and the present made him. The relation of it was very agreeable to his wife and children, who did not fail to return thanks to God for what providence had sent them by the hands of Sindbad.

Hindbad put on his best cloaths next day, and returned to the bountiful traveller, who received him with a pleasant air, and caressed him mightily. When all the guests were come, dinner was set upon the table, and continued a long time. When it was ended, Sindbad, addressing himself to the company, says, gentlemen, be pleased to give me audience, and listen to the adventures of my second voyage; they better deserve your attention than the first. Upon which every one held his peace, and Sindbad went on thus:

[1] The Turkish sequin is about 9s. sterling.*

The Second Voyage of Sindbad the Sailor

I DESIGNED, after my first voyage, to spend the rest of my days at Bagdad, as I had the honour to tell you yesterday; but it was not long ere I grew weary of a quiet life. My inclination to trade revived. I bought goods proper for the commerce I designed, and put to sea a second time with merchants of known probity. We embarked on board a good ship, and, after recommending ourselves to God, set sail: We traded from island to island, and exchanged commodities with great profit. One day we landed in an isle covered with several sorts of fruit-trees, but so desert, that we could neither see man nor horse upon it. We went to take a little fresh air in the meadows, and along the streams that watered them. Whilst some diverted themselves with gathering flowers, and others with gathering fruits, I took my wine and provisions, and sat down by a stream betwixt two great trees, which formed a curious shade. I made a very good meal, and afterwards fell asleep. I cannot tell how long I slept; but when I awakened, the ship was gone.

I was very much surprised to find the ship gone; I got up, looked about every where, and could not see one of the merchants who landed with me. At last I perceived the ship under sail, but at such a distance that I lost sight of her in a very little time.

I leave you to guess at my melancholy reflections in this sad condition. I was like to die of grief: I cried out sadly; I beat my head and breast, and threw myself down upon the ground, where I lay some time in a terrible agony, one afflicting thought being succeeded by another still more afflicting. I upbraided myself an hundred times, for not being content with the product of my first voyage, that might very well have served me all my life. But all this was in vain, and my repentance out of season.

At last I resigned myself to the will of God; and not knowing what to do, I climbed up to the top of a great tree, from whence I looked about on all sides, to see if there were any thing that could give me hopes. When I looked towards the sea, I could see nothing but sky and water; but, looking towards the land, I saw something white; and coming down from the tree, I took up what provision I had left, and went towards it, the distance being so great that I could not distinguish what it was.

When I came nearer, I thought it to be a white bowl, of a prodigious height and bigness; and when I came up to it, I touched it, and found it to be very smooth. I went round to see if it was open on any side, but saw it was not, and that there was no climbing up to the top of it was so smooth. It was at least fifty paces round.

By this time the sun was ready to set, and all of a sudden the sky became as dark as if it had been covered with a thick cloud. I was much astonished at this sudden darkness, but much more when I found it occasioned by a bird of monstrous size, that came flying towards me. I remembered a fowl, called Roc,[1] that I had often heard mariners speak of; and conceived that the great bowl, which I so much admired, must needs be its egg. In short, the bird lighted, and sat over the egg to hatch it. As I perceived her coming, I crept close to the egg, so that I had before me one of the legs of the bird, that was as big as the trunk of a tree; I tied myself strongly to it with the cloth that went round my turban, in hopes that when the roc flew away next morning, she would carry me with her out of this desert island. And after having passed the night in this condition, the bird actually flew away next morning as soon as it was day, and carried me so high, that I could not see the earth; she afterwards descended all of a sudden, with so much rapidity, that I lost my senses. But when the roc was sat, and that I found myself on the ground, I speedily untied the knot, and had scarce done, when the bird having taken up a serpent of a monstrous length in her bill, flew straight away.

The place where it left me was a very deep valley, encompassed on all sides with mountains so high that they seemed to reach above the clouds, and so full of steep rocks, that there was no possibility to get out of the valley. This was a new perplexity upon me; so that when I compared this place with the desert island the roc brought me from, I found that I had gained nothing by the change.

As I walked through this valley, I perceived it was strewed with diamonds, some of which were of a surprising bigness. I took a great deal of pleasure to look upon them; but speedily saw at a distance such objects as very much diminished my satisfaction, and which I could not look upon without terror; that was a great number of serpents, so big, and so long, that the least of them was capable of swallowing an elephant. They retired in the day time to their dens, where they hid themselves from the roc, their enemy, and did not come out but in the night time.

I spent the day in walking about the valley, resting myself at times in such places as I thought most commodious. When night came on, I went into a cave, where I thought I might be in safety; I stopped the mouth of it, which was low and strait, with a great stone, to preserve me from the serpents; but not so exactly fitted as to hinder light from coming in. I supped on part of my provisions; but the serpents, which began to appear, hissing about in the mean time, put me into such extreme fear, that you may easily imagine I did

[1] Mark Paul, in his Travels, and Father Martini, in his History of China, speak of this bird, and say it will take up an elephant and a rhinoceros.*

not sleep. When day appeared, the serpents retired, and I came out of the cave trembling; I can justly say, that I walked a long time upon diamonds, without having a mind to touch any of them. At last I sat down, and notwithstanding my uneasiness, not having shut my eyes during the night, I fell asleep, after having eat a little more of my provisions. But I had scarce shut my eyes, when something that fell by me with a great noise, wakened me, and that was a great piece of fresh meat; and at the same time I saw several others fall down from the rocks in different places.

I always looked upon it to be a fable, when I heard mariners and others discourse of the valley of diamonds, and of the stratagems made use of by some merchants to get jewels from thence; but then I found it to be true. For, in reality, those merchants come to the neighbourhood of this valley when the eagles have young ones, and throwing great joints into this valley, diamonds, upon whose points they fall, stick to them: the eagles, which are stronger in this country than any-where else, fall down with great force upon these pieces of meat, and carry them to their nests upon the top of the rocks, to feed their young eagles with; at which time the merchants running to their nests, frighten the eagles by their noise, and take away the diamonds that stick to the meat. And this stratagem they made use of to get the diamonds out of the valley, which is surrounded with such precipices that nobody can enter it.

I believed till then, that it was not possible for me to get out of this abyss, which I looked upon as my grave: but then I changed my mind; for the falling in of those pieces of meat put me in hopes of a way of saving my life.

I began to gather together the greatest diamonds that I could see, and put them into the leather-bag where I used to carry my provisions. I afterwards took the largest piece of meat I could find, tied it close round me with the cloth of my turban, and then laid myself upon the ground with my face downward, the bag of diamonds being tied fast to my girdle, so that it could not possibly drop off.

I had scarce laid me down, till the eagles came; each of them seized a piece of meat, and one of the strongest having taken me up, with the piece of meat on my back, carried me to his nest on the top of the mountain. The merchants fell straightway a shouting to frighten the eagles; and when they had obliged them to quit their prey, one of them came up to the nest where I was: He was very much afraid when he saw me; but recovering himself, instead of enquiring how I came thither, he began to quarrel with me, and asked, why I stole his goods? You will treat me, replied I, with more civility, when you know me better. Do not trouble yourself, I have diamonds enough for you and me too, more than all the other merchants together. If they have any, it is by chance; but I chose myself in the bottom of the valley all those which you see in this bag; and having spoke those words, I shewed him them. I had scarce done speaking, when the other merchants came trooping about us, very much astonished to see me; but they were much more surprised when I told them my story; yet they did not so much admire my stratagem to save myself, as my courage to attempt it.

They carried me to the place where they staid all together, and there having opened my bag, they were surprised at the largeness of my diamonds, and confessed, that in all the courts where they had been, they never saw any that came near them. I prayed the merchant, to whom the nest belonged whither I was carried, (for every merchant had his own,) to take as many for his share as he pleased: He contented himself with one, and that too the least of them; and when I pressed him to take more, without fear of doing me any injury, No, says he, I am very well satisfied with this, which is valuable enough to save me the trouble of making any more voyages, and to raise as great a fortune as I desire.

I spent the night with those merchants, to whom I told my story a second time, for the satisfaction of those who had not heard it. I could not moderate my joy, when I found myself delivered from the danger I have mentioned; I thought myself to be in a dream, and could scarce believe myself to be out of danger.

The merchants had thrown their pieces of meat into the valley for several days. And each of them being satisfied with the diamonds that had fallen to his lot, we left the place next morning all together, and travelled near high mountains, where there were serpents of a prodigious length, which we had the good fortune to escape. We took the first port we came at, and came to the isle of Ropha, where trees grow that yield camphire. This tree is so large, and its branches so thick, that a hundred men may easily sit under its shade. The juice of which the camphire is made, runs out from a hole bored in the upper part of the tree, is received in a vessel where it grows to a consistency, and becomes what we call camphire; and the juice thus drawn out, the tree withers and dies.

There is in this island the rhinoceros, a creature less than the elephant, but greater than the buffalo: they have a horn upon their nose, about a cubit long; this horn is solid, and cleft in the middle from one end to the other, and there is upon it white draughts, representing the figure of a man. The rhinoceros fights with the elephant, runs his horn into his belly, and carries him off upon his head; but the blood and the fat of the elephant running into his eyes, and making him blind, he falls to the ground; and that which is astonishing, the roc comes and carries them both away in her claws, to be meat for her young ones.

I pass over many other things peculiar to this island, lest I should be troublesome to you. Here I exchanged some of my diamonds for good merchandize. From thence we went to other isles, and at last, having touched at several trading towns of the firm land, we landed at Balsora; from whence I went to Bagdad. There I immediately gave great alms to the poor, and lived honourably upon the vast riches I had brought, and gained with so much fatigue. Thus Sindbad ended the story of his second voyage, gave Hindbad another hundred sequins, and invited him to come next day to hear the story of the third. The rest of the guests returned to their homes, and came again the next day at the same hour; and to be sure the porter did not fail, having by this time almost forgot his former poverty. When dinner was over, Sindbad demanded attention, and gave them an account of his third voyage, as follows.

The Third Voyage of Sindbad the Sailor

THE pleasures of the life which I then led, soon made me forget the risks I had run in my two former voyages; but being then in the flower of my age, I grew weary of living without business, and hardening myself against the thought of any danger I might incur, I went from Bagdad with the richest commodities of the country, to Balsora. There I embarked again with other merchants. We made a long navigation, and touched at several ports, where we drove a considerable commerce. One day, being out in the main ocean, we were attacked by a horrible tempest, which made us lose our course. The tempest continued several days, and brought us before the port of an island, where the captain was very unwilling to enter, but we were obliged to cast anchor there. When we had furled our sails, the captain told us, that this, and some other neighbouring islands, were inhabited by hairy savages, who would speedily attack us; and though they were but dwarfs, yet our misfortune was such, that we must make no resistance, for they were more in number than the locusts; and if we happened to kill one of them, they would all fall upon us, and destroy us.

This discourse of the captain put the whole equipage into a great consternation, and we found very soon, to our cost, that what he had told us was but too true; an innumerable multitude of frightful savages, covered all over with red hair, and about two feet high, came swimming towards us, and encompassed our ship in a little time. They spoke to us as they came near; but we understood not their language; they climbed up the sides of the ship with so much agility as surprised us. We beheld all this with a mortal fear, without daring to offer at defending ourselves, or to speak one word to divert them from their mischievous design. In short, they took down our sails, cut the cable, and hauling to the shore, made us all get out, and afterwards carried the ship into another island, from whence they came. All travellers carefully avoided that island where they left us, it being very dangerous to stay there, for a reason you shall hear anon; but we were forced to bear our affliction with patience.

We went forward into the island, where we found some fruits and herbs to prolong our lives as long as we could; but we expected nothing but death. As we went on, we perceived at a distance a great pile of building, and made towards it. We found it to be a palace, well built and very high, with a gate of ebony of two leaves, which we thrust open. We entered the court, where we saw before us a vast apartment, with a porch, having on one side a heap of men's bones, and on the other side a vast number of roasting spits. We trembled at this spectacle, and being weary with travelling, our legs failed under us, we fell to the ground, being seized with a mortal fear, and lay a long time immoveable.

The sun was set, and whilst we were in this lamentable condition just now mentioned, the gate of the apartment opened with a great noise, and there came out the horrible figure of a black man, as high as a palm tree. He had but one eye, and that in the middle of his forehead, where it looked as red as burning coal. His fore-teeth were very long and sharp, and came without his mouth, which was deep as that of a horse. His under lip hung down upon his breast. His ears resembled those of an elephant, and covered his shoulders; and his nails were as long and crooked as the talons of the greatest birds. At the sight of so frightful a giant, we lost all sense, and laid like dead men.

At last we came to ourselves, and saw him sitting in the porch looking at us: When he had considered us well, he advanced towards us, and laying his hand upon me, he took me up by the nape of my neck, and turned me round as a butcher would do a sheep's head; after having viewed me well, and perceiving me to be so lean that I had nothing but skin and bone, he let me go. He took up all the rest one by one, viewed them in the same manner: and the captain being the fattest, he held him with one hand, as I would do a sparrow, and thrusting a spit through him, kindled a great fire, roasted and eat him in his apartment for his supper; which being done, he returned to his porch, where he lay and fell asleep, snoring louder than thunder: he slept thus till morning; for our parts, it was not possible for us to enjoy any rest, so that we passed the night in the most cruel fear that could be imagined. Day being come, the giant awaked, got up, went out and left us in the palace.

When we thought him at a distance, then we broke the melancholy silence we had kept all night; and every one grieving more than another, we made the palace to resound with our complaints and groans. Though there were a great many of us, and that we had but one enemy, we had not at first the presence of mind to think of delivering ourselves from him by his death. This enterprise however, though hard to put into execution, was the only design we ought naturally to have formed.

We thought upon several other things, but determined nothing; so that, submitting to what it should please God to order concerning us, we spent the day in running about the island, for fruits and herbs to sustain our lives. When evening came we sought for a place to lie in, but found none; so that we were forced, whether we would or not, to return to the palace.

The giant failed not to come back, and supped once more upon one of our companions: After which he slept, and snored till day, and then went out and left us as formerly. Our condition was so very terrible, that several of my comrades designed to throw themselves into the sea, rather than die so strange a death; and those who were of this mind, argued with the rest to follow their example. Upon which one of the company answered, that we were forbid to destroy ourselves; but, allowing it to be lawful, it was more reasonable to think of a way to rid ourselves of the barbarous tyrant, who designed so cruel a death for us.

Having thought of a project for that end, I communicated the same to my comrades, who approved it. Brethren, said I, you know there is a great deal of timber floating upon the coast; if you will be advised by me, let us make several floats of it that may carry us, and when they are done, leave them there till we think fit to make use of them. In the mean time, we will execute the design to deliver ourselves from the giant; and if it succeed, we may stay here with patience till some ship pass by, that may carry us out of this fatal island; but if it happen to miscarry, we will speedily get to our floats, and put to sea. I confess, that, by exposing ourselves to the fury of the waves, we run a risk of losing our lives; but if we do, is it not better to be buried in the sea, than in the entrails of this monster, who has already devoured two of us? My advice relished, and we made floats capable of carrying three persons each.

We returned to the palace towards the evening, and the giant arrived a little while after. We were forced to conclude on seeing another of our comrades roasted. But at last revenged ourselves on the brutish giant thus. After he had made an end of his cursed supper, he lay down on his back, and fell asleep. As soon as we heard him snore,[1] according to his custom, nine of the boldest among us, and myself, took each of us a spit, and putting the points of them into the fire till they were burning hot, we thrust them into his eye all at once, and blinded him. The pain occasioned him to make a frightful cry, and to get up, and stretch out his hands, in order to sacrifice

[1] It would seem the Arabian author has taken this story from Homer's Odyssey.*

some of us to his rage; but we ran to such places as he could not find us, and, after having sought for us in vain, he groped for the gate, and went out howling dreadfully.

We went out of the palace after the giant, and came to the shore, where we had left our floats, and put them immediately into the sea. We waited till day, in order to get upon them in case the giant came towards us with any guide of his own species; but we hoped, if he did not appear by sun-rising, and give over his howling, which we still heard, that he would die; and if that happened to be the case, we resolved to stay in that island, and not to risk our lives upon the floats; but day had scarce appeared, when we perceived our cruel enemy, accompanied with two others almost of the same size, leading him; and a great number more coming before him, with a very quick pace.

When we saw this, we made no delay, but got immediately upon our floats, and rowed off from the shore. The giants, who perceived this, took up great stones, and running to the shore, entered the water up to the middle, and threw so exactly, that they sunk all the floats but that I was upon, and all my companions, except the two with me, were drowned. We rowed with all our might, and got out of the reach of the giants. But when we got out to sea, we were exposed to the mercy of the waves and winds, and tossed about sometimes on one side, and sometimes on another, and spent that night and the following day under a cruel uncertainty as to our fate; but next morning we had the good luck to be thrown upon an island, where we landed with much joy. We found excellent fruit there, that gave us great relief, so that we pretty well recovered our strength. In the evening we fell asleep on the bank of the sea; but were awaked by the noise of a serpent as long as a palm-tree, whose scales made a rustling as he creeped along. He swallowed up one of my comrades, notwithstanding his loud cries, and the efforts he made to rid himself from the serpent; which, shaking him several times against the ground, crushed him, and we could hear him gnaw and tear the poor wretch's bones, when we had fled at a great distance from him. Next day we saw the serpent again, to our great terror; when I cried out, O heaven, to what dangers are we exposed! We rejoiced yesterday at our having escaped from the cruelty of a giant, and the rage of the waves; and now are we fallen into another danger altogether as terrible.

As we walked about, we saw a large tall tree, upon which we designed to pass the following night, for our security; and having satisfied our hunger with fruit, we mounted it accordingly. A little while after, the serpent came hissing to the root of the tree, raised itself up against the trunk of it, and meeting with my comrade, who sat lower than I, swallowed him at once, and went off.

I staid upon the tree till it was day, and then came down more like a dead man than one alive, expecting the same fate with my two companions.—This filled me with horror, so that I was going to throw myself into the sea; but nature prompting us to a desire to live as long as we can, I withstood this temptation to despair, and submitted myself to the will of God, who disposes of our lives at his pleasure.

In the mean time, I gathered together a great quantity of small wood, brambles, and dry thorns, and making them up into faggots, made a great circle with them round the tree, and also tied some of them to the branches over my head. Having done this, when the evening came, I shut myself up within this circle, with this melancholy piece of satisfaction, that I had neglected nothing which could preserve me from the cruel destiny with which I was threatened. The serpent failed not to come at the usual hour, and went round the tree, seeking for an opportunity to devour me, but was prevented by the rampart I had made; so that he sat till day, like a cat watching in vain for a mouse that has retired to a place of safety. When day appeared he retired, but I dared not to leave my fort until the sun arose.

I was fatigued with the toil he had put me to, and suffered so much by his poisonous breath, that death seemed more eligible to me than the horror of such a condition. I came down from the tree, and, not thinking on the resignation I had made to the will of God the preceding day, I ran towards the sea, with a design to throw myself into it headlong. God took compassion on my desperate state; for just as I was going to throw myself into the sea, I perceived a ship at a considerable distance. I called as loud as I could, and taking the linen from my turban, displayed it, that they might observe me. This had the desired effect: all the crew perceived me, and the captain sent me his boat. As soon as I came aboard, the merchants and seamen flocked about me, to know how I came into that desert island; and after I had told them all that befel me, the oldest among them said to me, They had several times heard of the giants that dwelt in that island; that they were cannibals, and eat men raw as well as roasted: And as to the serpents, they added, that there were abundance in the isle, that hid themselves by day, and came abroad at night. After having testified their joy at my escaping so many dangers, they brought me the best of what they had to eat; and the captain seeing that I was all in rags, was so generous as to give me one of his own suits. We were at sea for some time, touched at several islands, and at last landed at that of Salabat, where there grows sanders, a wood of great use in physic. We entered the port, and came to an anchor. The merchants began to unload their goods, in order to sell or exchange them. In the mean time, the captain came to me, and said, Brother, I have here a parcel of goods that belonged to a merchant, who sailed some time on board this ship; and he being dead, I design to dispose of them for the benefit of his heirs, when I know them. The bales he spoke of lay on the deck; and shewing them to me, he says, There are the goods; I hope you will take care to sell them, and you shall have factorage. I thanked him that he gave me an opportunity to employ myself; because I hated to be idle.

The clerk of the ship took an account of all the bales, with the names of the merchants to whom they belonged. And when he asked the captain in whose name he should enter those he gave me the charge of, Enter them, says the captain, in the name of Sindbad the sailor. I could not hear myself named without some emotion; and looking stedfastly on the captain, I knew him to be the person, who, in my second voyage, had left me in the island where I fell asleep by a brook, and set sail without me, or sending to see for me. But I could not remember him at first, he was so much altered since I saw him.

And as for him, who believed me to be dead, I could not wonder at his not knowing me. But captain, says I, was the merchant's name, to whom those bales belonged, Sindbad? Yes, replies he, that was his name; he came from Bagdad, and embarked on board my ship at Balsora. One day, when we landed at an island to take water and other refreshments, I know not by what mistake, I set sail without observing that he did not reimbark with us; neither I nor the merchants perceived it till four hours after. We had the wind in our stern, and so fresh a gale, that it was not then possible for us to tack about for him. You believe him then to be dead, says I? Certainly, answers he. No, captain, says I, look upon me, and you may know that I am Sindbad, whom you left in that desert island; I fell asleep by a brook, and when I awaked, I found all the company gone. At these words the captain looked steadfastly upon me; and having considered me attentively, knew me at last, embraced me, and said, God be praised that fortune has supplied my defect. There are your goods, which I always took care to preserve, and to make the best of them at every port where I touched. I restore them to you with the profit I have made of them. I took them from him, and at the same time acknowledged how much I owed to him.

From the isle of Salabat, we went to another, where I furnished myself with cloves, cinnamon, and other spices. As we sailed from that island, we saw a tortoise that was twenty cubits in length and breadth. We observed also a fish which looked like a cow, and gave milk, and its skin is so hard, that they usually make bucklers* of it. I saw another which had the shape and colour of a camel. In short, after a long voyage, I arrived at Balsora, and from thence returned to this city of Bagdad, with so much riches, that I knew not what I had. I gave a great deal to the poor, and bought another great estate to what I had already.

Thus Sindbad finished the history of his third voyage; gave another hundred sequins to Hindbad, invited him to dinner again next day, and to hear the story of his fourth voyage. Hindbad and the company retired; and next day, when they returned, Sindbad, after dinner, continued the story of his adventures.

The Fourth Voyage of Sindbad the Sailor

THE pleasure, says he, and the divertisements I took after my third voyage, had not charms enough to divert me from another. I was again prevailed upon by my passion for traffic, and curiosity to see new things. I therefore put my affairs in order, and having provided a stock of goods fit for the places where I designed to trade, I set out on my journey. I took the way of Persia, of which I travelled several provinces, and then arrived at a port, where I embarked. We set sail, and having touched at several ports of Terra Firma, and some of the Easter islands, we put out to sea, and were seized by such a sudden gust of wind, as obliged the captain to furl his sails, and to take all other necessary precautions to prevent the danger that threatened us: But all was in vain; our endeavours took no effect; the sails were torn in a thousand pieces, and the ship was stranded, so that a great many of the merchants and seamen were drowned, and the cargo lost.

I had the good fortune with several of the merchants and mariners, to get a plank, and we were carried by the current to an island which lay before us. There we found fruit and fountain-water, which preserved our lives. We staid all night near the place where the sea cast us ashore, without consulting what we should do, our misfortune had dispirited us so much.

Next morning, as soon as the sun was up, we walked from the shore, and advancing into the island, saw some houses, to which we went: and as soon as we came thither, we were encompassed by a great number of blacks, who seized us, shared us among them, and carried us to their respective habitations.

I, and five of my comrades, were carried to one place; they made us sit down immediately, and gave us a certain herb, which they made signs to us to eat. My comrades, not taking notice that the blacks eat none of it themselves, consulted only the satisfying their own hunger, and fell a-eating with greediness. But I, suspecting some trick, would not so much as taste it, which happened well for me; for in a little time after, I perceived my companions had lost their senses, and that, when they spoke to me, they knew not what they said.

The blacks filled us afterwards with rice, prepared with oil of cocoas; and my comrades, who had lost their reason, eat of it greedily. I eat of it also; but very sparingly. The blacks gave us that herb at first, on purpose to deprive us of our senses, that we might not be aware of the sad destiny prepared for us; and they gave us rice on purpose to fatten us: for, being cannibals, their design was to eat us as soon as we grew fat. They did accordingly eat my comrades, who were not sensible of their condition: but my senses being entire, you may easily guess, gentlemen, that, instead of growing fat, as the rest did, I grew leaner every day. The fear of death, under which I laboured, turned all my food into poison. I fell into a languishing distemper, which proved my safety; for the blacks, having killed and eat up my companions, seeing me to be withered, lean, and sick, deferred my death till another time.

Meanwhile, I had a great deal of liberty, so that there was scarce any notice taken of what I did; and this gave me an opportunity one day to get at a distance from the houses, and to make my escape. An old man, who saw me and suspected my design, called to me as loud as he could to return; but, instead of obeying him, I redoubled my pace, and quickly got out of sight. At that time there was none but the old man about the houses, the rest being abroad, and not to come home till night, which was pretty usual with them. Therefore, being sure that they could not come time enough to pursue me, I went on till night, when I stopped to rest a little, and to eat some of the provisions I had taken care for; but I speedily set forward again, and travelled seven days, avoiding those places which seemed to be inhabited, and lived for the most part upon cocoa nuts, which served me both for meat and drink. On the eighth day I came near the sea, and saw all of a sudden white people, like myself, gathering of pepper, of which there was great plenty in that place; this I took to be a good omen, and went to them without any scruple.

The people who gathered pepper came to meet me: As soon as they saw me, and asked me, in Arabic, who I was, and whence I came? I was overjoyed to hear them speak in my own language, and willingly satisfied their curiosity, by giving them an account of my shipwreck, and how I fell into the hands of the blacks. Those blacks, replied they, eat men; and by what miracle did you escape their cruelty? I told them the same story I now told you, at which they were wonderfully surprised.

I staid with them till they had gathered their quantity of pepper, and then sailed with them to the island from whence they came. They presented me to their king, who was a good prince: he had the patience to hear the relation of my adventures, which surprised him; and he afterwards gave me cloaths, and commanded care to be taken of me.

The island was very well peopled, plentiful of every thing, and the capital was a place of great trade. This agreeable place of retreat was very comfortable to me after my misfortune, and the kindness of this generous prince towards me completed my satisfaction. In a word, there was not a person more in favour with him than myself, and by consequence every man in court and city sought how to oblige me; so that in a very little time I was looked upon rather as a native than a stranger.

I observed one thing which to me looked very extraordinary; all the people, the king himself not excepted, rode their horses without bridle or stirrups. This made me one day take the liberty to ask the king how that came to pass? His majesty answered, that I talked to him of things which nobody knew the use of in his dominions.

I went immediately to a workman, and gave him a model for making the stock of a saddle. When that was done, I covered it myself with velvet and leather, and embroidered it with gold. I afterwards went to a lock-smith, who made me a bridle according to the pattern I shewed him, and then he also made me some stirrups. When I had all things completed, I presented them to the king, and put them upon one of his horses. His majesty mounted immediately, and was so mightily pleased with them, that he testified his satisfaction by large presents to me. I could not avoid making several others for his ministers and principal officers of his household, who all of them made me presents that enriched me in a little time. I also made for the people of best quality in the city, which gained me great reputation and regard from every body.

As I made my court very exactly to the king, he says to me one day, Sindbad, I love thee; and all my subjects who know thee, treat thee according to my example. I have one thing to demand of thee, which thou must grant. Sir, answered I, there is nothing but what I will do, as a mark of my obedience to your majesty, whose power over me is absolute. I have a mind thou shouldest marry, replies he, that so thou mayest stay in my dominions, and think no more of thy own country. I dared not resist the prince's will, and he gave me one of the ladies of his court, a noble, beautiful, chaste, and rich lady. The ceremonies of marriage being over, I went and dwelt with the lady, and for some time we lived in perfect harmony. I was not, however, very well satisfied with my condition; and therefore designed to make my escape on the first occasion, and to return to Bagdad; which my present settlement, how advantageous soever, could not make me forget.

While I was thinking on this, the wife of one of my neighbours, with whom I had contracted a very strict friendship, fell sick, and died. I went to see and comfort him in his affliction; and finding him swallowed up with sorrow, I said to him as soon as I saw him, God preserve you, and grant you a long life. Alas! replies he, how do you think I should obtain that favour you wish me? I have not above an hour to live. Pray, says I, do not entertain such a melancholy thought; I hope it will not be so, but that I shall enjoy your company for many years. I wish you, says he, a long life; but for me, my days are at an end, for I must be buried this day with my wife. This is a law which our ancestors established in this island, and always observed it inviolably. The living husband is interred with the dead wife, and the living wife with the dead husband. Nothing can save me; every one must submit to this law.

While he was entertaining me with an account of this barbarous custom, the very hearing of which frightened me cruelly, his kindred, friends, and neighbours came in a body to assist at the funeral. They put on the corpse the woman's richest apparel, as if it had been her wedding day, and dressed her with all her jewels; then they put her into an open coffin, and lifting it up, began their march to the place of burial. The husband walked at the head of the company, and followed the corpse. They went up to an high mountain, and, when they came thither, took up a great stone, which covered the mouth of a very deep pit, and let down the corpse with all its apparel and jewels. Then the husband, embracing his kindred and friends, suffered himself to be put into another open coffin without resistance, with a pot of water, and seven little loaves, and was let down in the same manner they let down his wife. The mountain was pretty long, and reached to the sea. The ceremony being over, they covered the hole again with the stone, and returned.

It is needless, gentlemen, for me to tell you, that I was the only melancholy spectator of this funeral: whereas the rest were scarcely moved at it, the thing was so customary to them. I could not forbear speaking my thoughts of this matter to the king: Sir, says I, I cannot enough admire at the strange custom in this country, of burying the living with the dead. I have been a great traveller, and seen many countries, but never heard of so cruel a law. What do you mean, Sindbad? says the king; it is a common law; I shall be interred with the queen my wife, if she die first. But, sir, says I, may I presume to demand of your majesty, if strangers be obliged to observe this law? Without doubt, replies the king, (smiling at the occasion of my question,) they are not exempted, if they be married in this island.

I went home very melancholy at this answer; for the fear of my wife's dying first, and that I should be interred alive with her, occasioned me to have very mortifying reflections. But there was no remedy, I must have patience, and submit to the will of God. I trembled, however, at every little indisposition of my wife: but, alas! in a little time my fears came upon me all at once; for she fell sick, and died in a few days.

You may judge at my sorrow: To be interred alive, seemed to me as deplorable an end as to be devoured by cannibals. But I must submit; the king and all his court would honour the funeral with their presence, and the most considerable people of the city did the like. When all was ready for the ceremony, the corpse was put into a coffin, with all her jewels and magnificent apparel. The cavalcade was begun; and, as second actor in this doleful tragedy, I went next the corpse, with my eyes full of tears, bewailing my deplorable fate. Before I came to the mountain, I made an essay on the minds of the spectators; I addressed myself to the king in the first place, and then to all those who were round me, and bowing before them to the earth, to kiss the border of their garments, I prayed them to have compassion upon me. Consider, said I, that I am a stranger, and ought not to be subject to this rigorous law, and that I have another wife and children in my own country.[1] It was to no purpose for me to speak thus, no soul was moved at it; on the contrary, they made haste to let down my wife's corpse into the pit, and put me down the next moment in an open coffin, with a vessel full of water, and seven loaves. In short, the fatal ceremony being performed, they covered up the mouth of the pit, notwithstanding the excess of my grief, and my lamentable cries.

As I came near the bottom, I discovered, by help of the light that came from above, the nature of this subterranean place: it was a vast long cave, and might be about fifty fathom deep. I immediately smelt an insufferable stench, proceeding from the multitudes of dead corpses which I saw on the right and left; nay, I fancied that I heard some of them sigh out their last. However, when I got down, I immediately left my coffin, and getting at a distance from the corpse, held my nose, and lay down upon the ground, where I staid a long time, bathed in tears. Then reflecting on my sad lot, it is true, said I, that God disposes all things according to the decrees of his providence; but, poor Sindbad, art not thou thyself the cause of thy being brought to die so strange a death? Would to God thou hadst perished in some of those tempests which thou hast escaped! Then thy death had not been so lingering and terrible in all its circumstances. But thou hast drawn all this upon thyself by thy cursed avarice. Ah, unfortunate wretch! Shouldest thou not rather have staid at home, and quietly enjoyed the fruits of thy labour?

Such were the vain complaints with which I made the cave to echo, beating my head and stomach out of rage and despair, and abandoning myself to the most afflicting thoughts. Nevertheless, I must tell you, that, instead of calling death to my assistance in that miserable condition, I felt still an inclination to live, and to do all I could to prolong my days. I went

[1] He was a Mahometan, and they allow polygamy.*

groping about, with my nose stopped, for the bread and water that was in my coffin, and took some of it. Though the darkness of the cave was so great that I could not distinguish day and night, yet I always found my coffin again, and the cave seemed to be more spacious and fuller of corpses than it appeared to me at first. I lived for some days upon my bread and water; which being all spent, at last I prepared for death.

As I was thinking of death, I heard the stone lifted from the mouth of the cave, and immediately the corpse of a man was let down. When men are reduced to necessity, it is natural for them to come to extreme resolutions. While they let down the woman, I approached the place where her coffin was to be put, and as soon as I perceived they were covering the mouth of the cave, I gave the unfortunate wretch two or three great blows over the head, with a large bone that I found, which stunned, or, to say the truth, killed her. I committed this inhuman action merely for the sake of her bread and water that was in her coffin; and thus I had provisions for some days more. When that was spent, they let down another dead woman, and a live man; I killed the man in the same manner; and, as good luck would have it for me, there was then a sort of mortality in the town, so that by this means I did not want for provisions.

One day, as I had dispatched another woman, I heard something walking, and blowing or panting as it walked. I advanced towards that side from whence I heard the noise; and, upon my approach, the thing puffed and blew harder, as if it had been running away from me: I followed the noise, and the thing seemed to stop sometimes, but always fled and blew as I approached. I followed it so long, and so far, till at last I perceived a light, resembling a star: I went on towards that light, and sometimes lost sight of it, but always found it again; and at last discovered that it came through a hole in the rock, large enough for a man to get out at.

Upon this, I stopped some time to rest myself, being much fatigued with pursuing this discovery so fast: Afterwards coming up to the hole, I went out at it, and found myself upon the bank of the sea. I leave you to guess at the excess of my joy; it was such, that I could scarce persuade myself of its being real.

But when I was recovered from my surprise, and convinced of the truth of the matter, I found the thing which I had followed, and heard puff and blow, to be a creature which came out of the sea, and was accustomed to enter at that hole, to feed upon the dead carcases.

I considered the mountain, and perceived it to be situated betwixt the sea and the town, but without any passage or way to communicate with the latter, the rocks on the side of the sea were so rugged and steep. I fell down upon the shore to thank God for this mercy, and afterwards entered the cave again to fetch bread and water, which I did eat by day-light with a better appetite than I had done since my interment in the dark hole.

I returned thither again, and groped about among the biers for all the diamonds, rubies, pearls, gold bracelets, and rich stuffs I could find; these I brought to the shore, and tying them up neatly into bales, with the cords that let down the coffins, I laid them together upon the bank, waiting till some ship passed by, without any fear of rain, for it was not then the season.

After two or three days, I perceived a ship that had but just come out of the harbour, and passed near the place where I was. I made a sign with the linen of my turban, and called to them as loud as I could: They heard me, and sent a boat to bring me on board. When the mariners asked by what misfortune I came thither? I told them that I suffered shipwreck two days ago, and made shift to get ashore with the goods they saw. It was happy for me that those people did not consider the place where I was, nor enquire into the probability of what I told them, but without any more ado, took me on board with my goods. When I came to the ship, the captain was so well pleased to have saved me, and so much taken up with his own affairs, that he also took the story of my pretended shipwreck upon trust, and generously refused some jewels which I offered him.

We passed by several islands, and among others, that called the isle of Bells, about ten days sail from Serendib, with a regular wind, and six from that of Kela, where we landed. This island produces lead-mines, Indian canes, and excellent camphire.

The king of the isle of Bells,[1] which is about two days journey in extent, is also subject to him. The inhabitants are so barbarous, that they still eat human flesh. After we had finished our commerce in that island, we put to sea again, and touched at several other ports; at last I arrived happily at Bagdad with infinite riches, of which it is needless to trouble you with the detail. Out of thankfulness to God for his mercies, I gave great alms for the entertainment of several mosques, and for the subsistence of the poor, and employed myself wholly in enjoying my kindred and friends, and making good cheer with them.

Here Sindbad finished the relation of his fourth voyage, which was more surprising to the company than all the three former. He gave a new present of a hundred sequins to Hindbad, whom he prayed to return with the rest next day at the same hour, to dine with him and to hear the story of his fifth voyage. Hindbad and the rest of his guests took leave of him, and retired.

[1] Now Ceylon.*

Next morning when all met, they sat down at table; and when dinner was over, Sindbad began the relation of his fifth voyage.

The Fifth Voyage of Sindbad the Sailor

THE pleasures I enjoyed had again charms enough to make me forget all the troubles and calamities I had undergone, without curing me of my inclination to make new voyages. Therefore I bought goods, ordered them to be packed up and loaded, and set out with them for the best seaports; and there, that I might not be obliged to depend upon a captain, but have a ship at my own command, I staid till one was built on purpose, at my own charge. When the ship was ready, I went on board with my goods; but not having enough to load her, I took on board me several merchants of different nations with their merchandise.

We sailed with the first fair wind, and after a long navigation, the first place we touched at was a desart island, where we found an egg of a roc, equal in bigness with that I formerly mentioned. There was a young roc in it just ready to be hatched, and the bill of it began to appear.

The merchants, whom I had taken on board my ship, and who landed with me, broke the egg with hatchets, and made a hole in it, from whence they pulled out the young roc piece after piece, and roasted it. I had earnestly dissuaded them from meddling with the egg, but they would not listen to me.

Scarce had they made an end of their treat, when there appeared in the air, at a considerable distance from us, two great clouds. The captain whom I hired to sail my ship, knowing by experience what it meant, cried that it was the he and the she roc that belonged to the young one, and pressed us to reimbark with all speed, to prevent the misfortune which he saw would otherwise befal us. We made haste to do so, and set sail with all possible diligence.

In the mean time the two rocs approached with a frightful noise, which they redoubled when they saw the egg broke, and their young one gone. But having a mind to avenge themselves, they flew back towards the place from whence they came, and disappeared for some time, while we made all the sail we could, to prevent that which unhappily befel us.

They returned, and we observed that each of them carried between their talons stones, or rather rocks of a monstrous size. When they came directly over my ship, they hovered, and one of them let fall a stone; but by the dexterity of the steersman, who turned the ship with the rudder, it missed us, and falling by the side of the ship into the sea, divided the water so, that we almost could see to the bottom. The other roc, to our misfortune, threw the stone, so exactly upon the middle of the ship, that it split in a thousand pieces. The mariners and passengers were all killed by the stone or sunk. I myself, had the last fate; but as I came up again, I catched hold, by good fortune, of a piece of the wreck, and swimming sometimes with one hand, and sometimes with the other, but always holding fast my board, the wind and tide being for me, I came to an island, whose bank was very steep; I overcame that difficulty however, and got ashore.

I sat down upon the grass, to recover myself a little from my fatigue, after which I got up, and went into the island to view it. It seemed to be a delicious garden. I found trees every where, some of them bearing green and others ripe fruits, and streams of fresh pure water, with pleasant windings and turnings. I eat of the fruits, which I found excellent; and drank of the water, which was very pleasant.

Night being come, I lay down upon the grass, in a convenient place enough; but I could not sleep an hour at a time, my mind was so disturbed with the fear of being alone in so desart a place. Thus I spent best part of the night in fretting, and reproaching myself for my imprudence in not staying at home, rather than undertaking this last voyage. These reflections carried me so far, that I began to form a design against my own life; but day-light dispersed those melancholy thoughts, and I got up, and walked among the trees, but not without apprehensions of danger.

When I was a little advanced into the island, I saw an old man, who to me seemed very weak and feeble. He sat upon the bank of a stream, and at first I took him to be one who had been shipwrecked as myself. I went towards him, and saluted him; but he only bowed his head a little. I asked him what he did there; but instead of answering me, he made a sign for me to take him upon my back, and carry him over the brook, signifying that it was to gather fruit.

I believed him really to stand in need of my help, so I took him upon my back, and, having carried him over, bid him get down, and for that end stooped, that he might get off with ease; but instead of that, (which I laugh at every time I think on it) the old man, who to me appeared very decrepid, clasped his legs nimbly about my neck, and then I perceived his skin to be like that of a cow.—He sat astride me, upon my shoulders, and held my throat so strait, that I thought he would have strangled me, the fright of which made me faint away, and fall down.

Notwithstanding my fainting, the ill-natured old fellow kept fast about my neck, but opened his legs a little to give me time to recover my breath. When I had done so, he thrust one of his feet against my stomach, and struck me so rudely on the side with the other, that he forced me to rise up against my will. Being got up, he made me walk under the trees, and forced me now and then to stop to gather and eat such fruit as we found. He never left me all day; and when I lay down to rest me by night, he laid himself down with me, holding always fast about my neck. Every morning he pushed me, to make me awake; and afterwards obliged me to get up and walk, and pressed me with his feet. You may judge then, gentlemen, what trouble I was in, to be charged with such a burden as I could noways rid myself from.

One day, I found in my way several dry calabashes that had fallen from a tree; I took a large one, and, after cleaning it, pressed into it some juice of grapes, which abounded in the island; having filled the calabash, I set it in a convenient place, and coming hither again some days after, I took up my calabash, and setting it to my mouth, found the wine to be so good, that it made me presently not only forget my sorrow, but I grew vigorous, and was so light-hearted, that I began to sing and dance as I walked along.

The old man perceiving the effect which this drink had upon me, and that I carried him with more ease than I did before, made a sign for me to give him the calabash; and, the liquor pleasing his palate, he drank it all off. There being enough of it to fuddle him, he became drunk immediately: and the fumes getting up into his head, he began to sing after his manner, and to dance with his breech upon my shoulders. His jolting about made him vomit, and he loosened his legs from about me by degrees; so, finding that he did not press me as before, I threw him upon the ground, where he lay without motion, and then I took up a great stone, with which I crushed his head to pieces.

I was extremely rejoiced to be freed thus for ever from this cursed old fellow, and walked upon the bank of the sea, where I met the crew of a ship that had cast anchor to take in water, and refresh themselves. They were extremely surprised to see me, and to hear the particulars of my adventures. You fell, said they, into the hands of the Old Man of the Sea, and are the first that ever escaped strangling by him. He never left those he had once made himself master of, till he destroyed them; and he has made this island famous by the number of men he has slain, so that the merchants and mariners who landed upon it dared not to advance into the island but in numbers together.

After having informed me of those things, they carried me with them to the ship; the captain received me with great satisfaction, when they told him what had befallen me. He put out again to sea; and, after some days sail, we arrived at the harbour of a great city, whose houses were built with good stone.

One of the merchants of the ship, who had taken me into his friendship, obliged me to go along with him, and carried me to a place appointed for a retreat for foreign merchants. He gave me a great bag, and, having recommended me to some people of the town who used to gather cocoas, he desired them to take me with them to do the like: Go, says he, follow them, and do as you see them do, and do not separate from them, otherwise you endanger your life.—Having thus spoke, he gave me provisions for the journey, and I went with them.

We came to a great forest of trees, extreme straight and tall, and their trunks were so smooth that it was not possible for any man to climb up to the branches that bore the fruit. All the trees were cocoa trees; and when we entered the forest, we saw a great number of apes, of several sizes, that fled as soon as they perceived us, and climbed up to the tops of the trees with surprising swiftness.

The merchants with whom I was, gathered stones, and threw them at the apes on the tops of the trees. I did the same, and the apes out of revenge threw cocoa-nuts at us as fast, and with such gestures, as sufficiently testified their anger and resentment: we gathered up the cocoas, and from time to time threw stones to provoke the apes; so that by this stratagem we filled our bags with cocoa-nuts, which it had been impossible for us to have done otherwise.

When we had gathered our number, we returned to the city, where the merchant who sent me to the forest, gave me the value of the cocoas I brought: Go on, says he, and do the like every day, until you have got money enough to carry you home. I thanked him for his good advice, and insensibly gathered together so many cocoas as amounted to a considerable sum.

The vessel in which I came, sailed with the merchants, who loaded her with cocoas. I expected the arrival of another, which landed speedily for the like loading. I embarked on board the same all the cocoas that belonged to me; and when she was ready to sail, I went and took leave of the merchant who had been so kind to me; but he could not embark with me, because he had not finished his affairs.

We set sail towards those islands where pepper grows in great plenty. From thence we went to the isle of Comari,[1] where the best sort of wood of aloes grows, and whose inhabitants have made it an inviolable law to themselves to drink no wine, nor to suffer any place of debauch. I exchanged my cocoas in these two islands for pepper, and wood of aloes, and went with the other merchants a pearl-fishing. I hired divers, who fetched me up those that were very large and pure. I embarked joyfully in a vessel that happily arrived at Balsora; from thence I returned to Bagdad, where I made vast sums of my pepper, wood of aloes, and pearls. I gave the tenth of my gains in alms,

[1] This island, or peninsula, ends at the cape, which we now call cape Comoran. It is also called Comar, and Comor.*

as I had done upon my return from my other voyages, and endeavoured to ease myself from my fatigues by diversions of all sorts.

When Sindbad had done with his story, he ordered one hundred sequins to Hindbad, who retired with all the other guests; but next morning the same company returned to dine with rich Sindbad; who, after having treated them as formerly, demanded audience, and gave the following account of his sixth voyage.

The Sixth Voyage of Sindbad the Sailor

GENTLEMEN, says he, you long, without doubt, to know how, after being shipwrecked five times, and escaping so many dangers, I could resolve again to try my fortune, and expose myself to new hardships. I am astonished at it myself, when I think on it, and must certainly have been induced to it by my stars. But be that as it will, after a year's rest, I prepared for a sixth voyage, notwithstanding the prayers of my kindred and friends, who did all that was possible to prevent me.

Instead of taking my way by the Persian gulph, I travelled once more through several provinces of Persia, and the Indies, and arrived at a seaport, where I embarked aboard a ship, the captain of which was resolved on a long voyage.

It was very long indeed, but at the same time so unfortunate, that the captain and pilot lost their course, so as they knew not where they were. They found it at last, but we had no ground to rejoice at it. We were all seized with extraordinary fear, when we saw the captain quit his post, and cry out. He threw off his turban, pulled the hair of his beard, and beat his head like a madman. We asked him the reason, and he answered, that he was in the most dangerous place in all the sea; A rapid current carries the ship along with it; and we shall all of us perish in less than a quarter of an hour. Pray to God to deliver us from this danger; we cannot escape it, if he do not take pity on us. At these words he ordered the sails to be changed; but all the ropes broke, and the ship, without any possibility of helping it, was carried by the current to the foot of an inaccessible mountain, where she was run ashore, and broke to pieces, yet so as we saved our lives, our provisions, and the best of our goods.

This being over, the captain says to us, God has now done what he pleased; we may every man dig our grave here, and bid the world adieu: for we are all in so fatal a place, that none shipwrecked here, did ever return to their homes again. His discourse afflicted us mortally, and we embraced one another with tears in our eyes, bewailing our deplorable lot.

The mountain, at the foot of which we were cast, was the coast of a very long and large island. This coast was covered all over with wrecks; and by the vast number of men's bones we saw every where, and which filled us with horror, we concluded that abundance of people had died there. It is also incredible to tell, what a quantity of goods and riches we found cast ashore there. All those objects served only to augment our grief. Whereas, in all other places, rivers run from their channels into the sea, here a great river of fresh water runs out of the sea into a dark cave, whose entrance is very high and large.—What is most remarkable in this place is, that the stones of the mountain are of crystal, rubies, and other precious stones. Here is also a sort of fountain of pitch or bitumen, that runs into the sea, which the fishes swallow, and then vomit it up again turned into ambergris; and this the waves throw upon the beach in great quantities. Here grow also trees, most of which are wood of aloes, equal in goodness to those of Comari.

To finish the description of this place, which may well be called a gulph, since nothing ever returns from it, it is not possible for a ship to get off from it when once they come within such a distance of it. If they be drove thither by a wind from the sea, the wind and the current ruins them; and if they come into it when a land-wind blows, which might seem to favour their getting out again, the height of the mountain stops the wind, and occasions a calm, so that the force of the current runs them ashore, where they are broken in pieces, as ours was; and that which completes the misfortune is, that there is no possibility of getting to the top of the mountain, or getting out any manner of way.

We continued upon the shore like men out of their senses, and expected death every day. At first we divided our provisions as equally as we could, and so every one lived a longer or a shorter while, according to their temperance, and the use they made of their provisions.

Those who died first, were interred by the rest; and as for my part, I paid the last duty to all my companions. Nor are you to wonder at this; for besides that I husbanded the provision that fell to my share better than they, I had provisions of my own, which I did not share with my comrades; yet, when I buried the last, I had so little remaining, that I thought it could not hold out long. So that I dug a grave, resolving to lie down in it, because there was none left alive to inter me. I must confess to you at the same time, that while I was thus employed, I could not but reflect upon myself as the cause of my own ruin, and repented that I had ever undertaken this last voyage. Nor did I stop at reflections only, but had well nigh hastened my own death, and began to tear my hands with my teeth.

But it pleased God once more to take compassion on me, and put it in my mind to go to the bank of the river, which ran into the great cave; where, considering the river with great attention, I said to myself, this river, which runs thus under ground, must come out somewhere or other. If I make a float, and leave myself to the current, it will bring me to some inhabited country, or drown me. If I be drowned, I lose nothing, but only change one kind of death for another; and if I get out of this fatal place, I shall not only avoid the sad fate of my comrades, but perhaps find some new occasion of enriching myself. Who knows but fortune waits, upon my getting off this dangerous shelve, to compensate my shipwreck with usury.

After this, I immediately went to work on a float. I made it of good large pieces of timber and cables, for I had choice of them, and tied them together so strong, that I had made a very solid little float. When I had finished it, I loaded it with some bales of rubies, emeralds, ambergris, rock-crystal, and rich stuffs. Having balanced all my cargo exactly, and fastened them well to the float, I went on board it with two little oars that I had made; and leaving it to the course of the river, I resigned myself to the will of God.

As soon as I came into the cave, I lost all light, and the stream carried me I knew not whither. Thus I sailed some days in perfect darkness, and once found the arch so low, that it very nigh broke my head, which made me very cautious afterwards to avoid the like danger. All this while I eat nothing but what was just necessary to support nature; yet, notwithstanding this frugality, all my provisions were spent. Then a pleasing sleep seized upon me; I cannot tell how long it continued; but when I awaked, I was surprised to find myself in the middle of a vast country, at the brink of a river, where my float was tied, amidst a great number of negroes. I got up as soon as I saw them, and saluted them. They spoke to me, but I did not understand their language. I was so transported with joy, that I knew not whether I was asleep or awake; but being persuaded that I was not asleep, I recited the following words in Arabic aloud: Call upon the Almighty, and he will help thee; thou needest not perplex thyself about any thing else; shut thy eyes, and while thou art asleep, God will change thy bad fortune into good.

One of the blacks, who understood Arabic, hearing me speak thus, came towards me, and said, Brother, do not be surprised at us; we are inhabitants of this country, and came hither to-day to water our fields, by digging little canals from this river, which comes out of the neighbouring mountain. We perceived something floating upon the water, went speedily to see what it was, and perceiving your float, one of us swam into the river, and brought it hither, where we fastened it, as you see, until you should awake. Pray tell us your history, for it must be extraordinary; how did you venture yourself into this river, and whence did you come? I begged of them first to give me something to eat, and then I would satisfy their curiosity. They gave me several sorts of food; and when I had satisfied my hunger, I gave them a true account of all that had befallen me, which they listened to with admiration. As soon as I had finished my discourse, they told me, by the person who spoke Arabic, and interpreted to them what I said, that it was one of the most surprising stories they ever heard, and that I must go along with them, and tell it to their king myself; the thing is too extraordinary to be told by any other than the person to whom it happened. I told them I was ready to do whatever they pleased.

They immediately sent for a horse; which was brought them in a little time; and having made me get up upon him, some of them walked before me to shew me the way, and the rest took my float and cargo, and followed me.

We marched thus all together till we came to the city of Serendib, for it was in that island where I landed. The blacks presented me to their king. I approached his throne, and saluted him as I used to do the kings of the Indies; that is to say, I prostrated myself at his feet, and kissed the earth. The prince ordered me to rise up, received me with an obliging air, and made me come up and sit down near him. He first asked me my name; and I answered, they call me Sindbad the sailor, because of the many voyages I had undertaken; and that I was a citizen of Bagdad. But, replies he, how came you into my dominions, and from whence came you last?

I concealed nothing from the king; I told him all that I have now told you; and his majesty was so surprised and charmed with it, that he commanded my adventure to be written in letters of gold, and laid up in the archives of the kingdom. At last my float was brought him, and the bales opened in his presence; he admired the quantity of wood of aloes and ambergris, but, above all, the rubies and emeralds, for he had none in his treasury that came near them.

Observing that he looked on my jewels with pleasure, and viewed the most remarkable among them, one after another, I fell prostrate at his feet, and took the liberty to say to him, Sir, not only my person is at your majesty's service, but the cargo of the float, and I would beg of you to dispose of it as your own. He answered me with a smile, Sindbad, I will take care not to covet any thing of yours, nor to take any thing from you that God has given you; far from lessening your wealth, I design to augment it, and will not let you go out of my dominions without marks of my liberality. All the answer I returned was prayers for the prosperity of that prince, and commendations of his generosity and bounty. He charged one of his officers to take care of me, and ordered people to serve me at his own charge. The officer was very faithful in the execution of his orders, and made all the goods to be carried to the lodgings provided for me.

I went every day at a set hour to make my court to the king, and spent the rest of my time in seeing the city, and what was most worthy my curiosity.

The isle of Serendib[1] is situated just under the equinoctial line; so that the days and nights there are always of twelve hours each, and the island is eighty[2] parasangues in length, and as many in breadth.

The capital city stands in the end of a fine valley, formed by a mountain in the middle of the island, which is the highest in the world. It is seen three days sail off at sea. There are rubies and several sorts of minerals in it, and all the rocks for the most part emerald, a metalline stone made use of to cut and smooth other precious stones. There grow all sorts of rare plants and trees, especially cedars and cocoas. There is also a pearl fishing in the mouth of its river; and in some of its valleys there are found diamonds. I made, by way of devotion, a pilgrimage to the place where Adam was confined after his banishment from paradise, and had the curiosity to go to the top of it.

When I came back to the city, I prayed the king to allow me to return to my country, which he granted me in the most obliging and most honourable manner. He would needs force a rich present upon me; and when I went to take my leave of him, he gave me one much more considerable, and at the same time charged me with a letter for the commander of the faithful, our sovereign, saying to me, I pray you give this present from me, and this letter, to Caliph Haroun Alraschid, and assure him of my friendship. I took the present and letter in a very respectful manner, and promised his majesty punctually to execute the commission with which he was pleased to honour me. Before I embarked, this prince sent to seek for the captain and the merchants that were to go with me, and ordered them to treat me with all possible respect.

The letter from the king of Serendib was written on the skin of a certain animal of great value, because of its being so scarce, and of a yellowish colour. The characters of this letter were of azure, and the contents thus: 'The king of the Indies, before whom march 100 elephants, who lives in a palace that shines with 100,000 rubies, and who has in his treasury 20,000 crowns enriched with diamonds, to caliph Haroun Alraschid.

'Though the present we send you be inconsiderable, receive it, however, as a brother and a friend, in consideration of the hearty friendship which we bear for you, and of which we are willing to give you proof. We desire the same part in your friendship, considering that we believe it to be our merit, being of the same dignity with yourself. We conjure you this in quality of a brother. Adieu.'

[1] Geographers place it on this side of the line, in the first climate.*

[2] The eastern geographers make a parasangue longer than a French league.*

The present consisted, in the first place, of one single ruby made into a cup, about half a foot high, an inch thick, and filled with round pearls of half a dram each. 2. Of the skin of a serpent, whose scales were as large as an ordinary piece of gold, and had the virtue to preserve from sickness those who lay upon it. 3. Of 50,000 drams of the best wood of aloes, with 30 grains of camphire as big as pistachios. And, 4. A she slave, of ravishing beauty, whose apparel was all covered over with jewels.

The ship set sail, and, after a long and successful navigation, we landed at Balsora, from whence I went to Bagdad, where the first thing I did was to acquit myself of my commission.

I took the king of Serendib's letter, continued Sindbad, and went to present myself at the gate of the commander of the faithful, followed by the beautiful slave, and such of my own family as carried the presents. I gave an account of the reason of my coming, and was immediately conducted to the throne of the caliph. I made my reverence by prostration, and, after a short speech, gave him the letter and present. When he had read what the king of Serendib wrote to him, he asked me, if that prince were really so rich and potent as he had said in his letter? I prostrated myself a second time, and rising again, Commander of the faithful, says I, I can assure your majesty he doth not exceed the truth on that head, I am a witness of it. There is nothing more capable of raising a man's admiration than the magnificence of his palace. When the prince appears in public, he has a throne fixed on the back of an elephant, and marches betwixt two ranks of his ministers, favourites, and other people of his court: Before him, upon the same elephant, an officer carries a golden lance in his hand; and behind the throne there is another, who stands upright, with a column of gold, on the top of which there is an emerald half a foot long, and an inch thick: before him there marches a guard of 1000 men clad in cloth of gold and silk, and mounted on elephants richly caparisoned.

While the king is on his march, the officer, who is before him on the same elephant, cries, from time to time, with a loud voice, Behold the great monarch, the potent and redoubtable sultan of the Indies, whose palace is covered with 100,000 rubies, and who possesses 20,000 crowns of diamonds. Behold the crowned monarch, greater than the great Solima,[1] and the great Mihrage.[2] After he has pronounced those words, the officer behind the throne cries in his turn, This monarch, so great and so powerful, must die, must die, must die. And the officer before, replies, Praise be to him who lives for ever. Farther, the king of Serendib is so just, that there are no

[1] Solomon.*

[2] An ancient king of a great island of the same name in the Indies, and very much famed among the Arabians for his power and wisdom.*

judges in his dominions. His people have no need of them. They understand and observe justice exactly of themselves. The caliph was much pleased with my discourse. The wisdom of that king, says he, appears in his letter; and after what you tell me, I must confess that his wisdom is worthy of his people, and his people deserve so wise a prince. Having spoken thus, he discharged me, and sent me home with a rich present.

Sindbad left off speaking, and his company retired, Hindbad having first received one hundred sequins; and next day they returned to hear the relation of his seventh and last voyage as follows:

The Seventh and last Voyage of Sindbad the Sailor

BEING returned from my sixth voyage, I absolutely laid aside all thoughts of travelling any farther. For, besides that my years did now require rest, I was resolved no more to expose myself to such risks as I had run. So that I thought of nothing but to pass the rest of my days in quiet. One day, as I was treating a parcel of my friends, one of my servants came and told me that an officer of the caliph's asked for me. I rose from the table, and went to him. The caliph, says he, has sent me to tell you, that he must speak with you. I followed the officer to the palace; where being presented to the caliph, I saluted him by prostrating myself at his feet. Sindbad, says he to me, I stand in need of you; you must do me the service to carry my answer and present to the king of Serendib. It is but just I should return his civility.

This command of the caliph to me was like a clap of thunder. Commander of the faithful, replied I, I am ready to do whatever your majesty shall think fit to command me; but I beseech you most humbly to consider what I have undergone. I have also made a vow never to go out of Bagdad. Hence I took occasion to give him a large and particular account of all my adventures, which he had the patience to hear out.—As soon as I had finished, I confess, says he, that the things you tell me are very extraordinary; yet you must for my sake undertake this voyage which I propose to you. You have nothing to do but to go to the isle of Serendib, and deliver the commission which I give you. After that you are at liberty to return. But you must go; for you know it would be indecent, and not suitable to my dignity, to be indebted to the king of the island. Perceiving that the caliph insisted upon it, I submitted, and told him that I was willing to obey. He was very well pleased at it, and ordered me a thousand sequins for the charge of my journey.

I prepared for my departure in a few days; and as soon as the caliph's letter and present were delivered to me, I went to Balsora, where I embarked, and had a very happy voyage. I arrived at the isle of Serendib, where

I acquainted the king's ministers with my commission, and prayed them to get me speedily audience. They did so, and I was conducted to the palace in an honourable manner, where I saluted the king by prostration, according to custom. That prince knew me immediately, and testified very great joy to see me. O Sindbad, says he, you are welcome; I swear to you I have many times thought of you since you went hence; I bless the day upon which we see one another once more. I made my compliment to him, and after having thanked him for his kindness to me, I delivered him the caliph's letter and present, which he received with all imaginable satisfaction.

The caliph's present was a complete set of cloth of gold, valued at a thousand sequins; fifty robes of rich stuff, a hundred others of white cloth, the finest of Cairo, Suez,[1] Cusa, and Alexandria;[2] a royal crimson bed, and a second of another fashion; a vessel of agate, broader than deep, of an inch thick, and half a foot wide, the bottom of which represented, in bass-relief, a man with one knee on the ground, who held a bow and arrow, ready to let fly at a lion. He sent him also a rich table, which, according to tradition, belonged to the great Solomon. The caliph's letter was as follows:

'Greeting, in name of the sovereign guide of the right way, to the potent and happy sultan, from Abdallah Haroun Alraschid, whom God hath set in the place of honour, after his ancestors of happy memory.

'We received your letter with joy, and send you this from the council of our port, the garden of superior wits. We hope, when you look upon it, you will find our good intention, and be pleased with it. Adieu.'

The king of Serendib was mightily pleased that the caliph answered his friendship. A little time after this audience, I solicited leave to depart, and obtained the same with much difficulty. I got it, however, at last; and the king, when he discharged me, made me a very considerable present. I embarked immediately to return to Bagdad, but had not the good fortune to arrive there as I hoped. God ordered it otherwise.

Three or four days after my departure, we were attacked by corsairs,* who easily seized upon our ship, because it was no vessel of force. Some of the crew offered resistance, which cost them their lives. But for me and the rest, who were not so imprudent, the corsairs saved us on purpose to make slaves of us.

We were all stripped; and instead of our own clothes, they gave us sorry rags, and carried us into a remote island, where they sold us.

I fell into the hands of a rich merchant, who, as soon as he bought me, carried me to his house, treated me well, and clad me handsomely for a slave.

[1] A port on the Red sea.
[2] A town of Arabia.

Some days after, not knowing who I was, he asked me if I understood any trade? I answered, that I was no mechanic, but a merchant; and that the corsairs, who sold me, robbed me of all I had. But tell me, replies he, can you shoot with a bow? I answered, that the bow was one of my exercises in my youth, and I had not yet forgot it. Then he gave me a bow and arrows, and, taking me behind him upon an elephant, carried me to a vast forest some leagues from the town. We went a great way into the forest; and when he thought to stop, he bid me alight: then shewing me a great tree, Climb up that tree, says he, and shoot at the elephants as you see them pass by; for there is a prodigious number of them in this forest, and if any of them fall, come, and give me notice of it. Having spoke thus, he left me victuals, and returned to the town, and I continued upon the tree all night.

I saw no elephant during that night, but next morning, as soon as the sun was up, I saw a great number: I shot several arrows among them, and at last one of the elephants fell; the rest retired immediately, and left me at liberty to go and acquaint my patron with my booty. When I had told him the news, he gave me a good meal, commended my dexterity, and caressed me mightily. We went afterwards together to the forest, where we dug a hole for the elephant; my patron designing to return when it was rotten, and to take his teeth, &c. to trade with.

I continued this game for two months, and killed an elephant every day, getting sometimes upon one tree and sometimes upon another. One morning, as I looked for the elephants, I perceived, with an extreme amazement, that, instead of passing by me across the forest as usual, they stopped, and came to me with a horrible noise, in such a number that the earth was covered with them, and shook under them. They encompassed the tree where I was, with their trunks extended, and their eyes all fixed upon me. At this frightful spectacle I continued immoveable; and was so much frightened, that my bow and arrows fell out of my hand.

My fears were not in vain; for after the elephants had stared upon me some time, one of the largest of them put his trunk round the root of the tree, and pulled so strong, that he plucked it up, and threw it on the ground: I fell with the tree, and the elephant taking me up with his trunk, laid me on his back, where I sat more like one dead than alive, with my quiver on my shoulder. He put himself afterwards at the head of the rest, who followed him in troops, and carried me to a place where he laid me down on the ground, and retired with all his companions. Conceive, if you can, the condition I was in: I thought myself to be in a dream; at last, after having lain some time, and seeing the elephants gone, I got up, and found I was upon a long and broad hill, covered all over with the bones and teeth of elephants. I confess to you, that this object furnished me with abundance of reflections.

I admired the instinct of those animals; I doubted not but that was their burying place, and they carried me thither on purpose to tell me that I should forbear to persecute them, since I did it only for their teeth. I did not stay on the hill, but turned towards the city, and, after having travelled a day and a night, I came to my patron. I met no elephant in my way, which made me think they had retired farther into the forest, to leave me at liberty to come back to the hill without any obstacle.

As soon as my patron saw me; Ah, poor Sindbad, says he, I was in great trouble to know what was become of you. I have been at the forest where I found a tree newly pulled up, and a bow and arrows on the ground; and after having sought for you in vain, I despaired of ever seeing you more. Pray tell me what befel you, and by what good hap thou art alive? I satisfied his curiosity; and, going both of us next morning to the hill, he found to his great joy, that what I told him was true. We loaded the elephant upon which we came, with as many teeth as he could carry; and when we were returned, Brother, says my patron, for I will treat you no more as a slave, after having made such a discovery as will enrich me, God bless you with all happiness and prosperity; I declare before him, that I give you your liberty. I concealed from you what I am now going to tell you.

The elephants of our forest have every year killed us a great many slaves, whom we set to seek ivory. For all the cautions we could give them, those crafty animals killed them one time or other. God has delivered you from their fury, and has bestowed that favour upon you only. It is a sign that he loves you, and has use for your service in the world. You have procured me incredible gain. We could not have ivory formerly, but by exposing the lives of our slaves; and now our whole city is enriched by your means. Do not think I pretend to have rewarded you by giving you your liberty, I will also give you considerable riches. I could engage all our city to contribute towards making your fortune, but I will have the glory of doing it myself.

To this obliging discourse, I replied, Patron, God preserve you. Your giving me my liberty is enough to discharge what you owe me; and I desire no other reward for the service I have had the good fortune to do to you and your city, but leave to return to my own country. Very well, says he, the Mocon[1] will in a little time bring ships for ivory. I will send you home then, and give you wherewith to bear your charges. I thanked him again for my liberty, and his good intentions towards me. I staid with him expecting the Mocon; and during that time, we made so many journies to the hill, that we filled our warehouses with ivory. The other merchants who traded in it did the same thing, for it could not be long concealed from them.

[1] A regular wind that comes six months from the east and as many from the west.*

The ships arrived at last, and my patron himself having made choice of the ship wherein I was to embark, he loaded half of it with ivory on my account; he laid in provisions in abundance for my passage, and besides, obliged me to accept a present of the curiosities of the country, of great value. After I had returned him a thousand thanks for all his favours, I went aboard. We set sail; and as the adventure, which procured me this liberty, was very extraordinary, I had it continually in my thoughts.

We stopt at some islands to take in fresh provisions; our vessel being come to a port on the Terra Firma in the Indies, we touched there, and not being willing to venture by sea to Balsora, I landed my proportion of the ivory, resolving to proceed on my journey by land. I made vast sums of my ivory; I bought several rarities, which I intended for presents; and when my equipage was got ready, I set out in company with a large caravan of merchants. I was a long time on the way, and suffered very much; but endured all with patience, when I considered that I had nothing to fear from the seas, from pirates, from serpents, nor of the other perils I had undergone.

All these fatigues ended at last, and I came safe to Bagdad. I went immediately to call upon the caliph, and gave him an account of my embassy. That prince told me, he had been uneasy by reason I was so long a-returning, but that he always hoped God would preserve me. When I told him the adventure of the elephants, he seemed to be much surprised at it, and would never have given any credit to it had he not known my sincerity. He reckoned this story, and the other relations I had given him, to be so curious, that he ordered one of his secretaries to write them in characters of gold, and lay them up in his treasury. I retired very well satisfied with the honours I received, and the presents which he gave me; and after that I gave up myself wholly to my family, kindred, and friends.

Sindbad here finished the relation of his seventh and last voyage; and then, addressing himself to Hindbad, Well, friend, says he, did you ever hear of any person that suffered so much as I have done, or of any mortal that has gone through so many perplexities? Is it not reasonable, that, after all this, I should enjoy a quiet and pleasant life? As he said this, Hindbad drew near to him and kissing his hand, said, I must acknowledge, sir, that you have gone through terrible dangers; my troubles are not comparable to yours; if they afflict me for a time, I comfort myself with the thoughts of the profit I get by them. You not only deserve a quiet life, but are worthy besides of all the riches you enjoy, because you make such a good and generous use of them. May you therefore continue to live in happiness and joy till the day of your death. Sindbad gave him a hundred sequins more, received him into the number of his friends, and desired him to quit his porter's employment, and come and dine every day with him, that he might all his days have reason to remember Sindbad the sailor.

Scheherazade, perceiving it was not yet day, continued her discourse, and began another story.

The Story of the Three Apples

SIR, said she, I have already had the honour to entertain your majesty with a ramble which the caliph Haroun Alraschid made one night from his palace; I must give you an account of one more.

This prince one day commanded the grand visier Giafar, to come to his palace the night following.—Visier, said he, I will take a walk round the town, to inform myself what people say, and particularly how they are pleased with my officers of justice. If there be any against whom they have reason of just complaint, we will turn them out, and put others in their stead that shall officiate better: If, on the contrary, there be any that have gained their applause, we will have that esteem for them which they deserve. The grand visier being come to the palace at the hour appointed, the caliph, he, and Mesrour, the chief of the eunuchs, disguised themselves so as they could not be known, and went out all three together.

They passed through several places, and by several markets: and as they entered a small street, they perceived, by the light of the moon, a tall man, with a white beard, that carried nets on his head; he had a folding basket of palm-leaves on his arm, and a club in his hand. This old man, says the caliph, does not seem to be rich; let us go to him, and enquire into his circumstances. Honest man, said the visier, who art thou? The old man replied, Sir, I am a fisher, but one of the poorest and most miserable of the trade; I went from my house about noon to go a-fishing, and from that time to this I have not been able to catch one fish: and, at the same time, I have a wife and small children, and nothing to maintain them.

The caliph, moved with compassion, says to the fisherman, Hast thou the courage to go back and cast thy nets once more? We will give thee a hundred sequins for what thou shalt bring up. At this proposal, the fisherman, forgetting all his day's toil, took the caliph at his word; and, with him, Giafar and Mesrour, returned to the Tigris, saying to himself, These gentlemen seem to be too honest and reasonable not to reward my pains; and if they give me the hundredth part of what they promise me, it will be a great deal.

They came to the bank of the river; and the fisherman throwing in his net, when he drew it again, brought up a trunk, close shut, and very heavy.—The caliph made the grand visier pay him an hundred sequins immediately, and sent him away. Mesrour, by his master's orders, carried the trunk on his shoulder; and the caliph was so very eager to know what was in it, that he returned to the palace with all speed. When the trunk was opened, they found in it a large basket made of palm-leaves, shut up, and the covering of it sewed with red thread. To satisfy the caliph's impatience, they would not take time to unrip it, but cut the thread with a knife, and they took out of the basket a bundle wrapt up in a sorry piece of hanging, and bound about with a rope, which being untied, and the bundle opened, they found, to their great amazement, the corpse of a young lady, whiter than snow, all cut in pieces.

Your majesty may imagine a great deal better than I am able to express it, the astonishment of the caliph at this dreadful spectacle. His surprise was instantly changed into passion, and darting an angry look at the visier, Ah! thou wretch, said he, is this your inspection into the actions of my people? Do they commit such impious murders under thy ministry in my capital city, and throw my subjects into the Tigris, that they may cry for vengeance against me at the day of judgment? If thou dost not speedily revenge the murder of this woman, by the death of her murderer, I swear by heaven, that I will cause thee to be hanged, and forty more of thy kindred. Commander of the faithful, replied the grand visier, I beg your majesty to grant me time to make inquiry. I will allow thee no more, said the caliph, than three days; therefore thou must look to it.

The visier Giafar went home in great confusion of mind. Alas, said he, how is it possible that in such a vast and populous city as Bagdad, I should be able to detect a murderer, who undoubtedly committed the crime without witness, and perhaps may be already gone from hence? Any other person but I would take some wretched person out of prison, and cause him to die, to satisfy the caliph; but I will not burden my conscience with such a barbarous action; I will rather die than save my life at that rate.

He ordered the officers of the police and justice to make strict search for the criminal: they sent their servants about, and they themselves were not idle, for they were no less concerned in this matter than the visier. But all their endeavours turned to nothing; what pains soever they took, they could not find out the murderer: so that the visier concluded his life to be gone, unless some remarkable providence hindered it.

The third day being come, an officer came to this unfortunate minister, with a summons to follow him, which the visier obeyed. The caliph asked him for the murderer. He answered with tears in his eyes, Commander of the faithful, I have not found any person that could give me the least account of him. The caliph, full of fury and rage, gave him many reproachful words, and ordered that he and forty Barmicides[1] more should be hanged up at the gate of the palace.

In the mean while, the gibbets were preparing, and orders were sent to seize forty Barmicides more in their houses; a public crier was sent about the city to cry thus, by the caliph's order: Those who have a desire to see the grand visier Giafar hanged, and forty more Barmicides of his kindred, let them come to the square before the palace.

When all things were ready, the criminal-judge, and a great many officers belonging to the palace, brought out the grand visier with the forty Barmicides, and set each of them at the foot of the gibbet designed for them, and a rope was put about each of their necks. The multitude of people that filled the square could not without grief and tears behold this tragical sight, for the grand visier and the Barmicides were loved and honoured on account of their probity, bounty, and impartiality, not only in Bagdad, but through all the dominions of the caliph.

Nothing could prevent the execution of this prince's too severe and irrevocable sentence; and the lives of the honestest people in the city were just going to be taken away, when a young man of handsome mien, and good apparel, pressed through the crowd till he came where the grand visier was; and after he had kissed his hand, said, Most excellent visier, chief of the emirs of this court, and comfort of the poor, you are not guilty of the crime for which you stand here. Withdraw, and let me expiate the death of the lady that was thrown into the Tigris. It is I who murdered her, and I deserve to be punished for it.

Though these words occasioned great joy to the visier, yet he could not but pity the young man, in whose look he saw something, that, instead of being ominous, was engaging: But as he was about to answer him, a tall man, pretty well in years, who had likewise forced his way through the crowd, came up to him, saying, Sir, do not believe what this young man tells you; I killed that lady who was found in the trunk, and this punishment ought only to fall upon me. I conjure you, in the name of God, not to punish the innocent for the guilty. Sir, says the young man to the visier, I do protest that I am he who committed this vile act, and nobody else had any hand in it. My son, said the old man, it is despair that brought you hither, and you would anticipate your destiny. I have lived a long while in the world, and it is time for me to be gone; let me therefore sacrifice my life for yours. Sir, said he again to the visier, I tell you once more I am the murderer; let me die without any more ado.

[1] The Barmicides were a family come out of Persia, and of them the grand visier was descended.*

The controversy between the old man and the young one obliged the grand visier Giafar to carry them both before the caliph, which the judge-criminal consented to, being very glad to serve the visier. When he came before the prince, he kissed the ground seven times, and spake after this manner: Commander of the faithful, I have brought here before your majesty this old man and this young man, who both confess themselves to be the sole murderers of the lady. Then the caliph asked the criminals which of them it was that so cruelly murdered the lady, and threw her into the Tigris? The young man assured him it was he, but the old man maintained the contrary. Go, says the caliph, to the grand visier, and cause them both to be hanged. But, sir, says the visier, if only one of them be guilty, it would be unjust to take the lives of both. At these words the young man spoke again; I swear by the great God, who has raised the heavens so high as they be, that I am the man who killed the lady, cut her in quarters, and threw her into the Tigris about four days ago. I renounce my part of happiness among the just at the day of judgment, if what I say be not truth, therefore I am he that ought to suffer. The caliph being surprised at this oath, believed him; especially since the old man made no answer to this. Whereupon, turning to the young man, Thou wretch, said he, what was it that made thee to commit that detestable crime, and what is it that moves thee to offer thyself voluntarily to die? Commander of the faithful, said he, if all that has passed between that lady and me were set down in writing, it would be a history that might be very useful for other men. I command thee then to relate it, said the caliph. The young man obeyed, and began. His history was thus:

The Story of the Lady that was murdered, and of the young Man her Husband

COMMANDER of the faithful, your majesty may be pleased to know, that this murdered lady was my wife, the daughter of this old man you see here, who is my own uncle by the father's side. She was not above twelve years old when he gave her to me, and it is now eleven years ago. I have three children by her, all boys yet alive; and I must do her that justice to say, that she never gave me the least occasion of offence; she was chaste, of good behaviour, and made it her whole business to please me. And for my part, I loved her entirely, and rather prevented her in granting any thing she desired, than opposed it.

About two months ago she fell sick; I took all imaginable care of her, and spared nothing that could procure her a speedy recovery: After a month, she began to grow better, and had a mind to go to the bagnio. Before she went out of the house, Cousin, said she, (for so she used to call me out of familiarity) I long for some apples; if you could get me any, you would please me extremely; I have longed for them a great while, and, I must own, it is come to that height, that, if I be not satisfied very soon, I fear some misfortune will befal me. With all my heart, said I, I will do all that is in my power to make you easy.

I went immediately round all the markets and shops in the town to seek for apples, but I could not get one, though I offered to pay a sequin a-piece. I returned home very much dissatisfied at my disappointment. And for my wife, when she returned from the bagnio, and saw no apples, she became so very uneasy, that she could not sleep all night: I got up betimes in the morning, and went through all the gardens, but had no better success than the day before; only I happened to meet an old gardener, who told me that all my pains would signify nothing, for I could not expect to find apples any where but in your majesty's garden at Balsora. As I loved my wife passionately, and would not have any thing of neglect to satisfy her, chargeable upon me, I put myself in a traveller's habit, and after I had told her my design, I went to Balsora, and made my journey with so great diligence, that I returned at the end of fifteen days, with three apples, which cost me a sequin a-piece; there were no more left in the garden, so that the gardener would let me have them no cheaper. As soon as I came home, I presented them to my wife, but her longing was over; so she satisfied herself with receiving them, and laid them down by her. In the mean time she continued sickly, and I knew not what remedy to get for her.

Some few days after I returned from my journey, I was sitting in my shop, in the public place where all sorts of fine stuffs are sold, and saw an ugly, tall black slave, come in with an apple in his hand, which I knew to be one of those I had brought from Balsora. I had no reason to doubt it, because I was certain there was not one to be had in all Bagdad, nor in any of the gardens about it. I called to him, and said, Good slave, pray thee tell me where thou hadst this apple? It is a present (said he, smiling,) from my mistress. I was to see her to-day, and found her out of order. I saw three apples lying by her, and asked her where she had them? She told me, the good man, her husband, had made a fortnight's journey on purpose for them, and brought them her. We had a collation together; and, when I took my leave of her, I brought away this apple that you see.

This discourse put me out of my senses; I rose, shut up my shop, ran home with all speed, and going to my wife's chamber, looked immediately for the apples, and seeing only a couple, asked what was become of the third. Then my wife turning her head to the place where the apples lay, and perceiving there were but two, answered me coldly, Cousin, I know not what is become of it. At this answer I did verily believe what the slave told me to be true; and at the same time, giving myself up to madness and jealousy, I drew my knife from my girdle, and thrust it into the unfortunate creature's throat; I afterwards cut off her head, and divided her body into four quarters, which I packed up in a bundle, and hiding it in a basket, sewed it up with a thread of red yarn, put all together in a trunk, and when night came, I carried it on my shoulder down to the Tigris, where I sunk it.

The two youngest of my children were already put to bed, and asleep, the third was gone abroad; but at my return, I found him sitting by my gate, weeping very sore. I asked him the reason: Father, said he, I took this morning from my mother, without her knowledge, one of those three apples you brought her, and I kept it a long while; but, as I was playing some time ago with my little brother in the street, a tall slave that went by, snatched it out of my hands, and carried it with him: I ran after him, demanding it back; and besides, told him that it belonged to my mother, who was sick, and that you had made a fortnight's journey to fetch it; but all to no purpose, he would not restore it. And whereas I still followed him crying out, he turned and beat me; and then ran away as fast as ever he could from one lane to another, till at length I lost sight of him. I have since been walking without the town, expecting your return, to pray you, dear father, not to tell my mother of it, lest it should make her worse. And when he had said these words, he fell a-weeping again more bitterly than before.

My son's discourse afflicted me beyond all measure. I then found myself guilty of an enormous crime, and repented too late of having so easily believed the calumnies of a wretched slave, who, from what he had learned of my son, invented that fatal lie.

My uncle here present, came just at the time to see his daughter, but, instead of finding her alive, understood from me she was dead, for I did conceal nothing from him; and, without staying for his censure, declared myself the greatest criminal in the world.

Upon this, instead of reproaching me, he joined his tears with mine, and we wept three days together without intermission: he for the loss of a daughter whom he always loved tenderly; and I for the loss of a dear wife, of whom I deprived myself after so cruel a manner, by giving too easy a credit to the report of a lying slave.

This, commander of the faithful, is the sincere confession your majesty commanded from me. You have heard now all the circumstances of my crime, and I most humbly beg of you to order the punishment due for it; how severe soever it may be, I shall not in the least complain, but esteem it too easy and gentle.

The caliph was very much astonished at the young man's relation. But this just prince, finding he was rather to be pitied than condemned, began to speak in his favour: This young man's crime, said he, is pardonable before God, and excusable with men. The wicked slave is the sole cause of this murder: it is he alone that must be punished; wherefore, said he, looking upon the grand visier, I give you three days time to find him out; if you do not bring him within that space, you shall die in his stead. The unfortunate Giafar, who thought himself now out of danger, was terribly perplexed at this new order of the caliph: but as he durst not return any answer to this prince, whose hasty temper he knew too well, he departed from his presence, and retired to his house with tears in his eyes, persuading himself he had but three days to live; for he was so fully persuaded that he should not find the slave, that he made not the least inquiry about him. Is it possible, said he, that in such a city as Bagdad, where there is an infinite number of negro slaves, I should be able to find him out that is guilty? so that, unless God be pleased to bring it about, as he hath already detected the murderer, nothing can save my life.

He spent the two first days in mourning with his family, who sat round him weeping and complaining of the caliph's cruelty. The third day being come, he prepared himself to die with courage, as an honest minister, and one that had nothing to trouble his conscience; he sent for notaries and witnesses, who signed the last will he made in their presence. After which he took leave of his wife and children, and bid them the last farewell. All his family was drowned in tears, so that there never was a more sorrowful spectacle. At last the messenger came from the caliph to tell him that he was out of all patience, having heard nothing from him, nor concerning the negro slave, which he had commanded him to search for; I am therefore ordered, said he, to bring you before his throne. The afflicted visier made ready to follow the messenger; but as he was going out, they brought him his youngest daughter, about five or six years of age. The nurses that attended her presented her to her father to receive his last blessing.

As he had a particular love for that child, he prayed the messenger to give him leave to stop for a moment, and taking his daughter in his arms, he kissed her several times; as he kissed her, he perceived she had somewhat in her bosom that looked bulky, and had a sweet scent. My dear little one, said he, what hast thou in thy bosom? My dear father, said she, it is an apple, upon which is written the name of our lord and master the caliph; our slave Rihan[1] sold it me for two sequins.

[1] This word signifies in Arabic, Basilic, an odoriferous plant, and the Arabians call their slaves by this name, as the custom in France is to give the name to a footman.

At these words, Apple and Slave, the grand visier cried with surprise, intermixed with joy, and putting his hand into the child's bosom pulled out the apple! He caused the slave, who was not far off, to be brought immediately, and when he came, Rascal, said he, where hadst thou this apple? My lord, said the slave, I swear to you that I neither stole it in your house, nor where three or four small children were at play, one but the other day as was I going along a street, out of the commander of the faithful's garden; of them having it in his hand, I snatched it from him, and carried it away. The child ran after me, telling me it was none of his own, but belonged to his mother, who was sick; and that his father, to save her longing, had made a long journey, and brought home three apples, whereof this was one, which he had taken from his mother without her knowledge. He said what he could to make me give it him back, but I would not; and so brought it home, and sold it for two sequins to the little lady, your daughter; and this is the whole truth of the matter.

Giafar could not enough admire how the roguery of a slave had been the cause of an innocent woman's death, and almost of his own. He carried the slave along with him; and when he came before the caliph, he gave that prince an exact account of all that the slave had told him, and the chance that brought him to the discovery of his crime.

Never was any surprise so great as that of the caliph, yet he could not prevent himself from falling into excessive fits of laughter. At last he recovered himself, and, with a serious mien, told the visier, That since his slave had been the occasion of a strange accident, he deserved an exemplary punishment.—Sir, I must own it, said the visier, but his guilt is not irremissible. I remember a strange story of a visier of Cairo, called Noureddin[1] Ali, and Bedreddin[2] Hassan of Balsora, and since your majesty delights to hear such things, I am ready to tell it, upon condition, that, if your majesty finds it more astonishing than that which gives me occasion to tell it, you will be pleased to pardon my slave. I am content, said the caliph: but you undertake a hard task, for I do not believe you can save your slave, the story of the apples being so very singular. Upon this, Giafar began his story thus:

The Story of Noureddin Ali, and Bedreddin Hassan

COMMANDER of the faithful, there was in former days a sultan of Egypt, a strict observer of justice, gracious, merciful, and liberal; and his valour made him terrible to his neighbours. He loved the poor, and protected the learned,

[1] Noureddin signifies, in Arabic, the light of religion.
[2] And Bedreddin, the full moon of religion.

whom he advanced to the highest dignities. This sultan had a visier, who was prudent, wise, sagacious, and well versed in other sciences. This minister had two sons, very handsome men, and who in every thing followed his own footsteps. The eldest was called Schemseddin[1] Mohammed, and the younger Noureddin Ali. The last especially was endowed with all the good qualities that any man could have.

The visier their father being dead, the sultan sent for them; and after he had caused them both to put on the usual robes of a visier, I am as sorry, says he, for the loss of your father as yourselves; and because I know you live together, and love one another entirely, I will bestow his dignity upon you conjunctly; go, and imitate your father's conduct.

The two new visiers humbly thanked the sultan, and went home to their house, to make due preparation for their father's interment. They did not go abroad for a month, and then went to court, where they appeared continually on council-days; when the sultan went out a hunting, one of the brothers went along with him, and this honour they had by turns. One evening, as they were talking after supper, the next day being the elder brother's turn to go a hunting with the sultan, he said to his younger brother, Since neither of us is yet married, and that we live so lovingly together, a thought is come into my head: Let us both marry in one day, and let us chuse two sisters out of some family that may suit our quality: What do you think of this fancy? I must tell you, brother, answered Noureddin Ali, that it is very suitable to our friendship; there cannot be a better thought; for my part, I am ready to agree to any thing you shall think fit. But hold, this is not all, says Schemseddin Mohammed; my fancy carries me farther. Suppose both our wives should conceive the first night of our marriage, and should happen to be brought to bed on one day, yours of a son, and mine of a daughter, we will give them to one another in marriage, when they come to age. Nay, says Noureddin Ali aloud, I must acknowledge that this project is admirable; such a marriage will perfect our union, and I willingly consent to it. But then, brother, says he farther, if this marriage should happen, would you expect that my son should settle a jointure on your daughter? There is no difficulty in that, replied the elder; for I am persuaded, that, besides the usual articles of the marriage-contract, you will not fail to promise in his name at least three thousand sequins, three good manors, and three slaves. No, said the younger, I will not consent to that; are we not brethren, and equal in title and dignity? Do not you and I both know what is just? The male being nobler than the female, it is your part to give a large dowry with your daughter. By what I perceive, you are a man that would have your business done at another man's charge.

[1] That is to say, the sun of religion.

Although Noureddin Ali spoke these words in jest, his brother, being of an ill temper, was offended at it; and, falling into a passion, A mischief upon your son, said he, since you prefer him before my daughter; I wonder you had so much confidence, as to believe him worthy of her; you must needs have lost your judgment, to think you are my equal, and say we are colleagues; I would have you to know, you fool, that since you are so impudent, I would not marry my daughter to your son, though you would give him more than you are worth. This pleasant quarrel between two brothers about the marriage of their children before they were born, went so far, that Schemseddin Mohammed concluded with threatening: Were I not to-morrow, says he, to attend the sultan, I would treat you according as you deserve; but, at my return, I shall make you sensible that it does not become a younger brother to speak so insolently to his elder brother, as you have done to me. Upon this he retired to his apartment, and his brother went to bed.

Schemseddin Mohammed rose very early next morning, and goes to the palace to attend the sultan, who went to hunt about Cairo near the pyramids. As for Noureddin Ali, he was very uneasy all the night, and considering that it would not be possible for him to live longer with a brother who treated him with so much haughtiness, he provided a good mule, furnished himself with money, jewels, provisions and victuals; and having told his people that he was going on a private journey for two or three days, he departed.

When he was out of Cairo, he rode by the desert towards Arabia; but his mule happening to tire by the way, he was forced to continue his journey on foot. A courier that was going to Balsora, by good fortune overtaking him, took him up behind him. As soon as the courier came to Balsora, Noureddin Ali alighted, and returned him thanks for his kindness: As he went about to seek for a lodging, he saw a person of quality with a great retinue coming along, to whom all the people shewed a mighty respect, and stood still till he passed by, and Noureddin Ali stopped among the rest. This was the grand visier to the sultan of Balsora, who walked through the city to see that the inhabitants kept good order and discipline.

This minister casting his eye by chance on Noureddin Ali, found something extraordinary in his aspect, looked very attentively upon him, and as he came near him, and saw him in a traveller's habit, he stood still, asked him who he was, and from whence he came? Sir, said Noureddin Ali, I am an Egyptian, born at Cairo, and have left my country, because of the unkindness of a near relation, and am resolved to travel through the world, and rather to die than return home again. The grand visier, who was a reverend old gentleman, after hearing those words, says to him, Son, beware, do not pursue your design, there is nothing but misery in the world, you are not sensible of the hardships you must endure; come follow me, I may perhaps make you forget the thing that has forced you to leave your own country.

Noureddin Ali followed the grand visier, who soon perceived his good qualities, and fell so much in love with him, that one day he says to him in private, My son, I am, as you see, so far gone in years, that there is no likelihood I shall live much longer. Heaven has bestowed only one daughter upon me, who is as beautiful as you are handsome, and now fit for marriage. Several people of the greatest quality at this court have desired her for their sons, but I could not grant their request. I have a love for you, and think you so worthy to be received into my family, that, preferring you before all those that have sought her, I am ready to accept you for my son-in-law. If you like the proposal, I will acquaint the sultan my master that I have adopted you by this marriage, and I will pray him to grant you the reversion of my dignity of grand visier in the kingdom of Balsora. In the mean time, nothing being more requisite for me than ease in my old age, I will not only put you in possession of my estate, but leave the administration of public affairs to your management.

When the grand visier had made an end of this kind and generous proposal, Noureddin Ali fell at his feet, and expressing himself in terms that demonstrated his joy and gratitude, told the visier, that he was at his command in every thing. Upon this, the visier sent for his chief domestics, ordered them to furnish the great hall of his palace, and prepare a great feast; he afterwards sent to invite the nobility of the court and city to honour him with their company, and when they were all met, (Noureddin Ali having now told him who he was) he said to those lords, for he thought it proper to speak thus, on purpose to satisfy such of them to whom he had refused his alliance; I am now, my lords, to discover a thing to you, which hitherto I have kept secret. I have a brother, who is grand visier to the sultan of Egypt, as I am to the sultan of this kingdom. This brother has but one son, whom he would not marry in the court of Egypt, but sent him hither to marry my daughter, that both our branches may be re-united. His son, whom I knew to be my nephew as soon as I saw him, is this young gentleman I here present to you, and is to be my son-in-law. I hope you will do me the honour to be present at his wedding, which I am resolved to celebrate this day. The noblemen, who could not take it ill that he preferred his nephew before all the great matches that had been proposed to him, said, That he had very good reason for what he did, were willing to be witnesses to the ceremony, and wished that God might prolong his days to enjoy the satisfaction of the happy match.

The lords met at the visier of Balsora's house, having testified their satisfaction at the marriage of his daughter with Noureddin Ali, sat down to dinner, which lasted a long while; and the latter course was sweet-meats, of which every one, according to custom, took what they thought fit. The notaries came in with the marriage-contract, the chief lords signed it, and when the company departed, the grand visier ordered his servants to prepare a bagnio, and have every thing in readiness for Noureddin Ali to bathe. He had fine new linen, and every thing else provided for him in the most curious manner. When he had washed and dried himself, he was going to put on his former apparel, but had an extraordinary rich suit brought him. Being dressed and perfumed with the most odoriferous essence, he went to see the grand visier, his father-in-law, who was exceedingly well pleased with his genteel mien; and having made him sit down, My son, said he, you have declared unto me who you are, and the quality you had at the court of Egypt. You have also told me of a difference betwixt you and your brother, which occasioned you to leave your country. I desire you to make me your entire confidant, and to acquaint me with the cause of your quarrel; for now you have no reason either to doubt me, or to conceal any thing from me.

Noureddin Ali gave him an account of every circumstance of the quarrel; at which the visier burst out into a fit of laughter, and said, This is one of the oddest things that I ever heard: Is it possible, my son, that your quarrel should rise so high about an imaginary marriage? I am sorry you fell out with your elder brother upon such a frivolous matter; but I find he is in the wrong to be angry at what you only spoke in jest, and I ought to thank heaven for that difference which has procured me such a son-in-law. But, said the old gentleman, it is late, and time for you to retire; go to your bride, my son, she expects you: To-morrow I will present you to the sultan, and hope he will receive you in such a manner as shall satisfy us both.

Noureddin Ali took leave of his father-in-law, and went to his spouse's apartment. It is remarkable, continued Giafar, that Schemseddin Mohammed happened also to marry at Cairo the very same day that this marriage was solemnized at Balsora, the particulars of which are as follow.

After Noureddin Ali left Cairo, with an intention never to return, Schemseddin Mohammed, his elder brother, who was gone a-hunting with the sultan of Egypt, did not come back in a month: for the sultan loved that game extremely, and therefore continued the sport all that while. Schemseddin, at his return, ran to Noureddin Ali's apartment, but was much surprised when he understood, that, under pretence of taking a journey for two or three days, he went away on a mule the same day that the sultan went a-hunting, and never appeared since.

It vexed him so much the more, because he did not doubt but the hard words he had given him was the cause of his going away. He sent a messenger in search of him, who went to Damascus, and as far as Aleppo, but Noureddin was then at Balsora. When the courier returned, and brought word that he heard no news of him, Schemseddin Mohammed intended to make further inquiry after him in other parts, and in the mean time had a fancy to marry, and matched with the daughter of one of the greatest lords in Cairo, upon the same day his brother married the daughter of the grand visier of Balsora.

But this is not all, said Giafar; at the end of nine months, Schemseddin Mohammed's wife was brought to bed of a daughter at Cairo, and on the same day Noureddin's wife brought forth a son at Balsora, who was called Bedreddin Hassan.

The grand visier of Balsora testified his joy by great gifts and public entertainments for the birth of his grandson. And to show his son-in-law the great esteem he had for him, he went to the palace, and most humbly begged of the sultan to grant Noureddin Ali his office, that he might have the comfort before his death to see his son-in-law made grand visier in his stead.

The sultan, who had taken a great liking to Noureddin, when his father presented him after his marriage, and had ever since heard every body speak well of him, readily granted his father-in-law's request, and caused Noureddin immediately to put on the robe of a grand visier.

The next day, when the father saw his son-in-law preside in council, as he himself had done, and perform all the offices of a grand visier, his joy was complete. Noureddin Ali behaved himself so well in every thing, that one would have thought he had been all his lifetime employed in such affairs. He continued afterwards to assist in council every time, when the infirmities of age would not permit his father-in-law to appear.

The old gentleman died about four years after, with great satisfaction, to see a branch of his family that promised so fair to support the grandeur of it.

Noureddin Ali performed the last duty to him with all possible love and gratitude. And as soon as his son Bedreddin Hassan had attained to seven years of age, he provided him a most excellent tutor, who taught him such as became his birth. The child had a ready wit, and a genius capable of receiving all the good instructions that could be given.

After Bedreddin Hassan had been two years under the tuition of his master, who taught him perfectly to read, he learned the Alcoran by heart. His father Noureddin Ali put him afterwards to other tutors, by whom his mind was cultivated to such a degree, that when he was twelve years of age he had no more occasion for them. And then, as his physiognomy promised wonders, he was admired by all that looked upon him.

Hitherto Noureddin Ali had kept him to his study, and had not yet brought him into public; but now he carried him to the palace, on purpose to have the honour of kissing the sultan's hand, who received him very graciously. The people that saw him in the streets were charmed with his genteel mien, and gave him a thousand blessings.

His father proposing to make him capable of supplying his place, spared no cost for that end, and brought him up to business of the greatest moment, on purpose to qualify him betimes. In short he omitted nothing to advance a son he loved so well. But as he began to enjoy the fruits of his labour, he was all of a sudden taken with a violent fit of sickness; and finding himself past recovery, disposed himself to die like a good mussulman.

In that last and precious moment, he forgot not his son Bedreddin, but called for him, and said, My son, you see this world is transitory, there is nothing durable, but that which I shall speedily go to. You must, therefore, from henceforth, begin to fit yourself for this change, as I have done; you must prepare for it without murmuring, and so as to have no trouble of conscience for not acting the part of a real honest man. As for your religion, you are sufficiently instructed in it, by what you have learned from your tutors, and your own study; and as to what belongs to an honest man, I shall give you some instructions, which I hope you will make good use of. As it is a necessary thing to know one's self, and that you cannot come to that knowledge without you first understand who I am, I shall now tell it you.

I am (says he) a native of Egypt; my father, your grandfather, was first minister to the sultan of that kingdom. I myself had the honour to be visier to the same sultan, and so has my brother, your uncle, who I suppose is yet alive; his name is Schemseddin Mohammed. I was obliged to leave him, and come into this country, where I have raised myself to the high dignity I now enjoy. But you will understand all those matters more fully by a manuscript that I shall give you.

At the same time Noureddin Ali pulled out his pocket-book, which he had written with his own hand, and carried always about him, and giving it to Bedreddin Hassan, Take it (said he) and read it at your leisure; you will find, among other things, the day of my marriage, and that of your birth: these are such circumstances, as perhaps you may hereafter have occasion to know, therefore you must keep it very carefully.

Bedreddin Hassan being most afflicted to see his father in that condition, and sensibly touched with this discourse, could not but weep when he received the pocket-book, and promised, at the same time, never to part with it.

That very moment, Noureddin Ali fainted, so that it was thought he would have expired; but he came to himself again, and uttered these words:

My son, says he, the first instruction I give you, is, not to make yourself familiar with all sorts of people. The way to live happy is to keep your mind to yourself, and not tell your thoughts easily.

Secondly, Not to do violence to any body whatever; for in that case you will draw every body's hatred upon you. You ought to consider the world is a creditor, to whom you owe moderation, compassion, and forbearance.

Thirdly, Not to say a word when you are reproached; for, as the proverb says, He that keeps silence, is out of danger. And in this case particularly you ought to practise it; you also know what one of our poets says upon this subject, That silence is the ornament and safeguard of life; that our speech ought not to be like a storm of rain that spoils all: Never did any man yet repent of having spoke too little, whereas many have been sorry that they spoke too much.

Fourthly, To drink no wine, for that is the source of all vices.

Fifthly, To be frugal in your way of living; if you do not squander your estate away, it will maintain you in time of necessity. I do not mean you should be either too liberal or too niggardly; for though you have never so little, if you husband it well, and lay it out on proper occasions, you shall have many friends; but if, on the contrary, you have great riches, and make but a bad use of them, all the world will forsake you, and leave you to yourself.

In short, Noureddin Ali continued till the last moment of his breath to give good advice to his son; and when he was dead he was magnificently interred.

Bedreddin Hassan of Balsora, for so he was called, because born in that town, was so overwhelmed with grief for the death of his father, that, instead of a month's time to mourn, according to custom, he kept himself close shut up in tears and solitude about two months, without seeing any body, or so much as going abroad to pay his duty to the sultan of Balsora; who, being displeased at this neglect, looked upon it as a slight put upon his court and person, suffered his passion to prevail, and, in his fury, called for the new grand visier, (for he had created a new one as soon as Noureddin Ali died) commanded him to go to the house of the deceased, and seize upon it, with all his other houses, lands, and effects, without leaving any thing for Bedreddin Hassan, and to bring him prisoner along with him.

The new grand visier, accompanied with a great many messengers belonging to the palace, justices, and other officers, went immediately to execute his commission; but one of Bedreddin Hassan's slaves happening accidentally to come into the crowd, no sooner understood the visier's errand, but he ran before in all haste to give his master warning. He found him sitting in the porch of his house, as melancholy as if his father had but newly been dead. He fell down at his feet, out of breath, and after he had kissed the hem of his garment, cried out, My lord, save yourself immediately. Bedreddin Hassan, lifting up his head, asked, What is the matter, what news dost thou bring? My lord, said he, there is no time to be lost; the sultan is horribly incensed against you, and has sent people to take all you have, and also to seize your person.

The words of this faithful and affectionate slave put Bedreddin Hassan into great confusion; May not I have so much time, said he, as to take some money and jewels along with me? No, sir, replied the slave, the grand visier will be here this moment. Begone immediately, save yourself. Bedreddin Hassan rose up from his sofa in all haste, put his feet in his sandals, and after he had covered his head with the tail of his gown, that his face might not be known, he fled, without knowing what way to go, to avoid the impending danger.

The first thought that came in his head, was to get out of the next gate with all speed. He ran without stopping till he came to the public churchyard, and since it was growing dark, he resolved to pass that night on his father's tomb. It was a large edifice, in form of a dome, which Noureddin Ali built when he was alive. Bedreddin met a very rich Jew by the way, who was a banker and merchant, and was returning from a place where his affairs had called him, to the city.

The Jew, knowing Bedreddin, halted, and saluted him very courteously.

The caliph was very attentive to the grand visier's discourse, who went on after this manner. Isaac the Jew, after he had paid his respects to Bedreddin Hassan, by kissing his hand, says, My lord, dare I be so bold as to ask whither you are going at this time of night all alone, and so much troubled? Has any thing disquieted you? Yes, said Bedreddin, a while ago I was asleep, and my father appeared to me in a dream, looking very fiercely upon me, as if he were extraordinary angry: I started out of my sleep very much frightened, and came out immediately to go and pray upon his tomb.

My lord, said the Jew, (who did not know the true reason why Bedreddin left the town) your father of happy memory, and my good lord, had store of merchandise, in several vessels, which are yet at sea, and belong to you; I beg the favour of you to grant me the first refusal of them before any other merchant. I am able to lay down ready money for all the goods that are in your ships: And to begin, if you will give me those that happen to come in the first ship that arrives in safety, I will pay you down in part of payment, a thousand sequins. And drawing out a bag from under his gown, he showed it him sealed up with one seal.

Bedreddin Hassan being banished from home, and dispossessed of all that he had in the world, looked upon this proposal of the Jew as a favour from heaven, and therefore accepted it with a great deal of joy.—My lord, said the Jew, then you sell unto me for a thousand sequins, the lading of the first of your ships that shall arrive in port. Yes, answered Bedreddin, I sell it to you for a thousand sequins; it is done. Upon this the Jew delivered him the bag of a thousand sequins, and offered to count them; but Bedreddin Hassan saved him the trouble, and said, he would trust his word. Since it is so, my lord, said he, be pleased to favour me with a small note in writing of the bargain we have made. And having said this, he pulled his ink-horn from his girdle, and taking a small reed out of it, neatly cut for writing, he presented it to him, with a piece of paper he took out of his letter-case; and whilst he held the ink-horn, Bedreddin Hassan wrote these words:

This writing is to testify, that Bedreddin Hassan of Balsora has sold to Isaac the Jew, for the sum of one thousand sequins, received in hand, the lading of the first of his ships that shall arrive in this port.

BEDREDDIN HASSAN *of Balsora.*

This note he delivered to the Jew, who put it in his letter-case, and then took his leave of him.

While Isaac pursued his journey to the city, Bedreddin made the best of his way to his father Noureddin Ali's tomb. When he came to it, he bowed his face to the ground, and, with his eyes full of tears, deplored his miserable condition. Alas! said he, unfortunate Bedreddin, what will become of thee? Whither canst thou fly for refuge against the unjust prince that persecutes thee? Was it not enough to be afflicted for the death of so dear a father? Must fortune needs add new misfortunes to just complaints? He continued a long time in this posture; but at last rose up again, and leaning his head upon his father's sepulchre, his sorrows returned more violently than before; so that he sighed and mourned, till, overcome with heaviness, he stretched himself all along upon the floor, and fell asleep.

He had not slept long, till a genie, who had retired to that church-yard during the day, and was intending, according to custom, to range about the world at night, espying this young man in Noureddin Ali's tomb, he entered, and finding Bedreddin lying on his back, was surprised at his beauty.

When the genie had attentively considered Bedreddin Hassan, he said to himself, To judge of this creature by his good mien, he would seem to be an angel of the terrestrial paradise, whom God has sent to put the world in a flame with his beauty. At last, after he had satisfied himself with looking upon him, he took a flight into the air, where, meeting by chance with a fairy, they saluted one another; after which he said to her, Pray descend with me into the church-yard, where I stay, and I will show you a prodigious beauty, which is worthy your admiration as well as mine. The fairy consented, and both descended in an instant; they came into the tomb, Look ye, said the genie to the fairy, showing her Bedreddin Hassan, Did you ever see a young man of a better shape, and more beautiful than this?

The fairy, having attentively observed Bedreddin, returned to the genie; I must confess, said she, he is a very handsome man, but I just now came from seeing an object at Cairo more admirable than this; and if you will hear me, I will tell you a strange story concerning her. You will very much oblige me in so doing, answered the genie. You must know then, said the fairy, (for I will tell you it at length,) that the sultan of Egypt has a visier called Schemseddin Mohammed, who has a daughter of about twenty years of age, the most beautiful and complete person that ever was known. The sultan having heard of this young lady's beauty, sent the other day for her father, and told him, I understand you have a daughter to marry; I have a mind to marry her: Will not you consent to it? The visier, who did not expect this proposal, was troubled at it; and instead of accepting it joyfully, which another in his place would certainly have done, he answered the sultan; May it please your majesty, I am not worthy of the honour you confer upon me, and I most humbly beseech you to pardon me, if I do not agree to your request. You know I had a brother, called Noureddin Ali, who had the honour, as well as myself, to be one of your visiers: We had some difference together, which was the cause of his leaving me on a sudden, and since that time I have had no account of him till within these four days, that I heard he died at Balsora, being grand visier to the sultan of that kingdom.

He has left a son behind him; and there having been an agreement between us to match our children together, if ever we had any, I am persuaded he intended the match when he died; and being desirous to fulfil the promise on my part, I conjure your majesty to grant me leave: You have in your court many other lords, who have daughters as well as I, on whom you may be pleased to bestow that honour.

The sultan of Egypt, provoked at this bold denial of Schemseddin Mohammed, says to him in a passion which he could not restrain, Is this the way you requite my proposal to stoop so low as to desire your alliance? I know how to revenge your daring to prefer another to me, and I swear that your daughter shall be married to the most contemptible and ugly of all my slaves. And having spoke those words, he angrily bid the visier be gone; who went home to his house full of confusion, and extraordinary sad.

This very day the sultan sent for one of his grooms who was humpbacked, big-bellied, crook-legged, and as ugly as a hobgoblin; and after having commanded Schemseddin Mohammed to consent to marry his daughter to this ghastly slave, he caused the contract to be made out and signed by witnesses, in his own presence. The preparations for this fantastical wedding are all ready, and this very moment all the slaves belonging to the lords of the court of Egypt, are waiting at the door of a bagnio, each with a flambeau in his hand, for the crook-backed groom, who is bathing himself, to go along with them to his bride, who is already dressed to receive him; and when I departed from Cairo, the ladies, met for that purpose, were going to conduct her in all her nuptial attire to the hall, where she is to receive her hump-backed bridegroom, and is this minute now expecting him: I have seen her, and do assure you, that no person can look upon her without admiration.

When the fairy left off speaking, the genie says to her, Whatever you think or say, I cannot be persuaded that the girl's beauty exceeds that of this young man. I will not dispute it with you, answered the fairy, for I must confess he deserves to be married to that charming creature, whom they design for hump-back. And I think it were a deed worthy of us, to obstruct the sultan of Egypt's injustice, and put this young gentleman in the room of the slave. You are in the right, answered the genie; I am extremely obliged to you for so good a thought; let us deceive him. I consent to your revenge upon the sultan of Egypt; let us comfort a distressed father, and make his daughter as happy as she thinks herself miserable; I will do my utmost endeavour to make this project take, and I am persuaded you will not be backward; I will be at the pains to carry him to Cairo before he awake, and afterwards leave it to your care to carry him elsewhere, when we have accomplished our design.

The fairy and the genie having thus concerted what they had to do, the genie lifted up Bedreddin Hassan gently, and with an inconceivable swiftness carried him through the air, and set him down at the door of a public house next to the bagnio, whence hump-back was to come with the train of slaves that waited for him. Bedreddin Hassan awaked that very moment, and was mightily surprised to find himself in the middle of a city he knew not: He was going to cry out, and to ask where he was, but the genie touched him gently on the shoulder, and forbid him to speak a word. Then he put a torch in his hand, and bid him, Go and mix with the crowd at the bagnio door, and follow them till you come into a hall, where they are going to celebrate a marriage. The bridegroom is a hump-backed fellow, and by that you will easily know him. Put yourself at the right hand as you go in, and then immediately open the purse of sequins you have in your bosom, and distribute among the musicians and dancers as they go along; and when you are got into the hall, give money also to the female slaves you see about the bride, when they come near you; but every time you put your hand in the purse, be sure you take out a whole handful, and do not spare them. Observe to do every thing exactly as I have told you, with great presence of mind; be not afraid of any person or thing, and leave the rest to a superior power, who will order matters as he thinks fit.

Young Bedreddin being well instructed in all that he was to do, advanced towards the door of the bagnio; the first thing he did was to light his torch, as that of a slave; and then mixing among them as if he belonged to some nobleman of Cairo, he marched along as they did, and followed hump-back, who came out of the bagnio, and mounted a horse out of the sultan's own stable.

Bedreddin Hassan coming near to the musicians, and the men and women dancers, who went just before the bridegroom, pulled out, time after time, whole handfuls of sequins, which he distributed among them: And as he thus gave his money with an unparalleled grace, and engaging mein, all those that received it cast their eyes upon him; and, after they had a full view of his face, they found him so handsome and comely, that they could not look off again.

At last they came to Schemseddin Mohammed's gate, who was Bedreddin Hassan's uncle, and little thought his nephew was so near. The door-keepers, to prevent any disorder, kept back all the slaves that carried torches, and would not let them come in. Bedreddin was likewise refused; but the musicians, who had free entrance, stood still, and protested that they would not go in if they hindered him to go along with them; He is not one of the slaves, said they, look upon him, and you will soon be satisfied as to that; he is certainly a young stranger, who is curious to see the ceremonies observed at weddings in this city: And saying this, they put him in the midst of them, and carried him in, whether the porters would or no; they took his torch out of his hand, and gave it the first they met. Having brought him into the hall, they placed him at the right hand of the hump-backed bridegroom, who sat near the visier's daughter, on a throne richly adorned.

She appeared very lovely in all her dresses, but in her face there was nothing to be seen but vexation and mortal grief. The cause of this was easy to be guessed at, when she had by her a bridegroom so very deformed and so unworthy of her love. The throne of that ill-matched couple was in the midst of a sofa. The ladies of the emirs, visiers, and those of the sultan's bed-chamber, and several other ladies of the court and city, were placed on each side, a little lower, every one according to their quality, and all of them so fine and richly dressed, that it was one of the pleasantest sights that could be seen, each of them holding a large wax taper in their hand.

When they saw Bedreddin Hassan come into the room, they all fixed their eyes upon him, and admiring his shape and behaviour, and the beauty of his face, they could not forbear looking at him. When he was set down, every one left their seats, and came near to him, to have a full view of his face, and almost all of them, as they turned to their seats, found themselves moved with tender passion.

The disparity between Bedreddin Hassan, and the hump-backed groom, who made such a horrible figure, occasioned a great murmuring among the company, insomuch that the ladies cried out, We must give our bride to this handsome young gentleman, and not to this ugly hump-back.—Nor did they rest here, but uttered imprecations against the sultan, who, abusing his absolute power, would unite ugliness and beauty together. They did also upbraid the bridegroom, so as they put him out of countenance, to the great satisfaction of the spectators, whose shouts for some time put a stop to the concert of music in the hall. At last the musicians began again, and the women who dressed the bride came all about her.

Each time that the new bride changed her habit, she rose up from her seat, followed by her bride women, and passed by hump-back without giving him one look, and went towards Bedreddin Hassan, before whom she presented herself in her new attire. On this occasion, Bedreddin, according to the instructions given him by the genie, failed not to put his hand in his purse, and pulled out handfuls of sequins, which he distributed among the women that followed the bride: nor did he forget the players and dancers, but also threw money to them. It was pleasant to see how they pushed one another to gather it up. They showed themselves very thankful, and made him signs that the young bride should be for him, and not for the hump-backed fellow. The women that attended her, told her the same thing, and did not value whether the groom heard them or not; for they put a thousand tricks upon him, which very much pleased the spectators.

When the ceremony of changing habits was passed, the music ceased, and went away, but made a sign to Bedreddin Hassan to stay behind. The ladies did the same, and went all home, but those that belonged to the house. The bride went into a closet, whither her women followed to undress her, and none remained in the hall but the hump-backed groom, Bedreddin Hassan, and some of the domestics.

Hump-back, who was furiously mad at Bedreddin, suspecting him to be his rival, gave him a cross look, and said, And thou, what dost thou wait for? Why art not thou gone as well as the rest? Begone. Bedreddin having no pretence to stay, withdrew, not knowing what to do with himself. But he was not gone out of the porch, when the genie and fairy met and stopped him. Whither are you going? said the fairy, Stay, for Hump-back is not in the hall, he is gone out about some business; you have nothing to do but return, and introduce yourself into the bride's chamber: As soon as you are alone with her, tell her boldly, that you are her husband; that the sultan's intention was only to make sport with the groom; and, to make this pretended bridegroom some amends, you had caused to be prepared for him, in the stable, a good dish of cream: And then tell her all the fine things you can think on to persuade her; for being so handsome as you are, little persuasion will do: she will think herself happy in being deceived so agreeably. In the mean time we will take care that the hump-back shall not return, and let nothing hinder you to pass the night with your bride, for she is yours and none of his.

While the fairy thus encouraged Bedreddin, and instructed him how he should behave himself, hump-back was really gone out of the room; for the genie went to him in the shape of a great cat, mewing at a most fearful rate: The fellow called to the cat, and clapped his hands to make her flee; but instead of that, the cat stood upon her hinder feet, staring with her eyes like fire, looking fiercely at him, mewing louder than she did at first, and growing bigger, till she was as large as an ass. At this sight, hump-back would have cried out for help, but his fear was so great, that he stood gaping, and could not utter one word; and that he might have no time to recover, the genie changed himself immediately into a large buffalo, and in this shape called to him with a loud voice that redoubled his fear, Thou hump-backed villain! At these words the affrighted groom cast himself on the ground, and covering his face with his gown, that he might not see this dreadful beast: Sovereign prince of buffaloes, said he, what is it you want with me? Woe be to thee, replies the genie, hast thou the boldness to venture to marry my mistress? O my lord, said hump-back, I pray you to pardon me; if I am guilty, it is through ignorance. I did not know that this lady had a buffalo to her sweetheart; command me in any thing you please, I give you my oath that I am ready to obey you. By death, replied the genie, if thou goest out from hence, or speakest a word till the sun rises, I will crush thy head to pieces; but then I give thee leave to go from hence: I warn thee to make dispatch, and not to look back; but if thou hast the impudence to return, it shall cost thee thy life. When the genie had done speaking, he transformed himself into the shape of a man, took hump-back by the legs, and after having set him against the wall with his head downwards, If thou stir, said he, before the sun rise, as I have told thee already, I will take thee by the heels again, and dash thy head in a thousand pieces against the wall.

To return to Bedreddin Hassan, who being prompted by the genie and the presence of the fairy, he got into the hall again, from whence he slipt into the bride-chamber, where he sat down, expecting the success of his adventure. After a while, the bride arrived, conducted by an old matron, who came no farther than the door, exhorting the bridegroom to do his duty like a man, without looking in to see if it was hump-back or another; and then locked the door and retired.

The young bride was mightily surprised, instead of hump-back to find Bedreddin Hassan, who came up to her with the best grace in the world.

What! my dear friend, said she, by your being here at this time of night, you must be my husband's comrade? No, madam, (said Bedreddin,) I am of another sort of quality than that ugly hump-back. But, said she, you do not consider that you speak degradingly of my husband. He! your husband, madam, replies he, can you retain those thoughts so long? Be convinced of your mistake, madam, for so much beauty must never be sacrificed to the most contemptible of all mankind: It is I, madam, that am the happy mortal for whom it is reserved. The sultan had a mind to make himself merry, by putting this trick upon the visier, your father; but he chose me to be your real husband. You might have observed how the ladies, the musicians, the dancers, your women, and all the servants of your family, were pleased with this comedy. We have sent that hump-backed fellow to his stable again, where he is just now eating a dish of cream. And you may rest assured that he will never appear any more before your eyes.

At this discourse the visier's daughter, who was more like one dead than alive when she came into the bride-chamber, put on a gay air, which made her so handsome, that Bedreddin was perfectly charmed with her.

I did not expect, said she, to meet with so pleasing a surprise; and I had condemned myself to live unhappy all my days; but my good fortune is so much the greater, that I possess in you a man that is worthy of my tenderest affection.

Having spoke thus, she undressed herself, and stepped into bed. Bedreddin Hassan, overjoyed to see himself possessor of so many charms, made haste to follow her, and laid his cloaths upon a chair, with a bag that he got from the Jew, which, notwithstanding all the money he had pulled out, was still full.—He likewise laid off his turban, and put on a night-cap that had been ordained for hump-back, and so went to bed in his shirt and drawers.[1] His drawers were of blue sattin, tied with a lace of gold.

Whilst the two lovers were asleep, the genie, who had met again with the fairy, says to her, That it was high time to finish what was begun, and so successfully carried on hitherto; then let us not be overtaken by day-light, which will soon appear; go you and bring off the young man again without awaking him.

The fairy went into the bed-chamber, where the two lovers were fast asleep, and took up Bedreddin Hassan just as he was, that is to say, in his shirt and drawers; and, in company with the genie, with a wonderful swiftness, flew away with him to the gates of Damascus in Syria, where they arrived just at the time when the officers of the mosques, appointed for that end, were calling the people to come to prayers at break of day. The fairy

[1] All the eastern nations lie in their drawers, but this circumstance will stand him in stead in the sequel of the story.

laid Bedreddin Hassan softly on the ground, and leaving him close by the gate, departed with the genie.

The gate of the city being opened, and a great many people assembled to get out, they were mightily surprised to see Bedreddin Hassan lying in his shirt and drawers upon the ground. One said, he has been so hard put to it to get away from his mistress, that he could not get time to put on his cloaths. Look ye, says another, how people expose themselves; sure enough he has spent the most part of the night in drinking with his friends, till he has got drunk, and then, perhaps, having occassion to go out, instead of returning, is come this length, and not having his senses about him, was overtaken with sleep.—Others were of another opinion; but no body could guess what had been the occasion of his coming thither.

A small puff of wind happening to blow at the same time, uncovered his breast, that was whiter than snow. Every one being struck with admiration at the fineness of his complexion, they spoke so loud that it awaked the young man.

His surprise was as great as theirs, when he found himself at the gate of a city where he had never been before, and encompassed by a crowd of people gazing at him. Gentlemen, said he, for God's sake tell me where I am, and what you would have of me? One of the crowd spoke to him, saying, Young man, the gates of the city were just now opened, and as we came out, we found you lying here in this condition, and stood still to look on you: Have you lain here all night? And do not you know that you are at one of the gates of Damascus? At one of the gates of Damascus! answered Bedreddin; sure you mock me: When I lay down last night I was at Cairo. When he said these words, some of the people, moved with compassion for him, said, it is a pity such a handsome young man should have lost his senses; and so went away.

My son, says an old gentleman to him, you know not what you say: How is it possible that you, being this morning at Damascus, could be last night at Cairo? It is true, for all that, said Bedreddin; for I swear to you, that I was all day yesterday at Balsora. He had no sooner said these words, but all the people fell into a fit of laughter, and cried out, He is a fool, he is a madman. There were some, however, that pitied him because of his youth; and one among the company said to him, My son, you must certainly be crazed, you do not consider what you say: Is it possible that a man could yesterday be at Balsora, the same night at Cairo, and next morning at Damascus? Sure you are asleep still; come rouse up your spirits. What I say, answered Bedreddin Hassan, is so true, that last night I was married in the city of Cairo. All those that laughed before, could not forbear laughing again, when he said so: Call yourself to mind, says the same person that spoke before, you have sure enough dreamed all this, and that fancy still possesses your brain. I am sensible of what I say, answered the young man: Pray can you tell me how it was possible for me to go in a dream to Cairo, where I am very certain I was in person, and where my bride was seven times brought before me, each time dressed in a different habit, and where I saw an ugly hump-backed fellow to whom they intended to give her? Besides, I want to know what is become of my gown, my turban, and the bag of sequins I had at Cairo.

Though he assured them that all these things were matter of fact, yet they could not forbear to laugh at him, which put him into such a confusion, that he knew not well what to think of all those adventures.

After Bedreddin Hassan had confidently affirmed all that he said to be true, he rose up to go into the town, and every one that followed him, called out, A madman, a fool! Upon this, some looked out at their windows, some came to their doors, and others joined with those that were about him, calling out as they did, A madman; but not knowing for what. In this perplexity of mind, the young gentleman happened to come before a pastry-cook's shop, and went into it to avoid the rabble.

This pastry-cook had formerly been captain to a troop of Arabian robbers who plundered the caravans; and though he was become a citizen of Damascus, where he behaved himself to every one's content, yet he was dreaded by all those who knew him; wherefore, as soon as he came out to the rabble that followed Bedreddin, they dispersed.

The pastry-cook seeing them all gone, asked him what he was, and who brought him thither? Bedreddin Hassan told him all, not concealing his birth, nor the death of his father the grand visier: He afterwards gave him an account why he left Balsora; how, after he fell asleep the night following upon his father's tomb, he found himself when he awaked, at Cairo, where he had married a lady; and at last, in what amazement he was, when he found himself at Damascus, without being able to penetrate into all those wonderful adventures.

Your history is one of the most surprising (said the pastry-cook,) but if you will follow my advice, you shall let no man know those matters you have revealed to me, but patiently expect till heaven think fit to put an end to your misfortunes; you shall be free to stay with me till then; and since I have no children, I will own you for my son, if you consent to it; and after you are so adopted, you may freely walk up and down the city, without being exposed any more to the insults of the rabble.

Though this adoption was below the son of a grand visier, Bedreddin was glad to accept of the pastry-cook's proposals, judging it the best thing he could do, considering his then circumstances. The cook cloathed him, called for witnesses, and went before a notary, where he acknowledged him for his son. After this, Bedreddin staid with him by the name of Hassan, and learned the pastry trade.

Whilst this passed at Damascus, Schemseddin Mohammed's daughter awaked, and finding Bedreddin gone out of bed, supposed he had arisen softly for fear of disturbing her, but he would soon return: As she was in expectation of him, her father, the visier, (who was mightily vexed at the affront put upon him by the sultan,) came and knocked at her chamber-door, with a resolution to bewail her sad destiny. He called her by her name, and she knowing him by his voice, immediately got up, and opened the door: She kissed his hand, and received him with so much satisfaction in her countenance as surprised the visier, who expected to find her drowned in tears, and as much grieved as himself: Unhappy wretch, said he in a passion, do you appear before me thus? after the hideous sacrifice you have just consummated, can you see me with so much satisfaction.

The new bride, seeing her father angry at her pleasant countenance, said to him, For God's sake, sir, do not reproach me wrongfully; it is not the hump-backed fellow, whom I abhor more than death; it is not that monster I have married; every body laughed him so to scorn, and put him so out of countenance, that he was forced to run away and hide himself, to make room for a charming young gentleman who is my real husband. What fable do you tell me, said Schemseddin Mohammed, roughly: What! did not crook-back lie with you to-night? No, sir, said she, it was that young gentleman I told you of, who has large eyes and black eye-brows. At these words, the visier lost all patience, and fell into a terrible passion; Ah, wicked woman, says he, you will make me distracted! It is you, father, said she, that puts me out of my senses by your incredulity. So it is not true, replies the visier, that hump-back—Let us talk no more of hump-back, said she; a curse upon hump-back, must I always have him cast in my dish. Father, said she, I tell you once more, that I did not bed with him, but with my dear spouse, who I believe is not very far off.

Schemseddin Mohammed went out to seek him; but, instead of seeing him, was mightily surprised to find hump-back with his head on the ground, and his heels uppermost, as the genie had set him against the wall. What is the meaning of this? said he, who placed you thus? Crook-back, knowing it to be the visier, answered, Alas! alas! it is you then that would marry me to the mistress of a buffalo, the sweetheart of an ugly genie; I will not be your fool, you shall not put a trick upon me.

Schemseddin Mohammed, when he heard hump-back speak thus, thought he was raving, and bid him move, and stand upon his legs. I will take care how I do that, said hump-back, unless the sun be risen: Know, sir, that when

I came hither last night, on a sudden a black cat appeared to me, and in an instant grew as big as a buffalo: I have not forgot what he said to me, therefore you may go about your business, and leave me here. The visier, instead of going away, took him by the heels, and made him get up. Then hump-back ran as fast as he could, without looking behind him, and coming to the palace, presented himself to the sultan, who laughed heartily when he told him the story how the genie had served him.

Schemseddin Mohammed returned to his daughter's chamber, more astonished than before. Well then, my abused daughter, said he, can you give me no farther light into this matter? Sir, said she, I can give you no other account than what I have done already. Here are my husband's cloaths which he left upon the chair; perhaps you may find somewhat there that may solve your doubt. Then she shewed him Bedreddin's turban, which he took and examined narrowly on all sides. I should take this to be a visier's turban, if it were not made after the Moussoul[1] fashion: but perceiving somewhat to be sewed between the stuff and the lining, he called for scissars, and, having unripped it, found the paper which Noureddin Ali gave Bedreddin his son as he was dying, and he put it on his turban for more security.

Schemseddin Mohammed having opened the paper, knew his brother Noureddin's hand, and found this superscription, For my son Bedreddin Hassan. Before he could make any reflections upon it, his daughter delivered him the bag that lay under his cloaths, which he likewise opened, and found it full of sequins; for, as I told you before, notwithstanding all the liberality of Bedreddin, it was still kept full by the genie and fairy. He read these following words upon a note in the bag, A thousand sequins belonging to Isaac the Jew. And these lines underneath, which the Jew wrote before he parted from Bedreddin Hassan, 'Delivered to Bedreddin Hassan, for the cargo of the first of those ships that formerly belonged to Noureddin Ali his father, of worthy memory, sold unto me upon its arrival in this place.' He had scarce read these words, when he gave a shout, and fainted away.

The visier Schemseddin Mohammed being recovered from his fit by help of his daughter, and the women she called to her assistance; Daughter (said he) do not frighten yourself at this accident, the reason of it is such as you can scarcely believe: Your bridegroom is your cousin, the son of Noureddin Ali: The thousand sequins in the bag puts me in mind of a quarrel I had with my dear brother: it is without doubt the dowry he gives you. God be praised for all things, and particularly for this miraculous adventure, which demonstrates his almighty power. Then looking again upon his brother's writing, he kissed it several times, shedding abundance of tears.

[1] The town of Moussoul is in Mesopotamia, built over-against old Nineveh.

He looked over the book from one end to the other, where he found the date of his brother's arrival at Balsora, of his marriage, and of the birth of Bedreddin Hassan; and when he compared the same with the day of his own marriage, and the birth of his daughter at Cairo, he admired how every thing did agree so exactly.

This happy discovery put him into such a transport of joy, that he took up the book, with the ticket of the bag, and shewed it to the sultan, who pardoned what was past, and was so much pleased with the relation of this adventure, that he caused it, with all its circumstances, to be put in writing for the use of posterity.

Meanwhile, the visier, Schemseddin Mohammed, could not comprehend the reason why his nephew did not appear: he expected him every moment, and was impatient to have him in his arms. After he had expected him seven days in vain, he searched for him through all Cairo, but could hear no news of him, which perplexed him very much. This is the strangest adventure, said he, that ever man met with. And not knowing what alteration might happen, he thought fit to draw up in writing, with his own hand, after what manner the wedding had been solemnized; how the hall and his daughter's bed-chamber were furnished, and other circumstances. He likewise made the turban, the bag, and the rest of Bedreddin's things, into a bundle, and locked them up.

After some days were past, the visier's daughter perceived herself with child, and was brought to bed of a son after nine months. A nurse was provided for the child, besides other women and slaves to wait upon him; and his grandfather called him Agib.[1]

When young Agib had attained the age of seven, the visier, instead of learning him to read at home, put him to school with a master who was in great esteem; and two slaves were ordered to wait upon him. Agib used to play with his school-fellows; and, as they were all inferior to him in quality, they shewed him great respect, according to the example of their master, who many times would pass by faults in him that he would not pass by in the rest. This complaisance spoiled Agib so, that he became proud and insolent, would have his play-fellows bear all of him, and would bear nothing from them, but be master every where; and if any one took the liberty to thwart him, he would call them a thousand names, and many times beat them.

In short, all the scholars were weary of his company, and complained of him to their master: He answered, that they must have patience. But when he saw that Agib still grew more and more insolent, and occasioned him a great deal of trouble, Children, said he to his scholars, I find Agib is a little insolent gentleman; I will show you a way how to mortify him, so as he shall never torment you any more; nay, I believe it will make him leave the school:

[1] This word in Arabic signifies wonderful.

When he comes again to-morrow, and that you have a mind to play together, set yourselves round him, and do one of you call out, Come let us play, but upon condition, that they who desire to play, shall tell his own name, and the names of his father and mother; and they who refuse it shall be esteemed bastards, and not suffered to play in our company.

Next day, when they were gathered together, they failed not to follow their master's instructions; they placed themselves round Agib, and one of them called out, Let us begin a play, but on condition, that he who cannot tell his own name, and that of his father and mother, shall not play at all. They all cried out, and so did Agib, we consent to it. Then he that spoke first, asked every one the question, and all fulfilled the condition, except Agib, who answered, My name is Agib; my mother is called the lady of beauty, and my father Schemseddin Mohammed, visier to the sultan.

At these words all the children cried out, Agib, What do you say? That is not the name of your father, but your grandfather. A curse on you, said he in a passion: What! dare you say that the visier Schemseddin Mohammed is not my father? No, no, cried they, with great laughter, he is but your grandfather, and you shall not play with us: Nay, we will take care how we come into your company. Having spoke thus, they all left him, scoffing him, and laughing among themselves, which mortified Agib so much, that he wept.

The schoolmaster, who was near, and heard all that passed, came just at the nick of time, and speaking to Agib, says, Agib, do not you know that the visier Schemseddin Mohammed is none of your father, but your grandfather, and the father of your mother, the lady of beauty? We know not the name of your father no more than you do: We only know that the sultan was going to marry your mother to one of his grooms, a hump-backed fellow, but a genie lay with her. This is hard upon you, and ought to teach you to treat your school-fellows with less haughtiness than you have done hitherto.

Little Agib being nettled at this, ran hastily out of the school, and went home crying. He came straight to his mother's chamber, who being alarmed to see him thus grieved, asked him the reason? He could not answer for tears, his grief was so great; and it was but now and then he could speak plain enough to repeat what had been said to him, and occasioned his sorrow.

When he came to himself, Mother (said he,) for the love of God, be pleased to tell me who is my father? My son, (said she) Schemseddin Mohammed, that every day makes so much of you, he is your father. You do not tell me truth, (said he,) he is your father, and none of mine. But whose son am I? At this question, the lady of beauty calling to mind her wedding night, which had been succeeded by a long widowhood, began to shed tears, repining bitterly at the loss of so lovely a husband as Bedreddin.

Whilst the lady of beauty and Agib were both weeping, in comes the visier, who demanded the reason of their sorrow? The lady told him the shame Agib had undergone at school, which did so much afflict the visier, that he joined his tears with theirs; and judging from this, that the misfortune that had happened to his daughter was the common discourse of the town, he was quite out of patience.

Being thus afflicted, he went to the sultan's palace, and falling prostrate at his feet, most humbly prayed him to give him leave to make a journey into the provinces of the Levant, and particularly to Balsora, in search of his nephew Bedreddin Hassan; for he could not bear any longer that the people of the city should believe a genie had got his daughter with child.

The sultan was much concerned at the visier's affliction, approved his resolution, and gave him leave to go: He caused a passport also to be wrote for him, praying, in the most obliging terms that could be, all kings and princes, in whose dominions the said Bedreddin might sojourn, to grant that the visier might bring him along with him.

Schemseddin Mohammed, not knowing how to express his thankfulness to the sultan for this favour, thought it his duty to fall down before him a second time, and the floods of tears he shed, gave him sufficient testimony of his gratitude: At last, having wished the sultan all manner of prosperity, he took his leave, and went home to his house, where he disposed every thing for his journey; and the preparations for it were carried on with so much diligence, that in four days after, he left the city, accompanied with his daughter, the lady of beauty, and his grandson Agib.

They travelled nineteen days without stopping any where; but on the twentieth, arriving in a very pleasant mead, at a small distance from the gate of Damascus, they stopped there, and pitched their tents upon the banks of a river that runs through the town, and gives a very agreeable prospect to its neighbourhood.

The visier Schemseddin Mohammed declared he would stay in that pleasant place two days, and pursue his journey on the third: In the mean time, he gave leave to his retinue to go to Damascus; and almost all of them made use of it: Some influenced by curiosity to see a city they had heard so much of; and others by the opportunity of vending there the Egyptian goods they had brought with them, or buying stuffs, and the rarities of the country. The beautiful lady, desiring her son Agib might share in the satisfaction of viewing that celebrated city, ordered the black eunuch, that acted in the quality of his governor, to conduct him thither, and take care he came to no harm.

Agib, in magnificent apparel, went along with the eunuch, who had a large cane in his hand. They had no sooner entered the city, than Agib, fair and glorious as the day, attracted the eyes of the people: Some got out of their houses to gain a nearer and narrower view of him; others put their heads out of the windows; and those who passed along the streets, were not satisfied in stopping to look upon him, but kept pace with him, to prolong the pleasure of the agreeable sight: In fine, there was nobody that did not admire him, and bequeath a thousand benedictions to the father and mother that had given being to so fine a child. By chance, the eunuch and he passed by the shop where Bedreddin Hassan was, and there the crowd was so great that they were forced to halt.

The pastry-cook that had adopted Bedreddin Hassan, had died some years before, and left him his shop and all his estate; so Bedreddin became master of the shop, and managed the pastry-trade so dexterously, that he gained great reputation in Damascus. Bedreddin seeing so great a crowd before his door, that were gazing so attentively upon Agib and the black eunuch, stepped out to see them himself.

Bedreddin Hassan having cast his eyes particularly upon Agib, presently found himself moved, he knew not how, nor for what: He was not struck, like the people, with the shining beauty of the boy, it was another cause, unknown to him, that gave rise to the trouble and commotion he was in: It was the spring and force of the blood that worked in this tender father, who, laying aside all business, made up to Agib, and, with an engaging air, said to him, My little lord, who has won my soul, be so kind as to come into my shop, and eat a bit of such fare as I have; that during that time I may have the pleasure of admiring you at my ease: These words he pronounced with such tenderness, that tears trickled from his eyes. Little Agib was moved when he saw it, and turning to the eunuch, This honest man (says he) has a face that pleases me; he speaks in such an affectionate manner, that I cannot avoid complying with what he asks: let us step into the house and taste his pastry. Ay, in my troth, (replied the slave), it would be a fine thing to see the son of a visier, like you, go into a pastry-shop to eat; do not you imagine that I will suffer any such thing. Alas! my little lord, (cried Bedreddin,) it is a flaming piece of cruelty to trust your conduct in the hands of a person that treats you so harshly. Then applying himself to the eunuch, My good friend, (continued he,) pray do not hinder this young lord to grant me the favour I ask; do not put that piece of mortification upon me; rather do me the honour to walk in along with him, and by so doing you will give the world to know, that, though your outside is brown like a chesnut, your inside is as white as his: Do you know (continued he) that I am master of the secret to make you white, instead of being black, as you are? This set the eunuch a laughing, and then he asked Bedreddin what that secret was? I will tell you, replied Bedreddin; and so he repeated some verses in praise of black eunuchs; implying, that it was by their ministry that the honour of princes, and of all great men, was insured. The eunuch was so charmed with these verses, that without farther hesitation he suffered Agib to go into the shop, and went in with him himself.

Bedreddin Hassan was overjoyed in having obtained what he had so passionately desired; and falling about the work he had thus discontinued, I was making, said he, cream-tarts,* and you must, with submission, eat of them: I am persuaded you will find them very good; for my own mother, who makes them incomparably well, taught me to make them, and the people send to buy them of me from all quarters of the town. This said, he took a cream-tart out of the oven, and after strewing upon it some pomegranate-kernels and sugar, set it before Agib, who found it very delicious. Another was served up to the eunuch, and he gave the same judgment.

While they were both eating, Bedreddin Hassan minded Agib very attentively, and after looking upon him again and again, it came into his mind, that, for any thing he knew, he might have such a son by his charming wife, from whom he had been so soon and so cruelly separated; and the very thought drew tears from his eyes. He was thinking to have put some questions to little Agib about his journey to Damascus; but the child had no time to gratify his curiosity, for that the eunuch, pressing him to return to his grandfather's tents, took him away as soon as he had done eating. Bedreddin Hassan, not contented with looking after him, shut up his shop immediately, and went after him.

The eunuch perceiving he followed them, was extremely surprised: You impertinent fellow you, said he, with an angry tone, What do you want? My dear friend, replied Bedreddin, do not you trouble yourself: I have a little business out of town, that is just come into my head, and I must needs go and look after it. However, this answer did not all appease the eunuch, who, turning to Agib, said, This is all along of you; I foresaw I should repent of my complaisance; you would needs go into the man's shop; it was not wisely done in me to give you leave. Perhaps, replied Agib, he has real business out of town, and the road is free to every body. While this passed, they kept walking together, without looking behind them, till they came near the visier's tents, upon which they turned, to see if Bedreddin followed them: Agib perceiving he was within two paces of him, reddened and whitened alternately, according to the divers motions that affected him: He was afraid the grand visier, his grandfather, should come to know he had been in the pastry-shop, and had eat there. In this dread, he took up a pretty big stone that lay at his foot, and throwing it at Bedreddin Hassan, hit him in the forehead, which gave him such a wound that his face was covered with blood: Then he took to his heels, and ran under the eunuch's tent. The eunuch gave Bedreddin to understand, he had no reason to complain of a mischance that he had merited and brought upon himself.

Bedreddin turned towards the city, staunching the blood of this wound with his apron, which he had not put off. I was a fool, said he within himself, for leaving my house, to take so much pains about this brat; for doubtless he would never have used me after this manner, if he had not thought I had some fatal design against him. When he got home, he had his wound dressed, and softened the sense of his mischance, by the reflections that there was an infinite number of people upon the earth that were yet more unfortunate than he.

Bedreddin kept on the pastry-trade at Damascus, and his uncle Schemseddin Mohammed went from thence three days after his arrival.—He went by way of Emaus, Hanah, and Halep; then crossed the Euphrates, and, after passing through Mardin, Moussoul, Sengier, Diarbeker, and several other towns, arrived at last at Balsora; and, immediately after his arrival, desired audience of the sultan, who was no sooner informed of Schemseddin's quality, than he gave him audience, received him very favourably, and asked him the occasion of his journey to Balsora. Sir, replied the visier Schemseddin Mohammed, I come to know what is become of the son of Noureddin Ali, my brother, who has had the honour to serve your majesty. Noureddin Ali, said the sultan has been dead a long while; as for his son, all I can tell you of him is, that he disappeared all on a sudden, about two months after his father's death, and nobody has seen him since, notwithstanding all the inquiry I ordered to be made: But his mother, who is daughter of one of my visiers, is still alive. Schemseddin Mohammed desired leave of the sultan to see her, and carry her to Egypt; and having obtained his request, without tarrying till the next day for the satisfaction of seeing her, inquired after her place of abode, and that very hour went to her house, accompanied with his daughter and grandson.

The widow of Noureddin Ali lived in the same place where her husband had lived. It was a fine stately house, adorned with marble pillars: But Schemseddin did not stop to view it. At his entry, he kissed the gate, and the piece of marble upon which his brother's name was written in letters of gold: He asked to speak with his sister-in-law, and was told by her servants that she was in a small edifice in the form of a dome, which they shewed to him, in the middle of a very spacious court. The matter was, this tender mother used to spend the greatest part of day and night in that room which she had built for a representation of the tomb of Bedreddin Hassan, whom she took to be dead after so long absence. At that very minute she was pouring tears over the thoughts of that dear child, and Schemseddin Mohammed entering, found her buried in the last affliction.

He made his compliment, and after beseeching her to suspend her tears and groans, gave her to know he had the honour to be her brother-in-law, and acquainted her with the reason of his journey from Cairo to Balsora.

Schemseddin Mohammed, after acquainting his sister-in-law with all that passed at Cairo on his daughter's wedding night, after informing her of the surprisal occassioned by the discovery of the paper sewed up in Bedreddin's turban, presented to her Agib and the beautiful lady.

The widow of Noureddin Ali, who had still continued sitting like a woman moped, and weaned from the affairs of this world, no sooner understood by his discourse that her dear son, whom she lamented so bitterly, might still be alive, than she arose, and with repeated hugs, embraced the beautiful lady and her grandchild Agib; and perceiving in the youth the features of Bedreddin, shed tears of a quite different stamp from what she had been so long accustomed to shed. She could not forbear kissing the youth, who, for his part, received her embraces with all the demonstrations of joy he was capable of. Madam, said Schemseddin Mohammed, it is time to wipe off your tears, and cease your groans; you must think of going along with us to Egypt: The sultan of Balsora gives me leave to carry you thither, and I do not doubt but you will agree to it: I am hopeful we shall at last find out your son, my nephew; and if that comes to pass, the history of him, of you, of my own daughter, and of my own adventures, will deserve to be committed to writing, and so transmitted to posterity.

The widow of Noureddin Ali heard this proposal with pleasure, and from that very minute ordered the preparations to be made for her departure. While that was a-doing, Schemseddin Mohammed desired a second audience; and after taking leave of the sultan, who used him with ample marks of respect, and gave him a considerable present for himself, and another of great value for the sultan of Egypt, set out from Balsora for the city of Damascus.

When he arrived in the neighbourhood of Damascus, he ordered his tents to be pitched without the gate at which he designed to enter the city, and gave out he would tarry there three days, to give his equipage rest, and buy up the curiosities he could meet with, and such as were worthy of being presented to the sultan of Egypt.

While he was employed in looking upon, and picking out, the finest stuffs that the principal merchants had brought to his tents, Agib begged the black eunuch, his governor, to carry him through the city, in order to see what he had not leisure to view as he passed before; and to know what was become of the pastry-cook that he had wounded with a stone. The eunuch complying with his request, went along with him towards the city, after leave obtained of the beautiful lady, his mother.

They entered Damascus by the paradise gate, which lay next to the tents of the visier Schemseddin Mohammed. They walked through the great squares and the public places where the richest goods were sold, and took a view of the ancient mosque of the Ommiadæ,[1] at the hour of prayer, between noon[2] and sun-set. After that they passed to the shop of Bedreddin Hassan, whom they found still employed in making cream-tarts: I salute you, sir, says Agib; do you mind me? Do you remember you ever saw me before? Bedreddin hearing these words, cast his eyes upon him, and knowing him, (oh the surprising effect of paternal love!) found the same emotion within himself as when he saw him first of all: He was confused upon the matter, and, instead of making an answer, continued a long time without uttering one word: But after all, recalling his wits, My little lord, said he, be so kind as to come once more with your governor into my house, and taste a cream-tart. I beg your lordship's pardon for the trouble I gave you in following you out of town, I was at that time not myself, I did not know what I did. You dragged me after you, and the violence of the pull was so soft, that I could not withstand it.

Agib, astonished at what Bedreddin said, replied thus: There is an excess in the kindness you express, and, unless you engage under oath not to follow me when I go from hence, I will not enter into your house; if you give me your promise, and prove a man of your word, I will visit you again to-morrow, since the visier, my grandfather, is still employed in buying up things for a present to the sultan of Egypt. My little lord, replied Bedreddin, I will do whatever you would have me to do. This said, Agib and the eunuch went into the shop.

Presently after, Bedreddin set before them a cream-tart, that was full as good as what they had eat of when they saw him before. Come, says Agib, addressing himself to Bedreddin, sit down by me, and eat with us. Bedreddin sat down, and made offers to embrace Agib, as a testimony of the joy he conceived upon his sitting by him: But Agib shoved him off, desiring him to be easy, not to run his friendship too close, and to content himself with seeing and entertaining him.—Bedreddin obeyed, and fell a singing a song; the words of which he composed off-hand, in praise of Agib: He did not eat, but made it his business to serve his guests. When they had done eating, he brought them water to wash with,[3] and a very white napkin to wipe their hands.—Then he filled a large China cup with sherbet, and put snow into it;[4] and offering it to Agib, This, said he, is sherbet of roses, and the

[1] That is, of the caliphs that reigned after the four first successors of Mahomet, and were so named from one of their ancestors, whose name was Ommiam.*

[2] This prayer is always said two hours and a half before sun-set.*

[3] The Mahometans having a custom of washing their hands five times a day, when they go to prayers; they reckon they have no occasion to wash before eating, but they always wash after eating, because they eat without forks.

[4] This is done all the Levant over, for making their drink cool.

pleasantest you will meet with all the town over; I am sure you never tasted better. Agib having drank of it with pleasure, Bedreddin Hassan took the cup from him, and presented it to the eunuch, who drank it all off at one pull.

In fine, Agib and his governor having fared well, returned thanks to the pastry-cook for their good entertainment, and moved homewards, it being then lateish. When they arrived at the tents of Schemseddin Mohammed, they repaired immediately to the lady's tent. Agib's grandmother received him with transports of joy: her son Bedreddin ran always in her mind, and in embracing Agib, the remembrance of him drew tears from her eyes: Ah, my child! said she, my joy would be perfect if I had the pleasure of embracing your father, Bedreddin Hassan, as I now embrace you. Then sitting down to supper, she made Agib sit by her, and put several questions to him relating to the walk he had been taking along with the eunuch, and, complaining of his sorry stomach, gave him a piece of cream-tart, which she had made for herself, and was indeed very good, for I told you before, that she could make them better than the best pastry-cooks.—She likewise gave some to the eunuch, but both of them had eaten so heartily at Bedreddin's house, that they could not taste a bit.

Agib no sooner touched the piece of cream-tart that had been set before him, than he pretended he did not like it, and left it uncut; and Schaban,[1] such was the eunuch's name, did the same thing. The widow of Noureddin Ali observed with regret that her grandson did not like the tart: What! says she, does my child thus despise the work of my hands; be it known unto you, no one in the world can make such cream-tarts besides myself and your father Bedreddin Hassan, whom I myself taught to make them.—My good mother, replied Agib, give me leave to tell you, if you do not know how to make better, there is a pastry-cook in this town that goes beyond you in that point; we were at his shop but now, and eat of one that is much better than yours.

This said, the grandmother, frowning upon the eunuch, How now, Schaban, said she, was the care of my grandchild committed to you, to carry him to eat at pastry-shops like a beggar? Madam, replied the eunuch, it is true we did stop a little while and talked with the pastry-cook, but we did not eat with him. Pardon me, says Agib, we went into his shop, and there eat a cream-tart. Upon this, the lady more incensed against the eunuch than before, rose in a passion from the table, and running to the tent of Schemseddin Mohammed, informed him of the eunuch's crime, and that in such terms, as tended more to inflame the visier, than to dispose him to excuse it.

[1] The Mahometans give this name generally to the black eunuchs.

Schemseddin Mohammed, who was naturally passionate, did not fail on this occasion to display his anger: He went forthwith to his sister-in-law's tent, and making up to the eunuch, What! says he, you pitiful wretch, have you the impudence to abuse the trust I repose in you? Schaban, though sufficiently convicted by Agib's testimony, denied the fact still: But the child persisting in what he had affirmed, Grandfather, said he, I can assure you we not only eat, but we eat both of us so heartily, that we have no occasion for supper: Besides, the pastry-cook treated us also with a great bowl of sherbet. Well, cried Schemseddin, turning to Schaban, after all this, will you continue to deny that you entered the pastry-cook's house, and eat there? Schaban had still the imprudence to swear it was not true. Then you are a liar, said the visier, I believe my grandchild before I believe you; but, after all, says he, if you can eat up this cream-tart that is upon the table, I shall be persuaded you have truth on your side.

Though Schaban had crammed himself up to the throat before, he agreed to stand that test; and accordingly took a piece of tart; but his stomach rising against it, he was obliged to spit it out of his mouth: Yet he still pursued the lie, and pretended he had over-eat himself the day before, so that his stomach was not come to him. The visier, irritated with all the eunuch's frivolous pretences, and convinced of his guilt, ordered him to lie flat upon the ground, and to be soundly bastinadoed*. In undergoing this punishment, the poor wretch screeched out prodigiously, and at last confessed the truth; I own, cries he, that we did eat a cream-tart at the pastry-cook's, and that it was much better than that upon the table.

The widow of Noureddin Ali thought it was out of spite to her, and with a design to mortify her, that Schaban commended the pastry-cook's tart; and accordingly said, I cannot believe the cook's tarts are better than mine; I am resolved to satisfy myself upon that head. Where does he live? Go immediately and buy me one of his tarts. The eunuch having received of her what money was sufficient for that purchase, repaired to Bedreddin's shop, and addressed himself to Bedreddin, Good Mr pastry-cook, says he, take this money here, and let me have one of your cream-tarts: one of our ladies wants to taste of them. Bedreddin chose one of the best, and gave it to the eunuch: Take this, says he, I will engage it is an excellent one, and I can assure you, that no person is able to make the like, unless it be my mother, who perhaps is still alive.

Schaban returned speedily to the tents, and gave the tart to Noureddin's widow, and she, snatching it greedily, broke a piece off: but no sooner put it to her mouth, than she cried out and swooned away. Schemseddin Mohammed, who was present, was extremely surprised at the accident; he threw water himself upon her face, and was very active in succouring her.

As soon as she came to herself, My God! cried she, it must needs be my son, my dear Bedreddin, that made this tart.

When the visier Schemseddin Mohammed heard his sister-in-law say that the maker of the tart brought by the eunuch must needs be Bedreddin Hassan, he was overjoyed; but reflecting that his joy might prove groundless, and in all likelihood the conjecture of Noureddin's widow be false, Madam, said he, why are you of that mind? Do you think there may not be a pastry-cook in the world that knows how to make cream-tarts as well as your son? I own, replies she, there be many pastry-cooks that can make as good tarts as he, but forasmuch as I make them after a peculiar manner, and nobody but my son is let into the secret, it must absolutely be he that made this. Come, my brother, added she in a transport, let us call up mirth and joy; we have at last found what we have been so long looking for. Madam, said the visier in answer, I intreat you to moderate your impatience, for we shall quickly know the bottom of it. All we have to do, is to bring the pastry-cook hither; and then you and my daughter will readily distinguish whether it is Bedreddin or not: But you must both be hid, so as to have a view of Bedreddin while he cannot see you; for I would not have our interview and mutual discovery laid at Damascus. My design is to delay the discovery till we return to Cairo, where I propose to regale you with a very agreeable diversion.

This said, he left the ladies in their tent, and retired to his own, where he called for fifty of his men, and said to them, Take each of you a stick in your hands, and follow Schaban, who will conduct you to a pastry-cook's in this city. When you arrive there, break and dash in pieces all you find in the shop: If he asks you why you commit that disorder, only ask him again if it was not he that made the cream-tart that was brought from his house? If he says he is the man, seize his person, fetter him, and bring him along with you; but take care you do not beat him, nor do him the least harm. Go, and lose no time.

The visier's orders were immediately executed. The detachment, conducted by the black eunuch, went with expedition to Bedreddin's house, and broke in pieces the plates, kettles, copper-pans, tables, and all the other moveables and utensils they met with, and drowned the sherbet shop with cream and comfits. Bedreddin astonished at the sight, said, with a pitiful tone, Pray, good people, why do you serve me so? What is the matter? What have I done? Was it not you, said they, that sold this eunuch the cream-tart? Yes, replied he, I am the man, and who says any thing against it? I defy any one to make a better. Instead of giving him an answer, they continued to break all around him, and the oven itself was not spared.

In the mean time, the neighbours took the alarm, and, surprised to see fifty armed men commit such a disorder, asked the reason of such violence; and Bedreddin said once more to the actors of it, Pray tell me what crime I am guilty of, to have deserved this usage? Was it not you, replied they, that made the cream-tart you sold to the eunuch? Yes, yes, it was I, replied he, I maintain it is a good one; I do not deserve such usage as you give me. However, without listening to him, they seized his person, and snatching the cloth of his turban, tied his hands with it behind his back, and, after dragging him by force out of the shop, marched off.

The mob gathering, and taking compassion of Bedreddin, took his part, and offered opposition to Schemseddin's men; but that very minute up came some officers from the governor of the city, who dispersed the people, and favoured the carrying off of Bedreddin; for Schemseddin Mohammed had in the mean time gone to the governor's house to acquaint him with what orders he had given, and to demand the interposition of force to favour the execution; and the governor, who commanded all Syria in the name of the sultan of Egypt, was loth to refuse any thing to his master's visier. So Bedreddin was carried off, after all his cries and tears.

It was needless for Bedreddin Hassan to ask by the way, at those who carried him off, what fault had been found with his cream-tart? They gave him no answer. In short, they carried him to the tents, and made him stay there till Schemseddin Mohammed returned from the governor of Damascus's house.

Upon the visier's return, Bedreddin Hassan was brought before him. My lord, says Bedreddin, with tears in his eyes, pray do me the favour to let me know wherein I have displeased you? Why, you wretch you, says the visier, was it not you that made the cream-tart you sent me? I own I am the man, replied Bedreddin, but pray what crime is that? I will punish you according to your deserts, said Schemseddin; it shall cost you your life for sending me such a sorry tart. Good God! (cried Bedreddin) what news is this! Is it a capital crime to make a bad cream-tart? Yes, said the visier, and you are to expect no other usage from me.

While this interview lasted, the ladies, who were hid, minded Bedreddin narrowly, and readily knew him, notwithstanding he had been so long absent. They were so transported thereupon with joy, that they swooned away; and, when they recovered, would fain have ran up and fallen upon Bedreddin's neck, but the promise they had made to the visier of not discovering themselves, restrained the tender motions of love and of nature.

Schemseddin Mohammed, having resolved to set out that very night, ordered the tents to be struck, and the necessary preparations to be made for his journey: And as for Bedreddin, he ordered him to be clapped into a chest or box well locked, and laid on a camel. When every thing was got ready, the visier and his retinue began their march, and travelled the rest of that night, and all next day, without stopping. In the evening they halted, and Bedreddin was taken out of his cage, in order to be served with the necessary refreshments, but still carefully kept at a distance from his mother and his wife; and during the whole expedition, which lasted twenty days, was he served in the same manner.

When they arrived at Cairo, they encamped in the neighbourhood of that place; Schemseddin called for Bedreddin, gave orders, in his presence, to a carpenter to see for some wood with all expedition, and make a stake. Hey-day, says Bedreddin, what do you mean to do with a stake? Why, to nail you to it, replied Schemseddin, then to have you carried through all the quarters of the town, that the people may have the spectacle of a worthless pastry-cook, who makes cream-tarts without pepper. This said, Bedreddin cried out so comically, that Schemseddin had enough to do to keep his countenance; Good God! cried he, must I suffer death, as cruel as it is ignominious, for not putting pepper in a cream-tart?

Must I be rifled, and have all my goods in my house broken to pieces? Must I be imprisoned in a chest, and at last nailed to a stake, and all for not putting pepper in a cream-tart! Good God, who ever heard of such a thing? Are these the actions of mussulmen, of persons that make a profession of probity and justice, and practise all manner of good works? With these words he shed tears, and then renewing his complaint, No, continued he, never was man used so unjustly, nor so severely. Is it possible they should be capable of taking a man's life for not putting pepper into a cream-tart? Cursed be all the cream-tarts, as well as the hour in which I was born! Would to God I had died that minute!

Disconsolate Bedreddin did not cease to spin out his lamentations; and when the stake was brought, and nails to nail him to it, he cried out bitterly at the horrid sight. Heaven! said he, can you suffer me to die an ignominious and painful death? And all this for what crime? It is not for robbery or murder, or renouncing my religion, but for not putting pepper in a cream-tart.

Night being then pretty far advanced, the visier Schemseddin Mohammed ordered Bedreddin to be clapped up again in his cage, saying to him, Stay there till to-morrow; the day shall not be spent before I give orders for your death. Then the chest or cage was carried away, and laid upon the camel that had brought it from Damascus. At the same time all the other camels were loaded again; and the visier, mounting his horse, ordered the camel that carried his nephew to march before him, and so entered the city, with all his equipage at his back. After passing through several streets, where nobody appeared, every one being in bed, he arrived at his house, where he ordered the chest to be taken down, but not to be opened till farther orders.

While his retinue were unloading the other camels, he took Bedreddin's mother and his daughter aside, and addressed himself to the latter: God be praised, said he, my child, for this happy occasion of meeting your cousin and your husband. You remember, to be sure, what order your chamber was in on your wedding-night: Go and put every thing in the very same order they were then in; and in the mean time, if your memory do not serve you, I can supply by a written account, which I caused to be taken upon that occasion: As for what else is to be done, I will take care of that.

The beautiful lady went joyfully about her father's orders; and he, at the same time, began to put the things in the hall in the same order they were when Bedreddin Hassan was there with the sultan of Egypt's hunch-backed groom. As he went over his manuscript, his domestics placed every moveable accordingly: The throne was not forgot, nor yet the lighted wax candles. When every thing was put to rights in the hall, the visier went into his daughter's chamber, and put in their due place Bedreddin's cloaths, with the purse of sequins: This done, he said to the beautiful lady, Undress yourself, my child, and go to bed. As soon as Bedreddin enters your room, complain of his being from you so long, and tell him, that, when you awaked, you were astonished you did not find him by you: Press him to come to bed again: And to morrow morning you will divert your mother-in-law and me, in telling us what passes between you and him this night. This said, he went from his daughter's apartment, and left her to undress herself and go to bed.

Schemseddin Mohammed ordered all his domestics to depart the hall, excepting two or three, whom he ordered to stay there. These he commanded to go and take Bedreddin out of the chest, to strip him to his shirt and drawers, to conduct him in that condition to the hall, to leave him there all alone, and to shut the door upon him.

Bedreddin Hassan, though overwhelmed with grief, had been asleep all the time; insomuch that the visier's domestics had taken him out of the chest, and stripped him before he awaked; and carried him so suddenly into the hall, that they did not give him time to bethink himself where he was. When he found himself all alone in the hall, he looked round him, and the objects of his sight recalling to his memory the circumstances of his marriage, he perceived with astonishment that it was the same hall where he had seen the sultan's groom of the stables. His surprise was still the greater, when, approaching softly to the door of a chamber which he found open, he espied within, his own clothes, in the same place he remembered to have left them on his wedding night. My God! said he, rubbing his eyes, am I asleep or awake?

The beautiful lady, who, in the mean time, was diverting herself with his astonishment, opened the curtains of her bed all on a sudden, and, bending her head forward, My dear lord, said she, with a soft tender air, What do you do at the door? Prithee come to bed again! You have been out of bed a long time: I was strangely surprised when I awaked, in not finding you by me. Bedreddin Hassan's countenance changed, when he perceived that the lady who spoke to him was that charming person that he had lain with before: so he entered the room, but, calling up thoughts of all that had passed for ten years interval, and not being able to persuade himself that it could all have happened in the compass of one night, he went to the place where his cloaths lay, and the purse of sequins; and, after examining them very carefully, By the living God, cried he, these are things that I can by no means comprehend! The lady, who was pleased to see his confusion, said once more, My lord, come to bed again; what do you stand at? Then he stepped towards the bed, and said to her, Pray, madam, tell me, is it long since I left you? The question, answered she, surprises me! Did not you rise from me but now? Sure your thoughts are very busy. Madam, replied Bedreddin, I do assure you my thoughts are not very easy: I remember, indeed, to have been with you, but I remember, at the same time, that I have lived since ten years at Damascus: Now, if I was actually in bed with you this night, I cannot have been from you so long: These two things are inconsistent: Pray tell me what to think; whether my marriage with you is an illusion, or whether my absence from you is only a dream? Yes, my lord, cried she, doubtless you were light headed when you thought you were at Damascus. Upon this, Bedreddin laughed out heartily, and said, What a comical fancy is this? I assure you, madam, this dream of mine will be very pleasant to you: Do but imagine, if you please, that I was at the gate of Damascus in my shirt and drawers, as I am here now; that I entered the town with the haloo of a mob that followed and insulted me; that I fled to a pastry-cook's, who adopted me, taught me his trade, and left me all he had when he died; that, after his death, I kept a shop. In fine, madam, I had an infinity of other adventures, too tedious to recount; and that all I can say is, that it was not amiss that I awaked, for they were going to nail me to a stake. O Lord! and for what, cried the lady, feigning astonishment, would they have used you so cruelly? Sure you must have committed some enormous crime. Not in the least, replied Bedreddin, it was for nothing in the world but a mere trifle, the most ridiculous thing you can think of: All the crime I was charged with, was selling a cream-tart that had no pepper in it.—As for that matter, said the beautiful lady, laughing heartily, I must say they did you great injustice. Ah! madam, replied he, that was not all: for this cursed cream-tart was every thing in my shop broke to pieces, myself bound and fettered, and flung into a chest; where I lay so close, that methinks I am there still. In fine, a carpenter was called for, and he was ordered to get ready a stake for me: But, thanks be to God, all those things are no more than a dream.

Bedreddin was not easy all night: He awaked from time to time, and put the question to himself, whether he dreamed or was awake? He distrusted his felicity; and, to be sure whether it was true or not, opened the curtains, and looked round the room. I am not mistaken sure, said he, this is the chamber where I entered instead of the hunch-backed groom of the stables; and I am now in bed with the fair lady that was designed for him. Day-light, which then appeared, had not dispelled his uneasiness, when the visier, Schemseddin Mohammed, his uncle, knocked at the door, and at the same time went in to bid him good-morrow.

Bedreddin Hassan was extremely surprised to see, all on a sudden, a man that he knew so well, and that now appeared with a quite different air from that with which he pronounced the terrible sentence of death against him. Ah! cried Bedreddin, it was you that condemned me so unjustly, to a manner of death, the thoughts of which make me shrink still, and all for a cream-tart without pepper. The visier fell a-laughing, and, to put him out of suspence, told him, how, by the ministry of a genie, he had been at his house, and married his daughter, instead of the sultan's groom of the stables; then he acquainted him, that he had discovered him to be his nephew by a book written by the hand of Noureddin Ali; and, pursuant of that discovery, had gone from Cairo to Balsora in quest of him. My dear nephew, added he, with embraces and all the marks of tenderness, I ask your pardon for all I have made you undergo since I discovered you: I had a mind to bring you to my house before I told you your happiness, which ought now to be so much the dearer to you, that it has cost you so much perplexity and affliction. To atone for all your afflictions, comfort yourself with the joy of being in the company of those who ought to be dearest to you. While you are dressing yourself, I will go and acquaint your mother, who is beyond measure impatient to see you; and will likewise bring your son to you, whom you saw at Damascus, and for whom you shewed so much affection without knowing him.

No words are of sufficient energy to express the joy of Bedreddin when he saw his mother and his son. These three embraced, and shewed all the transports that love and a moving tenderness could inspire. The mother spoke to Bedreddin in the most moving terms; she mentioned the grief she had felt for his long absence, and the tears she had shed. Little Agib, instead of flying his father's embraces as at Damascus, received them with all the marks of pleasure:—And Bedreddin Hassan divided between two objects so worthy of his love, thought he could not give sufficient marks of his affection.

While this passed at Schemseddin Mohammed's, the visier was gone to the palace, to give the sultan an account of the happy success of his voyage: and the sultan was so charmed with the recital of the story, that he ordered it to be taken down in writing, and carefully preserved among the archives of the kingdom. After Schemseddin's return to his house, having prepared a noble feast, he sat down to table with his family, and all the household passed the day in solemnity and mirth.

The visier, Giafar, having thus made an end of the story of Bedreddin Hassan, told the caliph Haroun Alraschid, that this was what he had to relate to his majesty. The caliph found the story so surprising, that, without further hesitation, he granted his slave Rihan's pardon; and to condole the young man for the grief of having unhappily deprived himself of a woman whom he loved so tenderly, married him to one of his slaves; bestowed liberal gifts upon him, and entertained him till he died. But, sir, added Scheherazade, observing that day began to appear, though the story I have now told you be very agreeable, I have one still that is much more so. If your majesty pleases to hear it the next night, I am certain you will be of the same mind. Schahriar rose without giving any answer, and was in a quandary what to do. The good sultaness, said he, within himself, tells very long stories, and when once she begins one, there is no refusing to hear it out: I cannot tell whither I shall put her to death to-day or not: No sure, I will not; I will do nothing rashly: The story she promises is perhaps more diverting than all she has told yet; I will not deprive myself of the pleasure of hearing it, but when once she has told it, then she shall die.

Dinarzade did not fail to awaken the sultaness of the Indies before day, and the sultaness, after asking leave of the sultan, began the story she had promised, to the following purpose:

The Story of the Little Hunch-back

THERE was in former times at Casgar, upon the utmost skirts of Tartary, a taylor that had a pretty wife, whom he loved entirely, and was reciprocally loved by her. One day as he sat at work, a little hunch-back my lord came and sat down at the shop-door, and fell a-singing, at the same time played upon the tabor. The taylor took pleasure to hear him, and had a strong mind to take him into his house to make his wife merry: this little fellow, says he to his wife, will divert us both very agreeably. In fine, he invited my lord in, and he readily accepted the invitation; so the taylor shut up his shop and carried him home. The little gentleman being carried in, the taylor's wife covered the table, they sat down to supper, and had a good large dish of fish set before them; but as they eat heartily, unluckily the crooked gentleman swallowed a large bone, of which he died in a few minutes, notwithstanding all that the taylor and his wife could do to prevent it. Both the one and the other were mightily frightened at the accident, especially since it fell out in their house, and there was ground to fear that, if the justiciary magistrates came to hear it, they would be punished as assassins. However, the husband found an expedient to get rid of the corpse; He considered there was a Jewish doctor that lived just by, and so formed a project, in the execution of which, his wife and he took the corpse, the one by the feet, and the other by the head, and carried it to the physician's house:—They knocked at the door, from which ascended a steep pair of stairs to his chamber. As soon as they had knocked, the servant maid came down without any light, and opening the door, asked what they wanted? Prithee go up again, says the taylor, and tell your master we have brought him a man that is very sick and wants his advice. Here, says he, putting a piece of money into her hand, give him that before-hand, to convince him that we have no mind to make him lose his labour.—While the servant was gone up to acquaint her master with the welcome news, the taylor and his wife nimbly conveyed the hunch-backed corpse to the head of the stairs, and leaving it there, scoured off.

In the mean time, the maid having told the doctor that a man and a woman staid for him at the door, desiring he would come down and look upon a sick man they had brought with them; and the maid clapped the money she had received into his hand; the doctor was transported with joy; being paid beforehand, he thought it was a good chap, and should not be neglected. Light, light, cries he to the maid, follow me nimbly. However, without staying for the light, he gets to the stair-head, and that in such haste, that, stumbling against the corpse, he gave it such a kick as made it tumble quite down to the stair-foot: Nay, he had almost fallen himself, and tumbled down with my lord. A light, a light, cries he to the maid, quick, quick: At last the maid came with a light, and so he went down stairs with her; but when he saw the stumbling-block he had kicked down was a dead man, he was so frightened that he invoked Moses, Aaron, Joshua, and Esdras, and all the prophets of his law! Unhappy man that I am, said he, what made me offer to come down without a light? I have even made an end of the fellow that was brought me to be cured: Questionless, I am the cause of his death, and unless Esdras's ass[1] comes to assist me, I am ruined: Mercy on me, they will be here out of hand, and lug me out of my house for a murderer.

[1] Here the Arabian author plays upon the Jews; the ass is that which, as the Mahometans believe Esdras rid upon when he came from the Babylonian captivity to Jerusalem.*

But, notwithstanding the perplexity and jeopardy he was in, he had the precaution to shut his door, for fear any one passing by in the street should observe the mischance of which he reckoned himself the author: Then he took the corpse into his wife's chamber, upon which she swooned away. Alas, cried she, we are utterly ruined undone, undone, unless we fall upon some expedient or other to turn the corpse out of our house this night! Beyond all question, if we harbour it here till morning, our lives must pay for it. What a sad mischance is this. Why, how did you do to kill this man? That is not the question, replies the Jew, our business now is to find out a remedy for such a shocking accident.

The doctor and his wife consulted together how to get rid of this dead corpse that night: The doctor racked his brain in vain; he could not think of any stratagem to get clear; but his wife, who was more fertile in invention, said, I have a thought comes in my head; let us carry the corpse to the leads of our house, and tumble it down the chimney into the house of the mussulman, our next neighbour.

This mussulman, or Turk, was one of the sultan's purveyors, for furnishing oil, butter, and all sorts of fat, tallow, &c. and had a magazine* in his house, where the rats and mice made prodigious havoc.

The Jewish doctor approving the proposed expedient, his wife and he took the little hunch-back up to the roof of the house; and, clapping ropes under his arm-pits, let him down the chimney into the purveyor's chamber so softly and dexterously, that he stood upright against the wall as if he had been alive. When they found he stood firm, they pulled up the ropes, and left the gentleman in that posture. They were scarce gone down into their chamber when the purveyor went into his, being just come from a wedding-feast, with a lanthorn in his hand. He was mightily surprised, when, by the light of his lanthorn, he descried a man standing upright in his chimney; but being naturally a stout man, and apprehending it was a thief or robber, he took up a good lusty cane, and making straight up to the hunch-back, Ah, says he, I thought it was the rats and mice that ate my butter and tallow; and it is you come down the chimney to rob me, is it? I question if ever you come back again upon this errand. This said, he falls foul upon the man, and gives him a good many swinging thwacks with his cane: Upon that the corpse fell down, running its nose against the ground, and the purveyor redoubled his blows: But, observing the body not to move, he stood to consider a little; and, then perceiving it was a dead corpse, fear succeeded his anger. Wretched man that I am, said he, what have I done! I have killed a man dead: Alas, I have carried my revenge too far. Good God, unless thou pity me, my life is gone! Cursed, ten thousand times accursed, be the fat and the oil that gave occasion to this my commission of such a criminal action. In fine, he stood pale and thunderstruck; he thought he saw the officers already come to drag him to condign punishment, and could not think what resolution to take.

The sultan of Casgar's purveyor had never minded the little gentleman's hunch when he was beating him, but as soon as he perceived it, he threw out a thousand imprecations against him. Ah, you crooked hunch-back, cried he, you crooked son of a bitch, would to God you had robbed me of all my fat, and I had not found you here: If it had been so, I had not been so much perplexed as I now am, for the love of you and your nasty hunch. Oh! the stars that twinkle in the heavens, give light to none but me in this dangerous juncture. As soon as he had uttered these words, he took the little crooked corpse upon his shoulders, and carried him out of doors to the end of the street, where he set him upright, resting against a shop, and so trudged home again without looking behind him.

A few minutes before the break of day, a Christian merchant, who was very rich, and furnished the sultan's palace with most things it wanted; this merchant, I say, having sat up all night debauching, stepped then out of his house to go to bathe: Though he was drunk, he was sensible that the night was far spent, and the people would quickly be called to the morning-prayers that begin at the break of day; therefore he quickened his pace to get in time to the bath, for fear a Turk, meeting him in his way to the mosque, should carry him to prison for a drunkard. However, as he came to the end of the street, he stopped upon some necessary occasion, and leaned against the shop where the sultan's purveyor had put the hunch-backed corpse; and the corpse being jostled, tumbled upon the merchant's back. The merchant, thinking it was a robber that came to attack him, knocked him down with a swinging box on the ear, and, after redoubling his blows, cried out, Thieves!

The outcry alarmed the watch, who came up immediately, and finding a Christian beating a Turk, (for hunch-back was of our religion), What reason have you, said he, to abuse a mussulman after this rate? He would have robbed me, replied the merchant, and jumped upon my back, with an intent to take me by the throat. If he did, said the watch, you have revenged yourself sufficiently; come, get off him. At the same time he stretched out his hand to help little hunch-back up; but, observing he was dead; Ah! hey-day! said he, is it thus that a Christian dares to assassinate a mussulman? So he laid hold of the Christian, and carried him to the sheriff's house, where he was kept till the judge was stirring, and ready to examine him. In the mean time, the Christian merchant grew sober, and the more he reflected upon his adventure, the less could he conceive, how such single fisty-cuffs could kill the man.

The judge having heard the report of the watch, and viewed the corpse, which they had taken care to bring to his house, interrogated the Christian merchant upon it, and he could not deny the crime, though he had not committed it. But the judge, considering that little hunch-back belonged to the sultan, for he was one of his buffoons, would not put the Christian to death till he knew the sultan's pleasure. For this end, he went to the palace, and acquainted the sultan with what had happened, and received from the sultan this answer, I have no mercy to shew to a Christian that kills a Mussulman: Go, do your office. Upon this, the judge ordered a gibbet to be erected, and sent criers all over the city, to proclaim, that they were about to hang a Christian for killing a mussulman.

In fine, the merchant was brought out of gaol to the foot of the gallows; and the hangman having put the rope about his neck, was going to give him a swing, when the sultan's purveyor shoving through the crowd, made up to the gibbet, calling to the hangman to stop, for that the Christian had not committed the murder, but himself had done it. Upon that, the sheriff who attended the execution, put interrogatories to the purveyor, who told him every circumstance of his killing little crump-back, and conveying his corpse to the place where the Christian merchant found him. You were about, added he, to put to death an innocent person; for how can he be guilty of the death of a man who was dead before he came at him? My burden is sufficient in having killed a Turk, without loading my conscience with the additional charge of the death of a Christian that is not guilty.

The sultan of Casgar's purveyor having publicly charged himself with the death of the little hunch-backed man, the sheriff could not avoid doing justice to the merchant. Let the Christian go, said he, and hang this man in his room, since it appears by his own confession that he is guilty. Thereupon, the hangman released the merchant, and clapped the rope round the purveyor's neck; but, just when he was going to pull him up, he heard the voice of the Jewish doctor, earnestly entreating him to suspend the execution, and make room for him to come and throw himself at the gallows foot.

When he appeared before the judge, My lord, said he, this mussulman you are going to hang is not guilty: All the guilt lies at my door. Last night a man and a woman, unknown to me, came to my door with a sick man they had brought along; and they knocking at the door, my maid went and opened it without a light, and received from them a piece of money, with a commission to come and desire me, in their name, to step down and look upon a sick person. While she was delivering her message to me, they conveyed the sick person to the stair-head, and then disappeared. I went down, without staying for my servant to light a candle, and in the dark happened to stumble upon the sick person, and kick him down stairs. In fine, I saw he was dead, and that it was the crooked mussulman, whose death you are now about to avenge: So my wife and I took the corpse, and, after conveying it up to the leads of our house, shoved it to the roof of the purveyor, our next neighbour's house, and let it down the chimney into the chamber: The purveyor finding it in his house, took the little man for a thief, and, after beating him, concluded he had killed him. But that it was not so, you will be convinced by this my deposition; so that I am the only author of the murder, and though it was committed undesignedly, I have resolved to expiate my crime, by keeping clear of the charge of the death of two mussulmen, and hindering you to execute the sultan's purveyor, whose innocence I have now revealed. So pray dismiss him, and put me in his place, for I alone am the cause of the death of the little man.

The chief justice being persuaded that the Jewish doctor was the murderer, gave orders to the executioner to seize him, and release the purveyor: Accordingly, the doctor was just a-going to be hung up, when the taylor appeared, crying to the executioner to hold his hand, and make room for him, that he might come and make his confession to the lord justice. Room being made, My lord, said he to the judge, you have narrowly escaped taking away the lives of three innocent persons; but if you will have the patience to hear me, I will discover to you the real murderer of the crook-backed man: If his death is to be expiated by another, that must be mine. Yesterday, towards the evening, as I was at work in my shop, and had a mind to be merry, the little hunch-back came to my door half drunk, and sat down before it. He sung a little, and so I invited him to pass the evening at my house: Accordingly, he accepted of the invitation, and went in with me: We sat down to supper, and I gave him a plate of fish; but in eating, a bone stuck in his throat, and though my wife and I did our utmost to relieve him, he died in a few minutes. His death afflicted us extremely, and for fear of being charged with it, we carried the corpse to the Jewish doctor's house, and knocked at the door: The maid coming down and opening the door, I desired her to go up again forthwith, and ask her master to come down and give his advice to a sick person that we had brought along with us; and withal, to encourage him, I charged her to give him a piece of money, which I had put into her hand. When she was gone up again, I carried the hunch-back up stairs, and laid him upon the uppermost step; and then my wife and I made the best of our way home: The doctor coming down, made the corpse fall down stairs, and thereupon he took himself to be the author of his death. Now, this being the case, (continued he), release the doctor, and let me die in his room.

The chief justice, and all the spectators, could not sufficiently admire the strange emergencies that ensued upon the death of the little crooked gentleman. Let the Jewish doctor go, said the judge, and hang up the taylor, since he confesses the crime. It is certain, this history is very uncommon, and deserves to be recorded in letters of gold. The executioner having dismissed the doctor, made every thing ready to tie up the taylor.

While the executioner was making ready to hang up the taylor, the sultan of Casgar wanting the company of his crooked jester, asked where he was? and one of his officers told him what follows: The hunch-back, sir, whom you inquire after, got drunk last night, and, contrary to his custom, slipped out of the palace, and went a sauntering in the city, and this morning was found dead. A man was brought before the chief justice, and charged with the murder of him but, when he was going to be hanged, up came a man, and after him another, who took the charge upon themselves, and cleared one another. The examination has continued a long while, and the judge is now examining a third man that gives himself out for the real author of the murder.

Upon this intelligence the sultan of Casgar sent a hussar* to the place of execution. Go, said he to his messenger, make all the haste you can, and bring the arraigned persons before me immediately; and, withal, bring the corpse of poor hunch-back, that I may see him once more. Accordingly, the hussar went, and happened to arrive at the place of execution, at the same time that the executioner was going to tie up the taylor. So he cried aloud to the executioner to suspend the execution: The hangman knowing the hussar, did not dare to proceed, but untied the taylor, and then the hussar acquainted the judge with the sultan's pleasure: So the judge obeyed, and went straight to the palace, accompanied by the taylor, the Jewish doctor, and the Christian merchant; and made four of his men carry the hunch-corpse along with him.

When they appeared before the sultan, the judge threw himself at the prince's feet; and, after recovering himself, gave him a faithful relation of what he knew of the story of the crump-backed man. The sultan found the story so uncommon, that he ordered his private historians to write it with its circumstances. Then, addressing himself to all the audience, Did you ever hear, said he, such a surprising story as this, that has happened upon the account of my little crooked buffoon? Then the Christian merchant, after falling down and saluting the earth with his forehead, spoke in the following manner: Most puissant monarch, said he, I know a story yet more astonishing than that you have now spoke of; if your majesty will give me leave, I will tell it you: The circumstances are such, that nobody can hear them without being moved. Well, said the sultan, I give you leave; and so the merchant went on as follows:

The Story told by the Christian Merchant

SIR, before I commence the recital of the story you have allowed me to tell, I beg leave to acquaint you, that I have not the honour to be born in a place that pertains to your majesty's empire. I am a stranger, born at Cairo, in Egypt, one of the Coptic nations, and a professor of the Christian religion: My father was a broker, and got a good estate, which he left me at his death. I followed his example, and took up the same employment: And one day at Cairo, as I was standing in the public apartment for the corn-merchants, there comes up to me a young handsome man, well clad, and mounted upon an ass. He saluted me, and pulling out his handkerchief, where he had a sample of sesame and Turkey corn, asked me what a bushel of such sesame would fetch?

I examined the corn that the young man shewed me, and told him it was worth a hundred drams of silver per bushel. Pray, said he, look out for some merchant to take it at that price, and come to me at the Victory-gate,* where you will see a hut at a distance from the houses. So he left me, and I shewed the sample to several merchants, who told me, that they would take as much as I could spare, at an hundred and ten drams per bushel, so that I made an account to get ten drams per bushel for my brokerage. Full of the expectation of this profit, I went forthwith to the Victory-gate, where I found the young merchant staying for me, and he carried me into his granary, which was full of sesame. He had an hundred and fifty bushels of it, which I measured out, and having carried them off upon asses, sold them for five thousand drams of silver. Now, out of this sum, (said the young man), there is five hundred drams coming to you, at the rate of ten drams per bushel. I order you to take and apply it to your own use; and as for the rest, which is to come to me, do you take it out of the merchant's hand, and keep it till I call for it; for I have no occasion for it at present. I made answer, it should be ready for him whenever he pleased to call for it; and so took leave of him, with a grateful sense of his generosity.

It was a month after before he came near me; then he came and asked for his 4500 drams of silver. I told him they were ready, and should be told down to him in a minute: He was then mounted on his ass, and so I desired him to alight, and do me the honour to eat a mouthful with me before he received his money. No, said he, I cannot alight at present, I have urgent business that obliges me to be at a place just by here; but I will return this way, and then take the money, which I desire you will have in readiness. This said, he disappeared; and I still expected his return, but it was a full month before he came again. I thought to myself the young man reposed a great trust in me, leaving so great a sum in my hands without knowing me; another would have been afraid I should have run away with it. To be short, he came again at the end of the third month, and was still mounted on his ass; but finer in his clothes than before.

As soon as I saw the young man, I entreated him to alight, and asked him if he would not take his money. It is no matter for that, said he, with a pleasant easy air, I know it is in good hands; I will come and take it when my other money is all gone: Adieu, (continued he), I will come again towards the latter end of the week. With that he clapped his spurs to the ass, and away he went. Well, thought I to myself, he says he will see me towards the latter end of the week, but it is likely I may not see him for a great while; I will go and make the most of his money, and shall get a good penny by it.

And, as it happened, I was not out of my conjecture; for it was a full year before I saw my young merchant again. Then he appeared indeed with richer apparel than before, but was very thoughtful. I asked him to do me the honour to walk into my house: For this time, replied he, I will go in, but upon this condition, that you shall put yourself to no extraordinary charge upon my account. That shall be as you please, (said I) only do me the favour to alight and walk in. Accordingly, he complied, and I gave orders for some sort of entertainment; and while that was getting ready, we fell into discourse together. When the victuals were got ready, we sat down at table. When he eat the first mouthful, I observed he fed himself with the left hand, and not with the right: I could not tell what to think of it: I thought within myself, ever since I knew this young man, he always appeared very polite; is it possible he can do this out of contempt of me? What can the matter be, that he does not make use of his right hand!*

After we had done eating, and every thing was taken away, we sat down upon a sofa, and I presented him with a lozenge that was excellent for giving a sweet breath, and still he took it with his left hand. Then I accosted him in this manner; Sir, pray pardon the liberty I take in asking you what reason you have for not making use of your right hand. It is likely you have some disorder in that hand. Instead of answering, he fetched a deep sigh, and, pulling out his right arm, which he had hitherto kept under his garment, shewed me, to my great astonishment, that his hand had been cut off. Doubtless you were alarmed, said he, to see me feed myself with the left hand, but I leave you to judge whether it was in my power to do otherwise. May one ask you, said I, by what mischance it was that you lost your right hand? Upon that he fell into tears, and, after wiping his eyes, gave me the following relation:

You must know, said he, that I am a native of Bagdad, the son of a rich father, the most noted man in that city both for quality and for riches. I had scarce launched into the world, when, falling into the company of travellers, and hearing wonders told of Egypt, especially of Grand Cairo, I was moved by their discourse, and took a longing desire to travel thither; but my father was then alive, and had not given me leave. In fine, he died, and thereupon, being master of myself, I resolved to take a journey to Cairo. I laid out a large sum of money upon several sorts of fine stuffs of Bagdad and Moussoul, and so undertook my journey.

Arriving at Cairo, I went to the khan, called the khan of Mesrour, and there took lodgings, with a warehouse for my bales, which I brought along upon camels. This done, I retired to my chamber to rest myself after the fatigue of my journey, and ordered my servants to go and buy some provisions and dress them. After I had ate, I went and saw the castle, some mosques, public places, and the other things that were curious.

Next day I dressed myself pretty handsomely, and ordered some of the finest and richest of my bales to be picked out, and carried by my slaves to the Circassian Bezestein,[1] whither I went myself. I no sooner got thither than I was surrounded with brokers and criers that had heard of my arrival. I gave patterns of my stuffs to several of the criers, who went and carried them, and shewed them all over to the bezestein, but none of the merchants offered near so much as they had cost me in prime cost and carriage.—This vexed me, and the criers observing I was dissatisfied, If you will take our advice, said they, we will put you in a way of selling your stuffs without losing by them.

The brokers and the criers having thus promised to put me in a way of losing nothing by my goods, I asked them what course they would have me take? Divide your goods, said they, among several merchants, and they will sell them by retail; and twice a-week, that is on Mondays and Tuesdays, you may receive what money they take. By this means you will get, instead of losing, and the merchants will get by you: And in the mean time, you will have time to take your pleasure, and walk up and down the town, or to go upon the Nile.

I took their advice, and carried them to my warehouse; from whence I brought all my goods to the bezestein, and there divided them among the merchants that they represented as most reputable and able to pay; and the merchants gave me a formal receipt before witnesses, stipulating withal, that I should not make any demand upon them for the first month.

Having thus regulated my affairs, my mind was taken up with other sort of things than the ordinary pleasures. I contracted friendship with divers persons almost of the same age with myself, who took care I did not want

[1] A bezestein is a public place where silk stuffs, and other precious things, are exposed to sale.

company. After the first month expired, I began to visit my merchants twice a-week, taking along with me a public officer to inspect their books of sale, and a banker to see they paid me in good money, and to regulate the value of the several species; and so every pay-day I had a good sum of money to carry home to my lodging. I went nevertheless on the other days to pass the morning, sometimes at a merchant's house, and sometimes at some other person's. In fine, I diverted myself in conversing with one or an other, and seeing what passed in the bezestein.

One Monday, as I sat in a merchant's shop whose name was Bedreddin, a lady of quality, as one might easily perceive by her air, her habit, and her being attended by a she-slave in neat cloaths; this lady, I say, came into the shop and sat down by me: Her excellent appearance, joined to a natural grace that shined through all she did, inspired me with a longing desire to know her better than I did. I was at a loss to know whether she observed that I took pleasure in gazing upon her, but she tucked up the crape* that hung down over the muslin which covered her face, and so gave me the opportunity of seeing her large black eyes, which perfectly charmed me. In fine, she screwed my love to the height by the agreeable sound of her voice, and her genteel graceful carriage in saluting the merchant, and asking him how he did since she saw him last.

After entertaining him some-time upon indifferent things, she gave him to know that she wanted a sort of stuff with a ground of gold; that she came to his shop as affording the best choice of any in all the bezestein; and that, if he had any such as she asked for, he would oblige her in shewing them. Bedreddin shewed her several pieces, one of which she pitched upon, and he asked for it eleven hundred drams of silver. I agree, said she, to give you so much, but I have not money enough about me, so I hope you will give me credit till to-morrow, and in the mean time allow me to carry off the stuff. I shall not fail, added she, to send you to-morrow the eleven hundred drams I agreed for. Madam, said Bedreddin, I would give you credit with all my heart, and allow you to carry off the stuff if it were mine, but it belongs to that young man you see here, and this is the day on which we state our accounts. Why, said the lady in a surprise, why do you offer to use me so? Am not I a customer to your shop? And as often as I have bought of you, and carried home the things without paying ready money for them, did I ever fail to send you your money next morning? Madam, said the merchant, it is true, but this very day I have occasion for money. There, said she, throwing the stuff to him, take your stuff; may God confound you and all the merchants that are: You are all of you of one kidney, you respect nobody.—This said, she rose up in a passion, and walked out.

When I saw that the lady walked off, I found in my breast a great concern for her; so I called her back, saying, Madam, do me the favour to return, perhaps I can find a way to content you both. In fine, back she came, saying, it was for the love of me that she complied. Mr Bedreddin, said I to the merchant, what do you say you must have for this stuff that belongs to me? I must have, said he, eleven hundred drams; I cannot take less. Give it to the lady then, said I, let her take it home with her; I allow a hundred drams profit to yourself, and shall now write you a note impowering you to discount that sum upon the other goods you have of mine. In fine, I wrote, signed and delivered the note, and then handed the stuff to the lady: Madam, said I, you may take the stuff with you, and as for the money, you may either send it to-morrow or next day; or, if you will, accept the stuff as a present from me. I beg your pardon, sir, said she, I mean nothing of that: You use me so very civilly and obligingly, that I ought never to shew my face in the world again if I did not shew my gratitude to you. May God reward you in enlarging your fortune; may you live many years when I am dead; may the gate of heaven be opened to you when you remove to the other world, and may all the city proclaim your generosity.

These words inspired me with some assurance: Madam, said I, I desire no other reward for what service I have done to you than the happiness of seeing your face; that will repay me with interest. I had no sooner spoke, than she turned towards me, took off the muslim that covered her face, and discovered to my eyes a killing beauty. I was so struck with the surprising sight that I could not express my thoughts to her. I could have looked upon her for ever without being cloyed; but fearing any one should take notice, she quickly covered her face, and pulling down the crape, took up the piece of stuff, and went away, leaving me in a quite different sort of temper from what I was in when I came to the shop. I continued for some time in great disorder and perplexity. Before I took leave of the merchant, I asked him if he knew the lady? Yes, said he, she is the daughter of an emir, who left her an immense fortune at his death.

I went home and sat down to supper, but could not eat, neither could I shut my eyes all the night long: I thought it the longest night in my life-time. As soon as it was day I got up, in hopes to see once more the object that disturbed my repose; and, to engage her affection, I dressed myself yet more nicely than I had done the day before.

I had but just got to Bedreddin's shop, when I saw the lady coming in more magnificent apparel than before, and attended by her slave.—When she came in, she did not mind the merchant, but, addressing herself to me, Sir, said she, you see I am punctual to my word. I am come on purpose to pay the sum you was so kind as to pass your word for yesterday, though you had no knowledge of me: Such an uncommon piece of generosity I shall never forget. Madam, said I, you had no occasion to be so hasty: I was well satisfied as to my money, and am sorry you should put yourself to so much trouble about it. I had been very unjust, answered she, if I had abused your generosity. With these words, she clapped the money into my hand, and sat down by me.

Having this opportunity of conversing with her, I made the best use of it, and mentioned to her the love I had for her; but she rose and left me very abruptly, as if she had been angry with the declaration I had made; I followed her with my eyes as long as she was in sight; and as soon as she was out of sight, I took leave of the merchant, and walked out of the bezestein, without knowing where I went. I was musing upon this adventure, when I felt somebody pulling me behind; and, turning about to see who it was, I had the agreeable surprise to perceive it was the lady's slave. My mistress, said the slave, I mean the young lady you spoke with but now in the merchant's shop, wants to speak one word with you; so, if you please to give yourself the trouble to follow me, I will conduct you.—Accordingly I followed her, and found my mistress staying for me in a banker's shop.

She made me sit down by her, and spoke to this purpose: Dear sir, said she, do not be surprised that I left you so abruptly: I thought it not proper, before that merchant, to give a favourable answer to the discovery you made of your affection to me. But, to speak the truth, I was so far from being offended at it, that I was pleased when I heard it; and I account myself infinitely happy in having a man of true merit for my lover. I do not know what impression the first sight of me could make upon you, but, I assure you, I no sooner saw you than I had tender thoughts of you. Since yesterday I have done nothing but thought of what you said to me; and the haste I made to come and find you out this morning may convince you I have no small regard for you. Madam, said I, transported with love and joy, nothing can be more agreeable to me than what I now hear; no passion can be greater than that with which I love you: Since the happy moment I cast my eyes upon you, my eyes were then dazzled with so many charms, that my heart yielded without resistance. Do not let us trifle away the time in needless discourse, said she, interrupting me: I make no doubt of your sincerity, and you shall quickly be convinced of mine. Will you do me the honour to come to my home? Or, if you will, I will come to yours. Madam, said I, I am a stranger, lodged in a khan, which is not a proper place for the reception of a lady of your quality and merit. It is more proper, madam, for me to come to you at your home, if you will please to tell me where it is. The lady complying with this desire, I live, said she, in Devotion-street; come next Friday, after noon-prayers, and ask for the house of Abbon Schamain, sir-named Bercout, late master of the emirs; there you will find me. This said, we parted, and I passed the next day in great impatience.

On Friday, I got up betimes, and put on my best cloathes, with fifty pieces of gold in my pocket: Thus prepared, I mounted an ass, I had bespoke the day before, and set out, accompanied by the man that let me the ass. When we came to Devotion-street, I directed the owner of the ass to inquire for the house I wanted to be at: Accordingly he inquired, and conducted me thither. I paid him liberally, and sent him back; directing him to observe narrowly where he left me, and not to fail to come back with the ass to-morrow morning to carry me back again.

I knocked at the door, and presently two little girl-slaves, white as snow, and neatly dressed, came and opened it. Be pleased to come in, sir, said they, our mistress expects you impatiently; these two days she has spoke of nothing but you. So I entered the court, and saw a great pavilion raised upon seven steps, and surrounded with iron rails that parted it from a very pleasant garden. Besides the trees which embellished the prospect, and formed an agreeable shade, there was an infinite number of other trees, loaded with all manner of fruit. I was charmed with the warbling of a great number of birds, that joined their notes to the murmurings of a very high water-work in the middle of a ground plot enamelled with flowers. This water-work was a very agreeable sight:—Four large gilded dragons adorned the angles of the bason, which was of a square form; and these dragons spouted out water clearer than rock crystal. This delicious place gave me a charming idea of the conquest I had made. The two little slaves conducted me into a parlour magnificently furnished; and, while one of them went to acquaint her mistress with my arrival, the other tarried with me, and pointed out to me the ornaments of the hall.

I did not tarry long in the hall, said the young man of Bagdad, ere the lady I loved appeared, adorned with pearls and diamonds; but the splendour of her eyes did far outshine that of her jewels. Her shapes, which were now not disguised by the habit usual in the streets, were extremely fine and charming. I need not mention with what joy we received one another—that leaves all expression far behind it: I shall only tell you, that, when the first compliments were over, we sat both down upon a sofa, and there entertained one another with all imaginable satisfaction. After that, we had the most delicious messes served up to us; and after eating, continued our discourse till night. At night we had excellent wine brought up, and such fruit as is apt to promote drinking; and timed our cups to the sound of musical instruments joined to the voices of the slaves. The lady of the house sung herself, and by her songs screwed up my passion to the height. In fine, I passed the night in a full enjoyment of all manner of pleasure.

Next morning I slipped under the bolster of the bed the purse with the fifty pieces of gold I had brought with me, and took leave of the lady, who asked me when I would see her again? Madam, said I, I give you my promise to return this night. She seemed to be transported with my answer, and, conducting me to the door, conjured me at parting to be mindful of my promise.

The same man that had carried me thither waited for me with his ass to carry me home again; so I mounted the ass and went straight home; ordering the man to come to me again in the afternoon at a certain hour, to secure which I would not pay him till that time came.

As soon as I arrived at my lodging, my first care was to order my folks to buy a good lamb, and several sorts of cakes, which I sent by a porter as a present to the lady. When that was done, I minded my serious affairs till the owner of the ass came: Then I went along with him to the lady's house, and was received by her with as much joy as before, and entertained with equal magnificence.

Next morning I took leave, and left her another purse with fifty pieces of gold. I continued to visit the lady every day, and to leave her every time a purse of fifty pieces of gold, till the merchants whom I employed to sell my cloth, and whom I visited regularly twice a week, I continued these chargeable visits, I say, till the merchants owed me nothing. And, in short, I came at last to be moneyless, and hopeless of having any more.

In this desperate condition I walked out of my lodging, not knowing what course to take, and by chance steered towards the castle, where there was a great crowd of people to see the sultan of Egypt. As soon as I came up to them, I wedged in among the crowd, and by chance happened to stand by a cavalier well mounted, and handsomely cloathed, who had upon the bow of his saddle a bag half open, with a string of green silk hanging out of it. I clapped my hand to the bag, concluding the silk twist might be the string of a purse within the bag: In the mean time, a porter, with a load of wood upon his back, passed by the other side of the horse, so near that the gentleman on horseback was forced to turn his head towards him to avoid being rubbed by the wood. In that very minute did the devil tempt me; I took the string in one hand, and with the other laid open the mouth of the bag, and so pulled out the purse so dexterously that nobody perceived it. The purse was heavy, and so I did not doubt but there was gold or silver in it.

As soon as the porter had passed, the cavalier, who probably had some suspicion of what I had done while his head was turned, presently put his hand to his bag, and, finding his purse was gone, gave me such a blow that he knocked me down. This violence shocked all that saw it; some took hold of the horse's bridle to stop the gentleman, and know of him what reason he had to beat me, or how he came to treat a mussulman after that rate. Do not you trouble yourselves, said he, with a brisk tone, I had reason enough for what I did; this fellow is a thief. In fine, every one took my part, and cried he was a liar, for that it was incredible a young man, such as I, should be guilty of so foul an action; but while they were holding his horse by the bridle to favour my escape, unfortunately came by the justiciary judge, who, seeing such a crowd about the gentleman on horseback and me, came up and asked what the matter was? Every body reflected on the gentleman for treating me so unjustly upon the pretence of robbery.

The judge did not give ear to all that was said on my behalf; but asked the cavalier if he suspected any body else besides me? The cavalier told him he did not, and gave his reasons why he believed his suspicion not to be groundless. Upon this the judge ordered his followers to seize me, and search me, which they presently did; and, finding the purse upon me, exposed it to the view of all the people. The shame was so great I could not bear it, but I swooned away. In the mean time the judge called for the purse.

When the judge had got the purse in his hand, he asked the horseman if it was his, and how much money was in it? The cavalier knew it to be his own, and assured the judge he had put twenty sequins into it. Upon that the judge called me before him; Come, young man, said he, confess the truth. Was it you that took the gentleman's purse from him? Do not put yourself to the trouble of torture to extort confession. Then I looked down with my eyes, thinking within myself, that, if I denied the fact, they, finding the purse about me, would convict me of a lie; so, to avoid a double punishment, I looked up, and confessed it was I. I had no sooner made the confession than the judge called people to witness it, and ordered my hand to be cut off. This hard sentence was put in execution immediately upon the spot, to the great regret of all the spectators; nay, I observed, by the cavalier's countenance, that he was moved with pity as much as the rest. This judge would likewise have ordered my foot to be cut off, but I begged the cavalier to intercede for my pardon, which he did, and obtained it.

When the judge was gone, the cavalier came up to me, and holding out the purse, I see plainly, said he, that it was necessity put you upon an action so disgraceful and unworthy of such a handsome young man as you are. Here, take that fatal purse; I freely give it you, and am heartily sorry for the misfortune you have undergone. This said, he went away; and I being very weak, by reason of my loss of blood, some of the good people that lived that way had the charity to carry me into one of their houses, and gave me a glass of wine; they likewise dressed my arm, and wrapped up the dismembered hand in a cloth.

If I had returned to the khan where I lodged, I should not have found there such relief as I wanted; and to offer to go to the young lady's was running a great hazard, it being likely she would not look upon me after such an infamous thing had befallen me. However, I resolved to put it to the trial; and, to tire out the crowd that followed me, I turned down several by-streets, and at last arrived at my lady's, very weak, and so much fatigued, that I presently threw myself down upon a sofa, keeping my right arm under my coat, for I took great care to conceal my misfortune.

In the mean time, the lady hearing of my arrival, and that I was not well, came to me in all haste; My dear soul, said she, what is the matter with you? Madam, said I, I have got a violent pain in my head. The lady seemed to be mightily afflicted with my pretended illness, and asked me to sit down, for I had got up to receive her. Tell me, said she, how your illness came; the last time I had the pleasure to see you, you was very well: There must be something else that you conceal from me; prithee let me know what it is? I stood silent, and, instead of an answer, tears trickled down my cheeks. I cannot conceive, said she, what it is that afflicts you. Have I given you any occasion to be uneasy? or do you come on purpose to tell me you do not love me? It is not that, madam, said I, fetching a deep sigh, your unjust suspicion is an addition to my evil.

I could not think of discovering to her the true cause. When night came, supper was brought, and she pressed me to eat; but, considering I could only feed myself with my left hand, I begged to be excused, upon the plea of having no stomach. Your stomach will come to you, said she, if you would but discover what you so obstinately hide from me. Your inappetency, without doubt, is only owing to the aversion you have to a discovery. Alas! madam, said I, I find I must discover at last. I had no sooner spoke these words than she filled me a cup full of wine: Drink that, said she, it will give you assurance. So I reached out my left hand, and took the cup.

When I had got the cup in my hand, I redoubled my tears and sighs: Why do you sigh and cry so bitterly? said the lady; and why do you take the cup with your left hand rather than your right? Ah! madam, said I, excuse me, I beseech you, I have got a swelling in my right hand. Let me see that swelling, said she, I will open it. I desired to be excused upon that head, alledging the tumour was not ripe enough for opening; and drank the cupful, which was very large. In fine, the steams of the wine, joined to my weakness and weariness, set me asleep, and I slept very sound till next morning.

In the mean time, the lady, curious to know what ailment I had in my right hand, lifted up my coat that covered it, and saw, to her great astonishment, that it was cut off, and that I had brought it along with me, wrapped up in a cloth. She presently apprehended what was my reason for declining a discovery, notwithstanding all the pressing instances she made; and passed the whole night in the greatest uneasiness upon my disgrace, which she concluded had been occasioned by the love I bore to her.

When I awaked, I discerned by her countenance that she was extremely grieved. However, that she might not increase my uneasiness, she said never a word. She called for jelly broth of fowl, which she had ordered to be got ready, and made me eat and drink to recruit my strength. After that I offered to take leave of her, but she declared I should not go out of her doors:—Though you tell me nothing of the matter, said she, I am persuaded I am the cause of the misfortune that has befallen you: The grief that I feel upon that score will quickly make an end of me; but before I die, I must do one thing that is designed for your advantage. She had no sooner said the word than she called for a public notary and witnesses, and ordered a writing to be drawn up, entitling me to her whole estate. After this was done, and the men dispatched, she opened a large trunk, where lay all the purses I had given her from the commencement of our amours. There are they all entire, said she, I have not touched one of them: Here, take the key, the trunk is your's. After I had returned her thanks for her generosity and bounty, What I do for you, said she, is nothing at all: I shall not be satisfied unless I die, to shew how much I love you. I conjured her, by all the powers of love, to drop such a fatal resolution; but all my remonstrances were ineffectual; she was so afflicted to see me have but one hand, that she sickened, and died after five or six weeks illness.

After mourning for her death as long as was decent, I took possession of all her estate, a particular account of which she gave me before she died; and the corn you sold for me was part of it.

What I have now told you, will influence you to excuse me for eating with my left hand. I am mightly obliged to you for the trouble you have given yourself on my account. I can never make sufficient acknowledgment of your fidelity. Since God has still given me a competent estate, notwithstanding I have spent a great deal, I beg you to accept of the sum now in your hand as a present from me. Over and above this, I have a proposal to make to you, which is this: For as much as, by reason of this fatal accident, I am obliged to depart Cairo, I am resolved never to see it more. So, if you will please to accompany me, we will trade together as equal partners, and divide the profit.

I thanked the young man, said the Christian merchant, for the present he made me; and, as to the proposal of travelling with him, I willingly embraced it, assuring him that his interest should always be as dear to me as my own.

We set a day for our departure, and accordingly entered upon our travels. We passed through Syria and Mesopotamia, travelled all over Persia; and, after stopping at several cities, came at last, sir, to your metropolis. Some time after our arrival in this place, the young man having formed a design of returning to Persia, and settling there, we settled our accounts, and parted very good friends. So he went from hence, and I, sir, continue here at your majesty's service.—This, sir, is the story I had to tell you: Does not your majesty find it yet more surprising than that of the crooked buffoon?

The sultan of Casgar fell into a passion against the Christian merchant: You are very bold, said he, to tell me a story so little worth my hearing, and then to compare it to that of my jester. Can you flatter yourself so far, as to believe that the trifling adventures of a young rake can make such an impression upon me as those of my jester? Well, I am resolved to hang you all four to revenge his death.

This said, the purveyor fell down at the sultan's feet: Sir, said he, I humbly beseech your majesty to suspend your just wrath, and hear my story; and if my story appears to your majesty to be prettier than that of your jester, to pardon us all four. The sultan having granted his request, the purveyor began thus.

The Story told by the Sultan of Casgar's Purveyor

Sir, a person of quality invited me yesterday to his daughter's wedding; accordingly I went to his house at the hour appointed, and found there a large company of doctors, ministers of justice, and others of the best quality in the city. After the ceremony was over, we had a splendid treat; and, among other things set upon the table, there was a course with garlic-sauce, which indeed was very delicious and palatable to every body; only we observed that one of the guests did not offer to touch it, though it stood just before him, and thereupon we invited him to do as we did; but he conjured us not to press him upon that head: I will take care, said he, not to touch any thing that has garlic in it; I remember well what the tasting of such a thing cost me once before. We intreated him to tell us what was the occasion of his so strong aversion to garlic: But, before he had time to make answer, Is it thus, said the master of the house, that you honour my table? This ragout* is excellent, do not you pretend to be excused from eating of it; you must do me that favour as well as the rest. Sir, said the gentleman, who was a Bagdad merchant, I hope you do not think I refuse to eat it out of a mistaken nicety; if you will have me eat of it, I will do it; but still upon this condition, that, after eating of it, I may wash my hands, with your good leave, forty times with alcali,[1] forty times with the ashes of the same plant,

[1] This is called in English, salt-wort.*

and forty times again with soap. I hope you will not take it ill that I stipulate this condition, in pursuance of an oath I have made never to taste garlic without observing it.

The master of the house would not dispense with the merchant from eating of the ragout with garlic; and therefore ordered his servant to get ready a bason with water, together with alcali, the ashes of the same plant, and soap, that the merchant might wash as often as he pleased. When every thing was got ready, Now, said he to the merchant, I hope you will do as we do.

The merchant, displeased with the violence that was offered him, reached out his hand, and took up a bit, which he put to his mouth trembling, and ate with a reluctancy that surprised us all. But the greatest surprise of all was, that he had only four fingers and no thumb, which none of us observed before, though he had ate of other dishes. You have lost your thumb, said the master of the house, how came that about? It must have been occasioned by some extraordinary accident, a relation of which will be agreeable entertainment to the company. Sir, replied the merchant, I have not a thumb neither on the right nor on the left-hand. In speaking this, he shewed us his left-hand as well as his right. But this is not all, continued he, I have not a great toe on either of my feet. I hope you will take my word for it. I was maimed in this manner by an unheard-of accident, which I am willing to relate to you, if you will have the patience to hear me. The relation will equally astonish you, and affect you with pity; only suffer me to wash my hands first. With this he rose from the table, and, after washing his hands an hundred and twenty times, took his place again, and recounted the story as follows.

You must know, gentlemen, that, in the reign of the caliph Haroun Alraschid, my father lived at Bagdad, the place of my nativity, and was reputed one of the richest merchants in the city: But being a man mightily addicted to his pleasures, a man that loved an irregular life, and neglected his private affairs, instead of leaving me a plentiful fortune at his death, he left me in such a condition, that all the economy I could master was scarce sufficient to clear his debts. However, with much ado, I paid them all; and, through my industry and care, my little fortune began to look with a smiling countenance.

One morning as I opened my shop, a lady, mounted upon a mule, and attended by an eunuch and two women slaves, stopped near my shop-door, and, with the assistance of the eunuch, alighted. Madam, said the eunuch, I told you, you would be too soon, you see there is no body yet in the bezestein; if you had taken my advice, you might have saved yourself the trouble of waiting here. The lady looked all round her, and finding there was no shop open but mine, addressed herself to me, asking leave to sit in my shop till the rest of the merchants came: So I could do no less than return a civil answer, and invite the lady into my shop.

The lady sat down in my shop, and, observing there was nobody in the whole bezestein but the eunuch and I, uncovered her face to take the air; and, I must say, I never saw any thing so pretty in my life-time; I no sooner had a sight of her face than I loved her; in course I fixed my eyes upon her, and perceived that she was not displeased with my ogling, for she gave me a full opportunity to look upon her, and did not cover her face, but when she was afraid of being taken notice of.

After she had pulled down her veil again, she told me she wanted several sorts of the richest and finest stuffs, and asked me if I had them? Alas! madam, said I, I am but a young man, and just beginning the world, I have not stock enough for such great concerns; and it is a mortification to me that I have nothing to shew you such as you want: But, to save you the trouble of going from shop to shop, as soon as the merchants come, I will go, if you please, and fetch from them what you want, with the lowest prices; and so you may do your business without going any farther. She complied with my proposals, and entered into discourse with me, which continued so much the longer, that I still made her believe the merchants that could furnish what she wanted were not yet come.

I was no less charmed with her wit than I had been before with the beauty of her face; but there was a necessity of denying myself the pleasure of her conversation: I ran out to see for the stuffs she wanted, and, after she had pitched upon what she liked, we struck the price at five thousand drams of coined silver; so I wrapped up the stuffs in a small bundle, and gave it to the eunuch, who put it under his arm; this done, she rose and took leave: I still continued to look after her till she had got at the bezestein-gate, and mounted her mule again.

The lady had no sooner disappeared than I perceived that love is the cause of great oversights: It had so engrossed all my thoughts, that truly I did not mind that she went off without paying the money, neither had I the consideration to ask who she was, or where she dwelt. However, I considered I was accountable for a large sum to the merchants, who, perhaps, would not have the patience to stay for their money; and so I went to them and made the best excuse I could, pretending that I knew the lady; and then came home again equally affected with love, and with the burden of such a heavy debt.

I had desired my creditors to stay eight days for their money; and, when the eight days were past, they did not fail to dun me:* Then I entreated them to give me eight days more, which they agreed to, and the very next day I saw the lady come to the bezestein, mounted on her mule, with the same attendants as before, and exactly at the same hour of the day.

She came straight to my shop. I have made you stay some time, said she, but here is your money at last, carry it to a banker, and see it is all good. The eunuch, who brought me the money, went along with me to the banker's, and we found it very right: Then I came back again, and had the happiness of conversing with the lady till all the shops of the bezestein were open: Though we talked but of ordinary things, she gave them such a turn that they appeared new and uncommon, and convinced me that I was not mistaken in admiring her wit, when I conversed with her.

As soon as the merchants were come, and had opened their shops, I carried to the respective men the money that was due for their stuffs, and was readily entrusted with more, which the lady had desired to see. In short, the lady took stuffs to the value of an hundred pieces of gold, and carried them away again without paying for them; nay, without saying one word, or giving me to know who she was. I was astonished when I considered that at this rate she left me without any security of not being troubled if she never came again. She has paid me, thinks I to myself, a good round sum, but she leaves me in the lurch for another that runs much deeper. Sure she cannot be a cheat; it is not possible she can have any such design as to inveigle me to my ruin: The merchants do not know her, they will all come upon me. In short, my love was not so powerful as to guard off the uneasiness I was under when I reflected upon all circumstances: A whole month passed before I heard any thing of my lady again; and, during that time, the alarm grew higher and higher every day. The merchants were impatient for their money, and, to satisfy them, I was even going to sell off all I had, when the lady returned one morning with the same equipage as before.

Take your weights, said she, and weigh the gold I have brought you. These words dispelled my fear and inflamed my love. Before we told down the money, she asked me several questions, and, particularly, if I was married? I made answer, I never was. Then reaching out the gold to the eunuch, let us have your interposition, said she, to accommodate our matters: Upon which the eunuch fell a-laughing, and, calling me aside, made me weigh the gold: While I was weighing the gold, the eunuch whispered in my ear, I know by your eyes you love this lady, and I am surprised to find that you have not the assurance to disclose your love to her: She loves you more passionately than you do her. Do you imagine that she has any real occasion for your stuffs? She only makes an errand to come hither because you have inspired her with a violent passion. Do but ask her the question: It will be your own fault only, if you do not marry her. It is true, said I, I have had a love for her from the first moment that I cast my eyes upon her, but I durst not aspire to the happiness of thinking my love acceptable to her. I am entirely hers, and shall not fail to retain a grateful sense of your good offices in that matter.

In fine, I made an end of weighing the gold, and, while I was putting it into the bag, the eunuch turned to the lady, and told I was satisfied; that being the word they had both agreed upon between themselves. Presently after that, the lady rose and took leave; telling me she would send the eunuch to me, and that I should do what he directed me to do in her name.

I carried every one of the merchants their money, and waited some days with impatience for the eunuch. At last he came.

I entertained the eunuch very kindly, and asked him how his mistress did? You are, said he, the happiest lover in the world; she is quite sick of love for you; she covets extremely to see you; and, were she mistress of her own conduct, would not fail to come to you, and willingly pass all the moments of her life in your company. Her noble mien and graceful carriage, said I, gave me to know that she was a lady beyond the common level. The judgment you have formed upon that head, said the eunuch, is very just; she is the favourite of Zobeide, the caliph's lady, who has brought her up from her infancy, and entrusts her with all her affairs. Having a mind to marry, she has declared to the caliph's lady that she has cast her eyes upon you, and desired her consent. Zobeide told her she agreed to it, only she had a mind to see you first, in order to judge if she had made a good choice, the which, if she had, Zobeide meant to defray the charges of the wedding. Thus you see your felicity is certain; since you have pleased the favourite, you will be equally agreeable to the mistress, who seeks only to oblige her favourite, and would by no means thwart her inclination. In fine, all you have to do is to come to the palace. I am sent hither to call you, so you will please to come to a resolution. My resolve is formed already, said I, and I am ready to follow you whithersoever you please to conduct me. Very well, said the eunuch; but you know men are not allowed to enter the ladies' apartments in the palace, and so you must be introduced with great secrecy: The favourite lady has contrived the matter very well. Upon your side you are to act your part, and that very discreetly; for, if you do not, your life is at stake.

I gave him repeated assurances of a punctual performance of whatever should be enjoined me. Then, said he, in the evening you must be at the mosque built by the caliph's lady, on the bank of the Tigris, and stay there till one comes to call you. I agreed to all he proposed; and, after passing the day in great impatience, went in the evening to the prayer that is said an hour and a half after sun-set in the mosque,* and there I staid after all the people were gone.

Soon after, I saw a boat making up to the mosque, the rowers of which were all eunuchs, who came on shore, and put several large trunks into the mosque, and then retired; only one of them staid behind, whom I perceived to be the same eunuch that had all along accompanied the lady, and had been with me that morning. Much about the same time, I saw the lady enter the mosque; and, making up to her, told her I was ready to obey her orders. Come, come, said she, we have no time to lose; with that she opened one of the trunks, and bid me get into it, that being necessary both for her safety and mine. Fear nothing, added she, leave the management of all the rest to me. I considered with myself I had gone too far to look back, and so obeyed her orders, upon which she locked the trunk. This done, the eunuch that was her confidant called the other eunuchs who had brought in the trunks, and ordered them to carry them on board again. Then the lady and eunuch re-embarked, and the boatment rowed to Zobeide's apartment.

In the mean time, I reflected very seriously upon the danger to which I had exposed myself, and made vows and prayers, though it was then too late.

The boat put into the palace-gate, and the trunks were carried into the apartment of the officer of the eunuchs, who keeps the key of the ladies' apartments, and suffers nothing to enter without a narrow inspection. The officer was then in bed, and so there was a necessity of calling him up.

The officer of the eunuchs was angry that they should break his rest, and chid the favourite lady severely for coming home so late: You shall not come off so easily as you think; for, said he, not one of these trunks shall pass till I have opened them every one. At the same time he commanded the eunuchs to bring them before him, and open them one by one. The first they began with was that where I lay, which run me to the last degree of consternation.

The favourite lady, who had the key of that trunk, protested it should not be opened. You know very well, said she, I bring nothing hither but what is to serve Zobeide, your mistress and mine. This trunk, continued she, is filled with rich goods that I had from some merchants lately arrived, besides a number of bottles of Zemzem water sent from Mecca;[1] and if any of these should happen to break, the goods will be spoiled, and then you must answer for them: Zobeide will take care, I will warrant you, to resent your insolence. In fine, she stood up so tight to the matter, that the officer did not dare to take upon him to open any of the trunks. Let them go then, said he, carry them off. Upon that the lady's apartment was opened, and all the trunks were carried in.

They were scarce got in, when all on a sudden I heard the folks cry, Here is the caliph, here comes the caliph! This put me in such a fright, that I

[1] There is a fountain at Mecca, which, according to the Mahometans, is a spring that God shewed to Hagar, after Abraham was obliged to put her away. The water of this spring is drunk by way of devotion, and is sent in presents to princes and princesses.*

wonder I did not die upon the spot, for in effect it was the caliph. What hast thou got in these trunks, said he to the favourite? Some stuffs, said she, lately arrived, which your majesty's lady had a mind to see. Open them, cried he, and let me see them too. She pretended to excuse herself, alledging the stuffs were only proper for ladies, and that, by opening them, his lady would be deprived of the pleasure of seeing them first. I say, open them, cried the caliph, I have a mind to see them, and I will see them. She still represented that her mistress would be angry with her if she opened them: No, no, said he, I will engage she shall not say a word to you for so doing: Come, come, open them, I cannot stay.

There was a necessity of obeying, which gave me such shocking alarms, that I trembled every time I thought on it. Down sat the caliph; and the favourite ordered all the trunks to be brought before him, one after another. Then she opened them; and, to spin out the time, shewed all the beauties of each particular stuff, thinking thereby to tire out his patience; but her stratagem did not take. Being as loth as I to have the trunk where I lay opened, she left that to the last. So, when all the rest were viewed, Come, says the caliph, make an end; let us see what is in that one. I am at a loss to tell you whether I was dead or alive that moment, for I little thought of escaping so great a danger.

When Zobeide's favourite saw that the caliph would needs have the trunk opened where I lay, As for this trunk, says she, your majesty will please to dispense with the opening of it; there are some things in it which I cannot shew you without your lady be by. Well, well, says the caliph, since it is so, I am satisfied; order the trunks to be carried away. The word was no sooner spoken than the trunks were moved into her chamber, where I began to come to life again.

As soon as the eunuchs who had brought them were gone, she presently opened the trunk where I was prisoner. Come out, said she, go up these stairs that lead to an upper room, and stay there till I come. The door which led to the stairs she locked after I was in; and that was no sooner done than the caliph came and clapped him down upon the very trunk where I had been. The occasion of this visit was a motion of curiosity that did not respect me. He had a mind to discourse the lady about what she had seen or heard in the city. So they discoursed together a pretty while, and then he left her, and retired to his apartment.

When she found the coast clear, she came to the chamber where I was, and made many apologies for the alarms she had given me. My uneasiness, said she, was no less than yours; you cannot well doubt of that, since I have run the same risk out of love to you; perhaps another would not have had the presence of mind to manage matters so dexterously upon so tender an occasion; nothing less than the love I had for you could have inspired me with courage to do it. But come, take heart, now the danger is over. After some tender discourse between us, she told me it was time to go to bed, and that she would not fail to introduce me to Zobeide, her mistress, to-morrow, some hour of the day; for the caliph never sees her, added she, but at nights. Heartened by these words, I slept very well; or, at least, whatever interruptions happened to my sleep were agreeable disquietings, caused by the hopes of enjoying a lady that was blessed with such sparkling wit and beauty.

The next day, before I was introduced to Zobeide, her favourite instructed me how to behave before her, naming much the same questions as she put to me, and dictating the answers I was to give. This done, she carried me into a very magnificent and richly furnished hall; I was no sooner entered, than twenty she-slaves, in rich and uniform habits, came out of Zobeide's apartment, and placed themselves very modestly before the throne in two equal rows; they were followed by twenty other ladies, that looked younger, and were cloathed after the same manner, only their habits appeared somewhat gayer. In the middle of these appeared Zobeide, with a majestic air, and so loaded with jewels that she could scarce walk. Then Zobeide went and sat down on the throne, and the favourite lady, who had accompanied her, just by her, on her right-hand; the other ladies being placed at some distance on each side of the throne.

As soon as the caliph's lady was set down, the slaves that came in first made a sign for me to approach: So I advanced between the rows they had formed, and prostrated myself upon the tapestry that was under the princess's feet. She ordered me to rise, and did me the honour to ask my name, my family, and the condition of my fortune; upon all which I gave her satisfactory answers, as I perceived, not only by her countenance but by her words: I am very glad, said she, that my daughter (so she used to call the favourite lady, looking upon her as such, after the care she had taken of her education,) has made a choice that pleases me; I approve of it, and give consent to your marriage: I will give orders myself for what is to be done in solemnizing it, but I want to have her stay ten days with me before the solemnity; and in that time I will speak to the caliph, and obtain his consent: Meanwhile, do you stay here, you shall be taken care of.

Pursuant to the caliph's lady's orders, I staid ten days in the ladies' apartments, and, during that time, was deprived of the pleasure of seeing the favourite lady; but was so well used, by her orders, that I had no reason to be dissatisfied.

Zobeide told the caliph her resolution of marrying the favourite lady; and the caliph leaving to her the liberty of doing upon that head what she pleased, granted the favourite a considerable sum to help out her fortune.

When the ten days were expired, Zobeide ordered the contract of marriage to be drawn up; and the necessary preparations being made for the solemnity, the dancers (both men and women) were called in, and there were great rejoicings in the palace for nine days. The tenth day being appointed for the last ceremony of the marriage, the favourite lady was conducted to a bath, and I to another. At night I sat down to table, and had all manner of rarities served up to me, and, among other things, ragout with garlic, such as you have now forced me to eat of. This ragout I liked so well, that I scarce touched any other of the dishes. But such was my unhappiness, that, when I rose from the table, I only wiped my hands, instead of washing them well; a piece of negligence I had never been guilty of before.

Though it was then night, the whole apartment of the ladies was as light as day, by means of many illuminations. Nothing was to be heard all over the palace but musical instruments and acclamations of joy. My bride and I were introduced into a great hall, where we were placed upon two thrones. The women that attended her made her shift herself several times, and painted her face with different sorts of colours, according to the usual custom on wedding-days; and every time she changed her habit, they exposed her to my view.

In fine, all these ceremonies being over, we were conducted to the wedding-room; where, as soon as the company retired, I approached to embrace my mistress; but, instead of answering me with transports, she shoved me off, and cried out most fearfully; upon which all the ladies of the apartment came running into the chamber to know what she cried for; and, for my own part, I was so thunder-struck, that I stood like a post, without the power of so much as asking what she meant by it. Dear sister, said they to her, what is the matter? Let us know it, that we may try to relieve you. Take, said she, out of my sight that vile fellow. Why, madam, said I, wherein have I deserved your displeasure? You are a villain, said she, with furious passion: What, to eat garlic, and not wash your hands! Do ye think I would suffer such a filthy fellow to touch me? Down with him, down with him upon the ground, continued she, addressing herself to the ladies; and pray let me have a good bull's pizzle. In short, I was thrown upon the ground, and, while some held my hands, and others my feet, my wife, who was presently furnished with a weapon, laid on me most unmercifully, till I could scarce breathe: Then she said to the ladies, Take him, send him to the justiciary judge, and let the hand be cut off with which he fed upon the garlic ragout.

God bless my soul, cried I, must I be beat and bruised, and unmercifully mauled, and still, to complete my affliction, have my hand cut off, and all for eating of a ragout with garlic, and forgetting to wash my hands? What proportion is there between the punishment and the crime? Plague on the ragout, plague on the cook that dressed it, and may he be equally unhappy that served it up!

All the ladies that were by took pity of me, when they heard the cutting off of my hand spoken of.—Dear madam, dear sister, said they to the favourite lady, you carry your resentment too far. We own he is a man quite ignorant of the world, that he does not observe your quality, and the regards that are due to you: But we beseech you to overlook and pardon the fault he has committed. I have not received suitable satisfaction, said she; I will teach him to know the world, I will make him bear the sensible marks of his impertinence, and be cautious hereafter how he tastes a garlic ragout without washing his hands. However, they still continued their solicitations, and fell down at her feet, and kissing her fair hand; Good madam, said they, in the name of God, moderate your wrath, and grant the favour we request. She answered never a word, but got up, and, after throwing out a thousand hard words against me, walked out of the chamber, and all the ladies followed her, leaving me in inconceivable affliction.

I continued there ten days, without seeing any body but an old woman-slave that brought me victuals. I asked the old woman what was become of the favourite lady? She is sick, said the old woman, she is sick of the poisoned smell you infected her with. Why did you not take care to wash your hands after eating of that cursed ragout? Is it possible, thought I to myself, that these ladies can be so nice and so vindictive, for so small a fault! In the mean time, I loved my wife, notwithstanding all her cruelty.

One day the old woman told me my spouse was recovered, and gone to bathe, and would come to see me the next day; So, said she, I would have you to call up your patience, and endeavour to accommodate yourself to her humour. Besides, she is a woman of good sense and discretion, and entirely beloved by all the ladies about Zobeide's court.

In effect, my wife came next night, and accosted me thus: You see I am too good in seeing you again, after the affront you have offered me; but still I cannot stoop to be reconciled to you, till I have punished you according to your demerit, in not washing your hands after eating the garlic ragout. This said, she called the ladies, who, by her order, threw me upon the ground; and, after binding me fast, had the barbarity to cut off my thumbs and great toes themselves with a razor. One of the ladies applied a certain root to staunch the blood; but, what by bleeding and what by the pain, I swooned away.

When I came to myself, they gave me wine to drink to recruit my strength. Ah! madam, said I to my wife, if ever I eat of garlic ragout again, I solemnly swear to wash my hands a hundred and twenty times with the herb alcali, with the ashes of the same plant, and with soap. Well, replied my wife, upon that condition I am willing to forget what is past, and live with you as my husband.

This, continued the Bagdad merchant, addressing himself to the company, this is the reason why I refused to eat of the garlic ragout that is now upon the table.

To make an end of the Bagdad merchant's story, the ladies, said he, applied to my wounds, not only the root I mentioned to you, but likewise some balsam of Mecca, which they were morally assured was not adulterated, because they had it out of the caliph's own dispensatory: By virtue of that admirable balsam was I perfectly cured in a few days, and my wife and I lived together as agreeably as if I had never ate of the garlic ragout. But having been all my life-time used to the liberty of ranging abroad, I was very uneasy at the being confined to the caliph's palace; and yet I said nothing of it to my wife, for fear of displeasing her. However, she smelt it; and wanted nothing more herself than to get out, for it was gratitude alone that made her continue with Zobeide. In fine, being a very witty woman, she represented in lively terms to her mistress the constraint I was under in not living in the city with my fellow-companions, as I had always done: This she did so effectually, that the good princess chose rather to deprive herself of the pleasure of having her favourite about her, than not to grant what she equally desired.

In pursuance of this grant, about a month after our marriage, my wife came into my room with several eunuchs, carrying each of them a bag of silver.—When the eunuchs were gone, You never told me, said she, that you were uneasy in being confined to court, but I perceived it very well, and have happily found means to make you contented. My mistress Zobeide gives us leave to go out of the palace; and here are fifty thousand sequins of which she has made us a present, in order to enable us to live comfortable in the city. Prithee take ten thousand of them, and go and buy us a house.

I quickly found a house for the money, and, after furnishing it richly, we went and lived in it, and kept a great many slaves of both sexes, with a very pretty equipage. In short, we began to live after a very agreeable manner, but it did not last long. At a year's end my wife fell sick and died.

I might have married again, and lived honourably at Bagdad, but the curiosity of seeing the world put me upon other thoughts. I sold my house, and, after buying up several sorts of goods, I went with a caravan to Persia, from Persia I travelled to Samarcande, and from thence hither.

This, said the purveyor to the sultan of Casgar, this is the story that the Bagdad merchant told in a company where I was yesterday. This story, said the sultan, has something in it that is extraordinary, but it does not come near that of my little hunch-back. Then the Jewish physician prostrated himself before the sultan's throne, and rising again, addressed himself to that prince in the following manner: Sir, if you will be so good as to hear me, I flatter myself you will be pleased with a story I have to tell you. Well spoke, said the sultan, but if it is not more surprising than that of little hunch-back, do not you expect to live.

The Jewish physician, finding the sultan of Casgar disposed to hear him, gave the following relation.

The Story told by the Jewish Physician

SIR, when I was a student of physic, and just beginning the practice of that noble profession with some reputation, a man slave called me to see a patient in the governor of the city's family. Accordingly I went, and was carried into a room, where I found a very proper handsome young man mightily cast down with his condition: I saluted him, and sat down by him, but he made no return to my compliments, only a sign with his eyes that he heard me and thanked me. Pray, sir, said I, give your hand that I may feel your pulse. But, instead of stretching out his right, he gave me his left-hand, at which I was extremely surprised. This, thinks I to myself, is a gross piece of ignorance, that he does not know that people present their right-hand and not their left to a physician. However, I felt his pulse, and wrote him a receipt, and so took leave.

I continued my visits for nine days, and every time I felt his pulse, he still gave me the left hand; on the tenth day he seemed to be pretty well, and so I prescribed nothing for him but bathing. The governor of Damascus, who was by, did, in testimony of his being well satisfied with my service, invest me with a very rich robe, saying, he made me a physician of the city-hospital, and physician in ordinary to his house, where I might freely eat at his table when I pleased.

The young man likewise shewed me many civilities, and asked me to accompany him to the bath: Accordingly we went together; and when his attendants had undressed him, I perceived he wanted the right-hand, and that it had not been long cut off, which had been the occasion of his distemper, though concealed from me; for, while the people about him were applying proper medicines externally, they had called me to prevent the ill consequence of the fever he was then in. I was very much surprised and concerned on seeing his misfortune, which he observed by my countenance. Doctor, cried he, do not be astonished to see that my hand is cut off; some day or other I will tell you the occasion of it, and in that relation you will be entertained with very surprising adventures.

After we had done bathing, we sat down and ate; and after we had some other discourse together, he asked me if it would be any prejudice to his health, if he went and fetched a walk out of town in the governor's garden? I made answer, it would be so far from that, that it would benefit his health. Since it is so, said he, if you will let me have your company, I will tell you the history of my adventures. I replied, I was at his command for all that day. Upon which he presently called his servants to bring something for a collation; and so we went to the governor's garden. There we took two or three turns, and then sat down upon a carpet that his servants had spread under a tree, which gave a very pleasant shade. After we were set, the young man gave his history in the following terms.

I was born, said he, at Moussoul, and come of one of the most considerable families in the city. My father was the eldest of ten brothers that were all alive, and all married when my grandfather died. All the brothers were childless but my father; and he had never a child but me. He took a particular care of my education, and made me learn every thing that was proper for a child of my quality.

When I was grown pretty tall, and beginning to keep company with the world, I happened one Friday to be at noon-prayers with my father and my uncles in the great mosque of Moussoul. And after prayers were over, the rest of the company were going away, my father and my uncles continued sitting upon the best tapestry in the mosque, and I sat down by them. They discoursed of several things, but they fell insensibly, I do not know how, upon the subject of voyages. They extolled the beauties and peculiar rarities of some kingdoms, and of their principal cities: but one of my uncles said, that, according to the uniform report of an infinite number of voyagers, there was not in the world a pleasanter country than Egypt and the Nile; and the account he gave of them infused into me such a charming idea of them, that, from that very moment, I had a desire to travel. Whatever my other uncles said, by way of preference to Bagdad and the Tigris, in calling Bagdad the true residence of the mussulman religion, and the metropolis of all the cities of the earth, all this made no impression upon me. My father joined in his opinion with those who had spoken on the behalf of Egypt, which gave me a great deal of joy. Say what you will, said he, he that has not seen Egypt has not seen the greatest rarity in the world. All the land there is golden, I mean it is so fertile that it enriches its inhabitants: All the women of that country are charming, either in their beauty or in their agreeable carriage. If you speak of the Nile, pray where is there a more admirable river? What water was ever lighter or more delicious? The very slime it carries along in its overflowing, fattens a thousand times more than other countries that are cultivated with great labour. Do but mind what a poet said of the Egyptians, when he was obliged to depart Egypt: Your Nile loads you with good offices every day; it is for you only that it travels so far. Alas! in removing from you, my tears are going to run as abundantly as its water; you are to continue in the enjoyment of its sweetnesses, while I am condemned to rob myself of them against my will.

If you look, added my father, towards the island that is formed by the two great branches of the Nile, what variety of verdure have you there! What enamel of all sorts of flowers! What a prodigious number of cities, villages, canals, and a thousand other agreeable objects! If you cast your eyes on the other side, steering up towards Ethiopia, how many other objects of admiration! I cannot compare the verdure of so many plains, watered with the different canals of the island, better than to sparkling emeralds set in silver. Is not Great Cairo the largest, the most populous, and the richest city in the universe? What a prodigious number of magnificent edifices, both public and private! If you view the pyramids, you will be seized with astonishment: You will turn stiff and immoveable at the sight of these masses of stone of an extravagant thickness, which rise to the skies; and you will be obliged to profess, that the Pharaohs, who employed such riches and so many men in building them, must have surpassed all the monarchs that have appeared since, not only in Egypt, but all the world over, in magnificence and invention; so transcendant are the monuments they have left worthy of their memory: Monuments so ancient, that the learned cannot agree upon the time of their erection; and yet such as last to this day, and will last while ages are. I silently pass over the maritime cities of the kingdom of Egypt, such as Damietta, Rosetum, Alexandria, &c. where the Lord knows how many nations come for a thousand sorts of grain, seeds, cloth, and an infinite number of other things, calculated for the conveniency and the delight of men. What I speak of, I have some occasion to know; I spent some years of my youth there, which, as long as I live, I shall always reckon the most agreeable part of my life.

My uncles had no answer to give my father, and agreed to all he had said of the Nile, of Cairo, and of the whole kingdom of Egypt: As for my own part, I was so taken with it that I had never a wink of sleep that night. Soon after, my uncles declared of themselves how much they were touched with my father's discourse. They made a proposal to him that they should travel all together into Egypt. He accepted of the proposal; and, being rich merchants, they resolved to carry with them such goods as would go off there. I came to know that they were making preparations for their departure, and thereupon went to my father, and begged of him, with tears in my eyes, that he would suffer me to go along with him, and allow me some stock of goods to trade with by myself. You are too young yet, said my father, to travel into

Egypt; the fatigue is too great for you, and, besides, I am sure you will come off a loser in your traffic. However, these words did not cure me of the eager desire I had to travel. I made use of my uncles' interest with my father, who at last granted me leave to go as far as Damascus, where they would drop me till they went through their travels into Egypt. The city of Damascus, said my father, may likewise glory in its beauties, and it is very well if my son get leave to go so far. Though my curiosity to see Egypt was very pressing, I considered he was my father, and submitted to his will.

So I set out from Moussoul with him and my uncles. We travelled through Mesopotamia, passed the Euphrates, and arrived at Halep, where we staid some days. From thence we went to Damascus, the first sight of which was a very agreeable surprise to me. We lodged in one khan; and I had the view of a city that was large, populous, full of fine people, and very well fortified. We employed some days in walking up and down the delicious gardens that surrounded it; and we all agreed that Damascus was justly said to be seated in a paradise. At last my uncles thought of pursuing their journey; but took care, before they went, to sell my goods, which they did so advantageously for me, that I got five hundred per cent. This sale fetched me so considerable a sum, that I was transported to see myself possessor of it.

My father and my uncles left me in Damascus, and pursued their journey. After their departure, I used mighty caution not to lay out my money idly; but at the same time, I took a stately house all of marble, adorned with pictures of gold, and a pure branched work, and excellent water-works. I furnished it not so richly indeed as the magnificence of the place deserved, but at least handsomely enough for a young man of my condition. It had formerly belonged to one of the principal lords of the city, whose name was Modoun Adalraham: but then was the property of a rich jewel-merchant, to whom I paid for it only two sherriffs[1] a month. I had a good large number of domestics, and lived honourably; sometimes I gave entertainments to such people as I was acquainted with, and sometimes I went and was treated by them. Thus did I spend my time at Damascus, waiting for my father's return; no passion disturbed my repose, and my only employment was conversing with people of credit.

One day, as I sat taking the cool air at my gate, a very handsome fine lady came to me, and asked if I did not sell stuffs? but no sooner spoke the words than she went into my house.

When I saw that the lady had gone into the house, I rose, and, having shut the gate, carried her into a hall, and prayed her to sit down. Madam, said I, I have had stuffs that were fit to be shewn to you, but I have them not now, for which I am very sorry.—She took off the veil that covered her

[1] A sherriff is the same as a sequin. This word is in the ancient authors.

face, and made a beauty sparkle in my eyes, which affected me with such emotions as I had never felt before. I have no occasion for stuffs, said she, I only come to see you, and pass the evening with you; if you are pleased with it, all I ask of you is a light collation.

Transported with such happy luck, I ordered the folks to bring us several sorts of fruits, and some bottles of wine. They served us nimbly; and we eat and drank, and made merry till midnight. In short, I had not passed a night so agreeably all the while I had been there. Next morning I would have put ten sherriffs in the lady's hands, but she refused them: I am not come to see you, said she, from a design of interest; you affront me: I am so far from receiving money, that I desire you to take money of me, or else I will see you no more. In speaking this, she clapped her hand in her purse, took out ten sherriffs, and forced me to take them. You may expect me three days hence after sun-set. Then she took leave of me, and I felt that when she went she carried my heart along with her.

She did not fail to return at the appointed hour three days after; and I did not fail to receive her with all the joy of a person that waited impatiently for her arrival. The evening and the night we spent as before; and next day at parting she promised to return the third day after. However, she did not go without forcing me to take ten sherriffs more.

She returned a third time; and at that interview, when we were both warm with wine, she spoke thus: My dear heart, what do you think of me? Am I not handsome and agreeable? Madam, said I, all the marks of love with which I entertain you, ought to persuade you that I love you: I am charmed in seeing you, and more so in enjoying you. You are my queen, my sultaness; in you lies all the felicity of my life. Ah! sir, replied she, I am sure you would speak otherwise if you saw a certain lady of my acquaintance that is younger and handsomer than I: She is a lady of such a pleasant, jocund temper, as would make the most melancholy people merry. I must bring her hither; I spoke of you to her, and from the account I have given of you, she dies of desire to see you. She entreated me to gain her that pleasure, but I did not dare to humour her without speaking to you before-hand. Madam, said I, you shall do what you please; but, whatever you may say of your friend, I defy all her charms to tear my heart from you, to whom it is so inviolably tied, that nothing can disengage it. Do not be too positive, said she, I now tell you I am about to put your heart to a strange trial.

We staid together all night, and next morning at parting, instead of ten sherriffs, she gave me fifteen, which I was forced to accept. Remember, said she, that in two days you are to have a new guest; pray take care to give her a good reception: We will come at the usual hour, after sun-set. I took care to have my hall in great order, and a nice collation prepared, against they came.

I waited for the two ladies with impatience, and at last they arrived. They both unveiled themselves, and, as I had been surprised with the beauty of the first, I had reason to be much more so when I saw her friend. She had regular features, a lively complexion, and such sparkling eyes that I could hardly bear their splendour: I thanked her for the honour she did me, and intreated her to excuse me, if I did not give her the reception she deserved. No compliments, said she, it should be my part to make them to you for allowing my friend to bring me hither. But since you are pleased to suffer it, let us lay aside all ceremony, and think of nothing but being merry.

As soon as the ladies arrived, the collation was served up, and we sat down to supper. I sat opposite to the stranger lady, and she never left off looking upon me with a smile: I could not resist her conquering eyes, and she made herself mistress of my heart with such force, that I had not power to offer opposition. But, inspiring me, she took fire herself, and was equally touched; and was so far from shewing any thing of constraint in her carriage, that she told me very sensible, moving things.

The other lady, who minded us, did nothing at first but laugh at us. I told you, said she, addressing herself to me, you would find my friend full of charms; and I perceive you have already violated the oath you made of being faithful to me. Madam, said I, laughing as well as she, you would have reason to complain of me if I were wanting in civility to a lady that you brought hither, and one whom you are fond of; you might then upbraid me, both of you, for not knowing the measures of hospitality and entertainment.

We continued to drink on; but as the wine grew warm in our stomachs, the stranger lady and I ogled one another with so little reserve, that her friend grew jealous, and quickly gave us a dismal proof of her jealousy. She rose from the table and went out, saying, she would be with us presently again: But a few moments after, the lady that staid with me changed her countenance, fell into violent convulsions, and, in fine, expired in my arms, while I was calling to the people to come and assist me to relieve her. Immediately I went out, and asked for the other lady; and my people told me she had opened the street-door, and gone out of doors. Then I suspected what was really true, that she had been the cause of her friend's death. In fine, she had had the dexterity and the malice to put some very strong poison into the last glass, which she gave her out of her own hand.

I was afflicted to the last degree with the accident. What shall I do, thinks I within myself? What will become of me? I thought there was no time to lose, and so, it being then moon-light, made my servants quietly take up a great piece of marble, with which the yard of my house was paved; under that I made them dig a hole presently, and there inter the corpse of the young lady. After replacing the stone, I put on a travelling suit, and took what silver I had; and, having locked up every thing, affixed my own seal on the door of my house. This done, I went to see for the jewel-merchant, my landlord, paid him what rent I owed, with a year's rent more; and, giving him the key, prayed him to keep it for me: A very urging affair, said I, obliges me to be absent for some time; I am under a necessity of going to find out my uncles at Cairo. In fine, I took my leave of him, and that very moment mounted my horse, and set out with my equipage.

I had a good journey, and arrived at Cairo without any ill accident. There I met with my uncles, who were very much surprised to see me there. To excuse myself, I pretended I was tired of staying for them; and hearing nothing of them, was so uneasy that I could not be satisfied without coming to Cairo. They received me very kindly, and promised my father should not be angry with me for leaving Damascus without his permission. I lodged in the same khan with them, and saw all the curiosities of Cairo.

Having finished their traffic, they began to speak of returning to Moussoul, and to make preparations for their departure. But I having a mind to see something in Egypt that I had not yet seen, left my uncles, and went to lodge at a great distance from the khan, and did not appear till they were gone. They had sought for me all over the city; but, not finding me, they judged the remorse of having come to Egypt without my father's consent had put me upon returning to Damascus without saying any thing to them. So they began their journey, expecting to find me at Damascus, and there to take me up.

I continued at Cairo after their departure three years, to give full satisfaction to the curiosity I had of seeing all the wonders of Egypt. During that time I took care to send money to the jewel-merchant, ordering him to keep my house for me, for I had a design to return to Damascus, and stay there for some years. I had no adventure at Cairo worthy of your hearing; but doubtless you will be surprised at that I met with after my return to Damascus.

Arriving at this city, I went to the jewel-merchant's house, who received me joyfully, and would needs go along with me to my house, to shew me, that nobody had entered it whilst I was absent. In effect, the seal was still entire upon the lock; and when I went in, I found every thing in the same order in which I left it.

In sweeping and cleaning out my hall where I had used to eat, one of my servants found a gold chain necklace, with ten very large and very perfect pearls placed upon it at certain distances. He brought it to me, and I knew it to be the same I had seen upon the lady's neck that was poisoned; and concluded it had broke off and fallen when I did not perceive it. I could not look upon it without shedding tears, when I called to mind the lovely creature I had seen die in so fatal a manner; so I wrapped it up and put it in my bosom.

I passed some days to work off the fatigue of my voyage; after which I began to visit my former acquaintance. I abandoned myself to all manner of pleasure, and insensibly squandered away all my money: Being in this condition, instead of selling my moveables, I resolved to part with my necklace; but I had so little skill in pearls, that I took my measures very ill, as you shall hear.

I went to the bezestein, where I called a crier aside, and shewing him the necklace, told him I had a mind to sell it, and desired him to shew it to the principal jewellers. The crier was surprised to see such an ornament; What a pretty thing it is, cried he, staring upon it with admiration! Never did our merchants see any thing so rich: I am sure I shall oblige them in shewing it to them; and you need not doubt they will set a high price upon it in emulation with one another. He carried me to a shop, which proved to be my landlord's: Tarry here, says the crier, I will return presently, and bring you an answer.

While he was running about to shew the necklace, I sat with the jeweller, who was glad to see me; and we discoursed of common subjects. The crier returned, and calling me aside, instead of telling me the necklace was valued at two thousand sherriffs, he assured me nobody would give me more than fifty. The reason is, added he, the pearls are false; so see if you can part with it at that price. I took the crier to be an honest fellow; and, wanting money, Go, said I, I trust what you say, and they who know better than I; deliver it to them, and bring me the money immediately.

The crier had been ordered to offer me fifty sherriffs by one of the richest jewellers in town, who had made that offer only to sound me, and try if I was well acquainted with the value of the goods I exposed to sale. He had no sooner received my answer, than he carried the crier to the justiciary judge, and shewing him the necklace, Sir, said he, here is a necklace that was stolen from me, and the thief, under the character of a merchant, has had the impudence to offer it to sale, and is at this minute in the bezestein. He is willing to take fifty sherriffs for a necklace that is worth two thousand, which is a plain argument that it is stolen.

The judge sent immediately to seize me; and when I came before him, he asked me if the necklace he had in his hand was not the same that I had exposed to sale in the bezestein? I told him it was. Is it true, said he, that you are willing to deliver it for fifty sherriffs? I answered it was. Well, said he, in a scoffing way, give him the bastinado; he will quickly tell us, with all his fine merchant's cloaths, that he is only a downright thief; let him be beat till he confesses. The violence of the blows made me tell a lie: I confessed, though it was not true, that I had stolen the necklace; and presently the judge ordered my hand to be cut off.

This made a great noise in the bezestein, and I was scarce returned to my house, when my landlord came. My son, said he, you seem to be a young man well educated, and of good sense; how is it possible you could be guilty of such an unworthy action? you gave me an account of your estate yourself, and I do not doubt but the account is just. Why did not you ask money of me, and I would have lent it you? However, since the thing has happened, I cannot allow you to lodge longer in my house; you must go and see for other lodgings. I was extremely troubled at this; and entreated the jeweller, with tears in my eyes, to let me stay three days longer in his house, which he granted.

Alas! said I to myself, this misfortune and affront is insufferable; how shall I dare to return to Moussoul? There is nothing I can say to my father will persuade him that I am innocent.

Three hours after this fatal accident, my house was assaulted by the judge's officers, accompanied with my landlord and the merchant that had falsely accused me of having stolen the necklace. I asked them what brought them there? but, instead of giving me any answer, they bound me, calling me a thousand rogues, and telling me the necklace belonged to the governor of Damascus, who had lost it above three years ago, and whose daughter had not been heard of since that time. Judge you what thoughts rolled in my mind when I heard this news. However, I called all my resolution about me; I will tell, thinks I, I will tell the governor the truth; and so it will lie at his door either to put me to death, or to pardon me.

When I was brought before him, I observed he looked upon me with an eye of compassion, from whence I prophesied good things. He ordered me to be untied, and addressing himself to the jeweller who accused me, and to my landlord: Is this the man, said he, that sold the pearl-necklace? They had no sooner answered yes, than he said, I am sure he did not steal the necklace, and I am much astonished at the injustice that has been done him.——These words giving me courage, Sir, said I, I do assure you I am in effect very innocent; I am likewise fully persuaded the necklace never did belong to my accuser, whom I never saw, and whose horrible perfidiousness is the cause of my unjust treatment. It is true, I made a confession as if I had stolen it; but this I did contrary to my conscience, through the force of torture, and of another reason that I am ready to tell you, if you will be so good as to hear me. I know enough of it already, replied the governor, to do you one part of the justice that is due to you: Take from hence, continued he, take the false accuser, let him undergo the same punishment he caused to be inflicted on this young man, whose innocence is known to me.

The governor's orders were immediately put in execution; the jeweller was punished according to his demerit. Then the governor, having ordered all the company to withdraw, said to me, My child, tell me without fear how this necklace fell into your hands, conceal nothing of the matter from me. Then I told him plainly all that had passed, and declared I had chosen rather to pass for a thief, than to reveal that tragical adventure. Good God! said the governor, thy judgments are incomprehensible, and we ought to submit to them without murmuring. I receive, with an entire submission, the stroke thou hast been pleased to inflict upon me. Then directing his discourse to me, My child, said he, having now heard the cause of your disgrace, for which I am very much concerned, I will give you an account of the disgrace that befel me. Know then, that I am the father of these two young ladies you were speaking of but now.

I know that the first lady, who had the impudence to come to your house, was my eldest daughter. I had given her in marriage to one of her own cousins, my own brother's son, at Cairo. Her husband died, and she returned home, corrupted with all manner of wickedness which she had learned in Egypt. Before I took her home, her younger sister, who died in that deplorable manner in your arms, was a very prudent young woman, and had never given me any occasion to complain of her conduct. But after that, the eldest sister grew very intimate with her, and insensibly made her as wicked as herself.

The day after the death of the youngest, not finding her at table, I asked her eldest sister what was become of her? but she, instead of answering, fell a-crying bitterly, from whence I formed a fatal presage. I pressed her to inform me of what I asked her. My father, said she with sobs, I can tell you no more, but that my sister put on her best cloaths yesterday, and her fine necklace, and went abroad, and has not been heard of since. I made search for my daughter all over the town, but could learn nothing of her unhappy fate. In the mean time, the eldest, who doubtless repented of her jealous fury, took on very much, and bewailed the death of her sister; she denied herself all manner of food, and so put an end to her deplorable days.

Such, continued the governor, such is the state of mankind! such are the unlucky accidents to which they are exposed: However, my child, added he, since we are both of us equally unfortunate, let us unite our sorrow, and not abandon one another. I give you in marriage a third daughter I have still left; she is younger than her sisters, and takes after them in no manner of way in her conduct; besides, she is handsomer than they were, and, I assure you, is of a humour proper to make you happy: You shall have no other house but mine, and, after my death, you and she shall be my universal heirs. Sir, said I, I am ashamed of all your favours, and shall never be able to make a sufficient acknowledgment. That is enough, said he, interrupting me; let us not waste time in idle words. This said, he called for witnesses, ordered the contract of marriage to be drawn, and so he married his daughter without any ceremony.

He was not satisfied with punishing the jeweller that had falsely accused me, but confiscated, for my use, all his goods, which were very considerable. As for the rest, since you have been called to the governor's house, you have seen what respect they pay me there. I must tell you farther, that a man, who was sent by my uncles to Egypt on purpose to inquire for me there, passing through this city, found me out, and came last night and delivered me a letter from them. They gave me notice of my father's death, and invite me to come and take possession of his estate at Moussoul. But as the alliance and friendship of the governor have fixed me with him, and will not suffer me to remove from him, I have sent back the express, with an order which will secure to me what is my due. Now, after what you have heard, I hope you will pardon my incivility, during the course of my illness, in giving you my left instead of my right-hand.

This, said the Jewish physician, this is the story I heard from the young man of Moussoul. I continued at Damascus as long as the governor lived; after his death, being in the flower of my age, I had a curiosity to travel. Accordingly, I went over Persia to the Indies, and came at last to settle in this your capital, where I practise physic with reputation and honour.

The sultan of Casgar was pretty well pleased with this last story. I must say, said he to the Jew, the story you have told me is very odd; but I declare freely, that of the little hump is yet more extraordinary, and much more comical; so you are not to expect that I will give you your life no more than the rest; I will hang you all four. Pray, sir, stay a minute, said the taylor; and then prostrating himself at the sultan's feet, Since your majesty loves pleasing stories, I have one to tell you that is very comical. Well, I will hear thee too, said the sultan; but do not flatter thyself that I will suffer thee to live, unless thou tellest me some adventure that is yet more diverting than that of the hump-backed man. Upon this the taylor, as if he had been sure of his project, spake very briskly to the following purpose.

The Story told by the Taylor

A CITIZEN of this city did me the honour, two days ago, to invite me to a treat, which he was to give to his friends yesterday morning. Accordingly I went pretty early, and found there twenty persons.

The master of the house was gone out upon some business, but in a very little time he came home, and brought with him a young man, a stranger, very well dressed, and very handsome, but lame. When he came in, we all rose, and, out of respect to the master of the house, invited the young gentleman to sit down with us upon the sofa. He was going to sit down; but all on a sudden, spying a barber in our company, he flew backwards, and made towards the door. The master of the house, surprised at the action, stopped him; Where are you going, said he? I bring you along with me to do me the honour of being my guest among the rest of my friends; and here you are no sooner got into my house but you run away again. Sir, said the young man, for God's sake do not stop me, let me go, I cannot without horror look upon that abominable barber; though he is born in a country where all the natives are whites, he resembles an Ethiopian; and when all is come to all, his soul is yet blacker and yet more horrible than his face.

We were all surprised to hear the young man speak so, continued the taylor; and we began to have a very bad opinion of the barber, without knowing what ground the young man had for what he said. Nay, we protested we would not suffer any one to remain in our company, that bore so horrid a character. The master of the house intreated the stranger to tell us what reason he had for hating the barber. Gentlemen, said the young man, you must know this cursed barber is the cause of my being lame, and falling under the cruellest accident that any one can imagine: for this reason, I have made an oath to avoid all the places where he dwells. It was for this reason that I left Bagdad, where he then was; and travelled so far to settle in this city, in the heart of Great Tartary, a place where I flattered myself I should never see him. And now, after all, contrary to my expectation, I find him here. This obliges me, gentlemen, against my will, to deprive myself of the honour of being merry with you. This very day I take leave of your town, and will go, if I can, to hide my head where he shall not come. This said, he would have left us, but the master kept and intreated him to stay and tell the cause of his aversion for the barber, who all this while looked down, and said never a word. We joined with the master of the house in requesting him to stay; and at last the young man giving way to our intreaties, sat down upon the sofa; and, after turning his back to the barber, that he might not see him, gave us the following account:

My father's quality might have entitled him to the highest posts in the city of Bagdad, but he always preferred a quiet life to all the honours he might deserve. I was his only child; and when he died, I was already educated, and of age to dispose of the plentiful fortune he had left me; which I did not squander away foolishly, but applied it to such uses that every body respected me for my conduct.

I had not yet been disturbed with passion; I was so far from being sensible of love, that I acknowledge, perhaps to my shame, that I cautiously avoided the conversation of women. One day, walking in the streets, I saw a great company of ladies before me; and, that I might not meet them, turned down a narrow lane just by, and sat down upon a bench by a door. I sat over against a window where there stood a pot with pretty flowers, and I had my eyes fixed upon this, when, all on a sudden the window opened, and a young lady appeared, whose beauty was dazzling. Immediately she cast her eyes upon me; and, in watering the flower-pot with a hand whiter than alabaster, looked upon me with a smile that inspired me with as much love for her as I had formerly an aversion to all women. After having watered all her flowers, and darted upon me a glance full of charms that quite pierced my heart, she shut up the window again, and so left me in inconceivable trouble and disorder.

I had dwelt upon these thoughts long enough, if a noise that arose in the streets had not brought me to myself: Alarmed with the noise, I turned my head in a rising posture, and saw it was the upper cadis of the city, mounted on a mule, and attended by five or six servants; he alighted at the door of that house where the young lady had opened the window, and went in there; from whence I concluded he was the young lady's father.

I went home in a different sort of humour from what I brought with me; tossed with a passion which was so much the more violent that I had never felt its assaults before. In fine, I went to bed with a violent fever upon me, which all the family was mightily concerned at. My relations, who had a great love for me, were so alarmed with the sudden disorder I was in, that they came about me, and importuned me to know the cause; which I took care not to reveal to them. My silence created an uneasiness that the physicians could not dispel, because they knew nothing of my distemper, and, by the medicines they exhibited, rather inflamed than repaired it.

My relations began to despair of my life, when a certain old lady of our acquaintance, hearing I was ill, came to see me. She considered and examined every thing with great attention, and dived, I do not know how, into the real cause of my illness. Then she took my relations aside, and desired they would all retire out of the room but herself.

When the room was clear, she sat down on the side of my bed. My child, said she, you are very obstinate in concealing hitherto the cause of your illness; but you have no occasion to reveal it to me, I have experience enough to penetrate into a secret; you will not disown it yourself when I tell you it is love that makes you sick. I can find a way to cure you, if you will but let me know who that happy lady is that could move a heart so insensible as yours; for you have the name of a woman-hater, and I was not the last that perceived that such was your temper; but, in short, what I foresaw has just come to pass, and I am now glad of the opportunity to employ my talent in bringing you out of your pain.

The old lady having talked to me in this fashion, paused, expecting my answer; but, though what she had said made a strong impression upon me, I durst not lay open to her the bottom of my heart; I only turned to her, and fetched a deep sigh, without saying any thing. Is it bashfulness, said she, that keeps you from speaking? Or is it want of confidence in me? Do you doubt of the effect of my promise? I could mention to you an infinite number of young men of your acquaintance, that have been in the same condition with you, and have received relief from me.

In finc, the good lady told me so many things more, that I broke silence, declared to her my evil, pointed out to her the place where I had seen the object which caused it, and unravelled all the circumstances of my adventure: If you succeed, said I, and procure me the felicity of seeing that charming beauty, and revealing to her the passion with which I burn for her, you may depend upon it I will be grateful. My son, said the old woman, I know the lady you speak of; she is, as you judged right, the daughter of the first cadis of the city: I think it no wonder that you are in love with her; she is the handsomest comeliest lady in Bagdad; but what I most boggle at, is, that she is very proud, and of difficult access. You see how strict our judges are in adjoining the punctual observance of the severe laws that mew up women under such a burdensome constraint; and they are yet more strict in the observation of their own families: nay, which adds to all, the cadis you saw is more rigid in that than all the other magistrates put together. They are always preaching to their daughters what a heinous crime it is to shew themselves to men; and by this means the girls themselves are so possessed with the notion, that they make no other use of their own eyes but to conduct them along the streets, when necessity obliges them to go abroad. I do not say absolutely that the cadis's daughter is of that humour; but that does not hinder, but that I fear to meet with as great obstacles on her side as on her father's. Would to God you had loved any other lady, then I had not had so many difficulties to surmount. However, I shall employ all my wits to compass the thing; only time is required. In the mean time, do you take heart, and trust in me.

The old woman took leave of me; and, as I weighed within myself all the obstacles she had been talking of, the fear of her not succeeding in her enterprise inflamed my illness. Next day she came again, and I read in her countenance that she had no favourable news to impart. In effect, she spoke thus: My child, I was not mistaken in the matter, I have somewhat else to conquer besides the vigilance of a father; you love an indifferent insensible girl, that takes pleasure in making every one burn with love, that suffer themselves to be charmed by her; when she has once gained that point, she will not deign them the least comfort; she heard me with pleasure, when I spoke of nothing but the torment she made you undergo; but I no sooner began to enter upon the influencing her to allow you to see her, and converse with her, but, with a terrible look, You are very bold, said she, to make such a proposal to me; I discharge you ever to see me again with such discourse in your mouth.

Do not let this cast you down, continued she, I am not easily disheartened; and, if your patience does but hold out, I am hopeful I shall compass my end. To shorten my story, said the young man, this good procuress made several attempts on my behalf with the proud enemy of my rest. The fret I thereby underwent inflamed my distemper to that degree, that my physicians gave me quite over; so I was looked upon as a dead man, when the old woman came to give me life.

That nobody might hear what was said, she whispered in my ear, Remember now, you owe me a present for the good news I bring you. These words produced a marvellous effect; I raised myself to sit up in the bed, and, with transports, made answer, You shall not be without a present; but what are the news you bring me? Dear sir, said she, you shall not die this bout: I shall speedily have the pleasure to see you in perfect health, and very well satisfied with me. Yesterday being Monday, I went to see the lady you love, and I found her in very good humour. As soon as I came, I put on a sad countenance, and fetched many deep sighs, and began to squeeze out some tears: My good mother, said she, what is the matter with you? Why are you so cast down? Alas, my dear and honourable lady, said I, I have been just now with the young gentleman I spoke to you of the other day; his business is done; he is giving up his life for the love of you; it is a great injury, I will assure you, and there is a great deal of cruelty on your side. I am at a loss to know, replied she, for what you mean me to be the cause of his death. How can I have contributed to it? How, replied I, did not you tell me the other day that he sat down before your window when you opened it to water your flower-pot? He then saw that prodigy of beauty, those charms that your looking-glass represents to you every day. From that moment he languished, and his disease is risen to that height that he is reduced to that deplorable condition I have mentioned to you.

You remember well, added I, how rigorously you treated me the last time I was here, when I was offering to speak to you of his illness, and to propose a means to rescue him from the danger he was in; when I took leave of you, I went straight to his house, and he knew no sooner by my countenance that I had brought no favourable answer, than his distemper increased. From that time, madam, he is ready to die, and I do not know whether you can save his life now, though you should take pity on him. This is just what I said to her, continued the old woman. The fear of your death shaked her, and I saw her face change colour. Is it true what you say? said she. Has he actually no other disease but what is occasioned by the love of me? Ah madam, said I, that is too true; would to God it were false! Do you believe, said she, that the hopes of seeing me, would contribute any thing to rescue him from the danger he is in? Perhaps it may, said I, and, if you will give me orders, I will try the remedy. Well, said she sighing, make him hope to see me; but he can pretend to no other favours from me, unless he aspires to marry me, and my father give his consent to it. Madam, replied I, your goodness overcomes me: I will go and see for the young gentleman, and tell him he is to have the pleasure of an interview with you: The properest time I can think of, said she, for granting him that favour, is next Friday, at the time of noon-prayers. Let him take care to observe when my father goes out, and then to come and plant himself over against the house, if so be his health permits him to come abroad. When he comes I shall see him through my window, and shall come down and open the door to him; we shall then converse together during prayer-time; and he must be gone before my father returns.

It is now Tuesday, continued the old gentlewoman, you have from hence to Friday to recruit your strength, and make the necessary dispositions for the interview. While the good old gentlewoman was telling her story, I felt my illness decrease, or rather by that time she had done, I found myself perfectly well. Here, take this, said I, reaching out to her my purse, which was full, it is to you alone that I owe my cure. I reckon this money better employed than what I gave to the physicians, who have done nothing but tormented me during the whole course of my illness.

When the lady was gone, I found I had strength enough to get up: And my relations finding me so well, complimented me upon it, and went home.

Friday morning, the old woman came just when I was dressing myself, and laying out the finest cloaths I had: I do not ask you, says she, how you do; what you are about is intimation enough of your health; but will not you bathe before you go to the first cadis's house? That will take up too much time, said I, I will content myself with calling a barber to get my head and beard shaved. Presently I ordered one of my slaves to call a barber that could do his business cleverly and expeditiously.

The slave brought me this wretch you see here, who came in, and, after saluting me, Sir, said he, you look as if you were not well. I told him I was just recovered of a fit of sickness: I wish, said he, God may deliver you from all mischance; may his grace always go along with you. I hope, said I, he will grant your wish, for which I am very much obliged to you. Since you are recovering of a fit of sickness, said he, I pray God preserve your health: But now pray let us know what service I am to do; I have brought my razors and my lancets, do you desire to be shaved or to be bled? I replied, I am just recovered of a fit of sickness, I told you, and so you may readily judge I only wanted to be shaved: Come, make haste, do not lose time in prattling, for I am in haste, and precisely at noon am to be at a place.

The barber spent much time in opening his case and preparing his razors: Instead of putting water into the bason, he took a very handsome astrolabe out of his budget* and went very gravely out of my room to the middle of the yard to take the height of the sun; then he returned with the same grave pace; and, entering my room, Sir, said he, you will be pleased to know this day is Friday the 18th of the month Saffar, in the year 653,[1] from the retreat of our great prophet from Mecca to Medina, and in the year 7320[2] of the epocha of the great Iskender with two horns; and that the conjunction of Mars and Mercury signifies you cannot chuse a better time than this very day and this very hour for being shaved. But, on the other hand, the same conjunction is a bad presage to you. I learn from thence, that this day you run a great risque, not indeed of losing your life, but of an inconvenience which will attend you while you live. You are obliged to me for the advice I now give you to take care to avoid it; I should be sorry if it befel you.

You may guess, gentlemen, how vexed I was for having fallen into the hands of such a prattling impertinent barber; what an unseasonable adventure it was for a lover preparing for an interview! I was quite angry. I do not trouble my head, said I, in anger, with your advice and predictions; I did not call you to consult your astrology; you came hither to shave me, so pray shave me, or be gone, and I will call another barber. Sir, said he, with a dulness that put me out of all patience, what reason have you to be angry with me? You do not know that all barbers are not like me; and that you would scarce find such another, if you made it your business to search. You only sent for a barber, but here, in my person, you have the best barber in Bagdad, an experienced physician, a very profound chemist, an infallible astrologue, a finished grammarian, a complete orator, a subtile logician, a mathematician perfectly well versed in geometry, arithmetic, astronomy, and all the divisions of algebra; an historian, fully master of the histories of all the kingdoms of the universe: Besides, I know all parts of philosophy: I have all the traditions upon my finger ends. I am poet, I am architect, nay, what is it I am not? There is nothing in nature hidden from me. Your deceased

[1] This year 653 is one of the Hegira, the common epocha of the Mahometans, and answers to the year 1255, from the nativity of Christ; from whence we may conjecture that these computations were made in Arabia about that time.*

[2] As for the 7320, the author is mistaken in that computation.—The year 653 of the Hegira, and the 1255 of Christ, coincide only with the 1557 of the æra or epocha of the Seleucides, which is the same with that of Alexander the Great, who is called Iskender with two horns, according to the expression of the Arabians.

father, to whose memory I pay a tribute of tears every time I think of him, was fully convinced of my merit; he was fond of me, and spoke of me in all companies as the greatest man in the world. Out of gratitude and friendship for him, I am willing to take up with you, to take you into my protection, and guard you from all evils that your stars may threaten.

When I heard this stuff, I could not forbear laughing, notwithstanding my anger. You impertinent prattler, said I, will you have done, and begin to shave me?

Sir, replied the barber to me, you affront me in calling me a prattler; on the contrary, all the world gives me the honourable title of Silent. I had six brothers that you might justly have called prattlers; and that you may know them the better, the name of the first was Bacbouc, of the second, Barbarah, of the third, Bacbac, of the fourth, Barbarak, of the fifth, Alnascar, of the sixth, Schacabac.* These indeed were impertinent noisy fellows, but for me, who am a younger brother, I am grave and concise in my discourses.

For God's sake, gentlemen, do but suppose you had been in my place. What could I say when I saw myself so cruelly assassinated? Give him three pieces of gold, said I to the slave that was my housekeeper, and send him away, that he may disturb me no more; I will not be shaved this day. Sir, said the barber, what do you mean by that? I did not come to seek for you, it was you sent for me; and, since it is so, I swear by the faith of a mussulman I will not stir out of these doors till I have shaved you: If you do not know my value, that is not my fault. Your deceased father did me more justice: Every time he sent for me to let him blood, he made me sit down by him, and then he was charmed in hearing what fine things I talked of. I kept him in a continual strain of admiration; I ravished him, and when I had finished my discourses, My God, cried he, you are an inexhaustible source of sciences, no man can reach the depth of your knowledge. My dear sir, said I again, you do me more honour than I deserve: If I say any thing that is fine, it is owing to the favourable audience you vouchsafe me; it is your liberality that inspires me with the sublime thoughts that have the happiness to please you. One day, when he was charmed with an admirable discourse I had made him, Give him, says he, an hundred pieces of gold, and invest him with one of my richest robes. I received the present upon the spot, and presently I drew his horoscope, and found it the happiest in the world. Nay, I was grateful still, I let him blood with cupping-glasses.*

This was not all; he spinned out, besides, another harangue that was a large half-hour long. Fatigued in hearing him, and fretted at the loss of time, which was almost spent before I was half ready, I did not know what to say. No, said I, it is impossible there should be another such man in the world that takes pleasure as you do in making people mad.

I thought that I should succeed better if I dealt mildly with my barber. In the name of God, said I, leave off all your fine discourses, and dispatch me presently; I am called to attend an affair of the last importance, as I have told you already. Then he fell a laughing: It would be a laudable thing, said he, if our minds were always in the same strain; if we were always wise and prudent; however, I am willing to believe, that, if you are angry with me, it is your distemper has caused that change in your humour; and, for that reason, you stand in need of some instructions, and you cannot do better than to follow the example of your father and your grandfather. They came and consulted me upon all occasions, and I can say, without vanity, that they always extolled my counsel. Pray, mind it, sir, men never succeed in their enterprises without having recourse to the advice of quick-sighted men. The proverb tells you, a man cannot be wise without receiving advice from the wise. I am entirely at your service, and you have nothing to do but to command me.

What! cannot I prevail with you then? said I, interrupting him: Leave off these long discourses that tend to nothing but to split my head to pieces, and to detain me from the place where my business lies. Shave me, I say, or begone; with that I started up in a huff, stamping my foot against the ground.

When he saw I was angry in earnest, Sir, said he, do not be angry, we are agoing to begin soon. He washed my head, and fell a-shaving me, but he had not given me four sweeps of his razor when he stopped, saying, Sir, you are hasty, you should avoid these transports that come only from the devil. Besides, my merit speaks that you ought to have some more consideration for me, with respect to my age, my knowledge, and my shining virtues.

Go on and shave me, said I, interrupting him again, and do not speak. That is to say, replies he, you have some urgent business to go about: I will lay you a wager I guess right. Why I told you so these two hours, said I; you ought to have done before now. Moderate your passion, replied he, perhaps you have not maturely weighed what you are going about; when things are done precipitately they are generally repented of. I wish you would tell me what mighty business this is you are so earnest upon; I would tell you my opinion of it: Besides, you have time enough, since your appointment is not till noon, and it wants three hours of that yet. I do not mind that, said I; persons of honour, and of their word, are rather before their time than after. But I forget, that, in amusing myself with reasoning with you, I give into the faults of you prattling barbers; have done, have done, shave me.

The more haste I was in, the less haste he made. He laid down the razor, and took up his astrolabe; this done, he even laid down his astrolabe, and took up his razor again.

The barber quitted his razor again, and took up his astrolabe a second time; and so left me half shaved, to go and see precisely what o'clock it was. Back he came, and then, Sir, said he, I knew I was not mistaken, it wants three hours of noon, I am sure of it, or else all the rules of astronomy are false. Just heaven! cried I, my patience is at an end, I can forbear no longer. You cursed barber, you barber of mischief, I do not know what holds me from falling upon you and strangling you. Softly, sir, said he very calmly, without being moved by my passion: You are not afraid of a relapse; do not be in a passion, I am going to serve you this minute. In speaking these words, he clapped his astrolabe in his case, and took up his razor, which he had fixed to his belt, and fell a-shaving again; but all the while he shaved, the dog could not forbear prattling. If you please, sir, said he, to tell me what business it is you are going about at noon, I could give you some advice that may be of use to you. To satisfy the fellow, I told him I was going to meet some friends who were to regale me at noon, and make merry with me upon the recovery of my health.

When the barber heard me talk of regaling; God bless you this day as well as all other days, cried he, you put me in mind that yesterday I invited four or five friends to come and eat with me this day; indeed I had forgot it, and I have as yet made no preparation for them. Do not let that trouble you, said I, though I dine abroad, my house is always well provided. I make you a present of what is in it; nay, besides, I will order you as much wine as you have occasion for, for I have excellent wine in my cellar; only you must dispatch the shaving of me presently, and pray do not mind it; whereas my father made you presents to encourage you to speak, I give you mine to make you hold your peace.

He was not satisfied with the promise I made him: God reward you, sir, said he, for your kindness; but pray shew me these provisions now, that I may see if there will be enough to entertain my friends: I would have them satisfied with the good fare I make them. I have, said I, a lamb, six capons, a dozen of pullets, and enough to make four services of. I ordered a slave to bring all before him, with four great pitchers of wine. It is very well, said the barber, but we shall want fruit, and sauce for the meat. That I ordered likewise; but then he gave over shaving to look over every thing, one after another; and this survey lasted almost half an hour. I raged and stormed, and went mad, but it signified nothing, the coxcomb never troubled himself. However, he took up his razor again, and shaved me for some moments; then, stopping all on a sudden, I could not have believed, sir, that you would have been so liberal; I begin to perceive that your deceased father lives again in you: most certainly I do not deserve the favours with which you have loaded me; and I assure you I shall have them in perpetual remembrance.

For, sir, to let you know it, I have nothing but what comes from the generosity of honest gentlemen, such as you; in which point I am like to Zantout, that rubs the people in bathing; to Sali, that cries boiled pease in the streets; to Salout, that sells beans; to Akerscha, that sells greens; to Amboumecarez, that sprinkles the streets to lay the dust; and to Cassem, the caliph's life-guard-man. Of all these persons, not one is apt to be made melancholy; they are neither peevish nor quarrelsome; they are more contented with their lot than the caliph in the midst of his court; they are always gay, ready to dance and to sing, and have each of them their peculiar song and dance, with which they divert the city of Bagdad. But what I esteem most in them is, that they are no great talkers, no more than your slave that has now the honour to speak to you. Here, sir, that is the song and dance of Zantout, that rubs the people in baths; mind me, pray, and see if I do not imitate it exactly.

The barber sung the song, and danced the dance of Zantout; and, let me say what I could to oblige him to make an end of his buffooneries, he did not give over till he imitated, in like manner, the songs and dances of the other people he had named. After that, addressing himself to me, I am agoing, says he, to invite all these honest persons to my house; if you will take my advice, you will join in with us, and baulk your friends yonder, who perhaps are noisy prattlers, that will only teaze you to death with their nauseous discourses, and make you fall into a distemper, worse than that you so lately recovered of, whereas at my house you shall have nothing but pleasure.

Notwithstanding my anger, I could not forbear laughing at the fellow's impertinence. I wish I had no business upon my hands, said I, if I had not, I would accept of the proposal you make me; I would go with all my heart to be merry with you, but I beg to be excused, I am too much engaged this day: Another day I shall be more at leisure, and then we shall make up that company. Come, have done shaving me, and make haste to return home; perhaps your friends are already come to your house. Sir, said he, do not refuse me the favour I ask of you; come and be merry with the good company I am to have; if you were but once in our company, you would be so well pleased with it, you would forsake your friends to come to us. Let us talk no more of that, said I, I cannot be your guest.

I found I gained no ground upon him by mild terms. Since you will not come to my house, replied the barber, then pray let me go along with you: I will go and carry these things to my house, where my friends may eat of them if they like them, and I will return immediately: I would not be so uncivil as to leave you alone, you deserve this complaisance at my hands. Heavens! cried I, then I shall not get clear of this troublesome man this day: In the name of the living God, said I, leave off your unreasonable jargon; go to your friends, drink, eat, and be merry with them, and leave me at my liberty to go to mine. I have a mind to go alone, I have no occasion for company; besides, I must needs tell you, the place to which I go is not a place where you can be received; nobody must come there but I. You jest, sir, said he; if your friends have invited you to a feast, why should you hinder me to accompany you? You will please them, I am sure, by carrying thither a man that can speak comically like me, and knows how to divert company agreeably: But, say what you will, the thing is resolved upon; I will go along with you in spite of your teeth.

These words, gentlemen, made me very uneasy. How shall I get rid of this cursed barber, thought I to myself! If I do not snub him roundly, we shall never have done contesting. Besides, I heard then the first call to noon prayers, and it was time for me to go. In fine, I resolved to say nothing at all, and to make as if I consented to his proposal. By that time he had done shaving me; then I said to him, Take some of my servants to carry these provisions along with you, and return thither; I will stay for you, and shall not go without you. At last he went, and I dressed myself nimbly. I heard the last call to prayers, and made haste to set out; but the malicious barber, jealous of my intention, went with my servants only within sight of the house, and stood there till he saw them enter his house; having hid himself upon the turning of a street, with intent to observe and follow me. In fine, when I arrived at the cadis's door, I looked back, and saw him at the head of the street, which fretted me to the last degree.

The cadis's door was half open, and, as I went in, I saw an old woman waiting for me, who, after she had shut the door, conducted me to the chamber of the young lady I was in love with; but we had scarce began our interview, when we heard a noise in the streets. The young lady put her head to the window, and saw through the grate, that it was the cadis, her father, returning already from prayers. At the same time, I looked through the window, and saw the barber sitting over against the house, in the same place where I had seen the young lady before.

I had then two things to fear, the arrival of the cadis, and the presence of the barber. The young lady mitigated my fear of the first, by assuring me the cadis came but very seldom to her chamber; and, as she had foreseen that this misadventure might happen, she had contrived a way to convey me out safe: But the indiscretion of the accursed barber made me very uneasy; and you shall hear that this my uneasiness was not without ground.

As soon as the cadis was come in, he caned one of his slaves that deserved it. The slave made horrid shouts, which were heard in the streets; the barber thought it was I that cried out, and that I was mal-treated. Prepossessed with this thought, he screamed out most fearfully, rent his cloaths, and threw dust upon his head, and called the neighbourhood to his assistance. The neighbourhood came, and asked what ailed him, and what relief he wanted that they could give? Alas! cried he, they are assassinating my master, my dear patron; and, without saying any other thing, he ran all the way to my house with the very same cry in his mouth. From thence he returned, followed by all my domestics, armed with battons. They knocked with inconceivable fury at the cadis's door, and the cadis sent a slave to see what the matter was; but the slave being frightened, returned to his master, crying, Sir, above ten thousand men are going to break into your house by force.

Immediately the cadis ran himself, opened the door, and asked what they wanted? His venerable presence could not inspire them with respect: They insolently said to him, You cursed cadis, you dog of a cadis, what reason have you to assassinate our master? What has he done to you? Good people, replied the cadis, for what should I assassinate your master, whom I do not know, and who has done no offence? My house is open to you, come see and search.—You bastinadoed him, said the barber, I heard his cries not above a minute ago. But pray, replies the cadis, what offence could your master do to me, to oblige me to abuse him after that rate? Is he in my house? If he is, how came he in, or who could have introduced him? Ah! wretched cadis, cries the barber, you and your long beard shall never make me believe what you say: What I say, I know to be true; your daughter is in love with our master, and gave him a meeting during the time of noon-prayers; you, without doubt, have had notice of it; you returned home and surprised him, and made your slave bastinade him; but this your wicked action shall not pass with impunity; the caliph shall be acquainted with it, and he will give true and brief justice. Let him come out, deliver him to us immediately; or, if you do not, we will go in and take him from you, to your shame. There is no occasion for so many words, replied the cadis, nor to make so great a noise: If what you say is true, go in and find him out, I give you free liberty. Thereupon the barber and my domestics rushed into the house like furies, and looked for me all about.

When I heard all that the barber said to the cadis, I sought for a place to hide myself, and could find nothing but a great empty trunk, in which I lay down, and shut it upon me. The barber, after he had searched every where, came into the chamber where I was, and, opening the trunk, as soon as he saw me, he took it upon his head and carried it away. He came down a high stair-case into a court, which he went through very speedily, and got to the street.—While he carried me, the trunk unhappily opened, and I, not being able to endure to be exposed to the view and shouts of the mob that followed us, leaped out into the street with so much haste that I hurt my leg, so as I have been lame ever since. I was not sensible how bad it was at first, and therefore got up quickly to get away from the people, who laughed at me; nay, I threw handfuls of gold and silver among them, and, whilst they were gathering it up, I made my escape by cross-streets and alleys. But the cursed barber improving the stratagem that I made use of to get away from the mob, followed me close, crying, Stay, sir, why do you run so fast? If you knew how much I am afflicted at the ill treatment you received from the cadis, you, who are so generous a person, and to whom I and my friends are so much obliged! Did not I tell you truly that you would expose your life by your obstinate refusal to let me go with you? See now what has happened to you by your own fault; and, if I had not resolutely followed you to see whither you went, what would have become of you? Whither do you go then, sir? stay for me.

Thus the wretched barber cried aloud in the street; it was not enough for him to have occasioned so great a scandal in the quarter of the cadis, but he would have it be known through the whole town. I was in such a rage, that I had a great mind to have staid and cut his throat; but, considering that that would have perplexed me farther, I chose another course: For perceiving that his calling after me exposed me to vast numbers of people, who crowded to the doors or windows, or stopped in the street to gaze on me, I entered into a khan[1] or inn, the chamberlain of which knew me; and, finding him at the gate, whither the noise had brought him, I prayed him for the sake of heaven to hinder that madman from coming in after me. He promised to do so, and was as good as his word; but not without a great deal of trouble, for the obstinate barber would go in in spite of him, and did not retire without calling him a thousand ill names; and, after the chamberlain shut the gate, the barber continued telling the mob what great service he had done me. Thus I rid myself of that troublesome fellow. After that, the chamberlain prayed me to tell him my adventure, which I did, and then desired him to let me have an apartment until I was cured: But, sir, says he, won't it be more convenient for you to go home? I will not return thither, said I, for the detestable barber will continue plaguing me there, and I shall die of vexation to be continually teazed with him: Besides, after what is befallen me to-day, I cannot think of staying any longer in this town; I must go whither my ill fortune leads me. And actually, when I was cured, I took all the money I thought necessary for my travels, and gave the rest of my estate among my kindred.

[1] A public-house in the towns of the Levant, where strangers lodge.

Thus, gentlemen, I left Bagdad, and came hither. I had ground to hope that I should not meet this pernicious barber in a country so far from my own, and yet I found him amongst you: Do not be surprised then at my haste to begone; you may easily judge how unpleasant to me the sight of a man is, who was the occasion of my lameness, and of my being reduced to the melancholy necessity of living so far from my kindred, friends, and country. When he had spoke these words, the lame young man rose up and went out; the master of the house conducted him to the gate, and told him he was sorry that he had given him, though innocently, so great a subject of mortification.

When the young man was gone, continued the taylor, we were all astonished at the story, and turning to the barber, told him he was very much in the wrong, if what we had just now heard was true. Gentlemen, answers he, raising up his head, which, till then, he had held down, my silence during the young man's discourse is enough to testify that he advanced nothing that was not true: But, for all that he said to you, I maintain that I ought to have done what I did; I leave yourselves to be judges of it: Did not he throw himself into danger, and could he have come off so well without my assistance? He was too happy to get off with a lame leg. Did not I expose myself to a greater danger to get him out of a house where I thought he was ill treated? Has he any reason to complain of me, and to give me so many bad words? This is what one gets by serving unthankful people. He accuses me of being a prattling fellow; which is a mere slander: Of seven brothers there are of us, I am he who speaks the least, and have most wit for my share; and, to persuade you of it, gentlemen, I need only tell my own story and theirs. Honour me, I beseech you, with your attention.

The Story of the Barber

IN the reign of the caliph Monstancer Billah,[1] continues he, a prince so famous for his vast liberality towards the poor, ten highwaymen infested the roads about Bagdad, and for a long time committed unheard-of robberies and cruelties. The caliph having notice of this, sent for the judge of the police some days before the feast of Bairam, and ordered him, on pain of death, to bring all the ten to him.

The judge of the police used so much diligence, and sent so many people in pursuit of the ten robbers, that they were taken on the day of Bairam; I

[1] He was raised to this dignity in the year of the Hegira 623, and anno dom. 1226, and was the 36th caliph of the race of the Abassides.*

was walking then on the banks of the Tigris, and saw ten men richly apparelled go into a boat: I might have known they were robbers had I observed the guards that were with them; but I looked only to them, and thinking they were people that had a mind to spend the festival-day in jollity, I entered the boat with them without saying one word, in hopes they would allow me to be one of the company. We went down the Tigris, and landed before the caliph's palace: I had time then to consider with myself, and to find my mistake. When we came out of the boat, we were surrounded by a new troop of the judge of the police's guard, who tied us all, and carried us before the caliph. I suffered myself to be tied as well as the rest, without speaking one word: For to what purpose should I have spoke, or made any resistance? that had been the way to have been ill treated by the guards, who would not have listened to me, for they are brutish fellows that will hear no reason: I was with the robbers, and that was enough to make them believe me to be one.

When we came before the caliph, he ordered the ten highwaymens' heads to be cut off immediately. The executioner drew us up in a file within reach of his arm, and by good fortune I was the last. He cut off the heads of the ten highwaymen, beginning at the first; and when he came to me he stopped. The caliph perceiving that he did not meddle with me, he grew angry: Did not I command thee, says he, to cut off the heads of ten highwaymen, and why hast thou cut off but nine? Commander of the faithful, says he, heaven preserve me from disobeying your majesty's orders! here are ten corpses upon the ground, and as many heads which I cut off; your majesty may count them. When the caliph saw himself that what the executioner said was true, he looked upon me with amazement, and, perceiving that I had not the face of a highwayman, says to me, Good old man, how came you to be among those wretches who have deserved a thousand deaths? I answered, Commander of the faithful, I shall make a true confession: This morning I saw those ten persons, whose chastisement is a proof of your majesty's justice, take boat: I embarked with them, thinking they were men going to a treat, to celebrate this day, which is the most remarkable in our religion.

The caliph could not forbear laughing at my adventure; and, instead of treating me as a prattling fellow, as the lame young man did, he admired my discretion and constant silence. Commander of the faithful, said I, your majesty need not wonder at my keeping silence on such an occasion as would have made another apt to speak. I make a particular profession of holding my peace, and, upon that account, I have acquired the glorious title of Silent; thus I am called, to distinguish me from my six brothers. This is the effect of my philosophy; and, in a word, in this virtue consists my glory and happiness. I am very glad, says the caliph, smiling, that they gave you a title which you so well deserve, and know how to make such good use of. But tell me what sort of men were your brothers, were they like you? By no means, said I, they were all of them more given to prattling than another; and as to their persons, there was still a greater difference betwixt them and me. The first was hump-backed, the second had rotten teeth, the third had but one eye, the fourth was blind, the fifth had his ears cut, and the sixth had hare-lips. They had such adventures as would inform you of their characters, had I the honour to tell them to your majesty. And since the caliph seemed to desire no better than that I should tell him their stories, I went on without his order.

The Story of the Barber's eldest Brother

SIR, said I, my eldest brother, whose name was Bacbouc the hump-back, was a taylor by trade: When he came out of his apprenticeship, he hired a shop over against a mill, and, having but very little business, he could scarcely maintain himself. The miller, on the contrary, was very wealthy, and had a very handsome wife. One day, as my brother was at work in his shop, he lift up his head and saw the miller's wife looking out of the window, and was charmed with her beauty. The woman took no notice of him, but shut her window and came no more to it all that day, while the poor taylor did nothing but lift up his eyes towards the mill all day long. He pricked his finger oftener than once, and his work that day was not very regular. At night, when he was to shut his shop, he could scarce tell how to do it, because he still hoped the miller's wife would come to the window once more; but at last he was forced to shut up and go home to his little house, where he had but a very sorry night. He got up betimes in the morning, and ran to his shop, in hopes to see his mistress again; but he was no happier than the day before, for the miller's wife did not appear at the window above one moment all the day, but that moment made the taylor the most amorous that ever lived. The third day he had some more ground of satisfaction; for the miller's wife cast her eyes upon him by chance, and surprised him as he was gazing at her, of which she presently knew the reason.

No sooner did the miller's wife perceive my brother's mind, but, instead of being vexed at it, she resolved to make it her diversion: She looked upon him with a smiling countenance, and my brother looked upon her in the same manner, but after such an odd sort, that the miller's wife presently shut her window, lest her loud laughter should have made him sensible that she only ridiculed him. Poor Bacbouc interpreted her carriage to his own advantage, and flattered himself that she looked upon him with pleasure.

The miller's wife resolved to make sport with my brother: She had a piece of very fine stuff, with which she had a long time designed to make her a suit; she wrapped it up in a fine embroidered silk handkerchief, and sent it him by a young slave that she had; who, being taught her lesson, comes to the taylor's shop, and tells him, My mistress gives you her service, and prays you to make her a suit of this stuff according to this pattern; she changes her cloaths often, so that her custom will be profitable to you. My brother doubted not but the miller's wife loved him, and thought that she sent him work so soon after what had passed between them, only to signify that she knew his mind, and to confirm him that he had obtained her favour. My brother being of this opinion, charged the slave to tell her mistress, that he would lay aside all work for hers, and that the suit should be ready next morning. In effect, he worked at it with so much diligence, that he finished it the same day. Next morning the young slave came to see if the suit was ready; Bacbouc gave it to her neatly folded up, telling her, I am too much concerned to please your mistress to neglect her suit; I would engage her by my diligence to make use of no other but myself for the time to come. The young slave went some steps, as if she had intended to go away; and then coming back, whispered to my brother, I had forgot part of my commission, my mistress charged me to compliment you in her name, and to ask how you passed the night; for her, poor woman, she loves you so mightily that she could not sleep. Tell her, answers my silly brother, I have so strong a passion for her, that these four nights I have not slept one wink. After such a compliment from the miller's wife, my brother thought she would not let him languish in expectation of her favour.

About a quarter of an hour after, the slave returned to my brother with a piece of sattin: My mistress, says she, is very well pleased with her suit, nothing in the world can fit her better; and, since it is very fine, she would not wear it without a new petticoat, and she prays you to make her one as soon as you can of this piece of sattin. It is enough, says Bacbouc, I will do it before I leave my shop; you shall have it in the evening. The miller's wife shewed herself often at her window, was very prodigal of her charms, and, to encourage my brother, she made as if she took pleasure to see him work. The petticoat was soon made, and the slave came for it, but brought the taylor no money, neither for the trimming he had bought for the suit, nor for his labour. In the mean time, this unfortunate lover, whom they only amused, though he could not perceive it, had ate nothing all that day, and was forced to borrow money at night to buy his supper. Next morning, as soon as he arrived at his shop, the young slave came to tell him that the miller wanted to speak to him: My mistress, says she, has told him so much good of you when she shewed him your work, that he has a mind you should work also for him; she does it on purpose that the friendship she designs to form betwixt you and him may make you succeed in what you both equally desire. My brother was easily persuaded, and went to the mill with the slave. The miller received him very kindly, and shewed him a piece of cloth, told him he wanted shirts, bid him make twenty of that cloth, and give him again what was over and above.

My brother had work enough for five or six days to make twenty shirts for the miller, who afterwards gave him another piece of cloth to make him as many pair of drawers; when they were finished, Bacbouc carried them to the miller, who asked him what he must have for his pains? My brother answered he would be content with twenty drachms of silver. The miller immediately called the young slave, and bid her bring him the weights to see if his money was right. The slave, who had her lesson, looked upon my brother with an angry countenance, to signify to him that he would spoil all if he took any money: He knew her meaning, and refused to take any, though he wanted it so much, that he was forced to borrow money to buy the thread that sewed the shirts and drawers. When he left the miller, he came to me to borrow money to live on, and told me they did not pay him. I gave him some copper money I had in my pocket, and upon that he subsisted for some days. It is true, indeed, he lived upon nothing but broth, nor had he his fill of that.

One day he went to the miller, who was busy at his work, and, thinking my brother came for money, he offered him some; but the young slave being present, made him another sign not to take it, which he complied with, and told the miller he did not come for his money, but only to know how he did. The miller thanked him, and gave him an upper garment to make: Bacbouc carried it him next day. When the miller drew out his purse, the young slave gave my brother the usual sign, on which he said to the miller, Neighbour, there is no haste, we will reckon another time; so that the poor ninny went to his shop again, with three terrible distempers upon him, love, hunger, and want of money. The miller's wife was not only greedy, but ill-natured; for, not content to cheat my brother of his due, she provoked her husband to revenge himself upon him for making love to her, which they accomplished thus. The miller invited Bacbouc one night to supper, and after having given him a very sorry treat, says to him, Brother, it is too late for you to go home, you had best stay here all night; and then he carried him to a place in the mill where there was a bed; there he left him, and went to bed with his wife. About the middle of the night, the miller comes to my brother, and says, Neighbour, are you asleep? My mule is ill, and I have a great deal of corn to grind; you will do me a mighty kindness if you will turn the mill in her stead. Bacbouc, to shew his good nature, told him he was ready to do him that piece of service if he would shew him how. Then the miller tied him by the middle to the mule's place, and, whipping him over the back, says to him, Go, neighbour. Ho! says my brother, why do you beat me? It is to make you brisk, says the miller, for without a whip my mule won't go. Bacbouc was amazed at this sort of treatment, but durst not complain. When he had gone five or six rounds, he would fain have rested, but the miller gave him a dozen of sound lashes saying, Courage, neighbour, do not stop, pray: You must go on without taking your breath, otherwise you will spoil my meal.

The miller obliged my brother to turn the mill all night. About break of day, he left him without untying him, and went to his wife's chamber. Bacbouc continued there for some time, and at last the young slave came and untied him. Ah! says the treacherous wretch, how my mistress and I bemoaned you! We had no hand in this wicked trick which her husband has put upon you. Unhappy Bacbouc answered her never a word, he was so much fatigued with work and blows, but crept home to his house, resolving never to think more on the miller's wife.

The telling of this story, says the barber, made the caliph laugh. Go home, says he to me, I have ordered something to be given you instead of the good dinner you expected. Commander of the faithful, says I, I pray your majesty to stay till I tell the story of my other brothers. The caliph having signified by his silence that he was willing to hear me, I went on thus.

The Story of the Barber's second Brother

My second brother, who was called Backbarah the Toothless, going one day through the city, met an old woman in an out-street; she came to him presently, and says, I want one word with you, pray stop one moment. He did so, and asked her what she would have? If you will come along with me, says she, I will bring you into a stately palace, where you shall see a lady as fair as the day: She will receive you with abundance of pleasure, and give you a treat with excellent wine; I need say no more to you. But is what you say, true? replied my brother. I am no lying hussey, replies the old woman; I say nothing to you but what is true: But hark, I have something to ask of you: You must be wise, you must speak but little, and you must be mighty complaisant. Backbarah agreed to all this; the old woman went before, and he followed. After they came to the gate of a great palace, where there was abundance of officers and domestics, some of them would have stopped my brother, but no sooner did the old woman speak to them but they let him pass. Then, turning to my brother, she says to him, You must remember that the young lady I bring you to, loves good nature and modesty, and cannot endure to be contradicted; if you please her in that, you may be sure to obtain of her what you please. Backbarah thanked her for this advice, and promised to follow it.

She brought him into a fine apartment, which was a great square building, answerable to the magnificence of the palace. There was a gallery round it, and a very fine garden in the middle. The old woman made him sit down upon a sofa very well trimmed, and bid him stay a moment till she went to tell the young lady of his being come.

My brother, who had never been in such a stately palace before, gazed upon the fine things that he saw; and judging of his good fortune by the magnificence of the palace, he was scarcely able to contain himself for joy. By and by he heard a great noise, occasioned by a troop of merry slaves, who came towards him with loud fits of laughter, and in the middle of them he perceived a young lady of extraordinary beauty, who was easily known to be their mistress by the respect they paid her. Backbarah, who expected private conversation with the lady, was extremely surprised when he saw so much company with her. In the mean time, the slaves put on a grave countenance when they drew near; and when the young lady came up to the sofa, my brother rose up and made her a low bow. She took the upper-hand, prayed him to sit down, and says to him, with a smiling countenance, I am mighty glad to see you, and wish you all the happiness you can desire. Madam, replies Backbarah, I cannot desire a greater happiness than to be in your company.—You seem to be of a good humour, says she, and to have a mind that we should pass the time pleasantly together.

She forthwith commanded a collation to be brought, and immediately a table was covered with several baskets of fruit and confections. The lady sat down at the table with the slaves and my brother; and he being placed just over against her, when he opened his mouth to eat, she perceived he had no teeth; and, taking notice of it to her slaves, she and they laughed at him heartily. Backbarah, from time to time, lifted up his head to look at her, and perceiving her laugh, thought it was for joy of his company, and flattered himself that she would speedily send away her slaves, and be with him alone. She judged what was his mind, and, pleasing herself to flatter him in his mistake, she gave him abundance of sweet words, and presented him the best of every thing with her own hand. The treat being done, they rose from table, when ten slaves took musical instruments, and began to play and sing, and others went to dance. My brother, to make them sport, did likewise dance, and the lady danced with them. After they had danced some time, they sat down to take breath; and the young lady calling for a glass of wine, looked upon my brother with a smiling countenance, to signify that she was going to drink his health. He rose up and stood while she drank. When she had done, instead of giving back the glass, she ordered it to be filled, and presented it to my brother, that he might pledge her.

My brother took the glass from the young lady's hand, which he kissed at the same time, and stood and drank to her in acknowledgment of the favour she had done him. Then the young lady made him sit down by her, and began to caress him; she put her hand behind his head, and gave him some tips from time to time with her fingers: Ravished with those favours, he thought himself the happiest man in the world, and had a great mind to toy also with the charming lady, but durst not take that liberty before so many slaves, who had their eyes upon him, and laughed at their lady's wanton tricks. The young lady continued to tip him with her fingers, but at last gave him such a sound box on the ear, that he grew angry at it; the colour came in his face, and he rose up to sit at a greater distance from such a rude playfellow. Then the old woman, who brought him thither, gave him a look to let him know he was in the wrong, and that he had forgot the advice she gave him, to be very complaisant. He owned his fault, and, to make amends, he went near the young lady again, pretending that he did not go away out of any bad humour. She drew him by the arm, made him sit down by her again, and gave him a thousand malicious hugs. Her slaves came in for a part of the diversion; one gave poor Backbarah a fillip on the nose with all her strength; another pulled him by the ears, as if she would have plucked them off; and others boxed him so as might shew they were not in jest. My brother suffered all this with admirable patience, affected a gay air, and, looking to the old woman, says to her with a forced smile, You told me indeed, that I should find the lady very good, very pleasant, and very charming; I must own I am mightily obliged to you! All this is nothing, replies the old woman, let her go on, you will see another thing by and by. Then the young lady says to him, Brother, you are a brave man, I am glad to find you are of so good an humour, and so complaisant to bear with my little caprices; your humour is exactly like mine. Madam, replied Backbarah, who was charmed with this discourse, I am no more my own man, I am wholly yours, you may dispose of me as you please. Oh! how you oblige me, says the lady, by so much submission! I am very well satisfied with you, and will have you to be so with me; bring him perfume, says she, and rose-water: Upon this, two slaves went out, and returned speedily; one with a silver perfume-box, with the best of wood of aloes, with which she perfumed him; and the other with rose-water, which she threw on his hands and face. My brother was quite beside himself at this honourable treatment.—After this ceremony, the young lady commanded the slaves, who had already played on their instruments and sung, to renew their concerts. They obeyed, and, in the mean time, the lady called another slave, and ordered her to carry my brother with her, and do what she knew, and bring him back to her again. Backbarah, who heard this order, got up quickly, and, going to the old woman, who also rose up to go along with him and the slave, prayed her to tell him what they were to do with him? My mistress is only curious, replied the old woman softly; she has a mind to see how you look in a woman's dress, and this slave, who has orders to carry you with her, has orders to paint your eye-brows, to cut off your whiskers, and to dress you like a woman. You may paint my eye-brows as much as you please, says my brother, I agree to that, because I can wash it off again; but to shave me, you know I must not allow that. How can I appear abroad again without mustachios? Beware of refusing what is asked of you, says the old woman; you will spoil your affairs, which go on now as well as heart can wish: The lady loves you, and has a mind to make you happy; and will you, for a nasty whisker, renounce the most delicious favour that man can obtain? Backbarah listened to the old woman, and, without saying one word, went to a chamber with the slave, where they painted his eye-brows with red, cut off his whiskers, and went to do the like with his beard. My brother's patience then began to wear out; O! says he, I will never part with my beard. The slave told him, that it was to no purpose to have parted with his whiskers if he could not also part with his beard, which could never agree with a woman's dress: and she wondered that a man, who was upon the point to enjoy the finest lady in Bagdad, should have any regard to his beard. The old woman threatened him with the loss of the young lady's favour, so that at last he let them do what they would. When he was dressed like a woman, they brought him before the young lady, who laughed so heartily when she saw him, that she fell backwards on the sofa where she sat. The slaves laughed and clapped their hands, so that my brother was quite out of countenance. The young lady got up, and, still laughing, says to him, After so much complaisance for me, I should be very much in the wrong not to love you with all my heart; but there is one thing more you must do for me, and that is, to dance as we do. He obeyed, and the young lady and her slaves danced with him, laughing as if they had been mad. After they had danced some time with him, they all fell upon the poor wretch, and did so box and kick him, that he fell down like one out of his senses. The old woman helped him up again, and, that he might not have time to think of his ill treatment, she bid him take courage, and whispered in his ear, That all his sufferings were at an end, and that he was just about to receive his reward.

You have only one thing more to do, and that is but a small one: You must know that my mistress has a custom, when she has drank a little, as you see she has done to-day, to let nobody that she loves come near her, except they be stripped to their shirt; and when they have done so, she takes a little advantage of them, and sets a-running before them through the gallery, and from chamber to chamber, till they catch her. This is one more of her humours; what advantage soever she takes of you, considering your nimbleness, and inclination to the work, you will soon overtake her; strip yourself then to your shirt, and undress yourself without delay.

My silly brother, says the barber, had done too much to stick at any thing now. He undressed himself; and, in the mean time, the young lady was stripped to her shift and under-petticoat, that she might run the more nimbly. When they were ready to run, the young lady took the advantage of twenty paces, and fell a-running with surprising swiftness: My brother followed her as fast as he could; the slaves in the mean time laughing aloud and clapping their hands. The young lady, instead of losing ground, gained upon my brother; she made him run two or three times round the gallery; and then running into a long dark entry, got away by a passage which she knew. Backbarah, who still followed her, having lost sight of her in the entry, was obliged to slacken his pace because of the darkness of the place; at last, perceiving a light, he ran towards it, and went out at a door, which was immediately shut upon him. You may imagine that he was mightily surprised to find himself in a street inhabited by curriers, and they were no less surprised to see him in his shirt, his eye-brows painted red, and without beard or mustachios: They began to clap their hands and shout at him, and some of them ran after him, and lashed his buttocks with pieces of leather. Then they stopped, and set him upon an ass which they met by chance, and carried him through the town, exposed to the laughter of the people.

To complete his misfortune, as he went by the house of a justice of peace, he would needs know the cause of the tumult: The curriers told him, that they saw him come out in that condition at the gate of the apartment of the grand visier's lady, which opened into their street: Upon which the justice ordered unfortunate Backbarah to have a hundred blows with a cane on the soles of his feet, and sent him out of the town, with orders never to return again.

Thus, commander of the faithful, says I to the Caliph Monstancer Billah, I have given an account of the adventure of my second brother, who did not know that our greatest ladies divert themselves sometimes by putting such tricks upon young people, that are so foolish as to be catched in their snares.

The Story of the Barber's third Brother

COMMANDER of the faithful, says I to the caliph, my third brother, whose name was Bacbac, was blind, and his ill destiny reduced him to beg from door to door. He had been so long accustomed to walk through the streets alone that he had no need of one to lead him: He had a custom to knock at people's doors, and not to answer till they opened to him. One day he knocked thus at a door, and the master of the house, who was alone, cried, Who is there? My brother gave no answer, and knocked a second time: The master of the house asked again, Who is there? But to no purpose. My brother did not answer; upon which the man of the house came down, opened the door, and asked my brother what he wanted? That you would give me something for heaven's sake, says Bacbac. You seem to be blind, replied the master of the house. Yes, to my sorrow, says my brother. Give me your hand, says the master of the house. My brother did so, thinking he was going to give him alms; but he only took him by the hand to lead him up to his chamber; Bacbac thought he had been carrying him to dinner with him, as several other people had done. When they came up to the chamber, the man loosed his hand out of my brother's, and sitting down, asked him again, what he wanted? I have already told you, says Bacbac, that I want something for God's sake. Good blind man, replied the master of the house, all I can do for you is to wish that God may restore you your sight. You might have told me that at the door, says my brother, and not have given me the trouble to have come up. And why, fool, says the man of the house, do not you answer at first, when people ask you who is there? Why do you give any body the trouble to come and open the door when they speak to you? What will you do with me then? says my brother: I tell thee again, says the man of the house, I have nothing to give you. Help me down stairs then, replied Bacbac, as you helped me up. The stairs are before you, says the man of the house; and you may go down alone if you will. My brother went to go down, but, missing a step about the middle of the stairs, he fell down and hurt his head and his back: He got up again with a great deal of difficulty, and complained heavily of the master of the house, who laughed at his fall.

As my brother went out of the house, two blind men, his companions, were going by, knew him by his voice, and asked him what was the matter? He told what had happened to him, and afterwards said, I have ate nothing to-day; I conjure you to go along with me to my house, that I may take some of the money that we three have in common, to buy me something for supper. The two blind men agreed to it, and they went home with him.

You must know that the master of the house where my brother was so ill used, was a highwayman, and naturally cunning and malicious. He heard at his window what Bacbac had said to his companions, and therefore came down and followed them to my brother's house. The blind men being sat down, Bacbac says to them, Brethren, we must shut the door, and take care there be no stranger with us. At this the highwayman was much perplexed, but, perceiving by chance a rope hanging down from a beam, he catched hold of it, and hung by it while the blind men shut the door and felt about the room with their sticks. When they had done this, and had sat down again in their places, the highwayman left his rope, and sat down softly by my brother, who, thinking himself alone with his comrades, says to them, Brothers, since you have trusted me with the money which we all three gathered a long time, I will shew you that I am not unworthy of the trust that you repose in me. The last time we reckoned you know we had ten thousand drachms, and that we put them into ten bags; I will shew you that I have not touched one of them; and, having said so, he put his hand among some old lumber, and taking out the bags one after another, gave them to his comrades, saying, There they are, you may judge by their weight that they are whole, or you may tell them if you please. His comrades answered, there was no need, they did not mistrust him; so he opened one of the bags, and took out ten drachms, and each of the other blind men did the like.

My brother put the bags in their place again: After which, one of the blind men says to him, there is no need to lay out any thing for supper, for I have got as much victuals from good people as will serve us all three. At the same time he took out of his bag bread and cheese, and some fruit, and, putting all upon the table, they began to eat. The highwayman, who sat at my brother's right-hand, picked out the best, and ate with them; but whatever care he took to make no noise, Bacbac heard his chaps a-going, and cried out immediately, We are undone, there is a stranger among us! And, having said so, he stretched out his hand, and catching hold of the highwayman by the arm, cried out, Thieves! fell upon him, and boxed him. The other blind men fell upon him in like manner, and the highwayman defended himself as well as he could; and, being young and vigorous, and having the advantage of his eyes, he gave furious blows, sometimes to one, sometimes to another, as he could come at them, and cried out Thieves! louder than they did. The neighbours came running at the noise, broke open the door, and had much ado to separate the combatants; but having at last done it, they asked the cause of their quarrel? My brother, who still had hold of the highwayman, cried out, Gentlemen, this man I have hold on is a thief, and stole in with us on purpose to rob us of the little money we have. The thief, who shut his eyes as soon as the neighbours came, feigned himself also to be blind, and cries out, Gentlemen, he is a liar. I swear to you by heavens, and by the life of the caliph, that I am their companion, and they refuse to give me my just share: They have all three fallen upon me, and I demand justice. The neighbours would not meddle with their quarrel, but carried them all before a judge.

When they came before the magistrate, the highwayman, without staying to be examined, cried out, still feigning himself to be blind, Sir, since you are deputed to administer justice by the caliph, whom God prosper, I declare to you that we are all equally criminal, my three comrades and I; but we have all engaged upon oath, to confess nothing, except we be bastinadoed; so that, if you would know our crime, you need only order us to be bastinadoed, and begin with me. My brother would have spoke, but was not allowed to do so; and the highwayman was put under the bastinado.

The robber being under the bastinado, had the courage to bear twenty or thirty blows; when, seeming to be overcome with pain, he first opened one eye, and then the other, and, crying out for mercy, begged the judge would put a stop to the blows.—The judge perceiving that he looked upon him with his eyes open, was much surprised at it, and says to him, Rogue, what is the meaning of this miracle? Sir, replied the highwayman, I will discover to you an important secret, if you pardon me, and give me as a pledge that you will keep your word, the seal-ring* which you have on your finger. The judge agreed to it, gave him his ring, and promised him pardon. Upon this, says the highwayman, I must confess to you, sir, that I and my three comrades do all of us see very well. We feigned ourselves to be blind, that we might freely enter people's houses, and into women's apartments, where we might abuse their frailty. I must farther confess to you, that by this trick we have gathered together ten thousand drachms. This day I demanded of my partners 2500, that belong to me as my share; but they refused, because I told them I would leave them, and they were afraid I should accuse them. Upon my pressing still to have my share, they all three fell upon me; for which I appeal to those people who brought us before you. I expect from your justice that you will make them deliver me the 2500 drachms which is my due; and if you have a mind that my comrades should confess the truth, you must order them three times as many blows as I have had, and you will find they will open their eyes as well as I did.

My brother and the other two blind men would have cleared themselves of this horrid cheat, but the judge would not hear them: Villains, said he, do you feign yourselves blind then, and, under that pretext, cheat people, by begging their charity, and abusing poor women? He is a cheat, cried my brother, we take God to witness that none of us can see.

All that my brother could say was in vain, his comrades and he received each of them 200 blows. The judge looked always when they should have opened their eyes, and ascribed to their obstinacy what really they could not do. All the while the highwayman said to the blind men, Poor fools that you are, open your eyes, and do not suffer yourselves to be killed with blows. Then addressing himself to the judge, says, I perceive, sir, that they will be maliciously obstinate to the last, and will never open their eyes. They have a mind certainly to avoid the shame of reading their own condemnation in the face of every one that looks upon them; it were better, if you think fit, to pardon them, and send some person along with me for the ten thousand drachms they have hid.

The judge did so, gave the highwayman 2500 drachms, and kept the rest to himself; and, as for my brother and his two companions, he thought he shewed them a great deal of pity by sentencing them only to be banished. As soon as I heard what befel my brother, I ran after him; he told me his misfortune, and I brought him back secretly to the town. I could easily have justified him to the judge, and have got the highwayman punished as he deserved, but durst not attempt it, for fear of bringing myself into trouble. Thus I finished the sad adventure of my honest blind brother. The caliph laughed at it as much as at those he had heard before, and ordered again that something should be given me; but, without staying for it, I began the story of my fourth brother.

The Story of the Barber's fourth Brother

ALCOUZ was the name of the fourth brother, who came to lose one of his eyes upon an occasion that I shall acquaint your majesty with by-and-bye: He was a butcher by profession, and had a particular way of teaching rams to fight, by which he procured the acquaintance and friendship of the chief lords of the country who loved that sport; and, for that end, kept rams about their houses. He had, besides, a very good trade, and had his shop always full of the best meat, because he was very rich, and spared no cost for the best of every sort. One day, when he was in his shop, an old man, with a long white beard, came and bought six pounds of meat of him, gave him money for it, and went his way. My brother thought the money so fine, so white, and so well coined, that he put it apart by itself. The same old man came every day for five months together, bought a like quantity of meat, and paid for it in the same sort of money, which my brother continued to lay apart by itself.

At the end of five months, Alcouz having a mind to buy a parcel of sheep, and to pay for them in this fine money, opened his trunk; but, instead of finding his money, was extremely surprised to see nothing but a parcel of leaves clipped round in the place where he had laid it: He beat his head, and cried out aloud, which presently brought the neighbours about him, who were as much surprised as he, when he told them the story. O! cried my brother weeping, that this treacherous old fellow would come now with his hypocritical looks! He had scarce done speaking, when he saw him coming at a distance, ran to him, and laid hands on him; Mussulmen, cries he, as loud as he could, help! hear what a cheat this wicked fellow has put upon me; and at the same time told a great crowd of people, who came about him, what he had formerly told his neighbours. When he had done, the old man, without any passion, says to him very gravely, You would do well to let me go, and by that means make amends for the affront you have put upon me before so many people, for fear I should put a greater affront upon you, which I am not willing to do.—How, says my brother, what have you to say against me? I am an honest man in my business, and fear not you nor nobody. You would have me to tell it then, says the old man; and, turning to the people, says to them, Know, good people, that this fellow, instead of selling mutton as he ought to do, sells man's flesh! You are a cheat, says my brother. No, no, says the old man; good people, this very minute that I am speaking to him, there is a man with his throat cut hung up in his shop like a sheep: do any of you go thither, and see if what I say be not true.

Before my brother had opened his trunk, he had just killed a sheep, dressed it, and exposed it in the shop, according to custom; he protested that what the old man said was false; but, notwithstanding all his protestations, the mob being prejudiced against a man accused of such a heinous crime, would go to see whether the matter was true. They obliged my brother to quit the old man, laid hold of him, and ran like madmen to his shop, where they saw a man murdered and hung up, as the old man had told them; for he was a magician, and deceived the eyes of the people, as he did my brother, when he made him take leaves instead of money. At this spectacle, one of those who held Alcouz gave him a great blow with his fist, and says to him, Thou wicked villain, dost thou make us eat man's flesh instead of mutton? And at the same time, the old man gave him another blow, which beat out one of his eyes, and every body that could get near him beat him; and, not content with that, they carried him before a judge, with the pretended carcase of the man to be evidence against him. Sir, says the old magician to the judge, we have brought you a man who is so barbarous as to murder people and to sell their flesh instead of mutton: The public expects that you should punish him in an exemplary manner. The judge heard my brother with patience, but would believe nothing of the story of the money exchanged into leaves, called my brother a cheat, told him he would believe his own eyes, and ordered him to have five hundred blows. He afterwards made him tell him where his money was, took it all from him, and banished him for ever, after having made him ride three days through the town upon a camel, exposed to the insults of the people.

I was not at Bagdad when this tragical adventure befel my fourth brother, but he retired into a remote place, where he lay concealed till he was cured of the blows with which his back was terribly mauled. When he was able to walk, he went by night to a certain town, where nobody knew him; and there he took a lodging, from whence he seldom went out; but being weary of this life, he went to walk in one of the suburbs, where all of a sudden he heard a great noise of horsemen coming behind him. He was then by chance near the gate of a great house, and fearing, after what had befallen him, that these horsemen were pursuing him, he opened the gate in order to hide himself, and, after he had shut it, came into a great court, where immediately two servants came and took him by the neck, and said, Heaven be praised that you have come of your own accord to surrender yourself to us; you have frightened us so much these three last nights that we could not sleep; nor would you have spared our lives if you could have come at us. You may very well imagine my brother was much surprised at this compliment: Good people, says he, I know not what you mean, you certainly take me for another. No, no, replied they, you and your comrades are great robbers: You were not contented to rob our master of all that he had, and to reduce him to beggary, but you had a mind to take his life. Let us see a little if you have but a knife about you, which you had in your hand when you pursued us last night. And having said thus, they searched him, and found he had a knife. Ho! ho! cried they, laying hold of him, and dare you say you are not a robber? Why, says my brother, cannot a man carry a knife about him without being a highwayman? If you will hearken to my story, continues he, instead of having so bad an opinion of me, you will be touched with compassion at my misfortunes. But, far from hearkening to him, they fell upon him, trod him under foot, took away his clothes, and tore his shirt. Then, seeing the scars on his back, O dog, said they, redoubling their blows, would you have us to believe you are an honest man when your back shews us the contrary? Alas! says my brother, my faults must be very great, since, after having been abused already so unjustly, I am abused again a second time without being more culpable.

The two servants, no way moved with his complaint, carried him before the judge, who asked him how he durst be so bold as to go into their house, and pursue them with a drawn knife? Sir, replied poor Alcouz, I am the most innocent man in the world, and am undone if you will not be pleased to hear me patiently; nobody deserves more compassion. Sir, replies one of the domestics, will you listen to a robber who enters people's houses to plunder and murder them? If you will not believe us, only look upon his own back; and, when he said so, he uncovered my brother's back, and shewed it to the judge who, without any other information, commanded immediately to give him 100 lashes with a bull's pizzle over the shoulders, and made him afterwards be carried through the town on a camel, with one crying before him, Thus are such men punished as enter people's houses by force. After having treated him thus, they banished him the town, and forbid him ever to return to it again. Some people, who met him after the second misfortune, brought me word where he was; and I went and fetched him to Bagdad privately, and gave him all the assistance I could.

The caliph, continued the barber, did not laugh so much at this story as at the other. He was pleased to bewail the unfortunate Alcouz, and ordered something to be given me. But, without giving his servants time to obey his orders, I continued my discourse, and said to him, My sovereign lord and master, you see that I do not speak much: And, since your majesty has been pleased to do me the favour to listen to me so far, I beg you would likewise hear the adventures of my two other brothers: I hope they will be as diverting as those of the former. You may make a complete history of them, which will not be unworthy your library.

The Story of the Barber's fifth Brother

ALNASCHAR, as long as our father lived, was very lazy; instead of working for his living, he used to go a-begging in the evening, and to live upon what he got next day. Our father died in a very old age, and left among us 700 drachms of silver: We divided them equally among us, so that each of us had 100 to our share. Alnaschar, who had never so much money before in his life time, was very much perplexed to know what he should do with it. He consulted a long time with himself, and at last resolved to lay it out on glasses, bottles, and other glass work, which he bought of a great merchant. He put all in an open basket, and chose a very little shop, where he sat with the basket before him, and his back against the wall, expecting somebody would come and buy his ware. In this posture he sat with his eyes fixed on his basket, and began to rave. During which, he spoke as follows, loud enough to be heard by a neighbouring taylor: This basket, says he, cost me 100 drachms, which is all I have in the world; I shall make 200 of it by retailing my glass; and of these 200 drachms, which I will again lay out in glass, I shall make 400; and, going on thus, I shall at last make 4000 drachms; of 4000 I shall easily make 8000, and when I come to 10,000 I will leave off selling glass, and turn jeweller; I will trade in diamonds, pearls, and all sorts of precious stones. Then, when I am as rich as I can wish, I will buy a fine house, a great estate, slaves, eunuchs, horses, &c. I will keep a good house, and make a great figure in the world; I will send for all the musicians and dancers of both sexes in town. Nor will I stop here; I will, by the favour of heaven, go on till I get 100,000 drachms; and, when I have got so much, I will think myself as great as a prince, and send to demand the grand visier's daughter in marriage; and represent to that minister that I have heard very much of the wonderful beauty and modesty, wit, and all the other qualities of his daughter. In a word, that I will give him 1000 pieces of gold the first night we are married; and, if the visier be so uncivil as to refuse his daughter, which cannot be, I will go and take her before his face, and carry her to my house whether he will or no. As soon as I have married the grand visier's daughter, I will buy her ten young black eunuchs, the handsomest that can be had; I will clothe myself like a prince, and ride upon a fine horse, with a saddle of fine gold, with housings of cloth of gold finely embroidered with diamonds and pearls. I will march through the city, attended by slaves before and behind; and I will go to the visier's palace in the view of all sorts of people, who will all shew me a profound reverence. When I come to the foot of the visier's staircase, I will go up the same in the presence of all my people, ranged in files on the right and left; and the grand visier, receiving me as his son-in-law, shall give me the right-hand, and set me above him, to do me the more honour. If this comes to pass, as I hope it will, two of my people shall have each of them a purse of a thousand pieces of gold, which they shall carry with them. I will take one, and presenting it to the grand visier I will tell him, there is the thousand pieces that I promised the first night of marriage; and I will offer him the other, and say to him, there is as much more, to shew that I am a man of my word, and that I am better than my promise. After such an action as this, all the world will speak of my generosity. I will return to my own house in the same pomp. My wife shall send to compliment me by some officer, on the account of the visit I made to her father: I will honour the officer with a fine robe, and send him back with a rich present. If she thinks to send me one, I will not accept it, but dismiss the bearer. I will not suffer her to go out of her apartment, on any account whatever, without giving me notice! And, when I have a mind to come to her apartment, it shall be in such a manner as to make her respect me. In short, no house shall be better ordered than mine. I will be always richly clad. When I retire with my wife in the evening, I will sit on the upper hand; I will affect a grave air, without turning my head to one side or other: I will speak little; and whilst my wife, as beautiful as the full moon, stands before me in all her ornaments, I will make as if I did not see her. Her women about her, will say to me, Our dear lord and master, here is your spouse, your humble servant before you, she expects you would caress her, and is very much mortified that you do not so much as vouchsafe to look upon her: She is wearied with standing so long, bid her at least sit down. I will give no answer to this discourse, which will increase their surprising grief. They will lay themselves at my feet; and after they have done so a considerable time, begging me to relent, I will at last lift up my head, and give her a careless look: Afterwards I will return to my former posture; then will they think that my wife is not well enough, nor handsome enough dressed, and will carry her to her closet to change her apparel. At the same time I will get up, and put on a more magnificent suit than before: they will return, and hold the same discourse with me as before, and I will have the pleasure not so much as to look upon my wife, till they have prayed and entreated so long as they did at first. Thus I will begin, on the first day of marriage, to teach her what she is to expect during the rest of her life.

After the ceremonies of the marriage, says Alnaschar, I will take from one of my servants, who shall be about me, a purse of five hundred pieces of gold, which I will give to the tire-women,* that they may leave me alone with my spouse; when they are gone, my wife shall go to bed first: Then I will lie down by her with my back towards her, and will not say one word to her all night. The next morning she will certainly complain of my contempt of her, and of my pride, to her mother, the grand visier's wife, which will rejoice me at my heart. Her mother will come to wait upon me, respectfully kiss my hands, and say to me, Sir, (for she will not dare to call me son-in-law, for fear of provoking me by such a familiar style,) I pray you not to disdain my daughter, and refuse to come near her: I assure you that her chief business is to please you, and that she loves you with all her heart. But my mother-in-law had as good hold her peace. I will not answer her one word, but keep my gravity. Then she will throw herself at my feet, kiss them, and say to me, Sir, is it possible that you can suspect my daughter's chastity? I assure you, I never let her go out of my sight. You are the first man that ever saw her face; do not mortify her so much, do her the favour to look upon her, and confirm her in her good intentions to satisfy you in every thing: But nothing of this shall prevail with me. Upon which my mother-in-law will take a glass of wine, and, putting it in the hand of her daughter, my wife, will say, Go, present him this glass of wine yourself; perhaps he will not be so cruel as to refuse it from so fair a hand. My wife will come with the glass, and stand trembling before me; and when she finds that I do not look towards her, that I continue to disdain her, she will say to me, with tears in her eyes, My heart, my dear soul, my amiable lord, I conjure you, by the favours which heaven bestows upon you, to receive the glass of wine from the hand of your most humble servant; but I will not look upon her still, nor answer her. My charming spouse, she will say, redoubling her tears, and putting the glass to my mouth, I will never leave off till I prevail with you to drink. Then being fatigued with her entreaties, I will dart a terrible look at her, give her a good box on the cheek, and give her such a push with my foot, as will throw her quite off the alcove.

My brother was so full of these chimerical visions, that he acted with his foot as if she had been really before him, and by misfortune he gave such a push to his basket and glasses, that they were thrown down in the street, and broke in a thousand pieces.

A tailor, who was his neighbour, and heard his extravagant discourse, fell into a great fit of laughter when he saw the basket fall. O what an unworthy fellow art thou! says he to my brother: Ought you not to be ashamed to abuse thus a young spouse who gave you no cause of complaint? You must be a very brutish fellow to despise the tears and charms of such a beautiful lady. Were I the visier your father-in-law, I would order you a hundred lashes with a bull's pizzle, and send you through the town, with your character written on your forehead. My brother, on this fatal accident, came to himself, and perceiving that he had brought this misfortune upon himself by his insupportable pride, he beat his face, tore his clothes, and cried so loud, that the neighbours came about him; and the people, who were going to their noon-prayers, stopped to know what was the matter. Being on a Friday, more people went to prayers than usual; some of them took pity on Alnaschar, and others only laughed at his extravagancy. In the mean time, his vanity being dispersed, as well as his glasses, he bitterly bewailed his loss; and a lady of note passing by upon a mule, with rich caparisons, my brother's condition moved her compassion: She asked who he was, and what was the matter with him? They told her, that he was a poor man, who had laid out a little money he had in buying a basket of glasses, and that the basket falling, all his glasses were broke. The lady immediately turned to an eunuch, who attended her, and says to him, Give the poor man what you have about you. The eunuch obeyed, and put into my brother's hands five hundred pieces of gold: Alnaschar was like to die of joy when he received it: He gave a thousand blessings to the lady, and, shutting up his shop, where he had no more occasion to sit, he went to his house.

While he was making deep reflections upon his good luck, he heard one knock at his door; before he opened, he asked who it was? And knowing by the voice that it was a woman, he let her in. My son, says she, I have a favour to beg of you: The hour of prayer is come; pray let me wash myself, that I may be fit to say my prayers: Pray let me come into your house, and give me a bason of water. My brother looked upon her, and saw that she was a woman well advanced in years; though he knew her not, he granted what she required, and then sat down again, being still full of his new adventure. He put his gold in a long strait purse, proper to carry at his girdle. The old woman, in the mean time, said her prayers; and when she had done, came to my brother, and bowed to the ground twice, so low that she touched it with her forehead, as if she had been going to say her prayers; then rising up, she wished my brother all manner of happiness, and thanked him for his civility, being meanly clad, and was very humble to him. He thought she asked alms, upon which he offered her two pieces of gold. The old woman stepped back in a sort of surprise, as if my brother had done her an injury. Heavens! says she, what is the meaning of this? Is it possible, sir, says she, that you took me for an impudent beggar? Did you think I came so boldly into your house to ask alms? Take back your money, I have no need of it, thanks to heaven. I belong to a young lady of this city, who is a charming beauty, and very rich; she lets me want for nothing.

My brother was not cunning enough to perceive the craft of the old woman, who only refused the two pieces of gold that she might catch more. He asked her if she could not procure him the honour of seeing that lady? With all my heart, replied she, she will be very well satisfied to marry, and to put you in possession of her estate, by making you master of her person. Take up your money and follow me. My brother being ravished with his good luck of finding so great a sum of money, and almost at the same time a beautiful and rich wife, his eyes were shut upon all other considerations, so that he took his 500 pieces of gold, and followed the old woman. She walked before him, and he followed at a distance, to the gate of a great house, where she knocked. He came up to her just as a young Greek slave opened the gate. The old woman made him enter first, went cross a court very well paved, and introduced him into a hall, the furniture of which confirmed him in the good opinion he had conceived of the mistress of the house. While the old woman went to acquaint the lady, he sat him down, and the weather being hot, put off his turban, and laid it by him. He speedily saw the young lady come in, whose beauty and rich apparel perfectly surprised him; he got up as soon as he saw her. The lady, with a smiling countenance, prayed him to sit down again, and placed herself by him. She told him she was very glad to see him, and, after having spoke some engaging words to him, says, We do not sit here at our conveniency: Come, give me your hand. At these words she presented him hers, and carried him into an inner chamber, where she entertained him for some time. Then she left him, bidding him stay, she would be with him in a moment. He expected her; but instead of the lady, came in a great black slave, with a scymitar in his hand, and, looking upon my brother with a terrible aspect, says to him fiercely, What have you to do here? Alnaschar was so full of fear at the sight of the slave, that he had no power to answer. The black stripped him, carried off his gold, and gave him several cuts with his scymitar. My unhappy brother fell to the ground, where he lay without motion, though he had still the use of his senses. The black, thinking him to be dead, asked for salt; the Greek slave brought him a bason full: They rubbed my brother's wounds with it, who had so much command of himself, notwithstanding the intolerable pain it put him to, that he lay still without giving any sign of life. The black and the Greek slave being retired, the old woman, who drew my brother into the snare, came and dragged him by the feet to a trap-door, which she opened, and threw him into a place under ground among the corpses of several other people that had been murdered. He perceived this as soon as he came to himself; for the violence of the fall had taken away his senses. The salt rubbed into his wounds preserved his life, and he recovered strength by degrees, so as he was able to walk. After two days, he opened the trap during the night, and, finding a proper place in the court to hide himself, continued there till break of day, when he saw the cursed old woman open the gate, and go out and seek another prey. He staid in the place some time after she went out, that she might not see him, and then came to me for shelter, when he told me of his adventures.

In a month's time he was perfectly cured of his wounds by medicines that I gave him, and resolved to avenge himself of the old woman who had put such a barbarous cheat upon him: To this end he took a bag, large enough to contain five hundred pieces of gold, and filled it with pieces of glass.

My brother, continued the barber, fastened the bag of glass about him, disguised himself like an old woman, and took a scymitar under his gown. One morning he met the old woman walking through the town to seek her prey; he comes up to her, and, counterfeiting a woman's voice, says to her, Can you lend me a pair of scales? I am a woman newly come from Persia, have brought five hundred pieces of gold with me, and would know if they will hold out according to your weight. Good woman, answers the old hag, you could not have applied to a properer person: Follow me, I will bring you to my son, who changes money, and will weigh them himself, to save you the trouble: Let us make haste, for fear he go to his shop. My brother followed her to the house where she carried him the first time, and the Greek slave opened the door.

The old woman carried my brother to the hall, where she bid him stay a moment till she called her son. The pretended son came, and proved to be the villainous black slave. Come, old woman, says he to my brother, rise and follow me: Having spoke thus, he went before, to bring him to the place where he designed to murder him. Alnaschar got up, followed him, and, drawing his scymitar, gave him such a dexterous blow behind on the neck as cut off his head; which he took in one hand, and dragging the corpse with the other, threw them both into the place under ground before mentioned.

The Greek slave, who was accustomed to the trade, came presently with a bason of salt; but when she saw Alnaschar with the scymitar in his hand, and without his veil, she laid down the bason and fled; but my brother overtaking her, cut off her head also.—The wicked old woman came running at the noise, and my brother seizing her, says to her, Treacherous wretch, do not you know me? Alas! sir, answers she trembling, who are you? I do not remember that I ever saw you. I am, says he, the person to whose house you came the other day to wash and say your prayers. Hypocritical hag, do not you remember it? Then she fell on her knees to beg his pardon, but he cut her in four pieces.

There remained only the lady, who knew nothing of what had passed: He sought her out, and found her in a chamber, where she was ready to sink when she saw him: She begged her life, which he generously granted. Madam, says he, how could you live with such wicked people as I have so justly revenged myself upon now? I was, says she, wife to an honest merchant; and the cursed old woman, whose wickedness I did not know, used sometimes to come and see me: Madam, says she to me one day, we have a very fine wedding at our house, which you will be pleased to see if you give us the honour of your company: I was persuaded by her, to put on my best apparel, and took with me a hundred pieces of gold. I followed her; she brought me to this house, where the black has kept me since by force, and I have been three years here to my very great sorrow. By the trade which that cursed black followed, replied my brother, he must have gathered together a vast deal of riches. There is so much, says she, that you will be made rich for ever if you can carry them off. Follow me, and you shall see them, says she. Alnaschar followed her to a chamber, where she shewed him several coffers full of gold, which he beheld with admiration: Go, says she, fetch people enough to carry it all off. My brother needed not to be bid twice; he went out, and staid only till he got ten men together, and he brought them with him, and was much surprised to find the gate open, but more so when he found the lady and the coffers all gone; for she being more diligent than he, carried them all off. However, being resolved not to return empty-handed, he carried off all the goods he could find in the house, which was a great deal more than enough to make up the five hundred pieces of gold he was robbed of: But when he went out of the house, he forgot to shut the gate.—The neighbours, who saw my brother and the porters come and go, went and acquainted the magistrate with it; for they looked upon my brother's conduct as suspicious. Alnaschar slept well enough all night; but the next morning when he came out of his house, he found twenty of the magistrate's men, who seized him. Come along with us, said they, our master would speak with you. My brother prayed to have patience for a moment, and offered them a sum of money to let him escape: but, instead of listening to him, they bound him, and forced him to go along with them. They met in the street an old acquaintance of my brother's, who stopped them a while, and asked them why they seized my brother? and offered them a considerable sum to let him escape, and tell the magistrate they could not find him: But this would not do.

When the officers brought him before the magistrate, he asked him where he had the goods which he carried home last night? Sir, replied Alnaschar, I am ready to tell you all the truth; but allow me first to have recourse to your clemency, and to beg your promise that nothing shall be done to me. I give it you, says the magistrate. Then my brother told him the whole story without disguise, from the old woman coming into his house to say her prayers, to the time the lady made her escape, after he had killed the black, the Greek slave, and the old woman: And as for what he had carried to his house, he prayed the judge to leave him part of it for the five hundred pieces of gold that he was robbed off.

The judge, without promising him any thing, sent his officers to bring off all, and, having put the goods into his own wardrobe, commanded my brother to quit the town immediately, and never to return; for he was afraid, if my brother had staid in the city, he would have found some way to represent this injustice to the caliph. In the mean time, Alnaschar obeyed without murmuring, and left that town to go to another. By the way he met with highwaymen, who stripped him naked; and when the ill news was brought to me, I carried him a suit, and brought him in secretly again to the town, where I took the like care of him as I did of his other brothers.

The Story of the Barber's sixth Brother

I AM now only to tell the story of my sixth brother, called Schacabac with the hare lips. At first he was industrious enough to improve the hundred drachms of silver, which fell to his share, and became very well to pass; but a reverse of fortune forced him to beg his bread, which he did with a great deal of dexterity. He studied chiefly to get into great men's houses, by means of their servants and officers, that he might have access to their masters, and obtain their charity. One day, as he passed by a magnificent house, whose high gate shewed a very spacious court, where there was a multitude of servants, he went to one of them, and asked him to whom that house belonged? Good man, replies the servant, whence do you come, that you ask me such a question?

Does not all that you see make you understand that it is the palace of a Barmecide?[1] My brother, who very well knew the liberality and generosity of the Barmecides, addressed himself to one of his porters, for he had more than one, and prayed him to give him an alms. Go in, said they, nobody hinders you, and address yourself to the master of the house; he will send you back satisfied.

My brother, who expected no such civility, thanked the porters, and, with their permission, entered the palace, which was so large that it took him a considerable time to reach the Barmecide's apartment; at last he came to a fine square building of excellent architecture, and entered by a porch, through which he saw one of the finest gardens with gravel walks of several colours, extremely pleasant to the eye: The lower apartments round this square were most of them open, and were shut only with great curtains to keep out the sun, which were opened again when the heat was over.

Such an agreeable place struck my brother with admiration, and might well have done so to a man far above his quality. He went on till he came into a hall richly furnished, and adorned with painting of gold and azure foliage, where he saw a venerable man with a long white beard sitting at the upper end of an alcove; whence he concluded him to be the master of the house; and in effect it was the Barmecide himself, who said to my brother, in a very civil manner, that he was welcome; and asked him what he wanted? My lord, answers my brother, in a begging tone, I am a poor man, who stands in need of the help of such rich and generous persons as yourself. He could not have addressed himself to a fitter person than this lord, who had a thousand good qualities.

The Barmecide seemed to be astonished at my brother's answer, and, putting both his hands to his stomach, as if he would rend his clothes for grief, Is it possible, cries he, that I am at Bagdad, and that such a man as you is so poor as you say? This is what must never be. My brother, fancying that he was going to give him some singular mark of his bounty, blessed him a thousand times, and wished him all sort of happiness. It shall not be said, replied the Barmecide, that I will abandon you, nor will I have you to leave me. Sir, replied my brother, I swear to you I have not tasted a bit to-day. Is that true, replied the Barmecide, that you are fasting till now? Alas for thee, poor man! He is ready to die for hunger: Ho, boy, cries he with a loud voice, bring a bason and water presently, that we may wash our hands. Though no boy appeared that my brother saw, neither with water nor bason, the Barmecide fell a-rubbing his hands, as if one had poured water upon them, and bid my brother come and wash with him. Schacabac judged by that, that the Barmecide loved to be merry, and he himself understanding

[1] The Barmecides were a noble family of Persia, as has been said already, who settled themselves at Bagdad.

raillery, and knowing that the poor must be complaisant to the rich, if they would have any thing from them, he came forward and did as he did.

Come on, says the Barmecide, bring us something to eat, and do not let us stay for it. When he had said so, though nothing was brought, he began to cut as if something had been brought him upon a plate, and, putting his hand to his mouth, began to chew, and say to my brother, Come, friend, eat as freely as if you were at home; come eat, you said you were like to die of hunger, but you eat as if you had no stomach. Pardon me, my lord, says Schacabac, who perfectly imitated what he did, you see I lose no time, and that I do my part well enough. How like you this bread, says the Barmecide, do not you find it very good? O my lord, says my brother, who saw neither bread nor meat, I never ate any thing so white and so fine. Come eat your belly-full, says the Barmecide, I assure you the baker-woman that bakes me this bread, cost me five hundred pieces of gold to purchase her.

The Barmecide, after having boasted so much of his bread, which my brother ate only in idea, cries, Boy, bring us another dish; and, though no boy appeared, Come, my good friend, says he to my brother, taste this new dish; and tell me if ever you ate better mutton and barley-broth than this? It is admirably good, replies my brother, and therefore you see I eat heartily. You oblige me mightily, replies the Barmecide; I conjure you then, by the satisfaction I have to see you eat so heartily, that you eat all up, since you like it so well. A little while after, he calls for a goose and sweet sauce, vinegar, honey, dry raisins, grey pease, and dry figs, which were brought just in the same manner as the other was. The goose is very fat, says the Barmecide, eat only a leg and a wing, we must save our stomachs, for we have abundance of other dishes to come. He actually called for several other dishes, of which my brother, who was ready to die of hunger, pretended to eat; but what he boasted of more than all the rest, was a lamb fed with pistachio-nuts, which he ordered to be brought up in the same manner that the rest were. And here is a dish, says the Barmecide, that you will see at nobody's table but my own; I would have you eat your belly-full of it. Having spoke thus, he stretched out his hand as if he had a piece of lamb in it, and, putting it to my brother's mouth, There, says he, swallow that, and you will know whether I had not reason to boast of this dish. My brother thrust out his head, opened his mouth, and made as if he took the piece of lamb, and ate it with extreme pleasure. I knew you would like it, says the Barmecide. There is nothing in the world more fine, replies my brother; your table is a most delicious thing. Come, bring the ragout presently, I fancy you will like that as well as you did the lamb: Well, how do you relish it? says the Barmecide. O! it is wonderful, replies Schacabac; for here we taste, all at once, amber, cloves, nutmeg, ginger, pepper, and the most odoriferous herbs; and all these tastes are so well mixed, that one does not hinder but we may perceive the other: O how pleasant it is! Honour this ragout, says the Barmecide, by eating heartily of it. Ho, boy, cries he, bring us a new ragout. No, my lord, and it please you, replies my brother, for indeed I can eat no more.

Come, take away then, says the Barmecide, and bring the fruit. He staid a moment, as it were to give time to the servants to carry away; after which he says to my brother, Taste these almonds, they are fresh, new gathered. Both of them made as if they had peeled the almonds, and ate them; after this the Barmecide invited my brother to eat something else. Look you, says he, there is all sorts of fruits, cakes, dry sweetmeats, and conserves, take what you like; then stretching out his hand, as if he had reached my brother something, Look ye, says he, there is a lozenge very good for digestion. Schacabac made as if he ate it, and says, My lord, there is no want of musk here. These lozenges, says the Barmecide, are made at my own house, where there is nothing wanting to make every thing good. He still bid my brother eat, and says to him, Methinks you do not eat as if you had been so hungry as you said when you came. My lord, replies Schacabac, whose jaws ached with moving, and having nothing to eat, I assure you I am so full that I cannot eat one bit more.

Well then, friend, replies the Barmecide, we must drink now, after we have ate so well. You drink wine, my lord, replies my brother, but I will drink none, if you please, because I am forbid it.* You are too scrupulous, replies the Barmecide, do as I do. I will drink then out of complaisance, says Schacabac; for I see you will have nothing wanting to make your treat noble; but, since I am not accustomed to drink wine, I am afraid that I shall commit some error in point of breeding, and contrary to the respect that is due to you; and therefore I pray you once more to excuse me from drinking any wine, for I will be content with water. No, no, says the Barmecide, you shall drink wine; at the same time he commanded some to be brought in the same manner as the meat and fruit had been brought before. He made as if he poured out wine, and drank first himself, and then pouring out for my brother, presented him the glass; Drink my health, says he, and let us know if you think this wine good. My brother made as if he took the glass, and looked if the colour was good, and put it to his nose to try if it had a good flavour; then he made a low bow to the Barmecide, to signify that he took the liberty to drink his health; and making all the signs of a man that drinks with pleasure, My lord, says he, this is very excellent wine, but I think it is not strong enough. If you would have stronger, said the Barmecide, you need only speak, for I have several sorts in my cellar: Try how you like this. Upon which he made as if he poured out another glass to himself, and then to my brother; and did this so often, that Schacabac, feigning to be drunk with the wine, took up his hand, and gave the Barmecide such a box on the ear as made him fall down; he lifted up his hand to give him another blow, but the Barmecide holding up his hand to ward it off, cries to him, What, are you mad? Then my brother, making as if he had come to himself again, says, My lord, you have been so good as to admit your slave into your house, and give him a great treat; you should have been satisfied with making me eat, and not oblige me to drink wine; for I told you beforehand, that it might occasion me to come short in my respects: I am very much troubled at it, and beg you a thousand pardons.

Scarce had he finished these words, when the Barmecide, instead of being in a rage, fell a-laughing with all his might. It is a long time, says he, that I wanted a man of your character.

The Barmecide caressed Schacabac mightily, and told him, I not only forgive the blow you gave me, but I am willing henceforward we should be friends, and that you take my house for your home: You have been so complaisant as to accommodate yourself to my humour, and have had the patience to bear out the jest to the last; we will now eat in good earnest. When he had finished these words, he clapped his hands, and commanded his servants, who then appeared, to cover the table, which was speedily done, and my brother was treated with all those in reality which he ate before in fancy. At last they took away, and brought wine, and at the same time a number of handsome slaves, richly apparelled, came in and sung some agreeable airs to their musical instruments. In a word, Schacabac had all the reason in the world to be satisfied with the Barmecide's civility and bounty; for he treated him as his familiar friend, and ordered him a suit out of his wardrobe.

The Barmecide found my brother to be a man of so much wit and understanding, that, in a few days after, he trusted him with his household and all his affairs. My brother acquitted himself very well in that employment for twenty years; at the end of which this generous Barmecide died, and leaving no heirs, all his estate was confiscated to the use of the prince: Upon which my brother was reduced to his first condition, and joined a caravan of pilgrims going to Mecca, designing to accomplish that pilgrimage upon their charity; but by misfortune the caravan was attacked, and plundered by a number of Beduins,[1] superior to that of the pilgrims. My brother was then taken as a slave by one of the Beduins, who put him under the bastinado for several days, to oblige him to ransom himself. Schacabac protested to him, that it was all in vain. I am your slave, says he, you may dispose of me as you please; but I declare unto you, that I am extremely poor, and not able

[1] Or vagabond Arabians, who wander in the desarts, and plunder the caravans when they are not strong enough to resist them.*

to redeem myself. In a word, my brother discovered to him all his misfortunes, and endeavoured to soften him with his tears; but the Beduin had no mercy, and being vexed to find himself disappointed of a considerable sum, which he reckoned he was sure of, he took his knife, and slit my brother's lips, to avenge himself by this inhumanity for the loss that he thought he had sustained.

The Beduin had a handsome wife, and frequently, when he went on his courses, he left my brother alone with her, and then she used all her endeavours to comfort my brother under the rigour of his slavery; she gave him tokens enough that she loved him, but he durst not yield to her passion, for fear he should repent it; and therefore he shunned to be alone with her as much as she sought the opportunity to be alone with him. She had so great a custom of toying and jesting with the miserable Schacabac, whenever she saw him, that one day she happened to do it in presence of her husband. My brother, without taking notice that he observed them, so his sins would have it, jested likewise with her. The Beduin immediately supposing that they lived together in a criminal manner, fell upon my brother, in a rage, and after he had mangled him in a barbarous manner, he carried him on a camel to the top of a desert mountain, where he left him. The mountain was on the way to Bagdad, so that the passengers who passed that way, gave me an account of the place where he was. I went thither speedily, where I found unfortunate Schacabac in a deplorable condition: I gave him what help he stood in need of, and brought him back to the city.

This is what I told to the caliph Monstancer Billah, adds the barber: that prince applauded me with new fits of laughter. Now, says he, I cannot doubt but they justly give you the surname of Silent. Nobody can say the contrary; for certain reasons, however, I command you to depart the town immediately, and let me hear no more of your discourse. I yielded to necessity, and went to travel several years in far countries. I understood at last that the caliph was dead; I returned to Bagdad, where I found not one of my brethren alive. It was in my return to this town, that I did the important service to the same young man, which you have heard. You are, however, witness of his ingratitude, and of the injurious manner in which he treated me; instead of testifying his acknowledgment, he rather chose to fly from me, and to leave his own country. When I understood he was not at Bagdad, though nobody could tell me truly whither he was gone, yet I did not forbear to go and seek him. I travelled from province to province a long time; and, when I had given over all hopes, I met him next day, but I did not think to find him so incensed against me.

The tailor made an end of telling the sultan of Casgar the history of the lame young man, and the barber of Bagdad, after the manner I had the honour to tell your majesty.—When the barber had finished his story, we found that the young man was not to blame for calling him a great prattler. However, we were pleased that he would stay with us, and partake of the treat which the master of the house had prepared for us. We sat down to table, and were merry together till afternoon-prayers; till all the company parted, and I went to my shop; then it was time for me to return home.

It was during this interval that Hump-back came half-drunk before my shop, where he sung and tabored. I thought that by carrying him home with me, I should divert my wife, therefore I brought him along: My wife gave us a dish of fish, and I presented Hump-back with some, which he eat without taking notice of a bone. He fell down dead before us, and, after having in vain essayed to help him, in the trouble occasioned us by such an unlucky accident, and in the fear it occasioned to us, we carried the corpse out, and dexterously lodged him with the Jewish doctor. The Jewish doctor put him into the chamber of the purveyor, and the purveyor carried him forth into the street, where it was believed the merchant had killed him. This, sir, adds the tailor, is what I had to say to satisfy your majesty, who must pronounce whether we be worthy of mercy or wrath, life or death.

The sultan of Casgar looked with a contented air, and gave the tailor and his comrades their lives. I cannot but acknowledge, says he, that I am more amazed with the history of the young cripple, with that of the barber, and with the adventures of his brothers, than with the story of my jester: But, before I send you all four away, and before we bury Hump-back, I would see the barber who is the cause that I have pardoned you: Since he is in my capital, it is easy to satisfy my curiosity. At the same time, he sent a serjeant with the tailor to go and find him.

The serjeant and the tailor went immediately and brought the barber, whom they presented to the sultan: The barber was an old man of ninety years, his eye-brows and beard were as white as snow, his ears hanging down, and he had a very long nose. The sultan could not forbear laughing when he saw him. Silent man, says he to him, I understand that you know wonderful stories, will you tell me some of them? Sir, answered the barber, let us forbear the stories, if you please, at present. I most humbly beg your majesty to permit me to ask what that Christian, that Jew, that Mussulman, and that dead hump-back, who lies on the ground, do here before your majesty? The sultan smiled at the barber's liberty, and replied, Why do you ask? Sir, replied the barber, it concerns me to ask, that your majesty may know I am not so great a talker as some pretend, but a man justly called Silent.

The sultan of Casgar was so complaisant as to satisfy the barber's curiosity. He commanded them to tell him the story of the Hump-back, which he earnestly wished for. When the barber heard it, he shaked his head, as if he would say, there is something under this which he did not understand: Truly, cries he, this is a surprising story, but I am willing to examine Hump-back a little closely. He drew near him, sat down on the ground, and took his head between his knees, and, after he had looked upon him stedfastly, he fell into so great a fit of laughter, and had so little command of himself, that he fell backwards on the ground, without considering that he was before the sultan of Casgar. As soon as he came to himself, It is said, cries he, and not without reason, that no man dies without a cause. If ever any history deserved to be writ in letters of gold, it is this of Hump-back.

At this all the people looked on the barber as a buffoon, or a doting old man. Silent man, says the sultan, speak to me; Why do you laugh so hard? Sir, answered the barber, I swear by your majesty's good humours, that Hump-back is not dead; he is yet alive, and I shall be willing to pass for a madman if I do not let you see it this minute. Having said these words, he took a box, wherein he had several medicines that he carried about him to make use of on occasion; and he took out a small vial with balsam, with which he rubbed Hump-back's neck a long time; then he took out of his case a neat iron instrument, which he put betwixt his teeth, and after he had opened his mouth, he thrust down his throat a pair of small pincers, with which he took out a bit of fish and bone, which he shewed to all the people. Immediately Hump-back sneezed, stretched forth his arms and feet, and gave several other signs of life.

The sultan of Casgar and those with him, who were witnesses of this operation, were less surprised to see Hump-back revive, after he had passed a whole night, and great part of a day, without giving any signs of life, than at the merit and capacity of the barber, who performed this; and, notwithstanding all his faults, began to look upon him as a great person.—The sultan, ravished with joy and admiration, ordered the story of Hump-back to be writ down, with that of the barber, that the memory of it might, as it deserved, be preserved for ever. Nor did he stop here; but, that the tailor, Jewish doctor, purveyor, and Christian merchant, might remember the adventure which the accident of Hump-back had occasioned to them with pleasure, he did not send them away till he had given each of them a very rich robe, with which he caused them to be cloathed in his presence. As for the barber, he honoured him with a great pension, and kept him near his person.

Thus the sultaness finished this long train of adventures, to which the pretended death of Hump-back gave occasion; then held her peace, because day appeared. Upon which her sister Dinarzade says to her, My princess, my sultaness, I am so much the more charmed with the story you just now told, because it concludes with an incident I did not expect. I verily thought Hump-back was dead. This surprise pleases me, says Schahriar, as much as the adventures of the barber's brothers.—The story of the lame young man of Bagdad diverted me also very much, replies Dinarzade.

I am very glad of it, dear sister, says the sultaness; and, since I have had the good fortune not to tire out the patience of the sultan, our lord and master, if his majesty will still be so gracious as to preserve my life, I shall have the honour to give him an account to-morrow of the amours of Aboulhassen Ali Ebn Becar, and Schemselnihar, favourite of the caliph Haroun Alraschid, which is no less worthy of your notice than the history of Hump-back.—The sultan of the Indies, who was very well satisfied with the stories that Scheherazade had told him hitherto, was willing to hear that history which she promised. He rose however to go to prayers, and hold his council, without giving any signification of his pleasure towards the sultaness.

Dinarzade being always careful to awake her sister, called this night at the ordinary hour: My dear sister, says she, day will soon appear. I earnestly beg of you to tell us some of your fine stories. We need no other, said Schahriar, but that of the amours of Aboulhassen Ali Ebn Becar, and Schemselnihar, the favourite of caliph Haroun Alraschid. Sir, says Scheherazade, I will satisfy your curiosity; and began thus:

The History of Aboulhassen Ali Ebn Becar, and Schemselnihar, Favourite of Caliph Haroun Alraschid

IN the reign of the caliph Haroun Alraschid, there was at Bagdad a druggist called Alboussan Ebn Thaher, a very rich and handsome man.—He had more of wit and politeness than those of his profession ordinarily have: His integrity, sincerity, and jovial humour, made him to be loved and sought after by all sorts of people. The caliph, who knew his merit, had an entire confidence in him. He had so great an esteem for him, that he intrusted him with the care to provide the ladies, his favourites, with all things they stood in need of. He chose for them their clothes, furniture, and jewels, with admirable judgment.

His good qualities, and the favour of the caliph, made the sons of emirs, and other officers of the first rank, to be always about him: His house was the rendezvous of all the nobility of the court. But, among the young lords that went daily to visit him, there was one with whom he contracted a particular friendship, called Aboulhassen Ali Ebn Becar, originally of an ancient royal family of Persia. This family continued at Bagdad ever since the mussulmen made a conquest of that kingdom.*—Nature seemed to have taken pleasure to endue this young prince with many of the rarest qualities of body and mind: His face was so very beautiful, his shape so fine, and his physiognomy so engaging, that none could see him without loving him immediately. When he spoke, he expressed himself always in terms proper and well chosen, with a new and agreeable turn, and his voice charmed all that heard him; with this he had so much wit and judgment, that he thought and spoke of all subjects with admirable exactness. He was so reserved and modest, that he advanced nothing till after he had taken all possible precautions to avoid giving any ground of suspicion that he preferred his own opinion to that of others.

Being such a person as I have represented him, we need not wonder at Ebn Thaher distinguishing him from all the other young noblemen of the court, most of whom had vices contrary to his virtues. One day, when the prince was with Ebn Thaher, there came a lady mounted on a pyebald mule, in the midst of six women slaves, who accompanied her on foot, all very handsome, as far as could be judged by their air, and through the veils which covered their faces. The lady had a girdle of a rose-colour, four inches broad, embroidered with pearls and diamonds, of an extraordinary bigness; and as for beauty, it was easy to perceive that she surpassed all her women, as far as the full moon does that of two days old. She came to buy something, and when she had spoken to Ebn Thaher, she entered his shop, which was very neat and large, and he received her with all the marks of the most profound respect, entreating her to sit down, and shewing her with his hand the most honourable place.

In the mean time, the prince of Persia, not being willing to let such an occasion pass, to shew his good breeding and courtly temper, beat up the cushion of cloth of gold, for the lady to lean on; after which he retired speedily, that she might sit down; and having saluted her, by kissing the tapestry under her feet, he rose, and stood at the lower end of the sofa. It being her custom to be free with Ebn Thaher, she lifted up her veil, and then discovered to the prince of Persia such an extraordinary beauty, that he was struck with it to the heart. On the other hand, the lady could not contain herself from looking upon the prince, the sight of whom had made the same impression upon her. My lord, says she to him, with an obliging air, pray sit down. The prince of Persia obeyed, and sat down upon the edge of the sofa. He had his eyes constantly fixed upon her, and swallowed down large draughts of the sweet poison of love. She quickly perceived what passed in his heart, and this discovery served to inflame her the more towards him. She rose up, went to Ebn Thaher, and, after she had whispered to him thc cause of her coming, she asked the name and country of the prince? Madam, answered Ebn Thaher, this young nobleman's name is Aboulhassen Ali Ebn Becar, and he is a prince of the blood royal.

The lady was ravished to the heart that the person she already loved so passionately was of so high a quality. You mean certainly, says she, that he is descended of the kings of Persia? Yes, madam, replied Ebn Thaher, the last kings of Persia were his ancestors, and since the conquest of that kingdom, the princes of his family have always made themselves very acceptable at the court of our caliphs.—You will oblige me much, adds she, to make me acquainted with this young nobleman: When I send this woman, says she, pointing to one of her slaves, to give you notice to come and see me, pray bring him with you; I shall be very glad that he see the magnificence of my house, that he may see that avarice does not reign at Bagdad among persons of quality: You know very well what I mean; do not fail, otherwise I will be very angry with you, and never come hither again while I live.

Ebn Thaher was a man of too much penetration, not to perceive the lady's mind by these words: My princess, my queen, replied he, God preserve me from ever giving you any occasion of anger against me: I shall always make it a law to obey your commands. At this answer, the lady bowed to Ebn Thaher, and bad him farewell; and after she had given a favourable look to the prince of Persia, she remounted her mule, and went her way.

The prince of Persia was so deeply in love with the lady, that he looked after her as far as he could see her; and a long time after she was out of sight, he still looked that way. Ebn Thaher told him, that several persons observed him, and began to laugh to see him in this posture. Alas! said the prince to him, the world and you would have compassion on me, if you knew that the fine lady, who is just now gone from you, has carried with her the best part of me, and that the remaining part seeks for an opportunity to go after. Tell me, I conjure you, adds he, what cruel lady is this who forces people to love her, without giving them time to advise? My lord, answers Ebn Thaher, this is the famous Schemselnihar,[1] the principal favourite of the caliph our master. She is justly so called, adds the prince, since she is more beautiful than the sun at noon-day. That is true, replied Ebn Thaher, therefore the commander of the faithful loves, or rather adores her; he gave me express orders to furnish her all that she asked of me, and to prevent as much as possible every thing that she can desire of me.

He spoke after this manner, to hinder him from engaging in an amour which could not but prove unhappy to him; but this served only to inflame him the more. I was very doubtful, charming Schemselnihar, cries he, I should not be allowed so much as to think of you; I perceive well, however, that without hopes of being loved by you, I cannot forbear loving you; I will

[1] This word signifies the Sun of the Day.

love you then, and bless my lot that I am slave to an object fairer than the meridian sun.

While the prince of Persia was thus consecrating his heart to fair Schemselnihar, this lady, when she came home, thought upon a way how she might see and have free converse with him. She no sooner entered her palace, but she sent to Ebn Thaher the woman she had shewed him, and in whom she had put all her confidence, to tell him to come and see her without delay, and to bring the prince of Persia with him. The slave came to Ebn Thaher's shop while he was speaking with the prince, and, endeavouring to dissuade him, by very strong arguments, from loving the caliph's favourite. When she saw them together, Gentlemen, says she to them, my honourable mistress Schemselnihar, the chief favourite of the commander of the faithful, entreats you to come to her palace, where she waits for you. Ebn Thaher, to testify his obedience, got up immediately, without answering the slave, and followed her, not without some reluctancy. And the prince, he followed, without reflecting upon the danger there might be in such a visit. The company of Ebn Thaher, who had a liberty when he pleased to go to the favourite, made the prince very easy in the matter: They followed the slave, who went a little before them, and entered after her into the caliph's palace, and joined her at the gate of Schemselnihar's little palace, which was ready open. She introduced them into a great hall, where she prayed them to sit down.

The prince of Persia thought himself in one of those delicious palaces that are promised to us in the other world: He had never seen any thing that came near the magnificence of the palace he was in. The carpets, cushions, and other furniture of the sofa, the moveables, ornaments, and architecture, were surprisingly beautiful. A little time after Ebn Thaher and he sat down, a very handsome black slave brought them a table covered with several very fine dishes, the admirable smells of which made them judge of the delicacy of the sauce. While they were eating, the slave which brought them in waited upon them; she took care to invite them to eat of what she knew to be the greatest dainties. The other slaves brought them excellent wine after they had eaten. When they had done, there was presented to each of them a fine gold bason full of water to wash their hands; after which they brought them a golden pot full of the perfume of aloes, with which they perfumed their beards and clothes. Odoriferous water was not forgot, but served in a golden vessel enriched with diamonds and rubies, made particularly for this use, and it was thrown upon their beards and faces, according to custom. Then they went to their places; but they had scarce sat down when the slave entreated them to arise and follow her: She opened a gate of the hall where they were, and they entered into a large saloon of a marvellous structure. It was a dome of the most agreeable fashion, supported by an hundred pillars of marble, white as alabaster. The bases and chapiters* of the pillars were adorned with four-footed beasts, and birds of several sorts, gilded. The foot-carpet of this noble parlour consisted of one piece of cloth of gold, embroidered with garlands of roses in red and white silk, and the dome being painted in the same manner after the Arabian form, was one of the most charming objects that eye could behold. Betwixt each column there was a little sofa adorned in the same manner, and great vessels of china, crystal, jasper, jet, porphyry, agate, and other precious materials, garnished with gold and jewels: The spaces betwixt the columns were so many large windows, with jets high enough for one to lean on, covered with the same sort of stuff as the sofas, and looking out into the most delicious garden of the world; the walks were of little pebbles of different colours, which resembled the foot-carpet of the saloon; so that, looking upon the carpet within and without, it looked as if the dome, and the garden, with all its ornaments, had stood upon the same carpet. The prospect round was thus: At the end of the walks there were two canals of clear water, of the same circular figure as the dome, the one of which, being higher than the other, emptied its water into the lowermost, in form of a table-cloth; and curious pots of gilt brass, with flowers and greens, were set upon the banks of the canals at equal distances. Those walks lay betwixt great plots of ground, planted with straight and bushy trees, where there were a thousand birds, which formed a melodious concert, and diverted the view by their flying about, and sometimes by playing together, and, at other times, by fighting in good earnest in the air.

The prince of Persia and Ebn Thaher were a long time taken up in viewing the magnificence of the palace, and testified their surprise at every thing they saw, especially the prince, who had never seen any thing like it. Ebn Thaher, though he had been several times in that delicate palace, yet could not but observe many new beauties. In a word, they never grew weary in admiring so many singular things, and were thus agreeably employed, when they perceived a company of ladies richly apparelled, sitting without, at some distance from the dome, each of them upon a seat of Indian wood, inlaid with silver-wire in figures, with instruments of music in their hands, expecting orders to play. They went both to the jet, which fronted the ladies, and on the right they saw a great court, with a stair up from the garden, encompassed with beautiful apartments. The slave had left them, and, being alone, they discoursed together. For you, who are a wise man, says the prince of Persia, I doubt not but you look with a great deal of satisfaction upon all these marks of grandeur and power. For my part, I do not think there is any thing in the world more surprising. But when I consider that this is the glorious habitation of the lovely Schemselnihar, and that he is the greatest monarch of the earth who keeps her here, I confess to you that I look upon myself to be the most unfortunate of all mankind, and that no destiny can be more cruel than mine, to love an object possessed by my rival; and that too in a place where he is so potent that I cannot think myself sure of my life one moment.

Ebn Thaher, hearing the prince of Persia speak, says to him, Sir, I wish you could give me as good assurance of the happy success of your amours as I can give you of the safety of your life. Though this stately palace belongs to the caliph, who built it on purpose for Schemselnihar, called it the Palace of Eternal Pleasures, and that it makes part of his own palace, yet you must know, that this lady lives here at entire liberty; she is not besieged by eunuchs to be spies upon her; this is her particular house that is absolutely at her disposal. She goes into the city when she pleases, and returns again, without asking leave of any body; and the caliph never comes to see her but he sends Mesrour, the chief of his eunuchs, to give her notice, that she may be prepared to receive him. Therefore you may be easy, and give full attention to the concert of music, which I perceive Schemselnihar is preparing for you.

Just as Ebn Thaher had spoken these words, the prince of Persia and he saw the favourite's trusty slave come and give orders to the ladies to begin to sing, and play with the instruments: They all began immediately to play together, as a preludium, and, after they had played some time, one of them began to sing alone, and played at the same time admirably well upon her lute, being advertised before-hand upon what subject she was to sing. The words were so agreeable to the prince of Persia's sentiments, that he could not forbear to applaud her at the end of the stave: Is it possible, cries he, that you have the gift of knowing people's hearts, and that the knowledge of what is in my mind has occasioned you to give us a taste of your charming voice by those words? I should not express myself otherwise, were I to chuse. The lady replied nothing, but went on, and sung several other staves, with which the prince was so much affected, that he repeated some of them with tears in his eyes, which discovered plain enough that he applied them to himself. When she had made an end, she and her companions rose up, and sung all together, signifying by their words, that the full-moon was going to rise in all her splendour, and that they should speedily see her approach the sun: By which it was meant, that Schemselnihar was just a-coming, and that the prince of Persia should have the pleasure to see her.

And in effect, as they looked towards the court, they saw Schemselnihar's confidant coming towards them, followed by ten black women, who with much ado carried a throne of massy silver, curiously wrought, which they set down before them at a certain distance; after which the black slaves retired behind the trees to the entrance of a walk. After this came twenty handsome ladies, richly apparelled, all in one dress: They advanced in two rows, singing and playing upon instruments which each of them held in her hand; and, coming near the throne, ten of them sat down on each side of it.

All these things kept the prince of Persia and Ebn Thaher in so much the greater expectation, that they were curious to know how they would end. They then saw come out of the same gate from whence the ten black women came, ten other handsome ladies, very well dressed, who halted there a few moments expecting the favourite, who came out the last, and placed herself in the midst of them.

Schemselnihar was easily distinguished from the rest, by her fine shape and majestic air, as well as by a sort of mantle of a very fine stuff of gold and sky blue, fastened to her shoulders over her other apparel, which was the most handsome, best contrived, and most magnificent that could be thought on.

The pearls, and rubies, and the diamonds, which adorned her, were in very good order; not many in number, but well chosen, and of inestimable value: She came forward, with a majesty resembling the sun in its course amidst the clouds, which receive his splendour without hiding his lustre; and sat down upon the silver throne that was brought for her.

As soon as the prince of Persia saw Schemselnihar, he could look upon nothing else. We cease inquiring, says he to Ebn Thaher, after what we seek, when once we see it; and there is no doubt left remaining when once the truth makes itself manifest: Do you see this charming beauty? She is the cause of all my sufferings, which I hug, and will never forbear blessing them, how lasting soever they may be: At the sight of this object I am not my own master: my soul is disturbed and rebels, and I fancy it has a mind to leave me! Go then, my soul, I allow thee, but let it be for the welfare and preservation of this weak body. It is you, cruel Ebn Thaher, who is the cause of this disorder; you thought to do me a great pleasure in bringing me hither, and I perceive I am only come to complete my ruin. Pardon me, says he, interrupting himself, I am mistaken, I was willing to come, and can blame nobody but myself; and at these words broke out into tears. I am very well pleased, says Ebn Thaher, that you do me justice: When I told you at first that Schemselnihar was the caliph's chief favourite, I did it on purpose to prevent that fatal passion which you please yourself with entertaining in your breast: All that you see here ought to disengage you, and you are to think on nothing but of acknowledgment for the honour which Schemselnihar was willing to do you, by ordering me to bring you with me. Call in then your wandering reason, and put yourself in a condition to appear before her as good breeding requires. Lo! there she comes: Were the matter to begin again, I would take other measures, but, since the thing is done, I wish we may not repent it. What I have farther to say to you is this, that love is a traitor, who may throw you into a pit you will never get out of.

Ebn Thaher had not time to say more because Schemselnihar came, and, sitting down upon her throne, saluted them both with bowing her head; but she fixed her eyes on the prince of Persia, and they spoke to one another in a silent language, intermixed with sighs; by which, in a few moments, they spoke more than they could have done by words in a great deal of time. The more Schemselnihar looked upon the prince, the more she found by his looks that he was in love with her; and being thus persuaded of his passion, thought herself the happiest woman in the world. At last she turned her eyes from him, to command the women, who began to sing first, to come near; they got up, and, whilst they advanced, the black women, who came out of the walk into which they retired, brought their seats, and set them near the window, in the jet of the dome, where Ebn Thaher and the prince of Persia stood, and their seats were so disposed on each side the favourite's throne, that they formed a semicircle.

The women, who were sitting before she came, took each of them their places again, with the permission of Schemselnihar, who ordered them by a sign.—That charming favourite chose one of those women to sing, who, after she had spent some moments in tuning her lute, played a song, the meaning whereof was, That two lovers who entirely loved one another, whose affection was boundless, their hearts, though in two bodies, were one and the same; and, when any thing opposed their desires, could say, with tears in their eyes, If we love, because we find one another amiable, ought we to be blamed for this? Let destiny bear the blame.

Schemselnihar discovered so well by her eyes and gestures that those sayings ought to be applied to her and the prince of Persia, that he could not contain himself, but arose and came to a balluster, which he leaned upon, and obliged one of the women who came to sing, to observe him. When she was near him, Follow me, says he to her, and do me the favour to accompany with your lute a song which you shall hear forthwith. Then he sung with an air so tender and passionate as perfectly expressed the violence of his love. As soon as he had done, Schemselnihar following his example, said to one of the women, Follow me likewise, and accompany my voice: At the same time, she sung after such a manner as did farther pierce the heart of the prince of Persia, who answered her by a new air as passionate as the former.

Those two lovers declared their mutual affection by their songs. Schemselnihar yielded to the force of hers; she arose from her throne, and advanced towards the door of the hall. The prince, who knew her design, arose immediately, and went towards her in all haste. They met at the door, where they took one another by the hand, and embraced with so much passion that they fainted, and would have fallen, if the women who followed them had not helped them up. They supported them, and carried them to a sofa, where they were brought to themselves again by throwing odoriferous water upon their faces, and by giving them things to smell.

When they came to themselves, the first thing that Schemselnihar did, was to look about; and not seeing Ebn Thaher, she asked with a great deal of concern where he was? He had withdrawn out of respect whilst her women were applying things to recover her, and dreaded, not without reason, that some troublesome consequence might attend what had happened: but as soon as he heard Schemselnihar ask for him, he came forward, and presented himself before her.

Schemselnihar was very well pleased to see Ebn Thaher, and expressed her joy in these terms: Kind Ebn Thaher, I do not know how to make amends for the great obligations you have put upon me; without you, I should never have seen the prince of Persia, nor have loved that which is the most amiable thing in the world; but you may assure yourself, however, that I shall not die ungrateful, and that my acknowledgment, if possible, shall be equal to the obligation. Ebn Thaher answered this compliment by a low bow, and wished the favourite the accomplishment of all her desires.

Schemselnihar, turning towards the prince of Persia, who sat by her, and looking upon him with some sort of confusion, after what passed betwixt them, says to him, Sir, I am very well assured you love me, and how great soever your love may be to me, you need not doubt but mine is as great towards you. But let us not flatter ourselves; for though we be both agreed, yet I see nothing for you and me but trouble, impatience, and tormenting grief. There is no other remedy for our evils, but to love one another constantly, to refer ourselves to the disposal of heaven, and to expect till it shall determine our destiny. Madam, replies the prince of Persia, you will do me the greatest injustice in the world, if you doubt but one moment of the continuance of my love. It is so united to my soul, that I can justly say, it makes the best part of it, and that I shall persevere in it after death. Pains, torments, obstacles, nothing shall be capable of hindering me to love you. Speaking those words, he shed tears in abundance, and Schemselnihar was not able to restrain her's.

Ebn Thaher took this opportunity to speak to the favourite: Madam, says he, allow me to represent to you, that, instead of breaking forth into tears, you ought to rejoice that you are together. I understand not this grief. What will it be, when you are obliged to part? But why do I talk of that? We have been a long while here, and you know, madam, that it is time for us to be going. Ah! how cruel are you, replies Schemselnihar: You, who know the cause of my tears, have you no pity for my unfortunate condition? O sad fatality! What have I done to be subject to the severe law of not being able to enjoy the only thing I love!

She being persuaded that Ebn Thaher spoke to her only out of friendship, did not take amiss what he said to her, but made a good use of it. Then she made a sign to the slave, her confidant, who immediately went out, and in a little time brought a collation of fruits upon a small silver table, which she set down betwixt her mistress and the prince of Persia. Schemselnihar took some of the best, and presented to the prince, and prayed him to eat it for her sake: He took it, and put that part to his mouth which she touched; and then he presented some to her, which she took and ate in the same manner: She did not forget to invite Ebn Thaher to eat with them; but he, thinking himself not safe in that place, ate only out of complaisance. After the collation was taken away, they brought a silver bason, with water in a vessel of gold, and washed together; they afterwards returned to their places, and then three of the ten black women brought each of them a cup of rock crystal, full of curious wine, upon a golden salver, the which they set down before Schemselnihar, the prince of Persia, and Ebn Thaher. That they might be more private, Schemselnihar kept with her only ten black women, with ten others, who began to sing and play upon instruments; and, after she had sent away all the rest, she took up one of the cups, and holding it in her hand, sung some tender expressions, which one of her women accompanied with her lute. When she had done, she drank, and afterwards took up one of the other cups, and presented it to the prince, praying him to drink for the love of her, as she had drank for the love of him. He received the cup with a transport of love and joy; but, before he drank, he sung also a song, which another woman accompanied with an instrument; and as he sung, the tears fell from his eyes in such abundance, that he could not forbear expressing in his song, That he knew not whether he was going to drink the wine she had presented him, or his own tears. Schemselnihar at last presented the third cup to Ebn Thaher, who thanked her for her kindness, and for the honour she did him.

After this, she took a lute from one of her women, and sung to it in such a passionate manner as she seemed to be out of herself: The prince of Persia stood with his eyes fixed upon her, as if he had been enchanted. As these things passed, her trusty slave arrived all in a fright, and, addressing herself to her mistress, says, Madam, Mesrour and two other officers, with several eunuchs that attend them, are at the gate, and want to speak with you from the caliph. When the prince of Persia and Ebn Thaher heard these words, they changed colour, and began to tremble, as if they had been undone; but Schemselnihar, who perceived it, recovered their courage by a smile.

After Schemselnihar had quieted the prince of Persia and Ebn Thaher's fears, she ordered the slave, her confidant, to go and entertain Mesrour and the two other officers till she was in a condition to receive them, and send to her to bring them in. Immediately she ordered all the windows of the saloon to be shut, and the painted cloth on the side of the garden to be let down; and, after having assured the prince and Ebn Thaher, that they might continue there without any fear, she went out at the gate leading to the garden, and shut it upon them; but whatever assurance she had given them of their being safe, they were desperately afraid all the while they were there.

As soon as Schemselnihar was in the garden with the women who had followed her, she ordered all the seats which served the women who played on the instruments to be set near the window, where the prince of Persia and Ebn Thaher heard them; and having got things in order, she sat down upon a silver throne: then she sent notice by the slave, her confidant, to bring in the chief of the eunuchs, and his subaltern officers with him. They appeared, followed by twenty black eunuchs, all handsomely clothed, with scymitars by their sides, and gold belts of four inches broad. As soon as ever they perceived the favourite, Schemselnihar, at a distance, they made her a profound reverence, which she returned them from her throne. When they came near, she got up and went to meet Mesrour, who came first. She asked what news he brought? He answered, Madam, the commander of the faithful has sent me to signify, that he cannot live longer without seeing you; he designs to come and see you to-night, and I come before-hand to give you notice that you may be ready to receive him: He hopes, madam, that you long as much to see him, as he is impatient to see you.

Upon this discourse of Mesrour, the favourite Schemselnihar prostrated herself to the ground, as a mark of that submission with which she received the caliph's order; when she rose up again, she says, Pray tell the commander of the faithful, that I shall always reckon it my glory to execute his majesty's commands, and that his slave will do her utmost to receive him with all the respect that is due to him. At the same time, she ordered the slave, her confidant, to tell the black women appointed for that service, to get the palace ready to receive the caliph; and, dismissing the chief of the eunuchs, says to him, You see it requires some time to get all things ready, therefore I pray you to take care that his majesty may have a little patience, that when he arrives he may not find things out of order.

The chief of the eunuchs and his retinue being gone, Schemselnihar returned to the saloon extremely concerned at the necessity she was under of sending back the prince of Persia sooner than she thought to have done. She came up to him again with tears in her eyes, which heightened Ebn Thaher's fear, who thought it no good omen: Madam, says the prince to her,

I perceive you are come to tell me that we must part; provided there be nothing more to dread, I hope heaven will give me the patience which is necessary to support your absence. Alas! my dear heart, my dear soul, replies tender-hearted Schemselnihar, how happy do I think you, and how unhappy do I think myself, when I compare your lot with my sad destiny! No doubt you will suffer by my absence, but that is all, and you may comfort yourself with hopes of seeing me again: But as for me, just heaven! what a terrible trial am I brought to! I must not only be deprived of the sight of the only person whom I love, but I must be tormented with the sight of one whom you have made hateful to me: Will not the arrival of the caliph put me in mind of your departure? And how can I, when I am taken up with thinking on your sweet face, entertain that prince with that joy which he always observed in my eyes whenever he came to see me? I shall have my mind wavering when I speak to him, and the least complaisance which I shew to his love, will stab me to the heart like a dagger. Can I relish his kind words and caresses? Think, prince, to what torments I shall be exposed when I can see you no more. Her tears and sighs hindered her to go on; and the prince of Persia would have replied to her, but his own grief, and that of his mistress, made him incapable of doing it.

Ebn Thaher, whose chief business was to get out of the palace, was obliged to comfort them, and to exhort them to have patience; but the trusty slave interrupted them, saying to Schemselnihar, Madam, you have no time to lose, the eunuchs begin to arrive, and you know the caliph will be here immediately. O heavens! how cruel is this separation, cries the favourite. Make haste, says she to the confidant, carry them both to the gallery which looks into the garden on the one side, and to the Tigris on the other; and when the night grows dark, let them out by the back-gate, that they may retire with safety. Having spoken thus, she tenderly embraced the prince of Persia, without being able to say one word more, and went to meet the caliph in such a disorder as cannot well be imagined.

In the mean time, the trusty slave carried the prince and Ebn Thaher to the gallery, as Schemselnihar had appointed; and, having brought them in, left them there, and shut the door upon them, after having assured them that they had nothing to fear, and that she would come for them when it was time.

Schemselnihar's trusty slave leaving the prince of Persia and Ebn Thaher, they forgot she had assured them that they needed not to be afraid: They searched all the gallery, and were seized with extreme fear, because they knew no place where they might escape, in case the caliph or any of his officers should happen to come there.

A great light, which came all of a sudden from the side of the garden through the windows, caused them to approach to see from whence it came;

it was occasioned by a hundred flambeaux of white wax carried by as many young eunuchs; these were followed by more than one hundred others, who guarded the ladies of the caliph's palace, clothed, and armed with scymitars, in the same manner as those I spoke of before; and the caliph came after them betwixt Mesrour their captain on his right, and the vassif, their second officer, on his left-hand.

Schemselnihar waited for the caliph at the entry of an alley, accompanied with twenty women, all of surprising beauty, adorned with necklaces and ear-rings of large diamonds, and some of them had their whole heads covered with them; they played upon their instruments, and made a charming concert. The favourite no sooner saw the prince appear, but she advanced and prostrated herself at his feet; and, while she was doing this, prince of Persia, says she within herself, if your sad eyes bear witness to what I do, judge of my hard lot: If I was humbling myself before you, my heart should feel no reluctancy. The caliph was ravished to see Schemselnihar: Rise, madam, says he to her, come near; I am angry that I should have deprived myself so long of the pleasure of seeing you: As he spoke thus, he took her by the hand, and, after abundance of tender expressions, he went and sat down upon a silver throne, which Schemselnihar caused to be brought for him, and she sat down upon a seat before him, and the twenty women made a circle round them upon other seats, while the young eunuchs, who carried flambeaux, dispersed themselves at a certain distance from one another, that the caliph might enjoy the cool of the evening the better.

When the caliph sat down, he looked round him, and beheld with great satisfaction a great many other lights than those flambeaux the young eunuchs held; but, taking notice that the saloon was shut, was astonished thereat, and demanded the reason. It was done on purpose to surprise him; for he had no sooner spoken, but the windows were all open at once, and he saw it illuminated within and without, in a much better manner than ever he had seen it before. Charming Schemselnihar, cries he, at this sight, I understand you would have me to know there are as fine nights as days: After what I have seen I cannot disown it.

Let us return to the prince of Persia and Ebn Thaher, whom we left in the gallery. Ebn Thaher could not enough admire all that he saw: I am not very young, says he, and I have seen great entertainments in my time, but I do not think any thing can be seen so surprising and magnificent! All that is said of inchanted palaces does no way come near this prodigious spectacle we now see. O strange! What riches and magnificence together! The prince of Persia was not at all moved with those objects which were so pleasant to Ebn Thaher; he could look on nothing but Schemselnihar, and the presence of the caliph threw him into an inconceivable grief. Dear Ebn Thaher, says he, would to God I had my mind as free to admire those things as you! But, alas! I am in a quite different condition; all those objects serve only to increase my torment. Can I see the caliph cheek to cheek with her that I love, and not die of grief! Must such a passionate love as mine be disturbed with so potent a rival? O heavens! How cruel and strange is my destiny! It is but a moment since I esteemed myself the most fortunate lover in the world, and at this instant I feel my heart so struck, that it is like to kill me: I cannot resist it, my dear Ebn Thaher; my patience is at an end, my distemper overwhelms me, and my courage fails. While he was speaking these words, he saw something pass in the garden, which obliged him to keep silence, and to turn all his attention that way.

The caliph had ordered one of the women, who was near him, to play upon her lute, and she began to sing; the words that she sung were very passionate, and the caliph was persuaded that she sung thus by order of Schemselnihar, who had frequently entertained him with the like testimonies of her affection, therefore he interpreted all in his own favour. But this was not now Schemselnihar's meaning: She applied it to her dear Ali Ebn Becar, and was so sensibly touched with grief, to have before her an object whose presence she could no longer enjoy, that she fainted, and fell backwards upon her seat, which, having no arms to support her, she must have fallen down, had not some of the women helped her in time; after which, they took her up, and carried her into the saloon. Ebn Thaher, who was in the gallery, being surprised at this accident, turned towards the prince of Persia; but, instead of seeing him stand and look through the window as before, he was extremely amazed to see him fallen down at his feet, and without motion. He judged it to proceed from the violence of that prince's love to Schemselnihar, and admired the strange effect of sympathy, which put him into a mortal fear, because of the place they were in; in the mean time, he did all he could to recover the prince, but in vain. Ebn Thaher was in this perplexity, when Schemselnihar's confidant opened the gallery door, and came in out of breath, as one who knew not where she was. Come speedily, cries she, that I may let you out; all is in confusion here, and I fear this will be the last of our days. Ah! how would you have us go, replies Ebn Thaher with a mournful voice; come near, I pray you, and see what a condition the prince of Persia is in. When the slave saw him in a swoon, she ran for water in all haste, and returned in an instant.

At last the prince of Persia, after they had thrown water on his face, recovered his spirits. Prince, says Ebn Thaher to him, we run the risk of being destroyed if we stay here any longer, let us therefore endeavour to save our lives. He was so feeble that he could not rise alone; Ebn Thaher and the confidant lent him their hands, and supported him on each side. They came to a little iron gate, which opened towards the Tigris, went out at it, and came to the side of a little canal which had a communication with the river. The confidant clapped her hands, and immediately a little boat appeared, and came towards them, with one rower. Ali Ebn Becar and his comrade went aboard, and the trusty slave staid at the side of the canal. As soon as the prince sat down in the boat, he stretched one hand towards the palace, and laid his other upon his heart: Dear object of my soul, cries he, with a feeble voice, receive my faith with this hand, while I assure you with the other, that my heart shall for ever preserve the fire with which it burns for you. In the mean time, the boat-man rowed with all his might, and Schemselnihar's trusty slave accompanied the prince of Persia and Ebn Thaher, walking along the side of the canal until they came to the Tigris, and when she could go no farther, she took her farewell of them, and returned.

The prince of Persia continued very feeble: Ebn Thaher comforted him, and exhorted him to take courage. Consider, says he to him, that when we are landed, we have a great way to go before we come to my house, and I would not advise you to go to your lodgings, which are a great deal farther than mine, at this hour, and in this condition. At last they went out of the boat, but the prince had so little strength that he could not walk, which put Ebn Thaher into great perplexity. He remembered he had a friend in the neighbourhood, and carried the prince thither with great difficulty. His friend received them very cheerfully, and when he made them sit down, he asked them where they had been so late? Ebn Thaher answered him, I was this evening with a man that owed me a considerable sum of money, and designed to go a long voyage: I was unwilling to lose time to find him, and by the way I met with this young nobleman whom you see, and to whom I am under a thousand obligations; for, knowing my debtor, he would needs do me the favour to go along with me. We had a great deal of trouble to bring the man to reason; besides, we went out of the way, and that is the reason we are so late. In our return home, this good lord, for whom I have all possible respect, was attacked by a sudden distemper, which made me take the liberty to call at your house, flattering myself that you would be pleased to give us quarters for this night. Ebn Thaher's friend took all this for truth, told them they were welcome, and offered the prince of Persia, whom he knew not, all the assistance he could desire: But Ebn Thaher spoke for the prince, and said that his distemper was of that nature as required nothing but rest. His friend understood by this that they desired to go to bed. Upon which he conducted them to an apartment, where he left them.

Though the prince of Persia slept, he had troublesome dreams, which represented Schemselnihar in a swoon at the caliph's feet, and increased his affliction. Ebn Thaher was very impatient to be at home, and doubted not but his family was in great trouble, because he never used to lie abroad. He rose, and departed early in the morning, after he had taken leave of his friend, who rose at break of day to say his prayers. At last he came home, and the first thing the prince of Persia did, who had walked so far with much trouble, was to lie down upon a sofa, as weary as if he had gone a long journey. Being not in a condition to go home, Ebn Thaher ordered a chamber to be made ready for him, and sent to acquaint his friends with his condition, and where he was. In the mean time, he begged him to compose himself, to command in his house, and to order all things as he pleased. I thank you heartily for those obliging offers, says the prince of Persia; but that I may not be anywise troublesome to you, I conjure you to deal with me as if I were not at your house. I would not stay one moment, if I thought my presence would incommode you in the least.

As soon as Ebn Thaher had time to recollect himself, he told his family all that passed at Schemselnihar's palace, and concluded by thanking God, who had delivered him from the danger he was in. The prince of Persia's principal domestics came to receive his orders at Ebn Thaher's house, and in a little time there arrived several of his friends, who had notice of his indisposition. Those friends passed the greatest part of the day with him; and though their conversation could not extinguish those sad ideas which were the cause of his trouble, yet it gave him some relief. He would have taken his leave of Ebn Thaher towards the evening, but this faithful friend found him still so weak, that he obliged him to stay till next day; and, in the mean time, to divert him, he gave him a concert of vocal and instrumental music in the evening; but this concert served only to put him in mind of the preceding night, and renewed his trouble, instead of assuaging it; so that next day his distemper seemed to increase. Upon this, Ebn Thaher did not oppose his going home, but took care to accompany him thither; and, when he was with him alone in his chamber, he represented to him all those arguments which might influence him to a generous endeavour to overcome that passion, which in the end would neither prove lucky to himself nor to the favourite. Ah! dear Ebn Thaher, cries the prince, how easy it is for you to give this advice, but how hard is it for me to follow it! I am sensible of its importance, but am not able to profit by it. I have said it already, that I shall carry to the grave with me the love that I bear to Schemselnihar. When Ebn Thaher saw that he could gain nothing upon the prince, he took his leave of him, and would have retired, but the prince of Persia retained him, and said, kind Ebn Thaher, since I have declared to you that it is not in my power to follow your wise counsel, I beg you would not charge it on me as a crime, nor forbear to give me the usual testimonies of your friendship; you cannot do me a greater favour than to inform me of the destiny of my dear Schemselnihár when you hear any news of it: The uncertainty I am in concerning her fate, and the mortal apprehensions her fainting has occasioned in me, keeps me in this languishing condition you reproach me with. My lord, answered Ebn Thaher, you have reason to hope that her fainting was not attended with any bad consequences; her confidant will quickly come and inform me of the issue; and as soon as I know the particulars, I will not fail to impart them.

Ebn Thaher left the prince in this hope, and returned home, where he expected Schemselnihar's confidant all the rest of the day, but in vain, nor did she come next day: His uneasiness to know the state of the prince of Persia's health would not suffer him to stay any longer without seeing him; so he went to his lodgings to exhort him to patience, and found him lying on his bed as sick as ever, surrounded by a great many of his friends, and several physicians, who made use of all their art to discover the cause of his distemper. As soon as he saw Ebn Thaher, he looked upon him smiling, to signify that he had two things to tell him; the one, that he was glad to see him; the other, how much the physicians, who could not discover the cause of his distemper, were out in their reasonings.

His friends and physicians retired one after another, so that Ebn Thaher being alone with him, came near his bed to ask him how he did since he saw him? I must tell you, answers the prince, that my passion, which continually gathers new strength, and the uncertainty of the lovely Schemselnihar's destiny, augments my distemper every moment, and casts me into such a condition as afflicts my kindred and friends, and breaks the measures of my physicians, who do not understand it: You cannot think, adds he, how much I suffer to see so many people about me, who importune me, and whom I cannot in civility put away: It is your company alone that is comfortable to me; but, in a word, I conjure you not to dissemble with me: What news do you bring me of Schemselnihar? Have you seen her confidant? What says she to you? Ebn Thaher answered, that he had not seen her yet; and no sooner had he told the prince of Persia this sad news, but the tears came from his eyes, he could not answer one word, his heart was so oppressed. Prince, adds Ebn Thaher, suffer me to tell you that you are very ingenious in tormenting yourself: In the name of God wipe away your tears: If any of your people should come in just now, they would discover you by this, notwithstanding the care you ought to take to conceal your thoughts. Whatever this judicious confidant could say, it was not possible for the prince to refrain from weeping. Wise Ebn Thaher, says he, when he had recovered his speech, I may well hinder my tongue from revealing the secrets of my heart, but I have no power over my tears, upon such a direful subject as

Schemselnihar's danger: If that adorable and only object of my desires be no longer in the world, I shall not be one moment after her. Reject so afflicting a thought, replied Ebn Thaher; Schemselnihar is yet alive, you need not doubt it: If you have heard no news of her, it is because she could find no occasion to send to you, and I hope you will hear from her to-day. To this he added several other comfortable things, and then retired.

Ebn Thaher was scarce at his own house, when Schemselnihar's confidant arrived with a melancholy countenance, which he reckoned a bad omen. He asked news of her mistress. Tell me yours first, says the confidant, for I was in great trouble to see the prince of Persia go away in that condition. Ebn Thaher told her all that she desired to know; and when he had done, the slave began her discourse: If the prince of Persia, says she, has suffered, and does still suffer for my mistress, she suffers no less for him: After I departed from you, continues she, I returned to the saloon, where I found Schemselnihar not yet recovered from her swoon, notwithstanding all the help they endeavoured to give her. The caliph was sitting near her with all the signs of real grief: He asked all the women, and me in particular, if we knew the cause of her distemper, but we kept all secret, and told him we were altogether ignorant of it. In the mean time, we all wept to see her suffer so long, and forgot nothing that might any ways help her: In a word, it was almost midnight before she came to herself. The caliph, who had the patience to wait all the while, was very glad of her recovery, and asked Schemselnihar the cause of her distemper. As soon as she heard him speak, she endeavoured to recover her seat; and after she had kissed his feet, before he could hinder her, Sir, says she, I have reason to complain of heaven, that it did not allow me to expire at your majesty's feet, to testify thereby how sensible I am of your favours.

I am persuaded you love me, says the caliph to her, and I command you to preserve yourself for my sake. You have probably exceeded in something to-day, which has occasioned this indisposition; take heed, I pray you, abstain from it for the future; I am very glad to see you better, and I advise you to stay here to-night, and not to return to your chamber, for fear the motion disturb you. Upon this he commanded a little wine to be brought her, in order to strengthen her; and then, taking his leave of her, returned to his apartment.

As soon as the caliph was gone, my mistress gave me a sign to come near her. She asked me earnestly concerning you: I assured her that you had been gone a long time, which made her easy as to that matter. I took care not to speak of the prince of Persia's fainting, lest it should make her fall into the same condition from which we had so much trouble to recover her; but my precautions were all in vain, as you shall hear. Prince, says she, I henceforth renounce all pleasure as long as I am deprived of a sight of you. If I have understood your heart right, I only follow your example. Thou wilt not cease to weep until thou seest me again; it is but just that I weep and mourn till I see you. At these words, which she uttered in such a manner as expressed the violence of her passion, she fainted a second time betwixt my arms.

My comrades and I, says Schemselnihar's confidant, were a long time in recovering her; at last she came to herself; and then I said to her, Madam, are you resolved to kill yourself, and to make us also die with you? I beg of you be persuaded, in the name of the prince of Persia, for whom it is your interest to live, to save yourself, as you love yourself, as you love the prince, and for our sakes, who are so faithful to you. I am very much obliged to you, replied she, for your care, zeal, and advice; but alas! they are useless to me; you are not to flatter us with any hopes, for we can expect no end of our torment but in the grave. One of my companions would have diverted those sad thoughts by playing on her lute, but she commanded her to be silent, and ordered all of them to retire, except me, whom she kept all night with her. O heavens! what a night was it! She passed it in tears and groans, and always naming the prince of Persia; she lamented her lot, that had destined her to the caliph, whom she could not love, and not for him whom she loved so dearly.

Next morning, because she was not commodiously lodged in the saloon, I helped her to her chamber, where she no sooner arrived, than all the physicians of the palace came to see her, by order of the caliph, who was not long a-coming himself. The medicines which the physicians prescribed for Schemselnihar were to no purpose, because they were ignorant of the cause of her distemper, and the presence of the caliph augmented it. She got a little rest, however, this night, and as soon as she awoke, she charged me to come to you, to hear news of the prince of Persia. I have already informed you of his case, said Ebn Thaher; so return to your mistress, and assure her that the prince of Persia waits for news from her with the like impatience that she does from him: Besides, exhort her to moderation, and to overcome herself, for fear she drop some word before the caliph, which may prove fatal to us all. As for me, replied the confidant, I confess, I dread her transports; I have taken the liberty to tell her my mind, and am persuaded that she will not take it ill that I tell her this from you.

Ebn Thaher, who had but just come from the prince of Persia's lodgings, thought it not convenient to return so soon, and neglect his own important affairs, and therefore went not till the evening. The prince was alone, and no better than in the morning. Ebn Thaher, says he to him, as soon as he saw him, you have doubtless many friends, but they do not know your worth, which you discover to me by the zeal, care, and trouble, you give yourself to oblige me in my condition. I am confounded with all that you do for me with so great affection, and I know not how I shall be able to express my gratitude. Prince, answered Ebn Thaher, do not speak so, I entreat you; I am ready, not only to give one of my own eyes to save one of yours, but to sacrifice my life for you. But this is not the present business: I come to tell you that Schemselnihar sent her confidant to ask me about you, and at the same time to inform me of her condition. You may assure yourself that I said nothing but what might confirm the excess of your passion for her mistress, and the constancy with which you love her. Then Ebn Thaher gave him a particular account of all that had passed betwixt the trusty slave and him. The prince listened with all the different emotions of fear, jealousy, affection, and compassion, which his discourse could inspire him with; making, upon every thing which he heard, all the afflicting or comforting reflections that so passionate a lover was capable of.

Their conversation continued so long, that the night was far advanced, so that the prince of Persia obliged Ebn Thaher to stay with him. The next morning, as this trusty friend returned home, there came to him a woman, whom he knew to be Schemselnihar's confidant, and immediately she spoke to him thus: My mistress salutes you, and I am come to entreat you in her name to deliver this letter to the prince of Persia. The zealous Ebn Thaher took the letter, and returned to the prince, accompanied with the confidant slave.

When Ebn Thaher entered the prince of Persia's house with Schemselnihar's confidant, he prayed her to stay one moment in the drawing-room. As soon as the prince of Persia saw him, he asked earnestly what news he had? The best you can expect, answered Ebn Thaher; you are as dearly beloved as you love: Schemselnihar's confidant is in your drawing-room; she has brought you a letter from her mistress, and waits for your orders to come in. Let her come in, cries the prince, with a transport of joy; and, speaking thus, he sat down to receive her.

The prince's attendants went from him as soon as they saw Ebn Thaher, and left him alone with their master. Ebn Thaher went and opened the door, and brought in the confidant. The prince knew her, and received her very civilly. My lord, says she to him, I am sensible of the afflictions you have endured since I had the honour to conduct you to the boat which waited to bring you back; but I hope this letter I have brought will contribute to your cure: Upon this she presented him the letter. He took it, and, after he had kissed it several times, he opened it, and read as follows:

A Letter from Schemselnihar to Ali Ebn Becar, Prince of Persia.

The person who brings you this letter will give you a better account concerning me than I can do, for I have not been myself since I saw you. Being deprived of your presence, I sought to divert myself by entertaining you with these ill-writ lines, with the same pleasure as if I had the good fortune to speak to you.

It is said that patience is a cure for all distempers, but it sours mine instead of sweetening it. Although your picture be deeply engraven in my heart, my eyes desire constantly to see the original; and they will lose their light if they be any considerable time deprived of it. May I flatter myself that yours have the same impatience to see me? Yes, I can; their tender glances discovered it to me. How happy, prince, should you and Schemselnihar both be, if our agreeable desires were not crossed by invincible obstacles, which afflict me as sensibly as they do you.

These thoughts which my fingers write, and which I express with incredible pleasure, and repeat again and again, speak from the bottom of my heart, and from the incurable wound which you have made in it; a wound which I bless a thousand times, notwithstanding the cruel torment I endure for your absence. I would reckon all that opposes our love nothing, were I only allowed to see you sometimes with freedom; I would only enjoy you then, and what could I desire more?

Do not imagine that I say more than I think: Alas! whatever expressions I am able to use, yet I am sensible that I think no more than I can tell you. My eyes, which are continually watching and weeping for your return; my afflicted heart, which desires nothing but you alone; the sighs that escape me as often as I think on you, that is every moment; my imagination, which represents no other object to me than my dear prince; the complaints that I make to heaven for the rigour of my destiny; in a word, my grief, my trouble, my torments, which give me no ease ever since I lost the sight of you, are witnesses of what I write.

Am not I unhappy to be born to love, without hope of enjoying him whom I love? This doleful thought oppresses me so, that I should die, were I not persuaded that you love me; but this sweet comfort balances my despair, and preserves my life. Tell me that you love me always; I will keep your letter carefully, and read it a thousand times a-day: I will endure my afflictions with less impatience. I pray heaven may cease to be angry at us, and grant us an opportunity to say that we love one another without fear; and that we may never cease to love. Adieu. I salute Ebn Thaher, who has so much obliged us.

The prince of Persia was not satisfied to read the letter once; he thought he had read it with too little attention, and therefore read it again with more leisure; and as he read, sometimes he uttered sighs, sometimes he wept, and sometimes he discovered transports of joy and affection, as one who was touched with what he read. In a word, he could not keep his eyes off those characters drawn by so lovely a hand, and therefore began to read it a third time. Then Ebn Thaher told him that the confidant could not stay, and that he ought to think of giving an answer. Alas! cries the prince, how would you have me answer so kind a letter? In what terms shall I express the trouble that I am in? My spirit is tossed with a thousand tormenting things, and my thoughts destroy one another the same moment they are conceived, to make way for more; and so long as my body suffers by the impressions of my mind, how shall I be able to hold paper, or a reed[1] to write. Having spoke thus, he took out of a little desk, paper, cane, and ink.

The prince of Persia, before he began to write, gave Schemselnihar's letter to Ebn Thaher, and prayed him to hold it open while he wrote, that, by casting his eyes upon it, he might see the better what to answer. He began to write, but the tears that fell from his eyes upon the paper, obliged him several times to stop, that they might trickle down the more freely. At last he finished his letter, and, giving it to Ebn Thaher, Read it, I pray, says he to him, and do me the favour to see if the disorder of my mind has allowed me to give a reasonable answer. Ebn Thaher took it, and read as follows:

The Prince of Persia's Answer to Schemselnihar's Letter.

I was swallowed up with mortal grief when I received your letter; at the sight of which I was transported with unspeakable joy; and, at the view of the characters writ by your lovely hand, my eyes were enlightened more sensibly than they were darkened, when yours were closed on a sudden at the feet of my rival. These words, which your courteous letter contains, are so many rays of light, which have dispelled the darkness my soul was obscured with; they shew me how much you suffer by your love to me, and that you are not ignorant of what I endure for you, and thereby comfort me in my afflictions. On the one hand, they make me shed tears in abundance; and, on the other, they inflame my heart with a fire which supports it, and hinders me to die of grief. I have not had one moment's rest since our cruel separation. Your letter only gave me some ease: I kept a sorrowful silence till the moment I received it, and then it restored to me speech. I was buried in a profound melancholy, but it inspired me with joy, which immediately appeared in my eyes and countenance. But my surprise, at receiving a favour which I had not deserved, was so great, that I knew not which way to begin to testify my thankfulness for it. In a word, after having kissed it several times as a valuable pledge of your goodness, I read it over and over, and was confounded at the excess of my good fortune. You would have me to signify to you that I always love you. Ah, though I did not love you so perfectly as I do, I could not forbear adoring you, after all the marks you have given me of a love

[1] The Arabians, Persians, and Turks, when they write, hold the paper ordinarily upon their knee with their left hand, and write with their right, with a little reed or cane, cut as we do our pens; this cane is hollow, and resembles our reeds, but is harder.

so uncommon: Yes, I love you, my dear soul, and shall account it my glory to burn all my days with that sweet fire you have kindled in my heart. I will never complain of that brisk ardour with which I find it consumes me: And how rigorous soever the grief be which I suffer, I will bear it courageously, in hopes to see you some time or other. Would to heaven it were to-day, and that, instead of sending you my letter, I might be allowed to come and assure you that I die for love of you! My tears hinder me from saying any more. Adieu.

Ebn Thaher could not read those last lines without weeping. He returned the letter to the prince of Persia, and assured him it wanted no correction. The prince shut it, and, when he had sealed it, he desired the trusty slave to come near, and told her, This is my answer to your dear mistress; I conjure you to carry it to her, and to salute her in my name. The slave took the letter, and retired with Ebn Thaher.

After Ebn Thaher had walked some way with the slave, he left her, and went to his house, and began to think in earnest upon the amorous intrigue into which he found himself unhappily engaged. He considered, that the prince of Persia and Schemselnihar, notwithstanding their interest to conceal their correspondence, did manage themselves with so little discretion that it could not be long a secret. He drew all the consequences from it which a man of good sense ought to do. Were Schemselnihar, said he to himself, an ordinary lady, I would contribute all in my power to make her and her sweetheart happy; but she is the caliph's favourite, and no man can, without danger, undertake to displease him: His anger would fall at first upon Schemselnihar; it would cost the prince of Persia his life, and I should be embarked in his misfortune. In the mean time, I have my honour, my quiet, my family, and my estate to preserve; I must then deliver myself out of so great a danger while I can.

He was taken up with these thoughts all the day; next morning he went to the prince of Persia, with a design to use his utmost endeavours to oblige him to conquer his passion. He actually represented to him what he had formerly done in vain: that it would be much better for him to make use of all his courage to overcome his inclination for Schemselnihar, than to suffer himself to be conquered by it; and that his passion was so much the more dangerous, as his rival was the more potent. In a word, sir, if you will hearken to me, you ought to think of nothing but to triumph over your amour; otherwise you run a risk of destroying yourself with Schemselnihar, whose life ought to be dearer to you than your own. I give you this counsel as a friend, for which you will thank me some time or other.

The prince heard Ebn Thaher with a great deal of impatience, but suffered him however to speak out his mind, and then replied to him thus: Ebn

Thaher, do you think I can forbear to love Schemselnihar, who loves me so tenderly? She is not afraid to expose her life for me, and would you have me to regard mine? No, whatever misfortune befal me, I will love Schemselnihar to my last breath.

Ebn Thaher being offended with the obstinacy of the prince of Persia, left him hastily, and, going to his own house, recalled to mind what he thought on the other day, and began to think in earnest what he should do. At the same time a jeweller, one of his intimate friends, came to see him: this jeweller had perceived that Schemselnihar's confidant came oftener to Ebn Thaher than usual, and that he was constantly with the prince of Persia, whose sickness was known to every one, though not the cause of it: the jeweller began to grow suspicious, and, finding Ebn Thaher very pensive, he judged presently that he was perplexed with some important affair, and, fancying that he knew the cause, he asked what Schemselnihar's confidant wanted with him? Ebn Thaher being struck with this question, would have dissembled, and told him, that it was for a trifle she came so frequently to him. You do not tell me the truth, says the jeweller, and give me ground to think, by your dissimulation, that this trifle is a more important affair than at first I thought it to be. Ebn Thaher, perceiving that his friend pressed him so much, says to him, It is true, that it is an affair of the greatest consequence: I had resolved to keep it secret, but, since I know how much you are my friend, I choose rather to make you my confidant than to suffer you to be in a mistake about it. I recommend it to you to keep the secret, for you will easily judge, by what I am going to tell you, how important it is to keep it. After this preamble, he told him the amour between Schemselnihar and the prince of Persia. You know, continued he, in what esteem I am at court, in the city, and with lords and ladies of the greatest quality; what a disgrace would it be for me should this rash intrigue come to be discovered? But what do I say? Should not I and my family be quite destroyed? That is the thing perplexes my mind; but I have just now come to such a resolve as I ought to make: I will go immediately and satisfy my creditors, and recover my debts, and, when I have secured my estate, will retire to Balsora, and stay till the tempest, that I foresee, blows over. The friendship I have for Schemselnihar and the prince of Persia makes me very sensible to what dangers they are exposed. I pray heaven to discover it to themselves, and to preserve them; but, if their ill destiny will have their amours come to the knowledge of the caliph, I shall, at least, be out of the reach of his resentment; for I do not think them so wicked as to design to draw me into their own misfortunes. It would be extreme ingratitude in them to do so, and a sorry reward for the good service I have done them, and the good advice I have given them; particularly to the prince of Persia, who may save himself and his mistress both from this precipice, if he pleases: He may as easily leave Bagdad as I, and absence will insensibly disengage him from a passion which will only increase while he continues in this place.

The jeweller was extremely surprised at what Ebn Thaher told him. What you say to me, says he, is of so great importance, that I cannot understand how Schemselnihar and the prince have been capable to abandon themselves to such a violent amour; what inclination soever they may have for one another, instead of yielding to it, they ought to resist it, and make a better use of their reason. Is it possible they can be insensible of the dangerous consequences of their correspondence? How deplorable is their blindness! I perceive all the consequences of it as well as you, but you are wise and prudent, and I approve your resolution; that is the only way to deliver yourself from the fatal events which you have reason to fear. After this, the jeweller rose up, and took his leave of Ebn Thaher.

Before the jeweller retired, Ebn Thaher conjured him, by the friendship betwixt them, to speak nothing of this to any body. Be not afraid, says the jeweller, I will keep this secret on peril of my life.

Two days after, the jeweller went to Ebn Thaher's shop, and seeing it shut, he doubted not but he had executed the design he spoke of; but, to be sure, he asked a neighbour if he knew why it was shut? The neighbour answered, that he knew not, unless Ebn Thaher was gone a journey. There was no need of his inquiring farther, and immediately he thought on the prince of Persia: Unhappy prince, says he to himself, what grief will this be to you, when you hear this news? By what means will you now entertain your correspondence with Schemselnihar? I fear you will die of despair! I have compassion on you; I must make up the loss that you have of a too fearful confidant.

The business that obliged him to come abroad, was of no consequence; so that he neglected it: And though he had no knowledge of the prince of Persia, but only by having sold him some jewels, he went straight to his house: He addressed himself to one of the servants, and prayed him to tell his master that he desired to speak with him about a business of very great importance. The servant returned immediately to the jeweller, and introduced him to the prince's chamber, who was leaning on a sofa, with his head upon a cushion. As soon as the prince saw him, he rose up to receive him, said he was welcome, and entreated him to sit down; asked if he could serve him in anything, or if he came to tell him any thing concerning himself. Prince, answers the jeweller, though I have not the honour to be particularly acquainted with you, yet the desire of testifying my zeal, has made me take the liberty to come to your house, to impart to you some news that concerns you. I hope you will pardon my boldness because of my good intention.

After this introduction, the jeweller entered upon the matter, and pursued it thus: Prince, I shall have the honour to tell you, that it is a long time since the conformity of humour and several affairs we had together, united Ebn Thaher and me into strict friendship; I know you are acquainted with him, and that he has been employed in obliging you in all that he could; I am informed of this from himself, for he keeps nothing secret from me, nor I from him. I went just now to his shop, and was surprised to find it shut: I addressed myself to one of his neighbours to ask the reason; he answered me, that two days ago Ebn Thaher took his leave of him, and other neighbours, offering them his service at Balsora, whither he is gone, said he, about an affair of great importance. Not being satisfied with this answer, the concern that I have for whatever belongs to him, determined me to come and ask if you knew any thing particularly concerning this his sudden departure?

At this discourse, which the jeweller accommodated to the subject, that he might come the better to his design, the prince of Persia changed colour, and looked so as made the jeweller sensible that he was afflicted with the news. I am surprised at what you inform me, says he, there could not a greater misfortune befal me: Ah! says he, with tears in his eyes, I am undone, if what you tell me be true! Has Ebn Thaher, who was all my comfort, in whom I put all my confidence, left me! I cannot think of living after so cruel a blow.

The jeweller needed no more to convince him fully of the prince of Persia's violent passion, which Ebn Thaher told him of; mere friendship would not let him speak so; nothing but love could produce such feeling expressions.

The prince continued some moments swallowed up with those melancholy thoughts; at last he lifted up his head, and, calling one of his servants, Go, says he, to Ebn Thaher's house, and ask any of his domestics if he be gone to Balsora: Run, and come back quickly, and tell me what you hear. While the servant was gone, the jeweller endeavoured to entertain the prince of Persia with indifferent subjects, but the prince gave little heed to him. He was a prey to fatal grief: sometimes he could not persuade himself that Ebn Thaher was gone, and at other times he did not doubt of it, when he reflected upon the discourse he had with him the last time he saw him, and the angry countenance with which he left him.

At last the prince's servant returned, and reported that he had spoke with one of Ebn Thaher's servants, who assured him that he was gone two days before to Balsora. As I came from Ebn Thaher's house, adds the servant, a slave well arrayed came to me, and, after she had asked me if I had the honour to belong to you, she told me she wanted to speak with you, and begged at the same time that she might come along with me; she is in the outer-chamber, and I believe she has a letter to give to some person of note. The prince commanded immediately to bring her in; he doubted not but it was Schemselnihar's confidant slave, as indeed it was. The jeweller knew who she was, having seen her several times at Ebn Thaher's house. She could not have come in a better time to hinder the prince from despair. She saluted him, and the prince of Persia did likewise salute Schemselnihar's confidant. The jeweller arose as soon as he saw her appear, and stepped aside, to leave them at liberty to speak together. The confidant, after she had conversed some time with the prince, took her leave and departed. She left him quite another thing than before; his eyes appeared brighter, and his countenance more gay, which made the jeweller know that the good slave came to tell him some news that favoured his amour.

The jeweller having taken his place again near the prince, says to him, smiling, I see, prince, you have important affairs at the caliph's palace. The prince of Persia was astonished and alarmed at this discourse, and answered the jeweller, Why do you judge that I have affairs at the caliph's palace? I judge, replied the jeweller, by the slave who is gone forth. And to whom think you belongs this slave? replied the prince. To Schemselnihar, the caliph's favourite, answered the jeweller: I know, continues he, both the slave and her mistress, who has several times done me the honour to come to my house and buy jewels. Besides, I know that Schemselnihar keeps nothing secret from this slave; and I have seen her go and come for several days along the streets, very much troubled, as I thought; I imagined that it was for some affair of consequence concerning her mistress.

The jeweller's words did much trouble the prince of Persia. He would not say so, says he to himself, if he did not suspect, or rather know, my secret. He remained silent for some time, not knowing what to answer. At last he began, and said to the jeweller, You have told me those things which make me believe that you know yet more than you have acquainted me with; it will tend much to my quiet if I be perfectly informed; I conjure you therefore not to dissemble with me.

Then the jeweller, who desired no better, gave him a particular account of what had passed betwixt Ebn Thaher and himself; so that he let him know that he was informed of his correspondence with Schemselnihar; and forgot not to tell him that Ebn Thaher was afraid of the danger of being his confidant in the matter, which was partly the occasion of his retiring to Balsora, to stay there until the storm, which he feared, should be over. Thus he has done, adds the jeweller, and I am surprised how he could determine himself to abandon you in the condition he informed me you was in. As for me, prince, I confess I am moved with compassion towards you, and am come to offer you my service; and, if you do me the favour to accept of it, I engage myself to be as faithful to you as Ebn Thaher; besides, I promise to be more constant. I am ready to sacrifice my honour and life for you; and, that you may not doubt of my sincerity, I swear by all that is sacred in our religion, to keep your secret inviolable. Be persuaded then, prince, that you will find in me the friend which you have lost. This discourse encouraged the prince, and comforted him under Ebn Thaher's absence. I am very glad, says he to the jeweller, to find in you reparation of my loss: I want words to express the obligation I am under to you. I pray God to recompence your generosity, and I accept your obliging offer with all my heart. Believe it, continues he, that Schemselnihar's confidant came to speak to me concerning you; she told me that it was you who advised Ebn Thaher to go to Balsora; these were the last words she spoke to me, when she went away, and had almost persuaded me of it. But do not you resent it, for I doubt not but she is deceived, after what you have told me. Prince, replied the jeweller, I have had the honour to give you a faithful account of my conversation with Ebn Thaher. It is true, when he told me he would retire to Balsora, I did not oppose his design, but said he was a wise and prudent man; and that this may not hinder you to put your confidence in me, I am ready to serve you with all imaginable zeal, which, though you do otherwise, this shall not hinder me from keeping your secret religiously, according to my oath. I have already told you, replies the prince, that I would not believe what the confidant said: It is her zeal which inspired her with this groundless suspicion, and you ought to excuse it as I do.

They continued their conversation for some time, and consulted together of convenient means to entertain the prince's correspondence with Schemselnihar. They agreed to begin by disabusing the confidant, who was so unjustly prepossessed against the jeweller. The prince engaged to undeceive her the first time she returned, and to entreat her to engage herself to the jeweller, that she might bring the letters, or any other information, from her mistress to him. In effect, they agreed that she ought not to come so frequently to the prince's house, because thereby she might give an occasion to discover that which was of so great importance to conceal.—At last the jeweller arose, and, after having again prayed the prince of Persia to have an entire confidence in him, he retired.

The jeweller returned to his house, perceived before him a letter, which somebody had dropped in the street. He took it, and, since it was not sealed, he opened it, and found it conceived in these terms:

A Letter from Schemselnihar to the Prince of Persia

I am informed by my confidant of a piece of news, which troubles me no less than it does you: By losing Ebn Thaher, we have indeed lost much; but let not this hinder you, dear prince, from thinking to preserve yourself. If our confidant has abandoned us through a panic fear, let us consider that it is a misfortune which we could not avoid. I confess Ebn Thaher has left us at a time when we need him most; but let us fortify ourselves by patience against the unlooked-for accident, and let us not forbear to love one another constantly. Fortify your heart against this misfortune. Nobody can obtain what they desire without trouble. Let us not discourage ourselves, but hope that heaven will favour us, and that, after so many afflictions, we shall come to a happy accomplishment of our desires. Adieu.

While the jeweller was conversing with the prince of Persia, the confidant had time to return to the palace, and tell her mistress the ill news of Ebn Thaher's departure. Schemselnihar immediately wrote this letter, and sent back her confidant with it to the prince of Persia, but she negligently dropped it.

The jeweller was glad to find it, for it was a good way to set him right with the confidant, and bring him to the point he desired. When he had read it, he perceived the slave, who sought it with a great deal of uneasiness, looking about every where. He closed it again quickly, and put it into his bosom, but the slave took notice of it, and ran to him; Sir, says she, I have dropped a letter, which you had just now in your hand; I beseech you be pleased to restore it. The jeweller, taking no notice that he heard her, continued his way till he came to his house. He did not shut the door behind him, that the confidant, who followed him, might come in. She accordingly did so, and when she came to his chamber, Sir, says she to him, you can make no use of that letter you have found, and you would make no difficulty of returning it to me, if you knew from whom it came, and to whom it is directed. Besides, let me tell you, you cannot honestly keep it.

Before the jeweller answered the confidant, he made her sit down, and then he said to her, Is not this letter from Schemselnihar, and is it not directed to the prince of Persia? The slave, who expected no such question, blushed. The question puzzles you, replies he, but I assure you, I do not propose it rashly; I could have given you the letter in the street, but I suffered you to follow me on purpose that I might discourse with you: Is it just, tell me, to impute an unhappy accident to people who no ways contribute towards it? Yet this you have done, in telling the prince of Persia that it was I who counselled Ebn Thaher to leave Bagdad for his own safety. I do not pretend to lose time in justifying myself to you, it is enough that the prince of Persia is fully persuaded of my innocence in this matter. I will only tell you, that, instead of contributing to Ebn Thaher's departure, I have been extremely afflicted at it, not so much for my friendship to him, as out of compassion for the condition he left the prince of Persia in, whose correspondence with Schemselnihar he has discovered to me. As soon as I knew certainly that Ebn Thaher was gone from Bagdad, I went to present myself to the prince, in whose house you found me, to inform him of this news, and to offer him the same service which he did him; and provided you put the same confidence in me that you did in Ebn Thaher, you may serve yourself very well by my assistance. Inform your mistress of what I have told you, and assure her that, if I should die for engaging in so dangerous an intrigue, I will not repent to have sacrificed myself for two lovers so worthy of one another.

The confidant, after having heard the jeweller with great satisfaction, begged him to pardon the ill opinion she had conceived of him out of the zeal she had for her mistress. I am extremely glad, adds she, that Schemselnihar and the prince have found you, who are a man fit to supply Ebn Thaher's place. I will not fail to signify to my mistress the good-will you bear her.

After the confidant had testified to the jeweller her joy to see him so well disposed to serve Schemselnihar and the prince of Persia, the jeweller took the letter out of his bosom, and restored it to her, saying, Go, carry it quickly to the prince of Persia, and come back this way, that I may see the answer. Forget not to give him an account of our conversation. The confidant took the letter, and carried it to the prince, who answered it immediately. She returned to the jeweller's house to shew him the answer, which was thus:

The Prince of Persia's Answer to Schemselnihar.

Your precious letter had a great effect upon me, but not so great as I could wish. You endeavour to comfort me for the loss of Ebn Thaher; alas! for as sensible as I am of this, it is but the least of my troubles. You know my malady, and that it is only your presence can cure me. When will the time come that I shall enjoy it without fear of being deprived of it? O how long does it seem to me! But shall we rather flatter ourselves that we may see one another? You command me to preserve myself; I will obey, since I have renounced my own will to follow yours. Adieu.

After the jeweller had read this letter, he gave it again to the confidant, who said, when she was going away, I wili tell my mistress to put the same confidence in you she did in Ebn Thaher. You shall hear of me to-morrow. Accordingly next day she returned with a pleasant countenance. Your very looks, says he to her, inform me that you have brought Schemselnihar to what you wished for. That is true, says the confidant, and you shall hear how I effected it: I found yesterday, continues she, Schemselnihar expecting me with impatience: I gave her the prince of Persia's letter, and she read it with tears in her eyes; and, when she had done, I saw that she had abandoned herself to her ordinary sorrows; Madam, said I to her, this is doubtless Ebn Thaher's removal that troubles you; but suffer me to conjure you in the name of God to trouble yourself no farther concerning that matter: We have found another who offers to oblige you with as much zeal, and, what is yet more important, with greater courage. Then I spoke to her of you, continues the slave, and acquainted her with the motive which made you go to the prince of Persia's house: In short, I assured her that you would inviolably keep the secret betwixt her and the prince of Persia, and that you was resolved to favour their amours with all your might. She seemed to me to be much relieved by my discourse. Ah! what obligations, says she, are the prince of Persia and I under to that honest man you speak of! I must see him, that I may hear from his own mouth what you tell me, and thank him for such an unheard-of piece of generosity towards persons that he is no ways obliged to concern himself with. A sight of him will please me, and I will not omit any thing to confirm him in these good sentiments. Do not fail to bring him to me to-morrow. Therefore, pray, sir, go with me to the palace.

The confidant's discourse perplexed the jeweller. Your mistress, replies he, must allow me to say, that she has not thought well of what she requires of me. Ebn Thaher's access to the caliph gave him admission every where; and the officers who knew him, suffered him to go and come freely to Schemselnihar's palace; but as for me, how dare I enter? You see well enough that it is not possible: I entreat you to represent those reasons to Schemselnihar, which hinder me from giving her that satisfaction, and acquaint her with all the ill consequences that would attend it: If she consider it ever so little, she will find that it would expose me needlessly to very great danger.

The confidant endeavoured to encourage the jeweller: Believe me, says she, that Schemselnihar is not so unreasonable as to expose you to the least danger, from whom she expects so considerable services. Consider with yourself that there is not the least appearance of hazard: My mistress and I are too much interested in this affair, to involve you in any danger. You may depend upon me, and leave yourself to my conduct. After the thing is over, you will confess to me that your fear was groundless.

The jeweller hearkened to the confidant's discourse, and got up to follow her; but, notwithstanding his natural courage, he was seized with such terror, that his whole body trembled. In the condition you are in, says she, I perceive it will be better for you to stay at home, and that Schemselnihar take other measures to see you. It is not to be doubted, but that, to satisfy her desire, she will come hither herself: The case being so, sir, I would not have you to go; I am persuaded it will not be long ere you see her yourself. The confidant foresaw this very well, for she no sooner informed Schemselnihar of the jeweller's fear, but she made ready to go to his house.

He received her with all the marks of a profound respect. When she sat down, being a little fatigued with coming, she unveiled herself, and let the jeweller see such beauty as made him acknowledge that the prince of Persia was excusable in giving his heart to her. Then she saluted the jeweller with a graceful countenance, and said to him, I am informed with what zeal you have engaged in the prince of Persia's concerns and mine; but, without immediately forming a design to express my gratitude, I thank heaven, which has so soon made up Ebn Thaher's loss.

Schemselnihar said several other obliging things to the jeweller, after which she returned to her palace. The jeweller went immediately to give account of this visit to the prince of Persia, who said to him as soon as he saw him, I have expected you impatiently. The trusty slave has brought me a letter from her mistress, but she does not ease me; whatever the lovely Schemselnihar says, yet I dare not hope for any thing: My patience is at an end; I know not now what measures to take; Ebn Thaher's departure makes me despair: He was my only support; I lost all by losing him: I flattered myself with some hopes by reason of his access to Schemselnihar.

After these words, which the prince pronounced with so much eagerness, that he gave the jeweller no time to interrupt him, he said to the prince, No man can bear a greater share of your afflictions than I do; and, if you will have patience to hear me, you will perceive that I am capable of giving you ease. Upon this, the prince held his peace, and hearkened to him. I see very well, said the jeweller, that the only thing to give you satisfaction, is to fall upon a way that you may converse freely with Schemselnihar; this I will procure you, and to-morrow will set about it. You must by no means expose yourself to enter Schemselnihar's palace; you know by experience the danger of that: I know a very fit place for this interview, where you shall be safe. When the jeweller had spoken thus, the prince embraced him with a transport of joy. You revive, says he, by this charming promise, an unhappy lover, who was resolved to die; I see that you have fully repaired the loss of Ebn Thaher; whatever you do shall be well done, I will leave myself entirely to you.

After the prince had thanked him for his zeal, the jeweller returned home, and next morning Schemselnihar's confidant came to him; he told her that he had put the prince of Persia in hopes that he should see Schemselnihar speedily: I am come on purpose, answered she, to take measures with you for that end. I think, continued she, this house will be convenient enough for their interview: I could receive them very well here, replied he, but I think they will have more liberty in another house of mine, where nobody lives at present; I will quickly furnish it for receiving them.—Since the matter is so, replied the confidant, there remains nothing for me to do, but to make Schemselnihar consent to it. I will go and tell her, and return speedily with an answer.

She was as diligent as her promise, and, returning to the jeweller, told him that her mistress would not fail to keep the appointment in the evening. In the mean time, she gave him a purse of money, and told him it was to prepare a collation. He sent her immediately to the house where the lovers were to meet, that she might know whither to bring her mistress; and, when she was gone, he went to borrow from his friends vessels of gold and silver, tapestry, rich cushions, and other furniture, with which he furnished the house very magnificently; and, when he had put all things in order, he went to the prince of Persia.

You may easily conceive the prince of Persia's joy, when the jeweller told him that he came to conduct him to the house he had prepared to receive him and Schemselnihar: This news made him forget all his former trouble. He put on a magnificent robe, and went, without his retinue, along with the jeweller, who led him through several by-streets, that nobody might observe him, and at last brought him to the house, where they discoursed together until Schemselnihar came.

They did not stay long for this passionate lover. She came after evening-prayers, with her confidant and two other slaves. One cannot express the excess of joy that seized those two lovers when they saw one another; it is altogether impossible: They sat down together upon a sofa, looking upon one another for some time, without being able to speak, they were so much overjoyed; but, when their speech returned to them, they soon made up their silence: They expressed themselves with so much tenderness, as made the jeweller, the confidant, and the two other slaves weep.—The jeweller, however, restrained his tears to think upon the collation which he brought. The lovers ate and drank a little, after which they sat down again upon the sofa: Schemselnihar asked the jeweller if he had a lute, or any other instrument? The jeweller, who took care to provide all that might please them, brought her a lute: She took some time to tune it, and then played.

While Schemselnihar was charming the prince of Persia, and expressing her passion by words extempore, a great noise was heard; and immediately the slave which the jeweller had brought with him appeared all in a fright, and came to tell him that some people were breaking up the gate; that he asked who it was, but, instead of any answer, the blows were redoubled. The jeweller being alarmed, left Schemselnihar and the prince to go and inform himself of the truth of this bad news. There was already got into the court a company of men, armed with bayonets and scymitars, who had entered privily; and, having broke up the gate, came straight towards him. He stood close to a wall for fear of his life, and saw ten of them pass without being perceived by them; and, finding he could give no great help to the prince of Persia and Schemselnihar, he satisfied himself with bewailing them, and so fled for refuge to a neighbour's house, who was not yet gone to bed: He did not doubt but this unexpected violence was by the caliph's order, who, he thought, had been informed of his favourite's meeting with the prince of Persia. He heard a great noise in his own house, which continued till midnight; and, when all was quiet, as he thought, he prayed his neighbour to lend him a scymitar; and, being thus armed, went on till he came to the gate of his own house; he entered the court full of fear, and perceived a man, who asked him who he was; he knew by his voice that it was his own slave. How didst thou do, says he, to avoid being taken by the watch? Sir, answered the slave, I hid myself in a corner of the court, and I went out so soon as I heard the noise; but it was not the watch who broke into your house, they were highwaymen, who, within these few days, robbed another in this neighbourhood: They have doubtless had notice of the rich furniture you brought hither, and had that in their view.

The jeweller thought his slave's conjectures probable enough: He visited the house, and saw that the highwaymen had taken all the furniture out of the chamber where he received Schemselnihar and her lover: That they had also carried off the vessels of gold and silver, and, in a word, had left nothing. Being in this condition, O heaven, cries he, I am irrecoverably undone! what will my friends say, and what excuse can I make, when I shall tell them that the highwaymen have broke my house, and robbed me of all that they generously lent me? I shall never be able to make up their loss: Besides, what is become of Schemselnihar and the prince of Persia? This business will be so public, that it is impossible but it must reach the caliph's ears. He will get notice of this meeting, and I shall fall a sacrifice to his fury. The slave, who loved him, endeavoured to comfort him thus: As to Schemselnihar, says he, the highwaymen probably would content themselves to strip her, and you have reason to think that she is retired to her palace with her slaves: The prince of Persia is probably in the same condition, so that you have reason to hope that the caliph will never know of this adventure. As for the loss your friends have sustained, that is a misfortune that you could not avoid. They know very well the highwaymen are so numerous, that they have not only pillaged the house I have already spoken of, but many other houses of the principal noblemen of the court: And they are not ignorant, that, notwithstanding the orders given to apprehend them, nobody has yet been able to seize any of them. You will be acquitted by restoring your friends the value of the things that are stolen, and, blessed be God, you have enough left.

Waiting till day, the jeweller ordered the slave to mend the gate of the house, which was broke up, as well as he could: After which, he returned to his ordinary house with his slave, making sad reflections upon what had befallen him. Ebn Thaher, says he to himself, has been wiser than I; he foresaw the misfortune into which I have blindly thrown myself; would to God I had never meddled in this intrigue, which I fear will cost me my life.

It was scarce day when the report of the robbery spread through the city; and there came to his house a great many of his friends and neighbours to testify their grief for his misfortune, that were curious to know the particulars. He thanked them for their affection, and was so much the better satisfied that he heard no body speak of Schemselnihar or the prince of Persia, which made him believe they were at their own houses, or in some secret place.

When the jeweller was alone, his servants brought him something to eat, but he could not eat a bit.—About noon, one of his slaves came to tell him there was a man at the gate, whom he knew not, that desired to speak with him. The jeweller, not willing to receive a stranger in his house, rose up and went to speak with him. Though you do not know me, says the man, yet I know you, and I am come to talk with you about an important affair. The jeweller prayed him to come in. No, answered the stranger, if you please, rather take the trouble to go with me to your other house. How know you, replied the jeweller, that I have another house? I know well enough, answered the stranger, follow me, and do not fear any thing: I have something to communicate to you which will please you. The jeweller went immediately with him; and, after he had considered by the way how the house they were going to was robbed, he said to him that it was not fit to receive him.

When they were before the house, and the stranger saw the gate half broken down, he says to the jeweller, I see you have told me the truth,—I will carry you to a place which will be more convenient. When he said this, he went on, and walked all the rest of the day without stopping. The jeweller being weary with walking, vexed to see night approach, and that the stranger had walked all day without acquainting him where he was going, began to lose his patience. Then they came to a path which led them to the Tigris, and, as soon as they came to the river, they embarked in a little boat and went over. Then the stranger led the jeweller through a long street, where he had never been before; and, after he had brought him through I know not how many by-streets, he stopped at a gate, which he opened. He caused the jeweller to go in, and then he shut, and bolted the gate with a huge iron bolt, and conducted him to a chamber, where there were ten other men, all of them as great strangers to the jeweller as he that brought him hither.

These ten men received the jeweller without any compliments. They bid him sit down, of which he had great need, for he was not only out of breath with walking so far, but the fear he was in to find himself with people whom he thought he had reason to dread, would have disabled him to stand. They waited for their leader to go to supper, and as soon as he came, it was served up. They washed their hands, obliging the jeweller to do the like, and to sit at table with them. After supper, the man asked him if he knew whom he spoke to? He answered, No, and that he knew not the place he was in. Tell us your last night's adventure, said they to him, and conceal nothing from us. The jeweller being astonished at this discourse, answered, Gentlemen, it is probable you know it already. That is true, replied they; the young man and the young lady, who were at your house yesterday, told it us, but we would know it from your own mouth. The jeweller needed no more to inform him that he spoke to the highwaymen who had broke up and plundered his house. Gentlemen, says he, I am much troubled for that young man and the lady; can you tell me any thing of them?

Upon the jeweller's inquiry of the thieves if they knew any thing of the young man and the young lady, they answered, Be not concerned for them, they are safe enough, and in good health: Which saying, they shewed him two closets, where they assured him they were separately shut up. They added, We are informed you only know what relates to them, which we no sooner came to understand but we shewed them all imaginable respect, and were so far from doing them any injury, that we treated them with all the kindness we were capable of on your account. You may secure yourself of the like favour, proceeded they, in regard to your own person, and put all manner of confidence in us without the least reserve.

The jeweller being heartened at this, and overjoyed to hear that the prince of Persia and Schemselnihar were safe, resolved to engage the thieves yet farther in their interest. For this purpose, he commended them, flattered them, and gave them a thousand benedictions. Gentlemen, said he, I must confess I have not the honour to know you, yet it is no small happiness to me that I am not wholly unknown to you; and I can never be sufficiently grateful for the favours which that knowledge has procured me at your hands: Without mentioning so great an act of humanity as that I lately received from you, I must needs say, I am fully persuaded no person in the world can be so proper to trust a secret with, and none so fit to undertake a great enterprise, which you can best bring to a good issue by your zeal, courage, and intrepidity. In confidence of these great and good qualities, which are so much your due, I will not stick to relate to you my whole history, with that of those two persons you found in my house.

After the jeweller had thus secured, as he thought, the thieves' secrecy, he made no scruple to relate to them the whole amour of the prince of Persia and Schemselnihar, from the beginning of it to the time he received them into his house.

The thieves were greatly astonished at the surprising particulars they heard, and could not forbear crying out, How! is it possible that the young man should be the illustrious Ali Ebn Becar, prince of Persia, and the young lady the fair and celebrated beauty Schemselnihar? The jeweller assured them nothing was more certain, and that they needed not to think it strange, that persons of so distinguished a character should not care to be known.

Upon this assurance of their quality, the thieves went immediately, one after another, and threw themselves at their feet, imploring their pardon, and begging them to believe they would never have offered any violence to their persons had they but known who they were; and that, seeing they did not, they would, by their future conduct, do their best endeavours to make some recompence, at least, for the crime they had thus ignorantly committed. Thus said, and having made profound reverences, they turned to the jeweller, and told him they were heartily sorry they could not restore to him all that had been taken from him, some part being out of their possession; but as for what remained, if he would content himself with his plate, it should be forthwith put into his hands.

The jeweller was overjoyed at the favour done him, and, after the thieves had delivered the plate, they required of the prince, Schemselnihar, and him, to promise them upon oath that they would not betray them, and they would carry them to a place, whence they might easily go to their respective homes. The prince, Schemselnihar, and the jeweller, replied that they might rely on their words, but, since they desired an oath of them, they solemnly swore not to discover them, so long as they were with them. With this, the thieves being satisfied, immediately set out upon performing their promise.

By the way, the jeweller being concerned that he could not see the confidant and the two slaves, came up to Schemselnihar, and begged her to inform him what was become of them: She answered, she knew nothing of them, and that all she could tell him was, that she was carried away from his house, ferried over a river, and brought to the place from whence they were now come.

Schemselnihar and the jeweller had no farther discourse; they found themselves at the brink of a river, when the thieves immediately took boat, and carried them to the other side.

Whilst the prince, Schemselnihar, and the jeweller, were landing, they heard a noise, as of horse-guards, that were coming towards them. The thieves no sooner perceived the danger, but they took to their oars, and were over on the other side of the river in an instant.

The commander of the brigade demanded of the prince, of Schemselnihar, and the jeweller, who they were, and whence they came so late? This frightened them so at first, that they could not speak; but at length the jeweller found a tongue, and said, Sir, I can assure you we are very honest people, and that those rogues who have just landed us, and are got to the other side of the water, are thieves, who, having last night broke open the house that we were in, pillaged it, and afterwards carried us to an obscure inn, where, by some entreaty and good management, we prevailed on them to let us have our liberty; to which end they brought us hither. They have restored us part of the booty they had taken from us: At which words he shewed the plate he had recovered.

The commander, not being satisfied with what the jeweller had told him, came up to him and the prince of Persia, and, looking stedfastly at them, said, Tell me truly who is this lady? How came you to know her, and whereabouts do you live?

This demand surprised them strangely, and tied their tongues so much, that neither of them could answer; till at length Schemselnihar, taking the commander aside, told him frankly who she was; which he no sooner came to know, but he alighted, paid both her and the company great respect, and caused two boats to be got ready for their service.

When the boats were come, he put Schemselnihar into one, and the prince of Persia and jeweller into the other, with two of his people in each boat: They had orders to accompany them whithersoever they were bound. Being aboard, the two boats took different routs, but we shall at present speak only of that wherein were the prince and jeweller.

The prince, to save his guides trouble, bid them land the jeweller with him, and named the place whither he would go. The guides, mistaking his orders, stopped just before the caliph's palace, which put both him and the jeweller into a mortal fright, though he durst discover nothing of the matter; for, although they had heard the commander's orders to his men, they could not help imagining they were to be delivered up to the guard, to be brought before the caliph next morning.

This nevertheless was not the intention of the guides; for, after they had landed them, they, by their master's command, recommended them to an officer of the guard, who next morning assigned them soldiers to conduct them by land to the prince's chateau, which was at some distance from the river.

The prince being come home, what with the fatigue of his journey, and the affliction he conceived at being never likely to see Schemselnihar more, fell into a swoon on his sofa; whom, while the greatest part of his servants were endeavouring to recover, the other part gathered about the jeweller, and begged of him to tell them what had happened to the prince, their lord, whose absence had occasioned them such inexpressible disquiet.

The jeweller, who was sure to discover nothing to them that was not convenient for them to know, told them, that that was not a time for such a relation, and they would do better to go and assist their prince, than require any such thing of him, at that juncture especially. The prince by good fortune came to himself that very moment, when those, that but just before required this history with so much earnestness, began now to get at a distance, and pay that respect which was due from them.

Although the prince had in some measure recovered himself, yet he continued so weak, he could not open his mouth. He answered only by signs, and that even to his nearest relations that spoke to him. He remained in the same condition till next morning, when the jeweller came to take leave of him. His answer was only with a wink, and holding forth his right-hand; but when he saw he was laden with the bundle of plate the thieves had taken from him, he made a sign to his servants, that they should take it and carry it along with him to his house.

The jeweller had been expected home with great impatience by his family, the day he went forth with a man that came to ask for him, and whom he did not know: but now he was quite given over, and it was no longer doubted but some fatal disaster had befallen him. His wife, children, and servants, were under continual grief, and lamented him almost night and day: But at length, when they came to see him again, their joys were so great they could hardly contain themselves; yet they were still troubled, to find that his countenance was extremely altered from what it had been before, insomuch that he was hardly to be known. This was thought to have been occasioned by his great fatigue, and the fears he had undergone, which would not let him sleep. Finding himself something out of order, he continued within doors for two days, and would admit only one of his intimate friends to visit him.

The third day, perceiving himself somewhat better, he thought he might get strength by going abroad; and therefore went to the shop of a rich friend of his, with whom he continued long in discourse. As he was rising to go home, he observed a woman that made a sign to him, and whom he presently knew to be the confidant of Schemselnihar. Partly out of fear, and partly through joy, he made what haste he could away, without looking at her; but she followed him, as he very well knew she would, the place they saw each other in being by no means proper for their interview. As he walked a little faster than ordinary, she not being able to overtake him, every now and then called out to him to stay. He heard her, it is true, but, after what had happened, he did not think fit to take notice of her in public, for fear of giving cause to believe that he had been with Schemselnihar. In short, it was known to every one in Bagdad that this woman belonged to her, and therefore he thought it but prudent to conceal his having any knowledge of her. He continued the same pace, and at length came to a mosque, where he knew but few people came: There he entered, and she after him, where they had a long converse together, without any overhearing them.

But the jeweller and confidant expressed a great deal of joy for seeing each other, after the strange adventure occasioned by the thieves, and their reciprocal concern for each other's welfare, without mentioning a word of what related to their own particular persons.

The jeweller would needs have her relate to him how she escaped with the two slaves, and what she knew of Schemselnihar from the time he had left her; but so great were her importunities to know from him what had happened to him from the time of their unexpected separation, that he found himself obliged to comply with her. Having finished what she had desired, he told her he expected she would oblige him in her turn, which she did in the following manner.

When first I saw the thieves, said she, I imagined, before I rightly considered, that they were of the caliph's guard, who, being informed of the escape of Schemselnihar, had sent them to take away the lives of the prince and us all; but, being convinced of the error of that thought, I immediately got up to the leads of your house, at the same time that the thieves entered the chamber where the prince and Schemselnihar were, and was soon after followed by that lady's two slaves. From leads to leads, we came at last to a house of very honest people, who received us with a great deal of civility, and with whom we lodged that night. Next morning, after we had returned thanks to the master of the house for our good usage, we returned to Schemselnihar's hotel, where we entered in great disorder, and the rather, because we could not learn the fate of the two unfortunate lovers. The other women of Schemselnihar were astonished to see me return without their lady. We told them we had left her at a lady's house, one of her friends, and that she would send for us when she had a mind to come home; with which excuse they seemed well satisfied.

For my part, I spent the day in great uneasiness, and when night came, opening a little back-gate, I espied a boat driven along by the stream. Calling to the waterman, I desired him to row up the river, and see if he could meet a lady; and, if he found her, to bring her along with him. The two slaves and I waited impatiently for his return, and at length, about midnight, we saw the boat coming down with two men in it, and a woman lying along the stern: When the boat was come up, the two men helped the woman to rise, and then it was I knew her for Schemselnihar. I rejoiced so greatly to see her that my joy cannot be expressed.

I gave my hand to Schemselnihar to help her out of the boat: She had no small occasion for my assistance, for she could hardly stand. When she was ashore, she whispered me in the ear in an afflicted tone, and bid me go and take a purse of a thousand pieces of gold, and give it to the soldiers that had waited on her. I did as I was commanded, leaving her to be supported by the two slaves: and, having paid the waterman, shut the back-door.

I then followed my lady, said the confidant to the jeweller, who was hardly got up to her chamber before I overtook her. We undressed her, and put her to bed, where she had not long been before she was ready to give up the ghost; in which condition she continued the remainder of the night. The day following, her other women expressed a great desire to see her, but I told them she had been greatly fatigued, and wanted rest to restore her to her strength. We nevertheless (the other two slaves and I) gave her all the assistance we possibly could, and she reasonably expect. She persisted in taking nothing that we offered her; and we must have despaired of her life, if I had not at last persuaded her to drink a spoonful or two of wine, which had a sensible effect on her: By mere importunity we at length prevailed with her to eat also.

When she came to the use of her speech, (for she had hitherto only mourned, groaned, and sighed) I begged of her to tell me how she had escaped out of the hands of the thieves. Why should you require of me, said she, with a profound sigh, what will but renew my grief? Would to God the thieves had taken away my life rather than preserved it, since thereby my misfortunes would have had an end; whereas I now do but live to increase my torments.

Madam, replied I, I beg you would not refuse this favour; you cannot but know that unhappy people have a certain, I know not what consolation in venting their misfortunes; and, if you would but be pleased to relate yours, I doubt not but you would find some relief in it.

Why then, said she, lend your ear to a story the most afflicting that can be imagined. You must know, when I first saw the thieves entering with sword in hand, I believed that the last moment of my life; but dying did not then seem so shocking to me, since I thought I was to die with the prince of Persia: However, instead of murdering, two of the thieves were ordered to take care of us, whilst their companions were busied in packing up the goods they found in the house. When they had done, and got their bundles upon their backs, they went away, and carried us along them.

As we went, one of those that had the charge of us, demanded me briskly who I was? I answered, I was a dancer. He put the same question to the prince, who replied he was a shopkeeper.

When they were come to the place whither they were going, new fears came upon me, for they gathered about us, and, after having considered well my habit, and the rich jewels that I was adorned with, they seemed to doubt I had disguised my quality. Dancers, quoth they, do not use to be dressed as you are. Pray tell us truly who you are, said they to me; but, when they saw I answered nothing, they asked the prince once more who he was? for they told him they plainly perceived he was not the person he pretended to be. He did not satisfy them much more than I had done; he only told them he came to see the jeweller, who was the owner of that house where they found them. I know this jeweller, said one of the rogues, who seemed to have some authority over the rest; I have some obligations to him which yet he knows nothing of, and I take upon me to bring him hither to-morrow morning, from another house he has; but you must not expect to stir until he come and tell us who you are; though, in the mean time, I promise you there shall be no manner of injury offered to you.

The jeweller was brought next morning, as he said, who, thinking to oblige us, as he really did, declared to the rogues the whole truth of the matter. The thieves no sooner knew who we were, but they came and asked my pardon, and I believe did the like of the prince, who was shut up in another room. They protested to me they would not have broke open the jeweller's house had they but known whose it was. They soon after took us, (the prince, the jeweller, and myself,) and carried us to the river side, where, having put us aboard the boat, they rowed us across the water; but we were no sooner landed, than a party of the horse-guards came up to us, and then the rogues fled; but I took the commander aside, and told him my name, telling him, withal, that the night before I had been seized by robbers, who forced me along with them; but, having been told who I was, he released me, and the two persons that were with me, on my account. He alighted, and paid his respects to me; and, after having expressed a great deal of joy for being able to oblige me, he caused two boats to be brought, putting me and two of his soldiers, whom you have seen, into one, and the prince and the jeweller, with two others, into the other. My guides have conducted me hither, but what has become of the prince and his friend, I cannot tell.

I trust in heaven, added Schemselnihar, with a shower of tears, no harm has happened to them since our separation; and I do not doubt but the prince's concern for me is equal to mine for him. The jeweller, to whom we had been so much obliged, ought to be recompensed for the loss he has sustained upon our account. Do not you therefore fail, quoth she, (speaking to me) to take two purses of a thousand pieces of gold in each, and carry them to him to-morrow morning in my name, and, at the same time, be sure to enquire after the prince's welfare.

When my good mistress had done speaking, I endeavoured, as to the last article of enquiring into the prince's welfare, to calm her mind, which was in some disorder, and to persuade her not to yield so much to love, since the danger she had but lately escaped would be soon brought on again by such an indulgence. She bid me hold my tongue, and do what she had commanded me.

I was obliged to be silent, and am come hither to obey her commands without any farther scruple. I have been at your house, and not finding you at home, was about to have gone to wait on the prince of Persia, but did not dare to attempt so great a journey. I have left the two purses with a particular friend of mine, and, if you will have but patience, I will go and fetch them immediately.

The confidant returned quickly to the jeweller in the mosque, where she had left him. She gave him the two purses, and bid him accept them for her lady's sake. They are much more than is necessary, said the jeweller, and I can never be enough thankful for so great a present from so good and generous a lady; but I beseech you to acquaint her on my behalf, that I shall preserve an eternal remembrance of her bounties. He then agreed with the confidant, that she should find him at the first place she had seen him at, whenever she had occasion to impart any commands from Schemselnihar, or to know any thing of the prince of Persia: And so they parted.

The jeweller returned home very well satisfied, not only that he had got wherewithal plentifully to make up his losses, but also to think that no person in Bagdad could possibly come to know of the prince and Schemselnihar's being in his other house when it was robbed. It is true, he had acquainted the thieves with it, but their secrecy he thought he might very well depend on, especially in this particular; they, he imagined, had not sufficient converse in the world to give him any disturbance. He therefore hugged himself in his good fortune, paid his debts, and furnished both his houses to a nicety.—Thus he forgot all his past danger, and next morning set out to wait on the prince of Persia.

The prince's domestics told the jeweller, at his arrival, that he came in a very good time to make their lord speak, for they had not been able to get a word out of him ever since he was there last. They introduced him softly into his chamber, and he found him in such a condition as raised his pity: He was lying upon his bed, with his eye-lids shut; but when the jeweller saluted him, and exhorted him to take courage, he faintly opened his eyes, and looked upon him with such an aspect as sufficiently declared the greatness of his affliction. He nevertheless took and grasped him by the hand, to testify his friendship, and he told him, in a faint and weak tone, that he was extremely obliged to him for coming so far to seek one that was so exceedingly unhappy and miserable.

My lord, replied the jeweller, mention not, I beseech you, any obligations you have to me: I could wish with all my soul, the good offices I have endeavoured to do you had had a better effect: But at present let us discourse only of your health, which I fear you greatly injure by an unreasonable abstaining from proper nourishment.

The prince's servants hearing the jeweller say this, took occasion to let him know it was with the greatest difficulty they had prevailed on him to take in even the smallest matter; and that for some time he had taken nothing at all. This obliged the jeweller to beg of the prince to let his servants bring him something to eat, which favour he obtained with much intercession.

After the prince had eaten more largely than he had hitherto done, through the persuasion of the jeweller, he commanded the servants to quit the room, and leave him alone with his friend. When the room was clear, he said, In conjunction with my misfortune that distracts me, I have been exceedingly concerned to think of what you have suffered on my account; and as it is but just I should make you what recompence I can, so I shall be sure to take the first occasion of doing it: However, at present, begging only your pardon a thousand times, I must conjure you to tell me whether you have learned any thing of Schemselnihar since I had the misfortune to be parted from her.

Here the jeweller, upon the confidant's information, related to him all that he knew of Schemselnihar's arrival at her hotel, her state of health from the time he had left her, and how she had sent her confidant to him to inquire after his highness's welfare.

To all this the prince replied only with sighs and tears: Then he made an effort to get up, and, being assisted by the jeweller, made shift to rise: Being upon his legs, he called his servants, and made them open his wardrobe, whither he went in person; and, having caused several bundles of rich goods and plate to be packed up, he ordered them to be carried to the jeweller's house.

The jeweller would fain have withstood this kind offer; but, although he represented that Schemselnihar had already made him more than sufficient amends for what he had lost, the prince would be obeyed. The jeweller thought himself obliged to make all possible acknowledgments, and protested how much he was confounded at his highness's liberality. He would have taken his leave, but the prince would not let him; and so they passed away in discourse good part of the night.

Next morning the jeweller waited on the prince again, before he went away, but he would not let him stir: He must first sit down, and hear what he had to say to him. You know, said the prince, that there is an end proposed in all things: Now the end the lover proposes, is to enjoy the beloved object in spite of all opposition: If he loses that hope, he must not think to live. You also know that this is my hard case, for, when I have been twice at the very point of fulfilling my desires, I was all of a sudden tore from what I loved in the most cruel manner imaginable: I had then no more to do but to think of death; and I had certainly proved my own executioner, but that our holy law forbids us to be suicides. But there is no need of such violent means; death will soon do its own work in a sure though gentle method; I find myself in a manner gone, and that I have not long to wait the welcome blow. Here he was silent, and vented the rest of his passion only in groans, sighs, sobs, and tears, which came from him in great abundance.

The jeweller, who knew no better way of turning him from his despair than by bringing Schemselnihar into his mind, and giving him some hopes of enjoying her, told him, he feared the confidant might be come from her lady, and therefore thought it not proper to stay any longer from home. I will let you go, said the prince, but conjure you, that, if you see her, you recommend to her, to assure Schemselnihar, that if I die, as I expect to do every minute, I will bless her with my last breath, and love her to the last moment.

The jeweller returned home in expectation of seeing the confidant; and she came some few hours after, but all in tears, and in great affliction. He asked her, with great earnestness, what was the matter? She answered, that Schemselnihar, the prince, herself, and he, were all ruined. He demanded how? Hear the sad news, said she, as it was told me just upon entering our hotel, after I had left you.

Schemselnihar had, it seems, for some fault, chastised one of the slaves you saw with her in your other house; and the slave, enraged at the ill-treatment, ran presently away, and, finding the gate open, went forth; so that we have just reason to believe she has discovered all to an eunuch of the guard, who gave her protection, as we have since heard.

But this is not all; the other slave, her companion, is fled too, and has taken refuge in the caliph's palace, so that we may well fear she has acted her part in this discovery; for, just as I came away, the caliph had sent twenty of his eunuchs for Schemselnihar, and they had carried her to the palace. I just found means to come and tell you this; yet I fear no good will come of it; but, above all, I recommend it to you as a secret: And I think it would be most convenient for you to go and acquaint the prince with the whole affair, to the end he may be ready on all occasions, and contribute what he is able to the common cause. Saying this, she ran away in great haste, without speaking a word more, or staying for any answer.

What answer, however, could the jeweller have made in the deplorable condition he was in? He stood still as if he were thunderstruck, and had not a word to say. He was, nevertheless, sensible that the affair required expedition, and therefore immediately went to give the prince an account of it: He addressed himself to him with an air that sufficiently shewed the bad news he brought him.—Prince, said he, arm yourself with courage and patience, and prepare to receive the most terrible assault that was ever yet made on your nature.

Tell me in a few words, said the prince, what it is I must prepare to receive; for if it be death only, I am both ready and willing to undergo it.

Then the jeweller told him all that he had learned from the confidant: You see, continued he, your destruction is inevitable if you delay. Up, rise, save yourself by flight, for the time is precious. You, of all men, must not expose yourself to the anger of the caliph, and should much less confess any thing in the midst of torments.

At these words, the prince was almost ready to expire through grief, affliction, and fear; however, he recovered himself, and demanded of the jeweller what resolution he would advise him to take in this unhappy conjuncture. The jeweller told him he thought nothing more proper than that he should immediately take horse and haste away towards Anbar,[1] that he might get thither with all convenient speed. Take what servants and horses you think necessary, continued he, and suffer me to escape with you.

The prince, seeing nothing more adviseable, immediately gave orders for such an equipage as would be least troublesome; so, having put some money and jewels in his pocket, and taken leave of his mother, he departed in company of the jeweller and such servants as he had chosen.

[1] Anbar is a city on the Tigris, twenty leagues below Bagdad.

They travelled all that day, and the day following, without stopping, until at length, about the dusk of the evening, both their horses and themselves being greatly fatigued, they alighted at an inn to refresh themselves.

They had hardly sat down before they found themselves surrounded and assaulted by a huge knot of thieves. They defended their lives for some time courageously; but at length, the prince's servants being all killed, both he and the jeweller were obliged to yield at discretion. The thieves, however, spared their lives; but, after they had seized on the horses and baggage, they took away their clothes and left them naked.

Being in this condition, and the thieves gone from them, the prince said to the jeweller, What is to be done, my friend, in this conjuncture? Had I not better, think you, have tarried in Bagdad, and undergone any fate, rather than been reduced to this extremity? My lord, replied the jeweller, it is the decree of heaven that we should thus suffer: It has pleased God to add affliction to affliction, and we must not murmur at it, but receive his chastisements with submission. Let us stay no longer here, but go and look out for some place where we may be concealed and relieved. No, let me rather die, said the prince, for what signifies it whether I die here or elsewhere; for die I know I must very shortly. It may be this very minute that we are talking Schemselnihar is no more, and why should I endeavour to live after she is dead? The jeweller at length prevailed on him to do as he said; and they had not gone far before they came to a mosque, which, being open, they entered it, and passed there the remainder of the night.

At day-break, a single man came into the mosque to his devotion. When he had ended his prayer, and was turning to go out, he perceived the prince and the jeweller, who were sitting in a corner to conceal themselves. He came up to them, and, after having saluted them with a great deal of civility, said, By what I perceive, gentlemen, you seem to be strangers? The jeweller answered, You are not deceived, sir, we have been robbed to-night in coming from Bagdad, and are retired hither for shelter: If you can relieve us in our necessities, we should be very much obliged to you, for we know not any body here to make our addresses to. The man answered, If you shall think fit to come along with me to my house, I will do what I can for you. Upon this obliging offer, the jeweller turned to the prince, and said in his ear, This man, as far as I can perceive, sir, does not know us; therefore we had better go with him than stay here to be exposed to the sight of somebody that may. Do as you please, said the prince, I am willing to be guided by your discretion.

The man observing the prince and jeweller consulting together, thought they made some difficulty to accept his proposition; wherefore he demanded of them if they were resolved what to do? The jeweller answered, We are ready to follow you whither you please; all that we make a difficulty about, is to appear thus naked. Let not that trouble you, said the man; we will find wherewithal to clothe you, I warrant you; and they were no sooner got to the house, but he brought forth a very handsome suit for each of them. Next, as he thought they must needs be very hungry, and have a mind to go to bed, he had several plates of meat brought out to them by a slave; but they eat little, especially the prince, who was so dejected and dispirited as gave the jeweller cause to fear he would die. Then they went to bed, and their host left them to their repose; but they were no sooner laid down than the jeweller was forced to call him again to assist at the death of the prince. He found him breathe short, and with difficulty, which gave him just reason to fear he had but few minutes to live. Coming near him, the prince said, It is done, and I am glad you are by, to be witness of my last words. I quit this life with a great deal of satisfaction, but I need not tell you the reason, for you know it too well already. All the regret I have, is, that I cannot die in the arms of my dearest mother, who has always loved me with a tenderness not to be expressed, and for whom I had a reciprocal affection: She will undoubtedly not be a little grieved that she could not close my eyes and bury me with her own hands: But let her know how much I was concerned at this, and desire her in my name to have my corpse transported to Bagdad, that she may have an opportunity to bedew my tomb with her tears, and assist my departed soul with her prayers. He then took notice of the master of the house, and thanked him for the several favours he had received from him, desiring him to let his body be deposited with him till such time as it should be carried away to Bagdad. Having said all this, he turned aside and expired.

Next day after the prince's death, the jeweller took the opportunity of a numerous caravan that was going to Bagdad, and arrived there some time after in safety. He first went home to change his cloaths, and then hastened to the prince's palace, where every body was surprised to see their lord was not come with him. He desired them to acquaint the prince's mother that he must needs speak with her immediately; and it was not long before he was introduced to her, whom he found in a hall, with several of her women about her; Madam, said he to her, with an air that sufficiently denoted his ill news, God preserve your highness, and shower down the choicest of his blessings upon you: You cannot be ignorant that it is he alone that disposes of us all at his pleasure.

The princess would not give him leave to go on, but cried out, Alas! you bring me the deplorable news of my son's death. At which words she and her women set up such a hideous outcry as soon brought fresh tears into the jeweller's eyes. She thus tormented and grieved herself a long while before she would suffer the unfortunate messenger to go on. However, at length she gave a truce to her sighs and groans, and begged of him to continue the fatal relation, without concealing from her the least circumstance. He did as she commanded; and, when he had done, she farther demanded of him, if her son the prince had not given him in charge something more particular? He assured her his last words were, that it was the greatest concern to him that he must die so far distant from his dear mother; yet he earnestly entreated her, she would be pleased to have his corpse transported to Bagdad. Accordingly, next morning at day-break, the princess set out, with her women, and great part of her slaves, to bring her son's body to her own palace.

The jeweller having taken leave of her, returned home very sad and melancholy, to think he had lost so good a friend, and so accomplished a prince, in the flower of his age. As he came near his own house, dejected and musing, on a sudden lifting up his eyes, he saw a woman standing before him: He presently knew her to be the confidant, who had stood there grieving some time that she could not see him. At the sight of her, his tears began to flow afresh, but he said nothing to her; and, going into his own house, she followed him.

They sat down, when the jeweller, beginning the dismal discourse, asked the confidant, with a deep sigh, if she had heard nothing of the death of the prince of Persia, and if it was on his account that she grieved? Alas, answered she, what! is that charming prince then dead? He has not lived long after his dear Schemselnihar. Beauteous souls! continued she, in whatsoever place ye now are, ye ought to be pleased that your loves will no more be interrupted. Your bodies were before an obstacle to your wishes; but now, being delivered of them, ye may unite as closely as ye please.

The jeweller, who had heard nothing of Schemselnihar's death, and had not observed the confidant was in mourning, through his excessive grief that blinded him, was now anew afflicted, to hear this farther bad news. Is Schemselnihar then dead? cried he in great astonishment. She is dead, replied the confidant, weeping afresh; and it is for her I wear these weeds. The circumstances of her death were extraordinary, continued she, therefore it is requisite you should know them: But, before I give you an account of them, I beg you to let me know those of the prince of Persia, whom, in conjunction with my dearest friend and mistress, I shall lament as long as I live. The jeweller then gave the confidant that satisfaction she desired, and after he had told her all, even the departure of the prince's mother to bring her son's body to Bagdad, she began and said, You have not forgot, I suppose, that I told you the caliph had sent for Schemselnihar to his palace; and it is true, as we had all the reason in the world to believe, he had been informed of the amour betwixt her and the prince, by the two slaves, whom he had examined apart; now you will be apt to imagine he must of necessity be exceedingly enraged at Schemselnihar, and discover many tokens of jealousy and revenge against the prince: but I must tell you, he had neither one nor the other, and lamented only his dear mistress's forsaking him, which he, in some measure, attributed to himself, in giving her so much freedom to walk about the city without his eunuchs. This was all the resentment he shewed, as you will find by his carriage towards her, as follows:

He received her with an open countenance; and when he observed the sadness she was under, which nevertheless did not lessen her beauty, with a goodness peculiar to himself, he said, Schemselnihar, I cannot bear your appearing thus before me with an air of affliction: You must needs be sensible how much I have always loved you, by the continual demonstrations I have given you of it; and I can never change my mind, for even now I love you more than ever: You have enemies, Schemselnihar, proceeded he, and those enemies have done you all the wrong they can: For this purpose, they have filled my ears with stories against you, which have not yet made the least impression on me. Shake off then this melancholy, continued he, and prepare to entertain your lord this night after your accustomed manner. He said many other obliging things to her, and desired her to step into a magnificent apartment, and stay for him. The afflicted Schemselnihar was very sensible of the kindness the caliph had for her; but the more she thought herself obliged to him, the more she was concerned that she was so far off from the prince, without whom she could not live, and yet she was afraid she should never see him more.

This interview between the caliph and Schemselnihar, continued the confidant, was whilst I was come to speak with you, and I learned the particulars of it from my companions, who were present. But I had no sooner left you, proceeded she, than I went to my dear mistress again, and was eye-witness to what happened afterwards. I found her in the apartment I told you of; and, as she thought I came from you, she came up to me, and whispering me in the ear, said, I am much obliged to you for the service you have been doing me, but fear it will be the last. I took no notice of her words, and she said no more to me; but, if I had a mind to say any thing to comfort her, I was in a place that was not proper for it.

The caliph was introduced at night with the sound of instruments our women played upon, and the collation was immediately served up. He took his mistress by the hand, and made her sit down with him on the sofa; which she did with that regret, that she expired some few minutes after. In short, she was hardly set down, but she fell backwards, which the caliph believed to be only a swoon, and so we thought all; but, when we endeavoured to bring her to herself, we found she was quite gone, which you may imagine not a little afflicted us. The caliph did her the honour to weep over her, not being able to refrain from tears; and, before he left the room, ordered all the musical instruments to be broke, which was immediately executed. For my part, I staid with her corpse all night, and next morning bathed her with my tears, and dressed her for her funeral. The caliph had her interred soon after, in a magnificent tomb he had erected for her in her life time, in a place she had desired to be buried in.

Now since you tell me, said she, the prince of Persia's body is to be brought to Bagdad, I will use my best endeavours that he shall be interred in the same tomb, which may be some satisfaction at least to two such faithful lovers. The jeweller was somewhat surprised at this resolution of the confidant's, and said, Certainly you do not consider that this enterprize is in a manner impossible, for the caliph will be sure never to suffer it. Do not you be concerned at that, replied she, for you will undoubtedly be of another opinion, after I have told you that the caliph has given liberty to all her slaves in general, with a considerable pension to each for their subsistence; and as to my particular, has honoured me with the charge of my mistress's tomb, and allotted me an annual income for my maintenance. Moreover, you must needs think the caliph, who was not ignorant of the amour between Schemselnihar and the prince, as I have already told you, will not be a whit concerned, if now after her death he be buried with her.

To all this the jeweller had not a word to say, yet earnestly entreated the confidant to conduct him to her mistress's tomb, that he might say his prayers over her. When he came in sight of it, he was not a little surprised to find a vast number of people of both sexes, that were come thither from all parts of Bagdad. By reason he could not come near the tomb, he said his prayers at a distance; and then going to the confidant, who was waiting hard by, he said to her, I am altogether of a contrary opinion to what I was just now, for now I am so far from thinking that what you just now proposed cannot be put in execution, that you and I need only tell abroad what we know of the amour of this unfortunate couple, and how the prince died much about the same time with his mistress, and is now bringing up to be buried; and the people will bring the thing about, and not suffer that two such faithful lovers should be separated when dead, whom nothing could divide in affection whilst they lived. As he said, so it came to pass; for as soon as it came to be known that the corpse was within a day's journey of the city, the inhabitants almost of all sorts went forth, and met it above twenty miles off; and afterwards marched before it till it came to the city gate, where the confidant, waiting for that purpose, presented herself before the prince's mother, and begged of her, in the name of the whole city, that she would be pleased to consent that the bodies of the two lovers, who had but one heart whilst they lived, especially during their amour, might be buried in the same tomb now they were dead. The princess immediately consented; so the corpse of the prince, instead of being deposited in his own burying place, was laid by Schemselnihar's side, after it had been carried along in procession at the head of an infinite number of people of all conditions and degrees: nay from that very time, all the inhabitants of Bagdad, and even strangers, from such parts of the world as honoured the Mahometan religion, have had a mighty veneration for that tomb, and paid their devotion at it as often as opportunity would give them leave.

This, sir, said Scheherazade, who now perceived the day begin to approach, is what I had to relate to your majesty concerning the amour of the fair Schemselnihar, mistress to the caliph Haroun Alraschid, and the worthy Ali Ebn Becar, prince of Persia.

When Dinarzade observed her sister the sultaness had done speaking, she thanked her in the most obliging manner for her entertainment in a history so exceedingly agreeable. If the sultan will be but pleased to let me live till to-morrow, said Scheherazade, I will also relate that of prince Camaralzaman,[1] which you will find yet more agreeable. Here she stopped; and the sultan, who could not yet resolve on her death, permitted her to go on next night in the following manner.

The Story of the Amours of Camaralzaman, Prince of the Isles of the Children of Khaledan, and of Badoura, Princess of China

Sir, said she, about twenty days sail on the coast of Persia, there are islands in the main ocean, called the Islands of the Children of Khaledan: these islands are divided into four great provinces, which have all of them very flourishing and populous cities, and which make together a most potent kingdom. It is governed by a king, named Schahzaman,[2] who has four lawful wives, all daughters of kings, and sixty concubines.

Schahzaman thought himself the most happy monarch of the world, as well on account of his peaceful as prosperous reign. One thing only disturbed his happiness, which was, that he was pretty old, and had no children, though he had so many wives. He knew not what to attribute this barrenness to; and what increased his affliction was, that he was likely to leave his kingdom without a successor. He dissembled his discontent a long

[1] This word signifies in Arabic, the moon of the time, or the moon of the age.

[2] That is to say, in Persia, king of the time, or king of the age.

while; and what made it yet more uneasy to him, was, that he was forced to dissemble. However, at length he broke silence; and one day, after he had complained bitterly of his misfortune to his grand visier, he demanded of him if he knew any remedy for it? That wise minister replied, If what your majesty requires of me had depended on the ordinary methods of human wisdom, you had soon had an answer to your satisfaction; but, as my experience and knowledge are not sufficient to content you, I must advise you to have recourse to the Divine Power alone, who, in the midst of our prosperities, which often tempt us to forget him, is pleased so to limit our discernment that we may apply only to his omniscience for what we have occasion to know. Your majesty has subjects, proceeded he, who make a profession of loving and honouring God, and suffering great hardships for his sake; to them I would advise you to have recourse, and engage them by alms to join their prayers with your's: it may be, some among them may be so just and agreeable to God as to obtain what they pray for. King Schahzaman approved this advice very much, and thanked his visier for it: he immediately caused rich alms to be given to every monastery in his dominions: and, having sent for the superiors, declared to them his intention, and desired them to acquaint their monks with it.

The king, in short, obtained of heaven what he requested; for in nine months time he had a son born of one of his wives. In return for this favour, he sent new alms to the religious houses, and the prince's birth-day was celebrated throughout his dominions for a week together. The prince was brought to him as soon as born, and he found him so beautiful that he gave him the name of Camaralzaman, i.e. the moon of the age.

He was educated with all the care imaginable; and when he came to be old enough, his father appointed him a governor and able preceptors. These distinguished persons found him capable of receiving all the instructions that were proper to be given him, as well in relation to morals, as the other knowledge a prince ought to have. When he came to be somewhat older, he learned all his exercises, which he acquitted himself of with such grace and wonderful address, as charmed all that saw him, and particularly the sultan his father.

Having attained the age of fifteen years, the sultan, who loved him tenderly, thought of resigning his throne to him; and acquainted his grand visier with his intentions. I am afraid, says he, lest my son should lose those advantages in youth which nature and my education have given him; therefore, since I am somewhat advanced in age, and fit for a retreat, I have had thoughts of resigning the government to him, and passing the remainder of my days in the satisfaction of seeing him reign; I have undergone the fatigue of a crown a long while, and think it is now proper for me to retire.

The grand visier would not offer all the reasons he could have brought to dissuade the sultan from such a proceeding; on the contrary, he agreed with him in some measure. Sir, replied he, the prince is yet but young, and it would not be, in my humble opinion, wholly adviseable to burden him with the weight of a crown so soon. Your majesty fears, with a great deal of reason, his youth may be corrupted: but then, to remedy that, does not your majesty likewise think it would be proper to marry him? marriage being what would keep him within bounds, and confine his inclinations: moreover, your majesty might then admit him of your council, where he would learn by degrees the art of reigning, and so be fit to receive your power so soon as you should think proper to bestow it on him.

Schahzaman found this advice of his prime minister highly reasonable; therefore summoned the prince to appear before him at the same time that he dismissed the grand visier. The prince, who had been accustomed to see his father only at certain times, was a little startled at this irregular summons; therefore, when he came before him, he saluted him with great respect, and afterwards stood still, with his eyes fixed on the ground. The sultan perceiving his surprise, said to him in a mild way, Do you know, son, for what reason I have sent for you hither? Not I, and it please your majesty, answered the prince, modestly; God alone knows how to penetrate hearts: I should be glad to know of your majesty for what reason? Why, I sent for you, said the sultan, to let you know I design to marry you: what do you think of it?

Prince Camaralzaman heard this with great uneasiness; it quite surprised him, he was all in a sweat, and knew not what answer to make. After some few moments, however, he replied; Sir, I beseech your majesty to pardon me, if I seem surprised at the declaration you have made to me: I did not expect any such proposal to one so young as I am; and, besides, I know not whether I could ever prevail on myself to marry, not only on account of the troubles wives bring a man, and which I am very sensible of, though unmarried, but also by reason of their many impostures, wickednesses, and treacheries, which I have read of in authors. It may be, I may not always be of the same mind, yet I cannot but think I ought to have time to conclude on what your majesty requires of me.

Prince Camaralzaman's answer extremely afflicted his father. He was not a little grieved to see what an aversion he had to marriage, yet would not call his obedience in question, nor make use of his paternal authority: he contented himself with telling him he would not force his inclinations; and gave him time to consider of what he proposed to him; yet wished him to remember, that, as a prince designed to govern a great kingdom, he ought to take some care to leave a successor.

Schahzaman said no more to the prince; he admitted him into his council, and gave him all the reason to be satisfied that could be desired. About a year after, he took him aside, and said to him, Well, son, have you thoroughly considered of what I proposed to you about marrying last year? Will you still refuse me that satisfaction I desire, and let me die without seeing myself revive in your posterity? The prince seemed less astonished than before; he now briskly answered his father as follows: Sir, I have not neglected to consider of what you proposed to me; and, upon the whole matter, I am resolved to continue the state I am in, without concerning myself with marriage. In short, sir, the many evils I have read women have caused in the world, and the continual mischiefs I still hear and observe they do, has been the occasion of my resolution to have nothing to do with them; so that, sir, I hope your majesty will pardon me if I acquaint you, it will be to no purpose to solicit me any farther about that affair. Thus said, and making a low reverence, he went out briskly, without staying to hear what the sultan would answer.

Now any monarch but Schahzaman would have been in a wonderous passion at such a deportment of a son; but he took little notice of it, resolving to use all gentle methods before he proceeded to force. He communicated this new cause of discontent to his prime minister. I have followed your advice, says he, but Camaralzaman is farther off than ever from complying with my desires. He delivered his resolution in such arrogant terms, that I had all the occasion in the world for my reason and moderation to keep me from being in a passion. Fathers that desire favours of their children, which they nevertheless may command, are to blame themselves only, if they are disobeyed. But tell me, I beseech you, how I shall reclaim this hardy young prince, who proves so rebellious to my pleasure.

Sir, answered the grand visier, patience brings many things about that before seemed impracticable; but it may be this affair is of a nature not likely to succeed that way. However, in my judgment, your majesty would do well to give the prince another year to consider of the matter; and if, when that is expired, he still continues averse to your proposal, then your majesty may propose it to him in full council, as a thing that is highly necessary for the common good; and it is not likely he will refuse to comply with you before so grave an assembly, and on so necessary an account, whatever he has done before.

The sultan, who desired so passionately to see his son married, thought this long delay an age; however, though with much difficulty, he at length yielded to the grand visier's reasons, and which he could nowise disapprove.

After the grand visier was gone, sultan Schahzaman went to the apartment of the mother of prince Camaralzaman, to whom he had often discovered what an ardent desire he had to marry the prince: when he had told her, with tears in his eyes, how his son had refused to comply with him a second time; and that, nevertheless, through the advice of his grand visier, he was inclinable to wait yet a longer time for his compliance; he said, Madam, I know he will hearken more to you than me, therefore, I desire you would take your time to speak to him seriously of the matter, and to let him know, that, if he persists much longer in his obstinacy, he will oblige me to have recourse to extremities that may not be pleasing to him, and which may give him cause to repent of having disobeyed me.

Fatima, for so was the lady called, acquainted the prince the first time she saw him, that she had been informed of his second refusal to be married, and how much chagrin he had occasioned his father on that account. Madam, says the prince, I beseech you not to renew my grief upon that head, for if you do, I have reason to fear, in the disquiet I am under, that something may escape me which may not altogether correspond with the respect I owe you. Fatima knew by this answer, that it was not a proper time to speak to him, and, therefore, deferred what she had to say to another opportunity.

Some considerable while after, Fatima thought she had met with a more favourable occasion, which gave her hopes of being heard upon that subject; she therefore accosted him with all the eagerness imaginable; Son, said she, I beg of you, if it be not very irksome to you, to tell me what reason you have for your so great aversion to marriage? If you have no other than the badness and wickedness of some women, there can be nothing less reasonable and more weak: I will not undertake the defence of those that are bad, there are a great number of them undoubtedly; but it will be the greatest injustice imaginable to condemn all the sex for their sakes: Alas! son, you have met a great many bad women in your books, who have occasioned great disorders, and I will not excuse them; but you do not consider how many monarchs, sultans, and other princes, there have been in the world, whose tyrannies, barbarities, and cruelties, astonished those that read of them, and which I have done myself. Now, for one woman that is thus wicked, you will meet with a thousand of these tyrants and barbarians; and what torment do you think must a good woman undergo, for such there are, who is matched with any of these wretches? Madam, replied Camaralzaman, I doubt not but there are a great number of wise, virtuous, good, affable, and generous women in the world; and would to God they all resembled you! But what sticks with me, is the doubtful choice a man is obliged to make, and oftentimes one has not that liberty neither. Let us suppose then, madam, continued he, that I had a mind to marry, as the sultan, my father, so earnestly desires I should; what wife, think you, would he be likely to provide for me? Probably a princess whom he would demand of some neighbouring prince, and who would think it an honour done him to send him her. Fair or ugly, good or ill-humoured, she must go down; nay, suppose no other princess excelled her in beauty, yet who can be certain that her temper would be of equal goodness; that she would be affable, complaisant, entertaining, obliging, and the like; That her discourse would generally run on solid matters, and not on trifles, such as dress, adjustments, ornaments, and the like fooleries, which would disgust any man of sense? In a word, that she would not be haughty, proud, arrogant, impertinent, scornful, and waste a man's estate in frivolous expences, such as gaudy cloaths, unnecessary jewels, toys, and the like long train of magnificent follies? Thus you see, madam, continued he, how many reasons a man may have to be disgusted at marriage: Well, but to go farther; let this princess be never so perfect, accomplished, and irreproachable with any crimes, I have yet a great many more reasons not to desist from my sentiment, or depart from my resolution. What, son, replied Fatima, have you then more reasons after those you have already brought? I do not doubt but that I shall find wherewithal to answer them, and stop your mouth in a word. Very well, madam, replied the prince, and perhaps I may find wherewithal to reply to your answer. I mean, son, said Fatima, that it is easy for a prince, who has had the misfortune to marry such a wife as you describe, to get rid of her, and take such care that she may not prejudice his estate. Ah! but, madam, replied the prince, you do not consider what a mortification it would be to a person of so great quality, to be obliged to come to an extremity of that nature. Would it not have been better, think you, and much more for his honour and quiet, that he had never run such a risk?

But, son, said Fatima once more, after the manner you understand things, I apprehend you have a mind to be the last king of your race, who have nevertheless reigned so long and gloriously in the Isles of the Children of Khaledan. Madam, replied the prince, for my part, I do not desire to survive the king, my father; and if I should die before him, it would be no great matter of wonder, since so many children have died before their parents: But as for my leaving no successor, I am of opinion it is much better to be the last of one's race, than father to a bad prince, or husband to a bad wife.

From that time Fatima had frequent conferences with her son, the prince, on the same subject; and she omitted no opportunity or argument to endeavour rooting out his aversion to the fair sex; but he eluded all her reasonings by such as she could not well answer, and so continued in the same mind.

The year ran out, and, to the great regret of the sultan, prince Camaralzaman gave not the least proof of having changed his sentiments. So one day, when there was a great council held, the prime visier, the other visiers, the principal officers of the crown, and the generals of the army, being present, the sultan began to speak thus to the prince: Son, it is now a long while since I have earnestly desired to see you married, and I imagined you would have had more complaisance for a father, who required nothing unreasonable of you, than to oppose him so long: But after so great resistance on your part, which has almost worn out my patience, I have thought fit to propose the same thing once more to you in the presence of my council. Now, I would have you to consider, that the favour I desire, is not only to oblige me, but to comply with the earnest request of the estates of my dominions, who, for the common good of us all, in conjunction with me, require it of you: Declare then, before these lords present, whether you will marry or not; that according to your answer I may proceed, and take those measures which I ought. The prince answered with so little temper, or rather with so much heat, that the sultan, enraged to see himself affronted in full council, cried out, How, unnatural son! have you the insolence to talk thus to your father? Ho! guards, take him away. At which words, he was seized by the eunuchs, and carried to an old tower that had nobody in it for a long while, where he was shut up, with only a bed, a few moveables, some books, and one slave only to attend him.

Camaralzaman, thus deprived of liberty, was nevertheless pleased he had the freedom to converse with books, and that made him look on this confinement with some indifference. In the evening, he bathed and said his prayers; and after having read some chapters in the Alcoran, with the same tranquillity of mind as if he had been in the sultan's palace, he undressed himself and went to bed, leaving his lamp burning by him all the while he slept.

In this tower was a well, which served for a retreat to a certain fairy named Maimoune, daughter of Damriel, king or head of a legion of genies. It was about midnight when this Maimoune came forth silently, to wander about the world after her wonted custom: She was surprised to see a light in prince Camaralzaman's chamber. She entered there, and, without stopping at the slave who lay at the door, approached the bed, whose magnificence, though very great, she did not so much wonder at, as that there should be a man in it.

Prince Camaralzaman had but half covered his face with the bed-cloaths, by which Maimoune could perceive he was the finest young man she had seen in all her rambles through the world. What beauty, or rather what prodigy of beauty, said she within herself, will this youth appear, when his so well-formed eye-lids shall be open? What crime can he have committed to deserve being treated thus rigorously? She could not forbear admiring the prince, till, at length, having kissed him gently on both cheeks, and in the middle of the fore-head, without waking him, she laid the bed-cloaths in the order they were in before, and took her flight into the air. As she mounted to the middle region, she heard a great clapping of wings, which made her fly towards that side; and when she approached, she saw the genie that made the noise, but it was one of those that are rebellious to God. As for Maimoune, she belonged to that class whom the great Solomon forced to conform.

This genie, whose name was Danhasch, and son of Schamhourasch, knew Maimoune, but did not dare to take notice of her, in that he was sensible how much power she had over him, by her submission to the Almighty. He would fain have avoided her, but she was so near him, he must either fight or yield.

Brave Maimoune, said Danhasch, in the tone of a supplicant, swear to me in the name of the great power, that you will not hurt me, and I swear also, on my part, not to do you any harm.

Cursed genie, replied Maimoune, what hurt canst thou do me? I fear thee not; but, as thou hast desired that favour of me, I will swear not to do thee any harm. Tell me, then, wandering spirit, whence thou comest, what thou hast seen, and what mischief thou hast done this night? Fair lady, answered Danhasch, you meet me in a good time to hear something that is very wonderful.

I am come from the utmost limits of China, which look upon the last islands of this hemisphere.—But, charming Maimoune, said Danhasch, who trembled at the sight of this fairy, insomuch that he could hardly speak, promise me at least you will forgive me, and let me go on in my way after I have satisfied your demands. Go on, go on, cursed spirit, replied Maimoune, go on and fear nothing. Dost thou think I am as perfidious an elf as thyself, and that I am capable of breaking the serious oath I have made? No, you may depend on my promise, but be sure you tell nothing but what is true, or I shall clip your wings, and treat you as you deserve.

Danhasch, a little heartened at the words of Maimoune, said, My dear lady, I will tell you nothing but what is exceeding true, if you will but have the goodness to hear me. You must know then, the country of China, from whence I am come, is one of the largest and most powerful kingdoms of the earth, on which depend the utmost islands of this hemisphere, as I have already told you. The king of this country is at present Gaiour, who has a daughter the finest woman that ever the sun saw. Neither you nor I, nor your class nor mine, nor all mankind together, have expressions lively enough to give a sufficient description of this bright lady. Her hair is brown, and of so great a length, that it reaches far below her feet. Her forehead is as smooth as the best polished mirror, and of admirable symmetry. Her eyes are black, sparkling, and full of fire. Her nose is neither too long nor too short; and her mouth small and vermillion. Her teeth are like two rows of pearls, and surpass the finest of that sort for whiteness. When she moves her tongue, she forms a sweet and most agreeable voice; and expresses herself in such proper terms as sufficiently vindicate the vivacity of her wit. The whitest marble or alabaster is not fairer than her neck. In a word, by this perfect sketch, you may guess there is no beauty like to exceed her in the world. Any one that did not know the king, or father of this incomparable princess, would be apt to imagine, from the great respect and kindness he shews her, that he was in love with his daughter. Never did lover do more for a mistress the most endearing, than he has been seen to do for her: In a word, never was jealousy more watchful over one than he is over her; and to the end, her retreat, which he has resolved on, may not seem irksome to her, he has built seven palaces for her, the most uncommon and magnificent that ever were known. The first palace is of rock crystal, the second of brass, the third of fine steel, the fourth of another sort of brass more valuable than the foregoing, the fifth of touchstone, the sixth of silver, and the seventh of massy gold. He has furnished these palaces most sumptuously, and after a most unheard-of manner, with a matter not much unlike that they are built of. He has filled the gardens with parterres of grass and flowers, intermixed with all manner of water-works, such as jets-d'eau, canals, cascades, and the like. Then you have great groves of trees, where the eye is lost in prospect, and the sun never enters. King Gaiour, in a word, has made it appear that his paternal love exceeds all those of any other kind whatsoever.

Now, upon the fame of this incomparable princess' beauty, the most powerful neighbouring kings sent their ambassadors to request her in marriage.

The king of China received them all in a most obliging manner; but, as he resolved not to marry his daughter without her consent, so, as she did not like any of them, they were forced to return as they came, after having received great honours and civilities.

Sir, said the princess to the king her father, you have a mind to marry me, and think to oblige me by it; but where shall I find such stately palaces and delicious gardens as I have with your majesty? Under your good pleasure I am unconstrained in all things, and have the same honours done me that are paid to your own person. These are advantages I cannot expect to find any where else; to whatsoever husband I should give myself, men love ever to be masters, and I do not care to be commanded.

After divers more embassies on the same occasion, there came one from the most rich and potent king that had hitherto sent. This prince the king of China recommended to his daughter as a husband, both advantageous and proper for her: Yet him she refused for the same reasons as before; and begged of her father to dispense with her on that account. He pressed her to hearken to him; but, instead of complying, she lost all the respect and duty that were due to him. Sir, said she, in a great rage, trouble me no more with any talk of marriage, unless you would have me bury this poniard into my bosom to deliver myself from your importunities. The king at this, being greatly enraged, said, in a mighty passion, Daughter, you are mad, and I must use you as such; in a word, he had her shut up in a certain apartment of one of the seven palaces, and allowed her only ten old women to wait upon her, and keep her company, the chief whereof had been her nurse. And to the end, that the kings who had sent embassies to him on this account might not think any more of her, he dispatched envoys to them severally, to let them know how averse his daughter was to marriage; and, as he did not doubt but she was really mad, he gave them in charge to make known in every court, that, if there were any physician that would undertake to come and cure her, he should, if he succeeded, have her for his pains.

Fair Maimoune, said Danhasch, all is true that I have told you; and I, for my part, have not failed to go every day regularly to contemplate this incomparable beauty, whom I should be very far from doing any harm to, notwithstanding my natural bent that way. Now I would have you go and see her, continued he; I will assure you it would be worth your while, and do not doubt but you would think yourself obliged to me for the sight, when you come to find I am no liar; I am ready to wait on you as a guide, and you may command me as soon as you please.

Instead of answering Danhasch, Maimoune burst out into a violent laughter, which lasted for some time; and Danhasch, not knowing what might be the occasion of it, was not a little astonished. When she had laughed her laugh out, she cried, Good, good, very good, you would have me then believe all you have told me: I thought you designed to entertain me with something surprising and extraordinary, and you have been talking all this while of a driveller. Ah! fye, fye, what would you say if you had seen the fine prince that I am just come from seeing, and whom I love with a passion equal to his desert? I am confident you would soon give up the bell, and not compare your's with my choice. Agreeable Maimoune, replied Danhasch, may I presume to ask you how this prince is called? Know, answered Maimoune, he has had an accident happened to him much like that of your princess. The king his father would needs have married him against his will; but, after many importunities, he frankly told the old gentleman he would have nothing to do with a wife. This occasioned him to be confined in an old tower where I make my residence, and whence I came but just now from admiring him.

I will not absolutely contradict you, my pretty lady, replied Danhasch, but you must give me leave to be of opinion, till I have seen the prince, that no mortal upon earth can come near the beauty of my princess. Hold thy tongue, cursed spirit, replied Maimoune, I tell thee once more, that can never be. I will not contend with you, said Danhasch, but the way to be convinced, is to accept of the proffer I make you to go and see my princess, and after that, I will go with you to your prince. There is no need I should take such pains, replied Maimoune, there is another way to satisfy us both; and that is, for you to bring your princess, and place her at the prince's bed-side; by this means, it will be easy for us to compare them together, and see which is the handsomest. Danhasch consented to what Maimoune had proposed, and was resolved to set out immediately for China upon that errand; but Maimoune drew him aside, and told him, she must first shew him where the place was whither he was to bring the princess. They flew together to the tower, and when Maimoune had shewn whither he was to come, she cried, Go now, fetch your princess, and do it quickly, for you shall find me here.

Danhasch left Maimoune, and flew towards China, whence he soon returned with incredible speed, bringing the fair princess along with him asleep. Maimoune received him, and introduced him into the chamber of prince Camaralzaman, where they together placed the princess by the prince's side.

When the prince and the princess were thus laid together, all the while asleep, there arose a great contest between the genie and the fairy about the preference of their beauty. They were some time admiring and comparing them, but at length Danhasch broke silence, and said to Maimoune, You see, and I have already told you, my princess was handsomer than your prince; now I hope you are convinced of it. How convinced of it, replied Maimoune, I am not convinced of it; and you must be blind if you cannot see that my prince has the better of the comparison. The princess is fair, I do not deny it; but if you compare them together without prejudice, you will quickly see the difference. Though I should compare them never so often, said Danhasch, I could never change my opinion: I saw what I see now at first sight, and time will not be able to make me see more: However, this shall not hinder my yielding to you, charming Maimoune, if you desire it. Would I have you yield to me as a favour! I scorn it, said Maimoune, I would not receive a favour at such a wicked genie's hands; I refer the matter to an arbitrator, and if you will not consent, I shall get the better by your refusal.

Danhasch, who ever had a great deal of complaisance for Maimoune, immediately gave his consent, which he had no sooner done, but Maimoune stamping with her foot, the earth opened, and out came a hideous, hump-backed, blind, and lame genie, with six horns on his head, and claws on his hands and feet: As soon as he was come out, and the earth had closed up, he perceiving Maimoune, cast himself at her feet, and then, rising up on one knee, asked what she would please to have with him? Rise, Cascheasch, said Maimoune, I caused you to come hither to determine a difference between me and that cursed Danhasch there. Look on that bed, and tell me, without partiality, which is the handsomest of those two that lie there asleep, the young man or the young lady? Cascheasch looked on the prince and princess with great attention, admiration, and surprise; and after he had considered them a good while, without being able to determine whether was the handsomer, he turned to Maimoune, and said, Madam, I must needs confess I should deceive you, and betray myself, if I pretended to say one was a whit handsomer than the other: The more I examine them, the more it seems to me each possesses, in a sovereign degree, the beauty which is betwixt them; and if one has not the least defect, how can the other have any advantage? But if either has any thing amiss, it will be better discovered when they are awake, than now when they are asleep. Let them then be awaked one after another; and that person who shall express most love for the other, by ardour, eagerness, and passion, shall be deemed to have least beauty.

This proposal of Cascheasch's pleased equally both Maimoune and Danhasch. Maimoune then changed herself into a flea, and leaped on the prince's neck, where she stung him so smartly, that he awoke, and put up his hand to the place; but Maimoune skipped away as soon as she had done, and resumed her pristine form, which, like those of the two genies, was invisible, the better to observe what he would do.

In drawing back his hand, the prince chanced to let it fall on that of the princess of China. He opened his eyes, and was exceedingly surprised to find a lady lying by him; nay, a lady of the greatest beauty. He raised his head, and leaned on his elbow, the better to consider. Her blooming youth, and incomparable beauty, fired him in a moment; of which flame he had never yet been sensible, and from which he had even hitherto guarded himself with the greatest application.

Love seized on his heart in the most lively manner, insomuch that he could not help crying out, What beauty is this? What charms? O my heart! O my soul! In saying which, he kissed her forehead, both her cheeks, and her mouth, with so little caution, that she had certainly been awaked by it, had not she slept sounder than ordinary through the enchantment of Danhasch.

How, my pretty lady, said the prince, do you not awake at these testimonies of love given you by prince Camaralzaman? whosoever you are, I would have you to know he is not unworthy of your affection. He was going to awake her at that instant, but refrained himself all of a sudden. Is not this she, said he, that the sultan my father would have had me marry? He was in the wrong not to let me see her sooner. Had he so done, I should not have offended him by my disobedience, nor would he have had any occasion to use me as he has done.

The prince began to repent sincerely of the fault he had committed, and was once more upon the point of awaking the princess of China. It may be, said he within himself, the sultan my father has a mind to surprise me, and has sent this young lady to try if I had really that aversion for marriage which I pretended. Who knows, but, having thus laid her in the way, he is hid behind the hangings, to take an opportunity to appear, and make me ashamed of my dissimulation? This second crime would be yet much greater than my first. Upon the whole matter, I will content myself with this ring, which will at any time create in me a remembrance of this dear lady.

He then gently drew off a fine ring the princess had on her finger, and immediately put on one of his own in the place. After this, he turned his back, and was not long before he fell into a profounder sleep than before, through the enchantment of the genies.

As soon as prince Camaralzaman was sound asleep, Danhasch transformed himself into a flea likewise in his turn, and went and bit the princess so rudely on the lower hip, that she forthwith awoke, started, and clapped herself upon her breech, and, opening her eyes, was not a little surprised to see a man lying by her. From surprise she proceeded to admiration, and from admiration to a real joy, which she conceived at finding him so beautiful and young.

What! cried she, is it you the king my father has designed me for a husband? I am indeed most unfortunate for not knowing it before, for then I should not have put my lord and father in a rage, nor been so long deprived of a husband whom I cannot forbear loving with all my heart. Wake then, wake, my dear love! proceeded she, for it does not sure become a man that is married to sleep so soundly the first night of his nuptials. So saying, she took prince Camaralzaman by the arm, and shook him so violently as had been enough to have awaked the profoundest sleeper, had not Maimoune at that instant increased his sleep, and augmented his enchantment. She renewed this shaking several times, and finding it did not awake him, she cried out, What is come to thee, my dear? what jealous rival, envying thy happiness and mine, has had recourse to magic, to throw thee into this profound and insurmountable drowsiness, from whence I think thou wilt never recover? Then she snatched his hand, and, kissing it eagerly, perceived he had a ring upon his finger which greatly resembled her's, and which she found to be her own. So soon as she saw she had another upon her finger instead of it, she could not comprehend how this exchange could be made; but yet she did not doubt but it was a certain token of their marriage. At length, being tired with her fruitless endeavours to awake the prince, yet well assured he could not escape her when he awoke, she said, Since I find it is not in my power to awake thee, I will not trouble myself any farther about it, but bid thee good night, and so compose myself to rest. At these words, after having given him a hearty kiss on the cheeks and lips, she turned her back, and went again to sleep.

When Maimoune saw that she could now speak without fear of awaking the princess, she cried to Danhasch, Ah, cursed genie! dost thou not now see what thy contest is to come to? Art thou not now convinced how much thy princess is inferior to my prince in charms? At this she turned to Cascheasch, and, after having thanked him for his trouble, bid him, in conjunction with Danhasch, take the princess, and convey her back again to her bed, from whence he had taken her. Danhasch and Cascheasch did as they were commanded, and Maimoune retired to her well.

Prince Camaralzaman waking next morning, looked to see if the lady was by him whom he had seen the night before; but, when he found she was gone, he cried out, I thought indeed this was a trick the king my father designed to play me. I am obliged to him for the favour, yet have fairly escaped his trap. Then he awaked the slave, who was still asleep, and bid him come and dress him. The slave brought a bason of water, and after he had washed and said his prayers, he took a book and fell a reading.

After those ordinary exercises, he called the slave, and said to him, Come hither, and look you do not tell me a lie. How came the lady hither who lay with me to-night, and who brought her?

My lord, answered the slave, with great astonishment, I know not what lady your highness speaks of. I speak, said the prince, of her that came hither and lay with me to-night, or rather, that was brought for that purpose. My lord, replied the slave, I know of no such lady; and if there were any such, how should she come in without my knowledge, since I lay at the door?

Are you in the contrivance then, villain, replied the prince? Slave, you lie, for there was a lady here. In saying these words, he gave him a box on the ear, pushed him along upon the ground, and then stamped upon him for some time, till at length, taking the well-rope, and tying it under his arms, he plunged him several times into the water. I will drown thee, wretch, cried he, if thou dost not tell me speedily who this lady was, and who brought her.

The slave, half dead, said within himself, Doubtless my lord the prince must have lost his senses through grief, and I shall not know how to escape being murdered by him if I do not tell him a lie. My lord, then cried he in an humble and suppliant tone, I beseech your highness to spare my life, and I will tell you how the matter is.

Then the prince drew the slave up, and pressed him to begin. As soon as he was out of the well, My lord, said he, trembling, your highness may perceive it is not proper for me to relate any thing to you in this condition; I beg you to give me leave to go and change my clothes, and I will satisfy you all I am able. Do it then quickly, said the prince, and be sure you conceal nothing; for if you do, you must expect the worst of usage.

The slave being at liberty, went out, and having locked the door upon the prince, ran to the palace in the pickle he was in. The king was at that time in discourse with his prime visier, to whom he had just related the agonies he had undergone that night on account of his son's disobedience.

The wise minister endeavoured to comfort his master, by telling him he did not doubt but the prince would soon be reduced to obedience. Sir, said he, your majesty need not repent of having used your son after this rate; I dare promise it will contribute towards reclaiming him. Have but patience to let him continue a while in prison, and no doubt his heat of youth will abate, and he will submit entirely to your pleasure.

The grand visier had just made an end of speaking, when the slave came in, and cast himself at king Schahzaman's feet. My lord, said he, I am very sorry to be the messenger of ill news to your majesty, which I know must create you fresh affliction. My lord, the prince is distracted; he fancies a fine lady has lain with him all night, and has used me thus ill for questioning it. Then he proceeded to tell all the particulars of what prince Camaralzaman had said to him.

The king, who did not expect to hear any thing of this kind, said to the prime minister, Now you see how much you are mistaken in the remedy of a prison. This is very different from what hopes you gave me just now: run immediately and see what is the matter, and come and give me a speedy account.

The grand visier obeyed; and, coming into the prince's chamber, he found him sitting on his bed in good temper, and with a book in his hand, which he was reading.

After mutual salutations, the visier sat down by him, and said, My lord, I would willingly have a slave of yours punished, who has come to frighten the king your father with news that has put him under great disturbance.

What news is that, replied the prince, that could give my father so great uneasiness? I have much greater cause to complain of that slave.

My lord, answered the visier, God forbid that the news should be true which he has told your father concerning you, and which indeed I myself find to be false, by the good temper I observe you in, and which I pray God to continue. It may be, replied the prince, he did not make himself well understood; but since you are come, who ought to know something of the matter, give me leave to ask you, who was that lady that lay with me last night?

The grand visier was almost struck dumb at this demand: however, he recovered himself, and said, My lord, be not surprised at the confusion I was under upon your question. Is it possible, think you, my lord, any lady or other person in the world should penetrate by night into this place, without entering at the door, and walking over the belly of your slave? I beseech you, my lord, recollect yourself, and you will find this is only a dream which has made this impression on you.

I give no ear to what you say, said the prince, in an angry and high tone; I must know of you absolutely what is become of this lady; and if you scruple to obey me, I am in a place where I shall soon be able to force you to tell me.

At these stern words the grand visier began to be under greater confusion than before, and was thinking how to get away the best he could. He endeavoured to pacify the prince by good words, and begged of him, in the most humble manner, to tell him if he had seen this lady?

Yes, yes, answered the prince, I have seen her, and am very well satisfied you sent her to tempt me. She played the part you had given her admirably well, for I could not get a word out of her. She pretended to be asleep; but I was no sooner got into a slumber than she rose and left me. You know all this as well as I; for I do not doubt but she has been to make her report of her dexterity.

My lord, replied the visier, I swear to your highness, nothing of this has been acted which you seem to reproach me with; and I vow, by the head of our great prophet, neither your father, nor I, have sent this lady you speak of, if I may believe my royal master's protestations; and sure I am, I can answer for myself: I am confident, we never had either of us any such thought; permit me, therefore, to remember your highness once more this must needs be a dream.

What! do you come to affront and contradict me, said the prince, in a great rage, and to tell me to my face that what I have told you is a dream? You are an unbelieving varlet, cried he, and at the same time took him by the beard, and loaded him with so many thumps, that he was hardly able to stand under them.

The poor grand visier endured patiently all the brunt of his lord's indignation, and could not help saying within himself, Now am I even in as bad a condition as the slave, and shall think myself happy, if I can, like him, escape from any farther danger. In the midst of the blows that were given him, he cried out but for a moment's audience, which the prince, after he had near tired himself with banging him, consented to give him.

I own, my lord, said the grand visier, dissembling, there is something in what your highness suspects; but you cannot be ignorant under what necessity a minister is to obey his royal master's orders: yet, if your highness will but be pleased to set me at liberty, I will go and tell him any thing on your part that you shall think fit to command me. Go then, said the prince, and tell him from me, if he pleases, I will marry the lady he sent me, or rather, that was brought me last night. Do this quickly, and bring me a speedy answer. The grand visier made a profound reverence, and went away, not thinking himself altogether safe till he had got out of the tower, and shut the door upon the prince.

He came and presented himself before sultan Schahzaman with a countenance that sufficiently shewed he had been ill used. Well, said the king, in what condition did you find my son? Sir, answered the visier, what the slave reported to your majesty is but too true. He then began to relate what interview he had had with Camaralzaman, how he was in a passion upon his endeavouring to persuade him it was impossible any lady should get in to him, how he had used him very scurvily, and by what means he had made his escape.

Schahzaman was so much the more concerned, as he loved the prince with an exceeding tenderness, resolved to find out the truth of this matter, and therefore proposed to go and see his son in the tower himself, accompanied with the grand visier.

Prince Camaralzaman received the king, his father, in the tower, with great respect. The king sat down, and made his son, the prince, sit down by him, putting several questions to him, which he answered with a great deal of good sense. As they talked, the king every now and then looked on the grand visier, being as much as to say, he did not find his son had lost his wits, but rather thought he had lost his.

The king at length spoke of the lady to his son. Son, said he, I desire you to tell me what lady that was that lay with you the other night, as I have been told.

Sir, answered Camaralzaman, I beg of your majesty not to give me any more disturbance on that head, but rather to oblige me so far as to let me have her in marriage. Whatever aversion I may formerly have discovered for women, this young lady has charmed me to that degree that I cannot help betraying my weakness. I am ready to receive her at your majesty's hands, with all the acknowledgments imaginable.

King Schahzaman was surprised at this answer of the prince's, so remote, as he thought, from the good sense he had found in him before; therefore, said he to him, Son, you put me under the greatest consternation imaginable, by what you now say to me: I swear to you by my crown, that is to devolve upon you after me, I know not one word of what you mention about the lady; and if there has any such come to you, it was altogether without my knowledge or privity. But how could she get into this tower without my consent? For whatever my grand visier told you, it was only to appease you that he said it: It must, therefore, be a pure dream; and I beg of you not to believe any thing to the contrary.

Sir, replied the prince, I should be for ever unworthy of the good will of your majesty, if I did not give entire credit to what you are pleased to say. But I humbly beseech you, at the same time, to give ear to what I shall say to you, and then to judge whether what I have the honour to tell you be a dream or not.

Then prince Camaralzaman related to the king, his father, after what manner he had been awaked, exaggerating the beauty and charms of the lady he found by his side, the love he had for her at first sight, and the pains he took to awake her, without effect. He did not conceal what had obliged him to awake and fall asleep again, after he made the exchange of his ring with that of the lady: shewing the king the ring, he added, Sir, your majesty must needs know my ring very well, and you see I have it not on my finger, but another of a woman's instead of it. From this proof, therefore, I hope you will be pleased to be convinced that I have not lost my senses, as you had been almost made to believe I had.

King Schahzaman was so perfectly convinced of the truth his son had been telling him, that he had not a word to say, remaining astonished for some time, and not being able to utter a syllable.

The prince took advantage of this opportunity, and said farther, May it please your majesty, the passion I have conceived for this charming lady, whose precious image I bear continually in my mind, is so very great, I cannot live unless your majesty procures me the happiness of enjoying her, which I know you can well do, as not being ignorant who she is.

Son, replied the king, after what I have just heard, and what I see by the ring on your finger, I cannot doubt but your passion is real for this lady; and would to God I knew who she was, and I would make you happy from this moment. But what means have I to come at the knowledge of her? Where shall I find her, and how seek for her? How could she get in here, and by what conveyance, without my consent? Why did she come to sleep, only to inflame you with her beauty, and then leave you while you were in a slumber? These things, I must confess, are past my finding out: and if Heaven is not so favourable to give some light into them, we, I fear, must both go down to the grave together. Come then, my son, continued he, let us go and afflict ourselves in conjunction; you, for the hopes you have lost, and I, for seeing you grieve, and not being in a capacity to remedy your affliction.

King Schahzaman then led his son out of the tower, and conveyed him to the palace, where he was no sooner arrived, but he fell sick, and took to his bed; which made the king shut himself up with him, and grieve so bitterly, that he was not in a condition to take any cognizance of the affairs of his kingdom.

The prime minister, who was the only person had any admittance to him, came one day and told him, the whole court, and even the people, began to murmur at their not seeing him, and that he did not administer justice every day, as he was wont to do before this accident happened; which, he said, he knew not what disorders it might occasion. I humbly beg your majesty, therefore, to take some notice of what I humbly represent to you. I am sensible your majesty's company is a great comfort to the prince in his condition, and that his is no less assuaging to your grief; but then you must not run the risk of letting all be lost. I should think it were proper to be proposed to your majesty, that you would be pleased to suffer yourself to be transported to a castle you have in a little island over-against the port, where you may give audience to your subjects twice a-week; and where, during that function, the prince will be so agreeably amused with the beauty, prospect, and good air of the place, that he will be likely to bear your absence with less concern.

King Schahzaman approved this proposal; and after the castle, where he had now resided for some time, had been new furnished, he caused himself to be transported thither with the prince; where, excepting the times that he gave audience as aforesaid, he passed all his hours on his son's pillow, sometimes endeavouring to comfort him, but oftener afflicting himself with him.

Whilst matters passed thus in the capital of king Schahzaman, the two genies, Danhasch and Cascheasch, had carried the princess of China back to the palace where the king, her father, had shut her up, and laid her in her bed as before.

When she awaked next morning, and found, by looking to the right and the left, that prince Camaralzaman was not by her, she cried out with such a voice to her old woman as soon made them come to see what she wanted. Her nurse, who presented herself first, desired to be informed what her highness would please to have, and what had happened to her, that occasioned her to call out so earnestly.

Tell me, said the princess, what is become of the young man that has lain with me to-night, and whom I love with all my soul? Madam, replied the nurse, we know of no such person, and cannot pretend to understand your highness, unless you will please to explain yourself.

How do you mean? Explain myself! quoth the princess. Why, I had a lovely and most amiable young man that slept with me last night, whom, though I caressed never so much, I could not awake; I only ask you where he is?

Madam, answered the nurse, is it to jest and impose upon us, that your highness asks us these questions? I beseech your highness you would please to rise, and you shall be satisfied in all things that we are capable of satisfying you in. I am in earnest then, said the princess, and I must know where this young man is. Madam, insisted the nurse, you were alone when you went to bed last night; and how any man could come to you without our knowledge I cannot imagine, for we all lay about the door of the chamber, which was locked, and I had the key in my pocket.

At this, the princess lost all patience, and catching her nurse by the hair of the head, and giving her two or three sound cuffs, she cried, You shall tell me where this young man is, old sorceress, or I will beat your brains out.

The nurse struggled all she could to get from her, and at last she succeeded; when she went immediately with tears in her eyes, and her face all bloody, to complain to the queen her mother, who was not a little surprised to see the old woman in this condition.

Madam, began the nurse, you see what condition the princess has put me in; she had certainly murdered me if I had not had the good fortune to escape out of her hands. But for what, good nurse? replied the queen. What occasion did you give my daughter to use you ill? I gave her none, madam, answered the nurse; and so began to tell what had been the cause of all that passion and rage in the princess. The queen was mightily surprised to hear it, and could not guess how she came to be so infatuated as to take that for a reality which could be no other than a dream. Your majesty must conclude from all this, madam, continued the nurse, that my mistress the princess is out of her senses. I would beseech your majesty therefore to go and see her, and, you will find what I say to be but too true. The great love the queen bore the princess, soon made her comply with the nurse's proposal; so together they went to the princess's palace that very moment.

The queen of China sat down by her daughter's bed-side immediately upon her arrival in her apartment, and, after she had informed herself about her health, began to ask her what had made her so angry with her nurse, as to treat her after the manner she had done, which never great princesses had condescended to do before?

Madam, replied the princess, I plainly perceive your majesty is come to mock me, but I declare I will never let you rest until you consent I shall marry the young man that lay with me last night. You must needs know where he is; and therefore I beg of your majesty you would let him come to me again.

Daughter, answered the queen, you surprise me: I know nothing of what you talk of. Then the princess lost all manner of respect for the queen, and replied in a great passion, The king my father and you have all along persecuted me about marrying, when I had no mind to it, and now I have a mind, you would fain oppose me; but I must tell you, madam, I will have this young man I spoke of for a husband, or I will kill myself.

Here the queen endeavoured to calm the princess by soft words: Daughter, said she, you know well you are alone in this apartment, how then could any man come to you? This must be mere fancy, or a dream; for— Here the princess interrupted her, and was so far from hearkening to what she said, that she flew out into such extravagancies as obliged the queen to leave her, and retire in great affliction to inform her lord in what condition their daughter was.

The king hearing it, had a mind likewise to be satisfied in person; and, therefore, coming to his daughter's apartment, demanded of her, if what he had just heard was true? Sir, replied the princess, let us talk no more of that; I only beseech your majesty to grant me the favour that I may marry the young cavalier I lay with last night.

What! said the king, has any one lain with you last night? How, sir, replied the princess, without giving the king leave to go on, Do you ask me if any one lay with me last night? Your majesty knows that but too well. He was the finest and best made cavalier the sun ever saw. I desire him of you for my husband by all means, sir, and I beg you would not refuse me. But that your majesty may no longer doubt whether I have seen this cavalier, whether he has lain with me, whether I have caressed him, or whether I did not my utmost to awake him without succeeding, see, if you please, this ring. She then reached forth her hand, and shewed the king a man's ring on her finger. The king did not know what to make of all this; but as he had confined her for mad, so now he began to think her more mad than ever; therefore, without saying any thing more to her, for fear she might do violence on herself, or somebody else, he had her chained, and shut up more close than ever, allowing her only the nurse to wait on her, with a good guard at the door.

The king, exceedingly concerned at this indisposition of his daughter, sought all possible means to get her cured. He assembled his council, and, after having acquainted them what a condition she was in, he proffered any of them that would undertake her cure, the succession to his kingdom after his death, if they succeeded in their attempt.

The desire of enjoying a young princess, and the hopes of governing one day so powerful a kingdom as that of China, had a strong effect on an old emir, already advanced in age, and who was then present in council. As he was well skilled in magic, he offered the king to cure his daughter, and flattered himself with success. Very well, said the king; but I forgot to tell you one thing, and that is, that if you do not succeed, you shall lose your head. It would not be reasonable you should have so great a reward, and yet run no risk on your part: and what I say to you, continued the king, I say to all others that shall come after you, to let them consider beforehand what they undertake.

The emir however accepted the condition, and the king led him where the princess was. She covered her face as soon as she saw them come in, and cried out, Your majesty surprises me, in bringing a man along with you I do not know, and by whom my religion forbids me to let myself be seen. Daughter, replied the king, you need not be scandalized; it is only one of my emirs that is come to demand you of me in marriage. It is not, I perceive, he that you have already given me, replied the princess, and your majesty may rest assured I will never marry any other.

Now the emir expected the princess would have said or done some extravagant thing, and was not a little disappointed when he heard her talk so calmly and rationally; for he then knew her disease was nothing but a violent love-passion, which he was by no means able to cure. He therefore threw himself at his majesty's feet, and said, After what I have heard and observed, sir, it will be to no purpose for me to think of curing the princess, since I have no remedies proper for her malady; for which reason I humbly submit my life to your majesty's pleasure. The king, enraged at his incapacity, and the trouble he had given him, caused him immediately to be beheaded.

Some few days after, his majesty, unwilling to have it said that he had neglected his daughter's cure, put forth a proclamation in his capital city, importing, that if there were any physician, astrologer, or magician, who would undertake to restore the princess to her senses, he need only come and he should be employed, provided he would be willing to lose his head if he miscarried. He had the same thing published in the other principal cities and towns of his dominions, as likewise those of the neighbouring states.

The first that presented himself was both an astrologer and magician, whom the king caused to be conducted to the princess's prison by an eunuch. The astrologer, upon seeing his patient, drew forth, out of a bag he carried under his arm, an astrolabe, a small sphere, a chafing-dish, several sorts of drugs proper for fumigations, a brass pot, with many other things, and desired he might have a fire lighted.

The princess demanded what all these preparations were for? Madam, answered the eunuch, they are to exorcise the evil spirit that possesses you, and afterwards to shut him up in this pot, and throw him into the sea.

Foolish astrologer, replied the princess, I have no occasion for any of your preparations, but am in my perfect senses, and it is you alone are mad. If your art can bring him I love to me, I shall be obliged to you; otherwise you may go about your business, for I have nothing to do with you. Madam, said the astrologer, if your case be so, I shall desist from all my endeavours, believing the king your father can only remedy your disaster in this particular; so, putting up his trinkets again, he marched away, very much concerned that he had so easily undertaken to cure an imaginary sick person.

Coming to give an account to the king of what he had done, he would not suffer the eunuch to speak for him, but began thus himself: According to what your majesty published in your proclamation, and what you were pleased to confirm to me yourself, I thought the princess was distracted, and therefore had provided all I believed necessary to restore her to her senses, pursuant to the nostrums I have; but, to my great amazement, when I came to behold her, I found she had no other disease but that of love, over which the utmost extremity of my art has no power. Your majesty then may be pleased to consider that you alone are the physician can cure her, by giving her the person in marriage whom she desires. The king, upon hearing this, was very much enraged at the astrologer, and had his head cut off upon the spot.

Now, not to fatigue your majesty with long repetitions, proceeded Scheherazade to the sultan, I will acquaint you in a few words, that so many astrologers, physicians, magicians, and the like, came upon this account, that they in all amounted to about fifty, who nevertheless all underwent the same fate; and their heads were set upon poles on every gate of the city.

The princess of China's nurse, proceeded the sultaness, had a son, whose name was Marzavan, and who had been foster-brother to the princess. Their friendship was so great during their childhood, that they called each other, brother and sister, which even continued some time after their separation.

This Marzavan, among other studies, had from his youth been much addicted to judicial astrology, geomancy, and the like secret arts, wherein he became exceeding skilful. Not content with what he had learned from masters, he travelled, and there was hardly any person of note in any science but he knew him, so great was his thirst after knowledge.

After several years absence in foreign parts, on this account, he returned to the capital city of his native country, China, where, seeing so many heads on the gate by which he entered, he was exceedingly surprised; and coming to his lodging, demanded for what reason they had been placed there; but more especially he informed himself of the condition of the princess, his foster-sister, whom he had not forgot. As he could not be made acquainted with the one, without having an account of the other, he, for the present, satisfied himself with what he heard, until such time as he could learn more from his mother, the princess's nurse.

Although the nurse, mother to Marzavan, was very much employed about the princess, yet she no sooner heard her dear son was returned, but she found time to come and embrace, and stay with him a little. Having told him, with tears in her eyes, what a sad condition the princess was in, and for what reason the king her father had confined her, he desired to know of his mother, if she could not procure him the sight of her royal mistress without the king's knowing any thing of it. After some pause, she told him she could say nothing to the matter for the present; but if he would meet her next day at the same hour, she would give him her answer.

Now the nurse knowing none could approach the princess but herself without leave of the eunuch, who commanded the guard at the gate, she addressed herself to him, who she believed was ignorant of what had formerly passed at the court of China: You know, said she, I have brought up and suckled the princess, and may likewise have heard, that I had a daughter whom I brought up along with her. Now this daughter has been since married, yet the princess still does her the honour to remember her, and would fain see her, but she would do it without any body's perceiving her coming in or out.

The nurse would have gone on; but the eunuch cried, Say no more, it is sufficient, I will do any thing to oblige the princess; do you go and fetch your daughter, or send for her about midnight, and the gate shall be open to you.

As soon as night came, the nurse went to look for her son Marzavan, and having found him, dressed him so artificially in women's cloaths that nobody could know he was a man. She carried him along with her; and the eunuch verily believing it was a woman, admitted them without any more ado.

The nurse, before she thought fit to present Marzavan, went to the princess, and said, Madam, this is not a woman I have brought you, it is my son Marzavan, newly arrived from his travels, who having a great desire to kiss your hand, I hope your highness will admit him to that honour.

What! my brother Marzavan, said the princess, with a great deal of joy; come hither, my dear, cried she, and take off that veil; for it is not unreasonable sure, that a brother and a sister should see each other bare-faced.

Marzavan saluted her with profound respect, when she, without giving him leave to speak, cried out, I am rejoiced to see you returned in good health, after so many years absence, and without sending the least account all the while of your welfare to your good mother.

Madam, replied Marzavan, I am infinitely obliged to your highness for your goodness in rejoicing at my health; I also no sooner landed in my native country but I inquired after yours, and heard what to my great affliction I am now witness of; nevertheless, I cannot but rejoice that I am come seasonably enough to bring your highness that remedy for your cure which so many others have failed of; and though I should reap no other fruit of my long voyage, yet should I think myself considerably recompensed for my great charge and hazard by that one happiness.

Speaking these words, Marzavan drew forth a book, and other things out of his pocket, which he judged necessary to be used according to the relation he had had from his mother, of the princess's distemper. The princess seeing him make all these preparations, cried out, What! brother, are you then one of those that believe me mad? Undeceive yourself, and hearken to what I shall say to you.

The princess then began to relate to Marzavan all the particulars of her story, without omitting the least circumstance, even to the ring which was exchanged for her's, and which she shewed him. I have not concealed the least matter from you, quoth she, yet it is true there is something that I cannot comprehend, which has given occasion for some persons to think me mad; but as for the rest, I assure you it is literally as I tell you.

After the princess had done speaking, Marzavan, filled with wonder and astonishment, continued for some time with his eyes fixed on the ground without speaking a word; but at length he found his tongue, and having lifted up his head, said, If it be so as your highness says, and which I do not in the least doubt, I question not to procure you that satisfaction you desire; but I must first entreat your highness to arm yourself with patience, till such time as I shall return; for I am resolved to set out once more in quest of this person, and at my coming back, you may expect to have him you love not far from you. So saying, Marzavan took leave of the princess, and set out next morning on his intended voyage.

He travelled from city to city, from province to province, and from island to island; and in every place he passed through he could hear of nothing but the princess Badoura, (so was the princess of China's name,) and her history.

About four months after, our traveller arrived at Torf, a sea-port town, both great and populous, where he no more heard of the princess Badoura, but all the talk was of prince Camaralzaman, who was sick, and whose history was very like that of the princess. Marzavan was extremely glad to hear this, and informed himself of the place where the prince was to be found, to which one might go either by sea and land, or by sea only, which was the shortest way.

Marzavan chose the latter; so embarking on board a merchant ship, he arrived safe in sight of king Schahzaman's capital; but entering the port, his ship happened to strike against a rock, whereby being foundered, it sunk downright in sight of prince Camaralzaman's castle, where were at that time the king and his grand vizier.

Marzavan could swim very well, therefore he immediately cast himself into the sea upon the ship's sinking, and got safe on shore under the castle, where he was soon relieved by the grand visier's order. After he had changed his cloaths, and been well treated, he was introduced to the grand visier, who had sent for him.

Now Marzavan being a young man of good address, and a good air, this minister was very civil to him, especially when he heard him give such just and pertinent answers to what was asked of him. He also perceived he was learned; therefore said to him, For what I can understand, you have travelled a great way, and must needs have acquired much knowledge; but would to God you had learned any secret for curing a certain malady which has greatly afflicted this court for a long while.

Marzavan replied, If he knew what malady that was, he might perhaps find a remedy for it.

Then the grand visier related to him the whole story of prince Camaralzaman, taking it from its origin, and concealing nothing of his desired birth, his education, the inclination the king his father had to see him early married, his aversion to marriage, his disobeying his father in full council, his imprisonment, his pretended extravagancies in prison, which he said were afterwards changed into a violent passion for a certain unknown lady, who, he pretended, had exchanged a ring with him, though for his part he verily believed there was no such person in the world.

Marzavan gave great attention to all the grand visier said, and was infinitely rejoiced to find, that, by means of his shipwreck, he had fortunately lighted on the person he was looking after. He saw no reason to doubt but prince Camaralzaman was the man the princess of China was in love with; therefore, without discovering any thing farther to the visier, he desired to see him, whereby he said he might be better able to judge of his distemper. Follow me then, said the grand visier, and you will find the king with him, who has already desired I should introduce you to him.

The first thing that startled Marzavan at his entrance to the prince's chamber, was to find him upon his bed languishing, and with his eyes shut. Although he saw him in that condition, and although the king his father was sitting by him, he could not help crying out, Heaven! was there ever a greater resemblance than this! He meant in their faces; for it seems the princess and prince were much alike.

These words of Marzavan excited the prince's curiosity so far that he vouchsafed to open his eyes and look upon him. Marzavan who had a great deal of wit, laid hold of that opportunity, and made his compliment in verse extempore, which nevertheless he did in such a disguised manner, that neither the king nor grand visier understood any thing of the matter. However, he represented so nicely what had happened to the princess of China, that the prince had no room to doubt but he knew her, and could give him tidings of her. This made him so joyful, that the effects of it plentifully shewed themselves in his eyes and looks.

After Marzavan had finished his compliment in verse, which surprised prince Camaralzaman so agreeably, his highness took the liberty to make a sign to the king his father to go from the place where he was, and let Marzavan sit by him.

The king, overjoyed at this alteration, which gave him hopes of his son's speedy recovery, quitted his place, and taking Marzavan by the hand, led him to it, obliging him to sit in it. Then his majesty demanded of him who he was, and whence he came? And upon Marzavan's answering he was a subject of China, and came from that kingdom, the king cried out, Heaven grant you may be able to withdraw my son from this profound melancholy, and I shall have eternal obligations to you, which I will do my utmost to gratify beyond what was ever done. Having said thus, he left the prince to entertain himself with the stranger, whilst he went and rejoiced with the grand visier upon this happy rencounter.

Marzavan leaning down to the prince, spoke low in his ear thus: My lord, said he, it is high time your highness should cease to grieve. The lady on whose account you lament so bitterly, I know; it is the princess Badoura, daughter of Gaiour, king of China: this I can assure your highness, both on account of what she has told me of her adventure, and what I have learned of yours. You may also depend upon it, that she has undergone no less on your account than you have done on hers. Here he began to relate all that he knew of the princess, from the fatal time of their interview after that extraordinary manner. He omitted not to acquaint him how those had fared who had failed in their pretences to cure the princess of her indisposition.—But your highness is the only person, added he, that can cure her effectually; and therefore it were no matter how soon you set about it. However, before you undertake so great a voyage, I would have you perfectly recovered, and then we will take such measures as are necessary.

This discourse had a marvellous effect on the prince. He found so great benefit by it, through the hopes he conceived of speedily fulfilling his desires, that he had strength sufficient to rise; and accordingly begged leave of his father to dress himself before him, with such an air as gave the old king incredible satisfaction.

King Schahzaman immediately fell embracing Marzavan, without enquiring into the means that had wrought this wonderful effect; and, soon after, went out of the prince's chamber with the grand visier, to publish this agreeable news to his people. He, on this occasion, ordered public rejoicings for several days together; and, moreover, gave great largesses to his officers, alms to the poor, and caused the prisoners to be set at liberty throughout his kingdom. Every city resounded with joy, and every corner of his dominions felt the effect of his bounty.

Prince Camaralzaman, though he had been extremely weakened by almost continual watchings and abstinence, yet, contrary to all expectation, soon recovered his impaired health. When he found himself in a condition to undertake the voyage, he took Marzavan aside, and said, Dear Marzavan, it is now time to perform the promise you have made me: I burn with impatience to see the charming princess; and if you do not speedily give me an opportunity to put an end to her torments and my own, by setting out on our journey, I shall soon relapse into my former condition, and then perhaps you may not find it so easy to cure me as you have now done. But one thing still afflicts me, continued he, and that is, the difficulty I shall meet with in getting leave of my father to go. You see he scarce ever leaves me; therefore, if you do not assist me in that particular, I am undone.

At these words the prince fell a-weeping, and would not be comforted, till Marzavan said, Let not your highness be grieved at that, for I will warrant I will get your liberty, so that he shall not stop us. My principal design in this voyage was to deliver the princess of China, my mistress, from her grief; and I should fail in my duty to her if I did not do my best endeavour to effect it. This is then the means I have contrived to obtain your liberty: you have not stirred abroad for some time; therefore let the king your father understand you have a mind to take the air, and if he pleases, to go and hunt two or three days with me. No doubt he will grant your request which when he has done, order two good horses to be got ready in a certain place, and leave the rest to me.

Next day prince Camaralzaman did as he had been advised. He acquainted the king he was desirous to take the air, and if he pleased, would go and hunt two or three days with Marzavan. The king gave his consent, but bid him be sure not to lie out above one night, since too much exercise might injure his health, and too long absence create his majesty some uneasiness. He then ordered him the best horses in his stable, and took particular care that nothing should be wanting for his diversion. When all was ready, his majesty embraced the prince, and having recommended to Marzavan the care of him, he left them. Prince Camaralzaman and Marzavan were soon mounted; when, to amuse the two grooms that led the fresh horses, they made as if they would hunt, and so got as far off from the city, and out of the road, as was possible. When night began to approach, they alighted at a caravansary or inn, where they supped, and slept till about midnight, when Marzavan awaked the prince, without awaking the grooms, and desired his highness to let him have his suit, and to take another for himself, which was brought in his sumpter. Thus equipped, they mounted the fresh horses, and after Marzavan had taken one of the groom's horses by the bridle, they set out at a good round pace.

At day-break they were got into the forest, where, coming to the meeting of four roads, Marzavan went aside, and desired the prince to wait for him a little. He then cut the groom's horse's throat, and, after having torn the prince's suit he had on, besmearing it with blood, he threw it into the highway.

The prince demanded his reason for what he had done? He told his highness, he was sure the king his father would no sooner come to know that he was departed without the grooms, but he would suspect something, and immediately send in quest of them: Now, said Marzavan, to the end that when they come to this place they may stop, and think you devoured by wild beasts, I have done this; so that by this means we may have leisure to continue our journey without fear of pursuit. I must needs confess, continued Marzavan, this is a violent way of proceeding, to alarm an old father with the death of his son, whom he loves so passionately; but then, on the other hand, the news of your welfare, which he may soon have, will in a great measure alleviate his grief, and make some amends for your absence. Brave Marzavan, replied the prince, I cannot sufficiently admire your conduct, and I have all the obligations in the world to you for it.

This said, the prince and Marzavan, well provided with cash for their expences, continued their journey both by land and sea, and found no other obstacle but the length of the way, which they were forced to undergo. They however arrived at length at the capital of China, where Marzavan, instead of going to his lodging, carried the prince to a public inn. They tarried there *incognito* three days to rest themselves, during which time Marzavan caused an astrologer's habit to be made for the prince. The three days being expired, they went together to the bagnio, the prince putting on his astrologer's habit; and from thence Marzavan conducted him in sight of the king of China's palace, where he left him, to go and acquaint his mother, the princess Badoura's nurse, of his arrival; to the end she might give the like information to the princess her mistress.

Prince Camaralzaman, instructed by Marzavan what he was to do, and provided with all he wanted as an astrologer, came next morning to the gate of the king's palace, and cried aloud, I am an astrologer, and am come to effect a cure on the most beautiful princess Badoura, daughter of the most high and mighty monarch, Gaiour, king of China, on the conditions proposed by his majesty, to marry her if I succeed, or else to lose my life for my fruitless and presumptuous attempt.

Over and above the guards and porters at the gate, this novelty drew together a great number of people about prince Camaralzaman. There had no physician, astrologer, nor magician, appeared for a long time on this account, deterred by the many tragical examples of ill success that appeared before their eyes: it was therefore thought, there were either no more of these professions in the world, or at least that there were no more so mad as those that had gone before them.

The prince's good mien, noble air, and blooming youth, made every body pity him that saw him. What do you mean, sir, said some that were nearest him, to expose thus your life, that promises so much, to a certain death? Cannot the heads you see on all the gates of this city deter you from such an undertaking? In the name of God, consider what you do, and abandon this rash attempt.

The prince continued firm, notwithstanding the remonstrances made to him; and, as he saw nobody come to introduce him, he repeated the same cry, with a voice that made every body tremble. They all then cried, Let him alone, he is resolved to die; God have mercy upon his soul. He then proceeded to cry out a third time in the same manner, when the grand visier came in person, and introduced him to the king of China.

As soon as the prince came into the king's presence, he bowed and kissed the floor. The king, who, of all that had hitherto exposed their lives on this occasion, had not seen one worthy to cast his eyes upon before, had now a real compassion for prince Camaralzaman, on account of the danger he was about to undergo. But as he saw him more deserving than ordinary, he did him more honour, and made him come and sit by him. Young man, said he, I can hardly believe you at this age can have acquired experience enough to enable you to cure my daughter. I will give her to you with all my heart, on that account; nay, more willingly than I should have done to others that have offered themselves before you; but then I must declare to you at the same time, with a great deal of concern, that if you do not succeed in your attempt, notwithstanding your noble appearance, and exceeding beautiful youth, you must lose your head.

Sir, replied the prince, I have infinite obligations to your majesty for the honour you design me, though a stranger; but I desire your majesty to believe I would not have come from so remote a country as I have done, and which perhaps may be unknown in your dominions, if I had not been certain of the cure I propose. What might not be said of my inconstancy of temper, if, after so great fatigues and dangers as I have undergone on this account, I should abandon the generous enterprise I had engaged in? Even your majesty would soon lose that respect you have done me the honour to shew me, if I appeared so dastardly and mean-spirited. I beseech your majesty, therefore, to let me no longer delay the experiment I am certain of, but to give me leave to display the utmost of my art, which I doubt not will be to your majesty's satisfaction, as well as my great happiness.

Then the king commanded the eunuch, who had the guard of the princess, to introduce prince Camaralzaman into her apartment: but, before he would let him go, he was so kind as to remember him once more of the hazard he underwent; yet the prince seemed resolved: so the king suffered him to follow the eunuch.

When they came to a long gallery, at the end of which was the princess's apartment, the prince, through impatience to see once more the object of his vows, who had occasioned him so much grief, got before the eunuch, walking as fast as he could walk.

The eunuch, redoubling his pace, with much ado got up with him; when, taking him by the arm, he cried, Whither away so fast, sir? you cannot get in without me; and it should seem you have a great desire for death, that can run to it so headlong. Never any of all those many astrologers and magicians I have introduced before, made such haste as yourself to a place whither I fear you will come but too soon.

Friend, replied the prince, continuing his pace, and looking earnestly on the eunuch, this was because never any of your astrologers or magicians before me were so sure of their art as I am: they were certain, indeed, they should die if they did not succeed; but they had no certainty, at the same time, of their success, as I have. On this account, they had reason to tremble at approaching the place whither I go, and where I am sure to find my happiness. He had just spoke these words as he was at the door, which the eunuch opened, and introduced him into a great hall, whence there was an entrance into the princess's chamber, divided from it only by a piece of tapestry.

Prince Camaralzaman, speaking more softly to the eunuch, asked him before he entered, whether he would chuse that he should cure the princess in his presence, or where he was, without going any farther? telling him, in the same soft tone, that nobody might hear him in the princess's chamber, he made him that frank offer, to shew him it was not presumptuous caprice, nor heat of youth, which put him upon the enterprise.

The eunuch was very much amazed to hear the prince talk to him with such assurance: he left off insulting him, and said seriously to him, It is no matter whether you do it here or there, provided the business is done: cure her how you will, you will get immortal honour by it, not only in this court, but over all the world.

The prince replied, It will be best, then, to cure her without seeing her, that you may be witness of my skill; though I cannot without impatience put off my seeing a princess of her rank, who is to be my wife; yet, out of respect to you, I will deprive myself of that pleasure for a little while. He was furnished with every thing proper for an astrologer to carry about him; and, taking pen, ink, and paper, out of his pocket, wrote this billet to the princess.

Prince Camaralzaman to the Princess of China

Adorable princess!

The love-sick prince Camaralzaman will not trouble you with the pains that he has endured ever since that fatal night in which your charms deprived him of that liberty which he resolved to preserve as long as he lived: he only tells you, that he devoted his heart to you in your charming slumbers; those slumbers that hindered him from beholding the brightness of your piercing eyes, in spite of all his endeavours to oblige you to open them. He presumes to present you with his ring, as a token of his passion; and, in exchange, would be proud to receive yours, which he encloses in this billet. If you will condescend to return it, as a reciprocal assurance of your love, he will reckon himself the happiest of all lovers: if not, the sentence of death, which your refusal brings him, will be received with the more resignation, because he dies for love of you. He waits in your antichamber for your answer.

When the prince had finished his billet, he made it up, and inclosed with it the ring in a little packet, without letting the eunuch see what he did. When he had sealed it, he gave it to him. There, friend, says he, carry it to your mistress: if it does not cure her as soon as she reads it, and sees what is inclosed in it, I give you leave to tell every body that I am the most ignorant and impudent astrologer that ever was, is, or ever will be.

The eunuch, entering the princess of China's chamber, gave her the packet he received from prince Camaralzaman. Madam, says he, the boldest astrologer that ever lived, if I am not mistaken, is arrived here, and pretends, that, on reading this letter, and seeing what is in it, you will be cured; I wish he may prove neither a liar nor impostor.

The princess Badoura took this billet, and opened it with a great deal of indifference; but when she saw the ring, she had not patience to read it through: She rose hastily, broke the chain that held her down with struggling, ran and opened the door. She knew the prince as soon as she saw him, and he knew her. They presently embraced each other with all imaginable tenderness, and without being able to say a word for excess of joy. They looked on one another, admiring how they met again after their first interview. The princess's nurse, who ran to the door with her, made them come into her chamber, where the princess Badoura gave the prince her ring, saying, Take it, I cannot fairly keep it without restoring yours, which I will never part with; neither yours nor mine can be in better hands.

The eunuch went immediately to the king to tell him what had happened; Sir, says he, all the astrologers and doctors who have hitherto pretended to cure the princess, are a company of fools, in comparison of him who came last. He made use neither of schemes nor conjuration, of perfumes, or any thing else, but cured her without seeing her. Then he told the king how he did it. The monarch was agreeably surprised at the news, and going presently to the princess's chamber, embraced her; and then the king took his hand, and joined it to the princess's. Happy stranger, says the king, I will keep my word, and give you my daughter to wife; though, by what I see in you, it is impossible for me to believe you really what you would appear, and have me to believe you to be.

Prince Camaralzaman thanked the king in the most humble expressions, that he might the better shew his gratitude. As for my person, said he, I must own I am not an astrologer, as your majesty very judiciously guessed; I only put on the habit of one, that I might succeed more easily in my ambition to be allied to the most potent monarch in the world. I was born a prince, and the son of a king and of a queen. My name is Camaralzaman; my father is Schahzaman, who reigns over the islands that are well enough known by the name of the Islands of the Children of Khaledan. He then told him the adventures of his life, and how wonderful was the rise of his love; that the princess's was altogether as marvellous; and were both confirmed by the exchange of two rings.

When the prince had done speaking, the king said to him, This history is so extraordinary, it deserves to be known to posterity; an account shall be taken of it, and the original being deposited in my royal archives, I will spread copies of it abroad, that my own kingdoms and the kingdoms around me may know it.

The marriage was solemnized the same day, and the rejoicings for it were universal all over the empire of China. Nor was Marzavan forgotten; the king gave him an honourable post in his court immediately, and a promise to advance him higher afterwards.

Prince Camaralzaman and the princess Badoura enjoyed the fullness of their wishes in the sweets of marriage; and the king kept continual feasting for several months, to show his joy on the occasion.

In the midst of these pleasures, prince Camaralzaman dreamed one night that he saw his father on his death-bed ready to give up the ghost, and heard him speak thus to his attendants: My son, whom I so tenderly loved, my son, whom I bred with so much fondness, so much care, has abandoned me, and is himself the cause of my death. He awoke and sighed; his sighs awoke the princess, who asked him the reason of them. Alas! my love, cried the prince, perhaps in the very moment that I am speaking of it, my father is no more. He then acquainted her with his melancholy dream, and why that sad thought came into his head. The princess, who studied to please him in every thing, presently contrived a way to do it, and, fearing that he would take less delight in her company if he was kept from seeing his father, went to her own father that very day, and, finding him alone, kissed his hand, and thus addressed herself to him: Sir, I have a favour to beg of your majesty, and I beseech you not to deny me; but, that you may not believe I am put upon it by the prince my husband, I assure you, before-hand, he knows nothing of my asking it of you: It is, that you will give me leave to go and see the king Schahzaman, my father-in-law.

The king replied, Daughter, though I shall be very sorry to lose your company, and part with you for so long time as a journey to a place so distant will take up, yet I cannot disapprove of your resolution; it is worthy of yourself. Go, child, I give you leave, but on condition that you stay no longer than a year in king Schahzaman's court. I hope the king will be willing to come to this agreement with me, that we, in our turns, may see, he his son and daughter-in-law; and I, my daughter and my son-in-law.

The princess communicated the king of China's consent to prince Camaralzaman, who was transported to hear it, and gave her a thousand thanks for this new token of her love.

The king of China commanded preparations to be made for the journey; and, when all things were ready, he accompanied the prince and princess several leagues in their way. When they came to part, great was the weeping on all sides; the king embraced them, and desired the prince to be kind to his daughter, and to love her always with the same passion he now loved her; so he left them to go forward in their journey, and, to divert himself, hunted all the way as he returned to his capital city.

When the prince Camaralzaman and the princess Badoura had dried up their tears, and given over mourning for their parting with the king of China, they comforted themselves with the thoughts how glad king Schahzaman would be to see them, and how they should rejoice to see the king.

They travelled about a month incessantly; and, at last, came to a large field, planted with tall trees, at convenient distances, under whose shade they went on very pleasantly. The weather being very hot, and that day hotter than ordinary, Camaralzaman thought it best to stay there during the heat, and proposed it to Badoura, who readily consented to it. They alighted on one of the most agreeable places of the grove; a tent was presently set up; the princess, rising from the shade under which she sat down, entered it, and the prince ordered his servants to pitch their tents also, while they staid there, and went himself to give them directions how to do it. The princess, being weary with the fatigues of the journey, bid her women untie her girdle, which they laid down by her; and, she falling asleep, her attendants left her by herself.

Prince Camaralzaman having seen all things in order, came to the tent where the princess was sleeping; he entered, and sat down without making any noise, intending to take a nap himself; but observing the princess's girdle lying by her, he took it up, and looked upon the rubies and diamonds one by one. In doing it, he saw a little purse hanging to it, tied fast with a ribbon; he felt it, and found there was something in it. Being desirous to know what it was, he opened the purse, and took out a cornelian,* engraven with unknown figures and characters. This cornelian, says the prince to himself, must have something extraordinary in it, or my princess would not be at the trouble to carry it with her: And indeed it was Badoura's talisman, or a scheme of her nativity, drawn from the constellations of heaven, which the queen of China had given her daughter, as a charm that would keep her from any harm as long as she had it about her.

The prince, to see what the talisman was, took it out to the light, the tent being dark; and while he was holding it up in his hand, a bird darted down from the air, and snatched it away from him.

Your majesty will easily conceive the concern and grief of prince Camaralzaman, when he saw the bird fly away with the talisman.[1] He was more troubled at it than words can express, and cursed his unseasonable curiosity, by which means he had lost a treasure that was so precious, and so valued by his dear princess.

The bird having got her prize, pitched upon the ground not far off, with the talisman in her mouth. The prince drew near it, in hopes she would drop it; but, as he approached, the bird took wing, and pitched again on the ground farther off. Camaralzaman followed her, and the bird having swallowed the talisman, took a small flight farther off still. The prince, being very dexterous at a mark, thought to kill her with a stone, and still followed her; but the farther she flew, the more eager he grew in pursuing her, keeping her always in view. Thus the bird drew him along from hill to valley, and valley to hill, all day, every step leading him out of the way from the field where he left his camp and the princess Badoura; and, instead of perching at night on a bush, where he might probably have taken her, she roosted on a high tree, safe from his pursuit. The prince, vexing himself to the heart for taking so much pains to no purpose, thought of returning to the camp; but, alas! he thought of it too late: Whither shall he go? Which way return? How will he find out the untractable way of the mountains, and the untrodden paths of the valleys? Darkness spread over the heavens, and

[1] There is an adventure like this in the romance of Peter of Provence, and the fair Maguelonna, which was taken from the Arabic.*

night, and the fatigues of his day's labour, would not suffer him to undertake so soon to return the way he came, were there any hopes of his finding it. Ah! quoth the despairing lover, if I knew which way to return, how durst I appear before my princess without her talisman! Overwhelmed with such afflicting thoughts, and tired with his pursuit of the bird, sleep came upon him, and he lay down under a tree, where he passed the night.

He awoke the next morning before the bird had left the tree, and, soon as he saw her on the wing, followed her again that whole day with no better success than he had done the last, eating nothing but herbs and fruits all the way as he went. He did the same for ten days together, pursuing the bird, and keeping her in his eye from morning till night, lying always under the tree where she roosted. On the eleventh day, the bird still flying, and Camaralzaman observing her, he came near a great city; the bird made to it, flew over the walls, and the prince saw no more of her; so he despaired of ever recovering the princess Badoura's talisman.

Camaralzaman, whose grief was beyond expression, went to the city, which was built on the sea-side, and a fine port; he walked up and down the streets without knowing where he was or where to stop; at last he came to the port, in as great uncertainty as ever what he should do. Walking along the river-side, he perceived the gate of a garden open, and an old gardener at work in it. The good man, looking up, saw he was a stranger and a mussulman; so he asked him to come in and shut the door after him.

Camaralzaman entered, and as the gardener bade him shut the door, demanded of the gardener why he was so curious? Because, replied the old man, I see you are a stranger, and a mussulman newly arrived; and this city is inhabited, for the most part, by idolaters, who have a mortal aversion to us mussulmen, and use those few of us that are here with a great deal of barbarity. I suppose you did not know this, and it is a miracle you have escaped as you have done, considering how far you have come through them. These idolaters, being apt to fall upon mussulmen that are strangers, are instructed how to deal with them.

Camaralzaman thanked the honest gardener for his advice, and the security he offered him in his house. He would have said more, but the good man interrupted him, saying, Let us leave off complimenting, you are weary, and want to refresh yourself. Come in, eat what we have, and lie down to rest, you are very welcome. He conducted him into his little hut, clean, though small, and well defended from the injuries of the weather. He ordered the best provisions he had to be brought forth, and entertained the prince so heartily, that he was charmed with it; and, at his request, told him how he came there.

When he had ended his story, without hiding any part of it from him, he asked him which was the nearest way to his father's territories; for it is in vain for me to think of finding my princess where I left her, having been wandering eleven days, as I have been, from that place. Ah! continues he, how do I know she is alive! and saying this, burst out into tears, that would have melted the most cruel of the idolaters. The gardener replied, There was no possibility of his going thither by land, the ways were so difficult, and the journey so long; besides, there was no manner of convenience for his subsisting; or, if there were, he must necessarily pass through the countries of so many barbarous nations, that he would never reach his father's. That the quickest passage for him would be to go to the isle of Ebene, whence he might easily transport himself to the Isles of the Children of Khaledan; that there was a ship which sailed from the port where he was, every year to Ebene, and he might take that opportunity of returning to these islands. The ship departed, said he, but a few days ago, and it will be almost a year before it makes the voyage again. If you will accept of my house for your habitation so long, you will be as welcome to it as to your own.

Prince Camaralzaman was glad he had met with such an asylum, in a place where he had no knowledge of any man, nor any man of him, and where nobody could think it their interest to entertain or preserve him. He accepted of the offer, and lived with the gardener until the time came that the ship was to sail to the isle of Ebene. He spent his time all day in working in the garden, and all night in thinking of his dear princess Badoura, in sighs, tears, and complaints.

We must leave him in this place a while, to return to the princess, whom we left asleep in the tent.

The princess slept a long time, and when she awoke, wondered that prince Camaralzaman was not with her. She called her women, and asked them if they knew where he was gone? They told her they saw him enter the tent, but did not see him go out again. While they were talking to her, she spied her girdle, saw it had been meddled with, and, examining, found the little purse open, and that the talisman was lost. She did not doubt but Camaralzaman had taken it to see what it was, and that he would bring it back with him. She waited for him impatiently till night, and could not imagine what made him stay away from her so long.

When it was quite dark, and she could hear nothing of him, she fell into a violent passion of grief; she cursed the talisman, and him that made it; and, had she not been restrained by her duty, would have cursed her mother who gave it her. She was the more troubled, because she could not imagine how her talisman should have caused the prince's separation from her; however, amidst all her sorrow, she restrained her judgment, and came to a courageous resolution, not common with persons of her sex.

She, and her women only, knew of the prince's being gone, for his men were then asleep, or refreshing themselves in their tents. The princess, fearing they would betray her if they had any knowledge of it, first composed her mind a little, and moderated her grief, and forbid her women to say or do any thing that might make them suspect the truth: then she undressed herself, and put on prince Camaralzaman's suit, being so like him in it, that the next day, when she came abroad, his men took her for him.

She commanded them to pack up their baggage, and march forward; and, when all things were ready, she ordered one of her women to go into her sedan,* she herself getting on horseback, and riding by her side.

They travelled several months by land and sea; the princess continuing the journey under the name of Camaralzaman. They took the island of Ebene in their way to the Isles of the Children of Khaledan: they went to the capital of the island, where a king reigned whose name was Armanos. The persons that first landed, giving out, that they brought prince Camaralzaman, who was returning from a long voyage, towards his own country, and was forced to put in there by storm: the news of his arrival was presently carried to court.

King Armanos, accompanied by most of his courtiers, went immediately to wait on the prince, and met the princess just as she was landing, and going to the lodgings that had been taken up for her. He received her as the son of a king who was his friend, with whom he always kept a fair correspondence; and carried her to the palace, where an apartment was prepared for her and all her attendants; though she fain would have excused herself, and have lodged in a private house. Besides this, he was so courteous, that doing her common honours would not content him, he entertained her three days together with extraordinary magnificence and royal festivals.

The days of feasting being over, and king Armanos understanding that the princess, whom he still took for prince Camaralzaman, talked of going aboard again to proceed on her voyage; he was so charmed with the air and qualities of such an accomplished prince, as he took her to be, that he watched his opportunity when she was alone, and spoke to her in this manner: You see, prince, that I am old, and cannot hope to live long, it is my great trouble that I have not a son, to whom I may leave my crown. Heaven has only blessed me with one daughter, who cannot desire to be more happy than a prince of your virtues can make her, whose merit is equal with your birth.—Instead of going home, stay and take her from my hand; with her I will give you my kingdom, retreat myself to a quiet life, free from the business and cares of the world, having long enough had the weight of the crown upon me; and nothing could be a greater pleasure to me, in my retirement, than to consider what a worthy successor sits on my throne and rules my happy people.

The king of the isle of Ebene's generous offer to bestow his only daughter in marriage on the Princess Badoura, who could not accept of it, because she was a woman, gave her unexpected trouble, and she could not presently think of a way to extricate herself out of it: she thought it would not become a princess of her rank to deceive the king, and to own that she was not prince Camaralzaman, but his wife, when she had assured him she was he himself; whose part she had hitherto acted so well, that her sex was not the least suspected. She was also afraid to refuse him, seeing him so much bent upon the conclusion of the marriage, that there was reason to apprehend his kindness would turn to aversion and hatred, if the honour he offered her was rejected, and he might attempt something even against her life. Besides, she was not sure of finding prince Camaralzaman in the court of king Schahzaman, his father.

These considerations, added to the prospect of obtaining a kingdom for the prince her husband, in case she found him again, made her resolve to do what king Armanos would have her, and marry his daughter: So, after having stood silent for some minutes, she, with blushes, which the king took for a sign of her modesty, answered, Sir, I am infinitely obliged to your majesty for your good opinion of me, for the honour you do me, and the great favour you offer me, which I cannot pretend to merit, and dare not refuse.

But, sir, continued she, I cannot accept of this alliance on any other condition than that your majesty will assist me with your counsels, and that I do nothing without having first your approbation.

The marriage treaty being thus concluded and agreed on, the ceremony was put off till next day. In the mean time, princess Badoura gave notice to her officers, who still took her for prince Camaralzaman, what she was about to do, that they might not be surprised at it, assuring them the princess Badoura consented to it. She talked also to her women, and charged them to keep the secret she had entrusted them with, as they valued their lives.

The king of the isle of Ebene rejoiced that he had got him a son-in-law so much to his satisfaction. The next morning he summoned his council, and acquainted them with his design of marrying his daughter to prince Camaralzaman, whom he introduced to them, made him sit down by them, taking the princess Badoura for him; told them he resigned the crown to him, and required them to obey and swear fealty to him. Having said this, he descended from his throne, and the princess Badoura, by his order, mounted it. When she was placed, the lords of the court took an oath of allegiance. As soon as the council broke up, the new king was proclaimed through the city, several days of rejoicing were appointed, and couriers dispatched over all the kingdom to see the same ceremonies observed with the same demonstrations of joy.

At night there were extraordinary feastings at the palace-royal, and the princess Haiatalnefous[1] was led to the princess Badoura, whom every body took for a man: she was dressed like a royal bride. The wedding was solemnized with the utmost splendour, and the rites being performed, they were put to bed. In the morning, the princess Badoura went to receive the compliments of the nobility in a hall of audience, where they congratulated her on her marriage and accession to the throne. In the mean while, king Armanos and his queen went to the apartment of the new queen their daughter, and asked her how she spent the night: Instead of answering them, she held down her head, and by her looks they saw plain enough that she was not contented.

King Armanos, to comfort the princess Haiatalnefous, bid her not be troubled; prince Camaralzaman might be in haste to go to his father's court, and had not stopped at the isle of Ebene had it not been in his way thither: though we have engaged him to stay by arguments, with which he ought to be well satisfied, yet it is probable he grieves to be all at once deprived of the hopes of seeing either his father or any of his family. You must wait until those first emotions of tenderness are over, and his filial love wears off by degrees; he will then carry himself towards you as a good husband ought to do.

The princess Badoura, under the name and character of prince Camaralzaman, not only received the congratulatory addresses of the countries and the nobility of the kingdom, who were in and about the city, but she reviewed the regular troops of her household, and entered on the administration of affairs as king, with so much majesty and judgment, that gained her the general applause of all who were witnesses of her conduct.

It was evening before she returned to queen Haiatalnefous's apartment, and she perceived, by the reception she gave her, that the bride was not at all pleased with the wedding-night. She endeavoured to make her easy by a long discourse, in which she employed all the wit she had (and that was as much as any woman was mistress of) to persuade her she loved her entirely: She then gave her time to go to bed, and while she was undressing herself she went to her devotions: her prayers were so long, that queen Haiatalnefous was asleep before they were ended. She then gave over praying, and lay down softly by the new queen, without waking her, and was as much

[1] This is an Arabic word, which signifies life and soul.

afflicted at her being forced to act a part which did not belong to her, as in the loss of her dear Camaralzaman, for whom she ceased not to sigh. She rose as soon as it was day, before Haiatalnefous was awake, and being dressed in her royal robes, as king, went to council.

King Armanos, as he had done the day before, came early to visit the queen, his daughter, whom he found in sighs and tears; he wanted no more to be informed of the cause of her trouble: He began to resent the contempt, as he thought, which was put upon his daughter, and could not imagine what was the reason of it. Daughter, says he, have patience for another night. I raised your husband to the throne, and can pull him down again; depend upon it, I will drive him thence with shame, unless he gives you the satisfaction that he ought to do: His usage of you has provoked me so much, I cannot tell to what my resentment may transport me; the affront is as much to me as to you.

It was late again before the princess Badoura came to queen Haiatalnefous: She talked to her as she had done the night before; and after the same manner went to her devotions, desiring the queen to go to bed. But Haiatalnefous would not be so served; she held her back, and obliged her to sit down again: What, says she, you think to deal by me this night as you have done the two last: pray tell me, what can you dislike in a princess of my youth and beauty, who not only loves, but adores you, and thinks herself the happiest of all princesses in having so amiable a prince for her husband. Any body but me would be revenged of the slight, or, rather, the unpardonable affront you have put upon me, and abandon you to your evil destiny: However, though I did not love you so well as I do, yet out of pure good nature and humanity, which makes me pity the misfortunes of persons for whom I am nowise concerned, I cannot forbear telling you, that the king, my father, is enraged against you for your carriage towards me, and on the morrow will exert his fury in a manner I tremble to think of, if you still use me as you have done hitherto. Do not therefore throw a princess into despair, who, notwithstanding all your ill usage, cannot help loving you.

This discourse embarrassed the princess Badoura the most of any thing she had met with: she did not doubt of the truth of what Haiatalnefous had said. King Armanos's coldness to her the day before had given her but too much reason to see he was highly dissatisfied with her. The only way to justify her conduct was, to communicate her sex to the princess Haiatalnefous. She had foreseen she should be under a necessity of discovering it to her; yet, now she was about to make such a declaration, she was afraid how she would take it: but considering, that if Camaralzaman was alive, he must necessarily touch at the isle of Ebene, in his way to king Schahzaman his father's kingdom; that she ought to preserve herself for his sake; and it was impossible to do it if she did not let the princess Haiatalnefous know who and what she was; she resolved to venture, and try to get off that way.

The princess Badoura stood as one that was struck dumb; and Haiatalnefous being impatient to hear what she could say, was about to speak to her again, when she stopped her by these words: Lovely and too charming princess, I own I have been in the wrong, and I condemn myself for it; but I hope you will pardon me, and keep the secret I am going to reveal to you for my justification.

She then opened her bosom, and, shewing her breasts, proceeded thus: See, princess, if a woman, and a princess like yourself, does not deserve to be forgiven: I believe you will be so good, at least, when you know my story, and the terrible affliction that forced me to act the part you see.

The princess Badoura having discovered herself entirely to the princess of the isle of Ebene, she again prayed her to keep the secret, and to make as if she was really a husband to her, till prince Camaralzaman's arrival, which she hoped would be in a little time.

Princess, replied Haiatalnefous, your fortune is indeed strange, that a marriage so happy as yours was, should be rendered unhappy by so unaccountable an accident, your love being reciprocal, and full of wonders. Pray heaven you may meet with your husband again as soon as you desire; and assure yourself, I will keep the secret until he arrives. It will be the greatest pleasure to me in the world, to be the only person in the vast kingdom of the isle of Ebene who knows what and who you are, while you go on governing the people as happily as you have begun: I only ask of you to be your friend, than which nothing could be more to my satisfaction. Then the two princesses tenderly embraced each other, and, after a thousand vows of mutual friendship, lay down and took their rest.

According to the custom of the country, the tokens of the consummation of the marriage were to be produced and seen publicly. The two princesses found out a way to get over that difficulty: queen Haiatalnefous's women were next morning deceived by it themselves, and deceived king Armanos, his queen, and the whole court. From this time, the princess Badoura grew more and more in king Armanos's esteem and affection, governing the kingdom to his and his people's content, peaceably and prosperously.

While these things were transacting in the court of the isle of Ebene, prince Camaralzaman staid in the city of the idolaters with the gardener, who had offered him his house for a retreat till the ship sailed for that island.

One morning, when the prince was up early, and, as he used to do, was preparing to work in the garden, the gardener hindered him, saying, This day is a great festival among the idolaters; and, because they abstain from work themselves, to spend the time in their abominable mysteries and public rejoicings, they will not let the mussulmen work, who, to gain their favour, generally assist at their shows, which are worth seeing: wherefore there is nothing for you to do to-day: I leave you here; and the time approaching in which the ship uses to sail for the isle of Ebene, I will go to some of my friends, and know when it will depart, and secure you a passage in it. The gardener put on his best clothes, and went to the feast.

When prince Camaralzaman was alone, instead of going out to take part in the public joy of the city, the solitude he was in brought to his mind with more violence the loss of his dear princess. He walked up and down the garden, sighing and groaning, till the noise which two birds made on a neighbouring tree tempted him to lift up his head, and stop to see what was the matter.

Camaralzaman was surprised to behold a battle between these two birds, fighting with their beaks, and that in a very little while one of them fell down dead at the root of a tree; the bird that was victorious took wing again, and flew away.

In the instant, two other large birds that had seen the fight at a distance, came from the other side of the garden, and pitched on the ground, one at the feet, and the other at the head of the dead bird: they looked upon it some time, shaking their heads, as if they were grieved at the death of their departed friend; after which, they dug a grave with their talons, and interred the defunct.

When they had filled up the grave with the earth they had turned up to make it, they also flew away, and returned in a few minutes, bringing with them the bird that had committed the murder, the one holding one of her wings in his beak, and the other one of her legs; the criminal all the while crying out in a doleful manner, and struggling to escape. They carried him to the grave of the bird which he had lately sacrificed to his rage; and there they made a sacrifice of him to the manes of the dead bird; and striking him after with their beaks, at last they killed the murderer: they then opened his belly, tore out his entrails, left his body on the place unburied, and away they flew.

Camaralzaman remained in a great astonishment all the time that he stood beholding this fight. He drew near the tree where this scene had been acted; and, casting his eyes on the scattered entrails of the bird that was last killed, he spied something red hanging out of his body: he took it up, and found it was his beloved princess Badoura's talisman, which had cost him so much pains and sorrow, and so many sighs, since the bird snatched it out of his hand. Ah, cruel! said he to himself, still looking on the bird, thou tookest delight in doing mischief, so I have the less reason to complain of that which thou didst to me: but by how much the greater it was, by so much the more do I wish well to those that revenged my quarrel on thee, in punishing thee for the murder of one of their and thy own kind.

It is impossible to express prince Camaralzaman's joy. Dear princess, continued he to himself, this happy minute, which restores me a treasure that is so precious to thee, is without doubt a presage of our meeting again, and perhaps sooner than I think of. Thank Heaven, who sent me this good fortune, and gives me hope of the greatest felicity that my heart can desire.

Saying this, he kissed the talisman, wrapped it up in a ribbon, and tied it carefully about his arm. Until now, he had been almost every night a stranger to rest, his troubles always keeping him awake; but the next night he slept soundly: he rose somewhat later the next morning than he used to do, put on his working clothes, and went to the gardener for orders what he should go about: the good man bid him root up an old tree which stood in such a place, and was decaying.

Camaralzaman took an ax, and began his work: cutting off a branch of the root, he found his ax struck against something that resisted the blow and made a noise: he turned the earth up, and discovered a broad plate of brass, under which was a staircase of ten steps: he went down, and at the bottom saw a cave of above six yards square, with fifty brass urns placed in order around it, each with a cover to it: he opened them all, one after another, and there was not one of them which was not full of gold dust. He came out of the cave, rejoicing that he had found such a vast treasure: he put the brass plate on the staircase, and rooted up the tree against the gardener's coming to see what he had done.

The gardener had learned the day before, that the ship which was bound to the isle of Ebene would sail in a few days, but the certain time was not yet fixed: his friend promised to let him know the day, if he called upon him on the morrow; and while Camaralzaman was rooting up the tree, he went to have his answer. He returned with a joyful countenance, by which the prince guessed he brought him good news. Son, said the old man, (so he always called him, on account of the difference between his age and the prince's youth) be joyful, and prepare to embark; in three days, the ship will certainly set sail: I have taken passage for you, and agreed upon the price with the captain.

In the condition I am at present, replied Camaralzaman, you could not bring me more agreeable news; and in return, I have also tidings that will be as welcome to you: come along with me, and you shall see what good fortune heaven has in store for you.

The prince led the gardener to the place where he had rooted up the tree, shewed him the way into the cave, and, when he was there, let him see what a treasure he had discovered, thanking Providence for rewarding his virtue, and the pains he had been at for so many years. How, replied the gardener, do you imagine I will take these riches as mine which you found out? The property of them is yours: I have no right to them. For fourscore years, so long my father has been dead, I have done nothing but dug in this garden, and could not discover this treasure; which is a sign it was destined to you by fate, or heaven had revealed it to me. It agrees with your quality as a prince, and suits your age too better than mine: I am old, and have one foot in the grave, and cannot tell what to do with so much wealth: Providence has bestowed it upon you, at a time when you are returning to that country which will one day be your own, where you may make a good use of it, for the advantage of yourself, and the people over whom you are to reign.

Prince Camaralzaman would not be outdone in generosity by the gardener: they had a long dispute about who would refuse it, for neither of them would have it from the other: at last the prince solemnly protested that he would have none of it, unless the gardener would divide it with him, and take half. The good man consented to it, to please the prince: so they parted it between them, and each had twenty-five urns.

Having thus divided it, Son, said the gardener to the prince, it is not enough that you have got this treasure, we must now contrive how to carry it so privately aboard the ship that nobody may know any thing of the matter, otherwise you will run the risk of losing it. There are no olives in the isle of Ebene; those that are exported hence are a good commodity there: you know I have plenty of them, take what you will; fill fifty pots, half with the gold dust, and half with olives, which, being a common merchandise from this city to that island, none will mistrust there is any thing but olives in the pots.

The counsel was good; and Camaralzaman followed it. The rest of the day was taken up by him and the old man, in packing up the gold and the olives in the fifty pots; and the prince[1] fearing the talisman should come by any ill accident again, he carefully put it up in one of the pots, marking it with a particular mark, to distinguish it from the others. When they were all ready to be shipped, the prince retired into the gardener's hut with him, and, discoursing together, he related to him the battles of the birds, with the circumstance of that adventure, in which he had found the princess Badoura's talisman. The gardener was equally surprised and joyful to hear it, knowing what trouble the prince had been at for the loss of it. Whether the old man was quite worn out with age, or had spent himself too much that day, the gardener had a very bad night's rest: he grew worse the next day;

[1] This incident is also much the same with one in the romance of Peter of Provence and the fair Maguelonna.*

and on the third day, when the prince was to embark, was so bad that it was plain he was nigh his end. As soon as day broke, the captain of the ship came in person, with several seamen, to the gardener's: they knocked at the garden-door, and Camaralzaman opened it to them: they asked him where the passenger was that was to go with him? The prince answered, I am he: the gardener, who agreed with you for my passage, is sick, and cannot be spoke with: come in, and let your men carry these pots of olives, and a few other things, aboard for me: I will only take leave of the gardener, and follow you to the water side.

The seamen took up the pots and the baggage, and the captain bid the prince make haste, the wind being fair, and they staid for nothing but him.

When the captain and his men were gone, Camaralzaman went to the gardener to take his leave of him, and thank him for all his good offices; but he found him in the agonies of death, and had scarce time to bid him rehearse the articles of his faith, which all good mussulmen use to do before they die. The gardener did what he could towards it, and expired in his presence.

The prince being obliged to hasten his departure, was at a loss what to do: he was afraid he should lose his voyage, if he staid; and was loth to leave his dead benefactor, without paying him the last duty of a friend, according to their law. He washed him, buried him in his own garden, (for the Mahometans had no church-yard in the city of the idolaters, where they were only tolerated); and though he did it as fast as he could, having nobody to assist him, it was almost night before he had put him in the ground: but as soon as he had done it, he ran to the water side, carrying with him the key of the garden, designing, if he had time, to give it to the landlord; otherwise to deposit it in some trusty person's hand, before witnesses, that he might have it after he was gone. When he came to the port, he was told the ship sailed several hours before he came, and was already out of sight. It staid three hours for him, and the wind standing fair, the captain durst not stay longer.

It is easy to imagine that prince Camaralzaman was exceedingly grieved, to be forced to stay in that country a year longer, where he neither had, nor was willing to have, any acquaintance. It was a sad thing to him, to think that he must wait another twelvemonth for the opportunity he had lost; but what was the greatest affliction to him of all, was his missing the princess Badoura's talisman, which he gave over for lost. The only course that was left him to take, was to return to the garden from whence he came, to rent it of the landlord, and to go on with his gardening, that he might by himself deplore his misery and misfortunes. He hired a boy to help him to do some part of the drudgery; and that he might not lose the other half of the treasure, which came to him by the death of the gardener, who died without heirs, he put the gold dust in fifty other pots of olives, to be ready against the time of the ship's return, and making the same voyage.

While prince Camaralzaman began another year of labour, sorrow, and impatience, the ship having a fair wind, sailed before him to the isle of Ebene, where in due time she arrived at the capital city.

The palace royal being by the sea-side, the new king, or rather the princess Badoura, spying the ship as she was entering into the port, asked what vessel it was? she was answered, that it came from the city of idolaters, from whence it used to come every year about that time, and generally was richly laden.

The princess, who had always prince Camaralzaman in her mind, amidst the glories of her palace and power, imagined the prince might be aboard; on which thought, she resolved, since it might be so, to go aboard the ship and meet him, not to discover herself to him, (for she questioned whether he would know her again,) but to observe him, and take proper measures for their making themselves mutually known. Her pretence was, to see what merchandise was aboard, to have the first sight of the goods, and chuse the most valuable for herself. She commanded a horse to be brought her; she mounted and rode to the port, accompanied by several officers, who were waiting upon her at that time, and arrived at the port just as the captain came ashore: she ordered him to be brought before her, and asked him whence he came, how long he had been on his voyage, and what good or bad fortune he had met with in it, if he had no stranger of quality aboard, and with what his ship was laden?

The captain gave a satisfactory answer to all her demands; and as to passengers, assured her there was none but merchants in his ship who used to come every year, and bring rich stuffs from several parts of the world to trade with; calicoes, stained or unstained, diamonds, musk, ambergrease, camphire, civet, spices, drugs, and olives.

The princess Badoura loved olives extremely: when she heard the captain speak of them, Land them, says she; I will take them off your hands; as to the other goods, let the merchants bring them to me, and let me see them before they dispose of them, or shew them to any one.

The captain, taking her for the king of the isle of Ebene, replied, Sir, there are fifty pots of olives, but they belong to a merchant whom I was forced to leave behind; I gave him notice that I staid for him, but he not coming several hours afterwards, and the wind presenting, I was afraid of losing it, and so set sail. The princess answered: it is no matter, bring them ashore, we will drive a bargain for them however.

The captain sent his boat aboard, and in a little time it returned with the pots of olives. The princess demanded how much the fifty pots might be worth in the isle of Ebene? Sir, says the captain, the merchant is very poor, and your majesty will not pay too dear if you give him a 1000 pieces of silver.

To satisfy him, replied the princess, and because you tell me he is poor, I will order you 1000 pieces of gold for him, which do you take care to give him. The money was accordingly paid, and the pots carried to the palace.

Night drawing on, the princess withdrew into the inner palace, and went to the princess Haiatalnefous's apartment, ordering the olives to be brought thither; she opened one, to let the princess Haiatalnefous taste them, and to taste them herself. Great was her astonishment when she found the olives were mingled with gold dust. What can this mean! says she, it is wonderful beyond comprehension. Her curiosity increasing by so extraordinary an adventure, she ordered Haiatalnefous's women to open and empty all the pots in her presence; and her wonder was still greater, when she saw that the olives in all of them were mixed with gold dust; but, when she saw her talisman drop out of that in which the prince had put it, she was so surprised that she swooned away. The princess Haiatalnefous and her women brought the princess Badoura to life again, by throwing cold water on her face. When she recovered her sense, she took the talisman, and kissed it again and again; but not being willing that the princess Haiatalnefous's women should hear what she said, and it growing late, she dismissed them. Princess, says she to Haiatalnefous, as soon as they were gone, you who have heard my story, to be sure guessed it was at the sight of the talisman that I swooned. This is it, and the fatal cause of my losing my dear husband prince Camaralzaman; but as it was that which caused our separation, so I foresee it will be the means of our sudden meeting.

The next day, as soon as it was light, she sent for the captain of the ship; and when he came, spoke to him thus: I want to know more of the merchant to whom the olives belong that I bought of you yesterday; I think you told me you left him behind you in the city of the idolaters; can you tell me what he does there?

Yes, sir, replied the captain, I can speak on my own knowledge, and assure your majesty what I say is truth: I agreed for his passage with a gardener, a very old man, who told me I should find him in his garden where he worked under him; so he shewed me the place, and I went thither to call him, where I found what the gardener said to be true; and for that reason I told your majesty he was poor; I told him what haste I was in, spoke to him myself, and cannot be mistaken in the man.

If what you say is true, replied the princess Badoura, you must sail this very day for the city of the idolaters, and fetch me that gardener's man, who is my debtor, else I will not only confiscate all your and your merchants' goods, but your and their lives shall answer for his: I have ordered my seal to be put on all the warehouses where they are, which shall not be taken off till you bring me that man: this is all I have to say to you; go, and do as I command you.

The captain could make no reply to this order, though the obeying it was a very great loss to him and his merchants: He acquainted them with it; and they all considering that to lose their goods and their lives would be much greater, hastened him away as fast as they could. They set all hands at work to load provisions and fresh water for his voyage back; and were so diligent, that he was ready to set sail before night. Accordingly he weighed anchor, and made for the city of the idolaters, where he arrived in a short time, wind and weather favouring him all the way. When he was got as near the city as he thought convenient, he would not cast anchor, but let the ship ride off shore; and, going into his boat with as many hands as he wanted, he landed a little way off the port, whence he went directly to Camaralzaman's garden.

Though it was about midnight when he came there, the prince was not asleep. His separation from the fair princess of China, his wife, afflicted him after its usual manner, and he lay waking to bemoan his ill fortune. He cursed the minute in which his curiosity tempted him to touch the fatal girdle.

Thus did he pass those hours which are devoted to rest, and was in these mournful meditations when he heard somebody knock at the garden-door; he ran hastily to open it, half-dressed as he was; and he had no sooner done it but the captain and his seamen took hold of him, and carried him by force aboard his boat and so on ship-board, where, as soon as he was safe, they set sail immediately, and made the best of their ways to the isle of Ebene.

Hitherto Camaralzaman, the captain, and his men, had not said a word to one another; at last, the prince broke silence, and asked the captain, whom he knew again, why they had taken him away by force? The captain in his turn demanded of the prince whether he was not a debtor to the king of Ebene? I the king of Ebene's debtor, replied Camaralzaman in amazement; I do not know him; I had never any thing to do with him in my life, and never set foot in his kingdom. The captain answered, You should know that better than I; you will talk to him yourself in a little while, but till then, stay here and have patience.

The captain was not long on his voyage back to the isle of Ebene: though it was night when he cast anchor in the port, he landed immediately, and, taking prince Camaralzaman with him, hastened to the palace, where he demanded to be introduced to the king.

The princess Badoura was withdrawn into the inner palace: however, as soon as she had heard of the captain's return, and Camaralzaman's arrival, she came forth to speak to him. As soon as she cast her eyes on the prince, she knew the man for whom she had shed so many tears, who was in his gardener's habit. As for the prince, who trembled in the presence of a king, as he thought, to whom he was to answer for an imaginary debt, it could not enter into his thoughts that the person whom he so earnestly desired to see, stood before him. If the princess had followed the dictates of her inclination, she would have run to him, and by embracing, discovered herself to him; but she put a constraint on herself, believing that it was for both their interests that she should act the part of a king a little longer before she made herself known: she contented herself for the present to put him into the hands of an officer, who was then in waiting, charging him to take care of him, and use him well till next day.

When the princess Badoura had provided for prince Camaralzaman's entertainment, she turned about to the captain, whom she was now to gratify for the important service he had done her. She commanded another officer to go immediately, and take the seal off the ware-houses where his and his merchants' goods were, which she discharged; she also gave the master of the vessel a jewel worth much more than the expence he had been at in both his voyages: She, besides, bid him keep the thousand pieces of gold she had given him for the pots of olives, telling him she would make up the account with the merchant whom he had brought with him.

This done, she retired to the princess of the isle of Ebene's apartment, to whom she communicated her joy, praying her to keep the secret still. She told her how she intended to manage his and her discovering themselves to each other, and to the kingdom; adding, there was so vast a distance between a gardener and a great prince, as he is, that it may be dangerous to raise him at once from the lowest condition of the people to the highest degree, though it is but justice it should be done. The princess of the isle of Ebene was so far from betraying her, that she rejoiced with her, and entered into the design; assuring her she would contribute to it all that lay in her power, and do whatever she would desire of her to serve them.

The next morning the princess of China ordered prince Camaralzaman to be conducted to the royal baths, and then apparelled in the robes of an emir, or governor of a province. She then went to the council, with the name, habit, and authority of the king of the isle of Ebene. She commanded Camaralzaman to be introduced; and his fine mien and majestic air drew all the eyes of the lords there present upon him.

The princess Badoura herself was charmed to see him again as lovely as she had often seen him, and that pleasure inspired her to speak the more warmly in his praise. When she addressed herself to the council, having ordered the prince to take his seat among the emirs, she spoke to them thus: My lords, Camaralzaman, the man whom I have advanced to the same dignity with you, is not unworthy the honour that is done him. I have known enough of him in my travels to answer for him, and I can assure you he will make his merit known to all of you, as well by his valour, as by a thousand other shining qualities, which distinguish him from the rest of mankind.

Camaralzaman was extremely amazed to hear the king of the isle of Ebene, whom he was far from taking for a woman, much less for his dear princess, name him, and declare that he knew him, who, as he thought, was certain he had never seen him before in his life; and he was much more surprised when he heard him praise him so excessively. However, those praises, excessive as they were, did not confound him, though they came from the mouth of a king. He received them with such modesty as shewed that he deserved them, and did not grow vain upon it. He prostrated himself before the throne of the king, and then rising again, Sir, said he, I want words to express my gratitude to your majesty for the honour you have done me: I shall do all that lies in my power to render myself worthy of your royal favour.

From the council-board the prince was conducted to a palace which the princess Badoura had ordered to be fitted up for him; where he found officers and domestics ready to obey his commands, a stable full of fine horses, and every thing suitable to the quality of an emir. When he was in the closet, the steward of his household brought him a chest full of gold for his expences.

The less he conceived how it came about that he met with so much good fortune, the more he admired at it, never once imagining that he owed it to the princess of China.

Two or three days after, the princess Badoura made him lord-treasurer, which office became lately vacant, that he might be nearer her person. He behaved himself in his new charge with so much integrity, and was so obliging to every body, that he not only gained the friendship of the great, but also the affections of the people, by his uprightness and bounty.

Camaralzaman had been the happiest man in the world, being the reigning favourite of the king of the isle of Ebene, and in the esteem of all his subjects, if he had had his princess with him. In the midst of his good fortune he never ceased lamenting her, and grieving that he could hear no tidings of her, especially in a country where she must necessarily have come in her way to her father's court, and have arrived long before, had she met with no ill accident by the way. He had mistrusted something, had the princess Badoura still gone by the name of Camaralzaman, which she took with his habit; but on her accession to the throne, she changed it to take that of Armanos, in honour of the old king her father-in-law. There were very few courtiers who knew that she had ever been called Camaralzaman, which she assumed when she arrived at the court of the isle of Ebene; nor had Camaralzaman so much acquaintance with any of them yet, to inform himself further of her history.

The princess, fearing he might do it in time, and desiring that she should owe the discovery of herself to herself only, resolved to put an end to her torments and his; for she had observed, that, as often as she discoursed with him about the affairs of his office, he fetched such deep sighs as could be addressed to nobody but her. She herself lived in such a constraint that she could endure it no longer. Add to this, the friendship of the emirs and courtiers, with the zeal and affection of the people. In a word, every thing contributed to her putting the crown of the isle of Ebene on his head, without any obstacle.

The princess Badoura consulted the princess Haiatalnefous in this, as she had done in the other parts of the adventure, and they both agreeing to have it done, she one day took prince Camaralzaman aside, saying, I must talk with you about an affair, Camaralzaman, in which I want your advice; it will not be so proper to do it by day-light, for our discourse may be long, and I would not be observed. Come hither in the evening; do not let us wait for you; I will take care to provide you a bed.

Camaralzaman came punctually to the place at the hour appointed by the princess. She took him with her into the inner apartment, and having told the chief eunuch, who prepared to follow her, she had no occasion for his service, and that he should only keep the door shut, she carried him into a private apartment adjoining to the princess Haiatalnefous's, where she used to lie.

When she entered the chamber, where there was a bed, she shut the door, and taking the talisman out of her pocket, gave it to Camaralzaman, saying, It is not long since an astrologer presented me with this talisman; you being skilful in all things, pray tell me what it is good for?

Camaralzaman took the talisman, and drew near a lamp to view it. As soon as he knew it was the princess's, he was transported with pleasure, and she was no less pleased to see it. Sir, says the prince, your majesty asked me what this talisman is good for. Oh, king! it is only good to kill me with grief and despair, if I do not suddenly find the most charming and lovely princess in the world to whom it belongs, whose loss I was the occasion of, and of a strange adventure to me, the very recital of which will move your majesty to pity such an unfortunate husband and lover, if you would have patience to hear it.

You shall tell me that another time, replied the princess, I am very glad I know something of it already; stay here a little, and I will return to you in a moment.

At these words, she went into her closet, put off her royal turban, and in a few minutes dressed herself like a woman; and having the girdle round her, which she had on the day of her separation, she entered the chamber.

Prince Camaralzaman immediately knew his dear princess, ran to her, and tenderly embraced her, crying out, Ah! how much am I obliged to the king, who has so agreeably surprised me. Do not expect to see the king any more, replied the princess, with tears in her eyes: Let us sit down, and I will explain this enigma to you.

They sat down, and the princess told the prince the resolution she came to in the field where they encamped the last time they were together, as soon as she perceived she waited for him to no purpose: How she went through with it, till she arrived at the isle of Ebene, where she had been obliged to marry the princess Haiatalnefous, and accept of the crown, which king Armanos offered her as one of the conditions of the marriage: How the princess, whose merit she highly extolled, took her declaration of her sex; and how she found the talisman in the pots of olives, mingled with the gold dust, which she bought, and the finding it was the cause of her sending for him at the city of the idolaters.

When she had done telling her adventure, she obliged the prince to tell his. He informed her how the talisman occasioned their separation, and the rest of the story relating to him, as I have already told it. They then bemoaned one another's ill fortune, and rejoiced in their good; he complained of her with the most kind expressions love could invent, chiding her tenderly for her making him languish so long without her: She excused herself with the reasons I have already related; after which, it growing late, they went to bed.

The princess Badoura and prince Camaralzaman rose next morning as soon as it was light, but the princess would no more put on her royal robes as king; she dressed herself in her natural dress, that of a woman, and then sent the chief eunuch to king Armanos, her father-in-law, to desire he would give himself the trouble to come to her apartment.

When the king entered the chamber, he was amazed to see a lady there, who was unknown to him, and the lord treasurer with her, to whom it was not permitted to come within the inner palace, nor to any of the lords of the court. He sat down, and asked where the king was?

The princess answered, Yesterday I was king, sir, and to-day I am only princess of China, wife to the true prince Camaralzaman, the true son of king Schahzaman. If your majesty will have patience to hear both our histories, I hope you will not condemn me for putting an innocent deceit upon you. The king bid her go on, and heard her discourse from the beginning to the end, with astonishment. The princess finishing it, said to him, Sir, though our religion does not suffer us to have more wives than one, without some sort of scandal, and we women do not easily comply with the custom men have introduced to have several; yet if your majesty will give your consent to give your daughter, the princess Haiatalnefous, in marriage to the prince Camaralzaman, I will with all my heart yield up to her the rank and quality of queen, which of right belongs to her, and content myself with the second place after her. If this precedence was not her due, I would, however, give it her, being obliged to her for keeping the secret so faithfully as she has done. If your majesty approves of it, I am sure she will; and I will pass my word, that she shall obey you with joy.

King Armanos listened to the princess with admiration, and when she had done, turned about to prince Camaralzaman, saying, Son, since the princess Badoura, your wife, whom I have all along thought to be my son-in-law, through a deceit, of which I do not complain, assures me, that she will divide your bed with my daughter, I have nothing more to do, but to know of you if you are willing to marry her, and accept of the crown, which the princess Badoura would deservedly wear as long as she lived, if she did not quit it out of love to you. Sir, replied prince Camaralzaman, though I desire nothing so earnestly as to see my father, yet the obligations I have to your majesty and the princess Haiatalnefous are so weighty, I cannot deny you any thing that is in my power. Camaralzaman was proclaimed king, and married the same day with all possible demonstrations of joy; he being very well pleased with the princess Haiatalnefous's beauty and love for him.

The two queens lived together afterwards as friendly as they had done before, both being contented with king Camaralzaman's equal carriage towards them, and they alternately were taken to his bed.

The next year, each brought him a son at the same time, and the birth of the two princes was celebrated with extraordinary feastings. The first which the princess Badoura was delivered of, king Camaralzaman called D'Amgrad, (most glorious); and the other, which was born of queen Haiatalnefous, Assad, (most happy.)

The Story of the two Princes Amgrad and Assad

THE two princes were brought up with great care; and when they were old enough, had the same governor, and the same masters for the arts and sciences. King Camaralzaman would have them learn them, and that they should have each the same master for each exercise. The friendship which from their infancy they entered into, occasioned an uniformity of manners and inclinations, which increased with their years. When they were of years to keep each a separate court, they loved one another so tenderly, that they begged king Camaralzaman to let them live together: He consented to it; so they had the same officers, the same domestics, the same lodging, and the same table. Camaralzaman had so good an opinion of their capacity and justice, that he made no scruple of admitting them into his council at eighteen years old, and letting them, by turns, preside there, while he gave himself the diversion of hunting, or recreated himself with his queens at his houses of pleasure.

The two princes being equally handsome, both in their infancy, and now they were grown up, the two queens loved them with incredible tenderness, in such a manner, however, that the princes Badoura had a greater kindness for prince Assad, queen Haiatalnefous's son, than for her own; and queen Haiatalnefous loved Amgrad, the princess Badoura's son, better than her own son, Assad.

The two queens thought at first this inclination was nothing but a friendship which proceeded from an excess of their own for each other, which they still preserved: But as the two princes advanced in years, that friendship turned to a violent love; when the graces that appeared in their youth blinded their reason. They knew how criminal their passion was; they did all they could to resist it, and all they did proved in vain. They were accustomed to be familiar with them, to admire, to praise, to kiss, and caress them from their infancy, and could not leave it, when they grew up, which inflamed their desires to such a height that they could neither eat, nor drink, nor sleep. It was their and the princes' ill fortune that the latter, being used to be so treated by them, had not the least suspicion of their infamous fires.

The two queens had not made each other a confidant of the secret of their passion, nor had the boldness to tell each the prince she loved, by word of mouth, the guilty flame with which she burnt; they at last resolved to do it by billet, and made use of king Camaralzaman's absence to execute their wicked design, when he was gone a hunting, which would take him up three or four days.

Prince Amgrad presided at the council table the day of king Camaralzaman's departure, and heard causes till three or four o'clock in the afternoon; when he returned to the palace from the council-chamber, an eunuch took him aside, and gave him a billet from queen Haiatalnefous: Amgrad took it, and read it with horror. Traitor, says he to the eunuch, as soon as he had read it through, is this the fidelity thou owest thy master and thy king? At these words he drew his sabre, and cut off his head.

Having done this, he ran in haste to the princess Badoura his mother, bearing his resentment still in his looks, shewed her the billet, told her the contents of it, and from whom it came; but, instead of hearkening to him, she fell into a passion herself, and said, Son, it is all a calumny and imposture; queen Haiatalnefous is a very discreet princess, and you are very bold to talk to me after this rate. The prince was enraged at his mother, to hear her speak so of him: You are both bad alike, says he, and had it not been for the respect I owe my father, this day should have been the last of Haiatalnefous's life.

Queen Badoura might have imagined, by the example of her son Amgrad, that prince Assad, who was as virtuous as the other, would not be pleased with such a declaration of love as had been made to his brother; yet that did not hinder her persisting in so abominable a design: She wrote him a billet the next day, which she trusted with an old woman belonging to the palace, to convey to him.

The old woman watched her opportunity, and gave it him as he was coming from the council-chamber, where he presided that day in his turn; the prince took it, and reading it, fell into such a fury, that without finishing it, he drew his sabre, and punished the old woman as she deserved. He ran presently to his mother queen Haiatalnefous's apartment with the billet in his hand; he would have shewn it to her, but she did not give him time, crying out, I know what you would have with me; you are as impertinent as your brother Amgrad; so begone, and never come into my presence again.

Assad stood as one thunderstruck at these words, of which he could not comprehend the meaning. When he recollected himself, he was so transported with rage, that he had like to have given very fatal demonstrations of his anger; but he contained himself, and withdrew without making any reply, fearing if he staid he might say something or other unworthy the greatness of his soul. Amgrad had put the same constraint on himself, and guessing by his mother's carriage that she was altogether as criminal as queen Haiatalnefous, he went to his brother to chide him for not communicating that hated secret to him, and to mingle his sorrow with Assad's.

The two queens grew desperate when they found so much virtue in the two princes; and, instead of reforming themselves by it, they renounced all sentiments of mothers and nature, and conspired together to destroy them: They made their women believe the two princes had attempted to ravish them. They counterfeited the matter to the life by their tears, cries, and curses; and lay in the same bed, as if the resistance they had made had wasted them so much that they were almost at death's door.

When Camaralzaman returned to the palace from hunting, he was very much surprised to find them a-bed together, all in tears, acting the part of desponding ladies so well, that he was touched with compassion: He asked them with earnestness what had happened to them?

At this question, the dissembling queens wept and groaned more bitterly than before; and after he had pressed them again and again to tell him, queen Badoura at last answered him thus: Sir, our grief is so extraordinary, and so just, that we ought not to see the light of the sun, nor live a day, after the violence that has been offered us by the princes your sons: their brutality has been such, that they entered into a horrid design in your absence, and had the boldness and insolence to make attempts upon our honour: Your majesty will excuse us from saying any more; you may guess the rest by our affliction.

The king sent for the two princes, and had killed them both with his own hand, if old king Armanos, his father-in-law, who was by, had not held his hand; Son, said he, what are you going to do? Will you stain your hands and your palace with your own blood? There are other ways of punishing them, if they are really guilty.

He endeavoured thus to appease him, and desired him to examine the matter, and see whether they did indeed commit the crime of which they were accused.

It was no hard thing for Camaralzaman to be so much master of himself as not to butcher his own children: He ordered them to be put under arrest, and sent for an emir called Giendar, whom he commanded to carry them out of the city, and put them to death, as far off, and in what place he pleased; but not to see him again unless he brought their cloaths with him as a token of his having executed his orders.

Giendar travelled with them all night, and early next morning made them alight, telling them, with tears, the cruel commands he had received. Believe me, princes, said he, it is next to death to me to obey your father, who chose me to execute what he ordered concerning you; would to heaven I could avoid it. The princes replied, Do your duty: we know well enough you are not the cause of our deaths, and pardon you freely for it.

Then they embraced, and bid each other adieu with so much tenderness, that it was a long time before they could leave one another's arms. Prince Assad was the first who prepared himself for the fatal stroke. Begin with me, Giendar, said he, that I may not have the trouble to see my dear brother Amgrad die. Amgrad opposed him in it; and Giendar could not, without weeping more than before, be witness of this dispute between them; which shewed how perfect and sincere their friendship was.

They, in the end, thus determined the contest, desiring Giendar to tie them together, and put them in the most convenient posture for him to kill them both at one blow. Do not refuse two unfortunate brothers the poor comfort of dying together, said the generous princes; for all things, even our innocence, are in common between us.

Giendar agreed to it, and as they desired, tied them to each other, breast to breast, close; and when he had placed them so as he thought he might strike the blow with the more surety, to answer their request, and cut off their heads at once, he asked them if they had any thing to command him before they died?

We have only one thing to desire of you, replied the princes, which is, to assure our father at your return that we are innocent; but do not charge him with our deaths, knowing he is not well informed of the truth of the crime which we are accused of.

Giendar promised to do what they would have him, and drew his sabre; his horse being tied to a tree just by, started at the sight of the sabre, which glittered against the sun, broke his bridle, and ran away with all speed into the country.

Giendar set a great price upon him, for it was a very good horse, and was besides, so richly harnessed, that the emir could not well bear the loss of him. This accident so troubled him, that, instead of beheading the two princes, he threw away his sabre, and ran after his horse, to catch him again if he could.

The horse gallopped on before him, and led him several miles out of his way into a wood; Giendar followed him, and the horse's neighing roused a lion that was asleep not far off. The lion started up, and, instead of running after the horse, made directly towards Giendar, who thought no more of his beast, but how to save his life, and avoid the lion. He ran into the thickest of the wood, the lion pursuing him with more ease than he took his flight. Driven to this extremity, he said to himself, Heaven had not punished me in this manner, but to shew the innocence of the princes whom I was commanded to put to death, and now, to my misfortune, I have not my sabre to defend myself.

While Giendar was gone, the two princes were seized with a violent thirst, occasioned by the fear of death, notwithstanding their noble resolution to submit to the king their father's cruel order.

Prince Amgrad shewed the prince his brother a fountain not far off: Ah, brother, says Assad, we have so little while to live, what need have we to quench our thirst? We can bear it a few minutes longer.

Amgrad taking notice of his brother's remonstrance, unbound himself, and unbound his brother, whether he would or no. They went to the fountain, and, having refreshed themselves, heard the roaring of the lion, that, in pursuit of his prey, was come to the end of the wood where the princes were. They also heard Giendar's dreadful cries; at which Amgrad took up Giendar's sabre which lay on the ground, saying to Assad, Come, brother, let us go and help poor Giendar; perhaps we may come soon enough to deliver him from the danger in which he now is.

The two princes ran to the wood, and entered it just as the lion was going to fall on Giendar. The beast seeing prince Amgrad advancing towards him with a sabre in his hand, left his prey, and came against him with fury. The prince met him intrepidly, and gave him a blow so forcibly and dexterously, that it killed him on the spot.

When Giendar saw the two princes were the men who saved his life, he threw himself at their feet, and thanked them for the great obligation he had to them, in words which sufficiently shewed his gratitude. Princes, says he, rising up and kissing their hands, with tears, God forbid that ever I should attempt any thing against your lives, after you have so obligingly and bravely saved mine. It shall never be said that the emir Giendar was guilty of such a piece of ingratitude.

The service we have done you, answered the princes, ought not to hinder you to execute the orders you had received: let us catch your horse again, and then return to the place where you left us.—They were at no great trouble to take the horse, whose mettle was come down a little with running as he had done. When they had restored him to Giendar, and were near the fountain, they begged of him, and argued with him to do as their father had commanded him; but all to no purpose. I only take the liberty to desire you, says Giendar, and I pray you not to deny me, that you will divide my clothes between you, and give me yours; and to go so far, that the king your father may never hear a word of you more.

The princes were forced to comply with him. They each of them gave him his clothes, and covered themselves with what he could spare them of his. He also gave them all the gold he had about him, and took his leave of them.

When emir Giendar parted from the princes, he passed through the wood where Amgrad had killed the lion, in whose blood he dipped their clothes; which having done, he proceeded in his way to the capital city of the isle of Ebene.

At his arrival there, king Camaralzaman asked if he had done what he had ordered him? Giendar replied, See, sir, the faithful witnesses of my obedience; giving him at the same time the princes' clothes.

How did they take the punishment I commanded to be executed on them? Giendar answered, With wonderful constancy, sir, and a holy resignation to the decrees of heaven, which shewed how sincerely they made profession of their religion: but particularly they behaved themselves with great respect towards your majesty, and an entire submission to the sentence of death. We die innocent, said they: however, we do not murmur: we take our death as from the hand of heaven, and forgive our father; for we know very well he has not been rightly informed of the truth.

Camaralzaman was sensibly touched at emir Giendar's relation; and, putting his hand in prince Amgrad's pocket first, found a billet open, which he read. He no sooner knew that queen Haiatalnefous writ it, as well by a lock of her hair which was in it, as by her hand-writing, but he froze with horror: he then, trembling, put his hand into that of Assad, and finding there queen Badoura's billet, his surprise was so great and so lively, that he swooned away.

Never did man grieve like Camaralzaman. Barbarous father, as thou art, cried he, what hast thou done? thou hast murdered thy own children, thy innocent children. Did not their wisdom, their modesty, their obedience, their submission to thy will in all things; did not they all plead in their behalf? Blind and insensible father! dost thou deserve to live, after this execrable crime thou hast committed? I have brought this abomination on my own head; and heaven chastises me for not persevering in the aversion to woman with which I was born. And, Oh ye detestable wives! I will not, no, I will not, as ye deserve, wash off the guilt of your sins with your bloods; ye are unworthy my rage: but perdition seize me, if ever I see you more.

King Camaralzaman was a man of too much religion to break his vow: he commanded the two queens to be lodged in separate apartments that very day, where they were kept under strong guards; and he never saw them again as long as he lived.

While the king of the isles of Ebene afflicted himself for the loss of the princes his sons, which he thought he had been the author of, by his too rash condemning them; the royal youths wandered through deserts, endeavouring to avoid all places that were inhabited, and not to meet any human creature. They lived on herbs and wild fruits, and drank only stinking rain-water, which they found in the crevices of the rocks. They slept and watched by turns, at night, for fear of wild beasts.

When they had travelled about a month, they came to the foot of an high mountain, inaccessible for the craggedness of it, the stones being black, and so ragged, that it was impossible to ascend over them to the summit of a hill. They at last spied a sort of path, but so narrow and difficult that they durst not venture up it. This obliged them to go along by the foot of the mountain, in hopes to find a more easy way to reach the top of it. They went about it five days, but could see nothing like a path; so they were forced to return to that which they had neglected. They still thought it would be in vain for them to attempt going up by it: they deliberated what they should do a long time, and at last, encouraging one another, resolved to ascend the hill.

The more they advanced, they thought it was the higher, and the more steep, which made them think several times of giving over their enterprise.

When the one was weary, the other stopped, and they took breath together: sometimes they were both so tired that they wanted strength to go farther. Then, despairing of being able to reach the top, they thought they must lie down, and die of fatigue and weariness. A few minutes after, when they found they recovered a little strength, they animated one another, and went on.

Notwithstanding all their endeavours and their courage, they could not get to the top that day. Night came on; and prince Assad was so tired, and so spent, that he stopped, and said to prince Amgrad, I can go no farther, I am just a-dying. Stay as long as you will, replied prince Amgrad, let us rest ourselves, and have a good heart; it is but a little way to the top, and the moon befriends us.

They rested themselves about half an hour; and then Assad, putting on strength to it, once more ascended what remained of the way to the mountain's summit, where they both at last arrived, and lay down. Amgrad rose first, and advancing, saw a tree at a little distance: he went to it, and found it was a pomegranate-tree, which bare fruit upon it, and a fountain at the foot of it: he ran to his brother Assad to tell him the good news, and conduct him to the tree by the fountain side. They refreshed themselves there, by eating each a pomegranate; after which they fell asleep.

When they awoke next morning, Come, brother, says Amgrad to Assad, let us go on; I see the mountain is easier to be travelled over on this side than the other; all our way now is down-hill: but Assad was so tired with the last day's fatigue, that he wanted three or four days repose to recover himself.

They spent them as they had done many before, in discoursing on their mothers' inordinate desires, deploring their misfortunes: but, said they, since heaven has so visibly declared itself in our favour, we ought to bear them with patience, and comfort ourselves with hopes that we shall see an end of them.

At the end of three days rest, the two brothers continued their travels, and were five days in descending it before they came into the valley. They then discovered a great city, at which they were very joyful: Brother, says Amgrad to Assad, are not you of my opinion? which is, that you should stay in some place out of the city, where I may come to you again; while I go and learn the language, and inform myself what the name of the city is, and in what country we are; and when I come back I will bring provisions with me: It is not convenient for us to go there together; there may be danger in it; and so much notice will not be taken of one stranger as of two.

Brother, replied Assad, I approve of what you say; it is safe and prudent: but if one of us must part from the other on that account, I will not suffer that it shall be you; you must allow me to go; for what a trouble will it be to me, if any ill accident should happen to you!

Ah! but, brother, answered Amgrad, the same ill accident you fear for me, I am much afraid of for you: pray let me go, and do you stay here with patience. I will never yield to it, said Assad; if any ill happen to me, it will be some comfort to think you are safe. Amgrad was forced to submit, and Assad going towards the city, he staid in a grove at the foot of the mountain.

Prince Assad took the purse of money which Amgrad had in charge, and went forward towards the city. He had not gone far in the first street before he met with a reverend old man, with a cane in his hand: he was neatly dressed; and the prince took him for a man of note in the place, who would not put a trick upon him; so he accosted him thus:—Pray, my lord, which is the way to the market-place? The old man looked on prince Assad, smiling: Child, said he, it is plain you are a stranger, or you would not have asked that question of me.

Yes, my lord, I am a stranger, replied Assad. The old man answered, You are welcome then; our country will be honoured by the presence of so handsome a young man as you are: tell me what business you have at the market-place.

My lord, replied Assad, it is near two months since my brother and I parted from our own country, a great way from hence: we have not left off travelling ever since we set out first, and we arrived here but to-day; my brother, tired with such a long journey, stays at the foot of a mountain, and I am come to buy some provisions for him and me.

Son, says the old man, you could not have come in a better time, and I am glad of it for your and your brother's sake; I made a feast to-day for some friends of mine, and there is a great deal of victuals left untouched; come along with me, you shall eat as much as you please; and when that is done, I will give you enough to serve your brother and you several days: do not spend your money when there is no occasion for it; travellers are always in want of it: while you are eating, I will give you an account of our city, which nobody can do better than myself, who have borne all the honourable offices in it. It is well for you that you happened to light upon me; for, I must tell you, all our citizens cannot so well help and inform you as I can; I can assure you, some of them are very wicked. Come along; you shall see the difference between a real honest man, as I am, and such as boast to be so, and are not.

I am infinitely obliged to you, replied Assad, for your good-will towards me; I put myself entirely into your hands, and I am ready to go with you where you please.

The old man laughed in his sleeve to think he had got the prince in his clutches: he walked by the side of him, as close as he could, and all the way talked as civilly and plausibly as he could, to preserve the favourable opinion Assad had of him. Among other things, says he, It must be confessed it was your good fortune to meet with me, rather than with any other man: I thank God I met with you; you will know why I say it when you come to my house.

Thither they came before it was long; and the old man introduced Assad into a hall, where were forty such old fellows as himself, who made a circle round a flaming fire, which they adored. The prince was not more seized with horror, at the sight of so many men adoring the creature for the Creator, than with fear of finding himself betrayed, and in such an abominable place.

While Assad stood motionless with the surprise in which he was, the old cheat saluted the forty gray-headed men around the fire: Devout adorers of fire, said he to them, this is a happy day for us: where is Gazban? call him.

He spoke these words aloud; and a negro, who waited at the lower end of the hall, presently came up to him. This black was Gazban; who, as soon as he saw the disconsolate Assad, imagined for what he was called. He seized him immediately, and tied him hand and foot, with wonderful nimbleness. Carry him down, said the old man, when you have done, and bid my daughters, Bostama and Cavama, give him every day the bastinado, with a little bread, morning and night, for his sustenance, just enough to keep him alive till the next ship departs for the Blue Sea, and the Fiery Mountain: he shall then be offered up as an agreeable sacrifice to our divinity.

As soon as the old man had given the cruel order, Gazban carried prince Assad into a cellar under the hall, through several dark rooms, till they came to a dungeon, down to which were twenty steps; there he left him in chains of prodigious weight and bigness. When he had done, he went to give the old man's daughters notice of it; but he might have spared himself that labour, for their father had before sent for them, and given them their instructions himself. Daughters, said he to them, go down and give the mussulman I just now brought in the bastinado, as you know how to do it. Do not spare him; you cannot shew your zeal for our divinity, and that you adore the fire, any way better than by your severity to him.

Bostama and Cavama, who were bred up in their hatred to mussulmen, received this order with joy. They descended into the dungeon that very moment, stripped Assad, and bastinadoed him unmercifully, till the blood issued out of his wounds, and he was almost dead. After this cruel execution, they put a piece of bread and a pot of water by him, and retired.

Assad did not come to himself again for a long time; when he did, he broke out into a flood of tears, deploring his misery. His comfort, however, was, that this misfortune had not happened to his brother Amgrad.

The prince waited for his brother till evening, with impatience; when it was two, three, and four of the clock in the morning, and Assad did not return, he was like one desperate, sorrow so violently possessed him. He spent the night in that dismal condition; and as soon as it was day, went to the city. He admired, as soon as he entered it, to see but very few mussulmen. He accosted the first he met, and asked him the name of the place? He was told, It was the city of the magicians; so called, because of the great number of magicians that were there, who adored the fire, and that there were but very few mussulmen. Amgrad then demanded how far it was to the isle of Ebene? He was answered, Four months voyage by sea, and a year's journey by land. The man he talked to left him hastily, having satisfied him as to those two questions, and went about his business.

Amgrad, who was about six weeks coming from the isle of Ebene with his brother Assad, could not comprehend how they came to this city in so little a time, unless it was by enchantment, or that the way cross the mountain was much shortened, and not frequented, because of the difficulty to pass.

Going farther in the town, he stopped at a tailor's shop, whom he knew to be a mussulman by his habit, as he had known the man he had talked to before. Having saluted him, he sat down, and told him the occasion of the trouble he was in.

When prince Amgrad had done talking, the tailor replied, If your brother has fallen into the hands of some magicians, depend upon it you will never see him more; he is past all recovery; and I advise you to comfort yourself as well as you can, and to beware of falling into the same misfortune. To which end, if you will hearken to me, you shall stay at my house, and I will tell you all the tricks of these magicians, that you may take care of yourself when you go out. Amgrad, grievously afflicted for the loss of his brother, accepted the tailor's offer, and thanked him a thousand times for his kindness to him.

The Story of Prince Amgrad, and a Lady of the City of the Magicians

PRINCE Amgrad did not go out of the tailor's house for a month's time, except his host went with him. At last he ventured to go to the baths. As he was returning home through a street where there was nobody in it but himself and a lady, he was surprised to find her come up to him, and pull up her veil. The lady seeing a handsome young man, fresh come out of the bath, asked him, with a smiling air, whither he was going? and ogled him all the while so amorously, that Amgrad could not resist her charms. Madam, says he, I am going to my own house, or yours, as you please.

My lord, replied the lady, with an agreeable smile, ladies of my quality never carry men to their own houses; they always go to the men's.

Amgrad was very much confounded at this answer, which he did not expect. He durst not venture to take her home to his landlord's, fearing the good man would be scandalized at it, and he should have lost his protection, of which he stood in great need, considering he was in a place where he must always be upon his guard. He knew so little of it, that he could not tell where to carry her, and he did not care to lose so happy a minute. In this uncertainty, he resolved to throw himself upon chance; and, without making any answer, he marched before, and the lady followed him. Amgrad led her from street to street, through lanes and alleys, so long, that they were both weary with walking. At last they came to a street, at the end of which was a great gate, shut up, and they could go no farther; that gate opened to a house which fronted the street, and had a seat on each side of it. Amgrad sat down on one of them to take breath; and the lady, more weary than he, seated herself down on the other.

When she had taken her seat, she asked him if that was his house? Yes, madam, says Amgrad. Why do you not enter then? replied the lady. What do you stay for? Amgrad answered, Fair lady, I have not the key of the gate; I left it with my slave, when I sent him on an errand, and he cannot be come back yet. Besides, I ordered him to get something good for dinner; so that I am afraid we shall wait a long time for him.

The prince met with so many difficulties in satisfying her passion, that he began to repent he had undertaken it. He, therefore, contrived this answer, in hopes that the lady would, out of resentment, leave him, and seek out for a lover elsewhere; but he was mistaken.

This is a most impertinent slave, says madam, to make us stay so long. I will chastise him myself as he deserves, if you do not, when he comes back. It is not decent that I should sit here alone with a man at a gate. Saying this, she arose and took up a stone to break the lock, which was only of wood, and weak, according to the country fashion.

Amgrad did all he could to hinder her. What are you a-doing, madam? quoth the prince. For heaven's sake, stay a little! What are you afraid of, replies the lady, is it not your house? It is no great matter to break a lock; a new one will not cost much. The lock she accordingly broke; and, as soon as the door was open, entered the house, and walked before him.

Amgrad gave himself over for a lost man, when he saw the door forced open; he paused upon it, whether he should go into the house or not, or make off as fast as he could, to avoid the danger he believed was inevitable; and he was just going to fly when the lady returned.

Seeing he did not enter; Why do not you come into your house? says she. The prince answered, I am looking to see if my slave is coming, fearing we have nothing ready. Come in, come in, says madam, we had better wait for him within doors than without.

Amgrad, much against his will, followed her into the house. Passing through a spacious court newly paved, they mounted by several steps into piazzas, which led to a large open hall, very well furnished, where he and the lady saw a table ready spread with fruit, and a cistern full of bottles of wine.

When Amgrad saw every thing in such order, he doubted not but he was undone; the quality of the owner appearing by the richness of the feast. Poor Amgrad, said he to himself, thou wilt soon follow thy dear brother Assad.

On the contrary, the lady was transported at the sight, crying out, How, my lord, did you fear there was nothing ready? You see your slaves had done more than you expected; but, if I am not mistaken, these preparations were made for some other lady, and not for me. No matter, let her come, I promise you I will not be jealous; I only beg the favour of you that you will permit me to wait on her and you.

Amgrad, as much as he was troubled at this accident, could not help laughing at the lady's pleasantness. Madam, says he, thinking of something else besides what tormented him, there is nothing in what you fancy, this is my common dinner, and no extraordinary preparations, I assure you. He could not bring himself to sit down at a table which was not prepared for him, so he took his seat on a sofa;[1] but the lady would not let him alone. Come, sir, says she, you must be hungry after bathing, let us eat and enjoy ourselves.

Amgrad was forced to do what the lady would have him. They both sat down and fell to. The lady, having eat a bit, took a bottle and glass, poured out some wine, and drank to Amgrad; and, when she had drank herself, she filled another glass, and gave it to Amgrad, who pledged her. The more the prince thought of this adventure, the more he was amazed that the master of the house did not appear; and that so rich a house, and so well provided, should be left without a servant. It will be lucky, said he to himself, if the man of the house do not come until I am got clear of this intrigue. While he was thinking of this, and some other troublesome thoughts, she ate and drank heartily, and obliged him to do the same. They were almost come to the last course when the master of the house arrived.

It happened to be Bahader, master of the horse to the king of the magicians. This house belonged to him, but he commonly dwelt in another; and

[1] A Turkish bench, upon which matts and cushions are put.*

he seldom came here, unless it was to regale himself with two or three chosen friends. He always sent provisions from his other house on such occasions, and had done so this day by some of his servants, who were just gone as the lady and Amgrad entered it.

Bahader came, as he used to do, in disguise, and without attendants, and a little before the time appointed for his friends' coming. He was not a little surprised to see the door of his house broken open: he entered, making no noise, and, hearing some persons talking and making merry in the hall, he stole along under the wall, and put his head half-way within the door to see who they were.

Perceiving a young gentleman and a young lady eating at his table the victuals that had been provided for his friends and himself, and that there was no great harm done, he resolved to make a jest on it.

The lady's back was a little turned from him, and she did not see the master of the horse, but Amgrad saw him immediately; he had then the glass in his hand, and was going to drink it off. He changed colour at the sight of Bahader, who made a sign to him not to say a word, but to come and speak with him.

Amgrad drank and rose. Where are you going? says the lady. The prince answered, Pray, madam, stay here a little, I shall be back again in a minute, a small affair obliges me to go out at present. Bahader waited for him in the piazza, and led him into the court, to talk with him, without being heard by the lady.

When Bahader and prince Amgrad were in the court, Bahader demanded of the prince how the lady came into his house, and why they broke open his door? My lord, replied Amgrad, you may very reasonably think me guilty of a very unwarrantable action; but, if you will have patience to hear me, I hope my innocence will appear. He then told him, in a few words, what had happened to him, without disguising any part of the truth; and, to convince him that he was not capable of being so criminal as he might think him, he told him plainly he was a prince, and what was the reason of his coming to the city of the magicians.

Bahader, who naturally loved strangers, was transported with an opportunity of obliging one of Amgrad's rank and quality; for, by his air, his actions, his handsome discourse, and his noble looks, he did not in the least doubt of the truth of what he said. Prince, said Bahader, I am very glad I can oblige you in so pleasant an adventure as this; and shall be so far from disturbing the feast, it will be a pleasure to me to contribute to your satisfaction in any thing. Before I say any more on this subject, I am glad it may lie in my power to serve you; my name is Bahader, I am master of the horse to the king of the magicians. I commonly dwell in another house, which I have in this city, and come here sometimes to have the more liberty with my friends, for I cannot be so free at home among my children and domestics. You have made this lady believe you have a slave, though you have none. I will be your slave, and, to spare your excuses, I repeat it again, that it shall positively be so; and you will suddenly know my reason for it. Go into your place, and continue to divert yourself. When I return again, and come before you in a slave's habit, chide me for staying so long;—do not be afraid even to strike me. I will wait upon you all the while you are at table, till night; and you shall lie here, and so shall the lady; and, to-morrow morning, you may send her home with honour. I shall afterwards endeavour to do you more important services. Go, and lose no time. Amgrad would have made him an answer, but the master of the horse would not let him, forcing him to go to the lady. He had scarce got into the hall before Bahader's friends, whom he had invited, arrived. Bahader called them to him, and excused his not entertaining them that day, telling them they would approve of the reason of it when they knew it, which should be in due time. When they were gone, he also went forth, and dressed himself in a slave's habit.

Prince Amgrad came to the lady in a much better humour than when he left her, finding the house belonged to a man of quality, who had received him so courteously. When he sat down to the table again, he said, Madam, I beg a thousand pardons for my rudeness; I was vexed that my slave should tarry so long,—the rascal shall pay for it when he comes; I will teach him to make me stay so for him another time.

Let not that trouble you, says the lady, if he is guilty of any faults, let him pay for it; do not think of him, we will enjoy ourselves without him, I will warrant you so much.

They continued at the table with the more pleasure, by how much Amgrad was under no apprehensions of the consequence of the lady's indiscretion, who ought not to have broke open the door, though it had been Amgrad's own house. The prince was now as merry as the lady. They drank and laughed, and drank again, till Bahader arrived, disguised like a slave.

Bahader entered like a slave, who feared his master's displeasure for staying out when he had company with him. He fell down at his feet, and kissed the ground, to implore his clemency; and, when he had done, stood behind him with his hands across, in expectation of his commands.

Sirrah, says Amgrad, with a fierce tone and fiery look, is there such a slave as thou in all the world? Where have you been? What have you been doing that you came no sooner?

My lord, replied Bahader, I ask your pardon, I was endeavouring to do as you ordered me, and could not dispatch it before: besides, I did not think you would come home so early.

You are a rascal, says Amgrad, and I shall bang your sides for you, to teach you to lie, and to fail me another time. He then rose up, took a stick, and gave him two or three blows with it, so lightly that he hardly touched him; after which he sat down to table again.

The lady was not satisfied with the chastisement he bestowed on him; so that she also arose, took the stick, and fell upon Bahader so unmercifully that the tears came into his eyes. Amgrad, offended at the freedom she took, and that she should use one of the king's chief officers so ill, cried out, It is enough; but she struck on, and he called to her in vain. Let me alone with him, said she, I will give him enough, and teach him to be absent so long another time. She continued beating him, till Amgrad rose from the table, and forced the stick out of her hand, which she did not part with without struggling. When she found she could beat Bahader no longer, she sat down and railed at and cursed him.

Bahader wiped his eyes, and stood behind his pretended master to fill out wine. When he saw they had done eating and drinking, he took away the cloth, put every thing in its place; and, night coming on, lighted up the lamps. As often as he came by her, the lady muttered, and threatened him, and gave him abusive language, to Amgrad's great disliking, who would have hindered her, but he could not. When it was time for them to go to bed, Bahader prepared one for them, and withdrew into a chamber over-against that where they were to lie, where he laid himself down, and it was not long before he fell asleep, having been fatigued with his beating. Amgrad and the lady entertained one another a good half hour afterwards, and the lady wanted to go forth before she went to bed. Passing through the gallery that parted Bahader's chamber from theirs, she heard him snore, and, seeing a sabre hanging up by him, she turned back again, and said to prince Amgrad, Pray, my lord, as you love me, do me one favour. In what can I serve you? replied the prince. The lady answered, Oblige me so far as to take down your sabre, and cut off your slave's head with it. Amgrad was astonished at such a proposal from a lady, not doubting but it was the wine she had drank that moved it. Madam, says he, let my slave alone, he is not worthy of your notice; I have beat him, and you have beat him, it is sufficient; I am very well satisfied with him: he does not use to be guilty of such faults.

That will not do, replied the lady, in a violent fury, the rogue shall die; if not by your hands, by mine. Saying this, she ran and took down the sabre from the place where it hung, drew it out of the scabbard, and was going to execute her wicked design.

Amgrad, to prevent her, took the sabre out of her hand, saying, You shall be satisfied, madam, the slave shall die, since you will have it so; but I shall be sorry that any one besides myself should kill him. When she had given him the sabre, Come, follow me, says he, make no noise, for fear we wake him. They went into Bahader's chamber, where Amgrad, instead of striking him, struck at the lady, and cut off her head, which fell upon Bahader.

If the noise of the blow which Amgrad gave the lady in cutting off her head, had not waked Bahader, her head falling upon him would have done it. He was amazed to see Amgrad with a sabre all bloody, and the body of the lady lying headless on the ground. The prince told him what had passed; and, ending his discourse, said, I had no other way to hinder her from killing you, but to take away her life; she was so transported with fury against you. My lord, replied Bahader, full of gratitude, persons of your rank, and so generous as you, are not capable of doing such a wicked action as she desired of you. You are my deliverer, and I cannot enough thank you. After having embraced him, to shew him what sense he had of his obligations to him, he said, We must carry this corpse out before it is quite day; leave it to me, I will do it. Amgrad would not agree to that, saying, He would carry it away himself, since he had struck the blow. Bahader replied, You are a stranger in this city, and will not come off so well as one who is acquainted here; I must do it, if for no other reason, yet for both our safeties, to prevent our being questioned for her death. Stay you here, and if I do not come back again before day, you may be sure the watch has taken me; and, for fear of the worst, I will, by writing, give this house and furniture for your habitation while you stay in this city.

When he had written, signed, and delivered the paper to prince Amgrad, he put the lady's body in a bag, head and all, heaved it upon his shoulders, and went out with it from one street to another, taking the way to the sea-side. He had not gone far before he met with one of the judges of the city, who was going the rounds in person, as was usual for the chief magistrate to do there. Bahader was stopped by the judge's followers, who, opening the bag, found the body of a murdered lady, bundled up with the head. The judge, who knew the master of the horse, notwithstanding his disguise, had him home to his house, and, not daring to put him to death without telling the king of it, because of his quality, he carried him to court as soon as it was day. As soon as the king had heard from the judge what a foul action he had been guilty of, as appeared by the circumstances of the matter, he fell upon the master of the horse in these words: Is it thus then that thou murderest my subjects, to rob them, and then wouldst throw their dead bodies into the sea to hide thy villany? Let us rid the world of him, go hang him up immediately.

As innocent as Bahader was, he took the sentence of death with all imaginable resignation, and said not a word to justify himself. The judge carried him to his house, and while the gallows was preparing, he sent a crier to publish throughout the city, That, at noon, the master of the horse was to be hanged for a murder committed by him.

Prince Amgrad, who had in vain expected Bahader's return, was struck into a terrible consternation, when he heard the crier publish the approaching execution of the master of the horse. If, says he to himself, somebody should die for the death of such a wicked woman, it is I who must suffer, and not Bahader: I will never suffer an innocent man to be punished for the guilty; and, without deliberating any more about it, he hastened to the place of execution, whither the people were running from all parts.

When Amgrad saw the judge bringing Bahader to the gibbet, he went up to him and said, I am come to tell you, and to assure you, that the master of the horse, whom you are leading to execution, is wholly innocent of the lady's death. I am guilty of the crime, if it is one, to have killed the most detestable of women, who would have murdered Bahader. So he told him the thing as it happened.

The prince having informed the judge how he met her coming out of the bath; how she was the cause of going into the master of the horse's house of pleasure, and what had passed to the moment in which he was forced to cut off her head to save Bahader's life; the judge ordered the execution to be stopped, and conducted Amgrad to the king, taking the master of the horse with him.

The king had a mind to hear the story from Amgrad himself; and the prince, the better to prove his own innocence and the master of the horse's, took hold of that opportunity to discover who he was, and what had driven him and his brother Assad to that city, with all the accidents that had befallen them, from their departure from the capital of the isle of Ebene, to that time in which he talked to him.

The prince having done speaking, the king said to him, I rejoice that I have by this means come to the knowledge of you. I not only give you your own and my master of the horse's life, whom I commend for his civility to you, but I restore him to his office; and, as for you, prince, I declare you my grand visier, to make amends for your father's unjust usage of you, though it is also excusable; and I permit you to employ all the authority I now give you to find out prince Assad.

Prince Amgrad having thanked the king of the city and country of magicians for the honour he had done him, and taken possession of his office of grand visier, he ordered the common crier to promise a great reward to any one who should bring forth prince Assad, or tell any tidings of him. He sent men up and down the country to the same purpose; but, notwithstanding all his and their diligence, they could hear no news of him.

Assad, in the mean while, continued in the dungeon in chains; Bostama and Cavama, the cunning old conjurer's daughters, treating him daily with the same cruelty and inhumanity as at first.

The solemn festival of the adorers of fire approached; and a ship was fitted out for the Fiery Mountain, as usual. The captain's name was Behram, a great bigot to that religion. He loaded it with proper merchandise; and when it was ready to sail, he put Assad in a chest which was half full of goods, a few crevices being left for him to breathe enough to keep life in him. This chest was stowed in the bottom of the hold, for the greater security.

Before the ship sailed, the grand visier Amgrad, Assad's brother, who had been told that the adorers of fire used to sacrifice a mussulman every year on the Fiery Mountain, suspected that Assad might have fallen into their hands, and be designed a victim at that bloody sacrifice; wherefore he resolved to search the ship in person. He ordered all the passengers and seamen to be brought upon deck, and commanded his men to search all over the ship; which they did: and yet Assad could not be found, he was so well concealed.

When the grand visier had done searching the vessel, she sailed; and as soon as Behram was got out to sea, he ordered prince Assad to be taken out of the chest, and fettered, to secure him, fearing lest he should fling himself into the sea, since he knew he was going to be sacrificed.

The wind was very favourable two or three days, and then it turned contrary: after which there rose a furious storm; and the vessel was not only driven out of her course, but neither Behram nor his pilot knew where they were. They were afraid of splitting against the rocks; for they discovered land, and a dreadful shore before them. Behram saw he was driven into the port and capital of queen Margiana; which was a great mortification to him; for queen Margiana was a devout professor of the Mahometan religion, and a mortal enemy to the adorers of fire: she banished all of them out of her dominions, and would not let any of their ships touch at her ports: but Behram now could not help it: the tempest increased; and he was forced to put into the port of this queen's capital city, or else he had been dashed to pieces against the rocks that lay off the shore. In this extremity, he held a council with his pilot and seamen. My lads, says he, you see to what a necessity we are reduced; we must chuse one of these two things, either resolve to be swallowed up by the waves, or put into queen Margiana's port, whose hatred to all persons of our religion you very well know: she will certainly seize our vessel, and put us all to death without mercy. I see but one likely way to escape her; which is, to take off the fetters from the mussulman we have aboard, and dress him like a slave. When queen Margiana commands me to come before her, and asks what trade I use? I will tell her I deal in slaves; that I have sold all I had but one, whom I keep to be my clerk, because he can read and write. She will see him, to be sure; and he being handsome, and of her own religion, will have pity on him: no doubt, she will then ask to buy him of me; and I refusing, will not let us stay in her port till the weather is fair. If I sell him to her, perhaps she will give us leave to tarry, and let us be well used.

If any of you have any thing else to propose that will be of more advantage to us, I am ready to hearken to it. The pilot and seamen applauded his judgment, and agreed to follow his advice.

Behram commanded prince Assad's chains to be taken off; and had him dressed like a slave very neatly, as became one who was to pass for his clerk before the queen of the country. They had scarce time to fit every thing for their purpose, before the ship drove into the port, and they then dropped anchor.

Queen Margiana's palace was so near the sea-side that her garden extended down to the shore. She saw the ship sail by, and sent to the captain to come to her as soon as he moored his vessel. She was walking in her garden, and gave him to understand she staid there expecting him.

Behram, who knew he should be sent for, landed with prince Assad, whom he required to confirm what he had said of his being a slave, and his clerk. So he went to the palace-garden, and was introduced to the queen. He threw himself at her feet, and informed her of the necessity he was in to put into her port; that he dealt in slaves, and had sold all he had but one, which was Assad, there present, whom he kept for his clerk.

The queen was taken with Assad from the minute she first saw him, and was extremely glad to hear that he was a slave, resolving to buy him, cost what it would. She asked Assad what was his name?

Great queen, replied Assad, with tears, does your majesty ask what my name was formerly, or what it is now? The queen answered, Have you two names then? It is but too true, said Assad: I was once called Assad, (the most happy); and now my name is Motar, (devoted to be sacrificed).

Margiana, not being able to find out the depth of his meaning by his thought, his condition of a slave putting him upon mysterious answers, she perceived he had a great deal of wit. Since you are clerk to the captain, said she, no doubt you can write well; let me see your hand.

Behram had furnished Assad with pen, ink, and paper, as a token of his office, that the queen might take him for what he designed she should.

The prince stepped a little aside, and wrote as follows, suitable to his miserable circumstances:

'The blind man avoids the ditch into which the clear-sighted falls. Fools advance themselves to honours, by discourses which signify nothing; while men of sense and eloquence live in poverty and contempt. The mussulman with all his riches is miserable, the infidel triumphs; and we cannot hope things will be otherwise: the Almighty has decreed it should be so; and his will is not to be altered.'

Assad presented the paper to queen Margiana, who admired alike the sententiousness of the thoughts, and the goodness of the writing. She needed no more to have her heart set on fire, and to feel a sincere concern for his misfortunes. She had no sooner read it, but she addressed herself to Behram, saying, Do which you will, either sell me this slave, or make a present of him to me: perhaps it will turn most to your account to do the latter.

Behram answered insolently, That he could neither give nor sell him; that he wanted his slave, and would keep him.

Queen Margiana, provoked at his boldness, would not talk to him any more about it. She took the prince by the arm, and turned him before her to the palace, sending Behram word, that, if he staid a night in her port, she would confiscate his goods and burn his ship. So he was forced to go back to his vessel, and prepare her to put to sea again, notwithstanding the tempest was not yet laid.

Queen Margiana commanded supper to be got ready; and while it was providing, she ordered Assad to be brought into her apartment, where she bid him sit down. Assad would have excused himself: It does not belong to a slave, said he, to presume to this honour. To a slave! replied the queen: you shall not be so long: henceforward you are no more a slave. Sit down near me, and tell me the story of your life; for by what you wrote, and the inference of that slave-merchant, I guess there is something extraordinary in it.

Prince Assad obeyed her; and, sitting down, began thus: Mighty queen, your majesty is not mistaken in thinking there is something extraordinary in the story of my life: it is indeed more so than you can imagine. The ills, the incredible torments I have suffered, and the death to which I was devoted, and from which I am delivered by your generosity, will shew, when I have related them, that my obligation to you is infinite. But before I enter into the particulars of my miseries, which will strike horror into the hearts of all that hear it; to explain the occasion of them, I must trace the matter a little higher, and begin with the source of my misfortunes.

This preamble increased queen Margiana's curiosity. The prince then told her the whole of his royal birth; of his brother Amgrad, and their mutual friendship; of their mothers' criminal passion, which in a night turned into inveterate hatred, the cause of all their sufferings; of the king's rage; how miraculously they saved their lives; how he lost his brother; how he had been imprisoned, tortured, and was only sent then to be sacrificed on the Fiery Mountain.

When Assad had finished his discourse, the queen was more than ever enraged at the adorers of fire. Prince, said she, though I have always had an aversion to the adorers of fire, yet hitherto I have had some humanity for them; but after their barbarous usage of you, and their execrable design to sacrifice you, I will henceforth declare perpetual war with them.

She would have said more; but supper being served in, hindered her. She made prince Assad sit down at table with her, being charmed with his beauty and eloquence, and touched with a passion which she hoped suddenly to have an opportunity of letting him see. Prince, said she, we must make you amends for so many fasts and wretched meals which the pitiless adorers of fire forced you to make; you will want to be nourished after such sufferings. With these, and such like words, she began supper; and ordered the prince to be plied with wine, to recover his spirits; by which means he drank more than he could well carry.

The cloth being taken away, Assad wanting to go out, watched his time when the queen did not see him. He descended into a court, and seeing the garden-door open, went into it. Being tempted by the pleasantness of the place, he walked there a while: at last he came to a fountain, where he washed his face and hands, to refresh himself, and lying down on some grass-plots around the fountain, fell asleep.

It was almost night; and Behram, fearing the queen would do as she threatened, had weighed anchor, and was under sail, mightily troubled at the loss of Assad, by which he was disappointed of a most acceptable sacrifice. He comforted himself as well as he could, with the thoughts that the storm was over, and that a land-breeze favoured his getting off from that coast. He was towed out of the port; and as he was hoisting up more sail to hasten his course, he remembered he wanted some fresh water: My lads, says he to the seamen, we must put to shore again, and fill our water-casks. The sailors excused themselves, for that they did not know where to get water. Behram had observed, while he was talking to the queen in the garden, that there was a fountain at the end of it, near the port: Go, says he, to such a place of the palace-garden; the wall is not above breast-high, you may easily get over; there is a fountain, where you may fill all your barrels, and hand them aboard without difficulty.

The sailors accordingly went ashore at the place he directed them to, leaped over the wall, filled the barrels, and easily enough heaved them over also, when they returned to their boat.

As they were filling their casks, they perceived a man sleeping on the grass, and knew him to be Assad. They immediately divided themselves; and while some of the crew filled their barrels, others surrounded Assad, and observed him, lest he should awake and offer to run away.

He was fast, and slept on, giving them time to fill all their casks; which as soon as they had filled, they handed over the wall to others of their crew, who waited there to carry them aboard.

They afterwards seized Assad, and bore him away, asleep as he was. They got over the wall into their boat, and rowed to the ship. When they came near her, they cried out, Captain, sound your trumpets, beat your drums; we have brought you your slave again.

Behram, who could not imagine how the seamen could find and take him, and did not see Assad in the boat, it being night, waited their coming on board with impatience, to ask what they meant by their shouts; but seeing it was true, and that they had really got him, he could not contain himself, so great was his joy. He commanded him to be chained down again, not staying to enquire how they came at him; and, having hauled the boat on board, set sail for the Fiery Mountain.

In the mean while, queen Margiana was in a dreadful fright. She did not much concern herself at first, when she found prince Assad was gone out; because she did not doubt but he would return in a little time: when several minutes, and then an hour, was passed, without hearing any thing of him, she began to be uneasy, and commanded her women to look for him. They searched all about, without finding him; and night coming, she ordered them to search again with torches, which they did, and to as little purpose.

Queen Margiana was so impatient and frightened, that she went with lights all over the garden to seek for him herself; and, passing by the fountain, she spied a slipper, which she took up, and knew it to be prince Assad's: her women also said it was his: and the water being spilt about the cistern in which the fountain played, made her believe that Behram had carried him off again. She sent immediately to see if he was still in the port; and hearing he had set sail a little before it was dark; that he stopped some time off the shore, while he sent his boat for water from the fountain; she doubted no longer of the prince's ill fortune: so she commanded the commodore of ten men of war, who lay ready in the port to sail as occasion required, to prepare to put to sea, for she would embark herself next morning, as soon as it was day. The commodore ordered the captains, subalterns, seamen, and soldiers, aboard, and was ready to set sail at the time appointed: she embarked as she said she would, and when the squadron was at sea, told the commodore what was her intention. Make all the sail you can, said she, and give chase to the merchantman that sailed yesterday out of this port: I give it you to be plundered, if you take it; if not, your life shall answer it.

The ten ships chased Behram's two days entire, and could not come near her: the third day they got up with her, and encompassed her so about that she could not escape them.

As soon as cruel Behram spied the ten men of war, he did not doubt but it was queen Margiana's squadron in pursuit of him; and upon that, he ordered Assad to be bastinadoed; which he did every day, and had not missed once treating him so barbarously since he left the port of the city of the magicians; but on sight of these ships he used him more cruelly than before. He was very much puzzled what to do, when he found he was encompassed about. To keep Assad, was to declare himself guilty; to kill him, was as dangerous, for he feared some token or other of it might be seen: he therefore commanded him to be unfettered, and brought up from the bottom of the hold where he lay. When he came before him, It is thou, says he, that art the cause of my being pursued; and upon that he flung him into the sea.

Prince Assad knowing how to swim, by the help of his feet and hands, got safe to shore; the waves assisting him, by the art he had in making use of them. The first thing he did, after he landed, was to thank heaven, who had delivered him from so great danger, and once more rescued him out of the hands of the adorers of fire. He then stripped himself; and wringing the water off his clothes, he spread them on a rock, where, by the heat of the sun, and the rock together, they soon dried: after which, he lay down to rest himself, deploring his miserable condition, not knowing in what country he was, nor where to turn himself. He refreshed himself as well as he could with wild fruits and fair water, and then went on his way, keeping as near the sea-side as he could: at last he came to a sort of a path, which he followed, and travelled ten days through a country which was not inhabited, still living on herbs, plants, and fruits. On the eleventh day, he approached near a city, which he knew to be that of the magicians, where he had been so ill used, and where his brother Amgrad was grand visier. He was very glad of it, resolving not to come near any one of the adorers of fire, but only to converse with mussulmen; for he remembered he had seen some the first time he entered the town. It being late, and he knowing the shops were already shut, and few people in the streets, he resolved to stay in a church-yard near the city, where there were several tombs built in the form of mausoleums: he found the door of one of them open, entered it, and designed to pass the night there.

We must now return to Behram's ship, which was soon surrounded on all sides by queen Margiana's squadron, after he had thrown prince Assad over-board. Queen Margiana's ship, in which she was in person, first boarded him; and Behram being in no condition of defence against so many, lowered his sails, as a token of his yielding.

The queen herself came aboard him, and demanded where the clerk was, whom he had the boldness to take away from her out of her very palace?

Behram replied, O queen! I swear before your majesty he is not in my ship; you will, by searching it, see my innocence.

Margiana ordered the ship to be searched as narrowly as possible; but she could not find the man whom she so passionately longed to recover, as well out of love to him, as out of that generosity which was her distinguishing character. She was going to kill Behram with her own hand; but however did not, contenting herself with seizing his ship and cargo, and turning him and his men on shore.

Behram and his seamen arrived at the city of the magicians the same night that Assad did, stopped at the same church-yard, the city-gates being shut, intending to stay in some tomb till the next day, when they were opened again.

As Assad's ill luck would have it, Behram lighted upon that in which the prince was sleeping, with his head wrapped up in his coat: Assad awoke at the noise he made, and asked who was there?

Behram knew him again presently. Ha! ha! says he, thou art the man who has been my ruin for ever: thou hast escaped being sacrificed this year; but depend upon it, thou shalt not escape the next. Saying this, he flew upon him, clapped his handkerchief in his mouth, to prevent his making a noise, and, by the help of his seamen, bound him.

The next morning, as soon as the city-gates were open, Behram and his men easily carried Assad to the old man's house, where he had been so inhumanly treated. It was so early that they met nobody in the streets; and when he came to the old man's house, he was again thrown into the dungeon. Behram acquainted the wizard with the sad occasion of his return, and the ill success of his voyage: the old rascal, upon this, commanded his two furies, Bostama and Cavama, to treat him more cruelly than before, if possible.

Assad was in a terrible surprise to find himself in the hands of his old persecutors, from whom he had suffered so much, and hoped that he had been delivered: he bemoaned the rigour of his destiny, and trembled when he saw Bostama enter with a cudgel, a loaf, and a pitcher of water: he was almost dead at the sight of that unmerciful wretch, and the thoughts of the daily sufferings he was to endure for another year; after which he was to die the most horrible death.

Bostama dealt not so inhumanly to prince Assad as she had done on the first day of his confinement: his cries, complaints, and earnest prayers to her to spare him, joined with his tears, were so moving, that Bostama could not help being melted by them, and to weep as bitterly as himself. My lord, said she, covering his shoulders, which were always bare while he was under the bastinado, I ask a thousand pardons for my inhuman treatment of you formerly, and for what you felt at this time: until now, I was afraid of disobeying a father who is unjustly enraged against you, and resolved on your destruction; but, at last, I loath and abhor his barbarity. Be comforted, your bad days are over; I will endeavour to make amends for all my crimes, the enormity of which you will find I am convinced of, by my future usage. You have hitherto looked on me as an infidel; you must henceforth believe me one of your own religion, having been converted by a slave who is a mussulman. I hope your lessons will finish my conversion. To shew my good intentions, I first beg pardon of heaven for my sins in dealing so cruelly by you; and I trust that it will be put in my power to set you entirely at liberty.

The prince was transported to hear her talk at that rate: he thanked the Almighty for the change worked upon her, and for touching the heart of so barbarous a creature: he also thanked her for her good disposition towards him, and omitted no arguments which he thought would have any effect to confirm her in her new religion. He told her, as a sign of his confidence in her, his whole story, his high birth, and adventures to that time. When he began to believe she was in earnest, he asked her how she could hinder her sister Cavama's treating him as barbarously as she used to do? Let not that trouble you, replied Bostama, I know how to order matters so as she shall never come near you.

And as she said, she every day prevented her coming down into the dungeon, where she often visited the prince; and, instead of carrying him bread and water, she brought him the best wine, and the choicest victuals she could get, which was provided by her Mahometan slave. She eat with him herself, from time to time, and did her utmost to make him bear his confinement the more easily.

A few days afterwards, Bostama, as she stood at her father's door, heard the common crier making proclamation; but she could not hear what it was about, being too far off. He came up near her father's house when he had done; upon which she withdrew into it, holding the door half open, perceiving he marched before the grand visier Amgrad, brother to Assad, who was accompanied by several officers, and several attendants, walking before and behind him.

The crier going a few steps from the house, repeated the proclamation with a loud voice, as follows: 'The most excellent and illustrious lord the grand visier is come in person to seek for his dear brother, from whom he was separated about a year ago; he is a young man of such a make; if any one has him in keeping, or knows where he is, his excellency commands that they bring him forth, or give him notice where he shall find him, promising a great reward to the person that shall do so. If any one conceals him, and it be found out, his excellency declares he or they shall be punished with death, together with his or their children, and all that belong to him, and his, or their house or houses, be razed to the ground.' Bostama, as soon as she had heard this, shut the door as fast as she could, and ran to Assad in the dungeon. Prince, said she with joy, your troubles are at an end; follow me; come immediately, and be free. She had taken off his fetters several days before: so the prince followed her into the street, where she cried, There! there! and seemed transported at what she had done.

The grand visier, who was not far from the house, hearing the clamours, returned. Assad knew him to be his brother, ran to him, and embraced him. Amgrad, who presently saw it was his brother Assad, returned his embrace with all possible tenderness, made him mount one of his officers' horses, who alighted for that purpose, and conducted him to the palace, where he presented him to the king, by whom he was advanced to the post of a visier.

Bostama would not return to her father's house, which was the next day razed to the ground, but kept prince Assad in sight; and for the service she had done him was admitted into the queen's service.

The old man her father, and Behram, were brought before the king, who condemned them and all their families to be beheaded. They threw themselves at his feet, and implored his mercy. There is no mercy for you to expect, says the king, unless you renounce your adoration of fire, and profess the Mahometan religion.

They accepted the conditions, and were pardoned at the intercession of Assad, in consideration of Bostama's friendship; for whose sake, Cavama's life, and the lives of the rest of their families, were saved.

Amgrad, to reward Behram for turning mussulman, and recompence him for his losses, made him one of his officers, and lodged him in his house. Behram being informed of Amgrad and his brother Assad's story, proposed to his benefactor, to fit him a vessel to convey them to their father king Camaralzaman's court; for, says he, the king must certainly have heard of your innocence, and impatiently desire to see you ere this: otherwise we can easily inform ourselves of the truth before we land; and if he is still in the same mind, you can but return hither.

The two brothers liking the proposal, communicated it to the king of the city of the magicians, who approved of it, and commanded a ship to be equipped. Behram undertook the employment chearfully; and being master of the art of navigation and maritime affairs, he soon got in readiness to sail. The two princes, when they understood the ship was ready, waited upon the king one morning to take their leave of him. While they were reciprocally passing their compliments on that occasion, they were interrupted by a great noise and tumult in the city; and presently an officer came to give them notice that a numerous army was advancing against the city; nobody knowing who they were, or whence they came.

The king being mightily alarmed at the news, Amgrad addressed himself to him thus: Sir, though I am come to resign into your majesty's hands the dignity of your first minister, with which you were pleased to honour me, I am, however, ready to do you all the service that lies in my power: I desire, therefore, that you will be pleased to let me go and see who this enemy is that comes to attack you in your capital city, without having first declared war.

The king prayed him to do so; and Amgrad parted from him immediately, with a very small retinue, to see what enemy approached, and what was the reason of their coming.

It was not long before prince Amgrad descried the army, which approached nearer and nearer. The forlorn received him favourably, and conducted him to a princess, who stopped herself, and commanded her army to halt while she discoursed with the prince; who, bowing profoundly to her, demanded if she came as a friend or an enemy? if as an enemy, what cause of complaint she had against the king his master?

I am come as a friend, replied the princess, and have nothing to complain of against the king of the city of the magicians: his territories and mine are so situated, that it is almost impossible for our subjects to quarrel with one another, or we ourselves to have any disputes: I only come to require a slave, named Assad, to be delivered up to me. He was carried away by one Behram, a captain of a ship, the most insolent man in the world. I hope your king will do me justice, especially when he knows I am Margiana.

The prince answered, Mighty queen, the slave whom you take so much pains to seek for, is my brother. I lost him, and have found him again.—Come, madam, I will deliver him up to you myself; and will do myself the honour to tell you the rest of the story, as we go to the king my master's palace, who will rejoice to see you.

The queen ordered her army to pitch their tents, and encamp where they were; and accompanied prince Amgrad to the city and palace-royal, where he presented her to the king, who received her as became his dignity and hers. Assad, who was present, and knew her as soon as he saw her, also paid his duty to her. She shewed all the marks of transporting joy at the sight of him. And while they were thus busied, news came that an army, more powerful than the former, approached on another side of the city.

The king of the magicians was more frightened than before, understanding the second army was more numerous than the first; for the dust they made raised clouds in the air, so as to hide the face of the heavens. Amgrad, cried he, what shall we do now? a new army comes to destroy us.

Amgrad guessed what the king would have of him: so he mounted on horseback again, and gallopped towards this second army. He demanded of the advanced guards to speak with their general: they conducted him to a king, for such he was, he saw by the crown on his head. When he drew near him, he threw himself to the ground, and asked what he would have of the king his master?

The monarch replied, I am Gaiour, king of China; my desire to learn some tidings of a daughter, whose name is Badoura, whom I married to Camaralzaman, son of Schahzaman, king of the Isles of the Children of Khaledan, obliged me to leave my dominions. I suffered that prince to go and see his father king Schahzaman, on condition he came back in a year with my daughter: so long have I waited, and have heard nothing of them. Your king will lay an infinite obligation on an afflicted father, to tell him if he knows what is become of them.

Prince Amgrad perceiving by his discourse that this king was his grandfather, kissed his hand with tenderness, and answered him thus: Sir, I hope your majesty will pardon my freedom when you know I take it only to pay my duty to my grandfather; I am the son of Camaralzaman, king of the isle of Ebene, and of queen Badoura, for whom you are thus troubled, and I doubt not but they are both in good health in their kingdom.

The king of China, overjoyed to see his grandson, embraced him with extraordinary affection: such a meeting, so happy and unexpected, drew tears from both of them. The king enquiring on what occasion he came into a strange country, the prince told him all that had happened to him and his brother Assad. When he had ended his relation, My son, replied the king of China, it is not just that such innocent princes as you are should be longer ill used: Comfort yourself, I will carry you and your brother home, and make your peace. Return and acquaint your brother with my arrival.

While the king of China encamped in the same place where prince Amgrad met him, that prince returned to let the king of the magicians, who waited for him impatiently, know how he had succeeded.

The king was amazed that so mighty a king as he of China should undertake such a long and troublesome journey out of a desire to see his daughter; and, seeing he was so near his capital, he gave orders to make things ready for his reception, and went forth to meet him.

While these things were transacting, a great dust was seen from another quarter of the town: and suddenly news came of the arrival of a third army, which obliged the king to stop and to desire prince Amgrad once more to see who they were, and on what account they came.

Amgrad went accordingly, and prince Assad accompanied him. They found it was Camaralzaman, their father's army, with whom he was coming to seek for them. He was so grieved for the loss of his sons, that at last emir Giendar declared how he had saved their lives, and towards what country the two princes had travelled.

The sad father embraced the two princes with floods of joyous tears, which put an end to those he had a long time shed for grief.—The princes had no sooner told him the king of China, his father-in-law, was arrived, but he detached himself from the grand army, and, with a small party, among whom were his own sons, rode to wait upon him in his camp. They had not gone far before they saw a fourth army advancing in fair array, which seemed to come from Persia side.

Camaralzaman bid the two princes go and see what army it was, and he would, in the mean while, stay for them. They departed immediately, and, coming up to it, were presented to the king, whom they saluted with due reverence, and demanded on what design he approached so near the king of the magicians' capital? The grand visier, who was present, answered in the name of the king his master, The monarch to whom you speak is Schahzaman, king of the Isles of the Children of Khaledan, who has a long time travelled thus attended, to seek his son prince Camaralzaman, who left his dominions many years ago: if you know any thing of him, you cannot oblige him more than to acquaint him with it.

The princes only replied, that they would bring him an answer in a very little time, and, galloping back as fast as they could, told Camaralzaman it was king Schahzaman's army, and, that his father was with it in person.

Wonder, surprise, joy, and grief to have left the king his father without taking leave of him, had such an effect on king Camaralzaman, that he fell into a swoon as soon as he heard he was so near. Prince Amgrad and prince Assad so laboured to recover him, that at last he came to himself; and, when he was in a condition to ride to his father's tent, he threw himself at his feet.

Never was there a more moving interview: Schahzaman kindly complained of Camaralzaman's unkindness in so cruelly leaving him, and Camaralzaman discovered a hearty sorrow for the fault he had committed.

The three kings, and queen Margiana, staid three days at the court of the king of the magicians, who treated them magnificently.—Those three days were rendered the more remarkable by prince Assad's marriage with queen Margiana, and prince Amgrad's with Bostama, for the service she had done his brother Assad.

At last the three kings and queen Margiana, with her husband prince Assad, went to their several kingdoms. As for Amgrad, the king of the magicians had such a love for him, that he would not part with him, and, being very old, he resigned his crown to him. King Amgrad, when he had the supreme authority, did his utmost to exterminate the worship of fire, and establish the Mahometan religion throughout all his territories.

The Story of Noureddin and the Fair Persian

BALSORA was for many years the capital of a kingdom tributary to the caliphs of Arabia. The king who governed it in the days of caliph Haroun Alraschid, was named Zinchi. They were both cousins, the sons of two brothers. Zinchi not thinking it proper to commit the administration of his affairs to one single visier, made choice of two, Khacan and Saouy.

Khacan was of a sweet, generous, and affable temper, and took a wonderful pride in obliging those with whom he had any concern, to the utmost of his power, without the least hindrance or prejudice to justice, whenever it was demanded of him; so that he was universally respected both at court, in the city, and throughout the whole kingdom; and every body's mouth was full of the praises he so highly deserved.

Saouy was of a quite different character; he was always sullen and morose, and treated every body after a disrespectful manner, without any regard to their rank or quality; instead of making himself beloved and admired for his riches, he was so perfect a miser as to deny himself the necessaries of life. In short, nobody could endure him, and if ever any thing was said to him, to be sure it was something of ill. But what increased the people's hatred against him the more was his implacable aversion for Khacan; always interpreting in the worst sense the actions of that worthy minister, and endeavouring to do him all the ill offices imaginable with the king.

One day, after council, the king of Balsora diverted himself with his two visiers, and some other members of the council; they fell into discourse about the women-slaves, that with us are daily bought and sold, and are almost reckoned in the same rank with our wives. Some were of opinion, that it was enough if the slave that one bought was beautiful and well shaped, to make us amends for the wives, which, very often, upon the account of alliance or interest in families, we are forced to marry, who are not always the greatest beauties, nor mistresses of any perfection, either of mind or body. Others maintained, and amongst the rest Khacan, that neither beauty, nor a thousand other charming perfections of the body, were the only things to be coveted in a mistress, but they ought to be accompanied with a great deal of wit, prudence, modesty and agreeableness; and, if possible, abundance of sense and penetration. The reason they gave for it was, that nothing in the world could be more agreeable to persons on whom the management of important affairs depend, than, after having spent the day in that fatiguing employment, to have a companion in their retirement whose conversation is not only agreeable, but useful and diverting; for, in short, continued they, there is but little difference between brutes and those men who keep a mistress only to look upon her, and gratify a passion that we have in common with them.

The king was entirely of their opinion who spoke last, and he quickly gave some demonstration of it, by ordering Khacan to buy him a slave, one that was a perfect beauty, mistress of all those qualifications they had just mentioned, and especially very ingenious.

Saouy, jealous of the honour the king had done Khacan, and vexed at his being of a contrary opinion, Sir, says he, it will be very difficult to find a slave so accomplished as to answer your majesty's demand; and, should they light upon such a one, (as I scarce believe they will,) she will be a cheap bargain at ten thousand pieces of gold. Saouy, replied the king, I perceive plainly you think it too great a sum; it may be so for you, though not for me. Then turning to the chief treasurer, he ordered him to send the ten thousand pieces of gold to the visier's house.

Khacan, as soon as he came home, sent for all the courtiers who used to deal in women-slaves, and strictly charged them, that, if ever they met with a slave that answered the description he gave them, they should come and acquaint him with it. The courtiers, partly to oblige the visier, and partly for their own interest, promised to use their utmost endeavours to find out one to his liking. Accordingly there was scarce a day past but they brought him one, yet he always found some fault or other with them.

One day as Khacan was getting on horse-back very early in the morning to go to court, a courtier came to him, and, with a great deal of eagerness, catching hold of the stirrup, told him there was a Persian merchant arrived very late the day before, who had a slave to sell so surprisingly beautiful that she excelled all women that his eyes ever beheld; and as for her parts and learning, the merchant engages she shall cope with the finest wits and the most knowing persons of the age.

Khacan overjoyed at this news, which made him hope for a favourable reception at court, ordered him to bring the slave to his palace against his coming back, and so continued his journey.

The courtier failed not of being at the visier's at the appointed hour; and Khacan finding the lovely slave so much beyond his expectation, immediately gave her the name of the Fair Persian. As she had an infinite deal of wit and learning, he soon perceived by her conversation that it was in vain to search any farther for a slave that surpassed her in any of those qualifications required by the king, and therefore he asked the courtier at what rate the Persian merchant valued her.

Sir, replied the courtier, he is a man of few words in bargaining, and he tells me, that the very lowest rate he can part with her at, is ten thousand pieces of gold: he has also sworn to me, that without reckoning his pains and trouble from the time of his first taking care of her, he has laid out pretty near the sum upon her education, on masters to instruct and teach her, besides cloathes and maintenance, and, as he always thought her fit for a king, so from her very infancy, in which he bought her, he has not been sparing in any thing that might contribute towards advancing her to that high honour.—She plays on all sorts of instruments to perfection, she dances, sings, writes better than the most celebrated authors, understands poetry, and, in short, there is scarce any book but what she has read, so that there never was a slave of so vast a capacity heard of before.

The visier Khacan, who understood the merit of the fair Persian better than the courtier, that only reported what he had heard from the merchant, was unwilling to drive off the bargain to another time; and therefore he sent one of his servants to look after the merchant, where the courtier told him he was to be found.

As soon as the Persian merchant came, It is not for myself, but the king, says the visier Khacan, that I buy your slave; but however, you must let him have her at a more reasonable price than what you have already set upon her.

Sir, replied the merchant, I should do myself an unspeakable honour in offering her as a present to his majesty, were I able to make him one of so inestimable a value. I barely ask no more than what her education and breeding up has cost me; and all I have to say is, that I believe his majesty will be extremely pleased with the purchase.

The visier Khacan would stand no longer bargaining with the merchant, but paid him the money down immediately. Sir, says he to the visier, upon taking his leave of him, since the slave is designed for the king's use, give me leave to tell you, that being extremely fatigued with our long journey together, you see her at a great disadvantage, and though she has not her equal in the world for beauty, yet if you please to keep her at your own house but for a fortnight, and strive a little to please and humour her, she will appear quite another creature; after that, you may present her to the king with abundance of honour and credit; for which, I doubt not but you will think yourself much obliged to me. The sun, you see, has a little tarnished her complexion; but after two or three times bathing, and when you have dressed her according to the fashion of your country, she will appear to your eyes infinitely more charming than now.

Khacan was mightily pleased with the advice the merchant gave him, and was resolved to follow it; accordingly the Fair Persian was lodged in a particular apartment near his lady's, whom he desired to invite her to an entertainment, and henceforth to treat her as a mistress designed for the king: he also intreated his lady to get the richest cloaths for her that possibly could be had, and especially those that became her best. Before he took his leave of the Fair Persian, he says, Your happiness, madam, cannot be greater than what I am about to procure for you, since it is for the king himself I have bought you; and I hope he will be better pleased with the enjoyment of you, than I am in discharging the trust his majesty has laid upon me: however, I think it my duty to warn you of my son, who, though he has a tolerable share of wit, yet is a young, wanton, forward youth; and therefore have a care how you suffer him to come near you. The Fair Persian thanked him for his good advice, and after she had given him an assurance of her intention to follow it, he withdrew.

Noureddin, for so the visier's son was named, had all the liberty imaginable in his mother's apartment, with whom he usually ate: He was very genteel, young, agreeable, and bold; and being master of abundance of wit, and readiness of expression, he had the art of persuading people to whatever he pleased. He saw the Fair Persian; and from their first interview, though he knew his father had bought her purposely for the king, and he himself had declared the same, yet he never used the least endeavour to put a stop to the violence of his passion. In short, he resigned himself wholly to the power of her charms, by which his heart was at first conquered: and being ravished with her conversation, he was resolved to employ his utmost endeavours to get her from the king.

On the other hand, the Fair Persian had no dislike to Noureddin. The visier, says she to herself, has done me a particular honour in buying me for the king of Balsora; but I should have thought myself very happy if he had designed me only for his son.

Noureddin was not backward in making use of the advantage of seeing, entertaining, and conversing with a beauty he was so passionately in love with; for he would never leave her until his mother forced him to do it. My son, she would say, it is not proper for a young man, as you are, to be always amongst the ladies; go mind your studies, that in time you may be worthy to succeed your father in his high posts and honours.

It being a great while since the Fair Persian had bathed, on account of her late fatiguing journey, the visier's lady, five or six days after she was bought, ordered a private bath in her own house to be got ready purposely for her. She had a great many woman-slaves to wait upon her, who were charged by the visier's lady, to be as careful of her as of her own person, and after bathing, to put on her a very rich suit of cloaths that she had provided for her; and all this pains and care was taken purely to ingratiate herself the more into her husband's affection, by letting him see how much she concerned herself in every thing that contributed to his pleasure.

As soon as she came out of the bath, the Fair Persian, a thousand times more beautiful than ever she appeared to Khacan when he bought her, went to make a visit to his lady, who at first sight hardly knew her. After having saluted her in a very graceful manner, Madam, says she, I know not how you like me in this dress you have been pleased to order for me; but your women, who tell me it becomes me so extremely well they should scarce know me, are such gross flatterers, that it is from you alone I expect to hear the truth: but however, if what they say be really so, it is to you entirely, madam, that I owe the advantage it has given me.

Oh! my daughter, cries the visier's lady, quite transported with joy, you have no reason in the world to believe my women have flattered you: I am better skilled in beauty than they are, and, setting aside your dress, which becomes you admirably well, you appear so much handsomer than you did before your bathing, that I hardly knew you myself: If I thought the bath was yet hot enough, I would willingly take my turn, for I am now of an age that requires frequent use of it. Madam, replied the Fair Persian, I have nothing to say to the undeserved civilitics you have been pleased to shew me, but as for the bath, it is wonderfully fine, and if you design to go in, you must be quick, for there is no time to be lost, as your women can inform you as well as I.

The visier's lady, considering that she had not bathed for some days past, was willing to make use of that opportunity; and accordingly she acquainted her women with her intention, who immediately prepared all things necessary on such an occasion. The Fair Persian withdrew to her apartment; and the visier's lady, before she went to bathe, ordered two little slaves to stay with her, with a strict charge, that if Noureddin came they should not give him admittance.

While the visier's lady was bathing, and the fair slave alone in her apartment, in came Noureddin, and not finding his mother in her chamber, went directly to the Fair Persian's, where he found the two little slaves in the anti-chamber: He asked them where his mother was? They told him, in the bath. Where is the Fair Persian then? replied Noureddin. In her chamber, answered the slaves, but we have positive orders from your mother not to let you go in.

The entrance into the Fair Persian's chamber being only covered with a piece of tapestry, Noureddin went to lift it up in order to go in, but was opposed by the two slaves, who clapped themselves just before it on purpose to stop his passage; he presently caught hold of both their arms, and thrusting them out of the anti-chamber, locked the door upon them: Away they immediately ran with a great outcry to the bath, and with weeping eyes told their lady that Noureddin, having driven them away by force, was got into the Fair Persian's chamber.

The visier's lady received the astonishing news of her son's presumption with the greatest concern that could be; she immediately left off bathing, and dressing herself with all possible speed, came directly to the Fair Persian's chamber; but before she could get thither, Noureddin was fairly marched off.

The Fair Persian was extremely surprised to see the visier's lady enter her chamber all in tears, and in the utmost confusion imaginable; Madam, says she to her, may I presume to ask you the occasion of your concern; and what accident has happened in the bath, that makes you leave it so soon?

What! cries the visier's lady, can you so calmly ask that question, after your entertaining my son Noureddin alone in your chamber? or can there happen a greater misfortune either to him or me?

I beseech you, madam, says the fair slave, what injury can this action of Noureddin's do either to you or him?

How! replied the visier's lady, did not my husband tell you that you were designed for the king, and sufficiently cautioned you to have a care of Noureddin?

I have not forgot it, madam, replied the Fair Persian; but your son came to tell me the visier his father has changed his mind, and, instead of reserving me for the king, as he first designed, has made him a present of my person. I easily believed him, madam; for oh! think how a slave, as I am, accustomed from my infant years to the bonds of servitude, could have the heart and power to resist him! I must own I did it with the less unwillingness on account of a violent passion for him, which the freedom of conversation, and seeing one another daily, has raised in my soul; I could freely lose the hopes of ever being the king's, and think myself the happiest of creatures in spending my whole life with Noureddin.

At this discourse of the Fair Persian's, Would to God, cries the visier's lady, that what you say were true! for then I should have no reason to be concerned; but, believe me, Noureddin is an impostor, and you are deceived; for it is impossible his father should ever make him the present you spoke of: Ah! wretched youth, how miserable hast thou made me! but more thy father, by the dismal consequences we must all expect to share with him! Neither my prayers nor tears will be able to prevail, or obtain a pardon for him; but as soon as his father hears of his violence to you, he will inevitably sacrifice him to his just resentment. At the end of these words she fell a-weeping bitterly, and the slaves who had as tender a regard for Noureddin as herself, bore her company.

A little after this, in came the visier Khacan; and, being mightily surprised to find his lady and her slaves all in tears, and the Fair Persian very melancholy, asked the reason of it: but they, instead of answering him, kept on weeping, and making hideous lamentations. He was more astonished at this than he was before; at last, addressing himself to his wife, I command you, says he, to let me know the occasion of your tears, and to tell me the whole truth of the matter.

The poor disconsolate lady being forced to satisfy her husband, Sir, says she, you shall first promise not to use me unkindly upon the discovery of what you are desirous to know, since I tell you before-hand that what has happened has not been occasioned by any fault of mine. While I was bathing with my women, continued she, your son, laying hold of that fatal opportunity to ruin us both, came hither, and made the Fair Persian believe, that, instead of reserving her for the king, as you once designed, you had given her to him as a present: I do not say he has done this out of an ill design, but shall leave you to judge of it yourself: It is upon your account, and his, for whom I want confidence to implore your pardon, that I am so extremely concerned.

It is impossible to express the visier Khacan's distraction upon the hearing of the insolence of his son Noureddin: Ah! cried he, beating his breast, and tearing his beard, miserable son! unworthy of life! hast thou at last thrown thy father from the highest pinnacle of happiness into a misfortune that must inevitably involve thee also in its ruin! Neither will the king be satisfied with thy blood nor mine, but will revenge himself after a more severe manner for the affront offered to his royal person.

His lady used her utmost endeavours to comfort and assuage his sorrow. Concern yourself no more about the matter, my dear, said she; I will sell part of my jewels for ten thousand pieces of gold, with which you may buy another slave, handsomer, and more agreeable to the king's fancy, than this.

Ah! replied the visier, could you think me of so mean a spirit, as to be so extremely afflicted at the losing ten thousand pieces of gold? It is not that, nor the loss of all my goods, which I can easily part with, but the forfeiting of my honour, more precious than all the riches in the world, that torments and touches me so nearly. However, methinks, replied the lady, this can be no very considerable damage, since it is in the power of money to repair it.

How! cried the visier, you know Saouy is my mortal enemy, and as soon as this affair comes to his knowledge, do you think he will not insult over me, and mock my misfortunes before the king? Your majesty, he will say to him, is always talking of Khacan's zeal and affection for your service: but see what a proof he has lately given of his being worthy the respect you have hitherto shewn him. He has received ten thousand pieces of gold to buy a slave with, and, to do him justice, he has honourably performed that commission in buying the most beautiful that ever eyes beheld; but, instead of bringing her to your majesty, he has thought it better to make a present of her to his son: Here, my son, said he, take this slave, since thou art more worthy of her than the king. Then with his usual malice will he go on; His son has her now entirely in his possession, and every day revels in her arms, without the least disturbance: This, sir, is the whole truth of the matter, that I have done myself the honour of acquainting you with; and if your majesty questions the truth of it, you may easily satisfy yourself. Do you not plainly see, my dear, continued the visier, how, upon such a malicious insinuation as this, I am every moment liable to have my house forced open by the king's guards, and the Fair Persian taken from me, besides a thousand other misfortunes that will unavoidably follow? Sir, said the visier's lady to her husband, after he had finished his discourse, I am sensible the malice of Saouy is very great, and that, if he has had but the least intimation of this affair, he will certainly give it a turn very disadvantageous to your interest: but how is it possible that he or any body else should come to the knowledge of what has been privately transacted in your family? Suppose it comes to the king's ear, and he should ask you about it, cannot you say, that upon strict examination you did not think the slave so fit for his majesty's use as you did at the first view; that the merchant has cheated you; that, indeed, she has a great deal of beauty, but is nothing near so witty or agreeable as she was reported to be. The king will certainly believe what you say, and Saouy be vexed to the soul to see all his malicious designs of ruining you eternally disappointed: Take courage then, and, if you will follow my advice, send for all the courtiers, tell them you do not like the Fair Persian, and order them to be as expeditious as possible in getting another slave.

The visier Khacan, highly approving of this advice, was resolved to make use of it, and though his passion began to cool a little, yet his indignation against his son Noureddin was not in the least abated.

Noureddin came not in sight all that day; and, not daring to hide himself among his companions, lest his father should search their houses for him, he went a little way out of town, and took sanctuary in a garden where he had never been before, and where his person was utterly unknown. It was very late when he came back, being willing to stay till his father was a-bed, and then his mother's women opening the door very softly, let him in without any manner of noise. The next morning he went out before his father was stirring; and thus for a whole month was he put to his shifts, which was a terrible mortification to him. Indeed the women never flattered him, but told him plainly his father's anger was as great as ever, and if he came in his sight he would certainly kill him.

Though the visier's lady was informed by her women of Noureddin's lying every night in the house, yet she durst not presume to entreat her husband to pardon him: At last, one day, says she to him: I have hitherto been silent, not daring to take the liberty of talking to you about your son; but now give me leave to ask you what you design to do with him? Indeed it is impossible for a son to be more criminal towards a father than Noureddin has been towards you; he has robbed you of the honour and satisfaction of presenting the king with a slave so accomplished as the Fair Persian; but, after all, are you absolutely resolved to destroy him, and, instead of a light evil, draw upon yourself a far greater than perhaps you imagine at present? Are you not afraid that the world, which spitefully inquires after the reason of your son's absconding, should find out the true cause which you are so desirous of keeping secret? and if that should happen, you would justly fall into a misfortune which it is so much your interest to avoid.

Madam, said the visier, there is abundance of sound reasoning in what you have urged: however, I cannot think of pardoning Noureddin till I have humbled him a little more. He shall be sufficiently mortified, replied the lady, if you will put in execution what is just come into my mind: You must know then your son comes hither every night after you are a-bed, he lies here, and steals out every morning before you are stirring; you shall wait for his coming in to-night, make as if you designed to kill him; upon which, I will run to his assistance, and when he finds his life entirely owing to my prayers and entreaties, you may oblige him to take the Fair Persian on what condition soever you please. He loves her, and I am sensible the fair slave has no aversion for him.

Khacan was very willing to make use of this stratagem; so when Noureddin came at the usual hour, before the door was opened, he placed himself behind it: As soon as ever he entered, he rushed suddenly upon him, and got him down under his feet. Noureddin, lifting up his head, saw his father with a dagger in his hand, ready prepared to stab him.

In that very instant, in came his mother, and, catching hold of the visier's arm, Sir, cried she, what are you a-doing? Let me alone, replied the visier, that I may kill this base unworthy son. You shall kill me first, cried the mother; nor will I suffer you to imbrue your hands in your own blood: Speak to him, Noureddin, speak to him, and improve this tender moment. My father, cried he, with tears in his eyes, I implore your clemency and compassion; nor must you deny me pardon, since I ask it in his name, before whom we must all appear at the last day.

Khacan suffered the poniard to be taken out of his hand; and as soon as Noureddin was released, he threw himself at his father's feet, and kissed them, to shew how sincerely he repented of his having ever offended him.

Noureddin, said he, return your mother thanks, since it is purely for her sake I pardon you. I design also to give you the Fair Persian, on condition that you will oblige yourself by an oath not to look upon her any longer as a slave, but as your wife, that you will not sell her, nor ever be divorced from her; for she, having abundance of wit and prudence, besides much better conduct than you, I am persuaded she will be able to moderate those rash sallies of youth which are enough to ruin you.

Noureddin, who little expected to be treated after so kind and indulgent a manner, returned his father a thousand thanks, with all the gratitude and sincerity imaginable; and in the conclusion, the visier, the Fair Persian and he, were well pleased and satisfied with the match.

The visier Khacan would not stay in expectation of the king's asking him about the order he had given him, but took a particular care to mention it often, in representing to his majesty the many difficulties he met with in that affair, and how fearful he was of not acquitting himself to his majesty's satisfaction. In short, he managed the business with so much cunning and address, that the king insensibly forgot it; and, though Saouy had got some small information of the matter, yet Khacan was so much in the king's favour that he was afraid to speak of it.

It was now above a year that this nice affair had been kept with greater secrecy than at first the visier expected, when, being one day in the bath, and some important business obliging him to leave it all in a sweat, the air, which was then a little moist, struck a damp to his breast, caused a defluxion of rheum to fall upon his lungs, which threw him into a violent fever, and confined him to his bed. His illness growing every day worse, and perceiving he had but a few moments to live, he thus addressed himself to his son Noureddin, who never stirred from him during his whole sickness: My son, I know not whether I have made a good use of the riches heaven has blessed me with, but you see they are not able to save me from the hands of death; the last thing I desire of you, with my dying breath, is, that you would be mindful of the promise you made concerning the Fair Persian, and with a certainty of that, I shall die pleased and well contented.

These were the visier's last words, who, dying a few moments after, left his family, the court, and the whole city in great affliction for his death. The king lamented him, as having lost a wise, zealous, and faithful minister; and the whole city wept for him as their protector and benefactor. Never was there a funeral at Balsora solemnized with greater pomp and magnificence; the visiers and emirs, and, in general, all the grandees of the court, strove for the honour of bearing his coffin, one after another, upon their shoulders, to the place of burial; and both rich and poor accompanied him thither with tears.

Noureddin gave all the demonstration of a sorrow equal to the loss he had lately sustained, and lived a great while without ever seeing any company. At last, he admitted of a visit from an intimate friend of his. His friend endeavoured to comfort him all he could, and, finding him a little inclinable to hear reason, he told him, that, having paid what was due to the memory of his father, and fully satisfied all that custom and decency required of him, it was now high time to appear again in the world to converse with his friends, and maintain a character suitable to his birth and merit: For, continued he, we should sin both against the laws of nature and civility, and be thought insensible, if, upon the death of our fathers, we neglected to pay them what filial love and tenderness require at our hands; but having once performed that duty, and put it out of the power of any man to reproach us upon that account, we are obliged to return to our usual method of living. Dry up your tears then, and re-assume that wonted air of gaiety which always inspires with joy those that have the honour of your conversation.

This advice seeming very reasonable to Noureddin, he was easily persuaded to follow it; and, if he had been ruled by his friend in every thing, he would certainly have avoided all the misfortunes that afterwards befel him. He treated him very nobly; and, when he took his leave, Noureddin desired him to come the next day, and bring three or four friends of their acquaintance. By this means he insensibly fell into the society of about ten young gentlemen, pretty near his own age, with whom he spent his time in continual feasting and entertainments; and scarce a day came over his head but he made every one of them some considerable present.

Sometimes, to oblige his friends after a more particular manner, Noureddin would send for the Fair Persian to entertain them, who, notwithstanding her obedience to his command, never approved of his extravagant way of living; and often took the liberty of speaking her mind freely. Sir, said she, I question not but your father has left you abundance of riches; but, how great soever they are, be not angry with your slave for telling you that, at this rate of living, you will quickly see an end of them. We may indeed sometimes afford to treat our friends, and be merry with them, but, to make a daily practice of it, is certainly the high road to ruin and destruction. Therefore, for your own honour and reputation, you would do much better to follow the footsteps of your deceased father, that, in time, you may rise to that dignity by which he has acquired so much glory and renown.

Noureddin hearkened to the fair Persian's discourse with a smiling countenance; and, when she had done, My charmer, said he, with the same air of mirth, say no more of that; let us talk of nothing but mirth and pleasure. In my father's lifetime I was always under restraint, and I am now resolved to enjoy the liberty I so much sighed for before his death. It is time enough for me to think of leading a sober regular life; and a man of my age ought to taste the pleasures of youth.

What contributed very much towards ruining Noureddin's fortune, was his unwillingness to reckon with his steward; for, whenever he brought in his accounts, he still sent him away without examining them. Go, go, said he, I trust wholly to your honesty; therefore only take care to let me have wherewith to make merry.

You are the master, sir, replied he, and I but the steward; however, you would do well to think upon the proverb, He that spends much, and has but little, must at last insensibly be reduced to poverty. You are not contented with keeping an extravagant table, but you must lavish away your estate with both hands: and were your coffers as large as mountains, they would not be sufficient to maintain you. Begone, replied Noureddin, your grave lessons are needless; only take care to provide good eating and drinking, and trouble your head no farther about the rest.

In the mean time, Noureddin's friends were constant guests at his table, and never failed making some advantage of the easiness of his temper. They praised and flattered him, extolling his most indifferent actions to the very skies. But, above all, they took particular care to commend whatever belonged to him and his; and this, they found, turned to some account. Sir, says one of them, I came the other day by your estate that lies in such a place; certainly there is nothing so magnificent, or so handsomely furnished, as your house; and the garden belonging to it is a paradise upon earth. I am very glad it pleases you, says Noureddin. Here, bring me pen, ink, and paper: but, without more words, it is at your service, and I make you a present of it. No sooner had others commended his house, baths, and some public buildings erected for the use of strangers, the yearly revenue of which was very considerable, but he immediately gave them away. The Fair Persian could not forbear letting him know how much injury he did himself; but, instead of taking any notice of it, he continued his extravagancies, and upon the first opportunity squandered away the little he had left.

In short, Noureddin did nothing for a whole year together, but feasted and made himself merry, wasting and consuming, after a prodigal manner, the riches that his predecessors, and the good visier his father, had, with so much pains and care, heaped together and preserved.

The year was but just expired, when somebody, one day, knocked at the hall door, where he and his friends were at dinner together by themselves, having sent away their slaves, that they might enjoy a greater liberty and freedom of conversation.

One of his friends offered to rise, but Noureddin stepped before him, and opened the door himself. It seems it was the steward; and Noureddin going a little out of the hall to know his business, left the door half open.

The friend that offered to rise from his seat, seeing it was the steward, and being somewhat curious to know what he had to say to Noureddin, placed himself between the hangings and the door, where he plainly overheard the steward's discourse to his master. Sir, said the steward, I ask a thousand pardons for my coming to disturb you in the height of your joys; but this affair is of such importance that I thought myself bound in duty to acquaint you with it. I come, sir, to make up my last accounts, and to tell you that what I all along foresaw, and have often warned you of, is at last come to pass. Behold, sir, says he, (shewing him a small piece of money,) the remainder of all the sums I have received from you during my stewardship; the other funds you were pleased to assign me are all exhausted. The farmers, and those that owe you rent, have made it so plainly appear to me that you have assigned over to others, whatever remains in their hands due to you, that it is impossible for me to get any more off them upon your account. Here are my books, if you please, examine them; and if you think fit to continue me in the place I am now in, order me some other funds, or else give me leave to quit your service. Noureddin was so astonished at this discourse that he gave him no manner of answer.

The friend who had been listening all this while, and had heard every syllable of what the steward said, immediately came in and told the company what he had lately overheard. It is your business, gentlemen, says he, to make use of this caution; for my part, I declare it openly to you, this is the last visit I design ever to make Noureddin. Nay, replied they, if matters go thus, we have as little business here as you; and, for the future, shall take care not to trouble him with our company.

Noureddin returned presently after; yet, notwithstanding his carrying it pleasantly to his guests, by putting them into a merry humour again, he could not so handsomely dissemble the matter, but they plainly perceived the truth of what they had been informed of. He was scarce sat down in his place, but one of his friends rose up, saying, Sir, I am sorry I cannot have the honour of your company any longer; and, therefore, I hope you will excuse my rudeness of leaving you so soon. What urgent affair have you, replied Noureddin, that obliges you to be going? My wife, sir, said he, is brought to bed to-day, and upon such an occasion, you know, a husband's company is very acceptable: so, making a very low bow, away he went. A minute afterwards, a second took his leave upon another sham excuse. And so one after another, till at last not one of those ten friends that had hitherto kept Noureddin company, was left in the room.

As soon as they were gone, Noureddin, little suspecting the resolution they had made of never visiting him, went directly to the Fair Persian's apartment; to whom, in private, he related all the steward had told him, and seemed extremely concerned at the ill posture of his affairs. Sir, said the Fair Persian to him, you would never take my advice, but always managed your concerns after your own way, and now you see the fatal consequences of it. I find I was not mistaken, when I presaged to what a miserable condition you would bring yourself at last: but what afflicts me the more, is, that at present you do not see the worst of your misfortunes. Whenever I presumed freely to impart my thoughts to you, Let us be merry, said you, and in pleasures improve the time that fortune has kindly given us, perhaps she will not always be so prodigal of her favours: But was I now to blame in telling you that we are the makers or undoers of our own fortunes, by a prudent or foolish management of them? You indeed would never hearken to me; so, at last, much against my will, I was forced to desist, and let you alone.

I must own, replied Noureddin, I was extremely in the wrong in not following the advice that you, out of your abundance of prudence and discretion, was pleased to give me. It is true I have spent my estate, but do you not consider it is among friends of a long acquaintance, who, I am persuaded, have more generosity and gratitude in them than to abandon and forsake me in distress? Sir, replied the Fair Persian, if you have nothing but the gratitude of your friends to depend on, you are in a desperate condition; for, believe me, that hope is vain and ill-grounded, and you will tell me so yourself in a very little time.

To this Noureddin replied, Charming Persian, I have a better opinion of my friends' generosity than you. To-morrow I design to make a visit to them all, before the usual time of their coming hither, and you shall see me return with a vast sum, that they will raise among them to support me: I am resolved to change my way of living, and, with the money they lend me, set up for a merchant.

The next morning, Noureddin failed not to visit his ten friends, who lived in the very same street; he knocked at the first door he came at, where one of the richest of them lived. A slave came to the door; but, before he would open it, he asked who was there? Go to your master, says he to the slave, and tell him it is Noureddin, the late visier's son. Upon this, the slave opens the door, and shews him into a hall, where he left him to go and tell his master, who was in an inner room, that Noureddin was come to wait on him. Noureddin! cried he, in a disdainful tone, loud enough for Noureddin to hear it, with surprise:—Go, tell him I am not at home; and whenever he comes hither, be sure you give him the same answer. The slave came back, and told Noureddin he thought his master was within, but he was mistaken.

Noureddin came away in the greatest confusion in the world. Ah! base, ungrateful wretch! said he to himself, to treat me so basely to-day, after the vows and protestations of love and friendship that you made me yesterday! From thence he went to another door, but that friend ordered his slaves also to say he was gone out. He had the same answer at the third; and, in short, all the rest denied themselves, though every one of them was at home at the same time.

It was now that Noureddin began in earnest to reflect with himself, and be convinced of the folly of his too credulous temper, in relying so much upon the vows and protestations of amity, that his false friends in the time of his prosperity had solemnly made him. It is very true, said he to himself, that a fortunate man, as I was, may be compared to a tree loaden with fruit, which, as long as there is any remaining on its boughs, people will be crowding round; but, as soon as it is stripped of all, they immediately leave it, and go to another. He smothered his passions as much as possible while he was abroad; but, no sooner was he got home, but he gave loose to his sorrow, and resigned himself wholly to it.

The Fair Persian seeing him so extremely concerned, fancied he had not found his friends so ready to assist him as he expected. Well, sir, said she, you are now convinced of the truth of what I told you? Ah! cried he, my dear, thou hast been too true a prophetess; for not one of them would so much as know me, see me, or speak to me. Oh! who could ever have believed that persons so highly obliged to me as they are, and on whom I have spent my estate, could ever have used me so barbarously? I am distracted, and I fear committing some dishonourable action, below myself, in the deplorable condition I am reduced to, without the aid and assistance of your prudent advice. Sir, replied the Fair Persian, I see no other way of supporting yourself in your misfortunes, but selling off your slaves and moveables, and to live upon the money till heaven shall find out some other means to deliver you from your present misery.

Noureddin was very loth to make use of this expedient; but what could he do in the necessitous circumstance he was in? He first sold off his slaves; those unprofitable mouths, which were a greater expence to him than what his present condition could bear: he lived on the money for some time; and when all of it was spent, he ordered his goods to be carried into the market-place, where they were sold for half their worth; among which were several valuable things that cost immense sums. Upon this he lived for a considerable time; but that supply failing at last, he had nothing at all left by which he could raise any more money; of which he complained to the Fair Persian in the most tender expressions that sorrow could inspire.

Noureddin only waited to hear what answer this prudent creature would make him. Sir, said she, at last, I am your slave, and you know that the late visier your father gave ten thousand pieces of gold for me; perhaps I am a little sunk in value since that time, but I believe I shall sell pretty near that sum yet. Let me entreat you then instantly to carry me to the market, and expose me to sale; and with the money that you get for me, which will be very considerable, you may turn merchant in some city where you are unknown, and by that means find a way of living, if not in splendour, yet with happiness and content.

Ah! lovely and adorable Persian, cried Noureddin, is it possible you can entertain such a thought of me? Have I given you such slender proofs of my love, that you should think me capable of so base an action? But suppose me so vile a wretch, could I do it without being guilty of perjury, after the oath I have taken never to sell you? No, I could sooner die than part with you, whom I love infinitely beyond myself; though by the unreasonable proposition you have made me, it is plain your love is not so tender as mine.

Sir, replied the Fair Persian, I am sufficiently convinced that your passion for me is as violent as you say it is; and heaven, who knows with what reluctancy I have made this proposition that you dislike, is my witness, that mine is as great as yours; but, to silence reason at once, I need only bid you remember that necessity has no law. I love you to that degree, it is impossible for you to love me more; and be assured, that to what master soever I shall belong, my passion shall always continue the same: and if you are ever able to redeem me, as I hope you may, it will be the greatest pleasure in the world to be in your possession again. Alas! to what a fatal and cruel necessity are we driven! But I see no other way of freeing ourselves from the misery that involves us both.

Noureddin, who very well knew the truth of what the Fair Persian had spoken, and that there was no other way of avoiding a shameful poverty, was in the end forced to yield to her first request. Accordingly he led her to the market, where the women-slaves are exposed to sale, with a regret that cannot be easily expressed; he applied himself to a courtier named Hagi Hassan: Hagi Hassan, said he, here is a slave that I have a mind to sell, I pray thee see what they will give for her. Hagi Hassan desired Noureddin and the Fair Persian to walk into a room; and when she had pulled off the veil that covered her face, Sir, said Hagi Hassan to Noureddin, in a great surprise, if I am not mistaken, this is the slave your father, the late visier, gave ten thousand pieces of gold for. Noureddin assured him it was the same; and Hagi Hassan gave him some hopes of selling her at a good rate, and promised to use all his art and cunning to raise her price as high as it would bear.

Hagi Hassan and Noureddin went out of the room, and locked the Fair Persian in; after which Hagi Hassan went to look after the merchants; but they being busy in buying slaves that came from different countries, he was forced to stay till the market was done. When their sale was over, and the greatest part of them got together, My masters, said he to them, with an air of gaiety in his looks and actions, every thing that is round is not a nut, every thing that is long is not a fig; all that is red is not flesh, and all eggs are not fresh: It is true you have seen and bought a great many slaves in your lives, but you never yet saw one comparable to her I am going to tell you of; in short, she is the very pearl of slaves. Come, follow me, and you shall see her yourselves, and by that judge at what rate I shall cry her.

The merchants followed Hagi Hassan into the chamber where the Fair Persian was; and as soon as they beheld her, they were so surprised at her beauty, that at the first word they unanimously agreed that four thousand pieces of gold was the very lowest price that they could set upon her. The merchants then left the room, and Hagi Hassan, who came out with them, without going any farther, proclaimed with a loud voice, Four thousand pieces of gold for the Persian slave.

None of the merchants had yet offered any thing, and they were but just consulting together about what they might afford to give for her, when the visier Saouy, perceiving Noureddin in the market, appeared. Said he to himself, Noureddin has certainly made some more money of his goods, (for he knew of his exposing them to sale,) and is come hither to buy a slave with it. Upon this he advanced forward just as Hagi Hassan began to proclaim a second time, Four thousand pieces of gold for the Persian slave.

The visier Saouy concluding by the extravagancy of the price, that she must be some extraordinary piece of beauty, had a longing desire to see her; so spurring his horse forward, he rode directly up to Hagi Hassan, who was in the very middle of the merchants. Open the door, said he, and let me see this slave. It was never the custom to shew their slaves to any particular person, till after the merchants had seen her, and had the refusal: But Saouy being a person of so great authority, none of them durst dispute their right with him; and Hagi Hassan being forced to open the door, beckoned the fair slave to come forward, that Saouy might have a sight of her without the trouble of alighting from his horse.

The visier was astonished at the sight of so beautiful a slave; and knowing the courtier's name, (having formerly dealt with him,) Hagi Hassan, said he, is it not at four thousand pieces of gold that you cry her? Yes, sir, answered he, it is but a moment since I cried her at that price, and the merchants you see gathered together here are come to bid money for her; and I question not but they will give a great deal more than that.

If nobody offers any higher, I will give that sum, replied Saouy, looking upon the merchants at the same time with a countenance that forbid them to advance any more. In short, he was so universally dreaded, that nobody durst speak a word, not so much as to complain of his encroaching upon their privilege.

The visier Saouy having staid some time, and finding none of the merchants outbid him, What do you stay for? said he to Hagi Hassan: Go look after the seller, and strike a bargain with him at four thousand pieces of gold, or more if he demands it; not knowing yet the slave belonged to Noureddin.

Hagi Hassan having locked the chamber-door, went to confer notes with Noureddin: Sir, said he to him, I am very sorry to bring you the ill news of your slave's being just going to be sold for nothing. How so? replied Noureddin. Why sir, said Hagi Hassan, you must know that the business at first went on rarely; for as soon as the merchants had seen your slave, they ordered me to cry her at four thousand pieces of gold. Accordingly I cried her at that price; upon which the visier Saouy came, and his presence has stopped the mouths of all the merchants, who seemed inclinable to raise her, at least to the same price your deceased father gave for her. Saouy will give no more than four thousand pieces, and it is much against my inclination that I am come to tell you the despicable price he offers. The slave indeed is your own; but I will not advise you to part with her upon those terms, since you and every body else are sensible of her being worth infinitely more; besides, he is base enough to contrive a way to trick you out of the money.

Hagi Hassan, replied Noureddin, I am highly obliged to thee for thy advice; but do not think I will ever sell my slave to an enemy of our family. My necessities indeed are at present very great, but I would sooner die in the most shameful poverty, than ever consent to the delivering her up to his arms. I have only one thing to beg of thee, who art skilful in all the turns and shifts of life, that thou wouldst put me in a way to prevent the sale of her.

Sir, said Hagi Hassan, there is nothing more easy; you must pretend, that, being in a violent passion with your slave, you swore to expose her in the market, and for the sake of your oath you have now brought her hither, without any manner of intention of selling her. This will satisfy every body, and Saouy will have nothing to say against it. Come along with me then, and just as I am presenting her to Saouy, as if it were by your own consent, pull her to you, give her two or three blows, and send her home. I thank thee for thy council, said Noureddin, and thou shalt see I will make use of it.

Hagi Hassan went back to the chamber, and having in two words acquainted the Fair Persian with their design, that she might not be surprised at it, he took her by the hand, and led her to the visier Saouy, who was still on horseback at the door: Sir, said he, here is the slave, she is your's, pray take her.

These words were scarce out of Hagi Hassan's mouth, but Noureddin, catching hold of the Fair Persian, pulled her to him, and giving her a box on the ear, Come hither, impertinence, said he, and get you home again; for though your ill-humour obliged me to swear I should bring you hither, yet I never intended to sell you; I have business for you to do yet, and it will be time enough to part with you when I have nothing else left.

This action of Noureddin's put the visier Saouy into a violent passion. Miserable debauchee, cried he, wouldst thou have me believe thou hast any thing else left to make money of but thy slave? And at the same instant, spurring his horse directly against him, endeavoured to have carried off the Fair Persian. Noureddin nettled to the quick at the affront the visier had put upon him, quits the Fair Persian, and, laying hold of his horse's bridle, made him run two or three paces backwards. Vile dotard, said he to the visier, I would tear thy soul out of thy body this very moment, were it not for the crowd of people here present.

The visier Saouy being loved by nobody, but, on the contrary, hated by all, there was not one among them but was now pleased to see Noureddin mortifying him a little; and, by shrewd signs, they let him understand he might revenge himself upon him as much as he pleased, for nobody would meddle with their quarrel.

Saouy endeavoured all he could to make Noureddin quit the bridle; but he being a lusty vigorous man, and encouraged by those that stood by, pulled him off his horse, in the middle of a brook, gave him a thousand blows, and dashed his head against the stones till it was all of a gore of blood. The slaves that waited upon the visier would fain have drawn their scymitars and fallen upon Noureddin, but the merchants interposing prevented them from doing it. What do you mean, said they to them; do not you see the one is a visier, and the other a visier's son? Let them dispute their quarrel themselves; perhaps they will be reconciled one time or other; whereas, if you had killed Noureddin, your master, with all his greatness, could not have been able to protect you against the law.

Noureddin having given over beating the visier Saouy, left him in the middle of the brook, and taking the fair Persian, marched home with her, being attended by the people with shouts and acclamations for the action he had performed.

The visier Saouy, cruelly bruised with the strokes he had received, by the assistance of his slaves, made shift to get up, and had the mortification to see himself besmeared all over with blood and dirt. He leaned upon the shoulders of two slaves, and in that condition went straight to the palace, in the sight of all the people, with so much greater confusion, because nobody pitied him. As soon as he reached the king's apartment, he began to cry out, and call for justice, after a lamentable manner. The king ordered him to be admitted; and as soon as he came, he asked him who it was that had abused and put him into that miserable pickle. Sir, cried Saouy, your majesty ought to afford me a large share of your favour, and to take into your royal consideration my late abuse, since it was chiefly upon your account that I have been so barbarously treated. Say no more of that, replied the king, but let me hear the whole story, simply as it is, and who the offender is; and if he is in the wrong, you may depend upon it he shall be severely punished.

Sir, said Saouy then, telling the whole matter to his own advantage, having an occasion for a cook-maid, I went to the market of women-slaves to buy me one: when I came thither, there was a slave just cried at four thousand pieces of gold: I ordered them to bring the slave before me, and I think my eyes never did, nor ever will, behold a more glorious creature than she is. I had not time to examine her beauty thoroughly, but, however, I immediately asked to whom she belonged; and upon inquiry I found that Noureddin, son to the late visier Khacan, had the disposing of her.

Sir, you may remember, that, about two or three years ago, you gave that visier ten thousand pieces of gold, strictly charging him to buy you a slave with it. The money indeed was laid out upon this very slave; but instead of bringing her to your majesty, thinking his son deserved her better, he made him a present of her. Noureddin, since his father's death, having wasted his whole fortune in riot and feasting, has nothing left but this slave, which he intended to part with, and therefore she was to be sold in his name. I sent for him, and, without mentioning any thing of his father's baseness, or rather treachery, to your majesty, I very civilly said to him, Noureddin, the merchants, I perceive, have put your slave up at four thousand pieces of gold: and I question not, but in emulation of each other, they will raise the price considerably; let me have her for the four thousand pieces; I am going to buy her for the king, our lord and master; this will be a handsome opportunity of making your court to him, and his favour will be worth a great deal more than the merchants can propose to give you.

Instead of returning me a civil answer, as in good manners he ought to have done, the insolent wretch beholding me with an air of fierceness, Decrepid villain, said he, I would rather sell my slave to a Jew for nothing than to thee for money. Noureddin, replied I, without any manner of passion, though I had some reason to be a little warm, you do not consider that in talking at this rate you affront the king, who has raised your father and me to the honours we have enjoyed.

This admonition, instead of moving him to a compliance, provoked him to a higher degree; so that, falling upon me like a madman, he pulled me off my horse, beat me as long as he could stand over me, and has put me into this miserable plight your majesty sees me in; and therefore I beseech you, sir, to consider me, since it is upon your account I have been so openly affronted. At the end of these words, he bowed his head, and turning about, wept a plentiful shower of tears.

The abused king, highly incensed against Noureddin by this relation, full of malice and artifice, discovered by his countenance the violence of his anger; and, turning to the captain of his guards that stood near him, Take forty of your soldiers, said he, and immediately go plunder Noureddin's house; and, having ordered it to be razed to the ground, bring him and his slave along with you.

The captain of the guards was not gone out of the king's presence, when a gentleman-usher belonging to the court, who overheard the order that had been given, got before him. His name was Sangiar, and he had been formerly the visier Khacan's slave, by whose favour he was brought into the court-service, where by degrees he was advanced higher.

Sangiar, full of gratitude for his old master, and affection for Noureddin, with whom in his infancy he had often played, and being no stranger to Saouy's hatred of Khacan's family, could not hear the orders without concern and trembling. May be, said he to himself, this action of Noureddin's is not altogether so black as Saouy has represented it; but, however, the king is prejudiced against him, and will certainly put him to death without allowing him time to justify himself.

Sangiar made so much haste to Noureddin's house, as to get thither time enough to acquaint him with what had passed at court, and to desire him to provide for his own and the Fair Persian's safety. He knocked so violently loud at the door, that Noureddin, who had been a great while without any servant, ran immediately to open it: My dear lord, said Sangiar, here is no more staying for you in Balsora: if you design to save yourself, you must lose no time, but depart hence this very moment.

Why so? replied Noureddin; what is the reason I must begone so soon? Ah! sir, said Sangiar, make haste away, and take your slave with you; for, in short, Saouy has been just now acquainting the king, after his own way of telling it, all that happened between you and him; and the captain of the guards will be here in an instant, with forty soldiers, and seize you and the Fair Persian. Here, sir, take these forty pieces of gold, it is all I have about me, to assist you in finding out some other place of safety. Excuse my not staying any longer with you: I leave you with a great deal of unwillingness; but I do it for the good of us both. I have so much interest with the captain of the guards, that he will take no notice of me. Sangiar gave Noureddin but just time to thank him, and away he went.

Noureddin presently acquainted the Fair Persian with the absolute necessity of their going that moment. She only staid to put on her veil, and then they both stole out of the house together, and were so very lucky, as not only to get clear of the city, without the least notice being taken of their escape, but also safely to arrive at the mouth of the Euphrates, where they embarked in a vessel that lay ready to weigh anchor.

They were no sooner on ship-board but the captain came upon deck amongst his passengers; My children, said he to them, are you all here? have any of you any more business to do in the city? or have you left any thing behind you? They answered him they were all there, and ready prepared; so that he might set sail as soon as he pleased. When Noureddin came aboard, the first question he asked was, whither the ship was bound? and being told for Bagdad, he greatly rejoiced at it. And now the captain having weighed anchor, set sail, and the vessel with a very favourable wind lost sight of Balsora.

But now let us see how matters went at Balsora, in the mean time, while Noureddin and the Fair Persian made their escape from the fury of the enraged king.

The captain of the guards came to Noureddin's house and knocked at the door, but nobody coming to open it, he ordered his soldiers to break it down, who immediately obeyed him, and in they rushed in a full body. They searched every hole and corner of the house, but neither he nor the Fair Persian were to be found. The captain of the guards made them inquire of the neighbours, and he asked himself if they had seen them lately: it was all in vain; for, though they had seen him go out of his house, so universally beloved was Noureddin, that not one of them would have said the least word that might be injurious to him. As soon as they had rifled the house and levelled it to the ground, they went to acquaint the king with the news. Look for them, said he, in some other places, for I am resolved to have them found.

The captain of the guards made a second search after them; and the king dismissed the visier Saouy, with a great deal of honour. Go home, said he to him, trouble yourself no farther with Noureddin's punishment; for with my own hand I will revenge the insolence he has offered your person.

Without any farther delay, the king ordered the public criers to proclaim throughout the whole city a reward of a thousand pieces of gold for any person that should apprehend Noureddin and the Fair Persian, with a severe punishment upon whomsoever should conceal them. But after all this pains and trouble, there was no news to be heard of them; and the visier Saouy had only the comfort of seeing the king espouse his quarrel.

In the mean time, Noureddin and the Fair Persian, after a prosperous voyage, landed safe at Bagdad. As soon as the captain came within sight of that city, pleased that his voyage was at an end, Children, cried he to the passengers, chear up, and be merry! look, yonder is that great and wonderful city, where there is perpetual concourse of people from all parts of the world: there you shall meet with innumerable crowds every day, and never feel the extremity of cold in winter, nor the excess of heat in summer; but enjoy an eternal spring, always crowned with flowers, and the delicious fruits of autumn.

When the vessel came to anchor a little below the city, the passengers got ashore, and every body went to the place they designed to lie at that night. Noureddin gave the captain five pieces of gold for his passage, and went ashore also with the Fair Persian; but being a perfect stranger in Bagdad, he was at a loss for a lodging. They rambled a considerable time about the gardens that bordered on the Tigris, and keeping close to one of them that was inclosed with a very high wall, at the end of it, they turned into a street finely paved, where they perceived a garden door, and a charming fountain near it.

The door, which was very magnificent, happened to be shut, but the porch was open, in which there stood a sofa on each side. This is a very convenient place for us, said Noureddin to the Fair Persian, night comes on apace; and though we have eaten nothing since our landing, yet I believe we must even lie here to-night, and to-morrow we shall have time enough to get lodging; what say ye to it, my dear? Sir, replied the Fair Persian, you know very well I am never against what you propose, therefore let us go no farther, since you are willing to stay here. Each of them having drank a draught of water at the fountain, they laid themselves down upon one of the sofas, and after a little chat, being invited by the agreeable murmur of the water, they fell fast asleep.

The garden, it seems, belonged to the caliph, and in the middle of it there was a pavilion, called the pavilion of pictures, because its chief ornament was pictures, after the Persian manner, drawn by the most celebrated limners* in Persia, whom the caliph sent for on purpose. The stately hall beneath this pavilion was adorned with fourscore windows, and in every window a branched candlestick. The candles were never lighted but when the caliph came thither to spend the evening, which was never but when the weather was so very calm that not a breath of air was stirring. Then, indeed, they made a glorious illumination, and could be plainly discerned at a vast distance in the country on that side, and by the greatest part of the city.

There was but one person that had the charge of this fine garden, and the place was at this time enjoyed by a very ancient officer, named Scheich

Ibrahim, whom the caliph himself, for some important service, put into that employment, with a strict charge not to let all sorts of people in, but especially to suffer nobody either to sit or lie down on the sofas that stood at the outward door, that they might always be clean and handsome; and whenever he found any body there, to punish them severely.

Some business had obliged this officer to go abroad, and he was not as yet returned. When he came back, there was just day-light enough for him to discern two persons asleep upon one of the sofas, with both their heads under a piece of linen cloth, to secure them from the gnats. Very well, said Scheich Ibrahim to himself, here are brave people, to disobey the caliph's orders; but I shall take care to pay them handsomely what they deserve. Upon this, he opens the door very softly, and a moment after, returns with a swinging cane in his hand, and his sleeve tucked up to the elbow. He was just going to lay on them with all his force; but, withholding his arm, he began to reason with himself after this manner: Thou wast going to strike, without any consideration that those perhaps are strangers, destitute of a lodging, and utterly ignorant of the caliph's order; for that reason, it would be advisable in thee to know first who they are. Upon this, he gently lifts up the linen that covered their heads, and being wonderfully astonished to see two persons so mightily beautiful and well-shaped, waked Noureddin, with pulling him softly by the feet.

Noureddin presently lifting up his head, and seeing an old man with a long white beard standing at his feet, got up, and throwing himself upon his knees, Good father, said he, heaven preserve you! What do you want, my son, replied Scheich Ibrahim; who are you, and from whence came you? We are strangers newly arrived, answered Noureddin, and we would fain tarry here till to-morrow. This is not a proper place for you, said Scheich Ibrahim; but come in with me, and I will find one fitter for you to sleep in than this; and I fancy the sight of the garden, which is very fine, will please you, when you see it to-morrow by day-light. Is this garden your own? said Noureddin. Yes, replied Scheich Ibrahim; it is an inheritance left me by my father: pray walk in, for I am sure you will not repent your seeing it.

Noureddin rose up to thank Scheich Ibrahim for the civility he had shewn them, and afterwards the Fair Persian and he went into the garden. Scheich Ibrahim locked the door, and going before, led them to an eminence, from whence at one look they might almost take a view of the grandeur, order, and beauty of the whole garden.

Noureddin had seen very fine gardens in Balsora, but never any comparable to this. Having satisfied his curiosity in looking upon every thing worth taking notice of, as he was walking in one of the alleys, he turned about to the officer that was with him, and asked what his name was? As soon as he told him it was Scheich Ibrahim; Scheich Ibrahim, said he to him, I must confess this is a charming garden indeed. Heaven send you long to enjoy the pleasures of it; and we cannot sufficiently thank you for the favour of shewing us a place so worthy our seeing: however, it is but just that we should make you some amends for your kindness: therefore, here are two pieces of gold; take them, and get us something to eat, that we may be merry together before we part.

At the sight of the two pieces of gold, Scheich Ibrahim, who was a great admirer of that metal, laughed in his sleeve: he took them, and leaving Noureddin and the Fair Persian by themselves, went to provide what he was sent about. As soon as he was alone, said he to himself with abundance of joy, These are generous people; I should highly have injured myself, if, through imprudence or rashness, I had abused or driven them hence: the tenth part of the money will treat them like princes, and the rest I will keep for my pains and trouble.

While Scheich Ibrahim was gone to fetch something for his own supper, as well as for his guests, Noureddin and the Fair Persian took a walk in the garden, sometimes in one place, and sometimes in another, till at last they came to the pavilion of pictures that was in the middle of it. They stood a pretty while to admire its wonderful structure, beauty, and loftiness; and, after taking a full view of it on every side, they went up a great many steps of fine white marble, to the hall door, which they found locked.

They were but just got to the bottom of the steps as Scheich Ibrahim returned, loaded with provisions. Scheich Ibrahim, said Noureddin in a great surprise, did you not tell us that this was your garden? I did, replied Scheich Ibrahim, and do so still. And does this magnificent pavilion also belong to you? said Noureddin. Scheich Ibrahim was put to a nonplus, and would not hearken to any more questions: For, said he to himself, if I should say it is none of mine, he will presently ask me how I can be the master of the garden and not the pavilion? So, being willing to make them believe the garden was his, he said the same of the pavilion. My son, said he, the pavilion is not distinct from the garden, but they both belong to me. If so, said Noureddin, since you are willing to let us be your guests to-night, do us the favour to shew us the inside of it, for, if we may judge by the outward appearance, it must certainly be very splendid and magnificent.

It would have been a great piece of incivility in Scheich Ibrahim to have refused Noureddin that favour, after the returns he had made him: moreover, he considered that the caliph not having given any notice, according to the usual custom, it was likely he would not be there that night, and therefore resolved to treat his guests, and sup with them in that room. He laid the provisions upon the first step, while he went to his chamber to fetch the key. He soon returned with a light, and opened the door.

Noureddin and the Fair Persian entered the hall, and finding it so extravagantly surprising, could not forbear admiring the beauty and richness of the place. Indeed, without saying any thing of the pictures, which were admirably well drawn, the sofas were very noble and costly; and, besides the branched candlesticks that were fixed to every window, there was a silver spring between each cross-bar, with a wax candle in it. Noureddin could not behold those glorious objects, which put him in mind of his former greatness, without sighing.

In the mean time, Scheich Ibrahim was getting supper ready; and the cloth being laid upon a sofa, and every thing in order, Noureddin and the Fair Persian and he, sat down and ate together. When supper was done, and they had washed their hands, Noureddin opened the casement, and calling the Fair Persian to him, Come hither, my dear, said he, and with me admire the charming prospect and beauty of the garden by moon-light; for certainly nothing can be more agreeable. She came to him, and they both together diverted themselves with that lovely object, while Scheich Ibrahim was busy in taking away the cloth.

When Scheich Ibrahim came to his guests again, Noureddin asked him whether he had any good liquor in his lodgings to treat them with? What liquor would you have? replied Scheich Ibrahim.—Sherbet, I have the best in the world; but sherbet, you know, my son, is never drunk after supper.

I know that very well, said Noureddin; it is not sherbet, but another sort of liquor that we ask you for; and I am surprised at your not understanding me. It is wine that I perceive you speak of, said Scheich Ibrahim. You have hit right, replied Noureddin; and if you have any, pray let us have a bottle: you know a bottle after supper is a very proper companion to spend the hours with till bed-time.

Heaven defend me from keeping wine in my house, cried Scheich Ibrahim, and from ever coming to a place where any is to be sold! A man as I am, who has been a pilgrimage four times to Mecca, has renounced wine for ever.*

However, said Noureddin, you would do us a singular kindness in getting us a little for our own drinking: and if it be not too much trouble, I will put you in a way how you may do it, without ever going into the inn, or so much as laying your hand upon the vessel that contains it. Upon that condition, I will do it, replied Scheich Ibrahim; therefore pray let me know how I am to manage it.

Why then, said Noureddin to him, we just now saw an ass tied at the entrance of the garden, which certainly must be yours, and which you may make use of in this extremity. Here are two pieces of gold more; take them, and lead your ass with the panniers towards the next inn: you may stand at as great a distance as you please; only give something to the next passenger that comes by, and desire him to go with your ass to the inn, there load him with two pitchers of wine, one in one pannier, and another in another, which he must pay for out of the money we have given you; and so let him bring the ass back to you: you will have nothing to do but drive the beast hither before you; for we will take the wine out of the panniers; and by this means you will act nothing but what you may do without any scruple at all.

The two last pieces of gold that Scheich Ibrahim was going to receive, wrought wonderfully upon his temper. Ah! my son, cried he, after Noureddin had done speaking, you have contrived the matter rarely; and had it not been for your invention, I should never have found out a way of getting you some wine, without a little scruple of conscience.—Away he went to execute the orders he had received; and upon his return, which was in a little time, Noureddin went down stairs, and taking the wine out of the panniers, carried it into the hall.

Scheich Ibrahim having led the ass back to the place from whence he took him, came back again. Scheich Ibrahim, said Noureddin to him, we cannot enough thank you for the trouble we have already given you; but, my friend, we want something yet. What is that? replied Scheich Ibrahim; is it any thing that I can be farther serviceable to you in? Why, said Noureddin, we have no cups to drink out of; and a little choice fruit, if you have any, would be very acceptable to us. Do but say what you have a mind to, replied Scheich Ibrahim, and you shall have every thing to your heart's content.

Down went Scheich Ibrahim, and in a short time spread a table for them with porcelain dishes, full of all sorts of delicious fruits, besides a great number of gold and silver cups to drink out of; and having asked them if they wanted any thing else, he withdrew, though they pressed him earnestly to stay.

Noureddin and the Fair Persian sat down again, and after a cup a-piece, they were mightily pleased with the wine. Well, my dear, said Noureddin to the Fair Persian, are we not the most fortunate persons in the world, after so many dangers, to meet with so charming and agreeable a place? come, let us be merry, and think no more on the hardships of our voyage. Can my happiness be greater in this world, than to have you on one side of me, and my bottle on the other? They took off their cups pretty heartily, and diverted themselves very agreeably, in singing each of them a song.

Both of them having very fine voices, but especially the Fair Persian, Scheich Ibrahim, who had stood hearkening a great while on the steps, without discovering himself, was perfectly charmed with their songs. He could contain himself no longer; but, thrusting his head in at the door, Courage, sir, said he to Noureddin, whom he took to be quite drunk, I am overjoyed to see you so merry.

Ah! Scheich Ibrahim, cried Noureddin, turning to him, you are a glorious man, and we are extremely obliged to you. We dare not ask you to drink a cup; but pray walk in, and let us have the honour, at least, of your company. Excuse me, sir, said Scheich Ibrahim; the pleasure of hearing your songs is sufficient for me. Upon this, he immediately retired.

The Fair Persian perceiving Scheich Ibrahim, through one of the windows, standing upon the steps without the door, told Noureddin of it. Sir, said she, you see what an aversion he has for wine; yet I question not in the least to make him drink some, if you would do as I would have you. Noureddin asked her what it was? Do but say the word, replied he, and I am ready to do what you please. Prevail with him, then, only to come in and bear us company: some time after, fill up a bumper, and give it him; if he refuses it, drink it off, feign yourself to be asleep, and leave the rest to me.

Noureddin quickly finding out the drift of the Fair Persian's design, called to Scheich Ibrahim, who came again to the door: Scheich Ibrahim, said he, we are your guests; you have entertained us after the most obliging manner in the world; and will you now refuse us the honour of bearing us company? We do not ask you to drink, but only the favour of seeing you.

Scheich Ibrahim being at last prevailed upon, came into the hall, and sat down upon the edge of a sofa that stood the nearest to the door. You do not sit well there, said Noureddin; besides, you are too far off for us to converse with you; pray come nearer, and sit down by the lady, since she will have it so. I will obey you, replied Scheich Ibrahim; so, coming forward with a simpering countenance, to think he should be seated near so beautiful a creature, he placed himself at some distance from the Fair Persian. Noureddin desired a song of her, upon the account of the honour that Scheich Ibrahim had done them; and she sung one that charmed him to an extacy.

When the Fair Persian had ended her song, Noureddin poured out a cup of wine, and presented it to Scheich Ibrahim: Scheich Ibrahim, said he, here, drink this to our healths. Sir, replied he, starting back, as if the very sight of the wine had put him into a horror and confusion, I beseech you to excuse me; I have already told you, that I have forsworn the use of wine these many years. Then positively you will not drink our healths, said Noureddin; however, give me leave to drink yours.

While Noureddin was drinking, the Fair Persian cut a piece of apple, and presented it to Scheich Ibrahim. Though you refused drinking, said she, yet I believe you will not refuse eating this piece of apple, since it is a very good one. Scheich Ibrahim had no power to refuse it from so fair a hand; but taking it with a very low bow, kissed it, and put it in his mouth. She said a great many amorous things upon that occasion; and Noureddin tumbling back upon a sofa, pretended to fall fast asleep. The Fair Persian presently advanced towards Scheich Ibrahim; and speaking in a very low voice, See, said she, the sleepy sot! thus, in all our merry bouts, he constantly serves me; and no sooner has he drank a cup or two, but he falls asleep, and leaves me alone; but I hope you will have the goodness to keep me company till he awakes.

At this, the Fair Persian took a cup, and filling it to the brim with wine, offered it to Scheich Ibrahim: Here, said she, drink off this to my health: I am going to pledge you. Scheich Ibrahim made a great many difficulties of the matter at first, and begged her to excuse him from drinking; but, at last, overcome by her charms and entreaties, he took the cup, and drank every drop of the wine off.

The good old man loved a cheruping* cup to his heart, but was ashamed to drink among strangers. He often went to the tavern in private, as abundance of people do; and now his hand being once in, without any more ceremony, or round-about ways, as Noureddin had instructed him, he goes directly to the next inn, where he was very well known, and fetches some more wine (the night serving him instead of a cloak) with the money that Noureddin had ordered him to give the messenger that went for the first.

As soon as Scheich Ibrahim had taken off his cup, and made an end of the piece of apple, the Fair Persian filled him out another, which he received with less difficulty than the former, but made none at all at the third. In short, he drank four times before ever Noureddin discovered his pretended sleeping; but then bursting out into a violent fit of laughter, he rose up, and looking upon him, Ha! ha! said he, Scheich Ibrahim, are you caught at last? did you not tell me you had forsworn wine? and now you have drank it all up from me.

Scheich Ibrahim, not expecting to be surprised after that manner, blushed a little: however, that did not spoil his draught: but when he had done, Sir, said he to Noureddin, laughing, if there is any crime in what I have done, it lies at this fair lady's door, not mine; for who could possibly resist so many charms?

The Fair Persian, who knew well enough what Noureddin would be at, took Scheich Ibrahim's part: Let him talk, said she; Scheich Ibrahim, take no notice of him; but let us drink on, and be merry. A while after, Noureddin fills out a cup for himself and the Fair Persian; but when Scheich Ibrahim saw that Noureddin had forgot him in his turn, he took his cup, and presenting it to the Fair Persian, Madam, said he, do I pretend I cannot drink now?

At these words of Scheich Ibrahim's, Noureddin and the Fair Persian were ready to split their sides with laughing. Noureddin poured him out some wine; and there they sat laughing, chatting, and drinking, till pretty near midnight. About that hour, the Fair Persian began to take notice of there being but one candle upon the table. Scheich Ibrahim, said she to the good old officer, methinks you might have afforded us another candle, since there are so many wax-lights yonder: pray do us the favour to light some of them, that we may see a little better what we are doing here.

Scheich Ibrahim making use of the liberty that wine gives a man, when it gets up into the crown-office,* and not caring to be interrupted in his discourse with Noureddin, bid the Fair Persian light them herself: It is fitter for you to do it than I, said he: but, hark ye, be sure not to light above five or six; for this is enough. Up rose the Fair Persian immediately, and taking a wax-candle in her hand, lights it with that which stood upon the table; and, without any regard to Scheich Ibrahim's orders, set fire to the whole fourscore.

By and by, while Scheich Ibrahim was entertaining the Fair Persian with some other discourse, Noureddin took his turn to desire him to light up some of the candles in the branched candlesticks, not taking notice that all the wax-lights were already in a blaze: Certainly, replied Scheich Ibrahim, you are lazier, or less vigorous, than I am, that you are not able to light them yourself: get you gone; but be sure you light no more than three. To work he went; but, instead of that number, he lighted them all, and opened the shutters of the fourscore windows, before Scheich Ibrahim, who was deeply engaged with the Fair Persian, knew any thing of the matter.

The caliph Haroun Alraschid being not yet gone to bed, was in a parlour at his palace by the river Tigris, from whence he could take a side-view both of the garden and pavilion. By chance, he opened the casement, and seeing the pavilion was illuminated, was mightily surprised at it; and at first, by the greatness of the light, thought the city was on fire. The grand visier Giafar was still with him, who only waited for his going to rest, and then designed to go home too. The caliph, in a great rage, called the visier to him: Careless visier, said he, come hither, look upon the pavilion of pictures, and tell me the reason of its being illuminated, now I am not there.

The grand visier Giafar, upon this news, fell into a violent trembling, fearing something else was the matter; but, when he came nearer, and with his own eyes saw the truth of what the caliph had told him, he was more astonished than before. However, being obliged to make some excuse to appease the caliph's anger, he said, Commander of the true believers, all that I can say to your majesty about this matter is, that about five or six days ago, Scheich Ibrahim came to acquaint me, that he had a design to call an assembly of the ministers of his mosque, to assist at a ceremony he was ambitious of performing in your majesty's auspicious reign. I asked him if I could be any way serviceable to him in this affair; upon which he entreated me to get leave of your majesty to perform the ceremony in the pavilion. When he left me, I told him he might do it, and I would take care to acquaint your majesty with it; but indeed I had quite forgot it, and I heartily ask pardon. Scheich Ibrahim, continued he, has certainly made choice of this day for the ceremony; and after treating the ministers of his mosque, he was willing to divert them with the sight of this illumination.

Giafar, said the caliph, with a tone that plainly shewed his anger was a little mollified, according to thy own words, thou hast committed three faults that are unpardonable: the first, in giving Scheich Ibrahim leave to perform his ceremony in my pavilion; for a person in so mean an office as his, is not worthy of so great an honour: the second, in not acquainting me with it: and the third, in not diving into the bottom of the good old man's intention. For my part, I am persuaded he only did it to try if he could get any money towards bearing the charge of it; but perhaps that never came into thy head; and sure I shall not wrong him, in forgiving him the expence of the night's illumination, which will be some amends for thy presenting him with nothing.

The grand visier Giafar, overjoyed to hear the caliph put the matter upon that foot, very willingly owned the faults he reproached him with, and freely confessed he was to blame in not giving Scheich Ibrahim a few pieces of gold. Since the case is so, added the caliph, it is just that thou shouldst be punished for thy mistakes; but thy punishment shall be light: thou shalt spend the remainder of the night as I do, with these honest souls, whose company I am very well pleased with; and while I am putting on a citizen's habit, go thou and disguise thyself with Mesrour, and come both of you along with me. The visier Giafar told him it was late, and that all the company would be gone before he could get thither; but the caliph said he would positively go. The visier, who knew that not a syllable of what he said before was true, began to be in great consternation; but there was no reply to be made, and go he must.

The caliph then, disguised like a citizen, with the grand visier Giafar, and Mesrour chief of the eunuchs, stole out of the palace together. They rambled through the streets of Bagdad, till at last they came to the garden: the door, through the carelessness of Scheich Ibrahim, was open, having forgot to shut it when he came back from buying the wine. The caliph was very angry at it: Giafar, said he to the grand visier, what excuse have you for the door's being open at this unseasonable hour? Is it possible that Scheich Ibrahim makes a custom of leaving it thus all night? No; I rather believe the hurry of the feast has been the occasion of this neglect.

The caliph went into the garden; and when he came to the pavilion, resolving not to go into the hall till he knew what they were doing there, he consulted with the grand visier, whether it was not his best way to climb up into one of the trees that was near it, to make a discovery. The grand visier at last casting his eye upon the door, perceived it stood half open, and told the caliph of it. It seems Scheich Ibrahim had left it so, when he was prevailed upon to come in and bear Noureddin and the Fair Persian company.

The caliph laying aside his first design, stole softly up to the hall-door, which standing half open, he had the conveniency of seeing all the company that were within, without being discovered himself.

Never was any person so surprised as he, when he saw a lady of an incomparable beauty, and a young handsome fine-shaped man, sitting at the table, with Scheich Ibrahim by them. Scheich Ibrahim had just then got a cup in his hand: My dear creature, said he to the Fair Persian, a right toper* never drinks without singing a brisk tune first. If you please to hear, I will give you one of my best songs.

Scheich Ibrahim sung; and the caliph wondered at it more, because till that very moment he never knew any thing of his drinking wine, but always took him for a grave solid man, as he seemed to be to outward appearance. The caliph retired from the door with the same caution as he made his approach to it; and coming to the grand visier Giafar, who was standing upon the steps a little lower, Come up, said he to him, and see if those within yonder are the ministers of the mosque, as you would fain have me believe.

By the tone of the voice in which the caliph spoke these last words, the visier understood that things went ill on his side: however, he went up the steps; but when he had peeped in at the door, and saw them all three sitting, and in that condition, he fell a-trembling for fear of his life. He went back to the caliph, but in so great a confusion, that he had not a word to say to him. What riotous doings are here! said the caliph to him: Who are those people that have presumed to take the liberty of diverting themselves in my garden and pavilion? and how durst Scheich Ibrahim give them admittance, and partake of the diversion with them? However, I must confess, I never saw two persons more beautiful, or better paired, in my life; and therefore, before I discover my anger, I will inform myself a little better, and enquire who they are, and the reason of their being here. He went to the door again, to observe them more narrowly; and the visier, who followed, stood behind him, and fixed his eyes upon them. They both of them plainly heard every word that Scheich Ibrahim spoke to the Fair Persian. Is there any thing, my charming lady, wanting to render the pleasure of this night complete?

Nothing but a lute, replied the Fair Persian; and methinks, if you could get me one, all things would be very well. Can you play upon it? said Scheich Ibrahim. Fetch me one, replied the Fair Persian, and you shall hear whether I can or not.

Scheich Ibrahim, without stirring very far from his place, pulled a lute out of a cupboard, and presented it to the Fair Persian, who began to put it in tune. The caliph, in the mean time, turning to the grand visier; Giafar, said he, the young lady is going to play upon the lute; and if she performs well, I will forgive her, and the young man for her sake; but as for thee, thou mayest go hang thyself. Commander of the true believers, replied the grand visier, if that is your intention, I wish she may play ill. Why so? said the caliph. Because, replied the grand visier, the longer we live in this world, the more time we shall have to comfort ourselves with the hopes of dying in good social company. The caliph, who loved a jest dearly, began to laugh at this repartee; and putting his ear to the open side of the door, he listened to hear the Fair Persian play.

The Fair Persian made such artful flourishes upon the lute, that from the first moment of her touching it, the caliph perceived that she did it with a masterly hand. Afterwards, she began to sing; and suiting her voice, which was admirably fine, to the lute, she sung and played with so much skill and sweetness, that the caliph was quite ravished to hear her.

As soon as the Fair Persian had finished her song, the caliph went down the steps, and the visier Giafar after him. When he came to the bottom, By my soul, said he to the visier, I never heard a more charming voice, or a lute better touched in my life. Isaac,[1] that hitherto I thought the most skilful player in the world, does not come up to her. In short, I am so charmed with her music, that I must hear her play before me; and therefore contrive some way how to bring it about.

Commander of the true believers, said the grand visier, if you should go in, and Scheich Ibrahim chance to know you, he would infallibly die with the fright. I should be extremely concerned at that, replied the caliph, and should be loath to be the occasion of his death, after so many years service. But there is a thought just come into my head, how to compass my design: stay here with Mesrour, and wait for me in the next alley till I come.

The neighbourhood of the Tigris had given the caliph the conveniency of turning a sufficient quantity of water, under a stately bridge, well terrassed, into his garden, to make a fine canal, whither the choicest fish of the whole river used to retire. The fishermen knew it very well, and would have given the world to fish there; but the caliph had expressly charged Scheich Ibrahim, not to suffer any of them to come near it. However, that very night,

[1] A famous player on the lute, that lived at Bagdad at that time.*

a fisherman passing by the garden door, which the caliph had left open as he found it, made use of this opportunity, and going in, went directly to the canal.

The fisherman immediately fell to work with his casting-nets, and was just ready to draw them, when the caliph, fearing what would be the effect of Scheich Ibrahim's negligence, but willing to make use of it, to bring his design about, came to the same place. The fisherman, in spite of his disguise, knew him, and throwing himself at his feet, humbly implored his pardon, and excused himself upon account of his poverty. Rise, saith the caliph, and be not afraid; only draw your nets, that I may see what fish you have got.

The fisherman, recovered of his fright, quickly obeyed the caliph's orders. He drew out five or six very large fishes; and the caliph, chusing the two largest, tied them together by the head with a sprig of a tree. After this, said he to the fisherman, Give me thy clothes, and here take mine.—The exchange was soon made; and the caliph being dressed like a fisherman, even to his boots and turban, Take thy nets, said he to the fisherman, and get thee about thy business.

When the fisherman, very well pleased with his good fortune, was gone, the caliph, taking the two fishes in his hand, went to look after the grand visier Giafar, and Mesrour. He made a full stop at the grand visier, who, not knowing him, asked him what he wanted, and bid him go about his business. Upon this, the caliph fell a-laughing; by which the visier finding it to be him, Commander of the true believers, said he, is it possible it can be you? I knew you not; and I ask a thousand pardons for my rudeness: you are so strangely disguised now, that without any fear of being discovered by Scheich Ibrahim, you may venture into the hall. Stay you here with Mesrour, said the caliph, while I go yonder and play my part.

The caliph went up to the hall, and knocked at the door. Noureddin hearing him first, told Scheich Ibrahim of it, who asked who was there? The caliph opened the door, and stepping a little way into the hall, to shew himself, Scheich Ibrahim, said he, I am the fisherman Kerim, who being informed of your design to treat some of your friends, have brought two very large fishes, fresh caught, to see if you have any occasion for them.

Noureddin and the Fair Persian, mightily pleased to hear him name fish, Pray, said she to Scheich Ibrahim, let him come in, that we may look upon them. Scheich Ibrahim, by this time, was incapable of asking this counterfeit fisherman how or what way he came thither; but his whole design being only to oblige the Fair Persian, with much ado, he turns his head towards the door, being quite drunk, and in a stammering tone, calling to the caliph, whom he took to be a fisherman, Come hither, thou nightly thief, said he, and let us see what thou hast got.

The caliph went forwards, and counterfeiting all the humours and actions of a fisherman to a nicety, presented them with the two fishes. These are very fine ones indeed, said the Fair Persian; and if they were well ordered, and delicately dressed, I should be glad to eat some of them. The lady is in the right, answered Scheich Ibrahim; but what a plague can we do with your fish, unless it was dressed? Go, dress it thyself, and bring it to us; thou wilt find every thing necessary for thee in my kitchen.

The caliph went back to the grand visier: Giafar, said he, I have been very well received; but they want the fish to be dressed. I will take care to dress it myself, said the grand visier, and they shall have it in a moment. Nay, replied the caliph, so eager am I to accomplish my design, that I will take abundance of pains about it too; for since I have personated the fisherman so well, sure I can play the cook for once; besides, in my younger days, I dealt a little in cookery, and always came off with flying colours. In saying these words, he went directly towards Scheich Ibrahim's lodgings, and the grand visier and Mesrour followed him.

All three of them presently fell to work, and though Scheich Ibrahim's kitchen was not very large, yet there was every thing in it that they wanted. The fish was quickly cooked, and the caliph served it up, putting to every one's plate a lemon to squeeze, if they thought it proper, into the sauce. They all ate very heartily, but especially Noureddin and the Fair Persian; and the caliph sat down with them at the lower end of the table.

As soon as the repast was over, Noureddin looking upon the caliph, Fisherman, said he, never were better fish eaten, and you have done us the greatest favour in the world. At the same time putting his hand into his bosom, and pulling out a purse of thirty pieces of gold, the remainder of the forty that Sangiar, gentleman-usher to the king of Balsora, had given him just upon his departure: here, said he to him, take that, and if I had any more, thou shouldst have it: had I known thee in my prosperity, I would have taken care of securing thee from ever wanting: Do not refuse the small present I make thee, but accept of it as kindly as if it was much greater.

The caliph took the purse, and perceiving by the weightiness that it was all gold, Sir, said he, I cannot enough thank you for your liberality, and I think myself very fortunate in having to do with a person of your generosity; but before I take my leave, I have a favour to ask, which I beg you not to deny me. Yonder is a lute, which makes me believe that the lady understands playing upon it; and if you can prevail with her to play but one tune, I shall go away the best satisfied in the world; a lute, sir, is an instrument I greatly admire.

Fair Persian, said Noureddin, immediately addressing himself to her, I ask that favour of you, and I hope you will not refuse me. She took up the lute without more intreaties, and putting it presently in tune, played and sung with such an air as charmed the very soul of the caliph with its harmony. Afterwards she played upon the lute without singing, but with so much skill and softness that it transported him into an ecstasy of joy.

When the Fair Persian had given over playing, the caliph cried out, What a voice! What a hand! What skill is here! Was there ever finer singing, or better playing upon the lute? Never was there any heard or seen like it.

Noureddin, who was a person of breeding, and always returned the compliment that was made him; Fisherman, said he, I find thou hast some taste for music since thou art delighted with her performance; and if thou likest her she is thine; I make thee a present of her. At the same time he rose up, and taking his robe, which he had laid by, was for going away and leaving the pretended fisherman in possession of the Fair Persian.

The Fair Persian was extremely surprised at Noureddin's liberality; she took hold of him, and looking very wishfully at him, Whither, sir, are you going, said she? Sit down in your place, I intreat you, and hearken to the song I am going to sing and play. He did as she desired him, and then the Fair Persian touching her lute, and looking upon him with tears, sung some verses that she had made extempore to reproach him with his indifference, and the easiness as well as cruelty of resigning her to Kerim. She only hinted, without explaining herself any farther to the fisherman, for she was ignorant of his being the caliph, as well as Noureddin. When she had done playing she put the lute down by her, and clapped a handkerchief to her face to hide the tears she could not help shedding.

Noureddin made no answer to all these reproaches, but by his silence seemed to declare he did not repent of what he had done. The caliph surprised at what he had newly heard, Sir, said he, as far as I see, this beautiful lady, that so generously you have made me a present of just now, is your slave, and you are her master. It is very true, Kerim, replied Noureddin, and thou wouldst be more surprised than thou art now, should I tell thee all the misfortunes that have happened to me on her account. Ah! I beseech you, sir, replied the caliph, still behaving himself like a fisherman, oblige me so far as to let me hear part of your story.

Noureddin, who had already obliged him in several things of a higher nature than this, was so complaisant as to relate the whole story to him. He began with his father's buying the Fair Persian for the king of Balsora, and omitted nothing of what he had done, or what had happened to him, from that time to their arrival at Bagdad, and since, to that very moment he was talking to him.

When Noureddin had ended his story, Whither are you going now? said the caliph. Even where heaven shall direct me, answered Noureddin. Believe me, replied the caliph, you shall go no farther, but on the contrary, return to Balsora: I will go and write a short letter, which you shall give the king in my name; and you shall see upon the reading of it, he will give you a very handsome reception, and nobody will dare to speak against you.

Kerim, said Noureddin, what thou hast told me is very unaccountable and singular; didst thou ever hear that a poor fisherman, as thou art, had any correspondence with a king? Be not astonished at that, replied the caliph; you must know then, that we both studied together under the same masters, and were always the best friends in the world. It is true, fortune has not been equally favourable to us both; she has made him a king, and me but a fisherman. However, this inequality has not at all lessened our friendship; he has often expressed a readiness and desire to advance my fortune, but I always refused it; and am better pleased with the satisfaction of knowing that he never will deny me whatever I ask for the service and advantage of my friends: Let me do it then, and you shall see the success.

Noureddin consented to what the caliph had proposed; and there being every thing necessary for writing in the hall, the caliph wrote a letter to the king of Balsora; at the top of which, pretty near the edge of the paper, he placed this set form, in three small characters: 'In the name of the most merciful God,' to shew he would be absolutely obeyed.

The letter of Caliph Haroun Alraschid to the king of Balsora

Haroun Alraschid, son of Mandi, sends this letter to Mohammed Zinebi, his cousin, greeting. As soon as Noureddin, son to the late visier Khacan, the bearer, has delivered you this letter, and you have read it, pull off the royal mantle, put it on his shoulders, and place him in thy seat: fail not. So farewell.

The caliph folded up the letter, and sealed it, and giving it to Noureddin, without saying any thing of what was in it, Go, said he, and embark immediately in a vessel that is ready to go off, (as there did constantly every day at the same hour,) and you may sleep when you are aboard.

Noureddin took the letter, and away he went with the little money he had about him when Sangiar gave him his purse; and the Fair Persian, distracted with grief at his departure, retired by herself to one of the sofas, and fell a-weeping bitterly.

Noureddin was scarce gone out of the hall, when Scheich Ibrahim, who had been silent during the transaction of this affair, looking stedfastly upon the caliph, whom he still believed to be a fisherman, Hark you, said he, Kerim, thou hast brought us two fishes that are worth twenty pieces of leather or more, and thou hast got a purse and a slave; but dost thou think to have it all for thyself? I here declare that I will go halves with thee in the slave; and as for the purse, shew me what is in the inside; if it is silver, thou shalt have one piece for thyself; but if it is gold, I will have it all, and in exchange, give thee some pieces of leather I have in my pocket.

(For the better understanding of what follows, said Scheherazade, interrupting herself here, we must observe to you, that the caliph, before his serving up the fish, had dispatched the grand visier Giafar to his palace, with orders to get four slaves with a rich habit, and to wait on the other side of the pavilion till he gave a signal with his finger against the window. The grand visier receiving his commission, he, Mesrour and the four slaves waited at the appointed place, expecting the sign.)

The caliph, still personating the fisherman, answered Scheich Ibrahim very boldly, I know not what there is in the purse, gold or silver; whatever it is, you shall freely go my halves; but as to the slave, I will have her all to myself; and if you will not accept of these conditions, you shall have nothing at all.

Scheich Ibrahim, enraged to the last degree at this insolence, considering him only as a fisherman, snatched up one of the china dishes, and flung it at the caliph's head. The caliph easily avoided the blow, being thrown by a person in drink; but the dish striking against the wall was dashed into a thousand pieces. Scheich Ibrahim having missed his aim, grew more enraged, and catching up the candle that stood upon the table, rose from his seat, and staggering along, went down a back pair of stairs to look for a cane.

The Caliph made use of this opportunity, and striking his hands against the window, the grand visier, Mesrour, and the four slaves were with him in a trice, who quickly pulled off the fisherman's cloaths, and put on him the habit they had brought. They had not quite dressed the caliph, (who had seated himself upon the throne that was in the hall), but they were very busy about him, when Scheich Ibrahim, spurred on by interest, came back, with a swinging cane in his hand, with which he designed to pay the pretended fisherman soundly; but instead of finding him, he saw his cloaths in the middle of the hall, and the caliph upon his throne, with the grand visier and Mesrour on each side of him. He stood a while gazing upon this unexpected sight, doubting whether he was awake or asleep. The caliph fell a-laughing at his astonishment; and calling to him, Scheich Ibrahim, said he, what dost thou want, whom dost thou look after?

Scheich Ibrahim, no longer doubting that it was the caliph, immediately threw himself at his feet, with his face to the ground: Commander of the true believers, cried he, your vile slave has offended you; but he implores your clemency, and asks a thousand pardons for his offence. As soon as the slaves had made an end of dressing him, he came down from his throne, and advancing towards him, Rise, said he, I forgive thee.

Afterwards the caliph addressed himself to the Fair Persian, who had suspended her sorrow as soon as she understood that the garden and pavilion belonged to that prince, and not to Scheich Ibrahim, as he had all along made her believe, and that it was he himself disguised in the fisherman's cloaths. Fair Persian, said he, rise and follow me: by what you have lately seen, you ought to know who I am, and to believe that I am above taking any advantage of Noureddin's humour, who with a generosity not to be paralleled, has made me a present of your person: I have sent him to Balsora to be king there; and when I have dispatched some business necessary for his establishment, you shall also go thither and be a queen. In the mean time, I am going to order an apartment for you in my palace, where you shall be treated according to your desert.

This discourse put the Fair Persian in heart again, and comforted her after a very sensible manner. The joy of Noureddin's advancement, whom she passionately loved, to so high an honour, made her sufficient amends for her affliction. The caliph kept his promise, and recommended her to the care of his lady Zobeide, whom he acquainted with the esteem he had lately entertained for Noureddin.

Noureddin's return to Balsora was more fortunate and speedier by some days than he could have expected. Upon his arrival, without visiting any of his friends or relations, he went directly to the palace, where the king at that time was giving public audience. He pressed through the crowd with the letter held up in his hand, who presently made way for him to come forward, and deliver it. The king took and opened it; and his colour changed in reading it: he kissed it thrice, and was just about to obey the caliph's orders, when he bethought himself of shewing it to the visier Saouy, Noureddin's irreconcileable enemy.

Saouy, who had discovered Noureddin, and began to think with himself, with a great deal of uneasiness, what might be the design of his coming, was no less surprised than the king, at the order contained in the letter; and being as much concerned in it, he thought upon a way that very moment how to evade it. He pretended not to have read the letter quite through, and therefore desired a second view of it; he turned himself a little on one side, as if he wanted a better sight, and without being perceived by any body, dexterously tore off the set form that shewed the caliph would be absolutely obeyed, from the top of it, and putting it into his mouth, swallowed it down.

After this notorious piece of villainy, Saouy turned to the king, and giving him the letter, Sir, said he to him, in a low voice, what does your majesty intend to do? What the caliph has commanded me, replied the king. Have a care, sir, said the wicked visier, what you do: It is true, this is the caliph's hand; but the set form is not to it. The king had observed that very well, but in the confusion he was in, he thought his eyes deceived him, when he saw it was gone.

Sir, continued the visier, we have no reason to doubt, but that the caliph upon the complaints he has made against your majesty and me, has granted him this letter purely to get rid of him, not with any intention of having the order contained in it executed. Besides, we must consider, he has sent no express with a patent: and without that, the order is of no force: and since a king of your majesty's grandeur was never deposed without that formality, let who will bring such a letter as this, it ought not to be put in execution. Your majesty may depend upon what I have said; and how dangerous soever the consequence of disobeying this order may be, I will take it all upon myself.

King Zinebi, easily persuaded by this pernicious counsel, left Noureddin entirely to the discretion of the visier Saouy, who led him to his house, after a very insulting manner; where, after causing him to be bastinado'd till he was almost dead, he ordered him to a prison, where he commanded him to be put in the darkest dungeon, with a strict charge to the gaoler to give him nothing but bread and water.

When Noureddin, sadly bruised with the strokes, came to himself, and found what a nasty dungeon he was in, he bewailed his misfortunes after the most pathetic manner imaginable. Ah! fisherman, cried he, how hast thou cheated me; and how easy have I been in believing thee! Could I, after the civility I shewed thee, expect so inhuman and barbarous usage! However, may heaven reward thee: for I cannot persuade myself, that thy intention was so base, and I will with patience wait the end of my afflictions.

The poor disconsolate Noureddin remained six whole days in this miserable condition, and Saouy did not forget that he had confined him there, but being resolved to put him to a shameful death, and not daring to do it by his own authority, to accomplish his villainous design, he ordered some of his slaves to prepare some very rich presents, which he, at the head of them, went and presented to the king, saying, Behold, sir, what the new king hath sent you upon his accession to the crown, and begs your majesty to accept of it.

The king taking the matter just as Saouy intended it, What! replied he, is the wretch still living? I thought you had put him to death already. Sir, I have no power, answered the visier, to take any person's life away; that only belongs to your majesty. Go, said the king, behead him instantly; I give you full authority. Sir, replied the visier Saouy, I am infinitely obliged to your majesty for the justice you do me, but, since Noureddin has publicly affronted me, I humbly beg the favour that his execution may be performed before the palace, and, that the criers may publish it in every quarter of the city, that every body may be satisfied that he has made sufficient reparation for the affront. The king granted the request, and the criers in performing their office, diffused an universal sorrow through the whole city. The memory of his father's virtues being yet very fresh among them, there was no one could hear of the ignominious death the son was going to suffer through the villainy and instigation of the visier Saouy, without horror and indignation.

Saouy went in person to the prison, accompanied with twenty slaves his ministers of cruelty, who took Noureddin out of his dungeon, and put him on a shabby horse without a saddle. When Noureddin saw himself in the hands of his enemy; Thou triumphest now, said he, but thou abusest thy power.—Yet, I have still some confidence in the truth of what is written in one of our books: 'You judge unjustly, and in a little time you shall be judged yourself.' The visier Saouy, who really triumphed in his heart, What! insolent, said he, darest thou insult me yet? but go, I pardon thee, and care not whatever happens to me, so I have the pleasure of seeing thee lose thy head in the public view of all Balsora. Thou oughtest also to remember what another of our books says: 'What signifies dying the next day the death of his enemy?'

The visier, still implacable, and full of malice, surrounded by one part of his slaves in arms, ordered Noureddin to be conducted by the other towards the palace. The people were ready to fall upon him as they went along, and, if any body had set them the example, they would certainly have stoned him to death. When he had brought him to the place of suffering, which was in sight of the king's apartment, he left him in the executioner's hands, and went straight to the king, who was in his closet ready to glut his eyes with the bloody spectacle he had prepared.

The king's guard and the visier's slaves, who made a circle round Noureddin, had much ado to withstand the people, who made all the efforts possible, but in vain, to break through them and carry him off by force. The executioner coming up to him, Sir, said he, I hope you will forgive me; I am but a slave, and cannot help doing my duty. If you have no occasion for any thing, I beseech you prepare yourself, for the king is just going to give me orders to strike the blow.

The poor unfortunate Noureddin, at that cruel moment, looked round upon the people; Will no charitable body, cried he, bring me a little water to quench my thirst? which immediately they did, and handed it up to him upon the scaffold. The visier Saouy, perceiving this delay, called out to the executioner from the king's closet window, where he had planted himself, Strike, what dost thou stay for! At these barbarous and inhuman words the whole palace echoed with loud imprecations against him, and the king, jealous of his authority, made it appear, by ordering him to stay a while, that he was angry at his presumption. But there was another reason, for the king that very moment casting his eyes up into a large street that faced him and joined to the place of execution, he saw about the middle of it a troop of horsemen coming with full speed towards the palace. Visier, said the king immediately, look yonder, what is the meaning of those horsemen? Saouy, who knew not what it might be, earnestly pressed the king to give the executioner the sign. No, replied the king, I will first see who these horsemen are. It was the visier Giafar and his train, who came in person from Bagdad by the caliph's order.

To make the occasion of this minister's coming to Balsora a little plainer, we must observe that after Noureddin's departure with the caliph's letter, the caliph the next day, nor several days after, ever thought of sending the patent that he mentioned to the Fair Persian. He happened one day to be in the inner palace, which was the womens, and passing by the apartment, he heard the sound of a fine voice; he listened to it, and he had no sooner heard the words of one complaining for the absence of some body, but he asked the officer of his eunuchs that attended him, who that woman was that belonged to that apartment? The officer told him that it was the young stranger's slave, whom he had sent to Balsora to be king in the room of Mahommed Zinebi.

Ah! poor Noureddin, cried the caliph presently, I had forgot thee; but haste, said he to the officer, and bid Giafar come to me. The visier was with him in an instant. As soon as he came, Giafar, said he, I have hitherto neglected sending the patent to Noureddin which was to confirm him king of Balsora; but we have no time now to draw up one, therefore, immediately take post horses, and with some of your servants make what haste you can to Balsora. If Noureddin is dead, and put to death by them, order the visier Saouy to be hanged; but, if he be living, bring him to me with the king and the visier.

The grand visier staid no longer than just the time of getting on horseback, and being attended by a great train of officers belonging to his house, he set forward for Balsora, where he arrived after the manner, and at the time, above mentioned. As soon as he came to the palace-yard the people cleared the way for him, crying out, A pardon for Noureddin! and with his whole train he rode into the palace, even to the very stairs, where he alighted.

The king of Balsora knowing him to be the caliph's chief minister, went to meet him, and received him at the entrance of his apartment. The first question the visier asked was, If Noureddin was living? and if he was that he might be sent for. The king made answer, He was alive, and gave orders to have him brought in. Accordingly he soon made his appearance as he was, tied, and bound with cords. The grand visier Giafar caused him to be untied, and setting him at liberty, ordered the visier Saouy to be seized, and bound with the same cords.

The grand visier Giafar lay but one night in Balsora: The next day he set out again for Bagdad, and according to the order he had received, carried Saouy, the king of Balsora, and Noureddin along with him. As soon as he came to Bagdad, he presented them all to the caliph, and after he had given him an account of his journey, and particularly of the miserable condition he found Noureddin in, and that all his ill usage was purely by the advice and malice of Saouy; the caliph desired Noureddin to behead the visier himself. Commander of the true believers, said Noureddin, notwithstanding the injury this wicked man has done me, and the mischief he endeavoured to do my deceased father, I should think myself the basest of mankind if I had stained my hands with his blood. The caliph was extremely pleased with his generosity, and ordered justice to be done by the executioner's hand.

The caliph would fain have sent Noureddin back to Balsora to have been king there, but Noureddin humbly begged to be excused from accepting the offer, saying, Commander of the true believers, the city of Balsora, after the misfortunes that have happened to me there, is so much my aversion, and will always continue to be so, that I beseech your majesty to give me leave to keep the oath I have made of never returning thither again: and I shall think it my greatest glory to do you some services near your royal person, if you are pleased to do me the honour. The caliph consented to it, and placing him among the number of those courtiers who were his greatest favourites, restored the Fair Persian to him again. To all these favours he added a plentiful fortune, and he and the Fair Persian lived together to their dying day, with all the satisfaction they could both desire.

As for the king of Balsora, the caliph contented himself with only letting him see how careful he ought to be in the choice of his visiers, and so sent him back into his kingdom.

The Story of Beder, Prince of Persia, and Giahaure, Princess of Samandal

PERSIA is a country of so vast extent, that their ancient monarchs have, not without some colour of reason, assumed the haughty title of king of kings. For, not to mention those nations subdued by their arms, there are whole kingdoms and provinces whose kings are not only tributary, but also in as great subjection to them as petty governors in other nations are to kings.

Some ages ago one of these kings, who in the beginning of his reign had signalized himself by many glorious and successful conquests, enjoyed so profound and lasting a peace and tranquillity as rendered him the happiest of monarchs. The only thing in which he could be termed unfortunate was, that amongst all his mistresses not one of them ever brought him a son; and being now far advanced in years, he was desirous of an heir to succeed him after his death. However, he had above an hundred ladies all lodged in separate apartments, after a magnificent manner, with women-slaves and eunuchs to wait upon and take care of them.—Yet notwithstanding all his endeavours to please and humour them in every thing, there was not one that answered his expectation. He had women very often brought him from the most remote countries, and if they pleased him, he not only gave the merchants their full price at the first word, but treated them with all respect and civility imaginable, and by considerable presents obliged them still to bring others, flattering himself, that at last he might be so happy as to meet with one by whom he might have a son. There was scarce any act of charity but what he performed, fancying by that means to prevail with heaven. He gave immense sums to the poor, besides large donatives to the religious of his own persuasion, building for their use many noble colleges richly endowed, in hopes of obtaining by their prayers what he earnestly desired.

One day according to the custom of his royal predecessors, during their residence in their capital city, he gave his mistresses a ball, at which all the ambassadors, and strangers of quality about the court were present; and where they not only entertained one another with talking of news and politics, but also of learning, history, poetry, and whatever else was capable of diverting the understanding after the most agreeable manner. It was upon that day that an eunuch came to acquaint him with the arrival of a certain merchant from a far country, who, having brought a slave along with him, desired leave to shew her to his majesty. Give him admittance instantly, says the king, and after the ball is done I will talk with him: the merchant was introduced, and seated in a convenient place, from whence he might easily have a full view of the king, and hear him talk with abundance of familiarity to those that stood near his person. The king was extremely civil in his conversation with strangers, with a design, that by degrees they might grow acquainted with him; so that when they saw with what freedom and civility he addressed himself to the whole assembly, they took courage and began to discourse with him also, without being the least surprised at the dazzling pomp and splendour of his appearance, which was enough to deprive those of their power of speech that were not used to such glorious sights. He treated the ambassadors also after the same manner; first he ate with them, and during the repast, he asked them several questions concerning their health, of their voyage, and the affairs of their country; and after they had been encouraged by his generous entertainment, he gave them audience.

When the ball was over all the company retired; the merchant who was the only person left fell prostrate before the king's throne with his face to the earth, wishing his majesty an accomplishment of all his desires. As soon as he rose up, the king asked him if the news of his having brought a slave for him was true, and whether she was handsome?

Sir, replied the merchant, I doubt not in the least but your majesty has very beautiful women, since you search every corner of the earth for them; but I may boldly affirm, without over-valuing my merchandise, that you never saw a woman that could stand in competition with her for shape and beauty: besides a thousand other agreeable qualifications that she is mistress of. Where is she, says the king? bring her to me instantly. Sir, replied the merchant, I have delivered her into the hands of one of your chief eunuchs, and your majesty may send for her at your pleasure.

The fair slave was immediately brought in, and no sooner had the king cast his eyes on her, but the genteelness of her mien and shape charmed him. He went presently into his closet, whither the merchant, with a few eunuchs, followed him. The slave wore a red satin veil, striped with gold, over her face; and when the merchant had taken it off, the king of Persia beheld a lady that surpassed in beauty, not only his present mistresses, but even all that ever he had before; in short, he immediately fell passionately in love with her, and bid the merchant name his price.

Sir, said he, I gave a thousand pieces of gold to the persons of whom I bought her, and in my three years journey to your court, I have spent as much; but I shall forbear setting any price to so great a monarch; and therefore, if your majesty likes her, I humbly beg you would accept of her as a present. I am highly obliged to you, replied the king; but it is never my custom to treat merchants, who come hither purely for my pleasure, after so ungenerous a manner: I am going to order thee ten thousand pieces of gold, therefore speak, whether thou art pleased with that sum or not? Sir, answered the merchant, though I should have esteemed myself very happy in your majesty's acceptance of her for nothing, yet I dare not refuse so generous an offer. I shall take care to publish it, not only in my own country, but also in every place through which I pass. The money was presently paid him; and before he stirred out of his presence, the king made him put on a rich suit of cloth of gold.

The king caused the fair slave to be lodged in the finest apartment next his own, and gave particular orders to the matrons and to the women-slaves appointed to attend her, that after bathing they should dress her in the richest clothes the kingdom afforded. He also commanded them to carry her some pearl-necklaces, with abundance of diamonds, and other precious stones, that she might have the liberty of chusing those she liked best.

The officious matrons, whose only care it was to please the king, were astonished with admiration at her beauty; and being well skilled in that affair, they told his majesty, that, if he would allow them but three days, they would engage to make her so much handsomer than she was at present, that he should scarce know her again. The king at first was very loath to defer the pleasure of enjoyment so long, but at last he consented, upon condition they would be as good as their word.

The king of Persia's capital was situated in an island, and his palace, which was very magnificent was built upon the sea shore; his apartment looked upon that element: and the fair slave's, which was pretty near it, had also the same prospect, and it was the more agreeable, upon the account of the sea beating almost against the foot of the wall.

At the three days end, the fair slave, gloriously dressed and set off, was alone in her chamber, sitting upon a sofa, and leaning against one of the windows that faced the sea, when the king, being informed that he might visit her, came in. The slave hearing somebody walk in the room, with an air quite different from that of the women-slaves who had hitherto attended her, immediately turned her head about to see who it was. She knew him to be the king; but without discovering the least surprise, or so much as rising from her seat to salute or receive him, as if he had been the meanest person in the world, she put herself in the same posture again.

The king of Persia was extremely surprised to see a slave of so beauteous a form, so ignorant of the world. He attributed this piece of ill breeding to the narrowness of her education, and the little care that was taken of instructing her at first in the rules of civility and good manners. He went to her at the window, where, notwithstanding the coldness and indifferency with which she had just now received him, she suffered herself to be admired, caressed, and embraced as much as he pleased.

In the midst of these amorous embraces and tender endearments, this monarch paused a while, to gaze upon, or rather to devour her with his eyes: My goddess! my angel! my charmer! cried the king; whence came you? and where do those happy parents live that brought into the world so surprising a masterpiece of nature as you are? Ah! how I adore you, and my passion shall continue the same. Never did I feel for a woman what I now suffer for you: and though I have seen, and do see every day a vast number of beauties, yet never did my eyes behold so many charms in one single person, which have so transported me out of myself, that I am no longer at my own, but entirely at your disposal. My dearest life, continued he, you neither answer me, nor by any visible token give me the least reason to believe that you are sensible of the many demonstrations I have given you of the violence of my passion; neither will you turn your eyes on me, to afford mine the pleasure of meeting them with an amorous glance, and to convince you that it is impossible to love more than I do you. Why will you still keep this obstinate silence, which freezes me to death? and whence proceeds the seriousness, or rather sorrow, that torments me to the soul? Do you mourn for your country, your friends, or your relations? Alas! is not the king of Persia, who loves and adores you, capable of comforting and making you amends for the loss of every thing in the world?

What protestations of love soever the king of Persia made the fair slave to oblige her to speak to him, she continued her astonishing reservedness, and keeping her eyes still fixed on the ground, would not so much as open her lips.

The king of Persia charmed with the purchase he had made of a slave that pleased him so well, pressed her no farther, in hopes that by treating her civilly he might prevail upon her to change her mind. He presently gave the usual sign to the women that waited in an outward room: and as soon as they entered, he commanded them to bring in supper. When it was on the table, My dear, said he to the slave, come hither and sup with me. She rose up from her seat, and being placed over against the king, his majesty helped her, before he began eating himself; and so he did of every dish during the whole supper. The slave ate with down-cast eyes, and without speaking one word, though he often asked her how she liked the entertainment, and whether it was dressed to her taste.

The king willing to change the discourse, asked her what her name was, how she liked the clothes and the jewels she had on? what she thought of her apartment and the rich furniture? and whether the prospect of the sea was not very agreeable and charming? But to all these questions she answered not a word; so that the king was at a loss what to think of her silence. He imagined at first, that perhaps she might be dumb: But then, said he to himself, can it be possible that heaven should form a creature so beautiful, so perfect, and so accomplished, and yet at the same time with so great an imperfection? However, I cannot love with less passion than I do.

When the king of Persia rose from the table, he washed his hands on one side, while the fair slave washed hers on the other. He took that time to ask the women that held the bason and the towel, if ever they had heard her speak? One of them presently made answer, Sir, we have neither seen her open her lips, nor heard her speak, any more than your majesty has just now; we have taken care of her in the bath, we have combed and dressed her head, put on her clothes, and waited upon her in her chamber, but she has never opened her lips, so much as to say, that is well, or I like this. We have often asked her, Madam, do you want any thing? let us know what you would have? do but ask, and we are ready to get it for you? but we have never been able to draw a word from her; so that we cannot tell whether her silence proceeds from pride, sorrow, stupidity, or dumbness; and this is all we can inform your majesty of.

The king of Persia was more astonished at hearing this than he was before: however, believing the slave might have some reason for her sorrow, he was willing to endeavour to divert it, and make her merry. Accordingly, he made a very splendid ball, to which all the fine ladies of the court came, and those who were skilful in playing upon musical instruments shewed their parts, while others sung or danced, or did both together: in short, they played at a great many sorts of games, which mightily diverted the king. The fair slave was the only person that took no pleasure in those diversions; she never stirred out of her place, but with her eyes still fixed on the ground, without taking any notice of the entertainment, behaved herself with so much indifferency that all the ladies were no less surprised at it than the king. After the ball was done, every one retired to her apartment; and the king, who was left alone with the fair slave, lay with her that night.

The next morning the king of Persia arose more pleased than ever he had been with all the women he had seen before, and more enamoured with the fair slave than he was before. Indeed, he soon made it appear, by resolving henceforth to keep constant to her: and he performed his resolution. On the very same day he dismissed all his other women, giving every one of them their jewels, and other valuable things, besides a considerable fortune, with free leave to marry whom they thought fit, and only kept the matrons, and a few other old women, to wait upon and attend the fair slave.—However, for a whole year together, she never afforded him the pleasure of one single word, yet the king took abundance of pains to please her, and with all complaisance imaginable, to give her the most signal proofs of his violent passion.

The year was now expired, when the king, sitting one day by his mistress, protested to her that his love, instead of being diminished, grew every day more violent: My queen, said he, I cannot conceive what your thoughts are; but however, nothing is more true, and I swear to you the same, that in having the happiness of possessing you, there remains nothing for me to desire: I esteem my kingdom, great as it is, less than an atom, when I have the pleasure of beholding your eyes, and of telling you a thousand times how I adore you: you see I have given you some other proofs of my affection than bare words, and therefore surely you can never doubt of it, after the vast number of women I have sacrificed to your beauty. You may remember, it is about a year since I sent them away from my court, and I repent of it as little even now I am talking with you, as I did the first moment of their departure, and I believe I never shall. Nothing would be wanting to complete my happiness, and crown my joys for ever, would you speak but one single word to me, by which I might be assured that you thought yourself in some measure obliged to me; but how can you speak to me if you are dumb? and alas! how fearful I am lest it should be true! yet what reason have I to doubt of it, since you still torment me with silence, after a whole year's entreating you every hour to speak to me? However, if it is impossible for me to obtain that consolation, may heaven, at least, grant me the blessing of a son by you to succeed me after my death. I find myself growing old every day, and I begin to want one to assist me in bearing the weight of a crown. But still I cannot refrain from the desire I have of hearing you speak; for methinks something within me tells me you are not dumb; and therefore, dear madam, I beseech, I conjure you, to break through this obstinate humour, and speak but one word to me, and after that, I care not how soon I die.

At this discourse, the fair slave, who according to her usual custom, had hearkened to the king with down cast eyes, and had given him cause to believe, not only that she was dumb, but that she never had laughed in her life, began to look up and smile a little. The king of Persia perceived it with a surprise that made him break forth into an exclamation of joy, and no longer doubting but that she was going to speak, he waited for that happy moment with an eagerness and attention that cannot be easily expressed.

At last the fair slave, breaking her long kept silence, thus addressed herself to the king: Sir, said she, I have so many things to say to your majesty, that, having once broke silence, I know not where to begin. However, in the first place, I think myself obliged in duty to thank your majesty for all the favours and honours you have been pleased to confer upon me, and to implore the gods to bless and prosper you, to prevent the wicked designs and intentions of your enemies, and that they would not suffer you to die after hearing me speak; but to grant you a long and happy reign. After this, sir, I cannot give you a greater satisfaction than acquainting you with my being with child, and I wish as you do, it may be a son. Had it never been my fortune to have been breeding, I was resolved (I beg your majesty to pardon the sincerity of my intention) never to have loved you, as well as to have kept an eternal silence: But now I love and respect you as I ought to do.

The king of Persia, ravished to hear the fair slave not only speak, but at the same time to tell him such news, in which he was so nearly concerned, embraced her tenderly: Shining light of my eyes, said he, it is impossible for me to receive a greater joy than what you have now given me; you have spoken to me, and declared your being with child; so that I am fully satisfied in myself, that after these two signal occasions of joy, I ought to expect no other.

The king of Persia, in the transport of joy he was in, said no more to the fair slave: He left her; but after such a manner as made her perceive his intention was speedily to return: And being willing that the occasion of his joy should be made public, he declared it to his officers, and sent in all haste for the grand visier. As soon as he came, he ordered him to distribute a thousand pieces of gold among the holy men of his religion, who had made vows of poverty; as also among the hospitals and the poor, by way of returning thanks to heaven: And his will was obeyed, by the direction of that minister.

After the king of Persia had given this order, he came to the fair slave again: Madam, said he, pardon me for leaving you so abruptly, since you have been the occasion of it; but I hope you will entertain me some other time, since I am desirous to know of you several things of a much greater consequence. However, in the mean time, tell me, I beseech you, my dearest charmer, what were the powerful reasons that induced you to persist in that obstinate silence for a whole year together, though every day you saw me, heard me talk to you, ate and drank with me, and every night lay with me? I shall pass by your not speaking; but how you could carry yourself after such an indifferent manner, that I could never discover whether you were sensible of what I said to you, or no, I must confess it surpasses my understanding; and I cannot yet comprehend, how you could contain yourself so long; therefore I must conclude the occasion of it to be very extraordinary.

To satisfy the king of Persia's curiosity, this fair person replied, Think whether or no to be a slave, far from my own country, without any hopes of ever seeing it again, to have a heart torn with grief, for being separated from my mother, my brother, my friends, and my acquaintance, are not sufficient reasons for my keeping a silence your majesty has thought so strange and unaccountable? The love of our native country is as natural to us as that of our parents; and the loss of liberty is unsupportable to every one, who is not wholly destitute of sense and reason, and knows how to set a value on it. The body indeed may be enslaved, and under the subjection of a master who has the power and authority in his hands; but the will can never be conquered or domineered over, but still remains free and unconfined, depending on itself alone, and your majesty has found an example of it in me: And it is a wonder that I have not followed the example of abundance of unfortunate wretches, whom the loss of liberty has reduced to the mournful resolution of procuring their own deaths a thousand ways, rather than survive it, and wear out a wretched life in shameful slavery.

Madam, replied the king, I am now convinced of the truth of what you say; but till this moment I was of opinion, that a person beautiful, well-shaped, with a great deal of wit and good sense, such as yourself, whom her rigorous stars had destined to be a slave, ought to think herself very happy in meeting with a king for her master.

Sir, replied the fair slave, whatever the slave is, supposing her to be such as I have already mentioned to your majesty, there is no king on earth can tyrannise over her will. But however, when you speak of a slave, mistress of charms enough to captivate a monarch, and make him adore her, provided she is of a rank infinitely below him, I am of your opinion, she ought to think herself happy in her misfortune: But what happiness can it be when she considers herself only as a slave, torn from her parent's arms, and perhaps a lover's, for whom she has a passion that death only can extinguish? But when this very slave is in nothing inferior to the king that bought her, your majesty shall then judge yourself of the rigour of her destiny, of her misery, and of her sorrow, and to what desperate attempts the anguish of despair may drive her.

The king of Persia, astonished at this discourse, said, Madam, can it be possible that you are of royal blood, as by your words you seem to intimate? Explain the whole secret to me, I beseech you, and no longer augment my impatience: Ah! let me instantly know who are the happy parents of so great a prodigy of beauty, who are your brothers, your sisters, and your relations; but above all, what your name is?

Sir, said the fair slave, my name is Gulnare of the sea; and my father who is now dead, was one of the most potent monarchs of the ocean. When he died, he left his kingdom to a brother of mine, named Saleh, and to the queen my mother, who is also a princess, the daughter of another puissant monarch of the sea. We enjoyed a profound peace and tranquillity through the whole kingdom, till a neighbouring prince, an enemy to our repose, invaded our dominions with a mighty army; and penetrating as far as our capital made himself master of it; and we had but just time enough to save ourselves in a steep inaccessible place, with a few trusty officers, who were so generous as not to forsake us in our distress.

In this retreat, my brother was not negligent in contriving all manner of ways to drive the unjust invader from our dominions. While this affair was in agitation, one day taking me into his closet, Sister, said he, the events of the least undertakings in the world are always dubious: As for my own part, I am willing to die in the attempt I design to make to re-establish me in my kingdom. And I shall be less concerned for my own disgrace, than for what may possibly happen to you; and therefore to prevent it, and to secure you from whatever accident may befal you, I would fain see you married first. But in the miserable condition that our affairs are at present, I see no probability of matching you to any of the princes of the sea; and therefore I should be very glad if you would resolve to be of my opinion, and think of marrying to some of the princes of the earth. I am ready to contribute all that lies in my power towards it, and I am certain there is not one of them, considering the beauty you are mistress of, but would be proud of your accepting of their crown.

At this discourse of my brother's, I fell into a violent passion. Brother, said I, you know that I am descended, as well as you, by both father and mother's sides from the kings and queens of the sea, without any mixture of alliance with those of the earth; therefore I do not design to marry below myself, any more than they did: And I took an oath of it, as soon as I had understanding to inquire into the nobleness and antiquity of our family. The condition to which we are reduced shall never oblige me to alter my resolution, and if you perish in the execution of your design, I am prepared to fall with you, rather than to follow the advice, I so little expected from you.

My brother, who was still earnest for the marriage, endeavoured to make me believe that there were kings of the earth who were no ways inferior to those of the sea. This put me again into a violent passion, which occasioned him to speak several bitter reflecting things that nettled me to the quick. At last he left me, as much dissatisfied with myself, as he could possibly be; and in this peevish mood, I gave a spring from the bottom of the sea, directly up to the island of the moon.

Notwithstanding the violent discontent that made me cast myself upon that island, I lived pretty easy in a by-corner of it, where I retired for conveniency and safety. But alas! this happiness lasted not long, for in spite of all my endeavours to lie concealed in my beloved obscurity, a certain person of distinction and figure, attended by his servants, surprised me sleeping, and carried me to his own house: He made violent love to me, and omitted nothing which he thought might reasonably induce me to make a return to his passion. When he saw that fair means would prevail nothing upon me, he attempted to make use of force; but I soon made him repent of his insolence. So at last, finding that there was nothing to be done with me, he resolved to part with me, which he did to that very merchant who brought me hither and sold me to your majesty. He was a very prudent, courteous, obliging person; and during the whole journey, which was somewhat tedious, he never gave me the least reason to complain of his usage.

As for your majesty, Sir, continued the princess Gulnare, if you had not shewn me all the respect you have hitherto paid (for which I am extremely obliged to your goodness) and given me such undeniable marks of your affection, that I could no longer doubt of it; If you had not immediately sent away your women, give me leave to tell you plainly, sir, that I was positively resolved not to have lived with you; I would have thrown myself into the sea, out of this very window, where your majesty first saw me when you came into this apartment; and I would have gone in search after my mother, my brother, and the rest of my relations: I still persisted in that design, and I would infallibly have put it in execution, if, after a certain time, I had found myself deceived in the hopes of being with child: but now, in the condition I am in, I shall take care what I do. Should I tell my mother or my brother that I have been a slave, even to a king as mighty as you are, they would never believe it, but would for ever upbraid me with the crime I have committed against my honour, since it was a voluntary act of my own. However, sir, be it a prince or a princess that I bring into the world, it will be a pledge to engage me never to be parted from your majesty; and therefore I hope you will no longer look upon me as a slave, but as a princess worthy of your alliance.

It was after this manner that the princess Gulnare finished her story she had been telling the king of Persia. My charming and adorable princess, cried he, what wonders have I heard! and what an ample subject have you afforded my curiosity, of asking a thousand questions concerning those strange and unheard-of things which you have related to me! But, in the first place, I ought to thank you for your goodness and patience in making a trial of the truth and constancy of my passion. I must confess, I thought it impossible for me to love you more than I did: but since I know you to be so great a princess, I love you a thousand times more. What, did I say princess! Madam, you are no longer so; but you are my queen, the queen of Persia; and by that title you shall soon be proclaimed throughout the whole kingdom. To-morrow the ceremony shall be performed in my capital, with a pomp and magnificence that was never yet beheld; which will plainly shew, that you are both my queen and lawful wife. This should have been done long ago, had you sooner convinced me of my error; for from the first moment of my seeing you, I have been of the same opinion as now, to love you for ever, and never to place my affection on any other.

However, I am pleased with myself for having, in the mean time, paid you all the respect and civility I ought, that is due to your merit; and therefore, madam, I beseech you to inform me after a more particular manner, of the kingdoms and people of the sea, which are altogether unknown to me. I have heard much talk indeed of the inhabitants of the sea; but I always looked upon it as nothing but a pleasant tale or fable: however, by what you have told me, I am convinced there is nothing more true; and I have a very good proof of it in your own person, who are one of them, and are pleased to condescend to be my wife; which is an honour no other inhabitant on the earth can boast of besides myself. There is one thing yet, madam, which puzzles me a little; therefore I must beg the favour of you to explain it; that is, I cannot comprehend how it is possible for you to move, breathe, and walk up and down in the water, without being drowned. There are but few amongst us who have the art of staying under water; but they would surely perish there, if after a certain space of time, which is according to their skill, and constitution of their bodies, they did not come up again.

Sir, replied the queen Gulnare, I shall take a great deal of pleasure in satisfying the king of Persia, in any thing that lies in my power. You must know then, that we can walk at the bottom of the sea, with as much ease as you can upon the land; and can breathe in the water, as well as you do in the air: so that instead of suffocating us, as it does you, it is absolutely necessary for the preservation of our lives. What is yet more remarkable, is, that it never wets our clothes: so that when we have a mind to visit your upper world, we have no occasion of drying them. Our vulgar* language is the same in which the writing upon the seal of the great prophet Solomon, the son of David, was engraven.

I must not forget to tell you, that the water does not in the least hinder us from seeing in the sea; for we can open and shut our eyes when we please, without any manner of inconveniency: and as we have generally a very quick, piercing sight, so we can discern any object as clearly in the deepest part of the sea, as upon land. We have also a succession there of day and night; the moon affords us her light, and even the planets and the stars appear very visible to us. I have already spoken of their kingdoms; but as the sea is a great deal larger than the earth, so there are a greater number of them, and of vaster extent. They are divided into provinces, and in every province there are several great cities, well peopled; and, in short, there are an infinite number of nations, differing in manners and customs, as well as upon the earth.

The palaces of the kings and princes are very sumptuous and magnificent. There are some of them of marble of various colours; others of rock-crystal, mother of pearl, coral, and of other materials more valuable; gold, silver, and all sorts of precious stones, are more plentiful there than with you. I say nothing of the pearls, since the largest that ever was seen upon the earth would not be valuable amongst us; and none but the very lowest rank of citizens would wear them.

As we have a marvellous and almost incredible agility of transporting ourselves whither we please, in the twinkling of an eye, so we have no occasion for any coaches or horses: not but that every king has his stables, and his breed of sea-horses; but they seldom make use of them, but upon public feasts and rejoicing days. After they have been well managed, they set riders upon their backs, who shew their skill and dexterity in the art of riding: others are put to chariots of mother of pearl, adorned with an infinite number of shells of all sorts, of the liveliest colours in the world. These chariots are open; and in the middle there is a throne on which the king sits, and exposes himself to the public view of his subjects. The horses are trained up to draw by themselves; so that there is no occasion for a coachman to guide them. I pass over a thousand other particulars, relating to these sea-countries, full of wonder and curiosity, which would be very entertaining to your majesty: but I believe, sir, you will be pleased I should defer it, to speak of something of a much greater consequence; which is, that the method of delivering, and the way of managing the women of the sea in their lying in, is quite different from those of the women of the earth; and I am afraid to trust myself in the hands of the midwives of this country: therefore, sir, since my safe delivery is a thing which equally concerns us both, with your majesty's permission, I think it proper to send for my mother and my cousins to assist at my labour; at the same time to desire my brother's company, to whom I have a great desire to be reconciled. They will be very glad to see me again, after I have related my story to them, and when they understand that I am wife to the mighty king of Persia. I beseech your majesty to give me leave to send for them: I am sure they will be proud to pay their respects to you; and I dare say you will be extremely pleased to see them.

Madam, said the king of Persia, you are mistress, and so do whatever you please; I will endeavour to receive them with all the honours they deserve. But I would fain know how you would acquaint them with what you desire, and when they will arrive, that I may make some preparation for their reception, and go myself in person to meet them.

Sir, replied the queen Gulnare, there is no need of any of these ceremonies; they will be here in a moment; and if your majesty will be pleased but to step into the closet and look through the lattice, you shall see the manner of their arrival.

As soon as the king of Persia was gone into the closet, the queen Gulnare ordered one of her women to bring her a perfuming-pan,* with a little fire in it. After that, she bid her retire, and shut the door. When she was alone, she took a little piece of aloes out of a box, and put it into the perfuming-pan. As soon as she saw the smoke arise, she repeated some mystical words, utterly unknown to the king of Persia, who observed with great attention what she was doing: she had no sooner ended her charm, but the sea began to be disturbed. The closet that the king was in, was so contrived, that looking through the lattice, on the same side with the windows that faced the sea, he could plainly perceive it.

In short, the sea opened at some distance; presently there appeared a tall, handsome young man, with whiskers of a sea green colour; a little behind him, a lady well in years, but of a stately majestic air, attended by five young ladies, nothing inferior in beauty to queen Gulnare.

The queen Gulnare immediately came to one of the windows, and saw the king her brother, the queen her mother, and the rest of her relations, who at the same time perceived her also. The company came forward, not walking, but carried, as it were, upon the surface of the waves. When they came to the brink of the sea, they nimbly, one after another, leaped in at the window, from whence the queen Gulnare was retired, to make room for them. The king Saleh, the queen her mother, and the rest of her relations, embraced her tenderly, with tears in their eyes, upon their first entrance.

After the queen Gulnare had received them with all the honour imaginable, and placed them upon a sofa, the queen her mother addressed herself to her after a very tender manner. Daughter, said she, I am overjoyed to see you again, after so long an absence; and I am confident that your brother and your relations are no less so than I. Your leaving us, without acquainting any body with it, put us into an inexpressible concern; and it is impossible to tell you how many tears we have shed upon that account. We know of no other reason that could induce you to take such a surprising resolution, but the discourse that passed between your brother and you, of which he afterwards informed me. The advice he gave you seemed very advantageous to him at that time, for settling you handsomely in the world; and was then very suitable to the posture of our affairs. However, if you had not approved of his proposals, you ought not to have been so much alarmed; and give me leave to tell you, you took the thing quite otherwise than you ought to have done. But no more of this discourse, which serves only to renew the occasion of our sorrows and complaints, that we and you ought to bury for ever in oblivion. Give us now a relation of all that has happened to you since you left us, and also an account of the present circumstances you are in; but especially let us know if you are pleased and contented.

The queen Gulnare immediately threw herself at her mother's feet, and after rising up and kissing her hand, said, Madam, I own I have been guilty of a very great crime, and I shall be indebted to your goodness for the pardon which I hope you will be pleased to grant me. What I am going to say, in obedience to your commands, will soon convince you, that it is very often in vain for us to have an aversion for some certain things: I have experienced it myself; and the only thing I had an abhorrence to, either justly, or by the malice of my stars, has happened to me here. She began to relate the whole story of what had befallen her since her quitting the sea, in a violent passion, for the earth. As soon as she had made an end, and had acquainted them with her having been sold to the king of Persia, in whose palace she was at present; Sister, cried the king her brother, you have been mightily wronged in having so many affronts offered you; but you can blame nobody but yourself: you have it in your power now to free yourself; and I cannot but admire at your patience, that you could endure so long a slavery. Rise, and return with us into my kingdom, that I have re-conquered, and taken from the proud usurper that was once master of it.

The king of Persia, who heard these killing words from the closet where he stood, was in the utmost confusion imaginable. Ah! said he to himself, I am ruined and undone; and if my queen, my angel, leaves me, I shall surely die, for it is impossible for me to live without her; and will they be so barbarous as to deprive me of her? But the queen Gulnare soon put him out of his fears, and eased the sorrow of his heart.

Brother, said she, and smiled, what I have just now heard, gives me a greater proof than ever I had of the sincerity of your friendship for me; but as heretofore I could not brook your proposing a match between me and a prince of the earth, so now I can scarce forbear being angry with you, for advising me to break the engagement I have made with the most puissant and most renowned monarch in the world. I do not speak here of an engagement between a slave and her master; if that were all, it would be easy to return the ten thousand pieces of gold that I cost him; but I speak now of a contract between a woman and her husband, who has never given her the least reason to complain, or be discontented: besides, he is a king, wise, temperate, religious, and just, and has given me the most essential demonstrations of his love that possibly he could. What can be a greater instance of the violence of his passion, than sending away all his women (of which he had a great number) immediately upon my arrival, and confining himself only to me! I am now his wife, and he has lately declared me queen of Persia; and I am to sit with him in the council: besides, I am breeding; and if heaven shall be pleased to favour me with a son, that shall be another motive to engage my affections to him the more.

So, brother, continued the queen Gulnare, instead of following your advice, you see I have all the reason in the world, not only to love the king of Persia as passionately as I do, but also to live and die with him, more out of gratitude than duty. I hope, then, neither my mother, nor you, nor any of my cousins, will disapprove of the resolution and alliance I have made, which will be an equal honour to the kings of both the sea and earth. I ask a thousand pardons for giving you the trouble of coming hither from the bottom of the deep to partake of it; and I return you thanks for the pleasure of seeing you after so long a separation.

Sister, replied king Saleh, the proposition I made you of going back with us into my kingdom, upon the recital of your adventures, (which I could not hear without concern) was to let you see what a particular love and honour I had for you, and that nothing in the world was so dear to me as your welfare and happiness. Upon the same account, then, for my own part, I cannot condemn a resolution so reasonable, and so worthy of yourself, after what you have told me of the king of Persia, your husband, and the many obligations you have to him; and I am persuaded that the queen our mother will be of the same opinion.

The queen confirmed what her son had just spoken, and addressing herself immediately to her daughter, said, My dear, I am very glad to hear you are pleased; and I have nothing else to add to what your brother has already said to you. I should have been the first that would have condemned you, if you had not expressed all the gratitude you were capable of for a monarch that loves you so passionately, and has done such mighty things to oblige you.

As the king of Persia, who was still in the closet, had been extremely concerned for fear of losing his beloved queen, so now he was transported with joy at her resolution never to forsake him; and having no room to doubt of her love, after so open a declaration, he began to love her more than ever, and was resolved within himself to give her all the outward proofs of it, after the most sensible manner he possibly could.

While the king was entertaining himself with a pleasure that cannot easily be imagined, the queen Gulnare clapped her hands aloud, and presently in came some of her slaves, whom she had ordered to bring in a collation. As soon as it was served up, she invited the queen her mother, the king her brother, and her cousins, to sit down and take part of it. They began to consider, that, without ever asking leave, they were got into the palace of a mighty king, who had never seen or heard of them, and were all of the same opinion, that it would be a great piece of rudeness and incivility to eat at his table without him. This reflection raised a blush in their faces, and their eyes glowing with the concern they were in, they breathed nothing but flames at their mouths and nostrils.

This unexpected sight put the king of Persia, who was perfectly ignorant of the cause of it, into a most dreadful consternation. The queen Gulnare fancying that his majesty might be a little surprised at it, and finding her relations desirous of the honour of seeing him, rose from her seat, and told them she would be back in a moment. She went directly to the closet, and by her presence recovered the king of Persia from his surprise: Sir, said she, I doubt not but that your majesty is well pleased with the acknowledgment I have lately made of the many favours that I am still indebted to your goodness for. It was wholly in my power to have complied with my relations, who would fain have persuaded me to have forsaken you, and gone back with them into their dominions; but alas! I am not capable of being guilty of such ingratitude as I should have condemned in another. Ah! my queen, cried the king of Persia, speak no more of your obligations to me, for indeed you have none; it is I that am your debtor so much, that I am afraid I shall never be able to repay, or return you thanks equal to the favour you have done me; for I never thought it possible you could have loved me so tenderly as you do, and as you have made it appear to me, after the most signal manner in the world. Ah! Sir, replied the queen Gulnare, could I do less than I have done? I rather fear I have not done enough, considering all the honours and favours that your majesty has heaped upon me; and it is impossible for me to remain insensible of your passion, after so many convincing proofs as you have given me. But let us drop this, and give me leave to assure you of the sincere friendship that the queen my mother, and the king my brother, are pleased to honour you with; they earnestly desire to see you, and tell you themselves: I intended to have discoursed them a little before I introduced them to your majesty, and accordingly I have ordered a banquet for them, but they are very impatient to pay their respects to you; and therefore I desire your majesty would be pleased to walk in, and honour them with your presence.

Madam, said the king of Persia, I should be very glad to salute persons that have the honour to be so nearly related to you, but I am afraid of the flames that they breathe at their mouths and nostrils. Sir, replied the queen, laughing, you need not in the least be afraid of those flames, which are nothing but a sign of their unwillingness to eat in your palace without your honouring them with your presence, and eating with them.

The king of Persia taking heart at these words, went into his chamber with his queen Gulnare. She presented him to the queen her mother, to the king her brother, and to her other relations, who instantly threw themselves at his feet, with their faces to the ground. The king of Persia ran to them, and lifting them up, embraced them one after another after a very tender manner. After they were all seated, king Saleh began his speech: Sir, said he to the king of Persia, we are at a loss for words to express our joy, to think that the queen my sister, after all her hardships and affronts, should have the happiness of falling under the protection of so powerful a monarch as your majesty: We can assure you, sir, she is not unworthy of the high honour that you have been pleased to raise her to; and we have always had so much love and tenderness for her, that we could never think of parting with her, even to the most puissant princes of the sea, who have often demanded her in marriage before she came of age; but heaven has reserved her for you, sir, and, we have no better way of returning thanks for the favour it has done her, than beseeching it to grant your majesty a long and happy life with her, and to crown your days with content and satisfaction.

Certainly, replied the king of Persia, heaven reserved her purely for me, as you were pleased to observe; and I love her with so tender and violent a passion, that it is plain I never loved any woman till I saw her. Oh! how I am blessed and transported with her charms! and I cannot sufficiently thank either the queen her mother, or you, prince, or your whole family, for the matchless generosity with which you have consented to receive me into so glorious an alliance as your's. At the end of these words, he invited them to take part of the collation, and he and his queen sat down at his table with them. After the collation was over, the king of Persia entertained them with discourse till it was very late; and when they thought it convenient to retire, he waited upon them himself to the several apartments he had ordered to be prepared for them.

The king of Persia treated his illustrious guests for a great many days together; during which time, he omitted nothing that might shew his court in its greatest splendour and magnificence, and insensibly prevailed with them to stay there till the queen was brought to bed. When the time of her lying-in drew near, he gave particular orders to get every thing in readiness that was necessary upon such an occasion. At last there was a son born, to the great joy of the queen his mother, who, as soon as he was dressed in swaddling-clothes, which were very rich and costly, went and presented him to the king.

The king of Persia received the present with a joy easier to be imagined than expressed. The young prince being of a beautiful countenance, and all over charms, he thought no name so proper for him as that of Beder, which, in the Arabian language, signifies the Full Moon. By way of thanks to heaven, he was very liberal in his alms to the poor, and caused the prison-doors to be set open, and gave all the prisoners of both sexes their liberty. He distributed vast sums among the priests, and the holy men of his religion. He also gave large donatives to his courtiers, besides a great deal that was thrown amongst the people; and by a proclamation, ordered several rejoicing days to be kept publicly through the whole city.

One day after the queen's up-sitting,* as the king of Persia, queen Gulnare herself, the queen her mother, king Saleh her brother, and the princesses their relations, were discoursing together in her majesty's bed-chamber, the nurse chanced to come in with the young prince Beder in her arms. King Saleh no sooner saw him, but he ran to embrace him, and taking him in his arms, fell a kissing and caressing him, after a mighty rate. He took several turns with him about the room, dancing and dandling him about, when all of a sudden, through a transport of joy, the window being open, he leaped out, and plunged with him into the sea.

The king of Persia, who expected no such sight, set up a hideous cry, verily believing he should either see the dear prince his son no more, or that he should see him drowned; nay, he was like to give up the ghost amidst his so great grief and affliction. Sir, quoth queen Gulnare, with a quiet and undisturbed countenance, (the better to comfort him,) let your majesty fear nothing; the young prince is my son as well as your's, and I do not love him less than you do. You see I am not alarmed at the loss of him; neither in truth ought I to be so. In short, he runs no risk, and you will soon see the king his uncle appear with him again, who will return him to you safe and sound. Although he be born of your blood as well as mine, he will not fail to have the same advantage his uncle and I have, of living equally in the sea, and upon the land. The queen his mother, and the princesses his relations, confirmed the same thing; yet all was no great consolation to the king; he could not possibly recover from his fright till he saw prince Beder appear again as before.

The sea at length became troubled, when immediately king Saleh arose, with the young prince in his arms, and dancing and dandling him about, re-entered at the same window he went out at. The king of Persia, overjoyed to see prince Beder again, became as calm as before he lost sight of him. Then king Saleh said, Sir, was not your majesty in a great fright, when you first saw me plunge into the sea with the prince my nephew? Alas! prince, answered the king of Persia, I cannot express my concern: I thought him lost from that very moment, and you now restore life to me, by bringing him again. I thought as much, replied king Saleh, though you had not the least reason to apprehend any danger; for before I plunged into the sea with him, I pronounced certain mysterious words over him, which were engraven on the seal of the great Solomon the Son of David. We practise the like in relation to all those children that are born in the regions at the bottom of the sea, by virtue whereof, they receive the same privileges that we have over those people who inhabit the earth. Now, from what your majesty has observed, you may easily see what advantage your son prince Beder has acquired on the part of his mother queen Gulnare, my sister; for as long as he lives, and as often as he pleases, it shall be free for him to plunge into the sea, and traverse the vast empires it contains at its bottom.

Having so spoke, king Saleh, who had restored prince Beder to his nurse's arms, opened a box he had fetched from his palace in that little time he had disappeared, which was filled with three hundred diamonds, as large as pigeons' eggs; a like number of rubies, of extraordinary size; as many emerald wands, of half a foot long; and with thirty strings of necklaces of pearl, consisting each of ten pieces. Sir, said he to the king of Persia, presenting him with this box, when I was first summoned by the queen my sister, I knew not what part of the earth she was in, or that she had the honour to be married to so great a monarch as I now find: Wherefore I came empty handed; but now I understand how much we have been both obliged to your majesty, I beg you therefore to accept of this small token of gratitude in acknowledgment of the many particular favours you have been pleased to do us, and whereof I am not less sensible than she.

It cannot be imagined how greatly the king of Persia was surprised at the sight of so much riches inclosed in so little compass. What! prince, cried he, do you call so inestimable a present a small token of your gratitude, when you never have been indebted to me? I declare you have never been in the least obliged to me, neither you nor the queen your mother; I esteem myself but too happy in the consent you have been pleased to give to the alliance I have contracted with you. Madam, continued he, turning to Gulnare, the king, your brother, has put me into the greatest confusion in the world; and I would beg of him to retain his present, were it not that I fear to disoblige him. Do you therefore endeavour to obtain his leave, that I may be dispensed with on this occasion.

Sir, replied king Saleh, I am not at all surprised that your majesty thinks this present so extraordinary; I know you are not accustomed upon earth to see such, and so many fine stones; but if you knew, as I do, the mines from whence these jewels were taken, and that it is in my power to heap up a treasure much larger than those, of all the things of the earth, you would, it may be, wonder I should have the boldness to make you a present of so small a value. I beseech you therefore not to regard it in that respect, but on account of the sincere friendship I am obliged to offer to you, which I hope you will not give me the mortification to refuse. These engaging expressions obliged the king of Persia to accept the present, for which he returned many thanks, both to king Saleh and the queen his mother.

A few days after, king Saleh gave the king of Persia to understand that the queen his mother, the princesses, his relations, and himself could have no greater pleasure than to spend their whole lives at his court; but that having been absent from their own kingdom for some time, where their presence was absolutely necessary, they begged of him not to take it ill, if they took leave of him and queen Gulnare. The king of Persia assured them he was very sorry that it was not in his power to come and visit them in their dominions; but added, As I am verily persuaded you will not forget queen Gulnare, but come and see her now and then, I hope I shall have the honour to kiss your hands again many times before I die.

Many tears were shed on both sides upon their separation. King Saleh departed first; but the queen his mother, and the princesses his relations, were fain to force themselves, in a manner, from the embraces of queen Gulnare, who could not prevail with herself to let them go. This royal company were no sooner out of sight, but the king of Persia said to queen Gulnare, Madam, I should have looked upon that person as one who would have imposed on my credulity in the grossest manner, that had pretended to palm those wonders upon me for true, which I myself have been an eye witness of from the time I have been honoured with your illustrious family at my court: But I cannot escape conviction of this kind; and shall remember it as long as I live, and be always ready to bless heaven for directing you to me, preferably to any other prince.

Young prince Beder was brought up and educated in the palace, under the care of the king and queen of Persia, who both saw him grow and increase in beauty, to their great satisfaction. He gave them yet greater pleasure as he advanced in years, by his continued sprightliness, by his agreeable ways in whatever he did, and by the justness and vivacity of his wit in whatever he said; and they were the more sensible of this satisfaction, by reason king Saleh his uncle, the queen his grandmother, and the princesses his relations, came from time to time to take part of it.

He was easily taught to read and write, and was instructed with the same facility in all the sciences that became a prince of his rank.

When he arrived at fifteen, he acquitted himself of all his exercises with infinitely better address, and good grace, than any of his masters: He was withal very wise and prudent. The king, who had almost from his cradle discovered in him virtues so necessary for a monarch, and who moreover began to perceive the infirmities of old age coming upon himself, would not stay till death gave him the possession of his throne, but purposed to resign it to him immediately. He had no great difficulty to make his council consent to it; and the people heard this resolution with so much the more joy, as they conceived prince Beder worthy to govern them. In a word, as the king had not for a long time appeared in public, they had all the opportunity in the world to observe he had not that disdainful, proud, and crabbed air, which most princes, who look upon all below them with scorn and contempt, have. They saw, on the contrary, he treated all mankind with that goodness which invited them to approach him, that he heard favourably all who had any thing to say to him; that he answered every body with a goodness that was peculiar to him; and that he refused nobody any thing that had the least appearance of reasonableness.

The day for the ceremony was appointed, when in the midst of the whole assembly, which was then more numerous than ordinary, the king of Persia then sitting on his throne, came down from it, took the crown off his head, put it on that of prince Beder; and having seated him in his place, kissed his hand, as a token that he resigned his authority to him. After which, he ranged himself among the crowd of visiers and emirs.

Hereupon the visiers, emirs, and other principal officers, came immediately and threw themselves at the new king's feet, taking each the oath of fidelity, according to their degrees. Then the grand visier made a report of divers important matters; on which the young king gave judgment with that admirable prudence and sagacity that surprised all the council. He next turned out divers governors convicted of mal-administration, and put others in their room; which he did with that wonderful and just discernment as exacted the acclamations of every body, which were so much the more honourable, as flattery had no share in them. He at length left the council, accompanied by the late king his father, and went to wait on his mother queen Gulnare, at her apartment. The queen no sooner saw him coming with the crown upon his head, but she ran to embrace him with a great deal of tenderness, wishing him a long and prosperous reign.

The first year of his reign, king Beder acquitted himself of all his royal functions with great assiduity. Above all, he took care to instruct himself in affairs of state, and all that might any way contribute towards the happiness of his people. Next year, having left the administration to his council, under the direction of the old king his father, he went out of his capital city, under pretence of diverting himself with hunting; but his real intention was to visit all the provinces of his kingdom, that he might reform all abuses there, establish good order and discipline every where, and deprive all ill-minded princes, his neighbours, of any opportunities of attempting any thing against the security and tranquillity of his subjects, by appearing and shewing himself seasonably on his frontiers.

No less than a whole year sufficed this young king to put in practice a purpose so worthy of him. Soon after his return, the old king his father fell so dangerously ill, that he knew at first he should never recover: He waited for his last moment with great tranquillity, and his only care was to recommend to the ministers and other lords of his son's court to persist in the fidelity they had sworn to him; insomuch that there was not one but willingly renewed his oath as freely as at first. He died at length to the great grief of king Beder and queen Gulnare, who caused his corpse to be carried to a stately mausoleum, worthy of his rank and dignity.

When the funeral obsequies were ended, king Beder found no difficulty to comply with that ancient custom in Persia to mourn for the dead a whole month, and not to be seen by any body during all that time. He had mourned the death of his father his whole life, had he hearkened to his excessive affliction, and had it been permitted to so great a prince as he was, to amuse himself after that manner. During this interval, the queen, mother to queen Gulnare, and king Saleh, together with the princesses their relations, arrived at the Persian court, and shared in great part of their affliction, before they proposed any consolation.

Though the month was expired, the king could not prevail on himself to give admittance to the grand visier and the other lords of his court, who all besought him to lay aside his mourning habit, to shew himself to his subjects, and take upon him the administration of affairs as before.

He shewed so great unwillingness to their request, that the grand visier took upon him to speak in the following manner: Sir, it would be needless to represent to your majesty that it belongs only to women to persist in a perpetual mourning. We doubt not but you are sufficiently convinced of that, and that it is not your intention to follow their example. Neither our tears nor your's are capable of restoring life to the good king your father, though we should lament all our days. He has undergone the common fate of all men, which nobody can resist. Yet we cannot say absolutely that he is dead, since we see him reviving in the person of your sacred majesty. He did not himself doubt, when he was dying, but he should revive in you, and to your majesty it belongs to shew that he was not deceived.

King Beder could no longer oppose such pressing instances. He laid aside his mourning habit that very moment, and after he had resumed the royal ornaments he began to provide for the necessities of his subjects with the same assiduity as before his father's death. He acquitted himself with universal approbation; and, as he was exact in maintaining his predecessor's ordinances, the people perceived no alteration in their sovereign.

King Saleh who was returned to his dominions in the sea, with the queen his mother, and the princesses, no sooner saw that king Beder had resumed the government, but he came alone to visit him; and king Beder and queen Gulnare were overjoyed to see him. One day, as they rose from table, they fell to discoursing of several matters: King Saleh fell insensibly on the praises of the king his nephew, and the queen his sister, how glad he was to see him govern so prudently, which had acquired him so great reputation, not only among his neighbours, but more remote princes. King Beder, who could not bear to hear himself so well spoken of, and not being willing to interrupt the king his uncle, through good manners, turned on one side, and seemed to be asleep, leaning his head against a cushion that was behind him.

From these commendations, which regarded only the wonderful conduct and surprising wit of king Beder, king Saleh came to speak of the perfections of his body, which he extolled after a mighty rate, as having nothing equal to them, either upon the earth, or the kingdoms under the waters, which he was well acquainted with.

Sister, said he in an ecstacy, so beautiful as he is, and of such excellent endowments, I wonder you have not thought of marrying him ere this: If I mistake not, he is at present in his twentieth year; and at that age no prince ought to be suffered to be without a wife. I will think of a match for him myself, since you will not, and marry him to some princess of our lower world, that may be worthy of him.

Brother, replied queen Gulnare, you call to my remembrance a thing, I must own, I have never thought of to this very moment. As he never discovered any inclination for marriage, I never thought of mentioning it to him; and I am glad you have now spoke of it to me. I like your proposing one of your princesses; and I desire you to name one who may be beautiful and well accomplished, that the king my son may be obliged to love her.

I know one that will be proper, replied king Saleh, softly; but before I will tell you who she is, let us see if the king my nephew sleeps or not, and I will tell you afterwards why it is necessary we should take that precaution. Queen Gulnare then looked upon her son, and thought she had no reason to doubt but he was profoundly asleep, (king Beder nevertheless, very far from sleeping, redoubled his attention, as being unwilling to lose any thing the king his uncle said upon that subject.) There is no necessity for your speaking so low, said the queen to the king her brother; you may speak out with all freedom, without fear of being heard.

It is by no means proper, replied king Saleh, that the king my nephew should as yet have any knowledge of what I am going to say. Love, you know, sometimes enters the ear, and it is not necessary he should love this lady I am about to name, after that sort; in short, I see many difficulties to surmount in this case, not on the lady's part, as I hope, but on that of her father. I need only mention to you the princess Giauhara,[1] and the king of Samandal.

How, brother, replied queen Gulnare, is not the princess Giauhara yet married? I remember to have seen her a little before I left your palace; she was then about eighteen months old, and surprisingly beautiful, and must needs be the wonder of the world, if her charms have increased equal with her years. The few years she is older than the king my son, ought not to hinder our doing our utmost to bring the match about. Let me know but the difficulties that are to be surmounted, and I will warrant we will do well enough.

Sister, replied king Saleh, the greatest difficulty is, that the king of Samandal is insupportably vain, looking upon all others as his inferiors: It is not likely we shall easily get him to enter into this alliance. For my part, I will go to him in person, and demand the princess his daughter of him; and in case he refuses her, will address ourselves elsewhere, where we shall be like to be more favourably heard. For this reason, as you may perceive,

[1] Giauhara, in Arabic, signifies a precious stone.

added he, it is not proper for the king my nephew to know any thing of our design, lest he should fall in love with the princess Giauhara, and we afterwards not be able to obtain her for him. They discoursed a little longer upon this point, and before they parted, agreed that king Saleh should forthwith return to his own dominions, and demand the princess Giauhara, of the king of Samandal, her father, for the king of Persia, his nephew.

This done, queen Gulnare and king Saleh, who verily believed king Beder asleep, agreed to wake him; and he dissembled the matter so well, that he seemed to wake from a profound sleep. He had nevertheless heard every word they said; and the character they gave of the princess Giauhara had inflamed his heart with an unknown passion. He had conceived so bright an idea of her beauty, that he could not sleep a wink all night, but remained under continual inquietudes.

Next day king Saleh would needs take leave of queen Gulnare, and the king his nephew. The young king, who knew the king his uncle would not have departed so soon, but to go and promote his happiness, blushed when he heard him mention his departure. His passion was become so violent, it would not suffer him to wait so long for the sight of his mistress as would suffice to accomplish the marriage. He more than once resolved to desire his uncle to bring her away with him; but as he did not care to let the queen his mother understand he knew any thing of what had passed, he desired him only to stay with him a day or two, that they might hunt together, intending to make use of that occasion to discover his mind to him.

The day for hunting was set, and king Beder had many opportunities to declare his mind to his uncle; but he had not the courage so much as once to open his mouth to acquaint him with what he designed.

In the midst of the chase, when not only king Saleh, but all his attendants, had left him, he alighted near a spring; and having tied his horse to a tree that afforded a very plentiful shade, as did several others along the banks of the rivulet, he laid himself down on the grass, and gave a free course to his tears, which issued forth in great abundance, accompanied with many sobs and sighs. He remained in this condition, overwhelmed with thought, and not speaking so much as one word. King Saleh, in the mean time, missing the king his nephew, and not meeting with any one who could tell tidings of him, began to be much concerned to know what was become of him. He therefore left his company to go in search of him, and at length perceived him at a distance. He had observed the day before, and even more evidently that day, that he was not so merry as he used to be, that he was more pensive than ordinary, and that if he was asked a question, he either answered not at all, or nothing to the purpose; but he never so much as in the least suspected the cause of all this alteration, till he saw him lying in that disconsolate posture; when he immediately guessed he had not only heard what passed between him and the queen Gulnare, but was become passionately in love. He hereupon alighted, at some distance from him, and having tied his horse to a tree, took a compass, and came upon him so softly, that he heard him pronounce the following words:

Adorable princess of the kingdom of Samandal, cried he out, I have no doubt had but an imperfect sketch of your incomparable beauty, yet I hold you to be preferable to all the princesses in the world in charms, and to excel them as much as the sun does the moon and stars. I would this moment go and offer you my heart, if I but knew where to find you; it belongs to you, dear princess, and nobody shall be the possessor of it but you.

King Saleh would hear no more: he advanced immediately, and discovered himself to king Beder. From what I have understood, nephew, said he, you heard that which the queen your mother and I discoursed the other day of the Princess Giauhara. It was not our intention you should have known any thing, and we verily thought you were asleep. My dear uncle, replied king Beder, I heard every word you said, and have sufficiently experienced the effect you foretold; which it was not in your power to prevent. I detained you on purpose to acquaint you with my love before your departure; but the confusion I had to let you know my weakness, if it be any, to love so worthy a princess as this seems to be, altogether sealed my mouth. I beseech you then, by the friendship you profess for a prince that has the honour to be so nearly allied to you, that you would pity me, and not delay to procure me the consent of the king of Samandal, that I may marry his daughter, the adorable Giauhara, with all speed, unless you have a mind to see me die with love, before I have the sight of her.

These words of the king of Persia troubled king Saleh very much; he gave him to understand how difficult it was to give him the satisfaction he desired, and that he could not well do it without carrying him along with him; which might be of dangerous consequences, since his presence was so absolutely necessary in his kingdom, that the least absence might occasion his subjects to revolt. He conjured him therefore to moderate his passion till such time as he had put things into a better posture, assuring him he would use his utmost diligence to content him; and when he had brought matters to bear, he would come to acquaint him. But these reasons were not sufficient to satisfy the king of Persia. Cruel uncle, said he, I find you do not love me so much as you pretended, and that you had rather see me die than grant the first request that ever I made you.

I am ready to convince your majesty, replied king Saleh, that I would do any thing to serve you in reason; but as for carrying you along with me, I cannot do that till I have spoken to the queen your mother. What would she say if I should do this? if she consents, I am ready to do all you would have me. You cannot be ignorant, replied the king of Persia, that the queen my mother would never willingly part with me; and therefore this excuse of yours does but yet farther convince me of the hardness of your heart. If you do really love me, as you would have me to believe you do, you must return to your kingdom immediately, and carry me along with you.

King Saleh, finding himself in a manner obliged to yield to his nephew's importunity, drew a ring off his finger, which was engraved with the same mysterious names of God that were upon Solomon's seal, that had wrought so many wonders by their virtue. Here, take this ring, said he, put it upon your finger, and fear neither the waters of the sea, nor their depth. The king of Persia took the ring, and when he had put it on his finger, king Saleh said unto him, follow me; when at the same time they both mounted leisurely up into the air, and made towards the sea, which was not far off, where-into they jointly plunged.

The Sea-king was not long in going to his palace with the king of Persia, whom he immediately carried to the queen's apartment, and presented him to her. The king of Persia kissed the queen his grandmother's hands, and she embraced him with great demonstrations of joy. I do not ask you how you do, said she to him, I see you are well enough, and I am rejoiced at it; but I desire to know how my daughter, and your mother, queen Gulnare does? The king of Persia took great care not to let her know he came without her consent; and therefore told her the queen his mother was in perfect health, and had enjoined him to pay her duty to her. Then the queen presented him to the princesses; and while he was in conversation with them, she left him, and went with king Saleh into a closet. He there told her how the king of Persia was fallen in love with the princess Giauhara, upon the bare relation of her beauty, and, contrary to his intention, that he had brought him along with him, without being able to hinder it, and that he was going to concert measures to procure the princess for him in marriage.

Although king Saleh was, to do him justice, perfectly innocent of the king of Persia's passion, yet the queen could hardly forgive his indiscretion, in mentioning the princess Giauhara before him. Your imprudence is beyond parallel, said she to him: can you think that the king of Samandal, whose character is so well known, will have greater consideration for you than the many other kings he has refused his daughter to, with scorn and contempt! would you have him send you away with the same confusion he has done them?

Madam, replied king Saleh, I have told you it was contrary to my intention that the king my nephew heard what I related of the beauty of the princess Giauhara to the queen my sister. The fault, if it be one, is already committed, and we must consider what a violent passion he has for this princess, and that he will die with grief and affliction if we do not speedily obtain her for him, with whatever trouble we are to do it. For my part, I shall omit nothing that may contribute to it, since I was, though innocently, the cause of the malady: I will therefore do all that I can to remedy it. I hope, madam, you will approve of my resolution, to go and wait upon the king of Samandal, with a rich present of precious stones, and demand the princess his daughter of him, for the king of Persia, your grandson and my nephew. I have some reason to believe he will not refuse me, nor neglect to ally himself with one of the greatest potentates of the earth.

It were to have been wished, replied the queen, that we had not been under a necessity of making this demand, since the success of our attempt is not so certain as we could desire; but since my grandson's quiet and content totally depend upon it, I freely give my consent to it. But above all, I charge you, since you sufficiently know the humour of the king of Samandal, that you take care to shew him due respect, and not in any wise offend him by too presuming a behaviour.

The queen prepared the present herself, composing it of diamonds, rubies, emeralds, and strings of pearl; all which she put into a box, very neat, and very rich. Next morning, king Saleh took his leave of her majesty, and the king of Persia, and departed with a chosen but small troop of officers, and other attendants. He soon arrived at the capital and palace of the king of Samandal, who did not scruple to afford him audience immediately upon his arrival. He rose from his throne as soon as he perceived king Saleh, who, being willing to forget his character for some moments, knowing whom he had to deal with, prostrated himself at his feet, wishing him an accomplishment of whatever he desired. The king of Samandal immediately stooped to take him up, and after he had placed him by him on his left-hand, he told him he was welcome, and asked him if there was any thing he could do to serve him?

Sir, answered king Saleh, though I should have no other motive than that of rendering my respects to the most potent and most prudent prince in the world, yet would I endeavour to convince your majesty, though poorly, how much I honour and adore you. Were it possible you could penetrate into my inmost soul, you would soon be convinced of the great veneration I have had for you, and the ardent desire I entertain to pay you my most humble acknowledgments. Having spoken these words, he took the box of jewels from one of his servants, and having opened it, presented it to the king, imploring him to accept of it for his sake.

Prince, replied the king of Samandal, I hope you do not make me this present without requiring a proportional benefit from me. If there be any thing within the compass of my capacity, you may freely command it, and will do me signal honour in accepting it. Speak, and tell me frankly wherein I can serve you.

I must own ingenuously, replied king Saleh, I have a boon to ask of your majesty, but I shall take care to ask nothing but what is within your power to grant. The thing depends so absolutely on yourself, that it would be to no purpose to require it of any other. I ask it then with all possible earnestness, and I beg of you not to refuse it me. If it be so, replied the king of Samandal, you have nothing to do but to acquaint me what it is, and you shall see after what manner I can oblige people of desert.

Sir, then said king Saleh, after the confidence your majesty has been pleased to think I have put in your good-will, I will not dissemble any longer, that I came to beg of you to honour our house with your alliance by marriage, and by that means to fortify the good understanding that has always hitherto been between our two crowns.

At these words, the king of Samandal began to laugh heartily, falling back in his throne against a cushion that supported him; and soon after said, with an injurious and scornful air, to king Saleh; King Saleh, I have always hitherto thought you were a prince of great sense and wisdom; but now I find you just the contrary. Tell me, I beseech you, where was your wit or discretion, when you formed to yourself so great a chimera as you have just now proposed to me? Could you conceive a thought only of aspiring in marriage to so great a princess as my daughter? You ought to have considered better the great distance between us, and not to run the risk of losing in a moment the esteem I always had for your person.

King Saleh was extremely nettled at this affronting answer, and had much ado to restrain his just resentment: however, he replied with greater moderation than could be expected; God reward your majesty according as you deserve. I beg the honour to inform you, I do not demand the princess in marriage for myself: had I done so, your majesty, or the princess, ought to have been so far from being offended, that you might rather have taken it for an honour done to both. Your majesty knows well I am a king of the sea as well as yourself; that the kings my ancestors have no reason to yield in antiquity to any other royal families; and that the kingdom I inherit from them is no less potent and flourishing than it has ever been. If your majesty had not interrupted me, you had soon understood, that the favour I asked of you was not for myself, but for the young king of Persia, my nephew, whose power and grandeur, no less than his personal good qualities, cannot be unknown to you. Every body acknowledges the princess Giauhara to be one of the finest ladies under the heavens; but it is at the same time acknowledged by all, that the young king of Persia, my nephew, is as accomplished as any prince, either upon land, or under the water. Thus the favour that is asked, being likely to redound both to the honour of your majesty and the princess your daughter, you ought not to delay your consent to an alliance so equal, and which no doubt will be approved by the generality of people. The princess is worthy of the king of Persia, and the king of Persia is no less worthy of her. No king or prince in the world can deny me this.

The king of Samandal had not let king Saleh go on so long after this rate, had not the rage he put him in deprived him of all power of speech. He was moreover some time longer before he could find his tongue, so much was he transported with passion. At length, however, he broke out into outrageous and injurious expressions, unworthy of a king. Dog, says he aloud, dare you talk to me after this manner, and so much as once to mention my daughter's name in my presence? Can you think the son of your sister Gulnare worthy to come in competition with my daughter? Who are you? who was your father? who is your sister? and who your nephew? Was not his father a dog, and a son of a dog, like thee? Guards, seize the insolent wretch, and immediately cut off his head.

The few officers that were about the king of Samandal were immediately going to obey his orders, when king Saleh, who was in the flower of his age, nimble and vigorous, got from them before they could draw their sabres; and, having reached the palace gate, he there found a thousand men of his relations and friends, well armed and equipped, who were but just arrived. The queen his mother having considered the small number of attendants he took with him, and moreover foreseeing the bad reception he would probably have from the king of Samandal, she had sent these troops to protect and defend him, in case of danger. Those of his relations who were at the head of his troop immediately saw how seasonably they were arrived, when they beheld him and his companions come running in great disorder, and a small number of officers at their heels in pursuit of them. My lord, cried out his friends, at the moment he joined them, what is the matter? We are ready to revenge you; you need only command us.

King Saleh related his case to them in as few words as he could; and afterwards putting himself at the head of a large troop, he, whilst some seized on the gates, re-entered the palace as before. The few officers and guards who had pursued him being soon dispersed, he re-entered the king of Samandal's apartment, who, being abandoned by his attendants, was soon seized. King Saleh left sufficient guards to secure his person, and then went from apartment to apartment, to search after the princess Giauhara. But that princess, on the first noise of this alarm, had, together with her women, flung herself on the surface of the sea, and escaped to a desert island.

As matters passed thus in the palace of the king of Samandal, those of king Saleh's attendants, who had fled at the first menaces of the king, put the queen his mother into a terrible consternation, upon relating the danger her son was in. King Beder, who was by at that time, was the more concerned, in that he looked upon himself as the principal author of all the mischief that might ensue: therefore, not caring to abide the queen's presence any longer, he, whilst she was giving the necessary orders at that conjuncture, darted himself upwards from the bottom of the sea; and not knowing how to find his way to the kingdom of Persia, he happened to light on the same island where the princess Giauhara had saved herself.

The prince, not a little disturbed in mind, went and seated himself under the shade of a large tree, surrounded with divers others. Whilst he was endeavouring to recover his temper, he heard one that talked, but was too far off to understand what was said. He arose, and advanced softly towards the place whence the sound came, where, among the branches, he perceived a beauty that dazzled him. Doubtless, said he within himself, stopping, and considering her with great attention, this must be the princess Giauhara, whom fear has obliged to abandon her father's palace; or, if it be not, she is, at least, one that no less deserves my love and admiration. This said, he moved forward, and discovering himself, approached the princess with a profound reverence. Madam, said he, I can never sufficiently thank heaven for the favour it has done me, in regaling my eyes this day with so glorious a sight. A greater blessing could not be conferred on me than this opportunity to offer you my most humble services. I beseech you, therefore, madam, to accept them, it being impossible that a lady under such solitary circumstances should not want assistance.

True, my lord, replied Giauhara, very sorrowfully, it is not a little extraordinary for a lady of my quality to be found in this condition. I am a princess, daughter of the king of Samandal, and my name is Giauhara. As I was at ease in my father's palace, and my apartment, I all of a sudden heard a dreadful noise: news was immediately brought me, that king Saleh, I know not for what reason, had fired the palace, seized upon the king my father, and murdered all the guards that made any resistance. I had only time to save myself, and escape hither from his violence.

At these words of the princess, king Beder began to be concerned that he had quitted his grandmother so hastily, without staying to hear from her the news that had been brought her; but he was, on the other hand, overjoyed to find that the king his uncle had rendered himself master of the king of Samandal's person, not doubting but he would consent to give up the princess for his liberty. Adorable princess, continued he, your concern is most just; but it is easy to put an end both to that and your father's captivity. You will agree with me, when I shall tell you that I am Beder, king of Persia, and king Saleh is my uncle. I assure you, madam, he has no design to seize upon the king your father's dominions: his only intent is, to obtain of him that I may have the honour to be received for his son-in-law. I had already given my heart to you, upon the bare relation of your charming beauty; and now, very far from repenting of what I have done, I beg of you to accept it, and to be assured that I will love you as long as I live. I dare flatter myself you will not refuse this favour, but be ready to acknowledge, that a king that quitted his dominions purely on your account deserves some favour. Permit then, beauteous princess, that I may have the honour to go and present you to the king my uncle; and the king your father shall no sooner have consented to our marriage, but king Saleh will leave him sovereign of his dominions as before.

This declaration of king Beder had not all the success he could have desired. It is true the princess no sooner saw his person, and the good mien wherewith he accosted her, but she had some kindness for him; but when she came to understand from his own mouth that he had been the occasion of all the ill treatment her father had undergone, of the grief and fright she had endured, and especially the necessity she was reduced to in flying her country, to save her life, she looked upon him with that horror, that she considered him rather as an enemy than a friend, with whom she resolved to have no manner of converse. Moreover, whatever inclination she might by any means be thought to have, in regard to this marriage, she determined never to yield to it, in consideration, that one of the reasons her father might have against this match might be, that king Beder was son of a king of the earth; and therefore she proposed to obey her father, especially in that particular.

She nevertheless resolved to let king Beder know nothing of her resentment, and only sought an occasion to deliver herself dexterously out of his hands, seeming, in the mean time, to have a great kindness for him. Are you then, said she, with all possible civility, son of the queen Gulnare, so famous for her wit and beauty? I am highly glad of it, and moreover rejoice that you are the son of so worthy a mother. The king my father was much in the wrong for so strongly opposing our conjunction: he could no sooner have seen you but must have consented to have made us both happy. Saying these words, she reached forth her hand to him as a token of friendship.

King Beder, believing himself arrived at the very pinnacle of happiness, held forth his hand, and was stooping to take that of the princess to kiss it, when she, pushing him back, and spitting at him, said, Wretch, quit that form of a man, and take one of a white bird, with a red bill and feet. Upon her pronouncing these words, king Beder was immediately changed into a bird of that sort, to his great surprise and astonishment. Take him now, said she to one of her women, and carry him to the Desart Island. This island was only one frightful rock, where there was not a drop of water to be had.

The waiting-woman took the bird, and, in executing the princess's orders, had compassion on king Beder's destiny. It would be great pity, said she to herself, to let a prince, so worthy to live, die of hunger and thirst. The princess will, it may be, repent of what she has ordered, when she comes again to herself: it were better that I carried him to a place where he may die a natural death. She then carried him to a well-frequented island, and left him on a charming plain, planted with all sorts of fruit-trees, and watered by divers rivulets.

Let us now return to king Saleh, who, after he had sought a good while for the princess Giauhara, and ordered others to seek for her, to no purpose, caused the king of Samandal to be shut up in his palace, under a good guard; and, having given the necessary orders for governing the kingdom in his absence, he returned to give the queen his mother an account of what he had done. The first thing he asked, upon his arrival, was, Where was the king his nephew? and he was answered, to his great surprise and astonishment, that he disappeared soon after he left him. News being brought me, said the queen, of the danger you was in at the palace of the king of Samandal, while I was giving orders to send troops for you to revengc yourself, he disappeared. He must necessarily have been frightened at the hearing of your being in so great danger, and did not think himself in sufficient security with us.

This news exceedingly afflicted king Saleh, who now repented of his being so easily wrought upon by king Beder, as to carry him away with him without his mother's consent. He sent every where after him; but whatever diligence was used, he could hear no news of him; and instead of the joy he conceived at having carried on the marriage so far, which he looked upon as his own work, he felt a grief for this accident that was mortifying to him. While he was under suspence about his nephew, he left his kingdom to the administration of his mother, and went and governed that of the king of Samandal, whom he continued to keep with great vigilance, though with all due respect to his own character.

The same day that king Saleh returned to the kingdom of Samandal, queen Gulnare, mother to king Beder, arrived at the court of the queen her mother. The princess was not at all surprised to find her son did not return the same day he set out; because it was common for him to go farther than he proposed, in the heat of the chace: but when she saw he neither returned the next day, nor the day after that, she began to be alarmed, as may easily be imagined, from the kindness she professed for him. This alarm was considerably augmented, when the officers who had accompanied the king, and were retired, after they had for a long time sought in vain, both for him and his uncle, came and told her majesty they must of necessity have come to some harm, since, whatever diligence they had used, they could hear no tidings of them. Their horses, indeed, they had found; but as for their persons, they knew not where to look for them. The queen hearing this, dissembled, and concealed her affliction, bidding the officers go and search once more, with their utmost diligence; but in the mean time, saying nothing to any body, she went and plunged into the sea, to satisfy herself in the suspicion she had that king Saleh must have carried away his nephew along with him.

This great queen would have been the more affectionately received by the queen her mother, had she not, upon first sight of her, guessed the occasion of her coming. Daughter, said she, I plainly perceive you are not come hither to visit me; you come only to enquire after the king your son; and I can only tell you such news of him as will augment both your grief and mine. I must confess, I no sooner saw him arrive in your territories, but I greatly rejoiced: yet, when I came to understand he had come away without your knowledge, I began to partake with you in the concern you must needs have at it. Then she related to her with what zeal king Saleh went to demand the princess Giauhara in marriage for king Beder, and what happened upon it, till such time as her son disappeared. I have sent diligently after him, added she; and the king my son, who is just gone to govern the kingdom of Samandal, has done all that lay in his power, on his part. All our endeavours have hitherto proved unsuccessful; but we hope nevertheless to see him again, perhaps when we least expect it.

Comfortless queen Gulnare was not satisfied with this hope: she looked upon the king her dear son as lost; and she lamented him grievously, laying all the blame upon the king his uncle. The queen her mother made her to consider the necessity there was of her not yielding too much to her grief. The king your brother, said she, ought not, it is true, to have talked to you so inconsiderately about that marriage, nor ever have consented to carry away the king your son, without your privacy: yet, since it is not certain that the king of Persia is absolutely lost, you ought to neglect nothing to preserve his kingdom for him. Lose then no more time; but return to your capital: your presence there will be necessary; and it will not be hard for you to preserve the public peace, by causing it to be published that the king of Persia was gone to visit his grandmother.

This reason was sufficient to oblige queen Gulnare to submit to it. She took leave of the queen her mother, and was got back to the palace of her capital of Persia before she had been missed. She dispatched immediately persons to recal the officers she had sent after the king, and to tell them she knew where his majesty was, and that they should soon see him again. She also caused the same report to be spread throughout the city, and governed, in concert with the prime minister and council, with the same tranquillity as if the king had been present.

To return to king Beder, whom the princess Giauhara's waiting-woman had carried and left in the island before mentioned. That monarch was not a little surprised, when he found himself alone, and under the form of a bird. He esteemed himself more unhappy, in that he knew not where he was, nor in what part of the world the kingdom of Persia lay. But if he had known, and sufficiently knew the force of his wings to traverse so vast watery regions, what could he have gained by it, but the mortification to continue still in the same ill plight, not to be accounted so much as a man, in the lieu of being acknowledged for king of Persia? He was then in a manner constrained to remain where he was, and live upon such nourishment as birds of his kind were wont to have.

A few days after, a peasant, who was skilled in taking birds with nets, chanced to come to the place where he was; when, perceiving this fine bird, the like of which he had never seen, though he had used that sport for a long while, began greatly to rejoice. He employed all his art to become master of him; and at length used such proper methods, that he took him. Overjoyed at so great a prize, which he looked upon to be of more worth than all the other birds he commonly took, by reason of its being so great a rarity, he shut it up in a cage, and carried it to the city. As soon as he was come into the market, a citizen stopped him, and asked him how much he would have for that bird?

Instead of answering, the peasant demanded of the citizen what he would do with him in case he should buy him? What wouldst thou have me do with him, answered the citizen, but roast and eat him? Very well, replied the peasant; and so I suppose you would think me very well paid if you should give me the smallest piece of money for him: but know, I set a much greater value upon him; and you should not have him for a large piece of gold. Although I am pretty well advanced in years, I never saw such a bird in my life. I intend to make a present to the king of him; and sure he will know the worth of him better than you.

Without staying any longer in the market, the peasant went directly to the court, and placed himself exactly before the king's apartment. His majesty being at a window where he could see all that passed in the base-court, at length cast his eyes on this beautiful bird; and being charmed with the sight of it, he immediately sent the commander of his eunuchs to buy it for him. The officer going to the peasant, demanded of him how much he would have for that bird? If it be for his majesty, answered the peasant, I humbly beg of him to accept it of me as a present, and I desire you to carry it to him. Hereupon the officer took the bird, and brought it to the king, who found it so great a rarity, that he ordered the same officer to take ten pieces of gold, and carry them to the peasant, who departed very well satisfied with the market he had made. The king ordered the bird to be put into a magnificent cage, and gave it corn and water in rich vessels.

His majesty being then ready to mount on horseback, had not time to consider the bird, therefore had it brought to him as soon as he came back. The officer brought the cage; and the king, that he might the better view the bird, took it out himself, and perched it upon his hand. Looking earnestly upon it, he demanded of the officer if he had seen it eat? Sir, replied the officer, your majesty may observe his eating: the drawer is still full; and I believe he has hardly touched any of his meat, at least I did not see him. Then the king ordered him meat of divers sorts, that he might take what he liked best.

The table being spread, (for dinner happened to be served up just as the king had given these orders), and the plates being placed, the bird leaped off the king's hand, and clapping his wings, flew upon the table, where he began to peck the bread and victuals after an extraordinary rate. The king seeing this, was so surprised at it, that he immediately sent for the queen, to come and see this miracle. The person that was sent related the matter to her majesty, and she came forthwith: but she no sooner saw the bird, but she covered her face with her veil, and would have retired. The king, admiring her proceedings, in that there were none but the eunuchs of the chamber, and the women that waited on her, asked the reason of it.

Sir, answered the queen, your majesty will no longer admire at my proceeding, when you come to know that this bird, which you take to be such, is no bird, but a man. Madam, said the king, more astonished than before, you are pleased to banter me, I suppose; but you shall never persuade me that a bird can be a man. Sir, replied the queen, far be it from me to banter your majesty; yet nothing is more certain than what I have had the honour to tell you.

I can assure your majesty it is the king of Persia, named Beder, son of the celebrated Gulnare, princess of one of the largest kingdoms of the sea, nephew of Saleh, king of that kingdom, and grand-child of queen Farasche, mother of Gulnare and Saleh; and it was the princess Giauhara, daughter of the king of Samandal, who thus metamorphosed him into a bird. Moreover, that the king might no longer doubt of what she affirmed, she told him the whole story, as how, and for what reason, the princess Giauhara had thus revenged herself for the ill treatment which king Saleh had used towards the king of Samandal, her father.

The king had the less difficulty to believe this assertion of the queen's, in that he knew her to be a skilful sorceress, perhaps one of the greatest in the world. And as she knew every thing which passed in it, he was always timely informed of the designs of the kings his neighbours against him, and so prevented them. His majesty had compassion on the king of Persia, and therefore earnestly besought his queen to break the inchantment, that he might return to his own form.

The queen consented to it with great willingness. Sir, said she to the king, be pleased to take the bird into your closet, and I will shew you a thing worthy of the consideration you have for him. The bird, which had never minded eating, by reason of his attentiveness to what the king and queen said, would not give his majesty the trouble to take him, but hopped into the closet before him; and the queen came in soon after, with a pot full of water in her hand. She mumbled over the pot some words, unknown to the king, till such time as the water began to boil; when she took some of it in her hand, and sprinkling a little upon the bird, said, 'By virtue of these holy and mysterious words I am going to pronounce, and in the name of the Creator both of heaven and earth, who raises the dead, and maintains the universe in its distinct state, quit that form of a bird, and re-assume that form which thou receivedst from thy Creator.'

The words were scarce out of the queen's mouth, but, instead of a bird, the king saw a young prince of good shape, air and mien. King Beder immediately fell on his knees, and thanked God for the mercy that had been bestowed upon him. Then he took the king's hand, who helped him up, and kissed it as a token of his acknowledgment, but the king embraced him with a great deal of joy, and testified to him the great satisfaction he had to see him. He would then have paid his acknowledgments to the queen, but she was already retired to her apartment. The king made him sit at the table with him, and after supper was over, he prayed him to relate to him how the princess Giauhara had had the inhumanity to transform him into a bird, so agreeable and amiable a prince as he was; and the king of Persia immediately applied himself to satisfy him. When he had done, the king, disdaining the proceeding of the princess, could not help blaming her. It was commendable, said he, in the princess of Samandal, not to be insensible of the king her father's ill treatment; but to carry her vengeance so far, and especially against one that was not culpable, was by no means to be excused, and she will never be able to justify herself. But let us have done with this discourse, and tell me, I beseech you, in what I can farther serve you.

Sir, answered king Beder, my obligation to your majesty has been so great, that I ought to remain with you all my life-time to testify my acknowledgments: but since your majesty has set no limits to your generosity, I humbly entreat you to grant me one of your ships to transport me to Persia, where I fear my absence, which has been but too long, may have occasioned some disorder; and moreover, that the queen my mother, from whom I concealed my departure, may be dead of grief, under the uncertainty she must needs be of my life or of my death.

The king granted what he desired with all the good-will imaginable, and immediately gave orders for equipping one of his largest ships, and best sailors, in all his numerous fleet. The ship was soon furnished with all its complement of men, provisions and ammunition; and as soon as the wind became fair, king Beder embarked, after having taken leave of the king, and thanked him for all his favours.

The ship sailed before the wind for ten days together, which made it advance considerably. The eleventh day the wind changed, and becoming very violent, there followed a furious tempest. The ship was not only driven out of its course, but so grievously agitated, that all its masts were brought by the board: And driving along at the pleasure of the wind, it at length struck against a rock and bulged.

The greatest part of the people were drowned, though some few were saved by swimming, and others by getting on pieces of the wreck. King Beder was one of the last; when, after having been tossed about for some time under great uncertainty of his fate, he at length perceived himself near the shore, and not far from a city that seemed large.—He used his utmost endeavours to reach the land, and was at length so fortunate, to come so near as to be able to touch the ground with his feet. He then immediately abandoned his piece of wood which had been of so great service to him; but when he came pretty near the shore he was greatly surprised to see horses, camels, mules, asses, oxen, cows, bulls, and other animals, crowding towards the shore, and putting themselves in a posture to oppose his landing. He had all the difficulty in the world to conquer their obstinacy, and force his way; but at length he did it, which, when done, he sheltered himself among the rocks, till such time as he had recovered his breath, and dried his cloaths in the sun.

When the prince advanced to enter the city, he met with the same opposition from these animals, who seemed to intend to make him forego his design, and give him to understand it was dangerous to proceed.

King Beder, however, got into the city soon after, and saw many fair and spacious streets, but was surprised to find never a man there. This made him think it was not without a cause that so many animals had opposed his passage. Going forward, nevertheless, he observed divers shops open, which gave him reason to believe the place was not destitute of inhabitants, as he imagined. He approached one of these shops, where several sorts of fruits were exposed to sale, and saluted very courteously an old man that was sitting there.

The old man, who was busy about something, suddenly lifted up his head, and seeing a youth that shewed some grandeur in his air, started, and asked him whence he came? and what business had brought him hither? King Beder satisfied him in a few words; and the old man farther asked him, If he had met any body on the road? You are the first person I have seen, answered the king; and I cannot comprehend how so fine and large a city comes to be without inhabitants. Come in, sir, stay no longer on the threshold, replied the old man, or peradventure some misfortune may happen to you. I will satisfy your curiosity at leisure, and give you a reason why it is necessary you should take this precaution.

King Beder would not be bid twice: He entered the shop, and sat himself down by the old man. The old man, who had learned from him an account of his misfortunes, knew he must needs want nourishment, therefore immediately presented him with what was necessary to recover his spirits; and, although king Beder was very earnest to know why he gave him that precaution before he entered the shop, he would nevertheless not be prevailed upon to tell him any thing till he had done eating, for fear the sad things he had to relate might baulk his appetite. In a word, when he found he eat no longer, he said to him, You have great reason to thank God you got hither without any ill accident. Alas! why? replied king Beder, very much surprised and alarmed.

Because, answered he, this city is the city of enchantments, and governed not by a king, but a queen, who is not only one of the finest women of her sex, but likewise a dangerous sorceress. You will be convinced of this, added he, when you come to know that these horses, mules, and other animals that you have seen, are so many men like you and me, whom she has transformed by her diabolical art. And for young men like you only, that come to enter into the city, she has hired servants to stop, and bring them, either by good-will or force, before her. She receives them with all the seeming civility in the world: She caresses them, she treats and lodges them magnificently, and gives them so many reasons to believe that she loves them, that they think they cannot be mistaken. But she does not suffer them to enjoy long their happiness. Not one of them but she has transformed into some animal or bird, within the space of forty days. You told me those animals presented themselves to oppose your landing, and hinder your entering the city; and I must now tell you they were your friends, and what they did, was to make you comprehend the danger you were going to expose yourself to.

This account afflicted exceedingly the young king of Persia. Alas! cried he out aloud, to what extremities has my ill fortune reduced me! I am hardly freed from one enchantment, which I look back upon with horror, but I incur another much more terrible to me. This gave him occasion to relate his story to the old man much more at length, and to acquaint him of his birth and quality, his passion for the princess of Samandal, and her cruelty in changing him into a bird, the very moment he came to see and declare his love to her.

When the prince came to that passage where he spake of his good fortune in finding a queen that broke the enchantment, the old man said to him, Notwithstanding all I have told you of the magic queen being true, yet that ought not to give you the least disquiet, since I am generally beloved throughout the city, and am not even unknown to the queen herself, who has no small respect for me; therefore it was your peculiar happiness to address yourself to me rather than elsewhere. You are secure in my house, where I advise you to continue, if you think fit; and, provided you do not stray from hence, I dare assure you, you will have no just cause to complain of my breach of faith; so that you are under no sort of constraint whatsoever.

King Beder thanked the old man for his kind reception of him, and the protection he was pleased to afford him. Then he sat down at the entrance into the shop, where he no sooner appeared, but his youth and good mien drew the eyes of all that passed that way on him. Many stopped and complimented the old man, on his having so fine a slave, as they imagined the king to be, and they could not comprehend how so beautiful a youth could escape the queen's knowledge. Believe not, said the old man, this is a slave: You all know that I am not rich enough to have one of this consequence; he is my nephew, son of a brother of mine that is dead; and as I had no children of my own, I sent for him to keep me company. They all congratulated his good fortune, in having so fine a young man for his relation: but withal told him, they feared the queen would take him from him. You know her well, said they to him, and you cannot be ignorant of the danger you expose yourself and nephew to, after all the examples you have seen of the kind. How grieved would you be, if she should serve you as she has done so many others?

I am obliged to you, gentlemen, replied the old man, for your good-will towards me, and I thank you for the care you seem to take of my interest, but I shall never entertain the least thought that the queen will do me any injury, after all the kindness she has professed for me. In case she happens to hear of this young man, and speaks to me about him, I doubt not but she will be contented to excuse him, so soon as she comes to know he is my nephew.

The old man was exceedingly glad to hear the commendations they bestowed on the young king of Persia. He was as much affected with them as if he had been his own son; and he conceived such a kindness for him, as augmented every day during the stay he made with him. They lived about a month together, when king Beder sitting at the shop-door, after his ordinary manner, queen Labe (so was this magic queen's name,) happened to come by with great pomp. The young king no sooner perceived the guards coming, who marched before her, but he arose, and going into the shop, asked the old man what all that show meant? The queen is coming by, answered he, but stand you still, and fear nothing.

The queen's guards, clothed in purple, and well armed and mounted, marched in four files, with their sabres drawn, to the number of a thousand, and not one of their officers, but, as they passed by the shop, saluted the old man. Then followed a like number of eunuchs, habited in brocade silk, and better mounted, whose officers did the old man the like honours. Next came as many young ladies on foot, equally beautiful, richly dressed, and set off with precious stones. They marched gravely, with half pikes in their hands; and in the midst of them appeared queen Labe, on a horse all glittering with diamonds, with a golden saddle, and a housing* of inestimable price. All the young ladies saluted the old man, as they passed by him; and the queen, moved with the good mien of king Beder, stopped as soon as she came over-against the shop. Abdallah, (so was the old man's name) said she to him, tell me, I beseech thee, does that beautiful and charming slave belong to thee; and is it long that thou hast been in possession of him?

Abdallah, before he answered the queen, threw himself on the ground, and rising again, said, Madam, it is my nephew, son of a brother I had, who has been dead for some time. Having no children, I look upon him as my son, and sent for him to come and comfort me, intending to leave him what I have when I die.

Queen Labe, who had never yet seen any one that pleased her so well as king Beder, and who began to conceive a mighty passion for him, thought immediately of getting the old man to abandon him to her. Father, quoth she, will not you oblige me so far as to make me a present of this young man? Do not refuse me, I conjure you; and I swear by the fire and the light, I will make him as great and powerful as ever private man was in the world. Although my design be to do evil to all mankind, yet he shall be the sole exception. I trust you will grant me what I desire, more on account of the friendship you have for me, than the esteem you know I have always had, and shall ever have, for your person.

Madam, replied the good Abdallah, I am infinitely obliged to your majesty for all the kindness you have for me, and the honours you propose to do my nephew. He is not worthy to approach so great a queen, and I humbly beseech your majesty to excuse him.

Abdallah, replied the queen, I all along flattered myself you loved me, and I could never have thought you would have given me so evident a token of your slighting my request: but I swear once more by the fire and light, and even by whatsoever is most sacred in my religion, that I will pass on no farther until I have conquered thy obstinacy. I understand very well what raises fears in thee; but I here promise, thou shalt never have any occasion to repent thy having trusted me.

Old Abdallah was exceedingly grieved, in relation to king Beder and himself, for being in a manner forced to obey the queen. Madam, therefore, replied he, I would not willingly have your majesty have an ill opinion of the sincere respect I have for you, but would always contribute whatever I can to oblige you: I put an entire confidence in your royal word, and I do not in the least doubt but you will keep it: I only beg of your majesty to delay doing this great honour to my nephew till you shall again pass by this way. That shall be to-morrow, quoth the queen; and so saying, she inclined her head as a token of her being pleased, and so went forward towards her palace.

When queen Labe and all her attendants were out of sight, the good Abdallah said to king Beder, Son, (for so he was wont to call him, for fear of some time or other betraying himself in public) it has not been in my power, as you may have observed, to refuse the queen what she demanded of me with so great earnestness, to the end I might not force her to an extremity of employing her magic both against you and myself. But I have some reason to believe she will use you well, as she promised, on account of that particular esteem she professes for me. This you may have seen, by the respect both she and all her court paid me. She would be a cursed creature indeed, if she should deceive me; but in case she should, she shall not deceive me unrevenged, for I know how to be even with her.

All these assurances, which appeared very doubtful, were not sufficient to support king Beder's spirits. After all you have told me of this queen's wickedness, replied he, you cannot wonder if I am somewhat fearful to approach her: I should, it may be, slight all you could tell me of her, and suffer myself to be dazzled by the lustre of grandeur that surrounds her, if I had not already been at the mercy of a sorceress. The condition I was in, through the enchantment of the princess Giauhara, and from whence I was delivered only to enter anew into another, has made me to look upon such a fate with horror. His tears hindered him from going on any farther, and sufficiently shewed with what repugnance he held himself in a manner under a fatal necessity of being delivered to queen Labe.

Son, replied old Abdallah, do not afflict yourself; for though I must own there is no great stress to be laid upon the oaths and promises of so perfidious a queen, yet I must withal acquaint you, her power extends no farther than I am pleased to permit it: she knows it full well herself; and that is the reason, and no other, that she pays me so great respect. I can quickly hinder her from doing you the least harm, though she should be perfidious enough to attempt it. You may entirely depend upon me; and, provided you follow exactly the advice I shall give you before I abandon you to her, she shall have no more power over you than she has over me.

The magic queen did not fail to pass by the old man's shop the next day, with the same pomp she had done the day before; and Abdallah waited for her with great respect. Father, cried she, stopping just against him, you may judge of my impatience to have your nephew with me, by my punctual coming to put you in mind of your promise; I know you are a man of your word, and I cannot think you will break it with me.

Abdallah, who fell on his knees as soon as he saw the queen approaching, rose up when she had done speaking; and as he would have nobody hear what he had a mind to say to her, he advanced with great respect as far as her horse's head, and then said softly, Puissant queen! I am persuaded your majesty will not be offended at my seeming unwillingness to trust my nephew with you yesterday, since you cannot be ignorant of the reasons I had for it; but I conjure you to lay aside the secrets of that art which you possess in so wonderful a degree. I respect my nephew as my own son; and your majesty would reduce me to the utmost despair, if you should think fit to deal with him as you have done with others.

I promise you once more I will not, replied the queen; and I once more repeat the oath I made yesterday, that neither you nor your nephew shall have any cause to be offended at me. I see plainly, added she, you are not yet well enough acquainted with me: you never saw me yet but through a veil; but as I find your nephew worthy of my friendship, I will shew you I am not any-ways unworthy of his. With that she threw off her veil, and discovered to king Beder, who came near her with Abdallah, an incomparable face: but king Beder was little charmed. It is not enough, said he within himself, to be beautiful; one's actions ought to correspond in regularity with one's features.

While king Beder was making these reflections, with his eyes fixed on queen Labe, the old man turned towards him, and, taking him by the arm, presented him to her majesty, saying, Here he is, madam; and I beg of your majesty once more to remember he is my nephew, and to let him come and see me sometimes. The queen promised he should; and to give a farther assurance of her acknowledgment, she caused a bag of a thousand pieces of gold to be given him. He excused himself at first from receiving them; but she insisted absolutely upon it, and he could not refuse her. She had caused a horse to be brought, as richly harnessed and set out as her own, for the king of Persia. While he was mounting him, I forgot, said the queen to

Abdallah, to ask you your nephew's name; pray how is he called? He answered, his name was Beder, (The Full Moon); and her majesty replied, Sure his ancestors were mistaken; they ought to have given him the name of Shems, (The Sun).

When king Beder was mounted, he would have taken his post behind the queen; but she would not suffer him, and made him to ride on her left hand. She looked upon Abdallah; and after having made him an inclination with her head, she set forward on her march.

Instead of observing a satisfaction in the people's faces at the sight of their sovereign, king Beder took notice that they rather despised and cursed her. The sorceress, said some, has got a new subject to exercise her wickedness upon: will heaven never deliver the world from her tyranny? Poor stranger, cried out others, thou art much deceived, if thou thinkest thine happiness will last long: it is to render thy fall more terrible, that she has raised thee so high. This talk gave king Beder to understand Abdallah had told him nothing but the truth of queen Labe; but as he no longer depended on him, he had recourse to divine Providence to free him from the danger he was got into.

The magic queen arrived at her palace, whither she was no sooner come, but she alighted, and, giving her hand to king Beder, entered with him, accompanied by her women, and the officers of her eunuchs. She herself shewed him all her apartments, where there was nothing to be seen but massy gold, precious stones, and furniture of wonderful magnificence. When she had carried him into her closet, she led him out into a balcony, from whence he observed a garden of surprising beauty. King Beder commended all he saw, with a great deal of wit, but nevertheless in such a manner that he might not be discovered to be any other than old Abdallah's nephew. They discoursed of divers indifferent matters, till such time as news was brought the queen that dinner was upon the table.

The queen and king Beder arose, and went to place themselves at table, which was of pure massy gold, and the plates of the same. They began to eat, but did not drink till almost the desert came, when the queen caused a cup to be filled with excellent wine: she took it, and drank to king Beder's health; and then causing it to be filled again, presented it to him. King Beder received it with profound respect, and, by a very low bow, signified to her majesty that he likewise drank to her health.

Soon after, ten of queen Labe's women entered with musical instruments, with which, accompanied with their voices, they made an agreeable concert during the whole drinking, which continued till late at night. At length they began to be so heated with wine, that king Beder insensibly forgot he had to do with a magic queen, and looked upon her only as the finest woman he ever saw. As soon as the queen perceived she had wrought him to the pitch she desired, she made a sign to her eunuchs and women to retire. They obeyed; and king Beder and she went and lay together all night.

Next morning the queen and king Beder went to the bagnio; and as soon as they came out, the women who had served the king there, presented him with fine linen, and a magnificent habit. The queen likewise, who was more splendidly dressed than the day before, came to receive him, and they went together to her apartment, where they had a good repast brought before them, and spent the remainder of the day in walking and other amusements.

Queen Labe treated king Beder after this manner for forty days, as she had been accustomed to do all her lovers. The fortieth night, as they were lying together, she believing he was really asleep, arose, without making any noise; but he was awake, and perceiving she had some design upon him, watched all her motions. Being up, she opened a chest, from whence she took a little box, full of a certain yellow powder: Taking some of the powder, she laid a train of it across the chamber, and immediately flowed in a rivulet of water, to the great astonishment of king Beder. He trembled with fear, but still pretended to sleep, that he might not discover to the sorceress he was awake.

Queen Labe next took up some of the water in a pot and poured it into a bason, where there was flower; with which she made paste, and kneaded it for a long time: Then she mixed certain drugs with it, which she took from different boxes, and made a cake, and put it into a covered baking-pan. As she had taken care at first to make a good fire, she took some of the coals, and set the pan upon them; and as the cake was baking, she put up her pot and boxes again; and at the pronouncing of certain words, dismissed the rivulet, which appeared no more. When the cake was baked, she took it off the coals, and carried it into her closet, and afterwards returned to bed again to king Beder, who dissembled the matter so well with her, that she had not the least suspicion that he knew any thing of what she had done.

King Beder, whom the pleasures and delights of a court had made to forget his good host, Abdallah, began now to think of him again, and believed he had more than ordinary occasion for his advice at this juncture, since he saw all the queen had done that night. As soon as he was up, therefore, he expressed a great desire to go and see his uncle, and begged of her majesty to permit him. Alas! my dear Beder, cried the queen, are you then already tired, I will not say with the pleasures of so superfine a palace as mine is, but with the company of a queen who loves you so passionately as I do?

Great queen, answered king Beder, how can I be tired with so many favours and graces as your majesty perpetually heaps upon me? Very far from that, I desire this permission, madam, purely to go and give my uncle an account of the mighty obligations I have to your majesty. I must own likewise it is partly in this respect, that my uncle loving me so tenderly, as it is very well known he does, and I having been from him now forty days, without so much as once seeing him, he will surely take it very unkindly if I cannot afford him one visit. Go, said the queen, I consent to it; but you will not be long before you return, if you consider I cannot possibly live without you. This said, she ordered him a fine horse, richly caparisoned,* and so he departed.

Old Abdallah was overjoyed to see his dear adopted son again, insomuch that, without regard to his quality, he embraced him heartily, and king Beder returned the like, that nobody might doubt but that he was his nephew. As soon as they were sat down, Well, said Abdallah to the king, how do you do, sir? and how have you passed your time with that infidel sorceress?

Hitherto, answered king Beder, I must needs own she has been extraordinary kind to me, and has done all she could to persuade me that she loves me entirely; but I observed something last night, which gives me just reason to suspect that all her kindness hitherto is but dissimulation. Whilst she thought me asleep, although I was really awake, she stole from me with a great deal of precaution, which made me suspect her intention, and therefore I resolved to watch her. Going on with his discourse, he related to Abdallah how, and after what manner, he had seen her make the cake; and then added, Hitherto, said he, I must needs confess I had almost forgot, not only you, but all the advice you gave me concerning the wickedness of this queen: But this last action of her's gives me reason to fear she neither intends to observe any of her oaths or promises. I thought of you immediately, and esteem myself happy in that I have obtained permission to come to you.

You are not deceived in this wicked queen, replied old Abdallah with a smile, to shew he did not himself believe she would observe one word she spoke, or oath she made; nothing is capable to oblige a perfidious woman to mend her morals. But fear nothing, I have a way to make the mischief she intends you fall upon herself. You are become jealous in time; and you could not have done better than this, to have recourse to me. It is her ordinary practice to keep her lovers only forty days; and after that time, instead of sending them home, to turn them into animals, to stock her forests and parks; but I thought of measures yesterday to prevent her doing any harm. The earth has borne this monster long enough, and it is now high time she should be served as she deserves.

So saying, Abdallah put two cakes into king Beder's hands, bidding him keep them to make use of, as he should direct. You told me, continued he, the sorceress made a cake last night: it was for you to eat of, depend upon it; but take great care you do not touch it. Nevertheless, do not refuse to receive it when she offers it you; but, instead of tasting it, break off part of one of the two that I gave you, unobserved, and eat that. As soon as she thinks you have swallowed it, she will not fail to attempt transforming you into some animal, but she shall not succeed; which, when she sees, she will immediately turn the thing to pleasantry, as if what she had done was only to frighten you; but she will conceal a mortal aversion in her heart, and think her having failed proceeded only from the want of something in the composition of her cake. As for the cake she made, and which she will not know to be her own, you shall make a present of it to her, and press her to eat it; which she will not refuse to do, if it were only to convince you she does not mistrust you, though she has given you so much reason to mistrust her. When she has quite ate it, take a little water in the hollow of your hand, and throwing it in her face, say, Quit that form you now wear, and take that of such or such an animal, as you shall think fit; which done, come to me with the animal, and I will tell you what you shall do afterwards.

King Beder made all possible acknowledgments to old Abdallah, for the great obligations he had to him, for defending him from the wiles of a pestilent sorceress, who sought to ruin him; and after some little discourse, he took his leave of him and returned to the palace. Upon his arrival, he understood that the queen waited for him with great impatience in the garden. He went to pay his respects to her, and she no sooner perceived him, but she came in great haste to meet him. My dear Beder! said she, it is said, with a great deal of reason, that nothing moves more the force and excess of love than absence from the object beloved. I have had no quiet since I saw you, and the minutes I have been separated from you have seemed so many ages; nay, if you had staid ever so little longer, I was preparing to come and fetch you once more to my arms.

Madam, replied king Beder, I can assure your majesty that I have not been under less disquiets on your account; but I could not refuse to stay a little longer than ordinary with an uncle who loved me so dearly, and had not seen me for so long a while. He would have kept me still longer, but I tore myself away from him to come and pay my vows where they are so much due. Of all the collations he prepared for me, I have only brought away this cake, which I desire your majesty to accept. King Beder had wrapped up one of the two cakes in a handkerchief very neatly, took it out, and presented it to the queen, saying, I beg your majesty to accept of it, though it be so inconsiderable a present.

I do accept of it with all my heart, replied the queen, receiving it, and will eat it chearfully for your's and your good uncle's sake: but before I taste of it, I desire you will eat a piece of mine, which I have made for you during your absence. Fair queen, answered king Beder, receiving it with great respect, such hands as your majesty's can never make any thing but what is excellent, and the favour hereby done me will exact an eternal acknowledgment.

King Beder then substituted, in the place of the queen's cake, the other which old Abdallah had given him, and having broken off a piece, he put it to his mouth, and cried, while he was eating, Ah! queen, I never tasted any thing so charming in my life. They being near a cascade, the sorceress seeing him swallow one bit of the cake, and ready to eat another, she took a little water in the palm of her hand, and throwing it on the king's face, said, Wretch! quit that form of a man thou bearest, and take that of a vile horse, lame and blind.

These words not having the desired effect, the sorceress was strangely surprised to find king Beder still in the same form, and that he only started, being a little frightened. Blushes came suddenly into her cheeks, and as she saw that she had missed her aim, Dear Beder, cries she, this is nothing, recover thyself; I did not intend thee any harm; what I did, was only to see what thou wouldst say. I should be the most miserable and execrable of women, should I attempt aught against thy tranquillity; I do not only say, after all the oaths I made to the contrary, but even after so many testimonies of love I have given thee.

Puissant queen, replied king Beder, however well satisfied I were, that what your majesty did was only to divert yourself, yet I could not help being a little frightened with the surprise. Also, what could hinder me from being a little moved at the pronouncing of such terrible words, as are capable of making so strange a transformation? But, madam, continued he, let us set aside this discourse, and since I have ate of your cake, I desire you would do me the like favour, by tasting of mine.

Queen Labe, who could no better justify herself, than by putting this confidence in the king of Persia, broke off a piece of his cake and eat it; which she had no sooner done, but she appeared much troubled, and remained, as it were, motionless. King Beder seeing his time, took water out of the same bason she had done, and throwing it in her face, cried, Abominable sorceress! quit that form of a woman, and be turned instantly into a mare.

The same instant queen Labe was transformed into a very beautiful mare; and she was so concerned to find herself in that condition, that she shed tears in great abundance, which perhaps no mare before had been ever known to do. She bowed her head with great obeisance to king Beder, thinking to move him to compassion; but, though he could have been so moved, it was absolutely out of his power to repair the damage he had done her. He led her then into the stable belonging to the palace, and put her into the hands of a groom, to bridle and saddle; but of all the bridles he tried upon her, not one would fit her. This made him cause two horses to be saddled, one for the groom, and the other for himself; and the groom led the mare after him to old Abdallah's.

Abdallah seeing king Beder coming with the mare at a distance, doubted not but he had done what he advised him. Cursed sorceress, said he immediately to himself very joyfully, heaven has at length punished thee as thou deservest. King Beder alighted at Abdallah's door, and entered with him into the shop, embracing and thanking him for all the signal services he had done him. He related to him the whole matter, with all its circumstances; and moreover told him, he could find no bridle fit for the mare. Abdallah found one that fitted exactly; and as soon as king Beder had sent back the groom, he said to him, My lord, you have no reason to stay any longer in this city, take the mare, mount her, and return to your kingdom. I have but one thing more to recommend to you, and that is, if ever you should happen to part with the mare, be sure to deliver her bridle. King Beder promised to observe all his commands, and this especially; and so having taken leave of the good old man, he departed.

The young king of Persia no sooner got out of the city, but he began to reflect on the deliverance he had had, and to rejoice he had the sorceress in his power, who had given him so much cause to tremble. Three days after, he arrived at a great city, where, entering the suburbs, he met a venerable old man, walking on foot towards a pleasure-house he had hard by: Sir, said the old man to him, stopping, may I presume to ask from what part of the world you come? The king stopped to satisfy him, and, as they were discoursing together, an old woman chanced to come by, who stopping likewise, wept and sighed bitterly at the sight of the mare.

King Beder and the old man left off discoursing, to look on the old woman, whom the king asked, whom she had to lament so much? Alas! sir, replied she, it is because your mare resembles so perfectly one my son had, and which I still mourn the loss of on this account, and should think your's were the same, did I not know she was dead. Sell her to me, sir, I beseech you, and I will give you even more than she is worth, for the sake of the person that once owned her likeness.

Good woman, replied king Beder, I am heartily sorry I cannot comply with your request; my mare is not to be sold. Alas! sir, continued the old woman, do not refuse me this favour, for the love of God. I conjure you to do it out of pure charity, since my son and I shall certainly die with grief, if you do not grant it. Good mother, replied the king, I would grant it with all my heart, if I was disposed to part with so good a beast; but if I were so disposed, I believe you would hardly give a thousand pieces of gold for her, which is the lowest price I shall ever put upon her. Why should I not give so much? replied the old woman; if that be the lowest price, you need only say you will take it, and I will fetch you the money.

King Beder, seeing the old woman so poorly dressed, could not imagine she could find the money; therefore, to try her, he said, not thinking to part with his mare for all that, go fetch me the money and the mare is yours. The old woman immediately unloosed a purse she had fastened to her girdle, and desiring him to alight, bid him tell over the money: and, in case he found it came short of the sum demanded, her house was not far off, and she could quickly fetch the rest.

The surprise king Beder was in at the sight of this purse was not small. Good woman, said he, do you not perceive I have bantered* you all this while? I will assure you my mare is not to be sold.

The old man, who had been witness to all that was said, now began to speak: Son, quoth he to king Beder, it is necessary you should know one thing, which I find you are ignorant of; and that is, that in this city it is not permitted any one to lie, on any account whatsoever, and that on pain of death; now, you having made this bargain with this old woman, you must not refuse her money, and delivering your mare according to the agreement; and this you had better do without any noise, than expose yourself to what may ensue.

King Beder, sorely afflicted to find himself thus trapped by his rash proffer, was nevertheless forced to alight and perform his agreement. The old woman stood ready to seize the bridle, which, when she had done, she immediately unbridled the mare, and taking some water in her hand from a spring that ran in the middle of the street, she threw it in the mare's face, uttering these words; Daughter, quit that bestial form, and re-assume thy own. The transformation was effected in a moment; and king Beder, who swooned as soon as he saw queen Labe appear, would have fallen to the ground, if the old man had not hindered him.

The old woman, who was mother to queen Labe, and who had instructed her in all her magic, had no sooner embraced her daughter, but in an instant, she, by whistling, caused a genie to rise, of a gigantic form and stature: this genie immediately took king Beder on one shoulder, and the old woman, with the magic queen, on the other, and transported them in a few minutes to the palace of queen Labe, in the city of enchantments.

The magic queen immediately fell upon king Beder, reproaching him grievously, in the following manner: Is it thus, ungrateful wretch, that thy unworthy uncle and thou make me amends for all the kindnesses I have done for you? I shall soon be able to make you both feel what you so well deserve.

She said no more, but, taking water in her hand, threw it in his face, with these words, Come out of that form, and take that of a vile owl. These words were soon followed by the effect, and immediately she commanded one of her women to shut up the owl in a cage, and give him neither meat nor drink.

The woman took the cage, and, without regarding what the queen ordered, gave him both meat and drink. And being old Abdallah's friend, she sent him word privately how the queen had treated his nephew, and what design she had taken to destroy him and king Beder, in case he did not take timely measures to prevent it.

Abdallah knew no common measures would do with queen Labe; he therefore did but whistle after a certain manner, and there immediately rose a vast giant, with four wings, who presented himself before him, and asked what he would have with him? Lightning, said Abdallah to him, (for so was the genie's name), I command you to preserve the life of king Beder, son of the queen Gulnare. Go to the palace of the magic queen, and transport immediately to the capital of Persia the compassionate woman who has the cage in custody, that she may inform queen Gulnare of the danger the king her son is in, and the occasion he has of her assistance. Take care not to fright her when you come before her, and acquaint her from me what she ought to do.

Lightning immediately disappeared, and got in an instant to the palace of the magic queen. He instructed the woman, lifted her up into the air, and transported her to the capital of Persia, where he placed her on the terrace of the apartment where queen Gulnare was. She went down stairs to the apartment, and she there found queen Gulnare and queen Farasche, lamenting their mutual misfortunes. She made them a profound reverence, and, by the relation she gave them, they soon came to understand the great necessity king Beder was in of their assistance.

Queen Gulnare was so overjoyed at the news, that, rising from her seat, she went and embraced the good woman, telling her how much she was obliged to her for the service she had done her.

Then going immediately out, she commanded the trumpets to sound, and the drums to beat, to acquaint the city, that the king of Persia would suddenly return safe to his kingdom. She then went again, and found king Saleh her brother, whom Farasche had caused to come speedily thither, by a certain fumigation. Brother, said she to him, the king our nephew, and my dear son, is in the city of Enchantments, under the power of queen Labe. Both you and I must see what we can do to deliver him, for there is no time to be lost.

King Saleh forthwith assembled a puissant body of sea-troops, and even called to his assistance the genies his allies, who appeared with a much more numerous army. As soon as the two armies were joined, he put himself at the head of them, together with queen Farasche, queen Gulnare, and the princesses, who would all have their share in this glorious action. They then lifted themselves up into the air, and soon poured down on the palace and city of Enchantments, where the magic queen, her mother, and all the other adorers of fire, were destroyed in an instant.

Queen Gulnare had ordered the woman who brought her the news of queen Labe's transforming and imprisoning her son, to follow her close, and bid her, in her hurly-burly,* to take no other care, than to go and seize the cage, and bring it to her. She did as she was ordered, and queen Gulnare was no sooner in the possession of the cage, but she opened it, and took the owl out, saying, after she had sprinkled a little water upon him, My dear son, quit that foreign form which has been given thee, and resume thy natural one of a man. In a moment, queen Gulnare no more saw the hideous owl, but king Beder her son instead of him. She immediately embraced him with that excess of joy which is better expressed by actions than words. She could not find in her heart to let him go; and, if he had not been in a manner torn from her by queen Farasche, who had a mind to embrace him in her turn, for aught I know, they might not have parted till now, so great queen Gulnare's affection was for him. After the queen his grandmother had done with him, he was likewise embraced by the king his uncle, and the princesses his relations.

The next care queen Gulnare had, was to look out for old Abdallah, to whom she had been obliged for the recovery of the king of Persia; and who, being brought to her, she said to him, My obligations to you, sir, have been so great, that there is nothing within my power but I will freely do for you as a token of my acknowledgment. Do but satisfy me in what I can serve you; and you shall see I will immediately set about it. Great queen, replied Abdallah, if the lady next to your majesty will but consent to the marriage I offer her, and the king of Persia will give me leave to reside at his court, I will spend the remainder of my days in his service. The queen turned towards the lady, and finding by her modesty, that she was not against the match proposed, she caused them to join hands, and the king of Persia and she took care of their fortune.

This marriage occasioned the king of Persia to speak thus, addressing himself to the queen: Madam, I am heartily glad of this match which your majesty has just now made: There remains one more, which I desire you to think of. Queen Gulnare did not at first comprehend what marriage he meant; but, after a little considering, she said, Of yours do you mean, son? I consent to it with all my heart. Then, turning about, and looking on her brother's sea-attendants, and the genies, who were still present, she said, Go you, and traverse both the sea and land, to find out the most lovely and amiable princess, worthy of the king my son, and come and bring us word.

Madam, replied king Beder, it is to no purpose for them to take all that pains. You have, no doubt, heard that I have already given my heart to the princess of Samandal, upon the bare relation of her beauty. I have seen her, and do not repent of the present I then made her. In a word, neither earth, nor sea, in my opinion, can furnish a princess any thing like her. It is true, upon declaring my love to her, she used me after a rate that would have extinguished any flame less fierce than mine; but I hold her excused; for, after a rigorous treatment, and imprisoning the king her father, which I was in some measure the cause of, how could she use me more civilly? But, it may be, the king of Samandal may have changed his resolution; and his daughter, the princess, may consent to love me, when she sees her father has agreed to it.

Son, replied queen Gulnare, if only the princess Giauhara can make you happy in this world, I shall not make it my business to oppose you. The king your uncle need only have the king of Samandal brought, and we shall see whether he be still of the same untractable temper.

How strictly soever the king of Samandal had been kept during his captivity, by king Saleh's orders, yet he always had great respect shewn him, and was become very familiar with the officers that guarded him. In order to bring him, king Saleh caused a chaffing dish of coals to be brought, into which he threw a certain composition, uttering at the same time some mysterious words: As soon as the smoke began to arise, the palace shook, and immediately the king of Samandal, with king Saleh's officers, appeared. The king of Persia cast himself at the king of Samandal's feet, and then rising upon one knee, he said, It is no longer king Saleh that demands of your majesty the honour of your alliance for the king of Persia: it is the king of Persia himself that humbly begs that boon; and I persuade myself your majesty will never persist in being the cause of the death of a king, who can no longer live than he is in the possession of the adorable princess Giauhara.

The king of Samandal did not long suffer the king of Persia to remain on his knee; he took him up, and embracing him, said, I should be very sorry to have contributed in the least towards the death of a monarch who is so worthy to live. If it be true that so precious a life cannot be preserved, without being in possession of my daughter, live, sir, and live happy, she is yours. She has always hitherto been obedient to my will, and I cannot think she will now oppose it. Speaking these words, he ordered one of the officers that king Saleh had assigned him, to go and look for the princess Giauhara, and bring her to him immediately.

The princess continued all this while where the king of Persia had left her. The officer brought her with her women to attend her. The king of Samandal embraced her, and said, Daughter, I have provided a husband for you, it is the king of Persia you see there, the most accomplished monarch at this juncture in the universe. The preference he has given you to all other princesses obliges us both to make him suitable acknowledgments.

Sir, replied the princess Giauhara, your majesty well knows I have never presumed to disobey your will in any thing: I shall be always ready to obey you; and I hope the king of Persia will please to forget the ill treatment I gave him, and consider it was duty, not inclination, that forced me to it.

The nuptials were celebrated in the palace of the city of Enchantments, with so much the greater solemnity, that all the lovers of the magic queen, who resumed their pristine forms as soon as ever that queen ceased to live, assisted at them, and came to pay their acknowledgments to the king of Persia, queen Gulnare, and king Saleh. They were all either sons of kings, or princes of extraordinary merit.

King Saleh at length conducted the king of Samandal to his dominions, and put him once again in possession of them. The king of Persia having what he most desired, returned to his capital with queen Giauhara, queen Gulnare, queen Farasche, and the princesses; and queen Farasche and the princesses continued there till such time as king Saleh came to re-conduct them to his kingdom under the waves of the sea.

The History of Ganem, Son to Abou Ayoub, and known by the Surname of Love's Slave

THERE was formerly a merchant at Damascus, who had, by care and industry, acquired great wealth, on which he lived in a very honourable manner. His name was Abou Ayoub, and he had one son and a daughter. The son was at first called Ganem, but afterwards had the surname of Love's Slave. He was graceful as to his person, and the excellent natural qualities of his mind had been improved by able masters his father had taken care to provide him. The daughter's name was Alcolomb, signifying ravisher of hearts, because her beauty was so accomplished, that whosoever saw her could not but love her.

Abou Ayoub died, and left immense riches: An hundred loads of brocades, and other silks that lay in his warehouse, were the least part of it. The loads were ready made up, and on every bale was written, in large characters, 'For Bagdad.'

Mohammed, the son of Soliman, surnamed Zinebi, reigned at that time in Damascus, the capital of Syria. His kinsman Haroun Alraschid, whose residence was at Bagdad, had bestowed this kingdom on him as tributary to him.

Soon after the death of Abou Ayoub, Ganem, discoursing with his mother about their private affairs, among the rest, concerning the bales of merchandize that lay in the warehouse, asked her the meaning of what was written upon each bale? My son, answered his mother, your father used to travel sometimes into one province, and sometimes into another, and it was customary with him, before he set out, to write the name of the city he designed to repair to on every bale. He had provided all things to take a journey to Bagdad, and was upon the point of setting forwards, when death—She had not the power to proceed any farther; the lively remembrance of the loss of her husband would not permit her to say any more, and drew from her a shower of tears.

Ganem could not see his mother so sensibly affected, without relenting. Thus they continued some time in silence; but at length he recovered himself; and, as soon as he found his mother calm enough to listen to him, he directed his discourse to her, and said: Since my father designed these goods for Bagdad, and is no longer in being, to put his design in execution, I will prepare myself to perform that journey: And I am of opinion, it will be proper for me to expedite my departure, for fear those commodities should perish, or at least, that we lose the opportunity of selling them to the best advantage.

Abou Ayoub's widow, who tenderly loved her son, was much surprised at this resolution, and replied, My dear child, I cannot but commend you for designing to follow your father's example; but consider that you are too young, inexperienced, and altogether a stranger to the toils of travelling. Besides, can you think of leaving me, and by that means add to that sorrow with which I am already oppressed? Is it not better to sell those goods to the merchants of Damascus, and to take up with a moderate profit, than to expose yourself to the danger of perishing?

It was in vain for her to oppose Ganem's resolution by the strongest arguments, for they had no weight with him. An inclination to travel, and to accomplish himself by a thorough knowledge of the affairs of the world, urged him on to set out, and prevailed above all his mother's remonstrances, her entreaties, and even her tears. He went away to the market where the slaves are sold, and bought such as were able of body; hired 100 camels, and, having furnished all other necessaries, he entered upon his journey, with five or six merchants of Damascus, who were going to trade at Bagdad.

Those merchants, attended by all their slaves, and accompanied by several other travellers, made up such a considerable caravan, that they had no occasion to fear the Bedouins, that is, the Arabs, who made it their only profession to range the country, and to attack and plunder the caravans which are not strong enough to repulse them. Thus they had no other difficulty to encounter, but the usual fatigues of a long journey, which were easily forgot when they saw the city of Bagdad, where they arrived in safety.

They went to alight at the most magnificent and most resorted khan in the city; but Ganem, who had a mind to be lodged conveniently, and by himself, took no apartment there. He only left his goods in a warehouse for their greater security, and hired a very fine house in the neighbourhood, richly furnished; having a garden, which was very delightful, on account of the many water-works and shady groves that were in it.

Some days after this young merchant had been settled in his house, and perfectly recovered of the fatigue of his journey, he dressed himself genteelly, and repaired to the public place where the merchants meet to buy and sell their commodities, with a slave following him, carrying a parcel of fine stuffs and silks.

The merchants received Ganem very courteously, and their syndic, or chief, to whom he first made application, bought all his parcel, at the price set down in the ticket annexed to every piece of stuff. Ganem continued his trade so successfully, that he daily sold all the goods he exposed.

He had no more left but one bale, which he had caused to be carried from the warehouse to his own house, and then went to the public rendezvous, where he found all the shops shut. This seemed somewhat extraordinary to him, and, having asked the cause of it, was told, that one of the prime merchants, whom he knew, was dead, and that all his brother traders were gone to his funeral.

Ganem enquired after the mosque where the ceremony was to be performed, and whence the body was to be conducted to the grave; and having been told it, sent back his slaves with the goods, and walked towards the mosque. He got thither before the prayers were ended, which were said in a hall hung with black sattin. The corpse was taken up, and followed by the kindred, the merchants, and Ganem, to the place of burial, which was at a great distance without the city. It was a stone structure, like a dome, purposely built to receive the bodies of all the family of the deceased, and, being very small, they had pitched tents all about it, that all the company might be sheltered during the ceremony. The monument was opened, and the corpse laid into it, after which it was shut up again. Then the iman,* and other ministers of the mosque, sat down in a ring on carpets, in the largest tent, and said the rest of the prayers. They also read the chapters of the Alcoran appointed for the burial of the dead. The kindred and merchants sat round in the same manner behind the ministers.

It was near night before the whole was ended. Ganem, who had not expected such a long ceremony, began to be uneasy, and was the more so, when he saw meat served up in memory of the deceased, according to the custom of Bagdad. He was also told that the tents had been set up, not only against the heat of the sun, but also against the evening dew, because they should not return to the city before the next morning. These words perplexed Ganem: I am a stranger, said he to himself, and have the reputation of being a rich merchant: thieves may take this opportunity of my absence, and go rob my house: my very slaves may be tempted to make their advantage of so convenient a time; they may run away with all the gold I have received for my goods; and whither shall I look for them? His head being full of these thoughts, he eat a few mouthfuls hastily, and dexterously slipped away from the company.

He made all possible haste, to gain time; but, as it often happens, the more a man puts on, the less he advances; he mistook his way, and went astray in the dark; so that it was near midnight when he came to the city-gate; and, to add to this misfortune, that was shut. That disappointment was a fresh affliction to him; and he was obliged to think of finding some convenient place to pass the rest of the night in, and wait till the gate was opened. He went into a burial-place, so very spacious, that it reached from the city to the very place he was come from. He advanced to a parcel of pretty high walls, which inclosed a small field, being the peculiar burying-place of a family, and in which there was a palm-tree. There was an infinite number of other particular burial-places, the doors whereof they did not take much care to shut fast. Ganem, finding that this burial-place was open, went into it, and put to the door after him. He lay down on the grass, and did all he could to sleep; but the uneasiness he was under, for being absent from home, would not permit him. He got up; and, after having passed by the door several times, as he walked forwards and backwards, he opened it, without knowing why he did so, and immediately perceived a light at a distance, which seemed to come towards him. He was startled at that sight, put to the door, which had nothing to make it fast but a latch, and got up as fast as he could to the top of the palm-tree, looking upon that as the safest retreat under his present apprehensions. No sooner was he got up, than, by the help of the light which had frightened him, he plainly perceived three men, whom, by their habit, he knew to be slaves, come into the burial-place. One of them went foremost with a lanthorn, and the two others followed him, being loaded with a chest, between five and six feet long, which they carried on their shoulders. They laid it down, and then one of the three slaves said to his comrades, Brothers, if you will be advised by me, we will leave the chest here, and return to the city. No, no, replied another, that is not the way of doing what we were ordered by our mistress: we may have cause to repent our not doing as we were commanded: let us bury the chest, since we are so enjoined to do. The two other slaves complied with him; so they began to break ground with the tools they had brought for that purpose. When they had made a deep trench, they put the chest into it, and covered it with the earth they had taken out; then departed, and returned home.

Ganem, who, from the top of the palm-tree, had heard every word the slaves had spoken, could not tell what to think of that adventure. He concluded that chest must needs contain something of value, and that the person to whom it belonged had some particular reasons for causing it to be buried in that church-yard. He resolved immediately to satisfy his curiosity, came down from the palm-tree, his fear being gone with the slaves, and fell to work upon the pit, plying his hands and feet so well, that in a short time he discovered the chest, but found it secured with a great padlock. This new obstacle to the satisfying of his curiosity was no small mortification to him; yet he would not be discouraged; but the day beginning then to appear, he saw several great pebbles about the burial-place: he picked out one, with which he easily knocked off the padlock, and then, with much impatience, opened the chest. Ganem was strangely surprised, when, instead of finding money in it, he discovered a young lady of incomparable beauty. Her fresh and rosy complexion, and her gentle regular breathing, satisfied him that she was alive; but he could not conceive, why, if she were only asleep, she had not awaked at the noise he made in forcing off the padlock. Her habit was so costly, with bracelets and pendants of diamonds, and a necklace of true pearl, and so large, that he made not the least doubt of her being one of the prime ladies about the court. At the sight of so beautiful an object, not only natural inclination to relieve persons in danger, but also something more powerful, which Ganem could not then give an account of, prevailed on him to afford that young beauty all the assistance he was able.

He first shut the gate of the burial-place, which the slaves had left open, then returning, took the lady in his arms out of the chest, and laid her on the soft earth he had thrown off the chest. As soon as the lady was laid down, and had the benefit of the open air, she sneezed, and having made a motion in turning her head, there came from her mouth a liquor, which seemed to have been offensive to her stomach; then opening and rubbing her eyes, she, with such a voice as charmed Ganem, whom she did not see, cried out, Zohorob Bostan, Schragrom Matglon, Cassabos Soucear, Nouron Nihar, Nagmatos Sobi, Nour Hatos Zoman, why do you not answer? where are you? Those were the names of six female slaves that used to wait on her, and signified, Flower of the Garden, Branch of Coral, Sugar Cane, Light of the Day, Morning Star, and Delight of the Season. She called them, and wondered that nobody answered; but at length looking about, and perceiving she was in a burial-place, she was in a mighty fright. How now, cried she, much louder than before, is this the resurrection of the dead? Is the day of judgment come? What a wonderful change is this from night to morning!

Ganem did not think fit to leave the lady any longer in that confusion, but immediately appeared before her with all possible respect, and, in the most courteous manner, said, Madam, I am scarce able to express my joy, for having happened to be here to do you the service I have done, and for being present to offer you all the assistance you shall stand in need of, under your present circumstances.

In order to persuade the lady to repose all her confidence in him, he, in the first place, told her who he was, and what accident it was that had brought him into that place. Next, he acquainted her with the coming of the three slaves, and how they had buried the chest. The lady, who had covered her face with her veil as soon as Ganem appeared, was extraordinarily sensible of the obligations she owed him. I return thanks to God, said she, for having sent so worthy a person as you are to deliver me from death; but, since you have begun so charitable a work, I conjure you not to leave it imperfect. Let me beg of you to go into the city, and provide a muleteer to come with his mule, and carry me to your house in the chest; for, should I go in with you on foot, my dress being different from that of the city-ladies, some one might happen to take notice of it, and follow me, which it highly concerns me to prevent. When I shall be in your house, I will give you an account of myself; and, in the mean time, be assured that you have not obliged an ungrateful person.

Before the young merchant left the lady, he drew the chest out of the pit, which he filled up with earth, laid her again in the chest, and shut it in such a manner, that it did not look as if the padlock had been forced off; but, for fear of stifling her, he put it not quite close, leaving room for the air to get in. Going out of the burial-place, he drew the door after him; and the city-gate being then open, soon found what he sought for. He returned with speed to the burial-place, and helped the muleteer to lay the chest across his mule; telling him, to remove all causes of suspicion, that he came to that place the night before, with another muleteer, who, being in haste to return home, had laid down the chest in the burial-place.

Ganem, who had minded nothing but his business since his arrival at Bagdad, was still unacquainted with the power of love, and now felt the first sallies of it. It had not been in his power to look upon the young lady, without being disturbed; and the uneasiness he felt, following the muleteer at a distance, and the fear lest any accident might happen by the way that should deprive him of his conquest, taught him to unravel his intricate thoughts. It was an extraordinary satisfaction to him, when, being arrived safe at home, he saw the chest unloaded. He dismissed the muleteer; and having caused a slave to shut the doors of his house, he opened the chest, helped the lady out, gave her his hand, and conducted her to his apartment, lamenting how much she must have endured in that close confinement. If I have suffered, said she, I have satisfaction enough in what you have done for me, and in the pleasure of seeing myself out of danger.

Though Ganem's apartment was very richly furnished, the lady did not so much regard that, as she did the handsome presence and engaging mien of her deliverer, whose politeness and obliging behaviour highly heightened her gratitude. She sat down on a sofa; and, to begin to give the merchant to understand how sensible she was of the service done her, she took off her veil. Ganem, on his part, was sensible of the favour so lovely a lady did in uncovering herself, or rather felt he had already a most violent passion for her. Whatsoever obligations she owed him, he thought himself more than requited by so singular a favour.

The lady dived into Ganem's thoughts, yet was not at all surprised, because he appeared very full of respect. He, judging she might have occasion to eat, and not willing to trust any but himself with the care of entertaining so charming a guest, went out with a slave to an eating-house, to give directions for a treat. From thence he went to a fruit-seller, where he chose the finest and most excellent fruit; buying also the choicest wine, and some of the same bread that was eaten at the caliph's table.

As soon as he returned home, he, with his own hands, made a pyramid of the fruit he had bought, and served it up himself to the lady, in a large dish of the finest china ware, saying, Madam, be pleased to make choice of some of this fruit, while a more solid entertainment, and more worthy yourself, is made ready. He would fain have continued standing before her; but she declared she would not touch any thing, unless he sat down and eat with her. He obeyed; and when they had eaten some small matter, Ganem observing that the lady's veil, which she had laid down by her on a sofa, was embroidered along the edge with golden letters, begged leave of her to look upon that embroidery. The lady immediately took up the veil, and delivered it to him, asking him whether he could read? Madam, replied he, with a modest air, a merchant would be able to manage his business very ill, if he could not at least read and write. Well then, said she, read the words which are embroidered on that veil, which gives me an opportunity of telling you my story.

Ganem took the veil, and read these words, 'I am yours, and you are mine, thou descendant from the prophet's uncle.' That descendant from the prophet's uncle was the caliph Haroun Alraschid, who then reigned, and was descended from Abbas, Mahomet's uncle.

When Ganem perceived the sense of these words, Alas! madam, said he, in a melancholy tone, I have just saved your life, and this embroidery is my death! I do not comprehend all the mystery; but it makes me too sensible that I am the most unfortunate of men. Pardon the liberty I take, madam, of telling you so much. It was impossible for me to see you without giving you up my heart. You are not ignorant yourself, that it was not in my power to refuse it you; and that makes my presumption excusable. I proposed to myself to move yours by my respect, my diligence, my complaisance, my assiduity, my submission, and my constancy; and no sooner had I flattered myself with that design, than I am robbed of all my hopes. But be that as it will, I shall have the satisfaction of dying entirely yours. Proceed, madam, I conjure you, to give me a full information of my unhappy state.

He could not deliver those words without letting fall some tears. The lady was moved, but was so far from being displeased at the declaration he made, that she felt an inward joy, for her heart began to yield. However, she concealed it; and, as if she had not regarded what Ganem said, I would have been very cautious, answered she, of shewing you my veil, had I thought it would have made you so uneasy; and I do not perceive that what I have to say to you can make your condition so deplorable as you imagine.

You must understand, proceeded she, in order to acquaint you with my story, that my name is Fetnah, (which signifies a storm or tempest) which was given me at my birth, because it was judged that the sight of me would occasion many calamities. You cannot be a stranger to it, since nobody in Bagdad but knows that the caliph Haroun Alraschid, my sovereign lord and yours, has a favourite so called.

I was carried into his palace in my very tender years, and I have been brought up there with all the care that is usually taken with such persons of my sex as are designed to reside there. I made no ill advances in all they took the pains to teach me; and that, with some share of beauty, gained me the caliph's affection, who gave me a particular apartment adjoining to his own. That prince was not satisfied with such a mark of distinction: he appointed twenty women to wait on me, and as many eunuchs; and, ever since, he has made me such considerable presents, that I was once richer than any queen in the world. You may reasonably judge, by what I have said, that Zobeide, the caliph's wife and kinswoman, could not be but jealous of my happiness. Though Haroun has all the regard imaginable for her, she has used all her endeavours to ruin me.

Hitherto, I had secured myself against all her snares, but at length, I fell under the last effort of her jealousy; and, were it not for you, I had now been exposed to inevitable death. I do not question but that she had corrupted one of my slaves, who, last night, in some lemonade, gave me a drug, which causes such a deep sleep, that it is easy to dispose of those who have taken it; and that sleep is so profound, that nothing can dispel it for the space of seven or eight hours. I have the more reason to judge so, because naturally I am very light of sleep, and apt to wake at the least noise.

Zobeide, the better to put her design in execution, has laid hold of the opportunity of the absence of the caliph, who has been gone lately to put himself at the head of his troops, to chastise some neighbouring kings, who have presumed to join in league to make war on him. Were it not for this opportunity, my rival, courageous as she is, durst not have presumed to attempt any thing against my life. I know not what she will do to conceal this action from the caliph, but you see it highly concerns me that you should keep my secret. My life depends on it. I shall be safe in your house as long as the caliph is from Bagdad. It behoves you to keep my adventure private; for, should Zobeide know the obligation I owe you, she would punish you for having saved me.

When the caliph returns, I shall not need to be so much upon my guard. I shall find means to acquaint him with all that has happened, and I am fully persuaded he will be more earnest than myself to requite a service which restores me to his love.

As soon as Haroun Alraschid's beautiful favourite had done speaking, Ganem began, and said, Madam, I return you a thousand thanks for having given me the information I took the liberty to desire of you; and I beg of you to believe that you are here in safety; the sentiments you have inspired in me are a pledge of my secrecy.

As for my slaves, I own there is cause to suspect them; they may perhaps fail of the fidelity they owe me, should they know by what accident, and in what place I had the good fortune to find you; but it is impossible they should guess at that. Nay, I dare assure you that they will not have the curiosity to inquire after it. It is so natural for young men to purchase beautiful slaves, that it will be no way surprising to them to see you here, as believing you to be one, and that I have bought you. They will also believe that I had some particular reasons for bringing you home as I did. Set your heart therefore at rest as to that point, and remain satisfied that you shall be served with all the respect that is due to the favourite of so great a monarch as ours is. But how great soever he is, give me leave, madam, to declare, that nothing will be able to make me recall the present I have made you of my heart. I know, and shall never forget, that what belongs to the master is forbidden to the slave; but I loved you before you told me that you were engaged to the caliph; it is not in my power to overcome a passion, which, though now in its infancy, has all the force of a love strengthened by a perfect correspondence. I wish your august and most fortunate lover may revenge you against the malice of Zobeide, by calling you back to him; and, when you shall be restored to his wishes, that you may remember the unfortunate Ganem, who is no less your conquest than the caliph. As powerful as that prince is, I flatter myself he will not be able to blot me out of your memory. If love be your predominant passion, he cannot love you more passionately than I do; and I shall never cease to burn in your flames, whatsoever part of the world I go into to expire, after having lost you.

Fetnah perceived that Ganem was under the greatest of afflictions, and it moved her; but, considering the uneasiness she was likely to bring upon herself by prosecuting the discourse upon that subject, which might insensibly lead her to discover the inclination she felt in herself for him, she said, I perceive that this sort of conversation gives you too much trouble; let us change the discourse, and talk of the infinite obligations I owe you, I can never sufficiently express my satisfaction, when I consider, that, without your assistance, I had not beheld the light of the sun.

It was happy for them both that somebody just then knocked at the door: Ganem went to see who it was, and found it was one of his slaves to acquaint him that the entertainment was ready. Ganem, who, by way of precaution, would have none of his slaves to come into the room where Fetnah was, took what was brought, and served it up himself to his beautiful guest, whose soul was ravished to behold with what diligence and respect he attended her.

When they had eaten, Ganem took away, as he covered the table; and having delivered all things at the chamber-door to his slaves, he said to Fetnah, Madam, you may now perhaps desire to take some rest; I will leave you, and when you have reposed yourself, you shall find me ready to receive your commands.

Having spoken these words, he left her, and went to buy two women-slaves. He also bought two parcels, the one of linen, and the other of all such things as were proper to make up a toilet fit for the caliph's favourite. Having conducted home the two women slaves, he presented them to Fetnah, saying, Madam, a person of your quality cannot be without two maids, at least, to serve you; be pleased to allow me to give you these.

Fetnah, admiring Ganem's forecast, My lord, said she, I perceive you are not one that will do things by halves; you add by your courtesy to the obligations I owe you already; but I hope I shall not die ungrateful, and that heaven will soon put me in a condition to make acknowledgments for all your acts of generosity.

When the women slaves were withdrawn into a chamber adjoining, which the young merchant shewed them, he sat down on the sofa where Fetnah was; but at some distance from her, in token of the greater respect. He then began again to discourse of his passion, and spoke very moving things relating to the invincible obstacles which robbed him of all his hopes. I dare not so much as hope, said he, by my passion, to excite the least sensibility in a heart like your's, destined for the greatest prince in the world. Alas! it would be a comfort to me, if I could flatter myself that you have not looked upon the excess of my love with indifferency. My lord, answered Fetnah—Alas! madam, said Ganem, interrupting her at the word lord, this is a second time you have done me the honour to call me lord; the presence of the women slaves hindered me the first time from taking notice of it to you; in the name of God, madam, do not give me that title of honour, it does not belong to me; treat me, I beseech you, as your slave; I am, and shall never cease to be so.

No, no, replied Fetnah, interrupting him in her turn, I shall be cautious how I treat a man to whom I owe my life, after that manner. I should be ungrateful could I say or do any thing that did not become you. Leave me therefore to follow the dictates of my gratitude, and do not require it of me that I misbehave myself towards you, in return for the benefits I have received. I shall never be guilty of it; I am too sensible of your respectful behaviour, to abuse it; and I will not stick to own, that I do not look upon all your care with indifferency. You know the reason that condemns me to silence.

Ganem was ravished at that declaration, he wept for joy; and not being able to find expressions significant enough, in his own conceit, to return Fetnah thanks, was satisfied with telling her, that, as she knew what she owed to the caliph, he, on his part, was not ignorant, 'That what belongs to the master, is forbid to the servant.'

Night drawing on, he went out to fetch some light, which he brought in himself, as also some collation, as is the custom in the city of Bagdad; where, having made a good meal at noon, they, at night, are satisfied with eating some fruit, and drinking a glass of wine; so diverting the time till they go to bed.

They both sat down at table, and at first complimented each other, presenting the fruit reciprocally. The excellency of the wine insensibly drew them both on to drink, and, having drank two or three glasses, they agreed that neither should take another glass without singing some air first. Ganem sung verses he composed *extempore*, and which expressed the vehemency of his passion; and Fetnah, encouraged by his example, composed and sung verses relating to her adventure, and always containing something which Ganem might take in a sense that was favourable to him; bating, that she nicely observed the fidelity due to the caliph. The collation held till very late, and the night was far advanced, before they thought of parting. Ganem then withdrew to another apartment, leaving Fetnah where she was, and the women slaves he had bought coming in to wait upon her.

They lived together after this manner for several days. The young merchant went not abroad, unless upon business of the utmost consequence, and, even for that, took the time when his lady was at her rest; for he could not prevail upon himself to let slip a moment that might be spent in her company. All his thoughts were taken up with his dear Fetnah, who, on her side, giving way to her inclination, confessed she had no less affection for him than he had for her. However, as fond as they were of each other, their respect for the caliph kept them within those bounds that were due to him, which still heightened their passion.

While Fetnah, thus snatched from the jaws of death, passed her time so agreeably with Ganem, Zobeide was not without some apprehensions in Haroun Alraschid's palace.

As soon as the three slaves entrusted with the execution of her revenge, had carried away the chest, without knowing what was in it, or so much as the least curiosity to inquire into it, as being used to pay a blind obedience to her commands, she was seized with a tormenting uneasiness; a thousand perplexing thoughts disturbed her rest; sleep fled from her eyes, and she spent the night in contriving how to conceal her crime. My consort, said she, loves Fetnah more than ever he did any of his favourites. What shall I say to him at his return, when he inquires of me after her? Many contrivances occurred to her, but none were satisfactory: She still met with difficulties, and knew not where to fix. There lived with her an ancient lady, who had bred her up from her infancy: As soon as it was day, she sent for her, and having entrusted her with the secret, said, Dear mother, you have always been assisting to me with your advice; if ever I stood in need of it, it is now; when the business before you is to still my thoughts, distracted by a mortal concern, and to shew me some way to satisfy the caliph.

Dear Madam, replied the old lady, it had been much better not to have run yourself into the difficulties you labour under; but since the thing is done, the best way is to say no more of it: all that must now be thought of, is how to deceive the chief of believers; and I am of opinion that you must immediately cause a wooden image to be carved resembling a dead body: we will shroud it up in old linen; and when shut up in a coffin, it shall be buried in some part of the palace; then shall you immediately cause a marble monument to be built after the manner of a dome, over the burial place; and erect a figure which shall be covered with black cloth, and set about with great candlesticks, and large wax tapers. There is another thing, added the old lady, which ought not to be forgot: you must put on mourning, and cause the same to be done by all your own and Fetnah's women, your eunuchs, and all that belong to the palace: when the caliph returns, and sees you and all the palace in mourning, he will be sure to ask the occasion of it; then will you have an opportunity of insinuating yourself into his favour, saying, it was in respect to him, that you paid the last honours to Fetnah, snatched away by sudden death. You may also tell him you have caused a mausoleum to be built; and, in short, that you have paid all the dues to his favourite which he would have done himself had he been present. His passion for her being extraordinary, he will certainly go and shed some tears upon her grave; and perhaps, added the old woman, he will not believe she is really dead; and suspect you have turned her out of the palace through jealousy, and look upon all the mourning as an artifice to deceive him, and prevent his making search after her. It is likely he will cause the coffin to be taken up and opened, and it is certain he will be convinced of her death as soon as he shall see the figure of a dead body buried. He will be pleased with all you shall have done, and express his gratitude. As for the wooden image, I will undertake to have it cut myself by a carver, in the city, who shall not know what use it is to be put to. As for your part, madam, order Fetnah's woman, who yesterday gave her the lemonade, to give out that she had just found her mistress dead in her bed; and that they may only think of lamenting, without offering to go into her chamber, let her add, she has already acquainted you with it, and that you have ordered Mesrour to cause her to be laid out and buried.

As soon as the old lady had spoken these words, Zobeide took a rich diamond ring out of her casket, and putting it on her finger, and embracing her in a perfect transport of joy, said, How infinitely am I beholden to you, my dear mother! I should never have thought of so ingenious a contrivance. It cannot fail of success, and I perceive my peace of mind begins to be restored to me. I leave the care of the wooden figure to you, and I will go myself to order the rest.

The wooden image was got ready with as much expedition as Zobeide could have wished, and then conveyed by the lady herself into Fetnah's bedchamber, where she dressed it like a dead body, and put it into a coffin. Then Mesrour, who was much deceived by it, caused the coffin, and the representation of Fetnah, to be carried away; and buried it with the usual ceremonies, in the place appointed by Zobeide, the favourite's women weeping and lamenting, she who had given her the lemonade setting them an example by her cries and howlings.

That very day, Zobeide sent for the architect of the palace, and of the caliph's other houses, and, according to the orders he received from her, the mausoleum was finished in a very short time. Such potent princesses, as was this consort of a monarch whose power extended from east to west, are always punctually obeyed in whatsoever they command by all the court; so that the news of Fetnah's death was soon spread all over the town.

Ganem was one of the last who had heard of it; for, as I had before observed, he scarce went abroad. Being at length informed of it, Madam, said he to the caliph's fair favourite, you are thought to be dead in Bagdad, and I do not question but that Zobeide herself believes it: I bless heaven that I am the cause, and the happy witness of your being alive: and would to God, that, taking the advantage of this false report, you will share my fortune, and go far from hence to reign in my heart! But whither does this pleasing notion carry me? I do not consider that you are born to make the greatest prince in the world happy; and that only Haroun Alraschid is worthy of you. Supposing you could resolve to give him up for me, and that you would follow me, ought I to consent to it? No, it is my part always to remember, that, what belongs to the master, is forbidden to the slave.

The lovely Fetnah, though moved by the tenderness of the passion he expressed, yet prevailed with herself not to comply with it. My lord, said she to him, we cannot obstruct Zobeide's triumphing. I am not at all surprised at the artifice she makes use of to conceal her guilt: but let her proceed; I flatter myself, that sorrow will soon follow her triumph: the caliph will return, and we shall find means privately to inform him of all that has happened. In the mean time, let us be more cautious than ever, that she may not know I am alive. I have already told you the consequences.

Three months after, the caliph returned to Bagdad with honour, having vanquished all his enemies; he entered the palace with impatience to see Fetnah, and to lay all his laurels at her feet; but was amazed to see all the servants he had left behind him in mourning. It struck him without knowing the cause, and his concern was double, when, coming into the apartment of Zobeide, he spied that princess coming to meet him with all her women in mourning. He immediately asked her the cause of it, with much concern. Chief of the Believers, answered Zobeide, I am in mourning for your slave, Fetnah, who died so suddenly, that it was impossible to apply any medicine to her distemper. She would have proceeded, but the caliph did not give her time, being so surprised at the news, that he cried out, and then fell into a swoon in the arms of Giafar, his grand visier, who attended him. Coming soon after to himself, he, with a weak voice, which sufficiently expressed his concern, asked where his dear Fetnah had been buried? Sir, said Zobeide, I took care myself of her funeral, and spared for no cost to make it magnificent. I have caused a marble mausoleum to be built over her grave, and will attend you thither, if you desire it.

The caliph would not permit Zobeide to take that trouble, but was satisfied to have Mesrour to conduct him. He went thither just as he was, that is, in the camp-dress.* When he saw the figure covered with a black cloth, the lighted candles all about it, and the magnificence of the mausoleum, he was amazed that Zobeide should have performed the obsequies of her rival with so much magnificence; and, being naturally of a jealous temper, he suspected his wife's generosity, and fancied his mistress might perhaps be yet alive: that Zobeide, taking the advantage of his long absence, might have turned her out of the palace, ordering those she had intrusted with it to convey her so far off, that she might never more be heard of. This was all he suspected; for he did not think Zobeide wicked enough to have murdered his favourite.

The better to discover the truth himself, that prince ordered the figure to be removed, and caused the grave and the coffin to be opened in his presence: but when he saw the linen which wrapped up the wooden image, he durst not proceed any farther. That religious caliph thought it would be an irreligious act, to suffer the body of the dead lady to be touched; and this scruple prevailed above his love and curiosity. He caused the coffin to be shut up again, the grave to be filled, and the figure to be placed as it was before.

The caliph, thinking himself obliged to pay some respect to the tomb of his favourite, sent for the ministers of his religion, the officers of the palace, and the readers of the Alcoran; and, whilst they were calling together, he remained in the mausoleum, moistening the earth, that covered the phantom of his love, with his tears. When all the persons he had sent for were come, he stood before the figure, and they about it recited long prayers; after which the readers of the Alcoran read several chapters.

The same ceremony was performed every day during the whole month, morning and evening, the caliph being always present, with Giafar the grand visier, and the prime officers of the court, all of them in mourning, as well as the caliph himself, who all that while failed not to honour the memory of Fetnah with tears, and would not talk the least of any business.

The last day of the month, the prayers and reading of the Alcoran lasted from that morning till break of day the next morning; and at length, when all was done, every man returned home. Haroun Alraschid, being tired with sitting up all that time, went to take some rest in his apartment, and fell asleep on a sofa between two of the court-ladies, one of them sitting at the bed's head, and the other at the feet, who, whilst he slept, were working some embroidery, and observed a profound silence.

She who sat at the bed's head, and whose name was Nouron-Nihar, that is, Dawn of the Day, perceiving the caliph was asleep, whispered to the other, called Nagmatos-Sobi, signifying Morning-Star, There is great news! The chief of the believers, our master, will be overjoyed when he awakes and hears what I have to say to him: Fetnah is not dead, she is in perfect health. O heavens! cried Morning-Star, in a transport of joy, is it possible that the beautiful, the charming, the incomparable Fetnah should be still among the living? Morning-Star uttered these words with such a sprightly air, and so loud, that the caliph awaked. He asked why they had disturbed his rest? Alas! my sovereign lord, answered Morning-Star, pardon me this indiscretion, I could not contain myself. What then is become of her, said the caliph, if she is not dead? Chief of the Believers, replied Dawn of the Day, I this evening received a note, not signed, from a person unknown, but written with Fetnah's own hand, which gives me an account of her melancholy adventures, and orders me to acquaint you with it. I thought fit, before I fulfilled my commission, to let you take some few moments rest, believing you must stand in need of it after your fatigue.—Give me that note, said the caliph, interrupting her in a disorderly manner, you were in the wrong in deferring to deliver it to me.

Dawn of the Day immediately delivered him the note, which he opened with much impatience; and in it Fetnah gave a brief account of all that had befallen her, but enlarged a little too much on the care Ganem took of her. The caliph, who was naturally jealous, instead of being provoked at the inhumanity of Zobeide, was only concerned for the infidelity he fancied Fetnah had been guilty of towards him. Is it so? said he, after reading the note; the perfidious wretch has been four months with a young merchant, and has the impudence to boast of the respect he pays her. Thirty days are passed since my return to Bagdad, and she now bethinks herself of sending me this news. Ungrateful creature! while I spend the days in bewailing her, she passes them away in betraying me. Go to, let us take revenge of the false woman, and that bold youth who affronts me. Having spoken these words, that prince got up, and went into a great hall, where he used to appear in public, and to give audience to the great men of his court. The first gate was opened, and immediately all the courtiers, who expected him, that moment entered. The grand visier came in, and prostrated himself before the throne the caliph sat on. Then rising, he stood before his master, who, in a tone which denoted he would be instantly obeyed, said to him, Giafar, your presence is requisite for putting in execution an important affair I am about to commit to you. Take four hundred men out of my guards along with you, and first enquire where a merchant of Damascus lives, whose name is Ganem, the son of Abou Ayoub. When you have learned that, repair to his house, and cause it to be razed down to the foundation; but first secure Ganem, and bring him hither, with my slave Fetnah, who has lived with him these four months. I will punish her, and make an example of that insolent man, who has presumed to fail in respect to me.

The grand visier having received this positive command, made a low bow to the caliph, having his hand on his own head, as a token that he would rather lose it than disobey him, and departed. The first thing he did, was to send to the syndic, or head of the merchants, for some foreign stuffs, and fine silks, of the new ones brought by Ganem; with strict orders, above all things, to enquire after the street and house he lived in. The officer he sent with these orders brought him back word, that he had scarce been seen for some months, and no man knew what could keep him at home, if he was there. The same officer told Giafar where Ganem lived, and the name of the widow who had let him the house.

Upon this information, which could not fail, that minister, without losing any time, marched with the soldiers the caliph had ordered him to take, went to the mayor of the city, whom he also caused to bear him company; and being attended by a great number of carpenters and masons, with the necessary tools for razing of a house, came to that in which Ganem lived; and finding it stood alone, without being confined any way, he posted his soldiers quite round it, to prevent the young merchant making his escape.

Fetnah and Ganem had just then dined: the lady was sitting at a window next the street; and hearing a noise, she looked out through the lattice, when, seeing the grand visier draw near with all his attendants, she concluded his design was upon her as well as Ganem. She perceived her note had been received, but had not expected such an answer, having hoped that the caliph would have taken that business quite otherwise. She knew not how long that prince had been come home; and though she was acquainted with his jealous temper, yet she apprehended nothing on that account. However, the sight of the grand visier and the soldiers made her quake in reality, not for herself, but for Ganem: she did not question clearing herself, provided the caliph would but hear her. As for Ganem, whom she was kind to, rather out of gratitude than affection, she plainly foresaw that his rival, being incensed, would see, and might be apt to condemn him, upon account of his youth and mien. Being full of that thought, she turned to the young merchant, and said, Alas! Ganem, we are undone; it is you and I that are sought after. He presently looked through the lattice, and was seized with dread when he beheld the caliph's guards with their naked scymitars, and the grand visier, with the civil magistrate at the head of them. At that sight he stood motionless, and had not power to utter one word. Ganem, said the favourite, there is no losing of time: if you love me, put on the habit of one of your slaves immediately, and daub your face and arms with soot; then lay some of these dishes on your head: you may be taken for a servant belonging to the eating-house, and they will let you pass. If they happen to ask you where the master of the house is, answer, without any hesitation, that he is within. Alas! madam, answered Ganem, less concerned for himself than for Fetnah, you only take care of me; what will become of you? Let not that trouble you, replied Fetnah; it is my part to look to that. As for what you leave in this house, I will take care of it; and I hope it will be one day justly restored to you, when the caliph's anger is over; but do you avoid his fury; for the orders he gives in heat of passion are always fatal. The young merchant's affliction was so great, that he knew not what course to fix upon, and would certainly have suffered himself to have been seized by the caliph's soldiers, had not Fetnah pressed him to disguise himself. He was prevailed upon by her persuasions, to put on the habit of a slave, and daub himself with soot; and it was high time, for they were knocking at the door; and all they could do was to embrace each other lovingly: they were both so overwhelmed with sorrow, that they could not utter one word; and it was thus they parted. Ganem went out with some dishes on his head: he was taken for the servant of an eating-house, and nobody offered to stop him. On the contrary, the grand visier, who was the first that met him, gave him way to let him pass, being far from any thought that he was the man he looked for. Those who were behind the grand visier, made way as he had done, and thus favoured his escape. He got speedily to one of the city-gates, and so got clear away.

While he was making the best of his way from the grand visier Giafar, that minister came into the room where Fetnah was sitting on a sofa, and where there were many chests full of Ganem's equipage, and of the money he had made of his goods.

As soon as Fetnah saw the grand visier come into the room, she fell flat on her face, and continued in that posture, as it were, ready to receive her death. My lord, said she, I am ready to undergo the sentence passed against me by the chief of the believers; you need only make it known to me. Madam, answered Giafar, falling also down till she had raised herself, God forbid any man should presume to lay his profane hands on you: I do not design to offer you the least wrong: I have no farther orders, than to entreat you will be pleased to go with me to the palace, and to conduct you thither with the merchant that lives in this house. My lord, replied the favourite, let us go; I am ready to follow you. As for the young merchant, to whom I am indebted for my life, he is not here; he has been gone about a month since to Damascus, whither his business called him, and he has left these chests you see under my care till he returns. I conjure you to cause them to be secured, that I may perform the promise I made to take all possible care of them.

You shall be obeyed, said Giafar, and immediately sent for porters, whom he commanded to take up the chests, and carry them to Mesrour.

As soon as the porters were gone, he whispered the civil magistrate, committing to him the care of seeing the house razed, but first to cause diligent search to be made for Ganem, who, he suspected, might be hid, whatsoever Fetnah had told of him. Then he went out, taking the young lady with him, attended by the two slaves that waited on her. As for Ganem's slaves, they were not regarded; they ran in among the crowd, and it was not known what became of them.

No sooner was Giafar out of the house, than the masons and carpenters began to raze it; and did it so effectually, that in a few hours none of it remained. But the civil magistrate, not finding Ganem, after the strictest search, sent to acquaint the grand visier with it, before that minister reached the palace. Well, said Haroun Alraschid, seeing him come into his closet, have you executed my orders? Yes, sir, answered Giafar, the house Ganem lived in is levelled with the ground, and I have brought you your favourite Fetnah; she is at your closet-door, and I will call her in if you command me. As for the young merchant, we could not find him, though all places have been searched; and Fetnah affirms that he has been gone this month to Damascus.

Never was any man in such a passion as the caliph, when he heard that Ganem had made his escape. As for his favourite, being possessed that she had been false to him, he would neither see nor speak to her. Mesrour, said he to the chief of the eunuchs, who was there present, take the ungrateful, the perfidious Fetnah, and go shut her up in the dark tower. That tower was within the inclosure of the palace, and commonly served as a prison for the favourites who any way disgusted the caliph.

Mesrour being used to execute his sovereign's orders, though never so unjust, without making any objection, obeyed this with some reluctancy. He signified his concern to Fetnah, who was the more grieved at it, because she had reckoned, that the caliph would not refuse to speak to her. There was no remedy but to submit to her hard fate, and to follow Mesrour, who conducted her to the dark tower, and there left her.

In the mean time the caliph, being incensed, and only consulting his passion, writ the following letter, with his own hand, to the king of Syria, his cousin and tributary, who resided at Damascus.

The Letter from the Caliph Haroun Alraschid to Mohammed Zinebi, King of Syria

Cousin,

This is to inform you, that a merchant of Damascus, whose name is Ganem, the son of Abou Ayoub, has seduced the most amiable of my women-slaves, called Fetnah, and is fled. It is my will, that, when you have read my letter, you cause search to be made for Ganem, and secure him. When he is in your power, you shall cause him to be loaded with irons, and for three days successively he shall receive fifty strokes with a bull's pizzel. Then let him be led through all parts of the city, with a crier, crying, This is the smallest punishment the chief of the believers inflicts on him that offends his lord, and debauches one of his slaves. After that, you shall send him to me under a strong guard. It is my will that you cause his house to be plundered; and when it shall be razed, order the materials to be carried out of the city into the middle of the plain. Besides, if he has father, mother, sister, wives, daughters, or other kindred, cause them to be stripped; and when they are naked, expose them as a spectacle during three days to the whole city, forbidding any one, on pain of death, to afford them any shelter. I expect you will no way delay what I enjoin.

HAROUN ALRASCHID.

The caliph having writ this letter, sent it away by an express, ordering him to make all possible speed, and to take pigeons along with him, that he might the sooner hear what had been done by Mohammed Zinebi.

The pigeons of Bagdad have this particular quality, that, though they be carried never so far, they return to Bagdad as soon as they are turned loose, especially when they have young ones. A letter rolled up is made fast under their wing; and by that means, they have speedy advice from such places as they desire.

The caliph's express travelling night and day, as his master's impatience required, and being come to Damascus, went directly to king Zinebi's palace, who sat upon his throne to receive the caliph's letter. The express having delivered it, Mohammed looking upon it, and knowing the hand, stood up to shew his respect, kissed the letter, and laid it on his head, to denote he was ready submissively to obey the orders contained in it. He opened it, and having read it, immediately descended from his throne, and, without losing time, mounted on horseback, with the prime officers of his household. He also sent for the civil magistrate, who came to him; and then he went directly to Ganem's house, attended by all his guards.

That young merchant's mother had never heard or received any letter from him since he left Damascus; but the other merchants with whom he went to Bagdad were returned, and all of them told her they had left her son in perfect health. However, being he did not return himself, and neglected to write, the tender mother could not be persuaded but that he was dead, and was so fully convinced of it in her imagination, that she went into mourning. She bewailed Ganem as if she had seen him die, and had herself closed his eyes: never mother expressed greater sorrow. And so far was she from seeking any comfort, that she delighted in indulging her sorrow. She caused a dome to be built in the middle of the court belonging to her house, in which she placed a figure representing her son, and covered it with black cloth. She spent the greatest part of the days and nights in weeping under that dome, in the same manner as if her son had been buried there. The beautiful Alcolomb, or Ravisher of Hearts, her daughter, bore her company, and mixed her tears with hers.

It was now some time since they had thus devoted themselves to sorrow, and since the neighbourhood, hearing their cries and lamentations, pitied such loving relations, when king Mohammed Zinebi came to the door, which, being opened by a slave belonging to the family, he went into the house, enquiring for Ganem, the son of Abou Ayoub.

Though the slave had never seen king Zinebi, she easily guessed, by his retinue, that this must be one of the prime men of Damascus. My lord, said she, that Ganem you enquire for is dead: my mistress, his mother, is in that monument you see there, actually lamenting the loss of him. The king, not regarding what was said by the slave, caused all the house to be diligently searched by his guards for Ganem. Then he advanced towards the monument, where he saw the mother and daughter sitting on nothing but a mat, by the figure which represented Ganem, and their faces appeared to him bathed in tears. Those poor women immediately veiled themselves, as soon as they beheld a man at the door of the dome; but the mother, knowing the king of Damascus, got up, and ran to cast herself at his feet. My good lady, said he, I was looking for your son Ganem; is he here? Alas! sir, cried the mother, it is a long time since he has ceased to be; would to God I had at least put him into his shroud with my own hands, and had the comfort of having his bones in this monument! O, my son, my dear son!—She would have said more, but was oppressed with so violent sorrow, that she was not able.

Zinebi was moved, for he was a prince of a mild nature, and had much compassion for the sufferings of the unfortunate. If Ganem alone is guilty, thought he to himself, why should the mother and the daughters, who are innocent, be punished? Ah! cruel Haroun Alraschid, what a mortification do you put upon me, in making me the executioner of your vengeance, obliging me to persecute those persons who have not offended you!

The guards that the king ordered to search for Ganem, came and told him they had lost their labour. He was fully convinced: the tears of these two women would not leave him any room to doubt. It distracted him to be obliged to execute the caliph's order. My good lady, said he to Ganem's mother, come out of this monument with your daughter; it is no place of safety for you. They went out; and he, to secure them against any insult, took off his own robe, which was very large, and covered them both with it, bidding them be sure to keep close to him. Then he ordered the multitude to be admitted to plunder, which was performed with the utmost rapaciousness, and many shouts, which terrified Ganem's mother and sister the more, because they knew not the reason of it. The rabble carried off the richest goods, chests full of wealth, fine Persian and Indian carpets, cushions made of cloth of gold and silver, fine china ware. In short, all was taken away; nothing was left but the hard walls of the house: and it was certainly a dismal spectacle for the unhappy ladies, to see all their goods plundered, without knowing why they were so cruelly treated.

When the house was plundered, Mohammed ordered the civil magistrate to raze the house and monument; and, whilst that was doing, he carried away Alcolomb and her mother to his palace. There it was he redoubled their affliction, acquainting them with the caliph's will. He commands me, said he to them, to cause you to be stripped, and expose you naked for three days to the view of the people. It is with the utmost reluctance that I execute that cruel and ignominious sentence. The king delivered these words with such an air, as plainly made it appear his heart was really pierced with grief and compassion. Though the fear of being dethroned obstructed his following the dictates of his pity, yet he in some measure moderated the rigour of Haroun Alraschid's orders, causing coarse sacks, like smocks with sleeves, to be made of horse-hair, for Ganem's mother, and his sister Alcolomb, or Ravisher of Hearts.

The next day, these two victims of the caliph's rage were stripped of their clothes, and their horse-hair smocks put upon them; their head-dress was also taken away, so that their dishevelled hair hung upon their backs. Alcolomb had the finest hair in the world; and it hung down to the ground. In that condition, they were exposed to the people. The civil magistrate, attended by his officers, went along with them; and they were conducted throughout all the city. A crier went before them, who, every now and then, cried, This is the punishment due to those who have drawn on themselves the indignation of the chief of the believers.

When they walked in this manner along the streets of Damascus, with their arms and feet naked, clad in such a strange garment, and endeavouring to hide their shame under their hair, with which they covered their faces, all the people were dissolved in tears; more especially the ladies, looking on them as innocent persons, through their lattice-windows, and being particularly moved by Alcolomb's youth and beauty, made the air ring with their dreadful shrieks, as they passed before their houses. The very children, frighted at those shrieks, and at the spectacle that occasioned them, mixed their cries with that general lamentation, and added new horror to it. In short, had an enemy been at Damascus, and then putting all to fire and sword, the consternation could not have been greater.

It was near night when that dismal scene concluded. The mother and daughter were both conducted back to king Mohammed's palace. Not being used to walk bare-foot, they were so spent, that they lay a long time in a swoon. The queen of Damascus, highly afflicted at their misfortunes, notwithstanding the caliph's prohibition to relieve them, sent some of her women to comfort them with all sorts of refreshments, and wine to raise their spirits.

The queen's women found them still in a swoon, and almost past receiving any benefit by what they offered them. However, with much difficulty, they were brought to themselves. Ganem's mother immediately returned them thanks for their courtesy. My good lady, said one of the queen's ladies to her, we are highly concerned at your affliction; and the queen of Syria, our mistress, has done us a favour in employing us to assist you. We can assure you, that princess is much afflicted at your misfortunes, as well as the king her consort. Ganem's mother entreated the queen's women to return her majesty a thousand thanks from her and her daughter Alcolomb; and then, directing her discourse to the lady that spoke to her, she said, Madam, the king has not told me why the chief of the believers inflicts so many outrages on us; pray be pleased to tell us what crimes we have been guilty of? My good lady, answered the other, the origin of your misfortune proceeds from your son Ganem. He is not dead, as you imagine. He is accused of having stolen the beautiful Fetnah, the best beloved of all the king's favourites; and he having, by timely flight, withdrawn himself from that prince's indignation, the punishment is fallen on you. All mankind condemns the caliph's resentment; but all mankind fears him; and you see king Zinebi himself dares not contradict his orders, for fear of incurring his displeasure. So that all we can do is to pity and exhort you to have patience.

I know my son, answered Ganem's mother; I have educated him very carefully, and in that respect which is due to the commander of the believers. He has not committed the crime he is accused of; I dare answer for his innocency. But I will give over muttering and complaining, since it is for him that I suffer, and he is not dead. O Ganem! added she, in a transport of love and joy, my dear son Ganem, is it possible that you are still alive! I no longer am concerned for the loss of my goods; and how extravagant soever the caliph's orders may be, I forgive him all the severity of them, provided heaven has saved my son. I am only concerned for my daughter; her sufferings only afflict me; yet I believe her to be so good a sister as to follow my example.

At the hearing of these words, Alcolomb, who, till then, had appeared insensible, turned to her mother, and, clasping her arms about her neck, Yes, dear mother, said she, I will always follow your example, whatever extremity the love of my brother brings you to.

The mother and daughter thus interchanging their sighs and tears, continued a considerable time in such moving embraces. In the mean time, the queen's women, who were much moved at that spectacle, omitted no persuasions to prevail with Ganem's mother to take some sustenance. She ate a morsel out of complaisance, and Alcolomb did the like.

The caliph having ordered that Ganem's kindred should be exposed three days successively to the sight of the people, in the condition as has been said, Alcolomb and her mother afforded the same spectacle the second time next day, from morning till night. But that day and the following, things were not done after the same manner: the streets, which at first had been full of people, were left quite empty. All the traders, incensed at the ill usage of Abou Ayoub's widow and daughter, shut up their shops, and kept themselves close within their houses. The ladies, instead of looking through their lattice-windows, withdrew into the back parts of their houses. There was not one soul to be seen in the public places those unfortunate women were carried through. It looked as if all the inhabitants of Damascus had abandoned their city.

On the fourth day, king Mohammed Zinebi, who was resolved punctually to obey the caliph's orders, though he did not approve of them, sent criers into all quarters of the city to make proclamation, strictly forbidding all the inhabitants of Damascus, and strangers, of what condition soever, upon pain of death, and having their bodies cast to the dogs to be devoured, to receive Ganem's mother and sister into their houses, or to give them a morsel of bread, or a drop of water; and, in a word, to afford them the least support, or hold the least correspondence with them.

When the criers had performed what the king had enjoined them, that prince ordered the mother and the daughter to be turned out of the palace, and left to their choice to go where they thought fit. As soon as ever they appeared, all persons fled from them, so great an impression had the late prohibition made upon them all. They easily perceived that every body shunned them; but not knowing the reason of it, they were much surprised; and their amazement was the greater, when, coming into any street, or among several persons, they knew some of their best friends, who presently vanished with as much haste as the rest. What is the meaning of this, said Ganem's mother, do we carry the plague about us? Must the unjust and barbarous usage we have received render us odious to our fellow-citizens? Come, my child, added she, let us depart from Damascus with all speed; let us not stay any longer in a city where we are become frightful to our very friends.

The two wretched ladies, discoursing after this manner, came to one of the ends of the city, and retired to a ruined house, to pass the night. Thither some mussulmen, or believers, out of charity and compassion, resorted to them after the day was shut in. They carried them provisions, but durst not stay to comfort them, for fear of being discovered, and punished for disobeying the caliph's orders.

In the mean time, king Zinebi had let fly a pigeon, to give Haroun Alraschid an account of his exact obedience. He informed him of all that had been done, and conjured him to direct what he would have done with Ganem's mother and sister. He soon received the caliph's answer the same way, which was, that he banished them Damascus for ever. Immediately the king of Syria sent men to the old house, with orders to take the mother and the daughter, and to conduct them three day's journey from Damascus, and there to leave them, forbidding them ever to return to the city.

Zinebi's men executed their commission; but being less precise than their master, in the strictest performance of every tittle of Haroun Alraschid's orders, they in pity gave Alcolomb and her mother some small pieces of money to buy them some subsistence, and each of them a bag, which they hung about their necks, to carry their provisions.

In this miserable condition, they came to the first village. The peasants flocked about them; and as it appeared through their disguise that they were people of some fashion, they asked them what was the occasion of their travelling after that manner, in a habit that did not seem properly to belong to them? Instead of answering the question put to them, they fell a-weeping, which only served to heighten the curiosity of the peasants, and to move them to compassion. Ganem's mother told them what she and her daughter had endured; at which the good country-women were sensibly afflicted, and endeavoured to comfort them. They treated them as well as their poverty would permit; they took off their horse-hair smocks, which were very uneasy, and put on others they gave them, with shoes, and something to cover their heads, and save their hair.

Having expressed their gratitude to those charitable women, Alcolomb and her mother departed that village, taking short journeys towards Aleppo. They used at night to lie near the mosques, or in them, upon the mat, if there was any, or else on the bare pavement; and sometimes put up in the places appointed for the use of travellers. As for sustenance, they did not want; for they often came to places where bread, boiled rice, and other provisions, are distributed to all travellers who desire it.

At length they came to Aleppo, but would not stay there, and holding on their journey towards the Euphrates, crossed that river, and entered into Mesopotamia, which they traversed as far as Moussoul. Thence, notwithstanding all they had endured, they proceeded to Bagdad. That was the place they had fixed their thoughts upon, hoping to find Ganem there, though they ought not to have fancied that he was in a city where the caliph resided; but they hoped, because they wished it; their affection rather increasing than diminishing, in spite of all their misfortunes. Their discourse was generally about him, and they enquired for him of all they met. But let us leave Alcolomb and her mother, to return to Fetnah.

She was still confined close in the dark tower, ever since the day that had been so fatal to Ganem and her. However disagreeable as her prison was to her, it was much less grievous than the thoughts of Ganem's misfortune, the uncertainty of whose fate was a killing affliction to her. There was scarce a moment in which she did not lament him.

One night when the caliph was walking by himself, within the inclosure of his palace, as he frequently did; for he was the most prying prince in the world, and sometimes, by means of those night-walks, he came to the knowledge of things that happened in his palace, which would otherwise never have come to his ear: one of those nights, in his walk, he happened to pass by the dark tower, and fancying he heard somebody talk, he stopped, and drew near the door to listen, and distinctly heard these words, which Fetnah, whose thoughts were always on Ganem, uttered with a loud voice: O Ganem! too unfortunate Ganem! where are you at this time? whither has thy cruel fate led thee? Alas! it is I that have made you miserable! Why did you not let me perish unhappily, rather than afford me your generous relief? What a dismal reward have you received for your care and respect! The commander of the faithful, who ought to have requited, persecutes you; and in return for having always looked upon me as a person reserved for his bed, you lose all your goods, and are obliged to seek for safety in flight. O caliph! barbarous caliph, what will you say for yourself when you shall appear with Ganem before the tribunal of the Supreme judge, and the angels shall testify the truth before your face! All the power you are now invested with, and which makes the best part of the world quake, will not prevent your being condemned and punished for your violent and unjust proceedings. Here Fetnah ceased her complaint, her sighs and tears putting a stop to her tongue.

This was enough to bring the caliph to himself. He plainly perceived, that if what he had heard was true, his favourite must be innocent, and that he had been too rash in giving orders against Ganem and his family. Being resolved to be rightly informed in an affair which so nearly concerned him, in point of equity, on which he valued himself, he immediately returned to his apartment, and that moment ordered Mesrour to repair to the dark tower, and bring Fetnah to him.

By this command, and much more by the caliph's way of delivery, the chief of the eunuchs guessed that his master designed to pardon his favourite, and take her to him again. He was overjoyed at it, for he loved Fetnah, and had been much concerned at her disgrace; and therefore flying to the tower, Madam, said he to the favourite, with such an air as expressed his satisfaction, be pleased to follow me: I hope you will never more return to this vile dark tower: The commander of the faithful has a mind to speak with you, and I have reason to hope for a happy issue.

Fetnah followed Mesrour, who conducted her into the caliph's closet. She prostrated herself before that prince, and so continued, letting fall a shower of tears; Fetnah, said the caliph, without bidding her rise, I think you charge me with violence and injustice. Who is he, who notwithstanding the regard and respect he had for me, is in a miserable condition? Speak freely, you know how good-natured I am, and that I love to do justice.

By these words the favourite conceived that the caliph had heard what she had said, and laying hold on so favourable an opportunity to clear her dear Ganem, she said, Commander of the true believers, if I have let fall any word that is not agreeable to your majesty, I must humbly beseech you to forgive me; but he whose innocence and misfortune you desire to be acquainted with, is Ganem, the unhappy son of Abou Ayoub merchant in Damascus. He is the man that saved my life, and afforded me a safe sanctuary in his house. I must own, that from the first moment he saw me, he perhaps designed to devote himself to me, and conceived hopes of engaging me to admit of his service. I guessed at this, by the eagerness he shewed in entertaining, and giving me all the attendance which was requisite under the circumstances I was then in; but as soon as he heard that I had the honour to belong to you, 'Alas, madam,' said he, 'That which belongs to the master is forbidden to the slave.' From that moment, I owe this justice to his virtue, his behaviour was always suitable to his words. However, you well know with what rigour you have treated him, and you will answer for it before the tribunal of God.

The caliph was not displeased with Fetnah for the freedom of those words; But may I, answered he, rely on the assurances you give me of Ganem's virtue? Yes, replied Fetnah, you may; I would not for the world conceal the truth from you. And to make out to you that I am sincere, I must own one thing to you, which perhaps may displease you, but I beg pardon of your majesty beforehand. Speak, child, said Haroun Alraschid, I forgive all, provided you conceal nothing from me. Well then, replied Fetnah, let me inform you, that Ganem's respectful behaviour, together with all the good offices he did me, gained him my esteem. I went farther yet, you know the tyranny of love; I felt some tender inclination growing in my breast. He perceived it, but was still far from taking an advantage of my frailty: and notwithstanding the flame which consumed him, he still remained steady in his duty, and all his passion could force from him, was those words I have already told your majesty, 'That which belongs to the master is forbidden to the slave.'

This ingenious confession might have provoked any other man than the caliph; but it was the very thing which quite appeased that prince. He commanded her to rise, and making her sit by him, Tell me your story, said he, from the beginning to the end. She did so with much art and wit, slightly passing over what regarded Zobeide, and dilating on the obligations she owed Ganem, the expence he had been at for her; and, above all, she highly extolled his discretion, endeavouring by that means to make the caliph sensible that she had been under the necessity of lying concealed in Ganem's house, to deceive Zobeide. She concluded with the young merchant's escape, which she plainly told the caliph she had compelled him to, that he might avoid his indignation.

When she had done speaking, the caliph said to her, I believe all you have told me, but why was it so long before you let me hear from you? Was there any need of staying a whole month after my return, before you sent me word where you were? Commander of the true believers, answered Fetnah, Ganem went abroad so very seldom, that you need not wonder that we were none of the first that heard of your return. Besides that, Ganem, who took upon him to deliver the letter I wrote to Nouron Nihar, was a long time before he could find an opportunity of putting it into her own hands.

It is enough, Fetnah, replied the caliph, I own my fault, and would willingly make amends for it, by heaping favours on that young merchant of Damascus; Therefore consider what I can do for him: Ask what you think fit, and I will grant it. Hereupon the favourite fell down at the caliph's feet, with her face flat on the ground; and then rising again, said, Commander of the true believers, after returning your majesty thanks for Ganem, I most humbly intreat you to cause it to be published throughout all your dominions, that you pardon the son of Abou Ayoub, and that he may safely come to you. I will do more, rejoined that prince, in requital for having saved your life, and the respect he has bore to me, and to make amends for the loss of his goods; and in short, to repair the wrong I have done to his family, I give him to you for a husband. Fetnah had not words expressive enough to thank the caliph for his generosity: She then withdrew into the apartment she had before her dismal adventure. The same furniture was still in it, nothing had been removed; but that which pleased her most, was, to find there Ganem's chests and packs, which Mesrour had taken care to convey thither.

The next day Haroun Alraschid ordered the grand visier to cause proclamation to be made throughout all his dominions, that he pardoned the son of Abou Ayoub; but this proved of no effect, for a long time elapsed without any news of that young merchant. Fetnah concluded for certain, that he had not been able to survive the pain of losing her. A dreadful uneasiness seized her; but as hope is the last thing which forsakes lovers, she intreated the caliph to give her leave to seek for Ganem herself; which being granted, she took a purse with a thousand pieces of gold out of her basket, and one morning went out of the palace, mounted on a mule she had out of the caliph's stables, very richly accoutred. Black eunuchs attended her, with their hands on each side upon the mule's buttocks.

Thus she went from mosque to mosque, bestowing her alms among the devotees of the mahometan religion, desiring their prayers for obtaining the accomplishment of an affair on which the happiness of two persons, as she told them, depended. She spent the whole day and the thousand pieces of gold, in giving alms at the mosques, and returned to the palace in the evening.

The next day she took another purse of the same value, and in the like equipage as the day before, went to the place where all the jewellers shops were; and stopping at the door without alighting, sent one of her black eunuchs for the syndic, or chief of them. That syndic, who was an extraordinary charitable man, and spent above two thirds of his income in relieving poor strangers, whether they happened to be sick, or in distress, made not Fetnah stay, knowing by her dress that she was a lady belonging to the palace. I apply myself to you, said she, putting the purse into his hands, as a person whose piety is cried up throughout the city. I desire you to distribute that gold among the poor strangers you relieve, for I know you make it your business to assist poor strangers who have recourse to your charity. I am also satisfied that you prevent their wants, and that nothing is more agreeable to you, than to have an opportunity of easing their misery. Madam, answered the syndic, I shall obey your commands with pleasure; but if you desire to exercise your charity in person, and will be pleased to step to my house, you will there see two women worthy of your compassion: I met them yesterday as they were coming into the city; they were in a deplorable condition, and it moved me the more, because I thought they were persons of some quality. Through all the rags that covered them, and notwithstanding the impression the sun has made on their faces, I discovered a noble air, not to be commonly found in those poor people I relieve. I carried them both to my house, and delivered them to my wife, who was of the same opinion with me. She caused her slaves to provide them good beds, whilst she herself washed their faces, and gave them clean linen. We know not as yet who they are, because we will let them take some rest before we trouble them with our questions.

Fetnah, without being able to give any reason for it, had a curiosity to see them. The syndic would have conducted her to his house, but she would not give him the trouble, and was satisfied that a slave of his should go and shew her the way. She alighted at the door and followed the syndic's slave, who was gone before to give notice to his mistress, she being then in the chamber with Alcolomb and her mother, for they were the persons the syndic had been talking of to Fetnah.

The syndic's wife being informed by the slave, that a court-lady was in her house, was going out of the room to meet her; but Fetnah, who had followed close to the slave's heels, did not give her so much time, and coming into the chamber, the syndic's wife fell down before her, to express the respect she had for all that belonged to the caliph. Fetnah took her up, and said, My good lady, I desire you would let me speak with those two strangers that arrived at Bagdad last night. Madam, answered the syndic's wife, they lie in those two little beds you see close by each other. The favourite immediately drew near the mother's, and viewing her carefully, Good woman, said she, I come to offer you my assistance: I have a considerable interest in this city, and may be assisting to you and your companion. Madam, answered Ganem's mother, I perceive by your obliging offers that heaven has not quite forsaken us, though we have cause to believe it, after so many misfortunes as have befallen us. Having uttered these words, she wept so bitterly that Fetnah and the syndic's wife could not forbear letting fall some tears.

The caliph's favourite having dried up hers, said to Ganem's mother, Be so kind as to tell us your misfortunes, and recount your story. You cannot give the relation to any persons better disposed than we are, to use all possible means to comfort you. Madam, replied Abou Ayoub's disconsolate widow, a favourite of the commander of the true believers, a lady whose name is Fetnah, is the occasion of all our misfortunes. These words were like a thunder-bolt to the favourite: but suppressing her concern and uneasiness, she suffered Ganem's mother to proceed, who did it after this manner: I am the widow of Abou Ayoub, a merchant of Damascus; I had a son, called Ganem, who coming to trade at Bagdad, has been accused of having debauched that Fetnah. The caliph has caused search to be made for him every where, to put him to death; and not finding him, writ to the king of Damascus, to cause our house to be plundered and razed, and to expose my daughter and me three days successively, stark naked, to be seen by the people, and then to banish us out of Syria for ever.

But how unworthy soever our usage has been, I should still be comforted, were my son alive, and I could meet with him. What a pleasure would it be for his sister and me to see him again! Embracing him, we should forget the loss of our goods, and all the evils we have suffered for him. Alas! I am fully persuaded he is the innocent cause of them; and that he is no more guilty towards the caliph, than his sister and I.

No doubt of it, said Fetnah, interrupting her there, he is no more guilty than you are; I can assure you of his innocence, for I am that very Fetnah you so much complain of, who, through some fatality in my stars, have occasioned so many misfortunes. To me you must impute the loss of your son, if he is no more; but if I have occasioned your misfortune, I can in some measure relieve it. I have already cleared Ganem to the caliph, who has caused it to be proclaimed throughout his dominions, that he pardons the son of Abou Ayoub; and I do not question, but that he will do you as much good as he has done you harm. You are no longer his enemies: he expects Ganem, to requite the service he has done me, by uniting our fortunes: He gives me to him for his consort, therefore look on me as your daughter, and permit me to vow an eternal friendship to you. Having so said, she bowed down on Ganem's mother, who was so astonished that she could return no answer. Fetnah held her a long time in her arms, and only left her to run to the other bed to Alcolomb, who, sitting up, held out her arms to receive her.

When the caliph's charming favourite had given the mother and daughter all the tokens of affection they could expect from Ganem's wife, she said to them, cease both of you to afflict yourselves; the wealth Ganem had in this city is not lost, it is in my apartment in the palace; but I know all the treasure in the world cannot comfort you without Ganem; I judge so of his mother and sister, if I may judge of them by myself. Blood is no less powerful than love in great minds; but why should we despair of seeing him again? We shall find him: the good fortune of meeting with you makes me conceive fresh hopes; and perhaps this is the last day of your sufferings, and the beginning of a greater felicity than you enjoyed in Damascus when Ganem was with you.

Fetnah would have gone on, when the syndic of the jewellers came in, saying, Madam, I am come from seeing a very moving object, it is a young man, a camel-driver, who was carrying to the hospital of Bagdad: He was bound with cords on a camel, because he had not strength enough to sit him. They had already unbound, and were carrying him into the hospital, when I happened to be passing by. I went close up to the young man, viewed him carefully, and fancied his countenance was not altogether unknown to me. I asked him some questions concerning his family and his country; but all the answer I could get, consisted only in sighs and tears. I took pity on him, and perceiving, by being so much used to sick people, that he had great need to have particular care taken of him, I would not permit him to be put into the hospital; for I am too well acquainted with their way of looking to the sick, and am sensible of the incapacity of the physicians. I have caused him to be brought home to my house by my slaves, and they are now, by my orders, putting on some of my own linen, and serving him as they would do me, in a chamber for that purpose.

Fetnah's heart leaped at these words of the jeweller, and she felt a sudden emotion, for which she could not account: Shew me, said she to the syndic, into that sick man's room; I would gladly see him. The syndic conducted her, and whilst she was going thither, Ganem's mother said to Alcolomb, Alas! daughter, as wretched as that sick stranger is, your brother, if he be living, is not perhaps in a more happy condition.

The caliph's favourite coming into the chamber where the sick man was, drew near the bed, into which the syndic's slaves had already laid him. She saw a young man whose eyes were closed, his countenance pale, disfigured and bathed in tears. She gazed earnestly on him, her heart beat, and she fancied she beheld Ganem; but yet she would not believe her eyes. Though she found something of Ganem in the object she beheld, yet in other respects, he appeared so different, that she durst not imagine it was he that lay before her. However, not being able to withstand the earnest desire of being satisfied, Ganem, said she, with a quivering voice, is it you I behold? Having spoken these words, she stopped to give the young man time to answer; but observing that he seemed insensible, Alas! Ganem, added she, it is not you that I talk to! My imagination being over-charged with your image, has given this stranger a deceitful resemblance: The son of Abou Ayoub, though ever so sick, would know the voice of Fetnah. At the name of Fetnah, Ganem (for it was really he) opened his eyes, and turned his face towards the person that spoke to him, and knowing the caliph's favourite; Ah! Madam, said he, what miracle?—He could say no more; such a sudden transport of joy seized him that he fell into a swoon. Fetnah and the syndic did all they could to bring him to himself; but as soon as they perceived he began to revive, the syndic desired the lady to withdraw, for fear least the sight of her should heighten Ganem's distemper.

The young man having recovered his senses, looked all about, and not seeing what he looked for, cried out, what is become of you, charming Fetnah? did you really appear before mine eyes, or was it only an illusion? No, sir, said the syndic, it was no illusion. It was I that caused that lady to withdraw, but you shall see her again as soon as you are in a condition to bear her sight. You now stand in need of rest, and nothing ought to obstruct your taking it. The posture of your affairs is altered, since you are, as I suppose, that Ganem, in favour of whom the commander of the true believers has caused a proclamation to be made in Bagdad, declaring that he forgives him what is past. Be satisfied for the present, with knowing so much; the lady, who just now spoke to you, will acquaint you with the rest, therefore think of nothing but recovering your health; I will contribute all that shall be in my power towards it. Having spoke these words, he left Ganem to take his rest, and went himself to provide all such medicines for him as were proper to recover his strength, quite spent by want and toil.

During that time, Fetnah was in the room with Alcolomb and her mother, where almost the same scene was acted over again, for when Ganem's mother understood that the sick man the syndic had then newly brought into his house was Ganem himself, she was so overjoyed, that she also swooned away; and when, with the assistance of Fetnah and the syndic's wife, she was again come to herself, she would have got up to see her son: but the syndic coming in then hindered her, giving her to understand that Ganem was so weak and feeble that it would endanger his life, to excite in him those commotions which must be the consequence of the unexpected sight of a beloved mother and sister. There was no occasion for the syndic's making any long discourses to persuade Ganem's mother; as soon as she was told that she could not discourse to her son without hazarding his life, she ceased insisting to go and see him. Then Fetnah, turning the discourse, said, Let us bless heaven for having brought us all together into one place. I will return to the palace, to give the caliph an account of all these adventures, and to-morrow-morning I will return to you: This said, she embraced the mother and the daughter, and went away. As soon as she came to the palace, she sent Mesrour to desire to be admitted to the caliph in private, which was immediately granted; and being brought into that prince's closet, where he was alone, she prostrated herself at his feet, with her face on the ground, according to custom. He commanded her to rise, and having made her sit down, asked whether she had heard any news of Ganem? Commander of the true believers, said she, I have been so successful, that I have found him, as also his mother and sister. The caliph was curious to know how she could find them in so short a time, and she satisfied his curiosity, saying so many things in commendation of Ganem's mother and sister, that he desired to see them, as well as the young merchant.

Though Haroun Alraschid was passionate, and in his heat sometimes guilty of cruel actions; yet, to make amends, he was just, and the most generous prince in the world, as soon as his anger was over, and he was made sensible of the wrong he had done. Therefore, having no longer cause to doubt but that he had unjustly persecuted Ganem and his family, and having publicly wronged them, he resolved to make them public satisfaction. I am overjoyed, said he to Fetnah, that your search has proved so successful; it is a mighty satisfaction to me, not so much for your sake as for my own. I will keep the promise I have made you. You shall marry Ganem, and I here declare you are no longer my slave. Go back to that young merchant, and as soon as he has recovered his health, you shall bring him to me, with his mother and sister.

The next morning early, Fetnah repaired to the syndic of the jewellers, being impatient to hear of Ganem's health, and to tell the mother and daughter the good news she had for them. The first person she met was the syndic, who told her that Ganem had rested very well that night: and that his distemper altogether proceeded from melancholy, and the cause being removed, he would soon recover his health.

Accordingly the son of Abou Ayoub was much mended. Rest, and the good medicines applied to him, but above all, the easiness of his mind, had wrought so good an effect, that the syndic thought he might without danger see his mother, his sister, and his mistress, provided he was prepared to receive them; because there was ground to fear, that, not knowing his mother and sister were at Bagdad, the sight of them might occasion too great a joy and surprise. It was therefore resolved, that Fetnah should first go alone into Ganem's chamber, and then make a sign to the two other ladies to appear, when she thought fit.

Affairs being so ordered, the sick man was acquainted with Fetnah's coming, by the syndic, which was so ravishing a sight to him, that he was again near falling into a swoon. Well, Ganem, said she, drawing near to his bed, you have again found your Fetnah, whom you thought you had lost for ever. Ah! Madam, said he, interrupting her, what miracle has restored you to my sight? I thought you were in the caliph's palace; that prince has doubtless given ear to you. You have dispelled his jealousy, and he has restored you to his favour. Yes, my dear Ganem, answered Fetnah, I have cleared myself before the commander of the true believers, who, to make amends for the wrong he has done you, bestows me on you for a wife. These last words occasioned such an excess of joy in Ganem, that he knew not for a while how to express himself, otherwise than by that passionate silence so well known to lovers. At length he broke out with these words: Ah, beautiful Fetnah, may I give credit to what you tell me? May I believe that the caliph really resigns you to Abou Ayoub's son! Nothing is more certain, answered the lady. That prince, who before caused search to be made for you to take away your life, and who in his fury caused your mother and your sister to suffer a thousand indignities, desires now to see you, that he may reward the respect you had for him; and there is no question to be made, but that he will be profuse in his favours to your family.

Ganem asked what the caliph had done to his mother and sister, which Fetnah told him; and he could not forbear letting fall some tears at that relation, notwithstanding his thoughts were so full of the news he had heard of being married to his mistress. But when Fetnah informed him that they were actually in Bagdad, and in the same house with him, he appeared so impatient to see them, that the favourite could no longer defer giving him that satisfaction; and accordingly called them in: They were then at the door, only waiting that moment. They came in, made up to Ganem, and embracing him in their turns, gave him a thousand kisses. How many tears were shed amidst those embraces! Ganem's face was bathed with them, as well as his mother and sister's; and Fetnah let fall in abundance. The syndic himself, and his wife, being moved at the spectacle, could not forbear weeping, nor sufficiently admire the secret workings of providence, which brought together into their house four persons whom fortune had so cruelly parted.

When they had all dried up their tears, Ganem drew a fresh supply, by the recital of all he had suffered from the day he left Fetnah, till the moment the syndic brought him to his house. He told them, that having taken up in a small village, he there fell sick; that some charitable peasants had taken care of him, but finding he did not recover, a camel-driver had undertaken to carry him to the hospital at Bagdad. Fetnah, also, told them all the uneasiness of her imprisonment; how the caliph, having heard her talk in the tower, had sent for her into his closet, and how she had cleared herself. In the conclusion, when they had all related what accidents had befallen them, Fetnah said, Let us bless heaven, which has brought us all together again, and let us think of nothing but the happiness that attends us. As soon as Ganem has recovered his health, he must appear before the caliph, with his mother and sister; but because they are not in a condition to be seen, I will go and make some provision for them; so I desire you to stay a moment for me.

This said, she went away to the palace, and soon returned to the syndic's, with a purse containing a thousand pieces of gold, which she delivered to the syndic, desiring him to buy clothes for the mother and daughter. The syndic, who was a man of a good fancy, chose such as were extraordinary fine, and had them made up with all speed. They were finished in three days, and Ganem finding himself strong enough to go abroad, prepared for it; but on the day he had appointed to go and pay his respects to the caliph, when he was making ready, with his mother and sister, the grand visier Giafar came to the syndic's house.

That minister came on horseback, attended by a great number of officers. Sir, said he to Ganem, as soon as he came in, I am come from the Commander of the True Believers, my master and yours; the orders I have, differ very much from those which I do not care to revive in your memory. I am to bear you company, and to present you to the caliph, who is desirous to see you. Ganem returned no other answer to the visier's compliments than by profoundly bowing his head, and then mounted a horse brought from the caliph's stables, which he managed very gracefully. The mother and daughter were mounted on mules belonging to the palace; and whilst Fetnah led them a bye-way to the prince's court, Giafar conducted Ganem another way, and brought him into the presence-chamber. The caliph was there sitting on his throne, encompassed with emirs, visiers, and other attendants and courtiers, Arabs, Persians, Egyptians, Africans, and Syrians, of his own dominions, not to mention strangers.

When the visier had conducted Ganem to the foot of the throne, that young merchant paid his obeisance, prostrating himself with his face on the ground, and then rising, made his compliment in verse, which, though *extempore*, met with the approbation of the whole court.

After his compliment, the caliph caused him to draw near, and said to him, I am glad to see you, and desire to hear from your own mouth where you found my favourite, and all that you did for her. Ganem obeyed, and appeared so sincere, that the caliph was convinced of the reality of what he said. That prince ordered a very rich vest to be given him, according to the custom observed with those who are admitted to audience. After which, he said to him, Ganem, I will have you live in my court. Commander of the True Believers, answered the young merchant, a slave has no will but his master's, on whom his life and fortune depend. The caliph was highly pleased with Ganem's answer, and assigned him a considerable pension. Then that prince came down from his throne, and causing only Ganem and the grand visier to follow him, went into his own apartment. Not questioning but Fetnah was there, with Abou Ayoub's widow and daughter, he caused them to be called in. They fell down before him; He made them rise, and was so taken with Alcolomb's beauty, that, after viewing her very attentively, he said, I am so sorry for having treated your charms so unworthily, that I owe them such a satisfaction as may surpass the injury I have done them; I take you to wife; and by that means shall punish Zobeide, who shall become the first cause of your good fortune, as she was of your past sufferings. This is not all, added he, turning towards Ganem's mother, you are still young, I believe you will not disdain to be allied to my grand visier: I give you to Giafar. Let a cadi and witnesses be called, and the three contracts be drawn up and signed immediately. Ganem would have represented to the caliph, that it would be honour enough for his sister to be one of his favourites; but that prince was resolved to marry her.

He thought this such an extraordinary story, that he ordered a famous historian to commit it to writing with all its circumstances. It was afterwards laid up in his library, and many copies being transcribed from that original, it became public.

The History of Prince Zeyn Alasnam, and the King of the Genii

A KING of Balsora, who possessed great wealth and was well beloved by his subjects, had no children, which was a great affliction to him; and therefore he made presents to all the holy persons in his dominions to engage them to beg a son for him of heaven: And their prayers being effectual, the queen proved with child, and was happily delivered of a prince who was named Zeyn Alasnam, which signifies Ornament of the Statues.

The king caused all the astrologers in his kingdom to be assembled, and ordered them to calculate the infant's nativity. They found by their observations that he would live long, and be very brave; but that all his courage would be little enough to bear him through the misfortunes that would threaten him. The king was not daunted at the prediction; My son, said he, is not to be pitied, since he will be brave: It is fit that princes should have a taste of misfortunes; for adversity tries virtue, and they are the fitter to reign.

He rewarded the astrologers, and dismissed them; and caused Zeyn to be educated with the greatest care imaginable; appointing him able masters as soon as he was of age to receive their instructions. In short, he proposed to make him an accomplished prince, when on a sudden that good king fell sick of a distemper, which all the skill of his physicians could not cure. Perceiving his disease was mortal, he sent for his son, and among other things advised him, rather to endeavour to be beloved, than to be feared by his people; not to give ear to flatterers; to be as slow in rewarding as in punishing, because it often happens that monarchs, misled by false appearances, load wicked men with favours, and oppress the innocent.

As soon as king Zeyn was dead, prince Zeyn went into mourning, which he wore seven days, and the eighth he ascended the throne, taking his father's seal off the royal treasure, and putting on his own, beginning thus to taste the sweets of ruling, the pleasure of seeing all his courtiers bow down before him, and make it their whole business to shew their zeal and obedience. In a word, the sovereign power was too agreeable to him. He only regarded what his subjects owed to him, without considering what his duty was towards them, and consequently took little care to govern them well. He wallowed in all sorts of debauchery among the voluptuous youth, on whom he conferred the prime employments in the kingdom; so that there was nothing regular. Being naturally prodigal, he set no bounds to his grants, so that his women and his favourites insensibly drained his treasure.

The queen his mother was still living, a discreet, wise princess. She had several times unsuccessfully tried to give some check to her son's prodigality and debauchery; giving him to understand, that if he did not soon take another course, he would not only squander his wealth, but would also alienate the minds of his people, and occasion some revolution, which perhaps might cost him his crown and his life. What she had foretold was very near falling out: The people began to mutter against the government, and their muttering had certainly been followed by a general revolt, had not the queen by her dexterity prevented it. But that princess being informed of the ill posture of affairs, gave notice to the king, who at last suffered himself to be prevailed upon. He committed the government to discreet ancient men, who knew how to keep the people within the bounds of duty.

Zeyn, seeing all his wealth consumed, repented that he had made no better use of it. He fell into a dismal melancholy, and nothing could comfort him. One night he saw in a dream, a venerable old man, who came towards him, and with a smiling countenance, said, Know, Zeyn, that there is no sorrow but what is followed by mirth, no misfortune but what in the end brings some happiness. If you desire to see the end of your affliction, get up, set out for Egypt, go to Grand Cairo, a greater fortune attends you there.

The prince, when he awaked in the morning, reflected on his dream, and talked of it very seriously to his mother, who only laughed at it. My son, said she to him, would you now go into Egypt, upon belief of that fine dream? Why not, madam, answered Zeyn, do you imagine all dreams are chimerical? No, no, some of them are mysterious. My masters have told me a thousand stories, which will not permit me to doubt of it. Besides, though I were not otherwise convinced, I could not forbear giving some credit to it. The old man that appeared to me had something supernatural: He was not one of those men whom nothing but age makes venerable; there appeared a sort of divine air about his person. In short, he was such a one as our great prophet is represented; and if you will have me tell you what I think, I believe it was he, who, pitying my affliction, designs to ease it; I rely on the confidence he has inspired me with. I am full of his promises, and have resolved to follow his advice. The queen endeavoured to dissuade him, but it was in vain. The prince committed to her the government of the kingdom, set out one night very privately from his palace, and took the road to Cairo, without suffering any person to attend him.

After much trouble and fatigue, he arrived at that famous city, like which there are few in the world, either for extent or beauty. He alighted at the gate of a mosque, where, being spent with weariness, he lay down. No sooner was he fallen asleep, than he saw the same old man, who said to him, I am pleased with you, my son; you have given credit to my words. You are come hither, without being deterred by the length or the difficulties of the way; but take notice, that I have not put you upon undertaking such a long journey upon any other design than to make trial of you. I find you have courage and resolution. You deserve I should make you the greatest and richest prince in the world. Return to Balsora, and you shall find immense wealth in your palace. No king ever possessed so much as is there.

The prince was not pleased with that dream.—Alas! thought he to himself, when he awaked, how much was I mistaken! That old man, whom I took for our prophet, is no other than the product of my disturbed imagination. My fancy was so full of him, that it is no wonder I have seen him again. I had best return to Balsora; what should I do here any longer? It is very happy that I told none but my mother the occasion of my journey: I should become a jest to my people if they knew it.

Accordingly he set out again for his kingdom; and as soon as he arrived there, the queen asked him, whether he returned well pleased? He told her all that had happened, and was so much concerned for having been so credulous, that the queen, instead of adding to his vexation, by reproving or laughing at him, comforted him. Forbear afflicting yourself, my son, said she; if God has appointed you riches, you will have them without any trouble. Be easy: all that I recommend to you is, to be virtuous: renounce the delight of dancing, music, and high-coloured wine: shun all pleasures, they have already almost ruined you; apply yourself to the making of your subjects happy; and, securing their happiness, you will fix your own.

Prince Zeyn swore he would for the future follow his mother's advice, and be directed by the wise visiers she had made choice of to assist him in supporting the weight of the government. But the very first night after he returned to his palace, he the third time saw in a dream the old man, who said to him, Brave Zeyn, the time of your prosperity is come. To-morrow morning, as soon as you are up, take a little pick-axe, and go dig in your father's closet; you will there find a mighty treasure.

As soon as the prince awaked, he got up, ran to the queen's apartment, and with much earnestness told her the new dream of that night. Really, my son, said his mother, that is a very positive man: he is not satisfied with having deceived you twice; have you a mind to believe him again? No, madam, answered Zeyn, I give no credit to what he has said; but I will, for my own satisfaction, search my father's closet. I really fancied so, cried the queen, laughing out very heartily: go, my son, please yourself; my comfort is, that work is not so toilsome as the journey to Egypt.

Well, madam, answered the king, I must own that this third dream has restored my belief, for it agrees with the two others; and, in short, let us examine the old man's words. He first directed me to go into Egypt; there he told me, he had put me upon taking that journey only to try me. Return to Balsora, said he; that is the place where you are to find treasures: this night he has exactly pointed out to me the place where they are. These three dreams, in my opinion, are connected. After all, they may be chimerical; but I would rather search in vain, than blame myself as long as I live, for having perhaps missed of great riches, by being unseasonably too hard of belief.

Having spoken these words, he left the queen's apartment, caused a pick-axe to be brought him, and went alone into the late king's closet. He fell to breaking up the ground, and took up above half the square stones it was paved with, and yet not the least appearance of what he sought after. He ceased working, to take a little rest, thinking within himself, I am much afraid my mother had cause enough to laugh at me. However, he took heart, and went on with his labour: nor had he cause to repent; for, on a sudden, he discovered a white stone, which he took up, and under it found a door made fast with a steel padlock, which he broke with the pick-axe, and opened the door, which covered a stair-case of white marble. He immediately lighted a candle, and went down those stairs into a room, the floor whereof was laid with tiles of chinaware, and the roofs and walls were of crystal; but he particularly fixed his eyes on four places a little raised above the rest of the floor, on each of which there were ten urns of porphyry stone. He fancied they were full of wine: Well, said he, that wine must needs be very old; I do not question but it is excellent. He went up to one of the urns, took off the cover, and with no less joy than surprise, perceived it was full of pieces of gold. He searched all the forty, one after another, and found them full of the same coin, took out a handful, and carried it to the queen.

That princess was as much amazed as can be imagined, when the king gave her an account of what he had seen. Oh! my son, said she, take heed that you do not lavish away all that treasure foolishly, as you have already done the royal treasure: let not your enemies have so much occasion to rejoice. No, madam, answered Zeyn, I will from henceforward live after such a manner as shall be pleasing to you.

The queen desired the king her son to conduct her to that wonderful subterraneous place, which the late king her husband had made with such secrecy, that she had never heard the least account of it. Zeyn led her to the closet, down the marble stairs, and into the chamber where the urns were. She observed every thing with singular curiosity, and in a corner spied a little urn of the same sort of stone as the others. The prince had not before taken notice of it, but opening, found in it a golden key. My son, said the queen, this key certainly belongs to some other treasure; let us look all about, perhaps we may discover the use it is designed for.

They viewed all the chamber with the utmost exactness, and at length found a keyhole in one of the pannels of the wall, and guessed it to be that the key belonged to. The king immediately tried, and as readily opened the door, which led into a chamber, in the midst of which were nine pedestals of massy gold, on eight of which stood as many statues, each of them made of one single diamond, and from them came such a brightness that the whole room was perfectly light.

O heavens! cried Zeyn, in a wonderful surprise, where could my father find such rarities? The ninth pedestal redoubled their amazement, for it was covered with a piece of white sattin, on which were writ these words: 'Dear son, it cost me much toil to get these statues; but though they are extraordinary beautiful, you must understand that there is a ninth in the world which surpasses them all: that alone is worth more than a thousand such as these. If you desire to be master of it, go to the city of Cairo in Egypt: one of my old slaves, whose name is Morabec, lives there; you will easily find him; the first person you shall meet will shew you his house: go seek, and tell him all that has befallen you. He will know you to be my son, and he will conduct you to the place where that wonderful statue is, which you will get with safety.'

The prince having read those words, said to the queen, I will not be without that ninth statue; it must certainly be a very rare piece, since all these here are not of so great value together. I will set out speedily for Grand Cairo; nor do I believe, madam, that you will oppose my design. No, my son, answered the queen, I am not against it; you are certainly under the special protection of our great prophet; he will not suffer you to perish in this journey. Set out when you think fit; your visiers and I will take care of the government during your absence.—The prince made ready his equipage, but would take only a small number of slaves with him.

Nothing remarkable befel him by the way; but arriving at Cairo, he enquired for Morabec. The people told him he was one of the wealthiest inhabitants of the city; that he lived like a great lord, and that he kept open house, especially for strangers. Zeyn was conducted thither, knocked at the gate, which a slave opened, and said, What is it you want, and who are you? I am a stranger, answered the prince, and, having heard much of lord Morabec's generosity, am come to take up my lodging with him. The slave desired Zeyn to stay a while, and went to acquaint his master, who ordered him to desire the stranger to walk in. The slave returned to the gate, and told the prince he was welcome.

Zeyn went in, crossed a large court, and entered into a hall magnificently furnished, where Morabec expected him, and received him very courteously, returning thanks for the honour he did him in accepting of a lodging in his house. The prince having answered his compliments, said to Morabec, I am son to the late king of Balsora, and my name is Zeyn Alasnam. That king, said Morabec, was formerly my master; but, my lord, I never knew of any children he had: What age are you of? I am twenty years old, answered the prince. How long is it since you left my father's court? Almost two-and-twenty years, replied Morabec. But how can you convince me that you are his son? My father, replied Zeyn, had a subterraneous place under his closet, in which I have found forty porphyry urns full of gold. And what more is there? said Morabec. There are, answered the prince, nine pedestals of massy gold, on eight whereof are eight diamond statues, and on the ninth is a piece of white sattin, on which my father has writ what I am to do to get another statue, more valuable than all those together. You know where the statue is; for it is mentioned on the sattin that you will conduct me to it.

As soon as he had spoken these words, Morabec fell down at his feet, and, kissing one of his hands several times, said, I bless God for having brought you hither: I know you to be the king of Balsora's son. If you will go to the palace where the wonderful statue is, I will conduct you; but you must first rest here a few days. This day I treat the great men of the court: we were at table when word was brought me of your being at the door. Will you vouchsafe to come and be merry with us? I shall be very glad, replied Zeyn, to be admitted to your feast. Morabec immediately led him into a dome, where the company was, seated him at table, and served him on his knee. The great men of Cairo were surprised, and whispered to one another, Who is this stranger, to whom Morabec pays so much respect?

When they had dined, Morabec, directing his discourse to the company, said, Great men of Cairo, do not think much to see me serve this young stranger after this manner: be it known to you, that he is the son of the king of Balsora, my master. His father purchased me with his money, and died without making me free, so that I am still a slave, and consequently all I have of right belongs to this young prince, his sole heir. Here Zeyn interrupted him, saying, Morabec, I declare, before all these lords, that I make you free from this moment, and that I renounce all right to your person, and all you possess. Consider what you would have me do more for you. Morabec then kissed the ground, and returned the prince most hearty thanks. Wine was then brought in, which they drank all the day, and towards the evening presents were distributed among the guests, who then went away.

The next day, Zeyn said to Morabec, I have taken rest enough: I came not to Cairo to take my pleasure; my design is to get the ninth statue: it is time for us to set out in search of it. Sir, said Morabec, I am ready to comply with your desires; but you know not what dangers you must encounter to gain the precious conquest. Whatsoever the danger may be, answered the prince, I am resolved to undertake it; I will either perish or succeed. All that happens in this world is by God's direction: do you but bear me company, and let your resolution be equal to mine.

Morabec finding him resolved to set out, called his servants, and ordered them to make ready his equipage. Then the prince and he performed the ablution, or washing, and the prayer enjoined, which is called Farz;* and that done, they set out. By the way, they took notice of abundance of strange and wonderful things, and travelled many days; at the end whereof, being come to a delicious place, they alighted from their horses. Then Morabec said to all the servants that attended them, Do you stay in this place, and take care of our equipage till we return. Next, he said to Zeyn, Now, sir, let us two go on by ourselves: we are near the dreadful place where the ninth statue is kept. You will stand in need of all your courage.

They soon came to a lake; and Morabec sat down on the brink of it, saying to the prince, We must cross this sea. How can we cross it, answered Zeyn, when we have no boat? You will see one appear in a moment, replied Morabec: the enchanted boat of the king of the genii will come for us. But do not forget what I am going to say to you; you must observe a profound silence; do not speak to the waterman, though his figure seem never so strange to you: whatsoever you observe, say nothing; for I tell you beforehand, that if you utter the least word when you are embarked, the boat will sink down. I shall take care to hold my peace, said the prince: you need only tell me what I am to do, and I will strictly observe it.

Whilst they were talking, he spied on a sudden a boat in the lake, and it was made of red sanders. It had a mast of fine amber, and a blue sattin flag. There was only one waterman in it, whose head was like an elephant's, and his body like a tyger's. When the boat was come up to the prince and Morabec, the monstrous waterman took them up one after another with his trunk, and put them into the boat, and then carried them over the lake in a moment. He then again took them up with his trunk, set them ashore, and immediately vanished with his boat.

Now we may talk, said Morabec: the island we are on belongs to the king of the genii; there are no more such throughout the world. Look all about you, prince; can there be a more delightful place? It is certainly a lively representation of the charming place God has appointed for the faithful observers of our law. Behold the fields, adorned with all sorts of flowers and odoriferous plants: admire those fine trees, whose delicious fruit makes the branches hang down to the ground: enjoy the delight of those harmonious songs formed in the air by a thousand birds of as many various sorts, unknown in other countries. Zeyn could never sufficiently admire the beauty of those things that were about him, and still found something new, as he advanced farther into the island.

At length, they came before a palace all of fine emeralds, encompassed with a ditch, on the banks whereof, at certain distances, were planted such tall trees that they shaded the whole palace. Before the gate, which was of massy gold, was a bridge made of one single shell of a fish, though it was at least six fathoms long, and three in breadth. At the head of the bridge, stood a company of genii, of a prodigious height, who guarded the entrance into the castle with great clubs of china steel.

Let us go no farther, said Morabec, these genii will beat our brains out; and if we would prevent their coming to us, we must perform a magical ceremony. He then drew out of a purse he had under his garment four long stripes of yellow taffety; one he put about his middle, and laid the other on his back, giving the other two to the prince, who did the like. Then Morabec laid on the ground two large table-cloths, on the edges whereof he scattered some precious stones, musk, and amber. Then he sat down on one of those cloths, and Zeyn on the other; and Morabec said to the prince, I will now, sir, conjure the king of the genii, who lives in the palace that is before us, that he may come peaceably to us. I confess I am somewhat uneasy about the reception he is like to give us. If our coming into this island is displeasing to him, he will appear in the shape of a dreadful monster; but if he approves of our design, he will come in the shape of a handsome man. As soon as he appears before us, you must rise and salute him, without going off your cloth; for you would certainly perish, should you stir off it. You may say to him, Sovereign lord of the genii, my father, who was your servant, has been taken away by the angel of death; I wish your majesty may protect me, as you always protected my father. If the king of the genii ask you what favour you desire of him, you must answer, Sir, I most humbly beg of you to give me the ninth statue.

Morabec having thus instructed prince Zeyn, began his conjuration. Immediately their eyes were dazzled with a long flash of lightning, which was followed by a clap of thunder. The whole island was covered with a hideous darkness, a furious storm of wind blew, a dreadful cry was heard, the island felt a shock, and there was such an earthquake, as that which Asrasyel is to cause on the day of judgment.

Zeyn was somewhat startled, and began to look upon that noise as a very ill omen, when Morabec, who knew better than he what to think of it, began to smile, and said, Be not dismayed, my prince, all goes well. In short, that very moment the king of the genii appeared in the shape of a very handsome man, yet there was something of sternness in his air.

As soon as prince Zeyn had made him the compliment he had been taught by Morabec, the king of the genii, smiling, answered, My son, I loved your father, and every time he came to pay me his respects, I presented him with a statue, which he carried away with him. I have no less kindness for you. I obliged your father, some days before he died, to write that which you read on the piece of white sattin. I promised him to receive you under my protection, and to give you the ninth statue, which in beauty surpasses those you have already. I have begun to perform my promise to him. It was I whom you saw in a dream in the shape of an old man: I caused you to open the subterraneous place where the urns and the statues are: I have a great share in all that has befallen you, or rather am the occasion of it. I know the motive that brought you hither; and you shall obtain what you desire.—Though I had not promised your father to give it, I would willingly grant it you: but you must first swear to me by all that is sacred, that you will return to this island, and that you will bring a maid that is in her fifteenth year, and who has never known man, nor desired to know any. She must also be perfectly beautiful, and you so much master of yourself, as not even to desire to enjoy her, as you are conducting her hither.

Zeyn took the rash oath that was required of him. But, sir, said he, then suppose I should be so fortunate as to meet with such a maid as you require, how shall I know that I have found her? I own, answered the king of the genii smiling, that you might be mistaken in her mien: that knowledge is above the sons of Adam, and therefore I do not intend to depend upon your judgment in that particular; I will give you a looking-glass, which will be surer than your conjectures. When you shall have seen a maid of fifteen years of age, perfectly beautiful, you shall only need to look into the glass, in which you shall see the maiden's representation. If she be chaste, the glass will remain clean and unsullied; but if, on the contrary, it sullies, that will be a certain sign that she has not been always undefiled, or at least that she has desired to cease being so. Do not forget the oath you have taken; be sure to keep it, as becomes a man of honour, otherwise I will take away your life, as much kindness as I have for you. Prince Zeyn Alasnam protested over again that he would faithfully keep his word.

Then the king of the genii delivered to him a looking glass, saying, My son, you may return when you please: there is the glass you are to make use of. Zeyn and Morabec took leave of the king of the genii, and went towards the lake. The waterman with the elephant's head brought his boat, and carried them over the lake as he had done before. They joined their servants, and returned with them again to Cairo.

Prince Alasnam rested a few days at Morabec's house, and then said to him, Let us go to Bagdad, to seek a maiden for the king of the genii. Why, are we not at Grand Cairo? said Morabec: shall we not there find beautiful maidens enough? You are in the right, answered the prince; but how shall we do to find where they are? Do not trouble yourself about that, sir, answered Morabec; I know a very cunning old woman, whom I will entrust with that affair, and she will acquit herself well of it.

Accordingly the old woman found means to shew the prince a considerable number of beautiful maidens of fifteen years of age; but when he had viewed them, and came to consult his looking-glass, the fatal touchstone of their virtue, the glass always appeared sullied. All the maidens in the court and city, that were in their fifteenth year, underwent the trial one after another, and the glass never remained bright and clear.

When they saw there were no chaste maids to be found in Cairo, they went away to Bagdad, where they hired a magnificent palace in one of the chief corners of the city, and began to live splendidly.—They kept open house; and, after all people had eaten in the palace, the fragments were carried to the dervises, who by that means had convenient subsistence.

There lived in that quarter an iman, whose name was Boubekir Mouesm, a vain, haughty, and envious person: he hated the rich, only because he was poor, his misery incensing him against his neighbour's prosperity. He heard talk of Zeyn Alasnam, and of the plenty his house afforded. This was enough for him to take an aversion to that prince; and it proceeded so far, that one day after the evening-prayer, in the mosque, he said to the people, Brethren, I have been told a stranger is come to live in our ward, who is at a prodigious expence every day. What can we tell but that this unknown person is some villain, who has committed a great robbery in his own country, and comes hither to make much of himself? Let us take heed, brethren; if the caliph should happen to be informed that such a man is in our ward, it is to be feared that he will punish us for not acquainting him with it; I declare, for my part, I wash my hands of it, and if any thing should happen amiss, it shall not lie at my door. The multitude, who were easily led away, unanimously cried to Boubekir, It is your business, doctor, do you acquaint the council with it. The iman went home well pleased, and drew up a memorial, resolving to present it to the caliph the next day.

But Morabec, who had been at prayers, and heard all that was said by the doctor, as well as the rest of the company, put five hundred pieces of gold into a handkerchief, made up with a parcel of several silks, and went away to Boubekir's house. The doctor asked him in a harsh tone what he wanted? Doctor, answered Morabec, with an obliging air, and at the same time putting into his hand the gold and the silk, I am your neighbour and your servant; I come from Prince Zeyn, who lives in this ward. He has heard of your worth, and has ordered me to come and tell you, that he desires to be acquainted with you: and in the mean time, desires you to accept of this small present. Boubekir was transported with joy, and answered Morabec thus: Be pleased, sir, to beg the prince's pardon for me: I am ashamed I have not yet been to see him, but I will atone for my fault, and wait on him to-morrow.

Accordingly the next day, after morning-prayer, he said to the people, You must understand, brethren, that no man is without some enemies. Envy pursues those chiefly who are very rich. The stranger I spoke to you about yesterday in the evening is no ill man, as some ill-designing persons would have persuaded me: He is a young prince, endued with all manner of virtues. It behoves us to take care how we go about to give any ill account of him to the caliph.

Boubekir having thus wiped off the ill impression he had the day before given the people concerning Zeyn, returned home, put on his best apparel, and went to visit that young prince, who gave him a courteous reception. After several compliments had passed on both sides, Boubekir said to the prince, Sir, do you design to stay long at Bagdad? I shall stay, answered Zeyn, till I can find a maid fifteen years of age, perfectly beautiful, and so chaste, that she has not only never known a man, but even never desired to know him. You seek after a rarity, replied the iman; and I should be apt to fear your search would prove unsuccessful, did I not know where there is a maid of that character: Her father was formerly visier; but he has left the court, and lived a long time in a house out of the way, where he applies himself only to the education of his daughter. If you please, I will go ask her of him for you: I do not question but he will be overjoyed to have a son-in-law of your quality. Not so fast, said the prince, I shall not marry that maid before I know whether I like her. As for her beauty, I can depend on you: but what assurance can you give me in relation to her virtue? What assurance do you require? said Boubekir. I must see her face, answered Zeyn; that is enough for me to come to a resolution. You are skilful then in physiognomy? replied the iman smiling. Well, come along with me to her father's: I will desire him to let you see her one moment in his presence.

Mouesm conducted the prince to the visier's, who, as soon as he was acquainted with the prince's birth and design, called his daughter, and made her take off her veil. Never had the young king of Balsora beheld such a perfect and powerful beauty. He stood amazed; and, since he could then try whether the maid was as chaste as fair, he pulled out his glass, which remained bright and unsullied.

When he perceived he had at length found such a person as he desired, he entreated the visier to grant her to him. Immediately the lady was sent for, and came; the contract was signed, and the marriage-prayer said. After which ceremony Zeyn carried the visier to his house, where he treated him magnificently, and gave him considerable presents. Next, he sent a prodigious quantity of jewels to the bride by Morabec, who brought her to his house, where the wedding was kept with all the pomp that became Zeyn's quality. When all the company was dismissed, Morabec said to his master, Let us be gone, sir; let us not stay any longer at Bagdad, but return to Cairo: Remember the promise you made the king of the genii. Let us go, answered the prince, I must take care to perform it exactly; yet I must confess, my dear Morabec, that, if I obey the king of the genii, it is not without reluctancy. The person I have married is charming, and I am tempted to carry her to Balsora, and place her on the throne. Alas! sir, answered Morabec, take heed how you give way to your inclination: Make yourself master of your passions, and whatsoever it costs you, be as good as your word to the king of the genii: Well then, Morabec, said the prince, do you take care to conceal that lovely maid from me: let her never appear in my sight; perhaps I have already seen too much of her.

Morabec having made all ready for their departure, they returned to Cairo, and thence set out for the island of the king of the genii. When they were there, the maid, who had performed the journey in a horse-litter, and whom the prince had never seen since his wedding-day, said to Morabec, Where are we? shall we be soon in the dominions of the prince my husband? Madam, answered Morabec, it is time to undeceive you. Prince Zeyn married you, only in order to get you from your father; he did not engage his faith to you, to make you sovereign of Balsora, but to deliver you to the king of the genii, who has asked of him a virgin of your character. Hearing these words, she wept bitterly, which moved the prince and Morabec. Take pity on me, said she, I am a stranger, you will be accountable to God for your treachery towards me.

Her tears and complaints were of no effect, for she was presented to the king of the genii, who, having gazed on her very earnestly, said to Zeyn, Prince, I am satisfied with your behaviour; the virgin you have brought me is beautiful and chaste, and I am pleased with the force you have put upon yourself to be as good as your word to me. Return to your dominions, and when you shall enter the subterraneous room where the eight statues are, you shall find the ninth which I promised you. I will go and make my genii carry it thither. Zeyn thanked the king, and returned to Cairo with Morabec, but did not stay long there; his impatience to see the ninth statue made him hasten his journey. However, he could not but often think of the young virgin he married; and, blaming himself for having deceived her, he looked upon himself as the cause and instrument of her misfortune. Alas! said he to himself, I have taken her from a tender father to sacrifice her to a genie. O incomparable beauty! you deserve a better fate.

Prince Zeyn, disturbed with these thoughts, at length reached Balsora, where his subjects made extraordinary rejoicings for his return. He went directly to give his mother an account of his journey, who was in a rapture to hear he had obtained the ninth statue. Let us go, my son, said she, let us go and see it; for it is certainly in the chamber under ground, since the king of the genii told you you should find it there. The young king and his mother being both impatient to see that wonderful statue, went down into the subterraneous place, and into the room of the statues: but how great was their surprise, when, instead of a statue of diamonds, they spied on the ninth pedestal a most beautiful virgin, whom the prince knew to be the same he had conducted into the island of the genii! Prince, said the young maid, you are amazed to see me here; you expected to have found something more precious than me, and I question not but that you now repent having taken so much trouble: You expected a better reward. Madam, answered Zeyn, heaven is my witness, that I more than once thought to have broke my word with the king of the genii, to keep you to myself. Whatsoever the value of a diamond statue may be, is it worth the satisfaction of enjoying you? I love you above all the diamonds and wealth in the world.

Just as he had done speaking these words, a clap of thunder was heard, which made that subterraneous place shake. Zeyn's mother was frightened; but the king of the genii immediately appearing, dispelled her dread. Madam, said he to her, I protect and love your son: I had a mind to try whether, at his age, he could subdue his passions. I know the charms of this young lady have wrought on him, and that he did not punctually keep the promise he had made me, not to desire to enjoy her; but I am too well acquainted with the frailty of the human race. This is the ninth statue I designed for him; it is more rare and precious than the others. Live, said he, (directing his discourse to the young prince,) live happy, Zeyn, with this young lady, who is your wife; and, if you would have her true and constant to you, love her always, and love her alone. Give her no rival, and I will answer for her fidelity. Having spoke these words, the king of the genii vanished; and Zeyn, ravished with that young lady, consummated the marriage the same day, and caused her to be proclaimed queen of Balsora. Those two ever faithful and loving consorts lived together many years.

The History of Codadad and his Brothers

THOSE who have written the history of the kingdom of Diarbekir inform us, That there formerly reigned a most magnificent king in the city of Harran, who loved his subjects, and was equally beloved by them. He was endued with all virtues, and wanted nothing to complete his happiness but an heir. Though he had the finest women in the world in his seraglio, yet he was destitute of children. He continually prayed to heaven for them; and one night, in his sleep, a comely person, or rather a prophet, appeared to him, and said, Your prayers are heard; you have obtained what you desired: rise as soon as you awake, go to your prayers, and make two genuflections: then walk into the garden of your palace, call your gardener, and bid him bring you a pomegranate, eat as many of the seeds as you think fit, and your wishes shall be accomplished.

The king calling to mind his dream, when he awaked, returned thanks to heaven, got up, fell to his prayers, made two genuflections, and then went down into his garden, where he took fifty pomegranate-seeds, which he counted, and eat them. He had fifty wives who shared in his bed; they all proved with child: but there was one called Pirouze, who did not appear to be big-bellied. He took an aversion to that lady, and would have her put to death. Her barrenness, said he, is a certain token that heaven does not judge Pirouze worthy to bear a prince; it is my duty to deliver the world from an object that is odious to the Lord. He had taken this cruel resolution, but his visier diverted him from putting it in execution; representing to him, that all women were not of the same constitution, and that it was not impossible but that Pirouze might be with child, though it did not appear. Well, answered the king, let her live; but let her depart my court, for I cannot endure her. Your majesty, replied the visier, may send her to prince Samer, your cousin. The king approved of his advice: he sent Pirouze to Samaria, with a letter, in which he ordered his cousin to treat her well; and in case she proved with child, to give him notice of her being brought to bed.

No sooner was Pirouze arrived in that country, but it appeared that she was with child: and at length she was delivered of a most beautiful prince. The prince of Samaria wrote immediately to the king of Harran, to acquaint him with the birth of that son, and to congratulate him on that occasion. The king was much rejoiced at it, and answered prince Samer as follows: 'Cousin, all my other wives have also been delivered of each a prince; so that we have a great number of children here. I desire you to breed up that of Pirouze, to give him the name of Codadad, and to send him to me when I shall give you notice.'

The prince of Samaria spared nothing that might improve the education of his nephew. He taught him to ride, shoot with a bow, and all the other things becoming the son of a king; so that Codadad, at eighteen years of age, was looked upon as a prodigy. This young prince being inspired with a courage worthy his birth, said one day to his mother, Madam, I begin to grow weary of Samaria; I find myself inclined to gain renown; give me leave to go seek it amidst the perils of war. My father, the king of Harran, has many enemies: Some neighbouring princes make it their business to disturb him. Why does he not call me to his assistance? Why does he leave me here so long, like an infant? Must I spend my life here in sloth, when all my brothers have the good fortune to be fighting by his side? My son, answered Pirouze, I am no less impatient to have your name become famous; I could wish you had already signalized yourself against your father's enemies; but we must wait till he requires it. No, madam, replied Codadad, I have already waited but too long. I long to see the king, and am tempted to go to offer him my service as a young gentleman unknown. No doubt but he will accept of it, and I will not discover myself, till I have performed a thousand glorious actions: I design to merit his esteem before he knows who I am. Pirouze approved of his generous resolution; and Codadad one day departed Samaria, as if he had been going a-hunting, without acquainting prince Samer, for fear he should thwart his design.

He was mounted on a white horse, who had a gold bit and shoes; his housing was of blue sattin, embroidered with pearls; the hilt of his scymitar was of one entire diamond; and the scabbard of sandal-wood, all adorned with emeralds and rubies; and on his shoulder hung his bow and quiver. In this equipage, which added much to his good mien, he arrived at the city of Harran, and soon found means to offer his service to the king; who, being charmed with his beauty and lovely presence, and perhaps inspired by natural sympathy, gave him a favourable reception, and asked his name and quality. Sir, answered Codadad, I am son to an emir of Grand Cairo; an inclination to travel has made me quit my country; and, understanding, in my passage through your dominions, that you were engaged in war with some of your neighbours, I am come to your court to offer your majesty my service. The king shewed him extraordinary kindness, and employed him in his troops.

That young prince soon signalized his bravery. He gained the esteem of the officers, and was admired by the soldiers; and, having no less wit than courage, he so far advanced himself in the king's affection, as to become his favourite. All the ministers, and other courtiers, daily resorted to Codadad, and were so eager to purchase his friendship, that they neglected the king's other sons. Those princes could not but resent it; and, imputing it to the stranger, they all conceived an implacable hatred against him; but the king's affection daily increasing, he was never weary of giving him fresh testimonies of it. He always desired he should be near him: he admired his discourse, ever full of wit and discretion; and, to shew how much he was satisfied with his wisdom, he gave him the tuition of the other princes, though he was of the same age as they. Thus Codadad was made governor of his brothers;

which only served to heighten their hatred. Is it come to this, said they, that the king, not satisfied with loving a stranger more than us, will have him to be our tutor, and not allow us to do any thing without his leave? This is not to be endured: we must rid ourselves of this stranger. Let us go together, said one of them, and dispatch him. No, no, answered another, we had better be cautious how we sacrifice ourselves: his death would render us odious to the king, who, in return, would declare us all unfit to reign. Let us destroy the stranger artfully. We will ask leave to go a-hunting; and, when far from the palace, we will proceed to some other city, and stay there some time. The king will wonder at our absence; and, perceiving we do not return, he may perhaps put the stranger to death, or at least will turn him out of the court, for suffering us to leave the palace.

All the princes applauded this artifice, went together to Codadad, and desired him to give them leave to go and take the diversion of hunting, promising to return the same day. Pirouze's son was taken in the snare, and granted the leave his brothers desired. They went, but returned not. They had been three days absent, when the king asked Codadad where the princes were, for it was long since he had seen them. Sir, answered Codadad, they have been gone a-hunting these three days; but they promised me they would return sooner. The king grew uneasy, and much more when he perceived the princes did not return the next day. This provoked his passion: Indiscreet stranger, said he to Codadad, why did you let my sons go without bearing them company? Is it thus you discharge the trust I have reposed in you? Go seek them immediately, or you are a dead man.

These words pierced Pirouze's unfortunate son to the heart. He armed himself, went out of the city, and, like a shepherd who had lost his flock, searched all the country for his brothers, enquiring at every village whether they had been seen; and hearing no news of them, was grieved to the heart. Alas! my brothers, said he, what is become of you? Are you perhaps fallen into the hands of our enemies? Am I come to the court of Harran to be the occasion of giving the king so much trouble? He was altogether comfortless, for having given the princes leave to go a-hunting, or for not having borne them company.

After some days spent in a fruitless search, he arrived in a plain of prodigious extent, in the midst whereof was a palace all of black marble. He drew near, and at one of the windows spied a most beautiful lady, but set off with no other ornament than her own beauty; for her hair was dishevelled, her garments ragged, and on her countenance appeared all the tokens of the greatest affliction. As soon as she saw Codadad, and judged he might hear her, she directed her discourse to him, saying, Alas! young man, get away from this fatal place, or else you will soon fall into the hands of the monster that inhabits it. A black, who feeds only on human blood, resides in this palace. He seizes all persons whom their ill fate conducts to this plain, and shuts them up in his dark dungeons, whence they are never released but to be devoured by him.

Madam, answered Codadad, tell me who you are, and be not concerned for any more. I am a maid of quality, of Grand Cairo, replied the lady: I was passing by this castle yesterday, in my way to Bagdad, and met with the black, who killed all my servants, and brought me hither. I wish I had nothing but death to fear; but, to add to my calamity, this monster would persuade me to love him; and, in case I do not yield to-morrow to his brutality, I must expect the utmost violence. I tell you once more, added she, make your escape: the black will soon return: he is gone out to pursue some travellers he spied at a distance on the plain. Lose no time; nay, I know not whether a speedy flight will deliver you from him.

She had scarce done speaking these words before the black appeared. He was a man of a monstrous bulk, and of a dreadful aspect, mounted on a mighty Tartar horse, and wore such a large and heavy scymitar, that none but he could make use of it. The prince seeing him, was amazed at his monstrous mien, directed his prayers to heaven to assist him, then drew his scymitar, and stood still to expect the black; who, despising so inconsiderable an enemy, called to him to yield himself, with engaging words; but Codadad, by his behaviour, gave him to understand that he was resolved to defend his life; for he drew near and gave him a great cut on the knee. The black feeling himself wounded, gave such a dreadful shriek as made all the plain resound. He grew enraged, foamed at the mouth, and, raising himself on his stirrups, made at Codadad with his dreadful scymitar. The stroke was so violent, that no more would have been required to put an end to the prince, had not he, by a sudden spring he made his horse take, avoided it. The scymitar made a mighty hissing in the air; but, before the black could have leisure to second his blow, Codadad let fall one on his right arm with such fury, that he cut it off. The dreadful scymitar fell, with the hand that held it; and the black yielding under the violence of the stroke, lost his stirrups, and made the earth quake with his mighty fall. The prince alighted at the same time, and chopped off his enemy's head. Just then the lady, who had been a spectator of the combat, and was still offering up her vows to heaven for that young hero, whom she admired, gave a shriek for joy, and said to Codadad, Prince, (for the mighty victory you have obtained convinces me that you are of no ordinary extraction), finish the work you have begun: the black has the keys of this castle; take them, and deliver me out of prison. The prince searched the wretch's pockets, as he lay stretched out on the ground, and found several keys.

He opened the first door, and went into a court, where he met the lady coming to meet him: she would have cast herself at his feet, in token of her gratitude, but he would not permit her. She commended his valour, and extolled him above all the heroes in the world. He returned her compliments; and she appearing still more lovely to him near at hand than at a distance, I know not whether she was more joyful to be delivered from the desperate danger she had been in, than he for having done so considerable a service to so beautiful a person.

Their discourse was interrupted by dismal cries and groans. What is this I hear? said Codadad: Whence come those miserable cries which pierce our ears? Sir, said the lady to him, pointing to a little door there was in the court, they come from thence. There are I know not how many wretched persons, whom fate has made to fall into the hands of the black. They are all chained; and that monster drew out one every day to be devoured.

It is an addition to my joy, answered the young prince, to understand that my victory will save the lives of those unfortunate persons. Come along with me, madam, to partake in the satisfaction of giving them their liberty. You may guess by yourself how welcome we shall be to them. Having so said, they advanced towards the door of the dungeon; and the nearer they drew, the more distinctly they heard the complaints of the prisoners. Codadad pitying them, and impatient to put an end to their sufferings, put one of the keys into the key-hole, which proved not to be the right one at first, and therefore he took another; at which noise all those unfortunate creatures, concluding it was the black, who came, according to custom, to bring them some meat, and at the same time to seize one of them to eat himself, redoubled their cries and groans. Lamentable voices were heard, which sounded as if they had come from the centre of the earth.

In the mean time, the prince had opened the door, and went down a very steep staircase into a large and deep vault, which received some small light from a little window, and in which there were above an hundred persons, bound to stakes, and their hands tied. Unfortunate travellers, said he to them, wretched victims, who only expected the moment of an approaching cruel death, give thanks to heaven, which has this day delivered you by my means. I have slain the black by whom you were to be devoured, and am come to knock off your irons. The prisoners hearing these words, altogether gave a shout, occasioned by joy and surprise. Codadad and the lady began to unbind them; and as soon as any of them were loose, they helped to take off the fetters from the rest; so that in a short time they were all at liberty.

They then kneeled down, and having returned thanks to Codadad for what he had done for them, went out of the dungeon; and when they were come into the court, how surprising it was for the prince to see among the prisoners those he was in search of, and almost out of hopes to find. Princes, cried he, am I not deceived? is it not you I behold? May I flatter myself that it will be in my power to restore you to the king your father, who is inconsolable for the loss of you? But will he not have some one to lament? Are you all here alive? Alas! the death of one of you will suffice to damp all the joy I conceive for having delivered you.

The forty-nine princes all made themselves known to Codadad, who embraced them one after another, and told them how uneasy their father was on account of their absence. They gave their deliverer all the commendations he deserved, as did the other prisoners, who could not find words expressive enough to declare the gratitude they were sensible of. Next, Codadad, with them, took a view of the whole castle, where there was immense wealth; curious silks, gold brocades, Persian carpets, China sattins, and an infinite quantity of other goods, which the black had taken from the caravans he had plundered, a considerable part whereof belonged to the prisoners Codadad had then set free. Every man knew and reclaimed what belonged to him. The prince restored them their own, and divided the rest of the merchandize among them. Then he said to them, How will you do to carry away your goods? we are here in a desert place, and there is no likelihood of your getting horses. Sir, answered one of the prisoners, the black robbed us of our camels, as well as our goods, and perhaps they may be in the stables of this castle. That is not unlikely, replied Codadad, let us see after it. Accordingly they went to the stables, where they not only found the camels, but also the horses belonging to the king of Harran's sons. There were some black slaves in the stables, who, seeing all the prisoners released, and guessing thereby that their master had been killed, fled through by-ways well known to them. Nobody minded to pursue them. All the merchants, overjoyed that they had recovered their goods and camels, together with their liberty, thought of nothing but prosecuting their journey; but first repeated their thanks to their deliverer.

When they were gone, Codadad, directing his discourse to the lady, said, To what place, madam, do you desire to go? whither did you design when you was seized by the black? I intend to bear you company to the place you shall appoint, and I do not question but that all these princes will do the same. The king of Harran's sons protested to the lady they would not leave her till she was restored to her friends.

Princes, said she, I am of a country too remote from hence; and, besides that it would be an imposition on your generosity to oblige you to travel so far, I must own to you, that I am come from my native country for ever. I told you a while ago, that I was a lady of Grand Cairo; but since you have shewn me so much favour, and I am so highly obliged to you, added she, looking upon Codadad, I should be much in the wrong in concealing the truth from you. I am a king's daughter; an usurper has possessed himself of my father's throne, after having murdered him, and I have been forced to fly to save my life.

Then Codadad and his brothers desired the princess to tell them her story, assuring her they were highly concerned at her misfortunes, and fully disposed to spare for nothing that might contribute towards rendering her more happy. After thanks returned for their fresh protestations of readiness to serve her, she could not refuse satisfying their curiosity, and began the recital of her adventures in the following manner.

The History of the Princess of Deryabar

THERE is, in a certain island, a great city called Deryabar. It has been long governed by a potent, magnificent, and virtuous king. That prince had no children, which was the only thing wanting to make him happy. He continually addressed his prayers to heaven; but heaven granted his requests by halves; for the queen his wife, after a long expectation, brought forth a daughter.

I am the unfortunate princess. My father was rather troubled than pleased at my birth; but he submitted to the will of God, and caused me to be educated with all possible care, being resolved, since he had no son, to teach me the art of ruling, that I might supply his place after his death.

One day, when he was taking the diversion of hunting, he spied a wild ass, which he chased, lost his company, and was carried away so far in that heat, as to ride on till night, without reflecting that he was quite out of the way. He then alighted, and sat down at the edge of a wood, into which he had observed the ass had taken. No sooner was the day shut in, than he discovered a light among the trees, which made him conclude that he was not far from some village: he rejoiced at it, hoping that he might pass the night there, and find some person to send to his followers to acquaint them where he was; and accordingly he got up and walked towards the light, which served to guide him.

He soon found he had been deceived, that light being no other than a fire lighted in a hut: however, he drew near, and with amazement beheld a great black, or rather a dreadful giant, sitting on a sofa. Before the monster was a great pitcher of wine, and he was roasting a bullock he had newly killed.—Sometimes he drank out of the pitcher, and then cut slices off the bullock and ate them. But that which most drew the king my father's attention was a beautiful woman he saw in the hut. She seemed to be overwhelmed with grief; her hands were bound, and at her feet was a small child, about two or three years old, who, as if he was sensible of his mother's misfortunes, continually wept, and rent the air with cries.

My father being moved with that object of pity, thought at first to have gone into the hut, and attack the giant: but, considering it would be an unequal combat, he stopped, and resolved, since he had not strength enough to prevail by open force, to use art.

In the mean time, the giant having emptied the pitcher, and devoured above half the bullock, turned to the woman, and said, Beautiful Princess, why do you oblige me by your obstinacy to treat you with severity? It is in your own power to be happy. You need only to resolve to love and be true to me, and I shall express my affection to you. Thou hideous satyr, answered the lady, never expect that time should wear away the aversion I have for you. Thou wilt ever be a monster in my eyes. To these words she added so many reproaches, that the giant grew enraged. This is too much, cried he, in a furious tone; my love undervalued is turned into rage. Your hatred has at last caused mine; I find it prevails above my desires, and that I now wish your death rather than enjoyment. Having spoken these words, he took that wretched lady by the hair, held her up with one hand in the air, and, drawing his scymitar with the other, was just going to strike off her head, when the king my father let fly an arrow, which pierced the giant's breast, so that he staggered, and dropped down dead.

My father entered the hut, unbound the lady's hands, asked her who she was, and how she came thither? Sir, said she, there are some families of Saracens* along the sea-coast, who lived under a prince, who is my husband; this giant you have killed was one of his principal officers. The wretch fell desperately in love with me, but took special care to conceal it, till he could put in execution the designs he had laid of stealing me away. Fortune oftner favours wicked designs than the virtuous. The giant one day surprised me and my child in a bye place. He seized us both; and, to disappoint the search he well knew my husband would cause to be made on account of this rape, he removed far from the country inhabited by those Saracens, and brought us into this wood, where he has kept me some days. As deplorable as my condition is, it is still a great satisfaction to me, to think that the giant, though so brutal and amorous, never used force to obtain that which I always refused to his entreaties; not but that he has threatened me an hundred times that he would have recourse to the worst of extremities, in case he could not otherwise prevail upon me; and, I must confess to you, that a while ago, when I provoked his anger by my words, I was less concerned for my life than for my honour.

This, sir, said the prince of the Saracens wife, is the faithful account of my misfortunes; and I do not question, but that you will think me worthy enough of your compassion, not to repent your having so generously relieved me. Madam, answered my father, be assured your troubles have moved me, and I will do all that shall be in my power to make you happy again. To-morrow, as soon as the day appears, we will go out of this wood, and endeavour to fall into the road which leads to the great city of Deryabar, of which I am sovereign: and if you think fit, you shall be entertained in my palace, till the prince your husband shall come to reclaim you.

The Saracen lady accepted the offer, and the next day followed the king my father, who found all his retinue upon the skirts of the wood, they having spent the night in searching after, and being very uneasy for that they could not find him. They were no less joyful to meet their king, than amazed to see him with a lady, whose beauty surprised them. He told them how he had found her, and the danger he had run in drawing near to the hut, where he must certainly have lost his life had the giant espied him. One of his servants took up the lady behind him, and another carried the child.

Thus they arrived at the king my father's palace, who assigned the beautiful Saracen lady an apartment, and caused the child to be carefully educated. The lady was sensible of the king's goodness to her, and expressed as much gratitude as he could desire. She had at first appeared very uneasy and impatient, on account that her husband did not reclaim her; but by degrees she shook off that uneasiness: The respect my father paid her dispelled her impatience; and I am of opinion she would at last have blamed fortune more for restoring her to her kindred than she did for removing her from them.

In the mean time, the lady's son grew up; he was very handsome; and, not wanting wit, found the way to please the king my father, who had a great kindness for him. All the courtiers perceived it, and guessed that young man might in the end be my husband. Upon this conceit, and looking on him already as heir to the crown, they made their court to him, and every man endeavoured to gain his favour. He soon saw into their designs, grew conceited of himself, and, forgetting the distance there was between our conditions, flattered himself with the hopes that my father was fond enough of him to prefer him before all the princes in the world. Nay, he went farther, for the king not answering his expectation, in offering me to him as soon as he could have wished, he had the boldness to ask me of him. Whatsoever punishment his insolence deserved, my father was satisfied with telling him he had other thoughts in relation to me, and shewed him no farther dislike. The youth was incensed at this refusal; the vain fellow resented the contempt, as if he had asked some maid of indifferent extraction, or as if his birth had been equal to mine. Nor was he so satisfied, but resolved to be revenged on the king, and, with unparalleled ingratitude, conspired against him. In short, he murdered him, and caused himself to be proclaimed king of Deryabar, by a great number of malcontents, whom he supported. The first thing he did, after ridding himself of my father, was to come into my apartment with a great train of the conspirators. His design was either to take my life, or oblige me to marry him. Whilst he was busy murdering my father, the grand visier, who had been always loyal to his master, came to carry me away from the palace, and secured me in a friend's house, till a vessel he had provided was ready to sail. I then left the island, attended only by a governess and that generous minister, who chose rather to follow his master's daughter, and to partake of her misfortunes, than to submit to a tyrant.

The grand visier designed to carry me to the courts of the neighbouring kings, to implore their assistance, and excite them to revenge my father's death, but heaven did not give me a blessing to that resolution we thought so just. When we had been but a few days at sea, there arose such a furious storm, that, in spite of all the mariners' art, our vessel, carried away by the violence of the winds and waves, was dashed in pieces against a rock. I will not spend time in describing our shipwreck. I can but faintly represent to you how my governess, the grand visier, and all that attended me, were swallowed up by the sea. The dread I was seized with did not permit me to observe the horror of our condition. In fine, I lost my senses; and whether I was thrown upon the coast upon any part of the wreck of our ship, or whether heaven, which reserved me for other misfortunes, wrought a miracle in my deliverance, I found myself on shore, when my senses returned to me.

Misfortunes very often make us forget our duty; instead of returning thanks to God for so singular a mercy shewn me, I only lifted up my eyes to heaven, to complain because I had been saved. I was so far from bewailing the visier and my governess, that I envied their fate: and my dreadful imaginations by degrees prevailing above my reason, I resolved to cast myself into the sea. I was upon the point of doing so, when I heard behind me a great noise of men and horses. I looked about to see what it might be, and spied several armed horsemen, among whom was one mounted on an Arabian horse. He had on a garment embroidered with silver, a girdle set with precious stones, and a crown of gold on his head. Though his habit had not convinced me that he was the chief of the company, I should have judged it by the air of grandeur which appeared in his person. He was a young man extraordinary finely shaped, and perfectly beautiful. Being surprised to see a young lady alone in that place, he sent some of his officers to ask who I was? All my answer was weeping. The shore being covered with the wreck of our ship, they concluded some vessel had been cast away there, and that I was certainly some person that had saved my life: This conjecture, and my inconsolable condition, excited the curiosity of those officers, who began to ask me a thousand questions, with assurances that their king was a generous prince, and that I should receive all comfort in his court.

The king, impatient to know who I was, grew weary of expecting the return of his officers, and drew near to me. He gazed on me very earnestly, and observing that I did not give over weeping and afflicting myself, without being able to return an answer to their questions, he forbid them troubling me any more; and, directing his discourse to me, said, Madam, I conjure you to moderate your excessive affliction. Though heaven in its wrath has laid this calamity upon you, yet does it not behove you to despair. I beseech you, shew more courage; fortune, which has hitherto persecuted you, is inconstant, and may soon change. I dare assure you, that, if your misfortunes are capable of receiving any comfort, you shall find it in my dominions: My palace is at your service: You shall live with the queen my mother, who will endeavour by her kindness to ease your affliction. I know not as yet who you are; but I find I am already concerned for you.

I thanked the young king for his great goodness towards me, accepted of the obliging offers he made me; and, to convince him that I was not unworthy of him, told him my condition. I described to him the insolence of the young Saracen, and found it needless to do any more than barely to recount my misfortunes, to excite compassion in him, and all his officers who heard me. When I had done speaking, the prince began again, assuring me that he was highly concerned at my misfortune. Then he conducted me to his palace, and presented me to the queen his mother, to whom I am obliged again to repeat my misfortunes, and to renew my tears. The queen seemed very sensible of my troubles, and took an extraordinary liking to me. On the other hand, the king her son fell desperately in love with me, and soon offered me his person and his crown. I was still so entirely taken up with the thoughts of my calamities, that the prince, though so lovely a person, did not make so great an impression on me as he might have done at another time. However, gratitude prevailing on me, I did not refuse to make him happy, and our wedding was kept with all imaginable grandeur.

At the time when all the people were taken up with the celebration of their sovereign's nuptials, a neighbouring prince, who was his enemy, made a descent by night on the island with a great number of troops. That formidable enemy was the king Zanguebar: He surprised those people, and cut to pieces all the king my husband's subjects. We two escaped very narrowly, for he had already entered the palace with some of his followers; but we found means to slip away, and got to the sea-coast, where we took into a fishing-boat we had the good fortune to meet with. Two days we were drove about by the winds, without knowing what would become of us. The third day, we spied a vessel making towards us with all her sails aboard. We rejoiced at first, believing it had been a merchant-ship which might take us aboard; but were more astonished than I can express, when, as it drew near, we saw ten or twelve armed pirates appear on the deck. Being come up to us, five or six of them leaped into our boat, seized us, bound the prince, and conveyed us into their ship, where they immediately took off my veil. Instead of casting lots, every one of them claimed the preference, and me as his right. The controversy grew hot, and they came to blows about me, and fought like so many madmen. The deck was soon covered with dead bodies; and, in short, they were all killed but one, who, being left sole possessor of me, said, You are mine, I will carry you to Grand Cairo, to deliver you to a friend of mine, to whom I have promised a beautiful slave. But who, added he, looking upon the king my husband, is that man? What relation is he to you? Are you allied by blood or love? Sir, answered I, he is my husband. If so, replied the pirate, in pity I must rid myself of him; it would be too great an affliction to him to see you in my friend's arms. Having spoken these words, he took up the unhappy prince, who was bound, and threw him into the sea, notwithstanding all my endeavours to hinder him.

I shrieked in a dreadful manner at the sight of that cruel action, and had certainly cast myself headlong into the sea, had not the pirate held me. He plainly saw that was my design, and therefore bound me fast to the mainmast, and then hoisting sail, made towards the land, and there got ashore. He unbound and led me to a little town, where he bought camels, tents, and slaves, and then set out for Grand Cairo; designing, as he still said, to present me to his friend according to his promise.

We had been several days upon the road, when, as we were crossing this plain yesterday, we spied the black who inhabited this castle. At a distance, we took him for a tower; and when near us, could scarce believe him to be a man. He drew his vast scymitar, and summoned the pirate to yield himself up a prisoner, with all his slaves, and the lady he was conducting. The pirate was daring; and, being seconded by all his slaves, who promised to stand by him, he attacked the black. The fight lasted a considerable time; but at length the pirate fell under the enemy's deadly blows, as did all his slaves, who chose rather to die than forsake him. The black then conducted me to the castle, whither he also brought the pirate's body, which he did eat that night for his supper. After that inhuman meal, perceiving that I ceased not weeping, he said to me, Young lady, prepare to satisfy my desires, rather than continue thus to afflict yourself. Make a virtue of necessity, and comply: I give you till to-morrow to consider. Let me then find you comforted for all your misfortunes, and overjoyed for having been reserved for my bed. Having spoke these words, he conducted me to a chamber, and went to bed in his own, after locking up all the castle-doors. He opened them this morning, and presently locked them again, to pursue some travellers he perceived at a distance; but it is likely they made their escape, since he was coming alone, and without any booty, when you attacked him.

As soon as the princess had put an end to the recital of her adventures, Codadad declared to her that he was highly concerned at her misfortunes. But, madam, added he, it shall be your own fault if you do not live at ease for the future: the king of Harran's sons offer you a safe retreat in the court of the king their father; be pleased to accept of it. You will be there cherished by that prince, and respected by all other persons; and, if you do not disdain the person of your deliverer, permit me to make you a present of it, and to marry you before all these princes; let them be witnesses to our contract. The princess consented to it, and the marriage was concluded that very day in the castle, where they found all sorts of provisions. The kitchens were full of flesh, and other eatables, the black used to feed on when he was weary of feeding on human bodies. There was also a variety of fruits, very excellent in their kinds, and, to complete their satisfaction, abundance of delicious wine, and other liquors.

They all sat down to table; and, after having eaten and drank plentifully, they took along with them the rest of the provisions, and set out for the king of Harran's court. They travelled several days, encamping in the pleasantest places they could find; and they were within one day's journey of Harran, when, having halted, and drank all their wine, as being under no longer concern to make it hold out, Codadad directed his discourse to all his company thus: Princes, I have too long concealed from you who I am. Behold your brother Codadad! I have received my being, as well as you, of the king of Harran. The prince of Samaria has bred me, and the princess Pirouze is my mother. Madam, added he, applying himself to the princess of Deryabar, do you also forgive me, for having concealed my birth from you. Perhaps, by discovering it sooner, I might have prevented some disagreeable reflections which may have been occasioned by a match you may have thought unequal. No, sir, answered the princess, the opinion I at first conceived of you heightened every moment, and you did not stand in need of the extraction you now discover, to make me happy.

The princes congratulated Codadad on his birth, and expressed much satisfaction at the knowledge of it: but, in reality, instead of rejoicing, their hatred for so amiable a brother was redoubled. They met together at night in a bye-place, whilst Codadad and the princess his wife lay fast asleep in their tent. Those ungrateful, envious brothers, forgetting that, had it not been for the brave son of Pirouze, they must have been devoured by the black, agreed among themselves to murder him. We have no other course to chuse, said one of those wicked brethren; for the moment our father shall come to understand that this stranger he is already so fond of is our brother, and that he alone has been able to destroy a giant whom we could not all of us together conquer, he will bestow all his favour, and a thousand praises on him, and declare him his heir, in spite of all his brothers, who will be obliged to obey and fall down before him. Besides these, he added many other words, which made such an impression on their jealous minds, that they immediately repaired to Codadad, then fast asleep, stabbed him in a thousand places, and leaving him for dead in the arms of the princess Deryabar, proceeded on their journey for the city of Harran, where they arrived the next day.

The king their father conceived the greater joy at their return, because he had despaired of ever seeing them. He asked what had been the occasion of their stay? but they took care not to acquaint him with it, making no mention either of the black, or of Codadad; and only said, That, being curious to see the country, they had spent some time in the neighbouring cities.

In the mean time, Codadad lay in his tent drowned in his own blood, and little differing from a dead man, with the princess his wife, who seemed to be in no much better condition than he. She rent the air with her dismal shrieks, tore her hair, and, bathing her husband's body with her tears, Alas! Codadad, my dear Codadad, cried she, is it you whom I behold just departing this life? what cruel hands have put you into this condition? May I believe these are your brothers who have treated you so unmercifully? No, they are rather devils, who have taken those shapes to murder you. O barbarous wretches! whosoever you are, how could you make so ungrateful a return for the service he has done you? But why should I complain of your brothers, unfortunate Codadad! I alone am to blame for your death. You would tack your fate upon mine; and all the ill fortune that attends me since I left my father's palace has fallen upon you. O heaven! which has condemned me to lead a wandering life, and full of calamities, if you will not permit me to have a consort, why do you permit me to find any? Behold, you have now robbed me of two, just as I began to be endeared to them.

By these, and other moving expressions, the unhappy princess of Deryabar vented her sorrow, fixing her eyes on the deplorable Codadad, who could not hear her. But Codadad was not dead; and his consort observing that he still breathed, ran to a large open town she spied in the plain, to enquire for a surgeon. She was shewed one, who went immediately with her: but when they came to the tent, they could not find Codadad, which made them conclude he had been dragged away by some wild beast to devour him. The princess renewed her complaints and lamentations in a most dismal manner. The surgeon took compassion, and being unwilling to leave her in that miserable condition, proposed to her to return to the town, offering her his house and service.

She suffered herself to be prevailed on. The surgeon conducted her to his house, and, without knowing as yet who she was, treated her with all imaginable courtesy and respect. He used all his rhetoric to comfort her; but it was in vain to think of removing her sorrow, which was rather heightened than diminished. Madam, said he to her one day, be pleased to recount to me your misfortunes; tell your country and your condition; perhaps I may give you some advice, when I am acquainted with all the circumstances of your calamity. You do nothing but afflict yourself, without considering that remedies may be found for the most desperate diseases.

The surgeon's words were so efficacious, that they wrought on the princess, who recounted to him all her adventures; and when she had done, the surgeon directed his discourse to her, saying, Madam, since this is the posture of affairs, give me leave to tell you, that you ought not thus to give way to your sorrow; you ought rather to arm yourself with resolution, and to perform what the name and the duty of a wife require of you. You are obliged to revenge your husband: If you please I will wait on you as your squire: let us go to the king of Harran's court; he is a good and just prince: you need only represent to him, in a lively manner, how prince Codadad has been treated by his brothers: I am fully persuaded he will do you justice. I submit to your reasons, answered the princess; it is my duty to endeavour to revenge Codadad; and since you are so obliging and generous as to offer to bear me company, I am ready to set out. No sooner had she fixed this resolution, than the surgeon ordered two camels to be made ready, on which the princess and he mounted, and repaired to Harran.

They alighted at the first caravansary they found; and enquiring at the host what news at court? It is, said he, in very great confusion. The king had a son, who lived a long time with him as a stranger, and none can tell what is become of that young prince. One of the king's wives, called Pirouze, is his mother; she has made all possible enquiry, but to no purpose. All men are concerned at the loss of that prince, because he was very deserving. The king has forty-nine other sons, all of them born of several mothers; but not one of them has worth enough to comfort the king for the death of Codadad; I say his death, because it is impossible he should be alive, since no news have been heard of him, notwithstanding so much search has been made after him.

The surgeon having heard this account from the host, concluded that the best course the princess of Deryabar could take, was to wait upon Pirouze: but that method was not without some danger, and required much precaution; for it was to be feared, that if the king of Harran's sons should happen to hear of the arrival of their sister-in-law, and her design, they might cause her to be conveyed away before she could speak to Codadad's mother. The surgeon weighed all these particulars, and considered what risk he might run himself; and therefore, that he might manage the affair with discretion, he desired the princess to stay in the caravansary, whilst he went to the palace to observe which might be the safest way to conduct her to Pirouze.

He went accordingly into the city, and was walking towards the palace, like one led only by curiosity to see the court, when he spied a lady mounted on a mule richly accoutred. She was followed by several ladies mounted on mules, with a great number of guards and black slaves. All the people made a lane to see her pass along, and saluted her, prostrating themselves on the ground. The surgeon paid her the same respect, and then asked a calendar, who happened to stand by him, Whether that lady was one of the king's wives? Yes, brother, answered the calendar, she is one of the king's wives, and the most honoured and beloved by the people, because she is mother to prince Codadad, of whom I suppose you have heard.

The surgeon asked no more questions, but followed Pirouze to a mosque, into which she went to distribute alms, and assist at the public prayers the king had ordered to be made for the safe return of Codadad. The people, who were highly concerned for that young prince, ran in crowds to join their vows to the prayers of the priests, so that the mosque was quite full. The surgeon broke through the throng, and advanced as far as Pirouze's guards. He staid out the prayers; and when that princess went out, he stepped up to one of her slaves, and whispered him in his ear, saying, Brother, I have a secret of moment to impart to the princess Pirouze; may not I, by your means, be brought into her apartment? If that secret, answered the slave, be relating to prince Codadad, I dare promise you shall have audience of her this very day; but if it concerns not him, it is needless for you to endeavour to be introduced to her; for her thoughts are all upon her son, and she will not hear talk of any other subject. It is only about that dear son, replied the surgeon, that I would discourse to her. If so, said the slave, you need only follow us to the palace, and you shall soon speak to her.

Accordingly, as soon as Pirouze was returned to her apartment, that slave acquainted her that a person unknown had some important affair to communicate to her, and that it related to prince Codadad. No sooner had he uttered these words, than Pirouze expressed her impatience to see that stranger. The slave immediately conducted him into the princess's closet, who ordered all her women to withdraw, except two, from whom she concealed nothing. As soon as she saw the surgeon, she asked him abruptly what news he had to tell her of Codadad? Madam, answered the surgeon, after having prostrated himself on the ground, I have a long account to give you, and such as will be very surprising. Then he told her all the particulars of what had passed between Codadad and his brothers, which she listened to with an eager attention; but when he came to speak of the murder, that tender mother swooned away on her sofa, as if she had been herself stabbed like her son. Her two women used proper means, and soon brought her to herself. The surgeon continued his relation; and when he had ended it, Pirouze said to him, Go back to the princess of Deryabar, and assure her from me that the king shall soon own her for his daughter-in-law; and as for yourself, be assured that your service shall be well rewarded.

When the surgeon was gone, Pirouze remained on the sofa in such a state of affliction as is not easy to imagine; and, relenting at the thoughts of Codadad, O! my son, said she, I must never then expect to see you more! Alas! when I gave you leave to depart from Samaria, and you took leave of me, I did not imagine that so unfortunate a death had awaited you at such a distance from me. Unfortunate Codadad! why did you leave me? It is true, you would not have acquired so much renown; but you had been still alive, and had not cost your mother so many tears. Whilst she uttered these words, she wept bitterly, and her two confidants, moved by her sorrow, mixed their tears with hers.

Whilst they were all three in that affliction, the king came into the closet, and seeing them in that condition, asked Pirouze whether she had received any bad news concerning Codadad? Alas! sir, said she, all is over; my son has lost his life; and, to add to my sorrow, I cannot pay him the funeral rites; for, in all appearance, the wild beasts have devoured him. Then she told him all that she had heard from the surgeon, and did not fail to express herself fully at the inhuman manner in which Codadad had been murdered by his brothers.

The king did not give Pirouze time to finish her relation; but, being transported with anger, and giving way to his passion, Madam, said he to the princess, those perfidious wretches who cause you to shed these tears, and are the occasion of the mortal grief which oppresses their father, shall soon feel the punishment due to their guilt. The king having spoken these words, with indignation appearing in his countenance, went directly to the presence-chamber, where all his courtiers attended, and such of the people as had any petitions to present to him. They were all astonished to see him in that passion, and thought his anger had been kindled against his people.

Their hearts failed them for fear. He ascended the throne, and causing the grand visier to draw near, said, Hassan, I have some orders for you; Go immediately, take a thousand of my guards, and seize all the princes my sons; shut them up in the tower appointed for a prison for murderers; and let this be done in a moment. All that were present quaked at the hearing of this surprising command; and the grand visier, without answering one word, laid his hand on his head, to express his obedience, and went out of the presence to execute his orders, which were very surprising to him. In the mean time, the king dismissed those who attended to desire audience, and declared he would not dispatch any business for a month to come. He was still in the presence-chamber, when the visier returned. Are all my sons, said that prince, in the tower? They are, sir, answered the visier; I have obeyed your orders. This is not all, replied the king, I have farther commands for you; and so saying, he went out of the presence-chamber, and returned to Pirouze's apartment, with the visier following him. He asked that princess where Codadad's widow had taken up her lodging? Pirouze's women told him; for the surgeon had not forgot that in his relation. Then the king, turning to his minister, Go, said he, to that caravansary, and bring a young princess, who lodges there; but treat her with all the respect due to her quality.

The visier was not backward in performing what he was ordered. He mounted on horseback, with all the emirs and courtiers, and repaired to the caravansary where the princess of Deryabar was, whom he acquainted with his orders, and presented her, from the king, a fine white mule, whose saddle and bridle were adorned with gold, rubies, and diamonds. She mounted it, and went to the palace, attended by all those great men. The surgeon bore her company, mounted on a sprightly Tartar horse which the visier had provided for him. All the people were at their windows, or in the streets, to see that noble cavalcade; and it being given out that the princess, whom they conducted in such state to court, was Codadad's wife, the city resounded with acclamations, the air rung with shouts of joy, which would certainly have been turned into lamentations, had that prince's fatal adventure been known; so much was he beloved by all men.

The princess of Deryabar found the king at the palace gate, waiting to receive her. He took her by the hand, and led her to Pirouze's apartment, where a very moving scene was acted among them. Codadad's wife found her affliction redouble upon her at the sight of her husband's father and mother; as, on the other side, those parents could not look on their son's wife without being much concerned. She cast herself at the king's feet, and having bathed them with tears, was so overcome with grief, that she was not able to speak one word. Pirouze was in no better condition, she seemed to be stunned with her sorrows; and the king, moved by those dismal objects, gave way to his passion: those three persons, mixing their tears and sighs, for some time observed a silence, which appeared extraordinary moving and pitiful. At length the princess of Deryabar, being somewhat recovered, recounted the adventure of the castle and Codadad's disaster. Then she required justice for the treachery of the princes. Yes, madam, said the king to her, those ungrateful wretches shall perish, but Codadad's death must first be made public, that the punishment of his brothers may not cause my subjects to rebel; and, though we have not my son's body, we will not omit paying him the last duties. This said, he directed his discourse to the visier, and ordered him to build a dome of white marble in a delightful plain, in the midst of which the city of Harran stands; then he appointed the princess of Deryabar a fine apartment in his palace, acknowledging her for his daughter-in-law.

Hassan caused the work to be carried on with such diligence, and employed so many workmen, that the dome was soon finished. Within it was erected a monument, and on it was placed a figure representing Codadad. As soon as all was perfected, the king ordered prayers to be said, and appointed a day for the obsequies of his son.

On that day, all the inhabitants of the city went out upon the plain to see that ceremony performed; which was after this manner: The king, attended by his visier and the prime persons of the court, proceeded towards the dome; and being come to it, went in, and sat down with them on carpets laid on the ground, made of black sattin, with gold flowers. A great body of horse guards, hanging their heads, and looking down, drew up close about the dome, and marched round it twice, observing a profound silence; but at the third round, they halted before the door, and all of them with a loud voice pronounced these words; 'O prince, son to the king, could we by dint of sword and human valour, any way retrieve your misfortune, we would bring you back to life; but the King of kings has commanded, and the angel of death has obeyed.' Having uttered these words, they drew off, to make way for a hundred old men, all of them mounted on black mules, and wearing long grey beards.

These were anchorites,* who lived all their days concealed in caves. They never appeared in the sight of the world, but when they were to assist at the obsequies of the king of Harran, and of the princes of their family. Each of these venerable persons carried a book on his head, which he held with one hand. They took three turns round the dome without uttering one word; then stopping before the door, one of them said, 'O prince, what can we do for you? If you could be restored to life by prayers, or learning, we would rub our grey beards at thy feet, and recite prayers; but the King of the universe has taken you away for ever.'

This said, the old men removed at a distance from the dome, and immediately fifty young beautiful maids drew near to it: each of them was mounted on a little white horse: they wore no veils, and carried gold baskets full of all sorts of precious stones. Thus they did also ride thrice round the dome; and, halting at the same place as the others had done, the youngest of them spoke in the name of all as follows: 'O prince, once so beautiful, what relief can you expect from us? If we could restore you to life by our charms, we would become your slaves. But you are no longer sensible to beauty, and have no more occasion for us.'

When the young maids were withdrawn, the king and his courtiers arose, and, having walked thrice round the figure representing Codadad, the king spoke as follows: 'O my dear son, light of my eyes, I have then lost thee for ever.' These words were attended with sighs, and he watered the tomb with his tears; his courtiers weeping with him. Then the gate of the dome was shut, and all the people returned to the city. The next day, there were public prayers in all the mosques; and the same was continued for eight days successively. On the ninth, the king resolved to cause the princes his sons to be beheaded. All the people being incensed at their cruelty towards Codadad, impatiently expected to see them executed. The scaffolds were erecting; but the execution was respited, on account that, on a sudden, news was brought, that the neighbouring princes, who had before made war on king Harran, were advancing with more numerous forces than the first time, and were not then far from the city. It had been long known that they were preparing for war, but no great notice had been taken of it. This advice occasioned a general consternation, and gave new cause to lament the loss of Codadad, by reason that prince had signalized himself in the former war against those enemies. Alas! said they, were the brave Codadad alive, we should little value those princes who are coming to surprise us. The king, nothing dismayed, raised men with all possible speed, formed a considerable army, and, being too brave to expect the enemy to come and attack him within his walls, marched out to meet them. They, on their side, being informed by their advanced parties that the king of Harran was marching to engage them, halted in the plain, and formed their army.

As soon as the king discovered them, he also drew up his forces, and ranged them in order of battle. The signal was given, and he attacked them with extraordinary vigour. Nor was the opposition inferior, much blood was shed on both sides, and the victory remained long dubious; but at length it seemed to incline to the king of Harran's enemies, who, being more numerous, were about hemming him in, when a good body of horse appeared on the plain, and drew near the two armies in good order. The sight of that fresh party daunted both sides, as not knowing what to think of them: But their doubts were soon cleared; for those horsemen fell upon the flank of the king of Harran's enemies, giving such a furious charge, that they soon broke and put them to the rout; and not so satisfied, they pursued them, and cut most of them in pieces.

The king of Harran, who had nicely observed all the action, admired the bravery of those horsemen, whose unexpected arrival had given the victory to his side. But, above all, he was charmed with their chief, whom he had seen fighting with a more than ordinary valour. He longed to know the name of that generous hero. Being impatient to see and thank him, he advanced towards him, but perceived he was coming to prevent him. The two princes drew near, and the king of Harran finding Codadad in that brave warrior who had just then succoured him, or rather defeated his enemies, became motionless with the joy and surprise. Sir, said Codadad to him, you have sufficient cause to be astonished, seeing a man appear on a sudden before your majesty whom perhaps you concluded to be dead. I should have been so, had not heaven preserved me still against your enemies. O my son! cried the king, is it possible that you are restored to me? Alas! I despaired of seeing you any more. Having so said, he stretched out his arms to the young prince, who flew to his loving embraces.

I know all, my son, said the king again, after having long held him in his arms; I know what return my sons have made you for the service you did in delivering them out of the hands of the black; but you shall be revenged to-morrow. Let us now go to the palace; your mother, who has wept sufficiently for you, expects me, to rejoice with us for the defeat of our enemies. What a joy will it be to her to be informed that my victory is your handy-work! Sir, said Codadad, give me leave to ask you, how could you come to know the adventure of the castle? Has any of my brothers, repenting, owned the thing to you? No, answered the king, the princess of Deryabar has given us an account of all things; for she is in my palace, and come thither to demand justice against your brothers. Codadad was in a transport of joy, to understand that the princess his wife was at the court. Let us go, sir, cried he to his father in a rapture, let us go to see to my mother, who waits for us. I have an ardent desire to dry up her tears, as well as those of the princess Deryabar.

The king immediately returned to the city, with his army, which he dismissed; entering his palace victorious, amidst the acclamations of his people, who followed him in crowds, praying to heaven to prolong his life, and extolling Codadad to the skies. These two princes found Pirouze and her daughter-in-law waiting for the king to congratulate him; but there is no expressing the transport of joy they felt when they saw the young prince come with him: They dissolved in embraces, mixed with tears, but of a different sort from those they had before shed for him. When these four persons had performed all that the ties of blood and love demanded of them, the question was asked at Pirouze's son, by what miracle he came to be still alive? He answered, that a peasant, mounted on a mule, happening accidentally to come into the tent where he lay senseless, and perceiving him alone, and stabbed in several places, had made him fast on his mule, and carried him to his house, where he applied to his wounds certain herbs chewed, which had recovered him in a few days. When I found myself well, added he, I returned thanks to the peasant, and gave him all the diamonds I had. Then I drew near the city of Harran; but being informed by the way, that some neighbouring princes had gathered forces, and were coming to fall upon the king's subjects, I made myself known unto the villagers, and stirred up those people to stand upon their guard. I armed a good number of young men; and, heading them, happened to come in at that time when the two armies were engaged.

When he had done speaking, the king said, Let us return thanks to God for having preserved Codadad; but it is requisite that the traitors, who would have destroyed him, should perish this day. Sir, answered the generous son of Pirouze, though they are wicked and ungrateful, consider they are your own flesh and blood: they are my brothers; I forgive them the offence, and beg pardon of you for them. This generosity drew tears from the king, who caused the people to be assembled, and declared Codadad his heir. Then he ordered the princes, who were prisoners, to be brought, loaded with irons. Pirouze's son knocked off their chains, and embraced them all successively, with as much sincerity as he had done in the court of the black's castle. The people were charmed with Codadad's good-nature, and highly applauded him. Next he nobly rewarded the surgeon, to requite the service he had done the princess of Deryabar.

The sultaness Scheherazade having told the story of Ganem* with so much address, and in so agreeable a manner, that the sultan of the Indies could not forbear shewing the pleasure that relation gave him, said to that monarch, I doubt not but your majesty is very well satisfied to find the caliph Haroun Alraschid change his sentiments in favour of Ganem, his mother, and sister; and I believe you may be sensibly affected with their misfortunes, and the ill treatment they received: but am persuaded, if your majesty would hear the story of the Sleeper Awakened, it would, instead of exciting all those emotions of indignation and compassion in your breast, on the contrary, afford you all the mirth and diversion imaginable. The sultan, who promised himself some new adventures from the title of that story, would have heard it that morning; but, perceiving day approached, deferred it till next, when Dinarzade called upon her sister, who began her story as follows.

The Story of the Sleeper Awakened

In the reign of caliph Haroun Alraschid, there lived at Bagdad a very rich merchant, who, having married a woman pretty well in years, had but one son, whom he named Abon Hassan, and educated with great restraint. When this son was thirty years old, the merchant died, and left him his sole heir, and master of great riches, which his father had amassed together by his industry, frugality, and great application to business.

Abon Hassan, whose views and inclinations were very much different from those of his father, was resolved to make another use of his wealth; for, as his father had never allowed him any money but what was just necessary for subsistence, and he had always envied those young persons of his age who wanted none, and who debarred themselves from none of those pleasures to which youth are too much addicted, he resolved, in his turn, to signalize himself by extravagancies proportionable to his fortune. To this end, he divided his riches in two parts; with one half, he bought houses in town, and land in the country, with a promise to himself never to touch the income of his estate, which was considerable enough to live upon very handsomely, but lay it all by; with the other half, which he kept by him in ready money, he designed to make himself amends for the time he had lost in the severe restraint with which his father had always kept him.

With this intent, Abon Hassan associated himself in a few days with people of his age and condition, and thought of nothing more than how to spend their time agreeably. Every day he gave them splendid entertainments, at which the most exquisite and delicate wines flowed in plenty, while concerts of the best vocal and instrumental music heightened their pleasures; and then this young band of debauchees, with glasses in their hands, sung and joined with the music; and these feasts generally ended with balls at night, to which the best dancers of Bagdad, of both sexes, were invited. These entertainments, renewed every day, were so expensive to Abon Hassan, that he could not support the extravagance above one year; and, in short, the great sum which he had consecrated to this prodigality and the year ended together. As soon as he left off keeping this table, his friends forsook him; whenever they saw him, they avoided him; and if by chance he met any of them, and would stop them, they always excused themselves on some pretence or other.

Abon Hassan, touched more to the quick at this strange behaviour of his friends, who had forsaken him so basely and ungratefully, after all the protestations of friendship they had made him, and their inviolable attachment to his service, than all the money he had foolishly squandered away, went, melancholy and thoughtful, into his mother's apartment, and sat down on a sofa a good distance from her. What is the matter with you, son? said his mother, reading his grief in his countenance: why are you so altered, so dejected, and so much different from yourself? You could not certainly be more concerned if you had lost all you had in the world. I know you have lived very profusely, and believe all your money is spent; yet you have a good estate; and the reason that I did not so very much oppose your irregular way of living, was, I knew the wise precaution you had taken to preserve half your substance: therefore I do not see why you should plunge yourself into this deep melancholy.

At these words, Abon Hassan melted into tears, and in the midst of his sighs cried out, Ah! mother, I see at last, by sad experience, how insupportable poverty is: I am sensible that it deprives us of joy, as much as the setting sun does of light. In poverty, we have no commendations and fine things said unto us; we endeavour to conceal all our actions, and spend our nights in tears and sorrow. In short, a poor man is looked upon, both by friends and relations, as a stranger. You know, mother, how I have used my friends for this year past: I have entertained them with all imaginable generosity, till I have spent all my money; and now they have left me, when I can treat them no longer. For my estate, I thank heaven for having given me the grace to keep the oath I have made not to enter upon that; and now I shall know how to make a good use of it. But first, I will try the ingratitude of friends, who deserve not that I should call them so: I will go to them one after another, and when I have represented to them what I have done for their sakes, I will ask them to make me up a sum of money among them, to relieve me out of the miserable condition I am reduced to: these are the steps I intend to take, to try their gratitude.

I do not pretend, son, said Abon Hassan's mother, to dissuade you from executing your design; but I can tell you before-hand, that you have no ground for any hope; believe me, you will find no relief, but from the estate you have reserved. I see you do not, but will soon know those people, whom we generally call friends; and I wish to heaven you may, in the manner I desire; that is to say, for your own good. Mother, replied Abon Hassan, I am persuaded of the truth of what you say; but shall be certain of a fact which concerns me so nearly, when I shall inform myself better of their baseness. Upon this, Abon Hassan went immediately to his friends, whom he found at home, represented to them the great need he was in, and begged of them to loose their purse-strings to assist him. He promised to give every one bonds to pay them the money they lent him, as soon as his affairs were made up; giving them to understand, at the same time, that it was, in a great measure, upon their accounts that he was undone; and forgot not to allure them with the hopes of being once again entertained in the same manner as before.

Not one of his bottle companions was affected with the arguments which the afflicted Abon Hassan made use of to persuade them; and he had the mortification to find, that many of them told him plainly they scarce knew him.

He returned home again full of grief and rage; and, going into his mother's apartment, said, Ah! madam, you was in the right of it; instead of friends, I have found none but ungrateful, perfidious wretches, who deserve not my friendship; which I renounce, and promise never to see them more. He resolved to be as good as his word; and, to that end, took all possible precautions to avoid falling into the same inconvenience, taking an oath never to give an inhabitant of Bagdad any entertainment again. Afterwards, he opened a strong chest, in which he had put the rents he had received from his estate, and resolved to take every day a sum that was sufficient to defray the expence of a single person to sup with him; who, according to the oath he had taken, must be a stranger that came into Bagdad the same day, and must take his leave of him the next morning.

According to this project, Abon Hassan took care every morning to provide whatever he designed for night, and towards the close of the evening went and sat on Bagdad bridge; and, as soon as ever he saw a stranger, of whatever condition he was, he accosted him civilly, and invited him to sup and lodge with him that night; and, after having informed him of the law he had imposed upon himself, took him home with him. The repast with which Abon Hassan regaled his guests was not costly, but always plain and neat, with plenty of good wine, and generally lasted till the night was pretty well advanced; when, instead of entertaining his guest with the affairs of state, his family, or business, as it is too frequent, he affected to talk of indifferent subjects, and was naturally of so gay and pleasant a temper, that he could give the most agreeable turns in conversation, and make the most reserved and melancholy persons merry. When he saw his guest again the next morning, he always said to him, God preserve you from all sorrow wherever you go: when I invited you yesterday to come and sup with me, I informed you of the law I have made: therefore do not take it ill if I tell you that we must never see one another again, nor drink together, for reasons best known to myself; so God conduct you.

Abon Hassan was very exact in the observation of this oath, and never looked upon, or spoke to, any stranger he had once entertained, wherever he met them; and had lived for a long time after this manner, when one afternoon, a little before sun-set, as he was sitting upon the bridge, according to custom, the caliph Haroun Alraschid came by, so disguised that nobody could know him: for that monarch, though his chief ministers and officers of justice acquitted themselves of their duty very punctually, yet he would take notice of every thing himself; and, to that purpose, often disguised himself, and walked through the city and suburbs of Bagdad; and that day was dressed like a merchant of Moussel, who had but just disembarked, and was followed by a slave.

As the caliph had in his disguise a grave and awful air, Abon Hassan, who thought him to be a Moussel merchant, went directly to him, and, after having saluted him with a smiling countenance, and kissed his hand, said, Sir, I congratulate you on your happy arrival, and beg of you to do me the honour to go and sup with me, and repose yourself at my home this night, after the fatigue of your voyage. And, to oblige him not to deny him that favour, he told him his custom of entertaining the first stranger he met with. The caliph found something so odd and singular in Abon Hassan's taste, that he was very desirous to know the bottom, without quitting the character of a merchant; and told him, that he could not better answer that great civility, which he did not expect at his arrival at Bagdad, than by accepting the obliging offer that he made him.

Abon Hassan, who knew not that the guest which fortune presented to him was so very much above him, treated him as his equal, carried him home, and led him into a room very neatly furnished, where he set him on a sofa, at the upper end of a table that was ready laid for supper, which was soon after sent up by Abon Hassan's mother, who took upon herself the care of the kitchen, and consisting of three dishes. The first was a capon and four large pullets, which were set in the middle; and the second and third, placed on each side, were a fat roasted goose and boiled pigeons, all dressed very neatly, and with proper sauces.

Abon Hassan sat down over-against his guest, and he and the caliph began to eat heartily of what they liked best, without speaking or drinking, according to the custom of the country. When they had done eating, the caliph's slave brought them water to wash their hands; and in the mean time, Abon Hassan's mother sent up a desert of all sorts of dried sweetmeats, and all the fruits then in season, as grapes, peaches, apples, pears, &c. As soon as it grew dark, wax-candles were lighted, and Abon Hassan, after charging his mother to take care of the caliph's slave, brought bottles and glasses.

Then Abon Hassan, sitting down with the pretended Moussel merchant again, filled out a glass of wine, before he touched the desert; and holding it out in his hand, said to the caliph, You know, sir, that the cock never drinks before he calls to his hens to come and drink with him; so I invite you to follow my example. I do not know what you may think; for my part, I cannot reckon him a wise man who does not love wine: come, let us leave those sort of people to their dull melancholy humours, and seek for mirth, which is only to be found in a brimmer.

While Abon Hassan was drinking, the caliph, taking the glass that was set by him, said, Now I like you, you are an honest fellow; I am mightily taken with your pleasant temper, and expect you should fill me as much. Abon Hassan, as soon as he had drank, filled the caliph's glass, and giving it to him, Here, sir, said he, taste this wine; I will warrant it good. I am very well persuaded, replied the caliph, laughing, that you know how to make choice of the best. O, replied Abon Hassan, while the caliph was taking off his glass, one may easily find that you know what good living is, and have seen the world: Alas! how happy is my house in your presence, and how overjoyed am I for meeting with a man of so much merit!

The caliph, who was naturally a merry man, was mightily diverted with these sallies of Abon Hassan, and took great pleasure in promoting drinking, often asking for wine, thinking that when that began to work, he might penetrate so far into his discourse as to satisfy his curiosity. Therefore, to enter into conversation, he asked him his name, his business, and how he spent his life. My name, sir, replied he, is Abon Hassan: My father, whom I buried, was a merchant of Bagdad; and though he was not the richest, yet he lived very well. When he died, he left me enough in my station to live free from ambition; but, as he always kept a very strict hand over me in his life-time, I was willing, when he was gone, to make up the time I thought I had lost.

But notwithstanding, continued Abon Hassan, in this I was more prudent than most young people are, who give themselves unto debauchery without any thought, and who reduce themselves to the utmost poverty, and are forced to do penance all the rest of their lives after. Now I, to avoid this misfortune, divided what I had left me in two parts, and with one bought an estate, with a resolution not to finger my rents at that time; and kept the other in ready money to pursue my extravagancies with. I associated myself with young people of my age, and with my ready money, which I spent profusely, treated them every day; and, in short, spared for no sort of pleasure. But these feastings did not last long; for by that time the year was out, I had got to the bottom of my cash, and then all my friends vanished. I made a visit to every one of them, and represented to them the miserable condition I was in, but none of them would relieve me. Upon this, I renounced their friendship, and retrenched so far as to live within the compass of my income, and obliged myself to keep company with none but the first stranger I could meet with, coming that day into Bagdad, and to entertain him but one night. I have told you the rest before; and I thank my good fortune this day for meeting with a stranger of so much worth.

The caliph was very well satisfied with this information, and said to Abon Hassan, I cannot enough commend the measures you have taken, and the prudence with which you have acted, by forsaking your debauchery: a conduct rarely to be met with in young persons; and I esteem you the more for being so just to yourself as you have been. It was a slippery path you trode in; and I cannot enough admire, how, after having seen the end of your ready money, you had so great a command over yourself not to enter upon your estate. In short, I must own I envy your happiness; you are the only happy man in the world, to enjoy every day the company of some one honest man, with whom you can discourse freely and agreeably, and to whom you give an opportunity to declare, wherever he goes, how handsomely he was received by you. But we talk too long without drinking; come drink, and pour out to me.

In this manner the caliph and Abon Hassan entertained each other, drinking and talking of indifferent matters till the night was pretty far advanced; when the caliph, pretending to be fatigued after his voyage, told his host he stood in need of a little rest. But, added he, that I may not deprive you of yours, before we part, because to morrow I may be gone before you are stirring, I would be glad to shew you how sensible I am of your civility, and the kind and obliging hospitality you have shewn me. The only thing that troubles me is, that I know not which way to pay my acknowledgment; therefore I beg of you to let me understand how I may, and you shall see I will not be ungrateful; for certainly you must have some business in which you may be served, or must want something which you could wish for. Speak freely, and declare your mind; for, though I am but a merchant, it may be in mine or some friend's power to oblige you.

To these offers of the caliph, Abon Hassan, taking him still for a Moussel merchant, replied, I am very well persuaded, good sir, that it is not out of a compliment that you make me these generous tenders; but, upon the word of an honest man, I have nothing that troubles me, no business nor desires, and want not any thing. I have not the least ambition, as I told you before, but am very well satisfied with my condition. Therefore, I can only thank you for your obliging proffers, and the honour you have done me to come and take a slight repast with me. Yet I must tell you, pursued Abon Hassan, there is one thing gives me great uneasiness: You know the town of Bagdad is divided into several parts and divisions, to each of which there belongs a mosque, and an iman to read prayers at certain hours. The iman of the division I live in, is an old man, of an austere countenance, and the greatest hypocrite in the world. This man, and four old men of this neighbourhood, who are people of the same stamp, meet every day at the iman's house; there they vent their slander, calumny, and malice against me and the whole division, to the disturbance of the public peace of a neighbourhood, and the promotion of dissention.—Some they threaten, others they rail against; and, in short, would be lords paramount, and have every one govern himself according to their caprice; and, at the same time, know not how to govern themselves. Indeed, I would have them meddle with nothing but their Alcoran, and let the world live quietly.

Well, I suppose, said the caliph, you would willingly put a stop to this disorder? You have guessed it, answered Abon Hassan; and the only thing I should desire, would be to be caliph only for one day, in the stead of our sovereign lord and master Haroun Alraschid, the Commander of the Faithful. What would you do if you were, said the caliph? I would make them examples, answered Abon Hassan, to the satisfaction of all honest men. I would punish the four old men with each an hundred bastinadoes on the soles of their feet, and the iman with four hundred, to learn them not to disturb and abuse their neighbours any more.

The caliph was extremely well pleased with this thought of Abon Hassan's; and, as he was a prince who loved adventures, he fancied to make this a very singular one. Indeed, said he, I approve very much of your wish, which I see proceeds from an upright mind, that cannot bear to see the malice of wicked people to go unpunished: I could like to see it take effect, and that is not so impossible a thing as you imagine. I am persuaded that the caliph would willingly put his authority for twenty-four hours into your hands, if he knew your good intentions and the just use you would make of it. I see, said Abon Hassan, you laugh at my foolish fancy; and the caliph himself would laugh at my extravagance too if he knew it; but yet it would be a means of informing him of the iman's and his companions' behaviour, and he might chastise them.

Heaven forbid, replied the caliph, that I, who have been so handsomely entertained by you, should laugh at you; neither do I believe, as much a stranger as I am, that the caliph would be displeased. But let us lay this discourse aside; it is almost midnight, and time to go to bed. With all my heart, said Abon Hassan, I would not be any hinderance to your going to rest; but there is still some wine in the bottle, and, if you please, we will drink it off first. The only thing that I have to recommend to you is, that, when you go out in the morning, if I am not up, you will give yourself the trouble of shutting the door after you: which the caliph promised; and while Abon Hassan was talking, took the bottle and two glasses, and filled his own first, saying, Here is a cup of thanks to you; and then filling the other, put artfully a little powder, which he had about him, into it, and giving it to Abon Hassan, said, You have taken the pains to fill for me all this night, and it is the least I can do to save you the trouble once; come, drink to our good repose.

Abon Hassan took the glass, and, to shew his guest with how much pleasure he received the honour he did him, whipped it off at once; but had scarcely set the glass upon the table before the powder began to work, and he fell into so sound a sleep, that his head knocked against his knees. The caliph ordered the slave that he had brought along with him, and who came again into the room as soon as he had supped, to take him upon his back, and follow him; but to be sure to observe the house, that he might know it again when he should bring him back; and in this manner the caliph, followed by the slave with Abon Hassan on his back, went out of the house, but without shutting the door after him, as Abon Hassan desired him, and went directly to his palace, and, by a back-door, into his own apartment, where all the officers of his apartment were waiting for him, whom he ordered to undress him, and put him in his bed, which they immediately performed.

Then the caliph sent for all the officers and ladies of the palace, and said to them, I would have all those whose business it is to attend my levee, wait to-morrow morning upon this man who lies in my bed, and pay the same respect to him as to myself, and obey him in whatever he commands; let him be refused in nothing that he asks for, and be spoke to and answered in every thing he says or does, as if he was the Commander of the Faithful. In short, I expect you look upon him as the true caliph, and neglect not the least circumstance.

The officers and ladies presently understood that the caliph had a mind to divert himself, and made low bows to shew their obedience, and then withdrew, every one full of the part they were to act.

Then he sent for the grand visier: Giafar, said he, I have sent for you to instruct you, and to prevent your being surprised to-morrow when you come to an audience, to see this man, that is laid here in my bed, seated on my throne in my royal robes; accost him with the same reverence and respect you pay to myself; observe, and punctually execute, whatever he bids you do, the same as if I commanded you, even if his liberality should extend so far as to empty all the coffers in my treasury; and remember to acquaint all my emirs and huissirs, all the officers without the palace, to pay him the same honour at audience as the Commander of the Believers himself; and to carry on the matter so well, that he might not perceive the least thing that may interrupt this joke which I am diverting myself with.

Afterwards the grand visier retired, and the caliph went to bed in another apartment; and ordered Mesrour, the chief of his eunuchs, to take care to manage things so well, that he might see how Abon Hassan would use the power and authority of the caliph for the time he desired to have it; and, above all, charged him to awake him at the usual hour, before he awakened Abon Hassan, because he had a mind to be present when he rose.

Mesrour failed not to do as the caliph had commanded; and, as soon as the caliph went into the room where Abon Hassan lay, he placed himself in a little closet, from whence he could see all that passed. All the officers and ladies who were to attend Abon Hassan's levee, took their posts according to their rank, with great silence, and discharged themselves as punctually of their offices as if the caliph had been to rise.

As it was just day-break, and time to rise to morning-prayer before sunrise, the officer that stood nearest to the head of the bed put a spunge steeped in vinegar to Abon Hassan's nose; who presently turning his head about without opening his eyes, sneezed heartily, which was generally the effect of the caliph's powder, and which lasted longer or shorter in proportion to the dose. Then opening his eyes, he found himself, by the small light that appeared, in a stately room magnificently furnished, the ceiling of which was finely painted, and the floor covered with a rich silk tapestry, and surrounded by a great many young and handsome ladies, with all sorts of instruments of music in their hands, and black eunuchs richly clothed, all standing with great modesty and respect.—After casting his eyes on the quilt of the bed, he perceived it was cloth of gold, richly embossed with pearls and diamonds; and that there was laid by the bed an habit of the same stuff and trimmings, with a caliph's turban.

At the sight of these glittering objects, Abon Hassan was in the most inexpressible confusion and amazement, and looked upon all he saw as a dream. So, said he to himself, I am caliph; but, added he a little after, it is only a dream, the effect of the wish I entertained my guest with last night; and then he turned himself about to sleep again. At the same time, the eunuch said very respectfully, Commander of the Faithful, it is time for your majesty to rise to prayers, the morning begins to advance.

These words very much surprised Abon Hassan. Am I awake, or do I sleep? said he to himself. Ah! certainly I am asleep! continued he, keeping his eyes shut, there is no reason to doubt of it.

Immediately the eunuch, who saw he had no inclination to get up, and that he gave him no answer, said again, Your majesty I hope will not be angry, if I tell you once more that it is time to rise to morning-prayer, which you never neglect, and the sun is just upon rising. I am mistaken, said Abon Hassan presently: I am not asleep, but awake; for those that sleep do not hear, and I hear very distinctly. Then opening his eyes, he saw plainly by broad day-light, what appeared but uncertain before, and rising upon his breech, with a smiling countenance, like a man overjoyed at a sudden promotion, pleased the caliph, who penetrated into the bottom of his thoughts.

Then the ladies of the palace prostrated themselves with their faces to the ground before Abon Hassan, and those who had the instruments, of music in their hands, wished him a good-morrow, by a concert of soft flutes, hautboys, theorboes,* and other harmonious instruments, with which he was ravished, and was in such an ecstacy, that he knew not himself, nor where he was; but, recovering at last his first idea, he doubted whether what he saw was a dream, or matter of fact. He clapped his hands before his eyes, and lowering his head, said to himself, What means all this, where am I, and whom does this palace belong to? What can these eunuchs, officers, beautiful ladies, and musicians signify? How is it possible for me to distinguish whether I am in my right senses, or in a dream? When he took his hands from his eyes, the sun shone full in at the chamber-window; and at that instant, Mesrour, the chief of the eunuchs, came in, prostrated himself before Abon Hassan, and said, Commander of the Faithful, your majesty will excuse me for representing to you, that you used not to lie so long, and that the time of prayer is over; I am afraid your majesty has had an ill night, and has been indisposed, and may not be able to ascend your throne in council as usual; all your generals, governors, and other officers of state, wait your presence in the council-hall.

At this discourse of Mesrour's, Abon Hassan was verily persuaded that he was neither asleep nor in a dream; but at the same time, was very much embarrassed and confused: At last, looking earnestly at Mesrour, he said to him in a serious tone, Who is it you speak to, and call the Commander of the Faithful? For my part, I do not know you, and you mistake me for somebody else.

Any person but Mesrour would have been dashed at these questions of Abon Hassan's; but he had been so well instructed by the caliph, that he played his part to a wonder. My worthy lord and master, said he, your majesty only speaks thus to try me; is not your majesty the Commander of the Faithful, monarch of the world, and the prophet's vicar on earth? Mesrour, your slave, has not forgot you, after so many years that he has had the honour and happiness to serve and pay his respects to your majesty; and should think himself the most unhappy of all men if he has incurred your displeasure, and begs of you most humbly to remove his fears; but is apt to believe that you have been disturbed by some troublesome dream last night.

Abon Hassan burst out a-laughing at these words of Mesrour's, and fell backwards upon the bolster, which pleased the caliph so much, that he would have laughed as loud himself, if he had not been afraid of putting a stop to the pleasant scene he promised himself.

Abon Hassan, when he had tired himself with laughing, sat up again on his breech, and, speaking to a little black eunuch that stood by him, said, Hark ye, tell me who I am? Sir, answered the little boy modestly, your majesty is the Commander of the Believers, and God's vicar on earth. You are a liar, sooty face, said Abon Hassan. Then he called the lady that stood the nearest to him: Come hither, fair one, said he, holding out his hand, bite the end of my finger, that I may feel whether I am asleep or awake.

The lady, who knew the caliph saw all that passed, was overjoyed to shew how capable she was of diverting him, and went with a grave countenance, and putting his finger between her teeth, she bit so hard that he cried out; and snatching his hand quickly back again, said, I find I am awake, and not asleep. But by what miracle am I become caliph in a night's time? This is certainly the most strange and surprising thing in the world! Then addressing himself to the same lady, he said, I conjure you, for heaven's sake, not to hide the truth from me; am I really the Commander of the Faithful? It is so true, answered the lady, that we, who are your slaves, are amazed to find that you will not believe yourself to be so. Ah! you are a deceiver, replied Abon Hassan; I know very well who I am.

As the chief of the eunuchs perceived that Abon Hassan had a mind to rise, he lent him his hand, and helped him to get out of bed. No sooner were his feet set on the floor, but the chamber rang again with the repeated acclamations of the officers and ladies, who cried out, God preserve your majesty, and give you a good day. O heaven! cried Abon Hassan, what a strange thing is this! Last night I was Abon Hassan, and this morning I am the Commander of the Believers! I cannot comprehend this sudden and surprising change. Presently some of the officers began to dress him; and when they had done, Mesrour led him through all the eunuchs and ladies, who were ranged on both sides quite to the council-chamber door, which was opened by one of the huissirs. Mesrour walked before him to the foot of the throne, where he stopped, and putting one hand under one arm, while another officer did the same by the other, they helped him to ascend the throne.

The caliph, in the mean time, came out of the closet where he was hid, and went into another which looked into the council-hall, from whence he could hear all that passed, and see Abon Hassan, who filled his throne with all the gravity imaginable.

As soon as Abon Hassan had seated himself, the grand visier Giafar prostrated himself at the foot of the throne, and addressing himself to him, said, God shower down blessings on your majesty in this life, receive you into his paradise in the other world, and confound your enemies!

Abon Hassan, after all that had happened that morning, and these words of the grand visier, never doubted but he was caliph, as he wished to be; and so, without examining any farther, how, or by what adventure or sudden change of fortune, he immediately began to exercise his power, and looking very gravely upon the visier, asked him what he had to say? Commander of the Faithful, replied the grand visier, the emirs, visiers, and other officers who are of your majesty's council, wait at the door, until your majesty gives them leave to come in, and pay their usual respects to you. Abon Hassan presently bid that the door be opened, and the grand visier gave the sign to the huissir that waited for it.

When the door was opened, the visiers, emirs, and principal officers of the court, all dressed magnificently in their habits of ceremony, went in their order to the foot of the throne, and paid their respects to Abon Hassan; and bowing their heads down to the carpet, kneeling on one knee, saluted him with the title of Commander of the Faithful, according to the instruction of the grand visier, and afterwards took their seats.

When this ceremony was over, the grand visier, standing before the throne, began with papers in his hand to make his report of affairs, which at that time were of very little consequence. Nevertheless, Abon Hassan acquitted himself in his great post without the least embarrassment; and gave judgment so well in all matters, that the caliph could not help wondering at his address. But before the grand visier had finished his report, Abon Hassan called the judge of the police, whom he knew by sight, as he sat in his place: Hold, said he to the grand visier, I have something to order the judge of the police. The judge of the police perceiving that Abon Hassan looked at him, and hearing his name mentioned, arose from his seat, and went gravely to the foot of the throne, where he prostrated himself with his face to the ground. Judge of the police, said Abon Hassan, go immediately to such a division, and seize the iman of the mosque, and four old men, (whom he described,) and give each of the old men a hundred bastinadoes with a bull's pizzle, and the iman four hundred: After that, mount them all five on camels, with their faces to the tails; and lead them through the whole city, with a crier before them, who shall proclaim, This is the punishment of all those who trouble their heads with other people's affairs, and make it their business to create disturbances and misunderstandings in families in their neighbourhood. My intention is also, that you enjoin them to leave that division, and never to set a foot more in it; and while your lieutenant is conducting them through the town, return, and give me an account of the execution of my orders. The judge of the police laid his hand upon his head, to shew his obedience, and prostrating himself a second time, went away.

The caliph was extremely well pleased at this order; and perceived by Abon Hassan's strictness and expedition, that he was resolved not to lose the opportunity of punishing the iman and the other four old hypocrites. In the mean time, the grand visier went on with his report, and had just done when the judge of the police came back from executing his commission. He went to the throne with the usual ceremony, and said, Commander of the Faithful, I found the iman and his four companions; and for a proof that I have punctually obeyed your commands, I have brought an instrument signed by the principal inhabitants of that division: At the same time, he pulled out a paper, and presented it to the pretended caliph.

Abon Hassan took the paper, and reading over the names of the witnesses, who were all people that he knew very well, said to the judge of the police, It is very well; return to your seat. These old hypocrites, said he to himself, with a great deal of satisfaction in his looks, who must be censuring my actions, and finding fault with my entertaining honest people, deserved this punishment. The caliph all the time penetrated into his thoughts, and conceived a sensible joy in this expedition.

Then Abon Hassan, addressing himself afterwards to the grand visier, said, Go to the high treasurer for a purse of a thousand pieces of gold, and carry it to the mother of Abon Hassan, who is known by the name of The Debauchee; she lives in the same division into which I sent the judge of the police: return immediately.

The grand visier, after laying his hand upon his head, and prostrating himself before the throne, went to the high treasurer, who gave him the money; which he ordered a slave to take, and follow him to Abon Hassan's mother, to whom he gave it, saying only, The caliph makes you this present. She received it with the greatest surprise imaginable, and could not tell what to think of this liberality of the caliph's.

During the grand visier's absence, the judge of the police acted for him, in making the report, which lasted till the visier returned. As soon as he came into the council-chamber, and had assured Abon Hassan he had done as he had bid him, Mesrour, the chief of the eunuchs, who returned to the palace after he had conducted Abon Hassan to the council, came again, and made a sign to the visiers, emirs, and other officers, that the council was done, and that they might all retire; which they all did, by making the same reverence and obedience as when they entered.

Abon Hassan sat not long after them, but came down from the throne, supported in the same manner as he went up to it, by Mesrour and another eunuch, who attended him back again to the apartment from whence he came, preceded all the way by the grand visier: but before he reached the apartment, he was taken with a pressing occasion; upon which they shewed him into a convenient closet, paved with white marble; and while Abon Hassan was there, the grand visier went to acquaint the caliph with what had passed, though he had been an eye-witness all the time.

When Abon Hassan came out of the closet, Mesrour went before him, to shew him the way into an inner apartment, where there was a table spread. Several eunuchs ran before, to tell the musicians that the sham caliph was coming, who immediately began a concert of vocal and instrumental music, with which Abon Hassan was so charmed and transported, that he could not tell what to think at all he saw and heard. If this is a dream, said he, it is a long one: but certainly, continued he, it is no dream; for I can see and feel, walk, hear, and argue reasonably. Whatever it is, I trust in God: yet I cannot believe but I am the Commander of the Faithful; for no other person could live in this splendour. The honour and respect that is given me, and the obedience paid to my commands, are sufficient proofs.

In short, Abon Hassan took it for granted that he was caliph, and the Commander of the Faithful; and was fully convinced of it, when he entered that magnificent and spacious hall, which was finely painted. Seven bands of musicians were placed round the hall, and as many gold branches hung down from the ceiling, which was painted with blue and gold. In the middle of the hall there was spread a table, which was served up with all manner of rarities, in massy gold plates and dishes; and seven young beautiful ladies, dressed in the richest habits, of the most lively colours, stood round this table, each with a fan in her hand, to fan Abon Hassan when at dinner.

If ever mortal was charmed, Abon Hassan was: at every step he took in that stately hall, he could not help stopping to contemplate on all the wonders that regaled his eyes, and turned his head first on one side, and then again on the other, which made the caliph almost split his sides with laughing. At last he went and sat down at the table, and presently all the ladies that stood about it began to fan him. He looked first at one, and then at another, and admired the grace with which they acquitted themselves; and told them, with a smile, that he believed one fan was enough to cool him, and would have six of the ladies sit at table with him, three on his right hand, and three on his left; and as the table was round, which way soever he turned, his eyes might be saluted with agreeable objects.

The six ladies obeyed; and Abon Hassan taking notice, that, out of respect, they did not eat, helped them himself, and invited them to eat, in the most pressing and obliging terms. Afterwards, he asked their names; which they told him were, White Neck, Coral Lips, Fair Face, Sun Shine, Heart's Delight, Sweet Looks, and she who fanned him was Sugar Cane. The many soft things he said upon their names, shewed him to be a man of a sprightly wit, and very much increased the esteem which the caliph (who saw every thing) had for him.

When the ladies saw that Abon Hassan had done eating, one of them said to the eunuch who waited, The Commander of the Faithful will go into the next hall to the desert: bring some water. Upon which they all rose from the table, and taking from the eunuchs, one a gold bason, another an ewer, and a third a towel, kneeled down before Abon Hassan, and presented them to him, to wash his hands; who, as soon as he had done, got up, and after an eunuch had opened the door, went, preceded by Mesrour, who never left him, into another hall, as large as the former, adorned with the best paintings, gold vessels, silk tapestry, and other rich furniture. There seven other bands of music began a new concert, as soon as Abon Hassan appeared. In this hall there were seven gold branches, and a table full of dried sweetmeats, and the most choice and exquisite fruits, raised in pyramids, in seven gold basons, and seven ladies, more beautiful than the others, standing round it, with fans in their hands.

These new objects put Abon Hassan into a greater admiration than ever, who, after he had made a full stop, and given the most sensible marks of his surprise and astonishment, went directly to the table; where, sitting down, he gazed a considerable time at the seven ladies, with an embarrassment that plainly shewed he knew not which to give the preference to. At last he ordered them all to sit and eat with him, telling them that it was not so hot but he could spare them that trouble.

When the ladies were all placed about him, the first thing he did was to ask their names, which were different from the other seven, and expressed some perfection of either mind or body, which distinguished them from one another; and upon which he took an opportunity, when he presented them with fruit, &c. to say somewhat that was handsome. Take this fig, said he to Chain of Hearts, who sat on his right hand, and render the fetters with which you loaded me at first sight more supportable; and so went on to the rest. By these ways, Abon Hassan pleased and diverted the caliph more and more, who was resolved to carry on this scene, which entertained him so agreeably.

After Abon Hassan had tasted of all the fruits, &c. he got up and followed Mesrour into a third hall, much more magnificently furnished than the other two; where he was received by the same number of musicians and ladies, who stood about a table covered over with all manner of sweet-meats. After he had looked about him with new admiration, he advanced to the table, the music playing all the time, which ceased when he sat down. The seven ladies sat down with him, by his order, and helped themselves, as he desired them, to what they liked best; and afterwards he informed himself of their names, which pleased him as much as the others had done.

By this time the day began to close, and Abon Hassan was conducted into the fourth hall, much more stately and magnificently furnished, lighted with wax-candles, in seven gold branches and sconces, which were placed all around it; all which made a glorious light. Abon Hassan found the same number of musicians here as he had done in the other halls, and saw also as many ladies standing round a table, furnished with such things as were proper to promote drinking. There he saw a beaufet,* which he had not observed in any of the other halls, which was set out with seven large silver flaggons full of the choicest wines, and seven crystal glasses by them.

All the day long, Abon Hassan had drunk nothing but water, according to a custom observed at Bagdad, from the highest to the lowest, who never drink wine till the evening, it being accounted the most scandalous thing in the world to be seen drunk in the streets in the day-time.

As soon as Abon Hassan entered the fourth hall, he went directly to the table and sat down, and was a long time in a kind of extacy at the sight of those seven ladies, who were much more beautiful than all he beheld in the other halls. He was very desirous to know all their names; but the music playing then so very loud that he could not hear them speak, he made a sign for them to leave off playing: then taking one of the ladies who sat next to him by the hand, he made her sit down by him, and presenting her with some of those relishing viands before him, asked her name. Commander of the Faithful, said the lady, I am called Cluster of Pearls. No name, replied Abon Hassan, could have more properly expressed your worth; and indeed your teeth exceed the finest pearls. Cluster of Pearls, added he, since that is your name, oblige me with a glass of wine from your fair hand. The lady went presently to the beaufet, and brought him a glass, with a pleasant air. Abon Hassan took the glass with a smile, and looking passionately upon her, said, Cluster of Pearls, your health; I desire you to fill out as much for yourself, and pledge me. Accordingly she went to the beaufet, and returned with a glass in her hand: but before she drank, she sung a song, and by the sweetness of her voice ravished his senses.

After Abon Hassan had drank, he made another lady sit, and presenting her with some of the viands, asked her name, which she told him was Morning Star. Your bright eyes, said he, shine with greater lustre than that star you bear the name of. Do me the pleasure to bring me some wine; which she did, with an extraordinary grace. Then turning to the third lady, whose name was Daylight, he ordered her to do the same; and so on to the seventh, to the extreme satisfaction of the caliph.

When they had all filled him round, Cluster of Pearls went to the beaufet, poured out a glass of wine, and putting in a pinch of the same powder the caliph had used the night before, presented it to Abon Hassan. Commander of the Faithful, said she, I beg of your majesty to take this glass of wine; and before you drink it off, do me the favour to hear a song I have made to-day, and which may not displease you. With all my heart, said Abon Hassan, taking the glass; and, as Commander of the Faithful, I command you to sing it: for I am persuaded that so beautiful a lady as yourself must abound with wit and humour. The lady took a lute, and tuning it to her voice, sung with so much justness and grace, and with such delicate turns of thought and expression, that Abon Hassan was in perfect extacy all the time, and was so much delighted, that he ordered her to sing it again.

When the lady had done, Abon Hassan drank off his glass, and, turning his head towards her, to give her those praises which he thought due to her, fell fast asleep, with his mouth open, gaping, and his eyes close shut, just in the same condition as when the caliph brought him from home; who took a greater satisfaction in this scene, than he could have promised himself. One of the ladies stood ready to catch the glass, which fell out of his hand; and then the caliph, who was all along a spectator of what had passed, came into the hall to them, and ordered Abon Hassan to be dressed again in his own clothes, and to be carried back again to his own house by the same slave that brought him, charging him to lay him on a sofa in the same room, and to leave the door open.

The slave took Abon Hassan upon his shoulders, and carried him home by a back-door of the palace, and returned with speed to acquaint the caliph he had executed his commands. Well, said the caliph, Abon Hassan wished only to be caliph for one day, to punish the iman of the mosque, and the four scheiks, or old men of his division, who had displeased him: I have procured him the means, and he ought to be content.

In the mean time, Abon Hassan, who was laid upon a sofa by the slave, slept very late the next morning. When the powder was worked off, Abon Hassan opened his eyes, and finding himself at home, was in the utmost surprise. Cluster of Pearls! Morning Star! Coral Lips! Fair Face! cried he, calling the ladies of the palace by their names, as he remembered them: Where are you? Come hither.

Abon Hassan called so loud, that his mother, who was in her own apartment, heard, and running to him upon the noise he made, said, What do you mean, son? What is the matter? At these words, Abon Hassan lifted up his head, and looking haughtily at his mother, said, Good woman, who is it you call son? Why, you, answered his mother, very calmly; are not you Abon Hassan, my son? It is a strange thing that you have forgot yourself. I your son, old trull! replied Abon Hassan; thou art mad, and knowest not what thou sayest: I am not Abon Hassan, I tell you, but the Commander of the Faithful.

Hold your tongue, son, answered the mother; one would think you were a fool, to hear you talk thus. You are an old fool yourself, replied Abon Hassan; I tell you once more, I am the Commander of the Faithful, and God's vicar on earth. Ah! child, cried the mother, is it possible that I should hear you utter such words, that shew you are distracted? What evil genius possesses you to make you talk at this rate? God bless you, and preserve you from the power of Satan. You are my son Abon Hassan, and I am your mother.

After she had made use of all the arguments she could think of to bring him to himself, and to shew how great an error he was in, she said, do not you see that the room you are now in is your own, and is not like a chamber fit for the Commander of the Believers? think seriously of what I have said to you, and do not fancy things that are not, nor ever can be.

Abon Hassan heard all these remonstrances of his mother very patiently, holding down his eyes, and clapping his hands before his face, like one who was looking into himself to examine the truth of what he saw and heard. At last, said he to his mother, just as if he was come out of a deep sleep, and with his hands in the same posture, Methinks I am Abon Hassan, you are my mother, and I am in my own room. Then looking about him again, he added, I am Abon Hassan, there is no doubt of it, and I cannot comprehend how this fancy came into my head.

The mother really believed that her son was cured of that disorder of mind, and began to laugh, and ask him questions about his dream; when all on a sudden he started up on his breech, and looking crossly at his mother, said, Old sorceress, thou knowest not what thou sayest. I am not thy son, nor thou my mother, but the Commander of the Faithful, and thou shalt never persuade me to the contrary. For heaven's sake, son, said the mother, let us leave off this discourse, and talk of something else, for fear some misfortune should happen to us. I will tell you what fell out yesterday in our division to the iman of the mosque, and the four scheiks our neighbours: the judge of the police came and seized them, and gave each of them I do not know how many strokes with a bull's pizzle; and afterwards led them through all the streets, with a crier before them, who proclaimed, that that was the punishment of all those who troubled themselves about other folk's business, and set their neighbours at variance; and ordered them never to come into our division again. Abon Hassan's mother could not imagine that her son had any share in this adventure, and therefore turned the discourse this way to put him out of the conceit of being the Commander of the Faithful; but instead of effacing that idea, she rather strengthened it.

Abon Hassan no sooner heard this relation, but he cried out, I am neither thy son, nor Abon Hassan, but certainly the Commander of the Believers; I cannot doubt of it, after what you have told me. Know then, that it was by my order that the iman and the four scheiks were punished; and I tell you, I am certainly the Commander of the Faithful; therefore do not tell me any more of its being a dream. I was not asleep, but as much awake as I am now. You do me a pleasure to confirm what the judge of the police told me he had executed according to my order; and I am overjoyed that the iman and the four scheiks, those great hypocrites, were so chastised, and would be glad to know how I came here. God be praised for all things! I am certainly Commander of the Faithful, and all thy arguments shall not convince me to the contrary.

The mother, who could not divine or imagine why her son supported and maintained himself so strenuously to be caliph, never disputed but that he had lost his senses, when she found he insisted so much upon a thing that was so incredible; and in this thought said, I pray God to have mercy upon you, son! pray do not talk so madly. Beseech God to forgive you, and give you grace to talk more reasonably. What would the world say to hear you rave in this manner? Do not you know, they say walls have ears?

These remonstrances only enraged Abon Hassan the more; and he was so provoked at his mother, that he said, Old woman, I have bid you once already hold your tongue; if you do not, I shall rise and give you cause to repent it all your life-time. I am the caliph, and the Commander of the Believers; and you ought to believe me when I say so.

Then the good woman, perceiving that he was more lunatic than ever, abandoned herself to tears; and beating her face and breast, expressed the utmost grief and astonishment to see her son in that distraction. Abon Hassan, instead of appeasing and being moved by his mother's tears, on the contrary, lost all the respect due from a son to his mother; and getting up hastily, and laying hold of a cane, ran to his mother in great fury, and in a threatening manner said, Tell me presently, wicked woman, who I am. I do not believe, son, replied she, looking at him tenderly, and void of fear, that you are so abandoned by God as not to know your mother, who brought you into the world. Indeed you are my son Abon Hassan; and are very much in the wrong to arrogate to yourself the title of our sovereign lord the caliph Haroun Alraschid, after the noble and generous present that monarch made us yesterday. In short, I forgot to tell you, that the grand visier Giafar came to me yesterday, and putting a purse of a thousand pieces of gold into my hands, bid me pray for the Commander of the Faithful, who made me that present.

At these words, Abon Hassan grew quite mad. The circumstance of the caliph's liberality his mother told him of, persuaded him more than ever that he was caliph, remembering how he had sent the visier. Well, old hag, cried he, will you be convinced when I tell you that I sent you those thousand pieces of gold by my grand visier Giafar, who obeyed my commands, as I was Commander of the Faithful. But instead of believing me, thou endeavourest to distract me by thy contradictions, and maintainest with obstinacy that I am thy son; but thou shalt not go long unpunished. After these words, he was so unnatural, in the height of his frenzy, as to beat her cruelly with his cane.

The poor mother, who could not have thought that her son would have come so soon from words to blows, called out for help so loud, that the neighbours ran in to her assistance. But in the mean time, Abon Hassan, at every stroke, asked her if he was the Commander of the Faithful? To which she always answered tenderly, that he was her son.

By that time the neighbours came in, Abon Hassan's rage began to abate. The first who entered the room got between him and his mother; and taking the cane out of his hand, said to him, What are you doing, Abon Hassan? Have you no fear of God, nor reason? Did ever a son, so well brought up as you, ever dare to strike his mother? Are you not ashamed to treat yours so, who loves you so tenderly? Abon Hassan looked at him that spoke, without returning an answer; and then staring on all that followed him, said, Who is that Abon Hassan you speak of? Is it me you call by that name?

This question put the neighbours a little to the stand. How! said he that spoke first, do not you know your mother, who brought you up, and with whom you have always lived? Be gone; you are impertinent people, replied Abon Hassan; I neither know her nor you, and will not know you; I am not Abon Hassan; but will make you know, to your cost, I am the Commander of the Faithful.

At this discourse, the neighbours no longer doubted but that he was mad; and to prevent his being guilty of the like actions, seized him, notwithstanding his resistance, and bound him hand and foot, while one in the mean time ran for the keeper of the hospital for mad folks, who came presently with a bull's pizzle, chains, and handcuffs, and a great many attendants. When they entered the room, Abon Hassan, who little expected such treatment, endeavoured all he could to unloose himself; but after the keeper had given him two or three smart strokes upon his shoulders with the bull's pizzle, he lay so quiet, that the keeper and his people might do what they would with him; who, as soon as they had bound and manacled him, took him with them to the hospital; where, before the keeper put him into a room, he regaled him with fifty strokes of the bull's pizzle on his shoulders, which he repeated every day without pity for three weeks, bidding him to remember that he was not the commander of the faithful.

Abon Hassan's mother went every day to see her son, and could not forbear crying to see him fall away daily, and to hear him sigh and complain at the hardships he endured. In short, his shoulders, back, and sides, were so black and blue, and bruised, that he could not turn himself. His mother would willingly have talked with him, to comfort him, and to sound him whether he still retained the notion of being caliph; but whenever she opened her mouth, he rebuked her with so much fury, that she was forced to leave him, and return home disconsolate at his obstinacy.

At last those strong and lively ideas which Abon Hassan entertained of being clothed in the caliph's habit, and having used all his authority, and being obeyed very punctually, and treated like the true caliph, and which persuaded him when he awaked that he was so, all began to be insensibly effaced. Sometimes he would say to himself, If I was the caliph, and Commander of the Believers, how came I home dressed in my own apparel? Why should I not have been attended by eunuchs and ladies? Why should my grand visier Giafar, and all those emirs and governors of provinces, who prostrated themselves at my feet, forsake me? Undoubtedly if I had any authority over them, they would have delivered me all this time out of this miserable condition I am in: certainly I ought to look upon all this as a dream. It is true, I commanded the judge of the police to punish the iman, and four old men his companions: I ordered Giafar the grand visier to carry my mother a thousand pieces of gold; and all my commands were executed. All these things are obstacles to my believing it a dream; but yet there are so many things that I cannot comprehend, nor ever shall, that I will put my trust in God, who knows all things.

Abon Hassan was taken up with these thoughts and sentiments, when his mother came to see him; who found him so much altered and changed from what he had been, that she let fall a torrent of tears; in the midst of which she saluted him as she used to do, and he returned her salute, which he had never done before while he had been in the hospital. This civility she looked upon to be a good sign. Well, son, said she, how do you do, and how do you find yourself ? Have you renounced all those whims and fancies which some cursed demon had put into your head? Indeed, mother, replied Abon Hassan, very rationally and calmly, I acknowledge my error, and beg of you to forgive the execrable crime which I have been guilty of towards you, and which I detest. I ask pardon also of my neighbours whom I have abused. I have been deceived by a dream: but by so extraordinary a one, and so like to truth, that any other person, to whom such a thing might have happened, would have been guilty of as great extravagancies; and I am at this instant so much perplexed about it, that I can hardly persuade myself but that it was matter of fact: But whatever it was, I do and will always look upon it as a dream and illusion. I am convinced that I am not that shadow of a caliph and Commander of the Faithful, but Abon Hassan, your son; and shall never forget that fatal day which covered me with shame and confusion; but honour and respect you all my life as I ought.

At these sensible words, the mother of Abon Hassan changed the tears of her sorrow and affliction into those of joy, to find her son so well recovered. My dear child, said she, transported with pleasure, my satisfaction and comfort is inexpressible, to hear you talk so reasonably, and gives me so much joy as if I had brought you into the world a second time. But I must observe one thing in this adventure, which you may not have taken notice of; the stranger that you brought home one night to sup with you, went away without shutting the chamber-door after him, as you desired him; which I believe gave some demon an opportunity to enter, and put you into that horrible illusion you were in: and therefore, my son, you ought to return God thanks for your deliverance, and beseech him to keep you out of the snares of the evil spirit.

You have found out the source of my misfortunes, answered Abon Hassan; it was that very night I had this dream, which turned my brain. I bid the merchant expressly to shut the door after him; and now I find he did not do it. I am persuaded, as well as you, some devil came in, and filled my head full of these fancies. For they at Moussel are not so well convinced that the devil is the cause of troublesome dreams, as we are at Bagdad. But since, mother, you see I am so well recovered, for God's sake get me out of this hellish place. The mother, glad to hear her son so well cured of his foolish imagination of being caliph, went immediately to the keeper, and assuring him that he was very sensible and well, he came and examined him, and afterwards gave him his liberty.

When Abon Hassan came home, he staid within doors some days to comfort himself by better food and nourishment than what he had at the hospital. But when he had recovered his strength, and refreshed himself after his harsh treatment, he began to be weary with spending his evenings alone, and so entered again upon the same way of living as before; which was to provide enough every day to regale a stranger at night.

The day on which Abon Hassan renewed this custom, happened to be the first day of the month, which was the day that the caliph always sets apart to go disguised through the town, to observe what irregularities were committed in the government of the city. Towards the evening he went to the bridge, and sat himself on a bench which was fixed to the parapet; where, looking about him, he perceived the caliph disguised again like a Moussel merchant, and followed by the same slave: and, persuaded that all his misfortunes were owing to the caliph's leaving his door open, whom he took for a merchant, he swooned at the sight of him. God preserve me, said he to himself, if I am not deceived there is the magician again that enchanted me! and thereupon got up, and looked over the parapet into the river, that he might not see him.

The caliph, who had a mind to carry on his joke farther, had taken a great deal of care to inform himself of all that had happened when Abon Hassan waked at home, and conceived a great pleasure at the relation given him, especially at his being sent to a madhouse. But that monarch was both just and generous, and had taken a great liking to Abon Hassan: he designed, after he had carried on this scene, to take him into his palace; and to pursue this project, he had dressed himself again like a merchant of Moussel. He perceived Abon Hassan at the same time that he saw him, and presently guessed by his actions that he was angry with him, and wanted to shun him. This made him walk close to the parapet Abon Hassan leaned over; and when he came nigh him, he put his head over to look him in the face. Ho, brother Abon Hassan, said he, is it you, give me leave to embrace you. Not I, replied Abon Hassan roughly, without looking at the pretended Moussel merchant: I will not embrace you; I have nothing to say to you; go along.

What, answered the caliph, do you not know me? Do you not remember the evening we spent together at your house this day month, where you did me the honour to treat me very generously? No, replied Abon Hassan, I do not know you, nor what you talk about; go, I say again, about your business.

The caliph was not to be dashed with this rude behaviour of Abon Hassan's. He knew very well the law he had imposed on himself, never to have any commerce again with a stranger he had once entertained; and though Abon Hassan had declared so much to him, he pretended to be ignorant of it. I cannot believe, said he, but you must know me again; it is not possible that you should have forgot me in so short a time. Certainly some misfortune has befallen you, which gives you this aversion. However, you ought to remember, that I shew my acknowledgment by my good wishes; and that I have offered you my interest, which is not despicable, in an affair which you had very much at heart.

I do not know, replied Abon Hassan, what your interest may be, and I have no desire to make use of it; but I am sensible the utmost of your wishes were to make me mad. In God's name, I say once more, go your way, and trouble me no more.

Ah! brother Abon Hassan, replied the caliph, embracing him, I do not intend to part with you in this manner, since I have had the good fortune to meet with you a second time; you must exercise the same hospitality towards me again that you shewed me a month ago, when I had the honour to drink with you.

I have protested against it, said Abon Hassan, and have so much power over myself, not to receive such a man as you. You know the proverb, Take up your drum and be gone: Make the application to yourself. God be with you. You have been the cause of my misfortune, and I will not venture myself with you again. My good friend Abon Hassan, said the caliph, embracing him again, I beg of you not to treat me after this injurious manner, but be better persuaded of my friendship. Do me the favour to tell me what has happened to you; for I assure you, I wish you well, and would be glad of an opportunity to make you amends for the trouble I have caused you, if it has been actually my fault. Abon Hassan yielded to the pressing instances of the caliph, and bade him sit down by him. Your incredulity and importunity have tired my patience; and what I am going to tell you, will shew you that I do not accuse you wrongfully.

The caliph sat down by Abon Hassan, while he told him all that happened to him, from his waking in the palace to his waking again in his own house, all as a mere dream, with all the circumstances, which the caliph knew as well as himself, and which renewed his pleasure. He exaggerated afterwards upon the impression that dream of being caliph made upon him, which, he said, threw him into such extravagancies, that he was carried to the mad-house, and used very barbarously. But, said he, what will surprise you, and what you little think of, is, that it was altogether your fault that these things fell out; for, if you remember, I desired you to shut the door after you, which you neglected; and some devil finding it open, put this dream into my head, which, though it was very agreeable, was the cause of the misfortune I complain of; therefore you, for your negligence, are answerable for the horrid and detestable crime I was guilty of, for lifting my hand against my mother, whom I might have killed, and committed parricide, because she said I was her son, and she would not acknowledge me for the Commander of the Faithful: Besides, I blush when I think of it, and that all my neighbours were witnesses of my folly. In short, Abon Hassan complained of his misfortunes with great heat and vehemence, and did not forget the least circumstance; which pleased the caliph to find he had succeeded so well, who could not help bursting out a-laughing at the simplicity wherewith he related them.

Abon Hassan, who thought that his story should rather move compassion, and that every one ought to be as much concerned at it as himself, very much resented the pretended Moussel merchant's laughter. What! said he, do you make a jest of me, to laugh in my face, or do you believe that I do not speak seriously? If you want proofs for what I advance, look and see whether or no I tell you the truth: with that, stooping down, and baring his shoulders, he shewed the caliph the strokes and wheals the bull's pizzle had made.

The caliph could not behold these objects of horror, without pitying poor Abon Hassan, and being sorry for carrying the jest so far. Come, rise, dear brother, said he, hugging Abon Hassan friendly in his arms, let me go and enjoy the happiness of being merry with you to-night; and to-morrow, if it please God, all things will go well.

Abon Hassan, notwithstanding his resolution and oath, could not resist the caliph's caresses. I will consent, said he to the pretended merchant, if you will swear to shut my door after you, that no demon may come in to distract my brain again. The caliph promised that he would; upon which they both got up, and, followed by the caliph's slave, reached Abon Hassan's house by that time it was dark.

As soon as Abon Hassan entered the doors, he called for candles, and desired his guest to sit down upon a sofa, and then placed himself by him. A little time after, supper was brought up, and they both fell to without ceremony: afterwards there came up a small desert of fruit, wine and glasses. Abon Hassan first filled out his glass, and then the caliph's; and after they had drank some time, and talked of indifferent matters, the caliph perceiving that his host grew warm with liquor, began to talk of love, and asked him if he had never been sensible of that passion?

Brother, replied Abon Hassan familiarly, I never looked upon love or marriage but as bondage or slavery, to which I was always unwilling to submit; and must own to you, that I never loved any thing but good cheer and good wine; in short, to divert and entertain myself agreeably with my friends. But yet I do not tell you that I am so indifferent for marriage, or incapable of an inclination, if I could meet with a woman of such beauty, and sweetness of temper, as those I saw in my dream that fatal night I first saw you, and received you into my house, and you, to my misfortune, left my door open, who would pass the whole night with me, drinking, and singing, and playing on some instrument, and who would study to please and divert me: I believe, on the contrary, I should change all my indifference to a perfect attachment to such a person, and I believe should live very happily with her. But where is such a woman to be found, but in the caliph's palace, or in those of the grand visier, or some other great lords of the court, who want no money? I chuse rather to stick close to my bottle, which is a pleasure much cheaper, and which I can enjoy as well as they. In saying these words, he filled out his own and the caliph's glass, and said, Come, take your glass, and let us pursue this charming pleasure.

When they had drunk off their wine, It is a great pity, said the caliph, that so gallant a man as you, who owns himself not insensible of love, should lead so solitary a life. I prefer the easy quiet life I live, replied Abon Hassan, before the company of a wife, whose beauty might not please, and who, besides, might create me a great deal of trouble by her imperfections, and perhaps ill humour. This subject lasted a long time; and the caliph, seeing Abon Hassan had drank up to the pitch he wanted to have him, said, Let me alone; since you have so good a taste, I warrant you I will find you one that shall please you; and then taking Abon Hassan's glass, and putting a pinch of the same powder into it again, filled him up a bumper, and presenting it to him, said, Come, let us drink first the fair lady's health who is to make you happy.

Abon Hassan took the glass laughing, and shaking his head, said, Come, I will drink the lady's health you promised me, though I am very well contented as I am, and do not rely on your promise; but cannot be guilty of so great a piece of incivility, as to disoblige a guest of so much merit, in such a trifling matter. But as soon as he had drank off his liquor, he was seized with as deep a sleep as before; and the caliph ordered the same slave to take him and carry him to the palace, and in the mean time shut the door after him, as he had promised, and followed him.

When they arrived at the palace, the caliph ordered Abon Hassan to be laid on a sofa, in the fourth hall, from whence he was carried home: but first he bid them put him in the same habit which he acted the caliph in. After that, he charged all the eunuchs, officers, ladies, and musicians, who were in the hall when he drank the last glass of wine, to be there by day-break, and to take care to act their parts well; and then went to bed, charging Mesrour to wake him before they went into the hall, that he might hide himself in the closet as before.

Mesrour wakened the caliph at the hour appointed; who immediately rose, and went to the hall, where Abon Hassan was laid fast asleep; and when he had placed himself in his closet, Mesrour and the other officers and ladies placed themselves about the sofa, so that the caliph might see what passed.

Things being thus disposed, and the caliph's powder having had its effect, Abon Hassan began to stir, and the music to play a very agreeable concert. Abon Hassan was in a great surprise to hear that charming harmony; but when he opened his eyes, and saw the ladies and officers about him, and which he thought he knew again, his amazement was as great again. The hall that he was in seemed to be the same he dreamed of; and he observed the same branches, and the same furniture and ornaments.

When the concert was ended, he bit his finger, and cried, loud enough for the caliph to hear him, Alas! I am fallen again into the same dream and illusion that happened to me a month ago, and must expect again the bull's pizzle and mad-house. Almighty God, added he, I commit myself into the hands of thy divine providence. He was a wicked man that I entertained at my house last night, who has been the cause of this illusion, and the miserable hardships I must undergo. The base wretch swore to shut the door after him, and he did not do it; and the devil came in, and filled my head full of this wicked dream of being Commander of the Faithful, and other phantoms, which bewitch my eyes. May thou be confounded, Satan, and crushed under some mountain!

After these words, Abon Hassan closed his eyes, and remained some time thoughtful, and very much perplexed; then opening them again, and looking about him, cried out a second time, Great God! I commit myself into the hands of thy providence; preserve me from the temptation of Satan. Then shutting them again, he said, All that I know is, I will go and sleep till Satan leaves me, and returns as he came; when one of the ladies approached, and sitting down on a sofa by him, said to him, Commander of the Faithful, I beg of your majesty to forgive me for taking the liberty to tell you not to go to sleep; day appears, and it is time to rise. Be gone, Satan! answered Abon Hassan, raising his voice: but looking upon the lady, he said, Is it me you call the Commander of the Faithful? Certainly you take me for somebody else. It is your majesty I give that title, replied the lady, to whom it belongs, as you are sovereign of the world and the mussulmans, and I am your most humble slave. Undoubtedly your majesty, added she, pretends to have forgot yourself, or this is the effect of some troublesome dream; but if you would but open your eyes, the mists which may disturb your imagination will soon be dispelled, and you will find yourself in your own palace, surrounded by your officers and slaves, who all wait your commands: and that your majesty may not be surprised to find yourself in this hall, and not in bed, I beg leave to tell you, that you fell so suddenly asleep last night, that we were unwilling to wake you, to conduct you to your own chamber, but laid you carefully upon this sofa. In short, she urged so many things to him that were so very probable, that at last he sat upon his breech, and knew all the ladies again. Then she who spoke first, assuming the discourse, said, Commander of the Faithful, and the prophet's vicar on earth, be not displeased if I acquaint your majesty once more, that it is time to rise, for day appears.

You are very troublesome and importunate, replied Abon Hassan, rubbing his eyes: I am not the Commander of the Faithful, but Abon Hassan; and you shall not persuade me otherwise. We do not know that Abon Hassan your majesty speaks of, answered the lady; but know you to be the Commander of the Believers.

Abon Hassan looking about, and finding himself in the same hall, attributed all he saw and heard to be such a dream as he had before, and feared very much the dreadful consequences. Heaven have mercy on me! said he, lifting up his hands and eyes, like a man who knew not where he was; after what I have seen, there is no dispute but that devil who came into my chamber possesses me, and fills my imagination full of all these visions.

The caliph, who saw him all the time, and heard these exclamations, almost killed himself with laughing; and had much ado to forbear bursting out into so loud a laughter, but that the false caliph must have heard him.

Afterwards Abon Hassan laid himself down again, and shutting his eyes, the same lady said again, Since your majesty does not rise, after we have, according to our duty, told you it was day, and the dispatch of business requires your presence, we shall use the liberty you give us in such like cases.

Then taking him by one arm, and calling to one of the other ladies to do the same by the other, they lifted him up, and carried him into the middle of the hall, where they set him on his breech, and all taking hands, danced round him while the music played.

Abon Hassan was in an inexpressible perplexity of mind, and said, What! am I indeed caliph, and Commander of the Faithful? and in the uncertainty he was in, would have said something more, but the music was so loud that he could not be heard. At last he made a sign to two of the ladies who were dancing, that he wanted to speak with them; upon which they forbore, and went to him. Do not lie, now, said he, but tell me truly who I am?

Commander of the Faithful, replied one of the ladies, your majesty would either surprise us by asking this question, or else you must have had some very extraordinary dream to-night; which may very well be, considering that your majesty has slept longer to-night than ordinary: however, if you will give me leave, I will refresh your memory with what passed yesterday. Then she told him how he went to the council, punished the iman and the four old men, and sent a present by his grand visier, of a thousand pieces of gold, to the mother of one Abon Hassan: after that, continued she, your majesty dined in the three halls, and, in the fourth, did us the honour to make us sit down by you, to hear our songs, and receive wine from our hands, till your majesty fell so fast asleep, that you never awaked, contrary to custom, before day. All your slaves and officers can confirm what I say; and it is now time you should go to prayers.

Very well, replied Abon Hassan, shaking his head, you would have me believe all this; but I can tell you, you are all fools, or mad; and that is a great pity, for you are very handsome: for I can tell you, that since I saw you, I have been at home, where I used my mother so ill, that they sent me to a mad-house, and kept me three weeks, and beat me every day with a bull's pizzle; and yet you would make me believe all this to be a dream. Commander of the Faithful, answered the lady, we are all ready to swear by what your majesty holds most dear, that all you tell is a dream; for you never stirred out of this hall since yesterday, but slept here all night long.

The confidence with which the lady assured Abon Hassan that all she said was truth, and that he had never been out of the hall since that time, made him not to know what to believe, but bewildered his senses. O heaven! said he to himself, am I Abon Hassan, or the Commander of the Faithful? Almighty God, enlighten my understanding, and inform me of the truth. Then he bared his shoulders, and shewed the ladies the livid wheals. Look, and judge, said he, whether these strokes could come to me in a dream, or when I was asleep. For my part, I can affirm, that they were real blows; for I feel the smart of them yet, and that is a testimonial there is no room to doubt of. Now, if I received these strokes in my sleep, it is the most surprising and extraordinary thing in the world, and what I cannot understand.

In this uncertainty, Abon Hassan called to one of the officers that stood round him: Come hither, said he, and bite the tip of my ear, that I may know whether I am asleep or awake. The officer obeyed him, and bit so hard, that he made him cry out horridly: the music struck up at the same time, and the officers and ladies all began to dance, and skip about Abon Hassan, and made such a noise, that he was in a perfect enthusiasm, and played a thousand merry tricks. He tore off his caliph's habit, threw off his turban, and jumped up in his shirt and drawers, and taking hold of two of the ladies hands, fell a-dancing and singing, and jumping and cutting capers, that the caliph could not contain himself, but burst into so violent a laughter at this sudden pleasantry of Abon Hassan's, that he fell backwards, and made a greater noise than the musicians and all of them together, and lay in that condition for some time. At last he got up again, and putting out his head, cried out, Abon Hassan, Abon Hassan, what! have you a mind to kill me with laughing?

As soon as the caliph's voice was heard, every body was silent, and Abon Hassan among the rest; who, turning his head to see from whence the voice came, knew the caliph and the Moussel merchant, but was not in the least dashed; but, on the contrary, found that he was awake, and all that had happened to him was matter of fact, and not a dream. He entered into the caliph's pleasantry and intentions: Ha! ha! said he, looking at him with a good assurance, you are a merchant of Moussel, and complain that I would kill you, who have been the occasion of my using my mother so ill, and being sent to a mad-house. It was you who treated the iman and the four scheiks in the manner they were used, and not me; I wash my hands of it. It was you who have been the cause of all my disorders: in short, you are the aggressor, and I the injured person.

Indeed you are in the right of it, Abon Hassan, answered the caliph, laughing all the while; but to comfort thee, and make thee amends for all thy troubles, I call heaven to witness, I am ready and willing to make thee what reparation thou pleasest to ask. After these words, he came out of the closet into the hall, and ordered one of his most magnificent habits to be brought, and commanded the ladies to dress Abon Hassan in it; and when they had done so, he said, embracing him, Thou art my brother; ask what thou wilt, and thou shalt have it.

Commander of the Faithful, replied Abon Hassan, I beg of your majesty to do me the favour to tell me what you did to disturb my brain in that manner, and what was your design; for that is a thing of the greatest importance for me to know, that I may perfectly recover my senses.

The caliph promised to give him that satisfaction, and said, First you ought to know, that I often disguise myself, and particularly at night, to observe what irregularities are committed in Bagdad; besides, I set apart the first day of every month to make a tour about it, sometimes on one side, and sometimes on another, but always return by the bridge. That evening that you invited me to supper, I had been taking my rounds: and in our discourse you told me, that the only thing you wished for, was to be caliph for four-and-twenty hours, to punish the iman of your mosque, and his four counsellors. I fancied that this desire of thine would afford me a great deal of diversion, and thought immediately how I might procure thee that satisfaction. I had about me a certain powder, which throws immediately the person that takes it into a sound sleep for such a time. I put a dose of it, without being perceived by thee, into the last glass I presented to thee; upon which you fell fast asleep, and I ordered my slave to carry you to my palace, and came away without shutting the door. I have no occasion to repeat what happened at my palace when you waked: but after you had been regaled all day, one of the slaves, by my order, put another dose of the same powder at night into a glass she gave you; you fell asleep as before, and the same slave carried you home, and left the door open. You told me all that happened to you afterwards. I never imagined that you could have suffered so much as you have done. But as I have a great regard for you, I will make you amends; and that you may have no cause to remember your ill treatment, think of what would please you, and ask me boldly for it.

Commander of the Faithful, replied Abon Hassan, how great soever my tortures may have been, they were all blotted out of my remembrance, as soon as I understood my sovereign lord had any share in them, and doubt not in the least of your majesty's bounty: but as interest had never any sway over me, and I have the liberty to ask a favour, I beg that it may be that of having access to your person, to have the happiness of admiring, all my life-time, your grandeur.

This last proof of Abon Hassan's generosity completed the esteem the caliph had entertained for him. I am mightily pleased with thy request, said the caliph, and grant thee free access to my person at all times, and all hours. In short, he assigned him an apartment in the palace; and in regard to his pension, told him, that he would not have him to have any thing to do with his treasurer, but to come always to him for an order upon him.

Abon Hassan made a low bow, and the caliph left him, to go to council.

Abon Hassan made use of this time to go and inform his mother of his good fortune, and what had happened, which he told her was not a dream; for that he had actually been caliph, and had acted as such, and received all the honours; and that she had no reason to doubt of it, since he had it confirmed by the caliph himself.

It was not long before this new story of Abon Hassan was spread all about Bagdad, and was carried into all the provinces both far and near, and not one single circumstance scarce omitted.

The new favourite Abon Hassan was always with the caliph; for as he was a man of a pleasant temper, and created mirth by all his words and actions, the caliph could not live without him, and often carried him along with him to see his spouse Zobeide, to whom he told his story, and who was mightily pleased with him, and observed that every time he came with the caliph, he had his eyes always fixed upon one of her slaves, called Nouz-hatoul-aonadat, (which is to say, Renewed Pleasure), and resolved to tell the caliph of it. Commander of the Faithful, said that princess one day, you do not observe so well as me, that every time Abon Hassan attends you in your visits to me, he never keeps his eyes off Nouz-hatoul-aonadat, and makes her blush, which is almost a certain sign that she entertains no aversion for him. If you approve of it, we will make a match between them.

Madam, replied the caliph, you put me in mind of a thing which I ought to have done before now. I know Abon Hassan's taste of marriage from himself, and have always promised him a wife that should please him. I am glad you mentioned it; for I know not how I came to forget it. But it is better that Abon Hassan has followed his own inclination, and chose for himself; and if Nouz-hatoul-aonadat is not averse to it, we ought not to hesitate upon their marriage. And since they are both present, let them declare that they give consent.

Abon Hassan threw himself at the caliph's and Zobeide's feet, to shew the sense he had of their bounty; and, rising up, said, I cannot receive a wife from better hands, but dare not hope that Nouz-hatoul-aonadat will give me hers. After these words, he looked upon the princess's slave, who shewed, by her respectful silence, and the sudden blush that rose in her cheeks, that she was disposed to obey the caliph and her mistress Zobeide.

The marriage was solemnized, and the nuptials celebrated in the palace, with great rejoicings, which lasted several days. Zobeide, in respect to the caliph, made her slave considerable presents, and the caliph did the same to Abon Hassan. The bride was conducted to the apartment the caliph had assigned Abon Hassan, who waited for her with all the impatience of a bridegroom, and received her with sounding of trumpets, and all sorts of instruments, which played in concert, and made the air echo again their sweet and harmonious notes.

After these feasts and rejoicings, which lasted several days, the new-married couple were left to pursue their loves peaceably. Abon Hassan and his spouse were charmed with each other, and lived together in perfect union, and seldom were asunder, but when either he paid his respects to the caliph, or she to Zobeide. Indeed Nouz-hatoul-aonadat was endued with all the qualifications capable of gaining Abon Hassan's love and attachment, and was just such a wife as he desired; therefore they could want nothing to render their lives agreeable. They always eat the nicest and choicest rarities in season, and had the best meats tossed up in fricasees and ragouts, &c. by an excellent cook, who took upon him to provide every thing. Their beaufet was always stored with exquisite wines. At dinner they enjoyed themselves in this manner, and afterwards entertained each other with some pleasantry or other: and in the evenings, which they consecrated to mirth, they had generally some slight repast of dried sweet-meats, choice fruits, and other light meats, and invited each other, by songs and catches, to drink, and sometimes played to their voices on a lute, or other instruments which they could touch.

Abon Hassan and Nouz-hatoul-aonadat lived a long time in this manner, when the caterer, who disbursed the money for these expences, put them in mind that he had gone his length, and parted with all his money; which they found, but too late, to be so considerable a sum, that all the presents that the caliph and the princess Zobeide had given them at their marriage, were but just enough to pay him. This made them reflect on what was past, and which at that time they could not remedy. However, they agreed to pay the cook; and sent for him, and paid him all they owed him, without shewing the least trouble.

The caterer went away very well pleased to receive so large a sum of money, though Abon Hassan and his wife were not so over-well satisfied with seeing the bottom of their purse, but remained a long time silent and very much embarrassed, to find themselves reduced to that condition the first year of their marriage. Abon Hassan remembered very well that the caliph, when he took him into the palace, promised never to let him want any thing. But when he considered how prodigal he had been of his money in so short a time, he was unwilling to expose himself to the shame of telling the caliph the ill use he had made of what he had given him, and that he wanted more. Besides, he had made over his patrimony to his mother, as soon as the caliph had received him nigh his person; and was afraid to go to her, lest she should find that he had returned to the same extravagance he had been guilty of after his father's death. His wife, on the other hand, looked upon Zobeide's generosity, and the liberty she had given her to marry, as more than a sufficient recompence for her service, and thought she could not ask any more.

Abon Hassan at last broke silence, and looking upon his wife, said, I see you are in the same embarrassment as myself, and are thinking what we must do in this unhappy juncture. I do not know what your sentiments may be: but mine are, let what will happen, not to retrench our expences in the least; and I believe you will come into my opinion: the point is, how to support them without asking the caliph or Zobeide; and I fancy I have thought on the means; but we must both assist each other.

This discourse of Abon Hassan's very much pleased his wife, and gave her great hopes. I was thinking so as well as you, said she; but durst not explain my thoughts, because I did not know how to help ourselves; and must confess, that what you tell me gives me a great deal of pleasure. But since you say you have found out a way, and my assistance is necessary, you need but to tell me, and I will do all that lies in my power.

I believe, replied Abon Hassan, that you will not fail in this affair, which concerns us both; and therefore I must tell you, this want of money has made me think of a trick we will put upon the caliph and Zobeide, and at which, I am sure, they will both be pleased, and be diverted with the cheat; which is, you and I will both die. Not I indeed, interrupted Nouz-hatoul-aonadat; you may die by yourself, if you will. I am not so weary of this life; and whether you are pleased or not, will not die so soon. If you have nothing else to propose than that, you may do it by yourself; for I shall not meddle with it.

You are so quick and hasty, replied Abon Hassan, that you will not give me time to explain my meaning; have but a little patience, and you shall find that you will be ready enough; for sure you did not think I meant a real death? Well, said his wife, if it is but sham death you design, I am at your service, and you may depend on my zeal; for I must tell you truly, I am very unwilling to die as I apprehended you at first.

Be but easy a little, said Abon Hassan, and I will tell you what I propose. I will feign myself dead, and you shall lay me out on a white sheet, in the middle of my chamber, with my feet towards Mecca,* and my turban upon my face, just ready to be buried. When you have done so, you must cry and take on, as is usual in such cases, and tear your clothes, and with your hair loose about your ears, go to Zobeide. The princess will ask you the cause of your grief; and when you have told her, with words intermixed with sighs, she will pity you, and give you some money to defray the expence of my funeral, and a piece of gold brocade, to cover my body with, that my interment may be the more magnificent, and to make you an habit in the room of that you had tore. And as soon as you return with the money and the brocade, I will get up and lay you in my place, and go and act the same part with the caliph as you have done with Zobeide; and I dare say the caliph will be as generous to me as Zobeide will be to you.

Nouz-hatoul-aonadat liked this project very well, and said to Abon Hassan, Come, lose no time; strip to your shirt and breeches, while I prepare a sheet. Abon Hassan did as his wife bid him, and laid himself all along on his back, with his feet towards Mecca, on the sheet which his wife spread on the carpet, just in the middle of the room. And as soon as he had crossed his arms, his wife wrapped him up, and put a fine piece of muslin and his turban upon his face. After this, she pulled her hair over her face, and with a dismal crying and lamentation, ran across the court of Zobeide's apartment; who, hearing the voice of a person crying very loud, commanded some of her women to see who it was, who returned, and told her that it was Nouz-hatoul-aonadat, who was coming in a deplorable condition.

The princess, impatient to know what had happened to her, rose up immediately, and went to meet her at the door of the anti-chamber. Nouz-hatoul-aonadat played her part excellently well. As soon as she saw Zobeide, she redoubled her cries, tore her hair off by handfuls, beat her face and breast, and threw herself at her feet, bathing them with her tears.

Zobeide, amazed to see her slave in so extraordinary an affliction, asked her, what misfortune had happened to her? But instead of answering, she continued sighing and sobbing; and at last, feigning to strive to check them, said, with words intermixed with sighs, Alas! my most honoured lady and mistress, what greater misfortune could have befallen me than this, which obliges me to throw myself at your highness's feet? May God prolong your days, my most respectable princess, in perfect health, and grant you many happy years. Abon Hassan! poor Abon Hassan! whom you honoured with your esteem, and gave me for an husband, is no more!

Then Nouz-hatoul-aonadat redoubled her tears and sighs, and threw herself again at the princess's feet. Zobeide was extremely surprised at this news. Abon Hassan dead! cried she, that agreeable pleasant man! indeed I did not in the least expect his death so soon; he seemed to promise a long life, and well deserved one. Then she burst out also in tears, as did all her women, who had been often witnesses of Abon Hassan's pleasantries, when the caliph brought him to see the princess Zobeide, and continued a long time bewailing the loss of him. At last Zobeide broke silence, and ordered one of her slaves to go to her treasure, and fetch an hundred pieces of gold, and a piece of rich brocade.

The slave returned soon with a purse and piece of brocade, which, by Zobeide's order, she put into Nouz-hatoul-aonadat's hand; who threw herself again at the princess's feet, and thanked her with a great deal of satisfaction, to think she had succeeded so well. Go, said Zobeide, make use of that brocade to cover the corpse of thy husband, and with that money bury him handsomely, and as he ought to be. Moderate the transports of thy afflictions: I will take care of thee.

As soon as Nouz-hatoul-aonadat got out of the princess's presence, she dried up her tears, and returned with joy to Abon Hassan, to give him an account of her good success. When she came into her own apartment, and saw her husband still stretched out in the middle of the floor, she ran to him laughing, and bid him rise, and see the fruits of his project. Upon which he arose, and rejoiced with his wife at the sight of the purse and brocade, who, for her part, could not contain herself. Come, husband, said she laughing, let me act the dead part, and see if you can manage the caliph as well as I have done Zobeide.

That is the temper of all women, replied Abon Hassan, who, we may well say, have always the vanity to believe they can do things better than men, though, at the same time, what they do is by their advice. It would be odd indeed, if I, who laid this plot myself, could not carry it on likewise. But let us lose no time in idle discourse; lie down in my place, and see if I do not come off with as much applause.

Abon Hassan wrapped up his wife as she had done him; and with his turban undone, and set awry on his head, and like a man in the greatest affliction imaginable, he ran to the caliph, who was holding a private council with the grand visier Giafar, and some other visiers, and he having free access wheresoever he was, went with his handkerchief before his eyes, to hide the feigned tears which trickled down his cheeks, and striking his breast with the other, expressed an extraordinary grief.

The caliph, who was ever used to see Abon Hassan gay and merry, was very much surprised to behold him in that sorrowful state, and asked him the cause of his grief. Commander of the Faithful, answered Abon Hassan, with repeated sighings and sobbings, may God preserve your majesty on the throne, which you fill so gloriously! Alas! Nouz-hatoul-aonadat, whom you in your bounty gave me for a wife, is——At this exclamation, Abon Hassan pretended to have his heart so full that he could not utter one syllable more, but poured forth a flood of tears.

The caliph, who presently understood that Abon Hassan came to tell him of the death of his wife, seemed very much concerned, and said to him, God comfort thee; she was a good slave, and we gave her to thee with an intention to make thee happy: she deserved a longer life. Then the tears ran down his face, that he was obliged to pull out his handkerchief to wipe them off. In short, Abon Hassan dissembled so well, that the caliph, who did not in the least doubt of his sincerity, ordered his treasurer, who was then present, to give Abon Hassan a purse of an hundred pieces of gold, and a piece of brocade. Abon Hassan immediately cast himself at the caliph's feet, and thanked him for his present. Follow the treasurer, said that monarch; throw the brocade over the corpse, and with the money shew the last testimony of thy love for thy wife.

Abon Hassan made no reply to these obliging words of the caliph, but retired with a low bow, and followed the treasurer; and as soon as he had got the purse and piece of brocade, went home, very well pleased with having found out so quick and ready a way of supplying his necessity, which had given him some trouble.

Nouz-hatoul-aonadat, weary with lying so long in that posture, never waited till Abon Hassan bade her rise; but as soon as she heard the door open, got up and ran to her husband, and asked him if he had cheated the caliph as well as she did Zobeide? You see, said he, shewing her the stuff, and shaking the purse, that I can act a sorrowful husband as well as you can an afflicted wife. But for fear this trick of theirs should be attended with some ill consequences, he thought it would not be amiss to instruct his wife with what might happen, that they might act in concert. For, added he, the better we succeed in embarrassing the caliph and Zobeide, the more they will be pleased at last, and perhaps may shew their satisfaction by a greater liberality. And this last consideration induced them to carry on this scene further.

The caliph, though he had a great deal of business to transact in council, was nevertheless so impatient to go and condole with the princess upon the death of her slave, that he rose up as soon as Abon Hassan was gone, and put off the council to another day. Follow me, said he to Mesrour, who always attended him wherever he went, and let us go and share with the princess the grief which the death of her slave Nouz-hatoul-aonadat causes her.

Accordingly, they went to Zobeide's apartment, whom the caliph found set on a sofa, very much afflicted, and all in tears. Madam, said the caliph, going up to her, it is necessary to tell you how much I partake with you in your affliction; since you are not insensible that what gives you pleasure or trouble, has the same effect on me. But we are all mortals, and must surrender up to God that life he gives us, when he requires it. Nouz-hatoul-aonadat, your faithful slave, was endued with qualifications that deserved all your esteem, and I do not disapprove your expressing it after her death; but consider, all your grief will not bring her to life again. Therefore, Madam, if you love me, and would take my advice, be comforted for this loss, and take care of a life which you know is precious to me.

If the princess was charmed with these tender sentiments which the caliph expressed in his compliments, she was much more amazed to hear of Nouz-hatoul-aonadat's death. This news put her into so great a surprise, that she was not able to return an answer for some time. At last, recovering, she said, Commander of the Faithful, I am very sensible of all your tender sentiments; but cannot comprehend the news you tell me of the death of my slave, who is in perfect health. My affliction is for the death of Abon Hassan, her husband, your favourite, whom you was so kind to let me know, who often diverted me very agreeably, and for whom I have as great a value as you yourself. But, sir, the little concern you shew for his death, and your so soon forgetting a man in whom you have often told me you took a great deal of pleasure, amazes and surprises me very much; and this insensibility seems the greater, by your changing his death for that of my slave.

The caliph, who thought that he was perfectly well informed of the death of the slave, and had just reason to believe so, because he had both seen and heard Abon Hassan, fell a-laughing and shrugging up his shoulders, to hear Zobeide talk after this manner. Mesrour, said he, turning himself about to that eunuch, what dost thou think of the princess's discourse? Do not women sometimes lose their senses? for, in short, thou hast heard and seen all as well as myself. Then turning about to Zobeide, Madam, said he, do not shed any more tears for Abon Hassan, for I can assure you he is well; but rather bewail the death of your dear slave. It is not many moments since her husband came all in tears, and the most inexpressible affliction, to tell me of the death of his wife. I gave him a purse of an hundred pieces of gold, and a piece of brocade, to comfort him, and bury her with; and Mesrour here, who was by, can tell you the same.

The princess took this discourse of the caliph to be all a jest, and that he had a mind to impose upon her credulity. Commander of the Faithful, replied she, though you are used to banter, I must tell you this is not a proper time. What I tell you is very serious: I do not talk of my slave's death, but of Abon Hassan her husband's, whose fate I bewail, and so ought you too. Madam, said the caliph, putting on a grave countenance, I tell you, without raillery, that you are deceived; Nouz-hatoul-aonadat is dead, and Abon Hassan is alive, and in perfect health.

Zobeide was very much piqued at this answer of the caliph. Commander of the faithful, replied she smartly, surely you would make me think that you were mad; give me leave to repeat to you once more, that it is Abon Hassan who is dead, and that my slave Nouz-hatoul-aonadat is living; it is not an hour ago since she went from hence; she came here in so disconsolate a state, that the sight of her was enough to have drawn tears from my eyes, if she had not told me her affliction. All my women, who cried with me, can bear me witness, and tell you also, that I made her a present of an hundred pieces of gold, and a piece of brocade; and the grief which you found me in was upon the death of her husband; and just that instant that you came in, I was going to send you a compliment of condolence.

At these words of Zobeide, the caliph cried out, in a fit of laughter, This, madam, is a strange piece of obstinacy; but, continued he seriously, you may depend upon Nouz-hatoul-aonadat's being dead. I tell you not, sir, replied Zobeide instantly; it is Abon Hassan that is dead, and you shall never make me believe otherwise.

Upon this the caliph began to be angry, and set himself upon a sofa, some distance from the princess, and, speaking to Mesrour, said, Go immediately, and see which it is, and bring me word; for though I am certain that it is Nouz-hatoul-aonadat, I would rather take this way, than be any longer obstinately positive. For my part, replied Zobeide, I know very well that I am in the right, and you will find it to be Abon Hassan. And for mine, replied the caliph, I am so sure that it is Nouz-hatoul-aonadat, that I will lay you what wager you will, that Abon Hassan is well.

Do not think to come off there, said Zobeide: I accept of your wager, and I am so well persuaded of his death, that I would willingly lay the dearest thing in the world to me. You know what I have in my disposal, and what I value most; propose the bet, and I will stand to it.

Since it is come to that, said the caliph, I will lay my garden of pleasures against your palace of paintings, though the one is worth much more than the other. It is no matter for that, replied Zobeide; if your garden is more valuable, you have made choice of what you thought fit, and what belonged to me, as an equivalent against what you lay; and I say done to the wager, and will not turn back. The caliph said the same, and both waited until Mesrour returned.

While the caliph and Zobeide were disputing so earnestly, and with so much heat, Abon Hassan, who foresaw their difference, was very attentive to whatever might happen. As soon as he perceived Mesrour through a window, over-against which he sat, talking with his wife, and observed that he was coming directly to their apartment, he presently guessed what he was coming about, and bid his wife make haste to act the dead part once more, as they had agreed on; and, in short, they were so pinched for time, that Abon Hassan had much ado to wrap up his wife, and lay the piece of brocade upon her, before Mesrour came. As soon as he had done that, he opened the door of his apartment, and with a melancholy dejected countenance, and his handkerchief before his eyes, went and sat down at the head of the pretended deceased.

By that time he was seated, Mesrour came into the room. The dismal sight that saluted his eyes gave him a secret joy, on account of the errand the caliph sent him on. As soon as Abon Hassan perceived him, he rose up to meet him, and kissing his hand out of respect, said, sighing and groaning, You see me, sir, in the greatest affliction that ever could befal me; the death of my wife Nouz-hatoul-aonadat, whom you honoured with your favours.

Mesrour, softened by this discourse, could not refuse some tears to the memory of the deceased. He lifted up the pall a little at the head, which was uncovered, and peeping under it, let it down again, and said, with a deep sigh, There is no other god but God; we must all submit to his will, and return to him. Nouz-hatoul-aonadat, my good sister, added he, thy days have been very few: God have mercy on thee. Then turning to Abon Hassan, who was all the time in tears, We may well say, said he, that women sometimes have whims, and lose their senses; for Zobeide will maintain to the caliph that you are dead, and not your wife; and whatever the caliph can say to the contrary, he cannot persuade her otherwise. He called me to witness the truth of what he affirms; for you know I was by when you came and told him the sorrowful news: but all signifies nothing; they are both positive; and the caliph, to convince Zobeide, has sent me to know the truth: but I fear I shall not be believed; for when women once take a thing, they are not to be beat out of it.

God keep the Commander of the Faithful in the right use of his senses, replied Abon Hassan, still sighing and crying: you see how it is, and that I have not imposed upon his majesty; and I wish to heaven, continued he, to dissemble the better, that I had no occasion to tell him the melancholy and afflicting news. Alas! I cannot enough express my irreparable loss. That is true, replied Mesrour; and I can assure you, I have a great share in your affliction; but you must comfort, and not abandon yourself to your grief. I leave you against my will, to return to the caliph; but I beg the favour of you not to bury the corpse until I come again, for I will assist at the interment.

Abon Hassan waited on him to the door, and told him that he did not deserve the honour that he did him; and for fear Mesrour should return to say something else to him, he followed him with his eyes for some time, and then returned to his wife, and unloosed her. This is already, said he, a new scene of mirth; but I fancy it will not be the last; for certainly the princess Zobeide will not believe Mesrour, but laugh at him, since she has too substantial a reason to the contrary; therefore we must expect some new event. Whilst Abon Hassan and Nouz-hatoul-aonadat were talking thus, she had time enough to put on her clothes again; and both went and sat down on a sofa, opposite to the window, where they could see all that passed.

In the mean time, Mesrour reached Zobeide's apartment, and going into her closet laughing, clapped his hands, like one who had something very agreeable to tell.

The caliph, who was naturally impatient, would presently be informed of the truth of the matter; for he was piqued a little at the princess's diffidence: therefore, as soon as he saw Mesrour, Vile slave, said he, is this a time to laugh? Why do you not tell me which is dead, the wife or the husband?

Commander of the Faithful, answered Mesrour, putting on a serious countenance, it is Nouz-hatoul-aonadat who is dead; for the loss of whom Abon Hassan is as much afflicted as when he appeared before your majesty. The caliph, not giving him time to pursue his story, interrupted him, and cried out, laughing heartily, Good news; Zobeide was a moment ago mistress of the palace of paintings, which she staked against my garden of pleasures, since you went, and now it is mine; therefore thou couldst not have done me a greater pleasure: but give me a true account of what thou sawest.

Commander of the faithful, said Mesrour, when I came to Abon Hassan's apartments, I found the door open, and he bewailing the death of his wife Nouz-hatoul-aonadat. He was set at the head of the deceased, who was laid out in the middle of the room, with her feet towards Mecca, and was covered with that piece of brocade which your majesty made a present of to Abon Hassan. After I had expressed the share I had in his grief, I went and lifted up the pall at the head, and knew Nouz-hatoul-aonadat, though her face was very much swelled. I exhorted Abon Hassan the best I could to comfort himself; and when I came away, I told him I would attend at his wife's funeral, and desired him not to stir the corpse till I came. This is all I can tell your majesty. I ask no more, said the caliph, laughing heartily; and I am very well satisfied with thy exactness. Then addressing himself to Zobeide, Well, madam, said he, have you yet any thing to say against so certain a truth? Will you always believe that Nouz-hatoul-aonadat is alive, and that Abon Hassan is dead? And will you not own that you have lost your wager?

How, sir, replied Zobeide, who would not believe one word Mesrour said, do you think that I regard that impertinent slave, who knows not what he says? I am not so blind or mad. With these eyes, I saw Nouz-hatoul-aonadat in the greatest affliction; I spoke to her myself, and she told me that her husband was dead.

Madam, replied Mesrour, I swear to you by your own life, and that of the Commander of the Faithful, which are both dear to me, that Nouz-hatoul-aonadat is dead, and Abon Hassan is living.

Thou art a base despicable slave, said Zobeide, in a rage, and I will confound thee immediately; and thereupon she called her women, by clapping her hands together, who all came in. Come hither, said the princess to them, and speak the truth: Who was that who came and spoke with me a little before the caliph came here? The women all answered, that it was poor afflicted Nouz-hatoul-aonadat. And what, added she, addressing herself to her that was treasurer, did I order you to give her? Madam, answered the treasurer, I gave Nouz-hatoul-aonadat, by your orders, a purse of an hundred pieces of gold, and a piece of brocade, which she carried along with her. Well then, sorry slave, said Zobeide to Mesrour, in a great passion, what hast thou to say to all this? What dost thou think now, that I ought to believe thee, or my treasurer, my other women, or myself?

Mesrour did not want for arguments to contradict the princess; but, as he was afraid of provoking her too much, he chose rather to be silent, though he was satisfied within himself that the wife was dead, and not the husband.

All the time of this dispute between Zobeide and Mesrour, the caliph, who heard what was said on both sides, and was against the princess, because he had seen and spoke to Abon Hassan himself, laughed heartily to see Zobeide so exasperated against Mesrour. Madam, said he to Zobeide, I know not indeed who was the author of that saying, That women sometimes lose their wits; but I am sure you make it good. Mesrour came just now from Abon Hassan's, and tells you that he saw Nouz-hatoul-aonadat lying dead in the middle of the room, Abon Hassan alive, and sitting by her; and yet you will not believe this evidence, which nobody can reasonably refuse: I think it is very strange.

Zobeide would not hear what the caliph represented. Pardon me, Commander of the Faithful, replied she, if I suspect you: I see very well that you have contrived with Mesrour to chagrin me, and try my patience. And as I perceive that this report was concerted between you, I beg leave to send a person to Abon Hassan's, to know whether or no I am in the wrong.

The caliph consented, and the princess charged an old nurse, who had lived a long time with her, with that important commission. Hark ye, nurse, said she, you see the dispute between the caliph and me; therefore go to Abon Hassan's, or rather Nouz-hatoul-aonadat's, for he is dead, and clear up this matter. If thou bringest me good news, a handsome present is thy reward. Make haste, and return quickly.

The caliph was overjoyed to see Zobeide in this embarrassment; but Mesrour, extremely mortified to find the princess so angry with him, did all he could to appease her, insomuch that she and the caliph were both satisfied with him. He was overjoyed when Zobeide sent the nurse; because he was persuaded that the report she would make would agree with his, and would justify him, and restore him to her favour.

In the mean time, Abon Hassan, who watched the window, perceived the nurse at a distance, and guessing that she was sent by Zobeide, called his wife, and told her that the princess's nurse was coming to know the truth; therefore, said he, make haste and lay me out. Accordingly Nouz-hatoul-aonadat did so, and covered him with the piece of brocade Zobeide had given her, and put his turban upon his face. The nurse, eager to acquit herself of her commission, came a good round pace, and entering the room, perceived Nouz-hatoul-aonadat all in tears, her hair dishevelled, and set at the head of her husband, beating her breast, and expressing a violent grief.

The good old nurse went directly to the false widow. My dear Nouz-hatoul-aonadat, said she, with a sorrowful face, I come not to interrupt your grief and tears for a husband who loved you so tenderly. Ah! good mother, replied the counterfeit widow, you see my misfortune, and how unhappy am I by the loss of my beloved Abon Hassan. Abon Hassan, my dear husband! cried she, what have I done that you should leave me so soon? Have I not always rather obeyed your will than my own? Alas! what will become of poor Nouz-hatoul-aonadat?

The nurse was in a great surprise to see every thing quite the reverse of what the chief of the eunuchs had told the caliph. This black-faced Mesrour, said she, lifting up her hands, deserves to be impaled for having made so great a difference between my good mistress and the Commander of the Faithful, by the notorious lie he told them. I will tell you, daughter, said she, the wickedness of that villain Mesrour, who has asserted, with an inconceivable impudence, before my mistress's face, that you were dead, and Abon Hassan was alive.

Alas! my good mother, cried Nouz-hatoul-aonadat, I wish to heaven that it was true! I should not be in this sorrowful state, nor bewail a husband so dear to me. At these words she burst out into tears, and feigned a most desperate trouble.

The nurse was so much concerned for her tears, that she sat down by her, and cried too; then gently lifting up the turban and cloth, looked on the face of the corpse. Ah! poor Abon Hassan, cried she, covering the face again, God have mercy upon thee. Adieu, child, said she to Nouz-hatoul-aonadat; if I could stay longer with you, I would, with all my heart: but I am obliged to return immediately, to free my mistress from the uneasiness that black villain has given her by his impudent lie, assuring her with an oath that you was dead.

As soon as the nurse was gone, and had pulled the door after her, and Nouz-hatoul-aonadat thought she would not come back again, she wiped her eyes, and went and unloosed Abon Hassan, and then both went and sat down on a sofa against the window, expecting what would be the end of this cheat, and to be ready to act according as things should offer.

The nurse, in the mean time, made all the haste she could to Zobeide. The pleasure of carrying the princess good news, and hopes of a good reward, added wings to her feet; and running into the princess's closet, quite out of breath, there gave her a true account of all she had seen. Zobeide hearkened to the old woman's relation with a most sensible pleasure; and when she had done, she said, Repeat it once more before the caliph, who looks upon us all to be fools, and would make us believe we have no sense of religion, nor fear of God; and tell your story to that wicked black slave, who had the insolence to assert a falsity, and which I knew to be one.

Mesrour, who expected the nurse's report would prove favourable on his side, was very much mortified to find it so much the contrary. He was so vexed at the rage Zobeide expressed against him, for a thing he believed to be very true, that he was glad of having an opportunity of speaking his mind freely to the nurse, which he durst not do to the princess. Old toothless, said he to the nurse, thou tellest lies, and there is no truth in what thou sayest; for I saw Nouz-hatoul-aonadat, with these eyes, laid out in the midst of the room.

Thou art a notorious liar thyself, replied the nurse, with an insulting air, to dare to maintain before my face so great a falsity, since I saw Abon Hassan dead, and laid out, and left his wife alive. Thou art an impostor, replied Mesrour, and endeavourest to put us all into confusion.

There is impudence for you, said the nurse, to dare to tell me I lie, in the presence of their majesties, when I saw just now, with my own eyes, what I have had the honour to tell them. Indeed, nurse, answered Mesrour again, you had better hold your tongue, for you certainly doat.

Zobeide, who could not support this want of respect in Mesrour, who, without any regard to her, treated her nurse injuriously, without giving the nurse time to reply to so gross an affront, said to the caliph, Commander of the Faithful, I demand justice for this insolence in our presence; and could say no more, she was so enraged, and burst out into tears.

The caliph, who had heard all this dispute, thought it very intricate, and mused some time, and could not tell what to think of so many contradictions. The princess, for her part, as well as Mesrour, the nurse, and all the women slaves who were present, were as much puzzled, and remained silent. At last, the caliph taking up the cudgels, and addressing himself to Zobeide, said, I see very well we are all liars; myself first, and then you, Mesrour, and your nurse; or at least it seems not one can be believed before the other: therefore, let us go ourselves to know the truth; for I can see no other way to clear up these doubts.

After these words, the caliph got up, the princess followed him, and Mesrour went before, to open the doors. Commander of the Faithful, said he, I am overjoyed that your majesty has taken this course; and much more, when I shall make it plainly appear that the nurse doats, though the expression is displeasing to my good mistress.

The nurse, who wanted not to reply, said, Hold thy tongue, black face; thou doatest thyself.

Zobeide, who was very much provoked at Mesrour, could not bear to hear him attack her nurse again, without taking her part. Vile slave, said she, say what thou wilt, I maintain my nurse is in the right, and look upon thee as a liar. Madam, replied Mesrour, if the nurse is so very certain that Nouz-hatoul-aonadat is alive, and Abon Hassan is dead, I will lay her what she dares of it. The nurse was as ready as he; and, in short, they laid a piece of gold and silver stuff.

The apartment the caliph and Zobeide came out of, though it was a great way from Abon Hassan's, it was nevertheless just over against it, and Abon Hassan could perceive them coming, and told his wife, that the caliph and Zobeide, preceded by Mesrour, and followed by a great number of women, were coming to do them the honour of a visit. At this news she seemed frightened, and cried out, What shall we do? we are ruined! Fear nothing, replied Abon Hassan: What! have you forgot what we agreed on? We will both be dead, and you shall see all will go well. At the slow rate they come, we shall be ready before that time they get to the door. Accordingly Abon Hassan and his wife wrapped up and covered themselves with the piece of brocade, and waited patiently for their visitors.

Mesrour, who came first, opened the door, and the caliph and Zobeide, followed by their attendants, entered the room; but were extremely surprised, and stood motionless, at the dismal sight which saluted their eyes. At last Zobeide breaking silence, said to the caliph, Alas! they are both dead! You have done finely, continued she, looking at the caliph and Mesrour, to endeavour to make me believe that my slave was dead; and I find it true at last: it is dangerous jesting with edge-tools: the grief of losing her husband has certainly killed her. Say rather, madam, answered the caliph, prepossessed to the contrary, that Nouz-hatoul-aonadat died first, and the afflicted Abon Hassan could not survive his dear wife: therefore you ought to agree that you have lost your wager, and your palace of paintings is mine.

Hold there, answered Zobeide, animated with the same spirit of contradiction; I will maintain it, you have lost your garden of pleasures to me. Abon Hassan died first; since my nurse told you, as well as me, that she saw her alive, and crying for the death of her husband.

The dispute of the caliph and Zobeide brought on another between Mesrour and the nurse, who had wagered as well as they; and each pretended to win, and came at last to abuse each other very grossly.

After all, the caliph reflecting on what had passed, began to think that Zobeide had as much reason as himself to maintain that she had won. In the embarrassment he was, of not being able to find out the truth, he advanced towards the two corpses, and sat himself down at the head, searching after something that might gain him the victory over Zobeide. Well, cried he, presently after, I swear by the holy name of God, that I will give a thousand pieces of gold to him that can tell me which of these two died first.

No sooner were these words out of the caliph's mouth, but he heard a voice under Abon Hassan's pall, say, Commander of the Faithful, I died first, give me the thousand pieces of gold. At the same time, he saw Abon Hassan throw off the piece of brocade, and come and prostrate himself at his feet, while his wife did the same to Zobeide, keeping on her pall of brocade, out of decency. The princess at first shrieked out, and frightened all about her; but recovering herself at last, expressed a great joy to see her slave rise again alive. Ah! wicked Nouz-hatoul-aonadat, cried she, what affliction have I been in for thy sake! However, I forgive thee from my heart, and am glad to see thee well.

The caliph, for his part, was not so much surprised when he heard Abon Hassan's voice; but thought he should have died away with laughing at this unravelling of the mystery, and to hear Abon Hassan ask so seriously for the thousand pieces of gold. What, Abon Hassan, said he, hast thou conspired against my life, to kill me a second time with laughing? How came this thought into your head, to surprise Zobeide and me thus, when we least thought on such a trick?

Commander of the Faithful, replied Abon Hassan, I will declare to your majesty the whole truth, without the least reserve. Your majesty knows very well, that I always loved to eat and drink well; and the wife you gave me rather increased than restrained that inclination. With these dispositions, your majesty may easily suppose we might spend a good estate; and, to make short of my story, we were not the least sparing of what your majesty so generously gave us. This morning, accounting with our caterer, who took care to provide every thing for us, and paying what we owed him, we found we had nothing left. Then reflections of what was past, and resolutions to manage better for the future, crowded into our thoughts apace, and after them a thousand projects, all which we refused. At last, the shame of being reduced to so low a condition, and not daring to tell your majesty, made us contrive this trick to relieve our necessities, and to divert your majesty, hoping that you would be pleased to pardon us.

The caliph and Zobeide were very well satisfied with Abon Hassan's sincerity; and then Zobeide, who had all along been very serious, began to laugh, and could not help thinking of Abon Hassan's scheme; when the caliph, who had laughed his sides sore at the singularity of this adventure, rising up, said, Follow me both of you, and I will give you the thousand pieces of gold I promised you. Zobeide desired him to let her make her slave a present of that sum. By this means, Abon Hassan and his dear wife Nouz-hatoul-aonadat preserved the favour of the caliph Haroun Alraschid and the princess Zobeide; and by their liberalities were made capable of pursuing their pleasures.

The Story of Aladdin; or, the Wonderful Lamp

In the capital of one of the largest and richest provinces of the kingdom of China, there lived a taylor, whose name was Mustapha, who had no other distinction but that which his profession afforded him; and so poor, that he could hardly subsist himself and family, which consisted of a wife and son, by his daily labour.

His son, whom he called Aladdin, had been brought up after a very careless and idle manner, and by that means had contracted many vicious habits. He was wicked, obstinate, and disobedient to his father and mother, who, when he grew up, could not keep him within doors; but he would go out early in the morning, and stay out all day, playing in the streets and public places with blackguard boys, and such little vagabonds as himself.

When he was old enough to serve as an apprentice, his father not being able to put him out to any other trade, took him into his own shop, and shewed him how to use his needle: but neither good words, nor the fear of chastisement, were capable of fixing his mercurial genius. All that his father could do to keep him at home, and mind his work, was in vain; for no sooner was Mustapha's back turned, but Aladdin was gone for that day. Mustapha chastised him; but Aladdin was incorrigible; and his father, to his great grief, was forced to abandon him to his libertinism; and was so much troubled that he could not reclaim his son, that it threw him into a fit of sickness, of which he died in a few months after.

The mother finding that her son would not follow his father's trade, shut up the shop, and sold off the utensils of that trade, and with the money she got for them, and with what she could get by spinning cotton, thought to subsist herself and her son.

Aladdin, who was now no longer restrained by the fear of a father, and who cared so little for his mother, that whenever she chided him, he would fly in her face, gave himself entirely over to his folly, and was never out of the streets from his companions. This trade he drove till he was almost fifteen years old, without thinking in the least how to get his bread; when one day as he was playing, according to custom, in the streets, with his blackguard troop, a stranger passed by, who stood still to observe him.

The stranger was a famous magician, called by the author who writ his life, The African magician; and by that name I shall call him, since he was a native of Africa, and had been come but two days from thence.

Whether or no the African magician, who was a good physiognomist, had observed something in Aladdin's countenance, which was absolutely necessary for the execution of his design he came about, I cannot tell; but he informed himself who he was, and what were his inclinations; and when he had learned what he desired to know, he went up to him, and taking him aside from his comrades, said to him, Child, was not your father called Mustapha the taylor? Yes, answered Aladdin; but he has been dead a long time ago.

At these words, the African magician threw his arms about Aladdin's neck, and kissed him several times, with tears in his eyes. Aladdin, who observed his tears, asked him, what made him cry? Alas! my son, cried the African magician, with a sigh, how can I forbear? I am your uncle; your good father was my own brother: I have been a great many years abroad travelling, and now I am come home, big with the hopes of seeing him, you tell me he is dead! I assure you it is a sensible grief to me, to be deprived of the joy and comfort I expected. But it is some relief to my affliction, that as much as I can remember of him, I knew you at first sight, you are so like him; and I am not deceived. Then he asked Aladdin, putting his hand into his purse, where his mother lived? and as soon as Aladdin had informed him, he gave him a handful of small money, saying to him, Go, my brave boy, to your mother, and give my love and service to her; and tell her that I will come and see her to-morrow, if I have time, that I may have the satisfaction of seeing where my brother lived so long, and ended his days.

As soon as the African magician left his new-adopted nephew, Aladdin ran to his mother, overjoyed at the money his uncle had given him. Mother, said he, have I ever an uncle? No, child, replied his mother, you have no uncle, neither by your father's side nor mine. It is no matter for that, answered Aladdin; I am just now come from a gentleman, who says he is my uncle by my father's side, assuring me that he is his brother. He cried, and kissed me, when I told him my father was dead; and to shew you what I tell you is truth, added he, pulling out the money, see here what he has given me: he charged me to give his service to you, and to tell you, if he has any time to-morrow, he will come and pay you a visit, that he may see, at the same time, the house my father lived and died in. Indeed, child, replied the mother, your father had a brother; but he has been dead a long time, and I never heard of another.

The mother and son talked no more then of the African magician; but the next day Aladdin's uncle found him playing in the streets again among his companions, and embracing him as before, put two pieces of gold into his hand, and said to him, Carry this, child, to your mother, and tell her that I will come and sup with her to-night, and bid her get something for us to eat; but first shew me the house where you live.

After Aladdin had shewn the African magician the house, he carried the two pieces of gold to his mother; and when he had told her his uncle's intentions, she went out and bought provisions; and considering she wanted dishes and plates, and other conveniencies to dress the meat with, she went and borrowed them of her neighbours. She spent the whole day in this sort of work, and dressing the supper; and at night, when it was ready, she said to Aladdin, Perhaps your uncle knows not how to find our house; go and see for him, and bring him if you meet with him.

Though Aladdin had shewed the magician the house, he was very ready to go, when his uncle knocked at the door, which Aladdin immediately opened; and the magician came in, loaded with wine, and all sorts of fruits, which he brought for a desert.

After that the African magician had given what he brought into Aladdin's hand, he saluted his mother, and desired her to shew him the place of the sofa where his brother Mustapha used to sit; and when she had so done, he presently fell down and kissed it several times, crying out, with tears in his eyes, My poor brother! how unhappy am I, not to come soon enough to give him the last embrace! Aladdin's mother desired him to sit down in the same place; but he would not. No, said he, I shall take care how I do that; but give me leave to sit over-against it, that if I am deprived of the satisfaction of seeing the master of the family which is so dear to me, I may at least have the pleasure of seeing the place where he used to sit. Aladdin's mother pressed him no farther, but left him at his liberty to sit where he pleased.

When the magician had made choice of a place, he began to enter into discourse with Aladdin's mother. My good sister, said he, do not be surprised at your never having seen me all the time you have been married to my brother Mustapha. I have been forty years absent from this country, which is my native place, as well as my brother's; and during that time have travelled into the Indies, Persia, Arabia, Syria, and Egypt; and have resided in most of the finest towns of those countries; and afterwards crossed over into Africa, where I made a long abode. At last, as it is natural for a man, how distant soever it may be, to remember his native country, relations, and acquaintance, I was very desirous to see mine again, and to embrace my dear brother; and finding I had strength and courage enough to undertake so long a journey, I immediately made all necessary preparations for it, and so set forward. I will not tell you the length of time, all the obstacles I met with, and what fatigues I have endured, to come hither; but only, that nothing ever mortified or afflicted me so much as the hearing of my brother's death, for whom I always had a brotherly love and friendship. I observed his features in the face of my nephew your son, and distinguished him from among a number of children with whom he was at play; and he can tell you how I received the most melancholy news that ever reached my ears. But

God be praised for all things! it is a comfort to me to find him again in a son, who has his most remarkable features.

The African magician perceiving that Aladdin's mother began to weep at the remembrance of her husband, changed the discourse, and turning towards Aladdin, asked him his name. I am called Aladdin, said he. Well, Aladdin, replied the magician, what business do you follow? Are you any trade?

At this question Aladdin was a little dashed, when his mother made answer, Aladdin is an idle fellow; his father, when alive, strove all he could to learn him his trade, but could not do it; and since his death, notwithstanding all I can say to him, he does nothing but idle away his time in the streets, as you saw him, without considering he is no longer now a child; and if you do not make him ashamed of it, and leave it off, I despair of his ever coming to any good. He knows that his father left him no fortune, and sees me endeavour to get my bread by spinning cotton every day: for my part, I am resolved one of these days to turn him out of doors, and let him provide for himself.

After these words, Aladdin's mother burst out into tears; and the magician said, This is not well, nephew; you must think of helping yourself, and getting your livelihood. There are a great many sorts of trades; consider which you have the greatest inclination to; perhaps you did not like your father's trade: Come, do not disguise your sentiments from me: I will endeavour to help you. But finding that Aladdin returned no answer; If you have no mind, continued he, to learn any trade, and prove an honest man, I will take a shop for you, and furnish it with all sorts of fine stuffs and linens, and set you to trade with them; but you must be sure, with the money you take, to buy in fresh goods, and then you will live after an honourable way. Consult your own inclination, and tell me freely what you think of it: You shall always find me ready to keep my word.

This proposal very much flattered Aladdin, who hated working mortally, and had sense enough to know that such sort of shops were very much esteemed and frequented, and the owners very much honoured and respected. He told the magician he had a greater inclination to that business than to any other, and that he should be ever very much obliged to him. Since this profession is agreeable to you, said the African magician, I will carry you along with me to-morrow, and clothe you as richly and handsomely as the top merchants of the city, and after that, we will think of taking a shop.

Aladdin's mother, who never till then could believe that the magician was her husband's brother, thanked him for his good intentions; and after having exhorted Aladdin to render himself worthy of his uncle's favour, by his good behaviour, served up supper, at which they talked of several indifferent matters; and then the magician, who saw that the night was pretty far advanced, took his leave of the mother and son, and retired.

He came again the next day, as he promised, and took Aladdin along with him to a great merchant, who sold all sorts of habits ready made, and all sorts of fine stuffs, and bid Aladdin chuse those he liked best. Aladdin, charmed with the liberality of his new uncle, made choice of one; and the magician immediately bought it, and all things proper to it.

When Aladdin found himself so handsomely equipped, from top to toe, he returned his uncle all the thanks imaginable; who, on the other hand, promised never to forsake him, but always to take him along with him; which he did, to the most resorted places in the city, and particularly where the most topping merchants kept their shops. When he brought him into the street where they sold the richest stuffs and finest linens, he said to Aladdin, As you are soon to be a merchant as well as these here, it is proper you should frequent these shops, and be acquainted with them. Then he shewed him the largest and finest mosques, and carried him to the khans or inns, where the merchants and travellers lodge, and afterwards to the sultan's palace, where he had free access, and at last brought him to his own khan, where, meeting with some merchants he had got acquainted with since his arrival, he gave them a treat, to bring them and his pretended nephew acquainted.

This lasted till night, when Aladdin would have taken his leave of his uncle to go home: but the magician would not let him go by himself, but conducted him safe to his mother; who, as soon as she saw him so finely dressed, was transported with joy, and bestowed a thousand blessings upon the magician, for being at so great an expence upon her child. Generous relation, said she, I know not how to thank you for your liberality: I know that my son is not deserving of your favours; and was he never so grateful, and answered your good intentions, he would be unworthy of them. For my part, added she, I thank you with all my soul, and wish you may live long enough to be a witness of my son's gratitude, which he cannot better shew, than by regulating his conduct by your advice.

Aladdin, replied the magician, is a good boy, and minds me well enough, and I believe we shall do very well; but I am sorry for one thing, which is, that I cannot perform to-morrow what I promised, because it is Friday, and the shops will be shut up,* and therefore we cannot hire one, but must let it alone till Saturday. But I will call on him to-morrow, and take him a-walking in the gardens, where people of the best fashion generally walk. Perhaps he has never seen these diversions; he has only hitherto been among children; but now he must see men. Then the African magician took his leave of the mother and son, and retired. Nevertheless, Aladdin, who was overjoyed to be so well clothed, conceived a great deal of pleasure beforehand to walk in the gardens which lay about the town, and were very beautiful, and where he had never been in his life.

Aladdin rose early next morning, and dressed himself, to be ready against his uncle called on him; and after he had waited some time, he began to be impatient, and stood watching for him at the door; but as soon as he perceived him coming, he told his mother, took leave of her, and ran to meet him.

The magician caressed Aladdin when he came to him. Come along, my brave boy, said he, and I will shew you fine things. Then he led him out at one of the gates of the city, to some large fine houses, or rather palaces, to each of which belonged beautiful gardens, into which any body might go; and at every house he came to he asked Aladdin if he did not think it fine; and Aladdin was ready to answer according to his opinion. By this artifice, the cunning magician got Aladdin a pretty way into the country, and as he had a mind to carry him farther, to execute a design he had, he took an opportunity to sit down in one of the gardens by a fountain of clear water, pretending to be tired, the better to rest Aladdin. Come, nephew, said he, you must be weary as well as me; let us refresh ourselves, and we shall better be able to walk.

After they had sat down, the magician pulled out a handkerchief of cakes and sweetmeats, which he had provided on purpose, and laid it between them. Afterwards he broke a cake in two, and gave one half to Aladdin, and eat the other himself; and in regard to the sweetmeats, he left him at his liberty to take which sort he liked best; and during this short repast, he exhorted his nephew to break himself off his childish plays, and endeavour to keep men company and improve by their conversation; for, said he, you will soon be at man's estate, and must use yourself betimes to discourse gravely. When they had eat as much as they had a mind to, they got up, and pursued their walk through the gardens, which were only separated from one another by small ditches, which only marked out the limits, but never hindered the communication; so great was the confidence the inhabitants reposed in each other. By this means the African magician drew Aladdin insensibly beyond the gardens, and crossed the country, till they almost came to the mountains.

Then Aladdin, who had never been so far in his life before, began to find himself much tired with so long a walk, and said to the magician, Where are we going, uncle? We have left the gardens a great way behind us, and I see nothing but the mountains; if we go much farther, I do not know whether or no I shall be able to reach the town again? Never fear, nephew, said the false uncle; I will shew you a garden which surpasses all we have yet seen: it is not far off; it is but a little step; and when we come there, you will say that you would have been sorry to have been so nigh it, and not seen it. Aladdin was soon persuaded; and the magician, to make the way seem shorter, told him a great many stories.

At last they came between two mountains of a moderate height and equal size, divided by a little valley, which was the place where the magician intended to bring Aladdin, to put into execution a design that had brought him from Africa. We will go no farther now, said he to Aladdin; I will shew you here some things very extraordinary, and what nobody ever saw before; which, when you have seen them, you will thank me for: but while I strike fire, do you gather up all the loose dry sticks you can see, to light a fire with.

Aladdin found there so many dried sticks, that before the magician had lighted a match, he had gathered up a great heap. The magician presently set them on fire, and in a moment they were all in a blaze. The magician threw a perfume which he had about him into it, which raised a great cloud of smoke; then turning himself about, he pronounced several magical words, which Aladdin did not understand.

At the same time the earth trembled a little, and opened just before the magician and Aladdin, and discovered a stone about half a yard square, with a brass ring fixed into the middle of it to raise it up by. Aladdin was so frightened at what he saw, that he would have run away; but, as he was to be serviceable to the magician, he catched hold of him, and gave him such a blow upon the cheek, that he knocked him down, and had like to have beat his teeth down his throat. Poor Aladdin got up again trembling, and with tears in his eyes said to the magician, What have I done, uncle, to be treated after this severe manner? I have my reasons for it, replied the magician: I am your uncle, and supply the place of your father, and you ought to make no reply. But, child, added he, sweetening him, do not be afraid of any thing; for I shall not ask any thing of you, but that you may obey me punctually, if you would reap the advantages which I intended you should. These fair promises calmed Aladdin's fears and resentment; and when the magician saw that he was a little come to himself, he said to him, You see what I have done by the virtue of my perfume, and the words I pronounced. Know then, that under this stone there is hid a treasure, which is destined to be yours, and which will make you richer than the greatest monarchs in the world; therefore no other person but yourself is permitted to touch this stone, and pull it up, and go in: For I am forbid setting a foot into this treasure when it is opened; so you must without fail punctually execute what I tell you, for it is a matter of great consequence both to you and me.

Aladdin, amazed at all he saw and heard the magician say of the treasure which was to make him happy for ever, forgot what was past, and said to the magician, Well, uncle, what is to be done? command me; I am ready to obey you. I am overjoyed, child, said the African magician, embracing him, to see you act so prudently; here, take hold of the ring, and lift up that stone. Indeed, uncle, replied Aladdin, I am not strong enough to lift it; you must help me. You have no occasion for my assistance, answered the magician; if I help you, we shall be able to do nothing; you must lift it up yourself; take hold of the ring, and only pronounce the names of your father and grandfather, and lift it up, and you will find it will come easily. Aladdin did as the magician bade him, and raised the stone with a great deal of ease, and laid it by.

When the stone was pulled up, there appeared a cave of about three or four feet deep, and steps to go down lower. Observe, Aladdin, said the African magician, what I am going to say to you. Go down into that cave; and when you are at the bottom of those steps, you will find a door open, which will lead you into a large vaulted palace, divided into three great halls, in each of which you will see four large brass vessels placed on each side, full of gold and silver; but take care you do not meddle with them. Before you go into the first hall, be sure to tuck up your gown, and wrap it well about you; and then go through the second into the third, without stopping in the least. Above all things, have a care that you do not touch the walls, so much as with your clothes; for if you do, you die immediately. At the end of the third hall, you will find a door, which leads into a garden planted with fine trees, loaded with delicate fruit: walk directly across that garden, by a path which will carry you to five steps that will bring you upon a terrace-walk,* where you will see a niche before you, and in that niche a lighted lamp. Take the lamp down, and put it out; and when you have thrown away the wick, and poured out the liquor, put it in your breast, and bring it to me. Do not be afraid that the liquor will spoil your clothes, for it is not oil; and the lamp will dry as soon as it is thrown out. If you have a mind to any of the fruit of the garden, you may gather as much as you please.

After these words, the magician pulled a ring off his finger, and put it upon one of Aladdin's, telling him, that it was a preservative against all misfortunes, while he observed what was prescribed to him. After this instruction, he said, Go boldly, child, and we shall both be rich all our lives.

Aladdin jumped into the cave, went down the steps, and found the three halls just as the African magician had described them. He went through them with as much precaution as the fear of death could give him, and observed all that he was told very carefully; and, without stopping, crossed the garden, took down the lamp, threw out the wick and liquor, and put it in his bosom, as his uncle bid him. But as he came down from the terrace again, he stopped in the garden to observe the fruit, which he only had a glimpse of in crossing it. All the trees were loaded with extraordinary fine fruit, of different colours. Some trees bore fruit entirely white, and some clear and transparent as crystal; some pale red, and others deep; some green, blue, and purple, and others yellow: in short, there was fruit of all colours. The white were pearls; the clear and transparent, diamonds; the deepest red, rubies; the paler, bastard rubies;* the green, emeralds; the blue, turquoises; the purple, amethysts; and those that were upon the yellow cast, sapphires, &c. All these fruits were very large, and so beautiful, that nothing ever was seen like them. Aladdin was altogether ignorant of their value, and would have preferred figs and raisins before them: and though he took them only for coloured glass, yet he was so pleased with the variety of the colours, and the beauty and extraordinary size of the fruit, that he had a mind to gather some of every sort; and accordingly filled his two pockets, and the two new purses his uncle had bought him with his clothes, and fastened them to his girdle: some he wrapped up in the skirts of his gown, and crammed his breast as full as it could hold.

Aladdin, having thus loaded himself with riches he knew not the value of, returned through the three halls with the same precaution, and made all the haste he could, that he might not make his uncle wait, and soon arrived at the mouth of the cave, where the African magician expected him with the utmost impatience. As soon as Aladdin saw him, he cried out, Pray, uncle, lend me your hand, to help me up. Give me the lamp first, replied the magician; it will be troublesome to you. Indeed, uncle, answered Aladdin, I cannot now; it is not troublesome to me; but I will as soon as I am up. The African magician, provoked at this obstinate refusal of the lad, grew into a terrible passion, and threw a little of his perfume into the fire, which he had taken care to keep in; and no sooner pronounced two magical words, but the stone moved into its place, and the earth closed again, in the same manner as it had opened at the arrival of the magician and Aladdin.

This action of the African magician plainly shewed him to be neither Aladdin's uncle, nor Mustapha the taylor's brother, but a true African, as he was; for, as Africa is a country that delights the most in magic of any place in the whole world, he had applied himself to it from his youth; and after forty years experience in enchantments, works of geomancy, fumigations, and the reading of magic books, he had found out, that the possession of a wonderful lamp that there was in the world, would render him more powerful than the greatest prince in the world; and by a late operation which he made, he found out, that this lamp lay concealed in a subterraneous abode in the midst of China, which I have already described, with the circumstances attending it. Fully persuaded of the truth of this discovery, he set out from the farthest parts of Africa, and after a long and fatiguing journey came to the nearest town to this treasure. But though he had a certain knowledge of the place where the lamp was, yet he was not permitted to take it himself, nor to enter the subterraneous place where it was, but must receive it from the hands of another person. For this reason, he addressed himself to Aladdin, whom he looked upon as a young lad void of friends, and fit to serve his purpose; resolving, as soon as he got the lamp into his hands, to sacrifice poor Aladdin to his avarice and wickedness, by making the fumigation I mentioned before, and saying those two magical words, the effect of which was the removing the stone into its place again. The blow he gave Aladdin, and the authority he took upon him, was to use him to fear him, and to make him obey him the more readily, and that he should give him the lamp as soon as he asked for it. But his too great precipitation in executing his wicked intention on poor Aladdin, and his fear lest somebody should come that way during their dispute, made it fall out just the contrary of what he proposed to himself.

When the African magician saw that all his great hopes were frustrated for ever, he returned that same day for Africa; but went quite round the town, at the same distance from it, for fear lest some persons who had seen him walk out with the boy, should entertain any jealousy of him, and stop him.

According to all appearances, there was no expectations of hearing any more of Aladdin: but the magician, when he thought of Aladdin's death, had forgot that ring he gave him, which preserved him, though he knew not its virtue. And it is amazing to me, that the loss of that, together with the lamp, did not put the magician into the utmost despair: but magicians are used so much to misfortunes, and things falling out contrary to their desires, that they do not so much lay them to heart, but still feed themselves up with some new notions and chimeras.

As for Aladdin, who never in the least suspected this base usage from his pretended uncle, after all his caresses, and what he had done for him, his surprise is more easy to be imagined than expressed by words. As soon as he found he was so buried alive, he cried and called out to his uncle, to tell him he was ready to give him the lamp; but all in vain, since his cries could not be heard by him, and he must remain in this dark abode. At last, when he had quite tired himself with crying, he went to the bottom of the steps, with a design to get into the garden, where it was light; but the door, which was opened before by enchantment, was now shut. Then he redoubled his tears and lamentations, and sat down on the steps, without any hopes of ever seeing the light again, and in the expectation of a lingering death.

Aladdin remained in this state two days, without either eating or drinking, and on the third looked upon death as inevitable. Then clasping his hands with an entire resignation to the will of God, he said, The great and high God alone is all powerful. In this action of joining his hands, he rubbed the ring which the magician gave him, and which he had never thought of, nor knew not the use of; and immediately a genie, of an enormous size and frightful look, rose out of the earth, and said to him, What wouldst thou have with me? I am ready to obey thee as thy slave, and the slave of all who possess the ring on thy finger; I and the other slaves of that ring.

At another time, Aladdin, who had not been used to such visions, would have been so frightened, that he would not have been able to speak, at the sight of so extraordinary a figure; but the danger he was in made him answer without hesitation, Whoever thou art, deliver me from this place, if thou art able. He had no sooner made an end of these words, but the earth opened, and he found himself where the magician made his conjuration.

It was some time before Aladdin's eyes could bear the light, after having been so long in entire darkness: but after he had endeavoured by degrees to support it, and began to look about him, he was very much surprised not to find the earth open, and could not comprehend how he had got so soon from within its bowels. There was nothing to be seen but the place where the fire had been, by which he could judge pretty nigh whereabouts the cave was. Then turning himself about towards the town, he perceived it in the midst of fine gardens, and knew the way back to it; and then returning God thanks for his being alive, so contrary to his expectations, made the best of his way home. When he got within the doors, what with the joy to see his mother, and faintness for want of sustenance for three days, he fell into a swoon, and remained in it for a long time. His mother, who had given him over for dead, or lost, seeing him in this condition, omitted nothing to bring him to himself again. As soon as he recovered, the first words he spoke were, Pray, mother, give me something to eat, for I have not put a morsel of any thing in my mouth these three days. His mother brought what she had, and set it before him. My dear child, said she, do not be too eager, for it is dangerous; eat but a little at a time, and take care of yourself. Besides, I would not have you talk; you will have time enough to tell me what has happened to you when you are better recovered. It is a great comfort to me to see you again, after the grief I have been in since Friday, and the pains I have taken to learn what was become of you.

Aladdin took his mother's advice, and eat and drank but very moderately. When he had done, he said to her, I cannot help complaining of you for abandoning me so easily to the discretion of a man whose design was to kill me, and who at this very moment thinks my death certain. You believed he was my uncle, as well as I; and what other thoughts could we entertain of a man who was so kind to me, and made such advantageous proffers? But I must tell you, mother, he is a rogue and a cheat, and only did what he did, and made me all those promises, to accomplish my death; but for what reason, neither you nor I can guess. For my part, I can assure you, I never gave him any cause to deserve the least ill treatment from him. You shall judge of it yourself, when you have heard all that passed from the time I left you till he came to the execution of his wicked design.

Then Aladdin began to tell his mother all that had happened from the Friday, when the magician took him to see the palaces and gardens about the town, and what fell out in the way, till they came to the place where the great prodigy was to be performed; how, with a perfume which the magician threw into the fire, and some magical words, the earth opened, and discovered a cave, which led to an inestimable treasure. Among other things, he was sure to remember the blow the magician gave him; and then told her after what manner he sweetened him again, and engaged him by great promises, and putting a ring on his finger, to go down into the cave.

In short, he did not omit the least circumstance of what he saw in crossing the three halls, and the garden, and his taking the lamp, which he pulled out of his bosom, and shewed it to his mother, as well as the beautiful fruit which he had gathered in the garden, which she, who was as ignorant as her son as to the knowledge of jewels, looked upon as trifles, which were pretty enough to look at for the variety of the colours; notwithstanding, with the reflection of a lamp which was then burning, the room was as light as if the sun shone.

Aladdin put them underneath one of the cushions of the sofa he sat upon, and pursued his story; telling his mother, that when he returned and presented himself at the mouth of the cave, upon his refusal to give the magician the lamp till he was got out, the stone, by his throwing some perfume into the fire, and two or three magical words he used, stopped it up, and the earth closed again. Here he could not help bursting out into tears, at the representation of the miserable condition he was in, to find himself buried alive in a dismal cave, till, by the touching of his ring, the virtue of which he was then an entire stranger to, he, as I may properly say, came to life again. When he had thus made an end of his story, he said to his mother, This is my adventure, and the danger I have been exposed to since you saw me.

Aladdin's mother heard this surprising and wonderful relation with so much patience as not to interrupt him; notwithstanding, it could be no small affliction to a mother who loved her son tenderly, for all his faults: but yet, in places which were the most moving, and discovered the perfidy of the

African magician, she could not help shewing how much she detested him, by marks of the greatest indignation; and when Aladdin had quite finished his story, she let fly a thousand injurious names at that vile impostor. She called him perfidious traitor, barbarian, assassin, deceiver, magician, and an enemy and destroyer of mankind. Without doubt, child, added she, he is a magician; and they are plagues to the world, and by their enchantments and sorceries have commerce with the devil. Bless God for preserving you from his wicked designs; for your death would have been inevitable, if you had not called upon him, and implored his assistance. She said a great deal more concerning the magician's treachery; but finding that whilst she talked, her son Aladdin, who had not slept for three days and nights, nodded, she put him to bed, and soon after went to bed herself.

Aladdin, who had not had one wink of sleep while he was in the subterraneous abode, slept very soundly all that night, and never waked till late next morning: when the first thing he said to his mother, was, he wanted something to eat, and that she could not do him a greater pleasure than to give him his breakfast. Alas! child, said she, I have not a bit of bread to give you; you eat up all the provisions I had in the house yesterday; but have a little patience, and it shall not be long before I will bring you some: I have a little cotton, which I have spun; I will go and sell it, and buy bread, and something for our dinners. Mother, replied Aladdin, keep your cotton against another time, and give me the lamp I brought home with me yesterday; I will go and sell it, and the money I shall get for it will serve both for breakfast and dinner, and perhaps supper too.

Aladdin's mother took the lamp, and said to her son, Here it is, but it is very dirty; if it was a little cleaner, I believe it would bring something more. To that end she took a little fine sand and water to clean it; but had no sooner begun to rub it, but in an instant a hideous genie of gigantic size appeared before them, and said to her in a voice like thunder, What wouldst thou have? I am ready to obey thee as thy slave, and slave of all those who have that lamp in their hands; I, and the other slaves of the lamp.

Aladdin's mother was not able to speak at the sight of this frightful genie, but fell into a swoon; when Aladdin, who had once before seen such another, without losing time, or his senses, snatched the lamp out of his mother's hands, and said to the genie boldly enough, I am hungry, bring me something to eat presently. The genie disappeared immediately, and in an instant returned with a large silver bason on his head, and twelve covered plates of the same metal, which contained some nice and excellent meats; and two botles of wine, and two glasses in each hand. All these things he laid upon a table, and disappeared; and all this was done before Aladdin's mother came out of her swoon.

Aladdin went presently and fetched some water, and threw it in her face to recover her; but whether that, or the smell of the meats the genie brought, fetched her to life again, I cannot tell; but it was not long before she came to herself. Come, mother, said Aladdin, do not mind this, it is nothing at all; but get up, and come and eat: here is what will put you in heart, and, at the same time, satisfy my extreme hunger; do not let the meat be cold, but fall to.

His mother was very much surprised to see the great bason, twelve plates, six loaves, and the two bottles and glasses, and to smell the delicious odour which exhaled from the plates. O! child, said she to Aladdin, to whom are we obliged for this great plenty and liberality? Has the sultan been made acquainted with our poverty, and had compassion on us? It is no matter, mother, said Aladdin, sit down and eat; for you have almost as much need of a good breakfast as myself; when we have done, I will tell you. Accordingly, both mother and son sat down, and ate with as good stomachs as the table was well furnished. But all the time Aladdin's mother could not forbear looking at and admiring the bason and plates, though she could not well tell whether they were silver or any other metal, so little a judge was she and her son of such matters.

In short, the mother and son found that the excellency of the meats added such strength to their appetites, that they sat at breakfast till it was dinner-time, and then they thought it would be best to kill two birds with one stone, and put the two meals together; and yet found they should have enough left for supper, and two or three meals for the next day.

When Aladdin's mother had taken away and set by what was left, she went and sat down by her son on the sofa. Aladdin, said she, I expect now that you should satisfy my impatience, and tell me exactly what passed between the genie and you, while I was in the swoon: which he presently complied with.

She was in as great an amazement at what her son told her, as at the apparition of the genie, and said to him, But, son, how came that genie to address himself to me, and not to you, to whom he had appeared before in the cave? Mother, answered Aladdin, the genie you saw is not the same who appeared to me, though he resembles him in size; no, they had quite different miens and apparels; without doubt they belong to different masters. If you remember, he that I first saw called himself the slave of the ring on my finger, and this you saw called himself the slave of the lamp you had in your hand: but I believe you did not hear him, for I think you fainted away as soon as he began to speak.

What! cried the mother, was your lamp then the occasion of that cursed genie's addressing himself rather to me than to you? Ah, take it out of my sight, and put it where you please. I would rather you would sell it, than run the hazard of being frightened to death again by touching it; and if you would take my advice, you would part also with the ring, and not have any thing to do with genies, who, as our prophet has told us, are only devils.*

With your leave, mother, replied Aladdin, I shall now take care how I sell a lamp, as I was going to do, which may be so serviceable both to you and me. Have you not been an eye-witness of what it hath procured us, and it shall still continue to furnish us with what we have occasion for. You may well think that my false and wicked uncle would not have taken so much pains, and undertaken so long and tedious a journey, if it had not been to get this wonderful lamp into his possession, which he preferred before all the gold and silver which he knew was in the halls, and which these eyes of mine beheld. He knew too well the value and worth of this lamp, to ask for a greater treasure; and since chance hath discovered the virtue of it to us, let us make a profitable use of it, without making any great stir, and drawing the envy and jealousy of our neighbours upon us. However, since the genies frighten you so much, I will take it out of your sight, and put it where I may find it when I want it. As for the ring, I cannot resolve to part with that neither; for without that, you had never seen me again; and though I am alive now, perhaps, if it was gone, I might not be so some moments hence; therefore I hope you will give me leave to keep that, and to wear it always on my finger. Who knows what dangers you and I may be exposed to, which neither of us foresees, and which it may deliver us from. As Aladdin's arguments were just, and had a great deal of weight in them, his mother had nothing to say against them; but only replied, That he might do what he pleased, but for her part, she would have nothing to do with genies, but would wash her hands of them.

By the next night they had eaten all the provisions the genie had brought; and the next day Aladdin, who could not bear the thoughts of hunger, took one of the plates under his coat, and went out early to sell it, and addressing himself to a Jew, whom he met in the streets, and pulling out the plate, asked him if he would buy it? The cunning Jew examined the plate, and no sooner found that it was good silver, but he asked Aladdin, How much he asked for it? Aladdin, who knew not the worth of it, and never had been used to traffic, told him he would trust to his honour and generosity. The Jew was somewhat confounded at this plain dealing, and was doubtful whether Aladdin understood the full value of what he offered him to sell; however, he took a piece of gold out of his purse, and gave it him, though it was but the sixtieth part of the worth of the plate. Aladdin took the money very eagerly; and as soon as he got it in his pocket, retired with so much haste, that the Jew, not content with the exorbitancy of his profit, was vexed with himself in not penetrating into Aladdin's ignorance, and was for running after him, to endeavour to get some change out of the money, but that Aladdin had got so far, that it was hardly possible for him to overtake him.

Before Aladdin went home to his mother, he called at a baker's, bought a loaf, changed his money, and went home and gave his mother the rest, who went and bought other necessary provisions, which lasted them some time. After this manner they lived, till Aladdin had sold the twelve plates, one at a time, to the Jew, for the same money; who, after the first time, durst not offer him less, for fear of losing so good chap.* When he had sold the last plate, he had recourse to the bason, which weighed ten times as much as a plate, and would have carried it to his old purchaser, but that it was too large and cumbersome; therefore he was obliged to bring him home with him to his mother's, where, after the Jew had looked upon it, he laid him down ten pieces of gold, with which Aladdin was very well satisfied.

They lived on these ten pieces in a frugal manner a pretty while; and Aladdin, who had been used to an idle life, left off playing with young lads of his own age, after his adventure with the African magician. He spent his time in walking about, and discoursing with people with whom he had got acquainted. Sometimes he would stop at the most topping merchants shops,* where people of the best distinction met for the benefit of conversation, and listen, for improvement's sake, to their discourse, by which means he gained a little knowledge of the world.

When all the money was spent, Aladdin had recourse again to the lamp. He took it in his hand, looked for the same place where his mother had rubbed it with the sand, and rubbed it also, and the genie immediately appeared, and said, What wouldst thou have? I am ready to obey thee as thy slave, and the slave of all those who have that lamp in their hands; I and the other slaves of the lamp. I am hungry, said Aladdin; bring me something to eat. The genie disappeared, and presently returned with a bason and the same number of covered plates, &c. and set them down on a table, and vanished again.

Aladdin's mother, knowing what her son was going to do, went out at that time about some business; and when she returned, which was not long after, and found the table so furnished a second time, was almost as much surprised as before at the prodigious effect of the lamp. However, she sat down with her son, and when they had ate as much as they had a mind to, she set enough by to last them two or three days.

As soon as Aladdin found that their provisions were spent, he took one of these plates, and went to look for his Jew chapman again; but passing by a goldsmith's shop, who had the character of a very fair and honest man, the goldsmith perceiving him, called to him, and said, My lad, I have often observed you go by, loaded as you are at present, and talk with such a Jew, and then come back again empty handed. I imagine that you carry something that you sell to him; but perhaps you do not know what a rogue he is, and that he is the greatest cheat among all the Jews, and so well known, that nobody will have any thing to do with him. What I tell you is for your own good. If you have any thing to dispose of that lies in my way, I will give you the full worth of it; and if it be what I do not deal in, I will direct you to other merchants, who will not cheat you.

The hopes of getting more money for his plate, induced Aladdin to pull it presently from under his coat, and shew it to the goldsmith. The old man, who at first sight saw that it was made of the finest silver, asked him if he sold any such as that was to the Jew? and Aladdin told him plainly that he had sold him twelve such, for a piece of gold each. Ah, villain! cried the goldsmith; but added he, what is past cannot be recalled. But by shewing you the value of this plate, which is of the finest silver we use in our shops, I will let you see how much the Jew has cheated you.

The goldsmith took a pair of scales, weighed the plate; and after he had told Aladdin how much an ounce of his silver was worth, he demonstrated to him, that his plate was worth sixty pieces of gold, which he paid him down that minute. If you dispute my honesty, said he, you may go to any other of our trade, and if he gives you any more, I will be bound to forfeit twice as much: For what we gain by, is the fashion of the plate, and that is out of the way of the fairest dealing Jew of them all.

Aladdin thanked him for his good advice, and the favour he had done him; and never after went to any other person, but sold him all his plates, and the bason, and had as much for them as the weight came to.

Though Aladdin and his mother had an inexhaustible treasure in their lamp, and might have had whatever they had a mind to, yet they lived with the same frugality as before, only that Aladdin went more neat; but for his mother, she wore no clothes but what she earned by her spinning cotton. After their manner of living, we may easily suppose, that the full value of the plates and bason was sufficient to maintain them some years.

During this time, Aladdin, to accomplish himself and understand the world, very much frequented the great shops, where they sold cloth of gold and silver, and fine stuffs, silks and linens, and oftentimes entered into conversation with the best of people; and among other shops, he visited those of the top jewellers, and had got a pretty good acquaintance among them, and by that means came to know, that the fine fruit which he had gathered when he took the lamp, were not coloured glass, but jewels of an extraordinary value; for as he had seen all sorts of jewels bought and sold in their shops, but none that were so beautiful, or nigh so large as his, he found, that instead of coloured glass, he possessed an inestimable treasure; but was so prudent as not to say any thing of it, not so much as to his mother.

One day, as Aladdin was walking about the town, he heard an order of the sultan published, for all people to shut up their shops and houses, and keep within doors, while the princess Badroulbadour, (which is to say, the full moon of full moons,) the sultan's daughter, went to the baths and back again.

This public order inspired Aladdin with a great curiosity to see the princess's face, which he could not do without getting into the house of some acquaintance which stood in the way thither, and look through a window: But when he considered that the princess, when she went to the baths, had a veil on, he found his project would not take; but to satisfy his curiosity, he presently thought of one which would; which was to get behind the door of the baths, and then he could not fail of seeing her face.

Aladdin had not waited long before the princess came, and he could see her plainly without being seen. She was attended with a great crowd of ladies, slaves, and eunuchs, who walked on each side, and behind her. When she came within three or four yards of the door of the baths, she pulled off her veil, and gave Aladdin an opportunity of a full look at her.

Till then, Aladdin, who had never seen any woman's face but his mother's,* who was old, and never could boast of any such features, thought that all women were like her, and could hear people talk of the most surprising beauties without being the least moved; for whatever words are made use of to heighten the merit of a beauty, they can never make the same impression as the lady herself.

But as soon as Aladdin had seen the princess Badroulbadour, his sentiments were very much changed, and his heart could not withstand all those inclinations so charming an object inspires. The princess was the most lovely beautiful brown woman in the world: her eyes were large, lively, and sparkling; her looks sweet and modest; her nose was of a just proportion; her mouth small; her lips of a vermilion red and agreeable symmetry; in a word, all the features of her face were regular and beautiful; therefore nobody should be surprised, if Aladdin, who had never seen and was a stranger to so many charms, was dazzled, and his senses quite ravished. With all these perfections, the princess had so delicate a shape, so majestic an air, that the sight of her was sufficient to inspire respect.

After the princess had passed by Aladdin, and got into the baths, he remained some time astonished and confounded, and in a kind of extacy, in reflecting and imprinting the idea of so charming an object deeply in his mind: But at last considering that the princess was gone past him, and that when she returned from the bath her back would be towards him, and she veiled, he resolved to quit his post, and go home. But when he came there, he could not conceal his uneasiness so well, but that his mother perceived it, and was very much surprised to see him so much more thoughtful and melancholy than usual, and asked him what had happened to him to make him so? Aladdin returned no answer, but sat carelessly down on the sofa, and remained in the same condition, full of the image of the charming Badroulbadour. His mother, who was dressing supper, pressed him no more; but when it was ready, set it on the table before him; but perceiving that he gave no attention to it, bade him eat, which she had much ado to persuade him to; and when he did, it was with great indifference, and all the time cast down his eyes, and observed so great a silence, that she could not possibly get the least word out of him, to know the reason of so extraordinary an alteration.

After supper, she asked him again why he was so melancholy; but could have no other satisfaction, but that he would go to bed. Now, without examining how Aladdin passed the night, I shall only tell you, that as he sat next day over against his mother as she was spinning cotton, he spoke to her in these words: I perceive that my silence yesterday has very much troubled you; I was not, nor am not such as I fancy you believed; but I can tell you, that what I did then, and now endure, is worse than any disease. I cannot tell well what ails me, but yet do not doubt but what I am going to tell you will inform you.

It was published yesterday in another quarter of the town, and therefore you know nothing of it, that the princess Badroulbadour, the sultan's daughter, was to go to the baths after dinner; and, to pay all the respect that was due to that princess, all the shops were ordered to be shut up in her way thither, and every body to keep within doors, to give her and her attendants more liberty in the streets. As I was walking about, I heard this order of the sultan published; and as I was not then far off the baths, I had a great curiosity to see the princess's face; and a thought coming into my head, that the princess, when she should come nigh the door of the baths, would pull her veil off, I resolved to get behind that door; and as I imagined so it happened. The princess threw off her veil, and I had the happiness of seeing her lovely face with the greatest satisfaction imaginable. This, mother, was the cause of my melancholy and silence yesterday: I love the princess with so much violence, that I cannot express it; and as my lively passion increases every moment, I cannot live without the possession of the amiable princess Badroulbadour, and am resolved to ask her in marriage of the sultan her father.

Aladdin's mother gave a great deal of attention to what her son told her; but when he talked of asking the princess Badroulbadour in marriage of the sultan, she could not help bursting out into a loud laughter. Aladdin would have gone on with his discourse, but she interrupted him. Alas, child, said she, what are you thinking of? for you talk as if you were mad.

I can assure you, mother, replied Aladdin, that I am not mad, but in my right senses: I foresaw that you would reproach me thus foolishly and extravagantly; but I must tell you once more, that I am resolved to demand the princess Badroulbadour of the sultan in marriage, and your remonstrances shall not prevent me.

Indeed, son, replied the mother seriously, I cannot help telling you, that you have quite forgot yourself; and if you would put this resolution of yours in execution, I do not see who you can get to propose it for you. You yourself, replied he immediately. I go to the sultan! answered the mother, amazed and surprised; upon my word, I shall take care how I engage in such an affair. Why, who are you, son, continued she, that can have the impudence to think of your sultan's daughter? Have you forgot that your father was but a poor taylor, and that I am but of a mean extraction; and do not you know, that sultans never marry their daughters but to princes or sultans like themselves?

Mother, answered Aladdin, I have already told you, that I foresaw all that you have said, or can say; and tell you again, that none of your discourse nor remonstrances shall make me change my mind. I have told you, that you must ask the princess Badroulbadour in marriage for me: It is a favour I desire of you with all the respect I owe you; and I beg of you do not refuse me, unless you would rather see me in my grave, than by so doing give me new life.

The good old woman was very much embarrassed when she found Aladdin so obstinate as to persist so strongly in so foolish an undertaking. My dear child, said she again, it is true I am your mother, who brought you into the world; and there is nothing in the world that is reasonable, but I would do for you. If I was to go and treat about your marriage with some neighbour's daughter, whose circumstances were equal with yours, I would do it with all my heart; and then they would expect you should be of some trade, or have some little estate or fortune. When such poor folks as we are have a mind to marry, the first thing they ought to think of is to know how to live. But, without reflecting on the meanness of your birth, and the little merit you have to recommend you, you aim at the highest pitch of fortune; and your pretensions are no less than to demand the daughter of your sovereign in marriage, who, with one single word, can crush you in pieces. For your own part, I leave you to reflect on what you should do, and come now to consider on what you desire of me. How could so extraordinary a thought come into your head; for me to go and make a proposal to the sultan to give his daughter in marriage to you! Suppose I had, not to say the boldness, but the impudence, to make so extravagant a demand, to whom should I address myself to be introduced to his majesty? Do you think the first person I should speak to would not take me for a mad woman, and chastise me as I should deserve? Suppose there is no difficulty in presenting myself to an audience of the sultan, as I know there is none to those who go to ask justice, which he distributes equally among his subjects; or those who ask some favour for some signal service; how can I open my lips to offer such a proposal before his majesty and his whole court? What have you done to be worthy of such a favour? What have you done either for your prince or country? How have you distinguished yourself? And if you have done nothing to merit so great a favour, with what assurance shall I ask it? Besides, here is another reason which you do not think of, which is, nobody ever goes to ask a favour of the sultan without a present; for by a present they have this advantage, that if, for some particular reasons, the favour is denied, they are sure to be heard. But what presents have you to make? And if you had one that was worthy of the least attention of so great a monarch, what proportion could it bear to the favour you would ask? Therefore, son, reflect well on what you are about, and consider that you aspire to a thing which it is impossible for you to obtain.

Aladdin heard all that his mother could say to endeavour to dissuade him from his design very quietly; and after he had weighed that remonstrance in all points, he made answer: I own, mother, it is a great piece of rashness in me to dare to carry my pretensions so far; and a great piece of inconsideration, to ask you, with so much heat and precipitancy, to go and make that proposal of marriage to the sultan, without first taking proper measures to procure a favourable reception, and therefore beg your pardon. But be not surprised, that, through the violence of my passion, I did not at first sight see every thing that was necessary to be done to procure me that happiness I seek after. I love the princess Badroulbadour above all things that you can imagine; or rather I adore her, and shall always persevere in my design of marrying her; which is a thing I have determined and resolved on. I am obliged to you for the hint you have given me, and look upon it as the first step I ought to take to procure me the happy success I promise myself.

You say it is not customary to go to the sultan without a present, and that I have nothing worthy of his acceptance. As to what you say about the present, I agree with you, and own that I never thought of it: But as to what you say, that I have nothing fit to present him with, do not you think, mother, that what I brought home with me that day on which I was delivered from an inevitable death, may be an agreeable present? I mean those things you and I took for coloured glasses; but now I am undeceived, and can tell you that they are jewels of an inestimable value, and fit for the greatest of monarchs. I know the worth of them by frequenting the jewellers' shops; and you may take my word on it, all the jewels that I saw in the most topping jewellers' shops, were not to be compared to those we have, neither for size nor beauty, and yet they were valued at an excessive price. In short, neither you nor I know the value of ours; but be it as it will, by the little experience I have, I am persuaded that they will be received very favourably by the sultan. You have a large porcelain dish fit to hold them; go and fetch it, and let us see how they will look when we have ranged them according to their different colours.

Aladdin's mother fetched the china dish, and she took the jewels out of the two purses in which he had kept them all along, and placed them according to his fancy in the dish. But the brightness and lustre they had in the day-time, and the variety of colours, so dazzled the eyes, both of mother and son, that they were in the most agreeable surprise imaginable; for though Aladdin had seen them hang on the trees when he fetched the lamp, yet as he was then but a boy, he did not much take notice of them.

After they had admired this present some time, Aladdin said to his mother, Now you cannot excuse yourself from going to the sultan, under the pretext of not having a present to make him, since here is one which will gain you a favourable reception.

Though Aladdin's mother, notwithstanding the beauty and lustre of the present, did not believe it so valuable as her son esteemed it, she thought it might nevertheless be agreeable to the sultan, and found that she could not have any thing to say against it, but was very uneasy at Aladdin's demand in favour of his present. Child, said she, I cannot conceive that your present will have its desired effect, and that the sultan will look upon you with a favourable eye; and I am sure, that if I attempt to acquit myself of this message of yours, I shall have no power to open my mouth; and therefore I shall not only lose my labour, and the present, which you say is so extraordinary, but shall return home again in confusion, to tell you that your hopes are frustrated. Now I have told you the consequence, and you ought to believe me: But, added she, I will strive to please you, and endeavour to ask the sultan as you will have me; but certainly he will either laugh at me, and send me back like a fool, or be in so great a rage, as to make us both the victims of his fury.

She used a great many more arguments to endeavour to make him change his mind; but the charms of the princess Badroulbadour had made too great an impression on his heart, to dissuade him off his design. Aladdin persisted in his resolution; and she, as much out of tenderness, as for fear he should be guilty of a greater piece of extravagance, condescended to his request.

As it was too late to go that day to the sultan's palace, it was put off until the next. The mother and the son talked of indifferent matters the remaining part of the day; and Aladdin took a great deal of pains to encourage his mother in the task she had undertaken to go to the sultan, who, notwithstanding all his arguments, could not persuade herself she could ever succeed; and indeed there was room enough for her doubts. Child, said she to Aladdin, if the sultan should receive me as favourably as I could wish, for your sake, and would hear my proposal with great calmness, and after this kind reception should bethink himself, and ask me where lies your riches, and your estate, (for that is what he will sooner inquire after than your person,) if, I say, he should ask me the question, what answer would you have me return him?

Do not let us be uneasy, mother, replied Aladdin, at a thing which may never happen: first let us see how the sultan receives, and what answer he gives you. If it should so fall out that he will be informed of what you say, I have thought of an answer, and am confident that the lamp which hath subsisted us so long will not fail me at the last pinch.

Aladdin's mother could not say any thing against what her son then proposed; but reflected that the lamp might be capable of doing greater wonders than just providing victuals for them. This consideration gave her some satisfaction, and at the same time removed all the difficulties which might induce her not to undertake what she had promised her son; when Aladdin, who penetrated into his mother's thoughts, said to her, but, above all things, mother, be sure you keep this business secret, for thereon depends the success we ought to expect; and after this caution, Aladdin and his mother parted to go to bed. But violent love, and the great prospect of so immense a fortune, had so much possessed the son's thoughts, that he could not rest so well as he could have wished. He rose at day-break, and went presently and wakened his mother, who made all the haste she could to get herself dressed to go to the sultan's palace, and to get in before the grand visier and bashaws,* and other great officers of state, were sat in the divan, where the sultan always assisted in person.

When she was ready, she took the china dish, in which they had put the jewels the day before, tied up in a fine napkin at four corners, and set forwards for the sultan's palace, to the great joy and satisfaction of Aladdin. When she came to the gates, the grand visier, and the other visiers, and most distinguished lords of the court, were just gone in; and notwithstanding the crowd of people who had business at the divan was extraordinary great, she got into the divan, which was a large spacious hall, the entry into which was very magnificent. She placed herself just before the sultan, grand visier, and the great lords, who sat in that council, on their right and left hands. Several causes were called according to their order, and pleaded and adjudged, until the time the divan generally broke up; when the sultan rising, took his leave, and returned to his apartment, attended by the grand visier. The other visiers and ministers of state returned, as also did all those whose business called them thither; some pleased with gaining their causes, others dissatisfied at the sentence pronounced against them, and some in expectation of theirs being tried the next sitting.

Aladdin's mother seeing the sultan rise and retire, and all the people go away, judged that he would not come again that day, and so resolved to go home. When Aladdin saw her return with the present designed for the sultan, he knew not at first what to think of the success of this affair; and in the fear he was in, lest she should bring him some ill news, he had not courage enough to ask her any, till the mother, who had never set foot into the sultan's palace before, and knew not what was every day practised there, freed him from his embarrassment, and said to him, with a great deal of simplicity, Son, I have seen the sultan, and am very well persuaded he has seen me too; for I placed myself just before him, and nothing could hinder him from seeing me; but he was so much taken up with all those who talked on all sides of him, that I pitied him, and wondered at his patience to hear them. At last I believe he was heartily tired; for he rose up suddenly, and would not hear a great many who were ready prepared to speak to him, but went away; at which I was very well pleased, for indeed I began to lose all patience, and was extremely tired with staying so long. But, notwithstanding, I will go again to-morrow; perhaps the sultan may not be so busy.

Though Aladdin's passion was very violent, he was forced to be satisfied with this excuse, and to fortify himself with patience. However, he had the satisfaction to find that his mother had done her endeavour to get access to the sultan; and hoped that the example of those she saw speak to him, would embolden her to acquit herself the better of her commission when there was a favourable opportunity.

The next morning she went to the sultan's palace with the present, as early as the day before; but when she came there, she found the gates of the divan shut, and understood that the council sat but every other day, therefore she must come again the next. This news she carried her son, whose only relief was to guard himself with patience. She went six times afterwards on the days appointed, placed herself always directly before the sultan, but with as little success as the first time, and might have perhaps come a thousand times to as little purpose, if the sultan himself had not taken a particular notice of her; for it is probable that there were none there but who came with petitions to the sultan, and each pleaded their cause in his turn, and Aladdin's mother was none of that class.

That day, the council was broke up, when the sultan was in his own apartment, he said to his grand visier, I have for some time observed a certain woman, who comes constantly every day that I go into council, and has something wrapped up in a napkin: she always stays from the beginning to the breaking up of the council, and ever strives to place herself just before me. Do you know what she wants?

Sir, replied the grand visier, who knew no more than the sultan what she wanted, but had not a mind to seem short, your majesty knows that women often form complaints on trifles; perhaps this woman may come to complain to your majesty, that somebody had sold her some bad barley, or some such matter. The sultan was not satisfied with this answer, but replied, If this woman comes again next council-day, do not fail to call her, that I may hear what she has to say. The grand visier made an answer by kissing his hand, and lifting it up above his head, signifying his willingness to lose it if he failed.

By this time Aladdin's mother was so much used to go to the council, and stand before the sultan, that she did not think it any trouble in the least, if she could but satisfy her son that she neglected nothing that lay in her power to please him. So the next council-day she went to the divan, and placed herself before the sultan as usual; and before the grand visier had made his report of affairs, the sultan perceived her, and compassionating her for having waited so long, he said to the visier, Before you enter upon any business, remember the woman I spoke to you about; bid her come nigher, and let us hear and dispatch her first. The grand visier immediately called the chief of the huissirs, who stood ready to obey his commands; and pointing to her, bid him go to that woman, and tell her to come before the sultan.

The chief of the huissirs went to Aladdin's mother, and, by a sign he gave her, she followed him to the foot of the sultan's throne, where he left her, and retired to his place by the grand visier. Aladdin's mother, by the example of a great many others whom she saw salute the sultan, bowed her head down to the tapestry which covered the steps of the throne, and remained in that posture till the sultan bid her rise; which he had no sooner done, than the sultan said to her, Good woman, I have observed you to stand a long time, from the beginning to the rising of the divan: What is your business?

At these words, Aladdin's mother prostrated herself a second time; and when she got up again, said, Monarch of monarchs, before I tell your majesty the extraordinary and almost incredible affair which brings me before your high throne, I beg of you to pardon the boldness, or rather to say impudence, of the demand I am going to make; which is so uncommon, that I tremble, and am ashamed to propose it to my sultan. To give her the more freedom to declare what she had to say, the sultan ordered every body to go out of the divan but the grand visier, and then told her she might speak without restraint.

Aladdin's mother, not content with this favour of the sultan, to save her the trouble and confusion to speak before so many, was, notwithstanding, for securing herself against his anger, which, from the proposal she was going to make, she was not a little apprehensive of: therefore, assuming the discourse, she said, I beg of your majesty, that if you should think my demand the least injurious or offensive, to assure me first of your pardon and forgiveness. Well, replied the sultan, I will forgive you, be it what it will, and no hurt shall come to you: speak boldly.

When Aladdin's mother had taken all these precautions, for fear of the sultan's anger, she told him faithfully how Aladdin had seen the princess Badroulbadour, the violent love that fatal sight had inspired him with, the declaration he made to her of it when he came home, and what representations she had made to dissuade him from a passion no less injurious, said she, to your majesty as sultan, than the princess your daughter. But, continued she, my son, instead of taking my advice, and confessing his boldness, was so obstinate as to persevere in it, and to threaten me with some action of despair, if I refused to come and ask the princess in marriage of your majesty; which, after an extreme violence on myself, I was forced to be so complaisant to him; for which I beg of your majesty once more to pardon, not only me, but forgive Aladdin my son, for entertaining such a rash thought, as to aspire to so high an alliance.

The sultan hearkened to this discourse with a great deal of mildness, without shewing the least anger or passion: but before he gave her an answer, he asked her what she had tied up there in that napkin, which she had set down before she prostrated herself before him; upon which she unloosed it, and presented the china dish.

The sultan's amazement and surprise were inexpressible, when he saw so many, so considerably large, beautiful, and valuable jewels, in one dish. He was struck with so great admiration, that he was for some time motionless. At last, when he had recovered himself, he received the present from Aladdin's mother's hand, and crying out, in a transport of joy, How rich and beautiful is this! After he had admired and handled some of the jewels, he turned about to his grand visier, and shewing him the dish, said, Look here, and confess that your eyes never beheld any thing so rich and beautiful before. The visier was charmed. Well, continued the sultan, what sayest thou to such a present? Is it not worthy of the princess my daughter? and ought I not to bestow her on one who values her at so great a price?

These words put the grand visier into a strange agitation. Some time before, the sultan had signified to him his intention of bestowing the princess his daughter on a son of his; therefore he was afraid, and not without ground, that the sultan, dazzled by so rich and extraordinary a present, might change his mind. Thereupon, going up to him, and whispering him in the ear, said to him, Sir, I cannot disown but the present is worthy of the princess; but I beg of your majesty to grant me three months before you come to a resolution. I hope, before that time, my son, on whom you have had the bounty to look favourably, will be able to make a nobler present than Aladdin, who is an entire stranger to your majesty.

The sultan, though he was very well persuaded that it was not possible for the visier to provide so considerable a present for his son to make to the princess, yet he hearkened to him, and granted him that favour. So turning about to Aladdin's mother, he said to her, Good woman, go home, and tell your son that I agree to the proposal you have made me; but I cannot marry the princess my daughter, till some furniture I design for her be got ready, which cannot be finished these three months; but at the expiration of that time, come again.

Aladdin's mother returned home much more overjoyed than she could have ever imagined; for she looked upon her access to the sultan as a thing impossible and impracticable; and besides, the meeting with so favourable an answer, instead of the refusal and confusion she expected, ravished her senses. From two things, Aladdin, when he saw his mother return, judged that she brought him good news: the one was, that she returned sooner than ordinary; and the next was, the gayness of her countenance. Well, mother, said he to her, may I entertain any hopes, or must I die with despair? When she had pulled off her veil, and had set herself down on the sofa by him, she said to him, Not to keep you long in suspense, son, I will begin to tell you, that instead of thinking of dying, you ought to be very well satisfied. Then pursuing her discourse, she told him how that she had an audience before every body else, which made her come home so soon; the precautions she had taken lest she should have displeased the sultan, by making the proposal of marriage between him and the princess Badroulbadour; and the favourable answer she had from the sultan's own mouth; and that, as far as she could judge, the present wrought that powerful effect. But when I least expected it, said she, and he was going to give me an answer, the grand visier whispered him in the ear, and I am afraid might be some obstacle to his good intentions.

Aladdin thought himself the most happy of all men at the hearing of this news, and thanked his mother for all the pains she had taken in the pursuit of this affair, the good success of which was of so great importance to his quiet. Though, through his impatience to enjoy the object of his passion, three months seemed an age; yet he disposed himself to wait until then with patience, relying on the sultan's word, which he looked upon to be irrevocable. But all that time, he not only reckoned the hours, days, and weeks, but almost every moment. When two of the three months were past his mother one evening going to light the lamp, and finding no oil in the house, went to buy some; and when she came into the great streets, found them all illuminated, the shops shut up, and garnished with boughs, every body striving to shew their zeal by their rejoicings. The streets were crowded with officers in their habits of ceremony, mounted on horses richly caparisoned, each attended by a great many footmen. Aladdin's mother asked the oil-merchant what was the meaning of all those doings? Alas! good woman, said he, from whence came you, that you do not know that the grand visier's son is to marry the princess Badroulbadour, the sultan's daughter, to-night? She will presently return from the baths; and these officers you see there, are to assist at the cavalcade to the palace, where the ceremony is to be solemnized.

This was news enough for Aladdin's mother. She ran home in great haste, and when she came to her son, who little suspected any such thing happening, was quite out of breath. Child, cried she, you are quite undone! You depended upon the sultan's fine promises, but there is nothing in them. At these words Aladdin was terribly alarmed: Mother, replied he, how do you know the sultan has been guilty of a breach of promise? This night, answered the mother, the grand visier's son is to marry the princess Badroulbadour; and then she related all the circumstances, insomuch that he had no reason to dispute the truth of what she said.

At this account Aladdin was quite thunder-struck, till a secret motive of jealousy soon roused his spirits, and he bethought himself of the lamp which had till then been so useful to him; and without venting his rage in words against the sultan, visier, or his son, he only said, Perhaps, mother, the visier's son may not be so happy to-night as he promises himself; while I go into my chamber a moment, do you go and get supper ready. She accordingly went about it, and she guessed that her son was going to make use of the lamp, to prevent, if possible, the consummation of the marriage.

When Aladdin had got into his chamber, he took the lamp, and rubbed it in the same place as before, and immediately the genie appeared, and said to him, What wouldst thou have? I am ready to obey thee as thy slave, and the slave of all those who have that lamp in their hands; I, and the other slaves of the lamp. Hear me, said Aladdin; thou hast hitherto brought me whatever I wanted as to provisions; but now I have business of the greatest importance for thee to execute. I have demanded the princess Badroulbadour in marriage of the sultan her father; he promised her to me, but only asked three months time; and instead of keeping that promise, has this night, before the expiration of that time, married her to the grand visier's son. What I ask of thee is, That as soon as the new bride and bridegroom are in bed, that you bring them both hither in their bed. Master, replied the genie, I will obey you. Have you any other commands? None at present, answered Aladdin; and then the genie disappeared.

Aladdin went down stairs, and supped with his mother, with the same tranquillity of mind as usual; and after supper talked of the princess's marriage, as of an affair wherein he had not the least concern; and afterwards returned to his own chamber again, and left his mother to go to bed; but, for his own part, sat up till the genie had executed his orders.

In the mean time, every thing was prepared with the greatest magnificence, in the sultan's palace, to celebrate the princess's nuptials; and the evening was spent with all the usual ceremonies, and great rejoicings till midnight, when the grand visier's son, by a signal given him by the chief of the princess's eunuchs, slipped away from the company, and was introduced by that officer into the princess's apartment, where the nuptial bed was prepared. He went to bed first, and in a little time after, the sultaness, accompanied by her own women, and those of the princess, brought the bride, who, according to the custom of new-married ladies, made great resistance. The sultaness herself helped to undress her, put her into bed by force; and after having kissed her, and bid her good night, retired with all the women, and shut the door herself.

No sooner was the door shut, but the genie, as the faithful slave of the lamp, and punctual in obeying the command of them who possessed it, without giving the bridegroom the least time to caress his bride, to the great amazement of them both, took up the bed, and transported it into Aladdin's chamber, where he set it down.

Aladdin, who waited impatiently for this moment, could not bear to see the visier's son long in bed with the princess. Take this new bridegroom, said he to the genie, and put him in an house of office,* and come again to-morrow morning after day-break. The genie presently took the visier's son out of bed, and carried him in his shirt whither Aladdin bid him; and after he had breathed upon him, which prevented his stirring, he left him there.

Though Aladdin had a great love for the princess Badroulbadour, he did not talk much to her when they were alone; but only said, with a passionate air, Fear nothing, most adorable princess, you are here in safety; for notwithstanding the violence of my passion, which your charms have kindled, it shall never exceed the bounds of the profound respect I owe you. If I have been forced to come to this extremity, it is not with an intent of affronting you, but to prevent an unjust rival's possessing you, contrary to the sultan your father's promise in favour of me.

The princess, who knew nothing of these particulars, gave very little attention to what Aladdin could say. The fright and amazement of so surprising and unexpected an adventure, had put her into such a condition, that he could not get one word from her. However, he undressed himself, and got into the visier's son's place, and lay with his back to the princess, putting a sabre between himself and her, to shew that he deserved to be punished if he attempted any thing against her honour.

Aladdin, very well satisfied with having thus deprived his rival of the happiness he flattered himself with that night, slept very quietly, though the princess Badroulbadour never passed a night so ill in her life; and if we consider the condition the genie left the grand visier's son in, we may imagine that the new bridegroom spent his much worse.

Aladdin had no occasion the next morning to rub the lamp to call the genie; he came at the hour appointed, and just when he had done dressing himself, and said to him, I am here, master, what are your commands? Go, said Aladdin, fetch the visier's son out of the place where you left him, and put him into his bed again, and carry it from whence thou broughtest it. The genie presently returned with the visier's son; Aladdin took up his sabre; the new bridegroom was laid by the princess; and in an instant the nuptial-bed was transported into the same chamber of the palace from whence it was brought. But we must observe, that all this time the genie never appeared either to the princess or the grand visier's son. His hideous form would have made them die away with fear. Neither did they hear any thing of the discourse between Aladdin and him, but only perceived the motion of the bed, and their transportation from one place to another; which, as we may well imagine, was enough to frighten them.

As soon as the genie had set down the nuptial-bed in its proper place, the sultan, who was curious to know how the princess had spent the wedding-night, opened the door to bid her good morrow. The grand visier's son, who was almost perished with cold, by standing in his shirt all night, and had not had time to warm himself in bed, no sooner heard the door open, but he got out of bed, and ran into the wardrobe where he undressed himself the night before.

The sultan went to the bed-side, kissed the princess between the eyes, according to custom, wishing her a good morrow, and asked her, smiling, How she had passed the night? But looking at her most earnestly, he was extremely surprised to see her look so melancholy, and that neither by a blush, or any other sign, he could satisfy his curiosity. He said several things; but finding that he could not get a word from her, he attributed it to her modesty, and so retired. Nevertheless, he suspected that there was something extraordinary in this silence, and thereupon went immediately to the sultaness's apartment, and told her in what condition he found the princess, and how she received him. Sir, said the sultaness, your majesty ought not to be surprised at this behaviour; new married people always have a restraint upon themselves the next day; she will be quite another thing in two or three days time, and then she will receive the sultan her father as she ought. But I will go and see her, added she; I am very much deceived, if she uses me in the same manner.

As soon as the sultaness was dressed, away she goes to the princess's apartment, who was still in bed, undraws the curtain, bids her good morrow, and kissed her. But how great was her surprise, when she returned her no answer; and looking more attentively at her, she perceived her to be very much troubled, which made her judge that something had happened which she did not think of. How comes it, child, said the sultaness, that you do not return my caresses? ought you to use your mother after this manner? and do you think I do not know whatever may have happened in the circumstances you are in? But I am apt to believe you do not think so, and something extraordinary has happened; come, tell me freely, and do not make me any longer uneasy.

At last the princess Badroulbadour broke silence with a great sigh, and said, Alas! most honoured mother and madam, forgive me if I have failed in the respect I owe you. My mind is so full of the extraordinary things which have befallen me this night, that I have not yet recovered my amazement and fright, and scarce know myself. Then she told her, how, the instant after she and her spouse were in bed, the bed was transported into a dark ugly room, where he was taken from her, and carried away, where she knew not, and she was left alone with a young man, who, after he had said something to her, which, through her fright, she did not mind, laid himself down by her, in her husband's place, but first put his sabre between them; and in the morning her husband was brought to her again, and the bed was transported back to her own chamber. All this, said she, was but just done when the sultan, my father, came into my chamber. I was so overwhelmed with grief, that I had no power to make him one word of an answer; therefore I am afraid that he is enraged at the manner I received the honour he did me: but I hope he will forgive me, when he knows my melancholy adventure, and the miserable condition I am in at present.

The sultaness heard all the princess told very patiently, but would not believe it. You did well, child, said she, not to speak of this to your father: have a care, for the future, how you mention it to any body; for you will certainly be thought mad, if you talk at this rate. Madam, replied the princess, I can assure you I am in my right senses: ask my husband, and he will tell you the same story. Well, I will, said the sultaness; but if he should talk in the same manner, I shall not be one whit the better persuaded of the truth. Come, rise, and throw off this idle fancy; it will be a fine story indeed, if all the feasts and rejoicings in the kingdom should be interrupted by such a vision. Do not you hear the trumpets sounding, and drums beating, and concerts of the finest music? cannot all these inspire you with joy and pleasure, and make you forget all the whimsies and fancies you tell me of? At the same time the sultaness called the princess's women, and after she had seen her get up, and set at her toilet, she ran to the sultan's apartment, and told him that her daughter had got some odd notions in her head, but that there was nothing in them.

Then she sent for the visier's son, to know of him the bottom of what the princess had told her; but he thinking himself highly honoured to be allied to the sultan, was so prudent as to disguise the matter from her. Son-in-law, said the sultaness, are you as much infatuated as your wife? Madam, replied the visier's son, may I be so bold as to ask the reason of that question? O! that is enough, answered the sultaness; I see you are wiser than she.

The rejoicings lasted all that day in the palace; and the sultaness, who never left the princess, forgot nothing to divert her, and make her merry, and entertained her with all manner of diversions and sights; but she was so deeply struck with the ideas of what had happened to her that night, that it was easy to see her thoughts were entirely taken up about it; neither was the grand visier's son's affliction less, but that his ambition made him disguise it, and appear to be a happy bridegroom.

Aladdin, who was well acquainted with what passed in the palace, never disputed but that the new married couple were to lie together again that night, notwithstanding the troublesome adventure of the night before; and therefore, he having as great an inclination to disturb them, he had recourse to his lamp, and when the genie appeared, and offered his service, said to him, The grand visier's son and the princess Badroulbadour are to lie together again to-night; go, and, as soon as they are in bed, bring the bed hither, as thou didst yesterday.

The genie obeyed Aladdin as faithfully and exactly as the day before: the grand visier's son passed the night coldly and disagreeably as before, and the princess had the mortification again to have Aladdin for her bed-fellow, with the sabre between them. The genie, according to Aladdin's orders, came the next morning, and brought the bridegroom, and laid him by his bride, and then carried the bed and new married-couple back again to the palace.

The sultan, after the reception the princess Badroulbadour had given him that day, was very uneasy to know how she passed the second night, and if she would give him the same reception, and therefore went into her chamber as early as the morning before. The grand visier's son, more ashamed, and mortified with the ill success of this last night, no sooner heard him coming, but he jumped out of bed, and ran hastily into the wardrobe. The sultan went to the princess's bed-side, and after the caresses he had given her the former morning, bid her good morrow. Well, daughter, said he, are you in a better humour than you was yesterday morning? Still the princess was silent; and the sultan perceived her to be more troubled, and in greater confusion, than before, and never doubted but that something very extraordinary was the real cause; but provoked that his daughter should conceal it, he said to her in a rage, with his sabre in his hand, Daughter, either tell me what is the matter, or I will cut off your head immediately.

The princess, more frightened at the menaces and tone of the enraged sultan, than at the sight of the drawn sabre, at last broke silence, and said, with tears in her eyes, Dear father and sultan, I ask your majesty's pardon, if I have offended you, and hope, that out of your bounty and clemency you will have compassion on me, when I have told you in what a miserable condition I have spent this last night and the night before.

After this preamble, which appeased the sultan, she told him what had happened to her, in so moving a manner, that he, who loved her tenderly, was most sensibly grieved. And to confirm him into a belief of what she said, she added, If your majesty doubt of the truth of this account, you may inform yourself from my husband, who, I am persuaded, will tell you the same thing.

The sultan immediately entered into the great trouble so surprising an adventure ought to give the princess. Daughter, said he, you are very much to be blamed for not telling me this yesterday, since it concerns me as much as yourself. I did not marry you with an intention to make you miserable, but that you might enjoy all the happiness you deserve, and which you might hope for from a husband, who to me seemed agreeable to you. Efface all these troublesome ideas out of your memory: I will take care and give orders that you shall have no more such disagreeable and insupportable nights.

As soon as the sultan had got back to his own apartment, he sent for the grand visier. Visier, said he, have you seen your son, and has he told you nothing? The visier replied, No. Then the sultan related all that the princess Badroulbadour had told him, and afterwards said, I do not doubt but that my daughter has told me the truth; but nevertheless I should be glad to have it confirmed by your son; therefore go and ask him how it was.

The grand visier went immediately to his son, and communicated the sultan's pleasure to him, and enjoined him to conceal nothing from him, but to tell him the whole truth. I will disguise nothing from you, father, replied the son, for indeed all that the princess says is true; but what relates to my own self particularly, she knows nothing of. After my marriage, I have passed two such dismal nights as are beyond imagination or expression; not to mention the fright I was in, to feel my bed lifted up four times, and transported from one place to another, without being able to guess how it was done. You shall judge of the miserable condition I was in, to pass two whole nights in nothing but my shirt, in a kind of privy, unable to stir out of the place where I was put, or to make the least movement, though I could not perceive any obstacle to prevent me. Yet I must tell you, that all this ill usage does not in the least lessen those sentiments of love and respect I have for the princess, and of which she is so deserving; but I must confess, that, notwithstanding all the honour and lustre that attends my marrying my sovereign's daughter, I would much rather die than live so long in so great an alliance, if I must undergo what I have already endured. I do not doubt but that the princess entertains the same sentiments, and that she will readily agree to a separation, which is so necessary both for her repose and mine. Therefore, father, I beg you, by the same tenderness you had for me to procure me so great an honour, to get the sultan's consent that our marriage may be declared null and void.

Notwithstanding the grand visier's ambition to have his son allied to the sultan, the steady resolution he saw he had made to be separated from the princess, made him not think it proper to bid him have a little patience for a few days; but judged it most convenient to go and give the sultan an account of what he had told him; at which time he never waited till the sultan himself, whom he found pretty much disposed to it, spoke of breaking the marriage, but begged of him to give his son leave to retire from the palace; alledging for an excuse, that it was not just that the princess should be a moment longer exposed to so terrible a persecution upon his son's account.

The grand visier found it no great difficulty to obtain what he asked: from that very instant, the sultan, who had determined it already, gave orders to put a stop to all the rejoicings in the palace and town, and sent expresses to all parts of his dominions to countermand his first orders.

This sudden and unexpected change gave great room for various speculations and inquiries; but no other account could be given for it, but that the visier and his son went out of the palace both very much dejected. Nobody but Aladdin knew the secret, who rejoiced within himself for the happy success his lamp had procured him; which now he had no more occasion to rub, to produce the genie to prevent the consummation of the marriage, which he had certain information was broke off, and that his rival had left the palace. But what is most particular, neither the sultan nor the grand visier, who had forgot Aladdin, and his demand, had the least thought that he had any hand in the enchantment which caused the dissolution of the marriage.

Nevertheless, Aladdin let the three months be completed, which the sultan had appointed for the consummation of the marriage between the princess Badroulbadour and himself; but the next day sent his mother to the palace, to remind the sultan of his promise.

Aladdin's mother went to the palace, as her son had bid her, and stood before the divan in the same place as before. The sultan no sooner cast his eyes upon her, but he knew her again, and remembered her business, and how long he had put her off: therefore, when the grand visier was beginning to make his report, the sultan interrupted him, and said, Visier, I see the good woman who made me the present some months since; forbear your report, till I have heard what she has to say. The visier then looking about the divan, presently perceived Aladdin's mother, and sent the chief of the huissirs for her.

Aladdin's mother came to the foot of the throne, prostrated herself as usual, and when she had got up again, the sultan asked her what she would have? Sir, said she, I come to represent to your majesty, in the name of my son Aladdin, that the three months, at the end of which you ordered me to come again, are expired; and to put you in mind of your promise.

The sultan, when he set this time, little thought of hearing any more of a marriage, which he imagined would be very disagreeable to the princess, when he only considered the meanness of Aladdin's mother's dress; but yet this summons for him to be as good as his word, was somewhat embarrassing to him: thereupon he consulted his visier, and signified to him the little inclination he had to conclude a match with a stranger, whose fortune he supposed to be very mean.

The grand visier freely told the sultan his thoughts on the matter, and said to him, In my opinion, sir, there is an infallible way for your majesty to avoid a match so disproportionable, without giving Aladdin any cause of complaint; which is, for your majesty to set so high a value upon the princess, which, were he ever so rich, he could not come up to. This is the only way to make him desist from so bold, or, as I may say, rash an undertaking, which he never well thought of before he engaged in it.

The sultan approving of the grand visier's advice, turned about to Aladdin's mother, and after some short reflection, said to her, Good woman, it is true, sultans ought to be as good as their words, and I am ready to keep mine, by making your son happy by the marriage of the princess my daughter. But as I cannot marry her without some valuable consideration from your son, you may tell him, I will fulfil my promise, as soon as he shall send me forty basons of massy gold, full of the same things you have already made me a present of, and carried by the like number of black slaves, who shall be led by as many young and handsome white slaves, all dressed magnificently. On these conditions I am ready to bestow the princess my daughter on him; therefore, good woman, go and tell him so, and I will wait till you bring me his answer.

Aladdin's mother prostrated herself a second time before the sultan's throne, and retired. In her way home, she laughed within herself at her son's foolish imagination. Lack-a-day, said she, how can he get so many such large gold basons, and enough of that coloured glass to fill them? What, must he go again to that subterraneous abode, the entrance into which is stopped up, and gather them off the trees? But where will he get so many such slaves as the sultan requires? It is altogether out of his power, and I believe he will not be over-well satisfied with my embassage this time. When she came home, full of these thoughts, she said to her son, Indeed, child, I would not have you think any farther of your marriage with the princess Badroulbadour; though I must tell you too, the sultan received me very kindly, and I believe his intentions were very good, but, if I am not very much deceived, the grand visier has made him change his mind; therefore you may guess what I have to tell you. After I had represented to his majesty, that three months were expired, and begged of him to remember his promise, I observed that he whispered with his visier before he gave me his answer. Then she gave her son an exact account of what the sultan said to her, and the conditions on which he consented to the match. Afterwards, she said to him, The sultan expects your answer immediately; but, continued she, laughing, I believe he may wait long enough.

Not so long, mother, as you imagine, replied Aladdin: the sultan is mistaken, if he thinks by this exorbitant demand to prevent my entertaining thoughts of the princess. I expected greater difficulties, and that he would have set a higher price upon that incomparable princess. But I am very well pleased his demand is but a trifle to what I could have done for her. But while I think of satisfying his request, go and get us something for dinner.

As soon as Aladdin's mother was gone out to market, Aladdin took the lamp and rubbed it, and the genie appeared, and offered his service as usual. The sultan, said Aladdin to him, gives me the princess his daughter in marriage; but demands first of me forty large basons of massy gold, full of the fruits of the garden from whence I took this lamp thou art slave to: and these he expects to have carried by as many black slaves, each preceded by a young handsome white slave, richly clothed. Go, and fetch me this present as soon as possible, that I may send it to him before the divan breaks up. The genie obeyed his commands, and disappeared.

In a little time afterwards, the genie returned with forty black slaves, each with a bason on his head full of pearls, diamonds, rubies, and emeralds, all larger and more beautiful than those presented to the sultan before. Each bason was covered with a silver stuff, embroidered with flowers of gold. All these, and the white slaves, quite filled the house, which was but a small one, and the little yard before it, and a little garden behind. The genie asked Aladdin if he had any other commands? Aladdin told him that he wanted nothing farther then; and the genie disappeared.

When Aladdin's mother came from market, she was in a great surprise to see so many people, and such vast riches. As soon as she had laid down her provisions, she was going to pull off her veil; but Aladdin hindered her, and said, Mother, let us lose no time, but, before the sultan and the divan rise, I would have you return to the palace, and go with this present, as the dowry he asked for the princess Badroulbadour, that he may judge, by my diligence and exactness, of the ardent and sincere zeal I have to procure myself the honour of this alliance. Without waiting for his mother's making a reply, Aladdin opened the street door, and made the slaves walk out; a white slave followed always with a black one, with a bason on his head. When they were all got out, the mother followed the last black slave, and he shut the door, and then retired to his chamber, full of hopes that the sultan, after this present, would receive him as his son-in-law.

The first white slave that went out of the house made all the people who were going by, and saw him, stop; and before they were all got out of the house, the streets were crowded with spectators, who ran to see so extraordinary and noble a sight. The dress of each slave was so rich, both for the stuff and jewels, that those who were dealers in them valued each at no less than a million of money; besides the justness of the dress, the noble air and delicate shape of each slave was unparalleled. They marched slow, and in an equal distance from each other; and the jewels were large, and curiously set in their gold belts with just symmetry; and those in their hats were of so particular a taste and beautiful lustre, that the spectators were in so great an admiration that they could not forbear gazing at them, and following them with their eyes as far as possible; for, in short, the streets were so crowded with people that none could move out of the spot they stood on: but as they were to pass through a great many streets to go to the palace, a great part of the town had an opportunity of seeing them. As soon as the first of these slaves arrived at the palace-gates, the porters formed themselves into order, and took him for a king, by the richness and magnificence of his habit, and were going to kiss the hem of his garment; but the slave, who was instructed by the genie, prevented them, and said, We are only slaves; our master will appear at a proper time.

Then this slave, followed by the rest, advanced into the second court, which was very spacious, and in which stood the sultan's palace. The magnificence of the officers, who stood at the head of their troops, was very much eclipsed by Aladdin's slaves. Nothing was ever seen so shining and noble in the sultan's palace before, and all the bright and gay lords of his court were not to be compared to them.

As the sultan, who had been informed of their march and coming to the palace, had given orders for them to be admitted when they came, they met with no obstacle, but went into the divan in good order, one part filing to the right, and the other to the left. After they were all entered, and had formed a demi-circle before the sultan's throne, the black slaves laid the basons on the carpet, and all prostrated themselves, touching the carpet with their foreheads, and at the same time the white slaves did the same. When they all rose again, the black slaves uncovered the basons, and then all stood with their arms crossed over their breasts in great modesty.

In the mean time Aladdin's mother advanced to the foot of the throne, and having paid her respects, said to the sultan, Sir, my son Aladdin is sensible this present which he has sent your majesty is much below the princess Badroulbadour's worth; but hopes, nevertheless, that your majesty will accept of it, and make it agreeable to the princess; for that which gives him the greater confidence is, he has endeavoured to conform himself to the conditions you were pleased to impose on him.

The sultan was not able to give the least attention to this compliment of Aladdin's mother. The first moment he cast his eyes on the forty basons, full of the most precious and beautiful jewels he had ever seen, and the fourscore slaves, who appeared, by the richness and nobleness of their dress, to be so many kings, he was so struck, that he could not recover his admiration; but, instead of answering Aladdin's mother, addressed himself to the grand visier, who could not, any more than himself, comprehend from whence such profuse riches could come. Well, visier, said he aloud, what do you think of all this? Who can it be that has sent me so extraordinary a present, and neither of us know him? Do you think him worthy of the princess Badroulbadour my daughter?

The visier, notwithstanding his envy and grief to see a stranger preferred to be the sultan's son-in-law before his son, durst not disguise his sentiments. It was too visible that Aladdin's present was more than sufficient to merit his reception into that great alliance; therefore, diving into the sultan's thoughts, he returned this answer: I am so far, sir, from having any thoughts that the person who has made your majesty so noble a present is unworthy of the honour you would do him, that I should be so bold as to say he deserved much more, if I was not persuaded that the greatest treasure in the world ought not to be put in a balance with the princess. This advice was applauded by all the lords who were then in council.

The sultan never staid, nor thought of informing himself whether Aladdin was endued with all the qualifications fitting for one who aspired to be his son-in-law. The sight only of such immense riches, and Aladdin's diligence in satisfying his demand, without starting the least difficulty on the exorbitant conditions he had imposed on him, persuaded him easily that he could want nothing to render him accomplished. Therefore, to send Aladdin's mother back with all the satisfaction she could desire, he said to her, Good woman, go and tell your son, that I wait to embrace and receive him with open arms, and the more haste he makes to come and receive the princess my daughter from my hands, the greater pleasure he will do me.

As soon as Aladdin's mother was retired, as much overjoyed as a woman in her condition could be, to see her son rise, beyond all expectations, to such great fortune, the sultan put an end to the audience for that day; and rising from his throne, ordered that the princess's eunuchs should come and carry those basons into their mistress's apartment, whither he went himself to examine them with her at his leisure. The fourscore slaves were not forgot, but were conducted into the palace; and some time after, the sultan telling the princess Badroulbadour of their magnificence, ordered them to be brought before her apartment, that she might see he exaggerated not any thing in their praise.

In the mean time, Aladdin's mother got home, and shewed in her air and countenance the good news she brought her son. Child, said she to him, you have now all the reason in the world to be pleased. You are, contrary to my expectations, arrived at the height of your desires, and you know what I always told you. But not to keep you too long in suspense; the sultan, with the approbation of the whole court, has declared that you are worthy of possessing the princess Badroulbadour, and waits to embrace you, and conclude your marriage: therefore you must think of making some preparations for that interview, that may answer the great opinion he has of your person; and after the wonders I have seen you do, I am persuaded nothing can be wanting. But I must not forget to tell you, the sultan waits for you with great impatience; therefore lose no time.

Aladdin, charmed with this news, and full of the object which possessed his soul, made his mother very little reply, but retired to his chamber. There, after he had rubbed the lamp, which had never failed him in whatever he wished for, the obedient genie appeared. Genie, said Aladdin, I want to go to bathe immediately, and afterwards provide me the most rich and magnificent habit monarch ever wore. No sooner were the words out of his mouth, but the genie rendered him as well as himself invisible, and transported him into a fine marble bath of all sorts of colours; where first he was undressed, without seeing by whom, in a large spacious hall. From the hall he was led to the bath, which was of a moderate heat, and there rubbed and washed with all sorts of fine scented water. After he had passed through several degrees of heat, he got out, but quite a different man from what he was before. His skin was clear white and red, and his body lightsome and easy; and when he returned into the hall, he found, instead of his own, a noble habit, the magnificence of which very much surprised him. The genie helped him to dress, and when he had done, transported him back to his own chamber, where he asked him if he had any other commands? Yes, answered Aladdin; I expect you should bring me, as soon as possible, an horse that surpasses in beauty and goodness the best in the sultan's stables, with a saddle and housing, and other accoutrements, to the value of a million of money. I want also twenty slaves, as richly clothed as those presented to the sultan, to walk by my side, and follow me, and twenty more to go before me in two ranks. Besides these, bring six women slaves to wait on my mother, as finely dressed as any of the princess Badroulbadour's, each loaded with a complete suit fit for any sultaness; and after all these things, be sure do not forget to bring also ten thousand pieces of gold in ten purses; and make haste, and be diligent.

As soon as Aladdin had given these orders, the genie disappeared, and presently returned with the horse, forty slaves, ten purses of gold, and the six women slaves, each carrying on her head an habit for Aladdin's mother, wrapt up in a silver stuff, and presented them all to Aladdin.

Of the ten purses Aladdin took but four, which he gave to his mother, telling her, those were to supply her with necessaries; the other six he left in the hands of the slaves who brought them, with an order to throw handfuls among the people as they went to the sultan's palace. These six slaves, who carried the purses, he ordered likewise to march before him, three on the right and three on the left. Afterwards, he presented the six women slaves to his mother, telling her they were her slaves, and that the habits they had brought were for her use.

When Aladdin had thus disposed his affairs, he told the genie he would call him when he wanted him; and thereupon the genie disappeared. Then Aladdin's thoughts were more intent upon answering, as soon as possible, the desire the sultan had shewn to see him. He dispatched one of the forty slaves to the palace, with an order to address himself to the chief of the huissirs, to know when he might have the honour to come and throw himself at the sultan's feet. The slave soon acquitted himself of his message, and brought him word that the sultan waited for him with impatience.

Aladdin immediately mounted his horse, and began his march in the order he had appointed it; and though he never was on a horse's back before, he appeared with an extraordinary grace. The streets through which he was to pass were immediately crowded with an innumerable concourse of people, who made the air echo again with their acclamations, especially every time the six slaves, who carried the purses, threw handfuls of gold into the air. Neither did these acclamations and shouts of joy come only from those who scrambled for the money, but from a superior rank of people, who could not forbear commending publicly Aladdin's generosity. Besides, those who knew him once when he played in the streets like a vagabond, did not know him again; such were the effects of the lamp, as to procure by degrees, to those who possessed it, perfections agreeable to the high fortune the right use of it advanced them to. Much more attention was given to Aladdin's person, than to the pomp and magnificence of his attendants, which had been taken notice of the day before, in the march of the slaves with the present to the sultan. Nevertheless, the horse was very much admired by such as had good judgment, and knew how to discern his beauties, without being dazzled with the jewels and richness of the furniture. And when the report was every where spread about, that the sultan was going to give the princess Badroulbadour in marriage to him, nobody regarded his birth, nor envied his good fortune, so worthy he seemed of it.

When he arrived at the palace, every thing was prepared for his reception; and when he came to the second gate, he would have alighted from off his horse, to conform according to the custom observed by the grand visier, the generals of the armies, and governors of the provinces of the first rank: but the chief of the huissirs, who waited on him by the sultan's order, prevented him, and attended him to the council-hall, where he helped him to dismount; though Aladdin opposed him very much, but could not prevail. The huissirs formed themselves into two ranks at the entrance of the hall; the chief put Aladdin on his right hand, and, passing through the midst of them, led him to the sultan's throne.

As soon as the sultan perceived Aladdin, he was as much amazed to see him more richly and magnificently clothed than ever he had been himself, as surprised at his good mien, fine shape, and a certain air of grandeur, which was very much different from the meanness his mother appeared in; all which were contrary to his expectation. But notwithstanding, this amazement and surprise did not hinder him from rising off his throne, and stepping down two or three steps quick enough to prevent Aladdin's throwing himself at his feet: he embraced him with all the demonstrations of friendship. After this civility, Aladdin would have cast himself at his feet again; but he held him fast by the hand, and obliged him to sit between him and the grand visier.

Then Aladdin, assuming the discourse, said, I receive, sir, the honour which your majesty, out of your great bounty, is pleased to confer on me: but permit me to tell you, that I have not forgot that I am your slave; that I know the greatness of your power; and that I am not insensible how much my birth is below the splendour and lustre of the high rank to which I am raised. If any way, continued he, I could have merited so favourable a reception, I confess I cannot attribute it to my boldness, but to a mere chance, which made me raise my eyes, thoughts, and desires, to the divine princess who is the object of my wishes: I ask your majesty's pardon for my rashness, but I cannot dissemble. I should die with grief, if I should lose my hopes of seeing them accomplished.

Son, answered the sultan, embracing him a second time, you do me wrong to doubt the least of my sincerity; your life from this moment is too dear to me not to preserve it, by presenting you with a remedy which is in my disposal. I prefer the pleasure of seeing and hearing you before all your treasure and mine together.

After these words, the sultan gave a signal, and immediately the air echoed again with trumpets and hautboys, and other musical instruments: and at the same time the sultan led Aladdin into a magnificent hall, where there was prepared a noble feast. The sultan and Aladdin eat by themselves; the grand visier, and the great lords of the court, according to their dignity and rank, waited all the time. Their conversation was of indifferent matters; but all the while the sultan took so great a pleasure in seeing him, that he never hardly took his eyes off him; and throughout all their discourse, Aladdin shewed so much good sense, as confirmed the sultan in the good opinion he had of him.

After dinner, the sultan sent for the chief judge of his capital, and ordered him to draw up immediately a contract of marriage between the princess Badroulbadour his daughter and Aladdin. In the mean time, the sultan and he entered into another conversation, in the presence of the grand visier and the lords of the court, who all admired the solidity of his wit, the great ease and freedom wherewith he delivered himself, and the beautiful thoughts and delicacy of his expressing them.

When the judge had drawn up the contract in all the requisite forms, the sultan asked Aladdin if he would stay in the palace, and solemnize the ceremonies of marriage that day? To which he answered, Sir, though great is my impatience to enjoy your majesty's bounty, yet I beg of you to give me leave to defer it till I have built a palace fit to receive the princess in; I therefore desire you to grant me a convenient spot of ground nigh your palace, that I may come the more often to pay my respects to you, and I will take care to have it finished with all diligence. Son, said the sultan, take what ground you think proper; there is land enough before my palace; but consider, I cannot then see you so soon united with my daughter, which would complete my joy. After these words he embraced Aladdin again, who took his leave with as much politeness as if he had been bred up, and had always lived at court.

Aladdin mounted his horse again, and returned home in the same order he came, with the acclamations of the people, who wished him all happiness and prosperity. As soon as he dismounted, he retired to his own chamber, took the lamp, and called the genie as usual, who, in the like manner, made him tenders of his service. Genie, said Aladdin, I have all the reason in the world to commend thy exactness in executing hitherto punctually whatever I have asked thee to do; but now, if thou hast any regard for the lamp, thy mistress, thou must shew, if possible, more zeal and diligence than ever. I would have thee build me, as soon as thou canst, a palace over-against, and at a just distance from the sultan's, and fit it to receive my spouse the princess Badroulbadour. I leave the choice of the materials to thee, that is to say, porphyry, jasper, agate, lapis lazuli, fine marble, and the rest of the building. But I expect, that at the top of this palace thou shalt build me a large hall, with a dome, and four equal fronts; and that, instead of bricks, the walls be made of wedges of massy gold and silver, laid alternately; that each front shall contain six windows, all which, except one, which must be left unfinished and imperfect, shall be so enriched with art and symmetry, diamonds, rubies, and emeralds, that they shall exceed all things of that kind in the world. I would have an inward and outward court before this palace, and a curious garden; but, above all things, take care that there be laid in a place which thou shalt tell me of, a treasure of gold and silver coin. Besides, this palace must be well provided with kitchens and offices, storehouses, and rooms to keep choice furniture in, for all the seasons of the year. I must have stables full of the finest horses, equerries and grooms, and an hunting equipage. There must be officers to attend the kitchen and offices, and women slaves to wait on the princess. Thou understandest what I mean; therefore go about it, and come and tell me when all is done.

By that time Aladdin had instructed the genie with his intentions, and the building of his palace, the sun was set. The next morning, by break of day, Aladdin, whose love for the princess would not let him sleep, was no sooner up, but the genie presented himself, and said, Sir, your palace is finished, come and see if you like it. Aladdin had no sooner signified his consent, but the genie transported him thither in an instant, and he found it so much beyond his expectation, that he could not enough admire it. The genie led him through all the apartments, where he met with nothing but what was rich and magnificent, with officers and slaves, all dressed according to the rank and services for which they were appointed. Then the genie shewed him the treasury, which was opened by a treasurer, where Aladdin saw heaps of bags of money, of different sizes, piled up to the top of the ceiling. The genie assured him of the treasurer's fidelity; and thence led him to the stables, where he shewed him some of the finest horses in the world, and grooms carefully dressing them; and from thence they went to the store-houses, which were filled with all necessary provisions, both for the food and ornament of the horses.

When Aladdin had examined the palace from top to bottom, and particularly the hall with the four-and-twenty windows, and found it so much beyond whatever he could have imagined, he said to the genie, Genie, no one can be better satisfied than I am; and indeed I should be very much to blame, if I complained. There is only one thing wanting, which I forgot, that is, to lay, from the sultan's palace, to the door of the apartment designed for the princess, a piece of fine velvet for her to walk upon. The genie immediately disappeared, and Aladdin saw what he desired executed that minute. Then the genie returned, and carried Aladdin home, before the gates of the sultan's palace were opened.

When the porters, who had always been used to an open prospect, came to open the gates, they were amazed to find it limited, and to see a piece of velvet spread for a great way; but when they could discern Aladdin's palace distinctly, their surprise was very much increased. The news of so extraordinary a wonder was presently spread about the palace. The grand visier, who came soon after the gates were open, was no less amazed than other people at this novelty, but ran and acquainted the sultan, and endeavoured to make him believe it to be all enchantment. Visier, replied the sultan, why will you have it to be enchantment? You know as well as me that it is Aladdin's palace, which I gave him leave to build, to receive my daughter in. After the proof we have had of his riches, can we think it strange that he should build a palace in so short a time: he has a mind to surprise us, and let us see what wonders are to be done with ready money. Come, own sincerely, that what you mention of enchantment proceeds from your envy. It being then the hour of going to council, they had no farther discourse.

When Aladdin got home, and had dismissed the genie, he found his mother up, and dressing herself in one of those suits that were brought her. By that time the council generally broke up, Aladdin had disposed his mother to go to the palace with her slaves, and desired her, if she saw the sultan, to tell him she came to do herself the honour to attend the princess, towards the evening, to her palace. Accordingly she went with her slaves, who were dressed as fine as sultanesses; yet the crowd was nothing so great, because they were all veiled, and had each a surtout* on, agreeable to the richness and magnificence of their habits. For Aladdin, he mounted his horse, and took leave of his paternal house for ever, taking care not to forget his wonderful lamp, by the assistance of which he had reaped such advantages, and arrived at the utmost height of his wishes, and went to the palace in the same pomp as the day before.

As soon as the porters of the sultan's palace saw Aladdin's mother, they went and informed the sultan, who presently ordered the bands of trumpets and hautboys, &c. to play, and the drums to beat, so that the air rebounded the echoes, and inspired the whole city with joy; the tradesmen and merchants began to adorn their shops and houses with fine carpets and cushions, and bedeck them with boughs, and prepare illuminations against night. The handicraftsmen and workmen of all sorts, left their works, and all repaired to the great space between the sultan's and Aladdin's palace; which last gained all their attention, not only because it was new to them, but because there was no comparison between them. But the greatest part of their amazement was to comprehend by what unheard-of miracle so magnificent a palace should be so soon built, it being apparent to all that there were no such things as materials, or any foundation laid the day before.

Aladdin's mother was received in the palace with honour, and introduced into the princess Badroulbadour's apartment by the chief of the eunuchs. As soon as the princess saw her, she went and saluted her, and desired her to sit down on a sofa; and while her women made an end of dressing her, and adorning her with the jewels Aladdin had presented her with, a noble collation was served up. At the same time, the sultan, who had a mind to be as much with his daughter as possible before he parted with her, came and paid her great respect. Aladdin's mother had often talked to the sultan in public, but he had never seen her with her veil off, as she was then; and though she was somewhat advanced in years, she had the remains of a good face, which shewed what she had been in her youth. The sultan, who had always seen her dressed very mean and poor, was in admiration to find her as richly and magnificently clothed as the princess his daughter. This, when he came to a more serious reflection, made him think Aladdin equally prudent and wise in whatever he undertook.

When it was night, the princess took her leave of the sultan: their adieus were tender, and accompanied with tears: they embraced each other several times; and at last the princess left her own apartments, and set forwards for Aladdin's palace, with his mother on her left hand, followed by an hundred women slaves, dressed with surprising magnificence. All the bands of music, which played from the time Aladdin's mother arrived, joined together, led the procession, followed by an hundred chaoux,* and the like number of black eunuchs, in two files, with their officers at their head. Four hundred of the sultan's young pages carried flambeaux on each side, which, together with the illuminations of the sultan's and Aladdin's palaces, made it as light as day.

In this order the princess walked on the velvet, which was spread from the sultan's palace to Aladdin's, preceded by bands of musicians; who, joining with those on the terraces of Aladdin's palace, formed a concert, which, all extraordinary and confused as it appeared, increased the joy, not only of the crowd of people in the large place, but of all that were in the two palaces, the town, and a great way about it.

At last, when the princess arrived at the new palace, Aladdin ran with all the joy imaginable to the entry of the apartment, the place appointed for him to receive her. His mother had taken care to point him out to the princess, in the midst of the officers that surrounded him, who found him so handsome, she was charmed. Adorable princess, said Aladdin to her, accosting and saluting her respectfully, if I have the misfortune to have displeased you, by my boldness of aspiring to the possession of so lovely a princess, and my sultan's daughter, I must tell you, that you ought to blame your bright eyes and charms, not me. Prince, (as we may now call him,) answered the princess, I am obedient to the will of my father; and its enough for me to have seen you once, to tell you that I obey without reluctance.

Aladdin, charmed with so agreeable and obliging an answer, would not keep the princess standing, after she had walked so far, which was more than she was used to do; but took her by the hand, which he kissed with the greatest demonstration of joy, and led her into a large hall, illuminated with an infinite number of wax-candles, where, by the care of the genie, a noble feast was served up. The plates were all of massy gold, and contained the most delicate and costly meats. The vessels, basons, goblets, &c. with which the beaufet was furnished, were gold also, and of exquisite workmanship, and all the other ornaments and embellishments of the hall were answerable. The princess, dazzled to see so much riches in one place, said to Aladdin, I once thought, prince, that nothing in the world was so rich and beautiful as the sultan my father's palace; but the sight of this hall alone is sufficient to undeceive me.

Then Aladdin led the princess to the place appointed for her; and as soon as he and his mother were sat down, a band of the most harmonious instruments, accompanied with the voices of some beautiful ladies, began a concert, which lasted without intermission to the end of the repast. The princess was so charmed, that she declared she had never heard any thing like it in the sultan her father's court, but knew not that these musicians were fairies, which the genie had procured.

When the table was taken away, there entered a company of dancers, who danced, according to the custom of the country, several dances in figures, and performed their parts with a surprising lightness and activity, and shewed all the address they were capable of. About midnight, Aladdin, according to the custom of that time in China, presented his hand to the princess Badroulbadour to dance with her, and so finish the ceremonies of their nuptials; and, in short, both danced with so good a grace, that they were the admiration of all the company. When they left off, Aladdin did not let the princess's hand go, but led her to the apartment where the nuptial-bed was prepared. The princess's women helped to undress her, and put her to bed: Aladdin's officers did the same by him, and then all retired. Thus ended the ceremonies and rejoicings of Aladdin's and the princess Badroulbadour's marriage.

The next morning, when Aladdin waked, his valets-de-chambre presented themselves to dress him, and brought him another habit, as rich and magnificent as that he wore the day before. Then he ordered one of the horses appointed for his person to be got ready, mounted him, and went, in the midst of a large troop of slaves, to the sultan's palace. The sultan received him with the same honours as before, embraced him, placed him on the throne with him, and asked him to breakfast with him. To which Aladdin replied, I beg your majesty will dispense with me from accepting that honour to-day: I came to ask you to come and take a repast in the princess's palace, attended by your grand visier, and all the lords of the court. The sultan consented to it with pleasure, rose up immediately, and, as it was not far off, went thither on foot, with Aladdin on his right hand, the grand visier on his left, preceded by the chaoux, and principal officers of the palace, and followed by all the great lords of his court.

The nearer the sultan approached Aladdin's palace, the more he was struck with its beauty, but was much more amazed when he entered it, and could not forbear breaking out into exclamations. But when he came into the hall with the four-and-twenty windows, (to shew which Aladdin had invited him,) and had seen the ornaments, and, above all, cast his eyes on the windows, enriched with diamonds, rubies, emeralds, all large perfect stones; and when Aladdin had observed to him, that it was as rich on the outside, he was so much surprised, that he remained some time motionless. After he recovered himself, he said to his visier, Is it possible that there should be such a stately palace so nigh my own, and I be an utter stranger to it till now? Sir, replied the grand visier, your majesty may remember, that, the day before yesterday, you gave Aladdin whom you accepted for your son-in-law, leave to build a palace over-against your own; and that very night, before sun-set, there was nothing of it begun, and yesterday I had the honour to tell you first the palace was built and finished. I remember it, replied the sultan, but never imagined that that palace was one of the wonders of the world; for where, in all the world besides, shall we find walls built of massy gold and silver, instead of brick, stone, or marble; and diamonds, rubies, and emeralds set thick about the windows? Certainly there never was any thing like it in this world before.

The sultan would examine and admire the beauty of all the windows, and counting them, found that they were but three-and-twenty that were so richly adorned, and that the twenty-fourth was unfinished and imperfect. Visier, said he, (for that minister never left him,) I am surprised that a hall of this magnificence should be left thus imperfect. Sir, replied the grand visier, without doubt Aladdin has only wanted time to finish this window as well as the rest; for it is not to be supposed that he wants jewels for it, but that he will set about it the first opportunity.

Aladdin, who had left the sultan at the time of this discourse, to go and give some necessary orders, returned just as the visier had given the sultan his supposed reasons. Son, said the sultan to him, this hall is the most worthy of admiration of any hall in the world; there is only one thing that surprises me, which is to find one of the windows unfinished: it is certainly the forgetfulness or negligence of the workmen that they have not put the finishing stroke to so beautiful a piece of architecture. Sir, answered Aladdin, neither of these are the reasons why your majesty sees it in this condition: the thing was done with a design, and it was by my orders that the workmen left it thus, since I had a mind that your majesty should have the glory of finishing this hall, and the palace also; and I beg of you to approve of my good intention, that I may remember the favours I have received from you. If you did it with this intention, replied the sultan, I take it kindly, and will give orders about it immediately; and accordingly sent to the most topping jewellers and goldsmiths in his capital.

Afterwards, the sultan went out of this hall, and Aladdin led him into that where he had regaled the princess Badroulbadour on his wedding-day. The princess came immediately afterwards, and received the sultan her father with an air that shewed how much she was satisfied with her marriage. Two tables were immediately spread with the most delicious meats, served up in gold dishes. The sultan, princess, Aladdin, and the grand visier, sat down at the first, and all the lords of the court at the second, which was very long. The sultan was very much pleased with the meats, and owned they were very excellent, as well as the wines delicious. But what he most of all admired, was four large beaufets, profusely furnished with large flaggons, basons, and tumblers, all of massy gold beset with jewels. Besides, he was charmed with several bands of music, which were ranged along the hall, and formed most agreeable concerts.

When the sultan rose from table, he was informed that the jewellers and goldsmiths he had sent for, attended; upon which he returned to the hall, and shewed them the window which was unfinished. I sent for you, said he, to fit up this window in as great perfection as any of the rest; examine them well, and make all the dispatch you can.

The jewellers and goldsmiths examined the other three-and-twenty windows with great attention; and after they had consulted together, to know what each could furnish, they returned, and presented themselves before the sultan, whose principal jeweller undertaking to speak for the rest, said, Sir, we are all willing to use our utmost care and industry to obey your majesty; but among us all we cannot furnish jewels enough for so great a work. But then I can, said the sultan: come to my palace, and you shall chuse what are fitting.

When the sultan returned to his palace, he ordered his jewels to be fetched out; and the jewellers took a great quantity, particularly those which Aladdin had made him a present of; which they soon used, without making any great advance or shew in their work, and came again several times for more, and in a month's time had not finished half their work. In short, they used all the jewels the sultan had of his own, and borrowed of the visier, and yet the work was not half done.

Aladdin, at the same time, knew that all the sultan's endeavours to make this window like the rest were in vain; and therefore one day went into the hall to the jewellers and goldsmiths, and not only bid them desist from their work, but ordered them to undo what they had begun, and to carry the sultan all his jewels back again; and accordingly they undid in a few hours what they had been six weeks about, and then retired.

When they were all gone, and Aladdin was left alone, he took his lamp, and rubbed it, and presently the genie appeared. Genie, said Aladdin, I ordered thee to leave one of the four-and-twenty windows of this hall imperfect and unfinished, and thou didst execute my commands punctually; but now I would have thee make it like the rest. The genie immediately disappeared; Aladdin went out of the hall, and returning soon after into it, he found that window, as he wished it to be, like the others.

In the mean time, the jewellers and goldsmiths got to the palace, and were introduced into the sultan's presence, where the first jeweller presenting the jewels which he had brought back, said, in the name of all the rest, Sir, your majesty knows how long we have been upon the work you was pleased to set us about, in which we used all imaginable industry. It was pretty far advanced, when Aladdin obliged us not only to leave it off, but to undo what we had already begun, and bring your majesty your jewels back. The sultan asked them if Aladdin gave them any reason for so doing; and they answering that he had given them none, he ordered a horse to be brought to him presently, which he mounted, and rode to Aladdin's palace, with some few attendants on foot by his side. When he came there, he alighted at the stair-case which led up to the hall, and went directly up to it; but it happened that at that very juncture Aladdin was opportunely there, and had just time to receive him at the door.

The sultan, without giving Aladdin time to complain obligingly of his not giving him notice, that he might have acquitted himself with the more duty and respect, said to him, Son, I come myself to know the reason why you would leave so noble and magnificent an hall as this is, imperfect and unfinished.

Aladdin disguised the true reason, which was, that the sultan was not rich enough in jewels to be at so great an expence; but said, Indeed your majesty saw this hall unfinished, but I beg of you to see if any thing is wanting.

The sultan went directly to the window which was left imperfect; and when he found it like the rest, he fancied that he was mistaken, and examined the two windows on each side, and afterwards all the four-and-twenty; and when he was convinced that the window which several workmen had been so long about, was finished in so short a time, he embraced Aladdin, and kissed him between his eyes, saying to him, Certainly you are the most surprising of all men, to do things thus in the twinkling of an eye: there is not your fellow in the world; the more I know you, the more I admire you.

Aladdin received these praises of the sultan with a great deal of modesty, and replied in these words: Sir, it is a great honour to me to deserve your majesty's good will and approbation, and I assure you, I shall study to deserve them more.

The sultan returned to his palace, but would not let Aladdin go back with him. When he came there, he found his grand visier waiting for him, to whom he related the wonder he had been a witness of, with the utmost admiration, and in such terms, as left that minister no room to doubt but that the fact was as the sultan related it; though he was the more confirmed in his belief that Aladdin's palace was the effect of enchantment, as he told the sultan the first moment he saw that palace, and was going to repeat the same thing again; but the sultan interrupted him, and said, You told me so once before: I see, visier, you have not forgot your son's marriage to my daughter. The grand visier plainly saw how much the sultan was prepossessed; and therefore, to avoid any dispute, let him remain in his own opinion. The sultan, as soon as he rose in a morning, went into his closet to look at Aladdin's palace, and would go often in a day to contemplate and admire it.

All this time Aladdin did not confine himself in his palace, but took care to shew himself once or twice a-week in the town, by going sometimes to one mosque, and sometimes to another, to prayers, or going to pay the grand visier a visit, who affected to make great court to him, on certain days, on which he did the principal lords of the court the honour to regale them at his palace. Every time he stirred out, he caused two slaves, who walked by his side, to throw handfuls of money among the people as he passed through the streets, which were generally at that time crowded. Besides, no one came to his palace-gates to beg alms, but were sensible of his liberality.

Not a week passed, but Aladdin went either once or twice a-hunting, sometimes near the town, and sometimes farther off; at which time the villages through which he passed felt the effects of his generosity, which gained him so much the love and blessing of the people, that it was common for them to swear by his head. In short, without giving the sultan, to whom he gave all imaginable respect, the least umbrage, it might be said, that Aladdin, by his affable behaviour and liberality, had got the affection of the people, and was more beloved than the sultan himself. With all these good qualities, he shewed a great courage, and a commendable zeal for the public good; of both which he gave sufficient proofs in a revolt on the borders of that kingdom; for he no sooner understood that the sultan was levying an army to disperse the rebels, but he begged the command of it, which he found no difficulty to obtain. As soon as he got to the army, he marched the troops against the rebels, and was so quick in that expedition, that the sultan heard of the rebels' defeat before he had received an account of his arrival in the army. And though this action rendered his name famous throughout the kingdom, it never puffed up his heart with pride and vanity, but he was as affable after returning victor as before.

Aladdin had lived and behaved himself after this manner several years, when the African magician, who undesignedly had been the instrument of raising him to so high a pitch of fortune, bethought himself of him in Africa, whither, after his expedition, he returned. And though he was almost persuaded that Aladdin died miserably in the subterraneous abode where he left him, yet he had the curiosity to know his end certainly; and as he was a great necromancer, he took out of a cupboard a square box, which he made use of in his necromantic observations; then sat himself down on a sofa, and set it before him. After he had prepared and levelled the sand which was in it, with an intention to discover whether or no Aladdin died in the subterraneous abode, he cast figures, and formed a horoscope, by which, when he came to examine it, he found that Aladdin had escaped out of the cave, lived splendidly, was rich, had married a princess, and was very much honoured and respected.

The magician no sooner understood, by the rules of his diabolical art, that Aladdin had arrived to that height of good fortune, but a colour came into his face, and he cried out in a rage, This poor sorry taylor's son has discovered the secret and virtue of the lamp. I believed his death to be certain; but find too plainly he enjoys the fruit of my labour and study: but I will prevent his enjoying it long, or perish in the attempt. He was a great while deliberating on what he should do, but the next morning set forwards, and never stopped, but just to refresh himself, till he arrived at the capital of China, and took a lodging in a khan, and staid there the remainder of the day and the night, to refresh himself after so long a journey.

The next day, the first thing the magician did, was to enquire what people said of Aladdin; and taking a walk for that end through the town, he went to the most public and frequented places, where people of the best distinction met to drink a certain warm liquor, which he had drank often when he was there before. As soon as he sat down, he was presented with a glass, which he took, but listened at the same time to the discourse of the company, who were talking of Aladdin's palace. When he had drank off his glass, he joined them, and taking this opportunity, asked them particularly what palace that was they spoke so advantageously of? From whence come you? said the person to whom he addressed himself; you must certainly be a stranger, not to have seen or heard talk of prince Aladdin's palace, (for he was called so after his marriage with the princess Badroulbadour.) I do not say, continued the gentleman, that it is one of the wonders in the world, but the only wonder of the world, since there is nothing so grand, rich, and magnificent; certainly you must have come a great way off, not to have heard of it, for it is the greatest subject of conversation in this part of the world. Go and see, and then judge whether or no I have told you the truth. Forgive my ignorance, sir, replied the African magician; I arrived here but yesterday, and came from the farthest part of Africa, where the fame of this palace had not reached when I came away; for the affair which brought me hither was so urgent, that I made no stay in any place to be informed of news. But I will not fail to go and see it; and my impatience is so great, I will go immediately and satisfy my curiosity, if you will do me the favour to shew me the way thither.

The person to whom the African magician addressed himself, seeming to take a pleasure in shewing him the way to Aladdin's palace, got up, and went thither instantly. When he came to the palace, and had examined it on all sides, he made no dispute but that Aladdin had made use of the lamp to build it; and knew that none but the genies, the slaves of the lamp, the attaining of which he had missed, could have performed such wonders; and, piqued to the quick at Aladdin's grandeur, returned to the khan where he lodged.

The next thing he had to do was to know where the lamp was; if Aladdin carried it about with him, or where he kept it, and this he was to discover by his art of necromancy. As soon as he entered his lodging, he took his square box of sand, which he always carried along with him when he travelled, and after he had performed some operations, he knew that the lamp was in Aladdin's palace, and conceived an inexpressible joy at the discovery. Well, said he, I shall have the lamp, and I defy Aladdin's preventing it, and his falling into his original meanness, from whence he has taken so high a flight.

It was Aladdin's misfortune at this time to be gone a-hunting for eight days, which the magician came to know by this means. After he had performed this operation, which gave him so much joy, he went to the master of the khan, entered into a discourse with him on indifferent matters, and among the rest told him he had been to see Aladdin's palace; and after exaggerating on what was the most surprising, and most admired by the world, he added, But my curiosity leads me farther, and I shall not be easy till I have seen the person to whom this wonderful edifice belongs. That will be no difficult matter, replied the master of the khan; there is not a day passes but he will give you the opportunity; but now he is not at home; he has been gone these three days a hunting-match, which will last eight.

The magician wanted to know no more; he took his leave of the master of the khan, and returning to his own chamber, said to himself, This is an opportunity I ought by no means to let slip, but will make the best use of it. To that end, he went to a maker and seller of lamps, and asked for a dozen of copper lamps. The master of the shop told him he had not so many by him, but if he would have patience till the next day, he would get him so many against what time he had a mind to have them. The magician appointed his time, and bid him take care that they should be handsome and well polished.

The next day, the magician went for the twelve lamps, paid the man his full price for them, put them into a basket which he brought on purpose with him, hung the basket on his arm, and went directly with it to Aladdin's palace; and when he came near it, cried, Who will change old lamps for new ones? But as he went along, he gathered a crowd of children and apprentice boys about him, who thought him, as indeed a great many passing by did, mad, or a fool, to change new lamps for old ones, and therefore hollowed at him.

The African magician never minded all their scoffs and hollowings, or all they could say to him, but still cried, Who will change old lamps for new ones? Which he repeated so often about the princess Badroulbadour's palace, that the princess, who was then in the hall with the four-and-twenty windows, hearing a man cry something, and not being able to distinguish his words by reason of the hollowing of the mob about him, sent one of her women slaves to know what he cried.

The slave was not long before she returned, and ran into the hall, laughing so heartily that the princess could not forbear herself. Well, giggler, said the princess, will you tell me what you laugh at? Alas! madam, answered the slave, laughing still, who can forbear laughing, to see a fool with a basket on his arm, full of fine new lamps, ask to change them for old ones; which makes the children and mob make such a noise about him.

Another woman slave hearing this, said, Now you speak of lamps, I know not whether the princess may have observed it, but there is an old one upon the cornish, and whoever owns it, he will not be sorry to find a new one in its stead: if the princess has a mind, she may have the pleasure to try if this fool is so silly as to give a new lamp for an old one, without having any thing for the exchange.

Now the lamp this slave mentioned, happened to be Aladdin's wonderful lamp, which he, for fear of losing, had laid upon the cornish before he went a-hunting; which precaution he had made use of several times before, but neither the princess, their slaves or eunuchs, had ever taken notice of it. At all other times but hunting, he carried it about him; and then indeed he might have locked it up; but other people have been guilty of as great oversights.

The princess Badroulbadour, who knew not the value of this lamp, and the interest that Aladdin, not to mention her own, had to keep it, entered soon into the pleasantry, and bid an eunuch take it, and go and make that exchange. The eunuch obeyed, went out of the hall, and no sooner got to the palace gates, but he saw the African magician, called to him, and shewing him the old lamp, said to him, Give me a new lamp for this.

The magician never disputed but this was the lamp he wanted, since he had been informed that there were no such utensils in the palace but what were either gold or silver. He snatched it presently, and thrusting it as far as he could into his breast, offered him his basket, and bid him chuse which he liked best. The eunuch picked out one, and carried it to the princess Badroulbadour; but the exchange was no sooner made, but there was such a hollo, that the palace rung again; such a ridicule the children made of him.

The African magician gave every body leave to laugh as much as they pleased, but staid not long about Aladdin's palace, but made the best of his way, without crying any longer, New lamps for old ones, and by his silence got rid of the children and mob.

As soon as he got out of the space between the two palaces, he skulked down those streets which were the least frequented; and having no more occasion for his lamps or basket, set it down in the midst of the street when nobody saw him; then scouring down another street or two, he walked till he came to one of the city gates, and then pursuing his way through the suburbs, where he bought some provisions, he got into the fields, and turned into a road, which led to a lonely remote place, where he stopped for a time, to execute what he came about, never regretting his horse, which he left at the khan.

In this place the African magician passed the remainder of the day, till it was dark night, when he pulled out the lamp out of his breast, and rubbed it. Upon that summons the genie appeared, and said, What wouldst thou have? I am ready to obey thee as thy slave, and the slave of all those who have the lamp in their hands; both I and the other slaves of the lamp. I command thee, replied the magician, to transport me immediately, and the palace which thou and the other slaves of the lamp have built in this town, such as it is, and with all the people in it, to such a place in Africa. The genie made no reply, but with the assistance of the other genies, the slaves of the lamp, transported him and the palace entire immediately to the place he appointed in Africa; where we will leave the magician, palace, and the princess Badroulbadour, to speak of the surprise of the sultan.

As soon as the sultan rose the next morning, according to custom, he went into his closet, to have the pleasure of contemplating and admiring Aladdin's palace: but when he first looked that way, and saw an empty space instead of a palace, he thought at first he was mistaken, and rubbed his eyes; but when he looked again, and saw nothing of the palace any more the second time than the first, his amazement was so great that he stood for some time musing with himself, and reflecting how so large a palace as Aladdin's, which he saw plainly every day, and the night before, should vanish so soon, and not leave the least remains behind. Certainly, said he to himself, I am not mistaken; it stood there: if it had tumbled down, the materials would have lain in heaps; and if swallowed up in an earthquake, there would be some mark left. However, though he was convinced that no palace stood there, he could not help staying there some time, to see whether or no he might not be mistaken. At last he retired to his apartment, not without looking behind him, and ordered the grand visier to be fetched in all haste, and in the mean time sat down, but agitated by so many different thoughts, that he knew not what to resolve on.

The grand visier did not make the sultan wait long for him, but came in with so much precipitation, that neither he nor his attendants, as they passed by, missed Aladdin's palace; neither did the porters, when they opened the palace gates, observe any alteration.

When he came into the sultan's presence, he said to him, Sir, the hurry your majesty sent for me in, makes me believe something extraordinary has happened, since you know this is council-day, and I shall not fail attending you very soon. Indeed, said the sultan, it is something very extraordinary, as you say, and you will allow it to be so: tell me what is become of Aladdin's palace? Aladdin's palace! replied the grand visier in a great amazement; I think, as I passed by it, it stood in its usual place; such vast buildings are not easily removed. Go into my closet, said the sultan, and tell me if you can see it.

The grand visier went into the closet, where he was struck with no less amazement than the sultan had been. When he was well assured that there was not the least appearance, he returned to the sultan. Well, visier, said he, have you seen Aladdin's palace? Sir, answered the visier, your majesty may remember, that I had the honour to tell you, that that palace, which was the subject of your admiration, with all its immense riches, was only the work of magic and a magician; but your majesty then would not give the least attention to what I said.

The sultan, who could not disown what the grand visier had represented to him, for that reason flew into the greater passion. Where is that impostor, that wicked wretch, said he, that I may have his head cut off immediately? Sir, replied the grand visier, it is some days since he came to take his leave of your majesty; he ought to be sent to, to know what is become of his palace, since he cannot be ignorant of what has been transacted. That is too great an indulgence, replied the sultan; go and order a detachment of thirty horses, to bring him loaded with chains. The grand visier went and gave orders for a detachment of thirty horse, and instructed the officer that commanded them how he might take Aladdin. The detachment pursued their orders, and about six leagues from the town met him returning from hunting. The officer went up to him, and told him that the sultan was so impatient to see him, that he had sent them to accompany him home.

Aladdin had not the least suspicion of the true reason of their meeting him, but pursued his way; but when he came within half a league of the city, the detachment surrounded him, and the officer addressed himself, and said to him, Prince Aladdin, it is with great regret that I declare to you the sultan's order to arrest you, and to carry you before him as a criminal: I beg of you not to take it ill that I acquit myself of my duty, and to forgive me.

Aladdin, who thought himself innocent, was very much surprised at this declaration, and asked the officer if he knew what crime he was accused of; who replied, he did not. Then Aladdin, finding that his retinue was much inferior to this detachment, alighted off his horse, and said to the officer, Execute your orders, though I do not know any crime I have committed against the sultan's person or government. A large long chain was immediately put about his neck, and fastened round his body, so that both his arms were pinioned down; then the officer put himself at the head of the detachment, and one of the troopers taking hold of the end of the chain, obliged Aladdin to follow him a-foot into the town.

When this detachment entered the suburb, the people, who saw Aladdin thus led as a criminal, never disputed but that his head was to be cut off; and as he was generally beloved, some took sabres, and others arms; and those who had none, gathered stones, and followed the detachment. The last five of the detachment faced about to disperse them; but their numbers presently increased so much, that the detachment began to think that it would be well if they could get into the sultan's palace before Aladdin was rescued; to prevent which, as the streets were large, they extended themselves as far as possible. In this manner they arrived at the palace, and there drew up in a line, and faced about till the officer and troopers that led Aladdin had got within the gates.

Aladdin was carried before the sultan, who waited for him, attended by the grand visier, in a balcony; and as soon as he saw him, he ordered the executioner, who waited there on purpose, to cut off his head, without hearing him, or giving him leave to clear himself.

As soon as the executioner had taken off the chain that was fastened about Aladdin's neck and body, and laid down a skin stained with the blood of the many criminals he had executed, he made Aladdin kneel down, and tied a bandage over his eyes; then drawing his sabre, he flourished it three or four times in the air, waiting for the sultan's giving the signal to separate his head from his body.

At that instant, the grand visier perceiving that the populace had forced the guard of horse, and crowded the great square before the palace, and were scaling the walls in several places, he said to the sultan, before he gave the signal, I beg of your majesty to consider what you are going to do, since you will hazard your palace's being forced; and who knows what fatal consequence may attend it? My palace forced! replied the sultan, who can have that boldness? Sir, answered the grand visier, if your majesty casts but your eye towards the great square, and on the palace-walls, you will know what I mean.

The sultan was so frightened when he saw so great a mob, and perceived so enraged as they were, that he ordered the executioner to put up his sabre immediately in the scabbard, and to unbind Aladdin, and at the same time bid the chaoux declare to the people that the sultan had pardoned him.

Then all those who had already got upon the walls, and were witnesses of what passed, abandoned their posts, and got down, and, overjoyed that they had saved the life of a man whom they loved dearly, published the news among the rest, which was presently confirmed by the chaoux, which soon disarmed the populace of their rage; the tumult was soon abated, and the mob dispersed.

When Aladdin found himself at liberty, he turned towards the balcony, and perceiving the sultan, raised his voice, and said to him in a moving manner, I beg of your majesty to add one favour more to that which I have already received, which is, to let me know my crime? Thy crime! answered the sultan, perfidious wretch, dost thou not know it? Come up hither, and I will shew it thee.

Aladdin went up to the sultan, who, after he had paid his obedience, said to him, Follow me; and then led him into his closet. When he came to the door, he said to him, Thou oughtest to know whereabouts thy palace stood; look, and tell me what is become of it?

Aladdin, staring about him, perceived very well the spot of ground his palace stood on; but not being able to divine how it should disappear, he was in so great confusion and amazement, that he could not return one word of answer.

The sultan, growing impatient, said to him again, Where is thy palace, and what is become of my daughter? Then Aladdin, breaking silence, said to him, Sir, I see very well, and own that the palace which I have built is not in the same place where it was, but that it is vanished; neither can I tell your majesty where it may be, but can assure you I have no hand in it.

I am not so much concerned about thy palace, replied the sultan: I value my daughter a thousand times before it, and would have thee find her out, otherwise I will cause thy head to be struck off, and no consideration shall prevent it.

I beg of your majesty, answered Aladdin, to grant me forty days to make my inquiries in; and if in that time I have not the success I wish for, I will come again, and offer my head at the foot of your throne, and you may dispose of it at your pleasure. I give you the forty days you ask for, said the sultan; but do not think to abuse the favour I shew you, by thinking to escape my resentment; for I shall find ways to come at you, in whatsoever part of the world you go to.

Aladdin went out of the sultan's presence with great humiliation, and seemed worthy of pity. He crossed the courts of the palace, hanging down his head, and was in so great confusion he durst not lift up his eyes. The principal officers of the court, who had all professed themselves his friends, and whom he had never disobliged, turned their backs on him, instead of going up to him to comfort him, and offer him a place of retreat; which if they had done, he was so much distracted in his thoughts, he would not have known them; since he knew not himself, but had quite lost his senses, as it appeared, by asking every body he met if they had seen his palace, or could tell any news of it?

These questions made every body believe that Aladdin was mad: some laughed at him, but people of sense and humanity, particularly those he had dealt withal, and he had contracted some friendship with, really pitied him. For three days he rambled about the town after this manner, without coming to any resolution, or eating any thing but what some good people forced him to out of charity.

At last, when he was tired with wandering about the city in this manner, he strolled into the country, and after he had traversed several fields in a frightful uncertainty, at the close of the night he came to a river side: There, possessed by his despair, he said to himself, Where shall I seek my palace? In what province, country, or part of the world shall I find that, and my dear princess, whom the sultan expects from me? I shall never succeed: I had better free myself at once from so many fatigues, and such bitter griefs; and then was just going to throw himself into the river; but, as a good musselman, he thought first to say his prayers; and going to prepare himself, he went first to the river side to wash his hands and face, according to the custom. But that place being steep and slippery, by reason of the water's beating against it, he slides down, and had certainly fallen into the river, but for a little rock, which stood about two feet out of the earth: Besides, it was his happiness, that he still had the ring which the African magician put on his finger before he went down into the subterraneous abode to fetch the lamp; for by his falling down the bank, he rubbed the ring so hard by holding on the rock, that immediately the same genie appeared which he saw in the cave where the magician had left him. What wouldst thou have, said the genie? I am ready to obey thee as thy slave, and the slave of all those that have that ring on their finger; both I and the other slaves of the ring.

Aladdin, agreeably surprised at an apparition he so little expected in the despair he was in, replied, Save my life, genie, a second time, either by shewing me the place where the palace I have caused to be built now stands, or immediately transport it back where it first stood. That which you command me, answered the genie, is not in my power; I am only the slave of the ring; you must address yourself to the slaves of the lamp. If it be so, replied Aladdin, I command thee, by the power of the ring, to transport me to the place where my palace stands, in what part of the world soever it is, and set me down under the princess Badroulbadour's window. These words were no sooner out of his mouth, but the genie transported him into the midst of a large meadow in Africa, a small distance from a large city, where his palace stood, and set him exactly under the window of the princess's apartment, and then left him: All this he did almost in an instant.

Aladdin, notwithstanding the darkness of the night, knew his palace again very well, and the princess Badroulbadour's apartment; but as the night was pretty far advanced, and all was quiet in the palace, he retired some distance off, and sat down at the root of a large tree: There, full of hopes, and reflecting on his happiness, which he attributed to pure chance, he found himself in a much more peaceable situation than when he was arrested and carried before the sultan, and in danger of losing his life. He amused himself for some time with those agreeable thoughts; but not having slept for five or six days, he was not able to resist the drowsiness which came upon him, but fell fast asleep.

The next morning, as soon as day appeared, Aladdin was agreeably wakened, not only by the singing of the birds, which had roosted in the tree under which he had passed the night, but all those which had perched in the trees of the palace-garden. When he cast his eyes on that wonderful edifice, he conceived an inexpressible joy to think he should soon be master of it again, and once more possess his dear princess Badroulbadour. Pleased with these hopes, he immediately got up, and went to the princess's apartment, and walked under her window, in expectation of her rising, that he might see her. During this expectation, he began to consider with himself from whence the cause of his misfortune proceeded; and after he had well reflected on the matter, he never doubted but that it was owing to leaving his lamp behind him; upon which he accused himself of negligence, and the little care he took of it, to let it be a moment out of his sight. But what puzzled him most was, he could not imagine who had been so jealous of his happiness; but would soon have guessed, if he had then known that both he and his palace were in Africa, the very name of which would soon have made him remember the magician, his declared enemy; but the genie, the slave of the ring, had not made the least mention of the name of the place.

The princess Badroulbadour rose earlier that morning than ever she had done since her transportation into Africa by the African magician, whose presence she was forced to support once a day, because he was master of the palace, though, at the same time, she always treated him cruelly; and as she was dressing, one of the women looking through the window, perceived Aladdin, and presently ran and told her mistress. The princess, who could not believe the news, went that moment herself to the window, and seeing Aladdin, immediately opened it. The noise the princess made in opening the window made Aladdin turn his head that way, who, perceiving the princess, saluted her with an air that expressed his joy; who, to lose no time, said to him, I have sent to have the back-door opened for you; and then shut the window.

The back-door, which was just under the princess's apartment, was soon opened, and Aladdin was conducted into the princess's chamber. It is impossible to express the joy of those lovers to see each other, after a separation which they both thought was for ever. They embraced several times, and shewed all the marks of a sincere love and tenderness. After these embracings, and shedding some tears of joy, they sat down, and Aladdin assuming the discourse, said, I beg of you, princess, in God's name, before we talk of any thing else, to tell me, both for your own interest, the sultan your father's, and my own, what is become of an old lamp which I left upon the cornish in the hall of the four-and-twenty windows, before I went to the hunting-match.

Alas! dear husband, answered the princess, I am afraid that our misfortunes are owing to that lamp; and that which grieves me most is, that I have been the cause of it. Princess, replied Aladdin, do not blame yourself, since it was entirely my fault, and I ought to have taken care of it: But let us now think of repairing that neglect, and tell me what has happened, and into whose hands it has fallen.

Then the princess Badroulbadour gave Aladdin an account how she changed the old lamp for a new one, (which she ordered to be fetched, that he might see it,) and how the next morning she found herself in an unknown country, which was the same he and she were then in, which she was told was Africa by the traitor who had transported her hither by his magic art.

Princess, said Aladdin, interrupting her, you have informed me who the traitor is, by telling me we are in Africa. He is the most perfidious of all men: but this is neither a time nor place to give you a full account of his villanies. I desire you only to tell me what he has done with the lamp, and where he has put it. He carries it carefully wrapt up in his bosom, said the princess; and this I can assure you, because he pulled it out before me, and shewed it to me.

Princess, said Aladdin, do not be displeased that I trouble you with so many questions, since they are equally important both to you and me. But to come to what most particularly concerns me; tell me, I conjure you, how so wicked and perfidious a man treats you? Since I have been here, replied the princess, he comes once every day to see me; and I am persuaded the little satisfaction he receives from his visits, makes him come no oftener. All his discourse tends to persuade me to break that faith I have pledged to you, and to take him for an husband; giving me to understand, I ought not to entertain any hopes of ever seeing you again, for that you were dead, and had had your head struck off by the sultan my father's order. He added, that you was an ungrateful wretch; that your good fortune was owing to him; and a great many other things of that nature; but as he received no other answer from me but grievous complaints and tears, he was always forced to retire without the satisfaction he desired. I do not doubt but his intention is to allow me some time to vanquish my grief, in hopes afterwards that I may change my sentiments; and, if I persevere in an obstinate refusal, to use violence: But my dear spouse's presence removes all my disquiets.

I have a greater confidence, replied Aladdin, since my princess's fears are removed; and I believe I have thought of the means to deliver you from both your enemy and mine; to execute which design, it is necessary for me to go to that town. I shall return by noon, and then will communicate my project to you, and tell you what must be done to succeed in it. But that you may not be surprised, I think it proper to acquaint you, that I shall change my apparel, and beg of you to give orders that I may not wait long at the back-door, but that it may be opened at the first knock: All which the princess promised to observe.

When Aladdin was got out of the palace, he looked about him on all sides, and perceiving a country-fellow before him, who seemed not advancing towards, but going from the palace, he made all imaginable haste after him; and when he had overtaken him, made a proposal to him to change cloaths, which the fellow agreed to; and accordingly they went behind a hedge, and there made the exchange. Afterwards the country-man went about his business, and Aladdin to the town, where, traversing several streets, he arrived in that part of the town where all sorts of merchants and artizans had their particular streets, according to their trades: Among which, he found out that of the druggists; and going into one of the largest shops, asked the druggist if he had a certain powder, which he named.

The druggist looking upon Aladdin by his habit to be very poor, and that he had not money enough to pay for it, told him he had it, but that it was very dear; upon which, Aladdin penetrating into his thoughts, pulled out his purse, and shewing him some gold, asked for half a dram, which the druggist weighed, and wrapped it up in a piece of paper, and gave him, telling him the price was a piece of gold. Aladdin laid him down his money, and staying no longer in the town but just to get a little refreshment, returned to the palace, where he waited not long at the back-door. When he came into the princess's apartment, he said to her, Princess, it may be, the aversion you have for your ravisher may not render what I am going to propose to you very agreeable; but give me leave to tell you, it is proper that you should at this juncture dissemble a little, and constrain your inclinations, if you would deliver yourself from him, and give my lord the sultan, your father, the satisfaction of seeing you again.

If you would take my advice, continued he, dress yourself this moment in one of your richest habits, and when the African magician comes, receive him with an affable and open countenance, that he may imagine time may wear off your grief. In your conversation, let him understand that you strive to forget me; and that he may be the more fully convinced of your sincerity, invite him to sup with you, and seem to have a mind to taste of some of the best wines of this country: There is no doubt but he will be ready to fetch you some. During his absence, put into one of the cups this powder, and charge the slave you design that night to attend you, upon a signal you shall agree upon with her, to bring that cup to you. When the magician and you have eat and drank as much as you care for, give her the signal, and change cups with him, which he will take as a great favour; but no sooner will he have drank off the cup, but you will see him fall backwards. If you have any reluctance to drink out of his cup, you may pretend only to do it, without fear of being discovered; for the effect of the powder is so quick, that he will not have time enough to know whether you drink or not.

I own, answered the princess, I shall do myself a great violence in consenting to make the magician such advances, but I see they are absolutely necessary; and what cannot one resolve to do against a cruel enemy? Therefore I will follow your advice, since both our quiets depend on it. After the princess had thus agreed to the measures proposed by Aladdin, he took his leave of her, and went and spent the rest of the day about the palace till it was night, when he might safely approach the back-door.

The princess Badroulbadour, who was not only inconsolable to be separated from her dear husband, whom she loved from the first moment, more out of inclination than duty, but also from the sultan her father, who had always shewed a tender and paternal love for her, had, ever since that cruel separation, lived in great negligence of her person. She had almost, as one may say, forgot the neatness so agreeable to persons of her sex and quality, after the first time of the magician's paying her a visit, and that she understood by some of the women, who knew him again, that it was he who received the old lamp in exchange for a new one, which notorious cheat rendered the sight of him more horrible. However, the opportunity of taking the revenge he deserved, which offered sooner than she durst hope for, made her resolve to gratify Aladdin in his request; for as soon as he was gone, she sat down at her toilet, and was dressed by her women to the best advantage, in a most rich suit, and one the most agreeable to her design. Her girdle was of the finest and largest diamonds set in gold, which she suited with a necklace of thirty pearls, all of the same size, but so large, and of so beautiful a water, that the greatest sultanesses and queens would have been proud to have been adorned with only two of them. Her bracelets, which were diamonds and rubies intermixed, answered admirably the richness of the girdle and necklace.

When the princess Badroulbadour was thus entirely dressed, she consulted her glass and women upon her adjustment; and when she found she wanted no charms to flatter the foolish passion of the African magician, she sat down on a sofa, expecting his arrival.

The magician came at the usual hour; and as soon as he entered the great hall where the princess waited to receive him, she rose up, and pointed with her hand to the most honourable place, standing till he sat down; which was a piece of civility she had never shewn him before.

The magician, dazzled more with the lustre of the princess's eyes than the glittering of the jewels with which she was adorned, was very much surprised. Besides, the majestic and graceful air with which she received him, so opposite to her former behaviour, quite confounded him.

When he was set down, the princess, to free him from his embarrassment, broke silence first, and looking at him all the time in a manner that was sufficient to make him believe that he was not so odious to her as she had given him to understand before, said to him, Without doubt you are very much amazed to find me so much altered to-day from what I used to be; but when I have acquainted you, that I am naturally of a merry disposition, not inclined to melancholy and grief, your surprise will not be so great, and that I always strive to divert my afflictions when there is no other remedy to be had. I have reflected on what you mentioned to me of Aladdin's fate; and I know the sultan my father's temper so well, that I am persuaded with you that Aladdin could not escape feeling the effects of his rage: therefore, since my tears and complaints cannot recal him to life again, why should I grieve? for this reason, after I have done all that my love requires of me, I think I ought to endeavour to comfort myself. These are the motives of the change you see in me; and to begin to cast off all melancholy, and banish it entirely, I am persuaded you will bear me company to-night, and partake of a supper I have ordered to be dressed for us: but as I have no wine but what is of China, and have a great desire to taste of the product of Africa, I shall beg of you to get some of the best.

The African magician, who looked upon the happiness of coming so soon and easy into the princess Badroulbadour's good graces as a thing impossible, could not think of words expressive enough to testify how sensible he was of her favours; but to put an end the sooner to a conversation which would have embarrassed him, if he had engaged farther into it, he turned it upon the wines of Africa, and said, Of all the advantages Africa can boast of, that of producing the most excellent wines is the principal; at present I have some of seven years old, which has never been broached; and indeed not to praise it too much, it is the finest wine in the world. If my princess, added he, will give me leave, I will go and fetch two bottles, and return again quickly. I should be sorry to give you that trouble, replied the princess; you had better send for them. It is necessary I should go myself, answered the

African magician; for nobody but myself knows where the key of the cellar is laid, or has the secret to unlock the door. If it be so, said the princess, make haste back again; for the sooner you return, the less my impatience will be, and we shall sit down to supper.

The African magician, full of hopes of his expected happiness, rather flew than any thing else, and returned quickly with the wine. The princess, not doubting in the least but he would make haste, put the powder Aladdin gave her into the cup that was set apart for that purpose. When they sat down at the table, they placed themselves opposite to each other, the magician's back towards the beaufet. The princess presented him with the best at the table, and said to him, If you please, I will entertain you with a concert of music; but as we are only two, I think conversation may be more agreeable. This the magician took as a new favour.

After they had eat some time, the princess called for some wine, and drank the magician's health; and afterwards said to him, Indeed you was in the right to recommend your wine, since I never tasted of any so delicious in my life. Charming princess, said he, holding a cup in his hand, my wine becomes more exquisite by your approbation. Then drink my health, replied the princess; you will find I understand wines. Accordingly he drank the princess's health; and returning the cup, said, I think myself happy that I reserved this wine for so good an occasion, and own I never drank any so excellent before.

When they had drank two or three cups more a piece, the princess, who had quite charmed the magician by her obliging behaviour and civility, gave the slave who served them with wine the signal, bidding her at the same time bring the magician and herself a full cup. When they both had their cups in their hands, she said to him, How are you used here to express your loves when drinking together as we are? With us in China, the lover and his mistress reciprocally exchange cups, and drink each other's health. At the same time she presented her cup, and held out her hand to receive his; who, for his part made all imaginable haste to make the exchange, and did it with the more pleasure, because he looked upon this favour as the most certain token of an entire conquest over the princess. Before he drank, he said to her, with the cup in his hand all the time, Indeed we Africans are not so refined in the art of love as you Chinese; and the instructing me in a lesson I know nothing of, informs me how sensible I ought to be of the favour done me. I shall never, lovely princess, forget my recovering that life, in drinking out of your cup, which your cruelty, had it continued, made me despair of.

The princess Badroulbadour, who began to be tired with this barefaced declaration of the magician, interrupted him, and said, Come, drink first, and say what you will afterwards; and at the same time set the cup to her lips, while the African magician, who was eager to get his wine off first, drank up the very last drop. In the mean time, the princess kept hers only at her lips, until she saw his eyes turn in his head, and he fell backwards lifeless.

The princess had no occasion to order the back-door to be opened to Aladdin; for her women were so disposed from the great hall to the foot of the stair-case, that the word was no sooner given that the African magician was fallen backwards, but the door was opened that instant.

As soon as Aladdin entered the hall, he saw the magician stretched backwards on the sofa. The princess Badroulbadour got off her seat, and ran overjoyed to him to embrace him: but he stopped her, and said, Princess, this is not a proper time; oblige me by leaving me alone a moment, and retire to your own apartment, while I endeavour to transport you as soon back to China as you were brought from thence.

When the princess, her women and eunuchs, were gone out of the hall, Aladdin shut the door, and going directly to the dead body of the magician, opened his vest, and took out the lamp, carefully wrapped up, as the princess told him; and unfolding and rubbing it, the genie immediately appeared. Genie, said Aladdin, I call thee to command thee, on the part of thy mistress, this lamp here, to transport this palace presently into China, to the same place from whence it was brought hither. The genie made a bow with his head to shew his obedience, and then disappeared. Immediately the palace was transported into China; which was only to be felt by two little shocks, the one when it was lifted up, the other when set down, and both in a short interval of time.

Then Aladdin went down to the princess's apartment, and embracing her, said, I can assure you, princess, that your joy and mine shall be complete to-morrow morning. Afterwards the princess, who had not quite supped herself, guessing that Aladdin might be hungry, ordered the meats that were served up in the great hall, and were scarce touched, to be brought down. The princess and Aladdin eat as much as they thought fit, and drank in like manner of the African magician's old wine; during which time their discourse could not be any otherwise than satisfactory; and then retired to their own chamber.

From the time of the transportation of Aladdin's palace, and the princess Badroulbadour, the sultan, that princess's father, was inconsolable for the loss of her, as he imagined. He hardly slept night or day; and instead of diverting his affliction, he, on the contrary, indulged it; for whereas he used to go every morning into his closet, to please himself with that agreeable prospect, he went now often in the day-time to renew his tears, and plunge himself into the deepest melancholy, by reflecting on that which once gave him so much pleasure, and now he had lost what was the most dear to him in this world.

The first morning after the return of Aladdin's palace, the sultan went very early into his closet to indulge his sorrows, and being very pensive, cast his eyes in a melancholy manner towards the place where he remembered the palace once stood, expecting only to see an open space; but perceiving that vacancy filled up, at first imagined it to be the effect of a fog; but at last, looking more attentively, he made no doubt but that it was his son-in-law's palace. Then joy and gladness succeeded sorrow and grief. He returned immediately into his apartment, and ordered an horse to be saddled and brought to him in all haste, which he mounted that instant, thinking he could not make haste enough to get to Aladdin's palace.

Aladdin, who foresaw what would happen, rose that morning by day-break, put on one of the most magnificent habits his wardrobe afforded, and went up into the hall of twenty-four windows, from whence he perceived the sultan coming, and got down soon enough to receive him at the foot of the great stair-case, and to help him to dismount. Aladdin, said the sultan, I cannot speak to you till I have seen my daughter.

He led the sultan into the princess Badroulbadour's apartment, who, having been told by him when he arose, that she was no longer in Africa, but in the capital of the sultan her father, had just done dressing herself. The sultan embraced her with his face all bathed in tears of joy; and the princess, on her side, gave him all the testimonies of the pleasure the sight of him gave her.

The sultan was some time before he could open his lips; so great was his surprise and joy to find his daughter again after he had given her up for lost; and the princess, to see her father, let fall tears of joy.

At last, the sultan broke silence, and said, I would believe, daughter, your joy to see me makes you seem so little changed as if no misfortune had befallen you; yet I cannot be persuaded from thinking you have undergone a great deal; for a large palace cannot be so suddenly transported as yours has been, without great frights, and terrible anguish. I would have you tell me all that has happened, and not conceal any thing from me.

Hereupon, the princess, who took a great pleasure in giving the sultan the satisfaction he demanded, said, Sir, if I appear so little altered, I beg of your majesty to consider, that I received new life yesterday morning by the presence of my dear husband and deliverer, Aladdin, whom I looked upon and bewailed as lost to me; and the happiness of seeing and embracing of whom, has almost recovered me to my former state of health. But my greatest trouble was, not only to find myself forced from your majesty, and my dear husband, but the uneasiness I laboured under besides, was, my fear that he, though innocent, should feel the effects of your rage, to which I knew he was left exposed. I suffered but little from the insolence of my ravisher; for, having the ascendant over him, I always put a stop to his disagreeable discourse, and was as little restrained as at present.

As to what relates to my transportation, Aladdin had no hand in it; I myself was alone to blame, and he innocent. To persuade the sultan of the truth of what she said, she gave him a full account how the African magician disguised himself like a seller of lamps, and cried new lamps for old ones; and the pleasure she took in making that exchange; being entirely ignorant of the secret and importance of that lamp, by the means of which, the magician transported the palace and her into Africa, which she came to know by two of her women and the eunuch who made the exchange, when he first had the boldness to pay her the first visit, after the success of his audacious enterprise, to propose himself for her husband. After that, she made mention how he persecuted her till Aladdin's arrival; how he and she consulted together to get the lamp again, and the success they had; and particularly her dissimulation, and inviting him to supper, and giving the powder prepared for him. For the rest, added she, I leave it to Aladdin to give you an account of.

Aladdin, for his part, had not much to tell the sultan, but only said, When the back-door was opened, I went up into the great hall, where I found the magician dead, and extended upon the sofa; and as I thought it not proper for the princess to stay there any longer, I desired her to go down into her own apartment, with her women and eunuchs. As soon as I was alone, and had taken the lamp out of the magician's breast, I made use of the same secret he had done, to remove the palace and the princess; and by that means the palace was brought into the same place where it stood before; and I have the happiness to bring back the princess to your majesty, as you commanded me. But that your majesty may not think that I impose upon you, if you will give yourself the trouble to go up into the hall, you shall see the magician punished as he deserved.

The sultan, to be assured of the truth, rose up instantly, and went up into the hall, where, when he saw the African magician dead, and his face already livid by the strength of the poison, he embraced Aladdin with a great deal of tenderness, and said, Do not, son, take my proceedings against you ill, since they proceeded from my paternal love; and therefore you ought to excuse them. Sir, replied Aladdin, I have no reason to complain of your majesty's conduct, since you did nothing but what your duty required of you. This magician, the basest of all men, was the only cause of my misfortune. When your majesty has a leisure hour, I will give you an account of another villanous action he played me, which was no less black and base than this, from which I was preserved by the grace of God, in a very particular manner. I will take an opportunity, and that very shortly, replied the sultan, to hear it; but, in the mean time, let us think of mirth and rejoicings, and the removal of this odious object.

Aladdin ordered the magician's dead carcase to be removed, and thrown on the dung-hill, for the birds of the air to prey upon. In the mean time, the sultan commanded the drums to beat, and trumpets to sound, and a feast of ten days to be proclaimed, for joy of the princess Badroulbadour, and Aladdin and his palace's return.

Thus Aladdin escaped, a second time, the almost inevitable danger of losing his life; which was not the last, since he ran as great a hazard the third time, the circumstances of which I shall relate.

The African magician had a younger brother, who was as great a necromancer, and, I may say, surpassed him in villainy and pernicious designs. But as they did not live together, but at a great distance, they failed not every year to inform themselves, by their art of necromancy, where each other was, how they did, and whether they stood in need of each other's assistance.

Some time after the African magician had failed in his enterprise against Aladdin's happiness, his younger brother, who had not informed himself of him a year before, had a curiosity to know where he was, and how he did: And as he, as well as his brother, always carried a necromantic square instrument about him, he prepared the sand, cast figures, and found that he had been poisoned, and was in the capital of the kingdom of China; and that the person who poisoned him was of mean birth, and had married the princess, the sultan's daughter.

When the magician had, after this manner, informed himself of his brother's fate, he lost no time in useless regrets, which could not restore him to life again; but resolving immediately to revenge his death, he took horse, and set forwards for China; where, after crossing plains, rivers, mountains, deserts, and the sea, he arrived, after incredible fatigues.

When he came to the capital of China, he took a lodging, and the next day a walk through the town, not only to observe the beauties, which were indifferent to him, but with an intention to take proper measures to execute his pernicious designs; to which end, he introduced himself into the most public and frequented places, where he listened to every body's discourse. In one of these public places, where people resorted to divert themselves with all sorts of games, and as in such places some are conversing, while others play, he heard some gentlemen talk of the virtue and piety of a woman who was retired from the world, and called Fatima, and of the miracles she performed. As he fancied that this woman might be serviceable to him in some project he had in his head, he took one of the gentlemen aside, and desired him to tell him particularly who that woman was, and what sort of a miracle she performed.

What! said the person to whom he addressed himself, have you never seen nor heard talk of her? She is the admiration of the whole town, both of young and old, for her exemplary life; except Mondays and Fridays, she never stirs out of her little cell; and on those days on which she comes into the town, she does an infinite deal of good; for there is not a person that has the headache but is cured by her laying her hand upon them.

The magician wanted to know no more than this, but only asked the person in what part of the town this cell was. After the gentleman had shewn him it, and he had concluded and determined on the detestable design he had in his head, and that he might know the way again, he observed all the turnings and windings very carefully. When he had taken just observation of the place, he went to one of those houses where they sell a certain hot liquor, and where any person that pleases may be all night. About midnight, after the magician had satisfied the master of the house for what he had called for, he went directly away to the cell of Fatima the holy woman, the name she was known by throughout the town. It was no difficult matter for him to open the door, which was only fastened with a latch, which he lifted up without any noise; and when he entered the cell, perceived Fatima, by the moon-light, laid on a sofa, covered only by an old mat, with her head leaning against the wall, whom he awakened, and clapped a dagger to her breast.

The poor Fatima, opening her eyes, was very much surprised to see a man ready to stab her, and who said to her, If thou criest out, or makest the least noise, I will kill thee; but get up, and do as I bid thee.

Fatima, who had laid down in her cloaths, got up, trembling with fear. Do not be so much frightened, said the magician; I only want thy habit; give it me presently, and take mine. Accordingly Fatima and he changed cloaths. Then he said again, Colour my face as thine is, that I may be like thee; but perceiving that the poor creature could not help trembling, to encourage her, he said, I tell thee again, thou needest not fear any thing; I swear by the name of God, I will not take away thy life. Fatima lighted her lamp, and taking a pencil, and dipping it in a certain liquor, rubbed it over his face, and assured him the colour would not change, and that his face was of the same dye as her own. After which, she put on him a coif,* and shewed him how to hide his face as he passed through the town. After this, she put a long string of beads about his neck, which hung down to the middle of his body, and giving him the stick she was used to walk with in his hand, brought him a looking-glass, and bid him look, and see if he thought himself like her. The magician found himself disguised as he wished to be; but yet could not keep the oath he so solemnly swore to the good Fatima, but instead of stabbing her, for fear the blood might discover him, he strangled her, and when he found she was dead, threw her body into a cistern, just by the cell.

The magician, thus disguised like the holy woman Fatima, spent the remainder of the night in the cell, after he had committed so horrid a murder. The next morning, two hours after sun-rise, though it was not a day the holy woman used to go out on, he crept out of the cell, being well persuaded that nobody would ask him any questions about it; or if they would, knowing he had an answer ready for them. And as one of the first things he did after his arrival, was, to find out Aladdin's palace, where he was to execute his designs, he went directly thither.

As soon as the people saw the holy woman, as they imagined him to be, they presently gathered about him in a great crowd: some begged his blessing, others kissed his hand, and the most zealous the hem of his garment; while others, whether or no their heads ached, or they had a mind to be preserved against that distemper, stooped for him to lay his hands upon them; which he did, muttering some words in form of prayers; and, in short, counterfeited so well, that every body took him for her.

When he came to Aladdin's palace, the crowd was so great, that those who were the most zealous and strong, striving to keep the rest off from pressing too much upon him, there were such quarrels, and so great a noise, that the princess, who was in the hall of four-and-twenty windows, asked what was the matter; but nobody being able to give her an account, one of her women looked out of the window, and then told her it was a great crowd of people that were gathered about the holy woman that cured the headache.

The princess, who had heard a great deal of this holy woman, but had never seen her, conceived a great curiosity to have some discourse with her, which the chief of the eunuchs perceiving, told her it was an easy matter to bring her to her, if she desired and commanded it; and the princess shewing a desire, he immediately sent four eunuchs for her.

As soon as the crowd saw the eunuchs coming, they made way; and the magician perceiving also that they were coming for him, was overjoyed to find his plot took so well. Holy woman, said one of the eunuchs, the princess wants to see you, and has sent us for you. The princess does me too great an honour, replied the false Fatima: I am ready to obey her command, and at the same time followed the eunuchs to the palace.

When the magician, who under a holy garment disguised a wicked heart, was introduced into a great hall, and perceived the princess, he began a prayer, which contained a long enumeration of vows and well-wishes for the princess's health and prosperity, and that she might have every thing she desired. Then he made use of all his deceitful, hypocritical rhetoric, to insinuate himself into the princess's favour under the cloak of piety: which it was no hard matter for him to do; for as the princess herself was naturally good, she was easily persuaded that all the world was so besides, especially those who made the serving of God their profession, and for that end had chosen a solitary retreat.

When the pretended Fatima had made an end of his long harangue, the princess said to him, I thank you, good mother, for your prayers; I have great confidence in them, and hope God will hear them. Come, and sit by me. The false Fatima sat down with an affected modesty: then the princess resuming her discourse, said, My good mother, I have one thing to ask you, which you must not refuse me; which is, to stay with me, that you may entertain me with your way of living, and that I may learn from your good example how to serve God. Princess, said the counterfeit Fatima, I beg of you not to ask what I cannot consent to, without neglecting my prayers and devotion. That shall be no hindrance to you, answered the princess; I have a great many apartments out of use; you shall chuse which you like best, and shall have as much liberty to perform your devotions as if you were in your own cell.

The magician, who wanted nothing more than to introduce himself into Aladdin's palace, where it would be a much easier matter for him to execute his pernicious designs under the favour and protection of the princess, than if he had been forced to come and go from the cell to the palace, did not make any pressing instances to excuse accepting the obliging offer the princess made to him; but said, Princess, whatever resolution a poor miserable woman, as I am, may have made to renounce the pomp and grandeur of this world, I dare not be so bold to oppose the will and commands of so pious and charitable a princess.

Upon this the princess rising up, said, Come along with me; I will shew you what empty apartments I have, that you may make choice of which you like best. The magician followed the princess Badroulbadour, and of all the apartments she shewed him, made choice of that which was the worst furnished, saying, That it was too good for him, and that he only accepted of it to please her.

Afterwards the princess would have brought him back again into the great hall to make him dine with her; but he considering that he then should be obliged to shew his face, which he had always taken care to hide, and fearing that the princess should find out that he was not Fatima, he begged of her strenuously to dispense with him, telling her, That he never ate any thing but bread and dried fruits; and, at the same time, desired to eat that slight repast in his own apartment; which the princess granted him, saying, You may be as free here, good mother, as if you were in your own cell: I will order you a dinner, but remember I expect you as soon as you have finished your repast.

After the princess had dined, and the false Fatima had been informed, by one of the eunuchs, that she was risen from table, he was sure to wait upon her. My good mother, said the princess, I am overjoyed to have the company of so holy a woman as yourself, who will confer a blessing upon this palace. But now I am speaking of this palace, pray, how do you like it? and before I shew it you all, tell me first what you think of this hall?

Upon this question, the counterfeit Fatima, who, to act his part the better, affected to hang down his head, without so much as ever once lifting it up, at last looked up, and surveying the hall from one end to the other, and when he had examined it well, said he to the princess, As far as I can judge, who am not used to such fine buildings, there wants but one thing. And what is that, good mother, answered the princess Badroulbadour; tell me, I conjure you? For my part, I always believed, and have heard say, it wanted nothing; but if it does, it shall be supplied.

Princess, said the false Fatima, with a great deal of dissimulation, forgive me for the liberty I have taken; but my opinion is, if it can be of any importance, that if a roc's egg was hung up in the middle of this dome, this hall would have no fellow, and would be the wonder of the world.

My good mother, said the princess, what bird is that roc, and where may one get an egg? Princess, replied the pretended Fatima, it is a bird of a prodigious size, which inhabits the top of Mount Caucasus: the architect who built your palace can get you one.

After the princess Badroulbadour had thanked the false Fatima for her good advice, which she believed as such, she talked with her upon other matters; but could not forget the roc's egg, which she made account to tell Aladdin of, when he returned back from hunting. He had been gone six days, which the magician being no stranger to, had a mind to take the advantage of his absence, but returned that night, after the false Fatima had taken his leave of the princess, and retired to his apartment. As soon as he arrived, he went directly to the princess's apartment, kissed and embraced her, but fancied she received him coldly. My princess, said he, I think you are not so gay and merry as you used to be; has any thing happened during my absence, which has displeased you, or given you any trouble or dissatisfaction? In the name of God, do not hide any thing from me; I will leave nothing undone that is in my power to please you. It is a trifling matter, replied the princess, which concerns me so little, that I could not have thought you could have perceived any thing of it in my countenance: but since you have discovered some alteration in me, I will no longer disguise a matter of so little consequence from you.

I always believed, as well as you, continued the princess Badroulbadour, that our palace was the most noble, magnificent, and perfect in the world; but I will tell you now what I find fault with, upon examining the hall of four-and-twenty windows: Do not you think, as well as me, that it would be complete if a roc's egg was hung up in the midst of the dome? Princess, replied Aladdin, it is sufficient that you think there wants one; you shall see what diligence shall be used to repair that deficiency, since there is nothing shall be left undone for your sake.

Aladdin left the princess Badroulbadour that moment, and went up directly into the hall of four-and-twenty windows, where, pulling the lamp out of his bosom, which he always carried about him, after the danger he had been exposed to, he rubbed it; upon which the genie appeared. Genie, said Aladdin, there wants a roc's egg to be hung up in the midst of the dome; I command thee, in the name of this lamp, to repair the fault. Aladdin had no sooner pronounced these words, but the genie gave so terrible and loud a cry, that the hall shook so much, that Aladdin could scarce stand upright. What! miserable wretch, said the genie, in a voice that would have made the most undaunted man tremble, is it not enough that I and my companions have done every thing for thee; but thou, out of an unheard-of piece of ingratitude, must command me to bring my master, and hang him up in the midst of this dome? This attempt deserves that thou, thy wife and palace, should be immediately reduced to ashes: But thou art happy that thou art not the author of this request, and that it was not owing to thyself. Know then, that the true author is the brother of the African magician, thy enemy, whom thou hast used as he deserved: He is now in thy palace, disguised in the cloaths of the holy woman Fatima, whom he murdered; and it is he who has suggested to thy wife to make this pernicious demand: His design is to kill thee; therefore take care of thyself. After these words, the genie disappeared.

Aladdin lost not a word the genie said: He had heard talk of the holy woman Fatima, and how she pretended to cure the headache. He returned to the princess's apartment, and without mentioning a word of what had happened, complained very much of a great pain in his head; upon which the princess ordered the holy woman to be fetched presently, and then told him how that holy woman came to the palace, and that she had appointed her an apartment.

When the pretended Fatima came, Aladdin said, Come hither, good mother; I am very glad to see you here; I am very much tormented with a violent pain in my head, and demand your assistance, and hope you will not refuse me that favour which you do to so many persons afflicted with this distemper. After these words, he rose up, though, at the same time he held down his head. On the other hand, the counterfeit Fatima advanced towards him, with his hand all the time on a dagger he had in his girdle under his gown; which Aladdin observing, he seized his hand, before he had drawn it, and pierced him to the heart with his own dagger, and then tumbled him down on the floor.

What have you done, my dear husband, cried the princess in a surprise! You have killed the holy woman. No, my dear princess, answered Aladdin, without concern; I have not killed Fatima, but a wicked wretch that would have assassinated me if I had not prevented him. This wicked man, added he, uncovering his face, has strangled Fatima, whom you accused me of killing, and disguised himself in her cloaths, to come and murder me: But that you may know him better, he is brother to the African magician. Then Aladdin told her how he came to know those particulars, and afterwards ordered the dead body to be taken away.

Thus Aladdin was delivered from the persecution of two brothers who were magicians. Within a few years afterwards, the sultan died in a good old age, and as he left no male children, the princess Badroulbadour, as lawful heir of the crown, succeeding him, and communicating the power to Aladdin, they reigned together many years, and left a numerous and illustrious posterity behind them.

Sir, said the sultaness Scheherazade, after she had finished the story of the Wonderful Lamp, your majesty, without doubt, has observed in the person of the African magician a man abandoned to the passion of possessing immense treasures by the most horrid and detestable means. On the contrary, your majesty sees in Aladdin a person of mean birth raised to the royal dignity, by making use of the same treasures, which he never sought after, but just as he had an occasion for them; and in the sultan, what risks and dangers a just and equitable monarch runs of being dethroned, when, by an unjust fear, and against all the rules of equity, he dares, by an unreasonable precipitation, condemn an innocent person to death, without giving him leave to justify himself. In short, you must abominate those two wicked magicians, who sacrificed their lives, the one to attain great riches, the other to revenge him, and who both received the chastisement they deserved.

The sultan of the Indies signified to his spouse, the sultaness Scheherazade, that he was very much delighted with the prodigies he had heard of the wonderful lamp, and that all the stories which she told him every night gave him a great deal of pleasure. In short, they were all diverting, and, for the most part, seasoned with a good moral. He found that the sultaness knew how to introduce them very well, and was not sorry that she gave him an opportunity of suspending, by this means, the execution of the vow he had made never to keep a woman above one night, and put her to death the next day. And now he began to have no other thoughts, but to try if he could exhaust her store.

With this intention, the next morning he prevented Dinarzade, and waked the sultaness himself, asking her if she was at the end of her stories? At the end of my stories, sir, replied the sultaness! I am so far from that, that I cannot tell your majesty well how many I have left; but am more afraid you will be sooner tired with hearing, than I with telling them.

Do not let that fear disturb you, answered the sultan; but let us hear what you have new to tell me.

The sultaness Scheherazade, encouraged with these words, said, I have often entertained your majesty with the adventures of the famous Haroun Alraschid, who had a great many in his time; but, among the rest, I think none more worthy of your hearing than the following, which I shall here relate you.

The Adventures of the Caliph Haroun Alraschid

YOUR majesty cannot be insensible, but must have experienced, that we are sometimes in such extraordinary transports of joy, that we presently communicate that passion to those that come nigh us, or easily partake of theirs: And sometimes our melancholy is so great, that we are insupportable to ourselves, and are so incapable of giving any one a reason that should ask it, that we cannot account for it ourselves.

The caliph was one day in one of these moody fits, when his faithful and favourite grand visier, Giafar, came to him. That minister finding him alone, which was seldom, and perceiving, as he went nearer unto him, that he was in a very dull humour, and never lifted up his eyes, he made a full stop, till he should vouchsafe to look at him.

At last, the caliph cast his eyes upon Giafar, but presently turned them away again, and remained in the same posture of situation as before.

The grand visier, observing nothing in the caliph's eyes which regarded him personally, took the liberty to speak to him, and said, Commander of the Faithful, will your majesty give me leave to ask you from whence this melancholy proceeds, of which you always seemed to me so little susceptible?

Indeed, visier, answered the caliph, clearing up his countenance, I am very little subject to it, and had not perceived it but for you, and will remain no longer in it. If no new affair brought you hither, do me the pleasure to invent something to divert me.

Commander of the Faithful, replied the grand visier, my duty obliged me to wait on you, and I take the liberty to recommend to your majesty, that this is the day which you have appointed to inform yourself of the exact government of your capital city, and the little places about it; and this occasion very opportunely presents itself to dispel those clouds which could obscure your natural gaiety.

You do well to remember me of it, replied the caliph, for I had entirely forgot it; go and change your dress, while I do the same by mine.

They each put on the habit of a foreign merchant, and, in that disguise, went out by a back-door of the palace-garden, which led into the fields. After they had taken a round on the bank of the Euphrates, at a sufficient distance from the city-gates, on that side, without having observed any thing disorderly, they crossed the river in the first boat they met with, and making another tour on the other side, came over the bridge which made the communication betwixt the two parts of the town.

At the foot of the bridge, they met with an old blind man, who asked their alms: the caliph turned about, and put a piece of gold into his hand: the blind man presently catched hold of his hand, and stopped him, saying, Charitable person, whoever you are, that God hath inspired to bestow this alms, do not refuse the favour I ask you, to give me a box on the ear, for I deserve that, and a greater punishment. After these words, he let the caliph's hand go, that he might strike; but, for fear he should not, held him fast by his cloaths.

The caliph, surprised both at the request and action of the blind man, said, I cannot acquiesce with thy demand, and shall not lessen the merit of my charity, by treating thee as thou wouldst have me. After these words, he endeavoured to get away from the blind man.

The blind man, who expected the reluctancy of his benefactor, by the long experience he had had, did all he could to hold him. Sir, said he, forgive my boldness and importunity; I desire you would either give me a box on the ear, or take your alms back again, for I cannot receive it but on that condition, without breaking a solemn oath, which I made to God; and if you knew the reason, you would agree with me that the punishment is very slight.

The caliph, not caring to be detained any longer, yielded to the importunity of the blind man, and gave him a very light blow; whereupon, he immediately let him go, and thanked and blessed him. When the caliph and visier had got some small distance from the blind man, the caliph said to the visier, This blind man must certainly have some very substantial reasons which make him behave himself in this manner to all who give him alms: I should be glad to know them; therefore, return, and tell who I am, and bid him not fail to come to my palace about prayer-time in the afternoon, that I may have some talk with him.

The grand visier went back, bestowed his alms on the blind man, and after he had given him a box on the ear, told him the caliph's order, and then returned to him again.

When they came into the town, they found a great crowd of spectators in an open square, who were looking at a handsome, well-shaped young man that was mounted on a mare, which he rid full speed round the place, spurring and whipping the poor creature so barbarously, that she was all over in a lather and gore of blood.

The caliph, amazed at the inhumanity of the young man, asked the people if they knew why the young man used the mare so, but could learn nothing, but that, for some time past, he had every day, at the same hour, treated her after the same manner.

As they went along, the caliph bid the grand visier take particular notice of the place, and not fail to order the young man to come the next day, at the hour appointed to the blind man. But before the caliph got to his palace, he observed, in a street which he had not passed through for a long time before, an edifice newly built, which seemed to him to be the palace of some of the greatest lords of the court. He asked the grand visier if he knew to whom it belonged, who answered he did not, but would inquire; and thereupon asked a neighbour, who told him that house was one Cogia Hassan's, surnamed Alhabbal, upon account of his profession of rope-making, which he had seen him work at himself, when poor, and that, without knowing how fortune had favoured him, he had got such great riches, that he defrayed, honourably and splendidly, the expence he had been at in building, and lived very great.

The grand visier rejoined the caliph, and gave a full account of his intelligence. I must see this Cogia Hassan Alhabbal, said the caliph; therefore go and tell him, visier, to come to my palace at the same hour you ordered the other two. Accordingly the visier obeyed.

The next day, after afternoon prayers, the caliph returned to his own apartment, and the grand visier introduced the three persons we have been speaking of, and presented them to the caliph.

They all three prostrated themselves before the caliph; and when they rose up again, the caliph asked the blind man his name, who answered, Baba Abdalla.

Baba Abdalla, replied the caliph, thy manner of begging alms seemed so strange to me yesterday, that if it had not been for some certain considerations, I should not have complied with thy request, but should have prevented thee from giving scandal to the public. I ordered thee to come hither, to know from thyself what induced thee to make that indiscreet oath thou hast told me of, that I may judge whether thou hast done well, and if I ought to suffer thee to continue in the practice of a thing that sets so ill an example. Tell me freely, how so extravagant a thought came into thy head, and do not disguise any thing from me, for I will absolutely know the truth.

Baba Abdalla, intimidated by this reprimand, cast himself a second time at the foot of the caliph's throne, with his face to the ground; and when he rose up again, said, Commander of the Faithful, I most humbly ask your majesty's pardon for my boldness, in daring to require, and almost force you to do a thing which indeed appears so contrary to reason. I acknowledge my crime; but as I did not then know your majesty, I implore your clemency, and hope you will consider my ignorance.

As to the extravagancy of my action, I own it, and that it must seem strange to all mankind; but in the eye of God it is a very slight penance I have enjoined myself, for an enormous crime I am guilty of, and for which, if all the people in the world were each to give me a box on the ear, it would not be a sufficient atonement. Your majesty will judge of it yourself, when, in telling my story, in obedience to your commands, I shall let you know what that heinous crime was.

The Story of the Blind Man, Baba Abdalla

COMMANDER of the Faithful, continued Baba Abdalla, I was born at Bagdad, had a pretty fortune left me by my father and mother, who died soon after each other. Though I was then but very young, I did not squander away my fortune as most young men do, in idle expences and debauchery; but, on the contrary, neglected no opportunity to increase it by industry. At last I became rich enough to purchase fourscore camels, which I let out to merchants, who paid me very well for every journey I went with them throughout the extent of your majesty's dominions.

In the midst of this happiness, and with an ardent desire of growing much richer, as I was returning one day with my camels unloaded from Balsora, whither I had carried some merchandise that was to be embarked for the Indies, I met with a good pasturage, at a good distance from any habitation, and made a halt there, and let them graze for some time. While I was set down, a dervise, who had walked it from Balsora, came and sat down by me to rest himself. I asked him from whence he came, and where he was going;

and he did the same by me; and when we had satisfied each other's curiosity, we produced our provisions, and eat together.

During our repast, after we had talked of a great many indifferent things, the dervise told me that he knew of a treasure at a small distance from thence, where there were such immense riches, that if all my fourscore camels were loaded with gold and jewels, it would not be missed, and nobody could tell that any thing had been taken away.

This good news surprised and charmed me at the same time; and I was so overjoyed that I scarce knew myself. I could not believe that the dervise was capable of telling me a falsity; therefore I fell upon his neck, and said, Good dervise, I know you value not the riches of this world, therefore what service can the knowledge of this treasure be to you? You are alone, and cannot carry much of it away with you; shew me where it is; I will load all my camels, and, as an acknowledgment of the favour done me, will present you with one of them.

Indeed I offered a very small matter; but after he had communicated that secret to me, my desire of riches was become so violent, that I thought it a great deal, and looked upon the seventy-nine camel-loads which I reserved for myself, as nothing in comparison of what I allowed him.

The dervise, though he saw my avarice, was not however angry at the unreasonable proffer I had made him; but replied, without the least concern, You are sensible, brother, that what you offer me is not proportionable to the kindness you ask of me. I may chuse whether or no I will communicate my secret to you, and keep the treasure to myself. But what I have told you is sufficient to let you know my good intentions, and that it is still in my power to oblige you, and make you remember me, by making both our fortunes. But then I have one other proposition, more just and equitable, to make to you; it lies in your own breast, whether or no you will agree to it.

You say, continued the dervise, that you have fourscore camels: I am ready to carry you to the place where the treasure lies, and we will load them with as much jewels and gold as they well can carry, on condition that when they are so loaded, you will let me have one half, and you take the other; after which we will separate, and both go which way we think fit. You see here is nothing but reason and justice in this bargain; for if you give me forty camels, you will get by my means wherewithal to purchase thousands more.

I could not disown but there was a great deal of justice in what the dervise said; but without considering what riches I should gain in accepting of the conditions he proposed, I could not without reluctancy think of parting with my forty camels, especially when I considered that the dervise would then be as rich as myself. But as it was no time to hesitate long on such an affair, but I must either accept of the proposal, or resolve to repent all my life-time after, of losing an opportunity of obtaining a great fortune, that instant I went up and gathered up all my camels, and after we had travelled some time, we came into a large spacious valley, the entrance into which was so narrow, that two camels could not go a-breast. The two mountains which formed this valley were semicircular, but so high and craggy, that there was no fear of being seen by any body.

When we came between these two mountains, the dervise said to me, Stop your camels, and make them kneel down, that we may load them the easier, and I will proceed to discover the treasure.

I did as the dervise bid me; and going to him afterwards, found him with a match in one hand, and gathering sticks with the other, to light a fire; which he had no sooner done, but he cast a perfume into it, and pronouncing some words, which I did not understand, there arose a thick cloud presently. This cloud separated soon, and then a large rock, which stood between the two mountains, in the midst of the plain, and which was of a prodigious height, and seemed to be very solid, opened like two folding doors, and exposed to view a magnificent palace, built in the hollow of the rock, which was hewed, and seemed to be rather the workmanship of genies than men; for no man could ever have been so bold as to have undertaken such a surprising work.

But I must not forget to tell your majesty, I could not have patience to make any observation; I admired only the immense riches which I saw on all sides; and without staying to observe the just regularity in which the treasures were ranged, but like an eagle seizing her prey, I fell upon the first heap of golden money that I was near to, and began to fill the sack I had in my hand, as full as I thought I could carry it. The sacks were all large, and with my good will I would have filled them all; but I was obliged to proportion my burden to the strength of my camels. The dervise did the same; but I perceived he had got to an heap of jewels, upon which I followed his example, and we took away much more jewels than gold. At last, when we had filled our sacks, and loaded our camels, we had nothing left to do but to shut up the treasure, and go our way.

But before we departed, the dervise went again into the treasure, where there were a great many wrought vessels of gold, of different sorts and sizes, which contained things that were precious. I observed that he took out of one of these vessels a little box, of a certain wood which I knew not, and put it into his breast; but first shewed me that it contained only a kind of pomatum.*

The dervise used the same ceremony to shut the treasure as he had done to open it; and after he pronounced some certain words, the doors of the treasury shut again, and the rock seemed as whole and entire as before.

Then he divided our camels; I put myself at the head of the forty which I reserved for myself, and the dervise at the head of the rest. We came out of the valley by the same passage we went in, and travelled together till we came to the great road, where we were to part; the dervise to go to Balsora, and I to Bagdad. To thank him for so great a kindness, I made use of the most expressive terms, to testify my acknowledgment for the preference he had given me before all mankind, in letting me have a share of such riches. We embraced each other with a great deal of joy, and then took our leaves with an hearty adieu.

I had not gone many paces, before vile ingratitude and envy possessed my heart, and I deplored the loss of my forty camels, and much more the riches wherewith they were loaded. The dervise, said I to myself, has no occasion for all these riches; he is master of the treasure, and may have as much as he pleases: so I delivered myself up to the blackest ingratitude, and determined immediately to take the camels, as they were loaded, from him.

To execute this design, I first stopped my own, and afterwards ran after the dervise, and called on him as loud as I could, giving him to understand that I had something material to say to him, and made a sign to him to stop his, and stay for me; which he accordingly did.

When I came up to him, I said, Brother, I had no sooner parted from you, but a thought came into my head, which neither of us had reflected on before. You are a good dervise, used to live in tranquillity, disengaged from all the cares of the world, and intent upon serving God: You know not, perhaps, what trouble you have taken upon yourself, to take care of so many camels; if you would take my advice, I would have you to have but thirty; you will find it troublesome enough to manage them: take my word; I have had experience.

I believe you are in the right of it, replied the dervise, who found he was not able to contend with me; I own I never so much as thought of it; I begin already to be uneasy at what you have represented to me. Chuse which ten you please, and take them in God's name.

I set ten apart, and after I had turned them about, I put them in the road to follow my others. I could not have imagined that the dervise would be so easily persuaded to part with his camels, which increased my covetousness, and made me flatter myself, that it would be no hard matter to get ten more. Wherefore, instead of thanking him for his present, I said to him again, Brother, the interest I take in your repose is so great, that I cannot resolve to part with you without desiring you to consider once more, how difficult a thing it is to govern thirty loaded camels, especially you who are not used to such work: you will find it much better to return me as many more back as you have done already. What I tell you is not for my own sake and interest, but to do you the greater pleasure. Ease yourself then of the camels, and leave them to me, who can manage an hundred as well as one.

My discourse had the desired effect upon the dervise, who gave me, without any hesitation, the other ten camels; so that he had but twenty left, and I was master of sixty, and might boast of as great riches as most sovereign princes, but for all that could not be content; for as a person afflicted with a dropsy, the more he drinks, the more thirsty he is, so I became more greedy and desirous of the other twenty camels.

I redoubled my solicitations, prayers, and importunities, to make the dervise condescend to grant me ten of the twenty, which he did with a good grace; and as to the other ten he had left, I embraced him, kissed him, and caressed him, conjuring him not to refuse me, but to complete the obligation I should ever have to him, and crown my joy, by giving me them also. Make a good use of them, brother, said the dervise, and remember that God can take away riches as well as give them, if we do not assist the poor, whom he makes so on purpose that the rich may merit by their charity a greater recompence in the other world.

My blindness was then so great, that I could not profit by so wholesome advice; I was so far from it, that I was not content, though I had my forty camels again, and knew they were loaded with an inestimable treasure: But a thought came into my head, that the little box of pomatum which the dervise shewed me had something in it more precious than all the riches which I was obliged to him for: The place from whence the dervise took it, said I to myself, and his care to secure it, makes me believe there is something mysterious in it. I went and embraced him again, and bid him adieu; and as I turned about from him, said, What will you do with that little box of pomatum? It seems such a trifle, said I, it is not worth your carrying away; I desire you would make me a present of it; for what occasion has a dervise, as you are, who has renounced the vanities of the world, for pomatum?

I wish to heaven he had refused me that box; but if he had, I was stronger than him, and was resolved to have taken it from him by force, and, notwithstanding my obligation to him, not to have suffered him to have carried away the least thing of the treasure.

The dervise, far from denying me, presently pulled it out of his bosom, and presenting it to me with an extraordinary grace, said, Here, take it, brother, and be content; if I could do more for you, you needed but to have asked for it; you see I am ready and willing to satisfy you.

When I had the box in my hand, I opened it, and looking at the pomatum, said to him, Since you have hitherto been so good, I am sure you will not refuse me this one favour, which is, to tell me the particular use of this pomatum.

The use is very surprising and wonderful, replied the dervise: If you apply a little of this pomatum round the left eye, and upon the lid, you will see all the treasures contained in the bosom of the earth; but if you apply it to the right eye, it will make you blind.

I would make the experiment myself. Take the box, said I to the dervise, and apply some of this pomatum to my left eye; you understand how to do it better than I; for I long to make an experiment of a thing which seems so incredible to me. Accordingly I shut my left eye, and the dervise applied the pomatum. When he had done, I opened my eye, and saw immense treasures, and such prodigious riches, so diversified, that it is impossible for me to give an account of them: but as I was obliged to keep my right eye shut all the time with my hand, and that tired me, I desired the dervise to apply some of the pomatum to that eye.

I am ready to do it, said the dervise: but you ought to remember what I told you,—that if you put any of it upon your right eye, you will presently be blind; for such is the virtue of the pomatum.

Far from being persuaded of the truth of what the dervise said, I, on the contrary, imagined that there was some new mystery that he would hide from me. Brother, replied I smiling, it is unnatural that this pomatum should have two such contrary effects; I see you have only a mind to make me believe so.

The thing is as I tell you, replied the dervise, taking the name of God to bear witness; you ought to believe me, for I cannot disguise the truth.

However, I had not faith enough to believe the dervise, who spoke like an honest man: my insurmountable desire of seeing all the treasures in the world, and perhaps of enjoying what I had a mind to, had such an effect upon me, that I could not hearken to his remonstrances, nor be persuaded of a thing which was, however, but too much matter of fact, as I, to my great misfortune, soon experienced.

I imagined, that if that pomatum, by being applied to the left eye, had the virtue of shewing me all the treasures of the earth, by being applied to my right, it might have the power of putting them in my disposal. Possessed with this thought, I obstinately pressed the dervise to apply the pomatum to my right eye; but he as positively refused me. Brother, said he, after I have done you so much service, I cannot resolve to do you so great an injury: Consider with yourself what a misfortune it is to be deprived of one's eye-sight; therefore do not reduce me to the hard necessity of obliging you in a thing which you will repent of all your life-time after.

In short, my obstinacy was so prevailing, that I said to him, Brother, I earnestly desire you to lay aside all the difficulty you start: You have granted me generously all that I have asked of you hitherto, and would you have me go away unsatisfied at last, about a thing of so little consequence? For God's sake grant me this last favour; whatever happens, I will not lay the blame on you, but take it upon myself.

The dervise made all the resistance possible; but knowing that I was able to force him to do it, he said, Since you will absolutely have me, I will satisfy you; and thereupon took a little of the pomatum, and applied it to my right eye, which I kept shut: but, alas! when I came to open both my eyes, I could see nothing, but became as blind as you see me now.

Ah! dervise, cried I that moment, what you foretold me is but too true. Fatal curiosity, added I, insatiable desire of riches, into what abyss of miseries have you cast me! I am now sensible what a misfortune I have brought upon myself; but you, dear brother, cried I, addressing myself to the dervise, who are so charitable and good, examine into the wonderful secrets you know, and see if you have not one to restore me to my sight again.

Miserable wretch! answered the dervise, if thou wouldst have been advised by me, thou wouldst have avoided this misfortune; but thou hast thy deserts; the blindness of thy mind was the cause of the loss of thy eyes.—It is true I have secrets, and thou, in the little time I have been with thee, knowest I have, but none to restore thee to thy sight: pray to God, if thou believest there is one; it is he alone that can restore it to thee: he gave thee riches, of which thou wert unworthy, and takes them from thee again, and will by my hands give them to men not so ungrateful as thou.

The dervise said no more, and I had nothing to reply; he left me to myself, quite confounded, and plunged in inexpressible grief. After he had gathered my camels, he carried them away, and pursued the road to Balsora.

I desired him not to leave me in that miserable condition, but to conduct me to the first caravan; but he was deaf to my prayers and intreaties. Thus deprived of sight, and all I had in the world, I should have died of affliction and hunger, if, the next day, a caravan, returning from Balsora, had not received me charitably, and carried me to Bagdad.

After this manner I was reduced, without remedy, from a condition worthy the envy of princes, for riches and magnificence, though not for power, to beggary. I had no other way to subsist, but must resolve to ask charity, which I have done till now. But to expiate my offence against God, I enjoined myself, by way of penance, a box on the ear from every charitable person that should commiserate my condition.

This, Commander of the Faithful, is the motive which seemed so strange to your majesty yesterday, and for which I ought to incur your indignation. I ask your pardon once more as your slave, and submit to receive the chastisement I deserve. And if you vouchsafe to pronounce any thing on the penance I have imposed upon myself, I am ready to undergo it, since I am persuaded you think it too slight and too little for my crime.

When the blind man had made an end of his story, the caliph said, Baba Abdalla, thy sin is great; but God be praised, thou knowest both the enormity of that, and thy penance. As for the first, thou must ask God's pardon for it in every prayer thy religion obliges thee to say every day: and that thou mayest not be prevented by the care of getting thy living, I will settle a charity on thee during thy life, of four silver drachms a-day, which my grand visier shall give thee; therefore do not go till he has executed my orders.

At these words, Baba Abdalla prostrated himself before the caliph's throne, and rising up, returned him thanks, and wished him all happiness and prosperity.

The caliph Haroun Alraschid, very well satisfied with the story of Baba Abdalla and his dervise, addressed himself to the young man who used his mare so ill, and asked him his name; to which he replied, Sidi Nonman.

Sidi Nonman, then, said the caliph, I have seen horses exercised all my life, and have often exercised them myself, but never after so barbarous a manner as you yesterday treated your mare in the open square, to the great scandal of all the spectators, who murmured loudly against thee. In short, I myself was not much less displeased, and had like, contrary to my intention, to have discovered who I was, to have remedied that disorder. By thy air and behaviour, thou dost not seem to be so barbarous and cruel a man; and therefore I would believe that thou hadst a reason for what thou didst, since I am informed that this was not the first time, but that thou practisest the same thing every day: I would know what is the cause, and sent for thee for that purpose, that thou shouldst tell me the truth, and disguise nothing from me.

Sidi Nonman soon understood what the caliph demanded of him: The relation was painful to him: He changed colour several times, and could not help shewing how great an embarrassment he was in. However, he must resolve to tell his story; but before he spoke, he prostrated himself before the caliph's throne, and after he rose up again, endeavoured to speak, to satisfy the caliph, but was so confounded, not so much at the presence of the caliph, but the nature of his relation, that he was speechless.

The caliph, notwithstanding his natural impatience to be obeyed, shewed not the least anger at Sidi Nonman's silence: He saw plainly, that he either had not an assurance to speak before him, or was intimidated by the tone of his voice; or, in short, that he had a mind to conceal some things.

Sidi Nonman, said the caliph, to encourage him, do not be dashed, but tell me thy story as if thou wert speaking to thy most familiar friend. If there is any thing in thy relation which troubles thee, and thou thinkest I may be offended at it, I pardon thee now; therefore do not be uneasy, but speak boldly and freely, and disguise nothing.

Sidi Nonman, encouraged by these last words of the caliph, said, Commander of the Faithful, whatever apprehensions a man may be under at your majesty's presence, I am sensible that respectful apprehension would not deprive me of the use of my speech, and to fail in my obedience to you, in any other matter but this you ask of me. I dare not say I am the most perfect of men; yet I am not wicked enough to have committed, or to have had an intention of committing any thing against the laws, to fear their severity; and yet I cannot say I am exempt from sin, through ignorance: In this case, I would not depend upon your majesty's pardon, but will submit myself to your justice, and receive the punishment I deserve. I own, that the treatment of my mare, which I have used some time, and your majesty was a witness of, is very strange and cruel, and sets an ill example; but I hope you will think the motive well-grounded, and that I am more worthy of compassion than chastisement. But not to keep your majesty any longer in suspense by a long preamble, I will tell you my story.

The Story of Sidi Nonman

COMMANDER of the Faithful, said Sidi Nonman, I shall not trouble your majesty with my birth, which is not illustrious enough to merit your attention. For my fortune, my parents, by their good economy, left me enough to live on like an honest man, free from ambition, or being a charge to any one.

With these advantages, the only thing that I wanted to render my happiness complete, was a loving wife, who might partake of them with me; but that was a blessing that pleased God not to grant me: On the contrary, it was my misfortune to have one, who, the next day after our wedding, began to exercise my patience in a manner not to be conceived by any one that has not had the same trial.

As it is a custom for us to marry without seeing or knowing who we are to marry, your majesty is sensible that a husband has no reason to complain when he finds that the wife that is made choice of for him is not horribly ugly and deformed, and that her carriage, wit, and behaviour, correct any slight imperfections of the body.

The first time I saw my wife bare-faced, after she was brought home, with the usual ceremonies, to my house, I rejoiced to find that I had not been imposed upon in the description of her person, which pleased me, and was agreeable to my inclination.

The next day after our wedding, when our dinner was served up, which consisted of several dishes, I went into the room where the cloth was laid, and not finding my wife there, ordered her to be called, who, after she had made me wait a long time, at last came. I dissembled my impatience, and we sat down at table, and I began to eat rice with a spoon, as usual.

On the other hand, my wife, instead of making use of a spoon, pulled a little case out of her pocket, and took out of it an ear-picker,* with which she picked up the rice grain by grain.

Surprised at this manner of eating, I said to her, Amina, which was her name, are you used to eat rice so in your family, or do you do it because you are a little eater, or would you count the grains, that you may not eat more at one time than another? If you do it out of savingness, and to learn me not to be extravagant, you have no reason to fear that, and I can assure you we shall not ruin ourselves that way. We have, God be thanked, enough to live at our ease, without depriving ourselves of necessaries. Do not restrain yourself, my dear Amina, but eat as you see me eat. The affable manner in which I made these remonstrances might have gained some obliging answer; but she, without saying a word, continued to eat after the same manner. At last, to make me the more uneasy, she very seldom eat a grain of rice; and instead of eating any of the other meats with me, she now and then put some crumbs of bread into her mouth, but not so much as a sparrow would have ate.

I was very much provoked at her obstinacy; but yet, to excuse her, I imagined that she had not been used to eat with men, much more with a husband, before whom she might perhaps have been taught to be restrained, but, at the same time, thought she carried her simplicity too far. I fancied again that she might have breakfasted late, or that she might have a mind to eat alone, and at more liberty. These considerations prevented me from saying any more to her then, to ruffle her temper, or to shew any sign of dissatisfaction. After dinner I left her, but not with an air that shewed any displeasure.

At night, at supper, she did the same thing, and the next day, and every time we eat together, behaved herself after the same manner. I knew it was impossible for a woman to live on so little victuals, and that there was some mystery in it, which I did not understand. This made me resolve to dissemble: I seemed to take no notice of her actions, in hopes that time would bring her to live with me as I desired she should. But my hopes were in vain, and it was not long before I was convinced they were so.

One night when Amina thought me fast asleep, she got out of bed softly, dressed herself with great precaution, not to make a noise, for fear of waking me. I could not comprehend what her design was, but curiosity made me feign a sound sleep; and as soon as she had dressed herself, she crept softly out of the room.

When her back was turned, I got up, threw my gown over my shoulders, and had time enough to see her, by a window that looked into my court-yard, go out at the street door.

I ran presently down to the door, which she left half open, and followed her by moon-light, till she went into a burying-ground just by our house. I got to the end of the wall, taking care not to be seen, and looked over, and saw Amina with a goule.*

Your majesty knows that the goules of both sexes are wandering demons, which generally infest old buildings, from whence they rush out by surprise, on people that pass by, kill them, and eat their flesh, and, for want of prey, will sometimes go in the night into burying-grounds, and feed upon dead bodies that have been buried there.

I was in a terrible surprise to see my wife with this goule. They dug up a dead body which had been buried but that day, and the goule cut the flesh into several pieces, and they eat together by the grave-side, where they entertained each other very quietly during their so cruel and inhuman repast. But I was so far off, that it was impossible for me to hear their discourse, which, to be sure, was as strange as their repast, the remembrance of which makes me now shudder.

When they had made an end of this horrible feast, they threw the dead body into the grave again, and filled it up with the earth they had dug out. While they were doing that, I made haste home, and leaving the door as I found it, went into my chamber, and to bed again, where I pretended to be fast asleep.

Soon afterwards, Amina came, undressed herself without the least noise, and came to bed again, with all the joy imaginable, that she had succeeded so well without being discovered.

My mind was so full of the idea of so barbarous and abominable an action, that I had a great reluctancy to lie by a person who was guilty of it, and was a long time before I could fall asleep again. However, I got a short nap; but waked at the first call to public prayers at day-break, got up, dressed myself, and went to the mosque.

After prayers, I went out of the town, and spent the morning in walking in the gardens, to think what I should do to oblige my wife to change her manner of life: I rejected all the violent measures that came into my thoughts, and I resolved to use all gentle means to cure that unhappy inclination of hers: And these thoughts brought me insensibly home by dinner-time.

As soon as Amina saw me come in, she ordered dinner to be served up; and as I saw she persisted in the same manner of eating, I said to her, with all the moderation possible, You know, Amina, what reason I have to be surprised, when, the next day after our marriage, I saw you eat rice in so small a quantity, and odd manner, as would have made any other husband but me angry; you know also, I only acquainted you that I was uneasy at it, and desired you to eat of the other meats, which I ordered to be dressed several ways, to know your taste, and which you liked best; and I am sure my table did not want for variety. Besides, all my remonstrances have had no effect upon you, and you persist in your old way: I have never constrained you, and should be sorry now to say any thing to make you uneasy; but tell me, Amina, I conjure thee, are not the meats served up at my table better than dead flesh?

I had no sooner pronounced these last words, but Amina, who knew that I had watched her that night, flew into a rage beyond imagination. Her face was as red as scarlet, her eyes ready to start out of her head, and she foamed again with passion.

The terrible condition I saw her in, frightened me so much, that I stood as motionless as a stock or stone, and was not able to defend myself against the horrible wickedness she meditated against me, and which will surprise your majesty. In the violence of her passion, she dipped her hand into a bason of water which stood just by her; and muttering some words between her teeth, which I could not hear, she threw some water in my face, and said to me in a furious tone, Wretch, receive the punishment of thy curiosity, and become a dog.

No sooner had Amina, whom I knew not to be a sorceress till then, pronounced these diabolical words, but I was immediately changed into a dog. My amazement and surprise at so sudden and unexpected a change prevented my thinking at first of providing for my safety, till she took up a great stick to beat me, with which she laid on such heavy blows as were enough to kill me. I thought to have escaped her rage, by running into the yard, but she pursued me with the same fury; and notwithstanding all my activity, I could not avoid her blows. At last, when she was tired of beating me, and in despair that she had not killed me, as she desired, she thought of a new way to do it: She half opened the street door, that she might squeeze me to death between that and the wall. I was presently sensible of her pernicious design, and as present danger inspires a presence of mind, I looked her earnestly in the face, and took my opportunity so well, that I passed through quick enough to save my life, though she pinched the end of my tail.

The pain I felt made me cry out and howl, as I ran along the streets, which brought all the dogs about me, and I was bit by several of them, but, to avoid their pursuit, ran into the shop of a tripe-man, where I saved myself.

The tripe-man at first took my part with a great deal of compassion, by driving away the dogs that followed me, and would have worried me in his house. My first care was to run into the first hole I met with, to hide myself; but I was deceived in the sanctuary and protection I hoped for: my host was one of those extravagantly superstitious persons who think dogs unclean creatures, and if by chance one happen to touch them in the streets, cannot use soap and water enough to wash their garments clean. After the dogs who chaced me so far were all dispersed and gone, he did all he could to drive me out of his house that day; but I was hid, and out of his reach, and spent that night in his shop in spite of his teeth; and indeed I stood in need of rest, to recover Amina's ill treatment.

But not to weary your majesty with trifling circumstances, I shall not particularize the melancholy reflections I made on my metamorphosis; but only tell, that my host going out the next morning to lay in a stock of sheep-heads, and while he was laying out his goods, I crept out of my hole, and got among some other dogs of the neighbourhood, who had followed my host by the scent of his meat, and surrounded the shop, in expectation of having some thrown to them.

My host observing me among them in a begging posture, and considering that I had stole nothing while I lay in the shop, distinguished me from the rest, by throwing me larger pieces of meat, and oftener than the other dogs: after he had given me as much as he thought fit, I looked upon him earnestly, wagging my tail, and all to shew him I begged to come into the shop again. But he was inflexible, and opposed my entrance with a stick in his hand, so that I was forced to go and seek a new habitation.

Some houses farther, I stopped at a baker's shop, who was of a merry, gay temper, quite the reverse of the tripe-man, who was eaten up with melancholy. The baker was then at breakfast, and though I made no sign that I asked for any thing, he threw me a bit of bread. Instead of catching it up greedily, as most dogs do, I looked up first in his face, and wagged my tail to shew my acknowledgment: at which he was mightily pleased, and smiled. Afterwards, though I was not hungry, I eat the piece of bread, and he let me come into the shop. I turned myself about to the street, to shew him I only then wanted his protection; which he not only granted, but by his caresses assured me of, and shewed me a place where to lie, which I took possession of, and kept while I lived with him.

Whenever he breakfasted, dined, or supped, I had always my share of provisions; and, for my own part, I loved him, and was as faithful as gratitude required of me. I always had my eyes upon him, and he scarce stirred out of doors, but I was at his heels. I was the more exact, because I perceived my diligence pleased him; for whenever he went out, if I did not see him, he would call Chance, which was the name he gave me.

At this name I would jump and fly, and run round and round him, and never fawning on him till he went out; and then I always either followed him, or ran before him, often staring him in the face, to shew my joy.

I had lived some time with this baker, when a woman came one day into the shop to buy some bread, and giving my master a bad piece of money among some good, and he perceiving it, returned it back again, and asked for another.

The woman refused to take it again, and affirmed it to be good. The baker maintained the contrary, and told the woman that the piece of money was so visibly false, that his dog could distinguish it; upon which he called, Chance, Chance, and I jumped immediately on the counter, and the baker throwing the money down before me, said, See, and tell me which of these pieces is bad! I looked over all the pieces of money, and then set my paw upon that which was bad, separated it from the rest, and afterwards stared my master in the face, to shew him what I had done.

The baker, who never in the least thought of my pitching upon the bad money, but only called me to banter the woman, was very much surprised. The woman had nothing to say for herself, but changed the money, and gave another one in the stead of the bad one; and as soon as she was gone, my master called in some neighbours, and exaggerated very much upon my capacity, telling them what had happened.

The neighbours all desired to make the experiment, and of all the bad money they shewed me, mixed with good, I did not miss one piece, but separated the bad money from the good.

The woman, for her part, was sure to tell every body she met of my sense, and what had happened; insomuch, that the fame of my great capacity in distinguishing good money from bad, was not only spread throughout the neighbourhood, but all that part of the town, and insensibly through the whole city.

I had business enough every day, for I was obliged to shew my skill to all customers that came to buy bread of my master. In short, my reputation procured my master more business than he could manage, and brought him customers from the most distant parts of the town; and this run of business lasted so long, that my master owned to his neighbours that I was a treasure to him.

A great many people envied my master's good fortune, and laid a great many snares and traps to steal me away, which obliged him always to keep me in his sight. One day a woman came out of curiosity to buy some bread, and seeing me sit upon the counter, threw down among six pieces of money, one that was bad: I separated it presently from the good, and setting my paw upon it, looked in the woman's face, as much as to say, Is it not so? upon which the woman replied; Yes, thou art in the right of it, it is bad; and staying some time in the shop to look at and admire me, at last paid my master for his bread, and when she went out of the shop, made a sign, unknown to him, for me to follow her.

I was always attentive to any means to deliver myself out of so strange a metamorphosis, and had observed that the woman examined me with an extraordinary attention, and imagined that she might know something of my misfortune: However, I let her go, but all the time kept my eye fixed on her. Then walking two or three steps, she turned about, and seeing that I only looked at her, without stirring out of my place, she made me another sign to follow her.

Without deliberating any longer, and observing that my master the baker was busy cleaning bran, and did not mind me, I jumped off the counter, and followed the woman, who seemed overjoyed.

After I had gone some way, she stopped at a house, opened the door, and holding it in her hand, called to me to come in, saying, Thou wilt not repent thy following me. When I had got in, she shut the door, and carried me into a chamber, where I saw a young beautiful lady working embroidery. This lady, who was the charitable woman's daughter who had brought me from the baker's, was a very skilful magician, as I found afterwards.

Daughter, said the mother, I have brought you the famous baker's dog, that can tell good money from bad: You know that I gave you my thoughts on that matter when first I heard of him, and told you, I fancied he was a man changed into a dog. To-day, I bethought myself of going to buy some bread of that baker, and was myself a witness of the wonders performed by this dog, which has made such a noise in Bagdad. Now tell me, daughter, am I deceived in my conjectures? No, mother, you are not, answered the daughter, and I will make it appear so.

The young lady immediately got up, put her hand into a bason of water, which stood by her, and throwing some upon me, said, If thou art a dog, remain so, but if thou wert born a man, resume thy former shape, by the virtue of this water. At that instant, the enchantment was broke, and I became a man as before.

Penetrated with an acknowledgment of this great kindness, I threw myself at my deliverer's feet, and after I had kissed the hem of her garment, I said, My dear deliverer, I am so sensible of your exceeding and unparalleled goodness towards a stranger, as I am, that I beg of you to tell me yourself what I shall do to shew my gratitude; or rather, dispose of me as a slave, to whom you have a just right, since I am entirely yours: And that you may know who I am, I will tell you my story in as few words as possible.

After I had told her who I was, I gave her an account of my marriage with Amina, of the complaisance I shewed her, my patience in bearing her extraordinary behaviour, and the indignity with which she used me; and finished my story with my transformation, and thanking her mother for the inexpressible happiness she had procured me.

Sidi Nonman, said the daughter to me, let us not talk of obligations; it is enough to me, that I have done any service to so honest a man as you are; but let us talk a little of Amina your wife, with whom I was acquainted before your marriage; and, as I know her to be a magician, she is sensible that I understand that art as well as herself, since we had both the same mistress. We often meet at the baths, but as our tempers are different, I avoid all opportunities of contracting an intimacy with her, and she does the same by me. I am not at all surprised at her wickedness. But what I have already done for you is not sufficient; for I will complete what I have begun, and you shall punish her as she deserves, by going home again, and assuming the authority which belongs to you. Entertain and divert yourself a little with my mother, while I go and consult the proper means: I will come to you soon again.

My deliveress went into a closet; and while she was there, I expressed the sense of my obligation to the mother as well as daughter, who said to me, You see my daughter has as great knowledge in the magic art as Amina, but makes so good a use of it, that you would be surprised to know the good she has done, and daily does with it; and that induces me to let her practise it; for I should not permit her, was she to make an ill use of it.

Then the mother began to relate some of the wonders she had known her to do. When she came into the room again, with a little bottle in her hand, Sidi Nonman, said she, my books, which I have been consulting, tell me that Amina is now abroad, but will be at home presently. They also inform me, she pretended before your servants to be very uneasy at your absence, and made them believe that at dinner you remembered an affair which obliged you to go away immediately; and that as you went out, you left the door open, and a dog came in as far as the hall, where she was at dinner, and she beat him out with a great stick.

Take this little bottle, and go home immediately, and wait in your own chamber till she comes in: As soon as she comes home, run down into the yard, and meet her full-butt.* In her surprise to see you returned so unexpectedly, she will turn her back to run away; then be sure to have the bottle ready, and throw some of the liquor it contains upon her, pronouncing at the same time, these words boldly: Receive the chastisement of thy wickedness. I will tell you no more; you will see the effect.

After these words, I took my leave of my benefactress and her mother, with all the testimonies of a perfect acknowledgment, and a sincere protestation never to forget the obligation I had to them, and then went home.

All things happened as the young magician had foretold. Amina was not long before she came home: as she came up the yard, I went and met her with the water in my hand: as soon as she saw me, she shrieked out, and turned about to run to the door: I threw the liquor upon her, and pronouncing the words which the young magician taught me, she was presently changed into the same mare which your majesty saw me upon yesterday.

At that instant, in the surprise she was in, I seized her by the mane, and notwithstanding her resistance, led her into the stable, where I put an halter upon her head, and when I had tied her to the rack, I chastised her with a whip till I was tired, reproaching her all the time with her baseness; and punished her every day since after the same manner. I hope, Commander of the Faithful, continued Sidi Nonman, making an end of his story, your majesty will not disapprove of my conduct, and you will think I have shewn so wicked and pernicious a woman more indulgence than she deserved.

When the caliph found that Sidi Nonman had no more to say, he said to him, The story is very singular, and the wickedness of thy wife inexcusable; therefore I do not absolutely condemn the chastisement thou hast hitherto given her, but would have thee consider how great a punishment it is to be reduced into the number of the beasts, and I wish thou wouldst be content with that chastisement. Besides, I would order thee to go and address thyself to the young magician, to wave the enchantment and metamorphosis, but that I know the obstinacy and incorrigible cruelty of magicians who abuse their art, and was I not apprehensive that the second effect of thy wife's revenge would be more violent than the first.

The caliph, who was naturally mild and compassionate to all sufferers, after he had declared his mind to Sidi Nonman, addressed himself to the third person the grand visier Giafar had summoned to attend him. Cogia Hassan, said he, passing yesterday by thy house, it seemed so magnificent, that I had a curiosity to know whom it belongs to, and was told that thou, whose trade is so mean that a man can scarce get his bread by it, hast built it after thou hadst followed it some years. I was likewise informed, that thou makest a good use of the riches God has blessed thee with, and thy neighbours speak well of thee.

All this pleases me, added the caliph, and I am persuaded, that the means by which Heaven has bestowed these gifts on thee have been very extraordinary. I am curious to know them from thine own mouth, and sent for thee on purpose to have that satisfaction. Speak sincerely, that when I know thy story, I may rejoice in thy good fortune.

But that thou mayest not suspect my curiosity, and believe I have an interest in what you shall tell me, I declare, that far from having any pretensions, I give thee my word, thou shalt enjoy freely all thou hast got.

On these assurances of the caliph, Cogia Hassan prostrated himself before his throne, with his forehead down to the tapestry, and, when he rose up again, said, Commander of the Faithful, any other person but myself might have been concerned to have been summoned to appear before your majesty, but knowing that my conscience was clear, and that I had committed nothing against the laws nor your majesty, but, on the contrary, had always the most respectful sentiments, and the profoundest veneration for your person, my only fear was, I should not be able to support the lustre of your throne. But nevertheless, on the public fame of your majesty's receiving favourably, and hearing the meanest of your subjects, I took courage, and never doubted but I should have confidence enough to give you all the satisfaction you should require of me. Besides, your majesty has given me a proof of your goodness, by granting me your protection before you know whether I deserve it. Nevertheless, I hope I shall maintain the advantageous sentiments you have of me, when, in obedience to your command, I shall relate my adventures.

After this small compliment, to obtain the caliph's good will and attention, and after some moments, to recollect himself in his memory, Cogia Hassan resumed his discourse in the following manner.

The Story of Cogia Hassan Alhabbal

COMMANDER of the Faithful, said Cogia Hassan, that your majesty may the better understand by what means I arrived at the happiness I now enjoy, I ought to acquaint you, there are two intimate friends, citizens of Bagdad, now alive, who can testify the truth of what I shall tell you, and to whom, after God, the first author of all good, I owe my prosperity.

These two friends are called, the one Saadi, and the other Saad. Saadi, who is very rich, was always of opinion, that no man could be happy in this world without great riches, to live free from a dependance on any one.

Saad was of another opinion: He agreed that riches were necessary in life, but maintained, that the happiness of a man's life consisted in virtue, and no farther attachment to worldly goods than what were necessary in life, and to do good withal.

Saad himself is one of the number, and lives very happily and contentedly in his station; and though Saadi is infinitely more rich, their friendship is very sincere, and the richest values himself no more than the other. They never had any other dispute but on this point; in all other things their union is very strict.

One day as they were talking upon this subject, as I have since been informed by them both, Saadi affirmed that poverty proceeded from being born poor, or their spending their fortunes in luxury and debaucheries. My opinion is, said he, that most people's poverty is owing to their wanting at first a sufficient sum of money to employ their industry with, and by that means increase it: For, said he, if they once had such a sum, and made a right use of it, they would not only live well, but would infallibly grow rich in time.

Saad could not come into his sentiments. The way, said he, which you propose to make a poor man rich, is not so certain as you imagine. What you propose is very hazardous; and I can bring many good arguments against your opinion, but that they will carry us too far. I believe, and with as much probability on my side, that a man may become rich by other means as well as money: and there are people who have raised as great and surprising fortunes by mere chance, as others have done with great beginnings and good economy and management in business.

Sir, replied Saadi, I see we shall not come to any determination by my opposing my opinion against yours; but I will make an experiment to convince you, by giving, for example, a sum of money to some artisan whose generation has always been poor. If I have not the success I expect, you shall try if you will have better by the means you shall use.

Some days after this dispute, these two friends happened to walk out together, and passing through the street where I was at work in my stall, at my trade of rope-making, which I learned of my father, who learned it of his, and he of his ancestors before; and by my dress and equipage, it was no hard matter for them to guess at my poverty.

Saad, remembering Saadi's engagement, said, If you have not forgot what you said to me, there is a man, pointing to me, who I can remember a long time working at his trade of rope-making, and in the same poverty: He is a worthy subject for your liberality, and a proper person for you to make your experiment upon. I remember it so well, replied Saadi, that I have ever since carried a sufficient sum about me to do it, but only waited for an opportunity of our being together, that you might be a witness of the fact. Let us go to him, and know if he is really necessitous.

The two friends came to me, and, seeing that they had a mind to speak to me, I left off work. They both accosted me with a common salute, and Saadi taking upon him to speak, asked me my name.

I returned their salute, and answered Saadi's question, saying to him, Sir, my name is Hassan; but, by reason of my trade, I am commonly known by the name of Hassan Alhabbal.

Hassan, replied Saadi, as there is no trade but what a man may live by, I do not doubt but you may get enough to live well; and I am amazed that the long time you have worked at your trade you have not saved enough to lay in a good stock of hemp to employ more hands, by the profit of whose work you would soon increase.

Sir, replied I, you will be no longer amazed I have not saved money, and taken the way to be rich, when you come to know, that, let me work as hard as I can from morning till night, I can hardly get enough to keep my family in bread and pulse. I have a wife and five children, and not one of them old enough to do any thing: I must keep them and clothe them, and in our poor way of living, they still want a thousand necessaries, which they are forced to go without. And though hemp is not very dear, the first thing I do with any money I receive, is to lay by one part to lay in my small stock; otherwise, if I should neglect to do so, I and my family should starve.

Now judge, sir, added I, if it is possible that I should save any thing for myself and family: it is enough that we are content with the little God sends us, and that we have not the knowledge nor desire of what we want, but live as we have always been bred up, and are not reduced to beg charity.

When I had given Saadi this account, he said to me, I am not so much surprised as I was, and I comprehend what obliges you to be content in your station. But if I should make you a present of a purse of two hundred pieces of gold, would not you make a good use of it? And do not you believe, that with such a sum you could become soon as rich as the principal of your profession?

Sir, replied I, you seem to be so civil and honest a gentleman, that I am persuaded you would not make a sport of me, but that the offer you make me is serious; and I dare say, without presuming too much upon myself, that a sum much less would be enough to make me not only as rich as the principal of our profession, but in time I should be richer than them all of this city together, though Bagdad is so large and populous.

The generous Saadi shewed me immediately that what he said was serious: He pulled a purse out of his bosom, and putting it into my hands, said, Here, take this purse, you will find it contains two hundred pieces of gold: I pray God to bless you with them, and give you grace to make the good use of them I desire; and believe me, my friend Saad, whom you see here, and I, shall both take a great deal of pleasure to find they may contribute towards making you more happy than you now are.

When I had got the purse, the first thing I did was to put it into my bosom; but the transport of my joy was so great, and I was so much penetrated with acknowledgments, that my speech failed me, and I could give my benefactor no other tokens of my gratitude, but to catch hold of his garment and kiss it, which he drew from me, as he and his friend retired to pursue their walk.

As soon as they were gone, I returned to my work again, but could not think what I should do with my purse to keep it safe. I had neither box nor cupboard at home to lock it up in, and could not be sure it would not be discovered if I hid it.

In this perplexity, as I had been used, as a great many poor people are, to put the little money I had in the foldings of my turban, I left my work, and went into the house, under a pretext of wrapping my turban up anew, and took such precautions, that neither my wife nor children saw what I was doing. But first I laid apart ten pieces for present necessaries, and wrapped the rest up in the foldings of the linen which went about my cap.

The next thing I did that day, was to lay in a good provision of hemp, and afterwards, as my family had ate no flesh meat for a long time, I went to the shambles, and bought something for supper.

As I was carrying the meat I had bought home in my hand, a famished kite flew upon me, and would have taken away my meat, if I had not held it very fast; but, alas! I had better parted with it than lost my money: the faster I held my meat, the more the bird struggled, drawing me sometimes on one side, and sometimes on another, but would not quit the prize, till unfortunately, by making a sudden effort, my turban fell on the ground.

The kite immediately let go his hold, and seized upon my turban, before I could gather it up, and flew away with it. I cried out so loud, that I almost frightened all the men, women, and children in the neighbourhood, who joined their shouts and halloos to make the kite quit his prize; for by that means these sort of voracious birds are often frightened, and quit their prey. But it fell out otherwise in this case; for this kite carried off my turban, and we soon lost sight of him, and it was in vain for me to fatigue myself to run after him.

I went home very melancholy at the loss of my turban and money: and what would diminish the small remainder of the ten pieces, for I had laid out a deal in hemp, I was obliged to buy a new turban. Thus all my great hopes were quashed.

But that which troubled me most, was the little satisfaction I should be able to give my benefactor for his ill-placed generosity, who, when he should come to hear what a misfortune I had had, would perhaps look upon my story to be incredible, and by consequence an ill excuse.

While the remainder of the ten pieces lasted, my little family and I lived the better for it; but I soon fell again into the same poverty. However, I never murmured nor repined: God, said I, was pleased to give me riches when I least expected them, and has thought fit to take them from me again;

yet I will praise his name for all the benefits I have received, and submit myself entirely to his will.

These were my sentiments, while my wife, from whom I could not keep secret the loss I had sustained, was inconsolable. But yet I was so prudent in all my trouble as not to tell my neighbours, that when I lost my turban I lost an hundred and ninety pieces of gold, which if I had done, as they knew my poverty, and could not comprehend how I should have got so great a sum by my work, they would only have laughed at me.

About six months after this my misfortune, which I have related to your majesty, my two friends walking through that part of the town where I lived, the neighbourhood put Saad in mind of me. We are now, said he to Saadi, not far from the street where Hassan Alhabbal lives; let us call and see what use he has made of the two hundred pieces of gold you gave him, and what steps he has made towards the bettering of his fortune.

With all my heart, replied Saadi; I have been thinking of it some days; and it will be a greater pleasure and satisfaction to me, to have you with me: you will see a great alteration; we shall hardly know him again.

Just as Saadi said all this, these two friends turned the corner of the street; and Saad, who perceived me first at a distance, said to his friend, I believe you reckon without your host. I see Hassan Alhabbal, but can discern no change in his person, for he is as ill dressed as when we saw him before; the only difference that I can perceive, his turban looks something better. Observe him yourself, and see whether I am in the right or wrong.

As they drew nigher to me, Saadi saw me too, and found Saad was in the right, but could not tell to what he should attribute the little alteration he saw in my person; and was so much amazed, that he could not speak when he came up to me. Well, Hassan, said Saad, we do not ask you how affairs go since we saw you last; without doubt they carry a better face.

Gentlemen, replied I, addressing myself to them both, I have the great mortification to tell you, that your desires, wishes, and hopes, as well as mine, have not had the success you ought to expect, and I promised myself; you will scarce believe the extraordinary adventure that has befallen me. I assure you, nevertheless, on the word of an honest man, and you ought to believe me, for nothing is more true than what I am going to tell you. Then I related to them my adventures, with the circumstances I had the honour to tell your majesty.

Saadi rejected my discourse, and said, Hassan, you joke me, and would deceive me; for what you say is a thing incredible. What have kites to do with turbans? they only search for something to satisfy their hunger. You have done as most such sort of people as you are generally do. If they have made any extraordinary gain, or any good fortune happens to them, which they never expected, they throw aside their work, and divert themselves, and make merry while the money lasts, and when they have eat and drank it all out, are reduced to the same necessity as before. You would not be so miserable, but because you deserve it, and render yourself unworthy of any good action done to you.

Sir, replied I, I bear all these reproaches, and am ready to bear as many more, if they were more severe, and all with the more patience, because I do not think I deserve them. The thing is publicly known in this part of the town, and there is nobody scarce but what can satisfy you of the truth of it, if required; and you will find that I do not impose upon you. I own I never heard talk of kites flying away with turbans; but this is a thing that has happened, as a great many others do, which, though they do not fall out every day, are not the less probable.

Saad took my part, and told Saadi a great many as surprising stories of kites, some of which he affirmed he knew to be true, insomuch that at last he pulled his purse out of his bosom, counted out two hundred pieces of gold into my hand, which I put into my bosom, for want of a purse.

When Saadi had told me out that sum, he said to me, I make you a present of these two hundred pieces; but take care to put them in a safer place, that you may not lose them so unfortunately as you have done the others. I told him that the obligation of this his second kindness was much greater than I deserved, after what had happened, and that I should be sure to make a good use of his advice. I would have said a great deal more, but he would not permit me, but went away with his friend to make an end of their walk.

As soon as they were gone, I left off work, and went home; and finding neither my wife nor children within, I pulled out my money, put ten pieces by, and wrapped up the rest in a clean linen cloth; but then I was to consider where I should hide this linen cloth, that it might be safe. After I had considered some time, I bethought myself of laying it at the bottom of a great earthen vessel which stood full of bran in a corner, which I imagined that neither my wife nor children would look into: My wife came home soon after, and as I had but very little hemp in the house, I went out to buy some.

While I was out, a sand-man, who sells scouring sand, which women use to clean the baths with, passed through our street, and called, Any sand, ho? My wife who wanted some, called him; but as she had no money, she asked him, if he would make an exchange of some sand for some bran? The sand-man asked to see the bran. My wife shewed him the pot; the bargain was made; and the sand-man took the pot and bran along with him.

Not long after, I came home, loaded with as much hemp as I could carry, and followed by five porters loaded also. After I had satisfied them for their trouble, I sat down to rest myself, and looking about me, could not see the pot of bran.

It is impossible for me to express to your majesty my surprise, and the effect it had on me. I asked my wife hastily, what was become of it; and she told me the bargain she had made with the sand-man, which she thought to be a very good one.

Ah! unfortunate woman! cried I, you know not the injury you have done me, yourself, and our children, by making that bargain, which has ruined us quite. You thought only of selling the bran, but with the bran you have enriched the sand-man with an hundred and ninety pieces of gold, which Saadi, with his friend, came and made me a second present of.

My wife was like one stark mad, when she knew what a fault she had committed through ignorance. She cried and beat her breast, and tore off her hair and cloaths. Unhappy wretch that I am, cried she; am I fit to live after so horrid a mistake? Where shall I find this sand-man? I never saw him in our street before, and know him not. Oh! husband, added she, you was very much in the wrong to be so reserved in a matter of such importance! This had never happened, if you had communicated the secret to me. In short, I shall never make an end of my story, if I tell your majesty what her grief made her say; for women are often eloquent in their afflictions.

Wife, said I, moderate your grief; by your weeping and howling you will alarm the neighbourhood, and there is no occasion they should be informed of our misfortunes; they will only laugh at us, instead of pitying us; therefore we had best bear our loss patiently, and submit ourselves to the will of God, and bless him for the ten pieces of gold we have left, which will be of great service to us in our trade.

My wife at first did not relish all these my arguments; but as time softens the greatest misfortunes, and makes them more supportable, she at last grew easy, and had almost forgot them. It is true, said I to her, we live but poorly; but what signify riches? Do not we breathe the same air, enjoy the same light and warmth of the sun? Therefore what benefits have they more than we, that we should envy their happiness? They die as well as we. In short, while we live in the fear of God, as we all should do, the advantage they have over us is so very inconsiderable, that we ought not to regard it.

I will not tire your majesty any longer with my moral reflections. My wife and I comforted ourselves in this manner, and I followed my trade with as much alacrity as before these two mortifying losses. The only thing that troubled me sometimes, was, how I should look Saadi in the face, when he should come and ask me how much I had advanced my fortune with what he had so generously given me; though it was no fault of mine this time, no more than the other, but an accidental misfortune.

The two friends staid away longer this time than the former, though Saad had often spoke to Saadi, who always put it off; for, said he, the longer we stay away, the richer Hassan will be, and I shall have the greater satisfaction.

Saad, who had not the same opinion of the effect of his friend's generosity, made answer, You fancy, then, that your presents will turn to a better account now than before: I would advise you not to flatter yourself too much, for fear it should prove otherwise. Why, replied Saadi, kites do not fly away with turbans every day; and Hassan will be more cautious this time.

I do not doubt of it, replied Saad; but, added he, there are other accidents that neither you nor I can think of; therefore I say moderate your joy, and do not depend too much on Hassan's good success; for, to tell you what I think, and what I always thought, (whether you like it or not), I have a secret foresight, that you will be baulked in your expectations.

In short, one day when Saad and Saadi were together, and were disputing hard upon this subject, they resolved to take a walk, and inform themselves which of them was in the right. I saw them at a distance, was terribly concerned, and was just going to leave my work, and to run and hide myself. I seemed very earnest at my work, made as if I had not seen, and never lifted up my eyes till they were just by me, and had saluted me, and then I could not help it. After we had talked upon indifferent matters, I told them my last misfortunes, with all the circumstances, and that I was as poor as ever.

After that, I added, You may say that I ought to have hid my money in another place than in a pot of bran, (which was carried out of my house that same day), but that pot had stood there many years, and had never been removed until my wife parted with the bran; besides, could I guess that a sand-man should come by that very day, and my wife, having no money, should make such an exchange? Indeed you may allege, that I ought to have told my wife of it; but I will never believe that such prudent persons, as I am persuaded you are, would have given me that advice; and if I had put my money any where else, what certainty could I have that it would have been more safe?

I see, sir, said I, addressing myself to Saadi, that it has pleased God, whose ways are secret and impenetrable, that I should not be enriched by your liberality, and that I must be poor: however, the obligation is the same as if it had the desired effect.

After these words, I was silent, and Saadi replied, Though I would persuade myself, Hassan, that all you tell us is true, and not owing to your debauchery or ill economy, yet I must not be extravagant, and for the sake of an experiment to ruin myself. I do not regret, in the least, the four hundred pieces of gold I gave you to raise you in the world; I did it for God's sake, without expecting any recompence, but the pleasure of doing good; if any thing makes me repent, it is, that I did not address myself to another, who might have made a better use of my charity: Then turning about to his friend, Saad, continued he, you may know, by what I have said, that I do not give up my cause; you may now make your experiment, and let me see that there are ways, besides giving money, to make a poor man's fortune: let Hassan be the man; I dare say whatever you give him he will not be the richer. Saad had a piece of lead in his hand, which he shewed Saadi. You saw me, said he, take up this piece of lead, which I found on the ground; I will give it Hassan, and you shall see what it is worth.

Saadi burst out a-laughing at Saad. What is that bit of lead worth, said he; a farthing? What can Hassan do with that? Saad presented it to me, and said, take it, Hassan; let Saadi laugh; you will tell us some good news of it one time or other. I thought Saad was in jest, and had a mind to divert himself; but however, I put the lead in my pocket, and thanked him. The two friends pursued their walk, and I fell to work again.

At night, when I pulled off my cloaths to go to bed, the piece of lead, which I had never thought of from the time he gave it me, tumbled out of my pocket: I took it up, and laid it on the first place that was nearest me. The same night, it happened that a fisherman, a neighbour, mending his nets, found a piece of lead wanting; it being too late to buy any, since the shops were shut up, and he must either fish that night, or his family go without bread the next day, he called to his wife, and bid her inquire among the neighbours for a bit. She went from door to door, on both sides of the street, but could not get any, and came back again to her husband to tell him so. The fisherman seemed very much concerned, and scratching his head, asked her if she had been at Hassan Alhabbal's? No, indeed, said the wife; that was too far off, and I should but have lost my labour; for they never have any thing when one wants it. No matter for that, said the fisherman, you must go there, for though you have missed a hundred things before, you may chance to get what we want now.

The fisherman's wife, after grumbling and growling all the way, came and knocked at my door, and waked me out of a sound sleep. I asked her what she wanted? Hassan Alhabbal, said she, as loud as she could bawl, my husband wants a bit of lead to mend his nets with, and if you have a piece, desires you to give it him.

The piece of lead which Saad had given me was so fresh in my memory, that I could not well forget it. I told my neighbour, that if she would stay a moment, my wife should give her what she wanted. Accordingly, my wife, who was wakened as well as myself, got up, and groping about where I directed her, found the lead, opened the door, and gave it the fisherman's wife; who was so overjoyed, that she promised my wife, that, for the kindness she did her and her husband, we should have the first cast of the nets.

The fisherman was so much rejoiced to see the lead, which he so little expected, that he very much approved of his wife's promise, and mending his nets, went a-fishing two hours before day, according to custom. At the first throw he caught but one fish, about a yard long, and proportionable in thickness; and afterwards had a great many successful casts; but of all the fish he took, the first was the biggest.

When the fisherman had done fishing, he went home, where his first care was to think of me. I was extremely surprised, when at my work, to see him come to me with a large fish in his hand. Neighbour, said he, my wife promised you last night whatever fish I should catch at my first throw; and it pleased God to send me no more than this one, which, for the pleasure you did us, I desire you to accept; for all my other casts were very successful; and this is but a trifling present.

Neighbour, said I, the bit of lead which I gave you was worth so little, that it ought not to be valued at so high a rate: Neighbours should assist each other with what they want: I should have expected the same kindness from you, had I been in such a need; therefore I would refuse your present, if I was not persuaded you gave it me freely, and that I should anger you; and since you will have it so, I return you my hearty thanks.

After these compliments, I took the fish, and carried it home to my wife. Here, said I, take this fish, which the fisherman, our neighbour, has made me a present of, for the little bit of lead he sent for to us last night: I believe it is all that we can expect from the present Saad made me yesterday; and then I up and told her what passed between my two friends.

My wife was very much startled to see so large a fish. What would you have me do with it, said she? Our gridiron is only to broil small fish; and we have not a pot big enough to boil it. that is your business, answered I; dress it as you will, I shall like it either way; and then I went to my work again.

In cutting the fish, my wife found a large diamond; which, when she washed it, she took for a piece of glass: Indeed she had heard talk of diamonds, but had never seen one. She gave it to the children for a plaything, who handed it about from one to another, to admire the brightness and beauty of it.

At night, when the lamp was lighted, and the children were still playing with the diamond, they perceived that it gave a light, when my wife, who was getting them their supper, stood between them and the lamp; upon which they snatched it from one another to look at it; and the youngest fell a-crying that the eldest would not let him have it long enough: but as children always squabble and fall out, my wife and I took no notice of them; and all was quiet; for the great ones, who supped with us, had given the diamond in the mean time to the youngest.

After supper, when the children came together again, they began to make the same noise, and I called to the eldest to know what was the matter, who told me it was a piece of glass, which gave a light when his back was to the lamp; upon which I bid them bring it to me, and made the experiment myself; and it appeared so extraordinary to me, that I asked my wife what it was? who told me it was a piece of glass, which she found in gutting the fish.

I thought, no more than she, but that it was a bit of glass, but was resolved to make a farther experiment of it; and therefore bid my wife put the lamp in the chimney, and still found that it gave so great a light, that we might see to go to bed without the lamp; so I put it out, and placed the bit of glass upon the chimney to light us. Look, said I; this is another advantage that my friend Saad's piece of lead procures us; it will save us the expence of oil.

When the children saw the lamp was put out, and the bit of glass supplied its place, they hallooed out so loud, and made so great a noise, that it was enough to alarm the neighbourhood; and before my wife and I could quiet them, we were forced to augment it. After they were in bed, my wife and I, who lay just by them, went to bed too: and next morning, without thinking any more of the glass, I went to my work as usual; for it ought not to seem strange, that so ordinary a person as I was, who had never seen any diamonds should not know them, or their value.

But before I proceed, I must tell your majesty that there was but a very slight partition-wall between my next neighbour's house and mine, who was a very rich Jew, and a jeweller; and the chamber that he and his wife lay in joined to ours; and as they were both in bed, the noise my children made wakened them.

The next morning, the jeweller's wife came to mine to complain of being disturbed out of their first sleep. Good neighbour Rachel, (which was the Jew's name,) said my wife, I am very sorry for what happened, and hope you will excuse it; you are sensible it was the children, and they, you know, will laugh and cry for any thing: Come in, and I will shew you what was the occasion of all the noise.

The Jew went in with her; and my wife taking the diamond off the chimney-piece, gave it into her hands. See here, said she, it was this piece of glass that caused all the noise: and while the Jew, who understood all sorts of jewels, was examining this diamond with admiration, my wife had told her what had happened, and how she had found it in the fish's belly.

Indeed, Richaach, which was my wife's name, said the jeweller's wife, giving her the diamond again, I believe it is a piece of glass; but as it is more beautiful than common glass, and I have just such another piece at home, I will buy it, if you will sell it.

The children, who heard them talking of selling their play-thing, presently interrupted their conversation, crying and begging of their mother not to part with it, who, to quiet them, promised she would not.

The Jew being thus prevented in her bargain by my children, went away, but first whispered with my wife, who followed her to the door, that if she had a mind to sell it, not to shew it to any body before she had told her.

As soon as the Jew parted with my wife, she ran to the Jew her husband, who went out early in the morning to his shop, in that part of the town where the jewellers all resorted to, and told him the discovery she had made, and then gave him an account, as nigh as she could, of the size and weight of it, and of its beauty, water, and lustre.

The Jew sent his wife immediately to treat, and to offer her a trifle at first, as she should think fit, and then to raise her price by degrees, but to be sure to bring it, cost what it would. Accordingly his wife came again to mine, and bid her twenty pieces of gold for that piece of glass.

My wife finding the sum so considerable, would not make any bargain, but told her she could not part with it till she had spoken with me. In the mean time, I came from my work to dinner; and as they were a-talking at the door, my wife stopped me, and asked me if I would sell the piece of glass she had found in the fish's belly for twenty pieces of gold, which her neighbour offered her? I returned no answer, but reflected immediately on the assurance with which Saad, in giving me the piece of lead, told me it would make my fortune. The Jew woman, fancying that the low price she had offered was the reason I made no reply, said, I will give you fifty, neighbour, if that will do.

As soon as I found that she rose presently from twenty to fifty, I told her, that I expected a great deal more. Well, neighbour, said she, I will give you an hundred, and that is too much: I know not but my husband may be angry with me. At this new augmentation, I told her, I would have an hundred thousand pieces of gold: that I knew very well that the diamond was worth a great deal more, but to oblige her and her husband, as they were neighbours, I would limit myself to that price; and if they refused to give it, other jewellers should have it, who would give a great deal more.

The Jew confirmed me in this resolution, by being so eager to conclude the bargain, and by coming up, at several biddings, to fifty thousand pieces, which I refused. I can offer you no more, said she, without my husband's consent, who will be at home at night: and I would beg the favour of you to let him see it; which I promised.

At night when the Jew came home, his wife told him what she had done; that I refused fifty thousand pieces of gold, and that I had promised to stay till night. He observed the time I left off work, and came to me. Neighbour Hassan, said he, I desire you would shew me the diamond your wife shewed to mine. I bid him go in at the door with me, and he should. As it was pretty dark, and my lamp was not lighted, he knew presently, by the light the diamond cast, and by the lustre it had, that his wife had given him a just account. He looked at, and admired it a long time. Well, neighbour, said he, my wife tells me she has offered you fifty thousand pieces of gold; come, I will give you twenty thousand more.

Neighbour, said I, your wife can tell you that I value my diamond at an hundred thousand pieces, and I will take nothing less. He bartered a long time with me, in hopes that I would make some abatement; but finding at last that I was positive, and for fear that I should shew it to other jewellers, he came up to my price; but told me, that he had not so much then at home, but would pay it me all by that time to-morrow, and that very instant fetched two bags, of a thousand pieces each, as an earnest; and the next day, though I do not know how he raised the money, whether he borrowed it, or let some other jewellers in partners with him, he brought me the sum we agreed for, at the time appointed, and I gave him the diamond.

Having thus sold my diamond, and being infinitely rich, beyond my hopes, I thanked God for his bounty and liberality; and would have gone and thrown myself at Saad's feet, if I had known where he lived, as also Saadi's, to whom I was first obliged, though his good intention had not the same success.

Afterwards, I thought of the use I should make of so considerable a sum: My wife, with the vanity natural to her sex, proposed immediately to buy rich cloaths for her and her children, and to purchase a house, and furnish it handsomely. I told her we ought not to begin with such expences; for, said I, though the money is made to be spent, yet we must proceed to lay a good foundation, that we may not exhaust our stock; and began so to do the next morning.

I spent all that day, and the next, in going to the people of my own trade, who worked hard every day for their bread; and giving them money beforehand, engaged them to work for me in different sorts of rope-making, according to their ability, with a promise never to make them wait for their money, but to pay them as soon as their work was done.

By this means I engrossed almost all the business of Bagdad, and every body was pleased with my exactness and punctual payment.

Now, as so great a number of workmen must produce a great deal of work, I went and hired warehouses in several parts of the town, to hold my goods, and appointed a clerk over each, to sell by wholesale and retail; and by this economy received a considerable profit. Afterwards, to unite so many warehouses into one place, I bought a large house, which stood upon a great deal of ground, pulled it down, and built that which your majesty saw yesterday, which, though it makes so great an appearance, consists, for the most part, of warehouses for my business, with only what apartments are just necessary for me and my family.

Some time after I had left my poor old habitation, and removed to this new one, Saad and Saadi, who had scarce thought of me from the last time they had been with me, as they were one day walking together, and passing by our street, resolved to call upon me: But how great was their surprise, when they did not see me at work, as they used to find me! They asked what was become of me, and if I was alive or dead? But then their amazement was redoubled, when they were told I was become a great merchant, and was no longer called plain Hassan, but Cogia Hassan Alhabbal, which was to say, Merchant Hassan, rope-maker, and that I had built, in a street which they named, a house like a palace.

The two friends went directly to the street, and in the way, as Saadi could not imagine that the bit of lead which Saad had given me could be the raising of my fortune, he said to him, I am overjoyed to have made Hassan Alhabbal's fortune; but I cannot forgive the two lies he told me, to get four hundred pieces instead of two; for I, nor nobody else, can attribute it to the piece of lead that you gave him.

That is your thought, replied Saad, but not mine; and I do not see why you should do Cogia Hassan so much injustice as to take him for a liar. You will give me leave to believe that he told us the truth, and disguised nothing from us, and that the piece of lead which I gave him is the cause of his prosperity; and you will find he will presently tell us so.

In this discourse, the two friends came into the street where I live, and asked whereabouts my house stood; and being shewed it, and considering the front, they had much ado to believe it.

As soon as they had knocked at the door, my porter opened it; and Saadi, fearing to be rude, in taking the house of some noble lord for that he was inquiring after, said to the porter, I am afraid we are wrong, though they tell us this is Cogia Hassan Alhabbal's. You are very right, said the porter, opening the door wider, it is the same; and any of the slaves will tell him you attend.

I had no sooner set my eyes upon the two friends, but I knew them. I rose from my seat, and ran to them, and would have kissed the hem of their garments; but they would not let me, but embraced me. I invited them to sit down on a sofa, which was placed full against my gardens, and sat over-against them, assuring them at the same time, that I had not forgot that I was Hassan Alhabbal, nor the obligations I had to them.

Then Saadi, addressing himself to me, said, Cogia Hassan, I cannot express my joy to see you in the condition I wished you, when I made you the presents, without reproaching you, of twice two hundred pieces of gold; and I am persuaded, that those four hundred pieces have made this wonderful change in your fortune, which I see with pleasure; only there is one thing vexes me, which is, I cannot comprehend the reason why you should disguise the truth from me, alleging twice those misfortunes which seem incredible.

Saad heard this discourse of Saadi's with impatience, and, I may say, anger, which he shewed by casting down his eyes, and shaking his head; but, however, did not interrupt him. When he had done, he said to him, Forgive me, Saadi, if I prevent Cogia Hassan, before he answers you, to tell you, that I admire at your prejudice against his sincerity, and that you still persist in not believing the assurances he has already given you. I have told you before, and I repeat it to you once more, that I believe those two accidents which befel him, upon his bare relation; and whatever you may say, I am persuaded they are true: But let him speak himself, and tell which of us does him justice.

After this discourse of the two friends, I said, addressing myself to them both, Gentlemen, I should condemn myself to perpetual silence, on the clearing up of what you ask of me, if I was not certain the dispute you argue upon on my account cannot break that tie of friendship between you; therefore I will declare to you the truth, since you require it, and with the same sincerity as before. Then I told them every single accident, as your majesty has heard, without forgetting the least circumstance.

All my protestations had no effect on Saadi, to cure him of his prejudice. Cogia Hassan, replied Saadi, the adventure of the fish, and diamond found in his belly, appears to me as incredible as the kite's flying away with your turban, and the exchange of the scouring-sand. Be it as it will, I am convinced that you are no longer poor, but rich, as I intended you should, by my means, and I rejoice sincerely.

As it grew late, they got up to take their leave; when I, stopping them, said, Gentlemen, there is one favour I beg of you not to refuse to do me the honour of, that is, to stay and take a slight supper with me, and a bed to-night, and to-morrow I will carry you to a country-house I bought for the sake of the air, and we will return the same day on my horses. If Saad has no business that calls him elsewhere, said Saadi, I consent. Saad told him, that nothing should prevent his enjoying his company; and while they were talking about sending a slave to their homes, that they might not sit up for them, I went and ordered supper.

While supper was getting ready, I shewed my benefactors my house, and all my offices, which they found to be very large for my fortune: (I call them both benefactors, without distinction, because without Saadi, Saad would not have given me the piece of lead; and without Saad, Saadi would not have given me the four hundred pieces of gold, to which I attribute the rise of my good fortune); then I brought them back again into the hall, where they asked me several questions about my business; and I gave them such answers as satisfied them.

During this discourse, my servants came to tell me that supper was served up. I led them into another hall, where they admired the conveniency of it, the beaufet, and the meat I had provided: I regaled them also with a concert of vocal and instrumental music during the repast, and afterwards with a company of dancers, and other entertainments, endeavouring to shew them, as much as possible, my gratitude.

The next morning, as we had agreed to take a little fresh air, we went to the river side by sun-rise, and went on board a pleasure-boat that waited for us; and in less than an hour and a half's time, with six oars and the stream, we arrived at my country-house.

When we went ashore, my two friends stopped to observe the beauty of the outside of my house, and to admire its advantageous situation for the prospects, which were neither too much limited, nor too extensive, but very agreeable. Then I carried them into all the apartments, and shewed them all the outhouses and conveniencies; with all which they were very well pleased.

Afterwards we walked into the gardens, where what they were most taken with, was a grove of orange and lemon trees, loaded with fruit, which were planted at equal distances, and watered by a canal, which was cut from a pleasant river just by. The close shade, the fragrant smell which perfumed the air, the soft murmurings of the water, the harmonious notes of an infinite number of birds, and a great many other things which were agreeable, struck them in such a manner, that they hardly stirred a step but they expressed how much they were obliged to me for bringing them to so delightful a place, and sometimes to congratulate me upon my happiness and great acquisitions. Then I led them to the end of that grove, which was very long and large, where I shewed them a wood of large grown trees, which stood at the end of my gardens; and afterwards a summer-house, open on all sides, shaded with an host of palm-trees, but not so as to spoil the prospect; and then I invited them to walk in and repose themselves on a rich covered sofa.

There two of my boys, whom I had sent into the country, with a tutor, for the air, left us, to go into the wood a bird-nesting; and seeing one which was built pretty high, they bid the slave who waited on them climb the tree for it; who, when he came to it, was very much surprised to find it built in a turban: However, he took it, and brought it down with him, and, as he thought that I might like to see a thing that was so uncommon, he gave it to the eldest boy to bring to me.

I saw the children at a distance, coming back to us overjoyed to have a nest. Father, said the eldest lad, we have found a nest in a turban. The two friends and I were very much surprised at the novelty; but I much more, when I knew the turban to be that which the kite flew away with. After I had examined it well, and turned it about, I said to my two guests, Gentlemen, have you memories good enough to remember the turban I had on the day you did me the honour first to speak to me? I do not think, said Saad, that either my friend or I gave any attention to it; but if the hundred and ninety pieces of gold are in it, we cannot doubt of it.

Sir, replied I, there is no dispute but it is the same turban; for besides that I know it very well, it feels very heavy: Give yourself but the trouble to take it in your hand. Then after taking out the birds, and giving them to the children, I put it into his hands, and he gave it to Saadi. Indeed, said Saadi, I believe it to be your turban, which I shall be better convinced of when I see the money.

Now, sir, added I, taking the turban again, observe very well, before I touch it, that no human hand could have made such a nest; and the condition in which you see it, shews it not to be of a very fresh date, and is a sufficient proof that it has lain in the tree ever since that day the kite took it from off my head. I think it proper that I should make this remark, since it concerns me so much to remove your suspicions of my being deceitful. Saad backed me in what I urged, and said, Saadi, this regards you, and not me; for I am verily persuaded that Cogia Hassan does not impose upon us.

While Saad was talking, I pulled off the linen cloth which was wrapped about the cap, and took out the bag, which Saadi knew to be the same he gave me. I emptied it myself before them, and said, There, gentlemen, there is the money, count it, and see if it be right? which Saad did, and found it to be one hundred and ninety pieces of gold. Then Saadi, who could not deny so manifest a truth, addressing himself to me, said, I agree, Cogia Hassan, that this money could not be assisting to your enrichment, but the other hundred and ninety pieces, which you would make me believe you had in a pot of bran, might. Upon my word, sir, answered I, I have told you the truth in regard to both sums, and you would not have me retract, to make myself a liar.

Cogia Hassan, said Saad, leave Saadi to his own opinion; I consent, with all my heart, that he believes you are obliged to him for one part of your good fortune, by the means of the last sum he gave you, provided that he will agree that I contributed to the other half by the bit of lead, and will not pretend to dispute the diamond found in the fish's belly. I agree to it, answered Saadi, but still you must give me liberty to believe, that money is not to be amassed without money.

What, replied Saad, if chance should throw a diamond in my way worth fifty thousand pieces of gold, and I should have that sum given me for it, can it be said I got that sum by money?

They disputed no farther then, but we got up, and went into the house, just as dinner was ready. After dinner, I left my guests together, to pass away the heat of the day more at their liberty, while I went to give orders to my house-keeper and gardener. Afterwards I went to them again, and we talked of indifferent matters till it grew a little cooler, when we returned into the garden for fresh air, and staid till sun-set. Then we all mounted on horseback, and got to Bagdad by moon-light, two hours after, followed by one of my slaves.

It happened, by I do not know what negligence of my servants, that we were then out of oats, and the store-houses were all shut up; when one of my slaves seeking about the neighbourhood for some, met with a pot of bran in a shop, bought the bran, and brought the pot along with him, promising to carry it back again the next day. The slave emptied the bran into the manger, and dividing it with his hand among the horses, felt a linen cloth tied up, and very heavy: he brought the cloth to me in the condition that he found it, and presented it to me, telling me, that it might perhaps be the cloth he had often heard me speak of among my friends.

I ran overjoyed to my two benefactors. Gentlemen, said I, it has pleased God that you should not part from me before you should be fully convinced of the truth of what I have assured you; there is the other hundred and ninety pieces of gold, continued I, addressing myself to Saadi, which you gave me: I know it very well by the cloth, which I tied up with my own hands; and then I told out the money before them. I ordered the pot presently to be brought before me, and knew it to be the same, and sent it to my wife, who did so too at the first sight.

Saadi readily submitted, and renounced his incredulity, and said to Saad, I yield to you, and acknowledge, that money is not always the means of becoming rich.

When Saadi had done, I said to him, I dare not propose to return you the three hundred and eighty pieces of gold, which it hath pleased God should be found to undeceive you, and am persuaded, that you did not give them to me with an intention that I should return them; and for my part, I ought to be very well content, and do not design to make use of them, but, if you approve of it, to-morrow will give them to the poor, that God may bless us both.

The two friends lay with me that night too; and next day, after embracing me, went to their own homes, very well pleased with the reception I had given them, and to find I did not make an ill use of the riches Heaven had blessed me with. I thanked them both, and looked upon the leave they gave me to cultivate a friendship with them, and to visit them, as a great honour.

The caliph Haroun Alraschid was so attentive to Cogia Hassan's story, that he had not perceived the end of it, but by his silence. Cogia Hassan, said he, I have not heard any thing of a long time that has given me so much pleasure, to see the wonderful ways by which God gave thee thy riches, for which thou oughtest to continue to return him thanks, by the good use thou makest of his blessings. I am glad I can tell thee, that the same diamond which made thy fortune, is now in my treasury; and for my part, I am glad to know how it came there: But because there may remain in Saadi some doubts on the singularity of this diamond, which I look upon to be the most precious and valuable thing I am master of, I would have thee carry Saad and Saadi to my treasurer, who shall shew it them, to remove Saadi's unbelief, and to let them see that money is not the only certain means of making a poor man rich in a short time, without taking a great deal of pains. Besides, I would have thee tell the keeper of my treasury this story, that he may have it put into writing, and that it may be kept with the diamond.

After these words, the caliph signified to Cogia Hassan, Sidi Nonman, and Baba Abdalla, by bowing of his head, that he was satisfied with them, who all took their leaves, by prostrating themselves at the throne, and then retired.

The Story of Ali Baba, and the forty Thieves destroyed by a Slave

In a town in Persia, there lived two brothers, called Cassim and Ali Baba, who, though they were left equally alike by their father, whose substance was but small, yet they were not alike favourites of fortune.

Cassim married a wife, who, soon after their marriage, was left heir to a plentiful estate, and rich merchandizes; so that he became a rich and considerable merchant, and lived at his ease.

Ali Baba, on the other hand, who married a woman as poor as himself, lived very meanly, and was forced to maintain his wife and children by his daily labour, by cutting of wood in a forest hard by the town, and bringing it upon three asses, which were his whole substance, to town to sell.

One day, when Ali Baba was in the forest, and had just cut wood enough to load his asses, he saw at a distance a great cloud of dust, which seemed to approach towards him: He observed it very attentively, and distinguished a large body of horse; and though they did not talk much of thieves in that country, Ali Baba began to think that they might prove so, and without thinking what might become of his asses, he was resolved to save one, and to that end, climbed up a large, thick, and close-leafed tree, from whence he could see all that passed without being seen; and this tree stood at the bottom of a rock, which was very high, and so steep and craggy, that nobody could climb up it.

This troop, who were all well mounted and well armed, came to the foot of this rock, and there dismounted. Ali Baba counted forty of them, and, by their mien and equipment, never doubted but they were thieves, and was not mistaken in his opinion; for they were a troop of banditti, who robbed thereabouts, and made that place their rendezvous: what confirmed him in this opinion, was, every man unbridled his horse, and tied him to some shrub or other, and hung a bag of corn they brought behind them about his neck. Then each of them took his portmanteau, which seemed to Ali Baba to be gold and silver by the weight, and followed one who was most likely amongst them, and whom he took to be their captain, who, with his portmanteau too in his hand, came under the tree in which Ali Baba was hid, and traversing among some shrubs, pronounced these words distinctly, Sesame, (which is a sort of corn,) open. As soon as the captain of the robbers had said these words, a door opened; and after he had made all his troop go in, he followed them himself, and the door shut again.

The thieves staid some time within the rock, and Ali Baba, who feared that some one, or all of them together, should come and catch him, if he should endeavour to make his escape, sat very patiently on the tree, but was nevertheless tempted once or twice to get down and mount one of their horses, and lead another, and make all the haste he could to town; but the uncertainty of the event made him chuse the safest way.

At last the door opened again, and the forty robbers came out again: As the captain went in last, he came out first, and stood to see them all pass by him; and then Ali Baba heard him bid the door shut, by pronouncing these words, Shut Sesame. Every man went and bridled his horse, fastened his portmanteau, and mounted again; and when the captain saw them all ready, he put himself at their head, and returned the same way he came.

Ali Baba all this time never stirred out of the tree; for, said he to himself, they may have forgot something, and come back again, and then I shall be taken; but followed them with his eyes as far as he could see them; and after that, staid some time before he came down; and remembering the words the captain of the thieves made use of to cause the door to open and shut, he had the curiosity to try if his pronouncing of it would have the same effect. Accordingly, he went among the shrubs, and perceiving the door, he said, Open Sesame; and the door flew wide open.

Ali Baba, who expected a dark, dismal place, was very much surprised to see it light-some and spacious, cut out in the form of a vault by men, and receive the light from an opening at the top of the rock. He saw all sorts of provisions, and rich bales of merchandizes, of silks, stuffs, brocades, and fine tapestries, piled upon one another, and, above all, great heaps of gold and silver, and great bags, laid upon one another. This sight made him believe that this cave, by the riches it contained, had been possessed not years, but ages, by robbers, who succeeded one another.

Ali Baba did not stand long to consider what he should do, but went immediately into the cave, and as soon as he was in, the door shut again; which never disturbed him, because he knew the secret to open it again. He never regarded the silver, but made the best use of his time in carrying out as much of the gold, which was in bags, at several times, as he thought his three asses could carry. When he had done, he gathered up his asses, which were dispersed about, and when he had loaded them, covered the bags with green boughs; and pronouncing the words, Shut Sesame, the door closed after him, and he made the best of his way to the town.

When Ali Baba got home, he drove his asses into a little yard, and shut the gates carefully, threw off the wood that covered the bags, carried them into his house, and ranged them in order before his wife, who sat on a sofa.

His wife handled the bags, and finding them full of money, suspected that her husband had been robbing, insomuch, that when he had brought them all in, she could not help saying, Ali Baba, have you been so unhappy as to—Be quiet, wife, interrupted Ali Baba; do not fright yourself; I am no robber, unless he can be one who steals from thieves. You will no longer entertain an ill opinion of me, when I shall tell you my good fortune.

Then he emptied the bags, which raised such a great heap of gold as dazzled his wife's eyes; and when he had done, told her the whole adventure, from the beginning to the end; and, above all, recommended it to her to keep it secret.

The wife, recovered, and cured of her fears, rejoiced with her husband for their good luck, and would count all the gold, piece by piece. Wife, said Ali Baba, you do not know what you undertake, when you pretend to count the money; you will never have done: I will go and dig a hole, and bury it; there is no time to be lost. You are in the right of it, husband, replied the wife; but let us know as nigh as possible how much we have: I will go and borrow a small measure in the neighbourhood, and measure it while you dig the hole. What signifies it, wife, said Ali Baba; if you would take my advice, you had better let it alone; but be sure to keep the secret, and do what you please.

Away the wife ran to her brother-in-law, Cassim, who lived just by, but was not then at home; and addressing herself to his wife, desired her to lend her a measure for a little while. Her sister-in-law asked her whether she would have a great one or a small one? and being told a small one, bid her stay a little and she would fetch one.

As the sister-in-law knew very well Ali Baba's poverty, she was curious to know what sort of grain his wife wanted to measure, and bethought herself immediately of putting some suet at the bottom of the measure, and brought it to her, with an excuse, that she was sorry that she had made her stay so long, but that she could not find it sooner.

Ali Baba's wife went home, set the measure upon the heap of gold, and filled it and emptied it often, at a small distance, upon the floor: and she was very well satisfied to find the number of measures run so high as they did, and went to tell her husband, who had almost finished the hole he was digging; and while Ali Baba was burying the gold, his wife, to shew exactness and respect to her sister-in-law, carried the measure back again, but without taking notice of a piece of gold that stuck at the bottom. Sister, said she, giving it to her again, you see that I have not kept your measure long; I am obliged to you for it, and return it with thanks.

As soon as Ali Baba's wife's back was turned, Cassim's wife looked at the bottom of the measure, and was in an inexpressible surprise to find a piece of gold stuck to it. Envy immediately possessed her breast. What, said she, has Ali Baba gold so plentiful as to measure it? Where has that poor wretch got all this gold? Cassim, her husband, was not at home, as I said before, but at his shop, which he left always in the evening; which time she thought an age; so great was her impatience to tell him the news.

When Cassim came home, his wife said to him, Cassim, I warrant you, you think yourself rich, but you are much mistaken: Ali Baba is infinitely richer than you; he does not count his money, but measures it. Cassim bid her explain the riddle, which she did, by telling him the stratagem she had made use of to make the discovery, and shewed him the piece of money, which was so old a coin, that they could not tell in what prince's reign it was coined.

Cassim, instead of being pleased at his brother's prosperity, conceived a mortal jealousy, and could not sleep all that night for it, but went to him in the morning before sun-rise. Now Cassim, after he married the rich widow, never treated Ali Baba as a brother, but forgot that name. Ali Baba, said he, accosting him, you are very reserved in your affairs; you pretend to be miserably poor, and yet you measure gold. How, brother, replied Ali Baba,

I do not know what you mean: Explain yourself. Do not pretend ignorance, replied Cassim, shewing him the piece of gold his wife had given him. How many of these pieces, added he, have you? My wife found this at the bottom of the measure you borrowed yesterday.

By this discourse, Ali Baba perceived that Cassim and his wife, through his own wife's folly, knew what they had so much reason to keep secret: But what was done could not be recalled; therefore, without shewing the least surprise or trouble, he confessed all, and told him by what chance he had discovered this retreat of the thieves, and in what place it was, and offered him part of his treasure to keep the secret. That is not sufficient, replied Cassim, haughtily; I will know exactly where this treasure is, and the signs and tokens, that I may go to it myself when I have a mind; otherwise I will go and inform against you, and then you will lose all you have got, and I shall have half what you have, for my information.

Ali Baba, more out of his natural good temper than frightened by the insulting menaces of a barbarous brother, told him all he desired, and even the very words he was to make use of to go into the cave, and out again.

Cassim, who wanted no more of Ali Baba, left him soon after, resolving to be beforehand with him, and to get all the treasure to himself, He rose early the next morning, and a long time before the sun, and set out with ten mules loaded with great chests, which he designed to fill; proposing to carry more the next time, according to the riches he found; and followed the road which Ali Baba had told him. He was not long before he came to the rock, and found out the place, by the tree, and other marks his brother had given him. When he came to the door, he pronounced these words, Open Sesame, and it opened; and when he was in, it shut again. In examining the cave, he was in great admiration to find much more riches than he comprehended by Ali Baba's relation. He was so covetous, and desirous of riches, that he could have spent the whole day in feasting his eyes with so much treasure, if the thoughts of carrying some away with him, and loading his mules, had not hindered him. He laid as many bags of gold as he could carry at the door; and coming at last to open the door, his thoughts were so full of the great riches he should possess, that he could not think of the necessary word; but, instead of Sesame, said, Open Barley, and was very much amazed to find that the door did not open, but remained fast shut. Afterwards he named several sorts of grain, but all to no purpose.

Cassim never expected such an accident, and was so frightened at the danger he was in, that the more he endeavoured to remember the word Sesame, the more his memory was confounded, and he had as much forgot it as if he had never heard it in his life before; but walked and fretted about the cave, without having the least regard to all the riches that were about him; and in this miserable condition we will leave him, bewailing his fate, and undeserving of pity.

About midnight, the thieves returned to their cave, and at some distance from it found Cassim's mules straggling about the rock, with great chests and hampers on their backs. This novelty made them very uneasy, and made them gallop in full speed to the cave. The thieves never gave themselves the trouble to pursue the mules, which were drove away, but were more concerned to know who they belonged to: And while some of them searched about the rock, the captain and others went directly to the door, with their naked sabres in their hands, and pronouncing the words, it opened.

Cassim, who heard the noise of the horses feet trampling about the cave, never doubted of the coming of the thieves, and his approaching death, but was resolved to make one effort to escape from them. To this end, he stood ready at the door, and no sooner heard the word Sesame, which he had forgot, and saw the door open, but he jumped briskly out, and threw the captain down, but could not escape the other thieves, who with their sabres soon deprived him of life.

The thieves first care after this was to go into the cave, where they found all the bags which Cassim had brought to the door, to be the more ready to load his mules with, and carried them all back again, without perceiving what Ali Baba had taken away before; then holding a council, and deliberating upon this matter, they guessed that Cassim, when he was in, could not get out again; but then could not imagine how he got in. First, they thought that he might have got down by the top of the cave; but the opening by which it received light was so high, and the rock so inaccessible without, that they believed it impracticable; and, in short, none of them could imagine which way he entered; for they were all persuaded nobody knew their secret: But however it happened, it was a matter of the greatest importance to them to secure their riches; they therefore agreed to cut Cassim's body into four quarters, and to hang two on one side, and two on the other, within the door of the cave, to terrify any person that should attempt the same thing. They had no sooner taken this resolution, but they executed it: and when they had nothing more to detain them, they mounted their horses, and went to beat the roads again, and to attack the caravans they should meet.

In the mean time, Cassim's wife was very uneasy; when night came, and her husband was not returned, she ran to Ali Baba in a terrible fright, and said, I believe, brother-in-law, that you know that Cassim is gone to the forest, and upon what account; it is now night, and he is not returned; I am afraid some misfortune has come to him. Ali Baba, who never disputed but that his brother, after what he had said to him, would go to the forest, would not go himself that day, for fear of giving him any umbrage; therefore told her, without any reflection upon her husband's unhandsome behaviour, that she need not fright herself, for that certainly Cassim did not think it proper to come into the town till the night should be pretty far advanced.

Cassim's wife, considering how much it concerned her husband to keep this thing secret, was the more easily persuaded to believe him, and went home again, and waited patiently till midnight. Then her fear redoubled, with much more sensible grief, because she durst not shew it, but was forced to keep it secret from the neighbourhood. Then, if her fault had been reparable, she repented of her foolish curiosity, and cursed her desire of penetrating into the affairs of her brother and sister. She spent all that night in tears, and as soon as it was day went to them, telling them, by her tears, the cause of her coming.

Ali Baba never waited for his sister-in-law to desire him to go to see what was become of Cassim, but went immediately with his three asses, begging of her first to moderate her affliction. When he came near the rock, and having seen neither his brother nor the mules in his way, he was very much surprised to see some blood spilt by the door, which he took for an ill omen: But when he had pronounced the word, and the door opened, he was much more startled at the dismal sight of his brother's quarters. He was not long in thinking how he should pay the last duties to his brother, and without remembering the little brotherly friendship he had for him, went into the cave, to find something to wrap them in, and loaded one of his asses with them, and covered them over with green wood: The other two asses he loaded with bags of gold, covering them with boughs also; and then bidding the door shut, came away; but was so cautious as to stop some time at the end of the forest, that he might not go into the town before night. When he came home, he drove the two asses loaded with gold into his little yard, and left the care of unloading them to his wife, while he led the other to his sister-in-law's.

Ali Baba knocked at the door, which was opened by Morgiana, a cunning artful slave, so fruitful in her inventions, that she would succeed in the most difficult undertaking; and Ali Baba knew her to be such. When he came into the court, he unloaded his ass, and taking Morgiana aside, said to her, The first thing I ask of thee, is an inviolable secrecy, which you will find is necessary, both for thy mistress's sake and mine. Thy master's body is contained in both these two bundles, and our business is to bury him as if he died a natural death: Go, tell your mistress I want to speak with her; and mind what I say to you.

Morgiana went to her mistress, and Ali Baba followed her. Well, brother, said she with great impatience, what news do you bring me of my husband? I perceive no comfort in your countenance. Sister, answered Ali Baba, I cannot tell you any thing before you hear my story from the beginning to the end, without speaking a word; for it is of as great importance to you to keep what has happened secret, as to me. Alas! said she, this preamble lets me know that my husband is dead; but at the same time I know the necessity of the secrecy you require of me, and I must constrain myself: Say on; I will hear you.

Then Ali Baba told his sister the success of his journey, till he came to the finding of Cassim's body. Now, said he, sister, I have something to tell you, which will afflict you much the more, because it is what you so little expect: But it cannot now be remedied; and if any thing can comfort you, I offer to put that little which God hath sent me to what you have, and marry you; assuring you, that my wife will not be jealous, and that we shall live happily together. If this proposal is agreeable to you, we must think of acting so as that my brother should appear to have died a natural death: And I think fit to leave the management of it to the care of Morgiana, and will contribute myself all that lies in my power.

What could Cassim's widow do better than accept of this proposal? For though her first husband had left behind him a plentiful substance, this second was much richer, and by the discovery of this treasure might be much more. Instead of rejecting the offer, she looked upon it as a reasonable motive to comfort her; and drying up her tears, and suppressing her sighings and sobbings, shewed Ali Baba she approved of his proposition in this matter. Ali Baba left the widow, and also recommended to Morgiana to acquit herself well of what she had undertaken, and then returned home with his ass.

Morgiana went out at the same time to an apothecary's, and asked him for a sort of lozenges, which he prepared, and were very efficacious in the most dangerous distempers. The apothecary asked who was sick,—her master? And she replied, with a sigh, her good master, Cassim himself: That they knew not what his distemper was, but he could neither eat nor speak. After these words, Morgiana carried the lozenges home with her, and next morning went to the same apothecary's again, and, with tears in her eyes, asked for an essence with which they used to rub sick people when at the last extremity. Alas! said she, taking it from the apothecary, I am afraid that this remedy will have no better effect than the lozenges, and that I shall lose my good master.

On the other hand, as Ali Baba and his wife were often seen to go between Cassim's and their own house all that day, and to seem melancholy, nobody was much surprised in the evening to hear the lamentable shrieks and cries of Cassim's wife and Morgiana, who told it every where that her master was dead.

The next morning, soon after day appeared, Morgiana, who knew a certain old cobler that opened his stall early, before other people, went to him, and bidding him good-morrow, put a piece of gold into his hand. Well, said Baba Mustapha, which was his name, and who was a merry old fellow, looking on the gold, this is good handsel; what must I do for it?

Baba Mustapha, said Morgiana, you must take along with you your sewing tackle, and go with me; but I must tell you, we must blindfold you when you come to such a place.

Baba Mustapha seemed to boggle a little at these words. Ah! ah! replied he, you would have me do something against my conscience and honour. God forbid, said Morgiana, putting another piece of gold into his hand, that I should ask any thing that is contrary to your honour; only come along with me, and fear nothing.

Baba Mustapha went with Morgiana, who, after she had bound his eyes at the place she told him of, with an handkerchief, carried him home with her, and never unloosed his eyes till he came into the room where her master lay. Baba Mustapha, said she, you must make haste and sew these quarters together, and when we have done, I will give you another piece of gold.

After Baba Mustapha had done as she bid him, she blindfolded him again, gave him the gold she promised, recommending secrecy to him, carried him back to the place where she first bound his eyes, pulled off the band, and watched him that he returned to his stall, for fear he should have the curiosity to dodge her, and then went home.

By the time Morgiana had done all this, and warmed some water to wash the body, Ali Baba came with perfumes and incense to embalm it, with the usual ceremonies. Not long after, the joiner, according to Ali Baba's orders, brought the coffin, which Morgiana, that he might perceive nothing, received at the door, and helped Ali Baba to put the body into it; and as soon as he had nailed it up, went to the mosque to tell the iman that they were ready; telling the people of the mosque, whose business it was to wash the dead, and who offered to perform their duty, that it was done already.

Morgiana had scarce got home, before the iman and the other ministers of the mosque came. Four neighbours carried the corpse on their shoulders, and followed the iman, who recited some prayers, to the burying-ground. Morgiana, as a slave to the deceased, followed the corpse, beating her breast, and tearing her hair, and Ali Baba came after, with some neighbours, who walked two and two, and often relieved one another in carrying the corpse.

Cassim's wife staid at home to mourn, and receive visits from her neighbours' wives and acquaintance, who, according to the custom, during the time of the ceremony of the burial, came to bewail with the widow for her loss.

In this manner, Cassim's horrid murder was concealed, and managed so well by Ali Baba, his wife, Cassim's widow, and Morgiana, that nobody had the least knowledge or suspicion of it.

Three or four days afterwards, Ali Baba removed his goods to his brother's widow's house; but the money he had taken from the thieves he conveyed thither by night; and soon after, the marriage with his sister-in-law, (which is common in our religion), was blown about.

As for Cassim's shop, Ali Baba gave it to his eldest son, who had been some time out of his apprenticeship to a great merchant, promising him withal, that if he managed the stock well, he would give him a fortune to marry very advantageously.

Now let us leave Ali Baba, to enjoy the beginning of his good fortune, and return to the forty thieves.

They came again at the appointed time to visit their retreat, and were in a great surprise to find Cassim's body taken away, and some of their gold. We are certainly discovered, said the captain, and shall be undone, if we do not take care and apply some remedy; otherwise we shall insensibly lose all the riches which our ancestors have been so many years amassing together with so much pains and danger. What I think of this loss which we have sustained, is, that the thief whom we surprised had the secret of opening the door and we came luckily as he was coming out: But his body being removed, and the money which we miss, plainly shews that he has an accomplice; and it is likely that there were but two who had got this secret, and one we have catched; therefore we must look narrowly after the other. What say you to it, my lads?

All the thieves approved of it, and thought the captain's sentiments were very just, and agreed that they must lay all other enterprizes aside, to follow this closely, and not to depart till they had succeeded.

I expected no less, said the captain, from your courage and bravery: but first of all, we must make choice of one who is bold enough to go into the town, dressed like a traveller and stranger, to try if he can hear of any one's being barbarously murdered and massacred, and to endeavour to find out the house where he lived. This is a thing of the first importance for us to know, that we may do nothing we have reason to repent of, by discovering ourselves in a country where we have so much reason to continue. But to prevent our being deceived by any one who shall take upon himself the charge of this commission, and may come and give us a false report, which may be the cause of our ruin, I ask you all, if you do not think it fit, that, in that case, he shall submit to suffer death?

Without waiting for the suffrages of all his companions, one of the thieves started up, and said, I submit myself to this law, and think it an honour to expose my life by taking such a commission upon me; but remember, if I do not succeed, that, at least, I neither want courage nor good-will to serve my troop.

After this robber had received the thanks and commendations of the captain and his comrades, he disguised himself so that nobody would take him for what he was; and taking his leave of the troop that night, went into the town just at day-break, and walked up and down till he came to Baba Mustapha's stall, which was always open before any of the shops in the town.

Baba Mustapha was set on his seat, with an awl in his hand, just going to work. The thief saluted him, bidding him good-morrow; and perceiving that he was old, he said, Honest man, you begin to work very early: Is it possible that any one of your age can see so well? I question, if it was somewhat lighter, whether I can see to stitch.

Certainly, replied Baba Mustapha, you must be a stranger, and do not know me; for as old as I am, I have extraordinary good eyes; and perhaps you will not believe me when I tell you that I sewed a dead body together in a place where I had not so much light as I have now.

The thief was overjoyed to think that he had addressed himself at his first coming into the town to a man who gave him the intelligence he wanted, without asking him. A dead body! replied he with amazement, to make him explain himself. How do you say; stitched up a dead body! added he: you mean, you sewed up his winding-sheet. No, no, answered Baba Mustapha, I know what I say; you want to have me speak out; but you shall know no more.

The thief wanted no greater an insight to be persuaded that he had discovered what he came about: he put his hand into his pocket, and pulling out a piece of gold, putting it into Baba Mustapha's hand, said to him, I do not want to know your secret, though I can assure you I would not divulge it if you trusted me with it. The only thing which I desire of you, is, to do me the favour to shew the house where you stitched up the dead body.

If I would do you that favour which you ask of me, replied Baba Mustapha, holding the money in his hand, ready to give him again, I assure you I cannot do it; and you may believe me, for this reason: I was carried to a certain place, where they first blinded me, and then led me to the house, and brought me back again after the same manner; therefore you see the impossibility of doing what you desire.

Well, replied the thief, you may remember a little way that you was led blindfolded. Come, let me blind your eyes at the same place; perhaps you may remember some part of the way and turnings; and as every body ought to be paid for their trouble, there is another piece of gold for you; gratify me in what I ask you.

The two pieces of gold were great temptations to Baba Mustapha. He looked at them a long time in his hand, without saying one word, thinking with himself what he should do; but at last he pulled out his purse and put them in. I cannot assure you, said he to the thief, that I can remember the way exactly; but since you desire it, I will try what I can do. At these words, Baba Mustapha got off his seat, and without shutting up his shop, where he had nothing valuable to lose, he led the thief to the place where Morgiana bound his eyes. It was here, said Baba Mustapha, where I was blindfolded; and I turned this way. The thief, who had his handkerchief ready, tied it over his eyes, and walked by him till he stopped. I think, said Baba Mustapha, I went no further than here; and stopped directly at Cassim's house, where Ali Baba then lived: Upon which the thief, before he pulled off the band, marked the door with a piece of chalk, which he had ready in his hand; and when he pulled it off, he asked him if he knew whose house that was? to which Baba Mustapha replied, That as he did not live in that neighbourhood, he could not tell.

The thief, finding he could discover no more from Baba Mustapha, thanked him for the trouble he had given him, and left him to go back to his stall, while he returned to the forest, persuaded that he would be very well received.

A little after the thief and Baba Mustapha parted, Morgiana went out for something; and coming home again, and seeing the mark the thief had made, she stopped to observe it. What is the meaning of this mark, said she to herself? somebody intends my master no good, or else some boy has been playing the rogue; be what it will, added she, it is good to fence against the worst. Accordingly she went and fetched a piece of chalk, and marked two or three doors on each side theirs the same, without saying a word to her master.

In the mean time the thief rejoined his troop again in the forest, and told them the good success he had; expatiating upon his good fortune, in meeting with the only person so soon who could inform him of what he wanted to know. All the robbers listened to him with the utmost satisfaction; when the captain, commending his diligence, and addressing himself to them all, said, Comrades, we have no time to lose; let us go all armed; and that we may not give any suspicion, let one or two go privately into the town together, and appoint the rendezvous in the great square; and in the mean time, our comrades here, and I, will go and find out the house, and then we will consult what is best to be done.

This speech and method was approved by all; and according to it, they all got into the town without being in the least suspected. The captain and he that was the spy entered the last of all; and when they came to the street where Ali Baba lived, he shewed the captain one of the houses which Morgiana had marked, and said that it was it; but going a little farther, to prevent being taken notice of, the captain observed that the next door was chalked in the same manner and place; and shewing it to his guide, asked him which house it was, that or the first? The guide was so confounded, that he knew not what answer to make; and much more, when he and the captain saw five or six houses besides marked after the same manner. He assured the captain, with an oath, that he had marked but one, and could not tell who had chalked the rest so like that which he had marked, and owned, in that confusion he could not distinguish it.

The captain, finding that their design proved abortive, went directly to the place of rendezvous, and told the first of his troop that he met, that they had lost all their labour, and must return to their cave the same way as they came; and set them himself the example.

When the troop was all got together, the captain told them the reason of their returning; and presently the conductor was declared by all worthy of death, and with courage and resignation to their suffrages, kneeled down to receive the stroke from him that was appointed to give it.

But as, for the preservation of the troop, so great an injury was not to go unpunished, another of the gang, who promised himself that he should succeed better, presented himself, and his offer being accepted, he went and corrupted Baba Mustapha, as the other had done; and being shewed the house, marked it, in a place more remote from sight, with red chalk.

Not long after, Morgiana, whose eyes nothing could escape, went out, and seeing the red chalk, and arguing after the same manner with herself, marked the other neighbours' houses in the same place and manner.

The thief, at his return to his company, valued himself very much upon the precautions he had taken, which he looked upon as an infallible way of distinguishing Ali Baba's house from his neighbours; and the captain and all of them thought it would do. They conveyed themselves into the town in the same manner as before; and when the thief and his captain came to the street, they found the same difficulty; at which the captain was enraged, and the thief in as great confusion as his predecessor.

Thus the captain and his troop were forced to retire a second time, and much more dissatisfied; and the robber, as the author of the mistake, underwent the same punishment; which he willingly submitted to.

The captain having by this way lost two brave fellows of his troop, was afraid of diminishing it too much by pursuing it, and found, by their example, that their heads were not so good as their hands on such occasions; and therefore resolved to take upon himself this important commission.

Accordingly he went and addressed himself to Baba Mustapha, who did him the same piece of service he had done to the former. He never amused himself with setting any particular mark on the house, but examined and observed it so carefully, by passing often by it, that it was impossible for him to mistake it.

The captain, very well satisfied with his journey, and informed in what he wanted to know, returned to the forest; and when he came into the cave, where the troop waited for him, he said, Now, comrades, there is nothing can prevent our revenge; I am certain of the house, and in my way hither I have thought how to put it in execution; and if any one knows a better expedient, let him communicate it. Then he told them his contrivance; and as they approved of it, he ordered them to go into the towns and villages about, and buy nineteen mules, and eight-and-thirty large jars, and fill one of them full of oil.

In two or three days time, the thieves purchased the mules and jars; and the captain put his whole troop into the jars, all armed, leaving them room to breathe, by making holes under the place where they were tied at top, and rubbed the jars on the outside with oil.

Things being thus prepared, the nineteen mules were loaded with seven-and-thirty thieves in jars, and the jar of oil; and the captain, as their driver, set out with them, and got to the town by the dusk of the evening, as he intended. He led them through the streets till he came to Ali Baba's, at whose door he designed to have knocked, but was prevented by his sitting there, after supper, to take a little fresh air. However, he stopped his mules, and addressed himself to him, and said, I have brought some oil here a great way, to sell at to-morrow's market; and it is now so late, that I do not know where to lodge; if I should not be troublesome to you, do me the favour to let me lie with you, and I shall be very much obliged to you.

Though Ali Baba had seen the captain of the thieves, and had heard him speak, yet it was impossible for him to know him in the disguise of an oil-merchant. He told him he should be welcome, and immediately opened his gates, for the mules to go into the yard. At the same time, he called to a slave he had, and not only ordered him, when the mules were unloaded, to put them into the stable, but to give them corn and hay; and then went to Morgiana, to bid her get a good hot supper for his guest, and make him a good bed.

When the captain had unloaded his mules, and led them into the stable, and was looking for a place to lie in all night, Ali Baba went to him, and desired him to walk into the hall, telling him he would not by any means suffer him to lie in the yard all night. The captain excused himself very much, upon account of being troublesome, the better to disguise the matter, and at last, with much importunity, and with an inward satisfaction, consented. Ali Baba not only bore him company, but entertained him with a great many things to divert him; and when he had supped, told him, in taking his leave for that night, he might be free, and call for what he wanted.

The captain rose up at the same time, and went with him to the door; and while Ali Baba went into the kitchen to speak to Morgiana, he went into the yard, under a pretext of looking at his mules. Ali Baba, after charging Morgiana afresh to take care of his guest, said to her, To-morrow morning I design to go to the bath before day; take care my bathing-linen be ready, and give them to Abdalla, (which was the slave's name), and make me some broth against I come back. After this he went to bed.

In the mean time, the captain of the thieves went into the yard, to give his people orders what to do; and beginning at the first jar, and so on till the last, said, As soon as I throw some stones out of the chamber window where I lie, do not fail to cut the jar open with the knife you have about you, and come out, and I will be presently with you. After this he returned into the kitchen, and Morgiana, taking up a light, conducted him to his chamber, where, after she had asked him if he wanted any thing, she left him; and he, to avoid any suspicion, put the light out soon after, and laid himself down in his cloaths, that he might be the more ready to rise again.

Morgiana remembering Ali Baba's orders, got his bathing-linen ready, and ordered Abdalla, who was not then got to bed, to set on the pot for the broth; but while she scummed the pot, the lamp went out, and there were no candles, nor no more oil in the house; and what to do she did not know, for the broth must be made. Abdalla seeing her very uneasy, said, Do not fret and teaze yourself, but go into the yard, and take some oil out of some of the jars.

Morgiana thanked Abdalla for his advice; and while he went to bed, that he might be the better able to rise to follow Ali Baba to the bath, she took the oil-pot, and went into the yard; and as she came nigh the first jar, the thief within it said softly, Is it time?

Any other slave but Morgiana, to be surprised, as she was, to find a man in the jar instead of the oil she wanted, would have made a great noise, so as to have given an alarm, attended with ill consequences; whereas Morgiana, apprehending immediately the importance of keeping the secret, and the danger she, Ali Baba, and his family were in, and the necessity of applying a speedy remedy, without noise, conceived at once the means, and without shewing the least concern, answered, Not yet, but presently; and went in this manner to all the jars, giving the same answer, till she came to the jar of oil.

By this means, Morgiana found that her master Ali Baba, who thought that he had entertained an oil-merchant, had admitted eight-and-thirty thieves into his house: looking on the pretended merchant as their captain, she made what haste she could to fill her oil-pot, and returned into her kitchen, where, as soon as she had lighted her lamp, she took a great kettle, and went again to the oil-jar, filled it full, and set it on the fire to boil, and as soon as it boiled, went and poured enough into every jar to stifle and destroy the thief within.

When this action, worthy of the courage of Morgiana, was executed, without any noise, as she had projected, she returned into the kitchen, and shut the door; and having put out the great fire she had made to boil the oil, and leaving just enough to make the broth, put out also the lamp, and remained hushed, resolving not to go to bed till she had observed what was to follow.

She had not waited above a quarter of an hour, before the captain of the thieves waked, got up, and opened the window; and finding no light, and hearing no noise, nor any stirring in the house, gave the signal, by throwing stones at the copper jars, never disputing but that they would hear the sound they gave. Then he listened, and hearing nor perceiving nothing whereby he could judge that his companions stirred, he began to grow very uneasy, and threw again a second and third time, and could not comprehend the reason that none of them should answer to his signal. Cruelly alarmed, he went softly down into the yard, and going to the first jar, and asking the thief, whom he thought alive, if he was asleep? He smelled the hot boiling oil, which sent forth a steam out of the jar, and knew thereby that his plot was discovered; and examining all the jars, found that all his gang were dead; and by the oil he missed out of the last jar, he guessed at the means and manner of their deaths. Enraged, and in despair for having failed in his design, and to lose so many jolly companions, he forced the lock of a door that led from the yard to the garden, and tumbling over the walls of several gardens, at last made his escape.

When Morgiana heard no noise, and found, after waiting some time, that the captain did not return, she guessed that he chose rather to make his escape by the gardens than the street door, which was double-locked: satisfied and pleased to have succeeded so well, and secured the house, she went to bed.

Ali Baba rose before day, and, followed by his slave, went to the baths, entirely ignorant of the amazing accident that had happened at home; for Morgiana was in the right not to wake him before, for fear of losing the opportunity; and afterwards, she thought it needless to disturb him.

When he returned from the baths, and the sun was risen, he was very much surprised to see the oil-jars, and that the merchant was not gone with the mules, and asked Morgiana, who opened the door, and let all things stand as they were, the reason of it. My good master, answered she, God preserve you and your family; you will be better informed of what you desire to know, when you have seen what I have to shew you, if you will give yourself the trouble to follow me.

As soon as Morgiana had shut the door, Ali Baba followed her; and when she brought him into the yard, she bid him look into the first jar, and see if there was any oil. Ali Baba accordingly did so; and seeing a man, started backward, almost frightened out of his wits, and cried out. Do not be afraid, said Morgiana; the man that you see there can neither do you nor any body else any harm; he is dead. Ah! Morgiana! said Ali Baba, what is it you shew me? Explain the meaning of it to me. Moderate your astonishment, and do not excite the curiosity of your neighbours, replied Morgiana, and I will; for it is of great importance to keep this affair secret. Look into all the other jars.

Ali Baba examined all the other jars, one after another; and when he came to that which had the oil in it, he found it prodigiously sunk, and stood for some time motionless, sometimes looking on the jars and sometimes on Morgiana, without saying a word, so great was his surprise: At last, when he had recovered himself, he said, And what is become of the merchant?

Merchant! answered she, he is as much one as I am: I will tell you who he is, and what has become of him: but you had better hear the story in your own chamber; for it is time you had your broth, after your bathing.

While Ali Baba went into his chamber, Morgiana went into the kitchen to fetch the broth, and carry it to him; but before he would drink it, he first bid her satisfy his impatience, and tell him the story, with all the circumstances; and she obeyed him.

Last night, sir, said she, when you was gone to bed, I got your bathing-linen ready, and gave them to Abdalla; afterwards, I set on the pot for the broth; and as I was skimming the pot, the lamp, for want of oil, went out; and as there was not a drop more in the house, I looked for a candle, but could not find one. Abdalla seeing me vexed, put me in mind of the jars of oil which stood in the yard. I took the oil-pot, and went directly to the jar which stood nearest to me; and when I came to it, I heard a voice within it say, Is it time? I answered, without being dismayed, and comprehending immediately the malicious intention of the pretended oil-merchant, Not yet, but presently. Then I went to the next, and another voice asked me the same question, and I returned the same answer; and so on, till I came to the last, which I found full of oil; with which I filled my pot.

When I considered that there were seven-and-thirty thieves in your yard, who only waited for a signal to be given by the captain, whom you took to be an oil-merchant, and entertained so handsomely, I thought there was no time to be lost: I carried my pot of oil into the kitchen, lighted the lamp, and afterwards took the biggest kettle I had, went and filled it full of oil, and set it on the fire to boil, and then went and poured as much into each jar as was sufficient to prevent them executing the pernicious design they came about. After this I retired into the kitchen, and put out the lamp; but before I went to bed, I waited at the window to know what measures the pretended merchant would take.

After I had watched some time for the signal, he threw some stones against the jars, out of the window, and neither hearing nor perceiving any body stirring, after throwing three times, he came down, and I saw him go to every jar; after which, through the darkness of the night, I lost sight of him. I waited some time longer; and finding that he did not return, I never doubted but that, seeing he had missed his aim, he had made his escape over the walls of the garden.

This, said Morgiana, is the account you asked of me, and I am convinced it is the consequence of an observation which I had made for two or three days before, but did not think fit to acquaint you with: for when I came in one morning early, I found our street door marked with white chalk, and the next morning with red; and both times, without knowing what was the intention of those chalks, I marked two or three neighbours' doors on each hand after the same manner. If you reflect on this, and what has since happened, you will find it to be a plot of the thieves of the forest, of whose gang there are two wanting, and now they are reduced to three: All this shews, that they had sworn your destruction; and it is proper you should stand upon your guard, while there is one of them alive: for my part, I shall not neglect any thing necessary to your preservation, which I am in duty obliged to regard.

When Morgiana had left off speaking, Ali Baba was so sensible of the great service she had done him, that he said to her, I will not die without rewarding you as you deserve: I owe my life to thee, and for the first token of my acknowledgment, I give thee thy liberty from this moment. I am persuaded with thee that the forty thieves have laid all manner of snares for me. God, by thy means, has delivered me from them, and I hope will continue to preserve me from their wicked designs, and, by averting the danger which threatened me, will deliver the world from their persecution, and of that cursed race of people: All that we have to do, is to bury them immediately, and with all the secrecy imaginable; but that Abdalla and I will undertake.

Ali Baba's garden was very long, and shaded at the farther end by a great number of trees: thither he and the slave went and dug a trench long and wide enough to hold all the thieves, and were not long a-doing it, by reason that the earth was light. Afterwards they took the bodies out of the jars, pulled off their armour, carried them to the end of the garden, and then filled up the trench again. When this was done, Ali Baba hid the jars; and for the mules as he had no occasion for them, he sent them at different times to be sold.

While Ali Baba took these measures to prevent the world's knowing how he came by his riches in so short a time, the captain of the thieves returned to the forest in a most inconceivable mortification, and in the agitation, or rather confusion, he was in at his ill success, which proved so much contrary to what he had promised himself, he entered the cave, not being able all the way from the town to come to any resolution what to do to Ali Baba.

The loneliness of the place seemed frightful to him. Where are you, my brave lads, cried he, my old companions? What can I do without you? How unhappy am I to lose you by so fatal and so base a fate, and so unworthy your courage! Had you died with your sabres in your hands, like brave men, as you were, my regret had been the less. When shall I get so gallant a troop again? And if I could, can I undertake it without exposing so much gold and treasure to him who hath already enriched himself out of it? I cannot nor ought not to think of it, before I have taken away his life. Well, I will undertake that myself which I could not accomplish with so powerful assistance; and when I have taken care to secure this treasury from being pillaged, I will provide for it new masters and successors, who shall preserve and augment it to all posterity. This resolution being taken, he was not in the least embarrassed how to execute it, but easy in his mind, and full of hopes, slept all that night very quietly.

When he waked the next morning, which was pretty early, he dressed himself as he proposed, very agreeably to the project he had in his head, and went to the town, and took a lodging in a khan or inn; and as he expected what had happened at Ali Baba's might make a great noise in the town, he asked his host, by way of discourse, what news there was in the city? Upon which the innkeeper told him a great many things, which did not concern him in the least. He judged by this that the reason why Ali Baba kept this affair so secret, was for fear people should know where the treasure lay, and the means of coming to it; upon which account he sought his life; and this urged him the more to neglect nothing to rid himself of so dangerous a person, and by as secret a way.

The next thing that the captain had to do, was to convey a great many sorts of rich stuffs and fine linen to his lodgings, which he did by a great many journeys to the forest on a horse's back, but with all the necessary precautions imaginable; and to dispose of the merchandizes, when he had amassed them together, he took a shop, which happened to be opposite to that which was Cassim's, which Ali Baba's son traded in.

He took upon him the name of Cogia Houssain; and, as a new comer, was, according to custom, extremely civil and complaisant to all his neighbours: And as Ali Baba's son was young and handsome, and a man of good sense, and was often obliged to discourse with Cogia Houssain, he strove to cultivate his friendship, when, after two or three days, he understood whose son he was. To serve his ends, he caressed him after the most engaging manner, made him some small presents, and often asked him to dine and sup with him; and then treated him very handsomely.

Ali Baba's son did not care to lie under such obligations without making the like return; but was so much straitened for want of room in his lodging, that he could not entertain him so well as he could have wished; and therefore acquainted his father Ali Baba with his thoughts, and told him that it did not look well for him to receive such favours from Cogia Houssain, without inviting him again.

Ali Baba took care of the treat himself, with a great deal of pleasure. Son, said he, to-morrow is Friday, which is a day that the shops are shut up; get him to take a walk with you after dinner, and, as you come back, pass by my door, and call in; it will look better to have it happen accidentally, than if you give him a formal invitation. I will go and order Morgiana to provide a supper.

The next day, after dinner, Ali Baba's son and Cogia Houssain walked out, and as they returned, Ali Baba's son led Cogia Houssain through the street where his father lived; and when they came to the house, he stopped and knocked at the door. This, sir, said he, is my father's house, who, upon the account I have given him of your friendship, charged me to procure him the honour of your acquaintance; and I desire you to add this one favour more to those I am already indebted to you for.

Though it was the sole aim of Cogia Houssain to introduce himself into Ali Baba's house, that he might kill him without making any noise and hazarding his own life, yet he excused himself, and offered to take his leave; but a slave having opened the door, Ali Baba's son took him obligingly by the hand, and in a manner forced him in.

Ali Baba received Cogia Houssain with a smiling countenance, and in the most obliging manner he could wish for: he thanked him for all the favours he had done his son; adding withal, that he was a young man that could not very well know the world, and might profit by his example.

Cogia Houssain returned the compliment, by assuring Ali Baba, that though his son might not have the experience of older men, he had so much good sense as stood him in stead thereof: And after a little more conversation on different subjects, offered again to take his leave; when Ali Baba, stopping him, said, Where are you going, sir, in so much haste? I beg you would do me the honour to take a supper with me, though what I have to give you is not worthy your acceptance; but such as it is, you are heartily welcome to it. Sir, replied Cogia Houssain, I am thoroughly persuaded of your goodwill; and if I ask the favour of you not to take it ill that I do not accept of your obliging invitation, I beg of you to believe that it does not proceed from any slight, or intention of affront, but from a certain reason, which you would approve of if you knew it.

And what may that reason be, sir, replied Ali Baba, if I may be so bold as to ask you? It is, answered Cogia Houssain, that I can eat no victuals that have any salt in them; therefore judge how I should look at your table.* If that is the only reason, said Ali Baba, it ought not to deprive me of the honour of your company at supper: for, in the first place, there is no salt ever put into my bread, and for the meat we shall have to-night, I promise you there shall be none; I will go and take care of that; therefore you must do me the favour to stay: I will come again immediately.

Ali Baba went into the kitchen, and ordered Morgiana to put no salt to the meat that was to be dressed that night; and besides, to make two or three ragouts, but be sure to put no salt in them.

Morgiana, who was always ready to obey her master, could not help this time seeming somewhat dissatisfied at his new order. Who is this difficult man, said she, who eats no salt with his meat? Your supper will be spoiled if I keep it back so long. Do not be angry, Morgiana, replied Ali Baba; he is an honest man: therefore do as I bid you.

Morgiana obeyed, though with some reluctancy, and had a great curiosity to see this man who eat no salt. To this end, when she had done what she had to do in the kitchen, and Abdalla laid the cloth, she helped to carry up the plates; and looking at Cogia Houssain, knew him at the first sight to be the captain of the thieves, notwithstanding his disguise; and examining him very carefully, perceived that he had a dagger hid under his garment. I am not in the least amazed, said she to herself, that this wicked wretch, who is my master's greatest enemy, would eat no salt with him, since he intends to assassinate him; but I will prevent him.

When Morgiana had sent up the supper by Abdalla, while they were eating, she made the necessary preparations for executing one of the boldest acts which could be thought on, and had just done when Abdalla came again for the desert of fruit, which she carried up, and as soon as Abdalla had taken the meat away, set it upon the table; after that, she set a little table and three glasses by Ali Baba, and going out, took Abdalla along with her, to go to sup together, and to give Ali Baba the more liberty of conversation with his guest.

Then the pretended Cogia Houssain, or rather captain of the thieves, thought he had a favourable opportunity to kill Ali Baba. I will, said he to himself, make the father and son both drunk; and then the son, whose life I intend to spare, will not be able to prevent my stabbing his father to the heart; and while the slaves are at supper, or asleep in the kitchen, I can make my escape over the gardens, as before.

Instead of going to supper, Morgiana, who penetrated into the intentions of the counterfeit Cogia Houssain, would not give him leave to put his villanous design in execution, but dressed herself like a dancer, girded her waist with a silver-gilt girdle, to which there hung a poniard of the same metal, and put a handsome mask on her face. When she had thus disguised herself, she said to Abdalla, Take this tabor, and let us go and divert our master and his guests, as we are wont to do of a night when he is alone.

Abdalla took his tabor, and played before Morgiana all the way into the hall, who, when she came to the door, made a low courtesy, by way of asking leave to shew what she could do; and Abdalla seeing that his master had a mind to say something, left off playing. Come in, Morgiana, said Ali Baba, and let Cogia Houssain see what you can do, that he may tell us what he thinks of you: But, sir, said he, turning towards Cogia Houssain, do not think that I put myself to any expence to give you this diversion, since these are my slave, and my cook; and I hope you will not find the entertainment they shall give us disagreeable.

Cogia Houssain, who did not expect this diversion after supper, began to fear that he should not have the opportunity that be desired to have made use of; but hoped, if he missed it now, to have it another time, by keeping up a friendly correspondence; therefore, though he could have wished Ali Baba would have let it alone, he pretended to be obliged to him for it, and had the complaisance to express a pleasure which he could willingly have dispensed with.

As soon as Abdalla saw that Ali Baba and Cogia Houssain had done talking, he began to play on the tabor, and accompanied it with an air, to which Morgiana, who was an excellent dancer, danced after such a manner as would have created admiration in any other but Cogia Houssain, who was more attentive to his own designs.

After she had danced several dances with a great deal of justness, she drew the poniard, and holding it in her hand, danced a dance, which was very surprising for the many different figures and fine movements it required. Sometimes she presented the poniard to one's breast, and sometimes to another's, and often-times seemed to strike her own. At last, when she was just out of breath, she snatched the tabor from Abdalla with her left hand, and holding the dagger in her right, presented the side where there was a chink, after the manner of those who get their livelihoods by dancing, to try the liberality of the spectators.

Ali Baba put a piece of gold into the tabor, as did also his son; and Cogia Houssain seeing that she was coming to him, had pulled out his purse to make her a present too; but while he was putting his hand into it, Morgiana, with a courage and resolution worthy of herself, plunged the poniard into his heart.

Ali Baba and his son were very much frightened at this action. Ah! unhappy wretch, cried Ali Baba, what hast thou done, to ruin me and my family? It was to preserve you, and not to ruin you, answered Morgiana; for see here, said she, (opening Cogia Houssain's garment, and shewing the dagger,) what an enemy you had entertained! Look well at him, and you will find him to be both the pretended oil-merchant and the captain of the gang of the forty thieves. Remember too, that he would eat no salt with you; and what would you have more to inform you of his wicked design? Before I saw him, I suspected him, when you told me you had such a guest; and when I saw him, I found that my suspicion was not groundless.

Ali Baba, who was immediately sensible of the new obligation he had to Morgiana, for saving his life a second time, embraced her, saying, Morgiana, I gave thee thy liberty, and then promised thee, that my acknowledgment should not stop there, but that I would express it much farther; and now I will give a proof of it, by making thee my daughter-in-law. Then addressing himself to his son, he said to him, I believe you, son, to be so dutiful a child, that you will not refuse Morgiana to be your wife. You see that Cogia Houssain sought your friendship with a treacherous design to take away my life; and, if he had succeeded, there is no dispute but he would have sacrificed you too to his revenge. Consider that, by marrying Morgiana, you marry the support of my family and your own.

The son, far from shewing any dislike, readily consented to the marriage; not only because he would not disobey his father, but that his inclination prompted him to it.

After this, they thought of burying the captain of the thieves with his comrades, and did it so privately that nobody knew any thing of it till a great many years after, when not one had any concern in the publication of this remarkable history.

A few days afterwards, Ali Baba celebrated the nuptials of his son and Morgiana with great solemnity, and was very glad to see that his friends and neighbours, whom he invited, had no knowledge of the true motives of that marriage; but that those persons, who were not acquainted with Morgiana's good qualities, should commend his generosity.

Ali Baba forbore a long time after this marriage from going again to the thieves cave, (from the time he brought his brother Cassim, and some bags of gold on three asses,) for fear of being surprised by the other two thieves, whom he could give no account of, but whom he supposed to be alive.

But at the year's end, when he found they had not made any attempt to disturb him, he had a great inclination to make another journey, taking the most necessary precautions for his safety. Accordingly he mounted his horse; and when he came to the cave, and saw no footsteps of neither man nor horse, he looked upon it as a good sign: he alighted off his horse, and tied him to a tree; and presenting himself before the door, pronouncing these words, Open Sesame, the door opened; he went in, and by the condition he found things in, he judged that nobody had ever been there since the false Cogia Houssain, when he fetched the goods for his shop, and that the gang of forty thieves was quite destroyed; and never disputed but he was the only person in the world who had the secret of going into the cave, and that all the treasure was solely at his disposal; and having brought a valaise along with him, he put as much gold into it as his horse could carry, and then returned to town.

Afterwards, Ali Baba carried his son to the cave, taught him the secret, which they handed down to their posterity, and using this good fortune with moderation, lived in great honour and splendour, serving the greatest offices of the city.

The Story of Ali Cogia, a Merchant of Bagdad

In the reign of the caliph Haroun Alraschid, there lived at Bagdad a merchant, whose name was Ali Cogia, that was neither one of the richest nor the meanest sort. He was a bachelor, and lived master of his own actions, in the house which was his father's, very well content with the profit he made of his trading; but happening to dream for three nights together, that a venerable old man came to him, and, with a severe look, reprimanded him for not having made a pilgrimage to Mecca, he was very much troubled.

As a good mussulman, he knew he was obliged to undertake a pilgrimage; but as he had a house, shop, and goods, he always believed that they might stand for a sufficient reason to excuse him, endeavouring by his charity, and other good deeds, to atone for that neglect. But after this dream, his conscience was so much pricked, that the fear lest any misfortune should befal him, made him resolve not to defer it any longer; and, to be able to go that year, he sold off his household goods, his shop, and with it the greatest part of his merchandizes; reserving only some which he thought might turn to a better account at Mecca; and meeting with a tenant for his house, let that also.

Things being thus disposed, he was ready to go when the Bagdad caravan set out for Mecca; the only thing he had to do, was to secure a sum of a thousand pieces of gold, which would be troublesome to carry along with him, besides the money he had set apart to defray his expences. To this end, he made choice of a jar, of a proportionable size, put the thousand pieces of gold into it, and covered them over with olives. When he had closed the mouth of the jar, he carried it to a merchant, a particular friend of his, and said to him, You know, brother, that in two or three days time I set out with the caravan on my pilgrimage to Mecca; and I beg the favour of you, that you would take upon you the charge of keeping a jar of olives for me till I return. The merchant promised him he would, and in an obliging manner said, Here, take the key of my warehouse, and set your jar where you please; I promise you shall find it there when you come again.

On the day the caravan was to set out, Ali Cogia added himself to it, with a camel, (loaded with what merchandizes he thought fit to carry along with him,) which served him to ride on, and arrived safe at Mecca, where he visited, along with other pilgrims, the temple so much celebrated and frequented by all mussulmen every year, who come from all parts of the world, and observe religiously the ceremonics prescribed them; and when he had acquitted himself of the duties of his pilgrimage, he exposed the merchandizes he had brought with him, to sell or exchange them.

Two merchants passing by, and seeing Ali Cogia's goods, thought them so fine and choice, that they stopped some time to look at them, though they had no occasion for them; and when they had satisfied their curiosity, one of them said to the other, as they were going away, If this merchant knew to what profit these goods would turn at Cairo, he would carry them thither, and not sell them here, though this is a good market.

Ali Cogia heard these words; and as he had often heard talk of the beauties of Egypt, he was resolved to take the opportunity of seeing them, and take a journey thither; therefore, after having packed up his goods again, instead of returning to Bagdad, he set out for Egypt with a caravan of Cairo; and when he came thither, he found his account in his journey, and in a few days sold all his goods to a greater advantage than he hoped for. With this money he bought others, with an intent to go to Damascus; and while he waited for the opportunity of a caravan, which was to set forwards in six weeks, he saw all the rarities at Cairo, as the pyramids, &c. and rowing up and down the river Nile, viewed the most noble and charmingly situated towns on each side.

As the Damascus caravan took Jerusalem in their way, our Bagdad merchant had the opportunity of seeing the temple, looked upon by all the mussulmen to be the most holy, after that of Mecca.*

Ali Cogia found Damascus so delicious a place, abounding with fine meads, pleasantly watered, and delightful gardens, that it exceeded the descriptions given of it in history. Here he made a long abode, but nevertheless had not forgot his native Bagdad; for which place he set out, and arrived at Halep, where he made some stay; and from thence, after having passed the Euphrates, he went his course to Moussel, with an intention, in his return, to come down the Tigris.

When Ali Cogia came to Moussel, the Persian merchants, with whom he travelled from Halep, and had contracted a great friendship, had got so great an ascendant over him, by their civilities and agreeable behaviour, that they easily persuaded him not to leave them till they came to Schiraz, from whence he might easily return to Bagdad, with a considerable profit. They led him through the towns Sultania, Rei, Coam, Laschan, Ispahan, and from thence to Schiraz; from whence he was so complaisant as to bear them company to the Indies, and so came back again with them to Schiraz: insomuch that, accounting for the abode he made in every town, he was seven years absent from Bagdad, whither he then resolved to return.

All this time, his friend, with whom he had left his jar of olives, neither thought of him nor them; but just at the time when he was coming with a small caravan from Schiraz, one evening, when this merchant was supping at home with his family, and the discourse happening to fall upon olives, his wife was desirous to eat some, saying, that she had not tasted any for a long while. Now you talk of olives, said the merchant, you put me in mind of a jar which Ali Cogia left with me seven years ago, when he went to Mecca, and put it himself in my warehouse, for me to keep it for him against he returned; and what is become of him I know not; though, when the caravan came back, they told me he was gone for Egypt. Certainly he must be dead, since he has not returned in all this time; and we may eat the olives, if they prove good. Lend me a plate and a candle, and I will go and fetch some of them, and we will see.

For God's sake, good husband, said the wife, do not commit so base an action; you know that nothing is more sacred than what is committed to one's care and trust: you say Ali Cogia has been gone to Mecca, and is not returned; and they say, that he is gone to Egypt; and how do you know but that he may be gone farther? As you have no news of his death, he may return to-morrow, for any thing you can tell; and what a disgrace would it be to you and your family, if he should come, and you not restore him his jar in the same condition he left it? I declare I have no desire for the olives, and will not taste of them; for when I mentioned them, it was only by way of discourse; besides, do you think that they can be good, after they have been kept so long? They must be all mouldy, and spoiled; and if Ali Cogia should return, as I have a great fancy he will, and should find they have been opened, what will he think of your honour? I beg of you to let them alone.

The wife had not argued so long with her husband, but that she read his obstinacy in his face. In short, he never regarded what she said, but got up, took a candle and a platter, and went into the warehouse. Well, husband, said the wife again, remember I have no hand in this business, and that you cannot lay any thing to my charge if you should have cause to repent of this action.

The merchant's ears were deaf to these remonstrances of his wife, and he still persisted in his design. When he came into the warehouse, he opened the jar, and found the olives all mouldy; but, to see if they were all so at the bottom, he turned the jar topsy-turvy upon the plate; and by shaking the jar, some of the gold tumbled out.

At the sight of the gold, the merchant, who was naturally covetous, looked into the jar, and perceived that he had shaked out almost all the olives, and what remained was gold coin fast wedged in: he immediately put the olives into the jar again, and returned to his wife. Indeed, my dear, said he, you was in the right to say that the olives were all mouldy; for I have found it so, and have made up the jar just as Ali Cogia left it; so that he will not perceive that they have been touched, if he should return. You had better have taken my advice, said the wife, and not meddled with them: God grant that no mischief may come of it.

The merchant was not in the least affected with his wife's last words, but spent almost the whole night in thinking how he might appropriate Ali Cogia's gold to his own use, in case Ali Cogia should return, and ask him for the jar. The next morning he went and bought some olives of that year, took out the old, with the gold, and filled the jar with the new, covered it up, and put it in the same place.

About a month after the merchant had committed so base an action, (for which he ought to pay dear,) Ali Cogia arrived at Bagdad; and, as he had let his house, he alighted at a khan, chusing to stay there till he gave his tenant warning, that he might provide himself of another house.

The next morning, Ali Cogia went to pay a visit to the merchant his friend, who received him in the most obliging manner imaginable, and expressed a great deal of joy at his return, after so many years absence; telling him that he had begun to lose all hopes of ever seeing him again.

After the usual compliments on such a meeting, Ali Cogia desired the merchant to return him the jar of olives which he had left with him, and to excuse the liberty he had taken in giving him so much trouble.

My dear friend, Ali Cogia, replied the merchant, you are to blame to make all these apologies on such an occasion; I should have made as free with you; there, take the key of the warehouse, go and take it; you will find it in the same place where you left it.

Ali Cogia went into the merchant's warehouse, took his jar, and after having returned him the key, and thanks for the favour he had done, returned with it to the khan where he lodged; and opening the jar, and putting his hand down to the bottom, to see for his gold, was very much surprised to find none. At first he thought he might perhaps be mistaken; and, to discover the truth, poured out all the olives, without so much as finding one single piece of money. His astonishment was so great, that he then stood for some time motionless: lifting up his hands and eyes to heaven, he cried out, Is it possible that a man whom I took for my very good friend, should be guilty of so base an action.

Ali Cogia, cruelly frightened at so considerable a loss, returned immediately to the merchant. My good friend, said he, do not be surprised to see me come back so soon: I own the jar of olives to be the same put into your magazine; but with the olives I put a thousand pieces of gold into it, which I do not find: Perhaps you might have had an occasion for them, and used them in your traffic: if so, they are at your service; only put me out of my pain, and give me an acknowledgment, and pay me them again at your own convenience.

The merchant, who expected that Ali Cogia would come with such a complaint, had meditated upon a ready answer. Friend Ali Cogia, said he, when you brought your jar of olives to me, I never touched it, but gave you the key of my warehouse, whither you carried it yourself; and did not you find it in the same place, and covered in the same manner as when you left it? And if you put gold in it, you have found it again: You told me that they were olives, and I believed so. This is all I know of the matter; and you may believe me, if you please, for I never touched them.

Ali Cogia made use of all the mild ways he could think of, to oblige the merchant to do him right. I love peace and quietness, said he to him, and shall be very sorry to come to those extremities which will bring the greatest disgrace upon you: Consider, that merchants, as we are, ought to forsake all interest to preserve a good reputation. Once again, I tell you, I should be very much concerned, if your obstinacy should oblige me to force you to do me justice; for I would rather, almost, lose what is my right, than have recourse to law.

Ali Cogia, replied the merchant, you agree that you left the jar of olives with me; and now you have taken it away, you come and ask me for a thousand pieces of gold. Did you ever tell me that such a sum was in the jar? I knew nothing but that they were olives. I wonder you do not as well ask me for diamonds and pearls: Be gone about your business, and do not raise a mob about my shop.

These last words were pronounced in so great an heat and passion, as not only made those who stood about the shop already, stay longer, and created a great mob, but made the neighbouring merchants come out of their shops to see what was the difference between Ali Cogia and the merchant, and endeavour to reconcile them; and when Ali Cogia had informed them of his grievance, they asked the merchant what he had to say?

The merchant owned that he had kept the jar for Ali Cogia in his warehouse, but denied that ever he meddled with it, and swore, that he knew nothing but that it was full of olives, as Ali Cogia told him, and bid them all bear witness of the insult and affront offered him. You bring it upon yourself, said Ali Cogia, taking him by the arm; but since you use me so basely, I cite you according to the law of God: Let us see whether you will have the assurance to say the same thing before the cady.

The merchant could not refuse this summons, which every good mussulman is bound to observe, or be declared a rebel against his religion; but said, With all my heart, we shall soon see who is in the wrong.

Ali Cogia carried the merchant before the cady, before whom he accused him of cheating him of a thousand pieces of gold, which he had left with him. The cady asked him if he had any witnesses; to which he replied that he had not taken that necessary precaution, because he believed the person he trusted his money with, to be his friend, and always took him for an honest man.

The merchant made the same defence he had done before the merchants his neighbours, offering to make oath that he never had the money he was accused of, and that he did not so much as know there was such a sum; upon which the cady took his oath, and afterwards dismissed him.

Ali Cogia, extremely mortified to find that he must sit down with so considerable a loss, protested against the sentence the cady gave, declaring that he would appeal to the caliph Haroun Alraschid, who would do him justice; which protestation the cady only looked upon as the effect of the common resentment of all those who lose their cause; and thought he had done his duty, in acquitting a person accused without witnesses.

While the merchant returned home, triumphing over Ali Cogia, and overjoyed at his good fortune, Ali Cogia went to get a petition drawn up; and the next day, observing the time when the caliph came from prayers in the afternoon, he placed himself in the street he was to pass through; and holding out his hand with the petition, an officer appointed for that purpose, who always goes before the caliph, came and took it from him.

As Ali Cogia knew that it was the caliph's custom to read the petitions as he went into the palace, he went into the court, and waited till the officer came out of the caliph's apartment, who told him the hour the caliph had appointed to hear him; and then asking him where the merchant lived, he sent to him to signify the caliph's pleasure.

The same evening, the caliph, the grand visier Giafar, and Mesrour, the chief of the eunuchs, went all disguised through the town, as I have already told your majesty it was usual so to do; and passing through a street, the caliph heard a noise, and mending his pace, he came to a gate which led into a little court, where, through a hole, he perceived ten or twelve children playing by moon-light.

The caliph, who was curious to know at what play these children played, sat down upon a bench which he found just by; and still looking through the hole, he heard one of the briskest and liveliest of the children say, Come, let us play at the cady. I will be cady; bring Ali Cogia and the merchant who cheated him of the thousand pieces of gold before me.

These words of the child put the caliph in mind of the petition Ali Cogia had given him that day, and made him redouble his attention. As Ali Cogia's affairs and the merchant's made a great noise, and were in every body's mouth in Bagdad, it had not escaped the children, who all accepted the proposition with joy, and agreed on the parts each was to act; not one of them refused him that made the proposal to be cady; and when he had taken his seat, which he did with all the seeming gravity of a cady, another, as an officer of the court, presented two before him; one as Ali Cogia, and the other as the merchant against whom he complained.

Then the pretended cady, directing his discourse to the feigned Ali Cogia, asked him what he had to lay to that merchant's charge?

Ali Cogia, after a low bow, informed the young cady of the fact, and related every particular, and afterwards begged that he would use his authority, that he might not lose so considerable a sum of money.

Then the cady, turning about to the merchant, asked him why he did not return the money which Ali Cogia demanded of him?

The young merchant alledged the same reasons as the real merchant had done before the cady himself, and proffered to confirm it by an oath, that what he had said was truth.

Not so fast, replied the pretended cady; before you come to your oath, I should be glad to see the jar of olives. Ali Cogia, said he, addressing himself to the lad who acted that part, have you brought the jar? No, replied he: Then go and fetch it immediately.

The pretended Ali Cogia went immediately, and returning as soon, feigned to bring a jar before the cady, telling him, that it was the same he left with the accused person, and took away again. But to omit no part of the formality, the supposed cady asked the merchant if it was the same; and as, by his silence, he seemed not to deny it, he ordered it to be opened. He that represented Ali Cogia, seemed to take off the cover, and the pretended cady made as if he looked into it. They are fine olives, said he; let me taste them; and then pretending to eat of them, added, they are excellent: But, continued he, I cannot think that olives will keep seven years, and be so good: Send for two olive merchants, and let me hear what is their opinion. Then the two boys, as olive merchants, presented themselves. Are you olive merchants, said the sham cady? Tell me how long olives will keep to be fit to eat.

Sir, replied the two merchants, let us take what care we can, they will hardly be worth any thing at the third year; for they have neither taste nor colour. If it be so, answered the cady, look into that jar, and tell me how old those olives are?

The two merchants pretended to examine and to taste the olives, and told the cady they were new and good. You are deceived, said the young cady; there is Ali Cogia, who says they were put into the jar seven years ago.

Sir, replied the merchants, we can assure you they are of this year's growth; and we will maintain, there is not a merchant in Bagdad but will say the same.

The sham merchant that was accused would fain have objected against the evidence of the olive merchants; but the cady would not suffer him. Hold your tongue, said he; you are a rogue, and ought to be hanged. Then the children put an end to their play, by clapping their hands with a great deal of joy, and seizing the criminal, to carry him to execution.

I cannot express how much the caliph Haroun Alraschid admired the wisdom and sense of the boy who had passed so just a sentence, in an affair which was to be pleaded before him the next day; and rising up off the bench he sat on, he asked the grand visier, who heard all that passed, what he thought of it? Indeed, Commander of the True Believers, answered the grand visier Giafar, I am surprised to find so much sense in one so young.

But, answered the caliph, dost thou know one thing? I am to pronounce sentence in this very cause to-morrow, and that the true Ali Cogia presented his petition to me to-day: And do you think, continued he, that I can judge better? I think not, answered the visier, if the case is as the children represented it. Take notice then of this house, said the caliph, and bring the boy to me to-morrow, that he may judge of this affair in my presence; and also order the cady who acquitted the roguish merchant to attend, to take example by a child: Besides, take care to bid Ali Cogia bring his jar of olives with him, and let two olive merchants be present. After this charge, he pursued his rounds, without meeting with any thing worth his attention.

The next day, the visier went to the house where the caliph had been a witness of the children's play, and asked for the master of it; but he being abroad, his wife came to him. He asked her if she had any children? To which she answered, she had three; and called them. My brave boys, said the visier, which of you was the cady, when you played together last night? The eldest made answer, he was: But not knowing why he asked the question, coloured. Come along with me, child, said the grand visier, the Commander of the Faithful wants to see you.

The mother was in a great fright when she saw the grand visier would take her son with him, and asked him upon what account the caliph wanted him? The grand visier promised her that he should return again in an hour's time, when he would tell her; assuring her he should come to no harm. But pray, sir, said the mother, give me leave to dress him first, that he may be fit to appear before the Commander of the Faithful; which the visier readily complied with.

As soon as the child was dressed, the visier carried him, and presented him to the caliph, at the time he had appointed Ali Cogia and the merchant.

The caliph, who saw that the boy was dashed, to encourage him, said, Come to me, child, and tell me if it was you that determined the affair between Ali Cogia and the merchant that cheated him of his money? I saw and heard you, and am very well pleased with you. The boy answered modestly, that it was he. Well, my dear, replied the caliph, come and sit down by me, and you shall see the true Ali Cogia and the true merchant.

Then the caliph set him on the throne by him, and asked for the two parties. When they were called, they came and prostrated themselves before the throne, bowing their heads quite down to the tapestry. Afterwards, the caliph said to them, Plead both of you your causes before this child, who shall do you both justice; and if he be at any loss, I will rectify it.

Ali Cogia and the merchant pleaded one after the other, as before; but when the merchant proposed his oath, the child said, It is too soon; it is proper that we should see the jar of olives.

At these words, Ali Cogia presented the jar, placed it at the caliph's feet, and opened it. The caliph looked upon the olives, and took one, and tasted of it. Afterwards the merchants were called, who examined the olives, and reported that they were good, and of that year. The boy told them, that Ali Cogia assured him that it was seven years since he put them up; and they returned the same answer as the children who represented them the night before.

Though the merchant who was accused saw plainly that these merchants' opinion would condemn him, yet he would say something in his own justification: When the child, instead of ordering him to be hanged, looked upon the caliph, and said, Commander of the Faithful, this is no jesting matter; it is your majesty that must condemn him to death, and not me, though I did it yesterday in my play.

The caliph, fully satisfied of the merchant's villany, gave him into the hands of the ministers of justice, to be hanged; which sentence was executed upon him, after he had confessed where he had hid the thousand pieces of gold, which were restored to Ali Cogia. Then the monarch, who was all just and equitable, turning to the cady, bid him learn of the child how to acquit himself of his duty; and embracing the boy, sent him home with a purse of an hundred pieces of gold, as a token of his liberality.

The Story of the Enchanted Horse

ON the Novrouz,* that is to say, the new day, which is the first of the year and spring, an ancient and solemn feast is observed throughout all Persia, which has been continued from the time of idolatry to the introduction of our prophet's holy religion, which, as pure and true as it is, has not been able to abolish that heathenish custom, and the superstitious ceremonies, which are not only observed in the great cities, but celebrated, with extraordinary rejoicings, in every little village and hamlet.

But of all places, these rejoicings are the most extraordinary at the court, for the variety of new and surprising sights, insomuch that strangers are invited from the most remote parts of the world, by the king's rewards and liberality towards those who are the most excellent in their inventions. In short, nothing in the world can come nigh them in magnificence.

One of these feast days, after the most ingenious artisans had repaired to Schiraz, where the court then resided, and had entertained the king and all the court with their sights, and had been bountifully and liberally rewarded, according to their merit; when the assembly was just breaking up, an Indian appeared at the foot of the throne, with an artificial horse, richly bridled and saddled, and so well made, that at first sight he looked like a living horse.

The Indian prostrated himself before the throne, and then pointing to the horse, said to the king, Though, sir, I present myself the last before your majesty, yet I can assure you, that nothing that has been shewn to-day is so wonderful as this horse, on which I beg your majesty would be pleased to cast your eyes. I see nothing more in the horse, said the king, but the natural resemblance the workman has given him, and what another workman may do as well, or better.

Sir, replied the Indian, it is not his outward form and make that I intend your majesty should look upon as wonderful, but the use I know how to make of him, and what any other person, when I have communicated the secret to him, may do as well. Whenever I mount him, be it where it will, I can transport myself through the air, to the most distant part of the world, in a very short time. This, sir, is the wonder of my horse; a wonder which nobody ever heard speak of, and which I offer to shew your majesty, if you command me.

The king of Persia, who was fond of every thing that was curious, and after the many wonderful things he had seen, and desired to see, had never seen or heard of any thing like what the Indian proposed, told him, That nothing but the experience of the truth of what he told should convince him; and that withal he was ready to see him perform what he promised.

The Indian presently put his foot into the stirrup, and mounted his horse with a great deal of activity; and when he got the other foot into the stirrup, and had fixed himself in the saddle, he asked the king of Persia where he pleased to send him?

About three leagues from Schiraz, there was an high mountain, which affords a pleasant prospect to the large square which was before the palace, where the king and his court then were. Go to that mountain, said the king, pointing to the hill; it is far enough to judge of the haste thou canst make: But because it is not possible for the eye to follow thee so far, for a certain sign that thou hast been there, I expect that thou shouldst bring me a branch of a palm tree that grows at the bottom of the hill.

The king of Persia had no sooner declared his will, but the Indian turned a peg, which was in the hollow of the horse's neck, just by the saddle, and in an instant the horse flew into the air, to the admiration of the king and all the spectators; and was presently got so high, that those who had the strongest sight could not discern him; and within less than a quarter of an hour, they saw him come again with the palm-branch in his hand: But before he came quite down, he took two or three turns in the air, with the applauses and acclamations of all the people; then descended upon the same spot of ground, without receiving the least shock from the horse, to disorder him. Afterwards he dismounted, and going to the throne, prostrated himself, and laid the branch of the palm-tree at the king's feet.

The king of Persia, who was an eye-witness, with no less admiration than astonishment, of this unheard-of wonder of the Indian, conceived a great desire to have the horse; and as he persuaded himself that he should not find it a difficult matter to treat with the Indian about him, for whatever sum of money he should value him at, he began to look upon him as the most valuable thing in his treasury. To judge of the horse by his outward appearance, said he to the Indian, I did not think him worthy my consideration, till thou shewedst me his merit. I am obliged to thee for undeceiving me; and to shew thee how much I esteem him, I will buy him of thee, if he is to be sold.

Sir, replied the Indian, I never doubted but that your majesty, who has the character of the most judicious prince on earth, would set a just value on my horse, as soon as I had shewn him you, how worthy he was of your attention. I also foresaw, that you would not only praise and commend him, but would desire to have him. For my part, sir, though I know the true value of him, and that my being master of him will render my name immortal in the world; yet I am not so fond of it, but I can deprive myself of it to gratify that noble passion of your majesty: But in making this declaration, I have another thing to offer, without which I cannot resolve to part with him, and perhaps you may not approve of it.

Your majesty will not be displeased, continued the Indian, if I tell you, that I did not buy this horse, but obtained him of the maker, by giving him, at the same time, my only daughter in marriage, and promising, at the same time, never to sell him, but, if I parted with him, to exchange him for something that I should like.

The Indian would have gone on; but at the word exchange, the king of Persia interrupted him, saying, I am willing to give thee what thou wilt ask in exchange. Thou knowest my kingdom is large, and contains a great many large, rich, and populous cities; I will give you the choice of which you like best, and will grant thee the sovereignty for ever.

This exchange seemed royal and noble to the whole court, but was much below what the Indian proposed to himself, who had raised his thoughts much higher. I am infinitely obliged to your majesty for the offer you make me, answered he, and cannot thank you enough for your generosity; yet I must beg of you not to be angry with me, if I take the boldness to tell you, that I cannot let you have my horse, but by receiving the hand of the princess your daughter as my wife; for this is the only price I can sell my horse at.

The courtiers about the king of Persia could not forbear laughing out aloud at this extravagant demand of the Indian; but the prince Firouz Schah, the king's eldest son, and presumptive heir to the crown, could not hear it without indignation. The king was quite the reverse, and thought he might very well sacrifice the princess of Persia to the Indian, to satisfy his curiosity, and remained pensive for some time, considering what he should do.

Then the prince Firouz Schah, who saw his father hesitated on what answer he should make, began to fear least he should comply with the Indian's demand, which he looked upon as not only injurious to the royal dignity, and his sister, but also to himself; therefore, to prevent his father, he said, Sir, I hope your majesty will forgive me for daring to ask you if it is possible that your majesty should consider a moment what denial to give to so insolent a fellow, and scandalous a juggler, and that you should give him room to flatter himself a moment with being allied to one of the most powerful monarchs in the world? I beg of you to have regard to yourself, and the noble blood of your ancestors.

Son, replied the king of Persia, I very much approve of your remonstrance, and am very sensible of your zeal for preserving the lustre of our noble birth; but you do not consider enough the excellence of this horse, nor that the Indian, if I should refuse him, may make the proffer somewhere else, where this nice point of honour may be waved. I shall be in the utmost despair, if another prince should boast of having exceeded me in generosity, and deprived me of the glory of possessing a horse which I esteem as the most singular and wonderful thing in the world. I will not say, I will consent to grant him what he asketh; perhaps he may not insist upon his exorbitant demand, and I may make another agreement with him; but before I strike the bargain with him, I should be glad that you would examine the horse, and that you would try him yourself, and give me your opinion of him.

As it is natural for us to flatter ourselves in what we desire, the Indian fancied, by what he heard the king of Persia say, he was not entirely averse to his alliance, by taking the horse at his price, and that the prince, who seemed to be against it, might become more favourable, and not oppose the desire the king seemed to have; therefore he consented to it with a great deal of pleasure, and ran before the prince, to help him to mount, and shew him how to guide and manage him.

The prince mounted the horse with a wonderful address, without the Indian assisting him; and no sooner had he got his feet in both stirrups, but, without staying for the Indian's advice, he turned the peg he had seen him use before him, and in an instant mounted into the air, as quick as an arrow shot out of a bow; and in a few moments, the king, court, and the numerous assembly, lost sight of him; neither horse nor prince were to be seen; and the king of Persia made vain efforts to discern them: When the Indian, alarmed at what had happened, prostrated himself before the throne, and forced the king to look at him, and give attention to what he said. Sir, said he, your majesty yourself saw that the prince was so hasty that he would not permit me to give him the necessary instructions to govern my horse. He was too willing to shew his address, but knows not the way, (which I was going to shew him,) how to turn the horse about, and bring him back again; therefore, sir, the favour I ask of your majesty is, not to make me accountable for what accidents may befal him; you are too just to impute to me any misfortune that may attend him.

This discourse of the Indian very much surprised and afflicted the king of Persia, who comprehended the danger his son was in to be inevitable, if, as the Indian said, there was another secret to bring him back again, that was different from that which carried him away, and asked, in a passion, why he did not call him back the moment he went?

Sir, answered the Indian, your majesty saw, as well as I, with what swiftness the horse and prince flew away; the surprise I was in, and still am, deprived me of the use of my speech; and if I could have spoke, he was got too far to hear me, if I had: He knew not the secret to bring him back, which, through his impatience, he would not stay to learn: But, sir, added he, there is room to hope, that the prince, when he finds himself at a loss, will perceive another peg behind; and as soon as he touches that, the horse will light on the ground, and he may turn him which way he will.

Notwithstanding all these arguments of the Indian, which were not altogether groundless, the king of Persia was terribly frightened at the evident danger his son was in. I suppose, replied he, it is very uncertain whether my son perceives the other peg, and makes a right use of it; may not the horse, instead of lighting on the ground, fall upon some rock, from whence he may tumble into the sea?

Sir, replied the Indian, I can free your majesty from this apprehension, in assuring you, that the horse crosses seas without ever falling, and always carries his rider wherever he has a mind to go: And your majesty may assure yourself, that if the prince does but find out the other peg, I tell you the horse will carry him where he pleases to go; and is it to be thought that he will go any where but where he is well known, and will be well received?

Be it as it will, replied the king of Persia, as I cannot depend upon the assurance thou givest me, thy head shall answer for my son's life, if he does not return safe and sound in three days time, or that I can certainly hear that he is alive. Then he ordered his officers to secure his person, and keep him close prisoner; after which, he retired to his palace, extremely grieved that the feast of the Novrouz should afford him and his court so much sorrow.

In the mean time, the prince Firouz Schah was carried through the air with a prodigious swiftness, as I said before, and in less than an hour's time, he had got so high, that he could not distinguish any thing on the earth, but mountains and plains seemed confounded together. It was then he began to think of returning from whence he came, and thought to do it by turning the same peg the contrary way, and pulling the bridle at the same time: But when he found that the horse still rose with the same swiftness, his astonishment was extremely great. He turned the peg several times, one way and the other, but all in vain. It was then he grew sensible of his fault, in not taking the precautions to guide the horse before he mounted him. He immediately apprehended the great danger he was in; but the quickness of that apprehension did not deprive him in the least of his reason: He examined the horse from head to tail with great attention, and perceived another peg, smaller than the other, behind the horse's right ear; he turned that peg, and presently perceived, that he descended in the same oblique manner as he mounted, but not so swift.

Night had over-shadowed that part of the earth, almost half an hour, over which the prince then was when he found out the small peg; and as the horse descended, he by degrees lost sight of the sun, till he found it quite dark, insomuch, that, instead of chusing what place he would go to, he was forced to let the bridle lie upon the horse's neck, and wait patiently till he lighted, though not without the dread least it should be in a desert, river, or the sea.

At last the horse stopped, though it was first midnight, and the prince Firouz Schah dismounted, very faint and hungry, having eat nothing since the morning, when he came out of the palace with his father and the court. The first thing he had to do in this darkness of the night, was to endeavour to know where he was; when he found himself to be on the leads of a magnificent palace, surrounded with a balustrade of white marble, breast-high; and groping about, found a pair of stairs, which led down into the palace, and the door of the leads half open.

None but Prince Firouz Schah would have ventured to go down those stairs, so dark as it was, in regard to the danger he exposed himself to, from friends or foes; but no consideration could stop him. I do not come, said he to himself, to do any body any harm; and certainly, whoever meets or sees me first, will not attempt any thing against my life before they hear what I have to say for myself. After this reflection, he opened the door wider, without making any noise, and went softly down the stairs, that he might not awake any body; and when he came to the foot of the stair-case, he found the door of a great hall, that had a light in it, open.

The prince stopped at the door, and listening, heard no other noise than the snoring of some people who were asleep. He advanced a little into the room, and, by the light of a lanthorn, saw that those persons whom he heard snore were black eunuchs, with naked sabres laid by them; which was enough to inform him that this was the guard-chamber of some queen or princess; which latter it proved to be.

The next room to this he judged to be that wherein the princess lay, by the light he saw, which appeared (the door being open) through a thin silk curtain, which drew before the door-stead, whither Prince Firouz Schah advanced on his tiptoe, without waking the eunuchs. He put by the curtain, and went in; and without staying to observe the magnificence of the chamber, which was what he did not much regard, he gave his attention to something of greater importance: He saw a great many in bed, and among them, one laid on a sofa. The princess's women lay in the first, and she herself in the last.

This distinction was enough to direct the prince in his choice: He crept softly to the bed, without waking either the princess or her women, and beheld a beauty so extraordinary and surprising, that he was charmed and inflamed with love at first sight. O heavens! said he to himself, my fate hath brought me hither to deprive me of my liberty, which hitherto I have always preserved. How can I avoid a certain slavery when those eyes shall open, since, without doubt, they enliven and give a lustre to this stock of charms? I must quickly resolve; and yet I cannot stir without being my own murderer, for fate hath ordered it so.

After these reflections, and the prince had gazed on the princess's beauty, and examined the condition of his heart, he fell on his knees, and taking hold of the princess's shirt sleeve, pulled gently towards him an arm as white as snow; upon which the princess opened her eyes, and seeing a handsome, well-shaped man on his knees, she was in a great surprise, and remained for some time confounded, but yet seemed to shew no sign of fear.

The prince made use of this favourable moment, bowed his head down to the ground, and then said, Most beautiful princess, by the most extraordinary and wonderful adventure imaginable, you see here at your feet a suppliant prince, the son of a king of Persia, who was yesterday morning with his father in his court, at the celebration of a solemn feast, and is now in a strange country, in danger of my life, if you have not the goodness and generosity to give me your assistance and protection, which I implore, most adorable princess, with the confidence that you will not refuse it me; and have just ground to persuade myself that so much beauty and majesty cannot entertain the least inhumanity.

This princess, to whom Firouz Schah so happily addressed himself, was the princess of Bengal, and the king's eldest daughter, for whom he had built this palace, a small distance from his capital, whither she went often for air. After she had heard the prince, with all the candour he could desire, she replied, Prince, you may assure yourself that you are not in a barbarous country, since the same hospitality, humanity, and politeness, is to be met with in the kingdom of Bengal as in that of Persia: I shall not only grant you the protection you ask, and you will not only have it in my palace, but throughout the whole kingdom; you may believe me, and depend upon what I say.

The prince of Persia would have thanked the princess of Bengal for her obliging civility, and the favour she did him, and had already bowed down his head to return the compliment, but she would not give him leave to speak. Notwithstanding, I desire, said she, to know by what miracle you have come hither from the capital of Persia in so short a time; and by what enchantment you have been able to penetrate so far as to come to my apartment, and to have deceived the vigilance of my guards; yet, looking upon you as a guest that is welcome, and may want some refreshment, I will wave my curiosity, and give orders for my women to regale and shew you an apartment, that you may rest yourself after your fatigue, and be better able to satisfy my curiosity, as well as I to hear your story.

The princess's women, who awaked at the first words which the prince addressed to the princess, were in the utmost surprise to see a man at the princess's bolster, but could not conceive how he got thither without waking them or the eunuchs: However, as they comprehended the princess's intentions, they dressed themselves presently, and were ready to obey her commands as soon as she gave them. They each took a wax candle, of which there were great numbers lighted up in the room; and after the prince had taken his leave very respectfully, they went before him, and conducted him into a fine chamber, where, while some were preparing the bed, others went down into the kitchen to the cooks; for as it was at so unseasonable an hour, they did not make the prince Firouz Schah wait long, but brought him presently all sorts of meat; and when he had eat as much as he had a mind, and they had served him with whatever he had any desire for, they left him to taste the sweets of repose.

In the mean time, the princess of Bengal was so struck with the charms, wit, politeness, and other fine qualities which she discovered in that short conversation with the prince, that she could not sleep; but when her women came into her room, to go to bed, asked them if they had taken care of him, and if he wanted any thing, and, at last, what they thought of him?

The women, after they had satisfied her as to the first article, answered as to the last: We do not know what you may think of him; but, for our parts, we think you would be very happy if the king your father would marry you to him; for there is not a prince in all the kingdom of Bengal that is to be compared to him; nor can we hear that any of the neighbouring princes are worthy of you.

This flattering discourse was in no wise displeasing to the princess of Bengal, who, as she had no mind to declare her sentiments to them, imposed silence upon them, telling them they were mistaken, bidding them to go to bed, and let her sleep.

The next day, as soon as the princess was up, she sat down to her toilet, and took more pains in dressing and adjusting herself in the glass than ever she had done in her life. She never had tried her womens' patience so much before, by making them do and undo the same thing several times. Certainly, said she to herself, if the prince, as I perceived, was taken with me in my dishabille, he will be charmed with me when I am dressed. She adorned her head, neck, arms, and waist, with the finest and largest diamonds she had: The habit she made use of was one of the richest stuffs of the Indies, which was of a most beautiful colour, and made only for kings, princes, and princesses. After she had consulted her glass a long time, and asked her women, one after another, if nothing was wanting in her attire, she sent to know if the prince of Persia was awake; and as she never disputed but that, if he was up and dressed, he would ask leave to go and pay his respects to her, she charged the messenger, for some particular reason she had, to tell him she would make him the visit.

The prince of Persia, who had recovered by that night's rest the fatigue he had undergone the day before, had just dressed himself when he received the princess of Bengal's compliment; and without giving the lady who brought the message leave to make an end of what she had to say, asked her if it was proper for him then to go and pay his respects; and when the lady acquitted herself of her errand, he replied, As the princess thinks fit; I am solely at her pleasure.

As soon as the princess of Bengal understood that the prince of Persia waited for her, she immediately went to pay him a visit. After mutual compliments on both sides, the prince in asking pardon for having surprised and waked the princess out of a deep sleep, and the princess by asking after his health, and how he rested, the princess sat down on a sofa, as did also the prince, though at some distance, out of respect.

Then the princess, assuming the discourse, said, I would have received you, prince, in the chamber in which you found me in bed last night; but as the chief of my eunuchs has the liberty of coming into it, and never comes farther without my leave, through my impatience to hear the surprising adventure which procures me the happiness of seeing you, I chose to come hither, that we may not be interrupted; therefore I beg of you to give me that satisfaction, which will highly oblige me.

Prince Firouz Schah, to gratify the princess of Bengal, began his discourse with the solemn and annual feast of the Novrouz, relating all the sights, worthy of her curiosity, which were shown before the court of Persia, and the whole town of Schiraz; afterwards he came to the enchanted horse; the description of which, with the account of the wonders which the Indian performed on him before so august an assembly, convinced the princess that nothing of that kind in the world could be imagined more surprising. You may well think, charming princess, continued the prince of Persia, that the king my father, who values not what he gives for any thing that is rare and curious, would be very desirous to purchase such an horse, as indeed he was. He asked the Indian what he would have for him? who made an extravagant reply, telling him, that he never bought, but took him in exchange for his only daughter, and could not part with him but on the like condition, which was, to have his consent to marry the princess my sister.

The crowd of courtiers who stood about the king my father, hearing the extravagance of this proposal, all burst out a laughing; and I, for my part, conceived so great an indignation, that I could not disguise it; and the more, because the king my father was considering with himself what answer he should give him. In short, I believe he would have granted him what he asked, if I had not made a lively representation how injurious it would be to his honour; yet my remonstrance could not bring him entirely to quit his design of sacrificing the princess my sister to so despicable a person. He fancied he should bring me over to his opinion if once I could comprehend, as he imagined, the singular worth of this horse. With this view, he would have me look at him, and mount him, and make a trial of him myself.

To humour my father, I mounted the horse, and as I was got upon his back, I put my hand upon a peg, as I had seen the Indian do before me, to make the horse mount into the air, never staying to take instructions of the owner. The instant that I touched the peg, the horse mounted with me into the air, as swift as an arrow shot out of a bow, and I was presently got such a distance from the earth, that I could not distinguish any object. By the swiftness of the motion, I was for some time unapprehensive of the danger to which I was exposed; but when I grew sensible of it, I endeavoured to turn the peg the contrary way; but the experiment would not answer my expectation, and still the horse mounted with me, and carried me a greater distance from the earth. At last I perceived another peg, which I turned, and then I grew sensible that the horse declined towards the earth, and presently found myself so surrounded with darkness, that it was impossible for me to guide the horse. In this condition I laid the bridle on his neck, and trusted myself to the will of God to dispose of my fate.

Not long after the horse lighted, and I got off his back, and examining whereabouts I might be, perceived myself on the leads of this palace, and found the door of the staircase half open. I came softly down the stairs, and seeing a door open, by a small light, put my head into the room, and seeing some eunuchs asleep, and a great light in another room, the necessity I was in, notwithstanding the inevitable danger I was threatened with, if the eunuchs had waked, inspired me with boldness, or rather rashness, to cross that room to get to the other.

It is needless, madam, added the prince, to tell you the rest, since you are not unacquainted with all that passed afterwards; only I am obliged in duty to thank you for your goodness and generosity, and to beg of you to let me know how I may shew my acknowledgment. According to the law of nations, I am already your slave, and therefore cannot make you an offer of my person, but only of my heart: But, alas! princess, what is it I say? My heart is no longer my own; your charms have forced it from me, but in such a manner, as I will never ask for it again, but yield it up; therefore give me leave to declare you mistress both of my heart and person.

These last words of the prince Firouz Schah were pronounced with such an air and tone, that the princess of Bengal never doubted a moment of the effect she expected from her charms; neither did she seem to resent the precipitation of the prince of Persia's declaration, but only increased her beauty by a graceful blush, which completed her conquest.

As soon as she had recovered herself, she replied, Prince, you have given me a sensible pleasure, by telling me those surprising and wonderful things: But, on the other hand, I can hardly forbear shuddering, when I think on the height you was in the air; and though I have the good fortune to see you here safe and well, I was in pain till you came to that part where the Indian horse alighted on my palace-leads. I am glad that chance has given me the preference to the whole world, and the opportunity of letting you know, that fortune could not have conducted you any where, where you could have been received more agreeably, and with greater pleasure.

But, prince, continued she, I should be very angry with you, if I thought that what you mentioned of being my slave was serious, and it did not proceed from your abundance of civility, but from a sincerity of sentiment; for, by the reception I gave you yesterday, you might assure yourself you are here as in the midst of the court of Persia.

As to your heart, added the princess of Bengal, in a most sweet and obliging manner, as I am persuaded you have not lived so long without disposing of it, and that you could not fail of making choice of a princess of merit, I should be very sorry to give you an occasion to be guilty of an infidelity.

The prince Firouz Schah would have protested, that, when he left Persia, he was master of his own heart; but, at that instant, one of the princess's ladies in waiting came to tell her that dinner was served up.

This interruption delivered the prince and princess from an explanation which would have been equally embarrassing to both of them, and of which they stood in no need. The princess of Bengal was fully convinced of the prince of Persia's sincerity; and the prince, though the princess had not explained herself, judged, nevertheless, by some words she let fall, and the favourable manner she heard him, that he had no reason to complain.

As the lady held the door open, the princess of Bengal said to the prince of Persia, rising off her seat, as he did also from his, I am not used to dine so early; but as I fancied you might have had but an indifferent supper last night, I ordered dinner to be got ready sooner than ordinary. After this compliment, she led him into a magnificent hall, where a table was laid, and set off with great plenty of choice and excellent viands; and as soon as they were set down, a great many beautiful slaves of the princess's, who were richly dressed, began a most charming and agreeable concert of vocal and instrumental music.

This concert was so sweet and delicate, that it did not in the least prevent or interrupt the prince and princess's conversation. At dinner-time, their sole concern was to help and invite each other to eat: The prince, for his part, served the princess with the choicest of every thing, and strove to outdo her in civility, both by words and actions, which she returned again with a great many compliments; and in this reciprocal commerce of obliging each other, love made a great progress.

When they rose from the table, the princess carried the prince into a large and magnificent closet, finely embellished with paintings in blue and gold, of a just symmetry, and richly furnished. There they both sat down upon a sofa, which afforded a most agreeable prospect into the palace-garden, which prince Firouz Schah admired for the vast variety of flowers, shrubs, and trees, which were full as beautiful, but quite different, as those of Persia. Here, taking the opportunity of entering into a conversation with the princess, he said, I always believed, madam, that no part of the world but Persia afforded such stately palaces and beautiful gardens; but now I see that other great monarchs know as well how to build; and if there is a difference in the manner of building, there is none in the grandeur and magnificence.

Prince, replied the princess of Bengal, as I have no idea of the palaces of Persia, I cannot judge of the comparison you have made of mine, to tell you my opinion of it. But as sincere as you seem to be, I cannot hardly think it just, but believe it a compliment: However, I will not despise my palace before you; you discern too well, and have too good a taste to want sound judgment; but I assure you, I think it very indifferent, when I compare it with my father's, which far exceeds it for grandeur, beauty, and richness: You shall tell me yourself what you think of it; for since a chance has brought you so nigh to the capital of this kingdom, I do not doubt but you will see it, and make my father a visit, that he may pay you all the honour due to a prince of your rank and merit.

The princess flattered herself, that, by exciting in the prince of Persia a curiosity to see the palace of Bengal, and to visit her father, the king, seeing him so handsome, wise, and accomplished a prince, might perhaps take it in his head to propose an alliance with him, by offering her as a wife: And as she was very well persuaded she was not indifferent to the prince, and that he would be pleased with the proposal, she hoped to attain to the utmost of her wishes, and observe all the decorum agreeable to a princess who would appear to have all the regard to the will of her king and father which becomes a dutiful child: But the prince of Persia did not return her an answer according to her desire.

Princess, replied the prince, the preference which you give the king of Bengal's palace to your own, is enough for me to believe it much exceeds it. But as to the proposal of my going and paying my respects to the king your father, I should not only do myself a pleasure, but an honour in doing it. But judge, princess, yourself, would you advise me to present myself before so great a monarch at a venture, without attendance, and a train agreeable to my rank?

Prince, replied the princess, do not let that give you any pain; if you will but go, you shall want no money, or what train and attendance you please; I will furnish you; and we have traders here of all nations in great numbers, and you may make choice of as many as you please, to form your household.

Prince Firouz Schah penetrated into the princess of Bengal's intention, and this sensible mark she gave him of her love still augmented his passion, which, notwithstanding its violence, made him not forget his duty; but, without any hesitation, he replied, Princess, I should most willingly accept of the obliging offer you make me, for which I cannot enough shew my acknowledgment, if the uneasiness my father must be in, on account of my absence, did not prevent me. I should be unworthy of the bounty and tenderness he has always had for me, if I should not return soon to calm his fears. I know his temper so well, that while I have the happiness of enjoying the conversation of so lovely a princess, I am persuaded that he is plunged into the deepest grief, and has lost all hopes of seeing me again. I hope you will do me the justice to believe, I cannot, without ingratitude, and being guilty of a crime, dispense with going to restore that life to him, which a too long deferred return may have endangered.

After this, princess, continued the prince of Persia, if you will permit me, and think me worthy to aspire to the happiness of becoming your spouse, (as the king my father has declared that he never would constrain me in my choice,) I should find it no difficult matter to get leave to return, not as a stranger, but as a prince, to contract an alliance by our marriage; and I am persuaded that he will be overjoyed when I tell him with what generosity you received me, though a stranger.

The princess of Bengal was too reasonable, after what the prince of Persia had said, to insist any longer in persuading him to pay a visit to the king of Bengal, or to ask any thing of him contrary to his duty and honour, but was very much alarmed to find that he thought of so sudden a departure; fearing, that if he took his leave of her so soon, he would not remember his promise, but forget that ever he had seen her; but to put it off a little, she said to him, Prince, my intention of proposing a visit to my father was not to oppose so just an excuse as that you gave me, and which I did not foresee: I should have rendered myself an accomplice of the crime, had I thought of it: But I cannot approve of your thinking to go so soon as you propose; at least, grant me the favour I ask, of a little longer acquaintance; and since I had the happiness to have you alight in the kingdom of Bengal, rather than in the midst of a desert, or on the top of some steep craggy rock, from which it would have been impossible for you to descend, I desire you will make a little longer abode, that you may be able to give a better account at the court of Persia of what you have seen here.

The sole end the princess of Bengal had in this discourse was, that the prince of Persia, by a longer stay, might become insensibly more passionately taken with her charms; hoping thereby, that his ardent desire of returning would diminish, and then he might be brought to appear in public, and pay a visit to the king of Bengal. The prince of Persia could not well refuse her the favour she asked, after the kind reception she had given him, but was so complaisant as to condescend to her; whose only thoughts then were, how to render his abode agreeable, by all the diversions she could imagine.

Nothing went forwards for some days, but feasts, and balls, and concerts of music, which were always set off with magnificent collations. On other days, they went a-hunting deer in the palace-park, which abounded with all sorts, both stags, hinds, and fallow-deer: And after the chace, the prince and princess met in a convenient place in the park, where a carpet was spread, and cushions laid for them, to sit the more easy on, and rest themselves, after the violence of exercise. There they talked generally of indifferent matters; but the princess, for the most part, would intrude something about the grandeur, power, riches, and government of Persia, that, from Prince Firouz Schah's discourse, she might have an opportunity to talk of the kingdom of Bengal, and engage him to resolve to make a longer stay there; but she was baulked in her expectation.

In short, the prince of Persia, without making the least exaggeration, gave so advantageous an account of the largeness of the kingdom of Persia, its magnificence and riches, its military force, its commerce by sea and land, to the most remote parts of the world, the vast number of large and populous cities it contained, such as the king made his residence, where he had palaces ready furnished to receive him at all seasons of the year, so that at his choice he could always enjoy a perpetual spring, that, before he had done, the princess found the kingdom of Bengal to be very much inferior to that of Persia, in a great many instances. When he had finished his relation, he begged of her to entertain him with a description of Bengal; which, after a great deal of entreaty from the prince, she at last complied with.

The princess gave Prince Firouz Schah that satisfaction; but, by lessening a great many advantages the kingdom of Bengal had over that of Persia, she let him know the disposition she was in to accompany him, so that he believed she would consent to the first proposition he should make: But he thought it would not be proper then, till he had shewed her so much complaisance as to stay longer with her; but resolved to make it, in case she would keep him from returning to his father, as he was in duty bound to do.

Two whole months the prince Firouz Schah abandoned himself entirely to the will of the princess of Bengal, who neglected nothing to divert him. But, after that time, he declared seriously he could not stay any longer, and begged of her to give him leave to return to his father, repeating again the promise he had made her, to return soon, in an equipage worthy of her and himself, and in form to demand her in marriage of the king of Bengal.

And, princess, said the prince of Persia, that you may not suspect the truth of what I say, and that, by my asking this leave, you may not rank me among those false lovers who forget the object of their loves as soon as they are absent from them, but, to shew that my passion is real, and not feigned, and that my life cannot be agreeable to me when absent from so lovely a princess, I should be so bold, if I was not afraid you would be angry, to ask the favour of taking you along with me.

As the prince Firouz Schah saw that the princess blushed at these words, and that, without any mark of anger, she was determined what to do, he proceeded, and said, Princess, as for the king my father's consent, and the reception he will give you, he will receive you with pleasure into his alliance; and as for the king of Bengal, after all the love and tender regard he has always expressed for you, he must be the reverse of what you have described him, an enemy to your repose and happiness, if he should not receive the embassy friendly, which my father will send to him for his approbation of our marriage.

The princess of Bengal returned no answer to this discourse of the prince of Persia; but her silence, and the casting down of her eyes, were sufficient to inform him that she had no reluctance, but consented. The only difficulty she had to raise, was, that the prince knew not well enough how to govern the horse; which the prince soon removed, by assuring her, that, after the experience he had had, he defied the Indian himself to manage him better; upon which, they had nothing to do but concert measures so secretly, that nobody belonging to the palace should have the least suspicion of their design.

The next morning, a little before day-break, when all the palace were asleep, they went up on the leads of the palace; the prince turned the horse towards Persia, and placed him where the princess could easily get up behind him; which she had no sooner done, and was well settled, with her arms about his waist, for her better security, but he turned the peg, and the horse mounted into the air; and, in two hours time, the prince discovered the capital of Persia.

He would not light at the palace from whence he set out, nor in the sultan's palace, but directed his course towards a palace a little distance from the town. He led the princess into a fine apartment, where he told her, that, to do her all the honour that was due to her, he would immediately inform his father of their arrival. At the same time, he ordered the keeper of the palace, who was then present, to pay all imaginable respect to the princess, and provide her with whatever she had occasion for.

After the prince had taken his leave of the princess, he ordered an horse to be saddled presently, which he mounted, after he had charged the keeper, who attended him still, to carry the princess something for her breakfast, and then set forwards for the palace.—As he passed through the streets, he was received with acclamations of the people, who were overjoyed to see him again. The sultan, his father, was giving audience to his people, in the midst of his council, who, as well as the whole court, had been all in mourning ever since he had been absent. The sultan received, and, embracing him with tears of joy, asked him, What was become of the Indian's horse?

This question gave the prince an opportunity to tell him the embarrassment and danger he was in, when the horse had mounted into the air with him; how he arrived at last at the princess of Bengal's palace, and the kind reception he met with there; that the motive which obliged him to stay so long, was his complaisance to persuade her (after promising her marriage) to come with him into Persia. But, sir, added the prince, I have not only promised that princess marriage, but assured her of your consent, and brought her, by the Indian's horse, to a palace where your majesty often goes for your pleasure, and have left her there, till I could return and assure her that my promise was not in vain.

After these words, the prince prostrated himself before the sultan, who raised him up, embraced him a second time, and said unto him, Son, I will not only consent to your marriage with the princess of Bengal, but will go and meet her myself; I will thank her in particular for the obligation I have to her, and will bring her to my palace, and celebrate your nuptials this day.

Then the sultan gave orders for his court to go out of mourning, and make preparations for the princess's entry, and to fetch the Indian out of prison. When the Indian was brought before the sultan, he said to him, I secured thy person, that thy life, though not a sufficient victim to my rage and grief, might answer for that of the prince, my son, whom, thanks to God, I have found again: Go, take thy horse, and never let me see thy face more.

As the Indian had learned of those who fetched him out of prison that the prince Firouz Schah was returned, and had brought a princess behind him on his horse, and was also informed of the place where he had left her, and that the sultan was making preparations to go and bring her to his palace; as soon as he got out of the sultan's presence, he bethought himself of being before-hand with him and the prince, and, without losing any time, went directly to the palace, and addressing himself to the keeper, told him, That he came from the sultan and prince of Persia, to fetch the princess of Bengal, and to carry her behind him on his horse; telling him, at the same time, that they, and the whole court and city of Schiraz, waited for that wonderful sight.

The keeper, who knew the Indian, and how that the sultan had imprisoned him, gave the more credit to what he said, because he saw that he was at liberty, and presented him to the princess of Bengal, who no sooner understood that he came from the prince of Persia, but she consented, as she thought, to what that prince desired of her.

The Indian, overjoyed at his success, and the ease with which he had accomplished his villany, mounted his horse, took the princess behind him, with the assistance of the keeper, turned the peg, and presently the horse mounted into the air with him and the princess.

At the same time, the sultan of Persia, followed by his court, was on the road from his own palace to the palace where the princess of Bengal was left, and the prince of Persia was advanced before, to prepare the princess of Bengal to receive him, when the Indian, to brave them, and revenge himself for the ill treatment he had received, as he pretended, passed over their heads with his prize.

When the sultan of Persia saw the ravisher, he stopped; his surprise and affliction was much the more sensible, because it was not in his power to make him repent of so high and injurious an affront. He loaded him with a thousand imprecations, as also did all the courtiers, who were witnesses of so signal a piece of insolence, and unparalleled villany.

The Indian, little moved with their curses, which just reached his ears, continued on his way, while the sultan, extremely mortified at so great an injury, and to find he could not punish the author, returned back to his palace.

But, all this time, how violent was Prince Firouz Schah's grief, to see the Indian carry away the princess of Bengal, whom he loved so passionately, that he could not live without her? At the first sight of an object so little expected, he was quite thunderstruck, and, before he could deliberate with himself whether he should let fly all the injuries his rage could invent against the Indian, or bewail the deplorable state of the princess, or ask her pardon for not taking better precautions to preserve her, who had trusted herself so much to his care, as was sufficient to show her love, the horse was got out of sight. He could not well resolve what to do, whether he should return to the sultan's palace, and shut himself up in an apartment, to give himself entirely up to his affliction, without attempting to pursue the ravisher, to deliver the princess, and punish him as he deserved. But his generosity, love, and courage, would not permit him long to entertain such a thought; therefore he continued on his way to the palace where he left his princess.

When he came there, the keeper, sensible of the effect of his credulity, by which he was deceived by the Indian, threw himself at his feet, with tears in his eyes, and accused himself of the crime which he thought he had committed, and condemned himself to die by his hand: When the prince said to him, Rise up, I do not impute the loss of my princess to thee, but to my own simplicity: But, not to lose time, fetch me a dervise's habit, and take care you do not mention or give the least hint that it is for me.

Not far from this palace, there stood a convent of dervises, the scheik, or superior of which, was the palace-keeper's particular friend. According to the prince's orders, he went to this scheik, and telling him a story, that a considerable officer at court, and a man of worth, to whom he had been very much obliged, and was willing to serve, wanted the habit, in order to weather the sultan's rage, he easily got a complete dervise's habit, and carried it to the prince Firouz Schah. The prince immediately pulled off his own cloaths, and put it on; and, being so disguised and provided for his enterprise, with a box of jewels, which he brought as a present to the princess, he left the palace in the evening, uncertain which way to go, but resolved not to return till he had found out his princess again, and could bring her along with him.

But, to return to the Indian. He governed his horse so well that day, that he arrived pretty early in a wood, near the capital of the kingdom of Caschmire, where he was hungry himself, and judged that the princess might be the same: He alighted in that wood, in an open part of it, on a grass-plot, by a brook side, and there left the princess.

During the Indian's absence, the princess of Bengal, who knew that she was in the power of a base ravisher, whose violence she dreaded, thought of getting from him, and seeking out for some sanctuary; but as she had eat scarce any thing in the morning, she was so faint, she could not execute what she designed, but was forced to abandon her project, and to stay where she was, void of any other assistance than her own courage, and a firm resolution rather to suffer death than be unfaithful to the prince of Persia. When the Indian returned, she ate with him, and by that means recovered herself, and could answer, with courage enough, what he proposed to her, after they had done. After a great many threats, as she saw that the Indian intended to use violence, she got up to make a better resistance, and by cries and shrieks, drew a company of horsemen about them, which happened to be the sultan of Caschmire and his attendants, who, as they were returning from hunting, happily passed through that part of the wood, and ran to the princess of Bengal's assistance, at the noise she made.

The sultan addressed himself to the Indian, and asked him who he was, and what he had to do with the lady? The Indian replied, with a great deal of impudence, that she was his wife; and what had any one to do to concern themselves between them?

The princess, who neither knew the rank nor quality of the person who came so seasonably to her relief, told the Indian that he was a liar, and said to the sultan, Sir, whoever you are that heaven has sent to my assistance, have compassion on a princess, and give no credit to that impostor. Heaven forbid that I should be the wife of so vile and despicable an Indian, who is a wicked magician, that hath taken me away from the prince of Persia, to whom I was going to be married, and hath brought me hither on an enchanted horse.

The princess of Bengal had no occasion to say any more to persuade the sultan of Caschmire that what she told him was truth. Her beauty, majestic air, and her fears, spoke enough for her. The sultan of Caschmire, justly enraged at the insolence and villany of the Indian, ordered his guards to surround him, and cut off his head; which sentence was immediately executed.

The princess, though thus delivered from the persecution of the Indian, yet fell into another no less afflicting to her. The sultan, after he had ordered her an horse, carried her along with him to his palace, where he lodged her in the most magnificent apartment next his own, and gave her a great number of women slaves to attend her, and a guard of eunuchs. He led her himself into the apartment he assigned her, where, without giving her time to thank him for the great obligation she had to him, he said to her, As I am assured, princess, that you must want rest, I will here take my leave of you till to-morrow, when you will be better able to give me all the circumstances of this strange adventure; and then left her.

The princess of Bengal's joy was inexpressible, to find she was so soon freed from the violence of a man she could not look upon without horror. She flattered herself, that the sultan of Caschmire would be so generous as to send her back to the prince of Persia, when she told him her story, and asked that favour of him, but was very much deceived in these hopes; for the sultan of Caschmire resolved to marry her the next day; and for that end, had ordered rejoicings to be made by day-break, by beating of drums and sounding of trumpets, and other testimonials of joy; which not only echoed through the palace, but throughout the city.

The princess of Bengal was awakened by those tumultuous concerts, but could not tell what cause to attribute them to; when the sultan of Caschmire, who had given the slaves orders to tell him when the princess was ready to receive a visit, came to pay her one; and after he had informed himself of her health, he acquainted her that all those rejoicings were to render their nuptials more solemn; and, at the same time, desired her to approve of them: Which discourse put her into so great a consternation that she swooned away.

The women-slaves who were present ran to her assistance; and the sultan did all he could to bring her to herself again, though it was a long time before they could; but when she recovered, rather than be false, and break her promise she had made to Prince Firouz Schah, by consenting to marry the sultan of Caschmire, who had proclaimed their nuptials before he had asked her consent, she resolved to feign madness. To that end, she began to say the most extravagant things before the sultan, and even rose off her seat to fly upon him, insomuch that the sultan was very much surprised and afflicted that he had made such a proposal so unseasonably.

When he found that her frenzy rather increased than abated, he left her with her women, charging them never to leave her alone, but to take great care of her. He sent often that day to know how she did, but received no other answer, but that she was rather worse than better. In short, at night she seemed much worse than she had been all day, insomuch that the sultan of Caschmire was baulked in the happiness he so much promised himself.

This frenzy not only held the princess of Bengal the next day, but a great many more; so that the sultan sent for all the physicians belonging to his court, to talk with them about her disease, and to ask them if they could cure her.

The physicians all agreed that there were several degrees of this distemper, some curable, and others not, and told the sultan, that they could not judge of the princess of Bengal's, unless they saw her; upon which the sultan ordered the eunuchs to introduce them into the princess's chamber.

The princess, who foresaw what would happen, and feared, that, if she let the physicians come near her to feel her pulse, they would soon know that she was in a good state of health, and that her madness was only feigned, flew into such a rage and passion, that she was ready to tear out their eyes who came near her; so none of them durst go nigh her.

Some of them, who pretended to be more skilful than the rest, and boasted of judging of diseases only by sight, ordered her some potions, which they could by no means get her to take, she well knowing she could be sick or well at pleasure.

When the sultan of Caschmire saw that his physicians could not cure her, he called in the most noted and experienced of the city, who had all no better success. Afterwards he sent for the most famous in the kingdom, who met with no better reception from the princess; and what they ordered had no better effect than what was prescribed by the first. Afterwards, he dispatched expresses to the courts of neighbouring princes, with the case of the princess's distemper, to be distributed among the most famous physicians, with a promise to reward him or them well who should come and cure the princess of Bengal.

A great many physicians came from all parts to the capital of Caschmire, and undertook the cure; but none of them could boast of better success than their fellows, since it was a thing that did not depend on their skill, but on the will of the princess.

During this interval, the prince Firouz Schah, disguised in the habit of a dervise, had travelled through a great many large towns and provinces, full of grief; and having endured a great deal of fatigue, not knowing which way to direct his course next, to hear the news he sought, had made diligent inquiry after her at every place he came at; till at last, passing through a great town in India, he heard the people talk very much of a princess of Bengal, who ran mad on the day of the celebration of her nuptials with the sultan of Caschmire. At the name of the princess of Bengal, and supposing that there was no other princess of Bengal than she upon whose account he undertook his travels, he sets forward for the kingdom of Caschmire, on this common report; and at his arrival at the capital city, he went and lodged at a khan, where, the same day, he was told a story of the princess of Bengal, and the unhappy fate of the Indian, which he richly deserved. By all these circumstances, the prince knew he could not be deceived, but that she was the same princess he had sought so long after.

The prince of Persia, being informed of all these particulars, provided himself against the next day with a physician's habit, and having let his beard grow during his travels, passed for a physician, and, through the greatness of his impatience to see his princess, went to the sultan's palace, where, presenting himself to the chief of the huissars,* he told him, that perhaps it might be looked upon as a very bold undertaking in him to offer himself as a physician to attempt the cure of the princess, after so many had failed in it; but that he hoped some specifics, which he had had great experience of, and success from, would effect the cure. The chief of the huissars told him he was very welcome; that the sultan would receive him with a great deal of pleasure; and that, if he should have the good fortune to restore the princess to her former health, he might expect a considerable reward from the sultan his master's liberality; but, added he, stay a moment; I will come to you presently.

It had been a long time since any physician had offered himself; and the sultan of Caschmire, with great grief, had begun to lose all hopes of ever seeing the princess of Bengal restored to her former health, that he might marry her, as he so much wished to do; therefore he the sooner ordered the huissar who brought him the news, to bring the physician to him.

The prince of Persia was presented to the sultan of Caschmire in the habit and disguise of a physician; and the sultan, without wasting time in a long discourse, after having told him the princess of Bengal could not bear the sight of a physician without falling into the most violent transports, which increased her distemper, carried him into a closet, from whence, through a window, he might see her without being seen.

There Prince Firouz Schah saw his lovely princess, set carelessly, singing a song, with tears in her eyes, in which she deplored her unhappy fate, which deprived her, as she thought, for ever, of the object she loved so tenderly.

The prince was so sensibly affected at the melancholy condition he found his dear princess in, that he wanted no other signs to comprehend that her distemper was feigned, and that it was for the love of him that she was under so grievous a constraint. When he came out of the closet, he told the sultan, that he had discovered the nature of the princess's distemper, and that she was not incurable, but added withal, that he must speak with her in private, and by himself; and notwithstanding her violent fits at the sight of physicians, he hoped she would hear and receive him favourably.

The sultan ordered the princess's chamber-door to be opened, and Prince Firouz Schah went in.

As soon as the princess saw him, (for she took him by his habit to be a physician,) she rose up in a rage, threatening him, and giving him the most injurious language: Notwithstanding which, he made directly towards her, and when he was nigh enough for her to hear him, he said to her, in a low voice, and in a most respectful manner, Princess, I am not a physician, but the prince of Persia, who am come to procure you your liberty.

The princess, who presently knew the sound of the voice, and the upper features of his face, for all he had let his beard grow so long, grew calm at once, and a secret joy and pleasure spread over her face; her surprise was so agreeable, that it deprived her for some time of the use of her speech, and gave Prince Firouz Schah time to tell her how great and irresistible his despair was when he saw the Indian carry her away; the resolution he took afterwards, to leave every thing to find her out, wherever she was, and never to return home till he had found her, and forced her out of the hands of the perfidious wretch; and by what good fortune at last, after long fatiguing journeys, he had the satisfaction to find her in the palace of the sultan of Caschmire. Afterwards, he desired the princess to inform him of all that happened unto her, from the time she was taken away, till that happy moment; telling her, that it was of the greatest importance, that he might take the most proper measures to deliver her from the tyranny of the sultan of Caschmire.

The princess of Bengal told the prince how she was delivered from the Indian's violence by the sultan of Caschmire, as he was returning home from hunting; how ill she was treated the next day, by the declaration he had made of his love, and his precipitate design to marry her the next day, without so much as ever asking her consent; that this violent and tyrannical conduct put her into a swoon; after which she thought she had no other way than what she had taken, to preserve herself for a prince to whom she had given her heart and her faith; or die, rather than marry the sultan, whom she neither loved, nor could ever love.

Then the prince of Persia asked her if she knew what was become of the horse, after the Indian's death: To which she answered, that she knew not what orders the sultan had given about it; but believed, after the account she had given him of it, he would take care of it.

As Prince Firouz Schah never doubted but that the sultan had the horse, he communicated his design to the princess, of making use of it to carry them both back to Persia; and after they had consulted together on the measures they were to take, and that nothing might prevent the execution of them, they agreed that the princess should dress herself the next day, and receive the sultan civilly, when he brought him, but not to speak.

The sultan of Caschmire was overjoyed when the prince of Persia gave him an account what effect his first visit had towards the cure of the princess of Bengal: And the next day, when the princess received him after such a manner as persuaded him that her cure was far advanced, he looked upon him as the greatest physician in the world, and exhorted her to follow his directions, to complete what he had so well begun; and then retired.

The prince of Persia, who attended the sultan of Caschmire out of the princess's chamber, as he accompanied him, said to him, with all imaginable respect, Pray, sir, if I may be so bold as to ask you this question, how came the princess of Bengal into the dominions of Caschmire thus alone, since her own country lies so far off? This he said on purpose to introduce some discourse about the enchanted horse, and to know what was become of it.

The sultan of Caschmire, who could not penetrate into what motive the prince of Persia had to ask that question, made the matter no secret, but told him much the same story as the princess of Bengal had done; adding, that he had ordered the enchanted horse to be kept safe in his treasury, though he knew not the use of him.

Sir, replied the pretended physician, the information which your majesty gives me, affords me a means of curing the princess. As she was brought hither on a horse, and as that horse was enchanted, she hath contracted something of the enchantment, which I am sure I can remove. If your majesty would be pleased to entertain your court and people of your capital with the most surprising sight that ever was seen, let the horse be brought into the great square before the palace, and leave the rest to me: I promise to shew you, and that assembly, in a few moments of time, that the princess of Bengal shall be as well as ever she was in her life: But the better to effect what I propose, it will be proper that the princess should be as magnificently dressed as possible, and adorned with the best jewels your majesty has: Which, and much more difficult things, the sultan would have undertaken, to have arrived at the height of his desires, as he expected to do soon.

The next day the enchanted horse was, by his order, taken out of the treasury, and placed early in the great square before the palace; upon which a report was spread through the town, that there was something extraordinary to be seen, and crowds of people, of all sorts, flocked thither from all parts, insomuch that the sultan's guards were placed to prevent all disorders, and to make room enough round the horse.

The sultan of Caschmire, surrounded with all his nobles and ministers of state, was placed on a scaffold erected on purpose. The princess of Bengal, attended by a vast number of ladies which the sultan had assigned her, went directly up to the horse, and the women helped her to get upon his back. When she was fixed in the saddle, and had the bridle in her hand, the pretended physician placed a great many vessels full of fire, which he had ordered to be brought, round the horse; and going round about it several times, he cast a strong and grateful perfume into those pots; then casting down his eyes, and running, with his hand upon his breast, three times about the horse, he made as if he pronounced some certain words to himself. In the mean time, the pots sent forth a dark cloud, of a pleasant smell, and so surrounded the princess, that neither she nor the horse were to be discerned. At this juncture, the prince jumped nimbly up behind her, and reaching his hand to the peg, turned it; and while the horse mounted into the air, he pronounced these words, which the sultan heard distinctly, Sultan of Caschmire, when thou wouldst marry princesses who implore thy protection, learn first to get their consent.

Thus the prince of Persia recovered and delivered the princess of Bengal, and carried her that same day to the capital of Persia, where he alighted, in the midst of the palace, before the king his father's apartment, who deferred the solemnization of the marriage no longer than just to have time to make all the preparations necessary to render the ceremony pompous and magnificent.

After the days appointed for the rejoicings were over, the king of Persia's first care was to name and appoint an ambassador to go to give the king of Bengal an account of what was past, and to demand his approbation and ratification of the alliance contracted by this marriage; which the king of Bengal took as an honour, and granted with a great deal of pleasure and satisfaction.

The Story of Prince Ahmed and the Fairy Pari Banou[1]

THERE was a sultan who had peaceably filled the Indian throne several years, and had the satisfaction, in his old age, to have three sons, the imitators of his virtues, and a niece, who was the ornament of his court. The eldest of the princes was called Houssain, the second Ali, the youngest Ahmed, and the princess, his niece, Nouronnihar.[2]

The princess Nouronnihar was the daughter of the younger brother of the sultan, to whom the sultan in his lifetime allowed a considerable revenue: But that prince had not been married long, before he died, and left the princess very young. The sultan, in consideration that there was always a brotherly love and friendship between them, and that the prince, his brother, was attached to his person, took upon himself the care of his daughter's education, and brought her up in his palace with the three princes, where her wit and beauty, which were singular, and her virtue, distinguished her among all the princesses of her time.

The sultan, her uncle, proposed to marry her when she arrived at the proper age, and to contract an alliance with some neighbouring prince by that means; but when he perceived that the three princes his sons loved her passionately, he thought more seriously on that affair. He was very much concerned; but his grief did not proceed from their passions preventing his forming an alliance he designed; but the difficulty, he foresaw, was to make them agree, and that the two youngest should consent to yield her up to their elder brother. He spoke to each of them apart; and after having remon-

[1] Two Persian words, which signify the same, i.e. female fairy, or genie.

[2] The Arabian word that signifies day-light.

strated the impossibility of one princess being the wife of three, and the trouble they might create if they persisted in their passion, he did all he could to persuade them to come to stand to a declaration of the princess in favour of one of them; or to desist from their intentions, and to think of other matches among the neighbouring princes. But as he found them positively obstinate, he sent for them all together, and said to them, Children, since, for your good and quiet, I have not been able to persuade you no longer to aspire to the princess your cousin, and as I have no inclination to make use of my authority to give her to one preferable before the other two, I fancy I have thought of a proper expedient, which will please you all, and preserve the union among you, if you will but hear me, and do as I would have you. I think it would not be amiss, if every one travelled separately into different countries, so that you might not meet each other: And as you know I am very curious, and delight in every thing that is singular, I promise my niece in marriage to him that shall bring me the most extraordinary rarity; and for the purchase of the rarity you shall go in search after, and the expence of travelling, I will give you every one a sum of money agreeable to your birth; which shall not be laid out in equipage and attendants, which, by discovering who you are, would not only deprive you of the liberty to acquit yourselves of the inquiry you go about, but prevent your observing those things which merit the most of your attention, and may be the most useful to you.

As the three princes were always submissive and obedient to the sultan's will, and each flattered himself fortune might prove favourable to him, and give him the possession of the princess Nouronnihar, they all consented to it. The sultan paid them the money he promised them; and that very day they gave orders for the preparations for their travels, and took their leaves of the sultan, that they might be the more ready to go the next morning. Accordingly they all set out at the same gate of the city, each dressed like a merchant, attended by an officer of confidence, dressed like a slave, and all well mounted and equipped. They went the first day's journey together, and lay all at an inn, where the road was divided into three different tracts. At night, when they were at supper together, they all agreed to travel for a year, and to make that inn their rendezvous; and that the first that came should wait for the rest; that as they had all three taken their leaves together of the sultan, they might all return together. The next morning, by break of day, after they had embraced, and wished each other reciprocally good success, they mounted their horses, and took each a different road.

Prince Houssain, the eldest brother, who had heard wonders of the grandeur, strength, riches, and splendour of the kingdom of Bisnagar, bent his course towards the Indian coast, and, after three months travelling, (having joined himself to different caravans,) sometimes over deserts and barren mountains, and sometimes through rich fertile countries, arrived at Bisnagar, the capital of the kingdom of that name, and the residence of its king. He went and lodged at a khan appointed for foreign merchants; and having learned that there were four principal divisions where merchants of all sorts sold their commodities, and kept shops, and in the midst of which stood the castle, or rather the king's palace, on a large extent of ground, as the centre of the city, and surrounded with three works, and two leagues distant from one gate to the other, he went to one of these divisions the next day.

Prince Houssain could not view this division without admiration. It was large, and divided into several streets, all vaulted and shaded from the sun, and yet very light too. The shops were all of a size and just symmetry; and all that dealt in the same sort of goods lived in one street; as also the handicrafts-men, who kept their shops in the smaller streets.

The multitude of shops, stocked with all sorts of merchandizes, as the finest linens, from several parts of India, some painted in the most lively colours, and representing beasts, trees, and flowers; silks and brocades, from Persia, China, and other places; porcelain, both from Japan and China, and tapestries, surprised him so much, that he knew not how to believe his own eyes; but when he came to the goldsmiths and jewellers, (for those two trades were exercised by the same merchants,) he was in a kind of ecstacy, to behold such prodigious quantities of wrought gold and silver, and was dazzled by the lustre of the pearls, diamonds, rubies, emeralds, and other jewels, exposed to sale. But if he was so much amazed at the richness of one place, he was much more surprised when he came to judge of the wealth of the whole kingdom, by considering, that, except the bramins* and ministers of the idols, who profess a retired life, there was not an Indian, through the extent of that kingdom, man or woman, but what wore necklaces, bracelets, and ornaments about their legs and feet, of pearls, and other jewels, which appeared with the greater lustre, as they were blacks.

Another thing Prince Houssain particularly admired, was the great number of rose-sellers who crowded the streets; for the Indians are so great lovers of that flower, that not one will stir without a nosegay in his hand, or a garland on his head; and the merchants keep them in pots in their shops, so that the air is perfectly perfumed.

After Prince Houssain had run through that division, street by street, his thoughts fully employed on the riches he had seen, he was very much tired; which a merchant perceiving, civilly invited him to sit down in his shop; and he accepted of it; but had not been sat down long, before he saw a crier pass by with a piece of tapestry on his arm, about six foot square, and cried it at thirty purses. The prince called to the crier, and asked him to see the tapestry, which seemed to him to be valued at an exorbitant price, not only for the size of it, but the meanness of the stuff. When he had examined it well, he told the crier, that he could not comprehend how so small a piece of tapestry, and of so indifferent appearance, could be set at so high a price.

The crier, who took him for a merchant, replied, If this price seems so extravagant to you, your amazement will be greater, when I tell you I have orders to raise it to forty purses, and not to part with it under. Certainly, answered Prince Houssain, it must have something very extraordinary in it, which I know nothing of. You have guessed it, sir, replied the crier, and will own it, when you come to know, that whoever sits on this piece of tapestry may be transported in an instant where-ever he desires to be, without being stopped by any obstacle.

At this discourse of the crier, the prince of the Indies considering that the principal motive of his travel was to carry the sultan his father home some singular rarity, thought that he could not meet with any which could give him more satisfaction. If the tapestry, said he to the crier, has the virtue you assign it, I shall not think forty purses too much, but shall make you a present besides. Sir, replied the crier, I have told you the truth; and it is an easy matter to convince you of it, as soon as you have made the bargain for forty purses, on condition I shew you the experiment. But as I suppose you have not so much about you, and, to receive them, I must go with you to your khan where you lodge, with the leave of the master of the shop, we will go into the back-shop, and I will spread the tapestry, and when we have both sat down, and you have formed the wish to be transported into your apartment of the khan, if we are not transported thither, it shall be no bargain, and you shall be at your liberty. As to your present, though I am paid for my trouble by the seller, I shall receive it as a favour, and be very much obliged to you, and thankful.

On the credit of the crier, the prince accepted the conditions, and concluded the bargain; and having got the master's leave, they went into his back-shop: They both sat down on it; and as soon as the prince formed his wish to be transported into his apartment at the khan, he presently found himself and the crier there in the same situation; and as he wanted not a more sufficient proof of the virtue of the tapestry, he counted the crier out forty purses of gold, and gave him twenty pieces for himself.

In this manner Prince Houssain became the possessor of the tapestry, and was overjoyed, that, at his arrival at Bisnagar, he had found so rare a piece, which he never disputed would gain him the possession of Nouronnihar. In short, he looked upon it as an impossible thing for the princes, his younger brothers, to meet with any thing to be compared with it. It was in his power, by sitting on his tapestry, to be at the place of rendezvous that very day; but as he was obliged to stay there for his brothers, as they had agreed, and as he was curious to see the king of Bisnagar and his court, and to inform himself of the strength, laws, customs, and religion of the kingdom, he chose to make a longer abode there, and to spend some months in satisfying his curiosity.

It was a custom of the king of Bisnagar to give all strange merchants access to his person once a-week; and, by that title, Prince Houssain, who would not be known, saw him often; and as the prince was handsome, witty, and extremely polite, he easily distinguished himself among the merchants, and was preferred before them all by the sultan, who addressed himself to him to be informed of the sultan of the Indies' person, and of the government, strength, and riches of his dominions.

The rest of his time the prince spent in seeing what was most remarkable in and about the city; and among those things which were most worthy of admiration, he visited a temple of idols, which was built all of brass. It was about ten cubits square, and fifteen high; and that which was the greatest ornament to it was an idol, the height of a man, of massy gold: Its eyes were two rubies, set so artificially, that it seemed to look at those who looked at it, on which side soever they stood. Besides this, there was another, no less curious, in a village in the midst of a plain, of ten arches, which was a delicious garden, full of roses and the choicest flowers, surrounded with a small wall breast-high, to keep the cattle out. In the midst of this plain was raised a terrace, a man's height, so nicely paved, that the whole pavement seemed to be one single stone. A temple was erected in the middle of this terrace, with a dome about fifty cubits high, and might be seen for several leagues about. It was thirty cubits long, and twenty broad; the marble of which it was built was red, and extremely well polished. The inside of the dome was adorned with three rows of fine paintings; and, in short, there was not a place in the whole temple but what was embellished with basso-relievos,* and figures of idols, from top to bottom.

Every night and morning there were superstitious ceremonies performed in this temple, which were always succeeded with sports, concerts of music, dancing, singing, and feasts. The ministers of the temple, and the inhabitants of the place, had nothing to subsist on but the offerings of pilgrims, who came in numbers, from the most distant parts of the kingdom, to perform their vows.

Besides all this, Prince Houssain was a spectator of a solemn feast, which was celebrated every year at the court of Bisnagar, at which all the governors of provinces and fortified places, all governors and judges of towns, and the most celebrated bramins, were obliged to be present; and some lived so far off, that they were four months in coming. This assembly, composed of such innumerable multitudes of Indians, met in a plain of a vast extent, was a glorious sight. In the centre of this plain was erected a large scaffolding of nine rows of benches, inclosed on one side by a fine building, and supported by forty pillars. This place was raised for the king and his court, and those strangers he admitted to the audience once a-week: Within, it was adorned and furnished magnificently; and on the outside were painted fine landscapes, wherein all sorts of beasts, birds, and insects, even flies, were drawn very natural. Three other scaffolds, of about four or five benches, and painted almost all alike, formed the other three sides. But what was more particular in these scaffolds, they could make them change their situation every hour.

On each side of this place, at some distance from each other, were ranged great numbers of elephants, sumptuously harnessed, and each laden with a wooden castle upon his back, finely gilt, within each of which were musicians and stage-players. The trunks, ears, and bodies of these elephants were painted with cinnabar,* in which were represented grotesque figures.

But what Prince Houssain most of all admired, was the ingenious device and invention of the Indians, to make a large elephant stand with his four feet on a post, which was fixed into the earth, and stood out of it above two feet, and beat time with his trunk to the music. Besides this, there was another elephant, as big as this, and no less surprising, which being set upon a board, which was laid across a strong rail, about ten feet high, with a great weight at the other end, which balanced him, kept time, by the motions of his body and trunk, with the music, as well as the other elephant, and both in the presence of the king and the whole court.

Prince Houssain might have made a longer abode in the kingdom and court of Bisnagar, where he might have been agreeably diverted till the day he and his brothers had appointed to meet on, but he was so well satisfied with what he had seen, and his thoughts run so much upon the object of his love, that after his good success in meeting with this tapestry, the beauty and charms of the princess Nouronnihar increased every day the violence of his passion, and he fancied he should be the more easy and happy, the nearer he was to her. After he had satisfied the master of the khan for his apartment, and told him the hour he might come for the key, he shut his door, put the key on the outside, and spreading the tapestry, he and the officer he had brought with him sat down, and, as soon as he had formed his wish, were transported to the inn at which he and his brothers were to meet, and where he passed for a merchant till they came.

Prince Ali, Prince Houssain's second brother, who designed to travel into Persia, to conform himself to the intention of the sultan of the Indies, took the road, having, three days after he parted with his brother, joined a caravan, and, after four days travel. arrived at Schiraz, which was the capital of the kingdom of Persia; and having in the way contracted a friendship with some merchants, passed for a jeweller, and lodged in the same khan with them.

The next morning, while the merchants opened their bales of merchandizes, Prince Ali, who travelled only for his pleasure, and had brought nothing but just necessaries along with him, after he had dressed himself, took a walk into that part of the town which they at Schiraz called the bezestein; which was a spacious and well-built place; it being arched, and those arches supported by large pillars, round which, as well as the walls, there were fine furnished shops of jewellers, goldsmiths, and traders in gold and silver brocades, rich silks, fine linens, and other choice and valuable merchandizes. Prince Ali soon rambled through all the bezestein, and with admiration judged of the riches of the place by the prodigious quantities of the most precious merchandizes that were exposed to view.

But among all the criers who passed backwards and forwards with several sorts of goods, offering to sell them, he was not a little surprised to see one who held an ivory perspective-glass* in his hand, of about a foot in length, and the thickness of a man's thumb, and cried it at thirty purses. At first he thought the crier mad, and to inform himself, went to a shop, and said to the merchant, who stood at the door, Pray, sir, is not that man, pointing to the crier, who cried the ivory perspective-glass at thirty purses, mad? If he is not, I am very much deceived. Indeed, sir, answered the merchant, he was in his right senses yesterday, and I can assure you he is one of the ablest criers we have, and the most employed of any, he being to be confided in when any thing valuable is to be sold; and if he cries the ivory perspective-glass at thirty purses, it must be worth as much, or more, on some account or other. He will come by presently, and we will call him, and you shall be satisfied; in the mean time, sit down on my sofa, and rest yourself.

Prince Ali accepted of the merchant's obliging offer, and presently afterwards the crier passed by. The merchant called him by his name, and, pointing to the prince, said to him, Tell that gentleman, who asked me if you were in your right senses, what you mean by crying that ivory perspective-glass, which seems not to be worth much, at thirty purses! I should be very much amazed myself, if I did not know you. The crier, addressing himself to Prince Ali, said, Sir, you are not the only person that takes me for a madman, on the account of this perspective-glass; you shall judge yourself whether I am or no, when I have told you its property: And I hope you will value it at as high a price as those I have shewed it to already, who had as bad an opinion of me as you.

First, sir, pursued the crier, presenting the ivory pipe to the prince, observe that this pipe is furnished with a glass at both ends, and consider, by looking through one of them you see whatever object you wish to behold. I am, said the prince, ready to make you all imaginable reparation for the scandal I have thrown on you, if you will make the truth of what you advance appear: And as he had the ivory pipe in his hand, after he had looked at the two glasses, he said, Shew me at which of these ends I must look, that I may be satisfied. The crier presently shewed him, and he looked through, wishing, at the same time, to see the sultan his father, whom he immediately beheld in perfect health, set on his throne, in the midst of his council. Afterwards, as there was nothing in the world so dear to him, after the sultan, as the princess Nouronnihar, he wished to see her; and saw her at her toilet, laughing, and in a pleasant humour, with her women about her.

Prince Ali wanted no other proof to be persuaded that this perspective-glass was the most valuable thing in the world, and believed, that if he should neglect to purchase it, he should never meet again with such another rarity: Therefore he said to the crier, I am very sorry that I should have entertained so bad an opinion of you, but hope to make you amends by buying the glass, for I should be very well pleased with it; so tell me the just value, and the lowest price the seller has fixed on it; and do not give yourself any farther trouble to hawk it about, but go with me, and I will pay you the money. The crier assured him, with an oath, that his last orders were to take no less than forty purses; and if he disputed the truth of what he said, he would carry him to him. The prince believed him, took him with him to the khan where he lodged, and told him out the money, and received the perspective-glass.

Prince Ali was overjoyed at his bargain, and persuaded himself, that as his brothers would not be able to meet with any thing so rare and admirable, the princess Nouronnihar would be the recompense of his fatigue and trouble: He thought of nothing but visiting the court of Persia *incognito*, and seeing whatever was curious in Schiraz, and there-abouts, till the caravan with which he came returned back to the Indies. As soon as the caravan was ready to set out, the prince joined them, and arrived happily, without any accident or trouble, otherwise than the length of the journey, and fatigue of travelling, at the place of rendezvous, where he found Prince Houssain: and both waited for Prince Ahmed.

Prince Ahmed, who took the road of Samarcande, the next day after his arrival there, went, as his brothers had done, into the bezestein, where he had not walked long, before he heard a crier, who had an artificial apple in his hand, cry it at five-and-thirty purses: Upon which he stopped the crier, and said to him, Let me see that apple, and tell me what virtue and extraordinary properties it has, to be valued at so high a rate. Sir, said the crier, giving it into his hand, if you look at the outside of this apple, it is very inconsiderable; but if you consider its properties, virtues, and the use and benefit it is of to mankind, you will say it is no price for it, and that he who possesses it is master of a great treasure. In short, it cures all sick persons of the most mortal diseases, whether fevers, pleurisies, plagues, or other malignant distempers; and if the patient is dying, it will recover him immediately, and restore him to perfect health: And this is done after the easiest manner in the world, which is by the patient's smelling the apple.

If I may believe you, replied Prince Ahmed, the virtues of the apple are wonderful, and it is invaluable: But what ground have I for all you tell me, to be persuaded of the truth of this matter? Sir, replied the crier, the thing is known and averred by the whole city of Samarcande; but without going any farther, ask all these merchants you see here, and hear what they say; you will find several of them will tell you they had not been alive this day if they had not made use of this excellent remedy; and that you may the better comprehend what it is, I must tell you, it is the fruit of the study and experiments of a celebrated philosopher of this city, who applied himself all his life-time to the study and knowledge of the virtues of plants and minerals, and at last attended to this composition, by which he performed such surprising cures in this town, as will never be forgot; but died suddenly himself, before he could apply his sovereign remedy; and left his wife and a great many young children behind him, in very indifferent circumstances, who, to support her family, and provide for her children, is resolved to sell it.

While the crier informed Prince Ahmed of the virtues of this artificial apple, a great many persons came about them, and confirmed what he said; and one among the rest said he had a friend dangerously ill, whose life was despaired of; and that was a favourable opportunity to shew Prince Ahmed the experiment: Upon which Prince Ahmed told the crier he would give him forty purses, if he was sensible he cured the sick person.

The crier, who had orders to sell it at that price, said to Prince Ahmed, Come, sir, let us go and make the experiment, and the apple shall be yours; and I can assure you, that it will always have the desired effect. In short, the experiment succeeded, and the prince, after he had counted out to the crier forty purses, and he had delivered the apple to him, waited patiently for the first caravan that should return to the Indies. In the mean time, he saw all that was curious at and about Samarcande, and principally the valley of Soyda, so called from the river which waters it, and is reckoned by the Arabians to be one of the four paradises of this world, for the beauty of its fields and gardens, and fine palaces, and for its fertility in fruit.

At last, Prince Ahmed joined himself to the first caravan that returned to the Indies, and notwithstanding the inevitable fatigues in so long a journey, arrived in perfect health at the inn where the princes Houssain and Ali waited for him.

Prince Ali, who came there some time before Prince Ahmed, asked Prince Houssain, who got thither the first, how long he had been there? who told him, three months: To which he replied, Then certainly you have not been very far. I will tell you nothing now, said Prince Houssain, but only assure you, I was about three months travelling to the place I went to. But then, replied Prince Ali, you made a short abode there. Indeed, brother, said Prince Houssain, you are mistaken; I resided at one place above four or five months, and might have staid longer. Unless you flew back, replied Prince Ali again, I cannot comprehend how you can have been three months here, as you would make me believe.

I tell you the truth, added Prince Houssain, and it is a riddle which I shall not explain to you till our brother Ahmed comes, when I will let you know what rarities I have brought home from my travels. For your part, I know not what you have got, but believe it to be some trifle, because I do not perceive that your baggage is increased. And pray what have you brought? replied prince Ali; for I can see nothing but an ordinary piece of tapestry, with which you cover your sofa; and therefore I think I may return you your railing; and as you seem to make what you have brought a secret, you cannot take it amiss that I do the same.

I look upon the rarity I have purchased, replied Prince Houssain, to excel all others whatever, and should not make any difficulty to shew it to you, and make you own it to be so, and, at the same time, tell you how I came by it, without being in the least apprehensive that that which you have got is to be preferred to it; but it is proper that we should stay till our brother Ahmed arrives, that we may all communicate our good fortunes to each other.

Prince Ali would not enter into a dispute with Prince Houssain on the preference he gave his rarity, but was satisfied, and persuaded that if his perspective-glass was not preferable, it was impossible it should be inferior to it; and therefore agreed to stay till Prince Ahmed arrived, to produce their purchase.

When Prince Ahmed came to his two brothers, and they had embraced with tenderness, and complimented each other on the happiness of meeting together at the same place they set out at, Prince Houssain, as the elder brother, assumed the discourse, and said to them, Brothers, we shall have time enough hereafter to entertain ourselves with the particulars of our travels; but now let us come to that which is of the greatest importance for us to know; and as I do not dispute but that you remember, as well as me, the principal motive which engaged us to travel, therefore let us not conceal from each other our curiosities, but shew them, that we may guess and judge, as near as possible, to which the sultan our father may give the preference.

To set you an example, continued Prince Houssain, I will tell you, that the rarity which I have brought from my travels to the kingdom of Bisnagar is the tapestry on which I sit, which looks but ordinary, and makes no shew; but when I have declared its virtues to you, you will be struck with admiration, and will confess you never heard of any thing like it. In short, whoever sits on it, as we do, and desires to be transported to any place, be it ever so far off, is immediately carried thither. I made the experiment myself, before I paid down the forty purses which I gave for it; and when I had fully satisfied my curiosity at the court of Bisnagar, and had a mind to return, I made use of no other carriage than this wonderful tapestry for myself and servant, who can tell how long we were in coming hither: I will shew you both the experiment when you think fit; and now expect that you should let me know what you have brought, that is to be compared with this tapestry.

Here Prince Houssain made an end of commending the excellency of his tapestry; and Prince Ali, addressing himself to him, said, I must own, brother, that your tapestry is one of the most surprising things imaginable, if it has, as I do not doubt in the least, that property you speak of; but you must allow that there may be other things, I will not say more, but at least as wonderful, of another kind; and to shew you that there are, here is an ivory perspective-glass, which appears no more a rarity than your tapestry, and yet merits as much attention, and cost me as much; and you will be as just as to own that I am not bit, when you know, by experience, that by looking at one end, you see whatever object you wish to behold. I would not have you take my word, added Prince Ali, presenting the perspective-glass to him, but make trial of it yourself.

Prince Houssain took the glass from Prince Ali, and clapped that end to his eye which Prince Ali shewed him, with an intention to see the princess Nouronnihar, and to know how she did; when Prince Ali and Prince Ahmed, who kept their eyes fixed upon him, were extremely surprised to see his countenance change in such a manner as expressed an extraordinary surprise and affliction. Prince Houssain would not give them time to ask what was the matter, but cried out, Alas! princes, to what purpose have we undertaken so long and fatiguing journies, but with the hopes of being recompensed by the possession of the charming Nouronnihar, when, in a few moments, that lovely princess will breathe her last? I saw her in bed, surrounded by her women and eunuchs, who were all in tears, and seem to expect nothing less than her giving up the ghost: Take the glass; see yourselves the miserable state she is in; and mingle your tears with mine.

Prince Ali took the glass out of Prince Houssain's hand, and after he had seen the same object, with a sensible grief, presented it to Prince Ahmed, who took it, to behold the melancholy sight which so much concerned them.

When Prince Ahmed had taken the glass out of Prince Ali's hands, and saw that the princess Nouronnihar's end was so near, he addressed himself to his two brothers, and said, Princes, the princess Nouronnihar, equally the object of our vows, is indeed just at death's door; but provided we make haste, and lose no time, we may preserve her life. Then he took the artificial apple out of his bosom, and shewing it to the princes his brothers, said to them, This apple which you see here cost me as much, and more, than either the tapestry or perspective-glass; and the opportunity that presents itself to shew you its wonderful virtue, makes me not regret the price I gave for it: But, not to keep you longer in suspence, it has the virtue, if a sick person smells to it, though in the last agonies, to restore him to perfect health immediately: I have made the experiment, and can shew its wonderful effect on the person of the princess Nouronnihar, if you will make all the haste imaginable to assist her.

If that is all, replied Prince Houssain, we cannot make more, than by transporting ourselves instantly into her chamber, by the means of my tapestry. Come, lose no time, but sit down by me; it is large enough to hold us all three: But first let us give orders to our servants to set out immediately, and come to us to the palace.

As soon as the order was given, Prince Ali and Prince Ahmed went and sat down by Prince Houssain; and as their interest was the same, they all three formed the same wish, and were transported into the princess Nouronnihar's chamber.

The presence of the three princes, who were so little expected, frightened the princess's women and eunuchs, who could not comprehend by what enchantment three men should be among them; for they did not know them at first; and the eunuchs were ready to fall upon them, as people who had penetrated into the palace, where they were not allowed to come; but they presently recollected themselves, and found the mistake.

Prince Ahmed no sooner perceived himself in Nouronnihar's chamber, and perceiving that dying princess, but he rose off the tapestry, as did also the other two princes, and went to the bed-side, and put the apple under her nose: Some moments after, the princess opened her eyes, and turned her head from one side to another, looking at the persons who stood about her, and then rose up on end in the bed, and asked to be dressed, just as if she had waked out of a sound sleep. Her women having presently informed her, in a manner that shewed their joy, that she was obliged to the three princes for the sudden recovery of her health, and particularly to Prince Ahmed, she immediately expressed a joy to see them, and thanked them all together, and afterwards Prince Ahmed in particular. The princes told her how great a pleasure it was to them to come soon enough to contribute any thing towards relieving her out of the imminent danger she was in, and that they had made the most ardent wishes for her health; and afterwards, as she had called to be got up, they retired.

While the princess was dressing, the princes went to throw themselves at the sultan their father's feet, and pay their respects to him; but when they came before him, they found he had been informed of their arrival by the chief of the princess's eunuchs, and by what means the princess had been perfectly cured. The sultan received and embraced them with the greatest joy, both for their return and the recovery of the princess his niece, whom he loved as well as if she had been his own daughter, and who had been given over by the physicians. After the usual ceremonies and compliments, the princes presented each his rarity; Prince Houssain his tapestry, which he had taken care not to leave behind him in the princess's chamber; Prince Ali his ivory perspective-glass; and Prince Ahmed his artificial apple; and after each had commended their present, when they put it into the sultan's hands, they begged of him to pronounce their fate, and declare to which of them he would give the princess Nouronnihar for a wife, according to his promise.

The sultan of the Indies having heard, without interrupting them, all that the princes could represent farther about their rarities, and being well informed of what had happened in relation to the princess Nouronnihar's cure, remained some time silent, as if he was thinking on what answer he should make. At last he broke silence, and said to them, I would declare for one of you, children, with a great deal of pleasure, if I could do it with justice; but consider whether I can do it or no. It is true, Prince Ahmed, the princess my niece is obliged to your artificial apple for her cure; but I must ask you whether or no you could have been so serviceable to her, if you had not known by Prince Ali's perspective-glass the danger she was in, and Prince Houssain's tapestry had not brought you so soon. Your perspective-glass, Prince Ali, informed you and your brothers that you were like to lose the princess your cousin, and there you must own a great obligation. You must also grant, that that knowledge would have been of no service without the artificial apple and the tapestry. And lastly, Prince Houssain, the princess would be very ungrateful, if she should not shew her acknowledgment of the service of your tapestry, which was so necessary a means towards her cure. But consider, it would have been of little use, had you not been acquainted with the princess's illness by Prince Ali's glass, and Prince Ahmed had not applied his artificial apple. Therefore, as neither tapestry, ivory perspective-glass, nor artificial apple, have the least preference one before the other, but, on the contrary, there is a perfect equality, I cannot grant the princess to any one of you; and the only fruit you have reaped from your travels, is the glory of having equally contributed to restore her health.

If all this be true, added the sultan, you see that I must have recourse to other means to determine certainly in the choice I ought to make among you; and, as there is time enough between this and night, I will do it to-day. Go and get each of you a bow and arrow, and repair to the great plain where they exercise horses; I will soon come to you, and declare, I will give the princess Nouronnihar to him that shoots the farthest. But however, I do not forget to thank you all in general, and each in particular, for the present you brought me. I have a great many rarities in my closet already, but nothing comes up to the singularity of the tapestry, the ivory perspective-glass, and artificial apple, which shall have the first places among them, and shall be preserved carefully, not only for pure curiosity, but to make an advantageous use of them upon all occasions.

The three princes had nothing to say against the decision of the sultan. When they were out of his presence, they each provided themselves with a bow and arrow, which they delivered to one of their officers, and went to the plain appointed, followed by a great concourse of people.

The sultan did not make them wait long for him; and as soon as he arrived, Prince Houssain, as the eldest, took his bow and arrow, and shot first: Prince Ali shot next, and much beyond him; and Prince Ahmed last of all; but it so happened, that nobody could see where his arrow fell; and notwithstanding all the diligence that was used by himself and every body else, it was not to be found far or near: And though it was believed that he shot the farthest, and that he therefore deserved the princess Nouronnihar, it was, however, necessary that his arrow should be found, to make the matter more evident and certain; and notwithstanding his remonstrance, the sultan judged in favour of Prince Ali, and gave orders for preparations to be made for the solemnizing of the nuptials, which were celebrated a few days after, with great magnificence.

Prince Houssain would not honour the feast with his presence; his passion for the princess Nouronnihar was so sincere and lively, that he could scarce support with patience the mortification of seeing the princess in the arms of Prince Ali, who, he said, did not deserve her better, or love her truer, than himself. In short, his grief was so violent and unsupportable, that he left the court, and renounced all right of succession to the crown, to turn dervise, and put himself under the discipline of a famous scheik, who had gained a great reputation for his exemplary life, and had taken up his abode, and that of his disciples, whose number was great, in an agreeable solitude.

Prince Ahmed, urged by the same motive, did not assist at Prince Ali and the princess Nouronnihar's nuptials, any more than his brother Houssain, but did not renounce the world, as he had done. But as he could not imagine what could become of his arrow, he stole away from his attendants, and resolved to search after it, that he might not have any thing to reproach himself with. With this intent, he went to the place where the princes Houssain and Ali's were gathered up, and going straight forwards from thence, looking carefully on both sides of him, he went so far, that at last he began to think that his labour was all in vain; but yet could not help going forwards, till he came to some steep craggy rocks, which were bounds to his journey, and were situated in a barren country, about four leagues distant from whence he set out.

When Prince Ahmed came pretty nigh to these rocks, he perceived his arrow, which he took up, looked earnestly at it, and was in the greatest astonishment to find it was the same he shot away. Certainly, said he to himself, neither I, nor any man living, could throw an arrow so far; and finding it laid flat, not sticking into the ground, he judged that it had rebounded against the rock. There must be some mystery in this, said he to himself again, and it may be advantageous to me: Perhaps fortune, to make me amends for depriving me of what I thought the greatest happiness, may have reserved a greater blessing for my comfort.

As these rocks were very much indented, and some of those indentures were deep, the prince, full of these thoughts, entered into one, and looking about, cast his eyes on an iron door, which seemed to have no lock, but at the same time feared it was fastened; however, thrusting against it, it opened, and discovered an easy descent, but no steps, which he walked down, with his arrow in his hand. At first, he thought he was going into a dark obscure place, but presently a quite different light succeeded that which he came out of, and entering into a large spacious place, at about fifty or sixty paces distant, he perceived a magnificent palace, the structure admirable, which he had not then time enough to look at. At the same time, a lady of a majestic port and air, and of a beauty the richness of her cloaths and jewels was no advantage to, advanced as far as the porch, attended by a large troop of ladies, finely dressed, and so beautiful, that it was difficult to distinguish which was the mistress.

As soon as Prince Ahmed perceived the lady, he made all imaginable haste to go and pay his respects; and the lady, on her part, seeing him coming, prevented him from addressing his discourse to her first, but said to him, Come nearer, Prince Ahmed; you are welcome.

It was no small surprise to the prince to hear himself named in a place he had never heard of, though so nigh to his father's capital, and he could not comprehend how he should be known to a lady who was a stranger to him. At last he returned the lady's compliment, by throwing himself at her feet, and rising up again, said to her, Madam, I return you a thousand thanks for the assurance you give me of a welcome to a place where I believed my imprudent curiosity had made me penetrate too far. But, madam, may I, without being guilty of ill manners, dare to ask you by what adventure you know me, and that you, who live in the same neighbourhood with me, should be so great a stranger to me? Prince, said the lady, let us go into the hall, where I will gratify you in your request.

After these words, the lady led Prince Ahmed into the hall, the noble structure of which, and the gold and azure which embellished the dome, and the inestimable richness of the furniture, appeared so great a novelty to him, that he could not enough express his admiration, by crying out, that he had never in his life beheld any thing like it, and believed that never any thing was ever to be compared to it. I can assure you, replied the lady, that is the least piece of curiosity in my palace, and you will say so when you have seen all the apartments. Then she sat down on a sofa; and when the prince, by her intreaty, had done the same, she said, You are surprised, you say, that I should know you, and not be known by you; but you will no longer be surprised when I inform you who I am. You are undoubtedly sensible that your religion teaches you to believe that the world is inhabited by genies as well as men: I am the daughter of one of the most powerful and distinguished genies, and my name is Paribanon; therefore you ought not to be amazed that I know you, the sultan your father, the princes your brothers, and the princess Nouronnihar. I am no stranger to your lives and travels, of which I can give you all the circumstances, since it was I myself who exposed to sale the artificial apple which you bought at Samarcande; the tapestry which Prince Houssain met with at Bisnagar, and the ivory perspective-glass which Prince Ali brought from Schiraz. This is sufficient to let you know that I am not unacquainted with what relates to you. The only thing that I have to add, is, that you seemed to me worthy of a more happy fate than that of possessing the princess Nouronnihar; and that you might attain to it, I was present when you drew your arrow, and foresaw it would not go beyond Prince Houssain's: I took it in the air, and gave it the necessary motion to strike against the rocks, near which you found it; and tell you, that it lies in your power to make use of the favourable opportunity which presents itself to make you happy.

As the fairy Paribanon pronounced these last words with a different tone, and looked at the same time tenderly upon Prince Ahmed, with a modest blush on her cheeks, it was no hard matter for the prince to comprehend what happiness she meant. He presently considered that the princess Nouronnihar could never be his, and the fairy Paribanon excelled her infinitely in beauty, agreeableness, wit, and, as much as he could conjecture, by the magnificence of the palace, in immense riches. He blessed the moment that the thought of seeking after his arrow a second time, and yielding to his inclination, drew him towards the lovely object which had fired his heart. Madam, replied he, should I, all my life, have the happiness of being your slave, and the admirer of the many charms which ravish my soul, I should think myself the most blessed of men. Pardon in me the boldness which inspires me to ask this favour, and do not refuse to admit into your court a prince who is entirely devoted to you.

Prince, answered the fairy, as I have been a long time my own mistress, and have no dependence on my parents' consent, it is not as a slave that I would admit you into my court, but as a master of my person, and all that belongs to me, by pledging your faith to me, and taking me to be your wife. I hope you will not take my making this proposal amiss. I am mistress of my will, and must add, that the same customs are not observed among fairies as among other ladies, in whom it would not have been decent to have made such advances: But it is what we do, and you ought to be the more obliged to us for it.

Prince Ahmed made no answer to this discourse, but was penetrated with so much acknowledgment, that he could not better express it than by going to kiss the hem of her garment; which she would not permit him to do, but presented her hand, which he kissed a thousand times, and kept fast locked up in his. Well, Prince Ahmed, said she, will you not pledge your faith to me, as well as I give mine to you? Yes, madam, replied the prince, in an ecstasy of joy, what can I do better, and with greater pleasure? Yes, my sultaness, my queen, I will give you my heart, without the least reserve. Then, answered the fairy, you are my husband, and I am your wife: Our marriages are contracted with no other ceremonies, and yet are more firm and strict than those made by men, with all their formalities. But as I suppose, pursued she, that you have ate nothing to-day, a slight repast shall be served up for you, while preparations are making for our nuptial-feast at night, and then I will shew you the apartments of my palace, and you shall judge if this hall is not the meanest part of it.

Some of the fairy's women, who came into the hall with them, and guessed her intentions, went immediately out, and returned presently with some excellent meats and wines.

When Prince Ahmed had ate and drank as much as he cared for, the fairy Paribanon carried him through all the apartments, where he saw diamonds, rubies, emeralds, and all sorts of fine jewels, intermixed with pearls, agate, jasper, porphyry, and all sorts of the most precious marbles. But not to mention the richness of the furniture, which was inestimable, there was such profuseness throughout, that the prince, instead of ever having seen any thing like it, owned that he could not have imagined that there was any thing in the world that could come up to it. Prince, said the fairy, if you admire my palace so much, which indeed is very beautiful, what would you say to the palaces of the chief of our genies, which are much more beautiful, spacious, and magnificent? I could also charm you with my gardens, but we will let that alone till another time: Night draws near, and it will be time to go to supper.

The next hall which the fairy led the prince into, and where the cloth was laid for the feast, was the only apartment the prince had not seen, and not in the least inferior to the others. At his entrance into it, he admired the infinite number of sconces of wax-candles, perfumed with amber, the multitude of which, instead of being confused, were placed with so just a symmetry as formed an agreeable and pleasant sight. A large beaufet was set out with all sorts of gold plate, so finely wrought, that the workmanship was much more valuable than the weight of the gold. Several choruses of beautiful women, richly dressed, and whose voices were ravishing, began a concert, accompanied with all sorts of the most harmonious instruments; and when they were set down at table, the fairy Paribanon took care to help Prince Ahmed with the most delicate meats, which she named as she invited him to eat of them, and which the prince found to be so exquisitely nice, that he commended them without exaggeration, and said, that the entertainment far surpassed those of men. He found also the same excellence in the wines, which neither he nor the fairy tasted of till the desert was served up, which consisted of the choicest sweet-meats and fruits.

After the desert, the fairy Paribanon and Prince Ahmed rose from the table, which was immediately carried away, and sat down on a sofa, at their ease, with cushions of fine silk, curiously embroidered in all sorts of flowers, laid at their backs. Presently after, a great number of genies and fairies danced before them to the door of the chamber where the nuptial bed was made; and when they came there, they divided themselves into two rows, to let them pass, and after that, retired, leaving them to go to bed.

The nuptial feast was continued the next day; or rather, the days following the celebration were a continual feast, which the fairy Paribanon, to whom nothing was difficult, knew how to diversify by new ragouts and choice meats, and new concerts, dancings, plays, and other diversions; which were all so extraordinary, that Prince Ahmed, if he had lived a thousand years among them, could not have imagined.

The fairy's intention was not only to give the prince essential proofs of the sincerity of her love, and violence of her passion, but to let him see, that, as he had no pretensions at his father's court, or any where else, he could meet with nothing comparable to the happiness he enjoyed with her, and to attach him entirely to herself, that he might never leave her. In this scheme she succeeded so well, that Prince Ahmed's passion was not in the least diminished by possession, but increased so much, that, if he would, it was not in his power to forbear loving her.

At the end of six months, Prince Ahmed, who always loved and honoured the sultan his father, conceived a great desire to know how he did; and that desire could not be satisfied, without his absenting, and going himself: He told the fairy of it, and desired she would give him leave.

This discourse alarmed the fairy, and made her fear it was only an excuse to leave her; and thereupon said to him, What disgust can I have given, to oblige you to ask me this leave? Is it possible you should have forgot that you have pledged your faith to me, and that you no longer love one who is also passionately fond of you? Are not the proofs I have given you of it sufficient arguments?

My queen, replied the prince, I am very well convinced of your passion, and should be very unworthy of it, if I did not testify my acknowledgment by a reciprocal love. If you are offended at the leave I asked, I beg of you to forgive me, and I will make all the reparation I am capable of: I did not do it with an intention of displeasing you, but out of a pure motive of respect towards my father, whom I wish to free from the affliction my so long absence must have occasioned him; which must be the greater, as, I presume, he believes that I am dead: But since you do not consent that I should afford him that comfort, I will do what you will, and nothing to displease you.

Prince Ahmed, who did not dissemble, and loved her in his heart as much as he had assured her by word of mouth, no longer insisted on the leave he had asked; and the fairy expressed a great satisfaction thereat: But as he could not absolutely abandon the design he had formed to himself, he often took an opportunity to speak to her of the great qualifications of the sultan his father, and, above all, of his tenderness towards him.

All this he said with a design to move her compassion; for, as he judged, the sultan of the Indies, in the midst of all the rejoicings on account of Prince Ali's and princess Nouronnihar's nuptials, was sensibly afflicted at the absence of the other two princes his sons, though it was not long before he was informed of the resolution Prince Houssain had taken to forsake the world, and the place of retreat he had made choice of.

But as a good father's happiness consists in seeing his children about him, especially when they are deserving of his tenderness, he would have been better pleased had he stayed at his court; but as he could not so much disapprove of his choice, he supported his absence more patiently; though he made the most diligent search after Prince Ahmed, and dispatched couriers to all the provinces of his dominions, with orders to the governors to stop him, and oblige him to return to court: But all the care he took had not the desired success, and his trouble, instead of diminishing, increased. He would often talk with his grand visier about it, and say to him, Visier, thou knowest I always loved Ahmed the best of all my sons, and thou art not insensible of the means I have used to oblige him to return, without success. My grief is so lively, I shall sink under it, if thou hast not compassion on me; therefore, if thou hast any regard for the preservation of my life, I conjure thee to assist and advise me.

The grand visier, no less attached to the person of the sultan than zealous to acquit himself well of the administration of the affairs of state, considering on the means to give his sovereign some ease and relief, bethought of a sorceress of whom he had heard wonders, and proposed to send for her, to consult her. The sultan consented; and the grand visier, after he had sent for her, brought her to him himself.

The sultan said to the magician, The affliction I have been in since the marriage of my son Prince Ali to the princess Nouronnihar, my niece, on the account of the absence of Prince Ahmed, is so well known, and so public, that undoubtedly thou canst be no stranger to it: Therefore, by thy art and skill, canst thou tell me what is become of him? if he is alive; and where he is? what is he a-doing; and if I may hope ever to see him again? To this the sorceress made answer, It is impossible, sir, for me, though ever so skilful, to answer the questions your majesty asks me immediately; but if you give me till to-morrow, I will. The sultan granted her the time, and sent her away, with a promise to recompense her well, if her answer proved according to his desire.

The magician returned the next day, and the grand visier presented her a second time to the sultan. Sir, said she, notwithstanding all the diligence I have used, by applying myself to the rules of my art, to obey your majesty in what you desire to know, I have not been able to discover any thing more, than that Prince Ahmed is alive, but cannot find out where he is.

The sultan of the Indies was forced to be satisfied with this answer, which made him still as uneasy about the prince's fate.

But to return to Prince Ahmed: He so often entertained the fairy Paribanon with the sultan his father, without speaking any more of his desire to see him, that she comprehended at the same time what he meant; and perceiving this restraint he put upon himself, and fearing that her refusal might displease, she first inferred to herself, that his love for her was, by the many proofs she had at all times, sincere; and then considering the injustice she was guilty of, by opposing a son's tenderness for his father, and endeavouring to make him renounce that natural inclination, she resolved to grant him the leave which she saw he always so ardently desired; and one day said to him, Prince, the leave you have asked me to go and see the sultan your father, gave me a just fear that it was only a pretext to shew your inconstancy, and to leave me; and that was the motive which made me refuse you: But now I am so fully convinced, by your actions and words, that I can depend on your constancy and steady love, I change my resolution, and grant you that leave, upon condition that you swear to me first, that your absence shall not be long, and you will return soon. You ought not to be concerned at this condition, since I do not ask it out of a distrust, but to shew you the sincerity of my love.

Prince Ahmed would have thrown himself at the fairy's feet, to shew his acknowledgment; but she prevented him. My sultaness, said he, I am sensible of the great favour you grant me, but want words to return the thanks it deserves, and I conceive: Supply this defect, I conjure you, and whatever you can suggest to yourself, be persuaded I think much more. You may believe, that the oath you require is a pleasure to me, and I take it most willingly, since it is not possible for me to live without you. I go, but the haste I will make to return shall shew you that it is not for fear of being forsworn, but that I follow my inclination, which is to live with you for ever; and if I am absent some time with your consent, I shall always avoid the trouble a too long absence would create me.

Paribanon was the more charmed with these sentiments of Prince Ahmed, because they removed the suspicions she had entertained of him, fearing that his earnest desire to go to see the sultan his father, was only a pretext to break his faith with her. Prince, said she, go when you please: But first, do not take it amiss that I give you some advice how you shall behave yourself where you are going. First, I do not think it proper for you to tell the sultan your father of our marriage, nor of my quality, nor the place where you have been. Beg of him to be satisfied in knowing you are happy, and desire no more; and let him know, that the sole end of your visit is to make him easy, and inform him of your fate.

She appointed twenty gentlemen, well mounted and equipped, to attend him. When all was ready, Prince Ahmed took his leave of the fairy, embraced her, and renewed his promise to return soon. Then his horse, which was most finely caparisoned, and was as beautiful a creature as any in the sultan of the Indies' stables, was led to him, and he mounted him with an extraordinary grace, and pleasure to the fairy; and after he had bid her a last adieu, set forward on his journey.

As it was not a great way to his father's capital, Prince Ahmed soon arrived there. The people, glad to see him again, received him with acclamations of joy, and followed him in crowds to the sultan's apartment. The sultan received and embraced him with great joy, complaining, at the same time, with a fatherly tenderness, of the affliction his long absence had been to him, which, he said, was the more grievous, for that fortune having decided in favour of Prince Ali his brother, he was afraid he might have committed some rash action.

Sir, replied Prince Ahmed, I leave it to your majesty to consider, if, after having lost the princess Nouronnihar, who was the only object of my desires, I could resolve to be a witness of Prince Ali's happiness. If I had been capable of so mean a spirit, what would the court and town have thought of my love, or what your majesty? Love is a passion we cannot throw off when we will; it rules and governs us, and will not permit a true lover to have the right use of his reason. Your majesty knows, that when I shot my arrow, the most extraordinary thing that ever befel any body happened to me; that in so large and open a plain as that we shot in, my arrow was not to be found; upon which I lost the prize, though there was as much justice due to my love as that of the princes my brothers. Though thus vanquished by the caprice of fate, I lost no time in vain complaints, but, to satisfy my perplexed mind, in an adventure which I could not comprehend, I gave my attendants the slip, and returned back again alone to look for my arrow. I sought all about the place where Prince Houssain's and Prince Ali's were found, and where I imagined mine should fall, but all my labour was in vain. However, I was not dismayed, but continued my search in a direct line, and looked carefully about where I could guess it might fall, and, after this manner, had gone above a league, without being able to meet with any thing like an arrow.

When I reflected, that it was not possible that mine should fly so far, I stopped, to examine with myself whether or not I was in my right senses, to flatter myself with having strength enough to shoot an arrow so much farther than any of the greatest heroes in the world were able to do. After I had argued thus with myself, I was ready to abandon my enterprise, but when I was putting my resolution in execution, I found myself drawn forward almost against my will; and after having gone four leagues, to that part of the plain where it is bounded by the rocks, I perceived my arrow, ran and took it up, and knew it to be the same which I shot. But knowing that it was not found at a proper time or place, I was far from thinking your majesty had done me any injustice in declaring for my brother Prince Ali, but interpreted what had happened to me quite otherwise, and never doubted but there was a mystery in it to my advantage, the discovery of which I ought not to neglect, and which I found out, without going much farther. But as to what this mystery is, I must beg your majesty will not take it ill that I am silent, and that you will be satisfied to know from my own mouth, that I am happy, and content with my fate.

In the midst of all my happiness, the only thing that troubled me, or was capable of disturbing me, was the uneasiness I feared your majesty was in upon account of my leaving the court, and your not knowing what was become of me; therefore I thought it my duty to satisfy you in this point. This was the only motive which brought me hither; and the only favour I ask of your majesty is, to give me leave to come often, and pay you my respects, and to know how you do.

Son, answered the sultan of the Indies, I cannot refuse you the leave you ask me; but I should much rather you would resolve to stay with me; at least tell me where I may send to you, if you should fail to come, or when I may think your presence necessary. Sir, replied Prince Ahmed, what your majesty asks of me is part of the mystery I spoke to your majesty of; I beg of you to give me leave to remain silent on this head; for I shall come so frequently, that I am afraid I shall sooner be thought troublesome, than be accused of negligence in my duty.

The sultan of the Indies pressed Prince Ahmed no more, but said to him, Son, I penetrate no farther into your secrets, but leave you at your liberty, but can tell you, that you could not do me a greater pleasure than to come, and by your presence restore to me the joy I have not felt this long time; and that you shall always be welcome when you come, without interrupting your business or pleasure.

Prince Ahmed staid but three days at the sultan his father's court, and the fourth returned to the fairy Paribanon, who did not expect him so soon. His diligence made her condemn herself for suspecting his want of fidelity. She never dissembled in the least, but frankly owned her weakness to the prince, and asked his pardon. Thus the union of these two lovers became perfect.

A month after Prince Ahmed's return from paying a visit to his father, as the fairy Paribanon had observed that the prince, since the time that he gave her an account of his journey, his discourse with his father, and the leave he asked to go and see him often, had never talked of the sultan, as if there had been no such person in the world, whereas before he was always speaking of him; she thought he forebore on her account; therefore she took an opportunity to say to him one day, Prince, tell me, have you forgot the sultan your father? Do not you remember the promise you made to go and see him often? For my part, I have not forgot what you told me at your return, and so put you in mind of it, that you may not be long before you acquit yourself of your promise, the first time however.

Madam, replied Prince Ahmed, with the same mirth the fairy spoke to him, As I know I am not guilty of the forgetfulness you speak of, I rather chuse to be thus reproached, than exposed to a refusal, by shewing unseasonably a desire for a thing which you might not be pleased to grant me so readily. Prince, said the fairy, I would have you, in this affair, not have so much consideration for me, since it is a month since you have seen the sultan your father; pay him another visit to-morrow, and after that, go and see him once a-month, without speaking to me, or waiting for my leave.

Prince Ahmed went the next morning, with the same attendance as before, but much finer, and himself more magnificently mounted, equipped, and dressed, and was received by the sultan with the same joy and satisfaction. For several months he constantly paid his visits, and always in a richer and finer equipage.

At last some visiers, the sultan's favourites, who judged of Prince Ahmed's grandeur and power by the figure he made, abused the liberty the sultan gave them of speaking to him, by making him jealous of his son. They represented to him, that it was but common prudence to know where the prince retired, and how he could afford to live at such a rate, since he had no revenue nor income assigned him; and that he only came to court to brave him, and to shew that he wanted nothing of him to live like a prince; and it was to be feared he might inveigle himself into the people's favour, and dethrone him.

The sultan of the Indies, who was far from thinking that Prince Ahmed could be capable of so pernicious a design as his favourites would make him believe, said to them, You are mistaken; my son loves me, and I am certain of his tenderness and fidelity, as I have given him no reason to be disgusted.

Upon these last words, one of the favourites took an opportunity to say, Your majesty, in the opinion of people of most sense, could not have taken a better method than what you have done with the three princes, about their marriage with the princess Nouronnihar; but who knows whether Prince Ahmed has submitted to his fate with the same resignation as Prince Houssain? May not he imagine, that he only deserved her; and that your majesty, by leaving that matter to be decided by chance, has done him injustice?

Your majesty may say, added the malicious favourite, that Prince Ahmed has given no sign of a dissatisfaction; that our fears are vain; that we are too easily alarmed, and are in the wrong to entertain suspicions of this nature, which may have no ground, against a prince of his blood. But, sir, pursued the favourite, it may be also these suspicions are well grounded. Your majesty is sensible, that, in so nice and important an affair, you cannot be too much upon your guard. Consider, it is the prince's business to dissemble, amuse, and deceive you; and the danger is the greater, as the prince resides not far from your capital: And if your majesty gave but the same attention that we do, you may observe, that every time he comes, he and his attendants are fresh, and their cloaths and housings are clean and bright, as if they were come from the maker's hands; and their horses look as if they had only been walked out.

These are such sufficient signs that Prince Ahmed does not come a great way, that we should think ourselves wanting in our duty, if we did not make our humble remonstrances, that, for your own preservation, and the good of your people, you might take such measures as you should think fit.

When the favourite had made an end of this long speech, the sultan said, Be it as it will, I do not believe my son Ahmed is so wicked as you would persuade me he is; however, I am obliged to you for your good advice, and do not dispute but that it proceeds from your good intentions.

The sultan of the Indies said this, that his favourites might not know the impressions their discourses had made on his mind; which had so alarmed him, that he resolved to have Prince Ahmed watched, unknown to his grand visier. For this end, he sent for the magician, who was introduced by a back-door into his apartment. Thou toldest me the truth, said he, when thou assuredst me my son Ahmed was alive, for which I am obliged to thee; but now thou must do me another pleasure. I have seen him since, and he comes to my court every month, but I cannot learn from him where he resides, and I would not force his secret out of him, but believe thee capable of satisfying my curiosity, without letting him or any of my court know any thing of the matter. Thou knowest, that at present he is here with me, and is used to go without taking leave of me, or any of my court. Go immediately upon the road, and watch him so well, as to find out where he retires, and bring me word.

The magician left the sultan, and knowing the place where Prince Ahmed found his arrow, went immediately thither, and hid herself near the rocks, so that nobody could see her.

The next morning Prince Ahmed set out by day-break, without taking leave either of the sultan or any of his court, according to custom. The magician seeing him coming, followed him with her eyes, till, on a sudden, she lost sight of him and his attendants.

As the rocks were very steep and craggy, they were an insurmountable barrier, so that the magician judged that there were but two things for it; either that the prince retired into some cavern, or an abode of genies or fairies. Thereupon she came out of the place where she was hid, and went directly to the hollow way, which she traced till she came to the farther end, looking carefully about on all sides. But notwithstanding all her diligence, she could perceive no opening, not so much as the iron gate which Prince

Ahmed discovered, which was to be seen and opened to none but men, and only to such whose presence was agreeable to the fairy Paribanon.

The magician, who saw it was in vain for her to search any farther, was obliged to be satisfied with the discovery she had made, and returned to give the sultan an account. When she had told him what she had done, she added, Your majesty may easily understand, after what I have had the honour to tell you, it will be no hard matter to give you the satisfaction you desire of Prince Ahmed's conduct. I will not tell you now what I think, but chuse to let you know it when I can do it, and can give you a just account; to do which I only ask time, and that you will have patience, and give me leave to do it, without knowing first what measures I design to take.

The sultan was very well pleased with the magician's conduct, and said to her, Do you as you think fit; I will wait patiently the event of your promises; and, to encourage her, made her a present of a diamond of great value, telling her, it was only an earnest of the recompense she should have if she did him that important piece of service, which he left to her management.

As Prince Ahmed had obtained the fairy Paribanon's leave to go to the sultan of the Indies' court once a month, he never failed; and the magician knowing the time, went a day or two before to the foot of the rock where she lost sight of the prince and his attendants, and waited there, with an intention to execute the project she had in her head.

The next morning Prince Ahmed went out as usual, at the iron gate, with the same attendants as before, and passed by the magician, whom he knew not to be such, and seeing her lie with her head against the rock, and complaining as if she was in great pain, he pitied her, turned his horse about, and went to her, and asked her what was the matter with her, and what he could do to ease her?

The artful sorceress looked at the prince in a pitiful manner, without ever lifting up her head, and answered, in broken words and sighs, as if she could hardly fetch her breath, That she was going to the capital city, but in the way thither, she was taken with so violent a fever, that her strength failed her, and she was forced to lie down where he saw her, far from any habitation, and without any hopes of assistance.

Good woman, replied Prince Ahmed, you are not so far from help as you imagine: I am ready to assist you and convey you where you shall not only have all possible care taken of you, but where you will meet with a speedy cure; only get up, and let one of my people take you behind him.

At these words, the magician, who pretended sickness only to know where the prince lived, and what he did, refused not the charitable offer he made her; and that her actions might correspond with her words, she made many pretended vain endeavours to get up. At the same time, two of the prince's attendants, alighting off their horses, helped her up, and set her behind another, and mounted their horses again, and followed the prince, who turned back to the iron gate, which was opened by one of his retinue, who rode before: And when he came into the outward court of the fairy's, without dismounting himself, he sent to tell her he wanted to speak with her.

The fairy Paribanon came with all imaginable haste, not knowing what made Prince Ahmed return so soon; who, not giving her time to ask him the reason, said, Princess, I desire you would have compassion on this good woman, pointing to the magician, who was held up by two of his retinue; I found her in the condition you see her in, and promised her the assistance she stands in need of, and am persuaded that you, out of your own goodness, as well as upon my intreaty, will not abandon her.

The fairy Paribanon, who had her eyes fixed upon the pretended sick woman all the time that the prince was talking to her, ordered two of her women, who followed her, to take her from the two men that held her, and carry her into an apartment of the palace, and take as much care of her as herself.

Whilst the two women executed the fairy's commands, she went up to Prince Ahmed, and whispering him in the ear, said, Prince, I commend your compassion, which is worthy of you and your birth: I take a great pleasure in gratifying your good intention; but give me leave to tell you, I am afraid it will be but ill rewarded. This woman is not so sick as she pretends to be; and I am very much mistaken if she is not an impostor, who will be the cause of a great trouble to you. But do not be concerned; let what will be devised against you, be persuaded, that I will deliver you out of all the snares that shall be laid for you. Go and pursue your journey.

This discourse of the fairy did not in the least fright Prince Ahmed. My princess, said he, as I do not remember I ever did, or designed any body an injury, I cannot believe any body can have a thought of doing me one; but if they have, I shall not, nevertheless, forbear doing good, whenever I have an opportunity. After saying so, he took his leave of the fairy, and set forward again for his father's capital, where he soon arrived, and was received as usual by the sultan, who disguised, as much as possible, the trouble the discourse and suspicion of his favourites had given him.

In the mean time, the two women carried the magician into a very fine apartment, richly furnished. First they set her down upon a sofa, with her back supported with a cushion of gold brocade, while they made a bed on the same sofa before her, the quilt of which was finely embroidered with silk, the sheets of the finest linen, and the coverlid cloth of gold. When they had put her into bed, (for the old sorceress pretended that her fever was so violent she could not help herself in the least,) one of the women went out, and returned soon again, with a china dish in her hand, full of a certain liquor, which she presented to the magician, while the other helped her up on her breech. Drink this liquor, said she; it is the water of the fountain of lions, and a sovereign remedy against all fevers whatsoever. You will find the effect of it in less than an hour's time.

The magician, to dissemble the better, took it, after a great deal of intreaty, as if she was very much averse to take that potion; but at last she took the china dish, and holding back her head, swallowed down the liquor. When she was laid down again, the two women covered her up. Lie quiet, said she who brought her the china cup, and get a little sleep, if you can; we will leave you, and hope to find you perfectly cured when we come again an hour hence.

The magician, who came not to act a sick part long, but only to discover Prince Ahmed's retreat, and what made him leave his father's court, being fully satisfied in what she wanted to know, would willingly have declared that the potion had then had its effect, so great was her desire to return to the sultan, to inform him of the success of her commission: But as she had been told that the potion did not operate immediately, she was forced to wait the women's return.

The two women came again at the time they said they should, and found the magician got up and dressed, and set upon the sofa, who, when she saw them open the door of her apartment, cried out, O admirable potion! It has wrought its cure much sooner than you told me it would, and I have waited a long time with impatience, to desire you to carry me to your charitable mistress, to thank her for her kindness, for which I shall always be obliged to her, since being thus cured to a miracle. I shall not lose any time, but shall be able to prosecute my journey.

The two women, who were fairies as well as their mistress, after they had told the magician how glad they were that she was cured so soon, walked before her, and conducted her through several apartments, all more noble than that wherein she lay, into a large hall, the most richly and magnificently furnished of all the palace.

Paribanon was set, in this hall, on a throne of massy gold, enriched with diamonds, rubies, and pearls of an extraordinary size, and attended on each hand by a great number of beautiful fairies, all richly clothed. At the sight of so much majesty, the magician was not only dazzled, but was so amazed, that after she had prostrated herself before the throne, she could not open her lips to thank the fairy, as she proposed. However, Paribanon saved her the trouble, and said to her, Good woman, I am glad I had an opportunity to oblige you, and to see you are able to pursue your journey: I will not detain you, but perhaps you may not be displeased to see my palace; follow my women, and they will shew it you.

The old sorceress, who had not power nor courage to say a word, prostrated herself, with her head to the tapestry that covered the foot of the throne, a second time, and so took her leave, and was conducted by the two fairies through all the same apartments which were shewn to Prince Ahmed at his first arrival there, and examining all the riches and magnificence, she often made great exclamations. But what was the greatest subject of her admiration, was, that the two fairies told her, that all she saw and was surprised at was a mere trifle, in respect of their mistress's grandeur and riches; and that in the extent of her dominions she had so many palaces, that they could not tell the number of them, all of different models and architecture, and as magnificent and noble. In talking of a great many other particulars, they brought her at last to the iron gate at which Prince Ahmed brought her in, and which, after she had taken her leave of them, and thanked them for the pains they had taken, they opened, and wished her a good journey.

After the magician had gone a little way, she turned back again to observe the door, and know it again, but all in vain; for, as I have observed, it was invisible to her and all other women. Except in this circumstance, she was very well satisfied with executing the commission she had taken upon herself, and posted away to the sultan. When she came to the capital, she went a great many bye-ways to get privately to the back-door of the sultan's palace, who, being informed of her arrival, sent for her into his apartment, and perceiving a melancholy hang upon her countenance, he thought she had not succeeded, and said to her, By thy looks, I guess that thy journey has been to no purpose, and that thou hast not made the discovery I expected from thy diligence. Sir, replied the magician, your majesty must give me leave to represent to you, that you ought not to judge by my looks whether or no I have behaved myself well in the execution of the commands you were pleased to honour me with, but by the faithful reports I shall make you of all that has happened to me, and by which you will find that I have not neglected any thing that could render me worthy of your approbation. The melancholy you observe in my face proceeds from another cause than the want of success, which I hope your majesty will have all the reason in the world to be content with, and of which, if you will have patience, the relation I am going to give will inform you.

Then the magician related to the sultan of the Indies how she, pretending to be sick, Prince Ahmed, moved with compassion, had her carried into a subterraneous abode, and presented and recommended her himself to a fairy of an incomparable beauty, desiring her by her care to contribute towards her health. Then she told him with how much complaisance the fairy presently ordered two fairies that attended her to take care of her, and not to leave her till she had recovered; which great condescension, said she, could proceed from no other person but from a wife to a husband. Afterwards, the old sorceress exaggerated on her surprise at the front of the palace, which she said had not its fellow in the world; and gave him an account how the two fairies held her up by each arm, like a sick person, as she feigned to be, that could not walk or support herself; and made a long story of the care they took of her, after they had led her into an apartment; of the potion they made her drink, and the quickness of her cure; how she still pretended sickness, though she never doubted of the virtue of the draught: But, above all, she was sure not to forget the majesty of the fairy, seated on a throne that shined again with jewels, the value of which exceeded all the riches of the kingdom of the Indies; and that, in short, all the other riches which were included in that vast palace were immense.

Here the magician, finishing the relation of the success of her commission, and continuing her discourse, said, What does your majesty think of these unheard-of riches of the fairy? Perhaps you will say you are struck with admiration, and rejoice at the good fortune of Prince Ahmed your son, who enjoys them in common with the fairy. For my part, sir, I beg your majesty to forgive me, if I take the liberty to remonstrate to you, that I think otherwise, and to tell you, that I shudder when I consider the misfortune which may happen to you. And this is the melancholy which I could not so well dissemble, and you so soon perceived. I would believe that Prince Ahmed, of his own nature, is incapable of undertaking any thing against your majesty; but who can answer that the fairy, by her charms and caresses, and the influence she has already over him, may not inspire him with a pernicious design of dethroning your majesty, and seizing the crown of the Indies. This is what your majesty ought to consider as a serious affair, of the utmost importance.

Though the sultan of the Indies was very well persuaded that Prince Ahmed's natural disposition was good, yet he could not help being concerned at the discourse of the old sorceress, to whom, when she was taking her leave, he said, I thank thee for the pains thou hast taken, and thy wholesome advice: I am so sensible of the great importance it is to me, that I shall deliberate upon it in council.

Accordingly he returned to his favourites, with whom he was consulting when he was told of the magician's arrival, and ordered her to follow him. He acquainted them with what he had learned, and communicated to them all the reason he had to fear the fairy's influence over the prince; and asked them what measures they thought most proper to be taken to prevent so great a misfortune. To which one of the favourites, taking upon himself to speak for the rest, said, Your majesty knows who must be the author; and now he is in your court, and in your power, you ought to make no scruple to put him under arrest; and I will not say, take away his life, but make him a close prisoner while he lives. This advice all the other favourites unanimously applauded.

Then the magician, who thought it too violent, asked the sultan's leave to speak, which he granted her, and she said, Sir, I am persuaded the zeal of your counsellors for your majesty's interest makes them propose the arresting Prince Ahmed, but perhaps they will not take it amiss, if I offer to your and their consideration, that if you arrest the prince, you must also detain his retinue, who are all genies; and it is to be thought it will not be easy to seize and secure their persons. Is not their property such, as they can render themselves invisible, and transport themselves to the fairy, and give her an account of the insult offered her husband? and can it be supposed she will let it go unrevenged? But would it not be better, if, by any other means, which might not make so great a noise, the sultan could secure himself against any ill designs Prince Ahmed may have against him, and not injure his majesty's honour, or any body be suspected of giving evil counsel? If his majesty has any opinion of my advice, as genies and fairies can do things impracticable to men, it would pique Prince Ahmed in his honour, to engage him, by means of the fairy, to procure you certain advantages which he will be obliged to do: as, for example, every time your majesty goes into the field, you are obliged to be at a great expence, not only in pavilions and tents for your army, but likewise in mules and camels to carry their baggage. Now, might not you engage him to use his interest with the fairy to procure you a tent which might be carried in a man's hand, and which should be so large, as to shelter your whole army against bad weather?

I need say no more to your majesty: If the prince bring such a tent, you may make a great many other demands, of the same nature, that at last he may sink under the difficulties the impossibility of the executing of them will put him to, notwithstanding the power and fertile inventions of the fairy, who has enticed him from you by her enchantments; that at last he will be ashamed to appear, and will be forced to pass the rest of his life with the fairy, excluded from any commerce with the world; and then your majesty will have no reason to be afraid of any enterprises from him, and cannot be reproached with so detestable an action, as the shedding of a son's blood, or making him a prisoner for life.

When the magician had finished her speech, the sultan asked his favourites if they had any thing better to propose; and finding them all silent, determined to follow the magician's advice, as the most reasonable and most agreeable to his mild government.

The next day, when the prince came into his father's presence, who was talking with his favourites, and had sat down by him, after a conversation on different subjects, the sultan, addressing himself to Prince Ahmed, said, Son, when you came and dispelled those clouds of melancholy which your long absence had brought upon me, you made the place of your retreat a mystery to me. I was satisfied to see you again, and know that you was content with your condition, and would not penetrate farther into your secret; which I found you did not care I should. I do not know why you should use a father after this manner, who ever was, and will be glad of your happiness. However, I know your good fortune, and very much approve of your conduct in marrying a fairy so worthy of your love, and so rich and powerful; as I am informed, it was not possible for me to have procured so great a match for you. And now you are raised to so high a rank as to be envied by every body, but me your father, I not only desire you to preserve the good understanding between us we have lived in hitherto, but that you would use your credit with the fairy to obtain for me a little of her assistance, which I stand in need of in one circumstance, and therefore will make a trial of your interest.

You are not insensible what a great expence, not to mention the embarrassment to my generals and officers, the tents, pavilions, mules and camels which carry them, are to me every time I take the field. Now, if you would but give your attention to do me a pleasure, I am persuaded you could easily procure from her a pavilion that might be carried in a man's hand, and which would extend over a large army: Besides, when you let her know it is for me, though it may be a difficult thing, she will not refuse you: All the world knows fairies are capable of doing most extraordinary things.

Prince Ahmed never expected that the sultan his father would have asked such a thing, which at first appeared so difficult, not to say impossible. Though he knew not absolutely how great the power of genies and fairies was, he doubted whether it extended so far as to compass such a tent as his father desired; moreover, he had never asked any thing of the fairy Paribanon, but was satisfied with the continual and many proofs she had given him of her passion, which he studied to preserve, without any views of interest, farther than her love; therefore he was in the greatest embarrassment imaginable what answer to make. At last he replied, If, sir, after the finding my arrow, I have made my actions a secret to you, the reason was, that it was of no great importance to you to be informed of them; and though I know not how this mystery has been revealed to you, I cannot deny but your information is very just. I have married the fairy you speak of; I love her, and am persuaded she loves me; but can say nothing to the influence your majesty believes I have over her; it is what I have not yet made an experiment of, nor thought of; and should be very glad you would dispense with me for undertaking it; but let me enjoy the happiness of loving and being beloved, without any other views or interest. But the demand of a father is a command upon every child like me, who thinks it my duty to obey him in every thing. And though it is with the greatest reluctance imaginable, I will not fail to ask the favour of my wife your majesty desires, but will not promise you to obtain it; and if I should not have the honour to come again to pay you my respects, that shall be the sign that I have not had success: But, before-hand, I desire you to forgive me, and consider that you yourself have reduced me to this extremity.

Son, replied the sultan of the Indies, I should be very sorry what I ask of you should cause me the displeasure of never seeing you any more. I find you do not know the power a husband has over a wife; and yours would shew that her love to you was very indifferent, if she, with the power she has of a fairy, should refuse you so trifling a request as this I desire you to ask of her for my sake. Lay aside your fears, which proceed from your believing yourself not loved so well as you should be. Go and ask her only; you will find the fairy loves you better than you imagine; and remember, that people, for want of asking, often lose great advantages. Think with yourself, that as you love her, you would refuse her nothing; therefore, if she loves you, no more can she refuse you.

All this discourse of the sultan of the Indies could not persuade Prince Ahmed, who would rather he would have asked any thing else, than exposing him to the hazard of displeasing his dear Paribanon; and so great was his chagrin, that he left the court two days sooner than he used to do.

When he returned back to the fairy, to whom he always appeared with a very gay countenance, she asked him the cause of the alteration she perceived in his looks; and finding, that, instead of answering her, he enquired after her health, to avoid satisfying her, she said to him, I will answer your question when you have answered mine. The prince denied it, a long time, protesting that nothing was the matter with him; but the more he denied it, the more she teazed him, and said to him, I cannot bear to see you in this condition; tell me what makes you so concerned, that I may ease your trouble, whatever may be the cause of it; for it must be very extraordinary, if it is out of my power, unless it be the death of the sultan your father, and in that case, I will contribute all that lies in my power to comfort you.

Prince Ahmed could not long withstand the pressing instances of the fairy. Madam, said he, God prolong the sultan my father's life, and bless him: I left him alive, and in perfect health; therefore this is not the cause of the melancholy you perceive in me, though indeed the sultan is the occasion of my concern, because he has imposed upon me the necessity of being importunate to you. First, you know the care I have taken, with your approbation, to conceal from him the happiness I have to see you, love you, deserve your favour and love, and to have pledged my faith with you; but I cannot tell how he has been informed of it.

Here the fairy Paribanon interrupted Prince Ahmed, and said, If you do not know, I do: Remember what I told you of the woman who made you believe she was sick, on whom you took so much compassion: It is she who has acquainted the sultan your father with what you have taken so much care to hide from him. I told you that she was not sick, as she pretended to be; and she has made it appear so; for, in short, after the women whom I charged to take care of her had given her the sovereign water against all fevers, and which she had no occasion for, she pretended that the water had cured her, and came to take her leave of me, that she might go the sooner; and was in so much haste, that she would have gone away without seeing my palace, if I had not, by bidding my two women shew it her, thought it worth her seeing. But go on, and tell what is the necessity your father has imposed on you to be so importunate, which I desire you will be persuaded can never be.

Madam, pursued Prince Ahmed, you may have observed that hitherto I have been content with your love, and have never asked you any other favour: For what, after the possession of so lovely and charming a wife, can I desire more? But yet I know not how great your power may be, and have taken care not to make trial of it. Consider then, I conjure you, that it is not me, but the sultan my father, who indiscreetly, or at least I think so, begs of you a pavilion large enough to shelter him, his court, and army, from the violence of the weather, and which a man may carry in his hand; but remember it is the sultan my father that asks this favour.

Prince, replied the fairy, smiling, I am sorry that so small a matter should disturb you, and make you so uneasy as you appeared to me. I see two things have contributed towards it; one is, the law you have imposed upon yourself, to be content with loving, and being beloved by me, and to deny yourself the liberty of asking me the least favour that might try my power: the other, I do not doubt, whatever you may say, was, you thought that what your father asked of me was out of my power. As to the first, I commend you for it, and love you the better, if possible, for it; and for the second, I must tell you, that what the sultan your father asks of me is a trifle; and, upon occasion, I can do much more difficult things. Therefore be easy, and persuaded, that far from being importuned, I shall always take a great deal of pleasure in whatever you can desire me to do for your sake. Then the fairy sent for her treasurer, to whom, when she came, she said, Nourgihan, which was her name, bring me the largest pavilion in my treasury. Nourgihan returned presently with the pavilion, which she could not only hold in her hand, but in the palm of her hand, when she shut her fingers, and presented it to her mistress, who gave it to Prince Ahmed to look at.

When Prince Ahmed saw the pavilion which the fairy called the largest in her treasury, he fancied she had a mind to jest with him, and thereupon the marks of his surprise appeared presently in his countenance; which Paribanon perceiving, burst out a-laughing. What, prince, cried she, do you think I jest with you? You will see presently that I am in earnest. Nourgihan, said she to her treasurer, taking the tent out of Prince Ahmed's hands, go and set it up, that the prince may judge whether it might be large enough for the sultan his father.

The treasurer went out immediately with it out of the palace, and carried it a great way off; and when she had set it up, one end reached to the very palace: At which time, the prince thinking it small, found it large enough to shelter two greater armies than that of the sultan his father's, and then said to Paribanon, I ask my princess a thousand pardons for my incredulity; after what I have seen I believe there is nothing impossible to you. You see, said the fairy, that the pavilion is larger than what your father may have occasion for; for you must know, that it has one property, that it is larger or smaller, according to the army it has to cover.

The treasurer took down the tent again, reduced it, and brought it to the prince, who took it, and without staying any longer than till the next day, mounted his horse, and went with the same attendants to the sultan his father.

The sultan, who was persuaded that there could not be any such thing as such a tent as he asked for, was in a great surprise at the prince's diligence. He took the tent, and after he had admired its smallness, his amazement was so great that he could not recover himself. When the tent was set up in the great plain which we have before mentioned, he found it large enough to shelter any army twice as large as he could bring into the field; which he looking upon to be a superfluity that might be troublesome to him, Prince Ahmed told him, that for its size it would always be proportionable to his army.

To outward appearance, the sultan expressed a great obligation to the prince his son for so noble a present, desiring him to return his thanks to the fairy Paribanon, and ordered it to be carefully laid up in his treasury; but within himself, he conceived a greater jealousy than what his flattering favourites and the magician had harboured and suggested to him; considering, that, by the fairy's assistance, the prince his son might perform things that were infinitely out of his power, notwithstanding his grandeur and riches; and therefore he was the more intent upon his ruin, and went to consult the magician again, who advised him to engage the prince to bring him some of the water of the fountain of lions.

In the evening, when the sultan was surrounded as usual by all his court, and the prince came to pay his respects among the rest, he addressed himself to him in these words: Son, said he, I have already expressed to you how much I am obliged to you for the present of the tent you have procured me, that I look upon it as the most valuable thing in all my treasury; but you must do one thing more for me, which will be every whit as agreeable to me. I am informed, that the fairy your spouse makes use of a certain water called the water of the fountain of lions, which cures all sorts of fevers, even the most dangerous; and as I am perfectly well persuaded my health is dear to you, I do not doubt but you will ask her for a bottle of that water for me, and bring it to me as a sovereign medicine, which I may make use of when I have occasion. Do me this other important piece of service, and thereby complete the duty of a good son towards a tender father.

Prince Ahmed, who believed that the sultan his father would have been satisfied with so singular and useful a tent as that which he had brought, and that he would not have imposed any new task upon him, which might hazard the fairy's displeasure, was struck almost dumb at this new request, notwithstanding she had given him the assurance of granting him whatever lay in her power. After a long silence, he said, I beg of your majesty to be assured, that there is nothing I would not undertake to procure you, which may contribute to the prolonging your life, but I could wish it might not be by the means of my wife. For this reason, I dare not promise to bring the water; all I can do is, I will assure you I will ask it of her; but my reluctance is as great as when I asked her for the tent.

The next morning Prince Ahmed returned to the fairy Paribanon, and related to her, sincerely and faithfully, all that had passed at the sultan his father's court, (from the giving of the tent, which he told her he received with the utmost acknowledgment of the favour she had done him), to the new request he had charged him to make. And when he had done, he added: But, my princess, I only tell you this as a plain account of what passed between me and my father, but leave you to your own pleasure, whether you will gratify or reject this his new desire.

No, no, replied the fairy Paribanon, I am glad that the sultan of the Indies knows that you are not indifferent to me; I will satisfy him; and whatever advice the magician can give him, (for I see that he hearkens to her), he shall find no fault with you nor me: And yet there is a great deal of wickedness in this demand, as you will understand by what I am going to tell you. The fountain of lions is situated in the middle of a court of a great castle, the entrance into which is guarded by four fierce lions, two of which sleep alternately, while the other two are awake: but do not let that frighten you; I will give you means to pass by them without any danger.

The fairy Paribanon was at that time very hard at work; and as she had several clews of thread by her, she took up one, and presenting it to Prince Ahmed, said, First, take this clew* of thread; I will tell you presently the use of it. In the second place, you must have two horses; one you must ride yourself, and the other you must lead, which must be loaded with a sheep cut into four quarters, that must be killed to-day. In the third place, you must be provided with a bottle, which I will give you, to bring the water in: Set out early to-morrow morning, and when you have passed the iron gate, throw the clew of thread before you, which will roll till it comes to the gates of the castle: Follow it, and when it stops, as the gates will be open, you will see the four lions; the two that are awake will, by their roaring, wake the other two; but do not be frightened, but throw each of them a quarter of mutton, and then clap spurs to your horse, and ride to the fountain; fill your bottle without alighting, and then return with the same expedition: the lions will be so busy eating, they will let you pass by them.

Prince Ahmed set out the next morning at the time appointed him by the fairy, and followed her directions punctually. When he arrived at the gates of the castle, he distributed the quarters of mutton among the four lions, and passing through the midst of them with intrepidity, got to the fountain, filled his bottle, and returned as safe and sound back as he went. When he had got at a little distance from the castle-gates, he turned him about, and perceiving two of the lions coming after him, he drew his sabre, and prepared himself for defence. But as he went forwards, seeing one of them turned out of the road at some distance, and shewed, by his head and tail, that he did not come to do him any harm, but only to go before him, and that the other staid behind to follow, he put his sword up again in its scabbard. Guarded in this manner, he arrived at the capital of the Indies; but the lions never left him till they had conducted him to the gates of the sultan's palace; after which they returned the same way they came, though not without frightening all that saw them, for all they went in a very gentle manner, and shewed no fierceness.

A great many officers came to attend the prince while he dismounted his horse, and afterwards conducted him into the sultan's apartment, who was at that time surrounded with his favourites. He approached towards the throne, laid the bottle at the sultan's feet, and kissed the rich tapestry which covered his footstool, and then said, I have brought you, sir, the healthful water which your majesty desired so much to keep among your other rarities in your treasury; but, at the same time, wish you such extraordinary health, as never to have occasion to make use of it.

After the prince had made an end of his compliment, the sultan placed him on his right hand, and then said to him, Son, I am very much obliged to you for this valuable present; as also for the great danger you have exposed yourself to upon my account, (which I have been informed of by a magician who knows the fountain of lions;) but do me the pleasure, continued he, to inform me by what address, or rather by what incredible power, you have been secured.

Sir, replied Prince Ahmed, I have no share in the compliment your majesty is pleased to make me; all the honour is due to the fairy my spouse, whose good advice I followed. Then he informed the sultan what those directions were, and, by the relation of this his expedition, let him know how well he had behaved himself. When he had done, the sultan, who shewed outwardly all the demonstrations of great joy, but secretly became more jealous, retired into an inward apartment, where he sent for the magician.

The magician, at her arrival, saved the sultan the trouble to tell her of the success of Prince Ahmed's journey, which she had heard of before she came, and therefore was prepared with an infallible means, as she pretended. This means she communicated to the sultan, who declared it the next day to the prince, in the midst of all his courtiers, in these words: Son, said he, I have one thing more to ask of you; after which, I shall expect nothing more from your obedience, nor your interest with your wife. This request is, to bring me a man not above a foot and an half high, and whose beard is thirty feet long, who carries a bar of iron upon his shoulders of five hundred weight, which he uses as a quarter-staff.

Prince Ahmed, who did not believe that there was such a man in the world as his father described, would gladly have excused himself; but the sultan persisted in his demand, and told him, the fairy could do more incredible things.

The next day, the prince returned to his dear Paribanon, to whom he told his father's new demand, which, he said, he looked upon to be a thing more impossible than the two first; for, added he, I cannot imagine there can be such a man in the world: Without doubt, he has a mind to try whether or no I am so silly as to go about it, or he has a design on my ruin. In short, how can he suppose that I should lay hold on a man so well armed, though he is but little? What arms can I make use of to reduce him to my will? If there are any means, I beg you will tell them, and let me come off with honour this time.

Do not affright yourself, prince, replied the fairy: You ran a risk in fetching the water of the fountain of lions for your father; but there is no danger in finding out this man, who is my brother Schaibar; but is so far from being like me, though we both had the same father, that he is of so violent a nature, that nothing can prevent his giving bloody marks of his resentment for a slight offence; yet, on the other hand, is so good as to oblige any one in whatever they desire. He is made exactly as the sultan your father has described him, and has no other arms than a bar of iron of five hundred pounds weight, without which he never stirs, and which makes him respected. I will send for him, and you shall judge of the truth of what I tell you; but be sure to prepare yourself against being frightened at his extraordinary figure, when you see him. What! my queen, replied Prince Ahmed, do you say Schaibar is your brother? Let him be never so ugly or deformed, I shall be so far from being frightened at the sight of him, that, as our brother, I shall honour and love him.

The fairy ordered a gold chafing-dish to be set, with a fire in it, under the porch of her palace, with a box of the same metal, (which was a present to her;) out of which taking a perfume, and throwing it into the fire, there arose a thick cloud of smoke.

Some moments after, the fairy said to Prince Ahmed, See, there comes my brother. The prince immediately perceived Schaibar coming gravely, with his heavy bar on his shoulder, his long beard, which he held up before him, and a pair of thick mustacheos, which he tucked behind his ears, and almost covered his face; his eyes were very small, and deep set in his head, which was far from being of the smallest size, and on which he wore a grenadier's cap;* Besides all this, he was very much hump-backed.

If Prince Ahmed had not known that Schaibar was Paribanon's brother, he would not have been able to have looked at him without fear; but knowing first who he was, he stood by the fairy without the least concern.

Schaibar, as he came forwards, looked at the prince earnestly enough to have chilled his blood in his veins, and asked Paribanon, when he first accosted her, who that man was? to which she replied, He is my husband, brother; his name is Ahmed; he is son to the sultan of the Indies. The reason why I did not invite you to my wedding, was, I was unwilling to divert you from an expedition you was engaged in, and from which I heard, with pleasure, you returned victorious; and so took the liberty now to call for you.

At these words, Schaibar, looking on Prince Ahmed favourably, said, Is there any thing, sister, wherein I can serve him? It is enough to me that he is your husband, to engage me to do for him whatever he desires. The sultan his father, replied Paribanon, has a curiosity to see you; and I desire he may be your guide to the sultan's court. He needs but lead me the way; I will follow him. Brother, replied Paribanon, it is too late to go to-day; therefore stay till to-morrow morning; and, in the mean time, I will inform you of all that has passed between the sultan of the Indies and Prince Ahmed since our marriage.

The next morning, after Schaibar had been informed of the affair, he and Prince Ahmed set out for the sultan's court. When they arrived at the gates of the capital, the people no sooner saw Schaibar, but they ran and hid themselves; and some shut up their shops, and locked themselves up in their houses; while others, flying, communicated their fear to all they met, who staid not to look behind them, but ran too; insomuch that Schaibar and Prince Ahmed, as they went along, found the streets all desolate, till they came to the palace, where the porters, instead of keeping the gates, ran away too; so that the prince and Schaibar advanced without any obstacle to the council-hall, where the sultan was seated on his throne, and giving audience. Here likewise the huissirs, at the approach of Schaibar, abandoned their posts, and gave them free admittance.

Schaibar went boldly and fiercely up to the throne, without waiting to be presented by Prince Ahmed, and accosted the sultan of the Indies in these words: Thou hast asked for me, said he; see, here I am; what wouldst thou have with me?

The sultan, instead of answering him, clapped his hands before his eyes, to avoid the sight of so terrible an object; at which uncivil and rude reception Schaibar was so much provoked, after he had given him the trouble to come so far, that he instantly lifted up his iron bar, and killed him, before Prince Ahmed could intercede in his behalf. All that he could do, was to prevent his killing the grand visier, who sat not far from him, representing to him, that he had always given the sultan his father good advice. These are they, then, said Schaibar, who gave him bad; and as he pronounced these words, he killed all the other visiers and flattering favourites of the sultan, who were Prince Ahmed's enemies: Every time he struck, he killed some one or other; and none escaped but they who were so frightened as not to stand staring and gaping, and who saved themselves by flight.

When this terrible execution was over, Schaibar came out of the council-hall into the midst of the court-yard, with the iron bar upon his shoulder, and, looking hard at the grand visier, who owed his life to Prince Ahmed, he said, I know there is a certain magician who is a greater enemy of my brother-in-law than all these base favourites I have chastised: Let the magician be brought to me presently. The grand visier immediately sent for her; and as soon as she was brought, Schaibar said, at the time he fetched a stroke at her with his iron bar, Take the reward of thy pernicious counsel, and learn to feign sickness again.

After this, he said, This is not yet enough; I will use the whole town after the same manner, if they do not immediately acknowledge Prince Ahmed, my brother-in-law, for their sultan, and the sultan of the Indies. Then all that were there present made the air echo again with the repeated acclamations of Long life to Sultan Ahmed! and immediately after, he was proclaimed through the whole town. Schaibar made him be clothed in the royal vestments, installed him on the throne, and, after he had made all swear homage and fidelity to him, went and fetched his sister Paribanon, whom he brought with all the pomp and grandeur imaginable, and made her to be owned sultaness of the Indies.

As for Prince Ali and Princess Nouronnihar, as they had no hand in the conspiracy against Prince Ahmed, and knew nothing of any, Prince Ahmed assigned them a considerable province, with its capital, where they spent the rest of their lives. Afterwards he sent an officer to Prince Houssain, to acquaint him with the change, and make him an offer of which province he liked best; but that prince thought himself so happy in his solitude, that he bid the officer return the sultan his brother thanks for the kindness he designed him, assuring him of his submission, and that the only favour he desired of him was, to give him leave to live retired in the place he had made choice of for his retreat.

The Story of the Two Sisters who envied their younger Sister

THERE was a prince of Persia, named Khosrouschah, who, when he first came to his crown, to have a knowledge of the world, took a great pleasure in night adventures. He often disguised himself, attended by a trusty minister, disguised like him, and rambled through the whole city, and met with a great many particular adventures, which I shall not at present entertain your majesty with; but I hope you will hear with pleasure what happened to him upon his first ramble, which was in a little time after his accession to his father's throne, who, dying in a good old age, left him heir to the kingdom of Persia.

After the ceremonies of his deceased father's funeral rites and his own coronation were over, the new sultan Khosrouschah, as well through inclination as duty, went out one evening, attended by his grand visier, disguised like himself, to take notice of the regularity observed by the magistrates. Passing through a street in that part of the town where the meaner sort of people lived, he heard some people talking very loud; and going up close to the house from whence the noise came, and looking through a crack in the door, perceived the light, and three sisters on a sofa, who were entered into a chit-chat after supper. By what the eldest said, he presently understood the subject of their discourse was wishes; for, said she, since we have got upon wishes, mine shall be to have the sultan's baker for my husband; for then I shall eat my belly-full of that bread, which, by way of excellence, is called the sultan's bread: Now let us see if your tastes are as good as mine. For my part, replied the second sister, I wish I was the sultan's chief cook's wife, for then I should eat of the most excellent ragouts; and as I am persuaded that the sultan's bread is common in the palace, I should not want any of that: therefore you see, sister, addressing herself to her eldest sister, that I have a better fancy than you.

Then the youngest sister, who was very beautiful, and had more charms and wit than the two eldest, spoke in her turn. For my part, sisters, said she, I shall not limit my desires, but will take a higher flight; and, since we are upon wishing, I wish to be the sultan's wife: I would make him father of a prince, whose hair shall be gold on the one side of his head, and silver on the other; when he cries, the tears that fall from his eyes shall be pearls; and when he smiles, his vermillion lips shall look like a rose-bud fresh blown.

The three sisters' wishes, particularly the youngest's, seemed so singular to the sultan Khosrouschah, that he resolved to gratify them in their desires; and, without communicating this his design to his grand visier, he charged him only to take notice of the house, and bring the three sisters before him the next day.

The grand visier, in executing the sultan's orders, would but just give the three sisters time to dress themselves, and brought them to the palace, and presented them to the sultan, who said to them, Do you remember the wishes you made last night, when you were all in so pleasant a mood? Come, speak the truth; I must know what they were.

At this discourse the three sisters were very much confounded: They cast down their eyes, and blushed; and the colour which rose in the cheeks of the youngest quite captivated the sultan's heart; and out of modesty, and for fear they might have offended the sultan by their discourse, they remained silent. The sultan, guessing at their thoughts, to encourage them, said, Fear nothing; I did not send for you for any crime you have committed; and since I see that the question I ask you shocks you, and I know every one's wish, I will ease you of your fears. You, added he, that wished to be my wife, you shall have your desire this day; and you, continued he, addressing himself to the two eldest sisters, you shall also be married to my chief baker and cook.

As soon as the sultan had declared his pleasure, the youngest sister, setting her eldest an example, threw herself at the sultan's feet, to express her acknowledgment. Sir, said she, my wish, since it is come to your majesty's knowledge, was only made by way of discourse and amusement: I am unworthy of the honour you do me, and ask pardon for my boldness. The two other sisters would have excused themselves also; but the sultan, interrupting them, said, No, no, it shall be so; every one's wish shall be fulfilled.

The nuptials were all celebrated that day, as the sultan had resolved, but after a different manner. The youngest sister's were solemnized with all the rejoicings usual at the marriages of the sultans of Persia; and the other two sisters according to the quality and distinction of their husbands; the one as the sultan's chief baker, and the other as head cook.

The two elder sisters thought the disproportion of their marriages infinitely great; and this consideration made them far from being content, though they were arrived at the utmost height of their wishes, and much beyond their hopes. They were so much possessed with envy, that it not only disturbed their own joy, but was the cause of great troubles and afflictions to the sultaness their younger sister. But at that time they had not an opportunity to communicate their thoughts to each other upon the preference the sultan had given their younger sister to their prejudice, but were altogether employed in dressing themselves against the celebration of their marriages. Some days afterwards, when they had an opportunity of seeing each other at the public balls, the eldest sister said to the other, Well, sister, what say you to our sister's great fortune? Is not she a fine person to be a sultaness? I must own, said the other sister, I cannot conceive what charms the sultan could discover in her, to be so bewitched by a young jade: That because she was somewhat younger than us, was that a reason sufficient for him to prefer her? You were as worthy of his bed, and in justice he ought to have made choice of you.

Sister, said the elder, I should not have said any thing, if the sultan had but pitched upon you; but that he should chuse that pert slut, is what grieves me; but I will revenge myself; and you, I think, are as much concerned as me; therefore I would have us concert measures together, and communicate to me which way you can imagine to mortify her; while I, on my side, will inform you what my desire of revenge shall suggest to me.

After this wicked plot, the two sisters saw each other very frequently, and consulted how they might disturb and interrupt the happiness of the sultaness their youngest sister. They proposed a great many ways; but in deliberating about the manner of executing them, they found so many difficulties, that they durst not attempt them. In the mean time, they often went together to make her visits, with a detestable dissimulation, and every time gave her all the marks of friendship they could imagine, to persuade her how overjoyed they were to have a sister raised to so high a fortune. The sultaness, for her part, always received them with all the demonstrations of esteem and value they could expect from a sister who was not puffed up with her high dignity, and loved them as cordially as before.

Some months after their marriage, the sultaness found herself to be with child; upon which the sultan expressed great joy, which was communicated to all the court, and so spread throughout the capital city, and all Persia. Upon this news, the two sisters came to pay their compliments; and, entering into a discourse with their sister about her lying-in, they proffered their service to deliver her, desiring her, if she was not provided with a midwife, to accept of them.

The sultaness said to them, most obligingly, Sisters, I should desire no better, if it was absolutely in my power to make choice of you: however, I am obliged to you for your good will, but must submit to do as the sultan thinks fit. Let your husbands make interest, and get some courtier to ask this favour of the sultan; and if he speaks to me about it, be assured, that I shall not only express the pleasure he does me, but thank him for making choice of you.

The two husbands applied themselves to some courtiers, their patrons, and begged of them to use their interest to procure their wives the honour they aspired to. Those patrons interceded so much in their behalf, as that the sultan promised them to consider of it, and was as good as his word; for, in conversation with the sultaness on that affair, he told her, that he thought her sisters were the most proper persons to assist her in her labour, but did not think fit to name and appoint them to be her midwives before he asked her consent. The sultaness, sensible of the deference the sultan so obligingly paid her, said to him, Sir, I am ready to do as your majesty shall please to command me; but since you have been so kind as to think of my sisters, I thank you for that regard you have shewn them for my sake; and therefore I shall not dissemble with you, but tell you, I had rather have them than strangers.

Then the sultan Khosrouschah named the sultaness's two sisters to be her midwives; and from that time they passed to and fro to the palace, overjoyed at the opportunity they should have of executing the detestable wickedness they had meditated against the sultaness their sister.

When the sultaness's reckoning was out, she was safely delivered of a young prince, as bright as the day; but neither his innocence nor beauty were capable of moving the cruel hearts of the merciless sisters. They wrapped him up carelessly in his blankets, and put him into a little basket, which they abandoned to the stream of a small canal which ran under the sultaness's apartment, and declared she was delivered of a little dead dog, which they produced. This disagreeable news was presently told to the sultan, who conceived so much grief and anger thereat, as might have proved fatal to the sultaness, if his grand visier had not represented to him, that he could not, without injustice, make her answerable for the variations of nature.

In the mean time, the basket in which the little prince was exposed was carried by the stream beyond a wall which limited the prospect of the sultaness's apartment, and from thence floated with the current down the gardens. By chance the intendant of the sultan's gardens, one of the principal and most considerable of the officers of the kingdom, was walking by the side of this canal, and, perceiving a basket floating, called to a gardener, who was not far off, and bid him come presently to him, and reach him that basket, which he shewed him, that he might see what was in it. The gardener, with a spade he had in his hand, brought the basket to the side of the canal, and took it up, and gave it to him.

The intendant of the gardens was extremely surprised to see a child in the basket, which, though he easily knew it to be but just born, had very fine features. This intendant had been married several years, and though he had always been desirous of having children, Heaven had never blessed him with any. This accident interrupted his walk. He made the gardener follow him with the child; and when he came to his own house, which was situated at the entrance into the gardens of the palace, he went into his wife's apartment. Wife, said he, as we have no children of our own, God has sent us a boy here: I recommend him to you; provide him a nurse presently, and take as much care of him as if he were our own son; for, from this moment, I acknowledge him as such. The intendant's wife received the child with a great deal of joy, and took a great pleasure in having the care of him. The intendant himself would not inquire too narrowly from whence the child came; but knew very well it came not far off the sultaness's apartment, and that it was not his business to examine too far into secrets, nor to create disturbances.

The year after, the sultaness was brought to bed of another prince, on whom the ill-natured sisters had no more compassion than on his brother, but exposed him likewise in a basket, and set him adrift in the canal, pretending this time that the sultaness was delivered of a cat. It was happy also for this child that the intendant of the gardens was walking by the canal-side, who had it carried to his wife, and charged her to take as much care of it as of the first; which suited as well her inclination as it was agreeable to the intendant.

The sultan of Persia was more enraged this time against the sultaness than before, and she had felt the effects of his anger, if the grand visier, by his remonstrances, had not opposed him.

The third time the sultaness lay in, she was delivered of a princess; which innocent babe underwent the same fate as the princes her brothers, but was preserved from a certain death by the compassion and charity of the intendant, as well as the two princes her brothers.

To this inhumanity the two sisters added a lie, and used the same cheat as before. They produced a piece of wood, and affirmed it to be a mole, which the sultaness was delivered of.

The sultan Khosrouschah could no longer contain himself, when he was informed of the news. What! said he, this woman, unworthy of my bed, will fill my palace with monsters? Let her live! No, it shall not be, added he; she is a monster herself, and I will rid the world of her. He pronounced this sentence of death, and ordered the grand visier to take care to have her executed.

The grand visier and the courtiers who were present cast themselves at the sultan's feet, to beg of him to revoke that sentence. Your majesty, I hope, will give me leave, said the grand visier, to represent to you, that the laws which condemn persons to death were made to punish crimes: The three extraordinary lyings-in of the sultaness are no crimes; for in what can she be said to have contributed towards them? A great many other women have done, and do the same every day, and are to be pitied, but not punished. Your majesty may abstain from seeing her, and let her live: The affliction in which she will spend the rest of her life, after the loss of your favour, will be a punishment great enough.

The sultan of Persia considered with himself, and found that it was injustice in him to condemn the sultaness to death, and said, Let her live then; I will give her life; but it shall be on this condition, that she shall desire to die more than once a-day. Let a place be built for her at the gate of the principal mosque, with iron bars to the windows, and let her be put into it, in the coarsest habit; and every mussulman that shall go into the mosque to prayers shall spit in her face: If any one fail, I will have him exposed to the same punishment; and that I may be punctually obeyed, I charge you, visier, to appoint persons to see this done.

The sultan pronounced this last sentence in a tone of so much resolution, that the grand visier durst not open his mouth; and it was executed, to the great satisfaction of the two envious sisters. A cage or lodge was built, and the sultaness, truly worthy of compassion, as soon as her month was up, was put into it, and exposed ignominiously to the contempt of the people; which usage, as she did not deserve, she bore with a great deal of constancy and resolution, to the admiration, as well as compassion, of those who judged better things than the vulgar.

The two princes and the princess were nursed and brought up, by the intendant of the gardens and his wife, with all the tenderness of a true father and mother; and as they advanced in age, they all shewed marks of superior greatness; and the princess, in particular, a charming beauty, which increased the affections of the intendant and his wife, who called the name of the eldest prince, Bahman, and the second Perviz, both names of the most ancient sultans of Persia; and the princess, Parizade, whose name also had been borne by several sultanesses.

As soon as the two princes were old enough, the intendant provided proper masters to teach them to read and write; and the princess, their sister, who was often with them when they were learning their lessons, shewing a great desire to learn to read and write, though much younger than they, the intendant was so much taken with that disposition of hers, that he ordered the master to teach her also, who, by emulation, and her pretty, lively, and piercing wit, became, in a little time, as great a proficient as her brothers.

From that time, the brothers and sister had all the same masters in other arts and sciences, as geography, history, &c., all which came so easily to them, and, in a little time, they made so wonderful a progress, that their masters were amazed, and frankly owned, that if they held on so but a little longer, they could teach them no farther.

At the hours given them for their recreation, the princess learned to sing and play upon all sorts of instruments; and when the princes were learning to mount the managed horse, and to ride, she would not permit them to have that advantage over her, but went through all exercises with them, learning to ride the great horse, bend the bow, and dart the javelin, and oftentimes excelled in them.

The intendant of the gardens was so overjoyed to find his adopted children so accomplished in all the perfections of body and mind, and that they answered so well the charge he had been at upon their education, that he resolved to be still at a greater expence; for, whereas he had till then been content only with his house at the entrance of the garden, and kept no country-house, he, upon their account, purchased a country-seat, at a small distance from the town, and laid out a great sum of money there, in arable lands, meadows and woods. As the house was not fine, nor large enough, he pulled it down, and spared no expence to make it magnificent. He went every day to hasten, by his presence, the great number of workmen he had at work; and as soon as one apartment was finished, and fit to receive him, he staid there for several days together, when his presence was not necessary at court; and by his diligence, the house was finished answerable to the magnificence of the edifice. Afterwards he made gardens, according to the plan he had drawn out, and the manner of the great lords in Persia, and took in a large compass of ground for a park, which he walled round and stocked with fallow-deer, that the princes and princess might divert themselves with hunting when they pleased.

When the country-seat was finished, the intendant of the gardens went and cast himself at the sultan's feet, and after representing to him how long he had served him, and the infirmities he found growing upon him, he begged he might deliver up his charge and post, and retire. The sultan gave him leave, and the sooner, because he was satisfied of his long services, both in his father's reign and during his own; and before he went from him, he asked him what recompense he should give him? Sir, replied the intendant of the gardens, I have received so many obligations from your majesty, and the late sultan your father, of happy memory, that I desire no more than the honour of dying in your favour.

He took his leave of the sultan Khosrouschah, and afterwards returned to the country retreat he had built, with the two princes, Bahman and Perviz, and the princess Parizade: For his wife, she had been dead some years; and he himself had lived not above six months with them before he was surprised by so sudden a death, that he had not time to give the least account of their birth, which he had resolved to do that night. They lived as they always had done, and agreeable to the education he had given them.

The princes Bahman and Perviz, and the princess Parizade, who knew no other than that the intendant of the sultan's gardens was their father, regretted and bewailed him as such, and paid him all the honours in his funeral obsequies which their duty and gratitude required of them. They were content with the plentiful fortune he left them, and lived together in a perfect union, free from the ambition of distinguishing themselves at court, in places of great honour, which they might easily have compassed.

One day, when the two princes were at hunting, and the princess Parizade stayed at home, a religious old woman came to the gate, and desired leave to go in and say her prayers, it being then the hour. The servants went and asked the princess's leave, who ordered them to shew her into the oratory; which the intendant had taken care to fit up in this house, for want of a mosque in the neighbourhood; and bid them also, after she had done prayers, shew her the house and gardens, and then bring her to her.

The religious old woman went into the oratory, said her prayers, and when she came out again, two of the princess's women, who waited on her, invited her to see the house and gardens, which civility she accepted of, and followed them from one apartment to another, and observed, as a person who understood what belonged to furniture, the nice disposition of every thing. Afterwards she was conducted to the princess, who waited for her in the great hall, which, in propriety, beauty, and richness, exceeded all the apartments she had admired before.

As soon as the princess saw the devout woman, she said to her, Good mother, come near, and sit down by me; I am overjoyed at the happiness of having the opportunity of profiting for some moments by the good example and discourse of such a person as you, who has taken the right way, by dedicating yourself to the service of God: I wish every body were as wise.

The religious woman, instead of sitting upon a sofa, would only sit upon the edge of it; but the princess would not permit her to do so, but got off her seat, and taking her by the hand, obliged her to come and sit by her. The good woman, sensible of the civility, said, Madam, I ought not to have so much respect shewn me; but since you command me, I will obey you. When she had sat down, before they entered into any conversation, one of the princess's women brought a little table of mother-of-pearl and ebony, with a china dish of cakes upon it, and a great many others full of fruits in season, and wet and dry sweet-meats set round it.

The princess took up one of the cakes, and presenting her with it, said, Come, eat, good mother, and make choice of what you like best; you had need to have something on your stomach, after coming so far. Madam, replied the good woman, I am not used to eat such nice things; but will not refuse what God has sent me by so liberal a hand.

While the religious woman was eating, the princess ate something too, to bear her company, and asked her a great many questions upon the exercise of her devotion, and how she lived; all which questions she answered with great modesty. Talking of several things, at last she asked her how she liked the house?

Madam, answered the devotee, I must certainly have very bad judgment to disapprove of it, since it is beautiful, regular, and magnificently furnished, and all its ornaments well adjusted: Its situation is in an agreeable and pleasant part of the country, and no gardens can be more delightful; but yet if you will give me leave to speak my mind freely, I will take the liberty to tell you, that this house would be incomparable, if it had three things which I know of. My good mother, replied the princess Parizade, what are those three things? I conjure you, in God's name, to tell me what they are: I will spare nothing to have them, if it is possible to get them.

Madam, replied the devotee, the first of those three things is the Talking Bird, which is called Bulbulkezer, and is so singular a creature, that it can call all the singing-birds about it which come to accompany him with their songs. The second is the Singing Tree, the leaves of which are so many mouths, which form an harmonious concert, of different voices, and never ceases. The third thing is the Yellow Golden Water, a single pot of which being brought in a proper vessel, and poured into a large bason made for it in any garden, it fills immediately, and forms a fountain, which continually plays, and yet never overflows the bason.

Ah! my good mother, cried the princess, how much am I obliged to you for the knowledge of these things: They are surprising, and I never heard such curious and wonderful things before; but as I am well persuaded that you know where they are, I expect that you should do me the favour to tell me.

Madam, replied the good woman, I should be unworthy the hospitality you have with so much bounty shewed me, if I should refuse to satisfy your curiosity in that point, and am glad to have the honour to tell you, that these three things are to be met with on the confines of this kingdom, towards India: the road lies before your house; and whoever you send needs but to follow twenty days, and on the twentieth, let him but ask the first person he meets, where the talking bird, singing tree, and yellow water are, and he will be informed. After these words she rose from her seat, took her leave, and went her way.

The princess Parizade's thoughts were so taken up with what the religious woman had told her of the talking bird, singing tree, and yellow water, that she never perceived when she went her way, till she was going to ask her some questions for her better information; for she thought that what she had told her was not sufficient to expose herself to undertake a journey to no purpose; however, she would not send after her to bring her back, but endeavoured to remember all she had told her; and when she thought she had recollected every word, she took a great pleasure in thinking of the satisfaction she should have, if she could get these wonderful things into her possession; but then again, the difficulties she apprehended, and the fear of not succeeding, made her very uneasy.

She was lost in her thoughts when her brothers returned from hunting; who, when they entered the great hall, instead of finding her merry and brisk, as she used to be, were amazed to see her so pensive, and hang down her head, as if something troubled her.

Sister, said Prince Bahman, what is become of all your mirth and pleasantry? What! are you not well; or has some misfortune befallen you? Have you any reason to be so melancholy? Come, tell us, that we may do what is becoming us, and give you some relief: If any body has affronted you, we will revenge it.

The princess Parizade remained in the same posture some time, but at last lifted up her eyes to look at her brothers, and then held them down again, telling them nothing disturbed her.

Ah! sister, said Prince Bahman, you hide the truth from us: Then I am sure there is something extraordinary makes you so grave; it is impossible, for the short time we have been absent, we could observe so sudden a change, if nothing was the matter with you. You would not have us satisfied with the answer you have given us: Do not conceal any thing from us, unless you would have us believe that you renounce our friendship, and the strict union we have hitherto preserved from our infancy.

The princess, unwilling to break with her brothers, would not let them long entertain such a thought or suspicion, but said, When I told you nothing disturbed me, I meant nothing that was of any great importance, either to you or me; but since you press me to tell you by our strict union and friendship, I will: You think, and always believed so too, that this house, which our father has built, was complete in every thing; but this day I have learned that it wants three things, which would render it so perfect, that no country-seat could be compared with it. These three things are the talking bird, the singing tree, and the golden water; and after she had informed them of the excellency of these three rarities, a religious woman, added she, has made this discovery to me, and told me the place where they are to be found, and the way thither. Perhaps you may imagine these things trifles, and our house without these additions fine enough; but think what you please: for my part, I must tell you, that I am persuaded they are absolutely necessary; and I shall not be easy without them; therefore, whether you value them or not, I desire you to give me your opinion, what person you may think proper to send on this request.

Sister, replied Prince Bahman, nothing can concern you which we have not an equal interest in. It is enough you have a desire for the things you mention, to oblige us to endeavour to get them; but if you had not, we might: I am persuaded my brother is of my opinion; and therefore we ought to undertake this request, as you call it, for the importance and singularity, if it deserves that name; and I will take that charge upon myself: tell me only the place, and the way to it, and I will defer my journey no longer than till to-morrow.

Brother, said Prince Perviz, it is not convenient that you, who are the prop and stay of the family, should be absent so long; I desire my sister would join with me to oblige you to abandon your design, and think well of my going: I hope I may be able to acquit myself as well, and things will be more in order at home. I am persuaded, brother, of your good will, replied Prince Bahman, and that you will acquit yourself as well, or better, than me in this journey; but it is a thing I have resolved on, and will do, and I have no occasion to recommend to you the necessity of staying at home with our sister. The remainder of that day he spent in making provisions for his journey, and informing himself from the princess of the directions the devotee left her, that he might not miss his way.

The next morning early, Prince Bahman took horse, and Princess Parizade, who would see him set out, embraced, and wished him a good journey; but, in the midst of their adieus, the princess remembered one thing, which she never thought of before. Alas! brother, said she, I had quite forgot the accidents which attend travellers; who knows whether I shall ever see you again? Alight, I beseech you, and do not go this journey. I would rather be deprived of the sight and possession of the talking bird, singing tree, and yellow water, than run the risk of never seeing you more.

Sister, replied Prince Bahman, smiling at the sudden fears of the princess Parizade, my resolution is fixed; and were it not, I should determine upon it now. The accidents you speak of befal but those who are unfortunate. It is true, I may be of that number, but there are more who are not so, than who are; but as events are doubtful, and I may fail in this undertaking, all I can do is to leave you this knife.

Then Prince Bahman, pulling a knife out of his pocket, and presenting it in the sheath to the princess, said, Here, sister, take this knife, and give yourself the trouble sometimes to pull it out of the sheath: When you see it clean, as it is now, it shall be a sign that I am alive; but if you find it stained with blood, then you may believe me dead, and favour me with your prayers.

The princess Parizade could obtain nothing more of Prince Bahman, who bid her and Prince Perviz adieu for the last time, and rode away, well mounted, armed, and equipped; and when he got into the road, never turned to the right hand nor to the left, but went directly forwards towards India. The twentieth day, he perceived on the road side an old man, the sight of whom was frightful, who sat under a tree some small distance from a thatched house, which was his habitation.

His eye-brows were as white as snow, and so was the hair of his head; his mustachoes turned up to his nose, and, with his beard, which reached down to his waist, hid his mouth: the nails of his hands and feet were grown to an excessive length; his hat was slouched about his ears; he had no cloaths, but only a mat was thrown over his shoulders.

The good old man was a dervise, who had for many years retired from the world, and had neglected himself, and went in that manner to give himself up entirely to the service of God.

Prince Bahman, who had been all that morning very diligent to see if he could meet with any body that could give him information of the place he was going to, stopped when he came near the dervise, and alighted from off his horse, to be the more conformable to the directions the religious woman had given the princess Parizade, and leading his horse by the bridle, advanced towards him, and saluting him, said, God prolong your days, good father, and fulfil your desires.

The dervise returned the prince's salute, but so unintelligibly, that he could not understand one word he said. Prince Bahman perceiving that this obstruction of speech proceeded from the dervise's mustachoes hanging over his mouth, and at the same time unwilling to go any farther without the instructions he wanted, he pulled out a pair of scissars he had about him, having tied his horse fast to a tree, and said to the dervise, Honest friend, I want to have some talk with you, but your mustachoes prevent my understanding what you say; and if you will consent, I will cut off some part of them and your eye-brows, which disfigure you so much, that you look more like a bear than a man.

The dervise never opposed the prince, but let him do what he would; and when the prince had cut off as much hair as he thought fit, he perceived that the dervise had a good clear fresh skin, and that he was not so old as he appeared to be. Honest dervise, said he, if I had a glass, I would shew you how young you look; you are now a man, but before, nobody could tell what you were.

The caresses and behaviour of Prince Bahman made the dervise smile, and return his compliment. Sir, said he, whoever you are, I am infinitely obliged to you for the favour you have done me, and am ready to shew my acknowledgment, by doing any thing for you that lies in my power: You must have alighted here upon some account or other; therefore tell me what it is, and I will endeavour to serve you, if I can.

Good dervise, replied Prince Bahman, I have come a great way, and am in search after the talking bird, singing tree, and yellow water: I know these three things are not far from hence, but cannot tell exactly the place where they are to be found; if you know, I conjure you to shew me the way, that I may not mistake it, and lose my labour.

The prince, while he spoke, observed that the dervise changed countenance, held down his eyes, and looked very serious, and, instead of making any reply, remained silent; which obliged him to say to him again, Good dervise, I fancy you did not hear me; tell me whether you know what I asked you or not, that I may not lose my time, but inform myself somewhere else.

At last the dervise broke silence. Sir, said he to Prince Bahman, I know the way you ask of me; but the friendship which I conceived for you the first moment I saw you, and which is grown stronger by the favour you have done me, kept me in suspence, to know whether I should give you the satisfaction you desire. What motive can hinder it, replied the prince? and what difficulties do you find in it? I will tell you, replied the dervise; the danger you are going to expose yourself to is greater than you believe it to be. A great number of fine gentlemen, who have had as much bravery and courage as you can have, passed by here, and asked me the same question you do now; and when I had used all my endeavours to persuade them to desist, they would not believe me; at last I have yielded to their importunities, and, against my will, shewed them the way, and can assure you they have all perished, and not one came back again; therefore, if you have any regard for your life, take my advice; go no farther, but return home.

Prince Bahman persisted in his resolution. I am obliged to you, said he to the dervise, for the friendship you express for me, but will not believe that your advice is sincere; but whatever the danger may be you tell me of, nothing shall make me change my intent: Whoever attacks me, I am well armed, and can say I am as brave as any one. But they who shall attack you are not to be seen, replied the dervise, for there are a great many of them; how will you defend yourself against invisible persons? It is no matter what you say, answered the prince; you shall not persuade me from my design; and since you know the way, I conjure you once more to tell me, and not refuse me that favour.

When the dervise found he could not prevail upon Prince Bahman, and that he was obstinately bent to pursue his journey, notwithstanding the wholesome advice he gave him, he put his hand into a bag that lay by him, and pulled out a bowl,* which he presented to him, saying, Since I cannot get you to hear me, and take my advice, take this bowl, and when you are on horseback, throw it before you, and follow it to the foot of a mountain, where it will stop. As soon as the bowl stops, alight, and leave your horse with the bridle over his neck, and he will stand in the same place till you return. As you go up the hill, you will see, on your right and left hand, a great quantity of large black stones, and will hear on all sides of you confused voices, which will say a thousand injurious things to you, to discourage you, and prevent your climbing up the hill; but you must have a care, least you be afraid, and, above all things, not to turn your head, and look behind you; for in that instant that you do, you will be changed into such a stone as that you see, which are all so many gentlemen who have failed in this enterprize. If you escape the great danger which I give you but a slight description of, that you might think of it, and get to the top of the mountain, you will see a cage, and in that cage is this bird you seek; ask him for the singing tree and yellow water, and he will shew you where they are. I have nothing more to say, since I have told you what to do, and what danger you must avoid; but if you would believe me, you would take my advice, and not expose your life. Consider once more, when you have time, that the condition is insuperable, since it is almost impossible to arm yourself against that surprise, as you may well comprehend.

I am very much obliged to you for your advice, replied Prince Bahman, after he had received the bowl, but cannot follow it; however, I will endeavour to conform myself to that part of it which bids me not look behind me; and hope to come again soon, and thank you more when I have got what I am in search after. After these words, to which the dervise made no other answer than that he should be overjoyed to see him again, he mounted his horse, took his leave of the dervise, with a low bow, and threw the bowl before him.

The bowl rolled away, and at the last had as much strength as when Prince Bahman first delivered it out of his hand, which obliged him to put his horse to a good pace to follow it; and when it came to the foot of the mountain, it stopped, as the dervise said. The prince alighted from off his horse, which never stirred off the spot; and having first looked up the mountain, and seen the black stones, afterwards began to climb up it, but had not gone four steps before he heard the voices, though he could see nobody. Some said, Where is that rash man going? What would he have? Do not let him pass: others, Stop him, catch him, kill him; and others again, as loud as thunder, Ah! thief! murderer! ass! assassin! while some, in a gibing tone, cried, No, no, do not hurt him; let the pretty thing pass; we keep the bird and cage for him.

Notwithstanding all those troublesome voices, Prince Bahman mounted with courage and resolution; but the voices increasing their noise both behind and before him, at last he was frightened; his legs trembled under him; he reeled, and presently found that all his strength and courage failed him: He forgot the dervise's advice, turned about to run down the hill, and was that instant changed into a black stone, which metamorphosis had happened to many more besides him, who had attempted the same thing. His horse likewise underwent the same fate.

From the time of Prince Bahman's departure, the princess Parizade always wore the knife and sheath in her girdle, and pulled it out several times in a day, to know whether her brother was alive; and oftentimes she and Prince Perviz, who often asked her what news, discoursed together on that subject.

On the fatal day that Prince Bahman was metamorphosed into a stone, as Prince Perviz and the princess were talking together in the evening, as usual, the prince desired his sister to pull out the knife, to know how their brother did. The princess pulled out the knife, and looking upon it, and seeing the blood run down the point, was seized with so much horror and grief that she threw it down. Ah! my dear brother, cried she; I have been the cause of your death, and shall never see you more! How unhappy am I! Why did I tell you of the talking bird, singing tree, and yellow water; or rather, what matter of importance was it to me, to know whether the religious woman thought this house ugly or handsome, or complete or not? I wish to heaven she had never addressed herself to me. Deceitful hypocrite, added she, is this the return thou hast made me for the kind reception I gave thee? Why didst thou tell me of a bird, a tree, and a water, which are all imaginary, as I am persuaded they are, by my dear brother's death, yet disturb me, and all by thy enchantment!

Prince Perviz was as much afflicted at the death of Prince Bahman as the princess; but not to waste time in needless regrets, as he knew, by the princess's sorrow, that she still passionately desired the possession of the talking bird, singing tree, and the golden water, he interrupted her, and said, Our regret and tears for our brother Bahman are all vain and useless, since all our grief cannot restore him to life again; it is the will of Heaven, and we must submit to it, and adore the decrees of the Almighty, without searching into them. Why should you now doubt of the truth of what the holy woman told you? Do you think she spoke to you of three things that were not in being; and that she invented that story on purpose to deceive you, who had given her no cause to do so, since you received her with all the bounty and civility possible? Let us rather believe that our brother's death is owing to some fault or accident, which we cannot imagine; and therefore it ought not to prevent us from pursuing what we do and ought to wish for. I offered to go this journey, and am in the same mind and readiness still; his example has no effect upon my resolution: to-morrow I will go myself.

The princess did all she could to dissuade Prince Perviz off his journey, conjuring him not to expose her to the loss of two brothers; but he was resolved; and all the remonstrances she could urge had no effect upon him. Before he went, that she might know what success he had, he left her, as his brother had done, a knife, and a necklace of an hundred pearls, telling her, that if they would not run when she told them upon the string, but remain fixed, that should be a certain sign he had undergone the same fate as his brother; but at the same time told her, he hoped that would never happen, but that he should have the happiness to see her again, to her utmost satisfaction.

Prince Perviz, on the twentieth day from his setting out, met with the same dervise, in the same place his brother Bahman had done before him. He went directly up to him, and after he had saluted him, asked him if he could tell him where to find the talking bird, singing tree, and the golden water? The dervise made the same difficulties and remonstrances he had done to Prince Bahman, telling him, that a young gentleman, who very much resembled him, had been with him within a short time; that, overcome by his importunity and pressing influence, he had shewn him the way, by giving him a guide, and had told him how to behave himself to succeed; but withal, that he had never seen him since, and never disputed but he had the same fate as many more had undergone.

Good dervise, answered Prince Perviz, I know whom you speak of; he was my brother; and I am informed of the certainty of his death, but know not what it was. I can tell, replied the dervise: he was changed into a black stone, as all I speak of have been; and you ought to expect the same, unless you observe, more exactly than he has done, the good advice I gave him, in case you persist in your resolution, which I once more entreat you to desist from.

Dervise, said Prince Perviz, I cannot enough express how much I am obliged to you for the care you take of my life, since I am a stranger to you, and have done nothing to deserve so much good will; but I must tell you, I have deliberated too long upon this enterprize to quit it now; therefore beg of you to do me the same favour you have done my brother. Perhaps I may have better success, and may follow the directions I expect from you. Since I cannot prevail upon you, said the dervise, nor persuade you not to undertake what you have so obstinately resolved on, if my age did not prevent me, and I could stand, I would get up to reach you a bowl I have here, which will shew you the way.

Upon this the prince alighted from his horse, and went up to the dervise, who took a bowl out of his bag, in which he had a great many others, and gave it him, with the same directions he had given Prince Bahman.

Prince Perviz thanked the dervise, and when he had mounted his horse, and taken his leave, he threw his bowl. When the bowl came to the bottom of the hill, it stopped, and the prince got off his horse, and stood some time to recollect upon the dervise's directions, and then began to walk up, with a resolution to reach the top; but before he had gone above six steps, he heard a voice behind him, which seemed to be very near him, say, in an insulting tone, Stay, rash youth, that I may punish thee for thy boldness.

Upon this affront, the prince, forgetting the dervise's advice, clapped his hand upon his sword, and drew it, and turned about to revenge himself, but had scarce time to see that nobody followed him, before he and his horse were changed into black stones.

In the mean time, the princess Parizade, several times a-day, after her brother Perviz set out, flung over her necklace, which she generally held in her hand, and failed not every night she went to bed to do the same, and tie it about her neck, and in the morning count over the pearls again.

The day that Prince Perviz was changed into a stone, she was pulling over the pearls as she used to do, when, all of a sudden, she could not stir them, and never disputed but that it was a certain token that the prince her brother was dead: But as she had determined before what to do, in case it should so happen, she lost no time in outward shews of grief, which she disguised as much as possible; but having armed and disguised herself in men's apparel, she took horse the next morning, having told her servants she should return in two or three days, and took the same road her brothers had done before her.

The princess, who had been used to ride on horseback in hunting, supported the fatigue of so long a journey better than other ladies could have done; and as she made the same days journies as her brothers, she met with the dervise on the twentieth. When she came near him, she alighted off her horse, and leading him by the bridle, went and sat down by the dervise; and after she had saluted him, she said, Honest man, will you give me leave to sit by you; and do me the favour to tell me if you have not heard that there are, somewhere hereabouts, a talking bird, singing tree, and golden water?

Madam, answered the dervise, since, by your voice, I know you to be a woman disguised in man's apparel, I thank you for your compliment, and receive the honour you do me with a great deal of pleasure. I know the place very well where these things you speak of are to be found: But what makes you ask me this question?

Good dervise, replied the princess, I have had such an advantageous relation of them given me, that I have a great desire to have them. Madam, replied the dervise, you have been told the truth; these things are more singular and surprising than they have been represented to you; but you have not been acquainted with the unsurmountable difficulties to obtain them. If you had been informed of them, you would not certainly have undertaken so dangerous and troublesome an enterprize. Take my advice, and do not go any farther, and do not urge me to contribute towards your ruin.

Good father, said the princess, I have come a great way, and should be sorry to return back again without executing my design. You talk of difficulties, and of my running in danger of my life; but you do not tell me what those difficulties are, and wherein the danger lies, which is what I desire to know, that I may consider on it, and know whether I have courage and resolution enough to lead me to undertake it.

Then the dervise repeated to the princess Parizade what he had said to the princes Bahman and Perviz, exaggerating upon the difficulties of climbing up to the top of the mountain, where she was to make herself mistress of the bird, which would inform her of the singing tree and golden water; the noise and clamour of the terrible threatening voices, which she would hear on all sides of her, without seeing any body; and, in short, the great quantity of black stones, the only objects most capable of striking terror into her, or any other person; to reflect, that those stones were so many brave gentlemen, metamorphosed into that form or substance, for not observing the principal directions for a person to succeed in that undertaking, which was, not to look behind them before they had got possession of the bird and cage.

When the dervise had done, the princess replied, By what I comprehend from your discourse, the difficulty of succeeding in this affair, is, first, the getting up to the cage, without being frightened at the terrible voices I shall hear; and secondly, not to look behind me: For this last, I hope I shall be mistress enough of myself to observe it. As to the first, I own, that those voices, such as you represent them to be, are capable of striking terror into the most undaunted: But as in all enterprizes and dangers every one may use art and management, I desire to know of you if I may make use of one of great importance. And what is that management you would make use of, said the dervise? To stop my ears so hard with cotton, answered the princess, that I may not hear the voices, and by that means prevent the impression they may make upon my mind, and that I may not lose the use of my reason.

O, madam, replied the dervise, of all the persons who have addressed themselves to me, to know the way, I do not know that ever any one made use of what you propose: But this I know, they all perished. If you persist in your design, you may make the experiment; but I would not have you expose yourself to the danger.

What, replied the princess, not persist in my design! I am sure I shall succeed, and am resolved to try the experiment; therefore only want to know which way I must go, which is a favour I conjure you not to refuse me. The dervise exhorted her again to consider well what she was going to do; but finding her resolute, he took out a bowl, and presenting it to her, said, Take this bowl, and when you have mounted your horse again, throw it before you, and follow it till it stops at the bottom of the mountain, and there light off your horse: you know the rest; but be sure to remember what I have told you.

After the princess Parizade had thanked the dervise, and taken her leave of him, she mounted her horse, threw the bowl before her, and followed it till it stopt at the foot of the mountain.

The princess alighted off her horse, stopped her ears with cotton, and after she had well examined the way she was to go, to get up to the top, she began with a moderate pace, and walked up with intrepidity. She heard the voices, and perceived the great service the cotton was to her. The higher she went, the louder the voices seemed, but were not capable of making any impression on her. She heard a great many affronting, base things, which were very disagreeable to a woman, which she only laughed at. I mind not, said she to herself, all that can be said; I only laugh at them, and shall pursue my way. At last she got so high, that she began to perceive the cage and bird, which endeavoured, with the voices, to fright her, crying out, in a voice as loud as them, notwithstanding the smallness of its size, Retire, fool, and come no higher.

The princess, encouraged more by this object, redoubled her haste, when she saw herself just at her journey's end, and got to the top of the mountain, where the ground was all level and even; and running directly to the cage, and clapping her hand upon it, cried, Bird, bird, I have got three, in spite of thee; thou shalt not escape me.

While Princess Parizade was pulling the cotton out of her ears, the bird said to her, Brave lady, be not angry with me, for endeavouring to preserve my liberty; for, though kept in a cage, I was content with my condition; but since I am destined to be a slave, I would rather be yours than any other person's in the world, since you have obtained me so courageously: From this instant, I swear an universal fidelity to you, and an entire submission to your commands. I know who you are, and can tell you, it is what you do not know yourself; but the time will come, when I shall do you a piece of service, which, I hope, you will be obliged to me for; and for a proof of my sincerity, tell me what you desire, and I am ready to obey you.

The princess's joy was the more inexpressible, because the conquest she had made had cost her the lives of two beloved brothers, and given her more trouble and fatigue than she could have imagined, notwithstanding what the dervise had represented to her. Bird, said she, it was my intention to have told you I wish for a great many things, which are of the last importance to me; and am overjoyed that you have your own self prevented me first. I have been told that there is a golden water not far off, the property of which is very wonderful, and, above all things, I want to know where it is. The bird shewed her the place, which was just by; and she went and filled a silver flaggon she had brought along with her: Then she said to the bird, Bird, this is not enough, I want also the singing tree; tell me where it is. Turn about, said the bird, and you will see a wood behind you, where you will find the tree. The princess went into the wood, and, by the harmonious concert she heard, she soon knew the tree, which she found so large, that she said to the bird, which she always carried along with her, Well, now, bird, I have found this tree, I know not what to do with it, since I can neither carry it nor pull it up by the roots. The bird replied, it is enough that you break off a branch, and carry it to plant in your garden; it will take root as soon as it is clapt into the earth, and in a little time will grow to as fine a tree as this you see.

When the princess Parizade had the three things in her hand which the religious woman had told her of, and she conceived so great a desire for, she said again to the bird, All thou hast done for me yet, bird, is not enough; thou hast been the cause of the death of my two brothers, who ought to be among the black stones I saw as I came up the hill, and I want to take them home again with me.

The bird would fain have been dispensed with from satisfying the princess in this point, and indeed made some difficulty to do it. Bird, said the princess, remember you told me that you were my slave; and, in short, thou art so, and thy life is at my disposal. I cannot deny the truth, answered the bird; but although what you now ask of me is a more difficult thing than all the rest, yet I will do it for you. Cast your eyes about you, added he, and look if you can see a little pitcher. I see it already, said the princess. Take it then, said he, and, going down the hill, spill a little of the water that is in it upon every black stone, and that will be the way to find your brothers again.

The princess Parizade took up the pitcher, cage, and bird, flaggon of golden water, and the branch of the singing tree, and, as she went down the hill again, spilt a little of the water on every black stone, which was changed immediately either into a man or a horse; and as she did not miss one stone, she found both her brothers, as well as a great many fine gentlemen, and all their horses. She presently knew Prince Bahman and Prince Perviz, as they did likewise her; and all ran to embrace each other, expressing a great amazement. What do you here, brothers? said she. They told her they had been asleep. Yes, replied she, and if it had not been for me, perhaps might have slept for ever. Do not you remember that you came here to fetch the talking bird, singing tree, and yellow water; and did not you see, as you came along, a great many black stones? See if there be any now. If you desire to know how this miracle was performed, continued she, shewing the pitcher, which she set down at the foot of the mountain, it was done by virtue of the water which was in this pitcher, with which I sprinkled every stone; for, added she, after I had made this talking bird my slave, by his directions I found out the singing tree, a branch of which I have now in my hand, and the yellow water, which this flaggon is filled with; but, being still unwilling to return home without you, I constrained the bird, by the power I had over him, to afford me the means; upon which he told me where to find this pitcher, and the use I was to make of it.

Prince Bahman and Prince Perviz knew, by this discourse, the obligation they had to the princess their sister, and the other gentlemen were all so sensible of theirs to the princess, that, far from envying her happiness in the conquest she had made, and they all aspired to, they thought that they could not any otherwise acknowledge the favour she had done them, in restoring them to life again, than by declaring themselves all her slaves, and that they were ready to obey her in whatever she should command.

Gentlemen, replied the princess, if you had given any attention to my discourse, you might have observed that I had no other intention in what I have done than to find out my brothers again; therefore, if you have received any benefit, you have no obligation to me for it, and I have no other share in your compliment than what common civility requires, and return you my thanks, as I ought; moreover, I look upon you, in every particular, as free persons now, as you were before your misfortunes, and rejoice with you for the benefit and happiness which happened to you upon my account; but let us stay no longer in a place where we have nothing to detain us, but mount our horses, and return to our homes.

Then Princess Parizade shewed them the way first, and went and took her horse, which stood in the same place where she left him. Before she mounted, Prince Bahman, who would help her, desired her to give him the cage to carry. Brother, replied the princess, the bird is my slave, and I will carry him myself; but there is the branch of the singing tree, if you will take the pains to carry that; but hold the cage while I get on horseback.

When she had mounted her horse, and Prince Bahman had given her the cage, she turned about, and said to Prince Perviz, brother, I leave the golden water to your care, if it will not be too great a trouble for you to carry.

When Prince Bahman and Prince Perviz, and all the gentlemen, had mounted their horses, the princes Parizade waited for some of them to lead the way first. The two princes paid that compliment to the gentlemen, and they again to the princess, who, finding that none of them would accept of the honour, but that it was reserved for her, addressed herself to them, and said, Gentlemen, I expect that some of you should lead the way; to which one, in the name of the rest, replied, Madam, were we strangers to your being a woman, yet after what you have done for us, there is no honour we would not willingly pay you, notwithstanding all your modesty; therefore, desire you would not deprive us any longer of the happiness of following you.

Gentlemen, said the princess, I do not deserve the honour you do me, and accept of it only because you desire it. At the same time she led the way, and the two princes and gentlemen followed her, without the least distinction.

This illustrious company called upon the dervise as they passed by, to thank him for his good reception and wholesome advice, which they all found very sincere; but he was dead: But whether old age, or that he was no longer necessary to shew the way to the obtaining the three rarities which the princess Parizade was possessed of, they were doubtful in. Afterwards, they pursued their way, but lessened in their numbers every day; the gentlemen taking their leaves handsomely, and testifying their obligations to the princess, who, with her brothers, made the best of their way.

As soon as the princess came home, she placed the cage in the garden, just by the hall; and the bird no sooner began to sing, but he was surrounded by nightingales, chaffinches, goldfinches, larks, linnets, and a great many other sorts of birds. As for the branch of the singing tree, it was no sooner set in the midst of the parterre, some distance from the house, but it took root, and in a little time became a large tree, the leaves of which, in a short time, gave as harmonious a concert as those of the tree from which it was gathered. As to the flaggon of the yellow golden water, a large marble bason was made in the midst of another parterre, and when it was finished, the princess poured all the yellow water that was in the flaggon into it, which increased and swelled so much, that it soon reached up to the edges of the bason, and afterwards formed a fountain twenty feet high, which fell again into the bason, without a drop running over.

The news of these wonders was presently spread abroad in that neighbourhood; and as the doors of the house, and those of the garden, were shut to nobody, great bands of people came to admire them.

Some days after that, the princes Bahman and Perviz having recovered themselves of the fatigue of their journey, began to renew their former way of living; and as their greatest diversion was hunting, they mounted their horses, and went, not in their park, but two or three leagues from their own house; but as it happened that they had made choice of the same spot of ground where the sultan of Persia was then hunting, when they perceived it, they left off their chace, and retired, to avoid meeting him; but, for all their care and caution, they chanced to chop upon him in so strait and narrow a way that they could not turn back without being seen. In their surprise, they had only time to prostrate themselves before the sultan, without lifting up their heads to look at him. The sultan, who saw they were well mounted and dressed, had the curiosity to see their faces; therefore stopped, and commanded them to rise. The princes, when they rose up, stood before the sultan with so easy an air, and, at the same time, with so great modesty, that the sultan took some time to view them from head to foot, before he spoke; and after he had admired their good air and mien, he asked them who they were, and where they lived?

Sir, said Prince Bahman, we are the sons of your majesty's late intendant of your gardens; and we live in a house which he built a little before he died, for us to live in till we should be fit to serve your majesty.

By what I perceive by you, replied the sultan, you love hunting. Sir, answered Prince Bahman, it is our common exercise, and what your majesty's subjects, who intend to bear arms, or serve in your wars, ought not, according to the custom of the kingdom, to neglect. The sultan, charmed with so prudent an answer, said, Since it is so, I should be glad to see you hunt some wild beast; make choice of which you please.

The princes mounted their horses again, and followed the sultan, but had not gone far before they saw a great many wild beasts together. Prince Bahman chose a lion, and Prince Perviz a bear, and pursued them with so much intrepid courage, that the sultan was surprised. In short, they darted their javelins with so much skill and address, that they pierced, the one his lion, the other his bear, quite through and through, and the sultan saw them die with his own eyes. Immediately afterwards, Prince Bahman pursued a bear, and Prince Perviz another lion, and killed them in a short time, and would have beat out for fresh game, but the sultan, who would not let them, sent to them to come to him. When they came nigh enough that they could hear him, he said, If I would have given you leave, you would soon have destroyed all my game, but it is not that which I would preserve, but your persons; for I am very well assured of your bravery, which may, one time or other, be serviceable to me, so that from this moment your lives will be always dear to me.

The sultan Khosrouschah, in short, conceived so great a kindness for the two princes, that he invited them, at that time, to go and make him a visit; to which Prince Bahman replied, Your majesty does us an honour we do not deserve, and therefore we beg you will excuse us.

The sultan, who could not comprehend what reason the princes could have to refuse this token of his favour, asked and pressed them to tell him why they excused themselves. Sir, said Prince Bahman, we have a sister, with whom we live in so perfect an union, that we act nothing before we consult her, nor she any thing without asking our advice. I commend your brotherly agreement, answered the sultan; consult your sister, and meet me here to-morrow a-hunting, and give me an answer.

The princes went home, but not only forgot to speak of their adventure in meeting the sultan, and hunting with him, but to tell the princess how he had invited them to go home with him; but yet did not fail, the next morning, to meet him at the place appointed. Well, said the sultan, have you spoke to your sister, and has she consented to the pleasure I expect of seeing you at my palace? The two princes looked at each other, and blushed. Sir, said Prince Bahman, we beg of your majesty to excuse us, for both my brother and I forgot. Then remember to-day, replied the sultan, and be sure to bring me an answer tomorrow.

The princes were guilty of the same fault a second time; yet the sultan was so good-natured as to forgive their negligence; but to prevent their forgetfulness the third time, he pulled three golden bullets out of a purse, and put them into Prince Bahman's bosom. These bullets, said he, smiling, will prevent your forgetting a third time, since the noise they make, by falling on the floor when you undress yourself, will remind you, in case you should forget. And indeed the thing happened out as the sultan foresaw it would; and without these bullets, the princes had not thought of speaking to their sister of this affair; for as Prince Bahman unloosed his girdle to go to bed, the bullets dropt on the floor, and thereupon he ran into Prince Perviz's chamber, and both went into the princess Parizade's apartment, before she was got into bed; and after they had asked her pardon for coming at so unseasonable a time, they told her all the circumstances of their meeting the sultan.

The princess Parizade was something surprised at this news. Your meeting with the sultan, said she, is very happy and honourable, and in the end may be very advantageous to you, but may be ill for me. It was upon my account, I know, you refused the sultan, and I am infinitely obliged to you for it, and find your friendship is perfectly consistent with mine, since you would rather be guilty of ill manners towards the sultan, than break in upon the brotherly union we have sworn to each other: You judged right; for if you had once gone, you would insensibly have been engaged to leave me to go and pay your respects to him: But do not think it an easy matter absolutely to refuse the sultan what he so earnestly desires; for sultans will be obeyed in their desires, and it may be dangerous to oppose them; therefore, if, to follow my inclination, I should dissuade you from shewing the complaisance he expects from you, it may expose you to his resentment, and may render myself and you miserable. These are my sentiments; but before we conclude on any thing, let us consult the talking bird, and hear what he says; he is penetrating, and has promised his assistance in all difficulties.

The princess Parizade sent for the cage, and after she had related the fact to the bird, in the presence of her brothers, she asked him what they should do in these perplexed circumstances? The bird answered, the princes your brothers must conform with the sultan's pleasure, and in their turn invite him to come and see your house.

But, bird, replied the princess, my brothers and I love one another, and our friendship is unparalleled; will not this step be injurious to that friendship? Not at all, replied the bird, but it will become stronger thereby. Then, answered the princess, the sultan shall see them. The bird told her it was necessary he should, and that every thing would go better afterwards.

The next morning, the princes met the sultan a-hunting, who, when he came near enough to them to be heard, asked them if they had remembered to speak to their sister? and was answered by Prince Bahman, Sir, your majesty may dispose of us as you please; we are ready to obey you; for we have not only obtained our sister's consent with a great deal of ease, but she took it amiss that we should pay her that deference in a matter wherein our duty to your majesty was concerned: but you are so good, that if we have offended, we hope you will pardon us. Do not be uneasy upon that account, replied the sultan; I am so far from taking what you have done amiss, that I approve of it, and hope you will have the same deference and attachment to my person, for the little share I have in your friendship. The princes, confounded at the sultan's goodness, returned no other answer but by a low bow, to shew the great respect with which they received it.

The sultan, contrary to his usual custom, did not hunt long that day; he judged that the princes' wit was equal to their courage and bravery, and longed with impatience to be more at liberty to discourse with them: he made them ride on each side of him; which honour, without speaking of the principal courtiers, was envied by the grand visier, who was very much mortified to see them preferred before him.

When the sultan entered his capital, the eyes of the people, who stood in crowds in the streets, were fixed only upon the two princes, Bahman and Perviz; and they were earnest to know who they might be, whether foreigners or natives.

However, they all wished that the sultan had been blessed with two such handsome, lovely princes, and said, He might have had children as old, if the sultaness had not had misfortunes in her lyings-in.

The first thing that the sultan did when he arrived at his palace was, to carry the princes into the principal apartments; who praised, with judgment, the beauty and symmetry of the rooms, and the richness of the furniture and ornaments. Afterwards, a magnificent repast was served up, and the sultan made them sit at the same table with him; which they at first refused, but finding that it was his pleasure, they at last obeyed.

The sultan, who had himself had a great deal of wit, and had made a considerable progress in the arts and sciences, and particularly in history, foresaw that the princes, out of modesty and respect, would not take the liberty of beginning any conversation; therefore, to give them an opportunity, he furnished them with subjects all dinner-time; but whatever they talked on, they shewed so much wit, judgment, and discernment, that he was struck with admiration. Were these my own children, said he to himself, and I had given them all the education suitable to their births, they could not have been better instructed, or known more. In short, he took so great a pleasure in their conversation, that, after having sat at table longer than usual, he went into his closet, where he discoursed a long time with them, and at last said to them, I never believed that there were young gentlemen in the country who had so much wit and politeness; and I never was better pleased in my life with any conversation: But it is time now we should regale our senses with some diversion of my court, and nothing is more capable of enlivening the mind than music; you shall hear a vocal and instrumental concert, which may not be disagreeable to you.

The sultan no sooner spoke for them, but the musicians, who had orders to attend, entered, and answered very well the expectations the princes had entertained of their abilities. After the concert, an extraordinary play was acted, and the entertainment was concluded by some excellent dancers, both men and women.

The two princes seeing night draw on apace, prostrated themselves at the sultan's feet, and having first thanked him for the favours and honours they had received, asked his leave to retire; which was granted them by the sultan, who said, I give you my leave to go; but remember, I brought you to my palace myself to shew you the way, and the oftener you come, the welcomer you shall be, and you will do me the greater pleasure.

Before they went out of the sultan's presence, Prince Bahman said, Sir, shall we be so bold as to beg of your majesty to do us and our sister the favour, next time you pass near our house a-hunting, to call to rest and refresh yourself after your fatigue? It is not worthy your presence; but monarchs sometimes have vouchsafed to take shelter in a hut. Gentlemen, replied the sultan, your house cannot be otherwise than beautiful, and worthy of you. I will call and see it with pleasure, which will be the greater, to have you and your fair sister to be my hosts, who is already dear to me before I have seen her, from the account you give me of the rare qualities with which she is endowed; and this satisfaction I will defer no longer than to-morrow: Meet me to-morrow morning early, at the same place where I first saw you, and then you shall be my guides.

When the princes Bahman and Perviz went home, they gave the princess Parizade an account of the honourable reception the sultan had given them; and withal told her that they had invited him to do them the honour, as he passed by, to call at their house; and that he had appointed the next day.

If it be so, replied the princess, we must think presently of preparing a repast fit for his majesty; and for that end, I think it would be proper we should consult the talking bird; he will tell us, perhaps, what meats the sultan likes best. The princes approved of her thought; and after they retired, she consulted the bird alone. Bird, said she, the sultan will do us the honour to-morrow to come and see us, and our house, what shall we entertain him with? Tell us what we shall do to acquit ourselves in the most handsome manner possible.

Good mistress, replied the bird, you have excellent cooks, let them do the best they can; but, above all things, let them prepare a dish of cucumbers stuffed full of pearls, which must be set before the sultan in the first course, before all other meats.

Cucumbers stuffed full of pearls! cried Princess Parizade, with amazement; surely, bird, you do not know what you say; it is an unheard-of dish: The sultan may admire it for a piece of magnificence, but he will want something to eat, and not to admire pearls; but moreover, where shall I get pearls enough for such a dish?

Mistress, said the bird, do what I bid you, and do not be uneasy at what shall happen. As to the pearls, go early to-morrow morning to the foot of the first tree on your right hand in the park, and dig under it, and you will find what you want.

That night the princess ordered a gardener to be ready to wait on her, and the next morning early took him with her, and carried him to the tree the bird told her of, and bid him dig about a foot deep. When the gardener came to the depth, he found some resistance with the spade, and presently discovered a gold box, about a foot square, which he shewed the princess. This, said she, is what I brought thee for; take care not to hurt it with thy spade.

When the gardener took up the box, he gave it into the princess's hands, who, as it was only fastened with little hasps, soon opened it, and found it full of pearls of a moderate size. Very well satisfied with having found this treasure, after she had shut the box again, she clapt it under her arm, and went into the house, while the gardener threw the earth into the hole, and laid the green turf on again as before.

The princes Bahman and Perviz, who, as they were dressing themselves in their own apartments, saw the princess their sister in the garden earlier than usual, as soon as they could get dressed, went to go to her, and met her as she was coming back, and with a gold box under her arm, which very much surprised them. Sister, said Bahman, you carried nothing with you when we saw you before with the gardener, and now we see you have got a golden box: Was this treasure found by the gardener, and did he come and tell you of it?

No, brother, answered the princess, I carried the gardener to the place where the coffer was hid, and shewed him where to dig; but you will be more amazed when you see what it holds.

The princess opened the box, and when the princes saw the considerable quantity of pearls, which, though small, were of great value, they asked her how she came to the knowledge of this treasure? The princess, as they returned back to the house, gave them an account of her consulting the bird, as they had agreed she should, and the answer he gave her, to prepare a dish of cucumbers stuffed full of pearls, and how he had told her where to find this box. The princes and princess raised many conjectures to penetrate into what the bird could mean by such a dish; and though they could not by any means guess at his reason for so doing, they nevertheless followed his advice.

As soon as the princess got into the house, she called for the head cook, and after she had given him directions about the entertainment for the sultan, she said to him, Besides all this, you must dress an extraordinary dish for the sultan's own eating, which nobody else must touch besides yourself. This dish must be cucumbers stuffed with these pearls; and at the same time she opened the box, and shewed him the pearls.

The chief cook, who had never heard of such a dish, started back, and shewed by looks his thoughts; which the princess penetrating into, said, I see thou takest me to be mad, to order such a dish; but thou must know I have my reasons for so doing; therefore go and do the best thou canst, and bring me back what pearls are left. The cook made no reply, but took the box, and went away: and afterwards the princess gave directions to all the servants to have every thing in order, both in the house and gardens, to receive the sultan.

The two princes went to the place appointed; and as soon as the sultan of Persia came, they began a chace, which lasted till the heat of the sun obliged them to leave off; and while Prince Bahman staid to conduct the sultan to their house, Prince Perviz rode before, to inform the princess Parizade, who had been told by some servants before, and was ready to receive him.

When the sultan entered the court-yard, and alighted at the porch, the princess Parizade came and threw herself at his feet; and the two princes informed him she was their sister.

The sultan stooped to help her up, and after he had gazed some time on her beauty, and was dazzled with her good mien, noble air, and a *je ne scai quoi*,* which seemed foreign to a country life, he said, The brothers are worthy of the sister, and she worthy of them; and to judge of her sense by her person, I am not amazed that the brothers would do nothing without her consent: but, added he, I hope to be better acquainted with you, madam, after I have seen the house.

Sir, said the princess, it is only a plain country-house, and fit for none but such people as we are, who live retired from the world: It is not to be compared with the houses in great cities, much less with such a magnificent palace as yours. I am of another opinion, said the sultan, very obligingly; for, by its first appearance, it seems otherwise; however, I will not pass my judgment any farther upon it till I have seen it all; therefore be pleased to conduct me through the apartments.

Then the princess led the sultan through all the rooms but the hall; who, after he had considered them very attentively, was mightily taken both with them and their furniture. My fair one, said he to the princess Parizade, do you call this a country-house? The finest and largest cities would soon be deserted, if all country-houses were like yours. I am not at all surprised that you take so much delight in it, and despise the town so much: Now let me see if the gardens be answerable to the house.

The princess opened a door into the garden; and the first object which presented itself to the sultan's view was the golden fountain. Surprised at so rare a sight, he asked from whence that wonderful water, which gave him so much pleasure, had its rise; and by what art it was made to play so high, that nothing in the world was to be compared to it? and said, he would by and by take a nearer view of it.

Then the princess led him to the spot where the harmonious tree was planted; and there the sultan heard a concert, which was different from, and exceeded all the concerts he had ever heard in his life; and stopping to see where the musicians were, he could discern nobody, either far or near, but still heard the music distinctly, which ravished his senses. My fair one, said he to the princess Parizade, where are the musicians? Are they under ground, or invisible in the air? For certainly such excellent charming voices will not run the hazard of being seen, for fear they should please too much.

Sir, answered the princess, smiling, it is the tree your majesty sees before you, and not musicians, which forms this concert; and if you will give yourself the trouble to go a little nearer to it, you will not doubt of it, and the voices will be the more distinct.

The sultan went nearer, and was so charmed with the sweet harmony, that he could have staid for ever to hear it, but that his desire to see the fountain of yellow water nearer, forced him away. Fair one, said he, tell me, I pray you, whether this wonderful tree was found in your garden by chance, or if it was a present made you from some foreign country? For certainly it must have come a great way off, otherwise, curious as I am of these rarities, I should have heard of it. What name do you call it by?

Sir, replied the princess, this tree has no other name than that of the singing tree, and is not a native of this country. It will be too long to tell you here the adventures relating to it, the yellow water, and the talking bird, which your majesty may see after the golden water; but if it may be agreeable to your majesty, after you have refreshed yourself, and recovered the fatigue of hunting, which was the greater because of the sun's intent heat, you shall hear it.

My fair one, replied the sultan, my fatigue is so well recompensed by the wonders you have shewn me, that I am not in the least weary, but am impatient to see the yellow water, and admire the talking bird.

When the sultan came to the yellow water, his eyes were fixed so stedfastly upon the fountain, that he could not take them off: At last, addressing himself to the princess, he said, As you tell me, fair one, that this water has no spring nor communication hereabouts, by any means whatsoever, I apprehend that it is foreign, as well as the singing tree.

Sir, replied the princess, it is as your majesty says; and to let you know that this water has no communication with any spring, I must tell you that the bason is one entire stone, hewed out in that form: But what your majesty may think most wonderful is, that all this water proceeded but from one flaggon-full, which I threw into this bason, which increased of itself to the quantity you see, (a particular quality of this water,) and formed this fountain. Well, said the sultan, going from the fountain, this is enough for one time; I promise myself the pleasure to come and visit it very often: but now let us go and see the talking bird.

Going towards the hall, the sultan perceived a prodigious number of singing birds on the trees thereabouts, and asked why there were so many there, and none on the other trees in the garden? The reason, sir, answered the princess, is, because they come from all parts about, to keep the talking bird company, which your majesty may perceive in a cage just by the window of the hall we are going into; and if you do but mind, you will perceive that his notes are sweeter than all the other birds, even the nightingale's.

The sultan went into the hall; and as the bird kept singing, the princess raised her voice, and said, My slave, here is the sultan, pay your compliments to him. The bird left off singing that instant, and said, The sultan is welcome here: God prosper him, and prolong his life. To which the sultan replied, as he was sitting down at the table, Bird, I thank thee, and am overjoyed to find in thee the sultan and king of birds.

As soon as the sultan saw the dish of cucumbers set before him, he reached out his hand and took one; but when he cut it, he was in an extreme surprise to find it stuffed with pearls. What novelty is this, said he; and with what design were these cucumbers stuffed thus with pearls, since pearls are not to be ate? Then he looked at the two princes and princess, to ask them the meaning of it; when the bird, interrupting him, said, Can your majesty be in so great an astonishment at cucumbers stuffed with pearls, which you see with your own eyes, and yet could so easily believe that the sultaness your wife was delivered of a dog, a cat, and a piece of wood? I believe it, replied the sultan, because the midwives assured me of it. Those midwives, sir, replied the bird, were the sultaness's two sisters, who, envious of her happiness in being preferred by your majesty before them, to satisfy their envy and revenge, have abused your majesty so easily: If you interrogate them, they will confess their crime. The two brothers and the sister, whom you see before you, are your children, which were exposed, and received by the intendant of your gardens, who provided nurses for them, and took care of their education.

This discourse of the bird presently cleared up the sultan's understanding. Bird, cried he, I easily believe the truth which thou discoverest to me. The inclination and tenderness I have always had for them tell me but too plainly they are my own blood. Come then, my children, embrace me, and let me give you the first marks of a fatherly tenderness. Then he rose up, and after having kissed the two princes and the princess, and mingling his tears with theirs, he said, I now embrace you as my own children of the royal blood of the sultans of Persia, whose honour and glory I am persuaded you will maintain, and not as the children of the intendant of my gardens, to whom I have been very much obliged for preserving your lives.

After the two princes and the princess had embraced mutually, with an entirely new satisfaction, the sultan sat down at the table again with them, and pressed them to eat; and when they had done he said, My children, you know me to be your father; to-morrow I will bring the sultaness your mother; therefore prepare to receive her.

Afterwards the sultan mounted his horse, and returned in all haste to his capital, where the first thing he did, as soon as he alighted, was to command the grand visier to take out a process against the sultaness's two sisters, and take them and have them examined and interrogated separately; and accordingly they were tried and condemned to be quartered; which sentence was put in execution immediately.

In the mean time, the sultan Khosrouschah, followed by all the lords of his court, who were then present, went to the door of the great mosque; and after he had taken the sultaness out of the strict confinement she had languished under for so many years, he said to her, with tears in his eyes, and embracing her in the miserable condition she was then in, I come, madam, to ask your pardon for the injustice I have done you, and to make you the reparation I ought to do; which I have begun, by punishing the persons who put the abominable cheat upon me; and I hope you will look upon it as sufficient when I present to you two accomplished princes, and a charming, lovely princess, our children, and restore you to your former honours. All this was done and said before great crowds of people, who immediately spread the news throughout the town.

The next morning early, the sultan and sultaness, whose mournful weeds were changed into magnificent habits, went, with all their court, to the house built by the intendant of the gardens, where the sultan presented the princes Bahman and Perviz, and the princess Parizade, to the sultaness. These, madam, said he, are the two princes your sons, and this princess your daughter; embrace them with the same tenderness I have done, since they are worthy both of me and you. Then the tears flowed plentifully down their cheeks at these tender embraces, especially the sultaness's, for the joy of having two such princes for her sons, and such a princess for her daughter, after the afflictions she had endured upon their accounts.

The two princes and the princess prepared a magnificent repast for the sultan and sultaness, and their court. As soon as that was over, the sultan led the sultaness into the garden, and shewed her the harmonious tree and beautiful fountain. As for the bird, she had seen him in his cage; and the sultan had spared no panegyric in his praise during the repast.

When there was nothing to detain the sultan any longer, he took horse again, and with the princes Bahman and Perviz on his right and left hand, and the sultaness and the princess following them, preceded and followed by all the officers of his court, according to their posts, returned back to his capital. Crowds of people came out to meet them, and with acclamations of joy ushered them into the city, where all the people's eyes were not only upon the sultaness, the two princes, and the princess, but also upon the bird, which the princess carried before her in his cage, and who, by his sweet notes, had drawn flocks of all sorts of birds about him, which followed him, by flying from tree to tree, and from one house top to another: and nothing was to be seen or heard all that night but illuminations and acclamations of joy, from the palace to the utmost parts of the town.

The sultan of the Indies could not but admire the prodigious memory of the sultaness his wife, who had entertained and diverted him so many nights, with such new and agreeable stories, that he believed her stock inexhaustible.

A thousand and one nights had passed away in these agreeable and innocent amusements; which contributed so much towards removing the sultan's fatal prejudice against all women, and sweetening the violence of his temper, that he conceived a great esteem for the sultaness Scheherazade; and was convinced of her merit and great wisdom, and remembered with what courage she exposed herself voluntarily to be his wife, knowing the fatal destiny of the many sultanesses before her.

These considerations, and the many rare qualities he knew her to be mistress of, induced him at last to forgive her. I see, lovely Scheherazade, said he, that you can never be at a loss for these sort of stories to divert me; therefore I renounce in your favour the cruel law I had imposed on myself; and I will have you to be looked upon as the deliverer of the many damsels I had resolved to have sacrificed to my unjust resentment.

The sultaness cast herself at his feet, and embraced them with the marks of a most lively and sincere acknowledgment.

The grand visier was the first that learned this agreeable news from the sultan's own mouth, which presently was carried to all the towns and provinces, and gained the sultan and the lovely Scheherazade the blessings of all the people of the large empire of the Indies.

APPENDIX I

PRINCIPAL PLACE-NAMES IN THE *ARABIAN NIGHTS' ENTERTAINMENTS*

The transliteration of Eastern place-names in the earliest European editions of the *Arabian Nights' Entertainments* could at times be highly idiosyncratic. Galland and his anonymous English translator(s), however, seem conscientiously to retain the more precise and specific references—to locations both actual and imaginary—of their original documents, thus maintaining the distinctive and exotic oriental atmosphere of these originals as well. The following Appendix attempts to identify only the most important and frequently referred to countries, islands, cities, towns, and rivers in the text. Reference is usually given to the first appearance of the location in the volume.

ABYSSINIA: country of eastern Africa, south of Egypt, now Ethiopia. Sindbad, in recounting his first voyage, appears to refer generally to the Eastern coast of Africa as 'Abyssinia' (143).

ALEPPO: ancient city in northern Syria, about 30 miles south of what is now the Turkish border; for hundreds of years a principal market town at the crossroads of the great caravan routes (191).

ALEXANDRIA: ancient capital of Egypt, on the Mediterranean Sea at the Nile Delta, founded by Alexander the Great in 322 BC. Alexandria is vaguely footnoted in the earliest editions of Galland's *Nights* as 'a town of Arabia' (175).

ANBAR: noted in the text as 'a city on the Tigris, twenty leagues below Bagdad' (351); actually an ancient Mesopotamian (*q.v.*) town on the banks of the Euphrates River (*q.v.*), about 40 miles west of Baghdad (*q.v.*); an early capital of the Abbasid caliphs from AD 750–62 (351).

BAGDAD: i.e. Baghdad, ancient capital city located on the banks of the Tigris River at its closest point to the Euphrates *(qq.v.)*, in what is now central Iraq. The city dates from before the Arab conquest of Mesopotamia (*q.v.*) in AD 637. It was chosen by an early caliph of the Abbasid dynasty (al-Mansur), as his capital in 762, and was the spectacularly active economic and intellectual centre of the Arab world in the 8th and 9th centuries AD (66).

BALSORA: modern Basra, a busy port city south-east of Baghdad (*q.v.*) on the Shatt al-Arab (the waterway formed by the union of the Tigris and Euphrates rivers [*qq.v.*], dating from the mid-seventh century AD (132).

BELLS, ISLE OF: although the footnote identifies the Isle of Bells as Ceylon (a location later in the text called the isle of Serendib [*q.v.*]), the unidentified island kingdom referred to here may in fact have been located in the Malay peninsula, opposite Sumatra (163).

BENGAL: region in the north-east part of the Indian subcontinent (in the eighteenth century—from about 1764—a base for British expansion in India). In Galland's *Nights* Bengal is home to the princess beloved of Firouz Schah in 'The Story of the Enchanted Horse' (802).

BISNAGAR: i.e. Bisangarh or Visayanagar ('City of Victory'); an ancient Hindu capital in southern India (821).

BLACK ISLES: fictional kingdom ('which takes its name from the four little neighbouring mountains . . . formerly isles') enchanted and transformed by an evil Queen in 'The History of the young King of the Black Isles' (54).

CAIRO: 'Grand Cairo', ancient capital city of Egypt, the original settlement of which was on the eastern bank of the Nile River; a major centre of the Islamic world (175).

CASCHMIRE: i.e. Kashmir, area of the north-western Indian subcontinent, under Muslim rule from AD 1346 (813).

CASGAR: Kashghar or Kashgar; ancient oasis and trading centre located at the foot of the Pamir mountains in what is now western China (222).

CASSEL: fictional island referred to by Sindbad, alternately identified by later translators of the *Nights* as 'Kabil' and 'Poelsatta'. The island is said in Galland's translation to belong to king Mihrage (see p. 144 and note to page 173), and is rumoured by mariners to be the habitation of Dagial or 'al-Dajjal' (see p. 145 and note).

CAUCASUS, MOUNT: actually a mountain system—the Great Caucasus range—extending from the Black Sea to the Caspian Sea; referred to in the *Nights* as 'the bounds of the habitable world' (56).

CHINA: not necessarily used in the *Nights* to describe the area now covered by modern China, but often used to designate a vast empire extending eastward beyond Persia (1).

COAM: modern Qom or Qum; trading city in northern Iran, near Tehran (789).

COMARI, 'ISLE' OF: a reference, as the footnote to the original edition indicates, to Cape Comorin, south-eastern tip of the Indian subcontinent (167).

CUSA: actually Cufa or Kufah, an ancient city in what is now Iraq; a centre of Islamic civilization in the Middle Ages (175).

DAMASCUS: ancient trading city dating from the 3rd millenium BC; now capital of modern Syria (191).

DAMIETTA: ancient port city in the Nile Delta, a centre for textiles, now 8 miles from the Mediterranean Sea (253).

DERYABAR: fictional city 'in a certain island', home to the Princess of Deryabar, whose story is recited within the 'History of Codadad and his Brothers' (590).

DIARBEKER: i.e. Diyarbekir, province and city in south-eastern Turkey, situated on the Tigris river (*q.v.*), dating from the 3rd century AD (211).

EASTER ISLANDS: a mistranslation of Galland's *îles orientales* or Eastern Islands, carried into subsequent English editions; Easter Island or 'Rapanui', in the eastern Pacific Ocean, was not known to Europeans until 1722 (157).

EBENE, ISLE OF: the 'Ebony' Islands, also in later translations called the 'islands of Abrius'; an island kingdom mentioned both in 'The Story of the Second Calender, a King's Son', and in 'The Story of the Amours of Camaralzaman' (90).

EMAUS: probably Emmaus (ancient Nicopolis); modern Imwas, about 15 miles north-west of Jerusalem (*q.v.*), in what is now Israel (211).

EUPHRATES RIVER: largest river in western Asia (1,700 miles) extending south from the Armenian Plateau in Turkey to the Persian Gulf (211).

GANGES RIVER: Indian river held sacred by people of the Hindu faith, flowing 1,560 miles south-east from Uttar Pradesh, joined in what is now central Bangladesh by the Brahmaputra River, and emptying into the Bay of Bengal (1).

HALEP: i.e. Haleb; Aleppo (*q.v.*).

HANAH: i.e. Hama or Hamah; market city on the Orontes river in what is now Syria, on the caravan route between Damascus and Aleppo (*qq.v.*) (211).

HARRAN: ancient city on the Balikh river in the region of 'Diarbeker' (*q.v.*) in south-eastern Turkey (583).

HOMS: i.e. Hims, trading city in what is now western Syria, just over 100 miles north of Damascus (*q.v.*).

ISPAHAN: i.e. Isfahan or Esfahan; a city in what is now west central Iran, on the Zayadeh river, just over 200 miles south of Tehran. Ispahan was originally captured by the Arabs in AD 642 (789).

JERUSALEM: ancient middle-eastern city about 15 miles west of the Dead Sea and 35 miles east of the Mediterranean, now in the possession of Israel; a holy city for Jews, Christians, and Muslims. Jerusalem is the location of the Dome of the Rock (see p. 789 and note).

KELA, ISLE OF: alternately 'Kala' or 'Kulah', vaguely identified by later translators of the *Nights* as an area of the Malay Peninsula (163).

KHALEDAN, ISLANDS OF THE CHILDREN OF: identified by later translators of the *Nights* (including Sir Richard Frances Burton) as the 'Fortunate Isles'; the Canary Islands, in the eastern Atlantic Ocean (357).

MARDIN: Maridin, trading city in what is now eastern Turkey (211).

MECCA: city in what is now Saudi Arabia; birthplace of the prophet Muhammad, location of the Kaabba, and the holiest city in Islam (53).

MEDINA: city in western Saudi Arabia, site of the 'tomb of Muhammad'; one of the holiest cities in Islam (145).

MESOPOTAMIA: i.e. 'the Land Between the Rivers'; region between the Tigris and Euphrates Rivers (*qq.v.*) in central Asia, now Iraq (239).

MOUSSOL: i.e. Mosul, thriving commercial city on the Tigris River (*q.v.*) in what is now north-western Iraq, near the ancient Assyrian city of Nineveh (73).

PERSIA: kingdom of south-western Asia, now Iran; at times the designation 'Persia' is used in the West to refer to the whole of the Iranian Plateau (1).

REI: Rayy; ancient Iranian capital destroyed by the Mongols in AD 1220, near what is now Tehran (789).

ROPHA, ISLE OF: identified in Galland's original French translation as 'Roha'; later translators call the location 'Al-Rihah' or 'Jericho-town'; in the *Nights* an island kingdom famous for the production of camphor (150).

ROSETUM: i.e. Rosetta, modern Raschid; Egyptian maritime city at the Nile Delta near Alexandria (*q.v.*) (253).

SALABAT: i.e. Timor, mountainous island of the Malay Archipelago (155).

SAMARCANDE: i.e. Samarkand or Samarqand; 'metropolis' of 'Great Tartary' (*q.v.*), the capital city of the dominion of King Schahzenan, now a city in Uzbekistan (1).

SAMARIA: probably Samarra, a city on the Tigris river (*q.v.*) dating from the third century AD; a capital city of the Abbasid caliphate from AD 836–92 (584).

SCHIRAZ: historic trading centre in what is now south central Iraq (789).

SENGIER: i.e. Sinjar, city in northern Iraq located on the caravan route between Aleppo and Mosul (*qq.v.*) (211).

SERENDIB, ISLE OF: Ceylon, modern Sri Lanka, an island in the Indian Ocean, separated from peninsular India by Palk Strait (172).

SUEZ: Egyptian port city at the head of the Gulf of Suez (175).

TARSUS: harbour city in south central Turkey on the Tarsus river, near the Mediterranean Sea, dating from the eighth century BC (145 n.).

TARTARY, GREAT: vaguely defined central Asian territory, in the *Nights* the kingdom bestowed upon Schahzenan by his brother the sultan Schahriar, the capital city of which is Samarcande (*q.v.*) (1).

TIGRIS, RIVER: Asian river flowing south-eastward from what is now Turkey for 1,180 miles towards the Persian gulf; it meets, at the Shatt al-Arab, with the Euphrates (*q.v.*) (137).

VAKVAK, ISLES OF: identified in the earliest translations of the *Nights* as 'the isles of Japan' (143).

ZOUMAN: i.e. 'Rum' or 'Roum'; the Byzantine Empire (36).

APPENDIX II
PLOT SUMMARIES

Introductory Tale

The king of the Sassanians—'the ancient Kings of Persia'—has two sons: Schahriar and Schahzenan. Upon the death of their father, the elder Schahriar takes possession of the throne and grants his beloved brother the kingdom of Tartary. After having been separated for ten years the sultan wishes to see his brother once again and sends for him. Schahzenan has already left his capital city of Samarkand when he is possessed of a desire once more to 'embrace' his wife. He returns secretly, so that he may surprise her. To his horror he finds his wife in the arms of another man. He kills them both with his scimitar and resumes his journey to Persia.

Schahriar is overjoyed to see his brother, yet wonders why he is so melancholy. One day when Schahriar is out hunting Schahzenan sees his brother's wife and her women all in compromising positions with their slaves. Schahzenan suddenly perceives that his own situation is neither so unique nor so painful as he had originally supposed, and is returned to a good humour. Schahriar is happy to see this change in his brother and demands to know what has effected it. Schahzenan reluctantly tells him. The incredulous sultan insists on witnessing this infidelity with his own eyes. When he does see his wife's behaviour, he suggests that both he and his brother flee to an obscure place where they can conceal their misfortunes from the world. They travel until they reach the shores of a great sea, where they encounter a horrible genie who carries with him a large glass box which has been sealed with four locks. The box contains a beautiful lady of whom the genie is possessively jealous. While the genie sleeps with his head on the lady's lap, the lady in turn spies the two princes, who have attempted to conceal themselves in a nearby tree. She demands that they descend and give her their rings. She has many such tokens, she explains, and has collected them all from men whom she has encountered even while under the watchful eye of the genie who thinks he holds her secure. The brothers, having witnessed this cunning deceit, agree that there is 'no wickedness equal to that of women' and defeatedly resolve to return to their kingdoms and consider remarrying. Schahriar, however, believes that he has formulated a fool-proof scheme for ensuring that his wives remain faithful to him.

When he returns to Persia, Schahriar has his unfortunate sultaness strangled. He then embarks upon a plan of marrying anew each night and having each bride executed the following morning. His grand visier is particularly distressed by this plan, because he himself has two very beautiful daughters—Scheherazade and Dinarzade—neither of whom he wishes to lose to the sultan's brutality. Scheherazade, however, demands to be presented as one of the sultan's brides, telling her father that she knows how to put an end to the slaughter. In an attempt to dissuade her from this scheme, her father tells her:

The Fable of the Ass, the Ox, and the Labourer

There was once a farmer who was gifted with the ability to understand the language of animals, provided that he not reveal to others the substance of what he heard and understood. He one day overheard his ass advising his ox to feign sickness, in order not to be worked so hard in the fields. The advice backfired on the ass, however, as the farmer cunningly used the ass himself to perform the ox's usual labour. The wearied ass then advised the ox to act well again, pretending to have heard the farmer say that he would have the ox killed, rather than care for a sick, useless animal. The farmer laughed aloud when he overheard the ass's advice; his wife, who was standing beside him, demanded to know what he found so amusing. The farmer replied that he could not tell her. The wife responded by withholding all sexual favours from him until he did. The farmer's house was then thrown into great consternation, as the wife remained completely obstinate. The farmer then overheard the cock telling the dog that the only way to govern such a woman was to thrash her soundly. The farmer did this and succeeded in restoring order to his household. The grand visier suggests that the obstinate Scheherazade should be treated in much the same way by himself as the farmer treated his wife.

In spite of the visier's objections, however, Scheherazade is married to Schahriar and proceeds with her as-yet unspecified plan of keeping the sultan in a state of constant suspense by telling him a series of narratives, none of which is capable of being completed within the space of a single night. She first begins telling the sultan the story of:

The Merchant and the Genie

One day a merchant, throwing the pits of some dates he has been eating over his shoulder, unwittingly kills the son of a local genie. The angry genie commands the merchant to return to the same place in one year's time and forfeit his own life. The merchant dutifully returns exactly one year later. Before he meets the genie, however, he first encounters a man with a bitch, and then another man who brings with him two more black dogs. A third man also follows. When the genie appears and is about to claim the merchant's life the man's new-found companions beg the genie to carry out the intended execution only if their stories are not the most wonderful and surprising adventures he has ever heard. The genie agrees to this proposition and first listens to:

The History of the first Old Man, and the Bitch

The 'bitch' the man has brought with him is in reality his jealous wife. When he was on one occasion away from home on business this wife, who was a sorceress, maliciously transformed her stepson and the slave woman who had given birth to him into cows. Upon his return the old man almost had the two slaughtered. The man's late daughter-in-law, who was also versed in magic, restored the son and the slave to their proper human forms and in retribution transformed the wife herself into the very dog which now accompanies the man on his journey. For this story the genie forgives the merchant one third of his crime and then listens to:

The Story of the second Old Man, and the two black Dogs

These two 'dogs' are in fact the old man's brothers, whom he had in the past several times rescued from financial distress. When they had finally succeeded in engaging in a profitable trading venture with their brother's help the two nevertheless became jealous of his share in the profits and threw him overboard from the ship on which they were travelling. A fairy rescued the merchant, restored him to his home, and transformed the two ungrateful brothers into dogs for a period of five years. The merchant is now travelling with his canine brothers in quest of that fairy, since the five years have passed and he now generously seeks to have his brothers restored to their natural form.

Scheherazade does not tell the story of the third man. She instead begins:

The Story of the Fisherman

A fisherman one day rescues a genie from a bottle, only to find that the liberated genie has resolved in his long captivity to kill rather than reward the man who eventually sets him free. The genie is soon tricked back into the bottle by the clever fisherman, however, who claims that he does not understand how a genie now so large and intimidating could ever have fitted into such a small vessel. As the genie pleads for his liberty, the fisherman tells him:

The Story of the Grecian King and the Physician Douban

A physician named Douban one day cured a Grecian king of his mysterious illness, but an evil visier was subsequently jealous of the favour Douban then found in the king's eyes. The visier attempted to turn the king against the physician, but the king responded to his minister's allegations with the warning implicit in:

The Story of the Husband and Parrot

A certain man one day purchased a talking parrot in order to keep an eye on his wife while he was away from home. The wife foiled her husband's vigilance, however, by covering the bird's cage, pouring water over it, and creating a great deal of noise. When the farmer questioned the bird regarding what had passed in his house while he was away, the parrot consequently told the master that it had been a terrible, stormy night. The master, thinking the deceived bird to be telling a deliberate untruth, had the parrot killed. The visier responds in turn to the king's tale with:

The Story of the Visier that was punished

A young prince was almost killed one day by an ogress when he was out hunting. This was due to the negligence of a visier who, having been commanded never to lose sight of the prince, nevertheless allowed him to pursue game far into the forest unaccompanied. The moral of the tale warns against placing too much confidence in the advice of a single councillor.

The Grecian king was eventually convinced by the visier that Douban was indeed treacherous, and condemned the physician to death. Douban yet intrigued the king, however, by telling him that even after his head had been severed from his body, he would speak to the court, provided the king turn to a certain page in the physician's magic book. The king was anxious to see such a marvel and had Douban decapitated immediately. Douban's severed head did indeed talk to the king, but only to tell him that the pages of the enchanted book had been poisoned, so that the king, wetting his fingers the better to turn those pages, also died.

The History of the young King of the Black-Isles

The fisherman suggests that just as the king stubbornly rejected the pleas of the physician for life, so too the genie had before rejected his own pleas for mercy and must now likewise pay the consequence for his rash behaviour. In his desperation the genie finally promises to show the fisherman an enchanted lake where he can catch extraordinary fish. Having agreed to this scheme, the fisherman travels with the genie to the lake, catches some fish, and is told to take them to the nearby palace of the sultan. The fish are of four colours: white, red, blue, and yellow. The sultan's cook attempts to prepare the fish to be served at the royal table, but is each time interrupted at a certain point by the vision of a young lady—and on one occasion the vision of a gigantic slave—who magically appear and quiz the talking fish as they grill in the pan. Following the ritual the fish appear to have been burnt as black as coal and are unfit to be served. The sultan is amazed and asks to see the place where such strange fish can be caught. He travels with the fisherman to the lake and there discovers another palace. Inside the palace he meets the king of the Black Isles—a man whose lower body has been transformed into black marble. This king tells the sultan that while tracking his adulterous wife in her infidelity he had been able to deal her lover an incapacitating wound, but that his wife had in turn transformed his body into marble, and had then turned his kingdom into a lake. Moreover, she then transformed his subjects—respectively Muslims, Persians, Christians, and Jews—into the four types of fish which had been discovered in the pond. The queen has since placed her injured lover on a protected bier where she visits him regularly. The sultan undertakes to slay this lover for the king of the Black Isles, which he does, and then—disguised—places himself on the bier. When the queen arrives for her visit the sultan captures her and demands that she return both the king of the Black Isles and his kingdom to their former states. After she has done so the sultan sees that one effect of the enchanting transformation had been to make the Black Isles appear to be much closer to his own realm than they actually are. The restoration of the proper order of things brings the realization that he has a long journey to make before he can return to his own palace. He finally does return home, however, and rewards the fisherman for having provided him with a remarkable adventure.

Scheherazade tells the sultan that she knows even finer stories than this, and on the next night begins:

The Story of the three Calenders, Sons of Kings; and of the five Ladies of Bagdad

A porter who one day helps the beautiful maiden Safie collect and carry her goods home for a grand feast is allowed to remain with her that evening and with her even more beautiful sisters—Zobeide and Amine—and partake of the feast. The four have a wonderful time but are soon interrupted by three 'calenders' or mendicant monks. All three are blind in the right eye and have had their heads shaved. They are new to Baghdad and beg to stay with the sisters. They are soon joined by the caliph Haroun Alraschid, who enjoys wandering the streets of his capital incognito with his visier, Giafar, and the chief of his eunuchs, Mesrour. The one rule that the three sisters impose as the condition for their hospitality is that their guests not ask any questions regarding their behaviour in their own home. Yet, after the porter, the calenders, and the caliph witness the sisters mysteriously and ritualistically whip two dogs which are brought before them, and then observe that one of the sisters bears some very bad scars about her neck, they resolve to ask what has brought about such strange domestic behaviour. The minute they make their inquiries, however, they are surrounded by strong slaves and told that they are going to be killed. Only if they tell their own histories can they be spared. The porter immediately relates his own adventure of having met Safie in the market-place and then having asked to remain for the feast, and is spared. Following his brief account one of the calenders begins:

The History of the First Calender, a King's Son

A young prince had once assisted his friend and cousin in conducting an amorous affair. The cousin subsequently disappeared but the prince, who had taken an oath of secrecy in the matter, could not tell his uncle that he suspected just where his cousin had gone. The prince returned to his own country only to find that his father had been deposed. He eventually found his way back to his uncle's realm (having lost one of his eyes as a result of the usurper's cruelty) where he resolved finally to tell the grief-stricken king where he might find his son. When the two arrived at the place where the prince had left the lovers to rendezvous, they found both the cousin and his lover on a bier, burnt to cinders. The prince learned from his distraught uncle that his cousin's 'lover' was in fact that young man's own sister; the uncle felt that the two had been justly punished for conducting an incestuous affair. The prince was prevented from returning to his own kingdom by his father's enemies, and escaped to Baghdad only by disguising himself as a calender.

The Story of the Second Calender, a King's Son

The second calender tells them that he is in fact a young prince who has been living in hiding and disguised as a mere forester in the kingdom of one of his father's enemies. He one day stumbled upon a young woman who was being held captive by a hostile genie. The woman soon became romantically involved with the young prince.

When the genie discovered this relationship he threatened to kill the couple. The young prince asked for clemency by relating to the genie:

The Story of the envious Man, and of him that he envied

There was once a man who was so honest and fair-minded that in order to cure a neighbour of his envy he decided to move out of his own town and resettle elsewhere; the envious man would thus not have to witness the other's honesty and prosperity on a daily basis. Yet even this measure proved futile, as the incurably envious man one day had the opportunity to push his former neighbour down a well, and promptly did so. The generous man was not killed, however, but was rescued by the genies and fairies that lived in the well. Moreover, these fairies told him that on the very next day the sultan was going to come to him to ask his advice as to how to cure his daughter of her possession by an evil genie. What he must do, the fairies informed him, was to burn some of the white hairs taken from the tail of a black cat, and spot the head of the princess with the ashes. The man was able to climb from the well and on the next day rescued the princess from her possession in precisely this manner. The sultan eventually died without male heirs and left this generous man his kingdom. Enjoying such good fortune, the man not only forgave the neighbour who once envied him, but actually rewarded him.

Having heard this tale, the genie was persuaded only to the point of turning the young prince into an ape rather than killing him outright. Having been transformed into an ape the prince was taken in by a sultan who was promptly astonished at the animal's obvious intelligence, reasoning, and—more particularly—his ability to write. The sultan's daughter, who was well-versed in magic, told her father that this 'ape' was in fact a man who had been enchanted. The sultan asked his daughter to return the unfortunate prince to his natural form. The princess then conjured the genie who had transformed the young man. The two engaged in a spectacular battle in which they took upon themselves the forms of various animals. The genie finally transformed himself into fire, but even then the princess was able to withstand and vanquish him. She returned the prince, who had lost an eye in the battle, to his original form. She had herself been so weakened and poisoned by the fire, however, that she soon died. The grief-stricken sultan asked that the young prince leave his kingdom. The prince had thus outfitted himself as a calender and come to Baghdad.

The History of the third Calender, a King's Son

The third calender, a young man named Agib who also happens to be a prince, was once shipwrecked when the boat on which he was sailing drew too close to a mountain of black adamant. The adamant drew all the nails from the ship and the vessel split and sank. The prince alone survived the wreck. Stranded on a strange island, he was told in a dream that a man made entirely of metal would come to the island rowing a boat. The prince was instructed to get into the boat wherein, after ten days, he would be delivered to some further islands whence he would be able to return home. The only condition of this strange rescue was that he was not to express any thanks to God, or even mention the name of God. All the events revealed in the dream came to pass, except that just as they approached land the prince inadvertently thanked God for his rescue, and the boat in which he and the automaton had been travelling immediately sank. The prince then swam to another island, where he encountered a young man who had been immured in a subterranean cavern. The boy told the prince that he had been placed in the cavern by his father for his own safety, due to a prophecy which foretold that he would be killed at the end of forty days by the hand of one prince Agib. Agib, without telling the young man that he was himself that very prince, assured the boy that he would watch over him and keep him safe. On the fortieth day the two spent together, however, Agib accidentally killed the boy. The young man's father, who had returned to the island to retrieve his son, was devastated; prince Agib managed to remain hidden on the island. He was finally able to leave only when the level of water separating him from the mainland subsided. Once again on dry land, Agib encountered ten men—all blind in one eye—who lived in a great copper castle. Each night the ten berated and abased themselves for what they called their idleness and debaucheries. The prince was explicitly instructed not to ask what had happened to the men that they should so routinely humiliate themselves. When his curiosity got the better of him, however, he was told that he might endure what had happened to them for himself. He was first instructed to disguise himself as a sheep. Having done so, he was carried off by a giant bird called a roc, who in time deposited him at a strange castle. At this castle he for some time lived a pleasant life with forty beautiful young ladies, each of whom would in turn spend the night with him. After forty days they informed him that it would be necessary for them to leave him for a time, and told him that he might go anywhere within the castle while they were gone, except through one pair of golden doors. Agib, however, ignored this prohibition. Once opening the doors and entering the room beyond he encountered a magnificent black horse, who carried him back to the copper castle with the ten old men. When leaving, the horse swished its tail violently and blinded the prince in one eye. He was then told to journey to Baghdad, where he would meet with someone who would decide his destiny.

Zobeide is pleased with the stories, and decides that all the guests—including the caliph and his visier—will thus be spared. Yet the following morning the caliph, his own curiosity yet unsatisfied, has the women brought before him to explain their odd conduct.

The Story of Zobeide

Zobeide has had four sisters, the two who remain with her now—her half-sisters—and two full sisters. The latter came to live with her after bad marriages and the three of them subsequently engaged in trade together. On one trading voyage Zobeide decided to explore the place where they had landed. She soon discovered a city whose inhabitants—with the exception of a young man whom she discovered diligently reading the Koran—had all been turned into stone. It appeared that this lone survivor was the only one to have been spared the punishment placed upon the city for its failure to adhere to the 'true religion'. Zobeide took the young man with her and, on the voyage home (much to the consternation of her two sisters), resolved to marry him. The jealous sisters soon threw the couple overboard. The man drowned, but Zobeide herself was washed ashore and survived. She found herself upon a strand where she chanced to observe a large serpent being pursued by another winged serpent. Taking pity on the one pursued, she chased the second monster away with a rock. She then fell asleep and awoke to find beside her a beautiful woman holding two dogs that had been tied together. The woman, in fact a fairy, revealed herself to have been the very 'serpent' whom Zobeide had recently rescued from attack. She further informed Zobeide that the dogs were in reality her sisters, who had been thus punished and transformed because of their jealousy and malice. Zobeide was ordered to whip them without fail each night.

The Story of Amine

Amine was once married to a handsome man on the condition that she not speak to any other men. A month after her marriage she visited a silk merchant who demanded for his wares only the payment of a kiss. Amine was at first reluctant to grant the merchant's request but, convinced by her nurse that by this payment she would not, indeed, actually have spoken to a man, she eventually permitted it. The merchant, however, maliciously bit her. Amine attempted to hide her disfigured face from her husband, but he eventually learned the truth about the encounter. Rather than killing her, he beat her about the neck. Amine then sought out Zobeide, who now lived with her other half-sister, who had taken refuge with her after the death of her mother.

After all this is told to the caliph, Zobeide notes that the fairy who enchanted her sisters left with her a tuft of hair which, when burnt, would call her to Zobeide, wherever she might be at the time. The hair is burnt, and the genie appears. At the behest of the caliph, she transforms the dogs back into humans and removes the scars from the neck of Amine. The genie also tells the caliph that Amine's husband is none other than his own son Amin, who married her in secret. Amin is called to the assembly and again receives his wife. The caliph himself marries Zobeide, and the other three sisters are married to the three calenders.

The Story of Sindbad the Sailor

The porter Hindbad, who works hard for a living, one day sits down to rest and refresh himself outside a beautiful palace in Baghdad. He laments that while his condition is so fatiguing and deplorable, whoever owns the palace appears to live a life of continual pleasure and undeserved luxury. The owner of the house, the famous traveller Sindbad the Sailor, overhears Hindbad's remarks and invites him inside to partake of a sumptuous banquet. Sindbad then tells the weary porter his story:

His First Voyage

On his earliest voyage, Sindbad and his fellow sailors mistook the back of a large whale resting on the ocean surface for a small island. Eager for a brief respite from their voyage, the sailors disembarked and began eating and drinking on the whale's back. The whale soon 'trembled' and prepared to dive, however, and though some of his companions were able to make it back to their sloop, Sindbad soon found himself at the mercy of the waves. He survived an entire night at sea before being cast, exhausted, upon the shores of a strange island. He was there rescued by the grooms attending the horses of one King Mihrage. He later learned that the King's grooms every year brought the animals to an isolated point of the island kingdom, so that the mares could be mated with a powerful horse that rose out of the ocean. Sindbad was eventually able to return to Baghdad when he encountered the merchant who had originally abandoned him at sea, and who had subsequently given him up for lost. Sindbad's goods and the profits arising from them were thus restored to him.

The Second Voyage of Sindbad the Sailor

On his second outing Sindbad was mistakenly abandoned on an island. He there discovered the nest of a roc. After hiding in the roc's nest overnight, Sindbad thought to escape from the island by attaching himself to the bird so that when it flew away the following morning it would carry him away as well. The plan worked, and Sindbad was carried to a valley the floor of which was littered with huge diamonds. The valley was also home, however, to a species of serpents so large they seemed able to swallow an entire elephant. Sindbad was able to escape from the valley by observing the behaviour of some merchants and hunters who plundered its riches. The merchants threw huge chunks of meat into the valley from high precipices; when the pieces of meat hit the ground, the facets of the diamonds stuck to them. The chunks of meat were then carried out of the impenetrable valley by eagles, who grasped them in their talons and carried the diamonds away as well. The merchants could then raid the bird's eyries for the diamonds. Collecting the largest jewels he could find, Sindbad tied himself to a piece of meat and was soon carried out of the valley. He in time made his way to Baghdad via the island of Ropha, where he observed huge camphor trees and rhinoceroses.

The Third Voyage of Sindbad the Sailor

Sindbad's ship was on his third voyage attacked and raided by a tribe of small but fierce savages. Taking the ship, the savages then abandoned the crew on the shore of an island inhabited by a huge cyclops. The cyclops devoured several of Sindbad's companions before they were able to blind the monster and escape from their captivity by means of some hastily constructed rafts. The crew then landed on another island, only to find that it was home to a species of deadly serpent. The serpents soon ate Sindbad's remaining shipmates. Sitting high in a tree and lighting a fire about its base, Sindbad himself managed to escape. He then luckily encountered some merchants (including one member of the crew who had accidentally abandoned him on his preceding journey and had honestly preserved for him his goods and profits) who were able to return him to Baghdad. Thus, in spite of all his misfortunes, Sindbad's wealth was still increasing.

The Fourth Voyage of Sindbad the Sailor

Sindbad was on this voyage shipwrecked and captured by cannibals who drugged and ate all of his companions; Sindbad alone had the foresight not to swallow the drug. Soon grown lean and unappetizing, he was allowed some degree of freedom by his captors and was eventually able, with the help of some spice merchants, to escape from the island. These merchants carried him to a kingdom, the ruler of which so much admired Sindbad that he offered him his daughter's hand in marriage. Sindbad accepted the princess as his bride, but was soon horrified to learn of the local custom which dictated that a spouse must be immured with his or her dead mate when that mate died. Sindbad's wife promptly expired, and he was immured—alive and with only a few days' sustenance—with her corpse in the deep burial pit. He for some time survived by killing the living partners who subsequently descended into the darkness with their own dead husbands and wives, and appropriating their temporary provisions of bread and water. He eventually escaped via a hole in the cavern through which, he discovered, a sea-monster entered to consume the corpses. He was rescued by merchants with whom he again engaged in commerce before returning to Baghdad 'with infinite riches'.

The Fifth Voyage of Sindbad the Sailor

Sindbad was by now a captain of his own vessel, which had been built especially for him. Landing on a deserted island early in the voyage, the merchants who were travelling with him discovered the nest of a roc and stole the egg they found therein. They then ate the young roc which was just about to hatch. When the rocs returned to the nest and discovered the theft, they sank the ship by dropping huge boulders upon it. Sindbad again found himself shipwrecked on a desert island, on which he encountered an elderly man who was nevertheless in superb physical shape. This man managed to clasp his legs around Sindbad's neck and proceeded effectively to use him as a horse. Sindbad eventually managed to kill the old man by getting him drunk and dispatching him when he was thus incapacitated. Sindbad was later told by those who rescued him from the island that his captor had been the famous Old Man of the Sea, and that Sindbad himself was the first ever to have escaped his service. Sindbad again engaged in profitable trade with the merchants who rescued him and returned home.

The Sixth Voyage of Sindbad the Sailor

Sindbad's vessel was on this voyage drawn into a current which sucked passing ships into an immense gulf and destroyed them. Sindbad once more found himself the only survivor on a strange shore. He located a river which, he perceived, ran into an underground cavern, and resolved to follow it. He was rescued by a group of natives, one of whom spoke Arabic, and was taken to the city of Serendib. He enjoyed his stay there with the king, and was eventually sent back to Baghdad with messages and gifts of friendship from the ruler of Serendib for the caliph.

The Seventh and last Voyage of Sindbad the Sailor

Sindbad was soon sent back to Serendib with reciprocal gifts and a message from the caliph to the king, but on his return to Baghdad was captured and enslaved by corsairs or pirates. He was then sold in slavery to a merchant who engaged him to hunt elephants. Sindbad was successful in killing many elephants until the animals one day surrounded the tree he was hiding in and led him to a mysterious elephant graveyard. Sindbad reasoned that they discovered the place to him so that the merchant might still profit from the elephants' tusks and teeth, yet forbear killing those animals yet alive. Pleased with Sindbad's discovery, the merchant released him and he returned to Baghdad.

Having listened to Sindbad's many adventures, Hindbad acknowledges the teller's former hardships and is in time made a familiar of the household.

The Story of the Three Apples

The caliph Haroun Alraschid is once again travelling about the city of Baghdad at night with his visier to see what his subjects are doing. He encounters an honest-looking fisherman who has not had a catch all day. The caliph tells the fisherman that he will give him a rich reward for whatever he hauls out of the Tigris with his net. The man retrieves a sealed trunk which they soon discover contains the dismembered body of a young woman. The caliph is shocked at this discovery—so much so that he demands that his visier find out who committed such an outrage within three days, or the visier will have to pay for the crime with his own life. The visier's search proves fruitless, yet at the moment when he and forty members of his family are about to be executed, two men—one young, one old—simultaneously step forward and both confess to the crime. The young man swears that it was he who committed the act. He tells the caliph:

The Story of the Lady that was murdered, and of the young Man her Husband

The woman who has been found murdered had been the young man's wife. She had fallen ill and had requested as a refreshment some apples. The young husband tried everywhere to purchase apples but could not find a single one. It was finally necessary for him to travel as far as Balsora, where he was even then able to purchase only three. Soon after leaving the three apples by his wife's side, he encountered a slave who entered his shop with an apple in his hand. Knowing that the fruit was simply not to be had in Baghdad, he asked the slave how he had come by it. The slave replied that his mistress had given the apple to him, and that she had even informed him that her husband had taken a deal of trouble to get it. In a jealous rage the young man returned home, killed his wife, and then dumped her body in the river. Returning to his house, however, he encountered his eldest son, who told him that it was in fact he who had taken one of the apples, and that a slave had subsequently stolen it from him. The boy had pleaded with the slave, telling him how long it had taken his father to find the apple, but the slave had made off with the fruit none the less. The young man now realized that he had killed his wife wrongly. He had subsequently mourned with the old man, his wife's father, for three days.

Having listened to this tale the caliph decides that the person really at fault is the false and misleading slave. The visier is again threatened with death; this time it is the slave he must produce within three days. At the last minute he discovers that the culprit is a slave belonging to his own household, one Rihan. The visier asks for clemency for his servant from the caliph if he can entertain him with a yet more fabulous tale than that in which they have been involved. He then tells:

The Story of Noureddin Ali, and Bedreddin Hassan

The caliph's minister tells a lengthy tale of two brothers, the sons of a visier of Cairo, who early in life fell into a silly argument after they had decided that they would not only marry on the same day, but that their wives should likewise conceive on the same day, and bear their children on the same day. Moreover, they also agreed that the two children would themselves one day marry each other. After their dispute, however, one of the brothers—Noureddin Ali—left Cairo and travelled to Balsora, where he eventually married the visier's daughter and raised a son, whom he named Bedreddin Hassan. When Noureddin Ali died, the son was so grief-stricken that he mourned for a longer period than usual. The sultan, insulted by Bedreddin Hassan's neglect, ordered him seized. Bedreddin Hassan then decided to flee Balsora, and sought temporary refuge at his father's tomb. On the way he encountered a Jewish merchant. The merchant asked to purchase from him the first refusal on some of the cargoes of his father's ships which yet remained at sea. Seeing this as a way to obtain some sorely needed ready money, Bedreddin Hassan accepted the merchant's offer. Asleep by his father's tomb, he was then spotted by a genie and a fairy who declared him to be among the most beautiful of mortals. They together decided that he was deserving of a certain young woman of Cairo who was about to be married to an ill-suited groom as ugly as a 'hobgoblin'. The two then magically carried Bedreddin Hassan to Cairo, and contrived a plan by which he could outwit the groom, and himself marry and sleep with the young woman. In the morning, however, the genie and the fairy again magically removed him to Damascus. The father of the young woman was of course none other than Schemseddin Mohammed, the brother of Noureddin Ali introduced at the beginning of the story. The woman was eventually told that her husband was indeed her cousin, the son of Noureddin Ali. She eventually bore a son, Agib, who was shamed in school because he could not name his own father. Agib and his mother then left Cairo in search of Bedreddin Hassan, who had by then become a pastry-cook in Damascus. Through a complicated sequence of events, the three were eventually reunited, and Bedreddin Hassan was in turn reconciled with his long-lost uncle and father-in-law. The original plan of the two brothers—Schemseddin Mohammed and Noureddin Ali—had thus, in spite of their own efforts to hinder it, eventually come to pass.

The caliph is enchanted with his visier's story. He not only pardons the servant Rihan, but marries the young man who had mistakenly murdered his wife to one of his own slaves.

The Story of the Little Hunch-back

A tailor and his wife one day entertain a merry hunchback, who unfortunately chokes on a bone at their table and dies. Terrified of discovery, they shift the corpse to the house of a Jewish doctor, who kicks it downstairs in the dark and then thinks that it is in fact he who has killed the hunchback. The doctor in turn removes the body to the house of a Turk—one of the Sultan's purveyors—who mistakes the corpse for a thief and, assaulting him, believes himself to have killed him. The purveyor then props the hunchback in the street, where the body is soon assailed by a Christian merchant. The watchman sees this final desecration and hauls the merchant before a judge. As the Christian is about to be hanged, each of the guilty parties involved speaks up in turn. The hunchback turns out to be the sultan's own 'Crump-back', and the sultan finds the story exceedingly uncommon. The Christian Merchant however, hoping to mitigate the death sentence still placed upon him, offers to relate an even more astonishing tale. He tells:

The Story told by the Christian Merchant

The merchant had once encountered in Cairo a young man whose right hand had been cut off. The man had, he told the merchant, once fallen in love with a woman who had asked him after each of their encounters for a purse filled with fifty pieces of gold. This he was able to supply for some time but, finally having run out of money, he decided to steal a purse for her, and his hand had consequently been cut off. The woman, affected by this cruel sacrifice, nursed him back to health, returned all the money he had given her, and eventually married him.

The sultan is not pleased with this tale, however, so the Purveyor tells:

The Story told by the Sultan of Casgar's Purveyor

The purveyor had only the day before met a man at a wedding feast who perversely declined to eat a certain garlic sauce which had been set upon the table. Moreover, his thumbs and big toes had been severed. The man went on to explain to his host and to the purveyor that he had once fallen in love with a young favourite of the court, a wealthy aristocrat, and eventually agreed to meet with her in secret. The meeting, which was to occur in the ladies' apartments in the seraglio, was fraught with danger, but the relationship between the two was soon recognized by the young favourite's mistress, Zobeide, and the couple were permitted to be married. But on the last day of the wedding ceremonies the groom approached his bride without having washed his hands after eating a garlic sauce. Profoundly disgusted with his behaviour, she first had him beaten and then maimed. The two were eventually reconciled, but the man obviously retained to that day his aversion to a dish of stewed garlic.

The sultan notes that the story is indeed extraordinary, but still contends that that of his hunch-back is even more fascinating. The Jewish physician then tries his hand at appeasing the sultan with:

The Story told by the Jewish Physician

The physician too had once encountered a man whose hand had been severed. The man told the physician that when he was younger he had travelled to Damascus with his uncles, who were merchants. While staying in that city he had met two beautiful women who several times visited his home and feasted with him. On one such visit, however, one of the ladies dropped dead unexpectedly in his house. The man fled in fear to join his uncles, who had journeyed on to Cairo. After three years he returned to Damascus and in his former home found a necklace left by the woman who had so suddenly died. He attempted to sell the necklace but—since he was willing to accept such a low price for it—the merchants to whom it was offered assumed that he knew its true value and that it must have been stolen. As a penalty for the supposed theft his hand had thus been cut off. The governor of Damascus, however, recognized the necklace to have been among the possessions of his youngest daughter and informed the young man that her death had not, as he had assumed, been in any way his own fault, but that she had rather been killed by her own wicked sister. The governor later gave the young man another one of his daughters in marriage.

The sultan still considers the present adventure yet more extraordinary, but is offered one more occasion to change his mind by listening to:

The Story told by the Taylor

The tailor tells of having been invited two days before to the house of a certain gentleman for an early meal. The gentleman himself arrived home escorting a lame though handsome young man who refused to remain in the house when he espied among the company a certain barber. The young man explained that the garrulous barber had prevented him from keeping his liaison with a beautiful woman—the daughter of one of the most eminent cadis in the city—through his endless prattling, and that in the course of escaping from his ensuing misadventures, he had thus injured his leg. Having listened to the young man's account, the barber protested that there was little truth in the tale. As one of seven brothers, he further argued, it was he who, rather than speaking too much, was in fact the most reticent. As proof of this he tells:

The Story of the Barber

On one occasion the barber had mistakenly joined ten robbers on a barge on the Tigris, thinking that they were a merry company on their way together to celebrate a feast day. The ten men were in reality being taken to be executed. The ten were duly dispatched, but the executioner halted when he came to an unexpected eleventh prisoner: the barber himself. The barber offered this incident as proof of his constitutional inclination to silence, in so far as it demonstrated that even in such an extreme situation he could hold his tongue until the very moment of execution. His brothers, he further noted, were neither so wise nor so fortunate. He went on to relate:

The Story of the Barber's eldest Brother

Bacbouc, a hunchbacked tailor, fell in love with an avaricious and ill-natured miller's wife who, instead of returning his affection, abused him terribly. On one occasion she even contrived to have her husband hook Bacbouc up to the mill where he was humiliatingly whipped and used as a mule to grind the corn. The weary Bacbouc returned home and resolved never to think of the miller's wife again.

The Story of the Barber's second Brother

Backbarah (or Barbarah) the toothless, was made a fool of by a wealthy woman and her ladies. They on one occasion dressed him in women's clothing and exposed him to the ridicule of the town.

The Story of the Barber's third Brother

A third brother, Bacbac, was blind. A highwayman one day overheard him confiding the hiding place of his money to some of his blind companions. The highwayman then insinuated himself among the company, hoping eventually to gain access to the money. The group realized that there was a cheat among them and they captured him and called for a magistrate. The clever highwayman, however, then pretended that he too was blind. The frustrated magistrate had the entire company whipped. The highwayman then opened his eyes midway through the punishment, claiming that the others too were able to see, and would acknowledge it if they were only whipped enough. Thus they were all—including Bacbac—severely whipped and finally banished; the highwayman made away with most of Bacbac's money.

The Story of the Barber's fourth Brother

Alcouz (also called Barbarak), the barber's fourth brother, was a butcher who was cheated out of his business by a magician; his unscrupulous competitor deceived the community into thinking that Alcouz was selling the meat of humans rather than that of sheep. Alcouz was later mistaken for a highwayman and beaten.

The Story of the Barber's fifth Brother

Alnaschar (or Alnascar) set up as a merchant of glasswork and, upon his inheritance, began day-dreaming that he had married a rich visier's daughter who was obsequiously servile towards him. In the middle of his day-dreams he imagined kicking his wife, and in reality kicked over his merchandise and destroyed his shop. A tailor laughed at him, but a wealthy woman passing by reimbursed him for his loss. An old woman then passed by who promised to introduce him to her beautiful mistress. Rather than having any romantic encounter, however, he was instead led to a palace where he was beaten and robbed, had salt rubbed into his wounds, and was left for dead. He returned to the house seeking revenge, and killed the old woman and the slave who had actually wounded him. Having taken money from the house, however, he was brought before a magistrate and banished.

The Story of the Barber's sixth Brother

Schacabac, who was born with a hare lip, was a beggar. He encountered a wealthy though slightly crazed man who pretended to entertain him in a rich and generous manner, but instead offered him invisible food and drink. Schacabac was later captured by Bedouins on the way to Mecca.

The sultan asks to meet this barber who has provided the tailor with so many stories. The barber is produced and declares that the hunchback is not dead at all. Rubbing the victim's neck with balsam and extracting from his throat a bit of fish-bone, the barber revives him, and all ends happily.

The History of Aboulhassen Ali Ebn Becar, and Schemselnihar, Favourite of Caliph Haroun Alraschid

A prince of Persia named Ebn Becar is introduced by the sultan's favourite druggist—Aboulhassen Ebn Thaher—to a young woman named Schemselnihar. Schemselnihar, whose beauty is equal to her name, which means 'Sun of the Day', is the favourite mistress of the caliph. Although the druggist tries to warn him that such a romance will prove a dangerous undertaking, Ebn Becar soon falls passionately in love with Schemselnihar, and the couple are entertained at the druggist's home. Ebn Thaher eventually decides that the couple are acting far too indiscreetly, however, and informs a jeweller friend that he is going to retire to Balsora 'until the storm blows over' and the affair between the two has ended. The jeweller is himself intrigued by the couple's romance, however, and soon takes the place of Ebn Thaher as the pair's go-between. Borrowing elaborate decorations from some of his friends, he sets up a house in which the two can meet each other without the caliph's knowledge. This retreat is unfortunately broken into by highwaymen and the lovers themselves are taken captive. Although the couple are eventually freed, it becomes necessary for them to remain apart. They are able to communicate with each other for some time with the help of several confidants and loyal friends, but both soon die. They are finally buried together in a single, monumental tomb in Baghdad.

The Story of the Amours of Camaralzaman, Prince of the Isles of the Children of Khaledan, and of Badoura, Princess of China

Camaralzaman, a young prince of the Isles of the Children of Khaledan, refuses to marry any of the princesses presented to him by his father, the sultan Schahzaman. So too has Badoura, the princess of China, been so pampered by her father that she likewise refuses to be married. One night the couple are magically brought together through the efforts of two genies; both awaken the following morning claiming to be in love with the person who had been brought to their respective bedsides the night before. No one, however, can make any sense of their accounts of what has supposedly passed in the night. The princess of China is thought to be mad and astrologers are called in, unsuccessfully, to cure her. Marzavan—the foster-brother of the princess—returns home after many years of travelling and is shocked to find the kingdom in such an uproar. Seers and physicians alike are being executed because they cannot discover the cause of the princess's supposed illness. The princess herself tells Marzavan what has happened and he, believing her account, sensibly sets out to find a prince who claims to have had a similar experience. He eventually discovers Camaralzaman, who returns with him to China. Camaralzaman and the princess Badoura are thus finally brought together and married.

After some time has passed Camaralzaman desires to visit his father the sultan, whom he feels may soon die. Both he and his bride undertake the lengthy journey back to his native kingdom, which lies near Persia. After a month of continuous travelling they stop at a shady grove in order to rest and take some refreshment. While the princess is sleeping, the prince observes a talisman she has been carrying with her—one which he had never before noticed. He removes the small seal from her purse, but has no sooner begun to examine it, than it is snatched from his hands by a passing bird. In his efforts to retrieve the talisman the prince is imperceptibly led far away from his beloved. He eventually finds himself at a place called the City of the Idolaters, where he is befriended by a Muslim gardener and told that he will have to wait a year before there will be a ship leaving for the Isle of Ebene, whence he can finally travel to his native country.

The princess, meanwhile, is puzzled and heartbroken by the prince's sudden and unexplained departure. She decides to continue her journey in the guise of a man—in fact, of Prince Camaralzaman himself. She arrives at Ebene, where she is asked by the king to marry his daughter, the princess Haiatalnefous. Badoura reasons that such a match will eventually add to her husband's domains and agrees to the union. Initially the princess Haiatalnefous is distressed because her new 'husband' will not, understandably, consummate their marriage. After the princess of China perforce explains her situation, however, the two become fast friends.

A year has soon passed and Camaralzaman prepares to depart from the City of the Idolaters. Prior to leaving he has discovered a cave containing many urns filled with gold. He generously divides these riches between his host and himself. He is planning to have his share shipped with him, but the gardener's death causes him to miss the boat. Fortunately, the talisman of the princess has been mixed with the gold dust he has had transported to Ebene, and comes to the attention of the princess. She sends immediately for the 'merchant' who has shipped the goods, knowing that it must be her husband. The two are reunited, and the princess Haiatalnefous—to everybody's satisfaction—becomes the prince's second wife.

The Story of the two Princes Amgrad and Assad and The Story of Prince Amgrad, and a Lady of the City of Magicians

In a continuation of the preceding tale, the prince Camaralzaman has one son by each of his wives. The boys are named Amgrad and Assad. Each of the two wives, however—Badoura and Haiatalnafous—fall incestuously in love with the son of the other.

While the Prince is away on a hunting trip, the wives independently attempt to seduce their respective stepsons. The virtue of the two sons (who are the best of friends) is outraged. The wives decide to cover their guilt by turning the blame about, and claiming that it was the boys who had in fact pursued and attacked them. Upon his return the prince believes his wives, and peremptorily orders both of his sons executed. Yet when the two sons together save the appointed assassin from the attack of a lion, the assassin resolves not to complete the task, and lets the brothers go free. They wander for a month and arrive in the City of the Magicians, where Assad is taken captive by a people who worship fire rather than Muhammad, and intend to sacrifice him at the Blue Sea and the Fiery Mountain some time soon. He is nightly whipped by the two daughters of his captor, whose names are Bostava and Cavama.

Amgrad proceeds into the city, where he meets a woman who is obsessively amorous towards him. He lies and tells her he owns a rich house in town, to which he leads her. She sees it is locked and breaks the lock to enter. Amgrad is terrified that when the real owner arrives they will be taken into custody and killed, but the owner, named Bahader, sees the humour of the situation and pretends to be a slave and helps Amgrad. The woman is so incensed at the behaviour of this 'servant', however, that she almost kills him, and Amgrad ends up killing her instead in order to defend his new-found patron. Bahader tries to dispose of the body, but is stopped in the street and brought before the king, who almost executes him, notwithstanding the fact that he holds a court position. Amgrad arrives and explains what has happened. He is recognized as a prince by the king, and appointed grand visier.

Assad, meanwhile, is taken to be sacrificed, but the ship in which he is carried is forced to put into port at the capital of Queen Margiana, an enemy to the adorers of fire. In an effort to appease her, they sell her the 'Mohamatten' slave they have on board—Assad—but later steal him back. Queen Margiana pursues the ship for her handsome new prince; the fire-worshippers throw him overboard, and he makes his way back to the City of the Magicians. His captors are hard on his heels after Margiana has sunk their boat and placed them on land however, and Assad no sooner arrives in the city than he is captured again and returned to the basement to be whipped. The daughter Bostava has converted, however, and treats him well. When Amgrad, now grand visier, goes through the city publicly asking for his brother, Bostava presents him, and the two are reunited. At the very end of the story the king of China arrives looking for his daughter, who is said to be alive and well. Queen Margiana arrives seeking Assad. The army of Camaralzaman's father also arrives, and, finally, Camaralzaman himself. All return happily to their respective kingdoms. Assad marries Margiana, and Amgrad marries Bostava, for the services she has rendered his brother.

The Story of Noureddin and the Fair Persian

Zinchi, who is governing Balsora in the days of (and by the grace of) Haroun Alraschid, entrusts the administration of his city to two ministers: Khacan, who is affable and generous, and Saouy, who is sullen and morose. Khacan on one occasion purchases a slave of great beauty and rare education for the king. Yet at Khacan's home, where she is temporarily lodged, the slave encounters his son Noureddin, whom she admires and who soon tricks her into believing that she has now been designated not for the king, but for himself. Khacan is distraught because he knows his rival Saouy will place the blame for this misappropriation on him, and thus turn the king against him. He takes the advice of his wife who suggests that he merely tell the visier that, on closer examination, a mistake had been made and that the Fair Persian (as she is known) was simply not worthy of him. Khacan is also induced by his wife to pardon his son Noureddin, on the condition that the boy marry the Fair Persian and never rid himself of her. Khacan eventually dies and Noureddin, after a proper period of mourning, begins a life lived to excess. His wife the Fair Persian warns him that he is being a spendthrift, but he does not listen to her. In time, as his money runs out, his friends abandon him. At her own selfless insistence, the Fair Persian volunteers to be sold in the market so that her husband can rescue himself from debt. Khacan's old rival Saouy wishes to purchase her in the market, but Noureddin will not allow his father's former enemy to have her. They eventually fight. Saouy vows revenge, but Noureddin flees town with his wife. They travel to Baghdad, where they encounter one Scheich Ibrahim, the steward of the caliph Haroun Alraschid's garden and palace of pictures. Scheich Ibrahim welcomes the couple, drinking wine with them and pretending that the sultan's palace is in fact his own. Haroun Alraschid notices that the lights have been lit in his garden palace, and disguises himself as a fisherman to see what is going on. The 'fisherman' joins the group and soon plays and sings, and Noureddin, in his generous enthusiasm, offers him the Fair Persian. She is, of course, upset over her husband's seeming thoughtlessness. The disguised caliph tells Noureddin that he is an old friend of Zinchi, and will give him a sealed note that will more than return him to royal favour.

After Noureddin leaves, Haroun Alraschid is revealed to the conniving Scheich Ibrahim, who had wanted a share of Noureddin's generosity. Scheich Ibrahim is forgiven, and the Fair Persian is promised that she will soon be able to join Noureddin in Balsora, where he will reign as king. Upon Noureddin's return to Balsora Saouy attempts to have him killed; but the caliph's visier halts the execution. Noureddin finally begs to be released of the responsibilities of kingship, and lives a quieter life with the Fair Persian, in Baghdad.

The Story of Beder, Prince of Persia, and Giahaure, Princess of Samandal

The king of Persia purchases a gorgeous slave who perversely refuses to speak to him. After much patient wooing by the king, however, the slave finally agrees to tell her story. She informs him that her name is Gulnare and that she comes originally from one of 'the countries of the sea', where she was formerly a princess. She tells him, moreover, that there are many such kingdoms under the ocean. After a dispute with her brother, Saleh, she leapt out of the ocean as far as the moon, but was soon taken from there by someone whom she will identify only as 'a certain prince of distinction'. After rejecting the amorous desires of this 'person', she was eventually sold as a slave, hence her present position.

The king decides to marry Gulnare. He even receives her relatives, who arise, spectacularly, from the ocean to meet him. She eventually bears the king a beloved and generous son, whom she names Beder. In time the old king dies and Beder ascends the throne of Persia. When it is decided that it is time for Beder to seek a bride, his uncle Saleh suggests to Gulnare that he marry the princess Giauhara (or Guihare). The only objection to this scheme is that Giauhara's father—also a king in one of the 'countries of the sea', called Samandal—is insupportably vain, and will probably object to the match. Saleh suggests that he first test the ground, as it were, and not alert Beder himself to the possibilities of the match until something has been positively arranged. Having overheard simply the description of Giauhara, however, Beder has already fallen hopelessly in love with the princess and demands to be taken to see her. His uncle reluctantly brings him down to the kingdoms in the sea.

When they arrive in Samandal, the king is so outraged by the effrontery of the proposal that he peremptorily orders Saleh killed. Beder's mother has anticipated such a response, however, and has sent troops to protect her son. Thanks to these troops Saleh is able to capture the king and take over the palace. The princess Giauhara flees the palace during the attack and encounters Beder, who informs her of the reason for the commotion and protests his devotion to her. Like her father, however, Giauhara seems to resent the prince's impudence and promptly turns him into 'a white bird, with a red bill and feet'. A waiting woman, to whom he is committed in this form, has mercy on him, and places him not—as the princess has ordered—on a desolate rock, but in a field of plenty.

King Saleh cannot find his nephew and, back in Persia, queen Gulnare too becomes alarmed when she cannot locate her son. She seeks him in the kingdom of the sea, and is advised by her mother to return, for the time being, to Persia, and govern the country.

Beder, still a bird, is captured and given as a present to the king of Samandal. His queen, a powerful sorceress who knows what is going on throughout the world of magic, tells him that this is in fact Beder, the king of Persia, who has been transformed thus by his own daughter, the princess Giauhara. The king is rather distressed to hear just how far his daughter has taken her resentment of the young suitor, and asks his queen to transform Beder back into a man. When Beder is returned to his natural form, the king finds him to be charming. Beder asks to be returned to Persia. He is, however, shipwrecked on the way home, and is stranded upon a shore, near a great city, where a variety of animals attempt to prevent his landing. He enters the large city finally to meet one human—Abdallah—who tells him that he has landed in the kingdom of a sorceress who transforms all men into animals. This old man, who is alone respected by the sorceress, attempts to pass Beder off as his nephew.

This sorceress—Queen Labe—soon passes by, however, and demands Beder, for whom she has conceived a passion. She attempts to turn him into an animal, as she has turned all her other lovers into animals, but Beder does not swallow the necessary poison which she has baked into his food. He instead tricks her into eating it herself, and transforms her into a mare. Beder is on the way back to

Persia with the mare when he encounters an older woman who insists that he sell it to her. He tries to resist, but is told that he is in a city in which 'it is not permitted to lie'. He had told the shabbily dressed old woman, thinking her poor, that she could have the horse for a hundred pieces of gold. The woman produces the money, receives the horse, and quickly transforms it back into Queen Labe. The old woman turns out to be the sorceress's mother. Labe, outraged at Beder's clever treachery, transforms him into an owl. A compassionate servant brings him food, though instructed not to do so. Abdallah sees what has happened to Beder, so he conjures a genie, Lightning, to transport the good servant to the capital of Persia where she tells Queen Gulnare just where her son is, and how he stands in need of assistance. King Saleh and the others attack the city of Enchantments, and kill the queen. Gulnare transforms her son back into a man. Beder marries Samandal's princess.

The History of Ganem, Son to Abou Ayoub, and known by the Surname of Love's Slave

Ganem, son of the merchant Abou Ayoub of Damascus, travels to Baghdad following the death of his father in order to sell what remains of his father's goods. One evening he stumbles upon a group of slaves secretly and hurriedly burying a large chest under cover of darkness just outside the city walls. When the slaves depart Ganem retrieves the chest and, opening it, discovers Fetnah, the favourite of the caliph Haroun Alraschid, drugged and nearly dead inside. Ganem rescues her and takes her to recover at his own home in Baghdad. It soon becomes clear that Zobeide, the caliph's jealous wife, has had Fetnah poisoned with a sleeping potion and was the one responsible for attempting to have her buried alive. Fetnah realizes that she must for her own safety maintain a low profile while living with the merchant Ganem. Ganem, for his own part, has fallen hopelessly in love with the beautiful young favourite.

Zobeide has meanwhile told Haroun Alraschid that Fetnah has died. Even when Fetnah finally manages to communicate news of her whereabouts to the caliph, he believes her to have been perversely unfaithful to him. Rather than welcoming her back to court and rewarding her rescuer, Haroun orders his servants to kill Ganem and forcibly return his favourite to the palace. Disguised as a slave, Ganem manages to escape, but his house is levelled in the attack. Not content with this misplaced retribution, the caliph then orders that Ganem's relatives be located in Damascus. He instructs the sultan there—Mohammed Zinebi—to prosecute Ganem's mother and sister, Alcolomb. The two innocents are paraded through the streets, but a sympathetic populace refuses to jeer at or ridicule them. They are nevertheless disgraced in their home-town, and decide eventually to head for Baghdad.

Fetnah, meanwhile, has been imprisoned in a dark tower; only after a long incarceration does she have a chance to tell her story to Haroun and to plead Ganem's case. The caliph relents and wishes to forgive Ganem, but he cannot be found. Fetnah has in the meantime asked the syndic of some merchants to distribute money amongst the poor. This syndic tells her that two women—obviously noble but distraught—have recently arrived in Baghdad who seem to be particularly worthy of her charity.

Fetnah rescues the two, who are revealed to be Ganem's mother and sister. The caliph, who has by now been fully convinced of the extent of Zobeide's treachery, rejects his wife and marries Ganem's sister Alcolomb. He then offers Ganem's mother to Giafar, his grand visier. Ganem finally reappears in Baghdad, and he and Fetnah are happily reunited.

The History of Prince Zeyn Alasnam, and the King of the Genii

Prince Zeyn Alasnam ascends the throne of his father and, much to the distress of his wise mother, immediately begins spending his father's wealth. Having depleted all of his father's riches, he receives instructions in a dream to travel to Cairo. No sooner does he arrive in the city, however, but a second dream-vision instructs him to return home. A third vision tells him that there is a room filled with treasure hidden in his own palace. Undertaking to explore the residence, he does indeed find concealed in subterranean vaults within his father's chambers urns filled with gold and, more surprisingly, eight statues each cut from a single diamond mounted on pediments of solid gold; one pedestal alone remains unoccupied. The prince also discovers a message from his father which tells him that a faithful old household servant now living in Cairo by the name of Morabec can tell him where this ninth and most beautiful statue is now hidden. Zeyn Alasnam travels to Cairo and locates Morabec, who then takes him on a journey to the king of the Genii. The two summon this king who—before he will surrender the ninth statue—asks Zeyn Alasnam first to marry and then to deliver to him, the king, a 15-year-old virgin so pure of heart that she has 'never known man, nor desired to know any'. Moreover, Zeyn Alasnam must have so mastered his own passions that in the course of conducting this perfectly beautiful bride to the king of the Genies, he will himself not covet her nor desire to 'enjoy' her in the least. The prince is then given a magic mirror in which this pure woman will be revealed to him as unsullied; he then takes an oath that he will faithfully undertake what has been asked of him. He and Morabec search for this pure virgin among the women of Cairo, but cannot find her. They move to Baghdad, where they are finally introduced to a stunning young virgin whom the mirror reveals to be perfectly pure of heart. Zeyn marries the girl and, as instructed, carries her back to the king of the Genii. In his heart, however, Zeyn secretly regrets having to surrender her. He fulfils his vow, however, and the king tells him that when he returns to Baghdad he will find the ninth statue awaiting him. To his great astonishment and surprise he finds his recently married bride instead. It is then revealed that the whole episode has been a trial for Zeyn Alasnam conducted by the king of the Genii, who only wanted to be certain that the young prince, once an intemperate spendthrift, could master his passions and merit his good fortune.

The History of Codadad and his Brothers

The king of the city of Harran prays for a son; a prophet appears to him and soon thereafter all fifty of his wives are pregnant except one, Pirouze. Displeased with what he deems to be a stubborn infertility, the king sends Pirouze away to

Samaria. The prince of Samaria soon reports, however, that Pirouze has indeed been delivered of a child. The prince is asked to raise the child, who is named Codadad. Codadad, when grown, decides to fight by the side of his father and actively demonstrate his courage in battle before revealing his true identity. His brothers grow jealous of the new favourite (for so he soon becomes) and decide to disappear when they pretend to go hunting, hoping that Codadad will be held responsible for their absence. Codadad travels in search of his brothers, and rescues all forty-nine of them and a beautiful princess from a monstrous giant. The princess then tells her own story:

The History of the Princess of Deryabar

The princess's father had once rescued a lady and her son who had been taken from their own kingdom by a fearful genie. This son, raised as a privileged favourite in the court, grew up thinking that he would in time marry the princess and reign with her. When this did not come to pass, he angrily killed the king; the princess escaped only to be shipwrecked. She eventually met a young king who married her, but on the day of her nuptials the kingdom was invaded by one King Zanguebar, who 'cut to pieces all the king's subjects'. The princess and her husband escaped, but were soon attacked by pirates. The unfortunate prince was bound and thrown into the sea to drown. The pirates were in turn attacked on the way to Cairo by the giant from whom Codadad has just rescued her.

Codadad reveals his true identity to his brothers and offers to marry the princess. The brothers' resentment at Codadad's success, however, is now redoubled. They stab him many times and leave him for dead. The princess of Deryabar is hysterical and leaves his body only in order to find a physician. She soon returns, but is surprised to find that Codadad's body has disappeared. She and the physician assume that a wild beast has devoured him. The surgeon convinces the princess that it is her duty to travel to the court of Harran and avenge Codadad. The surgeon is eventually able to convey what little information he possesses about the young man's disappearance to Codadad's mother. On the basis of this evidence the treacherous princes are imprisoned and a huge monument is built in memory of Codadad. The princes are about to be executed when a neighbouring kingdom attacks. The king is rescued only by the unexpected arrival of some brave horsemen, the leader of whom turns out to be none other than Codadad himself, who had in fact been rescued by a peasant who had then ministered to his wounds. Codadad forgives his brothers and rewards the faithful surgeon.

The Story of the Sleeper Awakened

In the reign of the caliph Haroun Alraschid a merchant's son—Abon Hassan—spends half of his legacy in lavish entertainments only to realize that his friends desert him when his money runs out. Disappointed, he decides to allow only one person to dine with him each evening and never to eat with the same person twice. He meets his prospective guests on Baghdad bridge. One day the caliph, disguised as a Moussel merchant, is his guest. The caliph decides to trick Abon Hassan into believing that he is himself the Commander of the Believers and puts a sleeping draught in his glass. Upon awakening Abon Hassan falls for the deception; he is even incarcerated in a madhouse when he is finally returned to his own home and told that he is *not* the caliph. The caliph manages to repeat the trick, but eventually reveals his true identity to his dupe. Abon Hassan then becomes a favourite of the sultan. The caliph takes him to meet his wife Zobeide, and there Abon Hassan falls in love with Zobeide's slave Nouz-hatoul-aonadat. The two are married, and subsequently deceive the sultan and his wife each into thinking that they are dead, as a means of extracting money to continue their lavish life-style. The sultan is only impressed with Abon Hassan's ingenuity in perpetrating such a trick and rewards rather than punishes the pair for the deception.

The Story of Aladdin; or, the Wonderful Lamp

Aladdin is the spendthrift son of a tailor in a kingdom of China. After the death of his father an African magician arrives in the kingdom and poses as Aladdin's uncle. The uncle pretends to set Aladdin up as a merchant, but does so only in order to win the boy's trust and affection. One day he leads Aladdin far from the city and shows him a magic cave. Explaining that he cannot himself enter the cave, the magician tells Aladdin that he may remove from the underground cavern any jewels he wishes, but asks particularly that the boy bring to him a lamp which will be found prominently displayed within the cave. Aladdin passes safely through the enchanted cavern and soon finds the lamp but, when he does not immediately hand it over, the magician grows angry and shuts Aladdin within the cave. The impostor then returns to Africa and leaves Aladdin to die. The boy despairs for his life, but after two days rubs a ring which his supposed uncle had given him for protection while inside the cave. A genie appears and restores him to the outer world. Aladdin then returns to his mother. Planning to sell the lamp for food, Aladdin rubs it while preparing to polish it and yet another genie appears. Aladdin and his mother ask the genie for food, and subsequently live for some time by selling the silver plate on which the genie had delivered this sustenance.

One day Aladdin catches a forbidden glimpse of the face of the sultan's beautiful daughter, Badroulbadour, as she travels through the streets of the city on her way to the baths. He convinces his reluctant mother to ask the sultan, in his name, for Badroulbadour's hand in marriage. Aladdin's mother travels to the court, where she offers as a gift to the sultan many precious jewels which the genie of the lamp has retrieved from the cave. The sultan is stunned at the value of the jewels with which the seemingly impoverished woman presents him, and is ready to accept Aladdin's suit. His visier, however, who had hoped that one of his own sons might marry the sultan's daughter, asks his master to postpone the marriage for three months, by which time he promises that his own son will present the sultan and Badroulbadour with an even more impressive present. The sultan then appears to accept Aladdin's request for his daughter's hand in marriage, but asks that Aladdin return to the court in three months' time, at which point, he says, he expects some furniture which has been designed for Badroulbadour to be ready. Aladdin and his mother, unaware of the sultan's true design, anxiously wait for the three months to pass. Just before the allotted time has elapsed, however, they learn that the princess has been married that very evening to the visier's son. Aladdin is appalled at the sultan's treachery and calls on the genie of the lamp. He then has the genie transport the couple's nuptial bed to his own chamber, where he keeps the newly-weds apart from one another. The baffled bridegroom is transported magically from his bed to a privy where he is held captive until morning; Badroulbadour is so amazed that she is struck speechless. Aladdin so discomfits the two in this manner each evening that after a short while the marriage is finally broken off and the pair separate. After a further three months has expired Aladdin again sends his mother to court to claim the princess as his rightful bride. The sultan thinks that he can on this occasion rid himself of Aladdin by requiring of him forty large gold basins filled with jewels before Badroulbadour can be his. Aladdin not only supplies the sultan with the jewels, however, but further dazzles the court with his splendid retinue and with a massive palace of gold which the genie has constructed overnight beside the sultan's own residence. The sultan finally relents and Aladdin lives with his young bride in a magnificent manner—the son-in-law, ally, and friend of his monarch—for several years.

The African magician in time discovers through divination what Aladdin has accomplished with the aid of the lamp, however, and again resolves to have it for his own. He travels to China and—disguised now as a mad merchant—wanders through the streets of the city offering to exchange new lamps for old ones. One day, when Aladdin is away from home, the princess hears the magician's cry and—not knowing the true value of the lamp—exchanges it for a new one from the seemingly irrational merchant. With the magic lamp in his possession, the magician immediately commands the genie to transport the entire palace and its contents, including the princess, back with him to Africa.

The sultan is shocked to observe that the palace has disappeared and, blaming Aladdin for the abduction of his daughter, is about to have him executed. Aladdin requests that he be given a reprieve of forty days during which he might discover the whereabouts of the princess and rescue her. In his anxiety he accidentally twists the ring on his finger and again calls forth the forgotten genie of the ring, who is able to transport him to Africa. There he and the princess together outwit the magician, retrieve the lamp, and return the palace to China.

In a final episode, the younger and even more powerful brother of the African magician hears of his sibling's fate and travels to China to avenge him. When this brother arrives he first murders and then impersonates a local holy lady named Fatima, whom he perceives might have access to the princess Badroulbadour. At a time when Aladdin is again away from home the magician is admitted to the princess, and informs her that the only thing wanting to make her palace complete is a roc's egg hanging from the middle of its central dome. When Aladdin returns home the princess asks him to provide this novelty. The genie of the lamp is tremendously angered, however, that Aladdin would have the audacity to ask to have the genie's own true 'master' hung from the dome of his palace. Acknowledging that the request did not, however, originate from Aladdin himself, the genie tells him that the Fatima who has been admitted to the house is an impostor. The true identity of the magician's brother is revealed and he is killed. Aladdin and Badroulbadour finally live happily ever after.

The Adventures of the Caliph Haroun Alraschid

The caliph, in a melancholy mood, again dons his disguise and sets out to entertain himself in the great city of Baghdad. He soon encounters three things worthy of further inquiry: a blind man who perversely solicits from passers-by both alms and a box on the ear; a young man who—at a certain hour of each day—barbarously drives a horse around a central square; and a magnificent palace worthy of a great lord, but which in fact (he learns) belongs only to a simple rope-maker. On the next day at prayer time the caliph listens to each of their stories, beginning with:

The Story of the Blind Man, Baba Abdalla

A dervish had once revealed to the man—who at the time had been a prosperous merchant—the location of a cave in which was contained enough treasure to load all eighty of his camels. Baba Abdalla originally agreed to split the treasure evenly with the dervish, but little by little convinced his partner rather to give him *all* the treasure; he even coveted a little box of pomatum or pomade which the dervish had carried away. The generous dervish agreed to give Baba Abdalla even this, the last of his possessions, but warned him that although the application of the pomatum to one eye would allow him to see riches where they lay buried in the earth, application to both eyes would leave him blind. Baba Abdalla thinks the dervish is only deceiving him, applies the pomatum to both eyes, and is promptly blinded. He now solicits, as a punishment for his covetousness and his incredulity, the penalty of a box on the ear from all charitable people. The caliph then listens to:

The Story of Sidi Nonman

Sidi Nonman married a woman named Amina who, unknown to him, was a sorceress and a ghoul who ate human flesh. He followed her one night to the burying ground and discovered her true identity. When he confronted her, however, she transformed him into a dog. He lived in this form for some time with an honest baker, but was eventually returned to his human form by a good sorceress who likewise, in retribution, transformed his wife into a horse. The caliph suggests that the transformation of his wife was itself sufficient punishment for her crimes, and tells Sidi Nonman that he need no longer beat her. The caliph listens finally to:

The Story of Cogia Hassan Alhabbal

Two friends—one rich, Saadi, and one poor, Saad—wished one day to decide if either great riches or simple chance was, eventually, most productive of human felicity. As an experiment Saadi bestowed on a simple but honest rope-maker, Cogia Hassan Alhabbal, some money which was, through a series of bizarre misfortunes, taken from him. Saad in turn left the same rope-maker with a simple bar of lead. The rope-maker managed to transform this seemingly worthless gift into a monopoly of all the rope makers in Baghdad. Saad and Saadi thus decided that a man can in time become rich (and happy) without having had a large amount of capital to begin with; Cogia Hassan Alhabbal remained a very wealthy man with a spectacular palace in which to live.

The Story of Ali Baba, and the forty Thieves destroyed by a Slave

The brother of the poor Ali Baba is the rich and prosperous merchant Cassim. One day Ali Baba discovers a band of forty thieves who alight at a secret cave where, opening the massive cave door with the magic words 'Open Sesame', they deposit their loot. Ali Baba sneaks into the cave and takes some of the gold home. When Cassim learns of his brother's new-found prosperity, he demands that the honest Ali Baba tell him how he came by it. Cassim himself gains entrance to the cave, but once within forgets the magic password, and so remains trapped inside when the robbers return. The thieves find him and kill him, quartering his body and displaying it at the entrance of the cave as a warning to all who might follow. Ali Baba finds his brother's desecrated body and, with the help of the clever female servant Morgiana, has it sewn back together and properly buried. Ali Baba then marries his former sister-in-law and settles down to a temperate life. The thieves however—missing the body of Cassim at its entrance—see that their cave has again been violated and set out to find the person responsible. Two of the thieves lose their lives through the vigilance of the servant Morgiana, but finally the remaining thirty-eight are able to sneak into Ali Baba's house. The chief disguises himself as an oil merchant and conceals his followers in large oil jars. Morgiana discovers the infiltration and kills the thieves by pouring hot oil into each of the jars. The chief returns one more time and, again disguised as a merchant, insinuates himself into Ali Baba's home. Morgiana recognizes him and stabs him. Ali Baba's house prospers in succeeding generations.

The Story of Ali Cogia, a Merchant of Bagdad

The merchant Ali Cogia embarks upon a pilgrimage to Mecca. He then travels for seven years to such places as Cairo, Jerusalem, and Damascus. Before departing, he places his wealth in gold in a large jar. He adds a layer of olives to the top so that it looks like a simple jar of olives. This he entrusts to the care of a fellow merchant. He returns home only to find that this supposed friend has stolen the gold in his absence; the man denies ever having touched it. The caliph is scheduled to hear and decide the dispute between the two men when he overhears some children pretending to judge the case for themselves. He notes that the child playing the judge quite correctly points out that the original olives forming the top layer of the jug would have been seven years old and unfit to eat if they had not been tampered with. The caliph has the child himself brought to the court to judge the case. The dishonest merchant is hanged, the money is restored to Ali Cogia, and the perceptive young boy is rewarded for his judgement.

The Story of the Enchanted Horse

An Indian presents the king of Persia with a magic horse and demands in exchange to be married to the king's daughter. The king's son is outraged at the impertinence of the Indian, and asks to ride the horse in order to see its powers demonstrated for himself. He is soon transported by the magical horse to Bengal, where he falls in love with the princess of that country. The prince brings her back to Persia, but the treacherous Indian soon manages to abduct both the princess of Bengal and the horse. He flees to Caschmire where, attempting to pass the princess off as his own wife, he is killed. The princess is thrilled with this rescue, but is soon appalled to learn that the sultan of Caschmire himself now wants to marry her. She pretends to be insane, and the prince of Persia, who has been travelling in search of her, is finally able to sneak in to her disguised as a physician and take her back to Persia, where he finally marries her.

The Story of Prince Ahmed and the Fairy Pari Banou

The sultan of the throne of India has three sons: Houssain, Ali, and Ahmed. He also has a niece, Nouronnihar, who has been raised as one of his own children. All three sons wish to marry the niece, so the sultan decides to award her to the one who returns from his travels with the greatest wonder. Prince Houssain travels to Bisnagar, where he purchases a flying carpet which he is certain will win him the princess. Prince Ali travels to Persia, where he in turn purchases a perspective glass or telescope which will allow him to see whatever he wishes when he looks through it. Prince Ahmed travels to Samarcande, where he purchases an apple, the aroma of which, he is assured, will cure any illness. The brothers return to Persia and immediately find it necessary to use all three gifts in concert to cure a sickness into which the princess has fallen: they see her ill in the telescope, fly to her on the carpet, and cure her with the aroma of the apple.

His initial plan having proved inconclusive, the sultan now decides that he will award the princess to the prince who can shoot an arrow the farthest. The youngest son, Ahmed, in fact shoots his arrow far beyond those of his brothers, but his shaft cannot be found and the princess is instead given, by default, to Prince Ali. Ahmed pursues the path of his arrow and discovers the palace of a fairy named Paribanon (or Pari Banou), who is the daughter of 'one of the most powerful and distinguished genies'. Ahmed marries her and lives with her in her palace for six months.

The sultan, meanwhile, believes Ahmed to be lost and even dead. A sorceress in his court tells him that not only is his son still alive, but will soon return for a visit. The genie Paribanon does not want Ahmed to tell his father of their marriage, yet the sultan soon grows suspicious regarding the reasons for his son's long disappearance and after the visit has him followed by the sorceress back to Paribanon's palace. The sorceress, feigning illness, then gains access to the palace. When she returns to the sultan, she tells him that she suspects Paribanon of harbouring designs against him and his kingdom. She thus advises him to ask of Paribanon a series of wonderful things: a tent that can fit into the palm of one's hand, a bottle of water that cures all fevers, and a man 'not above a foot and a half high, and whose beard is thirty feet long, and who carries a bar of iron on his shoulder . . . which he uses as a quarter staff'. The genie Paribanon, however, is able to supply all of these things, including the precise dwarf described, who happens to be her brother. The dwarf travels to the sultan's court, kills the foolish sultan and his counsellors, and establishes Ahmed as sultan.

The Story of the Two Sisters who envied their younger Sister

The sultan of Persia, Khosrouschah, decides to grant the wishes he casually overhears of three sisters. The first sister desires to be married to the sultan's baker; the second wishes to be married to the sultan's cook; the youngest and most beautiful desires nothing less than to be married to the sultan himself. The first two sisters soon become jealous of their younger sibling's exalted status. On three occasions they act as midwives to the sultaness, and each time the healthy children to whom their sister has actually given birth are set adrift in a canal. The sisters claim that she has given birth instead to, respectively, a dog, a cat, and a mole. The sultaness is finally publicly humiliated and imprisoned. However, her three children—two boys and a girl—have been rescued from the canal and raised by an attendant in the sultan's gardens. Before dying, this attendant builds his foster-children a magnificent home or 'country-seat' outside the city.

One day several years later the young princess, Parizade, entertains a religious old woman who tells her that her house lacks only three things to be incomparable in Persia: the talking bird called Bulbulkezer, the Singing Tree ('the leaves of which are so many mouths, which form an harmonious concert'), and the 'Yellow Golden Water' which creates a self-sustaining fountain. These three rarities, the old woman tells Parizade, can be found not twenty days' distance from her own home. Both of the princess's brothers try to capture these ornaments, but are turned into stone in the attempt. Princess Parizade herself endeavours to retrieve them and succeeds. She is also able to return her brothers to their natural form. The three return home, where their marvellous possessions soon gain the attention of their father, the sultan. The talking bird eventually convinces Khosrouschah that Parizade and her brothers are in fact his own natural children. The sultaness is liberated from her long imprisonment and the family is once again united in the Persian capital, where they are received with great joy and celebration.

The volume finally returns to the frame story as the sultan Schahriar tells Scheherazade that she has succeeded in removing his 'fatal prejudice against all women', and that he has reconsidered his original intention to execute her. They are married and Scheherazade gains 'the blessings of all the people of the large empire of the Indies'.

EXPLANATORY NOTES

1 *the Susanians*: the Sassanians or Sassanid dynasty, an early Persian dynasty which ruled an area extending across what is now Iran and Iraq and into central Asia from about AD 226 until the Arabian conquest in AD 641. The Sassanian capital lay at Ctesiphon, in central Iraq. Many of the tales included in the *Nights*, however, are said to take place during later Islamic dynasties, most notably the Abbasid caliphate (*c.*AD 749–1258), a period famed for its economic prosperity, intellectual and cultural activity, and for the reign of the legendary Harun al-Raschid (786–809).

his prime visier: the visier or more properly *wazir* was the chief minister to the *caliph* (from the Arabic *khalifah* or 'successor' to the prophet Muhammad). The office emerged as an important post in the early years of the Abbasid caliphate (see note above).

2 *his scymetar*: i.e. scimitar, 'a short, curved, single-edged sword' (*OED*).

3 *a sofa or alcove*: see p. 422 and note. Not the free-standing sofas or couches of Western design, but a portion of the floor raised one or two feet, covered with carpets or cushions, and used for sitting and reclining.

8 *one of those malignant genies*: 'These beings are . . . normally invisible and have the power to take on many forms. Like men, but unlike the devils, the *jinn* [genies] may achieve eternal bliss if they follow the guidance sent in the Revelation, and many have done so. There are several different classes or types of *jinn*, the most powerful and most evil being the *'arafit* who may do violent harm to any whom they choose. The *'arafit* are sometimes associated with the souls of men who have died a violent death and who remain in this world to haunt and torment the living. Both popular folklore and Islamic literature in a variety of languages abound in stories of the *jinn* and their relations with men. It is commonly believed that men may and do contract marriages with the *jinn*, and there is highly developed lore among Muslims about the means that men may employ to have communication with the *jinn* and enlist these supernatural powers as their servants . . . An extensive literature in popular Islam shows Solomon as taming the *jinn* and using them (though they occasionally rebel against him) as a work-force in order for him to perform his many wonders. The belief in these spirits is all but universal among the generality of Muslims in our own day, and the art of seeking communication with the *jinn* is very much alive in many parts of the Islamic world.' See Charles J. Addams, 'Islamic Faith', in R. M. Savory (ed.), *Introduction to Islamic Civilization* (Cambridge, 1976), 42.

10 *a subaltern*: a person of inferior rank, a subordinate officer of the court.

13 *the currier*: 'one whose trade is the dressing and colouring of leather after it is tanned' (*OED*).

17 *factors*: a factor is a commission merchant, i.e. one who buys and sells goods for another person.

Mussulman: i.e. a Muslim. According to some Islamic traditions, Muslims are enjoined to wash their hands and face before and after eating, and to recite a short invocation or blessing (*Bismillah*, or, 'In the name of God') prior to the meal, and another short prayer (*Al-kamdu lillah*, or 'Glory be to God') after the meal.

23 *the festival of the great Bairam*: the 'greater' Bairam, the Islamic festival following (after seventy days) the fasting of the month of Ramadan (an obligation which is one of the five so-called 'Pillars of Islam'), and lasting four days.

mell: a heavy hammer or mallet.

26 *one thousand sequins*: see p. 146 and note.

27 *joined a caravan*: referring here to a caravan of merchants travelling together for the sake of collective security along well-established routes in the desert. Some main caravan and pilgrimage routes stretched from Baghdad towards Basra and Mecca in the south, and thence towards Jerusalem, Damascus, and Cairo.

31 *pannier*: a sack or basket, usually one used for carrying provisions.

32 *I pray you to render the sea . . . Moses*: referring to God's parting of the Red Sea for Moses and the Israelites in Exodus 14: 21–31. Perhaps also referring to the infant Moses's own rescue by the Pharaoh's daughter in Exodus 2: 1–10.

Solomon . . . the great prophet: the biblical King Solomon is often credited in Islamic literature and folklore with having tamed the *jinn* to perform miracles and wonders. He controlled them by means of his signet ring, the famous 'seal of Solomon' (see p. 142 and note).

36 *drenches*: medicinal drinks or potions.

42 *a Hogress . . . Hogres*: 'Hogres'—or more commonly ogres—were giant, man-eating monsters who, as the visier goes on to point out, were generally thought to hide in remote places and devour unsuspecting passers-by. This example cited in *OED*.

44 *emirs*: from the Arabic *amir*; originally (and as used here) a general or military commander, afterwards a title of honour held by independent rulers.

46 *as Imama treated Ateca formerly*: the story of these two women is no longer recorded.

47 *white, red, blue, and yellow*: the faith of each 'fish' in the pond (p. 60) can be identified by its colour, just as the colour of a turban worn in the East often marked its wearer's religion. Christians wore blue, Muslims white, Jews Yellow, and Zoroastrians (see p. 130 and note) red.

48 *my pendulum*: watch, clock.

50 *battoon*: baton, staff.

53 *massy*: massive, having great weight; the adjective becomes a favourite of English oriental writers in the eighteenth century.

56 *plat*: a small foot-bridge.

pallisadoes: i.e. palisados; a palisade is a defensive fence of wooden stakes.

60 *the Persians, who worshipped the fire*: Zoroastrians or Magians, commonly called 'fire worshippers'; see p. 130 and note.

ox pizzles: whips of ox-hide.

65 *ADVERTISEMENT*: all eighteenth-century editions of the *Nights* in Europe at some early point in their narratives abandon the introductory formulas of the frame story, and move seamlessly through each narrative until it is necessary for Scheherazade to introduce an entirely new body of tales. Galland's original French translation placed one such 'Advertisement' alerting readers to the subsequent omission of the Introductory Tale at the beginning of the third book of his (eventually) twelve-volume collection.

70 *drank first . . . custom of the Arabians*: a gesture of hospitality, perhaps to show that the wine was acceptable or had not been poisoned.

71 *calenders*: a mendicant order of dervishes (from the Persian *darwish*, meaning poor) in Turkey and Persia who dedicated themselves to a life of prayer and fasting. This example cited in *OED*.

73 *a khan (or inn)*: see p. 274 and note.

83 *branched candlesticks*: candelabras.

86 *the alcoran*: the Koran (Quran), the sacred text of Islam.

90 *a bagnio*: a bath; the term is sometimes used in the *Nights* in a more general sense of 'dressing room' or 'toilet'.

95 *a dervise's or monk's habit*: dervishes (see p. 71 and note) would often wear coarse woollen garments.

99 *six sorts of hands used among the Arabians*: different 'hands' or characters and styles of writing (e.g. *Rukai*, *Rayhani*, *Juls*, *Naskh*, etc.) with distinctive calligraphic characteristics, developed and cultivated independently of one another, would be appropriate for different kinds of documents and occasions.

102 *the character of Cleopatra*: Kufic or *Kufi*, an early variety of Arabic writing attributed to the scholars at Kufa or Kufah, a centre of Arabic culture in the Middle Ages.

110 *super-cargoes*: 'an officer on board a merchant ship whose business it is to superintend the cargo and the commercial transactions of the voyage' (*OED*).

115 *lamp-black*: a pigment made of almost pure carbon, usually used as paint or ink.

116 *a fowl of monstrous size, called a roc*: the 'roc' or *rukh* was a huge mythical bird of ancient Persian folklore (it is mentioned in the *Jatakas*, a collection of Indian folklore dating from the fourth century BC), capable of carrying in its talons creatures the size of an elephant with ease. See Douglas J. McMillan, 'The Roc', in Malcolm South (ed.), *Mythical and Fabulous Creatures: A Source Book and Research Guide* (New York, 1987), 75–83.

120 *that which our religion promises us after death*: the Islamic Garden of Paradise (*al-janna*), a heavenly mansion of deep fountains, fertile gardens, and beautiful dark-eyed maidens (the *Houris*), promised as the reward to all true believers.

121 *a large volary*: i.e. an aviary, a bird cage.

122 *sessems*: sesame; the *OED* notes that 'the modern currency and form of the word is due to translations of the *Arabian Nights* from [the French] (*sésame*)'.

129 *a nich . . . say our prayers*: the prayer niche (*mihrab*) in the prayer hall (*maqsurah*) of an Islamic house of worship is oriented towards Mecca.

130 *That prince . . . who rebelled against God*: i.e. Magians, a sect of ancient, Pre-Islamic Eastern philosophers who worshipped the deity under the emblem of fire; the sect, which later emphasized the dualism between good and evil, was reformed by the Iranian prophet Zoroaster in the sixth century BC.

135 *a cadis or scrivenor*: a cadis (from the Arabic *qadi*) is a civil judge among the Arabs, usually the judge of a town or village. The term 'scrivenor' or scrivener is generally used to designate a professional copyist or notary. Amine seems here to signify an official acting in a capacity similar to that of a local justice of the peace.

142 *the saying of the great Solomon . . . That death is more tolerable than poverty*: not, in fact, a saying generally attributed to Solomon.

143 *Arabia Felix*: 'fortunate Arabia', a familiar designation of South Arabia because of its reputation for fabulous wealth.

145 *Daigial . . . set round them* (footnote): i.e. Al-Dajjal or *al-Dadjdjal* ('the lying Christ' or 'the deceiver'), the Muslim Antichrist who according to Muslim eschatology (as the note indicates) would appear before the Day of Resurrection. According to some traditions he would be allowed to reign for a limited period of time before witnessing the universal conversion of the world to Islam.

146 *The Turkish sequin . . . 9s. sterling* (footnote): sequins were actually Venetian gold coins, although the term was also applied to the Turkish 'sultanin', and is a favourite of English writers of Oriental fiction in the eighteenth and nineteenth centuries.

148 *Mark Paul . . . a rhinoceros* (footnote): the *Travels* (*Il Milione*) of the Venetian merchant and explorer Marco Polo ('Mark Paul') in Asia, which included an account of his seventeen-year stay in China, were published soon after his return to Venice in 1295. He refers to the Roc or *rukh* (see p. 116 and note) when describing Madagascar, and detailing incidents in the life of Kublai Khan. Martinus Martini's popular *De bello Tartarico historia* had been translated into French (as *Histoire de la guerre des Tartares contre le chine*) and into English in 1654.

153 *It would seem . . . Homer's Odyssey* (footnote): See Homer, *Odyssey* ix, describing Odysseus' encounter with the Cyclops Polyphemos.

156 *bucklers*: small, round shields, often strapped directly to the arm.

161 *He was a Mahometan, and they allow polygamy* (footnote): 'Although it is found in many religious and cultural traditions, polygamy (or more precisely polygyny) is most often identified with Islam in the minds of Westerners. In fact, the Quran and Islamic law sought to control and regulate the number of wives rather than give free license . . . The Quran permits a man to marry up to four wives, provided he can support and treat them all equally. Muslims regard this Quranic command (4: 3) as strengthening the status of women and the family, for it sought to ensure the welfare of single women in a society whose male population was diminished by warfare, and to curb unrestricted polygamy.' See John L. Esposito, *Islam: The Straight Path* (Oxford, 1991), 95–6.

163 *Now Ceylon* (footnote): see App. I.

167 *This island . . . also called Comar, and Comor* (footnote): see App. I.

172 *Geographers place it . . . in the first climate* (footnote): Ceylon, or Sri Lanka, as the note insists, in fact lies north of the Equator.

The eastern geographers . . . French league (footnote): a 'parasangue' or parasang is 'a Persian measure of length, usually reckoned as equal to between three and three and a half miles' (*OED*). Sri Lanka, the island here called Serendip, is actually 272 miles long, with a maximum width of 140 miles.

173 *Solomon* (footnote): see p. 32 and note.

An ancient king . . . famed for his power and wisdom (footnote): the name is probably a corruption of maha-rajah (*Maharaj*), an Indian word for 'Great Chief' or 'Prince'.

175 *corsairs*: pirates or privateers, usually applied to the Mediterranean cruisers of Barbary, 'to whose attacks the ships and the coasts of the Christians were incessantly exposed' *(OED)*.

177 *A regular wind . . . from the west* (footnote): i.e. a monsoon, 'a seasonal wind prevailing in south Asia and especially in the Indian Ocean, which, during the period from April to October, blows approximately from the south-west' (*OED)*.

181 *The Barmecides . . . the grand visier was descended* (footnote): the Barmecides were an Iranian family of government officials that dominated political life of the Abbasid caliphate (see p. 1 and note) during the second half of the 8th century AD. The historical Giafir or 'Jiafir' was a descendant of this family. His father, Yahya, was tutor to the caliph Harun al-Raschid. In AD 803 the family was imprisoned, and Jiafir executed.

210 *cream-tarts*: a distinctly European substitution of Galland's, retained by subsequent English translators; in the Arabic original the confection is a cake of pomegranate seeds.

213 *That is . . . Ommiam* (footnote): the Umayyad dynasty—taking its name from an ancestor, Umayya—a caliphate which ruled the expanding Muslim empire from Damascus from AD 661 until 750. The first four caliphs, referred to in the note, are known as the *Rashidun* or 'rightly guided' caliphs, and reigned after Muhammad from AD 623 to 661.

213 *This prayer . . . before sun-set* (footnote): Islamic practice dictates that prayers (*salat*) be performed five times each day: once upon rising; early in the afternoon; late in the afternoon; at sunset; and immediately prior to going to bed in the evening.

215 *bastinadoed*: to be 'bastinadoed' was to be beaten with cudgels often on the soles of one's feet.

223 *Here . . . to Jerusalem* (footnote): a reference to the 'Esdras' or Ezra of the books of Ezra and Nehemiah in the Hebrew Bible, which relate the history of the Jews from 536 to 432 BC.

224 *a magazine*: storehouse, warehouse.

228 *hussar*: a mistranslation of Galland's *huissier*; an usher or messenger.

229 *the Victory-gate*: probably a reference to the Bab-el-Futuh (the 'Gate of Conquest' or 'Gate of Victories'), on the north side of Cairo's medieval city walls.

230 *he does not make use of his right hand*: the left hand would, according to custom, be used to cleanse one's self and would not, therefore, be considered hygienic; using the left hand to touch one's food would normally be considered bad manners or a mark of disrespect.

232 *crape*: thin silk fabric used as a veil.

240 *ragout*: a stewed dish of seasoned meat and vegetables.

This is called . . . salt-wort (footnote): 'saltwort' is actually a name generally applied to several types of maritime and salt-marsh plants.

242 *they did not fail to dun me*: to 'dun' someone is to demand payment for debts.

244 *the prayer that is said . . . in the mosque*: see p. 213 and note.

245 *There is a fountain at Mecca . . . present to princes and princesses* (footnote): pilgrims to Mecca ritually run from Safa to Marwa and back, commemorating Hagar's search for water for Ishmael, and then drink from the well of Zamzam, where Hagar is said to have found water gushing at Ishmael's feet.

267 *he took a very handsome astrolabe out of his budget*: an 'astrolabe' is an instrument used to observe the positions of heavenly bodies and solve problems of practical astronomy; a 'budget' is a pouch or wallet.

This year 653 . . . in Arabia about that time (foot note): the Muslim calendar dates from Muhammad's emigration (*hijra*) in AD 622 from Mecca to Medina. The Islamic year 653 according to the *Hijrah* lunar calendar would, as the note indicates, correspond to the year 1255 in the Common (Christian) Era.

268 *I had six brothers . . . Schacabac*: the spelling and even the actual names of the barber's brothers change later in the earliest English translations of his narrative. The second brother, for example, first identified as Barbarah, becomes Backbarah; the fourth—initially named Barbarak—becomes Alcouz; while the fifth is referred to first as Alnascar, and later as Alnashar.

cupping-glasses: glass vessels applied to the skin when drawing blood.

275 *He was raised . . . the Abbasides* (footnote): al-Mustansir, thirty-sixth and penultimate Abbasid caliph (AD 1226–42).

287 *seal-ring*: i.e. a signet, 'a finger ring used for bearing a seal' (*OED*).

293 *tire-women*: ladies' maids, dressers.

301 *You drink wine . . . because I am forbid it*: See p. 465 and note.

302 *Or vagabond Arabians . . . to resist them* (footnote): i.e. Bedouins; tribal Arab dwellers of the desert.

306 *This family . . . conquest of that kingdom*: Baghdad had become the centre of the Muslim caliphate under the Abbasids (see p. 1 and note) in the eighth century AD.

310 *chapiters*: i.e. chapters; the capitals of columns.

391 *cornelian*: a seal made of cornelian, a semi-transparent quartz, usually of a dull red colour.

There is an adventure . . . taken from the Arabic (footnote): a reference to the anonymous medieval romance *L'Ystoire du Vaillant Chevalier Piere Filz du Conte de Provence et de la Belle Maguelonne*, in which a bird similarly leads 'Piere' or Peter away from his beloved.

394 *sedan*: i.e. a sedan chair; a litter or closed vehicle seating one person.

401 *This incident . . . Maguelonna* (footnote): see p. 391 and note.

422 *A Turkish bench . . . cushions are put* (footnote): see p. 3 and note.

462 *limners*: painters, particularly water-colour artists.

465 *A Man as I am . . . has renounced wine forever*: the Koran several times (e.g. 2: 219; 5: 90) enjoins Muslims to refrain from the consumption of alcohol.

468 *cheruping*: i.e. chirruping; a 'chirruping cup' is a cheering glass of liquor producing merriment.

469 *the crown-office*: the head; brain.

471 *a right toper*: a hard drinker.

472 *A famous player . . . at Bagdad at that time* (footnote): Abu Ishak or Ishak al-Mawsili; a lute player living during the caliphate of Haroun al-Raschid.

493 *vulgar*: i.e. vernacular; the language commonly used by the people of a country.

494 *perfuming-pan*: a pot or vessel used for the burning of incense.

499 *up-sitting*: 'the occasion of a woman's first sitting up to receive company after a confinement' (*OED*).

522 *a housing*: i.e. a 'caparison' or cloth covering part of a horse or other animal for the purpose either of defence or ornament.

527 *caparisoned*: see p. 522 and note.

531 *bantered*: rallied, made fun of.

533 *hurly-burly*: confusion.

537 *iman*: an iman or *imam* (from the Arabic meaning 'leader') is the officiating priest in an Islamic mosque.

548 *camp-dress*: i.e. the military clothing in which he had returned to Baghdad.

577 *the prayer enjoined, which is called Farz*: such ablution and prayers are dictated by the Koran (e.g. 4: 43; 5: 5).

591 *Saracens*: a general term for Arabs and, by extension, Muslims.

602 *anchorites*: religious recluses.

605 *the story of Ganem*: the introductory frame reintroduced here reflects the confusing publication history of the *Nights* in the first decade of the eighteenth century, and the inclusion in the collection by Galland's publisher of several stories which were not part of the translator's original Syrian manuscript (see Introduction, p. xv).

614 *hautboys, theorboes*: 'hautboys' or oboes are double-reed wind instruments; theorboes were large lutes, popular in Europe in the seventeenth century.

620 *beaufet*: i.e. a buffet.

638 *I will feign myself dead . . . with my feet towards Mecca*: the bodies of some Islamic believers were actually lowered into the ground and buried with their faces, not their feet, oriented towards Mecca.

655 *because it is Friday . . . and the shops will be shut up*: 'Unlike the Sabbath in Judaism and Christianity, Friday was not traditionally a day of rest. However in many Muslim countries . . . it has replaced the Sunday holiday, usually instituted by colonial powers, and therefore often regarded as a Western, Christian legacy.' See Esposito, *Islam: The Straight Path*, 90.

658 *terrace-walk*: a raised walk in a garden.

659 *bastard rubies*: i.e. red stones resembling rubies.

665 *genies, who, as our prophet has told us, are only devils*: see p. 8 and note. Aladdin's mother is slightly mistaken in her description of the *jinn*, although some passages in the Koran do seem to connect the *jinn* with the demons or *shaytans* who lead men astray.

666 *chap*: custom or goods; a 'chapman' (p. 666) is a retail merchant.

the most topping merchants shops: i.e. the very best retail stands and stores.

668 *Aladdin, who had never seen any woman's face, but his mother's*: the customary veiling (*hijab*) and seclusion (*purdah*) of women in Islamic culture would have prevented Aladdin from ever having seen the face of a woman or young girl beyond the age of puberty.

673 *bashaws*: i.e. pashas; high-ranking military officers.

679 *an house of office*: a pantry or privy.

694 *a surtout*: a hooded cloak.

695 *the chaoux*: i.e. chiaus or chavushes; messenger, herald, guard.

720 *coif*: a close-fitting headdress or night-cap.

723 *it is a bird . . . Mount Caucasus*: see p. 116 and note; on Mount Caucasus see also App. I.

731 *pomatum*: i.e. pomade; a scented ointment for application to the skin.

738 *ear-picker*: an instrument for cleaning the ear of wax; tweezers.

739 *goule*: see description which follows; ghouls (the word *ghul* is of Arabic origin) were cannibalistic evil spirits who robbed graves and consumed their corpses.

744 *full-butt*: i.e. full in the face; directly.

784 *It is . . . at your table*: according to some Eastern customs a guest's loyalty towards his host was cemented when they ate salt at each other's table.

789 *the temple . . . the most holy, after that of Mecca*: the Dome of the Rock in Jerusalem, a shrine finished in AD 691, and built on the site of the Jewish Temple; the Dome of the Rock remains to this day a place of pilgrimage, and one of the most sacred sites in the Muslim world.

796 *Novrouz*: i.e. the *Nau-Ruz* or New Year's festival.

816 *huissars*: see p. 228 and note.

822 *bramins*: Brahmins; in the Hindu religion a member of the highest or priestly caste.

824 *basso-relievos*: 'relievos' or reliefs are sculptures which project from a background surface; in 'basso' or low reliefs the projection is minimal.

825 *cinnabar*: a mineral with a rich vermilion colour.

826 *perspective-glass*: a spyglass or telescope.

856 *clew*: i.e. a ball of thread.

858 *grenadier's cap*: the distinctive bonnet of a grenadier; a pointed cap.

873 *bowl*: i.e a ball.

888 *jene scai quoi*: i.e. *je ne sais quoi*, literally 'I know not what', here indicating specifically a certain, indescribable urbanity.